W9-AQA-129

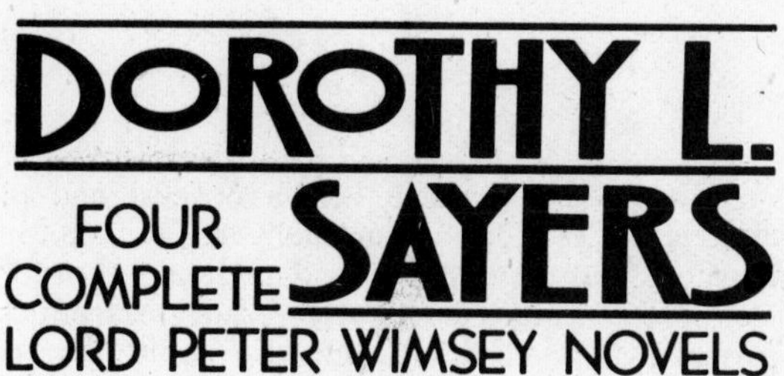
DOROTHY L.
SAYERS
FOUR
COMPLETE
LORD PETER WIMSEY NOVELS

Dorothy L. Sayers (1893–1957) was a British novelist and playwright best known for her detective stories. They are unusually well written for the genre and feature a detective who is both an aristocrat and a scholar—Lord Peter Wimsey.

Sayers was one of the first women ever to receive a degree from Oxford, and her field of study was medieval linguistics. Sayers also wrote plays concerned with Christian themes: *The Zeal of Thy House, The Man Born to Be King, The Devil to Pay,* and *Just Vengeance*. Her other works include critical essays on medieval literature and the translation for the Penguin Classics edition of Dante's *Divine Comedy.*

# DOROTHY L. SAYERS

## FOUR COMPLETE LORD PETER WIMSEY NOVELS

Whose Body?
Clouds of Witness
Murder Must Advertise
Gaudy Night

Complete & Unabridged

AVENEL BOOKS
New York

This edition was previously published in separate volumes
under the titles:

*Whose Body?* MCMXXIII by Dorothy Sayers
*Clouds of Witness* MCMXXVII by Dial Press, Inc.
*Murder Must Advertise* MCMXXXIII by Dorothy Leigh Sayers Fleming
*Gaudy Night* MCMXXXVI by Dorothy Leigh Sayers Fleming

This 1982 edition is published by Avenel Books,
distributed by Crown Publishers, Inc., by arrangement with
Harper & Row, Publishers, Inc.

Manufactured in the United States of America

**Library of Congress Cataloging in Publication Data**
Sayers, Dorothy L. (Dorothy Leigh), 1893-1957.
Dorothy L. Sayers 4 complete Lord Peter Wimsey
novels.

Contents: Whose body?—Clouds of witness—
Murder must advertise—[etc.]
1. Detective and mystery stories, English.
I. Title. II. Title: Dorothy L. Sayers four
complete Lord Peter Wimsey novels.
PR6037.A95A6 1982 823'.912 82-16300

ISBN: 0-517-395754

h g f e d c

# CONTENTS

Whose Body?
1

Clouds of Witness
107

Murder Must Advertise
261

Gaudy Night
459

# Whose Body?

To M.J.

Dear Jim:
This book is your fault. If it had not been for your brutal insistence, Lord Peter would never have staggered through to the end of this enquiry. Pray consider that he thanks you with his accustomed suavity.

Yours ever,
D.L.S.

# 1

"OH, DAMN!" said Lord Peter Wimsey at Piccadilly Circus. "Hi, driver!"

The taxi man, irritated at receiving this appeal while negotiating the intricacies of turning into Lower Regent Street across the route of a 19 'bus, a 38-B and a bicycle, bent an unwilling ear.

"I've left the catalogue behind," said Lord Peter deprecatingly. "Uncommonly careless of me. D'you mind puttin' back to where we came from?"

"To the Savile Club, sir?"

"No—110 Piccadilly—just beyond—thank you."

"Thought you was in a hurry," said the man, overcome with a sense of injury.

"I'm afraid it's an awkward place to turn in," said Lord Peter, answering the thought rather than the words. His long, amiable face looked as if it had generated spontaneously from his top hat, as white maggots breed from Gorgonzola.

The taxi, under the severe eye of a policeman, revolved by slow jerks, with a noise like the grinding of teeth.

The block of new, perfect and expensive flats in which Lord Peter dwelt upon the second floor, stood directly opposite the Green Park, in a spot for many years occupied by the skeleton of a frustrate commercial enterprise. As Lord Peter let himself in he heard his man's voice in the library, uplifted in that throttled stridency peculiar to well-trained persons using the telephone.

"I believe that's his lordship just coming in again—if your Grace would kindly hold the line a moment."

"What is it, Bunter?"

"Her Grace has just called up from Denver, my lord. I was just saying your lordship had gone to the sale when I heard your lordships's latchkey."

"Thanks," said Lord Peter; "and you might find me my catalogue, would you? I think I must have left it in my bedroom, or on the desk."

He sat down to the telephone with an air of leisurely courtesy, as though it were an acquaintance dropped in for a chat.

"Hullo, Mother—that you?"

"Oh, there you are, dear," replied the voice of the Dowager Duchess. "I was afraid I'd just missed you."

"Well, you had, as a matter of fact. I'd just started off to Brocklebury's sale to pick up a book or two, but I had to come back for the catalogue. What's up?"

"Such a quaint thing," said the Duchess. "I thought I'd tell you. You know little Mr. Thipps?"

"Thipps?" said Lord Peter. "Thipps? Oh, yes, the little architect man who's doing the church roof. Yes. What about him?"

"Mrs. Throgmorton's just been in, in quite a state of mind."

"Sorry, Mother, I can't hear. Mrs. Who?"

"Throgmorton–Throgmorton–the vicar's wife."

"Oh, Throgmorton, yes?"

"Mr. Thipps rang them up this morning. It was his day to come down, you know."

"Yes ?"

"He rang them up to say he couldn't. He was so upset, poor little man. He'd found a dead body in his bath."

"Sorry, Mother, I can't hear; found what, where?"

"A dead body, dear, in his bath."

"What?–no, no, we haven't finished. Please don't cut us off. Hullo! Hullo! Is that you, Mother? Hullo–Mother!–Oh, yes–sorry, the girl was trying to cut us off. What sort of body?"

"A dead man, dear, with nothing on but a pair of pince-nez. Mrs. Throgmorton positively blushed when she was telling me. I'm afraid people do get a little narrow-minded in country vicarages."

"Well, it sounds a bit unusual. Was it anybody he knew?"

"No, dear, I don't think so, but, of course, he couldn't give her many details. She said he sounded quite distracted. He's such a respectable little man–and having the police in the house and so on, really worried him."

"Poor little Thipps! Uncommonly awkward for him. Let's see, he lives in Battersea, doesn't he?"

"Yes, dear; 59, Queen Caroline Mansions; opposite the Park. That big block just round the corner from the Hospital. I thought perhaps you'd like to run around and see him and ask if there's anything we can do. I always thought him a nice little man."

"Oh, quite," said Lord Peter, grinning at the telephone. The Duchess was always of the greatest assistance to his hobby of criminal investigation, though she never alluded to it, and maintained a polite fiction of its non-existence.

"What time did it happen, Mother?"

"I think he found it early this morning, but, of course, he didn't think of telling the Throgmortons just at first. She came up to me just before lunch–so tiresome, I had to ask her to stay. Fortunately, I was alone. I don't mind being bored myself, but I hate having my guests bored."

"Poor old Mother! Well, thanks awfully for tellin' me. I think I'll send Bunter to the sale and toddle round to Battersea now an' try and console the poor little beast. So-long."

"Good-bye, dear."

"Bunter!"

"Yes, my lord."

"Her Grace tells me that a respectable Battersea architect has discovered a dead man in his bath."

"Indeed, my lord? That's very gratifying."

"Very, Bunter. Your choice of words is unerring. I wish Eton and Balliol had done as much for me. Have you found the catalogue?"

"Here it is, my lord."

"Thanks. I am going to Battersea at once. I want you to attend the sale for me. Don't lose time–I don't want to miss the Folio Dante* nor the de

Voragine—here you are—see? 'Golden Legend'—Wynken de Worde, 1493—got that?—and, I say, make a special effort for the Caxton folio of the 'Four Sons of Aymon'—it's the 1489 folio and unique. Look! I've marked the lots I want, and put my outside offer against each. Do your best for me. I shall be back to dinner."

"Very good, my lord."

"Take my cab and tell him to hurry. He may for you; he doesn't like me very much. Can I," said Lord Peter, looking at himself in the eighteenth-century mirror over the mantelpiece, "can I have the heart to fluster the flustered Thipps further—that's very difficult to say quickly—by appearing in a top-hat and frock-coat? I think not. Ten to one he will overlook my trousers and mistake me for the undertaker. A grey suit, I fancy, neat but not gaudy, with a hat to tone, suits my other self better. Exit the amateur of first editions; new motive introduced by solo bassoon; enter Sherlock Holmes, disguised as a walking gentleman. There goes Bunter. Invaluable fellow—never offers to do his job when you've told him to do somethin' else. Hope he doesn't miss the 'Four Sons of Aymon.' Still, there *is* another copy of that—in the Vatican.** It might become available you never know—if the Church of Rome went to pot or Switzerland invaded Italy—whereas a strange corpse doesn't turn up in a suburban bathroom more than once in a lifetime—at least, I should think not—at any rate, the number of times it's happened, *with* a pince-nez, might be counted on the fingers of one hand, I imagine. Dear me! it's a dreadful mistake to ride two hobbies at once."

He had drifted across the passage into his bedroom, and was changing with a rapidity one might not have expected from a man of his mannerisms. He selected a dark-green tie to match his socks and tied it accurately without hesitation or the slightest compression of his lips, substituted a pair of brown shoes for his black ones, slipped a monocle into a breast pocket, and took up a beautiful Malacca walking-stick with a heavy silver knob.

"That's all, I think," he murmured to himself. "Stay—I may as well have you—you may come in useful—one never knows." He added a flat silver matchbox to his equipment, glanced at his watch, and seeing that it was already a quarter to three, ran briskly downstairs, and, hailing a taxi, was carried to Battersea Park.

Mr. Alfred Thipps was a small, nervous man, whose flaxen hair was beginning to abandon the unequal struggle with destiny. One might say that his only really marked feature was a large bruise over the left eyebrow, which

*This is the first Florence edition, 1481, by Niccolo di Lorenzo. Lord Peter's collection of printed Dantes is worth inspection. It includes, besides the famous Aldine 8vo, of 1502, the Naples folio of 1477—"edizione rarissima," according to Colomb. This copy has no history, and Mr. Parker's private belief is that its present owner conveyed it away by stealth from somewhere or other. Lord Peter's own account is that he "picked it up in a little place in the hills," when making a walking-tour through Italy.

**Lord Peter's wits were wool-gathering. The book is in the possession of Earl Spencer. The Brocklebury copy is incomplete, the last five signatures being altogether missing, but is unique in possessing the colophon.

gave him a faintly dissipated air incongruous with the rest of his appearance. Almost in the same breath with his first greeting, he made a self-conscious apology for it, murmuring something about having run against the dining-room door in the dark. He was touched almost to tears by Lord Peter's thoughtfulness and condescension in calling.

"I'm sure it's most kind of your lordship," he repeated for the dozenth time, rapidly blinking his weak little eyelids. "I appreciate it very deeply, very deeply, indeed, and so would Mother, only she's so deaf, I don't like to trouble you with making her understand. It's been very hard all day," he added, "with the policemen in the house and all this commotion. It's what Mother and me have never been used to, always living very retired, and it's most distressing to a man of regular habits, my lord, and reely, I'm almost thankful Mother doesn't understand, for I'm sure it would worry her terribly if she was to know about it. She was upset at first, but she's made up some idea of her own about it now, and I'm sure it's all for the best."

The old lady who sat knitting by the fire nodded grimly in response to a look from her son.

"I always said as you ought to complain about that bath, Alfred," she said suddenly, in the high, piping voice peculiar to the deaf, "and it's to be 'oped the landlord'll see about it now; not but what I think you might have managed without having the police in, but there! you always were one to make a fuss about a little thing, from chicken-pox up."

"There now," said Mr. Thipps apologetically, "you see how it is. Not but what it's just as well she's settled on that, because she understands we've locked up the bathroom and don't try to go in there. But it's been a terrible shock to me, sir—my lord, I should say, but there! my nerves are all to pieces. Such a thing has never 'appened—happened to me in all my born days. Such a state I was in this morning—I didn't know if I was on my head or my heels—I reely didn't, and my heart not being too strong, I hardly knew how to get out of that horrid room and telephone for the police. It's affected me, sir, it's affected me, it reely has—I couldn't touch a bit of breakfast, nor lunch neither, and what with telephoning and putting off clients and interviewing people all morning, I've hardly known what to do with myself."

"I'm sure it must have been uncommonly distressin'," said Lord Peter, sympathetically, "especially comin' like that before breakfast. Hate anything tiresome happenin' before breakfast. Takes a man at such a confounded disadvantage, what?"

"That's just it, that's just it," said Mr. Thipps, eagerly. 'When I saw that dreadful thing lying there in my bath, mother-naked, too, except for a pair of eyeglasses, I assure you, my lord, it regularly turned my stomach, if you'll excuse the expression. I'm not very strong, sir, and I get that sinking feeling sometimes in the morning, and what with one thing and another I 'ad—had to send the girl for a stiff brandy, or I don't know *what* mightn't have happened. I felt so queer, though I'm anything but partial to spirits as a rule. Still, I make it a rule never to be without brandy in the house, in case of emergency, you know?"

"Very wise of you," said Lord Peter, cheerfully. "You're a very far-seein' man, Mr. Thipps. Wonderful what a little nip'll do in case of need, and the less you're used to it the more good it does you. Hope your girl is a sensible young woman, what? Nuisance to have women faintin' and shriekin' all over the place."

"Oh, Gladys is a good girl," said Mr. Thipps, "very reasonable indeed. She was shocked, of course; that's very understandable. I was shocked myself, and it wouldn't be proper in a young woman not to be shocked under the circumstances, but she is reely a helpful, energetic girl in a crisis, if you understand me. I consider myself very fortunate these days to have got a good, decent girl to do for me and Mother, even though she is a bit careless and forgetful about little things, but that's only natural. She was very sorry indeed about having left the bathroom window open, she reely was, and though I was angry at first, seeing what's come of it, it wasn't anything to speak of, not in the ordinary way, as you might say. Girls will forget things, you know, my lord, and reely she was so distressed I didn't like to say too much to her. All I said was: 'It might have been burglars,' I said, 'remember that, next time you leave a window open all night; this time it was a dead man,' I said, 'and that's unpleasant enough, but next time it might be burglars,' I said, 'and all of us murdered in our beds.' But the police-inspector—Inspector Sugg, they called him, from the Yard—he was very sharp with her, poor girl. Quite frightened her, and made her think he suspected her of something, though what good a body could be to her, poor girl, I can't imagine, and so I told the Inspector. He was quite rude to me, my lord—I may say I didn't like his manner at all. 'If you've got anything definite to accuse Gladys or me of, Inspector,' I said to him, 'bring it forward, that's what you have to do,' I said, but I've yet to learn that you're paid to be rude to a gentleman in his own 'ouse—house.' Reely," said Mr, Thipps, growing quite pink on the top of his head, "he regularly roused me, regularly roused me, my lord, and I'm a mild man as a rule."

"Sugg all over," said Lord Peter. "I know him. When he don't know what else to say, he's rude. Stands to reason you and the girl wouldn't go collectin' bodies. Who'd want to saddle himself with a body? Difficulty's usually to get rid of 'em. Have you got rid of this one yet, by the way?"

"It's still in the bathroom," said Mr. Thipps. "Inspector Sugg said nothing was to be touched till his men came in to move it. I'm expecting them at any time. If it would interest your lordship to have a look at it—"

"Thanks awfully," said Lord Peter. "I'd like to very much, if I'm not puttin' you out."

"Not at all," said Mr. Thipps. His manner as he led the way along the passage convinced Lord Peter of two things—first, that, gruesome as his exhibit was, he rejoiced in the importance it reflected upon himself and his flat, and secondly, that Inspector Sugg had forbidden him to exhibit it to anyone. The latter supposition was confirmed by the action of Mr. Thipps, who stopped to fetch the door-key from his bedroom, saying that the police had the other, but that he made it a rule to have two keys to every door, in case of accident.

The bathroom was in no way remarkable. It was long and narrow, the window being exactly over the head of the bath. The panes were of frosted glass; the frame wide enough to admit a man's body. Lord Peter stepped rapidly across to it, opened it and looked out.

The flat was the top one of the building and situated about the middle of the block. The bathroom window looked out upon the back-yards of the flats, which were occupied by various small outbuildings, coal-holes, garages, and the like. Beyond these were the back gardens of a parallel line of houses. On the right rose the extensive edifice of St. Luke's Hospital, Battersea, with its grounds, and, connected with it by a covered way, the residence of the famous surgeon, Sir Julian Freke, who directed the surgical side of the great new hospital, and was, in addition, known in Harley Street as a distinguished neurologist with a highly individual point of view.

This information was poured into Lord Peter's ear at considerable length by Mr. Thipps, who seemed to feel that the neighbourhood of anybody so distinguished shed a kind of halo of glory over Queen Caroline Mansions.

"We had him round here himself this morning," he said, "about this horrid business. Inspector Sugg thought one of the young medical gentlemen at the hospital might have brought the corpse round for a joke, as you might say, they always having bodies in the dissecting-room. So Inspector Sugg went round to see Sir Julian this morning to ask if there was a body missing. He was very kind, was Sir Julian, very kind indeed, though he was at work when they got there, in the dissecting-room. He looked up the books to see that all the bodies were accounted for, and then very obligingly came round here to look at this"—he indicated the bath—"and said he was afraid he couldn't help us—there was no corpse missing from the hospital, and this one didn't answer to the description of any they'd had."

"Nor to the description of any of the patients, I hope," suggested Lord Peter casually.

At this grisly hint Mr. Thipps turned pale.

"I didn't hear Inspector Sugg inquire," he said, with some agitation. "What a very horrid thing that would be—God bless my soul, my lord, I never thought of it."

"Well, if they have missed a patient they'd probably have discovered it by now," said Lord Peter. "Let's have a look at this one."

He screwed his monocle into his eye, adding: "I see you're troubled here with the soot blowing in. Beastly nuisance, ain't it? I get it too—spoils all my books, you know. Here, don't you trouble, if you don't care about lookin' at it."

He took from Mr. Thipps's hesitating hand the sheet which had been flung over the bath and turned it back.

The body which lay in the bath was that of a tall, stout man of about fifty. The hair, which was thick and black and naturally curly, had been cut and parted by a master hand, and exuded a faint violet perfume, perfectly recognisable in the close air of the bathroom. The features were thick, fleshy and strongly marked, with prominent dark eyes, and a long nose curving down to a heavy chin. The clean-shaven lips were full and sensual, and the dropped jaw showed teeth stained with tobacco. On the dead face the handsome pair of gold pince-nez mocked death with grotesque elegance; the fine gold chain carved over the naked breast. The legs lay stiffly stretched out side by side; the arms reposed close to the body; the fingers were flexed naturally. Lord Peter lifted one arm, and looked at the hand with a little frown.

"Bit of a dandy, your visitor, what?" he murmured. "Parma violet and manicure." He bent again, slipping his hand beneath the head. The absurd eye-glasses slipped off, clattering into the bath, and the noise put the last touch to Mr. Thipps's growing nervousness.

"If you'll excuse me," he murmured, "it makes me feel quite faint, it reely does."

He slipped outside, and he had no sooner done so than Lord Peter, lifting the body quickly and cautiously, turned it over and inspected it with his head on one side, bringing his monocle into play with the air of the late Joseph Chamberlain approving a rare orchid. He then laid the head over his arm, and bringing out the silver matchbox from his pocket, slipped it into the open mouth. Then making the noise usually written "Tut-tut," he laid the body down, picked up the mysterious pince-nez, looked at it, put it on his nose and looked through it, made the same noise again, readjusted the pince-nez upon the nose of the corpse, so as to leave no traces of interference for the irritation of Inspector Sugg, rearranged the body, returned to the window and, leaning out, reached upwards and sideways with his walking-stick, which he had somewhat incongruously brought along with him. Nothing appearing to come of these investigations, he withdrew his head, closed the window, and rejoined Mr. Thipps in the passage.

Mr. Thipps, touched by this sympathetic interest in the younger son of a duke, took the liberty, on their return to the sitting-room, of offering him a cup of tea. Lord Peter, who had strolled over to the window and was admiring the outlook on Battersea Park, was about to accept, when an ambulance came into view at the end of Prince of Wales Road. Its appearance reminded Lord Peter of an important engagement, and with a hurried "By Jove" he took his leave of Mr. Thipps.

"My mother sent kind regards and all that," he said, shaking hands fervently; "hopes you'll soon be down at Denver again. Good-bye, Mrs. Thipps," he bawled kindly into the ear of the old lady. "Oh, no, my dear sir, please don't trouble to come down."

He was none too soon. As he stepped out of the door and turned towards the station, the ambulance drew up from the other direction, and Inspector Sugg emerged from it with two constables. The Inspector spoke to the officer on duty at the Mansions, and turned a suspicious gaze on Lord Peter's retreating back.

"Dear old Sugg," said that nobleman, fondly, "dear, dear old bird! How he does hate me, to be sure."

## 2

"EXCELLENT, BUNTER," said Lord Peter, sinking with a sigh into a luxurious armchair. "I couldn't have done better myself. The thought of the Dante makes my mouth water–and the 'Four Sons of Aymon.' And you've saved me £60–that's glorious. What shall we spend it on, Bunter? Think of it–all ours, to do as we like with, for as Harold Skimpole so rightly observes, £60 saved is £60 gained, and I'd reckoned on spending it all. It's your saving, Bunter, and properly speaking, your £60. What do we want? Anything in your department? Would you like anything altered in the flat?"

"Well, my lord, as your lordship is so good"–the man-servant paused, about to pour an old brandy into a liqueur glass.

"Well, out with it, my Bunter, you imperturbable old hypocrite. It's no good talking as if you were announcing dinner–you're spilling the brandy. The voice is Jacob's voice, but the hands are the hands of Esau. What does that blessed darkroom of yours want now?"

"There's a Double Anastigmat with a set of supplementary lenses, my lord," said Bunter, with a note almost of religious fervour. "If it was a case of forgery now–or footprints–I could enlarge them right up on the plate. Or the side-angled lens would be useful. It's as though the camera had eyes at the back of its head, my lord. Look–I've got it here."

He pulled a catalogue from his pocket, and submitted it, quivering, to his employer's gaze.

Lord Peter perused the description slowly, the corners of his long mouth lifted into a faint smile.

"It's Greek to me," he said, "and £50 seems a ridiculous price for a few bits of glass. I suppose, Bunter, you'd say £750 was a bit out of the way for a dirty old book in a dead language, wouldn't you?"

"It wouldn't be my place to say so, my lord."

"No, Bunter, I pay you £200 a year to keep your thoughts to yourself. Tell me, Bunter, in these democratic days, don't you think that's unfair?"

"No, my lord."

'You don't. D'you mind telling me frankly why you don't think it unfair?"

"Frankly, my lord, your lordship is paid a nobleman's income to take Lady Worthington in to dinner and refrain from exercising your lordship's undoubted powers of repartee."

Lord Peter considered this.

"That's your idea is it, Bunter? Noblesse oblige–for a consideration. I daresay you're right. Then you're better off than I am, because I'd have to behave myself to Lady Worthington if I hadn't a penny. Bunter, if I sacked you here and now, would you tell me what you think of me?"

"No, my lord."

"You'd have a perfect right to, my Bunter, and if I sacked you on top of drinking the kind of coffee you make, I'd deserve everything you could say of me. You're a demon for coffee, Bunter–I don't want to know how you do it, because I believe it to be witchcraft, and I don't want to burn eternally. You can buy your cross-eyed lens."

"Thank you, my lord."

"Have you finished in the dining-room?"

"Not quite, my lord."

"Well, come back when you have. I have many things to tell you. Hullo! who's that?"

The doorbell had rung sharply.

"Unless it's anybody interestin' I'm not at home."

"Very good, my lord."

Lord Peter's library was one of the most delightful bachelor rooms in London. Its scheme was black and primrose. Its walls were lined with rare editions, and its chairs and Chesterfield sofa suggested the embraces of the houris. In one corner stood a black baby grand, a wood fire leaped on a wide old-fashioned hearth, and the Sèvres vases on the chimneypiece were filled with ruddy and gold chrysanthemums. To the eyes of the young man who was ushered in from the raw November fog it seemed not only rare and unattainable, but friendly and familiar, like a colourful and gilded paradise in a mediaeval painting.

"Mr. Parker, my lord."

Lord Peter jumped up with genuine eagerness.

"My dear man, I'm delighted to see you. What a beastly foggy night, ain't it? Bunter, some more of that admirable coffee and another glass and the cigars. Parker, I hope you're full of crime–nothing less than arson or murder will do for us tonight. 'On such a night as this–' Bunter and I were just sitting down to carouse. I've got a Dante, and a Caxton folio that is practically unique, at Sir Ralph Brocklebury's sale. Bunter, who did the bargaining, is going to have a lens which does all kinds of wonderful things with its eyes shut, and

> We both have got a body in a bath,
> We both have got a body in a bath–
> For in spite of all temptations,
> To go in for cheap sensations
> We insist upon a body in a bath–

Nothing less will do for us, Parker. It's mine at present, but we're going shares in it. Property of the firm. Won't you join us? You really must put *something* in the jack-pot. Perhaps you have a body. Oh, do have a body. Every body welcome.

> Gin a body meet a body
> Hauled before the beak,
> Gin a body jolly well knows who murdered
> a body and that old Sugg is on the
> wrong track,
> Need a body speak?

Not a bit of it. He tips a glassy wink to yours truly and yours truly reads the truth."

"Ah," said Parker, "I knew you'd been round to Queen Caroline Mansions. So've I, and met Sugg, and he told me he'd seen you. He was cross, too. Unwarrantable interference, he calls it."

"I knew he would," said Lord Peter. "I love taking a rise out of dear old Sugg, he's always so rude. I see by the *Star* that he has excelled himself by taking the girl, Gladys What's-her-name, into custody. Sugg of the evening, beautiful Sugg! But what were *you* doing there?"

"To tell you the truth," said Parker, "I went round to see if the Semitic-looking stranger in Mr. Thipp's bath was by any extraordinary chance Sir Reuben Levy. But he isn't."

"Sir Reuben Levy? Wait a minute, I saw something about that, I know! A headline: 'Mysterious disappearance of famous financier.' What's it all about? I didn't read it carefully."

"Well, it's a bit odd, though I daresay it's nothing really–old chap may have cleared for some reason best known to himself. It only happened this morning, and nobody would have thought anything about it, only it happened to be the day on which he had arranged to attend a most important financial meeting and do some deal involving millions–I haven't got all the details. But I know he's got enemies who'd just as soon the deal didn't come off, so when I got wind of this fellow in the bath, I buzzed round to have a look at him. It didn't seem likely, of course, but unlikelier things do happen in our profession. The funny thing is, old Sugg had got bitten with the idea it *is* him, and is wildly telegraphing to Lady Levy to come and identify him. But as a matter of fact, the man in the bath is no more Sir Reuben Levy than

Adolf Beck, poor devil, was John Smith. Oddly enough, though, he would be really extraordinarily like Sir Reuben if he had a beard, and as Lady Levy is abroad with the family, somebody may say it's him, and Sugg will build up a lovely theory, like the Tower of Babel, and destined so to perish."

"Sugg's a beautiful, braying ass," said Lord Peter. "He's like a detective in a novel. Well, I don't know anything about Levy, but I've seen the body, and I should say the idea was preposterous upon the face of it. What do you think of the brandy?"

"Unbelievable, Wimsey–sort of thing makes one believe in heaven. But I want your yarn."

"D'you mind if Bunter hears it, too? Invaluable man, Bunter–amazin' fellow with a camera. And the odd thing is, he's always on the spot when I want my bath or my boots. I don't know when he develops things–I believe he does 'em in his sleep. Bunter!"

"Yes, my lord."

"Stop fiddling about in there, and get yourself the proper things to drink and join the merry throng."

"Certainly, my lord."

"Mr. Parker has a new trick: The Vanishing Financier. Absolutely no deception. Hey, presto, pass! and where is he? Will some gentleman from the audience kindly step upon the platform and inspect the cabinet? Thank you, sir. The quickness of the 'and deceives the heye."

"I'm afraid mine isn't much of a story," said Parker. "It's just one of those simple things that offer no handle. Sir Reuben Levy dined last night with three friends at the Ritz. After dinner the friends went to the theatre. He refused to go with them on account of an appointment. I haven't yet been able to trace the appointment, but anyhow, he returned home to his house–9a, Park Lane–at twelve o'clock."

"Who saw him?"

"The cook, who had just gone up to bed, saw him on the doorstep, and heard him let himself in. He walked upstairs, leaving his greatcoat on the hall peg and his umbrella in the stand–you remember how it rained last night. He undressed and went to bed. Next morning he wasn't there. That's all," said Parker abruptly, with a wave of the hand.

"It isn't all, it isn't all. Daddy, go on, that's not *half* a story," pleaded Lord Peter.

"But it *is* all. When his man came to call him he wasn't there. The bed had been slept in. His pajamas and all his clothes were there, the only odd thing being that they were thrown rather untidily on the ottoman at the foot of the bed, instead of being neatly folded on a chair, as is Sir Reuben's custom–looking as though he had been rather agitated or unwell. No clean clothes were missing, no suit, no boots–nothing. The boots he had worn were in his dressing-room as usual. He had washed and cleaned his teeth and done all the usual things. The housemaid was down cleaning the hall at half-past six, and can swear that nobody came in or out after that. So one is forced to suppose that a respectable middle-aged Hebrew financier either went mad between twelve and six a.m.. and walked quietly out of the house in his birthday suit on a November night, or else was spirited away like the lady in the 'Ingoldsby Legends,' body and bones, leaving only a heap of crumpled clothes behind him."

"Was the front door bolted?"

"That's the sort of question you *would* ask, straight off; it took me an hour to think of it. No; contrary to custom, there was only the Yale lock on the door. On the other hand, some of the maids had been given leave to go to the theatre, and Sir Reuben may quite conceivably have left the door open under the impression they had not come in. Such a thing has happened before."

"And that's really all?"

"Really all. Except for one very trifling circumstance."

"I love trifling circumstances," said Lord Peter, with childish delight; "so many men have been hanged by trifling circumstances. What was it?"

"Sir Reuben and Lady Levy, who are a most devoted couple, always share the same room. Lady Levy, as I said before, is in Mentonne at the moment for her health. In her absence, Sir Reuben sleeps in the double bed as usual, and invariably on his own side–the outside–of the bed. Last night he put the two pillows together and slept in the middle, or, if anything, rather closer to the wall than otherwise. The housemaid, who is a most intelligent girl, noticed this when she went up to make the bed, and, with really admirable detective instinct, refused to touch the bed or let anybody else touch it, though it wasn't till later that they actually sent for the police."

"Was anybody in the house but Sir Reuben and the servants ?"

"No; Lady Levy was away with her daughter and her maid. The valet, cook, parlourmaid, housemaid and kitchenmaid were the only people in the house, and naturally wasted an hour or two squawking and gossiping. I got there about ten."

"What have you been doing since?"

"Trying to get on the track of Sir Reuben's appointment last night, since, with the exception of the cook, his 'appointer' was the last person who saw him before his disappearance. There may be some quite simple explanation, though I'm dashed if I can think of one for the moment. Hang it all, a man doesn't come in and go to bed and walk away again 'mid nodings on' in the middle of the night."

"He may have been disguised."

"I thought of that–in fact, it seems the only possible explanation. But it's deuced odd, Wimsey. An important city man, on the eve of an important transaction, without a word of warning to anybody, slips off in the middle of the night, disguised down to his skin, leaving behind his watch, purse, chequebook, and–most mysterious and important of all–his spectacles, without which he can't see a step, as he is extremely short-sighted. He–"

"That *is* important," interrupted Wimsey. "You are sure he didn't take a second pair?"

"His man vouches for it that he had only two pairs, one of which was found on his dressing-table, and the other in the drawer where it is always kept."

Lord Peter whistled.

"You've got me there, Parker. Even if he'd gone out to commit suicide he'd have taken those."

"So you'd think–or the suicide would have happened the first time he started to cross the road. However, I didn't overlook the possibility. I've got particulars of all today's street accidents, and I can lay my hand on my heart and say that none of them is Sir Reuben. Besides, he took his latchkey with him, which looks as though he'd meant to come back."

"Have you seen the men he dined with?"

"I found two of them at the club. They said that he seemed in the best of health and spirits, spoke of looking forward to joining Lady Levy later on–perhaps at Christmas–and referred with great satisfaction to this morning's business transaction, in which one of them—a man called Anderson of Wyndham's—was himself concerned."

"Then up till about nine o'clock, anyhow, he had no apparent intention or expectation of disappearing."

"None—unless he was a most consummate actor. Whatever happened to change his mind must have happened either at the mysterious appointment which he kept after dinner, or while he was in bed between midnight and 5.30 a.m."

"Well, Bunter," said Lord Peter, "what do you make of it?"

"Not in my department, my lord. Except that it is odd that a gentleman who was too flurried or unwell to fold his clothes as usual should remember to clean his teeth and put his boots out. Those are two things that quite frequently get overlooked, my lord."

"If you mean anything personal, Bunter," said Lord Peter, "I can only say that I think the speech an unworthy one. It's a sweet little problem, Parker mine. Look here, I don't want to butt in, but I should dearly love to see that bedroom tomorrow. 'Tis not that I mistrust thee, dear, but I should uncommonly like to see it. Say me not nay—take another drop of brandy and a Villar Villar, but say not, say not nay!"

"Of course you can come and see it—you'll probably find lots of things I've overlooked," said the other, equably, accepting the proffered hospitality.

"Parker, acushla, you're an honour to Scotland Yard. I look at you, and Sugg appears a myth, a fable, an idiot-boy, spawned in a moonlight hour by some fantastic poet's brain. Sugg is too perfect to be possible. What does he make of the body, by the way?"

"Sugg says," replied Parker, with precision, "that the body died from a blow on the back of the neck. The doctor told him that. He says it's been dead a day or two. The doctor told him that, too. He says it's the body of a well-to-do Hebrew of about fifty. Anybody could have told him that. He says it's ridiculous to suppose it came in through the window without anybody knowing anything about it. He says it probably walked in through the front door and was murdered by the household. He's arrested the girl because she's short and frail-looking and quite unequal to downing a tall and sturdy Semite with a poker. He'd arrest Thipps, only Thipps was away in Manchester all yesterday and the day before and didn't come back till late last night—in fact, he wanted to arrest him till I reminded him that if the body had been a day or two dead, little Thipps couldn't have done him in at 10.30 last night. But he'll arrest him tomorrow as an accessory—and the old lady with the knitting, too, I shouldn't wonder."

"Well, I'm glad the little man has so much of an alibi," said Lord Peter, "though if you're only gluing your faith to cadaveric lividity, rigidity, and all the other quiddities, you must be prepared to have some sceptical beast of a prosecuting counsel walk slapbang through the medical evidence. Remember Impey Biggs defending in that Chelsea tea-shop affair? Six bloomin' medicos contradictin' each other in the box, an' old Impey elocutin' abnormal cases from Glaister and Dixon Mann till the eyes of the jury reeled in their heads! 'Are you prepared to swear, Dr. Thingumtight, that the onset of rigor mortis indicates the hour of death without the possibility of error?' 'So far as my experience goes, in the majority of cases,' says the doctor, all stiff. 'Ah!' says Biggs, but this is a Court of Justice, Doctor, not a Parliamentary election. We can't get on without a minority report. The law, Dr. Thingumtight, respects the rights of the minority, alive or dead.' Some ass laughs, and old Biggs sticks his chest out and gets impressive. 'Gentlemen, this is no laughing matter. My client–an upright and honourable gentleman–is being tried for his life–for his life, gentlemen–and it is the business of the prosecution to show his guilt–if they can–without a shadow of doubt. Now, Dr. Thingumtight, I ask you again, can you solemnly swear, without the least shadow of doubt,–probable, possible shadow of doubt–that this unhappy woman met her death neither sooner nor later than Thursday evening? A probable opinion? Gentlemen, we are not Jesuits, we are straightforward Englishmen. You cannot ask a British-born jury to convict any man on the authority of a probable opinion.' Hum of applause."

"Biggs's man was guilty all the same," said Parker.

"Of course he was. But he was acquitted all the same, an' what you've just said is libel." Wimsey walked over to the bookshelf and took down a volume of Medical Jurisprudence. " 'Rigor mortis–can only be stated in a very general way–many factors determine the result.' Cautious brute. 'On the average, however, stiffening will have begun–neck and jaw–5 to 6 hours after death'–m'm–'in all likelihood have passed off in the bulk of cases by the end of 36 hours. Under certain circumstances, however, it may appear unusually early, or be retarded unusually long!' Helpful ain't it, Parker? 'Brown-Séquard states . . . 3½ minutes after death. . . . In certain cases not until lapse of 16 hours after death . . . present as long as 21 days thereafter.' Lord! 'Modifying factors–age–muscular state–or febrile diseases–or where temperature of environment is high'–and so on and so on–any bloomin' thing. Never mind. You can run the argument for what it's worth to Sugg. *He* won't know any better." He tossed the book away. "Come back to facts. What did *you* make of the body?"

"Well," said the detective, "not very much–I was puzzled–frankly. I should say he had been a rich man, but self-made, and that his good fortune had come to him fairly recently."

"Ah, you noticed the calluses on the hands–I thought you wouldn't miss that."

"Both his feet were badly blistered–he had been wearing tight shoes."

"Walking a long way in them, too," said Lord Peter, "to get such blisters as that. Didn't that strike you as odd, in a person evidently well off?"

"Well, I don't know. The blisters were two or three days old. He might have got stuck in the suburbs one night, perhaps–last train gone and no taxi–and had to walk home."

"Possibly."

"There were some little red marks all over his back and one leg I couldn't quite account for."

"I saw them."

"What did you make of them?"

"I'll tell you afterwards. Go on."

"He was very long-sighted–oddly long-sighted for a man in the prime of life; the glasses were like a very old man's. By the way, they had a very beautiful and remarkable chain of flat links chased with a pattern. It struck me he might be traced through it."

"I've just put an advertisement in the *Times* about it," said Lord Peter. "Go on."

"He had had the glasses some time–they had been mended twice."

"Beautiful, Parker, beautiful. Did you realize the importance of that?"

"Not specially, I'm afraid–why?"

"Never mind—go on."

"He was probably a sullen, ill-tempered man—his nails were filed down to the quick as though he habitually bit them, and his fingers were bitten as well. He smoked quantities of cigarettes without a holder. He was particular about his personal appearance."

"Did you examine the room at all? I didn't get a chance."

"I couldn't find much in the way of footprints. Sugg & Co. had tramped all over the place, to say nothing of little Thipps and the maid, but I noticed a very indefinite patch just behind the head of the bath, as though something damp might have stood there. You could hardly call it a print."

"It rained hard all last night, of course."

"Yes; did you notice that the soot on the windowsill was vaguely marked?"

"I did," said Wimsey, "and I examined it hard with this little fellow, but I could make nothing of it except that something or other had rested on the sill." He drew out his monocle and handed it to Parker.

"My word, that's a powerful lens."

"It is," said Wimsey, "and jolly useful when you want to take a good squint at somethin' and look like a bally fool all the time. Only it don't do to wear it permanently—if people see you full-face they say: 'Dear me! how weak the sight of that eye must be!' Still, it's useful."

"Sugg and I explored the ground at the back of the building," went on Parker, 'but there wasn't a trace."

"That's interestin'. Did you try the roof?"

"No."

"We'll go over it tomorrow. The gutter's only a couple of feet off the top of the window. I measured it with my stick—the gentleman-scout's vademecum, I call it—it's marked off in inches. Uncommonly handy companion at times. There's a sword inside and a compass in the head. Got it made specially. Anything more?"

"Afraid not. Let's hear your version, Wimsey."

"Well, I think you've got most of the points. There are just one or two little contradictions. For instance, here's a man wears expensive gold-rimmed pince-nez and has had them long enough to be mended twice. Yet his teeth are not merely discoloured, but badly decayed and look as if he'd never cleaned them in his life. There are four molars missing on one side and three on the other and one front tooth broken right across. He's a man careful of his personal appearance, as witness his hair and his hands. What do you say to that?"

"Oh, these self-made men of low origin don't think much about teeth, and are terrified of dentists."

"True; but one of the molars has a broken edge so rough that it had made a sore place on the tongue. Nothing's more painful. D'you mean to tell me a man would put up with that if he could afford to get the tooth filed?"

"Well, people are queer. I've known servants endure agonies rather than step over a dentist's doormat. How did you see that, Wimsey?"

"Had a look inside; electric torch," said Lord Peter. "Handy little gadget. Looks like a matchbox. Well—I daresay it's all right, but I just draw your attention to it. Second point: Gentleman with hair smellin' of Parma violet and manicured hands and all the rest of it, never washes the inside of his ears. Full of wax. Nasty."

"You've got me there, Wimsey; I never noticed it. Still—old bad habits die hard."

"Right oh! Put it down at that. Third point: Gentleman with the manicure and the brilliantine and all the rest of it suffers from fleas."

"By Jove, you're right! Flea-bites. It never occurred to me."

"No doubt about it, old son. The marks were faint and old, but unmistakable."

"Of course, now you mention it. Still, that might happen to anybody. I loosed a whopper in the best hotel in Lincoln the week before last. I hope it bit the next occupier!"

"Oh, all these things *might* happen to anybody—separately. Fourth point: Gentleman who used Parma violet for his hair, etc., etc., washes his body in strong carbolic soap—so strong that the smell hangs about twenty-four hours later."

"Carbolic to get rid of the fleas."

"I will say for you, Parker, you've an answer for everything. Fifth point: Carefully got-up gentleman, with manicured, though masticated, finger-nails, has filthy black toenails which look as if they hadn't been cut for years."

"All of a piece with habits as indicated."

"Yes, I know, but such habits! Now, sixth and last point: This gentleman with the intermittently gentlemanly habits arrives in the middle of a pouring wet night, and apparently through the window, when he has already been twenty-four hours dead and lies down quietly in Mr. Thipps's bath, unseasonably dressed in a pair of pince-nez. Not a hair on his head is ruffled—the hair has been cut so recently that there are quite a number of little short hairs stuck on his neck and the sides of the bath—and he has shaved so recently that there is a line of dried soap on his cheek—"

"Wimsey!"

"Wait a minute—and *dried soap in his mouth*."

Bunter got up and appeared suddenly at the detective's elbow, the respectful man-servant all over.

"A little more brandy, sir?" he murmured.

"Wimsey," said Parker, "you are making me feel cold all over." He emptied his glass—stared at it as though he were surprised to find it empty, set it down, got up, walked across to the bookcase, turned round, stood with his back against it and said:

"Look here, Wimsey—you've been reading detective stories; you're talking nonsense."

"No, I ain't," said Lord Peter, sleepily, "uncommon good incident for a detective story, though, what? Bunter, we'll write one, and you shall illustrate it with photographs."

"Soap in his—Rubbish!" said Parker. "It was something else—some discolouration—"

"No," said Lord Peter, "there were hairs as well. Bristly ones. He had a beard."

He took his watch from his pocket, and drew out a couple of longish, stiff hairs, which he had imprisoned between the inner and the outer case.

Parker turned them over once or twice in his fingers, looked at them close to the light, examined them with a lens, handed them to the impassible Bunter, and said:

"Do you mean to tell me, Wimsey, that any man alive would"—he laughed harshly—"shave off his beard with his mouth open, and then go and get killed with his mouth full of hairs? You're mad."

"I don't tell you so," said Wimsey. "You policemen are all alike—only one idea in your skulls. Blest if I can make out why you're ever appointed. He was shaved after he was dead. Pretty, ain't it? Uncommonly jolly little job for the barber, what? Here, sit down, man, and don't be an ass, stumpin' about the room like that. Worse things happen in war. This is only a blinkin' old shillin' shocker. But I'll tell you what, Parker, we're up against a criminal–*the* criminal–the real artist and blighter with imagination–real, artistic, finished stuff. I'm enjoyin' this, Parker."

# 3

Lord Peter finished a Scarlatti sonata, and sat looking thoughtfully at his own hands. The fingers were long and muscular, with wide, flat joints and square tips. When he was playing, his rather hard grey eyes softened, and his long, indeterminate mouth hardened in compensation. At no other time had he any pretensions to good looks, and at all times he was spoilt by a long, narrow chin, and a long, receding forehead, accentuated by the brushed-back sleekness of his tow-coloured hair. Labour papers, softening down the chin, caricatured him as a typical aristocrat.

"That's a wonderful instrument," said Parker.

"It ain't so bad," said Lord Peter, 'but Scarlatti wants a harpsichord. Piano's too modern–all thrills and overtones. No good for our job, Parker. Have you come to any conclusion?"

"The man in the bath," said Parker, methodically, "was not a well-off man careful of his personal appearance. He was a labouring man, unemployed, but who had only recently lost his employment. He had been tramping about looking for a job when he met with his end. Somebody killed him and washed him and scented him and shaved him in order to disguise him, and put him into Thipp's bath without leaving a trace. Conclusion: the murderer was a powerful man, since he killed him with a single blow on the neck, a man of cool head and masterly intellect, since he did all that ghastly business without leaving a mark, a man of wealth and refinement, since he had all the apparatus of an elegant toilet handy, and a man of bizarre, and almost perverted imagination, as is shown in the two horrible touches of putting the body in the bath and of adorning it with a pair of pince-nez.

"He is a poet of crime," said Wimsey. "By the way, your diffculty about the pince-nez is cleared up. Obviously, the pince-nez never belonged to the body."

"That only makes a fresh puzzle. One can't suppose the murderer left them in that obliging manner as a clue to his own identity."

"We can hardly suppose that; I'm afraid this man possessed what most criminals lack–a sense of humour."

"Rather macabre humour."

"True. But a man who can afford to be humourous at all in such circumstances is a terrible fellow. I wonder what he did with the body between the murder and depositing it chez Thipps. Then there are more questions. How did he get it there? And why? Was it brought in at the door, as Sugg of our heart suggests? or through the window, as we think on the not very adequate testimony of a smudge on the windowsill? Had the murderer accomplices? Is little Thipps really in it, or the girl? It don't do to put the notion out of course merely because Sugg inclines to it. Even idiots occasionally speak the truth accidentally. If not, why was Thipps selected for such an abominable practical joke? Has anybody got a grudge against Thipps? Who are the people in the other flats? We must find out that. Does Thipps play the piano at midnight over their heads or damage the reputation of the staircase by bringing home dubiously respectable ladies? Are there unsuccessful architects thirsting for his blood? Damn it all, Parker, there must be a motive somewhere. Can't have a crime without a motive, you know."

"A madman–" suggested Parker, doubtfully.

"With a deuced lot of method in his madness. He hasn't made a mistake–not one, unless leaving hairs in the corpse's mouth can be called a mistake. Well, anyhow, it's not Levy–you're right there. I say, old thing, neither your man nor mine has left much clue to go upon, has he? And there don't seem to be any motives knockin' about, either. And we seem to be two suits of clothes short in last night's work. Sir Reuben makes tracks without so much as a fig-leaf, and a mysterious individual turns up with a pince-nez, which is quite useless for purposes of decency. Dash it all! If only I had some good excuse for takin' up this body case officially–"

The telephone bell rang. The silent Bunter, whom the other two had almost forgotten, padded across to it.

"It's an elderly lady, my lord," he said. "I think she's deaf–I can't make her hear anything, but she's asking for your lordship."

Lord Peter seized the receiver, and yelled into it a "Hullo!" that might have cracked the vulcanite. He listened for some minutes with an incredulous smile, which gradually broadened into a grin of delight. At length he screamed: "All right! all right!" several times and rang off.

"By Jove!" he announced, beaming, "sportin' old bird! It's old Mrs. Thipps. Deaf as a post. Never used the 'phone before. But determined. Perfect Napoleon. The incomparable Sugg has made a discovery and arrested little Thipps. Old lady abandoned in the flat. Thipp's last shriek to her: 'Tell Lord Peter Wimsey.' Old girl undaunted. Wrestles with telephone book. Wakes up the people at the exchange. Won't take no for an answer (not bein' able to hear it), gets through, says: 'Will I do what I can?' Says she would feel safe in the hands of a real gentleman. Oh, Parker, Parker! I could kiss her, I reely could, as Thipps says. I'll write to her instead–no, hang it, Parker, we'll go round. Bunter, get your infernal machine and the magnesium. I say, we'll all go into partnership–pool the two cases and work 'em out together. You shall see my body tonight, Parker, and I'll look for your wandering Jew tomorrow. I feel so happy, I shall explode. O Sugg, Sugg, how art thou suggified! Bunter, my shoes, I say, Parker, I suppose yours are rubber-soled. Not? Tut, tut, you mustn't go out like that. We'll lend you a pair. Gloves? Here. My stick, my torch, the lampblack, the forceps, knife, pillboxes–all complete?"

"Certainly, my lord."

"Oh Bunter, don't look so offended. I mean no harm. I believe in you, I trust you–what money have I got? That'll do. I knew a man once, Parker, who let a world-famous poisoner slip through his fingers because the machine on the Underground took nothing but pennies. There was a queue at the booking office and the man at the barrier stopped him, and while they were arguing about accepting a five-pound-note (which was all he had) for a two-penny ride to Baker Street, the criminal had sprung into a Circle train, and was next heard of in Constantinople, disguised as an elderly Church of England clergyman touring with his niece. Are we all ready? Go!"

They stepped out, Bunter carefully switching off the lights behind them.

As they emerged into the gloom and gleam of Piccadilly, Wimsey stopped short with a little exclamation.

"Wait a second," he said. "I've thought of something. If Sugg's there he'll make trouble. I must short-circuit him."

He ran back, and the other two men employed the few minutes of his absence in capturing a taxi.

Inspector Sugg and a subordinate Cerberus were on guard at 59, Queen Caroline Mansions, and showed no disposition to admit unofficial inquirers. Parker, indeed, they could not easily turn away, but Lord Peter found himself confronted with a surly manner and what Lord Beaconsfield described as a masterly inactivity. It was in vain that Lord Peter pleaded that he had been retained by Mrs. Thipps on behalf of her son.

"Retained!" said Inspector Sugg, with a snort. "*She'll* be retained if she doesn't look out. Shouldn't wonder if she wasn't in it herself, only she's so deaf, she's no good for anything at all."

"Look here, Inspector," said Lord Peter, "what's the use of bein' so bally obstructive? You'd much better let me in—you know I'll get there in the end. Dash it all, it's not as if I was takin' the bread out of your children's mouths. Nobody paid me for finding Lord Attenbury's emeralds for you."

"It's my duty to keep out the public," said Inspector Sugg, morosely, "and it's going to stay out."

"I never said anything about your keeping out of the public," said Lord Peter, easily, sitting down on the staircase to thrash the matter out comfortably, "though I've no doubt pussyfoot's a good thing, on principle, if not exaggerated. The golden mean, Sugg, as Aristotle says, keeps you from bein' a golden ass. Ever been a golden ass, Sugg? I have. It would take a whole rose-garden to cure me, Sugg—

" 'You are my garden of beautiful roses,
My own rose, my one rose, that's you!' "

"I'm not going to stay any longer talking to you," said the harassed Sugg; "it's bad enough— Hullo, drat that telephone. Here, Cawthorn, go and see what it is, if that old catamaran will let you into the room. Shutting herself up there and screaming," said the Inspector, "it's enough to make a man give up crime and take to hedging and ditching."

The constable came back:

"It's from the Yard, sir," he said, coughing apologetically; "the chief says every facility is to be given to Lord Peter Wimsey, sir. Um!" He stood apart noncommittally, glazing his eyes.

"Five aces," said Lord Peter, cheerfully. "The Chief's a dear friend of my mother's. No go, Sugg, it's no good buckin'; you've got a full house. I'm goin' to make it a bit fuller."

He walked in with his followers.

The body had been removed a few hours previously, and when the bathroom and the whole flat had been explored by the naked eye and the camera of the competent Bunter, it became evident that the real problem of the household was old Mrs. Thipps. Her son and servant had both been removed, and it appeared that they had no friends in town, beyond a few business acquaintances of Thipps's, whose very addresses the old lady did not know. The other flats in the building were occupied respectively by a family of seven, at present departed to winter abroad, an elderly Indian colonel of ferocious manners, who lived alone with an Indian man-servant, and a highly respectable family on the third floor, whom the disturbance over their heads had outraged to the last degree. The husband, indeed, when appealed to by Lord Peter, showed a little human weakness, but Mrs. Appledore, appearing suddenly in a warm dressing-gown, extricated him from the difficulties into which he was carelessly wandering.

"I am sorry," she said, "I'm afraid we can't interfere in any way. This is a very unpleasant business, Mr.–I'm afraid I didn't catch your name, and we have always found it better not to be mixed up with the police. Of course, *if* the Thippses are innocent, and I am sure I hope they are, it is very unfortunate for them, but I must say that the circumstances seem to me most suspicious, and to Theophilus too, and I should not like to have it said that we had assisted murderers. We might even be supposed to be accessories. Of course you are young, Mr.–"

"This is Lord Peter Wimsey, my dear," said Theophilus mildly.

She was unimpressed.

"Ah, yes," she said, "I believe you are distantly related to my late cousin, the Bishop of Carisbrooke. Poor man! He was always being taken in by impostors; he died without ever learning any better. I imagine you take after him, Lord Peter."

"I doubt it," said Lord Peter. "So far as I know he is only a connection, though it's a wise child that knows its own father. I congratulate you, dear lady, on takin' after the other side of the family. You'll forgive my buttin' in upon you like this in the middle of the night, though, as you say, it's all in the family, and I'm sure I'm very much obliged to you, and for permittin' me to admire that awfully fetchin' thing you've got on. Now, don't you worry, Mr. Appledore. I'm thinkin' the best thing I can do is to trundle the old lady down to my mother and take her out of your way, otherwise you might be findin' your Christian feelin's gettin' the better of you some fine day, and there's nothin' like Christian feelin's for upsettin' a man's domestic comfort. Good-night, sir–good-night, dear lady–it's simply rippin' of you to let me drop in like this."

"Well!" said Mrs. Appledore, as the door closed behind him.

And–

"I thank the goodness and the grace
That on my birth have smiled,"

said Lord Peter, "and taught me to be bestially impertinent when I choose. Cat!"

Two a.m. saw Lord Peter Wimsey arrive in a friend's car at the Dower House, Denver Castle, in company with a deaf and aged lady and an antique portmanteau.

"It's very nice to see you, dear, said the Dowager Duchess, placidly. She was a small, plump woman, with perfectly white hair and exquisite hands. In feature she was as unlike her second son as she was like him in character; her black eyes twinkled cheerfully, and her manners and movements were marked with a neat and rapid decision. She wore a charming wrap from Liberty's, and sat watching Lord Peter eat cold beef and cheese as though his arrival in such incongruous circumstances and company were the most ordinary event possible, which with him, indeed, it was.

"Have you got the old lady to bed?" asked Lord Peter.

"Oh, yes, dear. Such a striking old person, isn't she? And very courageous. She tells me she has never been in a motorcar before. But she thinks you a very nice lad, dear—that careful of her, you remind her of her own son. Poor little Mr. Thipps—whatever made your friend the inspector think he could have murdered anybody?"

"My friend the inspector—no, no more, thank you, Mother—is determined to prove that the intrusive person in Thipps's bath is Sir Reuben Levy, who disappeared mysteriously from his house last night. His line of reasoning is: We've lost a middle-aged gentleman without any clothes on in Park Lane; we've found a middle-aged gentleman without any clothes on in Battersea. Therefore they're one and the same person, Q.E.D., and put little Thipps in quod."

"You're very elliptical, dear," said the Duchess, mildly. "Why should Mr. Thipps be arrested even if they are the same?"

"Sugg must arrest somebody," said Lord Peter, "but there is one odd little bit of evidence come out which goes a long way to support Sugg's theory, only that I know it to be no go by the evidence of my own eyes. Last night at about 9.15 a young woman was strollin' up the Battersea Park Road for purposes best known to herself, when she saw a gentleman in a fur coat and top-hat saunterin' along under an umbrella, lookin' at the names of all the streets. He looked a bit out of place, so, not bein' a shy girl, you see, she walked up to him, and said: 'Good-evening.' 'Can you tell me, please,' says the mysterious stranger, 'whether this street leads into Prince of Wales Road?' She said it did, and further asked him in a jocular manner what he was doing with himself and all the rest of it, only she wasn't altogether so explicit about that part of the conversation, because she was unburdenin' her heart to Sugg, d'you see, and he's paid by a grateful country to have very pure, high-minded ideals, what? Anyway, the old boy said he couldn't attend to her just then as he had an appointment. 'I've got to go and see a man, my dear,' was how she said he put it, and he walked on up Alexandra Avenue towards Prince of Wales Road. She was starin' after him, still rather surprised, when she was joined by a friend of hers, who said: 'It's no good wasting your time with him—that's Levy—I knew him when I lived in the West End, and the girls used to call him Peagreen Incorruptible'—friend's name suppressed, owing to implications of story, but girl vouches for what was said. She thought no more about it till the milkman brought news this morning of the excitement at Queen Caroline Mansions; then she went round, though not likin' the police as a rule, and asked the man there whether the dead gentleman had a beard and glasses. Told he had glasses but no beard, she incautiously said: 'Oh, then, it isn't him,' and the man said: 'Isn't who?' and collared her. That's her story. Sugg's delighted, of course, and quodded Thipps on the strength of it."

"Dear me," said the Duchess, "I hope the poor girl won't get into trouble."

"Shouldn't think so," said Lord Peter. "Thipps is the one that's going to get it in the neck. Besides, he's done a silly thing. I got that out of Sugg, too, though he was sittin' tight on the information. Seems Thipps got into a confusion about the train he took back from Manchester. Said first he got home at 10.30. Then they pumped Gladys Horrocks, who let out he wasn't back till after 11.45. Then Thipps, bein' asked to explain the discrepancy, stammers and bungles and says, first, that he missed the train. Then Sugg makes inquiries at St. Pancras and discovers that he left a bag in the cloak-room there at ten. Thipps, again asked to explain, stammers worse an' says he walked about for a few hours—met a friend—can't say who—didn't meet a friend–can't say what he did with his time–can't explain why he didn't go back for his bag–can't say what time he did get in–can't explain how he got a bruise on his forehead. In fact, can't explain himself at all. Gladys Horrocks interrogated again. Says, this time, Thipps came in at 10.30. Then admits she didn't hear him come in. Can't say why she didn't hear him come in. Can't say why she said first of all that she *did* hear him. Bursts into tears. Contradicts herself. Everybody's suspicion roused. Quod 'em both."

"As you put it, dear," said the Duchess, "it all sounds very confusing, and not quite respectable. Poor little Mr. Thipps would be terribly upset by anything that wasn't respectable."

"I wonder what he did with himself," said Lord Peter thoughtfully. "I really don't think he was committing a murder. Besides, I believe the fellow has been dead a day or two, though it don't do to build too much on doctors' evidence. It's an entertainin' little problem."

"Very curious, dear. But so sad about poor Sir Reuben. I must write a few lines to Lady Levy; I used to know her quite well, you know, dear, down in Hampshire, when she was a girl. Christine Ford, she was then, and I remember so well the dreadful trouble there was about her marrying a Jew. That was before he made his money, of course, in that oil business out in America. The family wanted her to marry Julian Freke, who did so well afterwards and was connected with the family, but she fell in love with this Mr. Levy and eloped with him. He was very handsome, then, you know, dear, in a foreign-looking way, but he hadn't any means, and the Fords didn't like his religion. Of course we're all Jews nowadays, and they wouldn't have minded so much if he'd pretended to be something else, like that Mr. Simons we met at Mrs. Porchester's, who always tells everybody that he got his nose in Italy at the Renaissance, and claims to be descended somehow or other from La Bella Simonetta–so foolish, you know, dear–as if anybody believed it; and I'm sure some Jews are very good people, and personally I'd much rather they believed something, though of course it must be very inconvenient, what with not working on Saturdays and circumcising the poor little babies and everything depending on the new moon and that funny kind of meat they have with such a slang-sounding name, and never being able to have bacon for breakfast. Still, there it was, and it was much better for the girl to marry him if she was really fond of him, though I believe young Freke was really devoted to her, and they're still great friends. Not that there was ever a real engagement, only a sort of understanding with her father, but he's never married, you know, and lives all by himself in that big house next to the hospital, though he's very rich and distinguished now, and I know ever so many people have tried to get hold of him–there was Lady Mainwaring wanted him for that eldest girl of hers, though I remember saying at the time it was no use expecting a surgeon to be taken in by a figure that was all padding–they have so many opportunities of judging, you know, dear."

"Lady Levy seems to have had the knack of makin' people devoted to her," said Peter. "Look at the peagreen incorruptible Levy."

"That's quite true, dear; she was a most delightful girl, and they say her daughter is just like her. I rather lost sight of them when she married, and you know your father didn't care much about business people, but I know everybody always said they were a model couple. In fact it was a proverb that Sir Reuben was as well loved at home as he was hated abroad. I don't mean in foreign countries, you know, dear–just the proverbial way of putting things–like 'a saint abroad and a devil at home'–only the other way on, reminding one of the *Pilgrim's Progress*."

"Yes," said Peter, "I daresay the old man made one or two enemies."

"Dozens, dear—such a dreadful place, the City, isn't it? Everybody Ishmaels together—though I don't suppose Sir Reuben would like to be called that, would he? Doesn't it mean illegitimate, or not a proper Jew, anyway? I always did get confused with those Old Testament characters."

Lord Peter laughed and yawned.

"I think I'll turn in for an hour or two," he said. "I must be back in town at eight—Parker's coming to breakfast."

The Duchess looked at the clock, which marked five minutes to three.

"I'll send up your breakfast at half-past six, dear," she said. "I hope you'll find everything all right. I told them just to slip a hot-water bottle in; those linen sheets are so chilly; you can put it out if it's in your way."

## 4

"—So THERE it is, Parker," said Lord Peter, pushing his coffee-cup aside and lighting his after-breakfast pipe; "you may find it leads you to something, though it don't seem to get me any further with my bathroom problem. Did you do anything more at that after I left?"

"No; but I've been on the roof this morning."

"The deuce you have—what an energetic devil you are! I say, Parker, I think this co-operative scheme is an uncommonly good one. It's much easier to work on someone else's job than one's own—gives one that delightful feelin' of interferin' and bossin' about, combined with the glorious sensation that another fellow is takin' all one's own work off one's hands. You scratch my back and I'll scratch yours, what? Did you find anything?"

"Not very much. I looked for any footmarks of course, but naturally, with all this rain, there wasn't a sign. Of course, if this were a detective story, there'd have been a convenient shower exactly an hour before the crime and a beautiful set of marks which could only have come there between two and three in the morning, but this being real life in a London November, you might as well expect foot-prints in Niagara. I searched the roofs right along—and came to the jolly conclusion that any person in any blessed flat in the blessed row might have done it. All the staircases open on to the roof and the leads are quite flat; you can walk along as easy as along Shaftesbury Avenue. Still, I've got evidence that the body did walk along there."

"What's that?"

Parker brought out his pocketbook and extracted a few shreds of material, which he laid before his friend.

"One was caught in the gutter just above Thipps's bathroom window, another in a crack of the stone parapet just over it, and the rest came from the chimney-stack behind, where they had caught in an iron stanchion. What do you make of them?"

Lord Peter scrutinized them very carefully through his lens.

"Interesting," he said, "damned interesting. Have you developed those plates, Bunter?" he added, as that discreet assistant came in with the post.

"Yes, my lord."

"Caught anything?"

"I don't know whether to call it anything or not, my lord," said Bunter, dubiously. "I'll bring the prints in."

"Do," said Wimsey. "Hallo! here's our advertisement about the gold chain in the *Times*–very nice it looks: 'Write, 'phone or call 110, Piccadilly.' Perhaps it would have been safer to put a box number, though I always think that the franker you are with people, the more you're likely to deceive 'em; so unused is the modern world to the open hand and the guileless heart, what?"

"But you don't think the fellow who left that chain on the body is going to give himself away by coming here and inquiring about it?"

"I don't, fathead," said Lord Peter, with the easy politeness of the real aristocracy; "that's why I've tried to get hold of the jeweller who originally sold the chain. See?" He pointed to the paragraph. "It's not an old chain–hardly worn at all. Oh, thanks, Bunter. Now, see here, Parker, these are the fingermarks you noticed yesterday on the window-sash and on the far edge of the bath. I'd overlooked them; I give you full credit for the discovery, I crawl, I grovel, my name is Watson and you need not say what you were just going to say, because I admit it all. Now we shall–Hullo, hullo, hullo !"

The three men stared at the photographs.

"The criminal," said Lord Peter, bitterly, "climbed over the roofs in the wet and not unnaturally got soot on his fingers. He arranged the body in the bath, and wiped away all traces of himself except two, which he obligingly left to show us how to do our job. We learn from a smudge on the floor that he wore india rubber boots, and from this admirable set of fingerprints on the edge of the bath that he had the usual number of fingers and wore rubber gloves. That's the kind of man he is. Take the fool away, gentlemen."

He put the prints aside, and returned to an examination of the shreds of material in his hand. Suddenly he whistled softly.

"Do you make anything of these, Parker?"

"They seemed to me to be ravellings of some coarse cotton stuff–a sheet, perhaps, or an improvised rope."

"Yes," said Lord Peter–"yes. It may be a mistake–it may be *our* mistake. I wonder. Tell me, d'you think these tiny threads are long enough and strong enough to hang a man?"

He was silent, his long eyes narrowing into slits behind the smoke of his pipe.

"What do you suggest doing this morning?" asked Parker.

"Well," said Lord Peter, "it seems to me it's about time I took a hand in your job. Let's go round to Park Lane and see what larks Sir Reuben Levy was up to in bed last night."

"And now, Mrs. Pemming, if you would be so kind as to give me a blanket," said Mr. Bunter, coming down into the kitchen, "and permit of me hanging a sheet across the lower part of this window, and drawing the screen across here, so–so as to shut off any reflections, if you understand me, we'll get to work."

Sir Reuben Levy's cook, with her eye upon Mr. Bunter's gentlemanly and well-tailored appearance, hastened to produce what was necessary. Her visitor placed on the table a basket, containing a waterbottle, a silver-backed hairbrush, a pair of boots, a small roll of linoleum, and the "Letters of A Self-made Merchant to His Son," bound in polished morocco. He drew an umbrella from beneath his arm and added it to the collection. He then advanced a ponderous photographic machine and set it up in the neighbourhood of the kitchen range; then, spreading a newspaper over the fair, scrubbed surface of the table, he began to roll up his sleeves and insinuate himself into a pair of surgical gloves. Sir Reuben Levy's valet, entering at the moment and finding him thus engaged, put aside the kitchenmaid, who was staring from a front-row position, and inspected the apparatus critically. Mr. Bunter nodded brightly to him, and uncorked a small bottle of grey powder.

"Odd sort of fish, your employer, isn't he?" said the valet, carelessly.

"Very singular, indeed," said Mr. Bunter. "Now, my dear," he added, ingratiatingly, to the kitchenmaid, "I wonder if you'd just pour a little of this grey powder over the edge of the bottle while I'm holding it—and the same with this boot—here, at the top—thank you, Miss—what is your name? Price? Oh, but you've got another name besides Price, haven't you? Mabel, eh? That's a name I'm uncommonly partial to—that's very nicely done, you've a steady hand, Miss Mabel—see that? That's the fingermarks—three there, and two here, smudged over in both places. No, don't you touch 'em, my dear, or you'll rub the bloom off. We'll stand 'em up here till they're ready to have their portraits taken. Now then, let's take the hairbrush next. Perhaps, Mrs. Pemming, you'd like to lift him up very carefully by the bristles."

"By the bristles, Mr. Bunter?"

"If you please, Mrs. Pemming—and lay him here. Now, Miss Mabel, another little exhibition of your skill, if you please. No—we'll try lampblack this time. Perfect. Couldn't have done it better myself. Ah! there's a beautiful set. No smudges this time. That'll interest his lordship. Now the little book—no, I'll pick that up myself—with these gloves, you see, and by the edges—I'm a careful criminal, Mrs. Pemming, I don't want to leave any traces. Dust the cover all over, Miss Mabel; now this side—that's the way to do it. Lots of prints and no smudges. All according to plan. Oh, please Mr. Graves, you mustn't touch it—it's as much as my place is worth to have it touched."

"D'you have to do much of this sort of thing?" inquired Mr. Graves, from a superior standpoint.

"Any amount," replied Mr. Bunter, with a groan calculated to appeal to Mr. Graves's heart and unlock his confidence. "If you'd kindly hold one end of this bit of linoleum, Mrs. Pemming, I'll hold up this end while Miss Mabel operates. Yes, Mr. Graves, it's a hard life, valeting by day and developing by night—morning tea at any time from 6.30 to 11, and criminal investigation at all hours. It's wonderful, the ideas these rich men with nothing to do get into their heads."

"I wonder you stand it," said Mr. Graves. "Now there's none of that here. A quiet, orderly, domestic life, Mr. Bunter, has much to be said for it. Meals at regular hours; decent, respectable families to dinner—none of your painted women—and no valeting at night, there's *much* to be said for it. I don't hold with Hebrews as a rule, Mr. Bunter, and of course I understand that you may find it to your advantage to be in a titled family, but there's less thought of that these days, and I will say, for a self-made man, no one could call Sir Reuben vulgar, and my lady at any rate is county—Miss Ford, she was, one of the Hampshire Fords, and both of them always most considerate."

"I agree with you, Mr. Graves—his lordship and me have never held with being narrow-minded—why, yes, my dear, of course it's a footmark, this is the washstand linoleum. A good Jew can be a good man, that's what I've always said. And regular hours and considerate habit have a great deal to recommend them. Very simple in his tastes, now, Sir Reuben, isn't he? for such a rich man, I mean."

"Very simple indeed," said the cook; "the meals he and her ladyship have when they're by themselves with Miss Rachel—well, there now—if it wasn't for the dinners, which is always good when there's company, I'd be wastin' my talents and education here, if you understand me, Mr. Bunter."

Mr. Bunter added the handle of the umbrella to his collection, and began to pin a sheet across the window, aided by the housemaid.

"Admirable," said he. "Now, if I might have this blanket on the table and another on a towel-horse or something of that kind by way of a background—you're very kind, Mrs. Pemming. . . . Ah! I wish his lordship never wanted valeting at night. Many's the time I've sat up till three and four, and up again to call him early to go off Sherlocking at the other end of the country. And the mud he gets on his clothes and his boots!"

"I'm sure it's a shame, Mr. Bunter," said Mrs. Pemming, warmly. "Low, I calls it. In my opinion, policework ain't no fit occupation for a gentleman, let alone a lordship."

"Everything made so difficult, too," said Mr. Bunter nobly sacrificing his employer's character and his own feelings in a good cause; "boots chucked into a corner, clothes hung up on the floor, as they say—"

"That's often the case with these men as are born with a silver spoon in their mouths," said Mr. Graves. "Now, Sir Reuben, he's never lost his good old-fashioned habit. Clothes folded up neat, boots put out in his dressing-room so as a man could get them in the morning, everything made easy."

"He forgot them the night before last, though."

"The clothes, not the boots. Always thoughtful for others, is Sir Reuben, Ah! I hope nothing's happened to him."

"Indeed, no, poor gentleman," chimed in the cook, "and as for what they're sayin', that he'd 'ave gone out surrepshous-like to do something he didn't ought, well, I'd never believe it of him, Mr. Bunter, not if I was to take my dying oath upon it."

"Ah!" said Mr. Bunter, adjusting his arc-lamps and connecting them with the nearest electric light, "and that's more than most of us could say of them as pays us."

"Five foot ten," said Lord Peter, "and not an inch more." He peered dubiously at the depression in the bed clothes, and measured it a second time with the gentleman-scout's vademecum. Parker entered this particular in a neat pocketbook.

"I suppose," he said, "a six-foot-two man *might* leave a five-foot-ten depression if he curled himself up."

"Have you any Scotch blood in you, Parker?" inquired his colleague, bitterly.

"Not that I know of," replied Parker. "Why?"

"Because of all the cautious, ungenerous, deliberate and cold-blooded devils I know," said Lord Peter, "you are the most cautious, ungenerous, deliberate and cold-blooded. Here am I, sweating my brains out to introduce a really sensational incident into your dull and disreputable little police investigation, and you refuse to show a single spark of enthusiasm."

"Well, it's no good jumping at conclusions."

"Jump? You don't even crawl distantly within sight of a conclusion. I believe if you caught the cat with her head in the cream-jug you'd say it was conceivable that the jug was empty when she got there."

"Well, it would be conceivable, wouldn't it?"

"Curse you," said Lord Peter. He screwed his monocle into his eye, and bent over the pillow, breathing hard and tightly through his nose. "Here, give me the tweezers," he said presently. "Good heavens, man, don't blow like that, you might be a whale." He nipped up an almost invisible object from the linen.

"What is it?" asked Parker.

"It's a hair," said Wimsey grimly, his hard eyes growing harder. "Let's go and look at Levy's hats, shall we? And you might just ring for that fellow with the churchyard name, do you mind?"

Mr. Graves, when summoned, found Lord Peter Wimsey squatting on the floor of the dressing-room before a row of hats arranged upside down before him.

"Here you are," said that nobleman cheerfully, "Now, Graves, this is a guessin' competition—a sort of three-hat trick to mix metaphors. Here are nine hats, including three top-hats. Do you identify all these hats as belonging to Sir Reuben Levy? You do? Very good. Now I have three guesses as to which hat he wore the night he disappeared, and if I guess right, I win; if I don't, you win. See? Ready? Go. I suppose you know the answer yourself, by the way?"

"Do I understand your lordship to be asking which hat Sir Reuben wore when he went out on Monday night, your lordship?"

"No, you don't understand a bit," said Lord Peter. "I'm asking if *you* know—don't tell me, I'm going to guess."

"I do know, your lordship," said Mr. Graves, reprovingly.

"Well," said Lord Peter, "as he was dinin' at the Ritz he wore a topper. Here are three toppers. In three guesses I'd be bound to hit the right one, wouldn't I? That don't seem very sportin'. I'll take one guess. It was this one."

He indicated the hat next the window.

"Am I right, Graves—have I got the prize?"

"That *is* the hat in question, my lord," said Mr. Graves, without excitement.

"Thanks," said Lord Peter, "that's all I wanted to know. Ask Bunter to step up, would you?"

Mr. Bunter stepped up with an aggrieved air, and his usually smooth hair ruffled by the focussing cloth.

"Oh, there you are, Bunter," said Lord Peter; "look here—"

"Here I am, my lord," said Mr. Bunter, with respectful reproach, "but if you'll excuse me saying so, downstairs is where I ought to be, with all those young women about—they'll be fingering the evidence, my lord."

"I cry your mercy," said Lord Peter, "but I've quarrelled hopelessly with Mr. Parker and distracted the estimable Graves, and I want you to tell me what finger-prints you have found. I shan't be happy till I get it, so don't be harsh with me, Bunter."

"Well, my lord, your lordship understands I haven't photographed them yet, but I won't deny that their appearance is interesting, my lord. The little book off the night table, my lord, has only the marks of one set of fingers—there's a little scar on the right thumb which makes them easy recognised. The hairbrush, too, my lord, has only the same set of marks. The umbrella, the toothglass and the boots all have two sets: the hand with the scarred thumb, which I take to be Sir Reuben's, my lord, and a set of smudges superimposed upon them, if I may put it that way, my lord, which may or may not be the same hand in rubber gloves. I could tell you better when I've got the photographs made, to measure them, my lord. The linoleum in front of the washstand is very gratifying indeed, my lord, if you will excuse my mentioning it. Besides the marks of Sir Reuben's boots which your lordship pointed out, there's the print of a man's naked foot—a much smaller one, my lord, not much more than a ten-inch sock, I should say if you asked me."

Lord Peter's face became irradiated with almost a dim, religious light.

"A mistake," he breathed "a mistake, a little one, but he can't afford it. When was the linoleum washed last, Bunter?"

"Monday morning, my lord. The housemaid did it and remembered to mention it. Only remark she's made yet, and it's to the point. The other domestics—"

His features expressed disdain.

"What did I say, Parker? Five-foot-ten and not an inch longer. And he didn't dare to use the hairbrush. Beautiful. But he *had* to risk the top-hat. Gentleman can't walk home in the rain late at night without a hat, you know, Parker. Look! what do you make of it? Two sets of finger-prints on everything, but the book and the brush, two sets of feet on the linoleum, and two kinds of hair in the hat!"

He lifted the top-hat to the light, and extracted the evidence with tweezers.

"Think of it, Parker—to remember the hairbrush and forget the hat—to remember his fingers all the time, and to make that one careless step on the tell-tale linoleum. Here they are, you see, black hair and tan hair—black hair in the bowler and the panama, and black and tan in last night's topper. And then, just to make certain that we're on the right track, just one little auburn hair on the pillow, on this pillow, Parker, which isn't quite in the right place. It almost brings tears to my eyes."

"Do you mean to say—" said the detective, slowly.

"I mean to say," said Lord Peter, "that it was not Sir Reuben Levy whom the cook saw last night on the doorstep. I say that it was another man, perhaps a couple of inches shorter, who came here in Levy's clothes and let himself in with Levy's latchkey. Oh, he was a bold, cunning devil, Parker. He had on Levy's boots, and every stitch of Levy's clothing down to the skin. He had rubber gloves on his hands which he never took off, and he did everything he could to make us think that Levy slept here last night. He took his chances, and won. He walked upstairs, he undressed, he even washed and cleaned his teeth, though he didn't use the hairbrush for fear of leaving red hairs in it. He had to guess what Levy did with boots and clothes; one guess was wrong and the other right, as it happened. The bed must look as if it had been slept in, so he gets in, and lies there in his victim's very pyjamas. Then, in the morning sometime, probably in the deadest hour between two and three, he gets up, dresses himself in his own clothes that he has brought with him in a bag, and creeps downstairs. If anybody wakes, he is lost, but he is a bold man, and he takes his chance. He knows that people do not wake as a rule—and they don't wake. He opens the street door which he left on the latch when he came in—he listens for the stray passer-by or the policeman on his beat. He slips out. He pulls the door quietly to with the latchkey. He walks briskly away in rubber-soled shoes—he's the kind of criminal who isn't complete without rubber-soled shoes. In a few minutes he is at Hyde Park Corner. After that—"

He paused, and added:

"He did all that, and unless he had nothing at stake, he had everything at stake. Either Sir Reuben Levy has been spirited away for some silly practical joke, or the man with the auburn hair has the guilt of murder upon his soul."

"Dear me!" ejaculated the detective, "you're very dramatic about it."

Lord Peter passed his hand rather wearily over his hair.

"My true friend," he murmured in a voice surcharged with emotion, "you recall me to the nursery rhymes of my youth—the sacred duty of flippancy:

There was an old man of Whitehaven
Who danced a quadrille with a raven,
But they said: It's absurd
To encourage that bird—
So they smashed that old man of Whitehaven.

That's the correct attitude, Parker. Here's a poor old buffer spirited away—such a joke—and I don't believe he'd hurt a fly himself—that makes it funnier. D'you know, Parker, I don't care frightfully about this case after all."

"Which, this or yours?"

"Both. I say, Parker, shall we go quietly home and have lunch and go to the Coliseum?"

"You can if you like," replied the detective; "but you forget I do this for my bread and butter."

"And I haven't even that excuse," said Lord Peter; "well, what's the next move? What would you do in my case?"

"I'd so some good, hard grind," said Parker. "I'd distrust every bit of work Sugg ever did, and I'd get the family history of every tenant of every flat in Queen Caroline Mansions. I'd examine all their boxrooms and rooftraps, and I would inveigle them into conversations and suddenly bring in the words 'body' and 'pince-nez' and see if they wriggled, like those modern psyo-what's-his-names."

"You would, would you?" said Lord Peter with a grin. "Well, we've exchanged cases, you know, so just you toddle off and do it. I'm going to have a jolly time at Wyndham's."

Parker made a grimace.

"Well," he said, "I don't suppose you'd ever do it, so I'd better. You'll never become a professional till you learn to do a little work, Wimsey. How about lunch?"

"I'm invited out," said Lord Peter, magnificently. "I'll run around and change at the club. Can't feed with Freddy Arbuthnot in these bags; Bunter!"

"Yes, my lord."

"Pack up if you're ready, and come round and wash my face and hands for me at the club."

"Work here for another two hours, my lord. Can't do with less than thirty minutes' exposure. The current's none too strong."

"You see how I'm bullied by my own man, Parker? Well, I must bear it, I suppose, Ta-ta!"

He whistled his way downstairs.

The conscientious Mr. Parker, with a groan, settled down to a systematic search through Sir Reuben Levy's papers, with the assistance of a plate of ham sandwiches and a bottle of Bass.

Lord Peter and the Honourable Freddy Arbuthnot, looking together like an advertisement for gents' trouserings, strolled into the dining-room at Wyndham's.

"Haven't seen you for an age," said the Honourable Freddy. "What have you been doin' with yourself?"

"Oh, foolin' about," said Lord Peter, languidly.

"Thick or clear, sir?" inquired the waiter of the Honourable Freddy.

"Which'll you have, Wimsey?" said that gentleman, transferring the burden of selection to his guest. "They're both equally poisonous."

"Well, clear's less trouble to lick out of the spoon," said Lord Peter.

"Clear," said the Honourable Freddy.

"Consommé Polonais," agreed the waiter. "Very nice, sir."

Conversation languished until the Honourable Freddy found a bone in the filleted sole, and sent for the head waiter to explain its presence. When this matter had been adjusted Lord Peter found energy to say:

"Sorry to hear about your gov'nor, old man."

"Yes, poor old buffer," said the Honourable Freddy; "they say he can't last long now. What? Oh! the Montrachet '08. There's nothing fit to drink in this place," he added gloomily.

After this deliberate insult to a noble vintage there was a further pause, till Lord Peter said: "How's 'Change?"

"Rotten," said the Honourable Freddy.

He helped himself gloomily to salmis of game.

"Can I do anything?" asked Lord Peter.

"Oh, no, thanks–very decent of you, but it'll pan out all right in time."

"This isn't a bad salmis," said Lord Peter.

"I've eaten worse," admitted his friend.

"What about those Argentines?" inquired Lord Peter. "Here, waiter, there's a bit of cork in my glass."

"Cork?" cried the Honourable Freddy, with something approaching animation; "you'll hear about this, waiter. It's an amazing thing a fellow who's paid to do the job can't manage to take a cork out of a bottle. What you say? Argentines? Gone all to hell. Old Levy bunkin' off like that's knocked the bottom out of the market."

"You don't say so," said Lord Peter. "What d'you suppose has happened to the old man?"

"Cursed if I know," said the Honourable Freddy; "knocked on the head by the bears, I should think."

"P'r'aps he's gone off on his own," suggested Lord Peter. "Double life, you know. Giddy old blighters, some of these City men."

"Oh, no," said the Honourable Freddy, faintly roused; "no, hang it all, Wimsey, I wouldn't care to say that. He's a decent old domestic bird, and his daughter's a charmin' girl. Besides, he's straight enough–he'd *do* you down fast enough, but he wouldn't *let* you down. Old Anderson is badly cut up about it."

"Who's Anderson?"

"Chap with property out there. He belongs here. He was goin' to meet Levy on Tuesday. He's afraid those railway people will get in now, and then it'll be all U.P."

"Who's runnin' the railway people over here?" inquired Lord Peter.

"Yankee blighter, John P. Milligan. He's got an option, or says he has. You can't trust these brutes."

"Can't Anderson hold on?"

"Anderson isn't Levy. Hasn't got the shekels. Besides, he's only one. Levy covers the ground–he could boycott Milligan's beastly railway if he liked. That's where he's got the pull, you see."

"B'lieve I met the Milligan man somewhere," said Lord Peter, thoughtfully. "Ain't he a hulking brute with black hair and a beard?"

"You're thinkin' of somebody else," said the Honourable Freddy. "Milligan don't stand any higher than I do, unless you call five-feet-ten hulking–and he's bald, anyway."

Lord Peter considered this over the Gorgonzola. Then he said: "Didn't know Levy had a charmin' daughter."

"Oh, yes," said the Honourable Freddy, with an elaborate detachment. "Met her and Mamma last year abroad. That's how I got to know the old man. He's been very decent. Let me into this Argentine business on the ground floor, don't you know?"

"Well," said Lord Peter, "you might do worse. Money's money, ain't it? And Lady Levy is quite a redeemin' point. At least, my mother knew her people."

"Oh, *she's* all right," said the Honourable Freddy, "and the old man's nothing to be ashamed of nowadays. He's self-made, of course, but he don't pretend to be anything else. No side. Toddles off to business on a 96 'bus every morning. 'Can't make up my mind to taxis, my boy,' he says. 'I had to look at every half-penny when I was a young man, and I can't get out of the way of it now.' Though, if he's takin' his family out, nothing's too good. Rachel–that's the girl–always laughs at the old man's little economies."

"I suppose they've sent for Lady Levy," said Lord Peter.

"I suppose so," agreed the other. "I'd better pop round and express sympathy or somethin', what? Wouldn't look well not to, d'you think? But it's deuced awkward. What am I to say?"

"I don't think it matters much what you say," said Lord Peter, helpfully. "I should ask if you can do anything."

"Thanks," said the lover, "I will. Energetic young man. Count on me. Always at your service. Ring me up any time of the day or night. That's the line to take, don't you think?"

"That's the idea," said Lord Peter.

Mr. John P. Milligan, the London representative of the great Milligan railroad and shipping company, was dictating code cables to his secretary in an office in Lombard Street, when a card was brought up to him, bearing the simple legend:

LORD PETER WIMSEY
*Marlborough Club*

Mr. Milligan was annoyed at the interruption, but, like many of his nation, if he had a weak point, it was the British aristocracy. He postponed for a few minutes the elimination from the map of a modest but promising farm, and directed that the visitor should be shown up.

"Good-afternoon," said that nobleman, ambling genially in, "it's most uncommonly good of you to let me come round wastin' your time like this. I'll try not to be too long about it, though I'm not awfully good at comin' to the point. My brother never would let me stand for the county, y'know–said I wandered on so nobody'd know what I was talkin' about."

"Pleased to meet you, Lord Wimsey," said Mr. Milligan. "Won't you take a seat?"

"Thanks," said Lord Peter, "but I'm not a peer, you know—that's my brother Denver. My name's Peter. It's a silly name, I always think, so old-world and full of homely virtue and that sort of thing, but my godfathers and godmothers in my baptism are responsible for that, I suppose, officially—which is rather hard on them, you know, as they didn't actually choose it. But we always have a Peter, after the third duke, who betrayed five kings somewhere about the Wars of the Roses, though come to think of it, it ain't anything to be proud of. Still, one has to make the best of it."

Mr. Milligan, thus ingeniously placed at that disadvantage which attends ignorance, manoeuvred for position, and offered his interrupter a Corona Corona.

"Thanks, awfully," said Lord Peter, "though you really mustn't tempt me to stay here burblin' all afternoon. By Jove, Mr. Milligan, if you offer people such comfortable chairs and cigars like these, I wonder they don't come an' live in your office." He added mentally: "I wish to goodness I could get those longtoed boots off you. How's a man to know the size of your feet? And a head like a potato. It's enough to make one swear."

"Say now, Lord Peter," said Mr. Milligan, "can I do anything for you?"

"Well, d'you know," said Lord Peter, "I'm wonderin' if you would. It's damned cheek to ask you, but fact is, it's my mother, you know. Wonderful woman, but don't realize what it means, demands on the time of a busy man like you. We don't understand hustle over here, you know, Mr. Milligan."

"Now don't you mention that," said Mr. Milligan; "I'd be surely charmed to do anything to oblige the Duchess."

He felt a momentary qualm as to whether a duke's mother were also a duchess, but breathed more freely as Lord Peter went on:

"Thanks—that's uncommonly good of you. Well, now, it's like this. My mother—most energetic, self-sacrificin' woman, don't you see, is thinkin' of gettin' up a sort of a charity bazaar down at Denver this winter, in aid of the church roof, y'know. Very sad case, Mr. Milligan—fine old antique—early English windows and decorated angel roof, and all that—all tumblin' to pieces, rain pourin' in and so on—vicar catchin' rheumatism at early service, owin' to the draught blowin' in over the altar—you know the sort of thing. They've got a man down startin' on it—little beggar called Thipps—lives with an aged mother in Battersea—vulgar little beast, but quite good on angel roofs and things, I'm told."

At this point, Lord Peter watched his interlocutor narrowly, but finding that this rigmarole produced in him no reaction more startling than polite interest tinged with faint bewilderment, he abandoned this line of investigation, and proceeded:

"I say, I beg your pardon, frightfully—I'm afraid I'm bein' beastly long-winded. Fact is, my mother is gettin' up this bazaar, and she thought it'd be an awfully interestin' side-show to have some lectures—sort of little talks, y'know—by eminent business men of all nations. 'How I Did It' kind of touch, y'know—'A Drop of Oil with a Kerosene King'—'Cash Conscience and Cocoa' and so on. It would interest people down there no end. You see, all my mother's friends will be there, and we've none of us any money—not what you'd call money, I mean—I expect our incomes wouldn't pay your telephone calls, would they?—but we like awfully to hear about the people who can make money. Gives us a sort of uplifted feelin', don't you know. Well, anyway, I mean, my mother'd be frightfully pleased and grateful to you, Mr. Milligan, if you'd come down and give us a few words as a representative American. It needn't take more than ten minutes or so, y'know, because the local people can't understand much beyond shootin' and huntin', and my mother's crowd can't keep their minds on anythin' more than ten minutes together, but we'd really appreciate it very much if you'd come and stay a day or two and just give us a little breezy word on the almighty dollar."

"Why, yes," said Mr. Milligan, "I'd like to, Lord Peter. It's kind of the Duchess to suggest it. It's a very sad thing when these fine old antiques begin to wear out. I'll come with great pleasure. And perhaps you'd be kind enough to accept a little donation to the Restoration Fund."

This unexpected development nearly brought Lord Peter up all standing. To pump, by means of an ingenious lie, a hospitable gentleman whom you are inclined to suspect of a peculiarly malicious murder, and to accept from him in the course of the proceedings a large cheque for a charitable object, has something about it unpalatable to any but the hardened Secret Service agent. Lord Peter temporized.

"That's awfully decent of you," he said. "I'm sure they'd be no end grateful. But you'd better not give it to me, you know. I might spend it, or lose it. I'm not very reliable, I'm afraid. The vicar's the right person–the Rev. Constantine Throgmorton, St. John-before-the-Latin-Gate Vicarage, Duke's Denver, if you like to send it there."

"I will," said Mr. Milligan. "Will you write it out now for a thousand pounds, Scoot, in case it slips my mind later?"

The secretary, a sandy-haired young man with a long chin and no eyebrows, silently did as he was requested. Lord Peter looked from the bald head of Mr. Milligan to the red head of the secretary, hardened his heart and tried again.

"Well, I'm no end grateful to you, Mr. Milligan, and so'll my mother be when I tell her. I'll let you know the date of the bazaar–it's not quite settled yet, and I've got to see some other business men, don't you know. I thought of askin' someone from one of the big newspaper combines to represent British advertisin' talent, what?–and a friend of mine promises me a leadin' German financier–very interestin' if there ain't too much feelin' against it down in the country, and I'll have to find somebody or other to do the Hebrew point of view. I thought of askin' Levy, y'know, only he's floated off in this inconvenient way."

"Yes," said Mr. Milligan, "that's a very curious thing, though I don't mind saying, Lord Peter, that it's a convenience to me. He had a cinch on my railroad combine, but I'd nothing against him personally, and if he turns up after I've brought off a little deal I've got on, I'll be happy to give him the right hand of welcome."

A vision passed through Lord Peter's mind of Sir Reuben kept somewhere in custody till a financial crisis was over. This was exceedingly possible, and far more agreeable than his earlier conjecture; it also agreed better with the impression he was forming of Mr. Milligan.

"Well, it's a rum go," said Lord Peter, "but I daresay he had his reasons. Much better not to inquire into people's reasons, y'know, what? Specially as a police friend of mine who's connected with the case says the old johnnie dyed his hair before he went."

Out of the tail of his eye, Lord Peter saw the red-headed secretary add up five columns of figures simultaneously and jot down the answer.

"Dyed his hair, did he?" said Mr. Milligan.

"Dyed it red," said Lord Peter. The secretary looked up. "Odd thing is," continued Wimsey, "they can't lay hands on the bottle. Somethin' fishy there, don't you think, what?"

The secretary's interest seemed to have evaporated. He inserted a fresh sheet into his looseleaf ledger, and carried forward a row of digits from the preceding page.

"I daresay there's nothin' in it," said Lord Peter, rising to go. "Well, it's uncommonly good of you to be bothered with me like this, Mr. Milligan—my mother'll be no end pleased. She'll write you about the date."

"I'm charmed," said Mr. Milligan. "Very pleased to have met you."

Mr. Scoot rose silently to open the door, uncoiling as he did so a portentous length of thin leg, hitherto hidden by the desk. With a mental sigh Lord Peter estimated him at six-foot-four.

"It's a pity I can't put Scoot's head on Milligan's shoulders," said Lord Peter, emerging into the swirl of the city. "And what *will* my mother say?"

# 5

MR. PARKER was a bachelor, and occupied a Georgian but inconvenient flat at No. 12A Great Ormond Street, for which he paid a pound a week. His exertions in the cause of civilization were rewarded, not by the gift of diamond rings from empresses or munificent cheques from grateful Prime Ministers, but by a modest, though sufficient, salary, drawn from the pockets of the British taxpayers. He awoke, after a long day of arduous and inconclusive labour, to the smell of burnt porridge. Through his bedroom window, hygienically open top and bottom, a raw fog was rolling slowly in, and the sight of a pair of winter pants, flung hastily over a chair the previous night, fretted him with a sense of the sordid absurdity of the human form. The telephone bell rang, and he crawled wretchedly out of bed and into the sitting-room, where Mrs. Munns, who did for him by the day, was laying the table, sneezing as she went.

Mr. Bunter was speaking.

"His lordship says he'd be very glad, sir, if you could make it convenient to step round to breakfast."

If the odour of kidneys and bacon had been wafted along the wire, Mr. Parker could not have experienced a more vivid sense of consolation.

"Tell his lordship I'll be with him in half an hour," he said, thankfully, and plunging into the bathroom, which was also the kitchen, he informed Mrs. Munns, who was just making tea from a kettle which had gone off the boil, that he should be out to breakfast.

"You can take the porridge home for the family," he added, viciously, and flung off his dressing-gown with such determination that Mrs. Munns could only scuttle away with a snort.

A 19 'bus deposited him in Piccadilly only fifteen minutes later than his rather sanguine impulse had prompted him to suggest, and Mr. Bunter served him with glorious food, incomparable coffee, and the *Daily Mail* before a blazing fire of wood and coal. A distant voice singing the "et iterum venturus est" from Bach's Mass in B minor proclaimed that for the owner of the flat cleanliness and godliness met at least once a day, and presently Lord Peter roamed in, moist and verbena-scented, in a bath-robe cheerfully patterned with unnaturally variegated peacocks.

"Mornin', old dear," said that gentleman. "Beast of a day, ain't it? Very good of you to trundle out in it, but I had a letter I wanted you to see, and I hadn't the energy to come round to your place. Bunter and I've been makin' a night of it."

"What's the letter?" asked Parker.

"Never talk business with your mouth full," said Lord Peter, reprovingly; "have some Oxford marmalade–and then I'll show you my Dante; they brought it round last night. What ought I to read this morning, Bunter?"

"Lord Erith's collection is going to be sold, my lord. There is a column about it in the *Morning Post*. I think your lordship should look at this review of Sir Julian Freke's new book on 'The Physiological Bases of the Conscience' in the *Times Literary Supplement*. Then there is a very singular little burglary in the *Chronicle*, my lord, and an attack on titled families in the *Herald*–rather ill-written, if I may say so, but not without unconscious humour which your lordship will appreciate."

"All right, give me that and the burglary," said his lordship.

"I have looked over the other papers," pursued Mr. Bunter, indicating a formidable pile, "and marked your lordship's after-breakfast reading."

"Oh, pray don't allude to it," said Lord Peter; "you take my appetite away."

There was silence, but for the crunching of toast and the crackling of paper.

"I see they adjourned the inquest" said Parker presently.

"Nothing else to do," said Lord Peter; "but Lady Levy arrived last night, and will have to go and fail to identify the body this morning for Sugg's benefit."

"Time, too," said Mr. Parker shortly.

Silence fell again.

"I don't think much of your burglary, Bunter," said Lord Peter. "Competent, of course, but no imagination. I want imagination in a criminal. Where's the *Morning Post*?"

After a further silence, Lord Peter said: "You might send for the catalogue, Bunter, that Apollonios Rhodios* might be worth looking at. No, I'm damned if I'm going to stodge through that review, but you can stick the book on the library list if you like. His book on crime was entertainin' enough as far as it went, but the fellow's got a bee in his bonnet. Thinks God's a secretion of the liver–all right once in a way, but there's no need to keep on about it. There's nothing you can't prove if your outlook is only sufficiently limited. Look at Sugg."

"I beg your pardon," said Parker. "I wasn't attending. Argentines are steadying a little, I see."

"Milligan," said Lord Peter.

*Apollonios Rhodios. Lorenzobodi Alopa. Firenze, 1496. (4to.) The excitement attendant on the solution of the Battersea Mystery did not prevent Lord Peter from securing this rare work before his departure for Corsica.

"Oil's in a bad way. Levy's made a difference there. That funny little boom in Peruvians that came on just before he disappeared has died away again. I wonder if he was concerned in it. D'you know at all?"

"I'll find out," said Lord Peter. "What was it?"

"Oh, an absolutely dud enterprise that hadn't been heard of for years. It suddenly took a little lease of life last week. I happened to notice it because my mother got let in for a couple of hundred shares a long time ago. It never paid a dividend. Now it's petered out again."

Wimsey pushed his plate aside and lit a pipe.

"Having finished, I don't mind doing some work," he said. "How did you get on yesterday?"

"I didn't," replied Parker. "I sleuthed up and down those flats in my own bodily shape and two different disguises. I was a gas-meter man and a collector for a Home for Lost Doggies, and I didn't get a thing to go on, except a servant in the top flat at the Battersea Bridge Road end of the row who said she thought she heard a bump on the roof one night. Asked which night, she couldn't rightly say. Asked if it was Monday night, she thought it very likely. Asked if it mightn't have been in that high wind on Saturday night that blew my chimney-pot off, she couldn't say but what it might have been. Asked if she was sure it was on the roof and not inside the flat, said to be sure they did find a picture tumbled down next morning. Very suggestible girl. I saw your friends, Mr. and Mrs. Appledore, who received me coldly, but could make no definite complaint about Thipps except that his mother dropped her h's, and that he once called on them uninvited, armed with a pamphlet about anti-vivisection. The Indian Colonel on the first floor was loud, but unexpectedly friendly. He gave me Indian curry for supper and some very good whisky, but he's a sort of hermit, and all *he* could tell me was that he couldn't stand Mrs. Appledore."

"Did you get nothing at the house?"

"Only Levy's private diary. I brought it away with me. Here it is. It doesn't tell one much, though. It's full of entries like: 'Tom and Annie to dinner'; and 'My dear wife's birthday; gave her an old opal ring'; 'Mr. Arbuthnot dropped in to tea; he wants to marry Rachel, but I should like someone steadier for my treasure.' Still, I thought it would show who came to the house and so on. He evidently wrote it up at night. There's no entry for Monday."

"I expect it'll be useful," said Lord Peter, turning over the pages. "Poor old buffer. I say, I'm not so certain now he was done away with."

He detailed to Mr. Parker his day's work.

"Arbuthnot?" said Parker. "Is that the Arbuthnot of the diary?"

"I suppose so. I hunted him up because I knew he was fond of fooling round the Stock Exchange. As for Milligan, he *looks* all right, but I believe he's pretty ruthless in business and you never can tell. Then there's the red-haired secretary–lightnin' calculator man with a face like a fish, keeps on sayin' nuthin'–got the Tarbaby in his family tree, I should think. Milligan's got a jolly good motive for, at any rate, suspendin' Levy for a few days. Then there's the new man."

"What new man?"

"Ah, that's the letter I mentioned to you. Where did I put it? Here we are. Good parchment paper, printed address of solicitor's office in Salisbury, and postmark to correspond. Very precisely written with a fine nib by an elderly business man of old-fashioned habits."

Parker took the letter and read:

CRIMPLESHAM AND WICKS,
*Solicitors*,
MILFORD HILL SALISBURY,
17 November, 192–.

Sir,

With reference to your advertisement today in the personal column of *The Times*, I am disposed to believe that the eyeglasses and chain in question may be those I lost on The L. B. & S. C. Electric Railway while visiting London last Monday. I left Victoria by the 5.45 train, and did not notice my loss till I arrived at Balham. This indication and the optician's specification of the glasses, which I enclose, should suffice at once as an identification and a guarantee of my bona fides. If the glasses should prove to be mine, I should be greatly obliged to you if you would kindly forward them to me by registered post, as the chain was a present from my daughter, and is one of my dearest possessions.

Thanking you in advance for this kindness, and regretting the trouble to which I shall be putting you, I am,

Yours very truly,
THOS. CRIMPLESHAM

Lord Peter Wimsey,
110 Piccadilly, W.
(Encl.)

"Dear me," said Parker, "This is what you might call unexpected."

"Either it is some extraordinary misunderstanding," said Lord Peter, "or Mr. Crimplesham is a very bold and cunning villain. Or possibly, of course, they are the wrong glasses. We may as well get a ruling on that point at once. I suppose the glasses are at the Yard. I wish you'd just ring 'em up and ask 'em to send round an optician's description of them at once–and you might ask at the same time whether it's a very common prescription."

"Right you are," said Parker, and took the receiver off its hook.

"And now," said the friend, when the message was delivered, "just come into the library for a minute."

On the library table, Lord Peter had spread out a series of bromide prints, some dry, some damp, and some but half-washed.

"These little ones are the originals of the photos we've been taking," said Lord Peter, "and these big ones are enlargements all made to precisely the same scale. This one here is the footmark on the linoleum; we'll put that by itself at present. Now these fingerprints can be divided into five lots. I've numbered 'em on the prints–see?–and made a list:

"A. The finger-prints of Levy himself, off his little bedside book and his hair-brush–this and this–you can't mistake the little scar on the thumb.

"B. The smudges made by the gloved fingers of the man who slept in Levy's room on Monday night. They show clearly on the water-bottle and on the boots–superimposed on Levy's. They are very distinct on the boots–surprisingly so for gloved hands, and I deduce that the gloves were rubber ones and had recently been in water.

"Here's another interestin' point. Levy walked in the rain on Monday night, as we know, and these dark marks are mud-splashes. You see they lie *over* Levy's finger-prints in every case. Now see: on this left boot we find the stranger's thumb-mark *over* the mud on the leather above the heel. That's a funny place to find a thumb-mark on a boot, isn't it? That is, if Levy took off his boots. But it's the place where you'd expect to see it if somebody forcibly removed his boots for him. Again, most of the stranger's fingermarks come *over* the mud-marks, but here is one splash of mud which comes on top of them again. Which makes me infer that the stranger came back to Park Lane, wearing Levy's boots, in a cab, carriage or car, but that at some point or other he walked a little way—just enough to tread in a puddle and get a splash on the boots. What do you say?"

"Very pretty," said Parker. "A bit intricate, though, and the marks are not all that I could wish a fingerprint to be."

"Well, I won't lay too much stress on it. But it fits in with our previous ideas. Now let's turn to:

"C. The prints obligingly left by my own particular villain on the further edge of Thipp's bath, where you spotted them, and I ought to be scourged for not having spotted them. The left hand, you notice, the base of the palm and the fingers, but not the tips, looking as though he had steadied himself on the edge of the bath while leaning down to adjust something at the bottom, the pince-nez perhaps. Gloved, you see, but showing no ridge or seam of any kind—I say rubber, you say rubber. That's that. Now see here:

"D and E come off a visiting-card of mine. There's this thing at the corner, marked F, but that you can disregard; in the original document it's a sticky mark left by the thumb of the youth who took it from me, after first removing a piece of chewing-gum from his teeth with his finger to tell me that Mr. Milligan might or might not be disengaged. D and E are the thumb-marks of Mr. Milligan and his red-haired secretary. I'm not clear which is which, but I saw the youth with the chewing-gum hand the card to the secretary, and when I got into the inner shrine I saw John P. Milligan standing with it in his hand, so it's one or the other, and for the moment it's immaterial to our purpose which is which. I boned the card from the table when I left.

"Well, now, Parker, here's what's been keeping Bunter and me up till the small hours. I've measured and measured every way backwards and forwards till my head's spinnin', and I've stared till I'm nearly blind, but I'm hanged if I can make my mind up. Question 1. Is C identical with B? Question 2. Is D or E identical with B? There's nothing to go on but the size and shape, of course, and the marks are so faint—what do you think?"

Parker shook his head doubtfully.

"I think E might almost be put out of the question," he said; "it seems such an excessively long and narrow thumb. But I think there is a decided resemblance between the span of B on the water-bottle and C on the bath. And I don't see any reason why D shouldn't be the same as B, only there's so little to judge from."

"Your untutored judgment and my measurements have brought us both to the same conclusion—if you can call it a conclusion," said Lord Peter, bitterly.

"Another thing," said Parker. "Why on earth should we try to connect B with C? The fact that you and I happen to be friends doesn't make it necessary to conclude that the two cases we happen to be interested in have any organic connection with one another. Why should they? The only person who thinks they have is Sugg, and he's nothing to go by. It would be different if there were any truth in the suggestion that the man in the bath was Levy, but we know for a certainty he wasn't. It's ridiculous to suppose that the same man was employed in committing two totally distinct crimes on the same night, one in Battersea and the other in Park Lane."

"I know," said Wimsey, "though of course we mustn't forget that Levy *was* in Battersea at the time, and now we know he didn't return home at twelve as was supposed, we've no reason to think he ever left Battersea at all."

"True. But there are other places in Battersea beside Thipps's bathroom. And he *wasn't* in Thipps's bathroom. In fact, come to think of it, that's the one place in the universe where we know definitely that he wasn't. So what's Thipps's bath got to do with it?"

"I don't know," said Lord Peter. "Well, perhaps we shall get something better to go on today."

He leaned back in his chair and smoked thoughtfully for some time over the papers which Bunter had marked for him.

"They've got you out in the limelight," he said. "Thank Heaven, Sugg hates me too much to give me any publicity. What a dull Agony Column! 'Darling Pipsey—Come back soon to your distracted Popsey'—and the usual young man in need of financial assistance, and the usual injunction to 'Remember thy Creator in the days of thy youth.' Hullo! there's the bell. Oh, it's our answer from Scotland Yard."

The note from Scotland Yard enclosed an optician's specification identical with that sent by Mr. Crimplesham, and added that it was an unusual one, owing to the peculiar strength of the lenses and the marked differences between the sight of the two eyes.

"That's good enough," said Parker.

"Yes," said Wimsey. "Then Possibility No. 3 is knocked on the head. There remain Possibility No. 1: Accident or Misunderstanding, and No. 2: Deliberate Villainy, of a remarkably bold and calculating kind—of a kind, in fact, characteristic of the author or authors of our two problems. Following the methods inculcated at that University of which I have the honour to be a member, we will now examine severally the various suggestions afforded by Possibility No. 2. This Possibility may be again subdivided into two or more Hypotheses. On Hypothesis 1 (strongly advocated by my distinguished colleague Professor Snupshed), the criminal, whom we may designate as X, is not identical with Crimplesham, but is using the name of Crimplesham as his shield, or aegis. This hypothesis may be further subdivided into two alternatives. Alternative A: Crimplesham is an innocent and unconscious accomplice, and X is in his employment. X writes in Crimplesham's name on Crimplesham's office-paper and obtains that the object in question, i.e., the eyeglasses, be despatched to Crimplesham's address. He is in a position to intercept the parcel before it reaches Crimplesham. The presumption is that X is Crimplesham's charwoman, office boy, clerk, secretary or porter. This offers a wide field of investigation. The method of inquiry will be to interview Crimplesham and discover whether he sent the letter, and if not, who has access to his correspondence. Alternative B: Crimplesham is under X's influence or in his power, and has been induced to write the letter by (*a*) bribery, (*b*) misrepresentation or (*c*) threats. X may in that case be a persuasive relation or friend, or else a creditor, blackmailer or assassin; Crimplesham, on the other hand, is obviously venal or a fool. The method of inquiry in this case, I would tentatively suggest, is again to interview Crimplesham, put the facts of the case strongly before him, and assure him in the most intimidating terms that he is liable to a prolonged term of penal servitude as an accessory after the fact in the crime of murder– Ah-hem! Trusting, gentlemen, that you have followed me thus far, we will pass to the consideration of Hypothesis No. 2, to which I personally incline, and according to which X is identical with Crimplesham.

"In this case, Crimplesham, who is, in the words of an English classic, a man-of-infinite-resource-and-sagacity, correctly deduces that, of all people, the last whom we shall expect to find answering our advertisement is the criminal himself. Accordingly, he plays a bold game of bluff. He invents an occasion on which the glasses may very easily have been lost or stolen, and applies for them. If confronted, nobody will be more astonished than he to learn where they were found. He will produce witnesses to prove that he left Victoria at 5.45 and emerged from the train at Balham at the scheduled time, and sat up all Monday night playing chess with a respectable gentleman well known in Balham. In this case, the method of inquiry will be to pump the respectable gentleman in Balham, and if he should happen to be a single gentleman with a deaf housekeeper, it may be no easy matter to impugn the alibi, since, outside detective romances, few ticket-collectors and 'bus-conductors keep an exact remembrance of all the passengers passing between Balham and London on any and every evening of the week.

"Finally, gentlemen, I will frankly point out the weak point of all these hypotheses, namely: that none of them offers any explanation as to why the incriminating article was left so conspicuously on the body in the first instance."

Mr. Parker had listened with commendable patience to this academic exposition.

"Might not X," he suggested, "be an enemy of Crimplesham's, who designed to throw suspicion upon him?"

"He might. In that case he should be easy to discover, since he obviously lives in close proximity to Crimplesham and his glasses, and Crimplesham in fear of his life will then be a valuable ally for the prosecution."

"How about the first possibility of all, misunderstanding or accident?"

"Well! Well, for purposes of discussion, nothing, because it really doesn't afford any data for discussion."

"In any case," said Parker, "the obvious course appears to be to go to Salisbury."

"That seems indicated," said Lord Peter.

"Very well," said the detective, "is it to be you or me or both of us?"

"It is to be me," said Lord Peter, "and that for two reasons. First, because, if (by Possibility No. 2, Hypothesis 1, Alternative A) Crimplesham is an innocent catspaw, the person who put in the advertisement is the proper person to hand over the property. Secondly, because, if we are to adopt Hypothesis 2, we must not overlook the sinister possibility that Crimplesham-X is laying a careful trap to rid himself of the person who so unwarily advertised in the daily press his interest in the solution of the Battersea Park mystery."

"That appears to me to be an argument for our both going," objected the detective.

"Far from it," said Lord Peter. "Why play into the hands of Crimplesham-X by delivering over to him the only two men in London with the evidence, such as it is, and shall I say the wits, to connect him with the Battersea body?"

"But if we told the Yard where we were going, and we both got nobbled," said Mr. Parker, "it would afford strong presumptive evidence of Crimplesham's guilt, and anyhow, if he didn't get hanged for murdering the man in the bath he'd at least get hanged for murdering us."

"Well," said Lord Peter, "if he only murdered me you could still hang him–what's the good of wasting a sound, marriageable young male like yourself? Besides, how about old Levy? If you're incapacitated, do you think anybody else is going to find him?"

"But we could frighten Crimplesham by threatening him with the Yard."

"Well, dash it all, if it comes to that, *I* can frighten him by threatening him with *you*, which, seeing you hold what evidence there is, is much more to the point. And, then, suppose it's a wild-goose chase after all, you'll have wasted time when you might have been getting on with the case. There are several things that need doing."

"Well," said Parker, silenced but reluctant, "why can't I go, in that case?"

"Bosh!" said Lord Peter. "I am retained (by old Mrs. Thipps, for whom I entertain the greatest respect) to deal with this case, and it's only by courtesy I allow you to have anything to do with it"

Mr. Parker groaned.

"Will you at least take Bunter?" he said.

"In deference to your feelings," replied Lord Peter, "I will take Bunter, though he could be far more usefully employed taking photographs or overhauling my wardrobe. When is there a good train to Salisbury, Bunter?"

"There is an excellent train at 10.50, my lord."

"Kindly make arrangements to catch it," said Lord Peter, throwing off his bath-robe and trailing away with it into his bedroom. "And, Parker–if you have nothing else to do you might get hold of Levy's secretary and look into that little matter of the Peruvian oil."

Lord Peter took with him, for light reading in the train, Sir Reuben Levy's diary. It was a simple, and in the light of recent facts, rather a pathetic document. The terrible fighter of the Stock Exchange, who could with one nod set the surly bear dancing, or bring the savage bull to feed out of his hand, whose breath devastated whole districts with famine or swept financial potentates from their seats, was revealed in private life as kindly, domestic, innocently proud of himself and his belongings, confiding, generous and a little dull. His own small economies were duly chronicled side by side with extravagant presents to his wife and daughter. Small incidents of household routine appeared, such as: "Man came to mend the conservatory roof," or "The new butler (Simpson) has arrived, recommended by the Goldbergs. I think he will be satisfactory." All visitors and entertainments were duly entered, from a very magnificent lunch to Lord Dewsbury, the Minister for Foreign Affairs, and Dr. Jabez K. Wort, the American plenipotentiary, through a series of diplomatic dinners to eminent financiers, down to intimate family gatherings of persons designated by Christian names or nicknames. About May there came a mention of Lady Levy's nerves, and further reference was made to the subject in subsequent months. In September it was stated that "Freke came to see my dear wife and advised complete rest and change of scene. She thinks of going abroad with Rachel." The name of the famous nerve-specialist occurred as a diner or luncher about once a month, and it came into Lord Peter's mind that Freke would be a good person to consult about Levy himself. "People sometimes tell things to the doctor," he murmured to himself. "And, by Jove! if Levy was simply going round to see Freke on Monday night, that rather disposes of the Battersea incident, doesn't it?" He made a note to look up Sir Julian and turned on further. On September 18th, Lady Levy and her daughter had left for the south of France. Then suddenly, under the date October 5th, Lord Peter found what he was looking for: "Goldberg, Skriner and Milligan to dinner."

There was the evidence that Milligan had been in that house. There had been a formal entertainment–a meeting as of two duellists shaking hands before the fight. Skriner was a well-known picture-dealer; Lord Peter imagined an after-dinner excursion upstairs to see the two Corots in the drawing-room, and the portrait of the oldest Levy girl, who had died at the age of sixteen. It was by Augustus John, and hung in the bedroom. The name of the red-haired secretary was nowhere mentioned, unless the initial S., occurring in another entry, referred to him. Throughout September and October, Anderson (of Wyndham's) had been a frequent visitor.

Lord Peter shook his head over the diary, and turned to the consideration of the Battersea Park mystery. Whereas in the Levy affair it was easy enough to supply a motive for the crime, if crime it were, and the difficulty was to discover the method of its carrying out and the whereabouts of the victim, in the other case the chief obstacle to inquiry was the entire absence of any imaginable motive. It was odd that, although the papers had carried news of the affair from one end of the country to the other and a description of the body had been sent to every police station in the country, nobody had as yet come forward to identify the mysterious occupant of Mr. Thipps's bath. It was true that the description, which mentioned the clean-shaven chin, elegantly cut hair and the pince-nez, was rather misleading, but on the other hand, the police had managed to discover the number of molars missing, and the height, complexion and other data were correctly enough stated, as also the date at which death had presumably occurred. It seemed, however, as though the man had melted out of society without leaving a gap or so much as a ripple. Assigning a motive for the murder of a person without relations or antecedents or even clothes is like trying to visualize the fourth dimension–admirable exercise for the imagination, but arduous and inconclusive. Even if the day's interview should disclose black spots in the past or present of Mr. Crimplesham, how were they to be brought into connection with a person apparently without a past, and whose present was confined to the narrow limits of a bath and a police mortuary?

"Bunter," said Lord Peter, "I beg that in the future you will restrain me from starting two hares at once. These cases are gettin' to be a strain on my constitution. One hare has nowhere to run from, and the other has nowhere to run to. It's a kind of mental D.T., Bunter. When this is over I shall turn pussyfoot, forswear the police news, and take to an emollient diet of the works of the late Charles Garvice."

It was its comparative proximity to Milford Hill that induced Lord Peter to lunch at the Minister Hotel rather than at the White Hart or some other more picturesquely situated hostel. It was not a lunch calculated to cheer his mind; as in all Cathedral cities, the atmosphere of the Close pervades every nook and corner of Salisbury, and no food in that city but seems faintly flavoured with prayer-books. As he sat sadly consuming that impassive pale substance known to the English as "cheese" unqualified (for there are cheeses which go openly by their names, as Stilton, Camembert, Gruyère, Wensleydale or

Gorgonzola, but "cheese" is cheese and everywhere the same), he inquired of the waiter the whereabouts of Mr. Crimplesham's office.

The waiter directed him to a house rather further up the street on the opposite side, adding: "But anybody'll tell you, sir; Mr. Crimplesham's very well known hereabouts."

"He's a good solicitor, I suppose?" said Lord Peter.

"Oh yes, sir," said the waiter, "you couldn't do better than trust to Mr. Crimplesham, sir. There's folk say he's old-fashioned, but I'd rather have my little bits of business done by Mr. Crimplesham than by one of these fly-away young men. Not but what Mr. Crimplesham'll be retiring soon, sir, I don't doubt, for he must be close on eighty, sir, if he's a day, but then there's young Mr. Wicks to carry on the business, and he's a very nice, steady-like young gentleman."

"Is Mr. Crimplesham really as old as that?" said Lord Peter. "Dear me! He must be very active for his years. A friend of mine was doing business with him in town last week."

"Wonderful active, sir," agreed the waiter, "and with his game leg, too, you'd be surprised. But there, sir, I often think when a man's once past a certain age, the older he grows the tougher he gets, and women the same or more so."

"Very likely," said Lord Peter, calling up and dismissing the mental picture of a gentleman of eighty with a game leg carrying a dead body over the roof of a Battersea flat at midnight. " 'He's tough, sir, tough, is old Joey Bagstock, tough and devilish sly,' " he added, thoughtlessly.

"Indeed, sir?" said the waiter "I couldn't say, I'm sure "

"I beg your pardon," said Lord Peter; "I was quoting poetry. Very silly of me. I got the habit at my mother's knee and I can't break myself of it."

"No, sir," said the waiter, pocketing a liberal tip. "Thank you very much, sir. You'll find the house easy. Just afore you come to Penny-farthing Street, sir, about two turnings off, on the right-hand side opposite."

"Afraid that disposes of Crimplesham-X," said Lord Peter. "I'm rather sorry; he was a fine sinister figure as I had pictured him. Still, his may yet be the brain behind the hands—the aged spider sitting invisible in the centre of the vibrating web, you know, Bunter."

"Yes, my lord," said Bunter. They were walking up the street together.

"There is the office over the way," pursued Lord Peter "I think, Bunter, you might step into this little shop and purchase a sporting paper, and if I do not emerge from the villain's lair—say within three-quarters of an hour, you may take such steps as your perspicuity may suggest."

Mr. Bunter turned into the shop as desired, and Lord Peter walked across and rang the lawyer's bell with decision.

"The truth, the whole truth and nothing but the truth is my long suit here, I fancy," he murmured, and when the door was opened by a clerk he delivered over his card with an unflinching air.

He was ushered immediately into a confidential-looking office, obviously furnished in the early years of Queen Victoria's reign, and never altered since. A lean, frail-looking old gentleman rose briskly from his chair as he entered and limped forward to meet him.

"My dear sir," exclaimed the lawyer, "how extremely good of you to come in person! Indeed, I am ashamed to have given you so much trouble. I trust you were passing this way, and that my glasses have not put you to any great inconvenience. Pray take a seat, Lord Peter." He peered gratefully at the young man over a pince-nez obviously the fellow of that now adorning a dossier in Scotland Yard.

Lord Peter sat down. The lawyer sat down. Lord Peter picked up a glass paper-weight from the desk and weighed it thoughtfully in his hand. Subconsciously he noted what an admirable set of fingerprints he was leaving upon it. He replaced it with precision on the exact centre of a pile of letters.

"It's quite all right," said Lord Peter. "I was here on business. Very happy to be of service to you. Very awkward to lose one's glasses, Mr. Crimplesham."

"Yes," said the lawyer, "I assure you I feel quite lost without them. I have this pair, but they do not fit my nose so well—besides, that chain has a great sentimental value for me. I was terribly distressed on arriving at Balham to find that I had lost them. I made inquiries of the railway, but to no purpose. I feared they had been stolen. There were such crowds at Victoria, and the carriage was packed with people all the way to Balham. Did you come across them in the train?"

"Well, no," said Lord Peter, "I found them in rather an unexpected place. Do you mind telling me if you recognized any of your fellow-travellers on that occasion?"

The lawyer stared at him.

"Not a soul," he answered. "Why do you ask?"

"Well," said Lord Peter, "I thought perhaps the—the person with whom I found them might have taken them for a joke."

The lawyer looked puzzled.

"Did the person claim to be an acquaintance of mine?" he inquired. "I know practically nobody in London, except the friend with whom I was staying in Balham, Dr. Philpots, and I should be very greatly surprised at his practising a jest upon me. He knew very well how distressed I was at the loss of the glasses. My business was to attend a meeting of shareholders in Medlicott's Bank, but the other gentlemen present were all personally unknown to me, and I cannot think that any of them would take so great a liberty. In any case," he added, "as the glasses are here, I will not inquire too closely into the manner of their restoration. I am deeply obliged to you for your trouble."

Lord Peter hesitated.

"Pray forgive my seeming inquisitiveness," he said, "but I must ask you another question. It sounds rather melodramatic, I'm afraid, but it's this. Are you aware that you have any enemy—anyone, I mean, who would profit by your—er—decease or disgrace?"

Mr. Crimplesham sat frozen into stony surprise and disapproval.

"May I ask the meaning of this extraordinary question?" he inquired stiffly.

"Well," said Lord Peter, "the circumstances are a little unusual. You may recollect that my advertisement was addressed to the jeweller who sold the chain."

"That surprised me at the time," said Mr. Crimplesham, "but I begin to think your advertisement and your behaviour are all of a piece."

"They are," said Lord Peter. "As a matter of fact I did not expect the owner of the glasses to answer my advertisement. Mr. Crimplesham, you have no doubt read what the papers have to say about the Battersea Park mystery. Your glasses are the pair that was found on the body, and they are now in the possession of the police at Scotland Yard, as you may see by this." He placed the specification of the glasses and the official note before Crimplesham.

"Good God!" exclaimed the lawyer. He glanced at the paper, and then looked narrowly at Lord Peter.

"Are you yourself connected with the police?" he inquired.

"Not officially," said Lord Peter. "I am investigating the matter privately, in the interest of one of the parties."

Mr. Crimplesham rose to his feet.

"My good man," he said, "this is a very impudent attempt, but blackmail is an indictable offence, and I advise you to leave my office before you commit yourself." He rang the bell.

"I was afraid you'd take it like that," said Lord Peter. "It looks as though this ought to have been my friend Detective Parker's job, after all." He laid Parker's card on the table beside the specification, and added: "If you should wish to see me again, Mr. Crimplesham, before tomorrow morning, you will find me at the Minster Hotel."

Mr. Crimplesham disdained to reply further than to direct the clerk who entered to "show this person out."

In the entrance Lord Peter brushed against a tall young man who was just coming in, and who stared at him with surprised recognition. His face, however, aroused no memories in Lord Peter's mind, and that baffled nobleman, calling out Bunter from the newspaper shop, departed to his hotel to get a trunk-call through to Parker.

Meanwhile, in the office, the meditations of the indignant Mr. Crimplesham were interrupted by the entrance of his junior partner.

"I say," said the latter gentleman, "has somebody done something really wicked at last? Whatever brings such a distinguished amateur of crime on our sober doorstep?"

"I have been the victim of a vulgar attempt at blackmail," said the lawyer; "an individual passing himself off as Lord Peter Wimsey–"

"But that *is* Lord Peter Wimsey," said Mr. Wicks, "there's no mistaking him. I saw him give evidence in the Attenbury emerald case. He's a big little pot in his way, you know, and goes fishing with the head of Scotland Yard."

"Oh, dear," said Mr. Crimplesham.

Fate arranged that the nerves of Mr. Crimplesham should be tried that afternoon. When, escorted by Mr. Wicks, he arrived at the Minster Hotel, he was informed by the porter that Lord Peter Wimsey had strolled out, mentioning that he thought of attending Evensong. "But his man is here, sir," he added, "if you'd like to leave a message."

Mr. Wicks thought that on the whole it would be well to leave a message. Mr. Bunter, on inquiry, was found to be sitting by the telephone waiting for a trunk-call. As Mr. Wicks addressed him the bell rang, and Mr. Bunter, politely excusing himself, took down the receiver.

"Hullo!" he said. "Is that Mr. Parker? Oh, thanks! Exchange! Exchange! Sorry, can you put me through to Scotland Yard? Excuse me, gentlemen, keeping you waiting–Exchange! all right–Scotland Yard–Hullo! Is that Scotland Yard?–Is Detective Parker round there?–Can I speak to him?–I shall have done in a moment, gentlemen.–Hullo! is that you, Mr. Parker? Lord Peter would be much obliged if you could find it convenient to step down to Salisbury, sir. Oh, no, sir, he's in excellent health, sir—just stepped round to hear Evensong, sir—oh, no, I think tomorrow morning would do excellently, sir, thank you, sir."

# 6

IT WAS, in fact, inconvenient for Mr. Parker to leave London. He had had to go and see Lady Levy towards the end of the morning, and subsequently his plans for the day had been thrown out of gear and his movements delayed by the discovery that the adjourned inquest of Mr. Thipps's unknown visitor was to be held that afternoon, since nothing very definite seemed forthcoming from Inspector Sugg's inquiries. Jury and witnesses had been convened accordingly for three o'clock. Mr. Parker might altogether have missed the event had he not run against Sugg that morning at the Yard and extracted the information from him as one would a reluctant tooth. Inspector Sugg, indeed, considered Mr. Parker rather interfering; moreover, he was hand-in-glove with Lord Peter Wimsey, and Inspector Sugg had no words for the interferingness of Lord Peter. He could not, however, when directly questioned, deny that there was to be an inquest that afternoon, nor could he prevent Mr. Parker from enjoying the inalienable right of any interested British citizen to be present. At a little before three, therefore, Mr. Parker was in his place, and amusing himself with watching the efforts of those persons who arrived after the room was packed to insinuate, bribe or bully themselves into a position of vantage. The Coroner, a medical man of precise habits and unimaginative aspect, arrived punctually, and looking peevishly round at the crowded assembly, directed all the windows to be opened, thus letting in a stream of drizzling fog upon the heads of the unfortunates on that side of the room. This caused a commotion and some expressions of disapproval, checked sternly by the Coroner, who said that with the influenza about again an unventilated room was a death-trap; that anybody who chose to object to open windows had the obvious remedy of leaving the court, and further, that if any disturbance was made he would clear the court. He then took a Formamint lozenge, and proceeded, after the usual preliminaries, to call up fourteen good and lawful persons and swear them diligently to inquire and a true presentment make of all matters touching the death of the gentleman with the pince-nez and to give a true verdict according to the evidence, so help them God. When an expostulation by a woman juror—an elderly lady in spectacles who kept a sweetshop, and appeared to wish she was back there—had been summarily quashed by the Coroner, the jury departed to view the body. Mr. Parker gazed round again and identified the unhappy Mr. Thipps and the girl Gladys led into an adjoining room under the grim guard of the police. They were soon followed by a gaunt old lady in a bonnet and mantle. With her, in a wonderful fur coat and a motor bonnet of fascinating construction, came the Dowager Duchess of Denver, her quick, dark eyes darting hither and thither about the crowd. The next moment they had lighted on Mr. Parker, who had several times visited the Dower House, and she nodded to him, and spoke to a policeman. Before long, a way opened magically through the press, and Mr. Parker found himself accommodated with a front seat just behind the Duchess, who greeted him charmingly, and said: "What's happened to poor Peter?" Parker began to explain, and the Coroner glanced irritably in their direction. Somebody went up and whispered in his ear, at which he coughed, and took another Formamint.

"We came up by car," said the Duchess–"so tiresome–such bad roads between Denver and Gunbury St. Walters–and there were people coming to lunch–I had to put them off–I couldn't let the old lady go alone, could I? By the way, such an odd thing's happened about the Church Restoration Fund–the Vicar–oh, dear, here are these people coming back again; well, I'll tell you afterwards–do look at that woman looking shocked, and the girl in tweeds trying to look as if she sat on undraped gentlemen every day of her life–I don't mean that–corpses of course–but one finds oneself being so Elizabethan nowadays–what an awful little man the coroner is, isn't he? He's looking daggers at me–do you think he'll dare to clear me out of the court or commit me for what-you-may-call-it?"

The first part of the evidence was not of great interest to Mr. Parker. The wretched Mr. Thipps, who had caught cold in gaol, deposed in an unhappy croak to having discovered the body when he went in to take his bath at eight o'clock. He had had such a shock, he had to sit down and send the girl for brandy. He had never seen the deceased before. He had no idea how he came there.

Yes, he had been in Manchester the day before. He had arrived at St. Pancras at ten o'clock. He had cloak-roomed his bag. At this point Mr. Thipps became very red, unhappy and confused, and glanced nervously about the court.

"Now, Mr. Thipps," said the Coroner, briskly, "we must have your movements quite clear. You must appreciate the importance of the matter. You have chosen to give evidence, which you need not have done, but having done so, you will find it best to be perfectly explicit."

"Yes," said Mr. Thipps faintly.

"Have you cautioned this witness, officer?" inquired the Coroner, turning sharply to Inspector Sugg.

The Inspector replied that he had told Mr. Thipps that anything he said might be used agin' him at his trial. Mr. Thipps became ashy, and said in a bleating voice that he 'adn't–hadn't meant to do anything that wasn't right.

This remark produced a mild sensation, and the Coroner became even more acidulated in manner than before.

"Is anybody representing Mr. Thipps?" he asked, irritably. "No? Did you not explain to him that he could–that he *ought* to be represented? You did not? Really, Inspector! Did you not know, Mr. Thipps, that you had a right to be legally represented?"

Mr. Thipps clung to a chair-back for support, and said, "No," in a voice barely audible.

"It is incredible," said the Coroner, "that so-called educated people should be so ignorant of the legal procedure of their own country. This places us in a very awkward position. I doubt, Inspector, whether I should permit the prisoner–Mr. Thipps–to give evidence at all. It is a delicate position."

The perspiration stood on Mrs. Thipps's forehead.

"Save us from our friends," whispered the Duchess to Parker. "If that cough-drop-devouring creature had openly instructed those fourteen people–and what unfinished-looking faces they have–so characteristic, I always think, of the lower middle-class, rather like sheep, or calves' head (boiled, I mean), to bring in wilful murder against the poor little man, he couldn't have made himself plainer."

"He can't let him incriminate himself, you know," said Parker.

"Stuff!" said the Duchess. "How could the man incriminate himself when he never did anything in his life? You men never think of anything but your red tape."

Meanwhile Mr. Thipps, wiping his brow with a handkerchief, had summoned up courage. He stood up with a kind of weak dignity, like a small white rabbit brought to bay.

"I would rather tell you," he said, "though it's reelly very unpleasant for a man in my position. But I reelly couldn't have it thought for a moment that I'd committed this dreadful crime. I assure you, gentlemen, I *couldn't bear* that. No. I'd rather tell you the truth, though I'm afraid it places me in rather a–well, I'll tell you."

"You fully understand the gravity of making such a statement, Mr. Thipps," said the Coroner.

"Quite," said Mr. Thipps. "It's all right–I–might I have a drink of water?"

"Take your time," said the Coroner, at the same time robbing his remark of all conviction by an impatient glance at his watch.

"Thank you, sir," said Mr. Thipps. "Well, then, it's true I got to St. Pancras at ten. But there was a man in the carriage with me. He'd got in at Leicester. I didn't recognize him at first, but he turned out to be an old schoolfellow of mine."

"What was this gentleman's name?" inquired the Coroner, his pencil poised.

Mr. Thipps shrank together visibly.

"I'm afraid I can't tell you that," he said. "You see–that is, you *will* see–it would get him into trouble, and I couldn't do that–no, I really couldn't do that, not if my life depended on it. No!" he added, as the ominous pertinence of the last phrase smote upon him, "I'm sure I couldn't do that."

"Well, well," said the Coroner.

The Duchess leaned over to Parker again. "I'm beginning quite to admire the little man," she said.

Mr. Thipps resumed.

"When we got to St. Pancras I was going home, but my friend said no. We hadn't met for a long time and we ought to–to make a night of it, was his expression. I fear I was weak, and let him overpersuade me to accompany him to one of his haunts. I use the word advisedly," said Mr. Thipps, "and I assure you, sir, that if I had known beforehand where we were going I never would have set foot in the place.

"I cloak-roomed my bag, for he did not like the notion of our being encumbered with it, and we got into a taxicab and drove to the corner of Tottenham Court Road and Oxford Street. We then walked a little way, and turned into a side street (I do not recollect which) where there was an open door, with the light shining out. There was a man at a counter, and my friend bought some tickets, and I heard the man at the counter say something to him about 'Your friend,' meaning me, and my friend said, 'Oh, yes, he's been here before, haven't you, Alf?' (which was what they called me at school), though I assure you, sir"–here Mr. Thipps grew very earnest–"I never had, and nothing in the world should induce me to go to such a place again.

"Well, we went down into a room underneath, where there were drinks, and my friend had several, and made me take one or two—though I am an abstemious man as a rule—and he talked to some other men and girls who were there—a very vulgar set of people, I thought them, though I wouldn't say but what some of the young ladies were nice-looking enough. One of them sat on my friend's knee and called him a slow old thing, and told him to come on—so we went into another room, where there were a lot of people dancing all these up-to-date dances. My friend went and danced, and I sat on a sofa. One of the young ladies came up to me and said, didn't I dance, and I said 'No,' so she said wouldn't I stand her a drink then. 'You'll stand us a drink then, darling,' that was what she said, and I said, 'Wasn't it after hours?' and she said that didn't matter. So I ordered the drink—a gin and bitters it was—for I didn't like not to, the young lady seemed to expect it of me and I felt it wouldn't be gentlemanly to refuse when she asked. But it went against my conscience—such a young girl as she was—and she put her arm round my neck afterwards and kissed me just like as if she was paying for the drink—and it reelly went to my 'eart," said Mr. Thipps, a little ambiguously, but with uncommon emphasis.

Here somebody at the back said, "Cheer-oh!" and a sound was heard as of the noisy smacking of lips.

"Remove the person who made that improper noise," said the Coroner, with great indignation. "Go on, please, Mr. Thipps."

"Well," said Mr. Thipps, "about half-past twelve, as I should reckon, things began to get a bit lively, and I was looking for my friend to say good-night, not wishing to stay longer, as you will understand, when I saw him with one of the young ladies, and they seemed to be getting on altogether too well, if you follow me, my friend pulling the ribbons off her shoulder and the young lady laughing—and so on," said Mr. Thipps, hurriedly, "so I thought I'd just slip quietly out, when I heard a scuffle and a shout—and before I knew what was happening there were half-a-dozen policemen in, and the lights went out, and everybody stampeding and shouting—quite horrid, it was. I was knocked down in the rush, and hit my head a nasty knock on a chair—that was where I got that bruise they asked me about—and I was dreadfully afraid I'd never get away and it would all come out, and perhaps my photograph in the papers, when someone caught hold of me—I think it was the young lady I'd given the gin and bitters to—and she said, 'This way,' and pushed me along a passage and out at the back somewhere. So I ran through some streets, and found myself in Goodge Street, and there I got a taxi and came home. I saw the account of the raid afterwards in the papers, and saw my friend had escaped, and so, as it wasn't the sort of thing I wanted made public, and I didn't want to get him into difficulties, I just said nothing. But that's the truth."

"Well, Mr. Thipps," said the Coroner, "we shall be able to substantiate a certain amount of this story. Your friend's name—"

"No," said Mr. Thipps, stoutly, "not on any account."

"Very good," said the Coroner. "Now, can you tell us what time you did get in?"

"About half-past one, I should think. Though reelly, I was so upset—"

"Quite so. Did you go straight to bed?"

"Yes, I took my sandwich and glass of milk first. I thought it might settle my inside, so to speak," added the witness, apologetically, "not being accustomed to alcohol so late at night and on an empty stomach, as you may say."

"Quite so. Nobody sat up for you?"

"Nobody."

"How long did you take getting to bed first and last?"

Mr. Thipps thought it might have been half-an-hour

"Did you visit the bathroom before turning in?"

"No."

"And you heard nothing in the night?"

"No. I fell fast asleep. I was rather agitated, so I took a little dose to make me sleep, and what with being so tired and the milk and the dose, I just tumbled right off and didn't wake till Gladys called me."

Further questioning elicited little from Mr. Thipps. Yes, the bathroom window had been open when he went in in the morning, he was sure of that, and he had spoken very sharply to the girl about it. He was ready to answer any questions; he would be only too 'appy–happy to have this dreadful affair sifted to the bottom.

Gladys Horrocks stated that she had been in Mr. Thipps's employment about three months. Her previous employers would speak to her character. It was her duty to make the round of the flat at night, when she had seen Mrs. Thipps to bed at ten. Yes, she remembered doing so on Monday evening. She had looked into all the rooms. Did she recollect shutting the bathroom window that night? Well, no, she couldn't swear to it, not in particular, but when Mr. Thipps called her into the bathroom in the morning it certainly *was* open. She had not been into the bathroom before Mr. Thipps went in. Well, yes, it had happened that she had left that window open before, when anyone had been 'aving a bath in the evening and 'ad left the blind down. Mrs. Thipps 'ad 'ad a bath on Monday evening. Mondays was one of her regular bath nights. She was very much afraid she 'adn't shut the window on Monday night, though she wished her 'ead 'ad been cut off afore she'd been so forgetful.

Here the witness burst into tears and was given some water, while the Coroner refreshed himself with a third lozenge.

Recovering, witness stated that she had certainly looked into all the rooms before going to bed. No, it was quite impossible for a body to be 'idden in the flat without her seeing of it. She 'ad been in the kitchen all evening, and there wasn't 'ardly room to keep the best dinner service there, let along a body. Old Mrs. Thipps sat in the drawing-room. Yes, she was sure she'd been into the dining-room. How? Because she put Mr. Thipps's milk and sandwiches there ready for him. There had been nothing in there–that she could swear to. Nor yet in her own bedroom, nor in the 'all. Had she searched the bedroom cupboard and the box-room? Well, no, not to say searched; she wasn't use to searchin' people's 'ouses for skelintons every night. So that a man might have concealed himself in the box-room or a wardrobe? She supposed he might.

In reply to a woman juror–well, yes, she was walking out with a young man. Williams was his name, Bill Williams,–well, yes, William Williams, if they insisted. He was a glazier by profession. Well, yes, he 'ad been in the flat sometimes. Well, she supposed you might say he was acquainted with the flat. Had she ever–no, she 'adn't, and if she'd thought such a question was going to be put to a respectable girl she wouldn't 'ave offered to give evidence. The vicar of St. Mary's would speak to her character and to Mr. Williams's. Last time Mr. Williams was at the flat was a fortnight ago.

Well, no, it wasn't exactly the last time she 'ad seen Mr. Williams. Well, yes, the last time was Monday–well, yes, Monday night. Well,if she must tell the truth, she must. Yes, the officer had cautioned her, but there wasn't any 'arm in it, and it was better to lose her place than to be 'ung, though it was a cruel shame a girl couldn't 'ave a bit of fun without a nasty corpse comin' in through the window to get 'er into difficulties. After she 'ad put Mrs. Thipps to bed, she 'ad slipped out to go to the Plumbers' and Glaziers' Ball at the "Black Faced Ram." Mr. Williams 'ad met 'er and brought 'er back. 'E could testify to where she'd been and that there wasn't no 'arm in it. She'd left before the end of the ball. It might 'ave been two o'clock when she got back. She'd got the keys of the flat from Mrs. Thipps's drawer when Mrs. Thipps wasn't looking. She 'ad asked leave to go, but couldn't get it, along of Mr. Thipps bein' away that night. She was bitterly sorry she 'ad be'aved so, and she was sure she'd been punished for it. She had 'eard nothing suspicious when she came in. She had gone straight to bed without looking round the flat. She wished she were dead.

No, Mr. and Mrs. Thipps didn't 'ardly ever 'ave any visitors; they kep' themselves very retired. She had found the outside door bolted that morning as usual. She wouldn't never believe any 'arm of Mr. Thipps. Thank you, Miss Horrocks. Call Georgiana Thipps, and the Coroner thought we had better light the gas.

The examination of Mrs. Thipps provided more entertainment than enlightenment, affording as it did an excellent example of the game called "cross questions and crooked answers." After fifteen minutes' suffering, both in voice and temper, the Coroner abandoned the struggle, leaving the lady with the last word.

'You needn't try to bully me, young man," said that octogenarian with spirit, "settin' there spilin' your stomach with them nasty jujubes."

At this point a young man arose in court and demanded to give evidence. Having explained that he was William Williams, glazier, he was sworn, and corroborated the evidence of Gladys Horrocks in the matter of her presence at the "Black Faced Ram" on the Monday night. They had returned to the flat rather before two, he thought, but certainly later than 1.30. He was sorry that he had persuaded Miss Horrocks to come out with him when she didn't ought. He had observed nothing of a suspicious nature in Prince of Wales Road at either visit.

Inspector Sugg gave evidence of having been called in at about half-past eight on Monday morning. He had considered the girl's manner to be suspicious and had arrested her. On later information, leading him to suspect that the deceased might have been murdered that night, he had arrested Mr. Thipps. He had found no trace of breaking into the flat. There were marks on the bathroom windowsill which pointed to somebody having got in that way. There were no ladder marks or footmarks in the yard; the yard was paved with asphalt. He had examined the roof, but found nothing on the roof. In his opinion the body had been brought into the flat previously and concealed till the evening by someone who had then gone out during the night by the bathroom window, with the connivance of the girl. In that case, why should not the girl have let the person out by the door? Well, it might have been so. Had he found traces of a body or a man or both having been hidden in the flat? He found nothing to show that they might *not* have been so concealed. What was the evidence that led him to suppose that the death had occurred that night?

At this point Inspector Sugg appeared uneasy, and endeavoured to retire upon his professional dignity. On being pressed, however, he admitted that the evidence in question had come to nothing.

*One of the jurors:* Was it the case that any fingermarks had been left by the criminal?

Some marks had been found on the bath, but the criminal had worn gloves.

*The Coroner:* Do you draw any conclusion from this fact as to the experience of the criminal?

*Inspector Sugg:* Looks as if he was an old hand, sir.

*The Juror:* Is that very consistent with the charge against Alfred Thipps, Inspector?

The Inspector was silent.

*The Coroner:* In the light of the evidence which you have just heard, do you still press the charge against Alfred Thipps and Gladys Horrocks?

*Inspector Sugg:* I consider the whole set-out highly suspicious. Thipps's story isn't corroborated, and as for the girl Horrocks, how do we know this Williams ain't in it as well?

*Williams Williams:* Now, you drop that. I can bring a 'undred witnesses—

*The Coroner:* Silence, if you please. I am surprised, Inspector, that you should make this suggestion in that manner. It is highly improper. By the way, can you tell us whether a police raid was actually carried out on the Monday night on any Night Club in the neighbourhood of St. Giles's Circus?

*Inspector Sugg* (sulkily): I believe there was something of the sort.

*The Coroner:* You will, no doubt, inquire into the matter. I seem to recollect having seen some mention of it in the newspapers. Thank you, Inspector, that will do.

Several witnesses having appeared and testified to the characters of Mr. Thipps and Gladys Horrocks, the Coroner stated his intention of proceeding to the medical evidence.

"Sir Julian Freke."

There was considerable stir in the court as the great specialist walked up to give evidence. He was not only a distinguished man, but a striking figure, with his wide shoulders, upright carriage and leonine head. His manner as he kissed the Book presented to him with the usual deprecatory mumble by the Coroner's officer, was that of a St. Paul condescending to humour the timid mumbo-jumbo of superstitious Corinthians.

"So handsome, I always think," whispered the Duchess to Mr. Parker; "just exactly like William Morris, with that bush of hair and beard and those exciting eyes looking out of it—so splendid, these dear men always devoted to something or other—not but what I think socialism is a mistake—of course it works with all those nice people, so good and happy in art linen and the weather always perfect—Morris, I mean, you know—but so difficult in real life. Science is different—I'm sure if I had nerves I should go to Sir Julian just to look at him—eyes like that give one something to think about and that's what most of these people want, only I never had any—nerves, I mean. Don't you think so?"

"You are Sir Julian Freke," said the Coroner, "and live at St. Luke's House, Prince of Wales Road, Battersea, where you exercise a general direction over the surgical side of St. Luke's Hospital?"

Sir Julian assented briefly to this definition of his personality.

"You were the first medical man to see the deceased?"

"I was"

"And you have since conducted an examination in collaboration with Dr. Grimbold of Scotland Yard?"

"I have"

"You are in agreement as to the cause of death?"

"Generally speaking, yes."

"Will you communicate your impressions to the Jury?"

"I was engaged in research work in the dissecting room at St. Luke's Hospital at about nine o'clock on Monday morning, when I was informed that Inspector Sugg wished to see me. He told me that the dead body of a man had been discovered under mysterious circumstances at 59 Queen Caroline Mansions. He asked me whether it could be supposed to be a joke perpetrated by any of the medical students at the hospital. I was able to assure him, by an examination of the hospital's books, that there was no subject missing from the dissecting room."

"Who would be in charge of such bodies?"

"William Watts, the dissecting-room attendant."

"Is William Watts present?" inquired the Coroner of the officer.

William Watts was present, and could be called if the Coroner thought it necessary.

"I suppose no dead body would be delivered to the hospital without your knowledge, Sir Julian?"

"Certainly not"

"Thank you. Will you proceed with your statement?"

"Inspector Sugg then asked me whether I would send a medical man round to view the body. I said that I would go myself."

"Why did you do that?"

"I confess to my share of ordinary human curiosity, Mr. Coroner."

Laughter from a medical student at the back of the room.

"On arriving at the flat I found the deceased lying on his back in the bath. I examined him, and came to the conclusion that death had been caused by a blow on the back of the neck, dislocating the fourth and fifth cervical vertebrae, bruising the spinal cord and producimg internal haemorrhage and partial paralysis of the brain. I judged the deceased to have been dead at least twelve hours, possibly more. I observed no other sign of violence of any kind upon the body. Deceased was a strong, well-nourished man of about fifty to fifty-five years of age."

"In your opinion, could the blow have been self-inflicted?"

"Certainly not. It had been made with a heavy, blunt instrument from behind, with great force and considerable judgment. It is quite impossible that it was self-inflicted."

"Could it have been the result of an accident?"

"That is possible, of course."

"If, for example, the deceased had been looking out of the window, and the sash had shut violently down upon him?"

"No; in that case there would have been signs of strangulation and a bruise upon the throat as well."

"But deceased might have been killed through a heavy weight accidentally falling upon him?"

"He might."

"Was death instantaneous, in your opinion?"

"It is difficult to say. Such a blow might very well cause death instantaneously, or the patient might linger in a partially paralyzed condition for some time. In the present case I should be disposed to think that deceased might have lingered for some hours. I base my decision upon the condition of the brain revealed in the autopsy. I may say, however, that Dr. Grimbold and I are not in complete agreement on the point."

"I understand that a suggestion has been made as to the identification of the deceased. *You* are not in a position to identify him?"

"Certainly not. I never saw him before. The suggestion to which you refer is a preposterous one, and ought never to have been made. I was not aware until this morning that it had been made, had it been made to me earlier, I should have known how to deal with it, and I should like to express my strong disapproval of the unnecessary shock and distress inflicted upon a lady with whom I have the honour to be acquainted."

*The Coroner:* It was not my fault, Sir Julian; I had nothing to do with it; I agree with you that it was unfortunate you were not consulted.

The reporters scribbled busily, and the court asked each other what was meant, while the jury tried to look as if they knew already.

"In the matter of the eyeglasses found upon the body, Sir Julian. Do these give any indication to a medical man?"

"They are somewhat unusual lenses, an oculist would be able to speak more definitely, but I will say for myself that I should have expected them to belong to an older man than the deceased."

"Speaking as a physician, who has had many opportunities of observing the human body, did you gather anything from the appearance of the deceased as to his personal habits?"

"I should say that he was a man in easy circumstances, but who had only recently come into money. His teeth are in a bad state, and his hands shows signs of recent manual labour."

"An Australian colonist, for instance, who had made money?"

"Something of that sort, of course, I could not say positively."

"Of course not. Thank you, Sir Julian."

Dr. Grimbold, called, corroborated his distinguished colleague in every particular, except that, in his opinion, death had not occurred for several days after the blow. It was with the greatest hesitancy that he ventured to differ from Sir Julian Freke, and he might be wrong. It was difficult to tell in any case, and when he saw the body, deceased had been dead at least twenty-four hours, in his opinion.

Inspector Sugg, recalled. Would he tell the jury what steps had been taken to identify the deceased?

A description had been sent to every police station and had been inserted in all the newspapers. In view of the suggestion made by Sir Julian Freke, had inquiries been made at all the seaports? They had. And with no results? With no results at all. No one had come forward to identify the body? Plenty of people had come forward; but nobody had succeeded in identifying it. Had any effort been made to follow up the clue afforded by the eyeglasses? Inspector Sugg submitted that, having regard to the interests of justice, he would beg to be excused from answering that question. Might the jury see the eyeglasses? The eyeglasses were handed to the jury.

William Watts, called, confirmed the evidence of Sir Julian Freke with regard to dissecting-room subjects. He explained the system by which they were entered. They usually were supplied by the workhouses and free hospitals. They were under his sole charge. The young gentlemen could not possibly get the keys. Had Sir Julian Freke, or any of the house surgeons, the keys? No, not even Sir Julian Freke. The keys had remained in his possession on Monday night? They had. And, in any case, the inquiry was irrelevant, as there was no body missing, nor ever had been? That was the case.

The Coroner then addressed the jury, reminding them with some asperity, that they were not there to gossip about who the deceased could or could not have been, but to give their opinion as to the cause of death. He reminded them that they should consider whether, according to the medical evidence, death could have been accidental or self-inflicted, or whether it was deliberate murder, or homicide. If they considered the evidence on this point insufficient, they could return an open verdict. In any case, their verdict could not prejudice any person; if they brought it in "murder," all the whole evidence would have to be gone through again before the magistrate. He then dismissed them, with the unspoken adjuration to be quick about it.

Sir Julian Freke, after giving his evidence, had caught the eye of the Duchess, and now came over and greeted her.

"I haven't seen you for an age," said that lady. "How are you?"

"Hard at work," said the specialist. "Just got my new book out. This kind of thing wastes time. Have you seen Lady Levy yet?"

"No, poor dear," said the Duchess. "I only came up this morning, for this. Mrs. Thipps is staying with me–one of Peter's eccentricities, you know. Poor Christine! I must run round and see her. This is Mr. Parker," she added, "who is investigating that case."

"Oh," said Sir Julian, and paused. "Do you know," he said in a low voice to Parker, "I am very glad to meet you. Have you seen Lady Levy yet?"

"I saw her this morning."

"Did she ask you to go on with the inquiry?"

"Yes," said Parker; "she thinks," he added, "that Sir Reuben may be detained in the hands of some financial rival or that perhaps some scoundrels are holding him to ransom."

"And is that *your* opinion?" asked Sir Julian.

"I think it very likely," said Parker, frankly.

Sir Julian hesitated again.

"I wish you would walk back with me when this is over," he said.

"I should be delighted," said Parker.

At this moment the jury returned and took their places, and there was a little rustle and hush. The Coroner addressed the foreman and inquired if they were agreed upon their verdict.

"We are agreed, Mr. Coroner, that deceased died of the effects of a blow upon the spine, but how that injury was inflicted we consider that there is not sufficient evidence to show."

Mr. Parker and Sir Julian Freke walked up the road together.

"I had absolutely no idea until I saw Lady Levy this morning," said the doctor, "that there was any idea of connecting this matter with the disappearance of Sir Reuben. The suggestion was perfectly monstrous, and could only have grown up in the mind of that ridiculous police officer. If I had had any idea what was in his mind I could have disabused him and avoided all this."

"I did my best to do so," said Parker, "as soon as I was called in to the Levy case–"

"Who called you in, if I may ask?" inquired Sir Julian.

"Well, the household first of all, and then Sir Reuben's uncle, Mr. Levy of Portman Square, wrote to me to go on with the investigation."

"And now Lady Levy had confirmed those instructions ?"

"Certainly," said Parker in some surprise.

Sir Julian was silent for a little time.

"I'm afraid I was the first person to put the idea into Sugg's head," said Parker, rather penitently. "When Sir Reuben disappeared, my first step, almost, was to hunt up all the street accidents and suicides and so on that had turned up during the day, and I went down to see this Battersea Park body as a matter of routine. Of course, I saw that the thing was ridiculous as soon as I got there, but Sugg froze on to the idea–and it's true there was a good deal of resemblance between the dead man and the portraits I've seen of Sir Reuben."

"A strong superficial likeness," said Sir Julian. "The upper part of the face is not an uncommon type, and as Sir Reuben wore a heavy beard and there was no opportunity of comparing the mouths and chins, I can understand the idea occurring to anybody. But only to be dismissed at once. I am sorry," he added, "as the whole matter has been painful to Lady Levy. You may know, Mr. Parker, that I am an old, though I should not call myself an intimate,friend of the Levys."

"I understood something of the sort."

"Yes. When I was a young man I–in short, Mr. Parker, I hoped once to marry Lady Levy." (Mr. Parker gave the usual sympathetic groan.) "I have never married, as you know," pursued Sir Julian. "We have remained good friends. I have always done what I could to spare her pain."

"Believe me, Sir Julian," said Parker, "that I sympathize very much with you and with Lady Levy, and that I did all I could to disabuse Inspector Sugg of this notion. Unhappily, the coincidence of Sir Reuben's being seen that evening in the Battersea Park Road–"

"Ah, yes," said Sir Julian. "Dear me, here we are at home. Perhaps you would come in for a moment, Mr. Parker, and have tea or a whisky-and-soda or something."

Parker promptly accepted this invitation, feeling that there were other things to be said.

The two men stepped into a square, finely furnished hall with a fireplace on the same side as the door, and a staircase opposite. The dining-room door stood open on their right, and as Sir Julian rang the bell a manservant appeared at the far end of the hall.

"What will you take?" asked the doctor.

"After that dreadfully cold place," said Parker, "what I really want is gallons of hot tea, if you, as a nerve specialist, can bear the thought of it."

"Provided you allow of a judicious blend of China in it," replied Sir Julian in the same tone, "I have no objection to make. Tea in the library at once," he added to the servant, and led the way upstairs.

"I don't use the downstairs rooms much, except the dining-room," he explained as he ushered his guest into a small but cheerful library on the first floor. "This room leads out of my bedroom and is more convenient. I only live part of my time here, but it's very handy for my research work at the hospital. That's what I do there, mostly. It's a fatal thing for a theorist, Mr. Parker, to let the practical work get behindhand. Dissection is the basis of all good theory and all correct diagnosis. One must keep one's hand and eye in training. This place is far more important to me than Harley Street, and some day I shall abandon my consulting practice altogether and settle down here to cut up my subjects and write my books in peace. So many things in this life are a waste of time, Mr. Parker."

Mr. Parker assented to this.

"Very often," said Sir Julian, "the only time I get for any research work–necessitating as it does the keenest observation and the faculties at their acutest–has to be at night, after a long day's work and by artificial light, which, magnificent as the lighting of the dissecting room here is, is always more trying to the eyes than daylight. Doubtless your own work has to be carried on under even more trying conditions."

"Yes, sometimes," said Parker; "but then you see," he added, "the conditions are so to speak part of the work."

"Quite so, quite so," said Sir Julian; "you mean that the burglar, for example, does not demonstrate his methods in the light of day, or plant the perfect footmark in the middle of a damp patch of sand for you to analyze."

"Not as a rule," said the detective, "but I have no doubt many of your diseases work quite as insidiously as any burglar."

"They do, they do," said Sir Julian, laughing, "and it is my pride, as it is yours, to track them down for the good of society. The neuroses, you know, are particularly clever criminals–they break out into as many disguises as–"

"As Leon Kestrel, the Master-Mummer," suggested Parker, who read railway-stall detective stories on the principle of the 'busman's holiday.

"No doubt," said Sir Julian, who did not, "and they cover up their tracks wonderfully. But when you can really investigate, Mr. Parker, and break up the dead, or for preference the living body with the scalpel, you always find the footmarks–the little trail of ruin or disorder left by madness or disease or drink or any other similar pest. But the difficulty is to trace them back, merely by observing the surface symptoms–the hysteria, crime, religion, fear, shyness, conscience, or whatever it may be; just as you observe a theft or a murder and look for the footsteps of the criminal, so I observe a fit of hysterics or an outburst of piety and hunt for the little mechanical irritation which has produced it."

"You regard all these things as physical?"

"Undoubtedly. I am not ignorant of the rise of another school of thought, Mr. Parker, but its exponents are mostly charlatans or self-deceivers. *'Sie haben sich so weit darin eingeheimnisst'* that, like Sludge the Medium, they are beginning to believe their own nonsense. I should like to have the exploring of some of their brains, Mr. Parker; I would show you the little faults and landslips in the cells–the misfiring and short-circuiting of the nerves, which produce these notions and these books. At least," he added, gazing sombrely at his guest, "at least, if I could not quite show you today, I shall be able to do so tomorrow–or in a year's time–or before I die."

He sat for some minutes gazing into the fire, while the red light played upon his tawny beard and struck out answering gleams from his compelling eyes.

Parker drank tea in silence, watching him. On the whole, however, he remained but little interested in the causes of nervous phenomena and his mind strayed to Lord Peter, coping with the redoubtable Crimplesham down in Salisbury. Lord Peter had wanted him to come: that meant, either that Crimplesham was proving recalcitrant or that a clue wanted following. But Bunter had said that tomorrow would do, and it was just as well. After all, the

Battersea affair was not Parker's case; he had already wasted valuable time attending an inconclusive inquest, and he really ought to get on with his legitimate work. There was still Levy's secretary to see and the little matter of the Peruvian Oil to be looked into. He looked at his watch.

"I am very much afraid–if you will excuse me–" he murmured.

Sir Julian came back with a start to the consideration of actuality.

"Your work calls you?" he said, smiling. "Well, I can understand that. I won't keep you. But I wanted to say something to you in connection with your present inquiry–only I hardly know–I hardly like–"

Parker sat down again, and banished every indication of hurry from his face and attitude.

"I shall be very grateful for any help you can give me," he said.

"I'm afraid it's more in the nature of hindrance," said Sir Julian, with a short laugh. "It's a case of destroying a clue for you, and a breach of professional confidence on my side. But since–accidentally–a certain amount has come out, perhaps the whole had better do so."

Mr. Parker made the encouraging noise which, among laymen, supplies the place of the priest's insinuating, "Yes, my son?"

"Sir Reuben Levy's visit on Monday night was to me," said Sir Julian.

"Yes?" said Mr. Parker, without expression.

"He found cause for certain grave suspicions concerning his health," said Sir Julian, slowly, as though weighing how much he could in honour disclose to a stranger. "He came to me, in preference to his own medical man, as he was particularly anxious that the matter should be kept from his wife. As I told you, he knew me fairly well, and Lady Levy had consulted me about a nervous disorder in the summer."

"Did he make an appointment with you?" asked Parker.

"I beg your pardon," said the other, absently.

"Did he make an appointment?"

"An appointment? Oh, no! He turned up suddenly in the evening after dinner when I wasn't expecting him. I took him up here and examined him, and he left me somewhere about ten o'clock, I should think."

"May I ask what was the result of your examination?"

'Why do you want to know?"

"It might illuminate–well, conjecture as to his subsequent conduct," said Parker, cautiously. This story seemed to have little coherence with the rest of the business, and he wondered whether coincidence was alone responsible for Sir Reuben's disappearance on the same night that he visited the doctor.

"I see," said Sir Julian. "Yes. Well, I will tell you in confidence that I saw grave grounds of suspicion, but as yet, no absolute certainty of mischief."

"Thank you. Sir Reuben left you at ten o'clock?"

"Then or thereabouts. I did not at first mention the matter as it was so very much Sir Rueben's wish to keep his visit to me secret, and there was no question of accident in the street or anything of that kind, since he reached home safely at midnight."

"Quite so," said Parker.

"It would have been, and is, a breach of confidence," said Sir Julian, "and I only tell you now because Sir Reuben was accidentally seen, and because I would rather tell you in private than have you ferretting round here and questioning my servants, Mr. Parker. You will excuse my frankness."

"Certainly," said Parker. "I hold no brief for the pleasantness of my profession, Sir Julian. I am very much obliged to you for telling me this. I might otherwise have wasted valuable time following up a false trail."

"I am sure I need not ask you, in your turn, to respect this confidence," said the doctor. "To publish the matter abroad could only harm Sir Reuben and pain his wife, besides placing me in no favourable light with my patients."

"I promise to keep the thing to myself," said Parker, "except of course," he added hastily, "that I must inform my colleague."

"You have a colleague in the case?"

"I have."

"What sort of person is he?"

"He will be perfectly discreet, Sir Julian."

"Is he a police officer?"

"You need not be afraid of your confidence getting into the records at Scotland Yard."

"I see that you know how to be discreet, Mr. Parker."

"We also have our professional etiquette, Sir Julian."

On returning to Great Ormond Street, Mr. Parker found a wire awaiting him, which said: "Do not trouble to come. All well. Returning tomorrow. Wimsey."

# 7

ON RETURNING to the flat just before lunchtime on the following morning, after a few confirmatory researches in Balham and the neighbourhood of Victoria Station, Lord Peter was greeted at the door by Mr. Bunter (who had gone straight home from Waterloo) with a telephone message and a severe and nursemaid-like eye.

"Lady Swaffham rang up, my lord, and said she hoped your lordship had not forgotten you were lunching with her."

"I have forgotten, Bunter, and I mean to forget. I trust you told her I had succumbed to lethargic encephalitis suddenly, no flowers by request."

"Lady Swaffham said, my lord, she was counting on you. She met the Duchess of Denver yesterday—"

"If my sister-in-law's there I won't go, that's flat," said Lord Peter.

"I beg your pardon, my lord, the Dowager Duchess."

"What's she doing in town?"

"I imagine she came up for the inquest, my lord."

"Oh, yes—we missed that, Bunter."

"Yes, my lord. Her Grace is lunching with Lady Swaffham."

"Bunter, I can't. I can't, really. Say I'm in bed with whooping cough, and ask my mother to come round after lunch."

"Very well, my lord. Mrs. Tommy Frayle will be at Lady Swaffham's, my lord, and Mr. Milligan—"

"Mr. who ?"

"Mr. John P. Milligan, my lord, and—"

"Good God, Bunter, why didn't you say so before? Have I time to get there before he does? All right. I'm off. With a taxi I can just—"

"Not in those trousers, my lord," said Mr. Bunter, blocking the way to the door with deferential firmness.

"Oh, Bunter," pleaded his lordship, "do let me—just this once. You don't know how important it is."

"Not on any account, my lord. It would be as much as my place is worth."

"The trousers are all right, Bunter."

"Not for Lady Swaffham's, my lord. Besides, your lordship forgets the man that ran against you with a milk-can at Salisbury."

And Mr. Bunter laid an accusing finger on a slight stain of grease showing across the light cloth.

"I wish to God I'd never let you grow into a privileged family retainer, Bunter," said Lord Peter, bitterly, dashing his walking-stick into the umbrella-stand. "You've no conception of the mistakes my mother may be making."

Mr. Bunter smiled grimly and led his victim away.

When an immaculate Lord Peter was ushered, rather late for lunch, into Lady Swaffham's drawing-room, the Dowager Duchess of Denver was seated on a sofa, plunged in intimate conversation with Mr. John P. Milligan of Chicago.

"I'm vurry pleased to meet you, Duchess," had been that financier's opening remark, "to thank you for your exceedingly kind invitation. I assure you it's a compliment I deeply appreciate."

The Duchess beamed at him, while conducting a rapid rally of all her intellectual forces.

"Do come and sit down and talk to me, Mr. Milligan," she said. "I do so love talking to you great business men—let me see, is it a railway king you are or something about puss-in-the-corner—at least, I don't mean that exactly, but that game one used to play with cards, all about wheat and oats, and there was a bull and a bear, too—or was it a horse?—no, a bear, because I remember one always had to try and get rid of it and it used to get so dreadfully crumpled and torn, poor thing, always being handed about, one got to recognise it, and then one had to buy a new pack—so foolish it must seem to you, knowing the real thing, and dreadfully noisy, but really excellent for breaking the ice with rather stiff people who didn't know each other—I'm quite sorry it's gone out."

Mr. Milligan sat down.

"Wal, now," he said, "I guess it's as interesting for us business men to meet British aristocrats as it is for Britishers to meet American railway kings, Duchess. And I guess I'll make as many mistakes talking your kind of talk as you would make if you were tryin' to run a corner in wheat in Chicago. Fancy now, I called that fine lad of yours Lord Wimsey the other day, and he thought I'd mistaken him for his brother. That made me feel rather green."

This was an unhoped-for lead. The Duchess walked warily.

"Dear boy," she said, "I am so glad you met him, Mr. Milligan. *Both* my sons are a *great* comfort to me, you know, though, of course, Gerald is more conventional—just the right kind of person for the House of Lords, you know, and a splendid farmer. I can't see Peter down at Denver half so well, though he is always going to all right things in town, and very amusing sometimes, poor boy."

"I was vurry much gratified by Lord Peter's suggestion," pursued Mr. Milligan, "for which I understand you are responsible, and I'll surely be very pleased to come any day you like, though I think you're flattering me too much."

"Ah, well," said the Duchess, "I don't know if you're the best judge of that, Mr. Milligan. Not that I know anything about business myself," she added. "I'm rather old-fashioned for these days, you know, and I can't pretend to do more than know a nice *man* when I see him; for the other things I rely on my son."

The accent of this speech was so flattering that Mr. Milligan purred almost audibly, and said:

"Wal, Duchess, I guess that's where a lady with a real, beautiful, old-fashioned soul has the advantage of these modern young blatherskites—there aren't many men who wouldn't be nice—to her, and even then, if they aren't rock-bottom she can see through them."

"But that leaves me where I was," thought the Duchess. "I believe," she said aloud, "that I ought to be thanking you in the name of the vicar of Duke's Denver for a very munificent cheque which reached him yesterday for the Church Restoration Fund. He was so delighted and astonished, poor dear man."

"Oh, that's nothing," said Mr. Milligan, "we haven't any fine old crusted buildings like yours over on our side, so it's a privilege to be allowed to drop a little kerosene into the worm-holes when we hear of one in the old country suffering from senile decay. So when your lad told me about Duke's Denver I took the liberty to subscribe without waiting for the Bazaar."

"I'm sure it was very kind of you," said the Duchess. "You are coming to the Bazaar, then?" she continued, gazing into his face appealingly.

"Sure thing," said Mr. Milligan, with great promptness. "Lord Peter said you'd let me know for sure about the date, but we can always make time for a little bit of good work anyway. Of course I'm hoping to be able to avail myself of your kind invitation to stop, but if I'm rushed, I'll manage anyhow to pop over and speak my piece and pop back again."

"I hope so very much," said the Duchess. "I must see what can be done about the date—of course, I can't promise—"

"No, no," said Mr. Milligan heartily. "I know what these things are to fix up. And then there's not only me—there's all the real big men of European eminence your son mentioned, to be consulted."

The Duchess turned pale at the thought that any one of the illustrious persons might some time turn up in somebody's drawing-room, but by this time she had dug herself in comfortably, and was even beginning to find her range.

"I can't say how grateful we are to you," she said; "it will be such a treat. Do tell me what you think of saying."

"Wal—" began Mr. Milligan.

Suddenly everybody was standing up and a penitent voice was heard to say:

"Really, most awfully sorry, y'know—hope you'll forgive me, Lady Swaffham, what? Dear lady, could I possibly forget an invitation from you? Fact is, I had to go an' see a man down in Salisbury—absolutely true, 'pon my word, and the fellow wouldn't let me get away. I'm simply grovellin' before you, Lady Swaffham. Shall I go an' eat my lunch in the corner?"

Lady Swaffham gracefully forgave the culprit.

"Your dear mother is here," she said.

"How do, Mother?" said Lord Peter, uneasily.

"How are you, dear?" replied the Duchess. "You really oughtn't to have turned up just yet. Mr. Milligan was just going to tell me what a thrilling speech he's preparing for the Bazaar, when you came and interrupted us."

Conversation at lunch turned, not unnaturally, on the Battersea inquest, the Duchess giving a vivid impersonation of Mrs. Thipps being interrogated by the Coroner.

" 'Did you hear anything unusual in the night?' says the little man, leaning forward and screaming at her, and so crimson in the face and his ears sticking out so—just like a cherubim in that poem of Tennyson's—or is a cherub blue?—perhaps it's a seraphim I mean—anyway, you know what I mean, all eyes, with little wings on its head. And dear old Mrs. Thipps saying, 'Of course I have, any time these eighty years,' and *such* a sensation in court till they found out she thought he'd said, 'Do you sleep without a light?' and everybody laughing, and then the Coroner said quite loudly, 'Damn the woman,' and she heard that, I can't think why, and said: 'Don't you get swearing, young man, sitting there in the presence of Providence, as you may say. I don't know what young people are coming to nowadays'—and he's sixty if he's a day, you know," said the Duchess.

By a natural transition, Mrs. Tommy Frayle referred to the man who was hanged for murdering three brides in a bath.

"I always thought that was so ingenious," she said, gazing soulfully at Lord Peter, "and do you know, as it happened, Tommy had just made me insure my life, and I got so frightened, I gave up my morning bath and took to having it in the afternoon when he was in the House—I mean, when he was *not* in the house—not at home, I mean."

"Dear lady," said Lord Peter, reproachfully, "I have a distinct recollection that all those brides were thoroughly unattractive. But it was an uncommonly ingenious plan—the first time of askin'—only he shouldn't have repeated himself."

"One demands a little originality in these days, even from murderers," said Lady Swaffham. "Like dramatists, you know—so much easier in Shakespeare's time, wasn't it? Always the same girl dressed up as a man, and even that borrowed from Boccaccio or Dante or somebody. I'm sure if I'd been a Shakespeare hero, the very minute I saw a slim-legged young page-boy I'd have said: 'Odsbodikins! There's that girl again!' "

"That's just what happened, as a matter of fact," said Lord Peter. "You see, Lady Swaffham, if ever you want to commit a murder, the thing you've got to do is to prevent people from associatin' their ideas. Most people don't associate anythin'—their ideas just roll about like so many dry peas on a tray, makin' a lot of noise and goin' nowhere, but once you begin lettin' 'em string their peas into a necklace, it's goin' to be strong enough to hang you, what?"

"Dear me!" said Mrs. Tommy Frayle, with a little scream, "what a blessing it is none of my friends have any ideas at all!"

"Y'see," said Lord Peter, balancing a piece of duck on his fork and frowning, "it's only in Sherlock Holmes and stories like that, that people think things out logically. Or'nar'ly, if somebody tells you somethin' out of the way, you just say. 'By Jove!' or 'How sad!' an' leave it at that, an' half the time you forget about it, 'nless somethin' turns up afterwards to drive it home. F'r instance, Lady Swaffham, I told you when I came in that I'd been down to Salisbury, 'n' that's true, only I don't suppose it impressed you much; 'n' I don't suppose it'd impress you much if you read in the paper tomorrow of a tragic discovery of a dead lawyer down in Salisbury, but if I went to Salisbury again next week 'n' there was a Salisbury doctor found dead the day after, you might begin to think I was a bird of ill omen for Salisbury residents; and if I went there again the week after, 'n' you heard next day that the see of Salisbury had fallen vacant suddenly, you might begin to wonder what took me to Salisbury, an' why I'd never mentioned before that I had friends down there, don't you see, an' you might think of goin' down to Salisbury yourself, an' askin' all kinds of people if they'd happened to see a young man in plum-coloured socks hangin' round the Bishop's Palace."

"I daresay I should," said Lady Swaffham.

"Quite. An' if you found that the lawyer and the doctor had once upon a time been in business at Poggleton-on-the-Marsh when the Bishop had been vicar there, you'd begin to remember you'd once heard of me payin' a visit to Poggleton-on-the-Marsh a long time ago, an' you'd begin to look up the parish registers there an' discover I'd been married under an assumed name by the vicar to the widow of a wealthy farmer, who'd died suddenly of peritonitis, as certified by the doctor, after the lawyer'd made a will leavin' me all her money, and *then* you'd begin to think I might have very good reasons for gettin' rid of such promisin' blackmailers as the lawyer, the doctor an' the bishop. Only, if I hadn't started an association in your mind by gettin' rid of 'em all in the same place, you'd never have thought of goin' to Poggleton-on-the-Marsh, 'n' you wouldn't even have remembered I'd ever been there."

"*Were* you ever there, Lord Peter?" inquired Mrs. Tommy, anxiously.

"I don't think so," said Lord Peter; "the name threads no beads in my mind. But it might, any day, you know."

"But if you were investigating a crime," said Lady Swaffham, "you'd have to begin by the usual things, I suppose–finding out what the person had been doing, and who'd been to call, and looking for a motive, wouldn't you?"

"Oh, yes," said Lord Peter, "but most of us have such dozens of motives for murderin' all sorts of inoffensive people. There's a lot of people I'd like to murder, wouldn't you?"

"Heaps," said Lady Swaffham. "There's that dreadful–perhaps I'd better not say it, though, for fear you should remember it later on."

"Well, I wouldn't if I were you," said Peter, amiably. "You never know. It'd be beastly awkward if the person died suddenly tomorrow."

"The difficulty with this Battersea case, I guess," said Mr. Milligan, "is that nobody seems to have any associations with the gentleman in the bath."

"So hard on poor Inspector Sugg," said the Duchess. "I quite felt for the man, having to stand up there and answer a lot of questions when he had nothing at all to say."

Lord Peter applied himself to the duck, having got a little behindhand. Presently he heard somebody ask the Duchess if she had seen Lady Levy.

"She is in great distress," said the woman who had spoken, a Mrs. Freemantle, "though she clings to the hope that he will turn up. I suppose you knew him, Mr. Milligan–know him, I should say, for I hope he's still alive somewhere."

Mrs. Freemantle was the wife of an eminent railway director, and celebrated for her ignorance of the world of finance. Her *faux pas* in this connection enlivened the tea parties of City men's wives.

"Wal, I've dined with him," said Mr. Milligan, good-naturedly. "I think he and I've done our best to ruin each other, Mrs. Freemantle. If this were the States," he added, "I'd be much inclined to suspect myself of having put Sir Reuben in a safe place. But we can't do business that way in your old country; no, ma'am."

"It must be exciting work doing business in America," said Lord Peter.

"It is," said Mr. Milligan. "I guess my brothers are having a good time there now. I'll be joining them again before long, as soon as I've fixed up a little bit of work for them on this side."

"Well, you mustn't go till after my bazaar," said the Duchess.

Lord Peter spent the afternoon in a vain hunt for Mr. Parker. He ran him down eventually after dinner in Great Ormond Street.

Parker was sitting in an elderly but affectionate armchair, with his feet on the mantelpiece, relaxing his mind with a modern commentary on the Epistle to the Galatians. He received Lord Peter with quiet pleasure, though without rapturous enthusiasm, and mixed him a whisky-and-soda. Peter took up the book his friend had laid down and glanced over the pages.

"All these men work with a bias in their minds, one way or other," he said; "they find what they are looking for."

"Oh, they do," agreed the detective; 'but one learns to discount that almost automatically, you know. When I was at college, I was all on the other side–Conybeare and Robertson and Drews and those people, you know, till I found they were all so busy looking for a burglar whom nobody had ever seen, that they couldn't recognise the foot-prints of the household, so to speak. Then I spent two years learning to be cautious."

"Hum," said Lord Peter, "theology must be good exercise for the brain then, for you're easily the most cautious devil I know. But I say, do go on reading–it's a shame for me to come and root you up in your off-time like this."

"It's all right, old man," said Parker.

The two men sat silent for a little, and then Lord Peter said:

"D'you like your job?"

The detective considered the question, and replied:

"Yes–yes, I do. I know it to be useful, and I am fitted to it. I do it quite well–not with inspiration, perhaps, but sufficiently well to take a pride in it. It is full of variety and it forces one to keep up to the mark and not get slack. And there's a future to it. Yes, I like it. Why?"

"Oh, nothing," said Peter. "It's a hobby to me, you see. I took it up when the bottom of things was rather knocked out for me, because it was so damned exciting, and the worst of it is, I enjoy it–up to a point. If it was all on paper I'd enjoy every bit of it. I love the beginning of a job–when one doesn't know any of the people and it's just exciting and amusing. But if it comes to really running down a live person and getting him hanged, or even quodded, poor devil, there don't seem as if there was any excuse for me buttin' in, since I don't have to make my livin' by it. And I feel as if I oughtn't ever to find it amusin'. But I do."

Parker gave this speech his careful attention.

"I see what you mean," he said.

"There's old Milligan, f'r instance," said Lord Peter. "On paper, nothin' would be funnier than to catch old Milligan out. But he's rather a decent old bird to talk to. Mother likes him. He's taken a fancy to me. It's awfully entertainin' goin' and pumpin' him with stuff about a bazaar for church expenses, but when he's so jolly pleased about it and that, I feel a worm. S'pose old Milligan has cut Levy's throat and plugged him into the Thames. It ain't my business."

"It's as much yours as anybody's," said Parker; "it's no better to do it for money than to do it for nothing."

"Yes, it is," said Peter stubbornly. "Havin' to live is the only excuse there is for doin' that kind of thing."

"Well, but look here!" said Parker. "If Milligan has cut poor old Levy's throat for no reason except to make himself richer, I don't see why he should buy himself off by giving £1,000 to Duke's Denver church roof, or why he should be forgiven just because he's childishly vain, or childishly snobbish."

"That's a nasty one," said Lord Peter.

"Well, if you like, even because he has taken a fancy to you."

"No, but–"

"Look here, Wimsey–do you think he *has* murdered Levy?"

"Well, he may have."

"But do you think he has?"

"I don't want to think so."

"Because he has taken a fancy to you?"

"Well, that biases me, of course–"

"I daresay it's quite a legitimate bias. You don't think a callous murderer would be likely to take a fancy to you?"

"Well–besides, I've taken rather a fancy to him."

"I daresay that's quite legitimate, too. You've observed him and made a subconscious deduction from your observations, and the result is, you don't think he did it. Well, why not? You're entitled to take that into account."

"But perhaps I'm wrong and he did do it."

"Then why let your vainglorious conceit in your own power of estimating character stand in the way of unmasking the singularly cold-blooded murder of an innocent and lovable man?"

"I know–but I don't feel I'm playing the game somehow."

"Look here, Peter," said the other with some earnestness, "suppose you get this playing-fields-of-Eton complex out of your system once and for all. There doesn't seem to be much doubt that something unpleasant has happened to Sir Reuben Levy. Call it murder, to strengthen the argument. If Sir Reuben has been murdered, is it a game? and is it fair to treat it as a game?"

"That's what I'm ashamed of, really," said Lord Peter. "It *is* a game to me, to begin with, and I go on cheerfully, and then I suddenly see that somebody is going to be hurt, and I want to get out of it."

"Yes, yes, I know," said the detective, "but that's because you're thinking about your attitude. You want to be consistent, you want to look pretty, you want to swagger debonairly through a comedy of puppets or else to stalk magnificently through a tragedy of human sorrows and things. But that's childish. If you've any duty to society in the way of finding out the truth about murders, you must do it in any attitude that comes handy. You want to be elegant and detached? That's all right, if you find the truth out that way, but it hasn't any value in itself, you know. You want to look dignified and consistent–what's that got to do with it? You want to hunt down a murderer for the sport of the thing and then shake hands with him and say, 'Well played–hard luck–you shall have your revenge tomorrow!' Well, you can't do it like that. Life's not a football match. You want to be a sportsman. You can't be a sportsman. You're a responsible person."

"I don't think you ought to read so much theology," said Lord Peter. "It has a brutalizing influence."

He got up and paced about the room, looking idly over the bookshelves. Then he sat down again, filled and lit his pipe, and said:

"Well, I'd better tell you about the ferocious and hardened Crimplesham."

He detailed his visit to Salisbury. Once assured of his bona fides, Mr. Crimplesham had given him the fullest details of his visit to town.

"And I've substantiated it all," groaned Lord Peter, "and unless he's corrupted half Balham, there's no doubt he spent the night there. And the afternoon was really spent with the bank people. And half the residents of Salisbury seem to have seen him off on Monday before lunch. And nobody but his own family or young Wicks seems to have anything to gain by his death. And even if young Wicks wanted to make away with him, it's rather far-fetched to go and murder an unknown man in Thipps's place in order to stick Crimplesham's eyeglasses on his nose."

"Where was young Wicks on Monday?" asked Parker.

"At a dance given by the Precentor," said Lord Peter, wildly. "David—his name is David—dancing before the ark of the Lord in the face of the whole Cathedral Close."

There was a pause.

"Tell me about the inquest," said Wimsey.

Parker obliged with a summary of the evidence. "Do you believe the body could have been concealed in the flat after all?" he asked. "I know we looked, but I suppose we might have missed something."

"We might. But Sugg looked as well."

"Sugg!"

"You do Sugg an injustice," said Lord Peter; "if there had been any signs of Thipps's complicity in the crime, Sugg would have found them."

"Why?"

"Why? Because he was looking for them. He's like your commentators on Galatians. He thinks that either Thipps, or Gladys Horrocks, or Gladys Horrocks's young man did it. Therefore he found marks on the window sill where Gladys Horrocks's young man might have come in or handed something in to Gladys Horrocks. He didn't find any signs on the roof, because he wasn't looking for them."

"But he went over the roof before me."

"Yes, but only in order to prove that there were no marks there. He reasons like this: Gladys Horrocks's young man is a glazier. Glaziers come on ladders. Glaziers have ready access to ladders. Therefore Gladys Horrocks's young man had ready access to a ladder. Therefore Gladys Horrocks's young man came on a ladder. Therefore there will be marks on the windowsill and none on the roof. Therefore he finds marks on the windowsill but none on the roof. He finds no marks on the ground, but he thinks he would have found them if the yard didn't happen to be paved with asphalt. Similarly, he thinks Mr. Thipps may have concealed the body in the box-room or elsewhere. Therefore you may be sure he searched the box-room and all the other places for signs of occupation. If they had been there he would have found them, because he was looking for them. Therefore, if he didn't find them it's because they weren't there."

"All right," said Parker, "stop talking. I believe you."

He went on to detail the medical evidence.

"By the way," said Lord Peter, "to skip across for a moment to the other case, has it occurred to you that perhaps Levy was going out to see Freke on Monday night?"

"He was; he did," said Parker, rather unexpectedly, and proceeded to recount his interview with the nerve-specialist.

"Humph!" said Lord Peter. "I say, Parker, these are funny cases, ain't they? Every line of inquiry seems to peter out. It's awfully exciting up to a point, you know, and then nothing comes of it. It's like rivers getting lost in the sand."

"Yes," said Parker. "And there's another one I lost this morning."

"What's that?"

"Oh, I was pumping Levy's secretary about his business. I couldn't get much that seemed important except further details about the Argentine and so on. Then I thought I'd just ask round in the City about those Peruvian Oil shares, but Levy hadn't even heard of them so far as I could make out. I routed out the brokers, and found a lot of mystery and concealment, as one always does, you know, when somebody's been rigging the market, and at last I found one name at the back of it. But it wasn't Levy's."

"No? Whose was it?"

"Oddly enough, Freke's. It seems mysterious. He bought a lot of shares last week, in a secret kind of way, a few of them in his own name, and then quietly sold 'em out on Tuesday at a small profit–a few hundreds, not worth going to all that trouble about, you wouldn't think."

"Shouldn't have thought he ever went in for that kind of gamble."

"He doesn't as a rule. That's the funny part of it."

"Well, you never know," said Lord Peter; "people do these things just to prove to themselves or somebody else that they could make a fortune that way if they liked. I've done it myself in a small way."

He knocked out his pipe and rose to go.

"I say, old man," he said suddenly, as Parker was letting him out, "does it occur to you that Freke's story doesn't fit in awfully well with what Anderson said about the old boy having been so jolly at dinner on Monday night? Would you be, if you thought you'd got anything of that sort?"

"No, I shouldn't," said Parker; "but," he added with his habitual caution, "some men will jest in the dentist's waiting-room. You, for one."

"Well, that's true," said Lord Peter, and went downstairs.

# 8

LORD PETER reached home about midnight, feeling extraordinarily wakeful and alert. Something was jigging and worrying in his brain; it felt like a hive of bees, stirred up by a stick. He felt as though he were looking at a complicated riddle, of which he had once been told the answer but had forgotten it and was always on the point of remembering.

"Somewhere," said Lord Peter to himself, "somewhere I've got the key to these two things. I know I've got it, only I can't remember what it is. Somebody said it. Perhaps I said it. I can't remember where, but I know I've got it. Go to bed, Bunter, I shall sit up a little. I'll just slip on a dressing-gown."

Before the fire he sat down with his pipe in his mouth and his jazz-coloured peacocks gathered about him. He traced out this line and that line of investigation–rivers running into the sand. They ran out from the thought of Levy, last seen at ten o'clock in Prince of Wales Road. They ran back from the picture of the grotesque dead man in Mr. Thipps's bathroom–they ran over the roof, and were lost–lost in the sand. Rivers running into the sand–rivers running underground, very far down–

Where Alph, the sacred river, ran
Through caverns measureless to man
Down to a sunless sea.

By leaning his head down, it seemed to Lord Peter that he could hear them, very faintly, lipping and gurgling somewhere in the darkness. But where? He felt quite sure that somebody had told him once, only he had forgotten.

He roused himself, threw a log on the fire, and picked up a book which the indefatigable Bunter, carrying on his daily fatigues amid the excitements of special duty, had brought from the Times Book Club. It happened to be Sir Julian Freke's "Physiological Bases of the Conscience," which he had seen reviewed two days before.

"This ought to send one to sleep," said Lord Peter; "if I can't leave these problems to my subconscious I'll be as limp as a rag tomorrow."

He opened the book slowly, and glanced carelessly through the preface.

"I wonder if that's true about Levy being ill," he thought, putting the book down; "it doesn't seem likely. And yet–Dash it all, I'll take my mind off it."

He read on resolutely for a little.

"I don't suppose Mother's kept up with the Levys much," was the next importunate train of thought. "Dad always hated self-made people and wouldn't have 'em at Denver. And old Gerald keeps up the tradition. I wonder if she knew Freke well in those days. She seems to get on with Milligan. I trust Mother's judgment a good deal. She was a brick about that bazaar business. I ought to have warned her. She said something once–"

He pursued an elusive memory for some minutes, till it vanished altogether with a mocking flicker of the tail. He returned to his reading.

Presently another thought crossed his mind aroused by a photograph of some experiment in surgery.

"If the evidence of Freke and that man Watts hadn't been so positive," he said to himself, "I should be inclined to look into the matter of those shreds of lint on the chimney."

He considered this, shook his head and read with determination.

Mind and matter were one thing, that was the theme of the physiologist. Matter could erupt, as it were, into ideas. You could carve passions in the brain with a knife. You could get rid of imagination with drugs and cure an outworn convention like a disease. "The knowledge of good and evil is an observed phenomenon, attendant upon a certain condition of the brain-cells, which is removable." That was one phrase; and again:

"Conscience in man may, in fact, be compared to the sting of a hive-bee, which, so far from conducing to the welfare of its possessor, cannot function, even in a single instance, without occasioning its death. The suvival-value in each case is thus purely social; and if humanity ever passes from its present phase of social development into that of a higher individualism, as some of our philosophers have ventured to speculate, we may suppose that this interesting mental phenomenon may gradually cease to appear; just as the nerves and muscles which once controlled the movement of our ears and scalps have, in all save a few backward individuals, become atrophied and of interest only to the physiologist."

"By Jove!" thought Lord Peter, idly, "that's an ideal doctrine for the criminal. A man who believed that would never–"

And then it happened–the thing he had been half-unconsciously expecting. It happened suddenly, surely, as unmistakably, as sunrise. He remembered–not one thing, nor another thing, nor a logical succession of things, but everything–the whole thing, perfect, complete, in all its dimensions as it were and instantaneously; as if he stood outside the world and saw it suspended in infinitely dimensional space. He no longer needed to reason about it, or even to think about it. He knew it.

There is a game in which one is presented with a jumble of letters and is required to make a word out of them, as thus:

COSSSSRI

The slow way of solving the problem is to try out all the permutations and combinations in turn, throwing away impossible conjunctions of letters, as:

SSSIRC

or

SCSRSO

Another way is to stare at the inco-ordinate elements until, by no logical process that the conscious mind can detect, or under some adventitious external stimulus, the combination:

SCISSORS

presents itself with calm certainty. After that, one does not even need to arrange the letters in order. The thing is done.

Even so, the scattered elements of two grotesque conundrums, flung higgledy-piggledy into Lord Peter's mind, resolved themselves, unquestioned henceforward. A bump on the roof of the end house–Levy in a welter of cold rain talking to a prostitute in the Battersea Park Road–a single ruddy hair–lint bandages–Inspector Sugg calling the great surgeon from the dissecting-room of the hospital–Lady Levy with a nervous attack–the smell of carbolic soap–the Duchess's voice–"not really an engagement, only a sort of understanding with her father"–shares in Peruvian Oil–the dark skin and curved, fleshy profile of the man in the bath–Dr. Grimbold giving evidence, "In my opinion, death did not occur for several days after the blow"–india-rubber gloves–even, faintly, the voice of Mr. Appledore, "He called on me, sir, with an anti-vivisectionist pamphlet"–all these things and many others rang together and made one sound, they swung together like bells in a steeple, with the deep tenor booming through the clamour:

"The knowledge of good and evil is a phenomenon of the brain, and is removable, removable, removable. The knowledge of good and evil is removable."

Lord Peter Wimsey was not a young man who habitually took himself very seriously, but this time he was frankly appalled. "It's impossible," said his reason, feebly; "*credo quia impossibile*," said his interior certainty with impervious self-satisfaction. "All right," said conscience, instantly allying itself with blind faith, "what are you going to do about it?"

Lord Peter got up and paced the room: "Good Lord!" he said. "Good Lord!" He took down "Who's Who" from the little shelf over the telephone and sought comfort in its pages:

FREKE, Sir Julian, Kt. *cr.* 1916; G.C.V.O. *cr.* 1919; K.C.V.O. 1917; K.C.B. 1918; M.D., F.R.C.P., F.R.C.S., Dr. en Méd. Paris; D. Sci. Cantab.; Knight of Grace of the Order of S. John of Jerusalem; Consulting Surgeon of St. Luke's Hospital, Battersea. *b.* Gryllingham, 16 March, 1872 *only son* of Edward Curzon Freke, Esq., of Gryll Court, Gryllingham, *Educ.* Harrow and Trinity Coll., Cambridge; Col. A.M.S.; late Member of the Advisory Board of the Army Medical Service. *Publications*: Some Notes on the Pathological Aspects of Genius, 1892; Statistical Contributions to the Study of Infantile Paralysis in England and Wales, 1894; Functional Disturbances of the Nervous System, 1899; Cerebro-Spinal Diseases, 1904; The Borderland of Insanity, 1906; An Examination into the Treatment of Pauper Lunacy in the United Kingdom, 1906; Modem Developments in Psycho-Therapy: A Criticism, 1910; Criminal Lunacy, 1914; The Application of Psycho-Therapy to the Treatment of Shell-Shock, 1917; An Answer to Professor Freud, with a Description of Some Experiments Carried Out at the Base Hospital in Amiens, 1919; Structural Modifications Accompanying the More Important Neuroses, 1920. *Clubs*: White's; Oxford and Cambridge; Alpine etc. *Recreations*: Chess, Mountaineering, Fishing. *Address*: 282, Harley Street and St. Luke's House, Prince of Wales Road, Battersea Park, S.W.11."

He flung the book away. "Confirmation!" he groaned. "As if I needed it!"

He sat down again and buried his face in his hands. He remembered quite suddenly how, years ago, he had stood before the breakfast table at Denver Castle–a small, peaky boy in blue knickers, with a thunderously beating heart. The family had not come down; there was a great silver urn with a spirit lamp under it, and an elaborate coffee-pot boiling in a glass dome. He had twitched the corner of the tablecloth–twitched it harder, and the urn moved ponderously forward and all the teaspoons rattled. He seized the tablecloth in a firm grip and pulled his hardest–he could feel now the delicate and awful thrill as the urn and the coffee machine and the whole of a Sèvres breakfast service had crashed down in one stupendous ruin–he remembered the horrified face of the butler, and the screams of a lady guest.

A log broke across and sank into a fluff of white ash. A belated motor-lorry rumbled past the window.

Mr. Bunter, sleeping the sleep of the true and faithful servant, was aroused in the small hours by a hoarse whisper, "Bunter!"

"Yes, my lord," said Bunter, sitting up and switching on the light.

"Put that light out, damn you!" said the voice. "Listen–over there–listen–can't you hear it?"

"It's nothing, my lord," said Mr. Bunter, hastily getting out of bed and catching hold of his master; "it's all right, you get to bed quick and I'll fetch you a drop of bromide. Why, you're all shivering–you've been sitting up too late."

"Hush! no, no–it's the water," said Lord Peter with chattering teeth; "it's up to their waists down there, poor devils. But listen! can't you hear it? Tap, tap, tap–they're mining us–but I don't know where–I can't hear–I can't. Listen, you! There it is again–we must find it–we must stop it. . . . Listen! Oh, my God! I can't hear–I can't hear anything for the noise of the guns. Can't they stop the guns?"

"Oh dear!" said Mr. Bunter to himself. "No, no–it's all right, Major–don't you worry."

"But I hear it," protested Peter.

"So do I," said Mr. Bunter stoutly; "very good hearing, too, my lord. That's our own sappers at work in the communication trench. Don't you fret about that, sir."

Lord Peter grasped his wrist with a feverish hand.

"Our own sappers," he said; "sure of that?"

"Certain of it," said Mr. Bunter, cheerfully.

"They'll bring down the tower," said Lord Peter.

"To be sure they will," said Mr. Bunter, "and very nice, too. You just come and lay down a bit, sir–they've come to take over this section."

"You're sure it's safe to leave it?" said Lord Peter.

"Safe as houses, sir," said Mr. Bunter, tucking his master's arm under his and walking him off to his bedroom.

Lord Peter allowed himself to be dosed and put to bed without further resistance. Mr. Bunter, looking singularly un-Bunterlike in striped pyjamas, with his stiff black hair ruffled about his head, sat grimly watching the younger man's sharp cheekbones and the purple stains under his eyes.

"Thought we'd had the last of these attacks," he said. "Been overdoin' of himself. Asleep?" He peered at him anxiously. An affectionate note crept into his voice. "Bloody little fool!" said Sergeant Bunter.

# 9

MR. PARKER, summoned the next morning to 110 Piccadilly, arrived to find the Dowager Duchess in possession. She greeted him charmingly.

"I am going to take this silly boy down to Denver for the week-end," she said, indicating Peter, who was writing and only acknowledged his friend's entrance with a brief nod. "He's been doing too much–running about to Salisbury and places and up till all hours of the night–you really shouldn't encourage him, Mr. Parker, it's very naughty of you–waking poor Bunter up in the middle of the night with scares about Germans, as if that wasn't all over years ago, and he hasn't had an attack for ages, but there! Nerves are such funny things, and Peter always did have nightmares when he was quite a little boy–though very often of course it was only a little pill he wanted; but he was so dreadfully bad in 1918, you know, and I suppose we can't expect to forget all about a great war in a year or two, and, really, I ought to be very thankful with both my boys safe. Still, I think a little peace and quiet at Denver won't do him any harm."

"Sorry you've been having a bad turn, old man," said Parker, vaguely sympathetic; "you're looking a bit seedy."

"Charles," said Lord Peter, in a voice entirely void of expression, "I am going away for a couple of days because I can be no use to you in London. What has got to be done for the moment can be much better done by you than by me. I want you to take this"—he folded up his writing and placed it in an envelope—"to Scotland Yard immediately and get it sent out to all the workhouses, infirmaries, police stations, Y.M.C.A.'s and so on in London. It is a description of Thipps's corpse as he was before he was shaved and cleaned up. I want to know whether any man answering to that description has been taken in anywhere, alive or dead, during the last fortnight. You will see Sir Andrew Mackenzie personally, and get the paper sent out at once, by his authority; you will tell him that you have solved the problems of the Levy murder and the Battersea mystery"—Mr. Parker made an astonished noise to which his friend paid no attention—"and you will ask him to have men in readiness with a warrant to arrest a very dangerous and important criminal at any moment on your information. When the replies to this paper come in, you will search for any mention of St. Luke's Hospital, or of any person connected with St. Luke's Hospital, and you will send for me at once.

"Meanwhile you will scrape acquaintance—I don't care how—with one of the students at St. Luke's. Don't march in there blowing about murders and police warrants, or you may find yourself in Queer Street. I shall come up to town as soon as I hear from you, and I shall expect to find a nice ingenuous Sawbones here to meet me." He grinned faintly.

"D'you mean you've got to the bottom of this thing?" asked Parker.

"Yes. I may be wrong. I hope I am, but I know I'm not."

"You won't tell me?"

"D'you know," said Peter, "honestly I'd rather not. I say I *may* be wrong—and I'd feel as if I'd libelled the Archbishop of Canterbury."

"Well, tell me—is it one mystery or two?"

"One."

"You talked of the Levy murder. Is Levy dead?"

"God—yes!" said Peter, with a strong shudder.

The Duchess looked up from where she was reading the *Tatler*.

"Peter," she said, "is that your ague coming on again? Whatever you two are chattering about, you'd better stop it at once if it excites you. Besides, it's about time to be off."

"All right, Mother," said Peter. He turned to Bunter, standing respectfully in the door with an overcoat and suitcase. "You understand what you have to do, don't you?" he said.

"Perfectly, thank you, my lord. The car is just arriving, your Grace."

"With Mrs. Thipps inside it," said the Duchess. "She'll be delighted to see you again, Peter. You remind her so of Mr. Thipps. Good-morning, Bunter."

"Good-morning, your Grace."

Parker accompanied them downstairs.

When they had gone he looked blankly at the paper in his hand—then, remembering that it was Saturday and there was need for haste, he hailed a taxi.

"Scotland Yard!" he cried.

Tuesday morning saw Lord Peter and a man in a velveteen jacket swishing merrily through seven acres of turnip-tops, streaked yellow with early frosts.

A little way ahead, a sinuous undercurrent of excitement among the leaves proclaimed the unseen yet ever-near presence of one of the Duke of Denver's setter pups. Presently a partridge flew up with a noise like a police rattle, and Lord Peter accounted for it very creditably for a man who, a few nights before, had been listening to imaginary German sappers. The setter bounded foolishly through the turnips, and fetched back the dead bird.

"Good dog," said Lord Peter.

Encouraged by this, the dog gave a sudden ridiculous gambol and barked, its ear tossed inside out over its head.

"Heel," said the man in velveteen, violently. The animal sidled up, ashamed.

"Fool of a dog, that," said the man in velveteen; "can't keep quiet. Too nervous, my lord. One of old Black Lass's pups."

"Dear me," said Peter, "is the old dog still going?"

"No, my lord; we had to put her away in the spring."

Peter nodded. He always proclaimed that he hated the country and was thankful to have nothing to do with the family estates, but this morning he enjoyed the crisp air and the wet leaves washing darkly over his polished boots. At Denver things moved in an orderly way; no one died sudden and violent deaths except aged setters—and partridges, to be sure. He sniffed up the autumn smell with appreciation. There was a letter in his pocket which had come by the morning post, but he did not intend to read it just yet. Parker had not wired; there was no hurry.

He read it in the smoking-room after lunch. His brother was there, dozing over the *Times*—a good, clean Englishman, sturdy and conventional, rather like Henry VIII in his youth; Gerald, sixteenth Duke of Denver. The Duke considered his cadet rather degenerate, and not quite good form; he disliked his taste for police-court news.

The letter was from Mr. Bunter.

110, Piccadilly,
W.1.

My Lord:

I write (Mr. Bunter had been carefully educated and knew that nothing is more vulgar than a careful avoidance of beginning a letter with the first person singular) as your lordship directed, to inform you of the result of my investigations.

I experienced no difficulty in becoming acquainted with Sir Julian Freke's man-servant. He belongs to the same club as the Hon. Frederick Arbuthnot's man, who is a friend of mine, and was very willing to introduce me. He took me to the club yesterday (Sunday) evening, and we dined with the man, whose name is John Cummings, and afterwards I invited Cummings to drinks and a cigar in the flat. Your lordship will excuse me doing this, knowing that it is not my habit, but it has always been my experience that the best way to gain a man's confidence is to let him suppose that one takes advantage of one's employer.

("I always suspected Bunter of being a student of human nature," commented Lord Peter. )

I gave him the best old port ("The deuce you did," said Lord Peter), having heard you and Mr. Arbuthnot talk over it. ("Hum!" said Lord Peter.)

Its effects were quite equal to my expectations as regards the principal matter in hand, but I very much regret to state that the man had so little understanding of what was offered to him that he smoked a cigar with it (one of your lordship's Villar Villars). You will understand that I made no comment on this at the time, but your lordship will sympathize with my feelings. May I take this opportunity of expressing my grateful appreciation of your lordship's excellent taste in food, drink and dress? It is, if I may say so, more than a pleasure–it is an education, to valet and buttle your lordship.

Lord Peter bowed his head gravely.

"What on earth are you doing Peter, sittin' there noddin' an' grinnin' like a what-you-may-call-it?" demanded the Duke, coming suddenly out of a snooze. "Someone writin' pretty things to you, what?"

"Charming things," said Lord Peter.

The Duke eyed him doubtfully.

"Hope to goodness you don't go and marry a chorus beauty," he muttered inwardly, and returned to the *Times*.

Over dinner I had set myself to discover Cummings's tastes, and found them to run in the direction of the music-hall stage. During his first glass I drew him out in this direction, your lordship having kindly given me opportunities of seeing every performance in London, and I spoke more freely than I should consider becoming in the ordinary way in order to make myself pleasant to him. I may say that his views on women and the stage were such as I should have expected from a man who would smoke with your lordship's port.

With the second glass I introduced the subject of your lordship's inquiries. In order to save time I will write our conversation in the form of a dialogue, as nearly as possible as it actually took place.

*Cummings:* You seem to get many opportunities of seeing a bit of life, Mr. Bunter.

*Bunter:* One can always make opportunities if one knows how.

*Cummings:* Ah, it's very easy for you to talk, Mr. Bunter. You're not married, for one thing.

*Bunter:* I know better than that, Mr. Cummings.

*Cummings*: So do I–*now*, when it's too late. (He sighed heavily, and I filled up his glass.)

*Bunter:* Does Mrs. Cummings live with you at Battersea?

*Cummings:* Yes, her and me we do for my governor. Such a life! Not but what there's a char comes in by the day. But what's a char? I can tell you it's dull all by ourselves in that d——d Battersea suburb.

*Bunter:* Not very convenient for the Halls, of course.

*Cummings:* I believe you. It's all right for you, here in Piccadilly, right on the spot as you might say. And I daresay your governor's often out all night, eh?

*Bunter:* Oh, frequently, Mr. Cummings.

*Cummings:* And I daresay you take the opportunity to slip off yourself every so often, eh?"

*Bunter:* Well, what do *you* think, Mr. Cummings?

*Cummings:* That's it; there you are! But what's a man to do with a nagging fool of a wife and a blasted scientific doctor for a governor, as sits up all night cutting up dead bodies and experimenting with frogs?

*Bunter:* Surely he goes out sometimes.

*Cummings:* Not often. And always back before twelve. And the way he goes on if he rings the bell and you ain't there. I give you *my* word, Mr. Bunter.

*Bunter:* Temper?

*Cummings:* No-o-o—but looking through you, nasty-like, as if you was on that operating table of his and he was going to cut you up. Nothing a man could rightly complain of, you understand, Mr. Bunter, just nasty looks. Not but what I will say he's very correct. Apologizes if he's been inconsiderate. But what's the good of that when he's been and gone and lost you your night's rest?

*Bunter:* How does he do that? Keeps you up late, you mean?

*Cummings:* Not him; far from it. House locked up and household to bed at half-past ten. That's his little rule. Not but what I'm glad enough to go as a rule, it's that dreary. Still, when I *do* go to bed I like to go to sleep.

*Bunter:* What does he do? Walk about the house?

*Cummings:* Doesn't he? All night. And in and out of the private door to the hospital.

*Bunter:* You don't mean to say, Mr. Cummings, a great specialist like Sir Julian Freke does night work at the hospital?

*Cummings:* No, no; he does his own work—research work, as you may say. Cuts people up. They say he's very clever. Could take you or me to pieces like a clock, Mr. Bunter, and put us together again.

*Bunter:* Do you sleep in the basement, then, to hear him so plain?

*Cummings:* No; our bedroom's at the top. But, Lord! what's that? He'll bang the door so you can hear him all over the house.

*Bunter:* Ah, many's the time I've had to speak to Lord Peter about that. And talking all night. And baths.

*Cummings:* Baths? You may well say that, Mr. Bunter. Baths? Me and my wife sleep next to the cistern-room. Noise fit to wake the dead. All hours. When d'you think he chose to have a bath, no later than last Monday night, Mr. Bunter?

*Bunter:* I've known them to do it at two in the morning, Mr. Cummings.

*Cummings:* Have you, now? Well, this was at three. Three o'clock in the morning we was waked up. I give you *my* word.

*Bunter:* You don't say so, Mr. Cummings.

*Cummings:* He cuts up diseases, you see, Mr. Bunter, and then he don't like to go to bed till he's washed the bacilluses off, if you understand me. Very natural, too, I daresay. But what I say is, the middle of the night's no time for a gentleman to be occupying his mind with diseases.

*Bunter:* These great men have their own way of doing things.

*Cummings:* Well, all I can say is, it isn't my way.

(I could believe that your lordship. Cummings has no signs of greatness about him, and his trousers are not what I would wish to see in a man of his profession.)

*Bunter:* Is he habitually as late as that, Mr. Cummings?

*Cummings:* Well, no, Mr. Bunter, I will say, not as a general rule. He apologized, too, in the morning, and said he would have the cistern seen to—and very necessary, in my opinion, for the air gets into the pipes, and the groaning and screeching as goes on is something awful. Just like Niagara, if you follow me, Mr. Bunter, I give you *my* word.

*Bunter:* Well, that's as it should be, Mr. Cummings. One can put up with a great deal from a gentleman that has the manners to apologize. And, of course, sometimes they can't help themselves. A visitor will come in unexpectedly and keep them late, perhaps.

*Cummings:* That's true enough, Mr. Bunter. Now I come to think of it, there *was* a gentleman come in on Monday evening. Not that he came late, but he stayed about an hour, and may have put Sir Julian behindhand.

*Bunter:* Very likely. Let me give you some more port, Mr. Cummings. Or a little of Lord Peter's old brandy.

*Cummings:* A little of the brandy, thank you, Mr. Bunter. I suppose you have the run of the cellar here. (He winked at me.)

"Trust me for that," I said, and I fetched him the Napoleon. I assure your lordship it went to my heart to pour it out for a man like that. However, seeing we had got on the right tack, I felt it wouldn't be wasted.

"I'm sure I wish it was always gentlemen that come here at night," I said. (Your lordship will excuse me, I am sure, making such a suggestion.)

("Good God," said Lord Peter, "I wish Bunter was less thorough in his methods.")

*Cummings:* Oh, he's that sort, his lordship, is he? (He chuckled and poked me. I suppress a portion of his conversation here, which could not fail to be as offensive to your lordship as it was to myself. He went on:) No, it's none of that with Sir Julian. Very few visitors at night, and always gentlemen. And going early as a rule, like the one I mentioned.

*Bunter:* Just as well. There's nothing I find more wearisome, Mr. Cummings, than sitting up to see visitors out.

*Cummings:* Oh, I didn't see this one out. Sir Julian let him out himself at ten o'clock or thereabouts. I heard the gentleman shout "Good-night" and off he goes.

*Bunter:* Does Sir Julian always do that?

*Cummings:* Well, that depends. If he sees visitors downstairs, he lets them out himself: if he sees them upstairs in the library, he rings for me.

*Bunter:* This was a downstairs visitor, then?

*Cummings:* Oh, yes. Sir Julian opened the door to him, I remember. He happened to be working in the hall. Though now I come to think of it, they went up to the library afterwards. That's funny. I know they did, because I happened to go up to the hall with coals, and I heard them upstairs. Besides, Sir Julian rang for me in the library a few minutes later. Still, anyway, we heard him go at ten, or it may have been a bit before. He hadn't only stayed about three-quarters of an hour. However, as I was saying, there was Sir Julian banging in and out of the private door all night, and a bath at three in the morning, and up again for breakfast at eight–it beats me. If I had all his money, curse me if I'd go poking about with dead men in the middle of the night. I'd find something better to do with my time, eh, Mr. Bunter–

I need not repeat any more of his conversation, as it became unpleasant and incoherent, and I could not bring him back to the events of Monday night. I was unable to get rid of him till three. He cried on my neck, and said I was the bird, and you were the governor for him. He said that Sir Julian would be greatly annoyed with him for coming home so late, but Sunday night was his night out and if anything was said about it he would give notice. I think he will be ill-advised to do so, as I feel he is not a man I could conscientiously recommend if I were in Sir Julian Freke's place. I noticed that his boot-heels were slightly worn down.

I should wish to add, as a tribute to the great merits of your lordship's cellar, that, although I was obliged to drink a somewhat large quantity both of the Cockbum '68 and the 1800 Napoleon I feel no headache or other ill effects this morning.

Trusting that your lordship is deriving real benefit from the country air, and that the little information I have been able to obtain will prove satisfactory, I remain.

With respectful duty to all the family,

Obediently yours,
MERVYN BUNTER.

"Y'know," said Lord Peter thoughtfully to himself, "I sometimes think Mervyn Bunter's pullin' my leg. What is it, Soames?"

"A telegram, my lord."

"Parker," said Lord Peter, opening it. It said:

"Description recognised Chelsea Workhouse. Unknown vagrant injured street accident Wednesday week. Died workhouse Monday. Delivered St. Luke's same evening by order Freke. Much puzzled. Parker."

"Hurray!" said Lord Peter, suddenly sparkling. "I'm glad I've puzzled Parker. Gives me confidence in myself. Makes me feel like Sherlock Holmes. 'Perfectly simple, Watson.' Dash it all, though! this is a beastly business. Still, it's puzzled Parker."

"What's the matter?" asked the Duke, getting up and yawning.

"Marching orders," said Peter, "back to town. Many thanks for your hospitality, old bird–I'm feelin' no end better. Ready to tackle Professor Moriarty or Leon Kestrel or any of 'em."

"I do wish you'd keep out of the police courts," grumbled the Duke. "It makes it so dashed awkward for me, havin' a brother makin' himself conspicuous."

"Sorry, Gerald," said the other; "I know I'm a beastly blot on the 'scutcheon."

"Why can't you marry and settle down and live quietly, doin' something useful?" said the Duke, unappeased.

"Because that was a wash-out as you perfectly well know," said Peter; "besides," he added cheerfully, "I'm bein' no end useful. You may come to want me yourself, you never know. When anybody comes blackmailin' you, Gerald, or your first deserted wife turns up unexpectedly from the West Indies, you'll realize the pull of havin' a private detective in the family. 'Delicate private business arranged with tact and discretion. Investigations undertaken. Divorce evidence a specialty. Every guarantee!' Come, now."

"Ass!" said Lord Denver, throwing the newspaper violently into his armchair. "When do you want the car?"

"Almost at once. I say, Jerry, I'm taking Mother up with me."

"Why should she be mixed up in it?"

"Well, I want her help."

"I call it most unsuitable," said the Duke.

The Dowager Duchess, however, made no objection.

"I used to know her quite well," she said, "when she was Christine Ford. Why, dear?"

"Because," said Lord Peter, "there's a terrible piece of news to be broken to her about her husband."

"Is he dead, dear?"

"Yes; and she will have to come and identify him."

"Poor Christine."

"Under very revolting circumstances, Mother."

"I'll come with you, dear."

"Thank you, Mother, you're a brick. D'you mind gettin' your things on straight away and comin' up with me? I'll tell you about it in the car."

# 10

MR. PARKER, a faithful though doubting Thomas, had duly secured his medical student: a large young man like an overgrown puppy, with innocent eyes and a freckled face. He sat on the Chesterfield before Lord Peter's library fire, bewildered in equal measure by his errand, his surroundings and the drink which he was absorbing. His palate, though untutored, was naturally a good one, and he realized that even to call this liquid a drink—the term ordinarily used by him to designate cheap whisky, post-war beer or a dubious glass of claret in a Soho restaurant—was a sacrilege; this was something outside normal experience: a genie in a bottle.

The man called Parker, whom he had happened to run across the evening before in the public-house at the corner of Prince of Wales Road, seemed to be a good sort. He had insisted on bringing him round to see this friend of his, who lived splendidly in Piccadilly. Parker was quite understandable; he put him down as a government servant, or perhaps something in the City. The friend was embarrassing; he was a lord, to begin with, and his clothes were a kind of rebuke to the world at large. He talked the most fatuous nonsense, certainly, but in a disconcerting way. He didn't dig into a joke and get all the fun out of it; he made it in passing, so to speak, and skipped away to something else before your retort was ready. He had a truly terrible manservant—the sort you read about in books—who froze the marrow in your bones with silent criticism. Parker appeared to bear up under the strain, and this made you think more highly of Parker; he must be more habituated to the surroundings of the great than you would think to look at him. You wondered what the carpet had cost on which Parker was carelessly spilling cigar ash; your father was an upholsterer—Mr. Piggott, of Piggott & Piggott, Liverpool—and you knew enough about carpets to know that you couldn't even guess at the price of this one. When you moved your head on the bulging silk cushion in the corner of the sofa, it made you wish you shaved more often and more carefully. The sofa was a monster—but even so, it hardly seemed big enough to contain you. This Lord Peter was not very tall—in fact, he was rather a small man, but he didn't look undersized. He looked right; he made you feel that to be six-foot-three was rather vulgarly assertive; you felt like Mother's new drawing-room curtains—all over great big blobs. But everybody was very decent to you, and nobody said anything you couldn't understand, or sneered at you. There were some frightfully deep-looking books on the shelves all round, and you had looked into a great folio Dante which was lying on the table, but your hosts were talking quite ordinarily and rationally about the sort of books you read yourself—clinking good love stories and detective stories. You had read a lot of those, and could give an opinion, and they listened to what you had to say, though Lord Peter had a funny way of talking about books, too, as if the author had confided in him beforehand, and told him how the story was put together, and which bit was written first. It reminded you of the way old Freke took a body to pieces.

"Thing I object to in detective stories," said Mr. Piggott, "is the way fellows remember every bloomin' thing that's happened to 'em within the last six months. They're always ready with their time of day and was it rainin' or not, and what were they doin' on such an' such a day. Reel it all off like a page of poetry. But one ain't like that in real life, d'you think so, Lord Peter?" Lord Peter smiled, and young Piggott, instantly embarrassed, appealed to his earlier acquaintance. "You know what I mean, Parker. Come now. One day's so like another, I'm sure I couldn't remember—well, I might remember yesterday, p'r'aps, but I couldn't be certain about what I was doin' last week if I was to be shot for it."

"No," said Parker, "and evidence given in police statements sounds just as impossible. But they don't really get it like that, you know. I mean, a man doesn't just say, 'Last Friday I went out at 10 a.m. to buy a mutton chop. As I was turning into Mortimer Street I noticed a girl of about twenty-two with black hair and brown eyes, wearing a green jumper, check skirt, Panama hat and black shoes, riding a Royal Sunbeam Cycle at about ten miles an hour turning the corner by the Church of St. Simon and St. Jude on the wrong side of the road riding towards the market place! ' It amounts to that, of course, but it's really wormed out of him by a series of questions."

"And in short stories," said Lord Peter, "it has to be put in statement form, because the real conversation would be so long and twaddly and tedious, and nobody would have the patience to read it. Writers have to consider their readers, if any, y'see."

"Yes," said Mr. Piggott, "but I bet you most people would find it jolly difficult to remember, even if you asked 'em things. I should—of course, I know I'm a bit of a fool, but then, most people are, ain't they? You know what I mean. Witnesses ain't detectives, they're just average idiots like you and me."

"Quite so," said Lord Peter, smiling as the force of the last phrase sank into its unhappy perpetrator; "you mean, if I were to ask you in a general way what you were doin'—say, a week ago today, you wouldn't be able to tell me a thing about it offhand?"

"No—I'm sure I shouldn't." He considered. "No. I was in at the Hospital as usual, I suppose, and, being Tuesday, there'd be a lecture on something or the other—dashed if I know what—and in the evening I went out with Tommy Pringle—no, that must have been Monday—or was it Wednesday? I tell you, I couldn't swear to anything."

"You do yourself an injustice," said Lord Peter gravely. "I'm sure, for instance, you recollect what work you were doing in the dissecting-room on that day, for example."

"Lord, no! not for certain. I mean, I daresay it might come back to me if I thought for a long time, but I wouldn't swear to it in a court of law."

"I'll bet you half-a-crown to sixpence," said Lord Peter, "that you'll remember within five minutes."

"I'm sure I can't."

"We'll see. Do you keep a notebook of the work you do when you dissect? Drawings or anything?"

"Oh, yes."

"Think of that. What's the last thing you did in it?"

"That's easy, because I only did it this morning. It was leg muscles."

"Yes. Who was the subject?"

"An old woman of sorts; died of pneumonia."

"Yes. Turn back the pages of your drawing book in your mind. What came before that?"

"Oh, some animals—still legs; I'm doing motor muscles at present. Yes. That was old Cunningham's demonstration on comparative anatomy. I did rather a good thing of a hare's legs and a frog's, and rudimentary legs on a snake."

"Yes. Which day does Mr. Cunningham lecture?"

"Friday."

"Friday; yes. Turn back again. What comes before that?"

Mr. Piggott shook his head.

"Do your drawings of legs begin on the right-hand page or the left-hand page? Can you see the first drawing?"

"Yes—yes—I can see the date written at the top. It's a section of a frog's hind leg, on the right-hand page."

"Yes. Think of the open book in your mind's eye. What is opposite to it?"

This demanded some mental concentration.

"Something round—coloured—oh, yes—it's a hand."

"Yes. You went on from the muscles of the hand and arm to leg- and foot-muscles?"

"Yes; that's right. I've got a set of drawings of arms.

"Yes. Did you make those on the Thursday?"

"No; I'm never in the dissecting-room on Thursday."

"On Wednesday, perhaps?"

"Yes; I must have made them on Wednesday. Yes; I did. I went in there after we'd seen those tetanus patients in the morning. I did them on Wednesday afternoon. I know I went back because I wanted to finish 'em. I worked rather hard—for me. That's why I remember."

"Yes; you went back to finish them. When had you begun them, then?"

"Why, the day before."

"The day before. That was Tuesday, wasn't it?"

"I've lost count—yes, the day before Wednesday—yes,Tuesday."

"Yes. Were they a man's arms or a woman's arms?"

"Oh, a man's arms."

"Yes; last Tuesday, a week ago today, you were dissecting a man's arms in the dissecting-room. Sixpence, please."

"By Jove!"

"Wait a moment. You know a lot more about it than that. You've no idea how much you know. You know what kind of man he was."

"Oh, I never saw him complete, you know. I got there a bit late that day, I remember. I'd asked for an arm specially, because I was rather weak in arms, and Watts—that's the attendant—had promised to save me one."

"Yes. You have arrived late and found your arm waiting for you. You are dissecting it—taking your scissors and slitting up the skin and pinning it back. Was it very young, fair skin?"

"Oh, no—no. Ordinary skin, I think—with dark hairs on it—yes, that was it."

"Yes. A lean, stringy arm, perhaps, with no extra fat anywhere?"

"Oh, no—I was rather annoyed about that. I wanted a good muscular arm, but it was rather poorly developed and the fat got in my way."

"Yes; a sedentary man who didn't do much manual work."

"That's right."

"Yes. You dissected the hand, for instance, and made a drawing of it. You would have noticed any hard calluses."

"Oh, there was nothing of that sort."

"No. But should you say it was a young man's arm? Firm young flesh and limber joints?"

"No–no."

"No. Old and stringy, perhaps."

"No. Middle-aged–with rheumatism. I mean, there was a chalky deposit in the joints, and the fingers were a bit swollen."

"Yes. A man about fifty."

"About that."

"Yes. There were other students at work on the same body."

"Oh, yes."

"Yes. And they made all the usual sort of jokes about it."

"I expect so–oh, yes!"

"You can remember some of them. Who is your local funny man, so to speak?"

"Tommy Pringle."

"What was Tommy Pringle's doing?"

"Can't remember."

"Whereabouts was Tommy Pringle working?"

"Over by the instrument cupboard–by sink C."

"Yes. Get a picture of Tommy Pringle in your mind's eye." Piggott began to laugh.

"I remember now. Tommy Pringle said the old Sheeny–"

"Why did he call him a Sheeny?"

"I don't know. But I know he did."

"Perhaps he looked like it. Did you see his head?"

"No."

"Who had the head?"

"I don't know–oh yes, I do, though. Old Freke bagged the head himself, and little Bouncible Binns was very cross about it, because he'd been promised a head to do with old Scrooger."

"I see. What was Sir Julian doing with the head?"

"He called us up and gave us a jaw on spinal haemorrhage and nervous lesions."

"Yes. Well, go back to Tommy Pringle."

Tommy Pringle's joke was repeated, not without some embarrassment.

"Quite so. Was that all?"

"No. The chap who was working with Tommy said that sort of thing came from over-feeding."

"I deduce that Tommy Pringle's partner was interested in the alimentary canal."

"Yes; and Tommy said, if he'd thought they'd feed you like that he'd go to the workhouse himself."

"Then the man was a pauper from the workhouse?"

"Well, he must have been, I suppose."

"Are workhouse paupers usually fat and well-fed?"

"Well, no–come to think of it, not as a rule."

"In fact, it struck Tommy Pringle and his friend that this was something a little out of the way in a workhouse subject?"

"Yes."

"And if the alimentary canal was so entertaining to these gentlemen, I imagine the subject had come by his death shortly after a full meal."

"Yes—oh, yes—he'd have had to, wouldn't he?"

"Well, I don't know," said Lord Peter. "That's in your department, you know. That would be your inference, from what they said."

"Oh, yes. Undoubtedly."

"Yes; you wouldn't, for example, expect them to make that observation if the patient had been ill for a long time and fed on slops."

"Of course not."

"Well, you see, you really know a lot about it. On Tuesday week you were dissecting the arm muscles of a rheumatic middle-aged Jew, of sedentary habits, who had died shortly after eating a heavy meal, of some injury producing spinal haemorrhage and nervous lesions, and so forth, and who was presumed to come from the workhouse?"

"Yes."

"And you could swear to those facts, if need were?"

"Well, if you put it that way, I suppose I could."

"Of course you could."

Mr. Piggott sat for some moments in contemplation.

"I say," he said at last, "I did know all that, didn't I?"

"Oh, yes—you knew it all right—like Socrates' slave."

"Who's he?"

"A person in a book I used to read as a boy."

"Oh—does he come in 'The Last Days of Pompeii'?"

"No—another book—I daresay you escaped it. It's rather dull."

"I never read much except Henty and Fenimore Cooper at school. . . . But—have I got rather an extra good memory, then?"

"You have a better memory than you credit yourself with."

"Then why can't I remember all the medical stuff? It all goes out of my head like a sieve."

"Well, why can't you?" said Lord Peter, standing on the hearthrug and smiling down at his guest.

"Well," said the young man, "the chaps who examine one don't ask the same sort of questions you do."

"No ?"

"No—they leave you to remember all by yourself. And it's beastly hard. Nothing to catch hold of, don't you know? But, I say—how did you know about Tommy Pringle being the funny man and—"

"I didn't, till you told me."

"No; I know. But how did you know he'd be there if you did ask? I mean to say—I say," said Mr. Piggott, who was becoming mellowed by influences themselves not unconnected with the alimentary canal—"I say, are you rather clever, or am I rather stupid?"

"No, no," said Lord Peter, "it's me. I'm always askin' such stupid questions, everybody thinks I must mean somethin' by 'em."

This was too involved for Mr. Piggott.

"Never mind," said Parker, soothingly, 'he's always like that. You mustn't take any notice. He can't help it. It's premature senile decay, often observed in the families of hereditary legislators. Go away, Wimsey, and play us the 'Beggar's Opera,' or something."

"That's good enough, isn't it?" said Lord Peter, when the happy Mr.

Piggott had been despatched home after a really delightful evening.

"I'm afraid so," said Parker. "But it seems almost incredible."

"There's nothing incredible in human nature," said Lord Peter; "at least, in educated human nature. Have you got that exhumation order?"

"I shall have it tomorrow. I thought of fixing up with the workhouse people for tomorrow afternoon. I shall have to go and see them first."

"Right you are; I'll let my mother know."

"I begin to feel like you, Wimsey, I don't like this job."

"I like it a deal better than I did."

"You are really certain we're not making a mistake ?"

Lord Peter had strolled across to the window. The curtain was not perfectly drawn, and he stood gazing out through the gap into lighted Piccadilly. At this he turned round:

"If we are," he said, "we shall know tomorrow, and no harm will have been done. But I rather think you will receive a certain amount of confirmation on your way home. Look here, Parker, d'you know, if I were you I'd spend the night here. There's a spare bedroom; I can easily put you up."

Parker stared at him.

"Do you mean–I'm likely to be attacked?"

"I think it very likely indeed."

"Is there anybody in the street?"

"Not now; there was half-an-hour ago."

"When Piggott left?"

"Yes."

"I say–I hope the boy is in no danger."

"That's what I went down to see. I don't think so. Fact is, I don't suppose anybody would imagine we'd exactly made a confidant of Piggott. But I think you and I are in danger. You'll stay?"

"I'm damned if I will, Wimsey. Why should I run away?"

"Bosh!" said Peter. "You'd run away all right if you believed me, and why not? You don't believe me. In fact, you're still not certain I'm on the right tack. Go in peace, but don't say I didn't warn you."

"I won't; I'll dictate a message with my dying breath to say I was convinced."

"Well, don't walk–take a taxi."

'Very well, I'll do that."

"And don't let anybody else get into it."

"No."

It was a raw, unpleasant night. A taxi deposited a load of people returning from the theatre at the block of flats next door, and Parker secured it for himself. He was just giving the address to the driver, when a man came hastily running up from a side street. He was in evening dress and an overcoat. He rushed up, signalling frantically.

"Sir–sir!–dear me! why, it's Mr. Parker! How fortunate! If you would be so kind–summoned from the club–a sick friend–can't find a taxi–everybody going home from the theatre–if I might share your cab–you are returning to Bloomsbury? I want Russell Square–if I might presume–a matter of life and death."

He spoke in hurried gasps, as though he had been running violently and far. Parker promptly stepped out of the taxi.

"Delighted to be of service to you, Sir Julian," he said; "take my taxi. I am going down to Craven Street myself, but I'm in no hurry. Pray make use of the cab."

"It's extremely kind of you" said the surgeon "I am ashamed–"

"That's all right," said Parker, cheerily. "I can wait." He assisted Freke into the taxi. "What number? 24 Russell Square, driver, and look sharp."

The taxi drove off. Parker remounted the stairs and rang Lord Peter's bell.

"Thanks, old man," he said. "I'll stop the night after all."

"Come in," said Wimsey.

"Did you see that?" asked Parker.

"I saw something. What happened exactly?"

Parker told his story. "Frankly," he said, "I've been thinking you a bit mad, but now I'm not quite so sure of it."

Peter laughed.

"Blessed are they that have not seen and yet have believed. Bunter, Mr. Parker will stay the night."

"Look here, Wimsey, let's have another look at this business. Where's that letter?"

Lord Peter produced Bunter's essay in dialogue. Parker studied it for a short time in silence.

"You know, Wimsey, I'm as full of objections to this idea as an egg is of meat."

"So'm I, old son. That's why I want to dig up our Chelsea pauper. But trot out your objections."

"Well–"

"Well, look here, I don't pretend to be able to fill in all the blanks myself. But here we have two mysterious occurrences in one night, and a complete chain connecting the one with another through one particular person. It's beastly, but it's not unthinkable."

"Yes, I know all that. But there are one or two quite definite stumbling-blocks."

"Yes, I know. But, see here. On the one hand, Levy disappeared after being last seen looking for Prince of Wales Road at nine o'clock. At eight next morning a dead man, not unlike him in general outline, is discovered in a bath in Queen Caroline Mansions. Levy, by Freke's own admission, was going to see Freke. By information received from Chelsea workhouse a dead man, answering to the description of the Battersea corpse in its natural state, was delivered that same day to Freke. We have Levy with a past, and no future, as it were; an unknown vagrant with a future (in the cemetery) and no past, and Freke stands between their future and their past."

"That looks all right–"

"Yes. Now, further: Freke has a motive for getting rid of Levy–an old jealousy."

"Very old–and not much of a motive."

'People have been known to do that sort of thing.* You're thinking that people don't keep up old jealousies for twenty years or so. Perhaps not. Not

*Lord Peter was not without authority for his opinion: "With respect to the alleged motive, it is of great importance to see whether there was a motive for committing such a crime, or whether there was not, or whether there is an improbability of its having been committed so strong as not to be overpowered by positive evidence. But *if there be any motive which can be assigned, I am bound to tell you that the inadequacy* just primitive, brute jealousy. That means a word and a blow. But the thing that rankles is hurt vanity. That sticks. Humiliation. And we've all got a sore spot we don't like to have touched. I've got it. You've got it. Some blighter said hell knew no fury like a woman scorned. Stickin' it on to women, poor devils. Sex is every man's loco spot–you needn't fidget, you know it's true–he'll take a disappointment, but not a humiliation. I knew a man once who'd been turned down–not too charitably–by a girl he was engaged to. He spoke quite decently about her. I asked what had become of her. 'Oh,' he said, 'she married the other fellow.' And then burst out–couldn't help himself. 'Lord, yes!' he cried. 'To think of it–jilted for a Scotchman!' I don't know why he didn't like Scots, but that was what got him on the raw. Look at Freke. I've read his books. His attacks on his antagonists are savage. And he's a scientist. Yet he can't bear opposition, even in his work, which is where any first-class man is most sane and openminded. Do you think he's a man to take a beating from any man on a side-issue? On a man's most sensitive side-issue? People are opinionated about side-issues, you know. I see red if anybody questions my judgment about a book. And Levy–who was nobody twenty years ago–romps in and carries off Freke's girl from under his nose. It isn't the girl Freke would bother about–it's having his aristocratic nose put out of joint by a little Jewish nobody.

"There's another thing. Freke's got another side-issue. He likes crime. In that criminology book of his he gloats over a hardened murderer. I've read it, and I've seen the admiration simply glaring out between the lines whenever he writes about a callous and successful criminal. He reserves his contempt for the victims or the penitents or the men who lose their heads and get found out. His heroes are Edmond de la Pommerais, who persuaded his mistress into becoming an accessory to her own murder, and George Joseph Smith of Brides-in-a-Bath fame, who could make passionate love to his wife in the night and carry out his plot to murder her in the morning. After all, he thinks conscience is a sort of vermiform appendix. Chop it out and you'll feel all the better. Freke isn't troubled by the usual conscientious deterrent. Witness his own hand in his books. Now again. The man who went to Levy's house in his place knew the house: Freke knew the house; he was a red-haired man, smaller than Levy, but not much smaller, since he could wear his clothes without appearing ludicrous: you have seen Freke–you know his height –about five-foot-eleven, I suppose, and his auburn mane; he probably wore surgical gloves: Freke is a surgeon; he was a methodical and daring man: surgeons are obliged to be both daring and methodical. Now take the other side. The man who got hold of the Battersea corpse had to have access to dead bodies. Freke obviously had access to dead bodies. He had to be cool and quick and callous about handling a dead body. Surgeons are all that. He had to be a strong man to carry the body across the roofs and dump it in at Thipps's window. Freke is a powerful man and a member of the Alpine Club. He probably wore surgical gloves and he let the body down from the roof with a surgical bandage. This points to a surgeon again. He undoubtedly

*of that motive is of little importance*. We know, from the experience of criminal courts, that atrocious crimes of this sort have been committed from very slight motives; *not merely from malice and revenge*, but to gain a small pecuniary advantage, and to drive off for a time pressing difficulities."–L. C. J. Campbell, summing up in Reg. v. Palmer, Shorthand Report, p. 308 C. C. C., May, 1856, Sess. Pa. 5. (Italics mine. D. L. S.)

lived in the neighbourhood. Freke lives next door. The girl you interviewed heard a bump on the roof of the end house. That is the house next to Freke's. Every time we look at Freke, he leads somewhere, whereas Milligan and Thipps and Crimplesham and all the other people we've honoured with our suspicion simply led nowhere."

"Yes; but it's not quite so simple as you make out. What was Levy doing in that surreptitious way at FrekEs on Monday night?"

"Well, you have Freke's explanation."

"Rot, Wimsey. You said yourself it wouldn't do."

"Excellent. It won't do. Therefore Freke was lying. Why should he lie about it, unless he had some object in hiding the truth?"

"Well, but why mention it at all?"

"Because Levy, contrary to all expectation, had been seen at the corner of the road. That was a nasty accident for Freke. He thought it best to be beforehand with an explanation–of sorts. He reckoned, of course, on nobody's ever connecting Levy with Battersea Park."

"Well, then, we come back to the first question: Why did Levy go there?"

"I don't know, but he was got there somehow. Why did Freke buy all those Peruvian Oil shares?"

"I don't know," said Parker in his turn.

"Anyway," went on Wimsey, "Freke expected him, and made arrangements to let him in himself, so that Cummings shouldn't see who the caller was."

"But the caller left again at ten."

"Oh, Charles! I did not expect this of you. This is the purest Suggery! Who saw him go? Somebody said 'Good-night' and walked away down the street. And you believe it was Levy because Freke didn't go out of his way to explain that it wasn't."

"D'you mean that Freke walked cheerfully out of the house to Park Lane, and left Levy behind–dead or alive–for Cummings to find?"

"We have Cummings's word that he did nothing of the sort. A few minutes after the steps walked away from the house, Freke rang the library bell and told Cummings to shut up for the night."

"Then–"

"Well–there's a side door to the house, I suppose–in fact, you know there is–Cummings said so–through the hospital."

"Yes–well, where was Levy?"

"Levy went up into the library and never came down. You've been in Freke's library. Where would you have put him?"

"In my bedroom next door."

"Then that's where he did put him."

"But suppose the man went in to turn down the bed?"

"Beds are turned down by the housekeeper, earlier than ten o'clock."

"Yes. . . . But Cummings heard Freke about the house all night."

"He heard him go in and out two or three times. He'd expect him to do that, anyway."

"Do you mean to say Freke got all that job finished before three in the morning?"

"Why not?"

"Quick work."

"Well, call it quick work. Besides, why three? Cummings never saw him again till he called him for eight o'clock breakfast."

"But he was having a bath at three."

"I don't say he didn't get back from Park Lane before three. But I don't suppose Cummings went and looked through the bathroom keyhole to see if he was in the bath."

Parker considered again.

"How about Crimplesham's pince-nez?" he asked.

"That is a bit mysterious," said Lord Peter.

"And why Thipps's bathroom?"

"Why, indeed? Pure accident, perhaps—or pure devilry."

"Do you think all this elaborate scheme could have been put together in a night, Wimsey?"

"Far from it. It was conceived as soon as that man who bore a superficial resemblance to Levy came into the workhouse. He had several days."

"I see."

"Freke gave himself away at the inquest. He and Grimbold disagreed about the length of the man's illness. If a small man (comparatively speaking) like Grimbold presumes to disagree with a man like Freke, it's because he is sure of his ground."

"Then—if your theory is sound—Freke made a mistake."

"Yes. A very slight one. He was guarding, with unnecessary caution, against starting a train of thought in the mind of anybody—say, the workhouse doctor. Up till then he'd been reckoning on the fact that people don't think a second time about anything (a body, say) that's once been accounted for."

"What made him lose his head?"

"A chain of unforeseen accidents. Levy's having been recognised—my mother's son having foolishly advertised in the *Times* his connection with the Battersea end of the mystery—Detective Parker (whose photograph has been a little prominent in the illustrated press lately) seen sitting next door to the Duchess of Denver at the inquest. His aim in life was to prevent the two ends of the problem from linking up. And there were two of the links, literally side by side. Many criminals are wrecked by over-caution."

Parker was silent.

# 11

"A REGULAR pea-souper, by Jove," said Lord Peter. Parker grunted, and struggled irritably into an overcoat.

"It affords me, if I may say so, the greatest satisfaction," continued the noble lord, "that in a collaboration like ours all the uninteresting and disagreeable routine work is done by you."

Parker grunted again.

"Do you anticipate any difficulty about the warrant?" inquired Lord Peter.

Parker grunted a third time.

"I suppose you've seen to it that all this business is kept quiet?"

"Of course."

"You've muzzled the workhouse people?"

"Of course."

"And the police?"

"Yes."

"Because, if you haven't there'll probably be nobody to arrest."

"My dear Wimsey, do you think I'm a fool?"

"I had no such hope."

Parker grunted finally and departed.

Lord Peter settled down to a perusal of his Dante. It afforded him no solace. Lord Peter was hampered in his career as a private detective by a public-school education. Despite Parker's admonitions, he was not always able to discount it. His mind had been warped in its young growth by "Raffles" and "Sherlock Holmes," or the sentiments for which they stand. He belonged to a family which had never shot a fox.

"I am an amateur," said Lord Peter.

Nevertheless, while communing with Dante, he made up his mind.

In the afternoon he found himself in Harley Street. Sir Julian Freke might be consulted about one's nerves from two till four on Tuesdays and Fridays. Lord Peter rang the bell.

"Have you an appointment, sir?" inquired the man who opened the door.

"No," said Lord Peter, "but will you give Sir Julian my card? I think it possible he may see me without one.

He sat down in the beautiful room in which Sir Julian's patients awaited his healing counsel. It was full of people. Two or three fashionably dressed women were discussing shops and servants together, and teasing a toy griffon. A big, worried-looking man by himself in a corner looked at his watch twenty times a minute. Lord Peter knew him by sight. It was Wintrington, a millionaire, who had tried to kill himself a few months ago. He controlled the finances of five countries, but he could not control his nerves. The finances of five countries were in Sir Julian Freke's capable hands. By the fireplace sat a soldierly-looking young man, of about Lord Peter's own age. His face was prematurely lined and worn; he sat bolt upright, his restless eyes darting in the direction of every slightest sound. On the sofa was an elderly woman of modest appearance, with a young girl. The girl seemed listless and wretched; the woman's look showed deep affection, and anxiety tempered with a timid hope. Close beside Lord Peter was another younger woman, with a little girl, and Lord Peter noticed in both of them the broad cheekbones and beautiful grey, slanting eyes of the Slav. The child, moving restlessly about, trod on Lord Peter's patent-leather toe, and the mother admonished her in French before turning to apologize to Lord Peter.

"*Mais je vous en prie*, madame," said the young man, "it is nothing."

"She is nervous, *pauvre petite*," said the young woman.

"You are seeking advice for her?"

"Yes. He is wonderful, the doctor. Figure to yourself, *monsieur*, she cannot forget, poor child, the things she has seen." She leaned nearer, so that the child might not hear. "We have escaped–from starving Russia–six months ago. I dare not tell you–she has such quick ears, and then, the cries, the tremblings, the convulsions–they all begin again. We were skeletons when we arrived–*mon Dieu!*–but that is better now. See, she is thin, but she is not starved. She would be fatter but for the nerves that keep her from eating. We who are older, we forget–*enfin, on apprend à ne pas y penser*–but these children! When one is young, *monsieur, tout ça impressionne trop*."

Lord Peter, escaping from the thraldom of British good form, expressed himself in that language in which sympathy is not condemned to mutism.

"But she is much better, much better," said the mother, proudly; "the great doctor, he does marvels."

"*C'est un homme précieux*," said Lord Peter.

"Ah, *monsieur, c'est un saint qui opère des miracles! Nous prions pour lui, Natasha et moi, tous les jours. N'est-ce pas, chérie?* And consider, *monsieur*, that he does it all, *ce grand homme, cet homme illustre*, for nothing at all. When we come here, we have not even the clothes upon our backs–we are ruined, famished. *Et avec ça que nous sommes de bonne famille–mais hélas! monsieur, en Russie, comme vous savez, ça ne vous vaut que des insultes–des atrocités. Enfin!* the great Sir Julian sees us, he says–'Madame, your little girl is very interesting to me. Say no more. I cure her for nothing–*pour ses beaux yeux,' a-t-il ajouté en raint. Ah, monsieur, c'est un saint, un véritable saint!* And Natasha is much, much better."

"*Madame, je vous en félicite.*"

"*And you, monsieur?* You are young, well, strong–you also suffer? It is still the war, perhaps?"

"A little remains of shell-shock," said Lord Peter.

"Ah, yes. So many good, brave, young men–"

"Sir Julian can spare you a few minutes, my lord, if you will come in now," said the servant.

Lord Peter bowed to his neighbour, and walked across the waiting-room. As the door of the consulting-room closed behind him, he remembered having once gone, disguised, into the staff-room of a German officer. He experienced the same feeling–the feeling of being caught in a trap, and a mingling of bravado and shame.

He had seen Sir Julian Freke several times from a distance, but never close. Now, while carefully and quite truthfully detailing the circumstances of his recent nervous attack, he considered the man before him. A man taller than himself, with immense breadth of shoulder, and wonderful hands. A face beautiful, impassioned and inhuman; fanatical, compelling eyes, bright blue amid the ruddy bush of hair and beard. They were not the cool and kindly eyes of the family doctor, they were the brooding eyes of the inspired scientist, and they searched one through.

"Well," thought Lord Peter, "I shan't have to be explicit, anyhow."

"Yes," said Sir Julian, "yes. You had been working too hard. Puzzling your mind. Yes. More than that, perhaps–troubling your mind, shall we say?"

"I found myself faced with a very alarming contingency."

"Yes. Unexpectedly, perhaps."

"Very unexpected indeed."

"Yes. Following on a period of mental and physical strain."

"Well–perhaps. Nothing out of the way."

"Yes. The unexpected contingency was–personal to yourself?"

"It demanded an immediate decision as to my own actions–yes, in that sense it was certainly personal."

"Quite so. You would have to assume some responsibility, no doubt."

"A very grave responsibility."

"Affecting others besides yourself?"

"Affecting one other person vitally, and a very great number indirectly."

"Yes. The time was night. You were sitting in the dark?"

"Not at first. I think I put the light out afterwards."

"Quite so–that action would naturally suggest itself to you. Were you warm?"

"I think the fire had died down. My man tells me that my teeth were chattering when I went in to him."

"Yes. You live in Piccadilly?"

"Yes."

"Heavy traffic sometimes goes past during the night, I expect."

"Oh, frequently."

"Just so. Now this decision you refer to–you had taken that decision."

"Yes."

"Your mind was made up?"

"Oh, yes."

"You had decided to take the action, whatever it was."

"Yes."

"Yes. It involved perhaps a period of inaction."

"Of comparative inaction–yes."

"Of suspense, shall we say?"

"Yes–of suspense, certainly."

"Possibly of some danger?"

"I don't know that that was in my mind at the time."

"No–it was a case in which you could not possibly consider yourself."

"If you like to put it that way."

"Quite so. Yes. You had these attacks frequently in 1918?"

"Yes–I was very ill for some months."

"Quite. Since then they have recurred less frequently?"

"Much less frequently."

"Yes–when did the last occur?"

"About nine months ago."

'Under what circumstances?"

"I was being worried by certain family matters. It was a question of deciding about some investments, and I was largely responsible."

"Yes. You were interested last year, I think, in some police case?"

"Yes–in the recovery of Lord Attenbury's emerald necklace."

"That involved some severe mental exercise?"

"I suppose so. But I enjoyed it very much."

"Yes. Was the exertion of solving the problem attended by any bad results physically?"

"None."

"No. You were interested, but not distressed."

"Exactly."

"Yes. You have been engaged in other investigations of the kind?"

"Yes. Little ones."

"With bad results for your health?"

"Not a bit of it. On the contrary. I took up these cases as a sort of distraction. I had a bad knock just after the war, which didn't make matters any better for me, don't you know."

"Ah! you are not married?"

"No."

"No. Will you allow me to make an examination? Just come a little nearer to the light. I want to see your eyes. Whose advice have you had till now?"

"Sir James Hodges'."

"Ah yes–he was a sad loss to the medical profession. A really great man–a true scientist. Yes. Thank you. Now I should like to try you with this little invention."

"What's it do?"

"Well–it tells me about your nervous reactions. Will you sit here?"

The examination that followed was purely medical. When it was concluded, Sir Julian said:

"Now, Lord Peter, I'll tell you about yourself in quite untechnical language–"

"Thanks," said Peter, "that's kind of you. I'm an awful fool about long words."

"Yes. Are you fond of private theatricals, Lord Peter?"

"Not particularly," said Peter, genuinely surprised. "Awful bore as a rule. Why?"

"I thought you might be," said the specialist, drily. "Well, now. You know quite well that the strain you put on your nerves during the war has left its mark on you. It has left what I may call old wounds in your brain. Sensations received by your nerve-endings sent messages to your brain, and produced minute physical changes there–changes we are only beginning to be able to detect, even with our most delicate instruments. These changes in their turn set up sensations; or I should say, more accurately, that sensations are the names we give to these changes of tissue when we perceive them: we call them horror, fear, sense of responsibility and so on."

"Yes, I follow you."

"Very well. Now, if you stimulate those damaged places in your brain again, you run the risk of opening up the old wounds. I mean, that if you get nerve-sensations of any kind producing the reactions which we call horror, fear, and sense of responsibility, they may go on to make disturbance right along the old channel, and produce in their turn physical changes which you will call by the names you were accustomed to associate with them–dread of German mines, responsibility for the lives of your men, strained attention and the inability to distinguish small sounds through the overpowering noise of guns."

"I see."

"This effect would be increased by extraneous circumstances producing other familiar physical sensations–night, cold or the rattling of heavy traffic, for instance."

"Yes."

"Yes. The old wounds are nearly healed, but not quite. The ordinary exercise of your mental faculties has no bad effect. It is only when you excite the injured part of your brain."

"Yes, I see."

"Yes. You must avoid these occasions. You must learn to be irresponsible, Lord Peter."

"My friends say I'm only too irresponsible already."

"Very likely. A sensitive nervous temperament often appears so, owing to its mental nimbleness."

"Oh!"

"Yes. This particular responsibility you were speaking of still rests upon you?"

"Yes, it does."

"You have not yet completed the course of action on which you have decided?"

"Not yet."

"You feel bound to carry it through?"

"Oh, yes–I can't back out of it now."

"No. You are expecting further strain?"

"A certain amount."

"Do you expect it to last much longer?"

"Very little longer now."

"Ah! Your nerves are not all they should be."

"No?"

"No. Nothing to be alarmed about, but you must exercise care while undergoing this strain, and afterwards you should take a complete rest. How about a voyage in the Mediterranean or the South Seas or somewhere?"

"Thanks. I'll think about it."

"Meanwhile, to carry you over the immediate trouble I will give you something to strengthen your nerves. It will do you no permanent good, you understand, but it will tide you over the bad time. And I will give you a prescription."

"Thank you."

Sir Julian got up and went into a small surgery leading out of the consulting room. Lord Peter watched him moving about–boiling something and writing. Presently he returned with a paper and a hypodermic syringe.

"Here is the prescription. And now, if you will just roll up your sleeve, I will deal with the necessity of the immediate moment."

Lord Peter obediently rolled up his sleeve. Sir Julian Freke selected a portion of his foream and anointed it with iodine.

"What's that you're goin' to stick into me. Bugs?"

The surgeon laughed.

"Not exactly," he said. He pinched up a portion of flesh between his finger and thumb. "You've had this kind of thing before, I expect."

"Oh, yes," said Lord Peter. He watched the cool fingers, fascinated, and the steady approach of the needle. "Yes–I've had it before–and, d'you know–I don't care frightfully about it."

He had brought up his right hand, and it closed over the surgeon's wrist like a vise.

The silence was like a shock. The blue eyes did not waver; they burned down steadily upon the heavy white lids below them. Then these slowly lifted; the grey eyes met the blue–coldly, steadily–and held them.

When lovers embrace, there seems no sound in the world but their own breathing. So the two men breathed face to face.

"As you like, of course, Lord Peter," said Sir Julian, courteously.

"Afraid I'm rather a silly ass," said Lord Peter, "but I never could abide these little gadgets. I had one once that went wrong and gave me a rotten bad time. They make me a bit nervous."

"In that case," replied Sir Julian, "it would certainly be better not to have the injection. It might rouse up just those sensations which we are desirous of avoiding. You will take the prescription, then, and do what you can to lessen the immediate strain as far as possible."

"Oh, yes–I'll take it easy, thanks," said Lord Peter. He rolled his sleeve down neatly. "I'm much obliged to you. If I have any further trouble I'll look in again."

"Do–do–" said Sir Julian, cheerfully. "Only make an appointment another time. I'm rather rushed these days. I hope your mother is quite well. I saw her the other day at that Battersea inquest. You should have been there. It would have interested you."

# 12

THE VILE, raw fog tore your throat and ravaged your eyes. You could not see your feet. You stumbled in your walk over poor men's graves.

The feel of Parker's old trench-coat beneath your fingers was comforting. You had felt it in worse places. You clung on now for fear you should get separated. The dim people moving in front of you were like Brocken spectres.

"Take care, gentlemen," said a toneless voice out of the yellow darkness, "there's an open grave just hereabouts."

You bore away to the right, and floundered in a mass of freshly turned clay.

"Hold up, old man," said Parker.

"Where is Lady Levy?"

"In the mortuary; the Duchess of Denver is with her. Your mother is wonderful, Peter."

"Isn't she?" said Lord Peter.

A dim blue light carried by somebody ahead wavered and stood still.

"Here you are," said a voice.

Two Dantesque shapes with pitchforks loomed up.

"Have you finished?" asked somebody.

"Nearly done, sir." The demons fell to work again with the pitchforks–no, spades.

Somebody sneezed. Parker located the sneezer and introduced him.

"Mr. Levett represents the Home Secretary. Lord Peter Wimsey. We are sorry to drag you out on such a day, Mr. Levett."

"It's all in the day's work," said Mr. Levett, hoarsely. He was muffled to the eyes.

The sound of the spades for many minutes. An iron noise of tools thrown down. Demons stooping and straining.

A black-bearded spectre at your elbow. Introduced. The Master of the Workhouse.

"A very painful matter, Lord Peter. You will forgive me for hoping you and Mr. Parker may be mistaken."

"I should like to be able to hope so too."

Something heaving, straining, coming up out of the ground.

"Steady, men. This way. Can you see? Be careful of the graves–they lie pretty thick hereabouts. Are you ready?"

"Right you are, sir. You go on with the lantern. We can follow you."

Lumbering footsteps. Catch hold of Parker's trench-coat again. "That you, old man? Oh, I beg your pardon, Mr. Levett–thought you were Parker."

"Hullo, Wimsey–here you are."

More graves. A headstone shouldered crookedly aslant. A trip and jerk over the edge of the rough grass. The squeal of gravel under your feet.

"This way, gentlemen, mind the step."

The mortuary. Raw red brick and sizzling gas-jets. Two women in black, and Dr. Grimbold. The coffin laid on the table with a heavy thump.

" 'Ave you got that there screw-driver, Bill? Thank 'ee. Be keerful wi' the chisel now. Not much substance to these 'ere boards, sir."

Several long creaks. A sob. The Duchess's voice, kind but peremptory.

"Hush, Christine. You mustn't cry."

A mutter of voices. The lurching departure of the Dante demons–good, decent demons in corduroy.

Dr. Grimbold's voice–cool and detached as if in the consulting room.

"Now–have you got that lamp, Mr. Wingate? Thank you. Yes, here on the table, please. Be careful not to catch your elbow in the flex, Mr. Levett. It would be better, I think, if you came on this side. Yes–yes–thank you. That's excellent."

The sudden brilliant circle of an electric lamp over the table. Dr. Grimbold's beard and spectacles. Mr. Levett blowing his nose. Parker bending close. The Master of the Workhouse peering over him. The rest of the room in the enhanced dimness of the gas-jets and the fog.

A low murmur of voices. All heads bent over the work.

Dr. Grimbold again–beyond the circle of the lamplight.

"We don't want to distress you unnecessarily, Lady Levy. If you will just tell us what to look for–the–? Yes, yes, certainly–and–yes–stopped with gold? Yes–the lower jaw, the last but one on the right? Yes–no teeth missing–no–yes? What kind of a mole? Yes–just over the left breast? Oh, I beg your pardon, just under–yes–appendicitis? Yes–a long one–yes–in the middle? Yes, I quite understand–scar on the arm? Yes, I don't know if we shall be able to find that–yes–any little constitutional weakness that might–? Oh, yes–arthitis–yes–thank you, Lady Levy–that's very clear. Don't come unless I ask you to. Now, Wingate."

A pause. A murmur. "Pulled out? After death, you think–well, so do I. Where is Dr. Colegrove? You attended this man in the workhouse? Yes. Do you recollect–? No? You're quite certain about that? Yes–we mustn't make a mistake, you know. Yes, but there are reasons why Sir Julian can't be present; I'm asking *you*, Dr. Colegrove. Well, you're certain–that's all I want to know. Just bring the light closer, Mr. Wingate, if you please. These miserable shells let the damp in so quickly. Ah! what do you make of this? Yes–yes–well, that's rather unmistakable, isn't it? Who did the head? Oh, Freke–of course. I was going to say they did good work at St. Luke's. Beautiful, isn't it, Dr. Colegrove? A wonderful surgeon–I saw him when he was at Guy's. Oh, no, gave it up years ago. Nothing like keeping your hand in. Ah–yes, undoubtedly that's it. Have you a towel handy, sir? Thank you. Over the head, if you please–I think we might have another here. Now, Lady Levy–I am going to ask you to look at a scar, and see if you recognise it. I'm sure you are going to help us by being very firm. Take your time–you won't see anything more than you absolutely must."

"Lucy, don't leave me."

"No, dear."

A space cleared at the table. The lamplight on the Duchess's white hair.

"Oh, yes–oh, yes! No, no–I couldn't be mistaken. There's that funny little kink in it. I've seen it hundreds of times. Oh, Lucy–Reuben!"

"Only a moment more, Lady Levy. The mole–"

"I–I think so–oh, yes, that is the very place."

"Yes. And the scar–was it three-cornered, just above the elbow?"

"Yes, oh, yes."

"Is this it?"

"Yes–yes–"

"I must ask you definitely, Lady Levy. Do you, from these three marks identify the body as that of your husband?"

"Oh! I must, mustn't I? Nobody else could have them just the same in just those places? It is my husband. It is Reuben. Oh–"

"Thank you, Lady Levy. You have been very brave and very helpful."

"But–I don't understand yet. How did he come here? Who did this dreadful thing?"

"Hush, dear," said the Duchess; "the man is going to be punished."

"Oh, but–how cruel! Poor Reuben! Who could have wanted to hurt him? Can I see his face?"

"No, dear," said the Duchess. "That isn't possible. Come away–you mustn't distress the doctors and people."

"No–no–they've all been so kind. Oh, Lucy!"

"We'll go home, dear. You don't want us any more, Dr. Grimbold?"

"No, Duchess, thank you. We are very grateful to you and to Lady Levy for coming."

There was a pause, while the two women went out, Parker, collected and helpful, escorting them to their waiting car. Then Dr. Grimbold again:

"I think Lord Peter Wimsey ought to see–the correctness of his deductions–Lord Peter–very painful –you may wish to see–yes, I was uneasy at the inquest–yes–Lady Levy–remarkably clear evidence–yes–most shocking case–ah, here's Mr. Parker–you and Lord Peter Wimsey entirely justified–do I really understand–? Really? I can hardly believe it–so distinguished a man–as you say, when a great brain turns to crime–yes–look here! Marvellous work–marvellous–somewhat obscured by this time, of course–but the most beautiful sections–here, you see the left hemisphere–and here–through the corpus striatum–here again–the very track of the damage done by the blow–wonderful–guessed it–saw the effect of the blow as he struck it, you know–ah, I should like to see *his* brain, Mr. Parker–and to think that–heavens, Lord Peter, you don't know what a blow you have struck at the whole profession–the whole civilized world! Oh my dear sir! Can you ask me? My lips are sealed of course–all our lips are sealed."

The way back through the burial ground. Fog again, and the squeal of wet gravel.

"Are your men ready, Charles?"

"They have gone. I sent them off when I saw Lady Levy to the car."

"Who is with them?"

"Sugg."

"Sugg?"

"Yes–poor devil. They've had him up on the mat at headquarters for bungling the case. All that evidence of Thipps's about the night club was corroborated, you know. That girl he gave the gin-and-bitters to was caught, and came and identified him, and they decided their case wasn't good enough, and let Thipps and the Horrocks girl go. Then they told Sugg he had overstepped his duty and ought to have been more careful. So he ought, but he can't help being a fool. I was sorry for him. It may do him some good to be in at the death. After all, Peter, you and I had special advantages."

"Yes. Well, it doesn't matter. Whoever goes won't get there in time. Sugg's as good as another."

But Sugg–an experience rare in his career–was in time.

Parker and Lord Peter were at 110 Piccadilly. Lord Peter was playing Bach and Parker was reading Origen when Sugg was announced.

"We've got our man, sir," said he.

"Good God!" said Peter. "Alive?"

"We were just in time, my lord. We rang the bell and marched straight up past his man to the library. He was sitting there doing some writing. When we came in, he made a grab for his hypodermic, but we were too quick for him, my lord. We didn't mean to let him slip through our hands, having got so far. We searched him thoroughly and marched him off."

"He is actually in gaol, then?"

"Oh, yes–safe enough–with two warders to see he doesn't make away with himself."

"You surprise me, Inspector. Have a drink."

"Thank you, my lord. I may say that I'm very grateful to you–this case was turning out a pretty bad egg for me. If I was rude to your lordship–"

"Oh, it's all right, Inspector," said Lord Peter, hastily. "I don't see how you could possibly have worked it out. I had the good luck to know something about it from other sources."

"That's what Freke says." Already the great surgeon was a common criminal in the inspector's eyes–a mere surname. "He was writing a full confession when we got hold of him, addressed to your lordship. The police will have to have it, of course, but seeing it's written for you, I brought it along for you to see first. Here it is."

He handed Lord Peter a bulky document.

"Thanks," said Peter. "Like to hear it, Charles?"

"Rather."

Accordingly Lord Peter read it aloud.

# 13

DEAR LORD Peter–When I was a young man I used to play chess with an old friend of my father's. He was a very bad, and a very slow, player, and he could never see when a checkmate was inevitable, but insisted on playing every move out. I never had any patience with that kind of attitude, and I will freely admit now that the game is yours. I must either stay at home and be hanged or escape abroad and live in an idle and insecure obscurity. I prefer to acknowledge defeat.

If you have read my book on "Criminal Lunacy," you will remember that I wrote: "In the majority of cases, the criminal betrays himself by some abnormality attendant upon this pathological condition of the nervous tissues. His mental instability shows itself in various forms: an overweening vanity, leading him to brag of his achievement; a disproportionate sense of the importance of the offence, resulting from the hallucination of religion, and driving him to confession; egomania, producing the sense of horror or conviction of sin, and driving him to headlong flight without covering his tracks; a reckless confidence, resulting in the neglect of the most ordinary precautions, as in the case of Henry Wainwright who left a boy in charge of the murdered woman's remains while he went to call a cab, or on the other hand, a nervous distrust of apperceptions in the past, causing him to revisit the scene of the crime to assure himself that all traces have been as safely removed as his *own judgment knows them to be*. I will not hesitate to assert that a perfectly sane man, not intimidated by religious or other delusions, could always render himself perfectly secure from detection, provided, that is, that the crime were sufficiently premeditated and that he were not pressed for time or thrown out in his calculations by purely fortuitous coincidence.

You know as well as I do, how far I have made this assertion good in practice. The two accidents which betrayed me, I could not by any possibility have foreseen. The first was the chance recognition of Levy by the girl in the Battersea Park Road, which suggested a connection between the two problems. The second was that Thipps should have arranged to go down to Denver on the Tuesday morning, thus enabling your mother to get word of the matter through to you before the body was removed by the police and to suggest a motive for the murder out of what she knew of my previous personal history. If I had been able to destroy these two accidentally forged links of circumstance, I will venture to say that you would never have so much as suspected me, still less obtained sufficient evidence to convict.

Of all human emotions, except perhaps those of hunger and fear, the sexual appetite produces the most violent, and, under some circumstances, the most persistent reactions; I think, however, I am right in saying that at the time when I wrote my book, my original sensual impulse to kill Sir Reuben Levy had already become profoundly modified by my habits of thought. To the animal lust to slay and the primitive human desire for revenge, there was added the rational intention of substantiating my own theories for the satisfaction of myself and the world. If all had turned out as I had planned, I should have deposited a sealed account of my experiment with the Bank of England, instructing my executors to publish it after my death. Now that accident has spoiled the completeness of my demonstration, I entrust the account to you, whom it cannot fail to interest, with the request that you will make it known among scientific men, in justice to my professional reputation.

The really essential factors of success in any undertaking are money and opportunity, and as a rule, the man who can make the first can make the second. During my early career, though I was fairly well-off, I had not absolute command of circumstance. Accordingly I devoted myself to my profession, and contented myself with keeping up a friendly connection with Reuben Levy and his family. This enabled me to remain in touch with his fortunes and interests, so that, when the moment for action should arrive, I might know what weapons to use.

Meanwhile, I carefully studied criminology in fiction and fact—my work on "Criminal Lunacy" was a side-product of this activity—and saw how, in every murder, the real crux of the problem was the disposal of the body. As a doctor, the means of death were always ready to my hand, and I was not likely to make any error in that connection. Nor was I likely to betray myself on account of any illusory sense of wrong-doing. The sole difficulty would be that of destroying all connection between my personality and that of the corpse. You will remember that Michael Finsbury, in Stevenson's entertaining romance, observes: "What hangs people is the unfortunate circumstance of guilt." It became clear to me that the mere leaving about of a superfluous corpse could convict nobody, provided that nobody was guilty in connection *with that particular corpse*. Thus the idea of substituting the one body for the other was early arrived at, though it was not till I obtained the practical direction of St. Luke's Hospital that I found myself perfectly unfettered in the choice and handling of dead bodies. From this period on, I kept a careful watch on all the material brought in for dissection.

My opportunity did not present itself until the week before Sir Reuben's disappearance, when the medical officer at the Chelsea workhouse sent word to me that an unknown vagrant had been injured that morning by the fall of a piece of scaffolding, and was exhibiting some very interesting nervous and cerebral reactions. I went round and saw the case, and was immediately struck by the man's strong superficial resemblance to Sir Reuben. He had been heavily struck on the back of the neck, dislocating the fourth and fifth cervical vertebrae and heavily bruising the spinal cord. It seemed highly unlikely that he could ever recover, either mentally or physically, and in any case there appeared to me to be no object in indefinitely prolonging so unprofitable an existence. He had obviously been able to support life until recently, as he was fairly well nourished, but the state of his feet and clothing showed that he was unemployed, and under present conditions he was likely to remain so. I decided that he would suit my purpose very well, and immediately put in train certain transactions in the City which I had already sketched out in my own mind. In the meantime, the reactions mentioned by the workhouse doctor were interesting, and I made careful studies of them, and arranged for the delivery of the body to the hospital when I should have completed my preparations.

On the Thursday and Friday of that week I made private arrangements with various brokers to buy the stock of certain Peruvian Oil-fields, which had gone down almost to wastepaper. This part of my experiment did not cost me very much, but I contrived to arouse considerable curiosity, and even a mild excitement. At this point I was of course careful not to let my name appear. The incidence of Saturday and Sunday gave me some anxiety lest my man should after all die before I was ready for him, but by the use of saline injections I contrived to keep him alive and, late on Sunday night, he even manifested disquieting symptoms of at any rate a partial recovery.

On Monday morning the market in Peruvians opened briskly. Rumours had evidently got about that somebody knew something, and this day I was not the only buyer in the market. I bought a couple of hundred more shares in my own name, and left the matter to take care of itself. At lunch time I made my arrangements to run into Levy accidentally at the corner of the Mansion House. He expressed (as I expected) his surprise at seeing me in that part of London. I simulated some embarrassment and suggested that we should lunch together. I dragged him to a place a bit off the usual beat, and there ordered a good wine and drank of it as much as he might suppose sufficient to induce a confidential mood. I asked him how things were going on 'Change. He said, "Oh, all right," but appeared a little doubtful, and asked me whether I did anything in that way. I said I had a little flutter occasionally, and that, as a matter of fact, I'd been put on to rather a good thing. I glanced round apprehensively at this point, and shifted my chair nearer to his.

"I suppose you don't know anything about Peruvian Oil, do you?" he said.

I started and looked round again, and leaning across to him, said, dropping my voice:

"Well, I do, as a matter of fact, but I don't want it to get about. I stand to make a good bit on it."

"But I thought the thing was hollow," he said; "it hasn't paid a dividend for umpteen years."

"No," I said, "it hasn't, but it's going to. I've got inside information." He looked a bit unconvinced, and I emptied off my glass, and edged right up to his ear.

"Look here," I said, "I'm not giving this away to everyone, but I don't mind doing you and Christine a good turn. You know, I've always kept a soft place in my heart for her, ever since the old days. You got in ahead of me that time, and now it's up to me to heap coals of fire on you both."

I was a little excited by this time, and he thought I was drunk.

"It's very kind of you, old man," he said, "but I'm a cautious bird, you know, always was. I'd like a bit of proof."

And he shrugged up his shoulders and looked like a pawnbroker.

"I'll give it to you," I said, 'but it isn't safe here. Come round to my place tonight after dinner, and I'll show you the report."

"How d'you get hold of it?" said he.

"I'll tell you tonight" said I. "Come round after dinner–any time after nine, say."

"To Harley Street?" he asked, and I saw that he meant coming.

"No," I said, "to Battersea–Prince of Wales Road; I've got some work to do at the hospital. And look here," I said, "don't you let on to a soul that you're coming. I bought a couple of hundred shares today, in my own name, and people are sure to get wind of it. If we're known to be about together, someone'll twig something. In fact, it's anything but safe talking about it in this place."

"All right," he said, "I won't say a word to anybody. I'll turn up about nine o'clock. You're sure it's a sound thing?"

"It can't go wrong," I assured him. And I meant it.

We parted after that, and I went round to the workhouse. My man had died at about eleven o'clock. I had seen him just after breakfast, and was not surprised. I completed the usual formalities with the workhouse authorities, and arranged for his delivery at the hospital at about seven o'clock.

In the afternoon, as it was not one of my days to be in Harley Street, I looked up an old friend who lives close to Hyde Park, and found that he was just off to Brighton on some business or other. I had tea with him, and saw him off by the 5.35 from Victoria. On issuing from the barrier it occurred to me to purchase an evening paper, and I thoughtlessly turned my steps to the bookstall. The usual crowds were rushing to catch suburban trains home, and on moving away I found myself involved in a contrary stream of travellers coming up out of the Underground, or bolting from all sides for the 5.45 to Battersea Park and Wandsworth Common. I disengaged myself after some buffeting and went home in a taxi; and it was not till I was safely seated there that I discovered somebody's gold-rimmed pince-nez involved in the astrakhan collar of my overcoat. The time from 6.15 to seven I spent concocting something to look like a bogus report for Sir Reuben.

At seven I went through to the hospital, and found the workhouse van just delivering my subject at the side door. I had him taken straight up to the theatre, and told the attendant, William Watts, that I intended to work there that night. I told him I would prepare the body myself–the injection of a preservative would have been a most regrettable complication. I sent him about his business, and then went home and had dinner. I told my man that I should be working in the hospital that evening, and that he could go to bed at 10.30 as usual, as I could not tell whether I should be late or not. He is used to my erratic ways. I only keep two servants in the Battersea house–the man-servant and his wife, who cooks for me. The rougher domestic work is done by a charwoman, who sleeps out. The servants' bedroom is at the top of the house, overlooking Prince of Wales Road.

As soon as I had dined I established myself in the hall with some papers. My man had cleared dinner by a quarter past eight, and I told him to give me the syphon and tantalus; and sent him downstairs. Levy rang the bell at twenty minutes past nine, and I opened the door to him myself. My man appeared at the other end of the hall, but I called to him that it was all right, and he went away. Levy wore an overcoat with evening dress and carried an umbrella. "Why, how wet you are!" I said. "How did you come?" "By 'bus," he said, "and the fool of a conductor forgot to put me down at the end of the road. It's pouring cats and dogs and pitch-dark–I couldn't see where I was." I was glad he hadn't taken a taxi, but I had rather reckoned on his not doing so. "Your little economies will be the death of you one of these days," I said. I was right there, but I hadn't reckoned on their being the death of me as well. I say again, I could not have foreseen it.

I sat him down by the fire, and gave him a whisky. He was in high spirits about some deal in Argentines he was bringing off the next day. We talked money for about a quarter of an hour and then he said:

"Well, how about this Peruvian mare's-nest of yours ?"

"It's no mare's-nest," I said; "come and have a look at it."

I took him upstairs into the library, and switched on the centre light and the reading lamp on the writing table. I gave him a chair at the table with his back to the fire, and fetched the papers I had been faking, out of the safe. He took them, and began to read them, poking over them in his short-sighted way, while I mended the fire. As soon as I saw his head in a favourable position I struck him heavily with the poker, just over the fourth cervical. It was delicate work calculating the exact force necessary to kill him without breaking the skin, but my professional experience was useful to me. He gave one loud gasp, and tumbled forward on to the table quite noiselessly. I put the poker back, and examined him. His neck was broken, and he was quite dead. I carried him into my bedroom and undressed him. It was about ten minutes to ten when I had finished. I put him away under my bed, which had been turned down for the night, and cleared up the papers in the library. Then I went downstairs, took Levy's umbrella, and let myself out at the hall door, shouting "Good-night" loudly enough to be heard in the basement if the servants should be listening. I walked briskly away down the street, went in by the hospital side door, and returned to the house noiselessly by way of the private passage. It would have been awkward if anybody had seen me then, but I leaned over the back stairs and heard the cook and her husband still talking in the kitchen. I slipped back into the hall, replaced the umbrella in the stand, cleared up my papers there, went up into the library and rang the bell. When the man appeared I told him to lock up everything except the private door to the hospital. I waited in the library until he had done so, and about 10.30 I heard both servants go up to bed. I waited a quarter of an hour longer and then went through to the dissecting-room. I wheeled one of the stretcher tables through the passage to the house door, and then went to fetch Levy. It was a nuisance having to get him downstairs, but I had not liked to make away with him in any of the ground-floor rooms, in case my servant should take a fancy to poke his head in during the few minutes that I was out house, or while locking up. Besides, that was a flea-bite to what I should have to do later. I put Levy on the table, wheeled him across to the hospital and substituted him for my interesting pauper. I was sorry to have to abandon the idea of getting a look at the latter's brain, but I could not afford to incur suspicion. It was still rather early, so I knocked down a few minutes getting Levy ready for dissection. Then I put my pauper on the table and trundled him over to the house. It was now five past eleven, and I thought I might conclude that the servants were in bed. I carried the body into my bedroom. He was rather heavy, but less so than Levy, and my Alpine experience had taught me how to handle bodies. It is as much a matter of knack as of strength, and I am, in any case, a powerful man for my height. I put the body into the bed–not that I expected anyone to look in during my absence, but if they should they might just as well see me apparently asleep in bed. I drew the clothes a little over his head, stripped, and put on Levy's clothes, which were fortunately a little big for me everywhere, not forgetting to take his spectacles, watch and other oddments. At a little before half-past eleven I was in the road looking for a cab. People were just beginning to come home from the theatre, and I easily secured one at the corner of Prince of Wales Road. I told the man to drive me to Hyde Park Corner. There I got out, tipped him well, and asked him to pick me up again at the same place in an hour's time. He assented with an understanding grin, and I walked on up Park Lane. I had my own clothes with me in a suitcase, and carried my own overcoat and Levy's umbrella. When I got to No. 9A there were lights in some of the top windows. I was very nearly too early, owing to the old man's having sent the servants to the theatre. I waited about for a few minutes, and heard it strike the quarter past midnight. The lights were extinguished shortly after, and I let myself in with Levy's key.

It had been my original intention, when I thought over this plan of murder, to let Levy disappear from the study or the dining-room, leaving only a heap of clothes on the hearth-rug. The accident of my having been able to secure Lady Levy's absence from London, however, made possible a solution more misleading, though less pleasantly fantastic. I turned on the hall light, hung up Levy's wet overcoat and placed his umbrella in the stand. I walked up noisily and heavily to the bedroom and turned off the light by the duplicate switch on the landing. I knew the house well enough, of course. There was no chance of my running into the man-servant. Old Levy was a simple old man, who liked doing things for himself. He gave his valet little work, and never required any attendance at night. In the bedroom I took off Levy's gloves and put on a surgical pair, so as to leave no tell-tale finger-prints. As I wished to convey the impression that Levy had gone to bed in the usual way, I simply went to bed. The surest and simplest method of making a thing appear to have been done is to do it. A bed that has been rumpled about with one's hands, for instance, never looks like a bed that has been slept in. I dared not use Levy's brush, of course, as my hair is not of his colour, but I did everything else. I supposed that a thoughtful old man like Levy would put his boots handy for his valet, and I ought to have deduced that he would fold up his clothes. That was a mistake, but not an important one. Remembering that well-thought-out little work of Mr. Bentley's, I had examined Levy's mouth for false teeth, but he had none. I did not forget, however, to wet his tooth-brush.

At one o'clock I got up and dressed in my own clothes by the light of my own pocket torch. I dared not turn on the bedroom lights, as there were light blinds to the windows. I put on my own boots and an old pair of goloshes outside the door. There was a thick Turkey carpet on the stairs and hall-floor, and I was not afraid of leaving marks. I hesitated whether to chance the banging of the front door, but decided it would be safer to take the latchkey. (It is now in the Thames. I dropped it over Battersea Bridge the next day.) I slipped quietly down, and listened for a few minutes with my ear to the letterbox. I heard a constable tramp past. As soon as his steps had died away in the distance I stepped out and pulled the door gingerly to. It closed almost soundlessly, and I walked away to pick up my cab. I had an overcoat of much the same pattern as Levy's, and had taken the precaution to pack an opera hat in my suitcase. I hoped the man would not notice that I had no umbrella this time. Fortunately the rain had diminished for the moment to a sort of drizzle, and if he noticed anything he made no observation. I told him to stop at 50 Overstrand Mansions, and I paid him off there, and stood under the porch till he had driven away. Then I hurried round to my own side door and let myself in. It was about a quarter to two, and the harder part of my task still lay before me.

My first step was to alter the appearance of my subject as to eliminate any immediate suggestion either of Levy or of the workhouse vagrant. A fairly superficial alteration was all I considered necessary, since there was not likely to be any hue-and-cry after the pauper. He was fairly accounted for, and his deputy was at hand to represent him. Nor, if Levy was after all traced to my house, would it be difficult to show that the body in evidence was, as a matter of fact, not his. A clean shave and a little hair-oiling and manicuring seemed sufficient to suggest a distinct personality for my silent accomplice. His hands had been well washed in hospital, and though calloused, were not grimy. I was not able to do the work as thoroughly as I should have liked, because time was getting on. I was not sure how long it would take me to dispose of him, and moreover, I feared the onset of *rigor mortis*, which would make my task more difficult. When I had him barbered to my satisfaction, I fetched a strong sheet and a couple of wide roller bandages, and fastened him up carefully, padding him with cotton wool wherever the bandages might chafe or leave a bruise.

Now came the really ticklish part of the business. I had already decided in my own mind that the only way of conveying him from the house was by the roof. To go through the garden at the back in this soft wet weather was to leave a ruinous trail behind us. To carry a dead man down a suburban street in the middle of the night seemed outside the range of practical politics. On the roof, on the other hand, the rain, which would have betrayed me on the ground, would stand my friend.

To reach the roof, it was necessary to carry my burden to the top of the house, past my servants' room, and hoist him out through the trap-door in the box-room roof. Had it merely been a question of going quietly up there myself, I should have had no fear of waking the servants, but to do so burdened by a heavy body was more difficult. It would be possible, provided that the man and his wife were soundly asleep, but if not, the lumbering tread on the narrow stair and the noise of opening the trap-door would be only too plainly audible. I tiptoed delicately up the stair and listened at their door. To my disgust I heard the man give a grunt and mutter something as he moved in his bed.

I looked at my watch. My preparations had taken nearly an hour, first and last, and I dared not be too late on the roof. I determined to take a bold step and, as it were, bluff out an alibi. I went without precaution against noise into the bathroom turned on the hot and cold water taps to the full and pulled out the plug.

My household has often had occasion to complain of my habit of using the bath at irregular night hours. Not only does the rush of water into the cistern disturb any sleepers on the Prince of Wales Road side of the house, but my cistern is afflicted with peculiarly loud gurglings and thumpings, while frequently the pipes emit a loud groaning sound. To my delight, on this particular occasion, the cistern was in excellent form, honking, whistling and booming like a railway terminus. I gave the noise five minutes' start, and when I calculated that the sleepers would have finished cursing me and put their heads under the clothes to shut out the din, I reduced the flow of water to a small stream and left the bathroom, taking good care to leave the light burning and lock the door after me. Then I picked up my pauper and carried him upstairs as lightly as possible.

The box-room is a small attic on the side of the landing opposite to the servants' bedroom and the cistern-room. It has a trap-door, reached by a short, wooden ladder. I set this up, hoisted up my pauper and climbed up after him. The water was still racing into the cistern which was making a noise as though it were trying to digest an iron chain, and with the reduced flow in the bathroom the groaning of the pipes had risen almost to a hoot. I was not afraid of anybody hearing other noises. I pulled the ladder through on to the roof after me.

Between my house and the last house in Queen Caroline Mansions there is a space of only a few feet. Indeed, when the Mansions were put up, I believe there was some trouble about ancient lights, but I suppose the parties compromised somehow. Anyhow, my seven-foot ladder reached well across. I tied the body firmly to the ladder, and pushed it over till the far end was resting on the parapet of the opposite house. Then I took a short run across the cistern-room and the box-room roof, and landed easily on the other side, the parapet being happily both low and narrow.

The rest was simple. I carried my pauper along the flat roofs, intending to leave him, like the hunchback in the story, on someone's staircase or down a chimney. I had got about half-way along when I suddenly thought "Why this must be about little Thipps's place," and I remembered his silly face, and his silly chatter about vivisection. It occurred to me pleasantly how delightul it would be to deposit my parcel with him and see what he made of it. I lay down and peered over the parapet at the back. It was pitch-dark and pouring with rain again by this time, and I risked using my torch. That was the only incautious thing I did, and the odds against being seen from the houses opposite were long enough. One second's flash showed me what I had hardly dared to hope–an open window just below me.

I knew those flats well enough to be sure it was either the bathroom or the kitchen. I made a noose in a third bandage that I had brought with me, and made it fast under the arms of the corpse. I twisted it into a double rope, and secured the end to the iron stanchion of a chimney-stack. Then I dangled our friend over. I went down after him myself with the aid of a drain-pipe and was soon hauling him in by Thipps's bathroom window.

By that time I had got a little conceited with myself, and spared a few minutes to lay him out prettily and make him shipshape. A sudden inspiration suggested that I should give him the pair of pince-nez which I had happened to pick up at Victoria. I came across them in my pocket while I was looking for a penknife to loosen a knot, and I saw what distinction they would lend his appearance, besides making it more misleading. I fixed them on him, effaced all traces of my presence as far as possible, and departed as I had come, going easily up between the drain-pipe and the rope.

I walked quietly back, re-crossed my crevasse and carried in my ladder and sheet. My discreet accomplice greeted me with a reassuring gurgle and thump. I didn't make a sound on the stairs. Seeing that I had now been having a bath for about three-quarters of an hour, I turned the water off, and enabled my deserving domestics to get a little sleep. I also felt it was time I had a little myself.

First, however, I had to go over to the hospital and make all safe there. I took off Levy's head, and started to open up the face. In twenty minutes his own wife could not have recognised him. I returned, leaving my wet goloshes and mackintosh by the garden door. My trousers I dried by the gas stove in my bedroom, and brushed away all traces of mud and brickdust. My pauper's beard I burned in the library.

I got a good two hours' sleep from five to seven, when my man called me as usual. I apologized for having kept the water running so long and so late, and added that I thought I would have the cistern seen to.

I was interested to note that I was rather extra hungry at breakfast, showing that my night's work had caused a certain wear-and-tear of tissue. I went over afterwards to continue my dissection. During the morning a peculiarly thick-headed police inspector came to inquire whether a body had escaped from the hospital. I had him brought to me where I was, and had the pleasure of showing him the work I was doing on Sir Reuben Levy's head. Afterwards I went round with him to Thipps's and was able to satisfy myself that my pauper looked very convincing.

As soon as the Stock Exchange opened I telephoned my various brokers, and by exercising a little care, was able to sell out the greater part of my Peruvian stock on a rising market. Towards the end of the day, however, buyers became rather unsettled as a result of Levy's death, and in the end I did not make more than a few hundreds by the transaction.

Trusting I have now made clear to you any point which you may have found obscure, and with congratulations on the good fortune and perspicacity which have enabled you to defeat me, I remain, with kind remembrances to your mother,

Yours very truly,
JULIAN FREKE

*Post-Scriptum:* My will is made, leaving my money to St. Luke's Hospital, and bequeathing my body to the same institution for dissection. I feel sure that my brain will be of interest to the scientific world. As I shall die by my own hand, I imagine that there may be a little difficulty about this. Will you do me the favour, if you can, of seeing the persons concerned in the inquest, and obtaining that the brain is not damaged by an unskilful practitioner at the post-mortem, and that the body is disposed of according to my wish?

By the way, it may be of interest to you to know that I appreciated your motive in calling this afternoon. It conveyed a warning, and I am acting upon it in spite of the disastrous consequences to myself. I was pleased to realize that you had not underestimated my nerve and intelligence, and refused the injection. Had you submitted to it, you would, of course, never have reached home alive. No trace would have been left in your body of the injection, which consisted of a harmless preparation of strychnine, mixed with an almost unknown poison, for which there is at present no recognised test, a concentrated solution of sn-

At this point the manuscript broke off.

"Well, that's all clear enough," said Parker.

"Isn't it queer?" said Lord Peter. "All that coolness, all those brains—and then he couldn't resist writing a confession to show how clever he was, even to keep his head out of the noose."

"And a very good thing for us," said Inspector Sugg, "but Lord bless you, sir, these criminals are all alike."

"Freke's epitaph," said Parker, when the Inspector had departed. "What next, Peter?"

"I shall now give a dinner party," said Lord Peter, "to Mr. John P. Milligan and his secretary and to Messrs. Crimplesham and Wicks. I feel they deserve it for not having murdered Levy."

"Well, don't forget the Thippses," said Mr. Parker.

"On no account," said Lord Peter, "would I deprive myself of the pleasure of Mrs. Thipps's company. Bunter!"

"My lord?"

"The Napoleon brandy."

# Clouds of Witness

THE SOLUTION OF

# THE RIDDLESDALE MYSTERY

WITH

A REPORT

OF THE TRIAL OF

# THE DUKE OF DENVER

BEFORE THE HOUSE OF LORDS

FOR

# MURDER

---

**The inimitable stories of Tong-king never have any real ending, and this one, being in his most elevated style, has even less end than most of them. But the whole narrative is permeated with the odour of joss-sticks and honourable high-mindedness, and the two characters are both of noble birth.**

***The Wallet of Kai-Lung***

# CONTENTS


1 "OF HIS MALICE AFORETHOUGHT" 109
2 THE GREEN-EYED CAT 124
3 MUDSTAINS AND BLOODSTAINS 137
4 ——AND HIS DAUGHTER, MUCH-AFRAID 151
5 THE RUE ST. HONORE AND THE RUE DE LA PAIX 160
6 MARY QUITE CONTRARY 169
7 THE CLUB AND THE BULLET 176
8 MR. PARKER TAKES NOTES 183
9 GOYLES 186
10 NOTHING ABIDES AT THE NOON 194
11 MERIBAH 202
12 THE ALIBI 212
13 MANON 222
14 THE EDGE OF THE AXE TOWARDS HIM 228
15 BAR FALLING 238
16 THE SECOND STRING 241
17 THE ELOQUENT DEAD 245
18 THE SPEECH FOR THE DEFENCE 249
19 WHO GOES HOME? 257

# 1

# "OF HIS MALICE AFORETHOUGHT"

*O, who hath done this deed?*

Othello

LORD PETER Wimsey stretched himself luxuriously between the sheets provided by the Hôtel Meurice. After his exertions in the unravelling of the Battersea Mystery, he had followed Sir Julian Freke's advice and taken a holiday. He had felt suddenly weary of breakfasting every morning before his view over the Green Park; he had realised that the picking up of first editions at sales afforded insufficient exercise for a man of thirty-three; the very crimes of London were oversophisticated. He had abandoned his flat and his friends and fled to the wilds of Corsica. For the last three months he had forsworn letters, newspapers, and telegrams. He had tramped about the mountains, admiring from a cautious distance the wild beauty of Corsican peasant-women, and studying the vendetta in its natural haunt. In such conditions murder seemed not only reasonable, but lovable. Bunter, his confidential man and assistant sleuth, had nobly sacrificed his civilised habits, had let his master go dirty and even unshaven, and had turned his faithful camera from the recording of finger-prints to that of craggy scenery. It had been very refreshing.

Now, however, the call of the blood was upon Lord Peter. They had returned late last night in a vile train to Paris, and had picked up their luggage. The autumn light, filtering through the curtains, touched caressingly the silver-topped bottles on the dressing-table, outlined an electric lampshade and the shape of the telephone. A noise of running water near by proclaimed that Bunter had turned on the bath (h. & c.) and was laying out scented soap, bath-salts, the huge bath-sponge, for which there had been no scope in Corsica, and the delightful flesh-brush with the long handle, which rasped you so agreeably all down the spine. "Contrast," philosophised Lord Peter sleepily, "is life. Corsica–Paris–then London. . . . Good morning, Bunter."

"Good morning, my lord. Fine morning, my lord. Your Lordship's bath-water is ready."

"Thanks," said Lord Peter. He blinked at the sunlight.

It was a glorious bath. He wondered, as he soaked in it, how he could have existed in Corsica. He wallowed happily and sang a few bars of a song. In a soporific interval he heard the valet de chambre bringing in coffee and rolls. Coffee and rolls! He heaved himself out with a splash, towelled himself luxuriously, enveloped his long-mortified body in a silken bath-robe, and wandered back.

To his immense surprise he perceived Mr. Bunter calmly replacing all the fittings in his dressing-case. Another astonished glance showed him the bags—scarcely opened the previous night—repacked, relabelled, and standing ready for a journey.

"I say, Bunter, what's up?" said his lordship. "We're stayin' here a fortnight y'know."

"Excuse me, my lord," said Mr. Bunter, deferentially, "but, having seen *The Times* (delivered here every morning by air, my lord; and very expeditious I'm sure, all things considered), I made no doubt your lordship would be wishing to go to Riddlesdale at once."

"Riddlesdale!" exclaimed Peter, "What's the matter? Anything wrong with my brother?"

For answer Mr. Bunter handed him the paper, folded open at the heading:

RIDDLESDALE INQUEST.
DUKE OF DENVER ARRESTED
ON MURDER CHARGE.

Lord Peter stared as if hypnotised.

"I thought your lordship wouldn't wish to miss anything," said Mr. Bunter, "so I took the liberty——"

Lord Peter pulled himself together.

"When's the next train?" he asked.

"I beg your lordship's pardon—I thought your lordship would wish to take the quickest route. I took it on myself to book two seats in the aeroplane *Victoria*. She starts at 11.30."

Lord Peter looked at his watch.

"Ten o'clock," he said. "Very well, You did quite right. Dear me! Poor old Gerald arrested for murder. Uncommonly worryin' for him, poor chap. Always hated my bein' mixed up with police-courts. Now he's there himself. Lord Peter Wimsey in the witness-box—very distressin' to feelin's of a brother. Duke of Denver in the dock—worse still. Dear me! Well, I suppose one must have breakfast."

"Yes, my lord. Full account of the inquest in the paper, my lord."

"Yes. Who's on the case, by the way?"

"Mr. Parker, my lord."

"Parker? That's good. Splendid old Parker! Wonder how he managed to get put on to it. How do things look, Bunter?"

"If I may say so, my lord, I fancy the investigations will prove very interesting. There are several extremely suggestive points in the evidence, my lord."

"From a criminological point of view I daresay it is interesting," replied his lordship, sitting down cheerfully to his *café au lait*, "but it's deuced awkward for my brother, all the same, havin' no turn for criminology, what?"

"Ah, well!" said Mr. Bunter, "they say, my lord, there's nothing like having a personal interest."

"The inquest was held to-day at Riddlesdale, in the North Riding of Yorkshire, on the body of Captain Denis Cathcart, which was found at three o'clock on Thursday morning lying just outside the conservatory door of the Duke of Denver's shooting-box, Riddlesdale Lodge. Evidence was given to show that deceased had quarrelled with the Duke of Denver on the preceding evening, and was subsequently shot in a small thicket adjoining the house. A pistol belonging to the Duke was found near the scene of the crime. A verdict of murder was returned against the Duke of Denver. Lady Mary Wimsey, sister of the Duke, who was engaged to be married to the deceased, collapsed after giving evidence, and is now lying seriously ill at the Lodge. The Duchess of Denver hastened from town yesterday and was present at the inquest. Full report on p. 12."

"Poor old Gerald!" thought Lord Peter, as he turned to page 12; "and poor old Mary! I wonder if she really was fond of the fellow. Mother always said not, but Mary never would let on about herself."

The full report began by describing the little village of Riddlesdale, where the Duke of Denver had recently taken a small shooting-box for the season. When the tragedy occurred the Duke had been staying there with a party of guests. In the Duchess's absence Lady Mary Wimsey had acted as hostess. The other guests were Colonel and Mrs. Marchbanks, the Hon. Frederick Arbuthnot, Mr. and Mrs. Pettigrew-Robinson, and the dead man, Denis Cathcart.

The first witness was the Duke of Denver, who claimed to have discovered the body. He gave evidence that he was coming into the house by the conservatory door at three o'clock in the morning of Thursday, October 14th, when his foot struck against something. He had switched on his electric torch and seen the body of Denis Cathcart at his feet. He had at once turned it over, and seen that Cathcart had been shot in the chest. He was quite dead. As Denver was bending over the body, he heard a cry in the conservatory, and, looking up, saw Lady Mary Wimsey gazing out horror-struck. She came out by the conservatory door, and exclaimed at once, "O God, Gerald, you've killed him!" (Sensation.)*

The Coroner: "Were you surprised by that remark?"

Duke of D.: "Well, I was so shocked and surprised at the whole thing. I think I said to her, 'Don't look,' and she said, 'Oh, it's Denis! Whatever can have happened? Has there been an accident?' I stayed with the body, and sent her up to rouse the house."

The Coroner: "Did you expect to see Lady Mary Wimsey in the conservatory?"

Duke of D.: "Really, as I say, I was so astonished all round, don't you know, I didn't think about it."

The Coroner: "Do you remember how she was dressed?"

Duke of D.: "I don't think she was in her pyjamas." (Laughter.) "I think she had a coat on."

The Coroner: "I understand that Lady Mary Wimsey was engaged to be married to the deceased?"

Duke of D.: "Yes."

The Coroner: "He was well known to you?"

*This report, though substantially the same as that read by Lord Peter in *The Times*, has been corrected, amplified and annotated from the shorthand report made at the time by Mr. Parker.

Duke of D.: "He was the son of an old friend of my father's; his parents are dead. I believe he lived chiefly abroad. I ran across him during the war, and in 1919 he came to stay at Denver. He became engaged to my sister at the beginning of this year."

The Coroner: "With your consent, and with that of the family?"

Duke of D.: "Oh, yes, certainly."

The Coroner: "What kind of man was Captain Cathcart?"

Duke of D.: "Well—he was a Sahib and all that. I don't know what he did before he joined in 1914. I think he lived on his income; his father was well off. Crack shot, good at games, and so on. I never heard anything against him—till that evening."

The Coroner: "What was that?"

Duke of D.: "Well—the fact is—it was deuced queer. He—— If anybody but Tommy Freeborn had said it I should never have believed it." (Sensation.)

The Coroner: "I'm afraid I must ask your grace of what exactly you had to accuse the deceased."

Duke of D.: "Well, I didn't—I don't—exactly accuse him. An old friend of mine made a suggestion. Of course I thought it must be all a mistake, so I went to Cathcart, and, to my amazement, he practically admitted it! Then we both got angry, and he told me to go to the devll, and rushed out of the house." (Renewed sensation.)

The Coroner: "When did this quarrel occur?"

Duke of D.: "On Wednesday night. That was the last I saw of him." (Unparalleled sensation.)

The Coroner: "Please, please, we cannot have this disturbance. Now, will your grace kindly give me, as far as you can remember it, the exact history of this quarrel?"

Duke of D.: "Well, it was like this. We'd had a long day on the moors and had dinner early, and about half-past nine we began to feel like turning in. My sister and Mrs. Pettigrew-Robinson toddled on up, and we were havin' a last peg in the billiard-room when Fleming—that's my man —came in with the letters. They come rather any old time in the evening, you know, we being two and a half miles from the village. No—I wasn't in the billiard-room at the time—I was lockin' up the gun-room. The letter was from an old friend of mine I hadn't seen for years—Tom Freeborn—used to know him at the House——"

The Coroner: "Whose house?"

Duke of D.: "Oh, Christ Church, Oxford. He wrote to say he'd seen the announcement of my sister's engagement in Egypt."

The Coroner: "In Egypt?"

Duke of D.: "I mean, *he* was in Egypt—Tom Freeborn, you see—that's why he hadn't written before. He engineers. He went out there after the war was over, you see, and, bein' somewhere up near the sources of the Nile, he doesn't get the papers regularly. He said, would I 'scuse him for interferin' in a very delicate matter, and all that, but did I know who Cathcart was? Said he'd met him in Paris during the war, and he lived by cheatin' at cards—said he could swear to it, with details of a row there'd been in some French place or other. Said he knew I'd want to chaw his head off—Freeborn's, I mean—for buttin' in, but he'd seen the man's photo in the paper, an' he thought I ought to know."

The Coroner: "Did this letter surprise you?"

Duke of D.: "Couldn't believe it at first. If it hadn't been old Tom

Freeborn I'd have put the thing in the fire straight off, and, even as it was, I didn't quite know what to think. I mean, it wasn't as if it had happened in England, you know. I mean to say, Frenchmen get so excited about nothing. Only there was Freeborn, and he isn't the kind of man that makes mistakes."

The Coroner: "What did you do?"

Duke of D.: "Well, the more I looked at it the less I liked it, you know. Still, I couldn't quite leave it like that, so I thought the best way was to go straight to Cathcart. They'd all gone up while I was sittin' thinkin' about it, so I went up and knocked at Cathcart's door. He said, 'What's that?' or 'Who the devil's that?' or somethin' of the sort, and I went in. 'Look here,' I said, 'can I just have a word with you?' 'Well, cut it short, then,' he said. I was surprised—he wasn't usually rude. 'Well,' I said, 'fact is, I've had a letter I don't much like the look of, and I thought the best thing to do was to bring it straight away to you an' have the whole thing cleared up. It's from a man—a very decent sort—old college friend, who says he's met you in Paris.' 'Paris!' he said, in a most uncommonly unpleasant way. 'Paris! What the hell do you want to come talkin' to me about Paris for?' 'Well,' I said, 'don't talk like that, because it's misleadin' under the circumstances.' 'What are you drivin' at?' says Cathcart. 'Spit it out and go to bed, for God's sake.' I said, 'Right oh! I will. It's a man called Freeborn, who says he knew you in Paris and that you made money cheatin' at cards.' I thought he'd break out at that, but all he said was, 'What about it?' 'What about it?' I said. 'Well, of course, it's not the sort of thing I'm goin' to believe like that, right bang-slap off, without any proofs.' Then he said a funny thing. He said, 'Beliefs don't matter—it's what one *knows* about people.' 'Do you mean to say you don't deny it?' I said. 'It's no good my denying it,' he said; 'you must make up your own mind. Nobody could *dis*prove it.' And then he suddenly jumped up, nearly knocking the table over, and said, 'I don't care what you think or what you do, if you'll only get out. For God's sake leave me alone!' 'Look here,' I said, 'You needn't take it that way. I don't say I do believe it—in fact,' I said, 'I'm sure there must be some mistake; only, you bein' engaged to Mary,' I said, 'I couldn't just let it go at that without looking into it, could I?' 'Oh!' says Cathcart, 'if that's what's worrying you, it needn't. That's off.' I said, 'What?' He said, 'Our engagement.' 'Off?' I said. 'But I was talking to Mary about it only yesterday.' 'I haven't told her yet,' he said. 'Well,' I said, 'I think that's damned cool. Who the hell do you think you are, to come here and jilt my sister?' Well, I said quite a lot, first and last. 'You can get out,' I said; 'I've no use for swine like you.' 'I will,' he said, and he pushed past me an' slammed downstairs and out of the front door, an' banged it after him."

The Coroner: "What did you do?"

Duke of D.: "I ran into my bedroom, which has a window over the conservatory, and shouted out to him not to be a silly fool. It was pourin' with rain and beastly cold. He didn't come back, so I told Fleming to leave the conservatory door open—in case he thought better of it—and went to bed."

The Coroner: "What explanation can you suggest for Cathcart's behaviour?"

Duke of D.: "None. I was simply staggered. But I think he must somehow have got wind of the letter, and knew the game was up."

The Coroner: "Did you mention the matter to anybody else?"

Duke of D.: "No. It wasn't pleasant, and I thought I'd better leave it till the morning."

The Coroner: "So you did nothing further in the matter?"

Duke of D.: "No. I didn't want to go out huntin' for the fellow. I was too angry. Besides, I thought he'd change his mind before long—it was a brute of a night and he'd only a dinner-jacket."

The Coroner: "Then you just went quietly to bed and never saw deceased again?"

Duke of D.: "Not till I fell over him outside the conservatory at three in the morning."

The Coroner: "Ah yes. Now can you tell us how you came to be out of doors at that time?"

Duke of D. (hesitating): "I didn't sleep well. I went out for a stroll."

The Coroner: "At three o'clock in the morning?"

Duke of D.: "Yes." With sudden inspiration: "You see, my wife's away." (Laughter and some remarks from the back of the room.)

The Coroner: "Silence, please. . . . You mean to say that you got up at that hour of an October night to take a walk in the garden in the pouring rain?"

Duke of D.: "Yes, just a stroll." (Laughter.)

The Coroner: "At what time did you leave your bedroom?"

Duke of D. : "Oh—oh, about half-past two, I should think."

The Coroner: "Which way did you go out?"

Duke of D.: "By the conservatory door."

The Coroner: "The body was not there when you went out?"

Duke of D.: "Oh, no!"

The Coroner: "Or you would have seen it?"

Duke of D.: "Lord, yes! I'd have had to walk over it."

The Coroner: "Exactly where did you go?"

Duke of D. (vaguely) : "Oh, just round about."

The Coroner: "You heard no shot?"

Duke of D.: "No."

The Coroner: "Did you go far away from the conservatory door and the shrubbery?"

Duke of D.: "Well—I was some way away. Perhaps that's why I didn't hear anything. It must have been."

The Coroner: "Were you as much as a quarter of a mile away?"

Duke of D.: "I should think I was—oh, yes, quite!"

The Coroner: "More than a quarter of a mile away?"

Duke of D.: "Possibly. I walked about briskly because it was cold."

The Coroner: "In which direction?"

Duke of D. (with visible hesitation): "Round at the back of the house. Towards the bowling-green."

The Coroner: "The bowling-green?"

Duke of D. (more confidently) : "Yes."

"The Coroner: "But if you were more than a quarter of a mile away, you must have left the grounds?"

Duke of D.: "I—oh, yes—I think I did. Yes, I walked about on the moor a bit, you know."

The Coroner: "Can you show us the letter you had from Mr. Freeborn?"

Duke of D.: "Oh, certainly—if I can find it. I thought I put it in my pocket, but I couldn't find it for that Scotland Yard fellow."

The Coroner: "Can you have accidentally destroyed it?"

Duke of D.: "No—I'm sure I remember putting it——Oh"—here the witness paused in very patent confusion, and grew red—"I remember now. I destroyed it."

The Coroner: "That is unfortunate. How was that?"

Duke of D.: "I had forgotten; it has come back to me now. I'm afraid it has gone for good."

The Coroner: "Perhaps you kept the envelope?"

Witness shook his head.

The Coroner: "Then you can show the jury no proof of having received it?"

Duke of D.: "Not unless Fleming remembers it."

The Coroner: "Ah, yes! No doubt we can check it that way. Thank you, your grace. Call Lady Mary Wimsey."

The noble lady, who was, until the tragic morning of October 14th, the fiancée of the deceased, aroused a murmur of sympathy on her appearance. Fair and slender, her naturally rose-pink cheeks ashy pale, she seemed overwhelmed with grief. She was dressed entirely in black, and gave her evidence in a very low tone which was at times almost inaudible.*

After expressing his sympathy, the coroner asked, "How long had you been engaged to the deceased?"

Witness: "About eight months."

The Coroner: "Where did you first meet him?"

Witness: "At my sister-in-law's house in London."

The Coroner: "When was that?"

Witness: "I think it was June last year."

The Coroner: "You were quite happy in your engagement?"

Witness : "Quite."

The Coroner: "You naturally saw a good deal of Captain Cathcart. Did he tell you much about his previous life?"

Witness: "Not very much. We were not given to mutual confidences. We usually discussed subjects of common interest."

The Coroner: "You had many such subjects?"

Witness : "Oh, yes."

The Coroner: "You never gathered at any time that Captain Cathcart had anything on his mind?"

Witness: "Not particularly. He had seemed a little anxious the last few days."

The Coroner: "Did he speak of his life in Paris?"

Witness: "He spoke of theatres and amusements there. He knew Paris very well. I was staying in Paris with some friends last February, when he was there, and he took us about. That was shortly after our engagement."

The Coroner: "Did he ever speak of playing cards in Paris?"

Witness: "I don't remember."

The Coroner: "With regard to your marriage—had any money settlements been gone into?"

Witness: "I don't think so. The date of the marriage was not in any way fixed."

The Coroner: "He always appeared to have plenty of money?"

Witness: "I suppose so; I didn't think about it."

The Coroner: "You never heard him complain of being hard up?"

Witness: "Everybody complains of that, don't they?"

The Coroner: "Was he a man of cheerful disposition?"

Witness: "He was very moody, never the same two days together."

*From the newspaper report—*not* Mr. Parker.

The Coroner: "You have heard what your brother says about the deceased wishing to break off the engagement. Had you any idea of this?"

Witness: "Not the slightest."

The Coroner: "Can you think of any explanation now?"

Witness: "Absolutely none."

The Coroner: "There had been no quarrel?"

Witness: "No."

The Coroner: "So far as you knew, on the Wednesday evening, you were still engaged to deceased with every prospect of being married to him shortly?"

Witness: "Ye-es. Yes, certainly, of course."

The Coroner: "He was not—forgive me this very painful question—the sort of man who would have been likely to lay violent hands on himself?"

Witness: "Oh, I never thought—well, I don't know—I suppose he might have done. That would explain it, wouldn't it?"

The Coroner: "Now, Lady Mary—please don't distress yourself, take your own time—will you tell us exactly what you heard and saw on Wednesday night and Thursday morning."

Witness: "I went up to bed with Mrs. Marchbanks and Mrs. Pettigrew-Robinson at about half-past nine, leaving all the men downstairs. I said good night to Denis, who seemed quite as usual. I was not downstairs when the post came. I went to my room at once. My room is at the back of the house. I heard Mr. Pettigrew-Robinson come up at about ten. The Pettigrew-Robinsons sleep next door to me. Some of the other men came up with him. I did not hear my brother come upstairs. At about a quarter past ten I heard two men talking loudly in the passage, and then I heard someone run downstairs and bang the front door. Afterwards I heard rapid steps in the passage, and finally I heard my brother shut his door. Then I went to bed."

The Coroner: "You did not inquire the cause of the disturbance?"

Witness (indifferently) : "I thought it was probably something about the dogs."

The Coroner: "What happened next?"

Witness: "I woke up at three o'clock."

The Coroner: "What wakened you?"

Witness: "I heard a shot."

The Coroner: "You were not awake before you heard it?"

Witness: "I may have been partly awake. I heard it very distinctly. I was sure it was a shot. I listened for a few minutes, and then went down to see if anything was wrong."

The Coroner: "Why did you not call your brother or some other gentleman?"

Witness (scornfully): "Why should I? I thought it was probably only poachers, and I didn't want to make an unnecessary fuss at that unearthly hour."

The Coroner: "Did the shot sound close to the house?"

Witness: "Fairly, I think—it is hard to tell when one is wakened by a noise—it always sounds so extra loud."

The Coroner: "It did not seem to be in the house or in the conservatory?"

Witness: "No, it was outside."

The Coroner: "So you went downstairs by yourself. That was very plucky of you, Lady Mary. Did you go immediately?"

Witness: "Not quite immediately. I thought it over for a few minutes; then

I put on walking-shoes over bare feet, a heavy covert-coat, and a woolly cap. It may have been five minutes after hearing the shot that I left my bedroom. I went downstairs and through the billiard-room to the conservatory."

The Coroner: "Why did you go out that way?"

Witness: "Because it was quicker than unbolting either the front door or the back door."

At this point a plan of Riddlesdale Lodge was handed to the jury. It is a roomy, two-storied house, built in a plain style, and leased by the present owner, Mr. Walter Montague, to Lord Denver for the season, Mr. Montague being in the States.

Witness (resuming) : "When I got to the conservatory door I saw a man outside, bending over something on the ground. When he looked up I was astonished to see my brother."

The Coroner: "Before you saw who it was, what did you expect?"

Witness: "I hardly know–it all happened so quickly, I thought it was burglars, I think."

The Coroner: "His grace has told us that when you saw him you cried out, 'O God! you've killed him!' Can you tell us why you did that?"

Witness (very pale): "I thought my brother must have come upon the burglar and fired at him in self-defence–that is, if I thought at all."

The Coroner: "Quite so. You knew that the Duke possessed a revolver?"

Witness : "Oh, yes–I think so."

The Coroner: "What did you do next?"

Witness: "My brother sent me up to get help. I knocked up Mr. Arbuthnot and Mr. and Mrs. Pettigrew-Robinson. Then I suddenly felt very faint, and went back to my bedroom and took some sal volatile."

The Coroner: "Alone?"

Witness: "Yes, everybody was running about and calling out. I couldn't bear it–I––"

Here the witness, who up till this moment had given her evidence very collectedly, though in a low voice, collapsed suddenly, and had to be assisted from the room.

The next witness called was James Fleming, the man-servant. He remembered having brought the letters from Riddlesdale at 9.45 on Wednesday evening. He had taken three or four letters to the Duke in the gun-room. He could not remember at all whether one of them had had an Egyptian stamp. He did not collect stamps; his hobby was autographs.

The Hon. Frederick Arbuthnot then gave evidence. He had gone up to bed with the rest at a little before ten. He had heard Denver come up by himself some time later–couldn't say how much later–he was brushing his teeth at the time. (Laughter.) Had certainly heard loud voices and a row going on next door and in the passage. Had heard somebody go for the stairs hell-for-leather. Had stuck his head out and seen Denver in the passage. Had said, "Hello, Denver, what's the row?" The Duke's reply had been inaudible. Denver had bolted into his bedroom and shouted out of the window, "Don't be an ass, man!" He had seemed very angry indeed, but the Hon. Freddy attached no importance to that. One was always getting across Denver, but it never came to anything. More dust than kick in his opinion. Hadn't known Cathcart long–always found him all right–no, he didn't *like* Cathcart, but he was all right, you know, nothing wrong about him that he knew of. Good lord, no, he'd never heard it suggested he cheated at cards! Well, no, of course, he didn't go about looking out for people cheating at cards–it wasn't

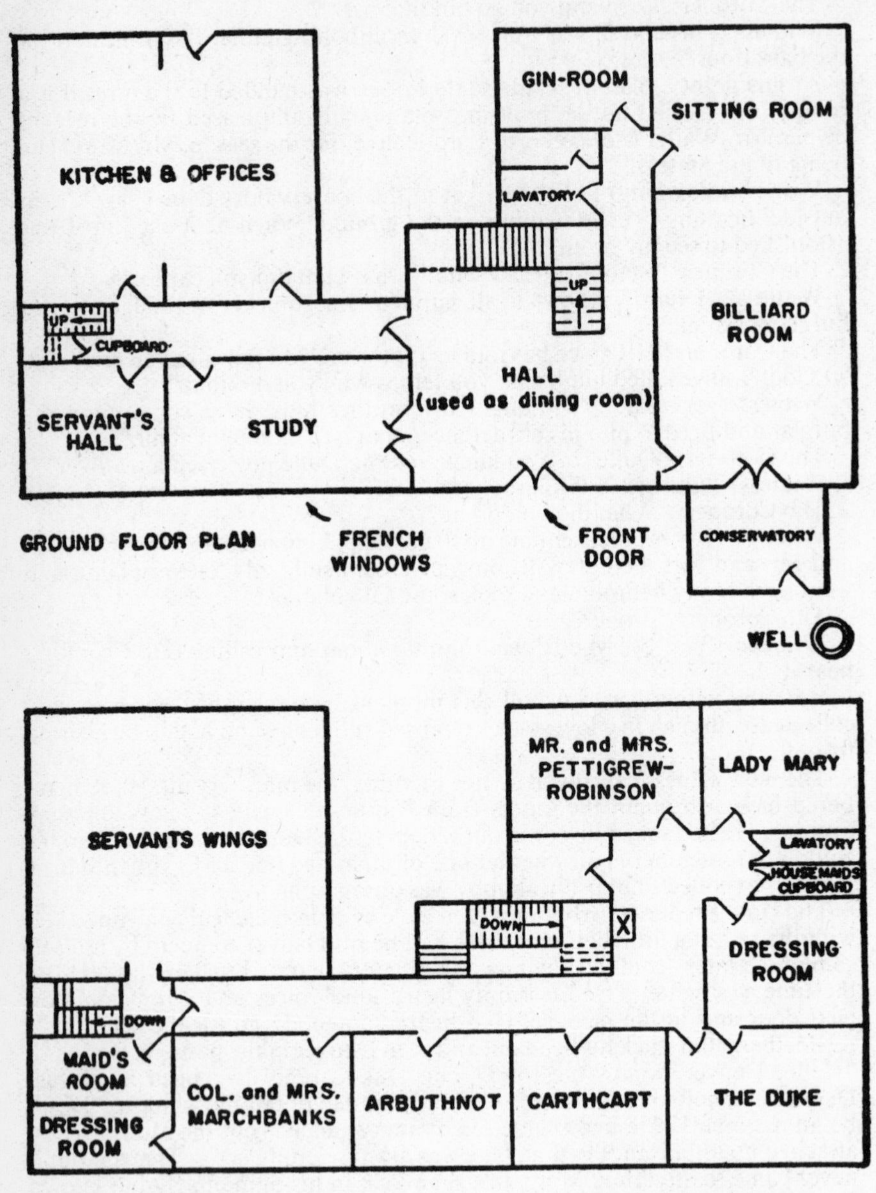
KITCHEN & OFFICES
GIN-ROOM
SITTING ROOM
LAVATORY
UP
BILLIARD ROOM
UP
CUPBOARD
HALL (used as dining room)
SERVANT'S HALL
STUDY
GROUND FLOOR PLAN
FRENCH WINDOWS
FRONT DOOR
CONSERVATORY
WELL
MR. and MRS. PETTIGREW-ROBINSON
LADY MARY
SERVANTS WINGS
LAVATORY
HOUSEMAIDS CUPBOARD
DOWN
X
DRESSING ROOM
DOWN
MAID'S ROOM
COL. and MRS. MARCHBANKS
ARBUTHNOT
CARTHCART
THE DUKE
DRESSING ROOM
SECOND FLOOR PLAN
X - Old Oak Chest

a thing one expected. He'd been had that way in a club at Monte once–he'd had no hand in bringing it to light–hadn't noticed anything till the fun began. Had not noticed anything particular in Cathcart's manner to Lady Mary, or hers to him. Didn't suppose he ever would notice anything; did not consider himself an observing sort of man. Was not interfering by nature; had thought Wednesday evening's dust-up none of his business. Had gone to bed and to sleep.

The Coroner: "Did you hear anything further that night?"

Hon. Frederick: "Not till poor little Mary knocked me up. Then I toddled down and found Denver in the conservatory, bathing Cathcart's head. We thought we ought to clean the gravel and mud off his face, you know."

The Coroner: "You heard no shot?"

Hon. Frederick: "Not a sound. But I sleep pretty heavily."

Colonel and Mrs. Marchbanks slept in the room over what was called the study–more a sort of smoking-room really. They both gave the same account of a conversation which they had had at 11:30. Mrs. Marchbanks had sat up to write some letters after the Colonel was in bed. They had heard voices and someone running about, but had paid no attention. It was not unusual for members of the party to shout and run about. At last the Colonel had said, "Come to bed, my dear, it's half-past eleven, and we're making an early start tomorrow. You won't be fit for anything." He said this because Mrs. Marchbanks was a keen sportswoman and always carried her gun with the rest. She replied, "I'm just coming." The Colonel said, "You're the only sinner burning the midnight oil–everybody's turned in." Mrs. Marchbanks replied, "No, the Duke's still up; I can hear him moving about in the study." Colonel Marchbanks listened and heard it too. Neither of them heard the Duke come up again. They had heard no noise of any kind in the night.

Mr. Pettigrew-Robinson appeared to give evidence with extreme reluctance. He and his wife had gone to bed at ten. They had heard the quarrel with Cathcart. Mr. Pettigrew-Robinson, fearing that something might be going to happen, opened his door in time to hear the Duke say, "If you dare to speak to my sister again I'll break every bone in your body," or words to that effect. Cathcart had rushed downstairs. The Duke was scarlet in the face. He had not seen Mr. Pettigrew-Robinson, but had spoken a few words to Mr. Arbuthnot, and rushed into his own bedroom. Mr. Pettigrew-Robinson had run out, and said to Mr. Arbuthnot, "I say, Arbuthnot," and Mr. Arbuthnot had very rudely slammed the door in his face. He had then gone to the Duke's door and said, "I say, Denver." The Duke had come out, pushing past him, without even noticing him, and gone to the head of the stairs. He had heard him tell Fleming to leave the conservatory door open, as Mr. Cathcart had gone out. The Duke had then returned. Mr. Pettigrew-Robinson had tried to catch him as he passed, and had said again, "I say, Denver, what's up?" The Duke had said nothing, and had shut his bedroom door with great decision. Later on, however, at 11:30 to be precise, Mr. Pettigrew-Robinson had heard the Duke's door open, and stealthy feet moving about the passage. He could not hear whether they had gone downstairs. The bathroom and lavatory were at his end of the passage, and, if anybody had entered either of them, he thought he should have heard. He had not heard the footsteps return. He had heard his travelling clock strike twelve before falling asleep. There was no mistaking the Duke's bedroom door, as the hinge creaked in a peculiar manner.

Mrs. Pettigrew-Robinson confirmed her husband's evidence. She had fallen asleep before midnight, and had slept heavily. She was a heavy sleeper at the beginning of the night, but slept lightly in the early morning. She had been annoyed by all the disturbance in the house that evening, as it had prevented her from getting off. In fact, she had dropped off about 10:30, and Mr. Pettigrew-Robinson had had to wake her an hour after to tell her about the footsteps. What with one thing and another she only got a couple of hours' good sleep. She woke up again at two, and remained broad awake till the alarm was given by Lady Mary. She could swear positively that she heard no shot in the night. Her window was next to Lady Mary's, on the opposite side from the conservatory. She had always been accustomed from a child to sleep with her window open. In reply to a question from the Coroner, Mrs. Pettigrew-Robinson said she had never felt there was a real, true affection between Lady Mary Wimsey and deceased. They seemed very off-hand, but that sort of thing was the fashion nowadays. She had never heard of any disagreement.

Miss Lydia Cathcart, who had been hurriedly summoned from town, then gave evidence about the deceased man. She told the Coroner that she was the Captain's aunt and his only surviving relative. She had seen very little of him since he came into possession of his father's money. He had always lived with his own friends in Paris, and they were such as she could not approve of.

"My brother and I never got on very well," said Miss Cathcart, "and he had my nephew educated abroad till he was eighteen. I fear Denis's notions were always quite French. After my brother's death Denis went to Cambridge, by his father's desire. I was left executrix of the will, and guardian till Denis came of age. I do not know why, after neglecting me all his life, my brother should have chosen to put such a responsibility upon me at his death, but I did not care to refuse. My house was open to Denis during his holidays from college, but he preferred, as a rule, to go and stay with his rich friends. I cannot now recall any of their names. When Denis was twenty-one he came into £10,000 a year. I believe it was in some kind of foreign property. I inherited a certain amount under the will as executrix, but I converted it all, at once, into good, sound, British securities. I cannot say what Denis did with his. It would not surprise me at all to hear that he had been cheating at cards. I have heard that the persons he consorted with in Paris were most undesirable. I never met any of them. I have never been in France."

John Hardraw, the gamekeeper, was next called. He and his wife inhabit a small cottage just inside the gate of Riddlesdale Lodge. The grounds, which measure twenty acres or so, are surrounded at this point by a strong paling; the gate is locked at night. Hardraw stated that he had heard a shot fired at about ten minutes to twelve on Wednesday night, close to the cottage, as it seemed to him. Behind the cottage are ten acres of preserved plantation. He supposed that there were poachers about; they occasionally came in after hares. He went out with his gun in that direction, but saw nobody. He returned home at one o'clock by his watch.

The Coroner: "Did you fire your gun at any time?"

Witness: "No."

The Coroner: "You did not go out again?"

Witness: "I did not."

The Coroner: "Nor hear any other shots?"

Witness: "Only that one; but I fell asleep after I got back, and was wakened up by the chauffeur going out for the doctor. That would be at about a quarter past three."

The Coroner: "Is it not unusual for poachers to shoot so very near the cottage?"

Witness: "Yes, rather. If poachers do come, it is usually on the other side of the preserve, towards the moor."

Dr. Thorpe gave evidence of having been called to see deceased. He lived in Stapley, nearly fourteen miles from Riddlesdale. There was no medical man in Riddlesdale. The chauffeur had knocked him up at 3:45 a.m., and he had dressed quickly and come with him at once. They were at Riddlesdale Lodge at half-past four. Deceased, when he saw him, he judged to have been dead three or four hours. The lungs had been pierced by a bullet, and death had resulted from loss of blood, and suffocation. Death would not have resulted immediately–deceased might have lingered some time. He had made a post-mortem investigation, and found that the bullet had been deflected from a rib. There was nothing to show whether the wound had been self-inflicted or fired from another hand, at close quarters. There were no other marks of violence.

Inspector Craikes from Stapley had been brought back in the car with Dr. Thorpe. He had seen the body. It was then lying on its back, between the door of the conservatory and the covered well just outside. As soon as it became light, Inspector Craikes had examined the house and grounds. He had found bloody marks all along the path leading to the conservatory, and signs as though a body had been dragged along. This path ran into the main path leading from the gate to the front door. (Plan produced.) Where the two paths joined, a shrubbery began, and ran down on both sides of the path to the gate and the gamekeeper's cottage. The blood-tracks had led to a little clearing in the middle of the shrubbery, about half-way between the house and the gate. Here the inspector found a great pool of blood, a handkerchief soaked in blood, and a revolver. The handkerchief bore the initials D. C., and the revolver was a small weapon of American pattern, and bore no mark. The conservatory door was open when the Inspector arrived, and the key was inside.

Deceased, when he saw him, was in dinner-jacket and pumps, without hat or overcoat. He was wet through, and his clothes, besides being much blood-stained, were very muddy and greatly disordered through the dragging of the body. The pocket contained a cigar-case and a small, flat pocket-knife. Deceased's bedroom had been searched for papers, etc., but so far nothing had been found to shed very much light on his circumstances.

The Duke of Denver was then recalled.

The Coroner: "I should like to ask your grace whether you ever saw deceased in possession of a revolver?"

Duke of D.: "Not since the war."

The Coroner: "You do not know if he carried one about with him?"

Duke of D.: "I have no idea."

The Coroner: "You can make no guess, I suppose, to whom this revolver belongs?"

Duke of D. (in great surprise): "That's my revolver–out of the study table drawer. How did you get hold of that?"–(Sensation.)

The Coroner: "You are certain?"

Duke of D.: "Positive. I saw it there only the other day, when I was hunting out some photos of Mary for Cathcart, and I remember saying then that it was getting rusty lying about. There's the speck of rust."

The Coroner: "Did you keep it loaded?"

Duke of D.: "Lord, no! I really don't know why it was there. I fancy I turned it out one day with some old Army stuff, and found it among my shooting things when I was up at Riddlesdale in August. I think the cartridges were with it."

The Coroner: "Was the drawer locked?"

Duke of D.: "Yes; but the key was in the lock. My wife tells me I'm careless."

The Coroner: "Did anybody else know the revolver was there?"

Duke of D.: "Fleming did, I think. I don't know of anybody else."

Detective-Inspector Parker of Scotland Yard, having only arrived on Friday, had been unable as yet to make any very close investigation. Certain indications led him to think that some person or persons had been on the scene of the tragedy in addition to those who had taken part in the discovery. He preferred to say nothing more at present.

The Coroner then reconstructed the evidence in chronological order. At, or a little after, ten o'clock there had been a quarrel between deceased and the Duke of Denver, after which deceased had left the house never to be seen alive again. They had the evidence of Mr. Pettigrew-Robinson that the Duke had gone downstairs at 11:30, and that of Colonel Marchbanks that he had been heard immediately afterwards moving about in the study, the room in which the revolver produced in evidence was usually kept. Again at this they had the Duke's own sworn statement that he had not left his bedroom till half-past two in the morning. The jury would have to consider what weight was to be attached to those conflicting statements. Then, as to the shots heard in the night; the gamekeeper had said he heard a shot at ten minutes to twelve, but he had supposed it to be fired by poachers. It was, in fact, quite possible that there had been poachers about. On the other hand, Lady Mary's statement that she had heard the shot at about three a.m. did not fit in very well with the doctor's evidence that when he arrived at Riddlesdale at 4:30 deceased had been already three or four hours dead. They would remember also that, in Dr. Thorpe's opinion, death had not immediately followed the wound. If they believed this evidence, therefore, they would have to put back the moment of death to between eleven p.m. and midnight, and this might very well have been the shot which the gamekeeper heard. In that case they had still to ask themselves about the shot which had awakened Lady Mary Wimsey. Of course, if they liked to put that down to poachers, there was no inherent impossibility.

They next came to the body of deceased, which had been discovered by the Duke of Denver at three a.m. lying outside the door of the small conservatory, near the covered well. There seemed little doubt, from the medical evidence, that the shot which killed deceased had been fired in the shrubbery, about seven minutes' distance from the house, and that the body of deceased had been dragged from that place to the house. Deceased had undoubtedly died as the result of being shot in the lungs. The jury would have to decide whether that shot was fired by his own hand or by the hand of another; and, if the latter, whether by accident, in self-defence, or by malice aforethought with intent to murder. As regards suicide, they must consider what they knew of deceased's character and circumstances. Deceased was a young man in the prime of his strength, and apparently of considerable fortune. He had had a meritorious military career, and was liked by his friends. The Duke of Denver had thought sufficiently well of him to consent to his own sister's engagement to deceased. There was evidence to show that the fiancés, though perhaps not demonstrative, were on excellent terms. The Duke affirmed that on the Wednesday night deceased had announced his intention of breaking off the engagement. Did they believe that deceased, without even communicating with the lady, or writing a word of explanation or farewell, would thereupon rush out and shoot himself? Again, the jury must consider the accusation which the Duke of Denver said he had brought against deceased. He had accused him of cheating at cards. In the kind of society to which the persons involved in this inquiry belonged, such a misdemeanour as cheating at cards was regarded as far more shameful than such sins as murder and adultery. Possibly the mere suggestion of such a thing, whether well-founded or not, might well cause a gentleman of sensitive honour to make away with himself. But was deceased honourable? Deceased had been educated in France, and French notions of the honest thing were very different from British ones. The Coroner himself had had business relations with French persons in his capacity as a solicitor, and could assure such of the jury as had never been in France that they ought to allow for these different standards. Unhappily, the alleged letter giving details of the accusation had not been produced to them. Next, they might ask themselves whether it was not more usual for a suicide to shoot himself in the head. They should ask themselves how deceased came by the revolver. And, finally, they must consider, in that case, who had dragged the body towards the house, and why the person had chosen to do so, with great labour to himself and at the risk of extinguishing any lingering remnant of the vital spark,* instead of arousing the household and fetching help.

If they excluded suicide, there remained accident, manslaughter, or murder. As to the first, if they thought it likely that deceased or any other person had taken out the Duke of Denver's revolver that night for any purpose, and that, in looking at, cleaning, shooting with, or otherwise handling the weapon, it had gone off and killed deceased accidentally, then they would return a verdict of death by misadventure accordingly. In that case, how did they explain the conduct of the person, whoever it was, who had dragged the body to the door?

The Coroner then passed on to speak of the law concerning manslaughter. He reminded them that no mere words, however insulting or threatening, can be an efficient excuse for killing anybody, and that the conflict must be sudden and unpremeditated. Did they think, for example, that the Duke had gone out, wishing to induce his guest to return and sleep in the house, and that deceased had retorted upon him with blows or menaces of assault? If so, and the Duke, having a weapon in his hand, had shot deceased in self-defence, that was only manslaughter. But, in that case, they must ask themselves how the Duke came to go out to deceased with a lethal weapon in his hand? And this suggestion was in direct conflict with the Duke's own evidence.

Lastly, they must consider whether there was sufficient evidence of malice to justify a verdict of murder. They must consider whether any person had a motive, means, and opportunity for killing deceased; and whether they could reasonably account for that person's conduct on any other hypothesis. And, if

*Verbatim.

they thought there *was* such a person, and that his conduct was in any way suspicious or secretive, or that he had wilfully suppressed evidence which might have had a bearing on the case, or (here the Coroner spoke with great emphasis, staring over the Duke's head) fabricated other evidence with intent to mislead—then all these circumstances might be sufficient to amount to a violent presumption of guilt against some party, in which case they were in duty bound to bring in a verdict of wilful murder against that party. And, in considering this aspect of the question, the Coroner added, they would have to decide in their own minds whether the person who had dragged deceased towards the conservatory door had done so with the object of obtaining assistance or of thrusting the body down the garden well, which, as they had heard from Inspector Craikes, was situate close by the spot where the body had been found. If the jury were satisfied that deceased had been murdered, but were not prepared to accuse any particular person on the evidence, they might bring in a verdict of murder against an unknown person, or persons; but, if they felt justified in laying the killing at any person's door, then they must allow no respect of persons to prevent them from doing their duty.

Guided by these extremely plain hints, the jury, without very long consultation, returned a verdict of wilful murder against Gerald, Duke of Denver.

# 2

# THE GREEN-EYED CAT

*And here's to the hound*
*With his nose unto the ground——*

Drink, Puppy, Drink

SOME PEOPLE hold that breakfast is the best meal of the day. Others, less robust, hold that it is the worst, and that, of all breakfasts in the week, Sunday morning breakfast is incomparably the worst.

The party gathered about the breakfast-table at Riddlesdale Lodge held, if one might judge from their faces, no brief for that day miscalled of sweet refection and holy love. The only member of it who seemed neither angry nor embarrassed was the Hon. Freddy Arbuthnot, and he was silent, engaged in trying to take the whole skeleton out of a bloater at once. The very presence of that undistinguished fish upon the Duchess's breakfast-table indicated a disorganised household.

The Duchess of Denver was pouring out coffee. This was one of her uncomfortable habits. Persons arriving late for breakfast were thereby made painfully aware of their sloth. She was a long-necked, long-backed woman, who disciplined her hair and her children. She was never embarrassed, and her anger, though never permitted to be visible, made itself felt the more.

Colonel and Mrs. Marchbanks sat side by side. They had nothing beautiful about them but a stolid mutual affection. Mrs. Marchbanks was not angry, but she was embarrassed in the presence of the Duchess, because she could not feel sorry for her. When you felt sorry for people you called them "poor old dear" or "poor dear old man." Since, obviously, you could not call the

Duchess poor old dear, you were not being properly sorry for her. This distressed Mrs. Marchbanks. The Colonel was both embarrassed and angry—embarrassed because, 'pon my soul, it was very difficult to know what to talk about in a house where your host had been arrested for murder; angry in a dim way, like an injured animal, because unpleasant things like this had no business to break in on the shooting-season.

Mrs. Pettigrew-Robinson was not only angry, she was outraged. As a girl she had adopted the motto stamped upon the school notepaper; *Quœcunque honesta*. She had always thought it *wrong* to let your mind *dwell* on anything that was not really nice. In middle life she still made a point of ignoring those newspaper paragraphs which bore such headlines as: "ASSAULT UPON A SCHOOLTEACHER AT CRICKLEWOOD" ; "DEATH IN A PINT OF STOUT"; £75 FOR A KISS"; or "SHE CALLED HIM HUBBYKINS." She said she could not see what *good* it did you to know about such things. She regretted having consented to visit Riddlesdale Lodge in the absence of the Duchess. She had never liked Lady Mary; she considered her a very objectionable specimen of the modern independent young woman; besides, there had been that very undignified incident connected with a Bolshevist while Lady Mary was nursing in London during the war. Nor had Mrs. Pettigrew-Robinson at all cared for Captain Denis Cathcart. She did not like a young man to be handsome in that obvious kind of way. But, of course, since Mr. Pettigrew-Robinson had wanted to come to Riddlesdale, it was her place to be with him. She was not to blame for the unfortunate result.

Mr. Pettigrew-Robinson was angry, quite simply, because the detective from Scotland Yard had not accepted his help in searching the house and grounds for footprints. As an older man of some experience in these matters (Mr. Pettigrew-Robinson was a county magistrate) he had gone out of his way to place himself at the man's disposal. Not only had the man been short with him, but he had rudely ordered him out of the conservatory, where he (Mr. Pettigrew-Robinson) had been reconstructing the affair from the point of view of Lady Mary.

All these angers and embarrassments might have caused less pain to the company had they not been aggravated by the presence of the detective himself, a quiet young man in a tweed suit, eating curry at one end of the table next to Mr. Murbles, the solicitor. This person had arrived from London on Friday, had corrected the local police, and strongly dissented from the opinion of Inspector Craikes. He had suppressed at the inquest information which, if openly given, might have precluded the arrest of the Duke. He had officiously detained the whole unhappy party, on the grounds that he wanted to re-examine everybody, and was thus keeping them miserably cooped up together over a horrible Sunday; and he had put the coping-stone on his offences by turning out to be an intimate friend of Lord Peter Wimsey's, and having, in consequence, to be accommodated with a bed in the gamekeeper's cottage and breakfast at the Lodge.

Mr. Murbles, who was elderly and had a delicate digestion, had travelled up in a hurry on Thursday night. He had found the inquest very improperly conducted and his client altogether impracticable. He had spent all his time trying to get hold of Sir Impey Biggs, K.C., who had vanished for the week-end, leaving no address. He was eating a little dry toast, and was inclined to like the detective, who called him "Sir," and passed him the butter.

"Is anybody thinking of going to church?" asked the Duchess.

"Theodore and I should like to go," said Mrs. Pettigrew-Robinson, "if it is not too much trouble; or we could walk. It is not so *very* far."

"It's two and a half miles, good," said Colonel Marchbanks.

Mr. Pettigrew-Robinson looked at him gratefully.

"Of course you will come in the car," said the Duchess. "I am going myself."

"Are you, though?" said the Hon. Freddy. "I say, won't you get a bit stared at, what?"

"Really, Freddy," said the Duchess, "does that matter?"

"Well," said the Hon. Freddy, "I mean to say, these bounders about here are all Socialists and Methodists. . . ."

"If they are Methodists," said Mrs. Pettigrew-Robinson, "they will not he at church."

"Won't they?" retorted the Hon. Freddy. "You bet they will if there's anything to see. Why, it'll be better'n a funeral to 'em."

"Surely," said Mrs. Pettigrew-Robinson, "one has a *duty* in the matter, whatever our private feelings may be—especially at the present day, when people are so terribly *slack*."

She glanced at the Hon. Freddy.

"Oh, don't you mind me, Mrs. P.," said that youth amiably. "All *I* say is, if these blighters make things unpleasant, don't blame me."

"Whoever thought of blaming you, Freddy?" said the Duchess.

"Manner of speaking," said the Hon. Freddy.

"What do you think, Mr. Murbles?" inquired her ladyship.

"I feel," said the lawyer, carefully stirring his coffee, "that, while your intention is a very admirable one, and does you very great credit, my dear lady, yet Mr. Arbuthnot is right in saying it may involve you in some—er—unpleasant publicity. Er—I have always been a sincere Christian myself, but I cannot feel that our religion demands that we should make ourselves conspicuous—er—in such very painful circumstances."

Mr. Parker reminded himself of a dictum of Lord Melbourne.

"Well, after all," said Mrs. Marchbanks, "as Helen so rightly says, does it matter? Nobody's really got anything to be ashamed of. There has been a stupid mistake, of course, but I don't see why anybody who wants to shouldn't go to church."

"Certainly not, certainly not, my dear," said the Colonel heartily. "We might look in ourselves, eh, dear? Take a walk that way I mean, and come out before the sermon. I think it's a good thing. Shows *we* don't believe old Denver's done anything wrong, anyhow."

"You forget, dear," said his wife, "I've promised to stay at home with Mary, poor girl."

"Of course, of course—stupid of me," said the Colonel. "How is she?"

"She was very restless last night, poor child," said the Duchess. "Perhaps she will get a little sleep this morning. It has been a shock to her."

"One which may prove a blessing in disguise," said Mrs. Pettigrew-Robinson.

"My dear!" said her husband.

"Wonder when we shall hear from Sir Impey," said Colonel Marchbanks hurriedly.

"Yes, indeed," moaned Mr. Murbles. "I am counting on his influence with the Duke."

"Of course," said Mrs. Pettigrew-Robinson, "he must speak out—for everybody's sake. He must say what he was doing out of doors at that time.

Or, if he does not, it must be discovered. Dear me! That's what these detectives are for, aren't they?"

"That is their ungrateful task" said Mr. Parker suddenly. He had said nothing for a long time, and everybody jumped.

"There," said Mrs. Marchbanks, "I expect you'll clear it all up in no time, Mr. Parker. Perhaps you've got the real mur—the culprit up your sleeve all the time."

"Not quite," said Mr. Parker, "but I'll do my best to get him. Besides," he added, with a grin, "I'll probably have some help on the job."

"From whom?" inquired Mr. Pettigrew-Robinson,

"Her grace's brother-in-law."

"Peter?" said the Duchess. "Mr. Parker must be amused at the family amateur," she added.

"Not at all," said Parker. "Wimsey would be one of the finest detectives in England if he wasn't lazy. Only we can't get hold of him."

"I've wired to Ajaccio—poste restante," said Mr. Murbles, "but I don't know when he's likely to call there. He said nothing about when he was coming back to England."

"He's a rummy old bird," said the Hon. Freddy tactlessly, "but he oughter be here, what? What I mean to say is, if anything happens to old Denver, don't you see, he's the head of the family, ain't he—till little Pickled Gherkins comes of age."

In the frightful silence which followed this remark, the sound of a walking-stick being clattered into an umbrella-stand was distinctly audible.

"Who's that, I wonder," said the Duchess.

The door waltzed open.

"Mornin', dear old things," said the newcomer cheerfully. "How are you all? Hullo, Helen! Colonel, you owe me half a crown since last September year. Mornin', Mrs. Marchbanks. Mornin', Mrs. P. Well, Mr. Murbles, how d'you like this bili-beastly weather? Don't trouble to get up, Freddy; I'd simply hate to inconvenience you. Parker, old man, what a damned reliable old bird you are! Always on the spot, like that patent ointment thing. I say, have you all finished? I meant to get up earlier, but I was snorin' so Bunter hadn't the heart to wake me. I nearly blew in last night, only we didn't arrive till 2 a.m. and I thought you wouldn't half bless me if I did. Eh, what, Colonel? Aeroplane *Victoria* from Paris to London—North-Eastern to Northallerton—damn bad roads the rest of the way, and a puncture just below Riddlesdale. Damn bad bed at the 'Lord in Glory'; thought I'd blow in for the last sausage here, if I was lucky. What? Sunday morning in an English family and no sausages? God bless my soul, what's the world coming to, eh, Colonel? I say, Helen, old Gerald's been an' gone an' done it this time, what? You've no business to leave him on his own, you know; he always gets into mischief. What's that? Curry? Thanks, old man. Here, I say, you needn't be so stingy about it; I've been travelling for three days on end. Freddy, pass the toast. Beg pardon, Mrs. Marchbanks? Oh, rather, yes; Corsica was perfectly amazin'—all black-eyed fellows with knives in their belts and jolly fine-looking girls. Old Bunter had a regular affair with the inn-keeper's daughter in one place. D'you know, he's an awfully susceptible old beggar. You'd never think it, would you? Jove! I am hungry. I say, Helen, I meant to get you some fetchin' crêpe-de-Chine undies from Paris, but I saw that old Parker was gettin' ahead of me over the bloodstains, so we packed up our things and buzzed off."

Mrs. Pettigrew-Robinson rose.

"Theodore," she said, "I think we ought to be getting ready for church."

"I will order the car," said the Duchess. "Peter, of course I'm exceedingly glad to see you. Your leaving no address was most inconvenient. Ring for anything you want. It is a pity you didn't arrive in time to see Gerald."

"Oh, that's all right," said Lord Peter cheerfully; "I'll look him up in quod. Y'know, it's rather a good idea to keep one's crimes in the family; one has so many more facilities. I'm sorry for poor old Polly, though. How is she?"

"She must not be disturbed today," said the Duchess with decision.

"Not a bit of it," said Lord Peter; "she'll keep. To-day Parker and I hold high revel. To-day he shows me all the bloody footprints–it's all right, Helen, that's not swearin', that's an adjective of quality. I hope they aren't all washed away, are they, old thing?"

"No," said Parker, "I've got most of them under flowerpots."

"Then pass the bread and squish," said Lord Peter, "and tell me all about it."

The departure of the church-going element had induced a more humanitarian atmosphere. Mrs. Marchbanks stumped off upstairs to tell Mary that Peter had come, and the Colonel lit a large cigar. The Hon. Freddy rose, stretched himself, pulled a leather armchair to the fireside, and sat down with his feet on the brass fender, while Parker marched round and poured himself out another cup of coffee.

"I suppose you've seen the papers," he said.

"Oh, yes, I read up the inquest," said Lord Peter. "Y'know, if you'll excuse my saying so, I think you rather mucked it between you."

"It was disgraceful," said Mr. Murbles, "disgraceful. The Coroner behaved most improperly. He had no business to give such a summing-up. With a jury of ignorant country fellows, what could one expect? And the details that were allowed to come out! If I could have got here earlier——"

"I'm afraid that was partly my fault, Wimsey," said Parker penitently. "Craikes rather resents me. The Superintendent at Stapley sent to us over his head, and when the message came through I ran along to the Chief and asked for the job, because I thought if there should be any misconception or difficulty, you see, you'd just as soon I tackled it as anybody else. I had a few little arrangements to make about a forgery I've been looking into, and, what with one thing and another, I didn't get off till the night express. By the time I turned up on Friday, Craikes and the Coroner were already as thick as thieves, had fixed the inquest for that morning–which was ridiculous–and arranged to produce their blessed evidence as dramatically as possible. I only had time to skim over the ground (disfigured, I'm sorry to say, by the prints of Craikes and his local ruffians), and really had nothing for the jury."

"Cheer up," said Wimsey. "I'm not blaming you. Besides, it all lends excitement to the chase."

"Fact is," said the Hon. Freddy, "that we ain't popular with respectable Coroners. Giddy aristocrats and immoral Frenchmen. I say, Peter, sorry you've missed Miss Lydia Cathcart. You'd have loved her. She's gone back to Golders Green and taken the body with her."

"Oh, well," said Wimsey. "I don't suppose there was anything abstruse about the body."

"No," said Parker, "the medical evidence was all right as far as it went. He was shot through the lungs, and that's all."

"Though, mind you," said the Hon. Freddy, "he didn't shoot himself. I didn't say anything, not wishin' to upset old Denver's story, but, you know, all that stuff about his bein' so upset and go-to-blazes in his manner was all my whiskers."

"How do you know?" said Peter.

"Why, my dear man, Cathcart'n I toddled up to bed together. I was rather fed up, havin' dropped a lot on some shares, besides missin' everything I shot at in the mornin', an' lost a bet I made with the Colonel about the number of toes on the kitchen cat, an' I said to Cathcart it was a hell of a damn-fool world, or words to that effect. 'Not a bit of it,' he said; 'it's a damn good world. I'm goin' to ask Mary for a date to-morrow, an' then we'll go and live in Paris, where they understand sex.' I said somethin' or other vague, and he went off whistlin'."

Parker looked grave. Colonel Marchbanks cleared his throat.

"Well, well," he said, "there's no accounting for a man like Cathcart, no accounting at all. Brought up in France, you know. Not at all like a straightforward Englishman. Always up and down, up and down! Very sad, poor fellow. Well, well, Peter, hope you and Mr. Parker will find out something about it. We mustn't have poor old Denver cooped up in gaol like this, you know. Awfully unpleasant for him, poor chap, and with the birds so good this year. Well, I expect you'll be making a tour of inspection, eh, Mr. Parker? What do you say to shoving the balls about a bit, Freddy?"

"Right you are," said the Hon. Freddy; "you'll have to give me a hundred, though, Colonel."

"Nonsense, nonsense," said that veteran, in high good humour; "you play an excellent game."

Mr. Murbles having withdrawn, Wimsey and Parker faced each other over the remains of the breakfast.

"Peter," said the detective, "I don't know if I've done the right thing by coming. If you feel——"

"Look here, old man," said his friend earnestly, "let's cut out the considerations of delicacy. We're goin' to work this case like any other. If anything unpleasant turns up, I'd rather you saw it than anybody else. It's an uncommonly pretty little case, on its merits, and I'm goin' to put some damn good work into it."

"If you're sure it's all right——"

"My dear man, if you hadn't been here I'd have sent for you. Now let's get to business. Of course, *I'm* settin' off with the assumption that old Gerald didn't do it."

"I'm sure he didn't," agreed Parker.

"No, no," said Wimsey, "that isn't your line. Nothing rash about you—nothing trustful. You are expected to throw cold water on my hopes and doubt all my conclusions."

"Right ho!" said Parker. "Where would you like to begin?"

Peter considered. "I think we'll start from Cathcart's bedroom," he said.

The bedroom was of moderate size, with a single window overlooking the front door. The bed was on the right-hand side, the dressing-table before the window. On the left was the fireplace, with an armchair before it, and a small writing-table.

"Everything's as it was," said Parker. "Craikes had that much sense."

"Yes," said Lord Peter. "Very well. Gerald says that when he charged Cathcart with bein' a scamp, Cathcart jumped up, nearly knockin' the table over. That's the writin'-table, then, so Cathcart was sittin' in the armchair.

Yes, he was–and he pushed it back violently and rumpled up the carpet. See! So far, so good. Now what was he doin' there? He wasn't readin', because there's no book about, and we know that he rushed straight out of the room and never came back. Very good. Was he writin'? No; virgin sheet of blottin'-paper——"

"He might have been writing in pencil," suggested Parker.

"That's true, old Kill-Joy, so he might. Well, if he was he shoved the paper into his pocket when Gerald came in, because it isn't here; but he didn't, because it wasn't found on his body; so he wasn't writing."

"Unless he threw the paper away somewhere else," said Parker. "I haven't been all over the grounds, you know, and at the smallest computation–if we accept the shot heard by Hardraw at 11:50 as *the* shot–there's an hour and a half unaccounted for."

"Very well. Let's say there is nothing to show he was writing. Will that do? Well, then——"

Lord Peter drew out a lens and scrutinised the surface of the armchair carefully before sitting down in it.

"Nothing helpful there," he said. "To proceed, Cathcart sat where I am sitting. He wasn't writing; he–you're sure this room hasn't been touched?"

"Certain."

"Then he wasn't smoking."

"Why not? He might have chucked the stub of a cigar or cigarette into the fire when Denver came in."

"Not a cigarette," said Parker, "or we should find traces somewhere–on the floor or in the grate. That light ash blows about so. But a cigar–well, he might have smoked a cigar without leaving a sign I suppose. But I hope he didn't."

"Why?"

"Because, old son, I'd rather Gerald's account had some element of truth in it. A nervy man doesn't sit down to the delicate enjoyment of a cigar before bed, and cherish the ash with such scrupulous care. On the other hand, if Freddy's right, and Cathcart was feelin' unusually sleek and pleased with life, that's just the sort of thing he would do."

"Do you think Mr. Arbuthnot would have invented all that, as a matter of fact?" said Parker thoughtfully. "He doesn't strike me that way. He'd have to be imaginative and spiteful to make it up, and I really don't think he's either."

"I know," said Lord Peter. "I've known old Freddy all my life, and he wouldn't hurt a fly. Besides, he simply hasn't the wits to make up any sort of a story. But what bothers me is that Gerald most certainly hasn't the wits either to invent that Adelphi drama between him and Cathcart."

"On the other hand," said Parker, "if we allow for a moment that he shot Cathcart, he had an incentive to invent it. He would be trying to get his head out of the–I mean, when anything important is at stake it's wonderful how it sharpens one's wits. And the story being so far-fetched does rather suggest an unpractised story-teller."

"True, O King. Well, you've sat on all my discoveries so far. Never mind. My head is bloody but unbowed. Cathcart was sitting here——"

"So your brother said."

"Curse you, *I* say he was; at least, somebody was; he's left the impression of his sit-me-down-upon on the cushion."

"That might have been earlier in the day."

"Rot. They were out all day. You needn't overdo this Sadducee attitude, Charles. I say Cathcart was sitting here, and–hullo ! hullo !"

He leaned forward and stared into the grate.

"There's some burnt paper here, Charles."

"I know. I was frightfully excited about that yesterday, but I found it was just the same in several of the rooms. They often let the bedroom fires go out when everybody's out during the day, and relight them about an hour before dinner. There's only the cook, housemaid, and Fleming here, you see, and they've got a lot to do with such a large party."

Lord Peter was picking the charred fragments over.

"I can find nothing to contradict your suggestion," he sadly said, "and this fragment of the *Morning Post* rather confirms it. Then we can only suppose that Cathcart sat here in a brown study, doing nothing at all. That doesn't get us much further, I'm afraid." He got up and went to the dressing-table.

"I like these tortoiseshell sets," he said, "and the perfume is '*Baiser du Soir*'–very nice too. New to me. I must draw Bunter's attention to it. A charming manicure set, isn't it? You know, I like being clean and neat and all that, but Cathcart was the kind of man who always impressed you as bein' just a little *too* well turned out. Poor devil! And he'll be buried at Golders Green after all. I only saw him once or twice, you know. He impressed me as knowin' about everything there was to know. I was rather surprised at Mary takin' to him, but, then, I know really awfully little about Mary. You see, she's five years younger than me. When the war broke out she'd just left school and gone to a place in Paris, and I joined up, and she came back and did nursing and social work, so I only saw her occasionally. At that time she was rather taken up with new schemes for puttin' the world to rights and hadn't a lot to say to me. And she got hold of some pacifist fellow who was a bit of a stumer, I fancy. Then I was ill, you know, and then I got the chuck from Barbara and didn't feel much like botherin' about other people's heart-to-hearts, and then I got mixed up in the Attenbury diamond case–and the result is I know uncommonly little about my own sister. But it looks as though her taste in men had altered. I know my mother said Cathcart had charm; that means he was attractive to women, I suppose. No man can see what makes that in another man, but mother is usually right. What's become of this fellow's papers?"

"He left very little here," replied Parker. "There's a cheque-book on Cox's Charing Cross branch, but it's a new one and not very helpful. Apparently he only kept a small current account with them for convenience when he was in England. The cheques are mostly to self, with an occasional hotel or tailor."

"Any pass-book?"

"I think all his important papers are in Paris. He has a flat there, near the river somewhere. We're in communication with the Paris police. He had a room at the Albany. I've told them to lock it up till I get there. I thought of running up to town to-morrow."

"Yes, you'd better. Any pocket-book?"

"Yes; here you are. About £30 in various notes, a wine-merchant's card, and a bill for a pair of riding-breeches."

"No correspondence?"

"Not a line."

"No," said Wimsey, "he was the kind, I imagine, that didn't keep letters. Much too good an instinct of self-preservation."

"Yes. I asked the servants about his letters, as a matter of fact. They said he got a good number, but never left them about. They couldn't tell me much about the ones he wrote, because all the outgoing letters are dropped into the post-bag, which is carried down to the post-office as it is and opened there, or handed over to the postman when—or if—he calls. The general impression was that he didn't write much. The housemaid said she never found anything to speak of in the waste-paper basket."

"Well, that's uncommonly helpful. Wait a moment. Here's his fountain-pen. Very handsome—Onoto with complete gold casing. Dear me! entirely empty. Well, I don't know that one can deduce anything from that, exactly. I don't see any pencil about, by the way. I'm inclined to think you're wrong in supposing that he was writing letters."

"I didn't suppose anything," said Parker mildly. "I daresay you're right."

Lord Peter left the dressing-table, looked through the contents of the wardrobe, and turned over the two or three books on the pedestal beside the bed.

"*La Rôtisserie de la Reine Pédaque, L'Anneau d'Améthyste, South Wind* (our young friend works out very true to type), *Chronique d'un Cadet de Coutras* (tut-tut, Charles!), *Manon Lescaut.* H'm! Is there anything else in this room I ought to look at?"

"I don't think so. Where'd you like to go now?"

"We'll follow 'em down. Wait a jiff. Who are in the other rooms? Oh, yes. Here's Gerald's room. Helen's at church. In we go. Of course, this has been dusted and cleaned up, and generally ruined for purposes of observation?"

"I'm afraid so. I could hardly keep the Duchess out of her bedroom."

"No. Here's the window Gerald shouted out of. H'm! Nothing in the grate here, naturally—the fire's been lit since. I say, I wonder where Gerald did put that letter to—Freeborn's, I mean."

"Nobody's been able to get a word out of him about it," said Parker. "Old Mr. Murbles had a fearful time with him. The Duke insists simply that he destroyed it. Mr. Murbles says that's absurd. So it is. If he was going to bring that sort of accusation against his sister's fiancé he'd want *some* evidence of a method in his madness, wouldn't he? Or was he one of those Roman brothers who say simply: 'As the head of the family I forbid the banns and that's enough'?"

"Gerald," said Wimsey, "is a good, clean, decent, thoroughbred public schoolboy, and a shocking ass. But I don't think he's so mediaeval as that."

"But if he has the letter, why not produce it?"

"Why, indeed? Letters from old college friends in Egypt aren't, as a rule, compromising."

"You don't suppose," suggested Parker tentatively, "that this Mr. Freeborn referred in his letter to any old—er—entanglement which your brother wouldn't wish the Duchess to know about?"

Lord Peter paused, while absently examining a row of boots.

"That's an idea," he said. "There were occasions—mild ones, but Helen would make the most of them." He whistled thoughtfully. "Still, when it come to the gallows——"

"Do you suppose, Wimsey, that your brother really contemplates the gallows?" asked Parker.

"I think Murbles put it to him pretty straight," said Lord Peter.

"Quite so. But does he actually realise—imaginatively—that it is possible to hang an English peer for murder on circumstantial evidence?"

Lord Peter considered this.

"Imagination isn't Gerald's strong point," he admitted. "I suppose they *do* hang peers? They can't be beheaded on Tower Hill or anything?"

"I'll look it up," said Parker; "but they certainly hanged Earl Ferrers in 1760."

"Did they, though?" said Lord Peter. "Ah, well, as the old pagan said of the Gospels, after all, it was a long time ago, and we'll hope it wasn't true."

"It's true enough," said Parker; "and he was dissected and anatomised afterwards. But that part of the treatment is obsolete."

"We'll tell Gerald about it," said Lord Peter, "and persuade him to take the matter seriously. Which are the boots he wore Wednesday night?"

"These," said Parker, "but the fool's cleaned them."

"Yes,' said Lord Peter bitterly. "M'm! a good heavy lace-up boat–the sort that sends the blood to the head."

"He wore leggings, too," said Parker; "these."

"Rather elaborate preparations for a stroll in the garden. But, as you were just going to say, the night was wet. I must ask Helen if Gerald ever suffered from insomnia."

"I did. She said she thought not as a rule, but that he occasionally had toothache, which made him restless."

"It wouldn't send one out of doors on a cold night, though. Well, let's get downstairs."

They passed through the billiard-room, where the Colonel was making a sensational break, and into the small conservatory which led from it.

Lord Peter looked gloomily round at the chrysanthemums and boxes of bulbs.

"These damned flowers look jolly healthy," he said. "Do you mean you've been letting the gardener swarm in here every day to water 'em?"

"Yes," said Parker apologetically, "I did. But he's had strict orders only to walk on these mats."

"Good," said Lord Peter. "Take 'em up, then, and let's get to work."

With his lens to his eye he crawled cautiously over the floor.

"They all came through this way, I suppose," he said.

"Yes," said Parker. "I've identified most of the marks. People went in and out. Here's the Duke. He comes in from outside. He trips over the body." (Parker had opened the outer door and lifted some matting, to show a trampled patch of gravel, discoloured with blood.) "He kneels by the body. Here are his knees and toes. Afterwards he goes into the house, through the conservatory, leaving a good impression in black mud and gravel just inside the door."

Lord Peter squatted carefully over the marks.

"It's lucky the gravel's so soft here," he said.

"Yes. It's just a patch. The gardener tells me it gets very trampled and messy just here owing to his coming to fill cans from the water-trough. They fill the trough up from the well every so often, and then carry the water away in cans. It got extra bad this year, and they put down fresh gravel a few weeks ago."

"Pity they didn't extend their labours all down the path while they were about it," grunted Lord Peter, who was balancing himself precariously on a small piece of sacking. "Well, that bears out old Gerald so far. Here's an elephant been over this bit of box border. Who's that?"

"Oh, that's a constable. I put him at eighteen stone. He's nothing. And this rubber sole with a patch on it is Craikes. He's all over the place. This squelchy-looking thing is Mr. Arbuthnot in bedroom slippers, and the goloshes are Mr. Pettigrew-Robinson. We can dismiss all those. But now here, just coming over the threshold, is a woman's foot in a strong shoe. I make that out to be Lady Mary's. Here it is again, just at the edge of the well. She came out to examine the body."

"Quite so," said Peter; "and then she came in again, with a few grains of red gravel on her shoes. Well, that's all right. Hullo!"

On the outer side of the conservatory were some shelves for small plants, and, beneath these, a damp and dismal bed of earth, occupied, in a sprawling and lackadaisical fashion, by stringy cactus plants and a sporadic growth of maidenhair fern, and masked by a row of large chrysanthemums in pots.

"What've you got?" inquired Parker, seeing his friend peering into this green retreat.

Lord Peter withdrew his long nose from between two pots and said: "Who put what down here?"

Parker hastened to the place. There, among the cacti, was certainly the clear mark of some oblong object, with corners, that had been stood out of sight on the earth behind the pots.

"It's a good thing Gerald's gardener ain't one of those conscientious blighters that can't even let a cactus alone for the winter," said Lord Peter, "or he'd've tenderly lifted these little drooping heads–oh! damn and blast the beastly plant for a crimson porcupine! *You* measure it."

Parker measured it.

"Two and a half feet by six inches," he said. "And fairly heavy, for it's sunk in and broken the plants about. Was it a bar of anything?"

"I fancy not," said Lord Peter. "The impression is deeper on the farther side. I think it was something bulky set up on edge, and leaned against the glass. If you asked for my private opinion I should guess that it was a suit-case."

"A suit-case!" exclaimed Parker. "Why a suit-case?"

"Why indeed? I think we may assume that it didn't stay here very long. It would have been exceedingly visible in the daytime. But somebody might very well have shoved it in here if they were caught with it–say at three o'clock in the morning–and didn't want it to be seen."

"Then when did they take it away?"

"Almost immediately, I should say. Before daylight, anyhow, or even Inspector Craikes could hardly have failed to see it."

"It's not the doctor's bag, I suppose?"

"No–unless the doctor's a fool. Why put a bag inconveniently in a damp and a dirty place out of the way when every law of sense and convenience would urge him to pop it down handy by the body? No. Unless Craikes or the gardener has been leaving things about, it was thrust away there on Wednesday night by Gerald, by Cathcart–or, I suppose, by Mary. Nobody else could be supposed to have anything to hide."

"Yes," said Parker, "one person."

"Who's that?"

"The Person Unknown."

"Who's he?"

For answer Mr. Parker proudly stepped to a row of wooden frames, carefully covered with matting. Stripping this away, with the air of a bishop unveiling a memorial, he disclosed a V-shaped line of footprints.

"These," said Parker, "belong to nobody–to nobody I've ever seen or heard of, I mean."

"Hurray!" said Peter.

> "Then downwards from the steep hill's edge
> They tracked the footmarks small

(only they're largish)."

"No such luck," said Parker. "It's more a case of:

> They followed from the earthy bank
> Those footsteps one by one,
> Into the middle of the plank;
> And farther there were none!"

"Great poet, Wordsworth," said Lord Peter; "how often I've had that feeling. Now let's see. These footmarks–a man's No. 10 with worn-down heels and a patch on the left inner side–advance from the hard bit of the path which shows no footmarks; they come to the body–here, where that pool of blood is. I say, that's rather odd, don't you think? No? Perhaps not. There are no footmarks under the body? Can't say, it's such a mess. Well, the Unknown gets so far–here's a footmark deeply pressed in. Was he just going to throw Cathcart into the well? He hears a sound; he starts; he turns; he runs on tiptoe–into the shrubbery, by Jove!"

"Yes," said Parker, "and the tracks come out on one of the grass paths in the wood, and there's an end of them."

"H'm! Well, we'll follow them later. Now where did they come from?"

Together the two friends followed the path away from the house. The gravel, except for the little patch before the conservatory, was old and hard, and afforded but little trace, particularly as the last few days had been rainy. Parker, however, was able to assure Wimsey that there had been definite traces of dragging and bloodstains.

"What sort of bloodstains? Smears?"

"Yes, smears mostly. There were pebbles displaced, too, all the way–and now here is something odd."

It was the clear impression of the palm of a man's hand heavily pressed into the earth of a herbaceous border, the fingers pointing towards the house. On the path the gravel had been scraped up in two long furrows. There was blood on the grass border between the path and the bed, and the edge of the grass was broken and trampled.

"I don't like that," said Lord Peter.

"Ugly, isn't it?" agreed Parker.

"Poor devil!" said Peter. "He made a determined effort to hang on here. That explains the blood by the conservatory door. But what kind of a devil drags a corpse that isn't quite dead?"

A few yards farther the path ran into the main drive. This was bordered with trees, widening into a thicket. At the point of intersection of the two paths were some further indistinct marks, and in another twenty yards or so they turned aside into the thicket. A large tree had fallen at some time and made a little clearing, in the midst of which a tarpaulin had been carefully spread out and pegged down. The air was heavy with the smell of fungus and fallen leaves.

"Scene of the tragedy," said Parker briefly, rolling back the tarpaulin.

Lord Peter gazed down sadly. Muffled in an overcoat and a thick grey scarf, he looked, with his long, narrow face, like a melancholy adjutant stork. The writhing body of the fallen man had scraped up the dead leaves and left a depression in the sodden ground. At one place the darker earth showed where a great pool of blood had soaked into it, and the yellow leaves of a Spanish poplar were rusted with no autumnal stain.

"That's where they found the handkerchief and revolver," said Parker. "I looked for finger-marks, but the rain and mud had messed everything up."

Wimsey took out his lens, lay down, and conducted personal tour of the whole space slowly on his stomach, Parker moving mutely after him.

"He paced up and down for some time," said Lord Peter.

"He wasn't smoking. He was turning something over in his mind, or waiting for somebody. What's this? Aha! Here's our No. 10 foot again, coming in through the trees on the farther side. No signs of a struggle. That's odd! Cathcart was shot close up, wasn't he?"

"Yes; it singed his shirt-front."

"Quite so. Why did he stand still to be shot at?"

"I imagine," said Parker, "that if he had an appointment with No. 10 Boots it was somebody he knew, who could get close to him without arousing suspicion."

"Then the interview was a friendly one——on Cathcart's side, anyhow. But the revolver's a difficulty. How did No. 10 get hold of Gerald's revolver?"

"The conservatory door was open," said Parker dubiously.

"Nobody knew about that except Gerald and Fleming," retorted Lord Peter. "Besides, do you mean to tell me that No. 10 walked in here, went to the study, fetched the revolver, walked back here, and shot Cathcart? It seems a clumsy method. If he wanted to do any shooting, why didn't he come armed in the first place?"

"It seems more probable that Cathcart brought the revolver," said Parker.

"Then why no signs of a struggle?"

"Perhaps Cathcart shot himself," said Parker.

"Then why should No. 10 drag him into a conspicuous position and then run away?"

"Wait a minute," said Parker. "How's this? No. 10 has an appointment with Cathcart–to blackmail him, let's say. He somehow gets word of his intention to him between 9:45 and 10:15. That would account for the alteration in Cathcart's manner, and allow both Mr. Arbuthnot and the Duke to be telling the truth. Cathcart rushes violently out after his row with your brother. He comes down here to keep his appointment. He paces up and down waiting for No. 10. No. 10 arrives and parleys with Cathcart. Cathcart offers him money. No. 10 stands out for more. Cathcart says he really hasn't got it. No. 10 says in that case he blows the gaff. Cathcart retorts, 'In that case you can go to the devil. I'm going there myself.' Cathcart, who has previously got hold of the revolver, shoots himself. No. 10 is seized with remorse. He sees that Cathcart isn't quite dead. He picks him up and part drags, part carries him to the house. He is smaller than Cathcart and not very strong, and finds it a hard job. They have just got to the conservatory door when Cathcart has a final hœmorrhage and gives up the ghost. No. 10 suddenly becomes aware that his position in somebody else's grounds, alone with a corpse at 3 a.m., wants some explaining. He drops Cathcart–and bolts. Enter the Duke of Denver and falls over the body. Tableau."

"That's good," said Lord Peter; "that's very good. But when do you suppose it happened? Gerald found the body at 3 a.m.; the doctor was here at 4:30, and said Cathcart had been dead several hours. Very well. Now, how about that shot my sister heard at three o'clock?"

"Look here, old man," said Parker, "I don't want to appear rude to your sister. May I put it like this? I suggest that that shot at 3 a.m. was poachers."

"Poachers by all means," said Lord Peter. "Well, really, Parker, I think that hangs together. Let's adopt that explanation provisionally. The first thing to do is now to find No. 10, since he can bear witness that Cathcart committed suicide; and that, as far as my brother is concerned, is the only thing that matters a rap. But for the satisfaction of my own curiosity I'd like to know: What was No. 10 blackmailing Cathcart about? Who hid a suit-case in the conservatory? And what was Gerald doing in the garden at 3 a.m.?"

"Well," said Parker, "suppose we begin by tracing where No. 10 came from."

"Hi, hi!" cried Wimsey, as they returned to the trail. "Here's something–here's real treasure-trove, Parker!"

From amid the mud and the fallen leaves he retrieved a tiny, glittering object–a flash of white and green between his finger-tips.

It was a little charm such as women hang upon a bracelet –a diminutive diamond cat with eyes of bright emerald.

# 3

# MUDSTAINS AND BLOODSTAINS

*Other things are all very well in their way, but give me Blood . . . We say, "There it is! that's Blood!" It is an actual matter of fact. We point it out. It admits of no doubt. . . . We must have Blood, you know.*

David Copperfield

"HITHERTO," SAID Lord Peter, as they picked their painful way through the little wood on the trail of Gent's No. 10's, "I have always maintained that those obliging criminals who strew their tracks with little articles of personal adornment–here he is, on a squashed fungus–were an invention of detective fiction for the benefit of the author. I see that I have still something to learn about my job."

"Well, you haven't been at it very long, have you?" said Parker. "Besides, we don't know that the diamond cat is the criminal's. It may belong to a member of your own family, and have been lying here for days. It may belong to Mr. What's-his-name in the States, or to the last tenant but one, and have been lying here for years. This broken branch may be our friend–I think it is."

"I'll ask the family," said Lord Peter, "and we could find out in the village if anyone's ever inquired for a lost cat. They're pukka stones. It ain't the sort of thing one would drop without making a fuss about—I've lost him altogether."

"It's all right—I've got him. He's tripped over a root."

"Serve him glad," said Lord Peter viciously, straightening his back. "I say, I don't think the human frame is very thoughtfully constructed for this sleuth-hound business. If one could go on all-fours, or had eyes in one's knees, it would be a lot more practical."

"There are many difficulties inherent in a teleological view of creation," said Parker placidly. "And here we are at the park palings."

"And here's where he got over," said Lord Peter, pointing to a place where the *chevaux de frise* on the top was broken away. "Here's the dent where his heels came down, and here's where he fell forward on hands and knees. Hum! Give us a back, old man, would you? Thanks. An old break, I see. Mr. Montague-now-in-the-States should keep his palings in better order. No. 10 tore his coat on the spikes all the same; he left a fragment of Burberry behind him. What luck! Here's a deep, damp ditch on the other side, which I shall now proceed to fall into."

A slithering crash proclaimed that he had carried out his intention. Parker, thus callously abandoned, looked round, and, seeing that they were only a hundred yards or so from the gate, ran along and was let out, decorously, by Hardraw, the gamekeeper, who happened to be coming out of the lodge.

"By the way," said Parker to him, "did you ever find any signs of any poachers on Wednesday night after all?"

"Nay," said the man, "not so much as a dead rabbit. I reckon t'lady wor mistaken, an 'twore the shot I heard as killed t'Captain."

"Possibly," said Parker. "Do you know how long the spikes have been broken off the palings over there?"

"A moonth or two, happen. They should 'a' bin put right, but the man's sick."

"The gate's locked at night, I suppose?"

"Aye."

"Anybody wishing to get in would have to waken you?"

"Aye, that he would."

"You didn't see any suspicious character loitering about outside these palings last Wednesday, I suppose?"

"Nay, sir, but my wife may ha' done. Hey, lass!"

Mrs. Hardraw, thus summoned, appeared at the door with a small boy clinging to her skirts.

"Wednesday?" said she. "Nay, I saw no loiterin' folks. I keep a look-out for tramps and such, as it be such a lonely place. Wednesday. Eh, now, John, that wad be t'day t'young mon caled wi' t'motor-bike."

"Young man with a motor-bike?"

"I reckon 'twas. He said he'd had a puncture and asked for a bucket o' watter."

"Was that all the asking he did?"

"He asked what were t'name o' t'place and whose house it were."

"Did you tell him the Duke of Denver was living here?"

"Aye, sir, and he said he supposed a many gentlemen came up for t'shooting."

"Did he say where he was going?"

"He said he'd coom oop fra' Weirdale an' were makin' a trip into Coomberland."

"How long was he here?"

"Happen half an hour. An' then he tried to get his machine started, an' I see him hop-hoppitin' away towards King's Fenton."

She pointed away to the right, where Lord Peter might be seen gesticulating in the middle of the road.

"What sort of a man was he?"

Like most people, Mrs. Hardraw was poor at definition. She thought he was youngish and tallish, neither dark nor fair, in such a long coat as motor-bicyclists use, with a belt round it.

"Was he a gentleman?"

Mrs. Hardraw hesitated, and Mr. Parker mentally classed the stranger as "Not quite quite."

"You didn't happen to notice the number of the bicycle"

Mrs. Hardraw had not. "But it had a side-car," she added.

Lord Peter's gesticulations were becoming quite violent, and Mr. Parker hastened to rejoin him.

"Come on, gossiping old thing," said Lord Peter unreasonably. "This is a beautiful ditch.

> From such a ditch as this,
> When the soft wind did gently kiss the trees
> And they did make no noise, from such a ditch
> Our friend, methinks, mounted the Troyan walls,
> And wiped his soles upon the greasy mud.

Look at my trousers!"

"It's a bit of a climb from this side," said Parker.

"It is. He stood here in the ditch, and put one foot into this place where the paling's broken away and one hand on the top, and hauled himself up. No. 10 must have been a man of exceptional height, strength, and agility. I couldn't get my foot up, let alone reaching the top with my hand. I'm five foot nine. Could you?"

Parker was six foot, and could just touch the top of the wall with his hand.

"I *might* do it–on one of my best days," he said, "for an adequate object, or after adequate stimulant."

"Just so," said Lord Peter. "Hence we deduce No. 10's exceptional height and strength."

"Yes," said Parker. "It's a bit unfortunate that we had to deduce his exceptional shortness and weakness just now, isn't it?"

"Oh!" said Peter. "Well–well, as you so rightly say, that is a bit unfortunate."

"Well, it may clear up presently. He didn't have a confederate to give him a back or a leg, I suppose?"

"Not unless the confederate was a being without feet or any visible means of support," said Lord Peter, indicating the solitary print of a pair of patched 10's. "By the way, how did he make straight in the dark for the place where the spikes were missing? Looks as though he belonged to the neighbourhood, or had reconnoitred previously."

"Arising out of that reply," said Parker, "I will now relate to you the entertaining 'gossip' I have had with Mrs. Hardraw."

"Humph!" said Wimsey at the end of it. "That's interesting. We'd better make inquiries at Riddlesdale and King's Fenton. Meanwhile we know where No. 10 came from; now where did he go after leaving Cathcart's body by the well?"

"The footsteps went into the preserve," said Parker. "I lost them there. There is a regular carpet of dead leaves and bracken."

"Well, but we needn't go through all that sleuth grind again," objected his friend. "The fellow went in, and, as he presumably is not there still, he came out again. He didn't come out through the gate or Hardraw would have seen him; he didn't come out the same way he went in or he would have left some traces. Therefore he came out elsewhere. Let's walk round the wall."

"Then we'll turn to the left," said Parker, "since that's the side of the preserve, and he apparently went through there."

"True, O King; and as this isn't a church, there's no harm in going round it widdershins. Talking of church, there's Helen coming back. Get a move on, old thing."

They crossed the drive, passed the cottage, and then, leaving the road, followed the paling across some open grass fields. It was not long before they found what they sought. From one of the iron spikes above them dangled forlornly a strip of material. With Parker's assistance Wimsey scrambled up in a state of almost lyric excitement.

"Here we are," he cried. "The belt of a Burberry! No sort of precaution here. Here are the toe-prints of a fellow sprinting for his life. He tore off his Burberry; he made desperate leaps–one, two, three–at the palings. At the third leap he hooked it on to the spikes. He scrambled up, scoring long, scrabbling marks on the paling. He reached the top. Oh, here's a bloodstain run into this crack. He tore his hands. He dropped off. He wrenched the coat away, leaving the belt dangling——"

"I wish you'd drop off," grumbled Parker. "You're breaking my collar-bone."

Lord Peter dropped off obediently, and stood there holding the belt between his fingers. His narrow grey eyes wandered restlessly over the field. Suddenly he seized Parker's arm and marched briskly in the direction of the wall on the farther side–a low erection of unmortared stone in the fashion of the country. Here he hunted along like a terrier, nose foremost, the tip of his tongue caught absurdly between his teeth, then jumped over, and, turning to Parker, said:

"Did you ever read *The Lay of the Last Minstrel?*"

"I learnt a good deal of it at school," said Parker. "Why?"

"Because there was a goblin page-boy in it," said Lord Peter "who was always yelling 'Found! Found! Found!' " at the most unnecessary moments. I always thought him a terrible nuisance, but now I know how he felt. See here."

Close under the wall, and sunk heavily into the narrow and muddy lane which ran up here at right angles to the main road, was the track of a side-car combination.

"Very nice too," said Mr. Parker approvingly. "New Dunlop tyre on the front wheel. Old tyre on the back. Gaiter on the side-car tyre. Nothing could be better. Tracks come in from the road and go back to the road. Fellow shoved the machine in here in case anybody of an inquisitive turn of mind should pass on the road and make off with it, or take its number. Then he went round on shank's mare to the gap he'd spotted in the daytime and got over. After the Cathcart affair he took fright, bolted into the preserve, and took the shortest way to his bus, regardless. Well, now."

He sat down on the wall, and, drawing out his note-book, began to jot down a description of the man from the data already known.

"Things begin to look a bit more comfortable for old Jerry," said Lord Peter. He leaned on the wall and began whistling softly, but with great accuracy, that elaborate passage of Bach which begins "Let Zion's children."

"I wonder," said the Hon. Freddy Arbuthnot, "what damn silly fool invented Sunday afternoon."

He shovelled coals on to the library fire with a vicious clatter, waking Colonel Marchbanks, who said, "Eh? Yes, quite right," and fell asleep again instantly.

"Don't *you* grumble, Freddy," said Lord Peter, who had been occupied for some time in opening and shutting all the drawers of the writing-table in a thoroughly irritating manner, and idly snapping to and fro the catch of the French window. "Think how dull old Jerry must feel. 'Spose I'd better write him a line."

He returned to the table and took a sheet of paper. "Do people use this room much to write letters in, do you know?"

"No idea," said the Hon. Freddy. "Never write 'em myself. Where's the point of writin' when you can wire? Encourages people to write back, that's all. I think Denver writes here when he writes anywhere, and I saw the Colonel wrestlin' with pen and ink a day or two ago, didn't you, Colonel?" (The Colonel grunted, answering to his name like a dog that wags its tail in its sleep.) "What's the matter? Ain't there any ink?"

"I only wondered," replied Peter placidly. He slipped a paper-knife under the top sheet of the blotting-pad and held it up to the light. "Quite right, old man. Give you full marks for observation. Here's Jerry's signature, and the Colonel's, and a big, sprawly hand, which I should judge to be feminine." He looked at the sheet again, shook his head, folded it up, and placed it in his pocket-book. "Doesn't seem to be anything there," he commented, "but you never know. 'Five something of fine something'–grouse, probably; 'oe–is fou'–is found, I suppose. Well, it can't do any harm to keep it." He spread out his paper and began:

"DEAR JERRY,–Here I am, the family sleuth on the trail, and it's damned exciting——"

The Colonel snored.

Sunday aftenoon. Parker had gone with the car to King's Fenton, with orders to look in at Riddlesdale on the way and inquire for a green-eyed cat, also for a young man with a side-car. The Duchess was lying down. Mrs. Pettigrew-Robinson had taken her husband for a brisk walk. Upstairs, somewhere, Mrs. Marchbanks enjoyed a perfect communion of thought with her husband.

Lord Peter's pen gritted gently over the paper, stopped, moved on again, stopped altogether. He leaned his long chin on his hands and stared out of the window, against which there came sudden little swishes of rain, and from time to time a soft, dead leaf. The Colonel snored; the fire tinkled; the Hon. Freddy began to hum and tap his fingers on the arms of his chair. The clock moved slothfully on to five o'clock, which brought teatime and the Duchess.

"How's Mary?" asked Lord Peter, coming suddenly into the firelight.

"I'm really worried about her," said the Duchess. "She is giving way to her nerves in the strangest manner. It is so unlike her. She will hardly let anybody come near her. I have sent for Dr. Thorpe again."

"Don't you think she'd be better if she got up an' came downstairs a bit?" suggested Wimsey. "Gets broodin' about things all by herself, I shouldn't wonder. Wants a bit of Freddy's intellectual conversation to cheer her up."

"You forget; poor girl," said the Duchess, "she was engaged to Captain Cathcart. Everybody isn't as callous as you are."

"Any more letters, your grace?" asked the footman, appearing with the post-bag.

"Oh, are you going down now?" said Wimsey. "Yes, here you are—and there's one other, if you don't mind waitin' a minute while I write it. Wish I could write at the rate people do on the cinema," he added, scribbling rapidly as he spoke. " 'DEAR LILIAN,—Your father has killed Mr. William Snooks, and unless you send me £1,000 by bearer, I shall disclose all to your husband.—Sincerely, EARL OF DIGGLESBRAKE.' That's the style; and all done in one scrape of the pen. Here you are, Fleming."

The letter was addressed to her grace the Dowager Duchess of Denver.

From the *Morning Post* of Monday, November—, 19—:

"ABANDONED MOTOR-CYCLE

"A singular discovery was made yesterday by a cattledrover. He is accustomed to water his animals in a certain pond lying a little off the road about twelve miles south of Ripley. On this occasion he saw that one of them appeared to be in difficulties. On going to the rescue, he found the animal entangled in a motor-cycle, which had been driven into the pond and abandoned. With the assistance of a couple of workmen he extricated the machine. It is a Douglas, with dark-grey side-car. The number-plates and licence-holder have been carefully removed. The pond is a deep one, and the outfit was entirely submerged. It seems probable, however, that it could not have been there for more than a week, since the pond is much used on Sundays and Mondays for the watering of cattle. The police are making search for the owner. The front tyre of the bicycle is a new Dunlop, and the side-car tyre has been repaired with a gaiter. The machine is a 1914 model, much worn"

"That seems to strike a chord," said Lord Peter musingly. He consulted a time-table for the time of the next train to Ripley, and ordered the car.

"And send Bunter to me," he added.

That gentleman arrived just as his master was struggling into an overcoat.

"What was that thing in last Thursday's paper about a number-plate, Bunter?" inquired his lordship.

Mr. Bunter produced, apparently by legerdemain, a cutting from an evening paper:

"NUMBER-PLATE MYSTERY

"The Rev. Nathaniel Foulis, of St. Simon's, North Fellcote, was stopped at six o'clock this morning for riding a motor-cycle without number-plates. The reverend gentleman seemed thunderstruck when his attention was called to the matter. He explained that he had been sent for in great haste at 4 a.m. to administer the

Sacrament to a dying parishioner six miles away. He hastened out on his motor-cycle, which he confidingly left by the roadside while executing his sacred duties. Mr. Foulis left the house at 5:30 without noticing that anything was wrong. Mr. Foulis is well known in North Fellcote and the surrounding country, and there seems little doubt that he had been the victim of a senseless practical joke. North Fellcote is a small village a couple of miles north of Ripley."

"I'm going to Ripley, Bunter," said Lord Peter.

"Yes, my lord. Does your lordship require me?"

"No," said Lord Peter, "but–who has been lady's maiding my sister, Bunter?"

"Ellen, my lord–the housemaid."

"Then I wish you'd exercise your powers of conversation on Ellen."

"Very good, my lord."

"Does she mend my sister's clothes, and brush her skirts, and all that?"

"I believe so, my lord."

"Nothing she may think is of any importance, you know, Bunter."

"I wouldn't suggest such a thing to a woman, my lord. It goes to their heads, if I may say so."

"When did Mr. Parker leave for town?"

"At six o'clock this morning, my lord."

* * * * *

Circumstances favoured Mr. Bunter's inquiries. He bumped into Ellen as she was descending the back stairs with an armful of clothing. A pair of leather gauntlets was jerked from the top of the pile, and, picking them up, he apologetically followed the young woman into the servants' hall.

"There," said Ellen, flinging her burden on the table, "and the work I've had to get them, I'm sure. Tantrums, that's what I call it, pretending you've got such a headache you can't let a person into the room to take your things down to brush, and, as soon as they're out of the way, 'opping out of bed and traipsing all over the place. 'Tisn't what I call a headache, would you, now? But there! I daresay you don't get them like I do. Regular fit to split, my head is sometimes–couldn't keep on my feet, not if the house was burning down. I just have to lay down and keep laying–something cruel it is. And gives a person such wrinkles in one's forehead."

"I'm sure I don't see any wrinkles." said Mr. Bunter, "but perhaps I haven't looked hard enough." An interlude followed, during which Mr. Bunter looked hard enough and close enough to distinguish wrinkles, "No," said he, "wrinkles? I don't believe I'd see any if I was to take his lordship's big microscope he keeps up in town."

"Lor' now, Mr. Bunter," said Ellen, fetching a sponge and a bottle of benzene from the cupboard, "what would his lordship be using a thing like that for, now?"

"Why, in our hobby, you see, Miss Ellen, which is criminal investigation, we might want to see something magnified extra big–as it might be handwriting in a forgery case, to see if anything's been altered or rubbed out, or if different kinds of ink have been used. Or we might want to look at the roots of a lock of hair, to see if it's been torn out or fallen out. Or take bloodstains, now; we'd want to know if it was animals' blood or human blood, or maybe only a glass of port."

"Now is it really true, Mr. Bunter," said Ellen, laying a tweed skirt out upon the table and unstoppering the benzene, "that you and Lord Peter can find out all that?"

"Of course, we aren't analytical chemists," Mr. Bunter replied, "but his lordship's dabbled in a lot of things—enough to know when anything looks suspicious, and if we've any doubts we send to a very famous scientific gentleman." (He gallantly intercepted Ellen's hand as it approached the skirt with a benzene-soaked sponge.) "For instance, now, here's a stain on the hem of this skirt, just at the bottom of the side-seam. Now, supposing it was a case of murder, we'll say, and the person that had worn this skirt was suspected, I should examine that stain." (Here Mr. Bunter whipped a lens out of his pocket.) "Then I might try it at one edge with a wet handkerchief." (He suited the action to the word.) "And I should find, you see, that it came off red. Then I should turn the skirt inside-out, I should see that the stain went right through, and I should take my scissors" (Mr. Bunter produced a small, sharp pair) "and snip off a tiny bit of the inside edge of the seam, like this" (he did so) "and pop it into a little pill-box, so" (the pill-box appeared magically from an inner pocket), "and seal it up both sides with a wafer, and write on the top 'Lady Mary Wimsey's skirt,' and the date. Then I should send it straight off to the analytical gentleman in London, and he'd look through his microscope, and tell me right off that it was rabbit's blood, maybe, and how many days it had been there, and that would be the end of that," finished Mr. Bunter triumphantly, replacing his nail-scissors and thoughtlessly pocketing the pill-box with its contents.

"Well, he'd be wrong, then," said Ellen, with an engaging toss of the head, "because it's bird's blood, and not rabbit's at all, because her ladyship told me so; and wouldn't it be quicker just to go and ask the person than get fiddling round with your silly old microscope and things?"

"Well, I only mentioned rabbits for an example," said Mr. Bunter. "Funny she should have got a stain down there. Must have regularly knelt in it."

"Yes. Bled a lot, hasn't it, poor thing? Somebody must 'a' been shootin' careless-like. 'Twasn't his grace, nor yet the Captain, poor man. Perhaps it was Mr. Arbuthnot. He shoots a bit wild sometimes. It's a nasty mess, anyway, and it's so hard to clean off, being left so long. I'm sure I wasn't thinking about cleaning nothing the day the poor Captain was killed; and then the Coroner's inquest—'orrid, it was—and his grace being took off like that! Well, there, it upset me. I suppose I'm a bit sensitive. Anyhow, we was all sixes and sevens for a day or two, and then her ladyship shuts herself up in her room and won't let me go near the wardrobe. 'Ow!' she says, 'do leave that wardrobe alone. Don't you know it squeaks, and my head's so bad and my nerves so bad I can't stand it,' she says. 'I was only going to brush your skirts, my lady,' I says. 'Bother my skirts,' says her ladyship, 'and do go away, Ellen. I shall scream if I see you fidgeting about there. You get on my nerves,' she says. Well, I didn't see why I should go on, not after being spoken to like that. It's very nice to be a ladyship, and all your tempers coddled and called nervous prostration. I know I was dreadfully cut up about poor Bert, my young man what was killed in the war—nearly cried my eyes out, I did; but, law! Mr. Bunter, I'd be ashamed to go on so. Besides, between you and I and the gate-post, Lady Mary wasn't that fond of the Captain. Never appreciated him, that's what I said to cook at the time, and she agreed with me. He had a way with him, the Captain had. Always quite the gentleman, of course, and never said anything as wasn't his place—I don't mean that—but I mean as it was a pleasure to do anything for him. Such a handsome man as he was, too, Mr. Bunter."

"Ah!" said Mr. Bunter. "So on the whole her ladyship was a bit more upset than you expected her to be?"

"Well, to tell you the truth, Mr. Bunter, I think it's just temper. She wanted to get married and away from home. Drat this stain! It's regular dried in. She and his grace never could get on, and when she was away in London during the war she had a rare old time, nursing officers, and going about with all kinds of queer people his grace didn't approve of. Then she had some sort of a love-affair with some quite low-down sort of fellow, so cook says; I think he was one of them dirty Russians as wants to blow us all to smithereens—as if there hadn't been enough people blown up in the war already! Anyhow, his grace made a dreadful fuss, and stopped supplies, and sent for her ladyship home, and ever since then she's been just mad to be off with somebody. Full of notions, she is. Makes me tired, I can tell you. Now, I'm sorry for his grace. I can see what he thinks. Poor gentleman! And then to be taken up for murder and put in gaol, just like one of them nasty tramps. Fancy!"

Ellen, having exhausted her breath and finished cleaning off the blood-stains, paused and straightened her back.

"Hard work it is," she said, "rubbing; I quite ache."

"If you would allow me to help you," said Mr. Bunter, appropriating the hot water, the benzene bottle, and the sponge.

He turned up another breadth of the skirt.

"Have you got a brush handy," he asked, "to take this mud off?"

"You're as blind as a bat, Mr. Bunter," said Ellen, giggling. "Can't you see it just in front of you?"

"Ah, yes," said the valet. "But that's not as hard a one as I'd like. Just you run and get me a real hard one, there's a dear good girl, and I'll fix this for you."

"Cheek!" said Ellen. "But," she added, relenting before the admiring gleam in Mr. Bunter's eye, "I'll get the clothes-brush out of the hall for you. That's as hard as a brick-bat, that is."

No sooner was she out of the room than Mr. Bunter produced a pocket-knife and two more pill-boxes. In a twinkling of an eye he had scraped the surface of the skirt in two places and written two fresh labels:

"Gravel from Lady Mary's skirt, about 6 in. from hem."

"Silver sand from hem of Lady Mary's skirt."

He added the date, and had hardly pocketed the boxes when Ellen returned with the clothes-brush. The cleaning process continued for some time, to the accompaniment of desultory conversation. A third stain on the skirt caused Mr. Bunter to stare critically.

"Hullo!" he said. "Her ladyship's been trying her hand at cleaning this herself."

"What?" cried Ellen. She peered closely at the mark, which at one edge was smeared and whitened, and had a slightly greasy appearance.

"Well, I never," she exclaimed, "so she has! Whatever's that for, I wonder? And her pretending to be so ill she couldn't raise her head off the pillow. She's a sly one, she is."

"Couldn't it have been done before?" suggested Mr. Bunter.

"Well, she might have been at it between the day the Captain was killed and the inquest," agreed Ellen, "though you wouldn't think that was a time to choose to begin learning domestic work. *She* ain't much hand at it, anyhow, for all her nursing. I never believed that came to anything."

"She's used soap," said Mr. Bunter, benzening away resolutely. "Can she boil water in her bedroom?"

"Now, whatever should she do that for, Mr. Bunter?" exclaimed Ellen, amazed. "You don't think she keeps a kettle? I bring up her morning tea. Ladyships don't want to boil water."

"No," said Mr. Bunter, "and why didn't she get it from the bathroom?" He scrutinised the stain more carefully still. "Very amateurish," he said; "distinctly amateurish. Interrupted, I fancy. An energetic young lady, but not ingenious."

The last remarks were addressed in confidence to the benzene bottle. Ellen had put her head out of the window to talk to the gamekeeper.

The Police Superintendent at Ripley received Lord Peter at first frigidly, and later, when he found out who he was, with a mixture of the official attitude to private detectives and the official attitude to a Duke's son.

"I've come to you," said Wimsey, "because you can do this combin'-out business a sight better'n an amateur like myself. I suppose your fine organisation's hard at work already, what?"

"Naturally," said the Superintendent, "but it's not altogether easy to trace a motor-cycle without knowing the number. Look at the Bournemouth Murder." He shook his head regretfully and accepted a Villar y Villar.

"We didn't think at first of connecting him with the number-plate business," the Superintendent went on in a careless tone which somehow conveyed to Lord Peter that his own remarks within the last half-hour had established the connection in the official mind for the first time. "Of course, if he'd been seen going through Ripley *without* a number-plate he'd have been noticed and stopped, whereas with Mr. Foulis's he was as safe as—as the Bank of England," he concluded in a burst of originality.

"Obviously," said Wimsey. "Very agitatin' for the parson, poor chap. So early in the mornin', too. I suppose it was just taken to be a practical joke?"

"Just that," agreed the Superintendent, "but, after hearing what you have to tell us, we shall use our best efforts to get the man. I expect his grace won't be any too sorry to hear he's found. You may rely on us, and if we find the man or the number-plates——"

"Lord bless us and save us, man," broke in Lord Peter with unexpected vivacity, "you're not goin' to waste your time lookin' for the number-plates. What d'you s'pose he'd pinch the curate's plates for if he wanted to advertise his own about the neighbourhood? Once you drop on them you've got his name and address; s'long as they're in his trousers pocket you're up a gum-tree. Now forgive me, Superintendent, for shovin' along with my opinion, but I simply can't bear to think of you takin' all that trouble for nothin'—draggin' ponds an' turnin' over rubbish-heaps to look for number-plates that ain't there. You just scour the railway-stations for a young man six foot one or two with a No. 10 shoe, and dressed in a Burberry that's lost its belt, and with a deep scratch on one of his hands. And look here, here's my address, and I'll be very grateful if you'll let me know anything that turns up. So awkward for my brother, y'know, all this. Sensitive man; feels it keenly. By the way, I'm a very uncertain bird—always hoppin' about; you might wire me any news in duplicate, to Riddlesdale and to town—110 Piccadilly. Always delighted to see you, by the way, if ever you're in town. You'll forgive me slopin' off now, won't you? I've got a lot to do."

* * * * *

Returning to Riddlesdale, Lord Peter found a new visitor seated at the tea-table. At Peter's entry he rose into towering height, and extended a shapely, expressive hand that would have made an actor's fortune. He was not an actor, but be found this hand useful, nevertheless, in the exploitation of dramatic moments. His magnificent build and the nobility of his head and mask were impressive; his features were flawless; his eyes ruthless. The Dowager Duchess had once remarked: "Sir Impey Biggs in the handsomest man in England, and no woman will ever care twopence for him." He was, in fact, thirty-eight, and a bachelor, and was celebrated for his rhetoric and his suave but pitiless dissection of hostile witnesses. The breeding of canaries was his unexpected hobby, and besides their song he could appreciate no music but revue airs. He answered Wimsey's greeting in his beautiful, resonant, and exquisitely controlled voice. Tragic irony, cutting contempt, or a savage indignation were the emotions by which Sir Impey Biggs swayed court and jury; he prosecuted murders of the innocent, defended in actions for criminal libel, and, moving others, was himself as stone. Wimsey expressed himself delighted to see him in a voice, by contrast, more husky and hesitant even than usual.

"You just come from Jerry?" he asked. "Fresh toast, please, Fleming. How is he? Enjoyin' it? I never knew a fellow like Jerry for gettin' the least possible out of any situation. I'd rather like the experience myself, you know; only I'd hate bein' shut up and watchin' the other idiots bunglin' my case. No reflection on Murbles and you, Biggs. I mean myself–I mean the man who'd be me if I was Jerry. You follow me?"

"I was just saying to Sir Impey," said the Duchess, "that he really must make Gerald say what he was doing in the garden at three in the morning. If only I'd been at Riddlesdale none of this would have happened. Of course, *we* all know that he wasn't doing any harm, but we can't expect the jurymen to understand that. The lower orders are so prejudiced. It is absurd of Gerald not to realise that he must speak out. He has *no* consideration."

"I am doing my very best to persuade him, Duchess," said Sir Impey, "but you must have patience. Lawyers enjoy a little mystery, you know. Why, if everybody came forward and told the truth, the whole truth, and nothing but the truth straight out, we should all retire to the workhouse."

"Captain Cathcart's death is very mysterious," said the Duchess, "though when I think of the things that have come out about him it really seems quite providential, as far as my sister-in-law is concerned."

"I s'pose you couldn't get 'em to bring it in 'Death by the Visitation of God,' could you, Biggs?" suggested Lord Peter. "Sort of judgment for wantin' to marry into our family, what?"

"I have known less reasonable verdicts," returned Biggs dryly. "It's wonderful what you can suggest to a jury if you try. I remember once at the Liverpool Assizes——"

He steered skilfully away into a quiet channel of reminiscence. Lord Peter watched his statuesque profile against the fire; it reminded him of the severe beauty of the charioteer of Delphi and was about as communicative.

* * * * *

It was not until after dinner that Sir Impey opened his mind to Wimsey. The Duchess had gone to bed, and the two men were alone in the library. Peter, scrupulously in evening dress, had been valeted by Bunter, and had been more than usually rambling and cheerful all evening. He now took a cigar, retired to the largest chair, and effaced himself in a complete silence.

Sir Impey Biggs walked up and down for some half-hour, smoking. Then he came across with determination, brutally switched on a reading-lamp right into Peter's face, sat down opposite to him, and said:

"Now, Wimsey, I want to know all you know."

"Do you, though?" said Peter. He got up, disconnected the reading-lamp, and carried it away to a side-table.

"No bullying of the witness, though," he added, and grinned.

"I don't care so long as you wake up," said Biggs, unperturbed. "Now then."

Lord Peter removed his cigar from his mouth, considered it with his head on one side, turned it carefully over, decided that the ash could hang on to its parent leaf for another minute or two, smoked without speaking until collapse was inevitable, took the cigar out again, deposited the ash entire in the exact centre of the ash-tray, and began his statement, omitting only the matter of the suit-case and Bunter's information obtained from Ellen.

Sir Impey Biggs listened with what Peter irritably described as a cross-examining countenance, putting a sharp question every now and again. He made a few notes, and, when Wimsey had finished, sat tapping his note-book thoughtfully.

"I think we can make a case out of this," he said, "even if the police don't find your mysterious man. Denver's silence is an awkward complication, of course." He hooded his eyes for a moment. "Did you say you'd put the police on to find the fellow?"

"Yes."

"Have you a very poor opinion of the police?"

"Not for that kind of thing. That's in their line; they have all the facilities, and do it well."

"Ah! You expect to find the man, do you?"

"I hope to."

"Ah! What do you think is going to happen to my case if you do find him, Wimsey?"

"What do I——"

"See here, Wimsey," said the barrister, "you are not a fool, and it's no use trying to look like a country policeman. You are really trying to find this man?"

"Certainly."

"Just as you like, of course, but my hands are rather tied already. Has it ever occurred to you that perhaps he'd better not be found?"

Wimsey stared at the lawyer with such honest astonishment as actually to disarm him.

"Remember this," said the latter earnestly, "that if once the police get hold of a thing or a person it's no use relying on my, or Murbles's, or anybody's professional discretion. Everything's raked out into the light of common day, and very common it is. Here's Denver accused of murder, and he refuses in the most categorical way to give me the smallest assistance."

"Jerry's an ass. He doesn't realise——"

"Do you suppose," broke in Biggs, "I have not made it my business to *make* him realise? All he says is, 'They can't hang me; I didn't kill the man, though I think it's a jolly good thing he's dead. It's no business of theirs what I was doing in the garden.' Now I ask you, Wimsey, is that a reasonable attitude for a man in Denver's position to take up?"

Peter muttered something about "Never had any sense."

"Had anybody told Denver about this other man?"

"Something vague was said about footsteps at the inquest, I believe."

"That Scotland Yard man is your personal friend, I'm told?"

"Yes."

"So much the better. He can hold his tongue."

"Look here, Biggs, this is all damned impressive and mysterious, but what are you gettin' at? Why shouldn't I lay hold of the beggar if I can?"

"I'll answer that question by another." Sir Impey leaned forward a little. "Why is Denver screening him?"

Sir Impey Biggs was accustomed to boast that no witness could perjure himself in his presence undetected. As he put the question he released the other's eyes from his, and glanced down with finest cunning at Wimsey's long, flexible mouth and nervous hands. When he glanced up again a second later he met the eyes passing, guarded and inscrutable, through all the changes expressive of surprised enlightenment; but by that time it was too late; he had seen a little line at the corner of the mouth fade out, and the fingers relax ever so slightly. The first movement had been one of relief.

"B'Jove!" said Peter. "I never thought of that. What sleuths you lawyers are. If that's so, I'd better be careful, hadn't I? Always was a bit rash. My mother says——"

"You're a clever devil, Wimsey," said the barrister. "I may be wrong, then. Find your man by all means. There's just one other thing I'd like to ask. Whom are *you* screening?"

"Look here, Biggs," said Wimsey, "you're not paid to ask that kind of question here, you know. You can jolly well wait till you get into court. It's your job to make the best of the stuff we serve up to you, not to give us the third degree. Suppose I murdered Cathcart myself——"

"You didn't."

"I know I didn't, but if I did I'm not goin' to have you askin' questions and lookin' at me in that tone of voice. However, just to oblige you, I don't mind sayin' plainly that I don't know who did away with the fellow. When I do I'll tell you."

"You will?"

"Yes, I will, but not till I'm sure. You people can make such a little circumstantial evidence go such a damn long way, you might hang me while I was only in the early stages of suspectin' myself."

"H'm!" said Biggs. "Meanwhile, I tell you candidly, I am taking the line that they can't make out a case."

"Not proven, eh? Well, anyhow, Biggs, I swear my brother shan't hang for lack of my evidence."

"Of course not," said Biggs, adding inwardly: "but you hope it won't come to that."

A spurt of rain splashed down the wide chimney and sizzled on the logs.

* * * * *

"Craven Hotel,
"Strand, W.C.,
"*Tuesday.*

"My Dear Wimsey,—A line as I promised, to report progress, but it's precious little. On the journey up I sat next to Mrs. Pettigrew-Robinson, and opened and shut the window for her and looked after her parcels. She mentioned that when your sister roused the household on Thursday morning she went first to Mr. Arbuthnot's room —a circumstance which the lady seemed to think odd, but which is natural enough when you come to think of it, the room being directly opposite the head of the staircase. It was Mr. Arbuthnot who knocked up the Pettigrew-Robinsons, and Mr. P. ran downstairs immediately. Mrs. P. then saw that Lady Mary was looking very faint, and tried to support her. Your sister threw her off—rudely, Mrs. P. says—declined 'in a most savage manner' all offers of assistance, rushed to her own room, and locked herself in. Mrs. Pettigrew-Robinson listened at the door 'to make sure,' as she says, 'that everything was all right,' but, hearing her moving about and slamming cupboards, she concluded that she would have more chance of poking her finger into the pie downstairs, and departed.

"If Mrs. Marchbanks had told me this, I admit I should have thought the episode worth looking into, but I feel strongly that if I were dying I should still lock the door between myself and Mrs. Pettigrew-Robinson. Mrs. P. was quite sure that at no time had Lady Mary anything in her hand. She was dressed as described at the inquest—a long coat over her pyjamas (sleeping suit was Mrs. P.'s expression), stout shoes, and a woolly cap, and she kept these garments on throughout the subsequent visit of the doctor. Another odd little circumstance is that Mrs. Pettigrew-Robinson (who was awake, you remember, from 2 a.m. onwards) is certain that just *before* Lady Mary knocked on Mr. Arbuthnot's door she heard a door slam somewhere in the passage. I don't know what to make of this—perhaps there's nothing in it, but I just mention it.

"I've had a rotten time in town. Your brother-in-law elect was a model of discretion. His room at the Albany is a desert from a detecting point of view; no papers except a few English bills and receipts, and invitations. I looked up a few of his inviters, but they were mostly men who had met him at the club or knew him in the Army, and could tell me nothing about his private life. He is known at several night-clubs. I made the round of them last night —or, rather, this morning. General verdict: generous but impervious. By the way, poker seems to have been his great game. No suggestion of anything crooked. He won pretty consistently on the whole, but never very spectacularly.

"I think the information we want must be in Paris. I have written to the Sûreté and the Crédit Lyonnais to produce his papers, especially his account and chequebook.

"I'm pretty dead with yesterday's and to-day's work. Dancing all night on top of a journey is a jolly poor joke. Unless you want me, I'll wait here for the papers, or I may run over to Paris myself.

"Cathcart's books here consist of a few modern French novels of the usual kind, and another copy of *Manon* with what the catalogues call 'curious' plates. He must have had a life somewhere, mustn't he?

"The enclosed bill from a beauty specialist in Bond Street may interest you. I called on her. She says he came regularly every week when he was in England.

"I drew quite blank at King's Fenton on Sunday—oh, but I told you that. I don't think the fellow ever went there. I wonder if he slunk off up into the moor. Is it worth rummaging about, do you think? Rather like looking for a needle in a bundle of hay. It's odd about that diamond cat. You've got nothing out of the household, I suppose?

It doesn't seem to fit No. 10, somehow–and yet you'd think somebody would have heard about it in the village if it had been lost. Well, so long,

"Yours ever,
"CH. PARKER."

# 4

# –AND HIS DAUGHTER, MUCH-AFRAID

*The women also looked pale and wan.*
The Pilgrim's Progress

MR. BUNTER brought Parker's letter up to Lord Peter in bed on the Wednesday morning. The house was almost deserted, everybody having gone to attend the police-court proceedings at Northallerton. The thing would be purely formal, of course, but it seemed only proper that the family should be fully represented. The Dowager Duchess, indeed, was there–she had promptly hastened to her son's side and was living heroically in furnished lodgings, but the younger Duchess thought her mother-in-law more energetic than dignified. There was no knowing what she might do if left to herself. She might even give an interview to a newspaper reporter. Besides, at these moments of crisis a wife's right place is at her husband's side. Lady Mary was ill, and nothing could be said about that, and if Peter chose to stay smoking cigarettes in his pyjamas while his only brother was undergoing public humiliation, that was only what might be expected. Peter took after his mother. How that eccentric strain had got into the family her grace could not imagine, for the Dowager came of a good Hampshire family; there must have been some foreign blood somewhere. Her own duty was clear, and she would do it.

Lord Peter was awake, and looked rather fagged, as though he had been sleuthing in his sleep. Mr. Bunter wrapped him solicitously in a brilliant Oriental robe, and placed the tray on his knees.

"Bunter," said Lord Peter rather fretfully, "your *café au lait* is the one tolerable incident in this beastly place."

"Thank you, my lord. Very chilly again this morning, my lord, but not actually raining."

Lord Peter frowned over his letter.

"Anything in the paper, Bunter?"

"Nothing urgent, my lord. A sale next week at Northbury Hall–Mr. Fleetwhite's library, my lord–a Caxton *Confessio Amantis*——"

"What's the good of tellin' me that when we're stuck up here for God knows how long? I wish to heaven I'd stuck to books and never touched crime. Did you send those specimens up to Lubbock?"

"Yes, my lord," said Bunter gently. Dr. Lubbock was the "analytical gentleman."

"Must have facts," said Lord Peter, "facts. When I was a small boy I always hated facts. Thought of 'em as nasty, hard things, all knobs. Uncompromisin'."

"Yes, my lord. My old mother——"

"Your mother, Bunter? I didn't know you had one. I always imagined you were turned out ready-made, so to speak. 'Scuse me. Infernally rude of me. Beg your pardon, I'm sure."

"Not at all, my lord. My mother lives in Kent, my lord, near Maidstone. Seventy-five, my lord, and an extremely active woman for her years, if you'll excuse my mentioning it. I was one of seven."

"That is an invention, Bunter. I know better. You are unique. But I interrupted you. You were goin' to tell me about your mother."

"She always says, my lord, that facts are like cows. If you look them in the face hard enough they generally run away. She is a very courageous woman, my lord."

Lord Peter stretched out his hand impulsively, but Mr. Bunter was too well trained to see it. He had, indeed, already begun to strop a razor. Lord Peter suddenly bundled out of bed with a violent jerk and sped across the landing to the bathroom.

Here he revived sufficiently to lift up his voice in "Come unto these Yellow Sands." Thence, feeling in a Purcellish mood, he passed to "I attempt from Love's Fever to Fly," with such improvement of spirits that, against all custom, he ran several gallons of cold water into the bath and sponged himself vigorously. Wherefore, after a rough towelling, he burst explosively from the bathroom, and caught his shin somewhat violently against the lid of a large oak chest which stood at the head of the staircase–so violently, indeed, that the lid lifted with the shock and shut down with a protesting bang.

Lord Peter stopped to say something expressive and to caress his leg softly with the palm of his hand. Then a thought struck him. He set down his towels, soap, sponge, loofah, bath-brush, and other belongings, and quietly lifted the lid of the chest.

Whether, like the heroine of *Northanger Abbey*, he expected to find anything gruesome inside was not apparent. It is certain that, like her, he beheld nothing more startling than certain sheets and counterpanes neatly folded at the bottom. Unsatisfied, he lifted the top one of these gingerly and inspected it for a few moments in the light of the staircase window. He was just returning it to its place, whistling softly the while, when a little hiss of indrawn breath caused him to look up with a start.

His sister was at his elbow. He had not heard her come, but she stood there in her dressing-gown, her hands clutched together on her breast. Her blue eyes were dilated till they looked almost black, and her skin seemed nearly the colour of her ash-blonde hair. Wimsey stared at her over the sheet he held in his arms, and the terror in her face passed over into his, stamping them suddenly with the mysterious likeness of blood-relationship.

Peter's own impression was that he stared "like a stuck pig" for about a minute. He knew, as a matter of fact, that he had recovered himself in a fraction of a second. He dropped the sheet into the chest and stood up.

"Hello, Polly, old thing," he said, "where've you been hidin' all this time? First time I've seen you. 'Fraid you've been havin' a pretty thin time of it."

He put his arm round her, and felt her shrink.

"What's the matter?" he demanded. "What's up, old girl? Look here, Mary, we've never seen enough of each other, but I am your brother. Are you in trouble? Can't I——"

"Trouble?" she said. "Why, you silly old Peter, of course I'm in trouble. Don't you know they've killed my man and put my brother in prison? Isn't that enough to be in trouble about?" She laughed, and Peter suddenly thought, "She's talking like somebody in a blood-and-thunder-novel." She went on more naturally. "It's all right, Peter, truly–only my head's so bad. I really don't know what I'm doing. What are you after? You made such a noise, I came out. I thought it was a door banging."

"You'd better toddle back to bed," said Lord Peter. "You're gettin' all cold. Why do girls wear such mimsy little pyjimjams in this damn cold climate? There, don't you worry. I'll drop in on you later and we'll have a jolly old pow-wow, what?"

"Not to-day–not to-day, Peter. I'm going mad, I think." ("Sensation fiction again," thought Peter.) "Are they trying Gerald to-day?"

"Not exactly trying," said Peter, urging her gently along to her room. "It's just formal, y'know. The jolly old magistrate bird hears the charge read, and then old Murbles pops up and says please he wants only formal evidence given as he has to instruct counsel. That's Biggy, y'know. Then they hear the evidence of arrest, and Murbles says old Gerald reserves his defence. That's all till the Assizes–evidence before the Grand Jury–a lot of bosh! That'll be early next month, I suppose. You'll have to buck up and be fit by then."

Mary shuddered.

"No–no! Couldn't I get out of it? I couldn't go through it all again. I should be sick. I'm feeling awful. No, don't come in. I don't want you. Ring the bell for Ellen. No, let go; go away! I don't want you, Peter!"

Peter hesitated, a little alarmed.

"Much better not, my lord, if you'll excuse me," said Bunter's voice at his ear. "Only produce hysterics," he added, as he drew his master gently from the door. "Very distressing for both parties, and altogether unproductive of results. Better to wait for the return of her grace, the Dowager."

"Quite right," said Peter. He turned back to pick up his paraphernalia, but was dexterously forestalled. Once again he lifted the lid of the chest and looked in.

"What did you say you found on that skirt, Bunter?"

"Gravel, my lord, and silver sand."

"Silver sand."

* * * * *

Behind Riddlesdale Lodge the moor stretched starkly away and upward. The heather was brown and wet, and the little streams had no colour in them. It was six o'clock, but there was no sunset. Only a paleness had moved behind the thick sky from east to west all day. Lord Peter, tramping back after a long and fruitless search for tidings of the man with the motor-cycle, voiced the dull suffering of his gregarious spirit. "I wish old Parker was here," he muttered, and squelched down a sheep-track.

He was making, not directly for the Lodge, but for a farmhouse about two and a half miles distant from it, known as Grider's Hole. It lay almost due north of Riddlesdale village, a lonely outpost on the edge of the moor, in a valley of fertile land between two wide swells of heather. The track wound down from the height called Whemmeling Fell, skirted a vile swamp, and crossed the little river Ridd about half a mile before reaching the farm. Peter had small hope of hearing any news at Grider's Hole, but he was filled with a sullen determination to leave no stone unturned. Privately, however, he felt convinced that the motor-cycle had come by the high road, Parker's investigations notwithstanding, and perhaps passed directly through King's Fenton without stopping or attracting attention. Still, he had said he would search the neighbourhood, and Grider's Hole was in the neighbourhood. He paused to relight his pipe, then squelched steadily on. The path was marked with stout white posts at regular intervals, and presently with hurdles. The reason for this was apparent as one came to the bottom of the valley, for only a few yards on the left began the stretch of rough, reedy tussocks, with slobbering black bog between them, in which anything heavier than a water-wagtail would speedily suffer change into a succession of little bubbles. Wimsey stooped for an empty sardine-tin which lay, horridly battered, at his feet, and slung it idly into the quag. It struck the surface with a noise like a wet kiss, and vanished instantly. With that instinct which prompts one, when depressed, to wallow in every circumstance of gloom, Peter leaned sadly upon the hurdles and abandoned himself to a variety of shallow considerations upon (1) The vanity of human wishes; (2) Mutability; (3) First love; (4) The decay of idealism; (5) The aftermath of the Great war; (6) Birth-control; and (7) The fallacy of free-will. This was his nadir, however. Realising that his feet were cold and his stomach empty, and that he had still some miles to go, he crossed the stream on a row of slippery steppingstones and approached the gate of the farm, which was not an ordinary five-barred one, but solid and uncompromising. A man was leaning over it, sucking a straw. He made no attempt to move at Wimsey's approach. "Good evening," said that nobleman in a sprightly manner, laying his hand on the catch. "Chilly, ain't it?"

The man made no reply, but leaned more heavily, and breathed. He wore a rough coat and breeches, and his leggings were covered with manure.

"Seasonable, of course, what?" said Peter. "Good for the sheep, I daresay. Makes their wool curl, and so on."

The man removed the straw and spat in the direction of Peter's right boot.

"Do you lose many animals in the bog?" went on Peter, carelessly unlatching the gate, and leaning upon it in the opposite direction. "I see you have a good wall all round the house. Must be a bit dangerous in the dark, what, if you're thinkin' of takin' a little evenin' stroll with a friend?"

The man spat again, pulled his hat over his forehead, and said briefly:

"What doost 'a want?"

"Well," said Peter, "I thought of payin' a little friendly call on Mr.—on the owner of this farm, that is to say. Country neighbours, and all that. Lonely kind of country, don't you see. Is he in, d'ye think?"

The man grunted.

"I'm glad to hear it," said Peter; "it's so uncommonly jolly findin' all you Yorkshire people so kind and hospitable, what? Never mind who you are, always a seat at the fireside and that kind of thing. Excuse me, but do you know you're leanin' on the gate so as I can't open it? I'm sure it's a pure oversight, only you mayn't realise that just where you're standin' you get the maximum of leverage. What an awfully charmin' house this is, isn't it? All so jolly stark and grim and all the rest of it. No creepers or little rose-grown porches or anything suburban of that sort. Who lives in it?"

The man surveyed him up and down for some moments, and replied, "Mester Grimethorpe."

"No, does he now?" said Lord Peter. "To think of that. Just the fellow I want to see. Model farmer, what? Wherever I go throughout the length and breadth of the North Riding I hear of Mr. Grimethorpe. 'Grimethorpe's butter is the best'; 'Grimethorpe's fleeces Never go to pieces'; 'Grimethorpe's pork Melts on the fork'; 'For Irish stews Take Grimethorpe's ewes'; 'A tummy lined with Grimethorpe's beef, Never, never comes to grief.' It has been my life's ambition to see Mr. Grimethorpe in the flesh. And you no doubt are his sturdy henchman and right-hand man. You leap from bed before the breaking-day, To milk the kine amid the scented hay. You, when the shades of evening gather deep, Home from the mountain lead the mild-eyed sheep. You, by the ingle's red and welcoming blaze, Tell your sweet infants tales of olden days! A wonderful life, though a trifle monotonous p'raps in the winter. Allow me to clasp your honest hand."

Whether the man was moved by this lyric outburst, or whether the falling light was not too dim to strike a pale sheen from the metal in Lord Peter's palm, at any rate he moved a trifle back from the gate.

"Thanks awfully, old bean," said Peter, stepping briskly past him. "I take it I shall find Mr. Grimethorpe in the house?"

The man said nothing till Wimsey had proceeded about a dozen yards up the flagged path, then he hailed him, but without turning round.

"Mester!"

"Yes, old thing?" said Peter affably, returning.

"Happen he'll set dog on tha."

"You don't say so?" said Peter. "The faithful hound welcomes the return of the prodigal. Scene of family rejoicing. 'My own long lost boy!' Sobs and speeches, beer all round for the delighted tenantry. Glees by the old fireside, till the rafters ring and all the smoked hams tumble down to join in the revelry. Good night, sweet Prince, until the cows come home and the dogs eat Jezebel in the portion of Jezreel when the hounds of spring are on winter's traces. I suppose," he added to himself, "they will have finished tea."

As Lord Peter approached the door of the farm his spirits rose. He enjoyed paying this kind of visit. Although he had taken to detecting as he might, with another conscience or constitution, have taken to Indian hemp—for its exhilarating properties—at a moment when life seemed dust and ashes, he had not primarily the detective temperament. He expected next to nothing from inquiries at Grider's Hole, and, if he had, he might probably have extracted all the information he wanted by a judicious display of Treasury notes to the glum man at the gate. Parker would in all likelihood have done so; he was paid to detect and to do nothing else, and neither his natural gifts nor his education (at Barrow-in-Furness Grammar School) prompted him to stray into side-tracks at the beck of an ill-regulated imagination. But to Lord Peter the world presented itself as an entertaining labyrinth of side-issues. He was a respectable scholar in five or six languages, a musician of some skill and more understanding, something of an expert in toxicology, a collector of rare editions, an entertaining man-about-town, and a common sensationalist. He had been seen at half-past twelve on a Sunday morning walking in Hyde Park in a top-hat and frock-coat, reading the *News of the World*. His passion for the unexplored led him to hunt up obscure pamphlets in the British

Museum, to unravel the emotional history of income-tax collectors, and to find out where his own drains led to. In this case, the fascinating problem of a Yorkshire farmer who habitually set the dogs on casual visitors imperatively demanded investigation in a personal interview. The result was unexpected.

His first summons was unheeded, and he knocked again. This time there was a movement, and a surly male voice called out:

"Well, let 'un in then, dang 'un–and dang *thee*," emphasised by the sound of something falling or thrown across the room.

The door was opened unexpectedly by a little girl of about seven, very dark and pretty, and rubbing her arm as though the missile had caught her there. She stood defensively, blocking the threshold, till the same voice growled impatiently:

"Well, who is it?"

"Good evening," said Wimsey, removing his hat. "I hope you'll excuse me droppin' in like this. I'm livin' at Riddlesdale Lodge."

"What of it?" demanded the voice. Above the child's head Wimsey saw the outline of a big, thick-set man smoking in the inglenook of an immense fireplace. There was no light but the firelight, for the window was small, and dusk had already fallen. It seemed to be a large room, but a high oak settle on the farther side of the chimney ran out across it, leaving a cavern of impenetrable blackness beyond.

"May I come in?" said Wimsey.

"If tha must," said the man ungraciously. "Shoot door, lass; what art starin' at? Go to thi moother and bid her mend thi manners for thee."

This seemed a case of the pot lecturing the kettle on cleanliness, but the child vanished hurriedly into the blackness behind the settle, and Peter walked in.

"Are you Mr. Grimethorpe?" he asked politely.

"What if I am?" retorted the farmer. "*I've* no call to be ashamed o' my name."

"Rather not," said Lord Peter, "nor of your farm. Delightful place, what? My name's Wimsey, by the way–Lord Peter Wimsey, in fact, the Duke of Denver's brother, y'know. I'm sure I hate interruptin' you–you must be busy with the sheep and all that–but I thought you wouldn't mind if I just ran over in a neighbourly way. Lonely sort of country, ain't it? I like to know the people next door, and all that sort of thing. I'm used to London, you see, where people live pretty thick on the ground. I suppose very few strangers ever pass this way?"

"None," said Mr. Grimethorpe, with decision.

"Well, perhaps it's as well," pursued Lord Peter. "Makes one appreciate one's home circle more, what? Often think one sees too many strangers in town. Nothing like one's family when all's said and done–cosy, don't you know. You a married man, Mr. Grimethorpe?"

"What the hell's that to you?" growled the farmer, rounding on him with such ferocity that Wimsey looked about quite nervously for the dogs before-mentioned.

"Oh, nothin'," he replied, "only I thought that charmin' little girl might be yours."

"And if I thought she weren't," said Mr. Grimethorpe, "I'd strangle the bitch and her mother together. What hast got to say to that?"

As a matter of fact, the remark, considered as a conversational formula, seemed to leave so much to be desired that Wimsey's natural loquacity suffered a severe check. He fell back, however, on the usual resource of the male, and offered Mr. Grimethorpe a cigar, thinking to himself as he did so: "What a hell of a life the woman must lead."

The farmer declined the cigar with a single word, and was silent. Wimsey lit a cigarette for himself and became meditative, watching his companion. He was a man of about forty-five, apparently, rough, harsh, and weather-beaten, with great ridgy shoulders and short, thick thighs–a bull-terrier with a bad temper. Deciding that delicate hints would be wasted on such an organism, Wimsey adopted a franker method.

"To tell the truth, Mr. Grimethorpe," he said, "I didn't blow in without any excuse at all. Always best to provide oneself with an excuse for a call, what? Though it's so perfectly delightful to see you–I mean, no excuse might appear necessary. But fact is, I'm looking for a young man–a–an acquaintance of mine–who said he'd be roamin' about this neighbourhood some time or other about now. Only I'm afraid I may have missed him. You see, I've only just got over from Corsica–interestin' country and all that, Mr. Grimethorpe, but a trifle out of the way–and from what my friend said I think he must have turned up here about a week ago and found me out. Just my luck. But he didn't leave his card, so I can't be quite sure, you see. You didn't happen to come across him by any chance? Tall fellow with big feet on a motor-cycle with a side-car. I thought he might have come rootin' about here. Hullo! d'you know him?"

The farmer's face had become swollen and almost black with rage.

"What day sayst tha?" he demanded thickly.

"I should think last Wednesday night or Thursday morning," said Peter, with a hand on his heavy malacca cane.

"I knew it," growled Mr. Grimethorpe. "——the slut, and all these dommed women wi' their dirty ways. Look here, mester. The tyke were a friend o' thine? Well, I wor at Stapley Wednesday and Thursday–tha knew that, didn't tha? And so did thi friend, didn't 'un? An' if I hadn't, it'd 'a' bin the worse for 'un. He'd 'a' been in Peter's Pot if I'd 'a' cot 'un an' that's where tha'll be thesen in a minute, blast tha! And if I find 'un sneakin' here again, I'll blast every boon in a's body and send 'un to look for thee there."

And with these surprising words he made for Peter's throat like a bull-dog.

"That won't do," said Peter, disengaging himself with an ease which astonished his opponent, and catching his wrist in a grip of mysterious and excruciating agony. " 'Tisn't wise, y'know–might murder a fellow like that. Nasty business, murder. Coroner's inquest and all that sort of thing. Counsel for the Prosecution askin' all sorts of inquisitive questions, and a feller puttin' a string round your neck. Besides, your method's a bit primitive. Stand still, you fool, or you'll break your arm. Feelin' better? That's right. Sit down. You'll get into trouble one of these days, behavin' like that when you're asked a civil question."

"Get out o' t'house," said Mr. Grimethorpe sullenly.

"Certainly," said Peter. "I have to thank you for a very entertainin' evenin', Mr. Grimethorpe. I'm sorry you can give me no news of my friend——"

Mr. Grimethorpe sprang up with a blasphemous ejaculation, and made for the door, shouting "Jabez!" Lord Peter stared after him for a moment, and then stared round the room.

"Something fishy here," he said. "Fellow knows somethin'. Murderous sort of brute. I wonder——"

He peered round the settle, and came face to face with a woman–a dim patch of whiteness in the thick shadow.

"You?" she said, in a low, hoarse gasp. "You? You are mad to come here.

Quick, quick! He has gone for the dogs."

She placed her two hands on his breast, thrusting him urgently back. Then, as the firelight fell upon his face, she uttered a stifled shriek and stood petrified—a Medusa-head of terror.

Medusa was beautiful, says the tale, and so was this woman; a broad white forehead under massed, dusky hair, black eyes glowing under straight brows, a wide, passionate mouth—a shape so wonderful that even in that strenuous moment sixteen generations of feudal privilege stirred in Lord Peter's blood. His hands closed over hers instinctively, but she pulled herself hurriedly away and shrank back.

"Madam," said Wimsey, recovering himself, "I don't quite——"

A thousand questions surged up in his mind, but before he could frame them a long yell, and another, and then another came from the back of the house.

"Run, run!" she said. "The dogs! My God, my God, what will become of me? Go, if you don't want to see me killed. Go, go! Have pity!"

"Look here," said Peter, "can't I stay and protect——"

"You can stay and murder me," said the woman. "Go!"

Peter cast Public School tradition to the winds, caught up his stick, and went. The brutes were at his heels as he fled. He struck the foremost with his stick, and it dropped back, snarling. The man was still leaning on the gate, and Grimethorpe's hoarse voice was heard shouting to him to seize the fugitive. Peter closed with him; there was a scuffle of dogs and men, and suddenly Peter found himself thrown bodily over the gate. As he picked himself up and ran, he heard the farmer cursing the man and the man retorting that he couldn't help it; then the woman's voice, uplifted in a frightened wail. He glanced over his shoulder. The man and the woman and a second man who had now joined the party, were beating the dogs back, and seemed to be persuading Grimethorpe not to let them through. Apparently their remonstrances had some effect, for the farmer turned moodily away, and the second man called the dogs off, with much whip-cracking and noise. The woman said something, and her husband turned furiously upon her and struck her to the ground.

Peter made a movement to go back, but a strong conviction that he could only make matters worse for her arrested him. He stood still, and waited till she had picked herself up and gone in, wiping the blood and dirt from her face with her shawl. The farmer looked round, shook his fist at him, and followed her into the house. Jabez collected the dogs and drove them back, and Peter's friend returned to lean over the gate.

Peter waited till the door had closed upon Mr. and Mrs. Grimethorpe; then he pulled out his handkerchief and, in the half-darkness, signalled cautiously to the man, who slipped through the gate and came slowly down to him.

"Thanks very much," said Wimsey, putting money into his hand. "I'm afraid I've done unintentional mischief."

The man looked at the money and at him.

" 'Tes t' master's way wi' them as cooms t'look at t'missus," he said. "Tha's best keep away if so be tha wutna' have her blood on tha heid."

"See here," said Peter, "did you by any chance meet a young man with a motor-cycle wanderin' round here last Wednesday or thereabouts?"

"Naay. Wednesday? T'wod be day t'mester went to Stapley, Ah reckon, after machines. Naay, Ah seed nowt."

"All right. If you find anybody who did, let me know. Here's my name, and I'm staying at Riddlesdale Lodge. Good night; many thanks."

The man took the card from him and slouched back without a word of farewell.

* * * * *

Lord Peter walked slowly, his coat collar turned up and his hat pulled over his eyes. This cinematographic episode had troubled his logical faculty. With an effort he sorted out his ideas and arranged them in some kind of order.

"First item," said he, "Mr. Grimethorpe. A gentleman who will stick at nothing. Hefty. Unamiable. Inhospitable. Dominant characteristic—jealousy of his very astonishing wife. Was at Stapley last Wednesday and Thursday buying machinery. (Helpful gentleman at the gate corroborates this, by the way, so that at this stage of the proceedings one may allow it to be a sound alibi.) Did not, therefore, see our mysterious friend with the side-car, *if* he was there. But is disposed to think he *was* there, and has very little doubt about what he came for. Which raises an interestin' point. Why the side-car? Awkward thing to tour about with. Very good. But if our friend came after Mrs. G. he obviously didn't take her. Good again.

"Second item, Mrs. Grimethorpe. Very singular item. By Jove!" He paused meditatively to reconstruct a thrilling moment. "Let us at once admit that if No. 10 came for the purpose suspected he had every excuse for it. Well! Mrs. G. goes in terror of her husband, who thinks nothing of knocking her down on suspicion. I wish to God—but I'd only have made things worse. Only thing you can do for the wife of a brute like that is to keep away from her. Hope there won't be murder done. One's enough at a time. Where was I?

"Yes—well, Mrs. Grimethorpe knows something—and she knows somebody. She took me for somebody who had every reason for not coming to Grider's Hole. Where was she, I wonder, while I was talking to Grimethorpe? She wasn't in the room. Perhaps the child warned her. No, that won't wash; I told the child who I was. Aha! wait a minute. Do I see light? She looked out of the window and saw a bloke in an aged Burberry. No. 10 is a bloke in an aged Burberry. Now, let's suppose for a moment she takes me for No. 10. What does she do? She sensibly keeps out of the way—can't think why I'm such a fool as to turn up. Then, when Grimethorpe runs out shoutin' for the kennel-man, she nips down with her life in her hands to warn her—her—shall we say boldly her lover?—to get away. She finds it isn't her lover, but only a gaping ass of (I fear) a very comin'-on disposition. New compromisin' position. She tells the ass to save himself and herself by clearin' out. Ass clears—not too gracefully. The next instalment of this enthrallin' drama will be shown in this theatre—when? I'd jolly well like to know."

He tramped on for some time.

"All the same " he retorted upon himself "all this throws no light on what No. 10 was doing at Riddlesdale Lodge."

At the end of his walk he had reached no conclusion.

"Whatever happens," he said to himself, "and if it can be done without danger to her life, I must see Mrs. Grimethorpe again."

# 5

# THE RUE ST. HONORÉ AND THE RUE DE LA PAIX

*I think it was the cat.*

H.M.S. Pinafore

MR. PARKER sat disconsolate in a small *appartement* in the Rue St. Honoré. It was three o'clock in the afternoon. Paris was full of a subdued but cheerful autumn sunlight, but the room faced north, and was depressing, with its plain, dark furniture and its deserted air. It was a man's room, well appointed after the manner of a discreet club; a room that kept its dead owner's counsel imperturbably. Two large saddlebag chairs in crimson leather stood by the cold hearth. On the mantelpiece was a bronze clock, flanked by two polished German shells, a stone tobacco-jar, and an Oriental brass bowl containing a long-cold pipe. There were several excellent engravings in narrow pearwood frames, and the portrait in oils of a rather florid lady of the period of Charles II. The windowcurtains were crimson, and the floor covered with a solid Turkey carpet. Opposite the fireplace stood a tall mahogany bookcase with glass doors, containing a number of English and French classics, a large collection of books on history and international politics, various French novels, a number of works on military and sporting subjects, and a famous French edition of the *Decameron* with the additional plates. Under the window stood a large bureau.

Parker shook his head, took out a sheet of paper, and began to write a report. He had breakfasted on coffee and rolls at seven; he had made an exhaustive search of the flat; he had interviewed the concierge, the manager of the Crédit Lyonnais, and the Prefect of Police for the Quartier, and the result was very poor indeed.

Information obtained from Captain Cathcart's papers:

Before the war Denis Cathcart had undoubtedly been a rich man. He had considerable investments in Russia and Germany and a large share in a prosperous vineyard in Champagne. After coming into his property at the age of twenty-one he had concluded his three years' residence at Cambridge, and had then travelled a good deal, visiting persons of importance in various countries, and apparently studying with a view to a diplomatic career. During the period from 1913 to 1918 the story told by the books became intensely interesting, baffling, and depressing. At the outbreak of war he had taken a commission in the 15th ——shires. With the help of the chequebook, Parker reconstructed the whole economic life of a young British officer–clothes, horses, equipment, travelling, wine and dinners when on leave, bridge debts, rent of the flat in the Rue St. Honoré, club subscriptions, and what not. This outlay was strictly moderate and proportioned to his income. Receipted bills, neatly docketed, occupied one drawer of the bureau, and a careful comparison of these with the cheque book and the returned cheques revealed no discrepancy. But, beyond these, there appeared to have been another heavy drain upon Cathcart's resources. Beginning in 1913, certain large cheques, payable to self, appeared regularly at every quarter, and sometimes at shorter intervals. As to the destination of these sums, the bureau preserved the closest discretion; there were no receipts, no memoranda of their expenditure.

The great crash which in 1914 shook the credits of the world was mirrored in little in the pass-book. The credits from Russian and German sources stopped dead; those from the French shares slumped to a quarter of the original amount, as the tide of war washed over the vineyards and carried the workers away. For the first year or so there were substantial dividends from capital invested in French *rentes*; then came an ominous entry of 20,000 francs on the credit side of the account, and, six months after, another of 30,000 francs. After that the landslide followed fast. Parker could picture those curt notes from the Front, directing the sale of Government securities, as the savings of the past six years whirled away in the maelstrom of rising prices and collapsing currencies. The dividends grew less and less and ceased; then, more ominous still, came a series of debits representing the charges on renewal of promissory notes.

About 1918 the situation had become acute, and several entries showed a desperate attempt to put matters straight by gambling in foreign exchanges. There were purchases, through the bank, of German marks, Russian roubles, and Roumanian lei. Mr. Parker sighed sympathetically, when he saw this, thinking of £12 worth of these delusive specimens of the engraver's art laid up in his own desk at home. He knew them to be wastepaper, yet his tidy mind could not bear the thought of destroying them. Evidently Cathcart had found marks and roubles very broken reeds.

It was about this time that Cathcart's pass-book began to reveal the paying in of various sums in cash, some large, some small, at irregular dates and with no particular consistency. In December, 1919, there had been one of these amounting to as much as 35,000 francs. Parker at first supposed that these sums might represent dividends from some separate securities which Cathcart was handling for himself without passing them through the bank. He made a careful search of the room in the hope of finding either the bonds themselves or at least some memorandum concerning them, but the search was in vain, and he was forced to conclude either that Cathcart had deposited them in some secret place or that the credits in question represented some different source of income.

Cathcart had apparently contrived to be demobilised almost at once (owing, no doubt, to his previous frequentation of distinguished governmental personages), and to have taken a prolonged holiday on the Riviera. Subsequently a visit to London coincided with the acquisition of £700, which, converted into francs at the then rate of exchange, made a very respectable item in the account. From that time on, the outgoings and receipts presented a similar aspect and were more or less evenly balanced, the cheques to self becoming rather larger and more frequent as time went on, while during 1921 the income from the vineyard began to show signs of recovery.

Mr. Parker noted down all this information in detail, and, leaning back in his chair, looked round the flat. He felt, not for the first time, a distaste for his profession, which cut him off from the great masculine community whose members take each other for granted and respect their privacy. He relighted his pipe, which had gone out, and proceeded with his report.

Information obtained from Monsieur Turgeot, the manager of the Crédit Lyonnais, confirmed the evidence of the passbook in every particular.

Monsieur Cathcart had recently made all his payments in notes, usually in notes of small denominations. Once or twice he had had an overdraft–never very large, and always made up within a few months. He had, of course, suffered a diminution of income, like everybody else, but the account had never given the bank any uneasiness. At the moment it was some 14,000 francs on the right side. Monsieur Cathcart was always very agreeable, but not communicative–*très correct.*

Information obtained from the concierge:

One did not see much of Monsieur Cathcart, but he was *très gentil.* He never failed to say, "*Bon jour, Bourgois,*" when he came in or out. He received visitors sometimes–gentlemen in evening dress. One made card-parties. Monsieur Bourgois had never directed any ladies to his rooms; except once, last February, when he had given a lunch-party to some ladies *très comme il faut* who brought with them his fiancée, *une jolie blonde.* Monsieur Cathcart used the flat as a *pied à terre*, and often he would shut it up and go away for several weeks or months. (He was *un jeune homme très rangé*). He had never kept a valet. Madame Leblanc, the cousin of one's late wife, kept his *appartement* clean. Madame Leblanc was very respectable. But certainly monsieur might have Madame Leblanc's address.

Information obtained from Madame Leblanc:

Monsieur Cathcart was a charming young man, and very pleasant to work for. Very generous and took a great interest in the family. Madame Leblanc was desolated to hear that he was dead, and on the eve of his marriage to the daughter of the English milady. Madame Leblanc had seen Mademoiselle last year when she visited Monsieur Cathcart in Paris; she considered the young lady very fortunate. Very few young men were as serious as Monsieur Cathcart, especially when they were so good-looking. Madame Leblanc had had experience of young men, and she could relate many histories if she were disposed, but none of Monsieur Cathcart. He would not always be using his rooms; he had the habit of letting her know when he would be at home, and she then went round to put the flat in order. He kept his things very tidy; he was not like English gentlemen in that respect. Madame Leblanc had known many of them, who kept their affairs *sens dessus dessous.* Monsieur Cathcart was always very well dressed; he was particular about his bath; he was like a woman for his toilet, the poor gentleman. And so he was dead. *Le pauvre garçon!* Really it had taken away Madame Leblanc's appetite.

Information obtained from Monsieur the Prefect of Police:

Absolutely nothing. Monsieur Cathcart had never caught the eye of the police in any way. With regard to the sums of money mentioned by Monsieur Parker, if monsieur would give him the numbers of some of the notes, efforts would be made to trace them.

Where had the money gone? Parker could think only of two destinations–an irregular establishment or a blackmailer. Certainly a handsome man like Cathcart might very well have a woman or two in his life, even without the knowledge of the concierge. Certainly a man who habitually cheated at cards–if he did cheat at cards–might very well have got himself into the power of somebody who knew too much. It was noteworthy that his mysterious receipts in cash began just as his economies were exhausted; it seemed likely that they represented irregular gains from gambling–in the casinos, on the exchange, or, if Denver's story had any truth in it, from crooked play. On the whole, Parker rather inclined to the blackmailing theory. It fitted in with the rest of the business, as he and Lord Peter had reconstructed it at Riddlesdale.

Two or three things, however, still puzzled Parker. Why should the blackmailer have been trailing about the Yorkshire moors with a cycle and side-car? Whose was the green-eyed cat? It was a valuable trinket. Had Cathcart offered it as part of his payment? That seemed somehow foolish. One could only suppose that the blackmailer had tossed it away with contempt. The cat was in Parker's possession, and it occurred to him that it might be worth while to get a jeweller to estimate its value. But the side-car was a difficulty, the cat was a difficulty, and, more than all, Lady Mary was a difficulty.

Why had Lady Mary lied at the inquest? For that she had lied, Parker had no manner of doubt. He disbelieved the whole story of the second shot which had awakened her. What had brought her to the conservatory door at three o'clock in the morning? Whose was the suit-case—if it was a suit-case—that had lain concealed among the cactus-plants? Why this prolonged nervous breakdown, with no particular symptoms, which prevented Lady Mary from giving evidence before the magistrate or answering her brother's inquiries? Could Lady Mary have been present at the interview in the shrubbery? If so, surely Wimsey and he would have found her footprints. Was she in league with the blackmailer? That was an unpleasant thought. Was she endeavouring to help her fiancé? She had an allowance of her own—a generous one, as Parker knew from the Duchess. Could she have tried to assist Cathcart with money? But in that case, why not tell all she knew? The worst about Cathcart—always supposing that card-sharping were the worst—was now matter of public knowledge, and the man himself was dead. If she knew the truth, why did she not come forward and save her brother?

And at this point he was visited by a thought even more unpleasant. If, after all, it had not been Denver whom Mrs. Marchbanks had heard in the library, but someone else—someone who had likewise an appointment with the blackmailer—someone who was on his side as against Cathcart—who knew that there might be danger in the interview. Had he himself paid proper attention to the grass lawn between the house and the thicket? Might Thursday morning perhaps have revealed here and there a trodden blade that rain and sap had since restored to uprightness? Had Peter and he found *all* the footsteps in the wood? Had some more trusted hand fired that shot at close quarters? Once again—*whose was the green-eyed cat?*

Surmises and surmises, each uglier than the last, thronged into Parker's mind. He took up a photograph of Cathcart with which Wimsey had supplied him, and looked at it long and curiously. It was a dark, handsome face; the hair was black, with a slight wave, the nose large and well shaped, the big, dark eyes at once pleasing and arrogant. The mouth was good, though a little thick, with a hint of sensuality in its close curves; the chin showed a cleft. Frankly, Parker confessed to himself, it did not attract him; he would have been inclined to dismiss the man as a "Byronic blighter," but experience told him that this kind of face might be powerful with a woman, either for love or hatred.

Coincidences usually have the air of being practical jokes on the part of Providence. Mr. Parker was shortly to be favoured—if the term is a suitable one—with a special display of this Olympian humour. As a rule, that kind of thing did not happen to him; it was more in Wimsey's line. Parker had made his way from modest beginnings to a respectable appointment in the C.I.D.

rather by a combination of hard work, shrewdness, and caution than by spectacular displays of happy guesswork or any knack for taking fortune's tide at the flood. This time, however, he was given a "leading" from above, and it was only part of the nature of things and men that he should have felt distinctly ungrateful for it.

He finished his report, replaced everything tidily in the desk and went round to the police-station to arrange with the Prefect about the keys and the fixing of the seals. It was still early evening and not too cold; he determined, therefore, to banish gloomy thoughts by a *café-cognac* in the Boul' Mich', followed by a stroll through the Paris of the shops. Being of a kindly, domestic nature, indeed, he turned over in his mind the idea of buying something Parisian for his elder sister, who was unmarried and lived a rather depressing life in Barrow-in-Furness. Parker knew that she would take pathetic delight in some filmy scrap of lace underwear which no one but herself would ever see. Mr. Parker was not the kind of man to be deterred by the difficulty of buying ladies' underwear in a foreign language; he was not very imaginative. He remembered that a learned judge had one day asked in court what a camisole was, and recollected that there had seemed to be nothing particularly embarrassing about the garment when explained. He determined that he would find a really Parisian shop, and ask for a camisole. That would give him a start, and then mademoiselle would show him other things without being asked further.

Accordingly, towards six o'clock, he was strolling along the Rue de la Paix with a little carton under his arm. He had spent rather more money than he intended, but he had acquired knowledge. He knew for certain what a camisole was, and he had grasped for the first time in his life that crêpe-de-Chine had no recognisable relation to crape, and was astonishingly expensive for its bulk. The young lady had been charmingly sympathetic, and, without actually insinuating anything, had contrived to make her customer feel just a little bit of a dog. He felt that his French accent was improving. The street was crowded with people, slowly sauntering past the brilliant shop-windows. Mr. Parker stopped and gazed nonchalantly over a gorgeous display of jewellery, as though hesitating between a pearl necklace valued at 80,000 francs and a pendant of diamonds and aquamarines set in platinum.

And there, balefully winking at him from under a label inscribed "*Bonne fortune*" hung a green-eyed cat.

The cat stared at Mr. Parker, and Mr. Parker stared at the cat. It was no ordinary cat. It was a cat with a personality. Its tiny arched body sparkled with diamonds, and its platinum paws, set close together, and its erect and glittering tail were instinct in every line with the sensuous delight of friction against some beloved object. Its head, cocked slightly to one side, seemed to demand a titillating finger under the jaw. It was a minute work of art, by no journeyman hand. Mr. Parker fished in his pocket-book. He looked from the cat in his hand to the cat in the window. They were alike. They were astonishingly alike. They were identical. Mr. Parker marched into the shop.

"I have here," said Mr. Parker to the young man at the counter, "a diamond cat which greatly resembles one which I perceive in your window. Could you have the obligingness to inform me what would be the value of such a cat?"

The young man replied instantly:

"But certainly, monsieur, the price of the cat is 5,000 francs. It is, as you perceive, made of the finest materials. Moreover, it is the work of an artist; it is worth more than the market value of the stones."

"It is, I suppose, a mascot?"

"Yes, monsieur; it brings great good luck, especially at cards. Many ladies buy these little objects. We have here other mascots, but all of this special design are of similar quality and price. Monsieur may rest assured that his cat is a cat of pedigree."

"I suppose that such cats are everywhere obtainable in Paris," said Mr. Parker nonchalantly.

"But no, monsieur. If you desire to match your cat I recommend you to do it quickly. Monsieur Briquet had only a score of these cats to begin with, and there are now only three left, including the one in the window. I believe that he will not make any more. To repeat a thing often is to vulgarise it. There will, of course, be other cats——"

"I don't want another cat," said Mr. Parker, suddenly interested. "Do I understand you to say that cats such as this are only sold by Monsieur Briquet? That my cat originally came from this shop?"

"Undoubtedly, monsieur, it is one of our cats. These little animals are made by a workman of ours—a genius who is responsible for many of our finest articles."

"It would, I imagine, be impossible to find out to whom this cat was originally sold?"

"If it was sold over the counter for cash it would be difficult, but if it was entered in our books it might not be impossible to discover, if monsieur desired it."

"I do desire it very much," said Parker, producing his card. "I am an agent of the British police, and it is of great importance that I should know to whom this cat originally belonged."

"In that case," said the young man, "I shall do better to inform monsieur the proprietor."

He carried away the card into the back premises, and presently emerged with a stout gentleman, whom he introduced as Monsieur Briquet.

In Monsieur Briquet's private office the books of the establishment were brought out and laid on the desk.

"You will understand, monsieur," said Monsieur Briquet, "that I can only inform you of the names and addresses of such purchasers of these cats as have had an account sent them. It is, however, unlikely than an object of such value was paid for in cash. Still, with rich Anglo-Saxons, such an incident may occur. We need not go back further than the beginning of the year, when these cats were made." He ran a podgy finger down the pages of the ledger. "The first purchase was on January 19th."

Mr. Parker noted various names and addresses, and at the end of half an hour Monsieur Briquet said in a final manner:

"That is all, monsieur. How many names have you there?"

"Thirteen," said Parker.

"And there are still three cats in stock—the original number was twenty—so that four must have been sold for cash. If monsieur wishes to verify the matter we can consult the day-book."

The seach in the day-book was longer and more tiresome, but eventually four cats were duly found to have been sold; one on January 31st, another on February 6th, the third on May 17th, and the last on August 9th.

Mr. Parker had risen, and embarked upon a long string of compliments and thanks, when a sudden association of ideas and dates prompted him to hand Cathcart's photograph to Monsieur Briquet and ask whether he recognised it.

Monsieur Briquet shook his head.

"I am sure he is not one of our regular customers," he said, "and I have a very good memory for faces. I make a point of knowing anyone who has any considerable account with me. And this gentleman has not everybody's face. But we will ask my assistants."

The majority of the staff failed to recognise the photograph, and Parker was on the point of putting it back in his pocket-book when a young lady, who had just finished selling an engagement-ring to an obese and elderly Jew, arrived, and said, without any hesitation:

"*Mais oui, je l'ai vu, ce monsieur-là*. It is the Englishman who bought a diamond cat for the *jolie blonde.*"

"Mademoiselle," said Parker eagerly, "I beseech you to do me the favour to remember all about it."

"*Parfaitement,*" she said. "It is not the face one would forget, especially when one is a woman. The gentleman bought a diamond cat and paid for it—no, I am wrong. It was the lady who bought it, and I remember now to have been surprised that she should pay like that at once in money, because ladies do not usually carry such large sums. The gentleman bought too. He bought a diamond and tortoiseshell comb for the lady to wear, and then she said she must give him something *pour porter bonheur*, and asked me for a mascot that was good for cards. I showed her some jewels more suitable for a gentleman, but she saw these cats and fell in love with them, and said he should have a cat and nothing else; she was sure it would bring him good hands. She asked me if it was not so, and I said, 'Undoubtedly, and monsieur must be sure never to play without it,' and he laughed very much, and promised always to have it upon him when he was playing."

"And how was she, this lady?"

"Blonde, monsieur, and very pretty; rather tall and svelte, and very well dressed. A big hat and dark blue costume. *Quoi encore? Voyons*—yes, she was a foreigner."

"English?"

"I do not know. She spoke French very, very well, almost like a French person, but she had just the little suspicion of accent."

"What language did she speak with the gentleman?"

"French, monsieur. You see, we were speaking together, and they both appealed to me continually, and so all the talk was in French. The gentleman spoke French *à merveille*, it was only by his clothes and a *je ne sais quoi* in his appearance that I guessed he was English. The lady spoke equally fluently, but one remarked just the accent from time to time. Of course, I went away from them once or twice to get goods from the window, and they talked then; I do not know in what language."

"Now, mademoiselle, can you tell me how long ago this was?"

"*Ah mon Dieu, ça c'est plus difficile. Monsieur sait que les jours se suivent et se ressemblent. Voyons.*"

"We can see by the day-book," put in Monsieur Briquet, "on what occasion a diamond comb was sold with a diamond cat."

"Of course," said Parker hastily. "Let us go back."

They went back and turned to the January volume, where they found no help. But on February 6th they read:

Peigne en écaille et diamants . . . f.7,500
Chat en diamants (Dessin C-5) . . f.5,000

"That settles it," said Parker gloomily.

"Monsieur does not appear content," suggested the jeweller.

"Monsieur," said Parker, "I am more grateful than I can say for your very great kindness, but I will frankly confess that, of all the twelve months in the year, I had rather it had been any other."

Parker found this whole episode so annoying to his feelings that he bought two comic papers and, carrying them away to Boudet's at the corner of the Rue Auguste Léopold, read them solemnly through over his dinner, by way of settling his mind. Then, returning to his modest hotel, he ordered a drink, and sat down to compose a letter to Lord Peter. It was a slow job, and he did not appear to relish it very much. His concluding paragraph was as follows:

"I have put all these things down for you without any comment. You will be able to draw your own inferences as well as I can—better, I hope, for my own are perplexing and worrying me no end. They may be all rubbish—I hope they are; I daresay something will turn up at your end to put quite a different interpretation upon the facts. But I do feel that they must be cleared up. I would offer to hand over the job, but another man might jump at conclusions even faster than I do, and make a mess of it. But of course, if you say so, I will be taken suddenly ill at any moment. Let me know. If you think I'd better go on grubbing about over here, can you get hold of a photograph of Lady Mary Wimsey, and find out if possible about the diamond comb and the green-eyed cat—also at exactly what date Lady Mary was in Paris in February. Does she speak French as well as you do? Let me know how you are getting on.

"Yours ever,

"Charles Parker."

He re-read the letter and report carefully and sealed them up. Then he wrote to his sister, did up his parcel neatly, and rang for the valet de chambre.

"I want this letter sent off at once, registered," he said, "and the parcel is to go to-morrow as a *colis postal*."

After which he went to bed, and read himself to sleep with a commentary on the Epistle to the Hebrews.

* * * * *

Lord Peter's reply arrived by return:

"Dear Charles,—Don't worry. I don't like the look of things myself frightfully, but I'd rather you tackled the business than anyone else. As you say, the ordinary police bloke doesn't mind whom he arrests, provided he arrests someone, and is altogether a most damnable fellow to have poking into one's affairs. I'm putting my mind to getting my brother cleared—that *is* the first consideration, after all, and really anything else would be better than having Jerry hanged for a crime he didn't commit. Whoever did it, it's better the right person should suffer than the wrong. So go ahead.

"I enclose two photographs—all I can lay hands on for the moment. The one in nursing-kit is rather rotten, and the other's all smothered up in a big hat.

"I had a damn' queer little adventure here on Wednesday, which I'll tell you about when we meet. I've found a woman who obviously knows more than she ought, and a most promising ruffian—only I'm afraid he's got an alibi. Also I've got a faint suggestion of a clue about No. 10. Nothing much happened at Northallerton, except that Jerry was of course committed for trial. My mother is here, thank God! and I'm hoping she'll get some sense out of Mary, but she's been worse the last two days—Mary, I mean, not my mother—beastly sick and all that sort of thing. Dr. Thingummy—who is an ass—can't make it out. Mother says it's as clear as noonday, and she'll stop it if I have patience a day or two. I made her ask about the comb and the cat. M. denies the cat altogether, but admits to a diamond comb bought in Paris—says she bought it herself. It's in town—I'll get it and send it on. She says she can't remember where she bought it, has lost the bill, but it didn't cost anything like 7,500 francs. She was in Paris from February 2nd to February 20th. My chief business now is to see Lubbock and clear up a little matter concerning silver sand.

"The Assizes will be the first week in November—in fact, the end of next week. This rushes things a bit, but it doesn't matter, because they can't try him there; nothing will matter but the Grand Jury, who are bound to find a true bill on the face of it. After that we can hang matters up as long as we like. It's going to be a deuce of a business, Parliament sitting and all. Old Biggs is fearfully perturbed under that marble outside of his. I hadn't really grasped what a fuss it was to try peers. It's only happened about once in every sixty years, and the procedure's about as old as Queen Elizabeth. They have to appoint a Lord High Steward for the occasion, and God knows what. They have to make it frightfully clear in the Commission that it *is* only for the occasion, because, somewhere about Richard III's time, the L.H.S. was such a terrifically big pot that he got to ruling the roost. So when Henry IV came to the throne, and the office came into the hands of the Crown, he jolly well kept it there, and now they only appoint a man *pro tem.* for the Coronation and shows like Jerry's. The King always pretends not to know there isn't a L.H.S. till the time comes, and is no end surprised at having to think of somebody to take on the job. Did you know all this? I didn't. I got it out of Biggy.

"Cheer up. Pretend you don't know that any of these people are relations of mine. My mother sends you her kindest regards and what not, and hopes she'll see you again soon. Bunter sends something correct and respectful; I forget what.

"Yours in the brotherhood of detection.

"P.W."

It may as well be said at once that the evidence from the photographs was wholly inconclusive.

# 6

# MARY QUITE CONTRARY

*I am striving to take into public life what any man gets from his mother.*
Lady Astor

ON THE opening day of the York Assizes, the Grand Jury brought in a true bill, against Gerald, Duke of Denver, for murder. Gerald, Duke of Denver, being accordingly produced in the court, the Judge affected to discover –what, indeed, every newspaper in the country had been announcing to the world for the last fortnight–that he, being but a common or garden judge with a plebeian jury, was incompetent to try a peer of the realm. He added, however, that he would make it his business to inform the Lord Chancellor (who also, for the last fortnight, had been secretly calculating the accommodation in the Royal Gallery and choosing lords to form the Select Committee). Order being taken accordingly, the noble prisoner was led away.

* * * * *

A day or two later, in the gloom of a London afternoon, Mr. Charles Parker rang the bell of a second-floor flat at No. 110 Piccadilly. The door was open by Bunter, who informed him with a gracious smile that Lord Peter had stepped out for a few minutes but was expecting him, and would he kindly come in and wait.

"We only came up this morning," added the valet, "and are not quite straight yet, sir, if you will excuse us. Would you feel inclined for a cup of tea?"

Parker accepted the offer, and sank luxuriously into a corner of the Chesterfield. After the extraordinary discomfort of French furniture there was solace in the enervating springiness beneath him, the cushions behind his head, and Wimsey's excellent cigarettes. What Bunter had meant by saying that things were "not quite straight yet" he could not divine. A leaping wood fire was merrily reflected in the spotless surface of the black baby grand; the mellow calf bindings of Lord Peter's rare editions glowed softly against the black and primrose walls; the vases were filled with tawny chrysanthemums; the latest editions of all the papers were on the table–as though the owner had never been absent.

Over his tea Mr. Parker drew out the photographs of Lady Mary and Denis Cathcart from his breast pocket. He stood them up against the teapot and stared at them, looking from one to the other as if trying to force a meaning from their faintly smirking, self-conscious gaze. He referred again to his Paris notes, ticking off various points with a pencil. "Damn!" said Mr. Parker, gazing at Lady Mary. "Damn–damn–damn––"

The train of thought he was pursuing was an extraordinarily interesting one. Image after image, each rich in suggestion, crowded into his mind. Of course, one couldn't think properly in Paris–it was so uncomfortable and the houses were central heated. Here, where so many problems had been unravelled, there was a good fire. Cathcart bad been sitting before the fire. Of course, he wanted to think out a problem. When cats sat staring into the fire they were thinking out problems. It was odd he should not have thought of that before. When the green-eyed cat sat before the fire one sank right down into a sort of rich, black, velvety suggestiveness which was most important. It was luxurious to be able to think so lucidly as this, because otherwise it would be a pity to exceed the speed limit–and the black moors were reeling by so fast. But now he had really got the formula he wouldn't forget it again. The connection was just there–close, thick, richly coherent.

"The glass-blower's cat is bompstable," said Mr. Parker aloud and distinctly.

"I'm charmed to hear it," replied Lord Peter, with a friendly grin. "Had a good nap, old man?"

"I–what?" said Mr. Parker. "Hullo! Watcher mean, nap? I had got hold of a most important train of thought, and you've put it out of my head. What was it? Cat–cat–cat––" he groped wildly.

"You *said* 'The glass-blower's cat is bompstable,' " retorted Lord Peter. "It's a perfectly rippin' word, but I don't know what you mean by it."

"Bompstable?" said Mr. Parker, blushing slightly. "Bomp–oh, well, perhaps you're right–I may have dozed off. But, you know, I thought I'd just got the clue to the whole thing. I attached the greatest importance to that phrase. Even now–– No, now I come to think of it, my train of thought doesn't seem quite to hold together. What a pity. I thought it was so lucid."

"Never mind," said Lord Peter. "Just back?"

"Crossed last night. Any news?"

"Lots."

"Good?"

"No."

Parker's eyes wandered to the photographs.

"I don't believe it," he said obstinately. "I'm damned if I'm going to believe a word of it."

"A word of what?"

"Of whatever it is."

"You'll have to believe it, Charles, as far as it goes," said his friend softly, filling his pipe with decided little digs of the fingers. "I don't say"–dig–"that Mary"–dig–"shot Cathcart"–dig, dig–"but she has lied"–dig–"again and again." –Dig, dig–"She knows who did it"–dig–"she was prepared for it"–dig–"she's malingering and lying to keep the fellow shielded"–dig–"and we shall have to make her speak." Here he struck a match and lit the pipe in a series of angry little puffs.

"If you can think," said Mr. Parker, with some heat, "that that woman"–he indicated the photographs–"had any hand in murdering Cathcart, I don't care what your evidence is, you–hang it all, Wimsey, she's your own sister."

"Gerald is my brother," said Wimsey quietly. "You don't suppose I'm exactly enjoying this business, do you? But I think we shall get along very much better if we try to keep our tempers."

"I'm awfully sorry," said Parker. "Can't think why I said that–rotten bad form–beg pardon, old man."

"The best thing we can do," said Wimsey, "is to look the evidence in the face, however ugly. And I don't mind admittin' that some of it's a positive gargoyle.

"My mother turned up at Riddlesdale on Friday. She marched upstairs at once and took possession of Mary, while I drooped about in the hall and teased the cat, and generally made a nuisance of myself. *You* know. Presently old Dr. Thorpe called. I went and sat on the chest on the landing. Presently the bell rings and Ellen comes upstairs. Mother and Thorpe popped out and caught her just outside Mary's room, and they jibber-jabbered a lot, and presently mother came barging down the passage to the bathroom with her heels tapping and her earrings simply dancing with irritation. I sneaked after 'em to the bathroom door, but I couldn't see anything, because they were blocking the doorway, but I heard mother say, 'There, now, what did I tell you'; and Ellen said, 'Lawks! your grace, who'd 'a' thought it?'; and my mother said, 'All I can say is, if I had to depend on you people to save me from being murdered with arsenic or that other stuff with the name like anemones *–you know what I mean–that that very attractive-looking man with the preposterous beard used to make away with his wife and mother-in-law (who was vastly the more attractive of the two, poor thing), I might be being cut up and analysed by Dr. Spilsbury now–such a horrid, distasteful job he must have of it, poor man, and the poor little rabbits, too.' " Wimsey paused for breath, and Parker laughed in spite of his anxiety.

"I won't vouch for the exact words," said Wimsey, "But it was to that effect–you know my mother's style. Old Thorpe tried to look dignified, but mother ruffled up like a little hen and said, looking beadily at him: 'In *my* day we called that kind of thing hysterics and naughtiness. *We* didn't let girls pull the wool over our eyes like that. I suppose *you* call it a neurosis, or a suppressed desire, or a reflex, and coddle it. You might have let that silly chlld make herself really ill. You are all perfectly ridiculous, and no more fit to take care of yourselves than a lot of babies–not but what there are plenty of poor little things in the slums that look after whole families and show more sense than the lot of you put together. I am very angry with Mary, advertising herself in this way, and she's not to be pitied.' You know," said Wimsey, "I think there's often a great deal in what one's mother says."

"I believe you," said Parker.

"Well, I got hold of mother afterwards and asked her what it was all about. She said Mary wouldn't tell her anything about herself or her illness; just asked to be left alone. Then Thorpe came along and talked about nervous shock–said he couldn't understand these fits of sickness, or the way Mary's temperature hopped about. Mother listened, and told him to go and see what the temperature was now. Which he did, and in the middle mother called him away to the dressing-table. But, bein' a wily old bird, you see, she kept her eyes on the looking-glass, and nipped round just in time to catch Mary stimulatin' the thermometer to terrific leaps on the hot-water bottle."

"Well, I'm damned!" said Parker.

"So was Thorpe. All mother said was, that if he wasn't too old a bird yet to be taken in by that hoary trick he'd no business to be gettin' himself up as a grey-haired family practitioner. So then she asked the girl about the sick fits–when they happened, and how often, and was it after meals or before, and so on, and at last she got out of them that it generally happened a bit after breakfast and occasionally at other times. Mother said she couldn't make it out at first, because she'd hunted all over the room for bottles and things, till at last she asked who made the bed, thinkin', you see, Mary might have

*Antimony? The Duchess appears to have had Dr. Pritchard's case in mind.

hidden something under the mattress. So Ellen said she usually made it while Mary had her bath. 'When's that?' says mother. 'Just before her breakfast,' bleats the girl. 'God forgive you all for a set of nincompoops,' says my mother. 'Why didn't you say so before?' So away they all trailed to the bathroom, and there, sittin' up quietly on the bathroom shelf among the bath salts and the Elliman's embrocation and the Kruschen feelings and the toothbrushes and things, was the family bottle of ipecacuanha–three-quarters empty! Mother said–well, I told you what she said. By the way, how do you spell ipecacuanha?"

Mr. Parker spelt it.

"Damn you!" said Lord Peter. "I *did* think I'd stumped you that time. I believe you went and looked it up beforehand. *No* decent-minded person would know how to spell ipecacuanha out of his own head. Anyway, as you were saying, it's easy to see which side of the famlly has the detective instinct."

"I didn't say so———"

"I know. Why didn't you? I think my mother's talents deserve a little acknowledgment. I said so to her, as a matter of fact, and she replied in these memorable words: 'My dear child, you can give it a long name if you like, but I'm an old-fashioned woman and I call it mother-wit, and it's so rare for a man to have it that if he does you write a book about him and call him Sherlock Holmes.' However, apart from all that, I said to mother (in private, of course), 'It's all very well but I can't believe that Mary has been going to all this trouble to make herself horribly sick and frighten us all just to show off. Surely she isn't that sort.' Mother looked at me as steady as an owl, and quoted a whole lot of examples of hysteria, ending up with the servant-girl who threw paraffin about all over somebody's house to make them think it was haunted, and finished up–that if all these new-fangled doctors went out of their way to invent subconsciousness and kleptomania, and complexes and other fancy descriptions to explain away when people had done naughty things, she thought one might just as well take advantage of the fact."

"Wimsey," said Parker, much excited, "did she mean she suspected something?"

"My dear old chap," replied Lord Peter, "whatever can be known about Mary by putting two and two together my mother knows. I told her all *we* knew up to that point, and she took it all in, in her funny way, you know, never answering anything directly, and then she put her head on one side and said: 'If Mary had listened to me, and done something useful instead of that V.A.D. work, which never came to much, if you ask me–not that I have anything against V.A.D.'s in a general way, but that silly woman Mary worked under was the most terrible snob on God's earth–and there were very much more sensible things which Mary might really have done well, only that she was so crazy to get to London–I shall always say it was the fault of that ridiculous club–what could you expect of a place where you ate such horrible food, all packed into an underground cellar painted pink and talking away at the tops of their voices, and never any evening dress–only Soviet jumpers and side-whiskers. Anyhow, I've told that silly old man what to say about it, and they'll never be able to think of a better explanation for themselves.' Indeed, you know," said Peter, "I think if any of them start getting inquisitive, they'll have mother down on them like a ton of bricks."

"What do you really think yourself?" asked Parker.

"I haven't come yet to the unpleasantest bit of the lot," said Peter. "I've only just heard it, and it did give me a nasty jar, I'll admit. Yesterday I got a letter from Lubbock saying he would like to see me, so I trotted up here and dropped in on him this morning. You remember I sent him a stain off one of Mary's skirts which Bunter had cut out for me? I had taken a squint at it myself, and didn't like the look of it, so I sent it up to Lubbock, *ex abundantia cauteloe;* and I'm sorry to say he confirms me. It's human blood, Charles, and I'm afraid it's Cathcart's."

"But–I've lost the thread of this a bit."

"Well, the skirt must have got stained the day Cathcart–died, as that was the last day on which the party was out on the moors, and if it had been there earlier Ellen would have cleaned it off. Afterwards Mary strenuously resisted Ellen's efforts to take the skirt away, and made an amateurish effort to tidy it up herself with soap. So I think we may conclude that Mary knew the stains were there, and wanted to avoid discovery. She told Ellen that the blood was from a grouse–which must have been a deliberate untruth."

"Perhaps," said Parker, struggling against hope to make out a case for Lady Mary, "she only said, 'Oh! one of the birds must have bled,' or something like that."

"I don't believe," said Peter, "that one could get a great patch of human blood on one's clothes like that and not know what it was. She must have knelt right in it. It was three or four inches across."

Parker shook his head dismally, and consoled himself by making a note.

"Well, now," went on Peter, "on Wednesday night everybody comes in and dines, and goes to bed except Cathcart, who rushes out and stays out. At 11:50 the gamekeeper, Hardraw, hears a shot which may very well have been fired in the clearing where the–well, let's say the accident–took place. The time also agrees with the medical evidence about Cathcart having already been dead three or four hours when he was examined at 4:30. Very well. At 3 a.m. Jerry comes home from somewhere or other and finds the body. As he is bending over it, Mary arrives in the most apropos manner from the house in her coat and cap and walking shoes. Now what is her story? She says that at three o'clock she was awakened by a shot. Now nobodv else heard that shot, and we have the evidence of Mrs. Pettigrew-Robinson, who slept in the next room to Mary, with her window open according to her immemorial custom, that she lay broad awake from 2 a.m. till a little after 3 a.m., when the alarm was given, and heard no shot. According to Mary, the shot was loud enough to waken her on the other side of the building. It's odd, isn't it, that the person already awake should swear so positively that she heard nothing of a noise loud enough to waken a healthy young sleeper next door? And, in any case, *if* that was the shot that killed Cathcart, he can barely have been dead when my brother found him–and again, in that case, how was there time for him to be carried up from the shrubbery to the conservatory?"

"We've been over all this ground," said Parker, with an expression of distaste. "We agreed that we couldn't attach any importance to the story of the shot."

"I'm afraid we've got to attach a great deal of importance to it," said Lord Peter gravely. "Now what does Mary do? Either she thought the shot——"

"There was no shot."

"I know that. But I'm examining the discrepancies of her story. She said she did not give the alarm because she thought it was probably only poachers. But, if it was poachers, it would be absurd to go down and investigate. So she explains that she thought it might be burglars. Now how does she dress to go and look for burglars? What would you or I have done? I think we would have taken a dressing-gown, a stealthy kind of pair of slippers, and perhaps a poker or a stout stick—not a pair of walking shoes, a coat, and a cap, of all things!"

"It was a wet night," mumbled Parker.

"My dear chap, if it's burglars you're looking for you don't expect to go and hunt them round the garden. Your first thought is that they're getting into the house, and your idea is to slip down quietly and survey them from the staircase or behind the dining-room door. Anyhow, fancy a present-day girl, who rushes about bareheaded in all weathers, stopping to embellish herself in a cap for a burglar-hunt—damn it all, Charles, it won't wash, you know! And she walks straight off to the conservatory and comes upon the corpse, exactly as if she knew where to look for it beforehand."

Parker shook his head again.

"Well, now. She sees Gerald stooping over Cathcart's body. What does she say? Does she ask what's the matter? Does she ask who it is? She exclaims: 'O God! Gerald, you've killed him,' and *then* she says, as if on second thoughts, 'Oh, it's Denis! What has happened? Has there been an accident?' Now, does that strike you as natural?"

"No. But it rather suggests to me that it wasn't Cathcart she expected to see there, but somebody else."

"Does it? It rather sounds to me as if she was pretending not to know who it was. First she says, 'You've killed him!' and then, recollecting that she isn't supposed to know who 'he' is, she says, 'Why, it's Denis!' "

"In any case, then, if her first exclamation was genuine, she didn't expect to find the man dead."

"No—no—we must remember that. The death *was* a surprise. Very well. Then Gerald sends Mary up for help. And here's where a little bit of evidence comes in that you picked up and sent along. Do you remember what Mrs. Pettigrew-Robinson said to you in the train?"

"About the door slamming on the landing, do you mean?"

"Yes. Now I'll tell you something that happened to me the other morning. I was burstin' out of the bathroom in my usual breezy way when I caught myself a hell of a whack on that old chest on the landin', and the lid lifted up and shut down, *plonk!* That gave me an idea, and I thought I'd have a squint inside. I'd got the lid up and was lookin' at some sheets and stuff that were folded up at the bottom, when I heard a sort of gasp, and there was Mary, starin' at me, as white as a ghost. She gave me a turn, by Jove, but nothin' like the turn I'd given her. Well, she wouldn't say anything to me, and got hysterical, and I hauled her back to her room. But I'd seen something on those sheets."

"What?"

"Silver sand."

"Silver——"

"D'you remember those cacti in the greenhouse, and the place where somebody'd put a suit-case or something down?"

"Yes."

"Well, there was a lot of silver sand scattered about—the sort people stick round some kinds of bulbs and things."

"And that was inside the chest too?"

"Yes. Wait a moment. After the noise Mrs. Pettigrew-Robinson heard, Mary woke up Freddy and then the Pettigrew-Robinsons—and then what?"

"She locked herself into her room."

"Yes. And shortly afterwards she came down and joined the others in the conservatory, and it was at this point everybody remembered noticing that she was wearing a cap and coat and walking shoes over pyjamas and bare feet."

"You are suggesting," said Parker, "that Lady Mary was already awake and dressed at three o'clock, that she went out by the conservatory door with her suit-case, expecting to meet the—the murderer of her—damn it, Wimsey!"

"We needn't go so far as that," said Peter; "we decided that she *didn't* expect to find Cathcart dead."

"No. Well, she went, presumably to meet somebody."

"Shall we say, *pro tem.*, she went to meet No. 10?" suggested Wimsey softly.

"I suppose we may as well say so. When she turned on the torch and saw the Duke stooping over Cathcart she thought—by Jove, Wimsey, I was right after all! When she said, 'You've killed him!' she meant No. 10—she thought it was No. 10's body."

"Of course!" cried Wimsey. "I'm a fool! Yes. Then she said 'It's Denis—what has happened?' That's quite clear. And, meanwhile, what did she do with the suit-case?"

"I see it all now," cried Parker. "When she saw that the body wasn't the body of No. 10 she realised that No. 10 must be the murderer. So her game was to prevent anybody knowing that No. 10 had been there. So she shoved the suit-case behind the cacti. Then, when she went upstairs, she pulled it out again, and hid it in the oak chest on the landing. She couldn't take it to her room, of course, because if anybody'd heard her come upstairs it would seem odd that she should run to her room before calling the others. Then she knocked up Arbuthnot and the Pettigrew-Robinsons—she'd be in the dark, and they'd be flustered and wouldn't see exactly what she had on. Then she escaped from Mrs. P., ran into her room, took off the skirt in which she had knelt by Cathcart's side, and the rest of her clothes, and put on her pyjamas and the cap, which somebody might have noticed, and the coat, which they *must* have noticed, and the shoes, which had probably left footmarks already. Then she could go down and show herself. Meantime she'd concocted the burglar story for the Coroner's benefit."

"That's about it," said Peter. "I suppose she was so desperately anxious to throw us off the scent of No. 10 that it never occurred to her that her story was going to help implicate her brother."

"She realised it at the inquest," said Parker eagerly. "Don't you remember how hastily she grasped at the suicide theory?"

"And when she found that she was simply saving her—well, No. 10—in order to hang her brother, she lost her head, took to her bed, and refused to give any evidence at all. Seems to me there's an extra allowance of fools in my family," said Peter gloomily.

"Well, what could she have done, poor girl?" asked Parker. He had been growing almost cheerful again. "Anyway, she's cleared——"

"After a fashion," said Peter, "but we're not out of the wood yet by a long way. Why is she hand-in-glove with No. 10 who is at least a blackmailer if not a murderer? How did Gerald's revolver come on the scene? And the green-eyed cat? How much did Mary know of that meeting between No. 10 and Denis Cathcart? And if she was seeing and meeting the man she might have put the revolver into his hands any time."

"No, no," said Parker. "Wimsey, don't think such ugly things as that."

"Hell!" cried Peter, exploding. "I'll have the truth of this beastly business if we all go to the gallows together!"

At this moment Bunter entered with a telegram addressed to Wimsey. Lord Peter read as follows:

"Party traced London; seen Marylebone Friday. Further information from Scotland Yard.–POLICE-SUPERINTENDENT GOSLING, Ripley."

"Good egg!" cried Wimsey. "Now we're gettin' down to it. Stay here, there's a good man, in case anything turns up. I'll run round to the Yard now. They'll send you up dinner, and tell Bunter to give you a bottle of Chateau Yquem–it's rather decent. So long."

He leapt out of the flat, and a moment later his taxi buzzed away up Piccadilly.

# 7

# THE CLUB AND THE BULLET

*He is dead, and by my hand. It were better that I were dead myself for the guilty wretch I am.*

Adventures of Sexton Blake

HOUR AFTER hour Mr. Parker sat waiting for his friend's return. Again and again he went over the Riddlesdale Case, checking his notes here, amplifying them there, involving his tired brain in speculations of the most fantastic kind. He wandered about the room, taking down here and there a book from the shelves, strumming a few unskilful bars upon the piano, glancing through the weeklies, fidgeting restlessly. At length he selected a volume from the criminological section of the bookshelves, and forced himself to read with attention that most fascinating and dramatic of poison trials–the Seddon Case. Gradually the mystery gripped him, as it invariably did, and it was with a start of astonishment that he looked up at a long and vigorous whirring of the door-bell, to find that it was already long past midnight.

His first thought was that Wimsey must have left his latchkey behind, and he was preparing a facetious greeting when the door opened–exactly as in the beginning of a Sherlock Holmes story–to admit a tall and beautiful young woman, in an extreme state of nervous agitation, with halo of golden hair, violet-blue eyes, and disordered apparel all complete; for as she threw back her heavy travelling-coat he observed that she wore evening dress, with light green silk stockings and heavy brogue shoes thickly covered with mud.

"His lordship has not yet returned, my lady," said Mr. Bunter, "but Mr. Parker is here waiting for him, and we are expecting him at any minute now. Will your ladyship take anything?"

"No, no," said the vision hastily, "nothing, thanks. I'll wait. Good evening, Mr. Parker. Where's Peter?"

"He has been called out, Lady Mary," said Parker. "I can't think why he isn't back yet. Do sit down."

"Where did he go?"

"To Scotland Yard–but that was about six o'clock. I can't imagine——"

Lady Mary made a gesture of despair.

"I knew it. Oh, Mr. Parker, what am I to do?"

Mr. Parker was speechless.

"I *must* see Peter," cried Lady Mary. "It's a matter of life and death. Can't you send for him?"

"But I don't know where he is," said Parker. "Please, Lady Mary——"

"He's doing something dreadful–he's all *wrong*," cried the young woman, wringing her hands with desperate vehemence. "I must see him–tell him—— Oh! did anybody ever get into such dreadful trouble! I–oh!——"

Here the lady laughed loudly and burst into tears.

"Lady Mary–I beg you–please don't," cried Mr. Parker anxiously, with a strong feeling that he was being incompetent and rather ridiculous. "Please sit down. Drink a glass of wine. You'll be ill if you cry like that. If it is crying," he added dubiously to himself. "It *sounds* like hiccups. Bunter!"

Mr. Bunter was not far off. In fact, he was just outside the door with a small tray. With a respectful "Allow me, sir," he stepped forward to the writhing Lady Mary and presented a small phial to her nose. The effect was startling. The patient gave two or three fearful whoops, and sat up, erect and furious.

"How *dare* you, Bunter!" said Lady Mary. "Go away at once!"

"Your ladyship had better take a drop of brandy," said Mr. Bunter, replacing the stopper in the smelling-bottle, but not before Parker had caught the pungent reek of ammonia. "This is the 1800 Napoleon brandy, my lady. Please don't snort so, if I may make the suggestion. His lordship would be greatly distressed to think that any of it should be wasted. Did your ladyship dine on the way up? No? Most unwise, my lady, to undertake a long journey on a vacant interior. I will take the liberty of sending in an omelette for your ladyship. Perhaps you would like a little snack of something yourself, sir, as it is getting late?"

"Anything you like," said Mr. Parker, waving him off hurriedly. "Now, Lady Mary, you're feeling better, aren't you? Let me help you off with your coat."

No more of an exciting nature was said until the omelette was disposed of, and Lady Mary comfortably settled on the Chesterfield. She had by now recovered her poise. Looking at her, Parker noticed how her recent illness (however produced) had left its mark upon her. Her complexion had nothing of the brilliance which he remembered; she looked strained and white, with purple hollows under her eyes.

"I am sorry I was so foolish just now, Mr. Parker," she said, looking into his eyes with a charming frankness and confidence, "but I was dreadfully distressed, and I came up from Riddlesdale so hurriedly."

"Not at all," said Parker meaninglessly. "Is there anything I can do in your brother's absence?"

"I suppose you and Peter do everything together?"

"I think I may say that neither of us knows anything about this investigation which he has not communicated to the other."

"If I tell you, it's the same thing?"

"Exactly the same thing. If you can bring yourself to honour me with your confidence——"

"Wait a minute, Mr. Parker. I'm in a difficult position. I don't quite know what I ought—— Can you tell me just how far you've got—what you have discovered?"

Mr. Parker was a little taken aback. Although the face of Lady Mary had been haunting his imagination ever since the inquest, and although the agitation of his feelings had risen to boiling-point during this romantic interview, the official instinct of caution had not wholly deserted him. Holding, as he did, proofs of Lady Mary's complicity in the crime, whatever it was, he was not so far gone as to fling all his cards on the table.

"I'm afraid," he said, "that I can't quite tell you that. You see, so much of what we've got is only suspicion as yet. I might accidentally do great mischief to an innocent person."

"Ah! You definitely suspect somebody, then?"

"*In*definitely would be a better word for it," said Mr. Parker with a smile. "But if you have anything to tell us which may throw light on the matter, I beg you to speak. We may be suspecting a totally wrong person."

"I shouldn't be surprised," said Lady Mary, with a sharp, nervous little laugh. Her hand strayed to the table and began pleating the orange envelope into folds. "What do you want to know?" she asked suddenly, with a change of tone. Parker was conscious of a new hardness in her manner—a something braced and rigid.

He opened his note-book, and as he began his questioning his nervousness left him: the official reasserted himself.

"You were in Paris last February?"

Lady Mary assented.

"Do you recollect going with Captain Cathcart—oh! by the way, you speak French, I presume?"

"Yes, very fluently."

"As well as your brother—practically without accent?"

"Quite as well. We always had French governesses as children, and mother was very particular about it."

"I see. Well, now do you remember going with Captain Cathcart on February 6th to a jeweller's in the Rue de la Paix and buying, or his buying for you, a tortoiseshell comb set with diamonds and a diamond and platinum cat with emerald eyes?"

He saw a lurking awareness come into the girl's eyes.

"Is that the cat you have been making inquiries about in Riddlesdale?" she demanded.

It being never worth while to deny the obvious, Parker replied "Yes."

"It was found in the shrubbery, wasn't it?"

"Had you lost it? Or was it Cathcart's?"

"If I said it was his——"

"I should be ready to believe you. *Was* it his?"

"No"—a long breath—"it was mine."

"When did you lose it?"

"That night."

"Where?"

"I suppose in the shrubbery. Wherever you found it. I didn't miss it till later."

"Is it the one you bought in Paris?"

"Yes."

"Why did you say before that it was not yours?"

"I was afraid."

"And now?"

"I am going to speak the truth."

Parker looked at her again. She met his eye frankly, but there was a tenseness in her manner which showed that it had cost her something to make her mind up.

"Very well," said Parker, "we shall all be glad of that, for I think there were one or two points at the inquest on which you didn't tell the truth, weren't there?"

"Yes."

"Do believe," said Parker, "that I am sorry to have to ask these questions. The terrible position in which your brother is placed——"

"In which I helped to place him."

"I don't say that."

"I do. I helped to put him in gaol. Don't say I didn't, because I did."

"Well," said Parker, "don't worry. There's plenty of time to put it all right again. Shall I go on?"

"Yes."

"Well, now, Lady Mary, it wasn't true about hearing that shot at three o'clock, was it?"

"No."

"Did you hear the shot at all?"

"Yes."

"When?"

"At 11:50."

"What was it, then, Lady Mary, you hid behind the plants in the conservatory?"

"I hid nothing there."

"And in the oak chest on the landing?"

"My skirt."

"You went out–why?–to meet Cathcart?"

"Yes."

"Who was the other man?"

"What other man?"

"The other man who was in the shrubbery. A tall, fair man dressed in a Burberry?"

"There was no other man."

"Oh, pardon me, Lady Mary. We saw his footmarks all the way up from the shrubbery to the conservatory."

"It must have been some tramp. I know nothing about him."

"But we have proof that he was there–of what he did, and how he escaped. For heaven's sake, and your brother's sake, Lady Mary, tell us the truth–for that man in the Burberry was the man who shot Cathcart."

"No," said the girl, with a white face, "that is impossible."

"Why impossible?"

"I shot Denis Cathcart myself."

* * * * *

"So that's how the matter stands, you see, Lord Peter," said the Chief of Scotland Yard, rising from his desk with a friendly gesture of dismissal. "The man was undoubtedly seen at Marylebone on the Friday morning, and, though we have unfortunately lost him again for the moment, I have no doubt whatever that we shall lay hands on him before long. The delay has been due to the unfortunate illness of the porter Morrison, whose evidence has been so material. But we are wasting no time now."

"I'm sure I may leave it to you with every confidence, Sir Andrew," replied Wimsey, cordially shaking hands. "I'm diggin' away too; between us we ought to get somethin'—you in your small corner and I in mine, as the hymn says—or is it a hymn? I remember readin' it in a book about missionaries when I was small. Did you want to be a missionary in your youth? I did. I think most kids do some time or another, which is odd, seein' how unsatisfactory most of us turn out."

"Meanwhile," said Sir Andrew Mackenzie, "if you run across the man yourself, let us know. I would never deny your extraordinary good fortune, or it may be good judgment, in running across the criminals we may be wanting."

"If I catch the bloke," said Lord Peter, "I'll come and shriek under your windows till you let me in, if it's the middle of the night and you in your little night-shirt. And talking of night-shirts reminds me that we hope to see you down at Denver one of these days, as soon as this business is over. Mother sends kind regards, of course."

"Thanks very much," replied Sir Andrew. "I hope you feel that all is going well. I had Parker in here this morning to report, and he seemed a little dissatisfied."

"He's been doing a lot of ungrateful routine work," said Wimsey, "and being altogether the fine, sound man he always is. He's been a damn good friend to me, Sir Andrew, and it's a real privilege to be allowed to work with him. Well, so long, Chief."

He found that his interview with Sir Andrew Mackenzie had taken up a couple of hours, and that it was nearly eight o'clock. He was just trying to make up his mind where to dine when he was accosted by a cheerful young woman with bobbed red hair, dressed in a short checked skirt, brilliant jumper, corduroy jacket, and a rakish green velvet tam-o'shanter.

"Surely," said the young woman, extending a shapely, ungloved hand, "it's Lord Peter Wimsey. How're you? And how's Mary?"

"B'Jove!" said Wimsey gallantly, "it's Miss Tarrant. How perfectly rippin' to see you again. Absolutely delightful. Thanks, Mary ain't as fit as she might be—worryin' about this murder business, y'know. You've heard that we're what the poor so kindly and tactfully call 'in trouble,' I expect, what?"

"Yes, of course," replied Miss Tarrant eagerly, "and, of course, as a good Socialist, I can't help rejoicing rather when a peer gets taken up, because it does make him look so silly, you know, and the House of Lords is silly, isn't it? But, really, I'd rather it was anybody else's brother. Mary and I were such great friends, you know, and of course, *you* do investigate things, don't you, not just live on your estates in the country and shoot birds? So I suppose that makes a difference."

"That's very kind of you," said Peter. "If you can prevail upon yourself to overlook the misfortune of my birth and my other deficiencies, p'raps you would honour me by comin' along and havin' a bit of dinner somewhere, what?"

"Oh, I'd have *loved* to," cried Miss Tarrant, with enormous energy, "but I've promised to be at the club to-night. There's a meeting at nine. Mr. Coke—the Labour leader, you know—is going to make a speech about converting the Army and Navy to Communism. We expect to be raided and there's going to be a grand hunt for spies before we begin. But look here, do come along and dine with me there, and, if you like, I'll try to smuggle you in to the meeting, and you'll be seized and turned out. I suppose I oughtn't to have told you anything about it, because you ought to be a deadly enemy, but I can't really believe you're dangerous."

"I'm just an ordinary capitalist, I expect," said Lord Peter, "highly obnoxious."

"Well, come to dinner, anyhow. I *do* so want to hear all the news."

Peter reflected that the dinner at the Soviet Club would be worse than execrable, and was just preparing an excuse when it occurred to him that Miss Tarrant might be able to tell him a good many of the things that he didn't know, and really ought to know, about his own sister. Accordingly, he altered his polite refusal into a polite acceptance, and, plunging after Miss Tarrant, was led at a reckless pace and by a series of grimy short cuts into Gerrard Street, where an orange door, flanked by windows with magenta curtains, sufficiently indicated the Soviet Club.

The Soviet Club, being founded to accommodate free thinking rather than high living, had that curious amateur air which pervades all worldly institutions planned by unworldly people. Exactly why it made Lord Peter instantly think of mission teas he could not say, unless it was that all the members looked as though they cherished a purpose in life, and that the staff seemed rather sketchily trained and strongly in evidence. Wimsey reminded himself that in so democratic an institution one could hardly expect the assistants to assume that air of superiority which marks the servants in a West End Club. For one thing, they would not be such capitalists. In the dining-room below the resemblance to a mission tea was increased by the exceedingly heated atmosphere, the babel of conversation, and the curious inequalities of the cutlery. Miss Tarrant secured seats at a rather crumby table near the serving-hatch, and Peter wedged himself in with some difficulty next to a very large, curly-haired man in a velvet coat, who was earnestly conversing with a thin, eager young woman in a Russian blouse, Venetian beads, a Hungarian shawl and a Spanish comb, looking like a personification of the United Front of the "Internationale."

Lord Peter endeavoured to please his hostess by a question about the great Mr. Coke, but was checked by an agitated "Hush!"

"*Please* don't shout about it," said Miss Tarrant, leaning across till her auburn mop positively tickled his eyebrows, "It's *so* secret."

"I'm awfully sorry," said Wimsey apologetically. "I say, d'you know you're dipping those jolly little beads of yours in the soup?"

"Oh, am I?" cried Miss Tarrant, withdrawing hastily. "Oh, thank you so much. Especially as the colour runs. I hope it isn't arsenic or anything." Then, leaning forward again, she whispered hoarsely :

"The girl next me is Erica Heath-Warburton—the writer, you know."

Wimsey looked with a new respect at the lady in the Russian blouse. Few books were capable of calling up a blush to his cheek, but he remembered that one of Miss Heath-Warburton's had done it. The authoress was just saying impressively to her companion :

"—ever know a sincere emotion to express itself in a subordinate clause?"

"Joyce has freed us from the superstition of syntax," agreed the curly man.

"Scenes which make emotional history," said Miss Heath-Warburton, "should ideally be expressed in a series of animal squeals."

"The D. H. Lawrence formula," said the other.

"Or even Dada," said the authoress.

"We need a new notation," said the curly-haired man, putting both elbows on the table and knocking Wimsey's bread on to the floor. "Have you heard Robert Snoates recite his own verse to the tom-tom and the penny whistle?"

Lord Peter with difficulty detached his attention from this fascinating discussion to find that Miss Tarrant was saying something about Mary.

"One misses your sister very much," she said. "Her wonderful enthusiasm. She spoke so well at meetings. She had such a *real* sympathy with the worker."

"It seems astonishing to me," said Wimsey, "seeing Mary's never had to do a stroke of work in her life."

"Oh," cried Miss Tarrant, "but she *did* work. She worked for us. Wonderfully! She was secretary to our Propaganda Society for nearly six months. And then she worked so hard for Mr. Goyles. To say nothing of her nursing in the war. Of course, I don't approve of England's attitude in the war, but nobody would say the work wasn't hard."

"Who is Mr. Goyles?"

"Oh, one of our leading speakers–quite young, but the Government are really afraid of him. I expect he'll be here to-night. He has been lecturing in the North, but I believe he's back now."

"I say, do look out," said Peter. "Your beads are in your plate again."

"Are they? Well, perhaps they'll flavour the mutton. I'm afraid the cooking isn't very good here, but the subscription's so small, you see. I wonder Mary never told you about Mr. Goyles. They were so *very* friendly, you know, some time ago. Everybody thought she was going to marry him–but it seemed to fall through. And then your sister left town. Do you know about it?"

"That was the fellow, was it? Yes–well, my people didn't altogether see it, you know. Thought Mr. Goyles wasn't quite the son-in-law they'd take to. Family row and so on. Wasn't there myself; besides, Mary'd never listen to *me*. Still, that's what I gathered."

"Another instance of the absurd, old-fashioned tyranny of parents," said Miss Tarrant warmly. "You wouldn't think it could still be possible–in post-war times."

"I don't know," said Wimsey, "that you could exactly call it that. Not parents exactly. My mother's a remarkable woman. I don't think she interfered. Fact, I fancy she wanted to ask Mr. Goyles to Denver. But my brother put his foot down."

"Oh, well, what can you expect?" said Miss Tarrant scornfully. "But I don't see what business it was of his."

"Oh, none," agreed Wimsey. "Only, owin' to my late father's circumscribed ideas of what was owin' to women, my brother has the handlin' of Mary's money till she marries with his consent. I don't say it's a good plan–I think it's a rotten plan. But there it is."

"Monstrous!" said Miss Tarrant, shaking her head so angrily that she looked like shock-headed Peter. "Barbarous! Simply feudal, you know. But, after all, what's money?"

"Nothing, of course," said Peter. "But if you've been brought up to havin' it it's a bit awkward to drop it suddenly. Like baths, you know."

"I can't understand how it could have made any difference to Mary," persisted Miss Tarrant mournfully. "She liked being a worker. We once tried living in a workman's cottage for eight weeks, five of us, on eighteen shillings a week. It was a *marvellous* experience–on the very *edge* of the New Forest."

"In the winter?"

"Well, no—we thought we'd better not *begin* with winter. But we had nine wet days, and the kitchen chimney smoked all the time. You see, the wood came out of the forest, so it was all damp."

"I see. It must have been uncommonly interestin'."

"It was an experience I shall *never* forget," said Miss Tarrant. "One felt so *close* to the earth and the primitive things. If only we could abolish industrialism. I'm afraid, though, we shall never get it put right without a 'bloody revolution,' you know. It's very terrible, of course, but salutary and inevitable. Shall we have coffee? We shall have to carry it upstairs ourselves, if you don't mind. The maids don't bring it up after dinner."

Miss Tarrant settled her bill and returned, thrusting a cup of coffee into his hand. It had already overflowed into the saucer, and as he groped his way round a screen and up a steep and twisted staircase it overflowed quite an amount more.

Emerging from the basement, they almost ran into a young man with fair hair who was hunting for letters in a dark little row of pigeon-holes. Finding nothing, he retreated into the lounge. Miss Tarrant uttered an exclamation of pleasure.

"Why, there *is* Mr. Goyles," she cried.

Wimsey glanced across, and at the sight of the tall, slightly stooping figure with the untidy fair hair and the gloved right hand he gave an irrepressible little gasp.

"Won't you introduce me?" he said.

"I'll fetch him," said Miss Tarrant. She made off across the lounge and addressed the young agitator, who started, looked across at Wimsey, shook his head, appeared to apologise, gave a hurried glance at his watch, and darted out by the entrance. Wimsey sprang forward in pursuit.

"Extraordinary," cried Miss Tarrant, with a blank face. "He says he has an appointment—but he can't surely be missing the——"

"Excuse me," said Peter. He dashed out, in time to perceive a dark figure retreating across the street. He gave chase. The man took to his heels, and seemed to plunge into the dark little alley which leads into the Charing Cross Road. Hurrying in pursuit, Wimsey was almost blinded by a sudden flash and smoke nearly in his face. A crashing blow on the left shoulder and a deafening report whirled his surroundings away. He staggered violently, and collapsed on to a second-hand brass bedstead.

# 8

# MR. PARKER TAKES NOTES

*A man was taken to the Zoo and shown the giraffe. After gazing at it a little in silence; "I don't believe it," he said.*

PARKER'S FIRST impulse was to doubt his own sanity; his next, to doubt Lady Mary's. Then, as the clouds rolled away from his brain, he decided that she was merely not speaking the truth.

"Come, Lady Mary," he said encouragingly, but with an accent of reprimand as to an over-imaginative child. "You can't expect us to believe that, you know."

"But you must," said the girl gravely; "it's a fact. I shot him. I did, really. I didn't exactly mean to do it; it was a—well, a sort of accident."

Mr. Parker got up and paced about the room.

"You have put me in a terrible position, Lady Mary," he said. "You see, I'm a police-officer. I never imagined——"

"It doesn't matter," said Lady Mary. "Of course you'll have to arrest me, or detain me, or whatever you call it. That's what I came for. I'm quite ready to go quietly—that's the right expression, isn't it? I'd like to explain about it, though, first. Of course I ought to have done it long ago, but I'm afraid I lost my head. I didn't realise that Gerald would get blamed. I hoped they'd bring it in suicide. Do I make a statement to you now? Or do I do it at the police-station?"

Parker groaned.

"They won't—they won't punish me so badly if it was an accident, will they?" There was a quiver in the voice.

"No, of course not—of course not. But if only you had spoken earlier! No," said Parker, stopping suddenly short in his distracted pacing and sitting down beside her. "It's impossible—absurd." He caught the girl's hand suddenly in his own. "Nothing will convince me," he said. "It's absurd. It's not like you."

"But an accident——"

"I don't mean that—you know I don't mean that. But that you should keep silence——"

"I was afraid. I'm telling you now."

"No, no, no," cried the detective. "You're lying to me. Nobly, I know; but it's not worth it. No man could be worth it. Let him go, I implore you. Tell the truth. Don't shield this man. If he murdered Denis Cathcart——"

"*No!*" The girl sprang to her feet, wrenching her hand away. "There was no other man. How dare you say it or think it! I killed Denis Cathcart, I tell you, and you *shall* believe it. I swear to you that there was no other man."

Parker pulled himself together.

"Sit down, please. Lady Mary, you are determined to make this statement?"

"Yes."

"Knowing that I have no choice but to act upon it?"

"If you will not hear it I shall go straight to the police."

Parker pulled out his note-book. "Go on," he said.

With no other sign of emotion than a nervous fidgeting with her gloves, Lady Mary began her confession in a clear, hard voice, as though she were reciting it by heart.

"On the evening of Wednesday, October 13th, I went upstairs at half-past nine. I sat up writing a letter. At a quarter past ten I heard my brother and Denis quarrelling in the passage. I heard my brother call Denis a cheat, and tell him that he was never to speak to me again. I heard Denis run out. I listened for some time, but did not hear him return. At half-past eleven I became alarmed. I changed my dress and went out to try and find Denis and bring him in. I feared he might do something desperate. After some time I found him in the shrubbery. I begged him to come in. He refused, and he told me about my brother's accusation and the quarrel. I was very much horrified, of course. He said where was the good of denying anything, as Gerald was determined to ruin him, and asked me to go away and marry him and live abroad. I said I was surprised that he should suggest such a thing in the circumstances. We both became very angry. I said, 'Come in now. To-morrow you can leave by the first train.' He seemed almost crazy. He pulled out a pistol and said that he'd come to the end of things, that his life was ruined, that we were a lot of hypocrites, and that I had never cared for him, or I shouldn't have minded what he'd done. Anyway, he said, if I wouldn't come with him it was all over, and he might as well be hanged for a sheep as a lamb–he'd shoot me and himself. I think he was quite out of his mind. He pulled out a revolver; I caught his hand; we struggled; I got the muzzle right up against his chest, and——either I pulled the trigger or it went off of itself–I'm not clear which. It was all in such a whirl."

She paused. Parker's pen took down the words, and his face showed growing concern. Lady Mary went on:

"He wasn't quite dead. I helped him up. We struggled back nearly to the house. He fell once——"

"Why," asked Parker, "did you not leave him and run into the house to fetch help?"

Lady Mary hesitated.

"It didn't occur to me. It was a nightmare. I could only think of getting him along. I think——*I think I wanted him to die.*"

There was a dreadful pause.

"He did die. He died at the door. I went into the conservatory and sat down. I sat for hours and tried to think. I hated him for being a cheat and a scoundrel. I'd been taken in, you see–made a fool of by a common sharper. I was glad he was dead. I must have sat there for hours without a coherent thought. It wasn't till my brother came along that I realised what I'd done, and that I might be suspected of murdering him. I was simply terrified. I made up my mind all in a moment that I'd pretend I knew nothing–that I'd heard a shot and come down. You know what I did."

"Why, Lady Mary," said Parker, in a perfectly toneless voice, "why did you say to your brother, 'Good God, Gerald, you've killed him'?"

Another hesitant pause.

"I never said that. I said, 'Good God, Gerald, he's killed, then.' I never meant to suggest anything but suicide."

"You admitted to those words at the inquest?"

"Yes——" Her hands knotted the gloves into all manner of shapes "By that time I had decided on a burglar story, you see."

The telephone bell rang and Parker went to the instrument. A voice came thinly over the wire:

"Is that 110 Piccadilly? This is Charing Cross Hospital. A man was brought in to-night who says he is Lord Peter Wimsey. He was shot in the shoulder, and struck his head in falling. He has only just recovered consciousness. He was brought in at 9:15. No, he will probably do very well now. Yes, come round by all means."

"Peter has been shot," said Parker. "Will you come round with me to Charing Cross Hospital? They say he is in no danger; still——"

"Oh, quick!" cried Lady Mary.

Gathering up Mr. Bunter as they hurried through the hall, detective and self-accused rushed hurriedly out into Pall Mall, and, picking up a belated taxi at Hyde Park Corner, drove madly away through the deserted streets.

# 9

# GOYLES

*"–and the moral of that is––" said the Duchess.*
Alice's Adventures in Wonderland

A PARTY of four was assembled next morning at a very late breakfast, or very early lunch, in Lord Peter's flat. Its most cheerful member, despite a throbbing shoulder and a splitting headache, was undoubtedly Lord Peter himself, who lay upon the Chesterfield surrounded with cushions and carousing upon tea and toast. Having been brought home in an ambulance, he had instantly fallen into a healing sleep, and had woken at nine o'clock aggressively clear and active in mind. In consequence, Mr. Parker had been dispatched in a hurry, half-fed and burdened with the secret memory of last night's disclosures, to Scotland Yard. Here he had set in motion the proper machinery for catching Lord Peter's assassin. "Only don't you say anything about the attack on me," said his lordship. "Tell 'em he's to be detained in connection with the Riddlesdale case. That's good enough for them." It was now eleven, and Mr. Parker had returned, gloomy and hungry, and was consuming a belated omelette and a glass of claret.

Lady Mary Wimsey was hunched up in the window-seat. Her bobbed golden hair made a little blur of light about her in the pale autumn sunshine. She had made an attempt to breakfast earlier, and now sat gazing out into Piccadilly. Her first appearance that morning had been made in Lord Peter's dressing-gown, but she now wore a serge skirt and jade-green jumper, which had been brought to town for her by the fourth member of the party, now composedly eating a mixed grill and sharing the decanter with Parker.

This was a rather short, rather plump, very brisk elderly lady, with bright black eyes like a bird's, and very handsome white hair exquisitely dressed. Far from looking as though she had just taken a long night journey, she was easily the most composed and trim of the four. She was, however, annoyed, and said so at considerable length. This was the Dowager Duchess of Denver.

"It is not so much, Mary, that you went off so abruptly last night–just before dinner, too–inconveniencing and alarming us very much–indeed, poor Helen was totally unable to eat her dinner, which was extremely distressing to her feelings, because, you know, she always makes such a point of never being upset about anything–I really don't know why, for some of the greatest men have not minded showing their feelings, I don't mean Southerners necessarily, but, as Mr. Chesterton very rightly points out–Nelson, too, who was certainly English if he wasn't Irish or Scotch, I forget, but United Kingdom, anyway (if that means anything nowadays with a Free State–such a ridiculous title, especially as it always makes one think of the Orange Free State, and I'm sure they wouldn't care to be mixed up with that, being so very green themselves). And going off without even proper clothes, and taking the car, so that I had to wait till the 1:15 from Northallerton–a ridiculous time to start, and such a bad train, too, not getting up till 10:30. Besides, if you *must* run off to town, why do it in that unfinished manner? If you had only looked up the trains before starting you would have seen you would have half an hour's wait at Northallerton, and you could quite easily have packed a bag. It's so much better to do things neatly and thoroughly—even stupid things. And it was very stupid of you indeed to dash off like that to embarrass and bore poor Mr. Parker with a lot of twaddle—though I suppose it was Peter you meant to see. You know, Peter, if you will haunt low places full of Russians and sucking Socialists taking themselves seriously, you ought to know better than to encourage them by running after them, however futile, and given to drinking coffee and writing poems with no shape to them, and generally ruining their nerves. And, in any case, it makes not the slightest difference; I could have told Peter all about it myself, if he doesn't know already, as he probably does."

Lady Mary turned very white at this and glanced at Parker, who replied rather to her than to the Dowager:

"No, Lord Peter and I haven't had time to discuss anything yet."

"Lest it should ruin my shattered nerves and bring a fever to my aching brow," added that nobleman amiably. "You're a kind, thoughtful soul, Charles, and I don't know what I should do without you. I wish that rotten old second-hand dealer had been a bit brisker about takin' in his stock-in-trade for the night, though. Perfectly 'straor'nary number of knobs there are on a brass bedstead. Saw it comin', y'know, an' couldn't stop myself. However, what's a mere brass bedstead? The great detective, though at first stunned and dizzy from his brutal treatment by the fifteen veiled assassins all armed with meat-choppers, soon regained his senses, thanks to his sound constitution and healthy manner of life. Despite the severe gassing he had endured in the underground room —eh? A telegram? Oh, thanks, Bunter."

Lord Peter appeared to read the message with great inward satisfaction, for his long lips twitched at the corners, and he tucked the slip of paper away in his pocket-book with a little sigh of satisfaction. He called to Bunter to take away the breakfast-tray and to renew the cooling bandage about his brow. This done, Lord Peter leaned back among his cushions, and with an air of malicious enjoyment launched at Mr. Parker the inquiry:

"Well, now, how did you and Mary get on last night? Polly, did you tell him you'd done the murder?"

Few things are more irritating than to discover, after you have been at great pains to spare a person some painful intelligence, that he has known it all along and is not nearly so much affected by it as he properly should be. Mr. Parker quite simply and suddenly lost his temper. He bounded to his feet, and exclaimed, without the least reason: "Oh, it's perfectly hopeless trying to do anything!"

Lady Mary sprang from the window-seat.

"Yes, I did," she said. "It's quite true. Your precious case is finished, Peter."

The Dowager said, without the least discomposure: "You must allow your brother to be the best judge of his own affairs, my dear."

"As a matter of fact," replied his lordship, "I rather fancy Polly's right. Hope so, I'm sure. Anyway, we've got the fellow, so now we shall know."

Lady Mary gave a sort of gasp, and stepped forward with her chin up and her hands tightly clenched. It caught at Parker's heart to see overwhelming catastrophe so bravely faced. The official side of him was thoroughly bewildered, but the human part ranged itself instantly in support of that gallant defiance.

"Whom have they got?" he demanded, in a voice quite unlike his own.

"The Goyles person," said Lord Peter carelessly. "Uncommon quick work, what? But since he'd no more original idea than to take the boat-train to Folkestone they didn't have much difficulty."

"It isn't true," said Lady Mary. She stamped. "It's a lie. He wasn't there. He's innocent. I killed Denis."

"Fine," thought Parker, "fine! Damn Goyles, anyway, what's he done to deserve it?"

Lord Peter said: "Mary, don't be an ass."

"Yes," said the Dowager placidly. "I was going to suggest to you, Peter, that this Mr. Goyles–such a terrible name, Mary dear, I can't say I ever cared for it, even if there had been nothing else against him–especially as he would sign himself Geo. Goyles–G. e. o. you know, Mr. Parker, for George, and I never *could* help reading it as Gargoyles–I very nearly wrote to you, my dear, mentioning Mr. Goyles, and asking if you could see him in town, because there was something, when I came to think of it, about that ipecacuanha business that made me feel he might have something to do with it."

"Yes," said Peter, with a grin, "you always did find him a bit sickenin', didn't you?"

"How can you, Wimsey?" growled Parker reproachfully, with his eyes on Mary's face.

"Never mind him," said the girl. "If you can't be a gentleman, Peter——"

"Damn it all!" cried the invalid explosively. "Here's a fellow who, without the slightest provocation, plugs a bullet into my shoulder, breaks my collar-bone, brings me up head foremost on a knobby second-hand brass bedstead and vamooses, and when, in what seems to me jolly mild, parliamentary language, I call him a sickenin' feller my own sister says I'm no gentleman. Look at me! In my own house, forced to sit here with a perfectly beastly headache, and lap up toast and tea, while you people distend and bloat yourselves on mixed grills and omelettes and a damn good vintage claret——"

"Silly boy," said the Duchess, "don't get so excited. And it's time for your medicine. Mr. Parker, kindly touch the bell."

Mr. Parker obeyed in silence. Lady Mary came slowly across, and stood looking at her brother.

"Peter," she said, "what makes you say that *he* did it?"

"Did what?"

"Shot–you?" The words were only a whisper.

The entrance of Mr. Bunter at this moment with a cooling draught dissipated the tense atmosphere. Lord Peter quaffed his potion, had his pillows re-arranged, submitted to have his temperature taken and his pulse counted, asked if he might not have an egg for his lunch, and lit a cigarette. Mr. Bunter retired, people distributed themselves into more comfortable chairs, and felt happier.

"Now, Polly, old girl," said Peter, "cut out the sob-stuff. I accidentally ran into this Goyles chap last night at your Soviet Club. I asked that Miss Tarrant to introduce me, but the minute Goyles heard my name, he made tracks. I rushed out after him, only meanin' to have a word with him, when the idiot stopped at the corner of Newport Court, potted me, and bunked. Silly-ass thing to do. I knew who he was. He couldn't help gettin' caught."

"Peter——" said Mary in a ghastly voice.

"Look here, Polly," said Wimsey. "I did think of you. Honest injun, I did. I haven't had the man arrested. I've made no charge at all—have I, Parker? What did you tell 'em to do when you were down at the Yard this morning?"

"To detain Goyles pending inquiries, because he was wanted as a witness in the Riddlesdale case," said Parker slowly.

"He knows nothing about it," said Mary, doggedly now. "He wasn't anywhere near. He is innocent of *that!*"

"Do you think so?" said Lord Peter gravely. "If you know he is innocent, why tell all these lies to screen him? It won't do, Mary. You know he was there—and you think he is guilty."

"No!"

"Yes," said Wimsey, grasping her with his sound hand as she shrank away. "Mary, have you thought what you are doing? You are perjuring yourself and putting Gerald in peril of his life, in order to shield from justice a man whom you suspect of murdering your lover and who has most certainly tried to murder me."

"Oh," cried Parker, in an agony, "all this interrogation is horribly irregular."

"Never mind him," said Peter. "Do you really think you're doing the right thing, Mary?"

The girl looked helplessly at her brother for a minute or two. Peter cocked up a whimsical, appealing eye from under his bandages. The defiance melted out of her face.

"I'll tell the truth," said Lady Mary.

"Good egg," said Peter, extending a hand. "I'm sorry. I know you like the fellow, and we appreciate your decision enormously. Truly, we do. Now, sail ahead, old thing, and you take it down, Parker."

"Well, it really started years ago with George. You were at the Front then, Peter, but I suppose they told you about it—and put everything in the worst possible light."

"I wouldn't say that, dear," put in the Duchess. "I think I told Peter that your brother and I were not altogether pleased with what we had seen of the young man—which was not very much, if you remember. He invited himself down one week-end when the house was very full, and he seemed to make a point of consulting nobody's convenience but his own. And you know, dear, you even said yourself you thought he was unnecessarily rude to poor old Lord Mountweazle."

"He said what he thought," said Mary. "Of course, Lord Mountweazle, poor dear, doesn't understand that the present generation is accustomed to discuss things with its elders, not just kow-tow to them. When George gave his opinion, he thought he was just contradicting."

"To be sure," said the Dowager, "when you flatly deny everything a person says it does sound like contradiction to the uninitiated. But all I remember saying to Peter was that Mr. Goyles's manners seemed to me to lack polish, and that he showed a lack of independence in his opinions."

"A lack of independence?" said Mary, wide-eyed.

"Well, dear, I thought so. What oft was thought and frequently much better expressed, as Pope says—or was it somebody else? But the worse you express yourself these days the more profound people think you—though that's nothing new. Like Browning and those quaint metaphysical people, when you never know whether they really mean their mistress or the Established Church, so bridegroomy and biblical—to say nothing of dear St.

Augustine—the Hippo man, I mean, not the one who missionised over here, though I daresay he was delightful too, and in those days I suppose they didn't have annual sales of work and tea in the parish room, so it doesn't seem quite like what we mean nowadays by missionaries—he knew all about it—you remember about that mandrake—or is that the thing you had to get a big black dog for? Manichee, that's the word. What was his name? Was it Faustus? Or am I mixing him up with the old man in the opera?"

"Well, anyway," said Mary, without stopping to disentangle the Duchess's sequence of ideas, "George was the only person I really cared about—he still is. Only it did seem so hopeless. Perhaps you didn't say much about him, mother, but Gerald said *lots*—dreadful things!"

"Yes," said the Duchess, "he said what he thought. The present generation does, you know. To the uninitiated, I admit, dear, it does sound a little rude." Peter grinned, but Mary went on unheeding.

"George had simply *no* money. He'd really given everything he had to the Labour Party one way and another, and he'd lost his job in the Ministry of Information: they found he had too much sympathy with the Socialists abroad. It was awfully unfair. Anyhow, one couldn't be a burden on him: and Gerald was a beast, and said he'd absolutely stop my allowance if I didn't send George away. So I did, but of course it didn't make a bit of difference to the way we both felt. I wlll say for mother she was a bit more decent. She said she'd help us if George got a job; but, as I pointed out, if George got a job we shouldn't *need* helping!"

"But, my dear, I could hardly insult Mr. Goyles by suggesting that he should live on his mother-in-law," said the Dowager.

"Why not?" said Mary. "George doesn't believe in those old-fashioned ideas about property. Besides, if you'd given it to me, it would be *my* money. We believe in men and women being equal. Why should the one always be the breadwinner more than the other?"

"I can't imagine, dear," said the Dowager. "Still, I could hardly expect poor Mr. Goyles to live on unearned increment when he didn't believe in inherited property."

"That's a fallacy," said Mary, rather vaguely. "Anyhow," she added hastily, "that's what happened. Then, after the war, George went to Germany to study Socialism and Labour questions there, and nothing seemed any good. So when Denis Cathcart turned up, I said I'd marry him."

"Why?" asked Peter. "He never sounded to me a bit the kind of bloke for you. I mean, as far as I could make out, he was Tory and diplomatic and—well, quite crusted old tawny, so to speak, I shouldn't have thought you had an idea in common."

"No; but then he didn't care twopence whether I had any ideas or not. I made him promise he wouldn't bother me with diplomats and people, and he said no, I could do as I liked, provided I didn't compromise him. And we were to live in Paris and go our own ways and not bother. And anything was better than staying here, and marrying somebody in one's own set, and opening bazaars and watching polo and meeting the Prince of Wales. So I said I'd marry Denis, because I didn't care about him, and I'm pretty sure he didn't care a halfpenny about me, and we should have left each other alone. I did so want to be left alone!"

"Was Jerry all right about your money?" inquired Peter.

"Oh, yes. He said Denis was no great catch—I do wish Gerald wasn't so vulgar, in that flat, early-Victorian way—but he said that, after George, he could only thank his stars it wasn't worse."

"Make a note of that, Charles," said Wimsey.

"Well, it seemed all right at first, but, as things went on, I got more and more depressed. Do you know, there was something a little alarming about Denis. He was so extraordinarily reserved. I know I wanted to be left alone, but–well, it was uncanny! He was correct. Even when he went off the deep end and was passionate–which didn't often happen–he was correct about it. Extraordinary. Like one of those odd French novels, you know, Peter: frightfully hot stuff, but absolutely impersonal."

"Charles, old man!" said Lord Peter.

"M'm?"

"That's important. You realise the bearing of that?"

"No."

"Never mind. Drive on, Polly."

"Aren't I making your head ache?"

"Damnably; but I like it. Do go on. I'm not sprouting a lily with anguish moist and fever-dew, or anything like that. I'm getting really thrilled. What you've just said is more illuminating than anything I've struck for a week."

"Really!" Mary stared at Peter with every trace of hostility vanished. "I thought you'd never understand that part."

"Lord!" said Peter. "Why not?"

Mary shook her head. "Well, I'd been corresponding all the time with George, and suddenly he wrote to me at the beginning of this month to say he'd come back from Germany, and had got a job on the *Thunderclap*–the Socialist weekly, you know–at a beginning screw of £4 a week, and wouldn't I chuck these capitalists and so on, and come and be an honest working woman with him. He could get me a secretarial job on the paper. I was to type and so on for him, and help him get his articles together. And he thought between us we should make £6 or £7 a week, which would be heaps to live on. And I was getting more frightened of Denis every day. So I said I would. But I knew there'd be an awful row with Gerald. And really I was rather ashamed–the engagement had been announced and there'd be a ghastly lot of talk and people trying to persuade me. And Denis might have made things horribly uncomfortable for Gerald–he was rather that sort. So we decided the best thing to do would be just to run away and get married first, and escape the wrangling."

"Quite so," said Peter. "Besides, it would look rather well in the paper, wouldn't it? 'PEER'S DAUGHTER WEDS SOCIALIST—ROMANTIC SIDE-CAR ELOPEMENT—"£6 A WEEK PLENTY," SAYS HER LADYSHIP.' "

"Pig!" said Lady Mary.

"Very good," said Peter, "I get you! So it was arranged that the romantic Goyles should fetch you away from Riddlesdale–why Riddlesdale? It would be twice as easy from London or Denver."

"No. For one thing he had to be up North. And everybody knows one in town, and–anyhow, we didn't want to wait."

"Besides, one would miss the Young Lochinvar touch. Well, then, why at the unearthly hour of 3 a.m.?"

"He had a meeting on Wednesday night at Northallerton. He was going to come straight on and pick me up, and run me down to town to be married by special license. We allowed ample time. George had to be at the office next day."

"I see. Well, I'll go on now, and you stop me if I'm wrong. You went up at

9:30 on Wednesday night. You packed a suit-case. You—did you think of writing any sort of letter to comfort your sorrowing friends and relations?"

"Yes, I wrote one. But I——"

"Of course. Then you went to bed, I fancy, or at any rate, turned the clothes back and lay down."

"Yes. I lay down. It was a good thing I did, as it happened——"

"True, you wouldn't have had much time to make the bed look probable in the morning, and we should have heard about it. By the way, Parker, when Mary confessed her sins to you last night, did you make any notes?"

"Yes," said Parker, "if you can read my shorthand."

"Quite so," said Peter. "Well, the rumpled bed disposes of your story about never having gone to bed at all, doesn't it?"

"And I thought it was such a good story!"

"Want of practice," replied her brother kindly. "You'll do better, next time. It's just as well, really that it's so hard to tell a long, consistent lie. *Did* you, as a matter of fact, hear Gerald go out at 11:30, as Pettigrew-Robinson (damn his ears!) said?"

"I fancy I did hear somebody moving about" said Mary, "but I didn't think much about it."

"Quite right," said Peter, "when I hear people movin' about the house at night, I'm much too delicate-minded to think anything at all."

"Of course," interposed the Duchess, "particularly in England, where it is so oddly improper to think. I will say for Peter that, if he can put a continental interpretation on anything, he will—so considerate of you, dear, as soon as you took to doing it in silence and not mentioning it, as you so intelligently did as a child. You were really a very observant little boy, dear."

"And still is," said Mary, smiling at Peter with surprising friendliness.

"Old bad habits die hard," said Wimsey. "To proceed. At three o'clock you went down to meet Goyles. Why did he come all the way up to the house? It would have been safer to meet him in the lane."

"I knew I couldn't get out of the lodge-gate without waking Hardraw, and so I'd have to get over the palings somewhere. I might have managed alone, but not with a heavy suit-case. So, as George would have to climb over, anyhow, we thought he'd better come and help carry the suit-case. And then we couldn't miss each other by the conservatory door. I sent him a little plan of the path."

"Was Goyles there when you got downstairs?"

"No—at least—no, I didn't see him. But there was poor Denis's body, and Gerald bending over it. My first idea was that Gerald had killed George. That's why I said, 'Oh, God! you've killed him!' " (Peter glanced across at Parker and nodded.) "Then Gerald turned him over, and I saw it was Denis—and then I'm sure I heard something moving a long way off in the shrubbery—a noise like twigs snapping—and it suddenly came over me, where was George? Oh, Peter, I saw everything then, so clearly. I saw that Denis must have come on George waiting there, and attacked him—I'm sure Denis must have attacked him. Probably he thought it was a burglar. Or he found out who he was and tried to drive him away. And in the struggle George must have shot him. It was awful !"

Peter patted his sister on the shoulder. "Poor kid," he said.

"I didn't know what to do," went on the girl. "I'd so awfully little time, you see. My one idea was that nobody must suspect anybody had been there. So I had quickly to invent an excuse for being there myself. I shoved my suitcase behind the cactus-plants to start with. Jerry was taken up with the body and didn't notice—you know, Jerry never *does* notice things till you shove them under his nose. But I knew if there'd been a shot Freddy and the Marchbankses must have heard it. So I pretended I'd heard it too, and rushed down to look for burglars. It was a bit lame, but the best thing I could think of. Gerald sent me up to alarm the house, and I had the story all ready by the time I reached the landing. Oh, and I was quite proud of myself for not forgetting the suit-case!"

"You dumped it into the chest," said Peter.

"Yes. I had a horrible shock the other morning when I found you looking in."

"Nothing like the shock I had when I found the silver sand there."

"Silver sand?"

"Out of the conservatory."

"Good gracious!" said Mary.

"Well, go on. You knocked up Freddy and the Pettigrew-Robinsons. Then you had to bolt into your room to destroy your farewell letter and take your clothes off."

"Yes. I'm afraid I didn't do that very naturally. But I couldn't expect anybody to believe that I went burglar-hunting in a complete set of silk undies and a carefully knotted tie with a gold safety-pin."

"No. I see your difficulty."

"It turned out quite well, too, because they were all quite ready to believe that I wanted to escape from Mrs. Pettigrew-Robinson—except Mrs. P. herself, of course."

"Yes; even Parker swallowed that, didn't you, old man?"

"Oh, quite, quite so," said Parker gloomily.

"I made a dreadful mistake about that shot," resumed Lady Mary. "You see, I explained it all so elaborately—and then I found that nobody had heard a shot at all. And afterwards they discovered that it had all happened in the shrubbery—and the time wasn't right, either. Then at the inquest I *had* to stick to my story—and it got to look worse and worse—and then they put the blame on Gerald. In my wildest moments I'd never thought of that. Of course, I see now how my wretched evidence helped."

"Hence the ipecacuanha," said Peter.

"I'd got into such a frightful tangle," said poor Lady Mary, "I thought I had better shut up altogether for fear of making things still worse."

"And did you still think Goyles had done it?"

"I—I didn't know what to think," said the girl. "I don't now. Peter, who else *could* have done it?"

"Honestly, old thing," said his lordship, "if he didn't do it, I don't know who did."

"He ran away, you see," said Lady Mary.

"He seems rather good at shootin' and runnin' away," said Peter grimly.

"If he hadn't done that to you," said Mary slowly, "I'd never have told you. I'd have died first. But of course, with his revolutionary doctrines—and when you think of red Russia and all the blood spilt in riots and insurrections and things—I suppose it does teach a contempt for human life."

"My dear," said the Duchess, "it seems to me that Mr. Goyles shows no especial contempt for his own life. You must try to look at the thing fairly. Shooting people and running away is not very heroic—according to *our* standards."

"The thing I don't understand," struck in Wimsey hurriedly, "is how Gerald's revolver got into the shrubbery."

"The thing I should like to know about," said the Duchess, "is, was Denis really a card-sharper?"

"The thing *I* should like to know about," said Parker, "is the green-eyed cat."

"Denis *never* gave me a cat," said Mary. "That was a tarradiddle."

"Were you ever in a jeweller's with him in the Rue de la Paix?"

"Oh, yes; heaps of times. And he gave me a diamond and tortoiseshell comb. But never a cat."

"Then we may disregard the whole of last night's elaborate confession," said Lord Peter, looking through Parker's notes, with a smile. "It's really not bad, Polly, not bad at all. You've quite a talent for romantic fiction—no, I mean it! Just here and there you need more attention to detail. For instance, you *couldn't* have dragged that badly wounded man all up the path to the house without getting blood all over your coat, you know. By the way, did Goyles know Cathcart at all?"

"Not to my knowledge."

"Because Parker and I had an alternative theory, which would clear Goyles from the worst part of the charge, anyhow. Tell her, old man; it was your idea."

Thus urged, Parker outlined the blackmail and suicide theory.

"That sounds plausible," said Mary—"academically speaking, I mean; but it isn't a bit like George—I mean, blackmail is so *beastly*, isn't it?"

"Well," said Peter, "I think the best thing is to go and see Goyles. Whatever the key to Wednesday night's riddle is, he holds it. Parker, old man, we're nearing the end of the chase."

# 10

# NOTHING ABIDES AT THE NOON

*"Alas!" said Hiya, "the sentiments which this person expressed with irreproachable honourableness, when the sun was high in the heavens and the probability of secretly leaving an undoubtedly well-appointed home was engagingly remote, seem to have an entirely different significance when recalled by night in a damp orchard, and on the eve of their fulfilment."*

The Wallet of Kai-Lung

*And his short minute, after noon, is night.*

*Donne*

Mr. Goyles was interviewed the next day at the police-station. Mr. Murbles was present, and Mary insisted on coming. The young man began by blustering a little, but the solicitor's dry manner made its impression.

"Lord Peter Wimsey identifies you," said Mr. Murbles, "as the man who made a murderous attack upon him last night. With remarkable generosity, he has forborne to press the charge. Now we know further that you were present at Riddlesdale Lodge on the night when Captain Cathcart was shot. You will no doubt be called as a witness in the case. But you would greatly assist justice by making a statement to us now. This is a purely friendly and private interview, Mr. Goyles. As you see, no representative of the police is present. We simply ask for your help. I ought, however, to warn you that, whereas it is, of course, fully competent for you to refuse to answer any of our questious, a refusal might lay you open to the gravest imputations."

"In fact," said Goyles, "it's a threat. If I don't tell you, you'll have me arrested on suspicion of murder."

"Dear me, no, Mr. Goyles," returned the solicitor. "We should merely place what information we hold in the hands of the police, who would then act as they thought fit. God bless my soul, no—anything like a threat would be highly irregular. In the matter of the assault upon Lord Peter, his lordship will, of course, use his own discretion."

"Well," said Goyles sullenly, "it's a threat, call it what you like. However, I don't mind speaking—especially as you'll be jolly well disappointed. I suppose you gave me away, Mary."

Mary flushed indignantly.

"My sister has been extraordinarily loyal to you, Mr. Goyles," said Lord Peter. "I may tell you, indeed, that she put herself into a position of grave personal inconvenience —not to say danger—on your behalf. You were traced to London in consequence of your having left unequivocal traces in your exceedingly hasty retreat. When my sister accidentally opened a telegram addressed to me at Riddlesdale by my family name she hurried immediately to town, to shield you if she could, at any cost to herself. Fortunately I had already received a duplicate wire at my flat. Even then I was not certain of your identity when I accidentally ran across you at the Soviet Club. Your own energetic efforts, however, to avoid an interview gave me complete certainty, together with an excellent excuse for detaining you. In fact, I'm uncommonly obliged to you for your assistance."

Mr. Goyles looked resentful.

"I don't know how you could think, George——" said Mary.

"Never mind what I think," said the young man, roughly. "I gather you've told 'em all about it now, anyhow. Well, I'll tell you my story as shortly as I can, and you'll see I know damn all about it. If you don't believe me I can't help it. I came along at about a quarter to three, and parked the 'bus in the lane."

"Where were you at 11:50?"

"On the road from Northallerton. My meeting didn't finish till 10:45. I can bring a hundred witnesses to prove it."

Wimsey made a note of the address where the meeting had been held, and nodded to Goyles to proceed.

"I climbed over the wall and walked through the shrubbery."

"You saw no person, and no body?"

"Nobody, alive or dead."

"Did you notice any blood or footprints on the path?"

"No. I didn't like to use my torch, for fear of being seen from the house. There was just light enough to see the path. I came to the door of the conservatory just before three. As I came up I stumbled over something. I felt it, and it was like a body. I was alarmed. I thought it might be Mary—ill or fainted or something. I ventured to turn on my light. Then I saw it was Cathcart, dead."

"You are sure he was dead?"

"Stone dead."

"One moment," interposed the solicitor. "You say you saw that it was Cathcart. Had you known Cathcart previously?"

"No, never. I meant that I saw it was a dead man, and learnt afterwards that it was Cathcart."

"In fact, you do not, now, know of your own knowledge, that it was Cathcart?"

"Yes—at least, I recognised the photographs in the papers afterwards."

"It is very necessary to be accurate in making a statement, Mr. Goyles. A remark such as you made just now might give a most unfortunate impression to the police or to a jury."

So saying, Mr. Murbles blew his nose, and resettled his pince-nez.

"What next?" inquired Peter.

"I fancied I heard somebody coming up the path. I did not think it wise to be found there with the corpse, so I cleared out."

"Oh," said Peter, with an indescribable expression, "that was a very simple solution. You left the girl you were going to marry to make for herself the unpleasant discovery that there was a dead man in the garden and that her gallant wooer had made tracks. What did you expect *her* to think?"

"Well, I thought she'd keep quiet for her own sake. As a matter of fact, I didn't think very clearly about anything. I knew I'd broken in where I had no business, and that if I was found with a murdered man it might look jolly queer for me."

"In fact," said Mr. Murbles, "you lost your head, young man, and ran away in a very foolish and cowardly manner."

"You needn't put it that way," retorted Mr. Goyles. "I was in a very awkward and stupid situation to start with."

"Yes," said Lord Peter ironically, "and 3 a.m. is a nasty, chilly time of day. Next time you arrange an elopement, make it for six o'clock in the evening, or twelve o'clock at night. You seem better at framing conspiracies than carrying them out. A little thing upsets your nerves, Mr. Goyles. I don't really think, you know, that a person of your temperament should carry fire-arms. What in the world, you blitherin' young ass, made you loose off that pop-gun at me last night? You *would* have been in a damned awkward situation then, if you'd accidentally hit me in the head or the heart or anywhere that mattered. If you're so frightened of a dead body, why go about shootin' at people? Why, why, why? That's what beats me. If you're tellin' the truth now, you never stood in the slightest danger. Lord! and to think of the time and trouble we've had to waste catchin' you—you ass! And poor old Mary, workin' away and half killin' herself, because she thought at least you wouldn't have run away unless there was somethin' to run from!"

"You must make allowance for a nervous temperament," said Mary in a hard voice.

"If you knew what it felt like to be shadowed and followed and badgered——" began Mr. Goyles.

"But I thought you Soviet Club people enjoyed being suspected of things," said Lord Peter. "Why, it ought to be the proudest moment of your life when you're really looked on as a dangerous fellow."

"It's the sneering of men like you," said Goyles passionately, "that does more to breed hatred between class and class——"

"Never mind about that," interposed Mr. Murbles. "The law's the law for everybody, and you have managed to put yourself in a very awkward position, young man." He touched a bell on the table, and Parker entered with a constable. "We shall be obliged to you," said Mr. Murbles, "if you will kindly have this young man kept under observation. We make no charge against him so long as he behaves himself, but he must not attempt to abscond before the Riddlesdale case comes up for trial."

"Certainly not, sir," said Mr. Parker.

"One moment," said Mary. "Mr. Goyles, here is the ring you gave me. Good-bye. When next you make a public speech calling for decisive action I will come and applaud it. You speak so well about that sort of thing. But otherwise, I think we had better not meet again."

"Of course," said the young man bitterly, "Your people have forced me into this position, and you turn round and sneer at me too."

"I didn't mind thinking you were a murderer," said Lady Mary spitefully, "but I *do* mind your being such an ass."

Before Mr. Goyles could reply, Mr. Parker, bewildered but not wholly displeased, manoeuvred his charge out of the room. Mary walked over to the window, and stood biting her lips.

Presently Lord Peter came across to her. "I say, Polly, old Murbles has asked us to lunch. Would you like to come? Sir Impey Biggs will be there."

"I don't want to meet him to-day. It's very kind of Mr. Murbles——"

"Oh, come along, old thing. Biggs is some celebrity, you know, and perfectly toppin' to look at, in a marbly kind of way. He'll tell you all about his canaries——"

Mary giggled through her obstinate tears.

"It's perfectly sweet of you, Peter, to try and amuse the baby. But I can't. I'd make a fool of myself. I've been made enough of a fool of for one day."

"Bosh," said Peter. "Of course, Goyles didn't show up very well this morning, but, then, he was in an awfully difficult position. *Do* come."

"I hope Lady Mary consents to adorn my bachelor establishment," said the solicitor, coming up. "I shall esteem it a very great honour. I really do not think I have entertained a lady in my chambers for twenty years–dear me, twenty years indeed it must be."

"In that case," said Lady Mary, "I simply *can't* refuse."

Mr. Murbles inhabited a delightful old set of rooms in Staple Inn, with windows looking out upon the formal garden, with its odd little flower-beds and tinkling fountain. The chambers kept up to a miracle the old-fashioned law atmosphere which hung about his own prim person. His dining-room was furnished in mahogany, with a Turkey carpet and crimson curtains. On his sideboard stood some pieces of handsome Sheffield plate and a number of decanters with engraved silver labels round their necks. There was a bookcase full of large volumes bound in law calf, and an oil-painting of a harsh-featured judge over the mantelpiece. Lady Mary felt a sudden gratitude for this discreet and solid Victorianism.

"I fear we may have to wait a few moments for Sir Impey," said Mr. Murbles, consulting his watch. "He is engaged in Quangle & Hamper v. *Truth*, but they expect to be through this morning–in fact, Sir Impey fancied that midday would see the end of it. Brilliant man, Sir Impey. He is defending *Truth*."

"Astonishin' position for a lawyer, what?" said Peter.

"The newspaper," said Mr. Murbles, acknowledging the pleasantry with a slight unbending of the lips, "against these people who profess to cure fifty-nine different diseases with the same pill. Quangle & Hamper produced some of their patients in court to testify to the benefits they'd enjoyed from the cure. To hear Sir Impey handling them was an intellectual treat. His kindly manner goes a long way with old ladies. When he suggested that one of them should show her leg to the Bench the sensation in court was really phenomenal."

"And did she show it?" inquired Lord Peter.

"Panting for the opportunity, my dear Lord Peter, panting for the opportunity."

"I wonder they had the nerve to call her."

"Nerve?" said Mr. Murbles. "The nerve of men like Quangle & Hamper has not its fellow in the universe, to adopt the expression of the great Shakespeare. But Sir Impey is not the man to take liberties with. We are really extremely fortunate to have secured his help.—Ah, I think I hear him!"

A hurried footstep on the stair indeed announced learned counsel, who burst in, still in wig and gown, and full of apology.

"Extremely sorry, Murbles," said Sir Impey. "We became excessively tedious at the end, I regret to say. I really did my best, but dear old Dowson is getting as deaf as a post, you know, and terribly fumbling in his movements.—And how are you, Wimsey? You look as if you'd been in the wars. Can we bring an action for assault against anybody?"

"Much better than that," put in Mr. Murbles; "attempted murder, if you please."

"Excellent, excellent," said Sir Impey.

"Ah, but we've decided not to prosecute," said Mr. Murbles, shaking his head.

"Really! Oh, my dear Wimsey, this will never do. Lawyers have to live, you know. Your sister? I hadn't the pleasure of meeting you at Riddlesdale, Lady Mary. I trust you are fully recovered."

"Entirely, thank you," said Mary with emphasis.

"Mr. Parker—of course your name is very familiar. Wimsey, here, can't do a thing without you, I know. Murbles, are these gentlemen full of valuable information? I am immensely interested in this case."

"Not just this moment, though," put in the solicitor.

"Indeed, no. Nothing but that excellent saddle of mutton has the slightest attraction for me just now. Forgive my greed."

"Well, well," said Mr. Murbles, beaming mildly, "let's make a start. I fear, my dear young people, I am old-fashioned enough not to have adopted the modern practice of cocktail-drinking."

"Quite right too," said Wimsey emphatically. "Ruins the palate and spoils the digestion. Not an English custom—rank sacrilege in this old Inn. Came from America—result, prohibition. That's what happens to people, who don't understand how to drink. God bless me, sir, why, you're giving us the famous claret. It's a sin so much as to mention a cocktail in its presence."

"Yes," said Mr. Murbles, "yes, that's the Lafite '75. It's very seldom, very seldom, I bring it out for anybody under fifty years of age—but you, Lord Peter, have a discrimination which would do honour to one of twice your years."

"Thanks very much, sir; that's a testimonial I deeply appreciate. May I circulate the bottle, sir?"

"Do, do—we will wait on ourselves, Simpson, thank you. After lunch," continued Mr. Murbles, "I will ask you to try something really curious. An odd old client of mine died the other day, and left me a dozen of '47 port."

"Gad!" said Peter. " '47! It'll hardly be drinkable, will it, sir?"

"I very greatly fear," replied Mr. Murbles, "that it will not. A great pity. But I feel that some kind of homage should be paid to so notable an antiquity."

"It would be something to say that one had tasted it," said Peter. "Like goin' to see the divine Sarah, you know. Voice gone, bloom gone, savour gone—but still a classic."

"Ah," said Mr. Murbles. "I remember her in her great days. We old fellows have the compensation of some very wonderful memories."

"Quite right, sir," said Peter, "and you'll pile up plenty more yet. But what was this old gentleman doing to let a vintage like that get past its prime?"

"Mr. Featherstone was a very singular man," said Mr. Murbles. "And yet—I don't know. He may have been profoundly wise. He had the reputation for extreme avarice. Never bought a new suit, never took a holiday, never married, lived all his life in the same dark, narrow chambers he occupied as a briefless barrister. Yet he inherited a huge income from his father, all of which he left to accumulate. The port was laid down by the old man, who died in 1860, when my client was thirty-four. He—the son, I mean—was ninety-six when he deceased. He said no pleasure ever came up to the anticipation, and so he lived like a hermit—doing nothing, but planning all the things he might have done. He wrote an elaborate diary, containing, day by day, the record of this visionary existence which he had never dared put to the test of actuality. The diary described minutely a blissful wedded life with the woman of his dreams. Every Christmas and Easter Day a bottle of the '47 was solemnly set upon his table and solemnly removed, unopened, at the close of his frugal meal. An earnest Christian, he anticipated great happiness after death, but, as you see, he put the pleasure off as long as possible. He died with the words, 'He is faithful that promised'—feeling to the end the need of assurance. A very singular man, very singular indeed—far removed from the adventurous spirit of the present generation."

"How curious and pathetic," said Mary.

"Perhaps he had at some time set his heart on something unattainable," said Parker.

"Well, I don't know," said Mr. Murbles. "People used to say that the dream-lady had not always been a dream, but that he never could bring himself to propose."

"Ah," said Sir Impey briskly, "the more I see and hear in the courts the more I am inclined to feel that Mr. Featherstone chose the better part."

"And are determined to follow his example—in that respect at any rate? Eh, Sir Impey!" replied Mr. Murbles, with a mild chuckle.

Mr. Parker glanced towards the window. It was beginning to rain.

Truly enough the '47 port was a dead thing; the merest ghost of its old flame and flavour hung about it. Lord Peter held his glass poised a moment.

"It is like the taste of a passion that has passed its noon and turned to weariness," he said, with sudden gravity. "The only thing to do is to recognise bravely that it is dead, and put it away." With a determined movement, he flung the remainder of the wine into the fire. The mocking smile came back to his face:

> "What I like about Clive
> Is that he is no longer alive—
> There is a great deal to be said
> For being dead.

What classic pith and brevity in those four lines!—However, in the matter of this case, we've a good deal to tell you, sir."

With the assistance of Parker, he laid before the two men of law the whole train of the investigation up to date, Lady Mary coming loyally up to the scratch with her version of the night's proceedings.

"In fact, you see," said Peter, "this Mr. Goyles has lost a lot by *not* being a murderer. We feel he would have cut a fine, sinister figure as a midnight assassin. But things bein' as they are, you see, we must make what we can of him as a witness, what?"

"Well, Lord Peter," said Mr. Murbles slowly, "I congratulate you and Mr. Parker on a great deal of industry and ingenuity in working the matter out."

"I think we may say we have made some progress," said Parker.

"If only negatively," added Peter.

"Exactly," said Sir Impey turning on him with staggering abruptness. "Very negative indeed. And, having seriously hampered the case for the defence, what are you going to do next?"

"That's a nice thing to say," cried Peter indignantly, "when we've cleared up such a lot of points for you!"

"I daresay," said the barrister, "but they're the sorts of points which are much better left muffled up."

"Damn it all, we want to get at the truth!"

"Do you?" said Sir Impey drily "I don't. I don't care twopence about the truth. I want a case. It doesn't matter to me who killed Cathcart, provided I can prove it wasn't Denver. It's really enough if I can throw reasonable doubt on its being Denver. Here's a client comes to me with a story of a quarrel, a suspicious revolver, a refusal to produce evidence of his statements, and a totally inadequate and idiotic alibi. I arrange to obfuscate the jury with mysterious footprints, a discrepancy as to time, a young woman with a secret, and a general vague suggestion of something between a burglary and a *crime passionel.* And here you come explaining the footprints, exculpating the unknown man, abolishing the discrepancies, clearing up the motives of the young woman, and most carefully throwing back suspicion to where it rested in the first place. What *do* you expect?"

"I've always said," growled Peter, "that the professional advocate was the most immoral fellow on the face of the earth, and now I know for certain."

"Well, well," said Mr. Murbles, "all this just means that we mustn't rest upon our oars. You must go on, my dear boy, and get more evidence of a positive kind. If this Mr. Goyles did not kill Cathcart we must be able to find the person who did."

"Anyhow, said Biggs, "there's one thing to be thankful for—and that is, that you were still too unwell to go before the Grand Jury last Thursday, Lady Mary"—Lady Mary blushed—"and the prosecution will be building their case on a shot fired at three a.m. Don't answer any questions if you can help it, and we'll spring it on 'em."

"But will they believe anything she says at the trial after that?" asked Peter dubiously.

"All the better if they don't. She'll be their witness. You'll get a nasty heckling, Lady Mary, but you mustn't mind that. It's all in the game. Just stick to your story and we'll deliver the goods. See!" Sir Impey wagged a menacing finger.

"I see," said Mary. "And I'll be heckled like anything. Just go on stubbornly saying, 'I am telling the truth now.' That's the idea, isn't it?"

"Exactly so," said Biggs. "By the way, Denver still refuses to explain his movements, I suppose?"

"Cat-e-gori-cally," replied the solicitor. "The Wimseys are a very determined family," he added, "and I fear that, for the present, it is useless to pursue that line of investigation. If we could discover the truth in some other way, and confront the Duke with it, he might then be persuaded to add his confirmation."

"Well, now," said Parker, "we have, as it seems to me, still three lines to go upon. First, we must try to establish the Duke's alibi from external sources. Secondly, we can examine the evidence afresh with a view to finding the real murderer. And thirdly, the Paris police may give us some light upon Cathcart's past history."

"And I fancy I know where to go next for information on the second point," said Wimsey suddenly. "Grider's Hole."

"Whew-w!" Parker whistled. "I was forgetting that. That's where that bloodthirsty farmer fellow lives, isn't it, who set the dogs on you?"

"With the remarkable wife. Yes. See here, how does this strike you? This fellow is ferociously jealous of his wife, and inclined to suspect every man who comes near her. When I went up there that day, and mentioned that a friend of mine might have been hanging about there the previous week, he got frightfully excited and threatened to have the fellow's blood. Seemed to know who I was referrin' to. Now, of course, with my mind full of No. 10–Goyles, you know –I never thought but what he was the man. But supposin' it was Cathcart? You see, we know now, Goyles hadn't even been in the neighbourhood till the Wednesday, so you wouldn't expect what's-his-name–Grimethorpe–to know about him, but Cathcart might have wandered over to Grider's Hole any day and been seen. And look here! Here's another thing that fits in. When I went up there Mrs. Grimethorpe evidently mistook me for somebody she knew, and hurried down to warn me off. Well, of course, I've been thinkin' all the time she must have seen my old cap and Burberry from the window and mistaken me for Goyles, but, now I come to think of it, I told the kid who came to the door that I was from Riddlesdale Lodge. If the child told her mother, she must have thought it was Cathcart."

"No, no, Wimsey, that won't do," put in Parker; "she must have known Cathcart was dead by that time."

"Oh, damn it! Yes, I suppose she must. Unless that surly old devil kept the news from her. By Jove! that's just what he would do if he'd killed Cathcart himself. He'd never say a word to her–and I don't suppose he would let her look at a paper, even if they take one in. It's a primitive sort of place."

"But didn't you say Grimethorpe had an alibi?"

"Yes, but we didn't really test it."

"And how d'you suppose he knew Cathcart was going to be in the thicket that night?"

Peter considered.

"Perhaps he sent for him," suggested Mary.

"That's right, that's right," cried Peter eagerly. "You remember we thought Cathcart must somehow or other have heard from Goyles, making an appointment–but suppose the message was from Grimethorpe, threatening to split on Cathcart to Jerry."

"You are suggesting, Lord Peter," said Mr. Murbles, in a tone calculated to chill Peter's blithe impetuosity, "that, at the very time Mr. Cathcart was betrothed to your sister, he was carrying on a disgraceful intrigue with a married woman very much his social inferior."

"I beg your pardon, Polly," said Wimsey.

"It's all right," said Mary, "I—as a matter of fact, it wouldn't surprise me frightfully. Denis was always—I mean, he had rather Continental ideas about marriage and that sort of thing. He'd probably have said there was a time and place for everything."

"One of those watertight compartment minds," said Wimsey thoughtfully. Mr. Parker, despite his long acquaintance with the seamy side of things in London, had his brows set in a gloomy frown of as fierce a provincial disapproval as ever came from Barrow-in-Furness.

"If you can upset this Grimethorpe's alibi," said Sir Impey, fitting his right-hand finger-tips neatly between the fingers of his left hand, "we might make some sort of a case of it. What do you think, Murbles?"

"After all," said the solicitor, "Grimethorpe and the servant both admit that he, Grimethorpe, was not at Grider's Hole on Wednesday night. If he can't prove he was at Stapley he may have been at Riddlesdale."

"By Jove!" cried Wimsey; "driven off alone, stopped somewhere, left the gee, sneaked back, met Cathcart, done him in, and toddled home next day with a tale about machinery."

"Or he may even have been to Stapley," put in Parker; "left early or gone late, and put in the murder on the way. We shall have to check the precise times very carefully."

"Hurray!" cried Wimsey. "I think I'll be gettin' back to Riddlesdale."

"I'd better stay here," said Parker. "There may be something from Paris."

"Right you are. Let me know the minute anything comes through. I say, old thing!"

"Yes?"

"Does it occur to you that what's the matter with this case is that there are too many clues? Dozens of people with secrets and elopements bargin' about all over the place——"

"I hate you, Peter," said Lady Mary.

# 11

# MERIBAH

*Oh-ho, my friend! You are gotten into Lob's pond.*
Jack the Giant-Killer

LORD PETER broke his journey north at York, whither the Duke of Denver had been transferred after the Assizes, owing to the imminent closing-down of Northallerton Gaol. By dint of judicious persuasion, Peter contrived to obtain an interview with his brother. He found him looking ill at ease, and pulled down by the prison atmosphere, but still unquenchably defiant.

"Bad luck, old man," said Peter, "but you're keepin' your tail up fine. Beastly slow business, all this legal stuff, what? But it gives us time, an' that's all to the good."

"It's a confounded nuisance," said his grace. "And I'd like to know what Murbles means. Comes down and tries to bully me—damned impudence! Anybody'd think he suspected me."

"Look here, Jerry," said his brother earnestly, "why can't you let up on that alibi of yours? It'd help no end, you know. After all, if a fellow won't say what he's been doin'——"

"It ain't my business to prove anything," retorted his grace, with dignity. "They've got to show I was there, murderin' the fellow. I'm not bound to say where I was. I'm presumed innocent, aren't I, till they prove me guilty? I call it a disgrace. Here's a murder committed, and they aren't taking the slightest trouble to find the real criminal. I give 'em my word of honour, to say nothin' of an oath, that I didn't kill Cathcart—though, mind you, the swine deserved it—but they pay no attention. Meanwhile, the real man's escapin' at his confounded leisure. If I were only free, I'd make a fuss about it."

"Well, why the devil don't you cut it short, then?" urged Peter. "I don't mean here and now to me"—with a glance at the warder, within earshot—"but to Murbles. Then we could get to work."

"I wish you'd jolly well keep out of it," grunted the Duke. "Isn't it all damnable enough for Helen, poor girl, and mother, and everyone, without you makin' it an opportunity to play Sherlock Holmes? I'd have thought you'd have had the decency to keep quiet, for the family's sake. I may be in a damned rotten position, but I ain't makin' a public spectacle of myself, by Jove!"

"Hell!" said Lord Peter, with such vehemence that the wooden-faced warder actually jumped. "It's you that's makin' the spectacle. It need never have started, but for you. Do you think *I* like havin' my brother and sister dragged through the Courts, and reporters swarmin' over the place, and paragraphs and news-bills with your name starin' at me from every corner, and all this ghastly business, endin' up in a great show in the House of Lords, with a lot of people togged up in scarlet and ermine, and all the rest of the damn-fool jiggery-pokery? People are beginnin' to look oddly at me in the Club, and I can jolly well hear 'em whisperin' that 'Denver's attitude looks jolly fishy, b'gad!' Cut it out, Jerry."

"Well, we're in for it now," said his brother, "and thank heaven there are still a few decent fellows left in the peerage who'll know how to take a gentleman's word, even if my own brother can't see beyond his rotten legal evidence."

As they stared angrily at one another, that mysterious sympathy of the flesh which we call family likeness sprang out from its hiding-place, stamping their totally dissimilar features with an elfish effect of mutual caricature. It was as though each saw himself in a distorting mirror, while the voices might have been one voice with its echo.

"Look here, old chap," said Peter, recovering himself, "I'm frightfully sorry. I didn't mean to let myself go like that. If you won't say anything, you won't. Anyhow, we're all working like blazes, and we're sure to find the right man before very long."

"You'd better leave it to the police," said Denver. "I know you like playin' at detectives, but I do think you might draw the line somewhere."

"That's a nasty one," said Wimsey. "But I don't look on this as a game, and I can't say I'll keep out of it, because I know I'm doin' valuable work. Still, I can—honestly, I can—see your point of view. I'm jolly sorry you find me such an irritatin' sort of person. I suppose it's hard for you to believe I feel anything. But I do, and I'm goin' to get you out of this, if Bunter and I both perish in the attempt. Well, so long—that warder's just wakin' up to say, 'Time, gentlemen.' Cheer-oh, old thing! Good luck!"

He rejoined Bunter outside.

"Bunter," he said, as they walked through the streets of the old city, "is my manner *really* offensive, when I don't mean it to be?"

"It is possible, my lord, if your lordship will excuse my saying so, that the liveliness of your lordship's manner may be misleading to persons of limited——"

"Be careful, Bunter!"

"Limited imagination, my lord."

"Well-bred English people never have imagination, Bunter."

"Certainly not, my lord. I meant nothing disparaging."

"Well, Bunter—oh, lord! there's a reporter! Hide me quick!"

"In here, my lord."

Mr. Bunter whisked his master into the cool emptiness of the Cathedral.

"I venture to suggest, my lord," he urged in a hurried whisper, "that we adopt the attitude and external appearance of prayer, if your lordship will excuse me."

Peeping through his fingers, Lord Peter saw a verger hastening towards them, rebuke depicted on his face. At that moment, however, the reporter entered in headlong pursuit, tugging a note-book from his pocket. The verger leapt swiftly on this new prey.

"The winder h'under which we stand," he began in a reverential monotone, "is called the Seven Sisters of York. They say——"

Master and man stole quietly out.

* * * * *

For his visit to the market town of Stapley Lord Peter attired himself in an aged Norfolk suit, stockings with sober tops, an ancient hat turned down all round, stout shoes, and carried a heavy ashplant. It was with regret that he abandoned his favourite stick—a handsome malacca, marked off in inches for detective convenience, and concealing a sword in its belly and a compass in its head. He decided, however, that it would prejudice the natives against him, as having a town-bred, not to say supercilious, air about it. The sequel to this commendable devotion to his art forcibly illustrated the truth of Gertrude Rhead's observation, "All this self-sacrifice is a sad mistake."

The little town was sleepy enough as he drove into it in one of the Riddlesdale dog-carts, Bunter beside him, and the under-gardener on the back seat. For choice, he would have come on a market-day, in the hope of meeting Grimethorpe himself, but things were moving fast now, and he dared not lose a day. It was a raw, cold morning, inclined to rain.

"Which is the best inn to put up at, Wilkes?"

"There's t' 'Bricklayers' Arms,' my lord—a fine, well-thought-of place, or t' 'Bridge and Bottle,' i' t' square, or t' 'Rose and Crown,' t'other side o' square."

"Where do the folks usually put up on market-days?"

"Mebbe 'Rose and Crown' is most popular, so to say—Tim Watchett, t' landlord, is a rare gossip. Now Greg Smith ower t'way at 'Bridge and Bottle,' he's nobbut a grimly, surly man, but he keeps good drink."

"H'm—I fancy, Bunter, our man will be more attracted by surliness and good drink than by a genial host. The 'Bridge and Bottle' for us, I fancy, and, if we draw blank there, we'll toddle over to the 'Rose and Crown,' and pump the garrulous Watchett."

Accordingly they turned into the yard of a large, stony-faced house, whose long-unpainted sign bore the dim outline of a "Bridge Embattled," which local etymology had (by a natural association of ideas) transmogrified into the "Bridge and Bottle." To the grumpy ostler who took the horse Peter, with his most companionable manner, addressed himself:

"Nasty raw morning, isn't it?"

"Eea."

"Give him a good feed. I may be here some time."

"Ugh!"

"Not many people about to-day, what?"

"Ugh!"

"But I expect you're busy enough market-days."

"Eea."

"People come in from a long way round, I suppose."

"Co-oop!" said the ostler. The horse walked three steps forward.

"Wo!" said the ostler. The horse stopped, with the shafts free of the tugs; the man lowered the shafts, to grate viciously on the gravel.

"Coom on oop!" said the ostler, and walked calmly off into the stable, leaving the affable Lord Peter as thoroughly snubbed as that young sprig of the nobility had ever found himself.

"I am more and more convinced," said his lordship, "that this is Farmer Grimethorpe's usual house of call. Let's try the bar. Wilkes, I shan't want you for a bit. Get yourself lunch if necessary. I don't know how long we shall be."

"Very good, my lord."

In the bar of the "Bridge and Bottle" they found Mr. Greg Smith gloomily checking a long invoice. Lord Peter ordered drinks for Bunter and himself. The landlord appeared to resent this as a liberty, and jerked his head towards the barmaid. It was only right and proper that Bunter, after respectfully returning thanks to his master for his half-pint, should fall into conversation with the girl, while Lord Peter paid his respects to Mr. Smith.

"Ah!" said his lordship, "good stuff, that, Mr. Smith. I was told to come here for real good beer, and, by Jove! I've been sent to the right place."

"Ugh!" said Mr. Smith, " 'tisn't what it was. Nowt's good these times."

"Well, I don't want better. By the way, is Mr. Grimethorpe here to-day?"

"Eh?"

"Is Mr. Grimethorpe in Stapley this morning, d'you know?"

"How'd I know?"

"I thought he always put up here."

"Ah!"

"Perhaps I mistook the name. But I fancied he'd be the man to go where the best beer is."

"Ay?"

"Oh, well, if you haven't seen him, I don't suppose he's come over today."

"Coom where?"

"Into Stapley."

"Doosn't 'e live here? He can go and coom without my knowing."

"Oh, of course!" Wimsey staggered under the shock, and then grasped the misunderstanding. "I don't mean Mr. Grimethorpe of Stapley, but Mr. Grimethorpe of Grider's Hole."

"Why didn't tha say so? Oh, him? Ay."

"He's here to-day?"

"Nay, I knaw nowt about 'un."

"He comes in on market-days, I expect."

"Sometimes."

"It's a longish way. One can put up for the night, I suppose?"

"Doosta want t'stay t'night?"

"Well, no, I don't think so. I was thinking about my friend Mr. Grimethorpe. I daresay he often has to stay the night."

"Happen a does."

"Doesn't he stay here, then?"

"Naay."

"Oh!" said Wimsey, and thought impatiently: "If all these natives are as oyster-like I *shall* have to stay the night. . . . Well, well," he added aloud, "next time he drops in say I asked after him."

"And who mought tha be?" inquired Mr. Smith in a hostile manner.

"Oh, only Brooks of Sheffield," said Lord Peter, with a happy grin. "Good morning. I won't forget to recommend your beer."

Mr. Smith grunted. Lord Peter strolled slowly out, and before long Mr. Bunter joined him, coming out with a brisk step and the lingering remains of what, in anyone else, might have been taken for a smirk.

"Well?" inquired his lordship. "I hope the young lady was more communicative than that fellow."

"I found the young person" ("Snubbed again," muttered Lord Peter) "perfectly amiable, my lord, but unhappily ill-informed. Mr. Grimethorpe is not unknown to her, but he does not stay here. She has sometimes seen him in company with a man called Zedekiah Bone."

"Well," said his lordship, "suppose you look for Bone, and come and report progress to me in a couple of hours' time. I'll try the 'Rose and Crown.' We'll meet at noon under that thing."

"That thing," was a tall erection in pink granite, neatly tooled to represent a craggy rock, and guarded by two petrified infantry-men in trench helmets. A thin stream of water gushed from a bronze knob half-way up, a roll of honour was engraved on the octagonal base, and four gas-lamps on cast-iron standards put the finishing touch to a very monument of incongruity. Mr. Bunter looked carefully at it, to be sure of recognising it again, and moved respectfully away. Lord Peter walked ten brisk steps in the direction of the "Rose and Crown," then a thought struck him.

"Bunter!"

Mr. Bunter hurried back to his side.

"Oh, nothing!" said his lordship. "Only I've just thought of a name for it."

"For——"

"That memorial," said Lord Peter. "I choose to call it 'Meribah.' "

"Yes, my lord. The waters of strife. Exceedingly apt, my lord. Nothing harmonious about it, if I may say so. Will there be anything further, my lord?"

"No, that's all."

* * * * *

Mr. Timothy Watchett of the "Rose and Crown" was certainly a contrast to Mr. Greg Smith. He was a small, spare, sharp-eyed man of about fifty-five, with so twinkling and humorous an eye and so alert a cock of the head that Lord Peter summed up his origin the moment he set eyes on him.

"Morning, landlord," said he genially, "and when did *you* last see Piccadilly Circus?"

" 'Ard to say, sir. Gettin' on for thirty-five year, I reckon. Many's the time I said to my wife, 'Liz, I'll tike you ter see the 'Olborn Empire afore I die.' But, with one thing and another, time slips aw'y. One day's so like another–blowed if I ever remember 'ow old I'm gettin', sir."

"Oh, well, you've lots of time yet," said Lord Peter.

"I 'ope so, sir. I ain't never wot you may call got used ter these Northerners. That slow, they are, sir–it fair giv' me the 'ump when I first come. And the w'y they speak–that took some gettin' used to. Call that English, I useter say, give me the Frenchies in the Chantycleer Restaurong, I ses. But there, sir, custom's everything. Blowed if I didn't ketch myself a-syin' 'yon side the square' the other day. Me!"

"I don't think there's much fear of your turning into a Yorkshire man," said Lord Peter, "didn't I know you the minute I set eyes on you? In Mr. Watchett's bar I said to myself, 'My foot is on my native paving-stones.' "

"That's raight, sir. And, bein' there, sir, what can I 'ave the pleasure of offerin' you? . . . Excuse me, sir, but 'aven't I seen you fice somewhere?"

"I don't think so," said Peter; "but that reminds me. Do you know one Mr. Grimethorpe?"

"I know five Mr. Grimethorpes. W'ich of 'em was you meanin', sir?"

"Mr. Grimethorpe of Grider's Hole."

The landlord's cheerful face darkened.

"Friend of yours, sir?"

"Not exactly. An acquaintance."

"There naow!" cried Mr. Watchett, smacking his hand down upon the counter. "I knowed as I knowed your fice! Don't you live over at Riddlesdale, sir?"

"I'm stayin' there."

"I knowed it," retorted Mr. Watchett triumphantly. He dived behind the counter and brought up a bundle of newspapers, turning over the sheets excitedly with a well-licked thumb. "There! Riddlesdale! That's it, of course."

He smacked open a *Daily Mirror* of a fortnight or so ago. The front page bore a heavy block headline: THE RIDDLESDALE MYSTERY. And beneath was a lifelike snapshot entitled, "*Lord Peter Wimsey, the Sherlock Holmes of the West End, who is devoting all his time and energies to proving the innocence of his brother, the Duke of Denver*." Mr. Watchett gloated.

"You won't mind my syin' 'ow proud I am to 'ave you in my bar, my lord.–'Ere, Jem, you attend ter them gentlemen; don't you see they're wytin'?–Follered all yer caises I 'ave, my lord, in the pipers–jest like a book they are. An' ter think——"

"Look here, old thing," said Lord Peter, "d'you mind not talkin' quite so loud. Seein' dear old Felix is out of the bag, so to speak, do you think you could give me some information and keep your mouth shut, what?"

"Come be'ind into the bar-parlour, my lord. Nobody'll 'ear us there," said Mr. Watchett eagerly, lifting up the flap. "Jem, 'ere! Bring a bottle of–what'll you 'ave, my lord?"

"Well, I don't know how many places I may have to visit," said his lordship dubiously.

"Jem, bring a quart of the old ale.–It's special, that's wot it is, my lord. I ain't never found none like it, except it might be once at Oxford. Thanks, Jem. Naow you get along sharp and attend to the customers. Now, my lord."

Mr. Watchett's information amounted to this. That Mr. Grimethorpe used to come to the "Rose and Crown" pretty often, especially on market-days. About ten days previously he had come in lateish, very drunk and quarrelsome, with his wife, who seemed, as usual, terrified of him. Grimethorpe had demanded spirits, but Mr. Watchett had refused to serve him. There had been a row, and Mrs. Grimethorpe had endeavoured to get her husband away. Grimethorpe had promptly knocked her down, with epithets reflecting upon her virtue, and Mr. Watchett had at once called upon the potmen to turn Grimethorpe out, refusing to have him in the house again. He had heard it said on all sides that Grimethorpe's temper, always notoriously bad, had become positively diabolical of late.

"Could you hazard, so to speak, a calculation as to how long, or since when?"

"Well, my lord, come to think of it, especially since the middle of last month—p'r'aps a bit earlier."

"M'm!"

"Not that I'd go for to insinuate anythink, nor your lordship, neither, of course," said Mr. Watchett quickly.

"Certainly not," said Lord Peter. "What about?"

"Ah!" said Mr. Watchett, "there it is, wot abaht?"

"Tell me," said Lord Peter, "do you recollect Grimethorpe comin' into Stapley on October 13th—a Wednesday, it was."

"That would be the day of the—ah! to be sure! Yes, I do recollect it, for I remember thinking it was odd him comin' here except on a market-day. Said he 'ad ter look at some machinery——drills and such, that's raight. 'E was 'ere raight enough."

"Do you remember what time he came in?"

"Well, naow, I've a fancy 'e was 'ere ter lunch. The waitress'd know. 'Ere, Bet!" he called through the side door, "d'yer 'appen to recollect whether Mr. Grimethorpe lunched 'ere October the 13th—Wednesday it were, the d'y the pore gent was murdered over at Riddlesdale?"

"Grimethorpe o' Grider's Hole?" said the girl, a well-grown young Yorkshire woman. "Yes! 'E took loonch, and coom back to sleep. Ah'm not mistook, for ah waited on 'un, an' took up 'is watter i' t'morning, and 'e only gied me tuppence."

"Monstrous!" said Lord Peter. "Look here, Miss Elizabeth, you're sure it was the thirteenth? Because I've got a bet on it with a friend, and I don't want to lose the money if I can help it. You're positive it was Wednesday night he slept here? I could have sworn it was Thursday."

"Naay, sir, t'wor Wednesday for I remember hearing the men talking o' t'murder i' t'bar, an' telling Mester Grimethorpe next daay."

"Sounds conclusive. What did Mr. Grimethorpe say about it?"

"There now," cried the young woman, " 'tis queer you should ask that; everyone noticed how strange he acted. He turned all white like a sheet, and looked at both his hands, one after the other, and then he pushes 'es hair off's forehead—dazed-like. We reckoned he hadn't got over the drink. He's more often drunk than not. Ah wouldn't be his wife for five hundred pounds."

"I should think not," said Peter; "you can do a lot better than that. Well, I suppose I've lost my money, then. By the way, what time did Mr. Grimethorpe come in to bed?"

"Close on two i' t'morning," said the girl, tossing her head. "He were locked oot, an' Jem had to go down and let 'un in."

"That so?" said Peter. "Well, I might try to get out on a technicality, eh, Mr.

Watchett? Two o'clock is Thursday, isn't it? I'll work that for all it's worth. Thanks frightfully. That's all I want to know."

Bet grinned and giggled herself away, comparing the generosity of the strange gentleman with the stinginess of Mr. Grimethorpe. Peter rose.

"I'm no end obliged, Mr. Watchett," he said. "I'll just have a word with Jem. Don't say anything, by the way."

"Not me," said Mr. Watchett; "I knows wot's wot. Good luck, my lord."

Jem corroborated Bet. Grimethorpe had returned at about 1:50 a.m. on October 14th, drunk, and plastered with mud. He had muttered something about having run up against a man called Watson.

The ostler was next interrogated. He did not think that anybody could get a horse and trap out of the stable at night without his knowing it. He knew Watson. He was a carrier by trade, and lived on Windon Street. Lord Peter rewarded his informant suitably, and set out for Windon Street.

But the recital of his quest would be tedious. At a quarter-past noon he joined Bunter at the Meribah memorial.

"Any luck?"

"I have secured certain information, my lord, which I have duly noted. Total expenditure on beer for self and witnesses 7*s*. 2*d*., my lord."

Lord Peter paid the 7*s*. 2*d*. without a word, and they adjourned to the "Rose and Crown." Being accommodated in a private parlour, and having ordered lunch, they proceeded to draw up the following schedule:

GRIMETHORPE'S MOVEMENTS. *Wednesday, October 13th to Thursday, October 14th.*

*October 13th* :

| | | |
|---|---|---|
| 12:30 | p.m. | Arrives "Rose and Crown." |
| 1:00 | p.m. | Lunches. |
| 3:00 | p.m. | Orders two drills from man called Gooch in Trimmer's Lane. |
| 4:30 | p.m. | Drink with Gooch to clinch bargain. |
| 5:00 | p.m. | Calls at house of John Watson carrier, about delivering some dog-food. Watson absent. Mrs. Watson says W. expected back that night. G. says will call again. |
| 5:30 | p.m. | Calls on Mark Dolby, grocer, to complain about some tinned salmon. |
| 5:45 | p.m. | Calls on Mr. Hewitt, optician, to pay bill for spectacles and dispute the amount. |
| 6:00 | p.m. | Drinks with Zedekiah Bone at "Bridge and Bottle." |
| 6:45 | p.m. | Calls again on Mrs. Watson. Watson not yet home. |
| 7:00 | p.m. | Seen by Constable Z15 drinking with several men at "Pig and Whistle." Heard to use threatening language with regard to some person unknown. |
| 7:20 | p.m. | Seen to leave "Pig and Whistle" with two men (not yet identified). |

*October 14th*:

| | | |
|---|---|---|
| 1:15 | a.m. | Picked up by Watson, carrier, about a mile out on road to Riddlesdale, very dirty and ill-tempered, and not quite sober. |
| 1:45 | a.m. | Let into "Rose and Crown" by James Johnson, potman. |

| | |
|---|---|
| 9:00 a.m. | Called by Elizabeth Dobbin. |
| 9:30 a.m. | In Bar of "Rose and Crown." Hears of man murdered at Riddlesdale. Behaves suspiciously. |
| 10:15 a.m. | Cashes cheque £129 17*s*. 8*d*. at Lloyds Bank. |
| 10:30 a.m. | Pays Gooch for drills. |
| 11:50 a.m. | Leaves "Rose and Crown" for Grider's Hole. |

Lord Peter looked at this for a few minutes and put his finger on the great gap of six hours after 7:20.

"How far to Riddlesdale, Bunter?"

"About thirteen and three-quarter miles, my lord."

"And the shot was heard at 10:55. It couldn't be done on foot. Did Watson explain why he didn't get back from his round till two in the morning?"

"Yes, my lord. He says he reckons to be back about eleven, but his horse cast a shoe between King's Fenton and Riddlesdale. He had to walk him quietly into Riddlesdale—about 3½ miles—getting there about ten, and knock up the blacksmith. He turned in to the 'Lord in Glory' till closing time, and then went home with a friend and had a few more. At 12:40 he started off home, and picked Grimethorpe up a mile or so out, near the cross roads."

"Sounds circumstantial. The blacksmith and the friend ought to be able to substantiate it. But we simply must find those men at the 'Pig and Whistle.' "

"Yes, my lord. I will try again after lunch."

It was a good lunch. But that seemed to exhaust their luck for the day, for by three o'clock the men had not been identified, and the scent seemed cold.

Wilkes, the groom, however, had his own contribution to the inquiry. He had met a man from King's Fenton at lunch, and they had, naturally, got to talking over the mysterious murder at the Lodge, and the man had said that he knew an old man living in a hut on the Fell, who said that on the night of the murder he'd seen a man walking over Whemmeling Fell in the middle of the night. "And it coom to me, all of a sooden, it mought be his grace," said Wilkes brightly.

Further inquiries elicited that the old man's name was Groot, and that Wilkes could easily drop Lord Peter and Bunter at the beginning of the sheep-path which led up to his hut.

Now, had Lord Peter taken his brother's advice, and paid more attention to English country sports than to incunabula and criminals in London—or had Bunter been brought up on the moors, rather than in a Kentish village—or had Wilkes (who was a Yorkshire man bred and born, and ought to have known better) not been so outrageously puffed up with the sense of his own importance in suggesting a clue, and with impatience to have that clue followed up without delay—or had any of the three exercised common sense—this preposterous suggestion would never have been made, much less carried out, on a November day in the North Riding. As it was, however, Lord Peter and Bunter left the trap at the foot of the moor-path at ten minutes to four, and, dismissing Wilkes, climbed steadily up to the wee hut on the edge of the fell.

* * * * *

The old man was extremely deaf, and, after half an hour of interrogation, his story did not amount to much. On a night in October, which he thought might be the night of the murder, he had been sitting by his peat fire when–about midnight, as he guessed–a tall man had loomed up out of the darkness. He spoke like a Southerner, and said he had got lost on the moor. Old Groot had come to his door and pointed out the track down towards Riddlesdale. The stranger had then vanished, leaving a shilling in his hand. He could not describe the stranger's dress more particularly than that he wore a soft hat and an overcoat, and, he thought, leggings. He was pretty near sure it was the night of the murder, because afterwards he had turned it over in his mind and made out that it might have been one of yon folk at the Lodge——possibly the Duke. He had only arrived at this result by a slow process of thought, and had not "come forward," not knowing whom or where to come to.

With this the inquirers had to be content, and, presenting Groot with half a crown, they emerged upon the moor at something after five o'clock.

"Bunter," said Lord Peter through the dusk, "I am absobally-lutely positive that the answer to all this business is at Grider's Hole."

"Very possibly, my lord."

Lord Peter extended his finger in a south-easterly direction. "That is Grider's Hole," he said. "Let's go."

"Very good, my lord."

So, like two Cockney innocents, Lord Peter and Bunter set forth at a brisk pace down the narrow moor-track towards Grider's Hole, with never a glance behind them for the great white menace rolling silently down through the November dusk from the wide loneliness of Whemmeling Fell.

* * * * *

"Bunter!"

"Here, my lord!"

The voice was close at his ear.

"Thank God! I thought you'd disappeared for good. I say, we ought to have known."

"Yes, my lord."

It had come on them from behind, in a single stride, thick, cold, choking–blotting each from the other, though they were only a yard or two apart.

"I'm a fool, Bunter," said Lord Peter.

"Not at all, my lord."

"Don't move; go on speaking."

"Yes, my lord."

Peter groped to the right and clutched the other's sleeve.

"Ah! Now what are we to do?"

"I couldn't say, my lord, having no experience. Has the–er–phenomenon any habits, my lord?"

"No regular habits, I believe. Sometimes it moves. Other times it stays in one place for days. We can wait all night, and see if it lifts at daybreak."

"Yes, my lord. It is unhappily somewhat damp."

"Somewhat–as you say," agreed his lordship, with a short laugh.

Bunter sneezed, and begged pardon politely.

"If we go on going south-east," said his lordship, "we shall get to Grider's Hole all right, and they'll jolly well *have* to put us up for the night–or give us an escort. I've got my torch in my pocket, and we can go by compass–oh, hell!"

"My lord?"

"I've got the wrong stick. This beastly ash! No compass, Bunter–we're done in."

"Couldn't we keep on going downhill, my lord?"

Lord Peter hesitated. Recollections of what he had heard and read surged up in his mind to tell him that uphill or downhill seems much the same thing in a fog. But man walks in a vain shadow. It is hard to believe that one is really helpless. The cold was icy. "We might try," he said weakly.

"I have heard it said, my lord, that in a fog one always walked round in a circle," said Mr. Bunter, seized with a tardy diffidence.

"Not on a slope, surely," said Lord Peter, beginning to feel bold out of sheer contrariness.

Bunter, being out of his element, had, for once, no good counsel to offer.

"Well, we can't be much worse off than we are," said Lord Peter. "We'll try it, and keep on shouting."

He grasped Bunter's hand, and they strode gingerly forward into the thick coldness of the fog.

How long that nightmare lasted neither could have said. The world might have died about them. Their own shouts terrified them; when they stopped shouting the dead silence was more terrifying still. They stumbled over tufts of thick heather. It was amazing how, deprived of sight, they exaggerated the inequalities of the ground. It was with very little confidence that they could distinguish uphill from downhill. They were shrammed through with cold, yet the sweat was running from their faces with strain and terror.

Suddenly–from directly before them as it seemed, and only a few yards away–there rose a long, horrible shriek–and another–and another.

"My God! What's that?"

"It's a horse, my lord."

"Of course." They remembered having heard horses scream like that. There had been a burning stable near Poperinghe——

"Poor devil," said Peter. He started off impulsively in the direction of the sound, dropping Bunter's hand.

"Come back, my lord," cried the man in a sudden agony. And then, with a frightened burst of enlightenment:

"For God's sake stop, my lord–the bog!"

A sharp shout in the utter blackness.

"Keep away there–don't move–it's got me!"

And a dreadful sucking noise.

# 12

# THE ALIBI

*When actually in the embrace of a voracious and powerful wild animal, the desirability of leaving a limb is not a matter to be subjected to lengthy consideration.*

The Wallet of Kai-Lung

"I TRIPPED right into it," said Wimsey's voice steadily, out of the blackness. "One sinks very fast. You'd better not come near, or you'll go too. We'll yell a bit. I don't think we can be very far from Grider's Hole."

"If your lordship will keep shouting," returned Mr. Bunter, "I think–I can–get to you," he panted, untying with his teeth the hard knot of a coll of string.

"Oy!" cried Lord Peter obediently. "Help! Oy! Oy!"

Mr. Bunter groped towards the voice, feeling cautiously before him with his walking-stick.

"Wish you'd keep away, Bunter," said Lord Peter peevishly. "Where's the sense of both of us——?" He squelched and floundered again.

"Don't do that, my lord," cried the man entreatingly. "You'll sink farther in."

"I'm up to my thighs now," said Lord Peter.

"I'm coming," said Bunter. "Go on shouting. Ah, here's where it gets soggy."

He felt the ground carefully, selected a tussocky bit which seemed reasonably firm, and drove his stick well into it.

"Oy! Hi! Help!" said Lord Peter, shouting lustlly.

Mr. Bunter tied one end of the string to the walking-stick, belted his Burberry tightly about him, and, laying himself cautiously down upon his belly, advanced, clue in hand, like a very Gothic Theseus of a late and degenerate school.

The bog heaved horribly as he crawled over it, and slimy water squelched up into his face. He felt with his hands for tussocks of grass, and got support from them when he could.

"Call out again, my lord!"

"Here!" The voice was fainter and came from the right. Bunter had lost his line a little, hunting for tussocks. "I daren't come faster," he explained. He felt as though he had been crawling for years.

"Get out while there's time," said Peter. "I'm up to my waist. Lord! this is rather a beastly way to peg out."

"You won't peg out," grunted Bunter. His voice was suddenly quite close. "Your hands now."

For a few agonising minutes two pairs of hands groped over the invisible slime. Then:

"Keep yours still," said Bunter. He made a slow, circling movement. It was hard work keeping his face out of the mud. His hands slithered over the slobbery surface–and suddenly closed on an arm.

"Thank God!" said Bunter. "Hang on here, my lord."

He felt forward. The arms were perilously close to the sucking mud. The hands crawled clingingly up his arms and rested on his shoulders. He grasped Wimsey beneath the armpits and heaved. The exertion drove his own knees deep into the bog. He straightened himself hurriedly. Without using his knees he could get no purchase, but to use them meant certain death. They could only hang on desperately till help came–or till the strain became too great. He could not even shout; it was almost more than he could do to keep his mouth free of water. The dragging strain on his shoulders was intolerable; the mere effort to breathe meant an agonising crick in the neck.

"You must go on shouting, my lord."

Wimsey shouted. His voice was breaking and fading.

"Bunter, old thing," said Lord Peter, "I'm simply beastly sorry to have let you in for this."

"Don't mention it, my lord," said Bunter, with his mouth in the slime. A thought struck him.

"What became of your stick, my lord?"

"I dropped it. It should be somewhere near, if it hasn't sunk in."

Bunter cautiously released his left hand and felt about.

"Hi! Hi! Help !"

Bunter's hand closed over the stick, which, by a happy accident, had fallen across a stable tuft of grass. He pulled it over to him, and laid it across his arms, so that he could just rest his chin upon it. The relief to his neck was momentarily so enormous that his courage was renewed. He felt he could hang on for ever.

"Help!"

* * * * *

Minutes passed like hours.

* * * * *

"See that?"

A faint, flickering gleam somewhere away to the right. With desperate energy both shouted together.

"Help! Help! Oy! Oy! Help!"

An answering yell. The light swayed–came nearer–a spreading blur in the fog.

"We *must* keep it up," panted Wimsey. They yelled again.

"Where be?"

"Here!"

"Hello!" A pause. Then:

"Here be stick," said a voice, suddenly near.

"Follow the string!" yelled Bunter. They heard two voices, apparently arguing. Then the string was twitched.

"Here! Here! Two of us! Make haste!"

More consultation.

"Hang on, canst a?"

"Yes, if you're quick."

"Fetchin' hurdle. Two on 'ee, sayst a?"

"Yes."

"Deep in?"

"One of us."

"Aw reet. Jem's comin'."

A splattering noise marked the arrival of Jem with a hurdle. Then came an endless wait. Then another hurdle, the string twitching, and the blur of the lantern bobbing violently about. Then a third hurdle was flung down, and the light came suddenly out of the mist. A hand caught Bunter by the ankle.

"Where's t'other?"

"Here–nearly up to his neck. Have you a rope?"

"Aye, sure. Jem! T'rope!"

The rope came snaking out of the fog. Bunter grasped it, and passed it round his master's body.

"Now–coom tha back and heave."

Bunter crawled cautiously backwards upon the hurdle. All three set hands upon the rope. It was like trying to heave the earth out of her course.

"'Fraid I'm rooted to Australia," panted Peter apologetically. Bunter sweated and sobbed.

"It's aw reet—he's coomin'!"

With slow heavings the rope began to come towards them. Their muscles cracked.

Suddenly, with a great *plop!* the bog let go its hold. The three at the rope were hurled head over heels upon the hurdles. Something unrecognisable in slime lay flat, heaving helplessly. They dragged at him in a kind of frenzy, as though he might be snatched back from them again. The evil bog stench rose thickly round them. They crossed the first hurdle—the second—the third—and rose staggeringly to their feet on firm ground.

"What a beastly place," said Lord Peter faintly. " 'Pologise, stupid of me to have forgotten—what'sy name?"

"Well, tha's loocky," said one of their rescuers. "We thowt we heerd someun a-shouting. There be few falks as cooms oot o' Peter's Pot dead or alive, I reckon."

"Well, it was nearly potted Peter that time," said his lordship, and fainted.

* * * * *

To Lord Peter the memory of his entry that night into the farmhouse at Grider's Hole always brought with it a sensation of nightmare. The coils of fog rolled in with them as the door opened, and through them the firelight leapt steamily. A hanging lamp made a blur. The Medusa-head of Mrs. Grimethorpe, terribly white against her black hair, peered over him. A hairy paw caught her by the shoulder and wrenched her aside.

"Shameless! A mon—ony mon—that's a' tha thinks on. Bide till tha's wanted. What's this?"

Voices—voices—ever so many fierce faces peering down all round.

"Peter's Pot? An' what were 'ee a-wanting on t'moor this time night? No good. Nobbody but a fool or a thief 'ud coom oop 'ere i' t'fog."

One of the men, a farm labourer with wry shoulders and a thin, malicious face, suddenly burst into tuneless song:

"I been a'courtin' Mary Jane
On Ilkla' Moor bar t'at."

"Howd toong!" yelled Grimethorpe, in a fury. "Doost want Ah should break ivery bwoan i' thi body?" He turned on Bunter. "Tak thesen off, Ah tell tha. Tha'rt here for no good."

"But, William——" began his wife. He snapped round at her like a dog, and she shrank back.

"Naay now, naay now," said a man, whom Wimsey dimly recognised as the fellow who had befriended him on his previous visit, "tha mun' taak them in for t' night, racken, or there'll be trouble wi' t' folk down yonder at t' Lodge, lat aloan what police 'ull saay. Ef t' fellow 'm coom to do harm, 'ee's doon it already—to 'unself. Woan't do no more to-night—look at 'un. Bring 'un to fire, mon," he added to Bunter, and then, turning to the farmer again, " 'Tes tha'll be in Queer Street Street ef'e wor to goo an' die on us wi' noomony or rhoomaticks."

This reasoning seemed partly to convince Grimethorpe. He made way, grumbling, and the two chilled and exhausted men were brought near the fire. Somebody brought two large, steaming tumblers of spirits. Wimsey's brain seemed to clear, then swim again drowsily, drunkenly.

* * * * *

Presently he became aware that he was being carried upstairs and put to bed. A big, old-fashioned room, with a fire on the hearth and a huge, grim four-poster. Bunter was helping him out of soaked clothes; rubbing him. Another man appeared from time to time to help him. From below came the bellowing sound of Grimethorpe's voice, blasphemously uplifted. Then the harsh, brassy singing of the wry-shouldered man:

"Then woorms will coom an' ate thee oop
On Ilkla' Moor bar t'at. . . .

Then doocks will coom an' ate oop woorms
On Ilkla' Moor. . . ."

Lord Peter rolled into bed.

"Bunter–where–you all right? Never said thank you–dunno what I'm doing–anywhere to sleep–what?"

He drifted away into oblivion. The old song came up mockingly, and wound its horrible fancies into his dreams:

"Then we shall coom an' ate oop doocks
On Ilkla' Moor bar t'at. . . .

An' that is how–an' that is how–is how . . . ."

* * * * *

When Wimsey next opened his eyes a pale November sun was struggling in at the window. It seemed that the fog had fulfilled its mission and departed. For some time he lay, vaguely unaware of how he came to be where he was; then the outlines of recollection straightened themselves, the drifting outposts of dreams were called back, the burden of his preoccupation settled down as usual. He became aware of an extreme bodily lassitude, and of the dragging pain of wrenched shoulder muscles. Examining himself perfunctorily, he found a bruised and tender zone beneath the armpits and round his chest and back, where the rescuing rope had hauled at him. It was painful to move, so he lay back and closed his eyes once more.

Presently the door opened to admit Bunter, neatly clothed and bearing a tray from which rose a most excellent odour of ham and eggs.

"Hullo, Bunter!"

"Good morning, my lord! I trust your lordship has rested."

"Feel as fit as a fiddle, thanks–come to think of it, why fiddle?–except for a general feeling of havin' been violently massaged by some fellow with cast-iron fingers and knobbly joints. How about you?"

"The arms are a trifle fatigued, thank you, my lord; otherwise, I am happy to say, I feel no trace of the misadventure. Allow me, my lord."

He set the tray tenderly upon Lord Peter's ready knees.

"They must be jolly well dragged out of their sockets," said his lordship, "holdin' me up all that ghastly long time. I'm so beastly deep in debt to you already, Bunter, it's not a bit of use tryin' to repay it. You know I won't forget, anyhow, don't you? All right, I won't be embarrassin' or anything—thanks awfully, anyhow. That's that. What? Did they give you anywhere decent to sleep? I didn't seem to be able to sit up an' take notice last night."

"I slept excellently, I thank your lordship." Mr. Bunter indicated a kind of truckle-bed in a corner of the room. "They would have given me another room, my lord, but in the circumstances, I preferred to remain with your lordship, trusting you would excuse the liberty. I told them that I feared the effects of prolonged immersion upon your lordship's health. I was uneasy, besides, about the intention of Grimethorpe. I feared he might not feel altogether hospitably disposed, and that he might be led into some hasty action if we were not together."

"I shouldn't wonder. Most murderous-lookin' fellow I ever set eyes on. I'll have to talk to him this morning—or to Mrs. Grimethorpe. I'd take my oath she could tell us something, what?"

"I should say there was very little doubt of it, my lord."

"Trouble is," pursued Wimsey, with his mouth full of egg, "I don't know how to get at her. That jolly husband of hers seems to cherish the most unpleasant suspicions of anything that comes this way in trousers. If he found out we'd been talkin' to her, what you may call privately, he might, as you say, be hurried by his feelin's into doin' something regrettable."

"Just so, my lord."

"Still, the fellow must go an' look after his bally old farm some time, and then, p'raps, we'll be able to tackle her. Queer sort of woman—damn fine one, what? Wonder what she made of Cathcart?" he added musingly.

Mr. Bunter volunteered no opinion on this delicate point.

"Well, Bunter, I think I'll get up. I don't suppose we're altogether welcome here. I didn't fancy the look in our host's eye last night."

"No, my lord. He made a deal of opposition about having your lordship conveyed to this room."

"Why, whose room is it?"

"His own and Mrs. Grimethorpe's, my lord. It appeared most suitable, there being a fireplace, and the bed already made up. Mrs. Grimethorpe showed great kindness, my lord, and the man Jake pointed out to Grimethorpe that it would doubtless be to his pecuniary advantage to treat your lordship with consideration."

"H'm. Nice, graspin' character, ain't he? Well, it's up and away for me. O Lord! I *am* stiff. I say, Bunter, have I any clothes to put on?"

"I have dried and brushed your lordship's suit to the best of my ability, my lord. It is not as I should wish to see it, but I think your lordship will be able to wear it to Riddlesdale."

"Well, I don't suppose the streets will be precisely crowded," retorted his lordship. "I *do* so want a hot bath. How about shavin' water?"

"I can procure that from the kitchen, my lord."

Bunter padded away, and Lord Peter, having pulled on a shirt and trousers with many grunts and groans, roamed over to the window. As usual with hardy country dwellers, it was tightly shut, and a thick wedge of paper had been rammed in to keep the sash from rattling. He removed this and flung up the sash. The wind rollicked in, laden with peaty moor scents. He drank it in gladly. It was good to see the jolly old sun after all—he would have hated to die a sticky death in Peter's Pot. For a few minutes he stood there, returning thanks vaguely in his mind for the benefits of existence. Then he withdrew to finish dressing. The wad of paper was still in his hand, and he was about to fling it into the fire, when a word caught his eye. He unrolled the paper. As he read it his eyebrows went up and his mouth pursed itself into an indescribable expression of whimsical enlightenment. Bunter, returning with the hot water, found his master transfixed, the paper in one hand, and his socks in the other, and whistling a complicated passage of Bach under his breath.

"Bunter," said his lordship, "I am, without exception, the biggest ass in Christendom. When a thing is close under my nose I can't see it. I get a telescope, and look for the explanation in Stapley. I deserve to be crucified upside-down, as a cure for anæmia of the brain. Jerry! Jerry! But, naturally, of course, you rotten ass, isn't it obvious? Silly old blighter. Why couldn't he tell Murbles or me?"

Mr. Bunter advanced, the picture of respectful inquiry.

"Look at it—look at it!" said Wimsey, with a hysterical squeak of laughter. "O Lord! O Lord! Stuck into the window-frame for anybody to find. *Just* like Jerry. Signs his name to the business in letters a foot long, leaves it conspicuously about, and then goes away and is chivalrously silent."

Mr. Bunter put the jug down upon the washstand in case of accident, and took the paper.

It was the missing letter from Tommy Freeborn.

No doubt about it. There it was—the evidence which established the truth of Denver's evidence. More—which established his alibi for the night of the 13th.

Not Cathcart—Denver.

Denver suggesting that the shooting party should return in October to Riddlesdale, where they had opened the grouse season in August. Denver sneaking hurriedly out at 11.30 to walk two miles across the fields on a night when Farmer Grimethorpe had gone to buy machinery. Denver carelessly plugging a rattling sash on a stormy night with an important letter bearing his title on it for all to see. Denver padding back at three in the morning like a homing tom-cat, to fall over his guest's dead body by the conservatory. Denver, with his kind, stupid, English-gentleman ideas about honour, going obstinately off to prison, rather than tell his solicitor where he had been. Denver misleading them all into the wildest and most ingenious solutions of a mystery which now stood out clear as seven sunbeams. Denver, whose voice the woman had thought she recognised on the memorable day when she flung herself into the arms of his brother. Denver calmly setting in motion the enormous, creaking machinery of a trial by his noble peers in order to safeguard a woman's reputation.

This very day, probably, a Select Committee of lords was sitting "to inspect the journals of this House upon former trials of peers in criminal cases in order to bring the Duke of Denver to a speedy trial, and to report to the House what they should think proper thereupon." There they were: moving that an address be presented to His Majesty by the lords with white staves, to acquaint His Majesty of the date proposed for the trial; arranging for fitting up the Royal Gallery at Westminster; humbly requesting the attendance of a sufficient police force to keep clear the approaches leading to the House; petitioning His Majesty graciously to appoint a Lord High Steward; ordering, in sheeplike accordance with precedent, that all lords be summoned to attend in their robes; that every lord, in giving judgment, disclose his opinion upon his honour, laying his right hand upon his heart; that the Sergeant-at-Arms be within the House to make proclamations in the King's name for keeping silence—and so on, and on, unendingly. And there, jammed in the window-sash, was the dirty little bit of paper which, discovered earlier, would have made the whole monstrous ceremonial unnecessary.

Wimsey's adventure in the bog had unsettled his nerves. He sat down on the bed and laughed, with the tears streaming down his face.

Mr. Bunter was speechless. Speechlessly he produced a razor—and to the end of his days Wimsey never knew how or from whom he had so adequately procured it—and began to strop it thoughtfully upon the palm of his hand.

Presently Wimsey pulled himself together and staggered to the window for a little cooling draught of moor air. As he did so, a loud hullabaloo smote his ear, and he perceived, in the courtyard below, Farmer Grimethorpe striding among his dogs; when they howled he struck at them with a whip, and they howled again. Suddenly he glanced up at the window, with an expression of such livid hatred that Wimsey stepped hurriedly back as though struck.

While Bunter shaved him he was silent.

* * * * *

The interview before Lord Peter was a delicate one; the situation, however one looked at it, unpleasant. He was under a considerable debt of gratitude to his hostess; on the other hand, Denver's position was such that minor considerations really had to go to the wall. His lordship had, nevertheless, never felt quite such a cad as he did while descending the staircase at Grider's Hole.

In the big farm kitchen he found a stout country-woman, stirring a pot of stew. He asked for Mr. Grimethorpe, and was told that he had gone out.

"Can I speak to Mrs. Grimethorpe, please?"

The woman looked doubtfully at him, wiped her hands on her apron, and, going into the scullery, shouted, "Mrs. Grimethorpe!" A voice replied from somewhere outside.

"Gentleman wants see tha."

"Where is Mrs. Grimethorpe?" broke in Peter hurriedly.

"I' t'dairy, recken."

"I'll go to her there," said Wimsey, stepping briskly out. He passed through a stone-paved scullery, and across a yard, in time to see Mrs. Grimethorpe emerging from a dark doorway opposite.

Framed there, the cold sunlight just lighting upon her still, dead-white face and heavy, dark hair, she was more wonderful than ever. There was no trace of Yorkshire descent in the long, dark eyes and curled mouth. The curve of nose and cheekbones vouched for an origin immensely remote; coming out of the darkness, she might have just risen from her far tomb in the Pyramids, dropping the dry and perfumed grave-bands from her fingers.

Lord Peter pulled himself together.

"Foreign," he said to himself matter-of-factly. "Touch of Jew perhaps, or Spanish, is it? Remarkable type. Don't blame Jerry. Couldn't live with Helen myself. Now for it."

He advanced quickly.

"Good morning," she said, "are you better?"

"Perfectly all right, thank you—thanks to your kindness, which I do not know how to repay."

"You will repay any kindness best by going at once," she answered in her remote voice. "My husband does not care for strangers, and 'twas unfortunate the way you met before."

"I will go directly. But I must first beg for the favour of a word with you."

He peered past her into the dimness of the dairy. "In here, perhaps?"

"What do you want with me?"

She stepped back, however, and allowed him to follow her in.

"Mrs. Grimethorpe, I am placed in a most painful position. You know that my brother, the Duke of Denver, is in prison, awaiting his trial for a murder which took place on the night of October 13th?"

Her face did not change. "I have heard so."

"He has, in the most decided manner, refused to state where he was between eleven and three on that night. His refusal has brought him into great danger of his life."

She looked at him steadily.

"He feels bound in honour not to disclose his whereabouts, though I know that, if he chose to speak, he could bring a witness to clear him."

"He seems to be a very honourable man." The cold voice wavered a trifle, then steadied again.

"Yes. Undoubtedly, from his point of view, he is doing the right thing. You will understand, however, that, as his brother, I am naturally anxious to have the matter put in its proper light."

"I don't understand why you are telling me all this. I suppose, if the thing is disgraceful, he doesn't want it known."

"Obviously. But to us—to his wife and young son, and to his sister and myself—his life and safety are matters of the first importance."

"Of more importance than his honour?"

"The secret is a disgraceful one in a sense, and will give pain to his family. But it would be an infinitely greater disgrace that he should be executed for murder. The stigma in that case would involve all those who bear his name. The shame of the truth will, I fear, in this very unjust society of ours, rest more upon the witness to his alibi than upon himself."

"Can you in that case expect the witness to come forward?"

"To prevent the condemnation of an innocent man? Yes, I think I may venture to expect even that."

"I repeat—why are you telling me all this?"

"Because, Mrs. Grimethorpe, you know, even better than I, how innocent my brother is of this murder. Believe me, I am deeply distressed at having to say these things to you."

"I know nothing about your brother."

"Forgive me, that is not true."

"I know nothing. And surely, if the Duke will not speak, you should respect his reasons."

"I am not bound in any way."

"I am afraid I cannot help you. You are wasting time. If you cannot produce your missing witness, why do you not set about finding the real murderer? If you do so you surely need not trouble about this alibi. Your brother's movements are his own business."

"I could wish," said Wimsey, "You had not taken up this attitude. Believe me, I would have done all I could to spare you. I have been working hard to find, as you say, the real murderer, but with no success. The trial will probably take place at the end of the month."

Her lips twitched a little at that, but she said nothing.

"I had hoped that with your help we might agree on some explanation—less than the truth, perhaps, but sufficient to clear my brother. As it is, I fear I shall have to produce the proof I hold, and let matters take their course."

That, at last, struck under her guard. A dull flush crept up her cheeks; one hand tightened upon the handle of the churn, where she had rested it.

"What do you mean by proof?"

"I can prove that on the night of the 13th my brother slept in the room I occupied last night," said Wimsey, with calculated brutality.

She winced. "It is a lie. You cannot prove it. He will deny it. I shall deny it."

"He was not there?"

"No."

"Then how did this come to be wedged in the sash of the bedroom window?"

At sight of the letter she broke down, crumpling up in a heap against the table. The set lines of her face distorted themselves into a mere caricature of terror.

"No, no, no! It is a lie! God help me!"

"Hush!" said Wimsey peremptorily. "Someone will hear you." He dragged her to her feet. "Tell the truth, and we will see if we can find a way out. It is true–he was here that night?"

"You know it."

"When did he come?"

"At a quarter past twelve."

"Who let him in?"

"He had the keys."

"When did he leave you?"

"A little after two."

"Yes, that fits in all right. Three quarters of an hour to go and three quarters to come back. He stuck this into the window, I suppose, to keep it from rattling?"

"There was a high wind–I was nervous. I thought every sound was my husband coming back."

"Where was your husband?"

"At Stapley."

"Had he suspected this?"

"Yes, for some time."

"Since my brother was here in August?"

"Yes. But he could get no proof. If he had had proof he would have killed me. You have seen him. He is a devil."

"M'm."

Wimsey was silent. The woman glanced fearfully at his face and seemed to read some hope there, for she clutched him by the arm.

"If you call me to give evidence," she said, "he will know. He *will* kill me. For God's sake, have pity. That letter is my death-warrant. Oh, for the mother that bore you, have mercy upon me. My life is a hell, and when I die I shall go to hell for my sin. Find some other way–you can–you must."

Wimsey gently released himself.

"Don't do that, Mrs. Grimethorpe. We might be seen. I am deeply sorry for you, and, if I can get my brother out of this without bringing you in, I promise you I will. But you see the difficulty. Why don't you leave this man? He is openly brutal to you."

She laughed.

"Do you think he'd leave me alive while the law was slowly releasing me? Knowing him, do you think so?"

Wimsey really did not think so.

"I will promise you this, Mrs. Grimethorpe. I will do all I can to avoid having to use your evidence. But if there should be no other way, I will see that you have police protection from the moment that the subpoena is served on you."

"And for the rest of my life?"

"When you are once in London we will see about freeing you from this man."

"No. If you call upon me, I am a lost woman. But you will find another way?"

"I will try, but I can promise nothing. I will do everything that is possible to protect you. If you care at all for my brother——"

"I don't know. I am so horribly afraid. He was kind and good to me. He was—so different. But I am afraid—I'm afraid."

Wimsey turned. Her terrified eyes had seen the shadow cross the threshold. Grimethorpe was at the door, glowering in upon them.

"Ah, Mr. Grimethorpe," exclaimed Wimsey cheerfully, "there you are. Awfully pleased to see you and thank you, don'tcherknow, for puttin' me up. I was just saying so to Mrs. Grimethorpe, an' asking her to say good-bye to you for me. Must be off now, I'm afraid. Bunter and I are ever so grateful to you both for all your kindness. Oh, and I say, could you find me the stout fellows who hauled us out of that Pot of yours last night—if it is yours. Nasty, damp thing to keep outside the front door, what? I'd like to thank 'em."

"Dom good thing for unwelcome guests," said the man ferociously. "An' tha'd better be off afore Ah throws thee out."

"I'm just off," said Peter. "Good-bye again, Mrs. Grimethorpe, and a thousand thanks."

He collected Bunter, rewarded his rescuers suitably, took an affectionate farewell of the enraged farmer, and departed, sore in body and desperately confused in mind.

# 13

# MANON

*"That one word, my dear Watson, should have told me the whole story, had I been the ideal reasoner which you are so fond of depicting."*

Memoirs of Sherlock Holmes

"Thank God," said Parker. "Well, that settles it."

"It does—and yet again, it doesn't," retorted Lord Peter. He leaned back against the fat silk cushion in the sofa corner meditatively.

"Of course, it's disagreeable having to give this woman away," said Parker sensibly and pleasantly, "but these things have to be done."

"I know. It's all simply awfully nice and all that. And Jerry, who's got the poor woman into this mess, has to be considered first. I know. And if we don't restrain Grimethorpe quite successfully, and he cuts her throat for her, it'll be simply rippin' for Jerry to think of all his life. . . . Jerry! I say, you know, what frightful idiots we were not to see the truth right off! I mean—of course, my sister-in-law is an awfully good woman, and all that, but Mrs. Grimethorpe

—whew! I told you about the time she mistook me for Jerry. One crowded, split second of glorious all-overishness. I ought to have known then. Our voices are alike, of course, and she couldn't see in that dark kitchen. I don't believe there's an ounce of any feeling left in the woman except sheer terror—but, ye gods! what eyes and skin! Well, never mind. Some undeserving fellows have all the luck. Have you got any really good stories? No? Well, I'll tell you some—enlarge your mind and all that. Do you know the rhyme about the young man at the War Office?"

Mr. Parker endured five stories with commendable patience, and then suddenly broke down.

"Hurray!" said Wimsey. "Splendid man! I love to see you melt into a refined snigger from time to time. I'll spare you the really outrageous one about the young housewife and the traveller in bicycle-pumps. You know, Charles, I really *should* like to know who did Cathcart in. Legally, it's enough to prove Jerry innocent, but, Mrs. Grimethorpe or no Mrs. Grimethorpe, it doesn't do us credit in a professional capacity. 'The father weakens, but the governor is firm'; that is, as a brother I am satisfied—I may say light-hearted—but as a sleuth I am cast down, humiliated, thrown back upon myself, a lodge in a garden of cucumbers. Besides, of all defences an alibi is the most awkward to establish, unless a number of independent and disinterested witnesses combine to make it thoroughly air-tight. If Jerry sticks to his denial, the most they can be sure of is that *either* he *or* Mrs. Grimethorpe is being chivalrous."

"But you've got the letter."

"Yes. But how are we going to prove that it came that evening? The envelope is destroyed. Fleming remembers nothing about it. Jerry might have received it days earlier. Or it might be a complete fake. Who is to say that I didn't put it in the window myself and pretend to find it. After all, I'm hardly what you would call disinterested."

"Bunter saw you find it."

"He didn't, Charles. At that precise moment he was out of the room fetching shaving-water."

"Oh, was he?"

"Moreover, only Mrs. Grimethorpe can swear to what is really the important point—the moment of Jerry's arrival and departure. Unless he was at Grider's Hole before 12:30 at least, it's immaterial whether he was there or not."

"Well," said Parker, "can't we keep Mrs. Grimethorpe up our sleeve, so to speak——"

"Sounds a bit abandoned," sald Lord Peter, "but we will keep her with pleasure if you like."

"—and meanwhile," pursued Mr. Parker, unheeding, "do our best to find the actual criminal?"

"Oh, yes," said Lord Peter, "and that reminds me. I made a discovery at the Lodge—at least, I think so. Did you notice that somebody had been forcing one of the study windows?"

"No, really?"

"Yes; I found distinct marks. Of course, it was a long time after the murder, but there were scratches on the catch all right—the sort of thing a penknife would leave."

"What fools we were not to make an examination at the time!"

"Come to think of it why should you have? Anyhow, I asked Fleming about it, and he said he did remember, now he came to think of it, that on the Thursday morning he'd found the window open, and couldn't account for it. And here's another thing. I've had a letter from my friend Tim Watchett. Here it is:

"My Lord.—About our conversation. I have found a Man who was with the Party in question at the 'Pig and Whistle' on the night of the 13th ult. and he tells me that the Party borrowed his bicycle, and same was found afterwards in the ditch where Party was picked up with the Handlebars bent and wheels buckled.

"Trusting to the Continuance of your esteemed favour.

"Timothy Watchett."

"What do you think of that?"

"Good enough to go on," said Parker. "At least, we are no longer hampered with horrible doubts."

"No. And, though she's my sister, I must say that of all the blithering she-asses Mary is the blitheringest. Taking up with that awful bounder to start with——"

"She was jolly fine about it," said Mr. Parker, getting rather red in the face. "It's just because she's your sister that you can't appreciate what a fine thing she did. How should a big, chivalrous nature like hers see through a man like that? She's so sincere and thorough herself, she judges everyone by the same standard. She wouldn't believe anybody could be so thin and wobbly-minded as Goyles till it was *proved* to her. And even then she couldn't bring herself to think ill of him till he'd given himself away out of his own mouth. It was wonderful, the way she fought for him. Think what it must have meant to such a splendid, straight-forward woman to——"

"All right, all right," cried Peter, who had been staring at his friend, transfixed with astonishment. "Don't get worked up. I believe you. Spare me. I'm only a brother. All brothers are fools. All lovers are lunatics—Shakespeare says so. Do you want Mary, old man? You surprise me, but I believe all brothers are always surprised. Bless you, dear children!"

"Damn it all, Wimsey," said Parker, very angry, "you've no right to talk like that. I only said how greatly I admired your sister—everyone must admire such pluck and staunchness. You needn't be insulting. I know she's Lady Mary Wimsey and damnably rich, and I'm only a common police official with nothing a year and a pension to look forward to, but there's no need to sneer about it."

"I'm not sneering," retorted Peter indignantly. "I can't imagine why anybody should want to marry my sister, but you're a friend of mine and a damn good sort, and you've my good word for what it's worth. Besides—dash it all, man!—to put it on the lowest grounds, do look what it might have been! A Socialist Conchy of neither bowels nor breeding, or a card-sharping dark horse with a mysterious past! Mother and Jerry must have got to the point when they'd welcome a decent, God-fearing plumber, let alone a policeman. Only thing I'm afraid of is that Mary, havin' such beastly bad taste in blokes, won't know how to appreciate a really decent fellow like you, old son."

Mr. Parker begged his friend's pardon for his unworthy suspicions, and they sat a little time in silence. Parker sipped his port, and saw unimaginable visions warmly glowing in its rosy depths. Wimsey pulled out his pocket-book, and began idly turning over its contents, throwing old letters into the fire, unfolding and refolding memoranda, and reviewing a miscellaneous series of other people's visiting-cards. He came at length to the slip of blotting-paper from the study at Riddlesdale, to whose fragmentary markings he had since given scarcely a thought.

Presently Mr. Parker, finishing his port and recalling his mind with an effort, remembered that he had been meaning to tell Peter something before the name of Lady Mary had driven all other thoughts out of his head. He turned to his host, open-mouthed for speech, but his remark never got beyond a preliminary click like that of a clock about to strike, for, even as he turned, Lord Peter brought his fist down on the little table with a bang that made the decanters ring, and cried out in the loud voice of complete and sudden enlightenment:

"*Manon Lescaut!*"

"Eh?" said Mr. Parker.

"Boil my brains!" said Lord Peter. "Boil 'em and mash 'em and serve 'em up with butter as a dish of turnips, for it's damn well all they're fit for! Look at me!" (Mr. Parker scarcely needed this exhortation.) "Here we've been worryin' over Jerry, an' worryin' over Mary, an' huntin' for Goyleses an' Grimethorpes and God knows who–and all the time I'd got this little bit of paper tucked away in my pocket. The blot upon the paper's rim a blotted paper was to him, and it was nothing more. But Manon, Manon! Charles, if I'd had the grey matter of a woodlouse that book ought to have told me the whole story. And think what we'd have been saved!"

"I wish you wouldn't be so excited," said Parker. "I'm sure it's perfectly splendid for you to see your way so clearly, but I never read *Manon Lescaut*, and you haven't shown me the blotting-paper, and I haven't the foggiest idea what you've discovered."

Lord Peter passed the relic over without comment.

"I observe," said Parker, "that the paper is rather crumpled and dirty, and smells powerfully of tobacco and Russian leather, and deduce that you have been keeping it in your pocket-book."

"No!" said Wimsey incredulously. "And when you actually saw me take it out! Holmes, how do you do it?"

"At one corner," pursued Parker, "I see two blots, one rather larger than the other. I think someone must have shaken a pen there. Is there anything sinister about the blot?"

"I haven't noticed anything."

"Some way below the blots the Duke has signed his name two or three times–or, rather, his title. The inference is that his letters were not to intimates."

"The inference is justifiable, I fancy."

"Colonel Marchbanks has a neat signature."

"He can hardly mean mischief," said Peter. "He signs his name like an honest man! Proceed."

"There's a sprawly message about five something of fine something. Do you see anything occult there?"

"The number five may have a cabalistic meaning, but I admit I don't know what it is. There are five senses, five fingers, five great Chinese precepts, five books of Moses, to say nothing of the mysterious entities hymned in the Dilly Song–'Five are the flamboys under the pole.' I must admit that I have always panted to know what the five flamboys were. But, not knowing, I get no help from it in this case."

"Well, that's all, except a fragment consisting of 'oe' on one line, and 'is fou–' below it."

"What do you make of that?"

" 'Is found,' I suppose."

"Do you?"

"That seems the simplest interpretation. Or possibly 'his foul'–there seems to have been a sudden rush of ink to the pen just there. Do you think it is 'his foul'? Was the Duke writing about Cathcart's foul play? Is that what you mean?"

"No, I don't make that of it. Besides, I don't think it's Jerry's writing."

"Whose is it?"

"I don't know, but I can guess."

"And it leads somewhere?"

"It tells the whole story."

"Oh, cough it up, Wimsey. Even Dr. Watson would lose patience."

"Tut, tut! Try the line above."

"Well, there's only 'oe.' "

"Yes, well?"

"Well, I don't know. Poet, poem, manoeuvre, Loeb edition, Citroen–it might be anything."

"Dunno about that. There aren't lashings of English words with 'oe' in them–and it's written so close it almost looks like a diphthong at that."

"Perhaps it isn't an English word."

"Exactly; perhaps it isn't."

"Oh! Oh, I see. French?"

"Ah, you're gettin' warm."

*"Sœur–œuvre–œuf–bœuf——"*

"No, no. You were nearer the first time."

*"Sœur–cœur!"*

*"Cœur.* Hold on a moment. Look at the scratch in front of that."

"Wait a bit*–er–cer——*"

"I believe you're right. *'Percer le cœur.'* "

"Yes. Or *'perceras le cœur.'* "

"That's better. It seems to need another letter or two."

"And now your 'is found' line."

*"Fou!"*

"Who?"

"I didn't say 'who'; I said '*fou*.' "

"I know you did. I said who?"

"Who?"

"Who's *fou?*"

"Oh, *is*. By Jove, '*suis*'! '*Je suis fou.*' "

"*A la bonne heure!* And I suggest that the next words are '*de douleur*,' or something like it."

"They might be."

"Cautious beast! I say they are."

"Well, and suppose they are?"

"It tells us everything."

"Nothing!"

"Everything, I say. Think. This was written on the day Cathcart died. Now who in the house would be likely to write these words, '*Perceras le cœur . . . je suis fou de douleur*'? Take everybody. I know it isn't Jerry's fist, and he wouldn't use those expressions. Colonel or Mrs. Marchbanks? Not Pygmalion likely! Freddy? Couldn't write passionate letters in French to save his life."

"No, of course not. It would have to be either Cathcart or—Lady Mary."

"Rot! It couldn't be Mary."

"Why not?"

"Not unless she changed her sex, you know."

"Of course not. It would have to be '*Je suis folle.*' Then Cathcart——"

"Of course. He lived in France all his life. Consider his bank-book. Consider——"

"Lord! Wimsey, we've been blind."

"Yes."

"And listen! I was going to tell you. The Sûreté write me that they've traced one of Cathcart's banknotes."

"Where to?"

"To a Mr. François who owns a lot of house property near the Etoile."

"And lets it out in *appartements!*"

"No doubt."

"When's the next train? Bunter!"

"My lord!"

Mr. Bunter hurried to the door at the call.

"The next boat-train for Paris?"

"Eight-twenty, my lord, from Waterloo."

"We're going by it. How long?"

"Twenty minutes, my lord."

"Pack my toothbrush and call a taxi."

"Certainly, my lord."

"But, Wimsey, what light does it throw on Cathcart's murder? Did this woman——"

"I've no time," said Wimsey hurriedly. "But I'll be back in a day or two. Meanwhile——"

He hunted hastily in the bookshelf.

"Read this."

He flung the book at his friend and plunged into his bedroom.

At eleven o'clock, as a gap of dirty water disfigured with oil and bits of paper widened between the *Normannia* and the quay; while hardened passengers fortified their sea-stomachs with cold ham and pickles, and the more nervous studied the Boddy jackets in their cabins; while the harbour lights winked and swam right and left, and Lord Peter scraped acquaintance with a second-rate cinema actor in the bar, Charles Parker sat, with a puzzled frown, before the fire at 110 Piccadilly, making his first acquaintance with the delicate masterpiece of the Abbé Prévost.

# 14

# THE EDGE OF THE AXE TOWARDS HIM

*Scene 1. Westminster Hall. Enter as to the Parliament, Bolingbroke, Aumerle, Northumberland, Percy, Fitzwater, Surrey, the Bishop of Carlisle, the Abbot of Westminster, and another Lord, Herald, Officers, and Bagot.*

BOLINGBROKE: Call forth Bagot.
Now, Bagot, freely speak thy mind;
What thou dost know of noble Gloucester's death;
Who wrought it with the king, and who performed
The bloody office of his timeless end.

BAGOT: Then set before my face the Lord Aumerle.

*King Richard II*

THE HISTORIC trial of the duke of Denver for murder opened as soon as Parliament reassembled after the Christmas vacation. The papers had leaderettes on "Trial by his Peers," by a Woman Barrister, and "The Privilege of Peers: should it be abolished?" by a Student of History. The *Evening Banner* got into trouble for contempt by publishing an article entitled "The Silken Rope" (by an Antiquarian), which was deemed to be prejudicial, and the *Daily Trumpet*–the Labour organ–inquired sarcastically why, when a peer was tried, the fun of seeing the show should be reserved to the few influential persons who could wangle tickets for the Royal Gallery.

Mr. Murbles and Detective Inspector Parker, in close consultation, went about with preoccupied faces, while Sir Impey Biggs retired into a complete eclipse for three days, revolved about by Mr. Glibbery, K.C., Mr. Brownrigg-Fortescue, K.C., and a number of lesser satellites. The schemes of the Defence were kept dark indeed–the more so that they found themselves on the eve of the struggle deprived of their principal witness, and wholly ignorant whether or not he would be forthcoming with his testimony.

Lord Peter had returned from Paris at the end of four days, and had burst in like a cyclone at Great Ormond Street "I've got it," he said, "but it's touch and go. Listen!"

For an hour Parker had listened, feverishly taking notes.

"You can work on that," said Wimsey. "Tell Murbles. I'm off."

His next appearance was at the American Embassy. The Ambassador, however, was not there, having received a royal mandate to dine. Wimsey damned the dinner, abandoned the polite, horn-rimmed secretaries, and leapt back into his taxi with a demand to be driven to Buckingham Palace. Here a great deal of insistence with scandalised officials produced first a higher official, then a very high official, and, finally, the American Ambassador and a Royal Personage while the meat was yet in their mouths.

"Oh, yes," said the Ambassador, "of course it can be done——"

"Surely, surely," said the Personage genially, "we mustn't have any delay. Might cause an international misunderstanding, and a lot of paragraphs about Ellis Island. Terrible nuisance to have to adjourn the trial—dreadful fuss, isn't it? Our secretaries are everlastingly bringing things along to our place to sign about extra policemen and seating accommodation. Good luck to you, Wimsey! Come and have something while they get your papers through. When does your boat go?"

"To-morrow morning, sir. I'm catching the Liverpool train in an hour—if I can."

"You surely will," said the Ambassador cordially, signing a note. "And they say the English can't hustle."

So, with his papers all in order, his lordship set sail from Liverpool the next morning, leaving his legal representatives to draw up alternative schemes of defence.

* * * * *

"Then the peers, two by two, in their order, beginning with the youngest baron."

Garter King-of-Arms, very hot and bothered, fussed unhappily around the three hundred or so British peers who were sheepishly struggling into their robes, while the heralds did their best to line up the assembly and keep them from wandering away when once arranged.

"Of all the farces!" grumbled Lord Attenbury irritably. He was a very short, stout gentleman of a choleric countenance, and was annoyed to find himself next to the Earl of Strathgillan and Begg, an extremely tall, lean nobleman, with pronounced views on Prohibition and the Legitimation question.

"I say, Attenbury," said a kindly, brick-red peer, with five rows of ermine on his shoulder, "is it true that Wimsey hasn't come back? My daughter tells me she heard he'd gone to collect evidence in the States. Why the States?"

"Dunno," said Attenbury; "but Wimsey's a dashed clever fellow. When he found those emeralds of mine, you know, I said——"

"Your grace, your grace," cried Rouge Dragon desperately, diving in, "Your grace is out of line again."

"Eh, what?" said the brick-faced peer. "Oh, damme! Must obey orders, I suppose, what?" And was towed away from the mere earls and pushed into position next to the Duke of Wiltshire, who was deaf, and a distant connection of Denver's on the distaff side.

The Royal Gallery was packed. In the seats reserved below the Bar for peeresses sat the Dowager Duchess of Denver, beautifully dressed and defiant. She suffered much from the adjacent presence of her daughter-in-law, whose misfortune it was to become disagreeable when she was unhappy—perhaps the heaviest curse that can be laid on man, who is born to sorrow.

Behind the imposing array of Counsel in full-bottomed wigs in the body of the hall were seats reserved for witnesses, and here Mr. Bunter was accommodated—to be called if the defence should find it necessary to establish the alibi—the majority of the witnesses being pent up in the King's Robing-Room, gnawing their fingers and glaring at one another. On either side, above the Bar, were the benches for the peers—each in his own right a judge both of fact and law—while on the high dais the great chair of state stood ready for the Lord High Steward.

The reporters at their little table were beginning to fidget and look at their watches. Muffled by the walls and the buzz of talk, Big Ben dropped eleven slow notes into the suspense. A door opened. The reporters started to their feet; counsel rose; everybody rose; the Dowager Duchess whispered irrepressibly to her neighbour that it reminded her of the Voice that breathed o'er Eden; and the procession streamed slowly in, lit by a shaft of wintry sunshine from the tall windows.

The proceedings were opened by a Proclamation of Silence from the Sergeant-at-Arms, after which the Clerk of the Crown in Chancery, kneeling at the foot of the throne, presented the Commission under the Great Seal to the Lord High Steward,* who, finding no use for it, returned it with great solemnity to the Clerk of the Crown. The latter accordingly proceeded to read it at dismal and wearisome length, affording the assembly an opportunity of judging just how bad the acoustics of the chamber were. The Sergeant-at-Arms retorted with great emphasis, "God Save the King," whereupon Garter King-of-Arms and the Gentleman Usher of the Black Rod, kneeling again, handed the lord High Steward his staff of office. ("So picturesque, isn't it?" said the Dowager—"quite High Church, you know.")

The Certiorari and Return followed in a long, sonorous rigmarole, which, starting with George the Fifth by the Grace of God, called upon all the Justices and Judges of the Old Bailey, enumerated the Lord Mayor of London, the Recorder, and a quantity of assorted aldermen and justices, skipped back to our Lord the King, roamed about the City of London, Counties of London and Middlesex, Essex, Kent, and Surrey, mentioned our late Sovereign Lord King William the Fourth, branched off to the Local Government Act one thousand eight hundred and eighty-eight, lost its way in a list of all treasons, murders, felonies, and misdemeanours by whomsoever and in what manner soever done, committed or perpetrated and by whom or to whom, when, how and after what manner and of all other articles and circumstances concerning the premises and every one of them and any of them in any manner whatsoever, and at last, triumphantly, after reciting the names of the whole Grand Jury, came to the presentation of the indictment with a sudden, brutal brevity.

"The Jurors for our Lord the King upon their oaths present that the most noble and puissant prince Gerald Christian Wimsey, Viscount St. George, Duke of Denver, a Peer of the United Kingdom of Great Britain and Ireland, on the thirteenth day of October in the year of Our Lord one thousand nine hundred and twenty–in the Parish of Riddlesdale in the County of Yorkshire did kill and murder Denis Cathcart."

"After which, Proclamation** was made by the Sergeant-at-Arms for the Gentleman Usher of the Black Rod to call in Gerald Christian Wimsey, Viscount St. George, Duke of Denver, to appear at the Bar to answer his indictment, who, being come to the Bar, kneeled until the Lord High Steward acquainted him that he might rise."

The Duke of Denver looked very small and pink and lonely in his blue serge suit, the only head uncovered among all his peers, but he was not without a certain dignity as he was conducted to the "Stool placed within the Bar," which is deemed appropriate to noble prisoners, and he listened to the Lord High Steward's rehearsal of the charge with a simple gravity which became him very well.

*The Lord Chancellor held the appointment on this occasion as usual.

**For Report of the procedure see House of Lords Journal for the dates in question.

"Then the said Duke of Denver was arraigned by the Clerk of the Parliaments in the usual manner and asked whether he was Guilty or Not Guilty, to which he pleaded Not Guilty."

Whereupon Sir Wigmore Wrinching, the Attorney-General, rose to open the case for the Crown.

After the usual preliminaries to the effect that the case was a very painful one and the occasion a very solemn one, Sir Wigmore proceeded to unfold the story from the beginning: the quarrel, the shot at 3 a.m., the pistol, the finding of the body, the disappearance of the letter, and the rest of the familiar tale. He hinted, moreover, that evidence would be called to show that the quarrel between Denver and Cathcart had motives other than those alleged by the prisoner, and that the latter would turn out to have had "good reason to fear exposure at Cathcart's hands." At which point the accused was observed to glance uneasily at his solicitor. The exposition took only a short time, and Sir Wigmore proceeded to call witnesses.

The prosecution being unable to call the Duke of Denver, the first important witness was Lady Mary Wimsey. After telling about her relations with the murdered man, and describing the quarrel, "At three o'clock," she proceeded, "I got up and went downstairs."

"In consequence of what did you do so?" inquired Sir Wigmore, looking round the Court with the air of a man about to produce his great effect.

"In consequence of an appointment I had made to meet a friend."

All the reporters looked up suddenly, like dogs expecting a piece of biscuit, and Sir Wigmore started so violently that he knocked his brief over upon the head of the Clerk to the House of Lords sitting below him.

"Indeed! Now, witness, remember you are on your oath, and be very careful. What was it caused you to wake at three o'clock?"

"I was not asleep. I was waiting for my appointment."

"And while you were waiting did you hear anything?"

"Nothing at all."

"Now, Lady Mary, I have here your deposition sworn before the Coroner. I will read it to you. Please listen very carefully. You say, 'At three o'clock I was wakened by a shot. I thought it might be poachers. It sounded very loud, close to the house. I went down to find out what it was.' Do you remember making that statement?"

"Yes, but it was not true."

"Not true?"

"No."

"In the face of that statement, you still say that you heard nothing at three o'clock?"

"I heard nothing at all. I went down because I had an appointment."

"My lords," said Sir Wigmore, with a very red face, "I must ask leave to treat this witness as a hostile witness."

Sir Wigmore's fiercest onslaught, however, produced no effect, except a reiteration of the statement that no shot had been heard at any time. With regard to the finding of the body, Lady Mary explained that when she said, "Oh, God! Gerald, you've killed him," she was under the impression that the body was that of the friend who had made the appointment. Here a fierce wrangle ensued as to whether the story of the appointment was relevant. The Lords decided that on the whole it was relevant; and the entire Goyles story came out, together with the intimation that Mr. Goyles was in court and could be produced. Eventually, with a loud snort, Sir Wigmore Wrinching gave up the witness to Sir Impey Biggs, who, rising suavely and looking extremely handsome, brought back the discussion to a point long previous.

"Forgive the nature of the question," said Sir Impey, bowing blandly, "but will you tell us whether, in your opinion, the late Captain Cathcart was deeply in love with you?"

"No, I am sure he was not; it was an arrangement for our mutual convenience."

"From your knowledge of his character, do you suppose he was capable of a very deep affection?"

"I think he might have been, for the right woman. I should say he had a very passionate nature."

"Thank you. You have told us that you met Captain Cathcart several times when you were staying in Paris last February. Do you remember going with him to a jeweller's–Monsieur Briquet's in the Rue de la Paix?"

"I may have done; I cannot exactly remember."

"The date to which I should like to draw your attention is the sixth."

"I could not say."

"Do you recognise this trinket?"

Here the green-eyed cat was handed to witness.

"No; I have never seen it before."

"Did Captain Cathcart ever give you one like it?"

"Never."

"Did you ever possess such a jewel?"

"I am quite positive I never did."

"My lords, I put in this diamond and platinum cat. Thank you, Lady Mary."

James Fleming, being questioned closely as to the delivery of the post, continued to be vague and forgetful, leaving the Court, on the whole, with the impression that no letter had ever been delivered to the Duke. Sir Wigmore, whose opening speech had contained sinister allusions to an attempt to blacken the character of the victim, smiled disagreeably, and handed the witness over to Sir Impey. The latter contented himself with extracting an admission that witness could not swear positively one way or the other, and passed on immediately to another point.

"Do you recollect whether any letters came by the same post for any of the other members of the party?"

"Yes; I took three or four into the billiard-room."

"Can you say to whom they were addressed?"

"There were several for Colonel Marchbanks and one for Captain Cathcart."

"Did Captain Cathcart open his letter there and then?"

"I couldn't say, sir. I left the room immediately to take his grace's letters to the study."

"Now will you tell us how the letters are collected for the post in the morning at the Lodge?"

"They are put into the post-bag, which is locked. His grace keeps one key and the post-office has the other. The letters are put in through a slit in the top."

"On the morning after Captain Cathcart's death were the letters taken to the post as usual?"

"Yes, sir."

"By whom?"

"I took the bag down myself, sir."

"Had you an opportunity of seeing what letters were in it?"

"I saw there was two or three when the postmistress took 'em out of the bag, but I couldn't say who they was addressed to or anythink of that."

"Thank you."

Sir Wigmore Wrinching here bounced up like a very irritable jack-in-the-box.

"Is this the first time you have mentioned this letter which you say you delivered to Captain Cathcart on the night of his murder?"

"My lords," cried Sir Impey, "I protest against this language. We have as yet had no proof that any murder was committed."

This was the first indication of the line of defence which Sir Impey proposed to take, and caused a little rustle of excitement.

"My lords," went on Counsel, replying to a question of the Lord High Steward, "I submit that so far there has been no attempt to prove murder, and that, until the prosecution have established the murder, such a word cannot properly be put into the mouth of a witness."

"Perhaps, Sir Wigmore, it would be better to use some other word."

"It makes no difference to our case, my lord; I bow to your lordships' decision. Heaven knows that I would not seek, even by the lightest or most trivial word, to hamper the defence on so serious a charge."

"My lords," interjected Sir Impey, "if the learned Attorney-General considers the word murder to be a triviality, it would be interesting to know to what words he does attach importance."

"The learned Attorney-General has agreed to substitute another word," said the Lord High Steward soothingly, and nodding to Sir Wigmore to proceed.

Sir Impey, having achieved his purpose of robbing the Attorney-General's onslaught on the witness of some of its original impetus, sat down, and Sir Wigmore repeated his question.

"I mentioned it first to Mr. Murbles about three weeks ago."

"Mr. Murbles is the solicitor for the accused, I believe."

"Yes, sir."

"And how was it," inquired Sir Wigmore ferociously, settling his pince-nez on his rather prominent nose, and glowering at the witness, "that you did not mention this letter at the inquest or at the earlier proceedings in the case?"

"I wasn't asked about it, sir."

"What made you suddenly decide to go and tell Mr. Murbles about it?"

"He asked me, sir."

"Oh, he asked you; and you conveniently remembered it when it was suggested to you?"

"No, sir. I remembered it all the time. That is to say, I hadn't given any special thought to it, sir."

"Oh, you remembered it all the time, though you hadn't given any thought to it. Now I put it to you that you had not remembered about it at all till it was suggested to you by Mr. Murbles."

"Mr. Murbles didn't suggest nothing, sir. He asked me whether any other letters came by that post, and then I remembered it."

"Exactly. When it was suggested to you, you remembered it, and not before."

"No, sir. That is, if I'd been asked before I should have remembered it and mentioned it, but, not being asked, I didn't think it would be of any importance, sir."

"You didn't think it of any importance that this man received a letter a few hours before–his–decease?"

"No, sir. I reckoned if it had been of any importance the police would have asked about it, sir."

"Now, James Fleming, I put it to you again that it never occurred to you that Captain Cathcart might have received a letter the night he died till the idea was put into your head by the defence."

The witness, baffled by this interrogative negative, made a confused reply, and Sir Wigmore, glancing round the house as much as to say, "You see this shifty fellow," proceeded:

"I suppose it didn't occur to you either to mention to the police about the letters in the post-bag?"

"No, sir."

"Why not?"

"I didn't think it was my place, sir."

"Did you think about it at all?"

"No, sir."

"Do you ever think?"

"No, sir–I mean, yes, sir."

"Then will you please think what you are saying now."

"Yes, sir."

"You say that you took all these important letters out of the house without authority and without acquainting the police?"

"I had my orders, sir."

"From whom?"

"They was his grace's orders, sir."

"Ah! His grace's orders. When did you get that order?"

"It was part of my regular duty, sir, to take the bag to the post each morning."

"And did it not occur to you that in a case like this the proper information of the police might be more important than your orders?"

"No, sir."

Sir Wigmore sat down with a disgusted look; and Sir Impey took the witness in hand again.

"Did the thought of this letter delivered to Captain Cathcart never pass through your mind between the day of the death and the day when Mr. Murbles spoke to you about it?"

"Well, it did pass through my mind, in a manner of speaking, sir."

"When was that?"

"Before the Grand Jury, sir."

"And how was it you didn't speak about it then?"

"The gentleman said I was to confine myself to the questions, and not say nothing on my own, sir."

"Who was this very peremptory gentleman?"

"The lawyer that came down to ask questions for the Crown, sir."

"Thank you," said Sir Impey smoothly, sitting down, and leaning over to say something, apparently of an amusing nature, to Mr. Glibbery.

The question of the letter was further pursued in the examination of the Hon. Freddy. Sir Wigmore Wrinching laid great stress upon this witness's assertion that deceased had been in excellent health and spirits when retiring to bed on the Wednesday evening, and had spoken of his approaching marriage. "He seemed particularly cheerio, you know," said the Hon. Freddy.

"Particularly what?" inquired the Lord High Steward.

"Cheerio, my lord," said Sir Wigmore, with a deprecatory bow.

"I do not know whether that is a dictionary word," said his lordship, entering it upon his notes with meticulous exactness, "but I take it to be synonymous with cheerful."

The Hon. Freddy, appealed to, said he thought he meant more than just cheerful, more merry and bright, you know.

"May we take it that he was in exceptionally lively spirits?" suggested Counsel.

"Take it in any spirit you like," muttered the witness, adding, more happily, "Take a peg of John Begg."

"The deceased was particularly lively and merry when he went to bed," said Sir Wigmore, frowning horribly, "and looking forward to his marriage in the near future. Would that be a fair statement of his condition?"

The Hon. Freddy agreed to this.

Sir Impey did not cross-examine as to witness's account of the quarrel, but went straight to his point.

"Do you recollect anything about the letters that were brought in the night of the death?"

"Yes; I had one from my aunt. The Colonel had some, I fancy, and there was one for Cathcart."

"Did Captain Cathcart read his letter there and then?"

"No, I'm sure he didn't. You see, I opened mine, and then I saw he was shoving his away in his pocket, and I thought——"

"Never mind what you thought," said Sir Impey. "What did you do?"

"I said, 'Excuse me, you don't mind do you?' And he said, 'Not at all'; but he didn't read his; and I remember thinking——"

"We can't have that, you know," said the Lord High Steward.

"But that's why I'm so sure he didn't open it," said the Hon. Freddy, hurt. "You see, I said to myself at the time what a secretive fellow he was, and that's how I know."

Sir Wigmore, who had bounced up with his mouth open, sat down again.

"Thank you, Mr. Arbuthnot," said Sir Impey, smiling.

Colonel and Mrs. Marchbanks testified to having heard movements in the Duke's study at 11:30. They had heard no shot or other noise. There was no cross-examination.

Mr. Pettigrew-Robinson gave a vivid account of the quarrel, and asserted very positively that there could be no mistaking the sound of the Duke's bedroom door.

"We were then called up by Mr. Arbuthnot at a little after 3 a.m.," proceeded witness, "and went down to the conservatory, where I saw the accused and Mr. Arbuthnot washing the face of the deceased. I pointed out to them what an unwise thing it was to do this, as they might be destroying valuable evidence for the police. They paid no attention to me. There were a number of footmarks round about the door which I wanted to examine, because it was my theory that——"

"My lords," cried Sir Impey, "we really cannot have this witness's theory."

"Certainly not!" said the Lord High Steward. "Answer the questions, please, and don't add anything on your own account."

"Of course," said Mr. Pettigrew-Robinson. "I don't mean to imply that there was anything wrong about it, but I considered——"

"Never mind what you considered. Attend to me, please. When you first saw the body, how was it lying?"

"On its back, with Denver and Arbuthnot washing its face. It had evidently been turned over, because——"

"Sir Wigmore," interposed the Lord High Steward, "You really must control your witness."

"Kindly confine yourself to the evidence," said Sir Wigmore, rather heated. "We do not want your deductions from it. You say that when you saw the body it was lying on its back. Is that correct?"

"And Denver and Arbuthnot were washing it."

"Yes. Now I want to pass to another point. Do you remember an occasion when you lunched at the Royal Automobile Club?"

"I do. I lunched there one day in the middle of last August–I think it was about the sixteenth or seventeenth."

"Will you tell us what happened on that occasion?"

"I had gone into the smoke-room after lunch, and was reading in a high-backed armchair, when I saw the prisoner at the Bar come in with the late Captain Cathcart. That is to say, I saw them in the big mirror over the mantelpiece. They did not notice there was anyone there, or they would have been a little more careful what they said, I fancy. They sat down near me and started talking, and presently Cathcart leaned over and said something in a low tone which I couldn't catch. The prisoner leapt up with a horrified face, exclaiming, 'For God's sake, don't give me away, Cathcart–there'd be the devil to pay.' Cathcart said something reassuring–I didn't hear what, he had a furtive sort of voice–and the prisoner replied, 'Well, don't, that's all. I couldn't afford to let anybody get hold of it.' The prisoner seemed greatly alarmed. Captain Cathcart was laughing. They dropped their voices again, and that was all I heard."

"Thank you."

Sir Impey took over the witness with a Belial-like politeness.

"You are gifted with very excellent powers of observation and deduction, Mr. Pettigrew-Robinson," he began, "and no doubt you like to exercise your sympathetic imagination in a scrutiny of people's motives and characters?"

"I think I may call myself a student of human nature," replied Mr. Pettigrew-Robinson, much mollified.

"Doubtless, people are inclined to confide in you?"

"Certainly. I may say I am a great repository of human documents."

"On the night of Captain Cathcart's death your wide knowledge of the world was doubtless of great comfort and assistance to the family?"

"They did not avail themselves of my experience, sir," said Mr. Pettigrew-Robinson, exploding suddenly. "I was ignored completely. If only my advice had been taken at the time——"

"Thank you, thank you," said Sir Impey, cutting short an impatient exclamation from the Attorney-General, who thereupon rose and demanded:

"If Captain Cathcart had had any secret or trouble of any kind in his life, you would have expected him to tell you about it?"

"From any right-minded young man I might certainly have expected it," said Mr. Pettigrew-Robinson blusteringly; "but Captain Cathcart was disagreeably secretive. On the only occasion when I showed a friendly interest in his affairs he was very rude indeed. He called me——"

"That'll do," interposed Sir Impey hastily, the answer to the question not having turned out as he expected. "What the deceased called you is immaterial."

Mr. Pettigrew-Robinson retired, leaving behind him the impression of a man with a grudge—an impression which seemed to please Mr. Glibbery and Mr. Brownrigg-Fortescue extremely, for they chuckled continuously through the evidence of the next two witnesses.

Mrs. Pettigrew-Robinson had little to add to her previous evidence at the inquest. Miss Cathcart was asked by Sir Impey about Cathcart's parentage, and explained, with deep disapproval in her voice, that her brother, when an all-too-experienced and middle-aged man of the world, had nevertheless "been entangled by" an Italian singer of nineteen, who had "contrived" to make him marry her. Eighteen years later both parents had died. "No wonder," said Miss Cathcart, "with the rackety life they led," and the boy had been left to her care. She explained how Denis had always chafed at her influence, gone about with men she disapproved of, and eventually gone to Paris to make a diplomatic career for himself, since which time she had hardly seen him.

An interesting point was raised in the cross-examination of Inspector Craikes. A penknife being shown him, he identified it as the one found on Cathcart's body.

By Mr. Glibbery: "Do you observe any marks on the blade?"

"Yes, there is a slight notch near the handle."

"Might the mark have been caused by forcing back the catch of a window?"

Inspector Cralkes agreed that it might, but doubted whether so small a knife would have been adequate for such a purpose. The revolver was produced, and the question of ownership raised.

"My lords," put in Sir Impey, "we do not dispute the Duke's ownership of the revolver."

The Court looked surprised, and, after Hardraw the gamekeeper had given evidence of the shot heard at 11:30, the medical evidence was taken.

Sir Impey Biggs: "Could the wound have been self-inflicted?"

"It could, certainly."

"Would it have been instantly fatal?"

"No. From the amount of blood found upon the path it was obviously not immediately fatal."

"Are the marks found, in your opinion, consistent with deceased having crawled towards the house?"

"Yes, quite. He might have had sufficient strength to do so."

"Would such a wound cause fever?"

"It is quite possible. He might have lost consciousness for some time, and contracted a chill and fever by lying in the wet."

"Are the appearances consistent with his having lived for some hours after being wounded?"

"They strongly suggest it."

Re-examining, Sir Wigmore Wrinching established that the wound and general appearance of the ground were equally consistent with the theory that deceased had been shot by another hand at very close quarters, and dragged to the house before life was extinct.

"In your experience is it more usual for a person committing suicide to shoot himself in the chest or in the head?"

"In the head is perhaps more usual."

"So much as almost to create a presumption of murder when the wound is in the chest?"

"I would not go so far as that."

"But, other things being equal, you would say that a wound in the head is more suggestive of suicide than a body-wound?"

"That is so."

Sir Impey Biggs: "But suicide by shooting in the heart is not by any means impossible?"

"Oh, dear, no."

"There have been such cases?"

"Oh, certainly; many such."

"There is nothing in the medical evidence before you to exclude the idea of suicide?"

"Nothing whatever."

This closed the case for the Crown.

# 15

# BAR FALLING

*Copyright by Reuter, Press Association Exchange Telegraph, and Central News.*

WHEN SIR Impey Biggs rose to make his opening speech for the defence on the second day, it was observed that he looked somewhat worried–a thing very unusual in him. His remarks were very brief, yet in those few words he sent a thrill through the great assembly.

"My lords, in rising to open this defence I find myself in a more than usually anxious position. Not that I have any doubt of your lordships' verdict. Never perhaps has it been possible so clearly to prove the innocence of any accused person as in the case of my noble client. But I will explain to your lordships at once that I may be obliged to ask for an adjournment, since we are at present without an important witness and a decisive piece of evidence. My lords, I hold here in my hand a cablegram from this witness–I will tell you his name; it is Lord Peter Wimsey, the brother of the accused. It was handed in yesterday at New York. I will read it to you. He says: 'Evidence secured. Leaving tonight with Air Pilot Grant. Sworn copy and depositions follow by S.S. *Lucarnia* in case accident. Hope arrive Thursday.' My lords, at this moment this all-important witness is cleaving the air high above the wide Atlantic. In this wintry weather he is braving a peril which would appal any heart but his own and that of the world-famous aviator whose help he has enlisted, so that no moment may be lost in freeing his noble brother from this terrible charge. My lords, the barometer is falling."

An immense hush, like the stillness of a black frost, had fallen over the glittering benches. The lords in their scarlet and ermine, the peeresses in their rich furs, counsel in their full-bottomed wigs and billowing gowns, the Lord High Steward upon his high seat, the ushers and the heralds and the gaudy kings-of-arms, rested rigid in their places. Only the prisoner looked across at his counsel and back to the Lord High Steward in a kind of bewilderment, and the reporters scribbled wildly and desperately stop-press announcements –lurid headlines, picturesque epithets, and alarming weather predictions, to halt hurrying London on its way: "PEER'S SON FLIES ATLANTIC"; "BROTHER'S DEVOTION"; "WILL WIMSEY BE IN TIME"; "RIDDLESDALE MURDER CHARGE: AMAZING DEVELOPMENT." This was news. a million tape-machines ticked it out in offices and clubs, where clerks and messenger-boys gloated over it and laid wagers on the result; the thousands of monster printing-presses sucked it in, boiled it into lead, champed it into slugs, engulfed it in their huge maws, digested it to paper, and flapped it forth again with clutching talons; and a blue-nosed, ragged veteran of Vimy Ridge, who had once assisted to dig Major Wimsey out of a shell-hole, muttered: "Gawd 'elp 'im, 'e's a real decent little blighter," as he tucked his newspapers into the iron grille of a tree in Kingsway and displayed his placard to the best advantage.

After a brief statement that he intended, not merely to prove his noble client's innocence but (as a work of supererogation) to make clear every detail of the tragedy, Sir Impey Biggs proceeded without further delay to call his witnesses.

Among the first was Mr. Goyles, who testified that he had found Cathcart already dead at 3 a.m., with his head close to the water-trough which stood near the well. Ellen, the maid-servant, next confirmed James Fleming's evidence with regard to the post-bag, and explained how she changed the blotting-paper in the study every day.

The evidence of Detective-Inspector Parker aroused more interest and some bewilderment. His description of the discovery of the green-eyed cat was eagerly listened to. He also gave a minute account of the footprints and marks of dragging, especially the imprint of a hand in the flower-bed. The piece of blotting-paper was then produced, and photographs of it circulated among the peers. A long discussion ensued on both these points, Sir Impey Biggs endeavouring to show that the imprint on the flower-bed was such as would have been caused by a man endeavouring to lift himself from a prone position, Sir Wigmore Wrinching doing his best to force an admission that it might have been made by deceased in trying to prevent himself from being dragged along.

"The position of the fingers being towards the house appears, does it not, to negative the suggestion of dragging?" suggested Sir Impey.

Sir Wigmore, however, put it to the witness that the wounded man might have been dragged head foremost.

"If, now," said Sir Wigmore. "I were to drag you by the coat-collar–my lords will grasp my contention——"

"It appears," observed the Lord High Steward, "to be a case for *solvitur ambulando*." (Laughter.) "I suggest that when the House rises for lunch, some of us should make the experiment, choosing a member of similar height and weight to the deceased." (All the noble lords looked round at one another to see which unfortunate might be chosen for the part.)

Inspector Parker then mentioned the marks of forcing on the study window.

"In your opinion, could the catch have been forced back by the knife found on the body of the deceased?"

"I know it could, for I made the experiment myself with a knife of exactly similar pattern."

After this the message on the blotting-paper was read backwards and forwards and interpreted in every possible way, the defence insisting that the language was French and the words "*Je suis fou de douleur*," the prosecution scouting the suggestion as far-fetched, and offering an English interpretation, such as "is found" or "his foul." A handwriting expert was then called, who compared the handwriting with that of an authentic letter of Cathcart's, and was subsequently severely handled by the prosecution.

These knotty points being left for the consideration of the noble lords, the defence then called a tedious series of witnesses: the manager of Cox's and Monsieur Turgeot of the Crédit Lyonnais, who went with much detail into Cathcart's financial affairs; the concierge and Madame Leblanc from the Rue St. Honoré; and the noble lords began to yawn, with the exception of a few of the soap and pickles lords, who suddenly started to make computations in their notebooks, and exchanged looks of intelligence as from one financier to another.

Then came Monsieur Briquet, the jeweller from the Rue de la Paix, and the girl from his shop, who told the story of the tall, fair, foreign lady and the purchase of the green-eyed cat—whereat everybody woke up. After reminding the assembly that this incident took place in February, when Cathcart's fiancée was in Paris, Sir Impey invited the jeweller's assistant to look round the house and tell them if she saw the foreign lady. This proved a lengthy business, but the answer was finally in the negative.

"I do not want there to be any doubt about this," said Sir Impey, "and, with the learned Attorney-General's permission, I am now going to confront this witness with Lady Mary Wimsey."

Lady Mary was accordingly placed before the witness, who replied immediately and positively: "No, this is not the lady; I have never seen this lady in my life. There is the resemblance of height and colour and the hair bobbed, but there is nothing else at all—not the least in the world. It is not the same type at all. Mademoiselle is a charming English lady, and the man who marries her will be very happy, but the other was *belle à se suicider*—a woman to kill, suicide one's self, or send all to the devil for, and believe me, gentlemen" (with a wide smile to her distinguished audience), "we have the opportunity to see them in my business."

There was a profound sensation as this witness took her departure, and Sir Impey scribbled a note and passed it down to Mr. Murbles. It contained the one word, "Magnificent!" Mr. Murbles scribbled back:

"Never said a word to her. Can you beat it?" and leaned back in his seat smirking like a very neat little grotesque from a Gothic corbel.

The witness who followed was Professor Hébert, a distinguished exponent of international law, who described Cathcart's promising career as a rising young diplomat in Paris before the war. He was followed by a number of officers who testified to the excellent war record of the deceased. Then came a witness who gave the aristocratic name of du Bois-Gobey Houdin, who perfectly recollected a very uncomfortable dispute on a certain occasion when playing cards with le Capitaine Cathcart, and having subsequently mentioned the matter to Monsieur Thomas Freeborn, the distinguished English engineer. It was Parker's diligence that had unearthed this witness, and he looked across with an undisguised grin at the discomfited Sir Wigmore Wrinching. When Mr. Glibbery had dealt with all these the afternoon was well advanced, and the Lord High Steward accordingly asked the lords if it was their pleasure that the House be adjourned till the next day at 10.30 of the clock in the forenoon, and the lords replying "Aye" in a most exemplary chorus, the House was accordingly adjourned.

A scurry of swift black clouds with ragged edges was driving bleakly westward as they streamed out into Parliament Square, and the seagulls screeched and wheeled inwards from the river. Charles Parker wrapped his ancient Burberry closely about him as he scrambled on to a 'bus to get home to Great Ormond Street. It was only one more drop in his cup of discomfort that the conductor greeted him with "Outside only!" and rang the bell before he could get off again. He climbed to the top and sat there holding his hat on. Mr. Bunter returned sadly to 110 Piccadilly, and wandered restlessly about the flat till seven o'clock, when he came into the sitting-room and switched on the loud speaker.

"London calling," said the unseen voice impartially. "2LO calling. Here is the weather forecast. A deep depression is crossing the Atlantic, and a secondary is stationary over the British Isles. Storms, with heavy rain and sleet, will be prevalent, rising to a gale in the south and south-west. . . ."

"You never know," said Bunter. "I suppose I'd better light a fire in his bedroom."

"Further outlook similar."

# 16

# THE SECOND STRING

*O, when he came to broken briggs*
*He bent his bow and swam,*
*And whan he came to the green grass growin'*
*He slacked his shoone and ran.*

*O, whan he came to Lord William's gates*
*He baed na to chap na ca',*
*But set his bent bow till his breast,*
*An' lightly lap the wa'.*

Ballad of Lady Maisry

LORD PETER peered out through the cold scurry of cloud. The thin struts of steel, incredibly fragile, swung slowly across the gleam and glint far below, where the wide country dizzied out and spread like a revolving map. In front the sleek leather back of his companion humped stubbornly, sheeted with rain. He hoped that Grant was feeling confident. The roar of the engine drowned the occasional shout he threw to his passenger as they lurched from gust to gust.

He withdrew his mind from present discomforts and went over that last, strange, hurried scene. Fragments of conversation spun through his head.

"Mademoiselle, I have scoured two continents in search of you."

"*Voyons*, then, it is urgent. But be quick for the big bear may come in and be grumpy, and I do not like *des histoires*."

There had been a lamp on a low table; he remembered the gleam through the haze of short gold hair. She was a tall girl, but slender, looking up at him from the huge black-and-gold cushions.

"Mademoiselle, it is incredible to me that you should ever–dine or dance–with a person called Van Humperdinck."

Now what had possessed him to say that–when there was so little time, and Jerry's affairs were of such importance?

"Monsieur van Humperdinck does not dance. Did you seek me through two continents to say that?"

"No, I am serious."

"*Eh bien*, sit down."

She had been quite frank about it.

"Yes, poor soul. But life was very expensive since the war. I refused several good things. But always *des histoires*. And so little money. You see, one must be sensible. There is one's old age. It is necessary to be provident, *hein?*"

"Assuredly." She had a little accent–very familiar. At first he could not place it. Then it came to him–Vienna before the war, that capital of incredible follies.

"Yes, yes, I wrote. I was very kind, very sensible. I said, '*Je ne suis pas femme à supporter de gros ennuis.' Cela se comprend, n'est-ce pas?*"

That was readily understood. The 'plane dived sickly into a sudden pocket, the propeller whirring helplessly in the void, then steadied and began to nose up the opposite spiral.

"I saw it in the papers–yes. Poor boy! Why should anybody have shot him?"

"Mademoiselle, it is for that I have come to you. My brother, whom I dearly love, is accused of the murder. He may be hanged."

"Brr!"

"For a murder he did not commit."

"*Mon pauvre enfant*——"

"Mademoiselle, I implore you to be serious. My brother is accused, and will be standing his trial——"

Once her attention had been caught she had been all sympathy. Her blue eyes had a curious and attractive trick–a full lower lid that shut them into glimmering slits.

"Mademoiselle, I implore you, try to remember what was in his letter."

"But, *mon pauvre ami*, how can I? I did not read it. It was very long, very tedious, full of *histoires*. The thing was finished–I never bother about what cannot be helped, do you?"

But his real agony at this failure had touched her.

"Listen, then; all is perhaps not lost. It is possible the letter is still somewhere about. Or we will ask Adèle. She is my maid. She collects letters to blackmail people–oh, yes, I know! But she is *habile comme tout pour la toilette*. Wait–we will look first."

Tossing out letters, trinkets, endless perfumed rubbish from the little gimcrack secretaire, from drawers full of lingerie ("I am so untidy–I am Adèle's despair"), from bags–hundreds of bags–and at last Adèle, thin-lipped and wary-eyed, denying everything till her mistress suddenly slapped her face in a fury, and called her ugly little names in French and German.

"It is useless, then," said Lord Peter. "What a pity that Mademoiselle Adèle cannot find a thing so valuable to me."

The word "valuable" suggested an idea to Adèle. There was Mademoiselle's jewel-case which had not been searched. She would fetch it.

"*C'est cela que cherche monsieur?*"

After that the sudden arrival of Mr. Cornelius van Humperdinck, very rich and stout and suspicious, and the rewarding of Adèle in a tactful, unobtrusive fashion by the elevator shaft.

Grant shouted, but the words flipped feebly away into the blackness and were lost. "What?" bawled Wimsey in his ear. He shouted again, and this time the word "juice" shot into sound and fluttered away. But whether the news was good or bad Lord Peter could not tell.

* * * * *

Mr. Murbles was aroused a little after midnight by a thunderous knocking upon his door. Thrusting his head out of the window in some alarm, he saw the porter with his lantern steaming through the rain, and behind him a shapeless figure which for the moment Mr. Murbles could not make out.

"What's the matter?" said the solicitor.

"Young lady askin' urgently for you, sir."

The shapeless figure looked up, and he caught the spangle of gold hair in the lantern-light under the little tight hat.

"Mr. Murbles, please come. Bunter rang me up. There's a woman come to give evidence. Bunter doesn't like to leave her–she's frightened–but he says it's *frightfully* important, and Bunter's always right, you know."

"Did he mention the name?"

"A Mrs. Grimethorpe."

"God bless me! Just a moment, my dear young lady, and I will let you in."

And, indeed, more quickly than might have been expected, Mr. Murbles made his appearance in a Jaeger dressing-gown at the front door.

"Come in, my dear. I will get dressed in a very few minutes. It was quite right of you to come to me. I'm very, very glad you did. What a terrible night! Perkins, would you kindly wake up Mr. Murphy and ask him to oblige me with the use of his telephone?"

Mr. Murphy–a noisy Irish barrister with a hearty manner–needed no waking. He was entertaining a party of friends, and was delighted to be of service.

"Is that you Biggs? Murbles speaking. That alibi––"

"Yes?"

"Has come along of its own accord."

"My God! You don't say so!"

"Can you come round to 110 Piccadilly?"

"Straight away."

It was a strange little party gathered round Lord Peter's fire–the white-faced woman, who started at every sound; the men of law, with their keen, disciplined faces; Lady Mary; Bunter, the efficient. Mrs. Grimethorpe's story was simple enough. She had suffered the torments of knowledge ever since Lord Peter had spoken to her. She had seized an hour when her husband was drunk in the "Lord in Glory," and had harnessed the horse and driven in to Stapley.

"I couldn't keep silence. It's better my man should kill me, for I'm unhappy enough, and maybe I couldn't be any worse off in the Lord's hand–rather than they should hang him for a thing he never done. He was kind, and I was desperate miserable, that's the truth, and I'm hoping his lady won't be hard on him when she knows it all."

"No, no," said Mr. Murbles, clearing his throat. "Excuse me a moment, madam. Sir Impey––"

The lawyers whispered together in the window-seat.

"You see," said Sir Impey, "she has burnt her boats pretty well now by coming at all. The great question for us is, Is it worth the risk? After all, we don't know what Wimsey's evidence amounts to."

"No, that is why I feel inclined–in spite of the risk–to put this evidence in," said Mr. Murbles.

"I am ready to take the risk," interposed Mrs. Grimethorpe starkly.

"We quite appreciate that," replied Sir Impey. "It is the risk to our client we have to consider first of all."

"Risk?" cried Mary. "But surely this clears him!"

"Will you swear absolutely to the time when his grace of Denver arrived at Grider's Hole, Mrs. Grimethorpe?" went on the lawyer, as though he had not heard her.

"It was a quarter past twelve by the kitchen clock–'tis a very good clock."

"And he left you at——"

"About five minutes past two."

"And how long would it take a man, walking quickly, to get back to Riddlesdale Lodge?"

"Oh, wellnigh an hour. It's rough walking, and a steep bank up and down to the beck."

"You mustn't let the other counsel upset you on those points, Mrs. Grimethorpe, because they will try to prove that he had time to kill Cathcart either before he started or after he returned, and by admitting that the Duke had something in his life that he wanted kept secret we shall be supplying the very thing the prosecution lack–*a motive for murdering anyone who might have found him out*."

There was a stricken silence.

"If I may ask, madam," said Sir Impey, "has any person any suspicion?"

"My husband guessed," she answered hoarsely. "I am sure of it. He has always known. But he couldn't prove it. That very night——"

"What night?"

"The night of the murder–he laid a trap for me. He came back from Stapley in the night, hoping to catch us and do murder. But he drank too much before he started, and spent the night in the ditch, or it might be Gerald's death you'd be inquiring into, and mine, as well as the other."

It gave Mary an odd shock to hear her brother's name spoken like that, by that speaker and in that company. She asked suddenly, apropos of nothing, "Isn't Mr. Parker here?"

"No, my dear," said Mr. Murbles reprovingly, "this is not a police matter."

"The best thing we can do, I think," sald Sir Impey, "is to put in the evidence, and, if necessary, arrange for some kind of protection for this lady. In the meantime——"

"She is coming round with me to mother," said Lady Mary determinedly.

"My dear lady," expostulated Mr. Murbles, "that would be very unsuitable in the circumstances. I think you hardly grasp——"

"Mother said so," retorted her ladyship. "Bunter, call a taxi."

Mr. Murbles waved his hands helplessly, but Sir Impey was rather amused. "It's no good, Murbles," he said. "Time and trouble will tame an advanced young woman, but an advanced old woman is uncontrollable by any earthly force."

So it was from the Dowager's town house that Lady Mary rang up Mr. Charles Parker to tell him the news.

# 17

# THE ELOQUENT DEAD

*Je connaissais Manon: pourquoi m'affliger tant d'un malheur que j'avais dû prévoir.*

Manon Lescaut

THE GALE had blown itself out into a wonderful fresh day, with clear spaces of sky, and a high wind rolling boulders of cumulus down the blue slopes of air.

The prisoner had been wrangling for an hour with his advisers when finally they came into court, and even Sir Impey's classical face showed flushed between the wings of his wig.

"I'm not going to say anything," said the Duke obstinately. "Rotten thing to do. I suppose I can't prevent you callin' her if she insists on comin'—damn' good of her—makes me feel no end of a beast."

"Better leave it at that," said Mr. Murbles. "Makes a good impression, you know. Let him go into the box and behave like a perfect gentleman. They'll like it."

Sir Impey, who had sat through the small hours altering his speech, nodded.

The first witness that day came as something of a surprise. She gave her name and address as Eliza Briggs, known as Madame Brigette of New Bond Street, and her occupation as beauty specialist and perfumer. She had a large and aristocratic clientele of both sexes, and a branch in Paris.

Deceased had been a client of hers in both cities for several years. He had massage and manicure. After the war he had come to her about some slight scars caused by grazing with shrapnel. He was extremely particular about his personal appearance, and, if you called that vanity in a man, you might certainly say he was vain. Thank you. Sir Wigmore Wrinching made no attempt to cross-examine the witness, and the noble lords wondered to one another what it was all about.

At this point Sir Impey Biggs leaned forward, and, tapping his brief impressively with his forefinger, began:

"My lords, so strong is our case that we had not thought it necessary to present an alibi——" when an officer of the court rushed up from a little whirlpool of commotion by the door and excitedly thrust a note into his hand. Sir Impey read, coloured, glanced down the hall, put down his brief, folded his hands over it, and said in a sudden, loud voice which penetrated even to the deaf ear of the Duke of Wiltshire:

"My lords, I am happy to say that our missing witness is here. I call Lord Peter Wimsey."

Every neck was at once craned, and every eye focused on the very grubby and oily figure that came amiably trotting up the long room. Sir Impey Biggs passed the note down to Mr. Murbles, and, turning to the witness, who was yawning frightfully in the intervals of grinning at all his acquaintances, demanded that he should be sworn.

The witness's story was as follows:

"I am Lord Peter Wimsey, brother of the accused. I live at 110 Piccadilly. In consequence of what I read on that bit of blotting-paper which I now identify, I went to Paris to look for a certain lady. The name of the lady is Mademoiselle Simone Vonderaa. I found she had left Paris in company with a man named Van Humperdinck. I followed her, and at length came up with her in New York. I asked her to give me the letter Cathcart wrote on the night of his death. (Sensation). I produce that letter, with Mademoiselle Vonderaa's signature on the corner, so that it can be identified if Wiggy there tries to put it over you. (Joyous sensation, in which the indignant protests of prosecuting counsel were drowned.) And I'm sorry I've given you such short notice of this, old man, but I only got it the day before yesterday. We came as quick as we could, but we had to come down near Whitehaven with engine trouble, and if we had come down half a mile sooner I shouldn't he here now." (Applause, hurriedly checked by the Lord High Steward.)

"My lords," said Sir Impey, "your lordships are witnesses that I have never seen this letter in my life before. I have no idea of its contents; yet so positive am I that it cannot but assist my noble client's case, that I am willing–nay, eager–to put in this document immediately, as it stands, without perusal, to stand or fall by the contents."

"The handwriting must be identified as that of the deceased," interposed the Lord High Steward.

The ravening pencils of the reporters tore along the paper. The lean young man who worked for the *Daily Trumpet* scented a scandal in high life and licked his lips, never knowing what a much bigger one had escaped him by a bare minute or so.

Miss Lydia Cathcart was recalled to identify the handwriting, and the letter was handed to the Lord High Steward, who announced:

"The letter is in French. We shall have to swear an interpreter."

"You will find," said the witness suddenly, "that those bits of words on the blotting-paper come out of the letter. You'll 'scuse my mentioning it."

"Is this person put forward as an expert witness?" inquired Sir Wigmore witheringly.

"Right ho!" said Lord Peter. "Only, you see, it has been rather sprung on Biggy as you might say.

"Biggy and Wiggy
Were two pretty men,
They went into court
When the clock––"

"Sir Impey, I must really ask you to keep your witness in order."

Lord Peter grinned, and a pause ensued while an interpreter was fetched and sworn. Then, at last, the letter was read, amid a breathless silence:

"Riddlesdale Lodge,
"Stapley,
"N.E. Yorks.
"*le 13 Octobre, 192–*

"SIMONE,–Je viens de recevoir ta lettre. Que dire? Inutiles, les prières ou les reproches. Tu ne comprendras–tu ne liras même pas.

"N'ai-je pas toujours su, d'ailleurs, que tu devais infailliblement me trahir? Depuis huit ans déjà je souffre tous les torments que puisse infliger la jalousie. Je comprends bien que tu n'as jamais voulu me faire de la peine. C'est tout justement cette insouciance, cette légèreté, cette façon séduisante d'être malhonnête, que j'adorais en toi. J'ai tout su, et je t'ai aimée.

"Ma foi, non, ma chère, jamais je n'ai eu la moindre illusion. Te rappelles-tu cette première rencontre, un soir au Casino? Tu avais dix-sept ans, et tu étais jolie à ravir. Le lendemain tu fus à moi. Tu m'as dit, si gentiment, que tu m'aimais bien, et que j'étais, moi, le premier. Ma pauvre enfant, tu en as menti. Tu riais, toute seule, de ma naïveté—il y avait bien de quoi rire! Dès notre premier baiser, j'ai prévu ce moment.

"Mais écoute, Simone. J'ai la faiblesse de vouloir te montrer exactement ce que tu as fait de moi. Tu regretteras peut-être en peu. Mais, non—si tu pouvais regretter quoi que ce fût, tu ne serais plus Simone.

"Il y a huit ans, la veille de la guerre, j'étais riche—moins riche que ton Américain, mais assez riche pour te donner l'éstablissement qu'il te fallait. Tu étais moins exigeante avant la guerre, Simone—qui est-ce qui, pendant mon absence, t'a enseigné le goût du luxe? Charmante discrétion de ma part de ne jamais te le demander! Eh bien, une grande partie de ma fortune se trouvant placée en Russie et en Allemagne, j'en ai perdu plus des trois-quarts. Ce que m'en restait en France a beaucoup diminué en valeur. Il est vrai que j'avais mon traitement de capitaine dans l'armée britannique, mais c'est peu de chose, tu sais. Avant même la fin de la guerre, tu m'avais mangé toutes mes économies. C'était idiot, quoi? Un jeune homme qui a perdu les trois-quarts de ses rentes ne se permet plus une maîtresse et un appartement Avenue Kléber. Ou il congédie madame, ou bien il lui demande quelques sacrifices. Je n'ai rien osé demander. Si j'étais venu un jour te dire, 'Simone, je suis pauvre'—que m'aurais-tu répondu?

"Sais-tu ce que j'ai fait? Non—tu n'as jamais pensé à demander d'où venait cet argent. Qu'est-ce que cela pouvait te faire que j'ai tout jeté—fortune, honneur, bonheur—pour te posséder? J'ai joué, désespérément, éperdument—j'ai fait pis: j'ai triché au jeu. Je te vois hausser les épaules—tu ris—tu dis, 'Tiens, c'est malin, ça!' Oui, mais cela ne se fait pas. On m'aurait chassé du régiment. Je devenais le dernier des hommes.

"D'ailleurs, cela ne pouvait durer. Déjà un soir à Paris on m'a fait une scène désagréable, bien qu'on n'ait rien pu prouver. C'est alors que je me suis fiancé avec cette demoiselle dont je t'ai parlé, la fille du duc anglais. Le beau projet, quoi! Entretenir ma maîtresse avec l'argent de ma femme! Et je l'aurais fait—et je le ferais encore demain, si c'était pour te reposséder.

"Mais tu me quittes. Cet Américain est riche—archiriche. Depuis longtemps tu me répètes que ton appartement est trop petit et que tu t'ennuies à mourir. Cet 'ami bienveillant' t'offre les autos, les diamants, les mille-et-une nuits, la lune! Auprès de ces merveilles, évidemment, que valent l'amour et l'honneur?

"Enfin, le bon duc est d'une stupidité très commode. Il laisse traîner son révolver dans le tiroir de son bureau. D'ailleurs, il vient de me demander une explication à propos de cette histoire de cartes. Tu vois qu'en tout cas la partie était finie. Pourquoi t'en vouloir? On mettra sans doute mon suicide au compte de cet exposé. Tant mieux, je ne veux pas qu'on affiche mon histoire amoureuse dans les journaux.

"Adieu, ma bien-aimée—mon adorée, mon adorée, ma Simone. Sois heureuse avec ton nouvel amant. Ne pense plus à moi. Qu'est-ce tout cela peut bien te faire? Mon Dieu, comme je t'ai aimée—comme je t'aime toujours, malgré moi. Mais c'en est fini. Jamais plus tu ne me perceras le coeur. Oh! J'enrage—je suis fou de douleur! Adieu.

"DENIS CATHCART."

## TRANSLATION

"SIMONE,—I have just got your letter. What am I to say? It is useless to entreat or reproach you. You would not understand, or even read the letter.

"Besides, I always knew you must betray me some day. I have suffered a hell of jealousy for the last eight years. I know perfectly well you never meant to hurt me. It was just your utter lightness and carelessness and your attractive way of being dishonest which was so adorable. I knew everything, and loved you all the same.

"Oh, no, my dear, I never had any illusions. You remember our first meeting that night at the Casino. You were seventeen, and heartbreakingly lovely. You came to me the very next day. You told me, very prettily, that you loved me and that I was the first. My poor little girl, that wasn't true. I expect, when you were alone, you laughed to think I was so easily taken in. But there was nothing to laugh at. From our very first kiss I foresaw this moment.

"I'm afraid I'm weak enough, though, to want to tell you just what you have done for me. You may be sorry. But no—if you could regret anything, you wouldn't be Simone any longer.

"Eight years ago, before the war, I was rich—not so rich as your new American, but rich enough to give you what you wanted. You didn't want quite so much before the war, Simone. Who taught you to be so extravagant while I was away? I think it was very nice of me never to ask you. Well, most of my money was in Russian and German securities, and more than three-quarters of it went west. The remainder in France went down considerably in value. I had my captain's pay, of course, but that didn't amount to much. Even before the end of the war you had managed to get through all my savings. Of course, I was a fool. A young man whose income has been reduced by three-quarters can't afford an expensive mistress and a flat in the Avenue Kléber. He ought either to dismiss the lady or to demand a little self-sacrifice. But I didn't dare demand anything. Suppose I had come to you one day and said, 'Simone, I've lost my money'—what would you have said to me?

"What do you think I did? I don't suppose you ever thought about it at all. You didn't care if I was chucking away my money and my honour and my happiness to keep you. I gambled desperately. I did worse, I cheated at cards. I can see you shrug your shoulders and say, 'Good for you!' But it's a rotten thing to do—a rotter's game. If anybody had found out they'd have cashiered me.

"Besides, it couldn't go on for ever. There was one row in Paris, though they couldn't prove anything. So then I got engaged to the English girl I told you about—the duke's daughter. Pretty, wasn't it? I actually brought myself to consider keeping my mistress on my wife's money! But I'd have done it, and I'd do it again, to get you back.

"And now you've chucked me. This American is colossally rich. For a long time you've been dinning into my ears that the flat is too small and that you're bored to death. Your 'good friend' can offer you cars, diamonds—Aladdin's palace—the moon! I admit that love and honour look pretty small by comparison.

"Ah, well, the Duke is most obligingly stupid. He leaves his revolver about in his desk drawer. Besides, he's just been in to ask what about this card-sharping story. So you see the game's up, anyhow. I don't blame you. I suppose they'll put my suicide down to fear of exposure. All the better. I don't want my love-affairs in the Sunday Press.

"Good-bye, my dear—oh, Simone, my darling my darling, good-bye. Be happy with your new lover. Never mind me—what does it all matter? My God—how I loved you, and how I still love you in spite of myself. It's all done with. You'll never break my heart again. I'm mad—mad with misery! Good-bye.

# 18

# THE SPEECH FOR THE DEFENCE

*"Nobody; I myself; farewell"*

Othello

AFTER THE reading of Cathcart's letter even the appearance of the prisoner in the witness-box came as an anti-climax. In the face of the Attorney-General's cross-examination he maintained stoutly that he had wandered on the moor for several hours without meeting anybody, though he was forced to admit that he had gone downstairs at 11:30, and not at 2:30, as he had stated at the inquest. Sir Wigmore Wrinching made a great point of this, and, in a spirited endeavour to suggest that Cathcart was blackmailing Denver, pressed his questions so hard that Sir Impey Biggs, Mr. Murbles, Lady Mary, and Bunter had a nervous feeling that learned counsel's eyes were boring through the walls to the side-room where, apart from the other witnesses, Mrs. Grimethorpe sat waiting. After lunch Sir Impey Biggs rose to make his plea for the defence.

"My lords,—Your lordships have now heard—and I, who have watched and pleaded here for these three anxious days, know with what eager interest and with what ready sympathy you have heard—the evidence brought by my noble client to defend him against this dreadful charge of murder. You have listened while as it were from his narrow grave, the dead man has lifted his voice to tell you the story of that fatal night of the thirteenth of October, and I feel sure you can have no doubt in your hearts that that story is the true one. As your lordships know, I was myself totally ignorant of the contents of that letter until I heard it read in Court just now, and, by the profound impression it made upon my own mind, I can judge how tremendously and how painfully it must have affected your lordships. In my long experience at the criminal bar, I think I have never met with a history more melancholy than that of the unhappy young man whom a fatal passion—for here indeed we may use that well-worn expression in all the fulness of its significance—whom a truly fatal passion thus urged into deep after deep of degradation, and finally to a violent death by his own hand.

"The noble peer at the Bar has been indicted before your lordships of the murder of this young man. That he is wholly innocent of the charge must, in the light of what we have heard, be so plain to your lordships that any words from me might seem altogether superfluous. In the majority of cases of this kind the evidence is confused, contradictory; here, however, the course of events is so clear, so coherent, that had we ourselves been present to see the drama unrolled before us, as before the all-seeing eye of God, we could hardly have a more vivid or a more accurate vision of that night's adventures. Indeed, had the death of Denis Cathcart been the sole event of the night, I will venture to say that the truth could never have been one single moment in doubt. Since, however, by a series of unheard-of coincidences, the threads of Denis Cathcart's story became entangled with so many others, I will venture to tell it once again from the beginning, lest, in the confusion of so great a cloud of witnesses, any point should still remain obscure.

"Let me, then, go back to the beginning. You have heard how Denis Cathcart was born of mixed parentage—from the union of a young and lovely southern girl with an Englishman twenty years older than herself: imperious, passionate, and cynical. Till the age of 18 he lives on the Continent with his parents, travelling from place to place, seeing more of the world even than the average young Frenchman of his age, learning the code of love in a country where the *crime passionel* is understood and forgiven as it never can be over here.

"At the age of 18 a terrible loss befalls him. In a very short space of time he loses both his parents—his beautiful and adored mother and his father, who might, had he lived, have understood how to guide the impetuous nature which he had brought into the world. But the father dies, expressing two last wishes, both of which, natural as they were, turned out in the circumstances to be disastrously ill-advised. He left his son to the care of his sister, whom he had not seen for many years, with the direction that the boy should be sent to his own old University.

"My lords, you have seen Miss Lydia Cathcart, and heard her evidence. You will have realised how uprightly, how conscientiously, with what Christian disregard of self, she performed the duty entrusted to her, and yet how inevitably she failed to establish any real sympathy between herself and her young ward. He, poor lad, missing his parents at every turn, was plunged at Cambridge into the society of young men of totally different upbringing from himself. To a young man of his cosmopolitan experience the youth of Cambridge, with its sports and rags and naïve excursions into philosophy o' nights, must have seemed unbelievably childish. You all, from your own recollections of your Alma Mater, can reconstruct Denis Cathcart's life at Cambridge, its outward gaiety, its inner emptiness.

"Ambitious of embracing a diplomatic career, Cathcart made extensive acquaintances among the sons of rich and influential men. From a worldly point of view he was doing well, and his inheritance of a handsome fortune at the age of twenty-one seemed to open up the path to very great success. Shaking the academic dust of Cambridge from his feet as soon as his Tripos was passed, he went over to France, established himself in Paris, and began, in a quiet, determined kind of way, to carve out a little niche for himself in the world of international politics.

"But now comes into his life that terrible influence which was to rob him of fortune, honour, and life itself. He falls in love with a young woman of that exquisite, irresistible charm and beauty for which the Austrian capital is world-famous. He is enthralled body and soul, as utterly as any Chevalier des Grieux, by Simone Vonderaa.

"Mark that in this matter he follows the strict, continental code: complete devotion, complete discretion. You have heard how quietly he lived, how *rangé* he appeared to be. We have had in evidence his discreet banking-account, with its generous cheques drawn to self, and cashed in notes of moderate denominations, and with its regular accumulation of sufficient 'economies' quarter by quarter. Life has expanded for Denis Cathcart. Rich, ambitious, possessed of a beautiful and complaisant mistress, the world is open before him.

"Then, my lords, across this promising career there falls the thunderbolt of the Great War—ruthlessly smashing through his safeguards, overthrowing the edifice of his ambition, destroying and devastating here, as everywhere, all that made life beautiful and desirable.

"You have heard the story of Denis Cathcart's distinguished army career. On that I need not dwell. Like thousands of other young men, he went gallantly through those five years of strain and disillusionment, to find himself left, in the end, with his life and health indeed, and, so far, happy beyond many of his comrades, but with his life in ruins about him.

"Of his great fortune–all of which had been invested in Russian and German securities–literally nothing is left to him. What, you say, did that matter to a young man so well equipped, with such excellent connections, with so many favourable openings, ready to his hand? He needed only to wait quietly for a few years, to reconstruct much of what he had lost. Alas! my lords, he could not afford to wait. He stood in peril of losing something dearer to him than fortune or ambition; he needed money in quantity, and at once.

"My lords, in that pathetic letter which we have heard read nothing is more touching and terrible than that confession: 'I knew you could not be unfaithful to me.' All through that time of seeming happiness he knew–none better–that his house was built on sand. 'I was never deceived by you,' he says. From their earliest acquaintance she had lied to him, and he knew it, and that knowledge was yet powerless to loosen the bands of his fatal fascination. If any of you, my lords, have known the power of love exercised in this irresistible–I may say, this predestined manner–let your experience interpret the situation to you better than any poor words of mine can do. One great French poet and one great English poet have summed the matter up in a few words. Racine says of such a fascination:

*C'est Vénus tout entière à sa proie attachée.*

And Shakespeare has put the lover's despairing obstinacy into two piteous lines:

If my love swears that she is made of truth
I will believe her, though I know she lies.

My lords, Denis Cathcart is dead; it is not our place to condemn him, but only to understand and pity him.

"My lords, I need not put before you in detail the shocking shifts to which this soldier and gentleman unhappily condescended. You have heard the story in all its cold, ugly details upon the lips of Monsieur du Bois-Gobey Houdin, and, accompanied by unavailing expressions of shame and remorse, in the last words of the deceased. You know how he gambled, at first honestly–then dishonestly. You know from whence he derived those large sums of money which came at irregular intervals, mysteriously and in cash, to bolster up a bank-account always perilously on the verge of depletion. We need not, my lords, judge too harshly of the woman. According to her own lights, she did not treat him unfairly. She had her interests to consider. While he could pay for her she could give him beauty and passion and good humour and a moderate faithfulness. When he could pay no longer she would find it only reasonable to take another position. This Cathcart understood. Money he must have, by hook or by crook. And so, by an inevitable descent, he found himself reduced to the final deep of dishonour.

"It is at this point, my lords, that Denis Cathcart and his miserable fortunes come into the life of my noble client and of his sister. From this point begin all those complications which led to the tragedy of October 14th, and which we are met in this solemn and historic assembly to unravel.

"About eighteen months ago Cathcart, desperately searching for a secure source of income, met the Duke of Denver, whose father had been a friend of Cathcart's father many years before. The acquaintance prospered, and Cathcart was introduced to Lady Mary Wimsey, at that time (as she has very frankly told us) 'at a loose end,' 'fed up,' and distressed by the dismissal of her fiancé, Mr. Goyles. Lady Mary felt the need of an establishment of her own, and accepted Denis Cathcart, with the proviso that she should be considered a free agent, living her own life in her own way, with the minimum of interference. As to Cathcart's object in all this, we have his own bitter comment, on which no words of mine could improve: 'I actually brought myself to consider keeping my mistress on my wife's money.'

"So matters go on until October of this year. Cathcart is now obliged to pass a good deal of his time in England with his fiancée, leaving Simone Vonderaa unguarded in the Avenue Kléber. He seems to have felt fairly secure so far; the only drawback was that Lady Mary, with a natural reluctance to commit herself to the hands of a man she could not really love, had so far avoided fixing a definite date for the wedding. Money is shorter than it used to be in the Avenue Kléber, and the cost of robes and millinery, amusements and so forth, has not diminished. And, meanwhile, Mr. Cornelius van Humperdinck, the American millionaire, has seen Simone in the Bois, at the races, at the opera, in Denis Cathcart's flat.

"But Lady Mary is becoming more and more uneasy about her engagement. And at this critical moment, Mr. Goyles suddenly sees the prospect of a position, modest but assured, which will enable him to maintain a wife. Lady Mary makes her choice. She consents to elope with Mr. Goyles, and by an extraordinary fatality the day and hour selected are 3 a.m. on the morning of October 14th.

"At about 9:30 on the night of Wednesday, October 13th, the party at Riddlesdale Lodge are just separating to go to bed. The Duke of Denver was in the gunroom, the other men were in the billiard-room, the ladies had already retired, when the manservant, Fleming, came up from the village with the evening post. To the Duke of Denver he brought a letter with news of a startling and very unpleasant kind. To Denis Cathcart he brought another letter—one which we shall never see, but whose contents it is easy enough to guess.

"You have heard the evidence of Mr. Arbuthnot that, before reading this letter, Cathcart had gone upstairs gay and hopeful, mentioning that he hoped soon to get a date fixed for the marriage. At a little after ten, when the Duke of Denver went up to see him, there was a great change. Before his grace could broach the matter in hand Cathcart spoke rudely and harshly, appearing to be all on edge, and entreating to be left alone. Is it very difficult, my lords, in the face of what we have heard to-day—in the face of our knowledge that Mademoiselle Vonderaa crossed to New York on the *Berengaria* on October 15th—to guess what news had reached Denis Cathcart in that interval to change his whole outlook upon life?

"At this unhappy moment, when Cathcart is brought face to face with the stupefying knowledge that his mistress has left him, comes the Duke of Denver with a frightful accusation. He taxes Cathcart with the vile truth—that this man, who has eaten his bread and sheltered under his roof, and who is about to marry his sister, is nothing more nor less than a card-sharper. And when Cathcart refuses to deny the charge—when he, most insolently, as it seems, declares that he is no longer willing to wed the noble lady to whom he is affianced—is it surprising that the Duke should turn upon the impostor and forbid him ever to touch or speak to Lady Mary Wimsey again? I say, my lords, that no man with a spark of honourable feeling would have done otherwise. My client contents himself with directing Cathcart to leave the house next day; and when Cathcart rushes madly out into the storm he calls after him to return, and even takes the trouble to direct the footman to leave open the conservatory door for Cathcart's convenience. It is true that he called Cathcart a dirty scoundrel, and told him he should have been kicked out of his regiment, but he was justified; while the words he shouted from the window—'Come back, you fool,' or even, according to one witness, 'you b—— fool'—have almost an affectionate ring in them. (Laughter.)

"And now I will direct your lordships' attention to the extreme weakness of the case against my noble client from the point of view of motive. It has been suggested that the cause of the quarrel between them was not that mentioned by the Duke of Denver in his evidence, but something even more closely personal to themselves. Of this contention not a jot or tittle, not the slightest shadow of evidence, has been put forward except, indeed, that of the extraordinary witness, Robinson, who appears to bear a grudge against his whole acquaintance, and to have magnified some trifling allusion into a matter of vast importance. Your lordships have seen this person's demeanour in the box, and will judge for yourselves how much weight is to be attached to his observations. While we on our side have been able to show that the alleged cause of complaint was perfectly well founded in fact.

"So Cathcart rushes out into the garden. In the pelting rain he paces heedlessly about, envisaging a future stricken at once suddenly barren of love, wealth, and honour.

"And, meanwhile, a passage door opens, and a stealthy foot creeps down the stair. We know now whose it is—Mrs. Pettigrew-Robinson has not mistaken the creak of the door. It is the Duke of Denver.

"That is admitted. But from this point we join issue with my learned friend for the prosecution. It is suggested that the Duke, on thinking matters over, determines that Cathcart is a danger to society and better dead—or that his insult to the Denver family can only be washed out in blood. And we are invited to believe that the Duke creeps downstairs, fetches his revolver from the study table, and prowls out into the night to find Cathcart and make away with him in cold blood.

"My lords, is it necessary for me to point out the inherent absurdity of this suggestion? What conceivable reason could the Duke of Denver have for killing, in this cold-blooded manner, a man of whom a single word has rid him already and for ever? It has been suggested to you that the injury had grown greater in the Duke's mind by brooding—had assumed gigantic proportions. Of that suggestion, my lords, I can only say that a more flimsy pretext for fixing an impulse to murder upon the shoulders of an innocent man was never devised, even by the ingenuity of an advocate. I will not waste my time or insult you by arguing about it. Again it has been suggested that the cause of quarrel was not what it appeared, and the Duke had reason to fear some disastrous action on Cathcart's part. Of this contention I think we have already disposed; it is an assumption constructed *in vacuo*, to meet a set of circumstances which my learned friend is at a loss to explain in conformity with the known facts. The very number and variety of motives suggested by the prosecution is proof that they are aware of the weakness of their own case. Frantically they cast about for any sort of explanation to give colour to this unreasonable indictment.

"And here I will direct your lordships' attention to the very important evidence of Inspector Parker in the matter of the study window. He has told you that it was forced from outside by the latch being slipped back with a knife. If it was the Duke of Denver, who was in the study at 11:30, what need had he to force the window? He was already inside the house. When, in addition, we find that Cathcart had in his pocket a knife, and that there are scratches upon the blade such as might come from forcing back a metal catch, it surely becomes evident that not the Duke, but Cathcart himself forced the window and crept in for the pistol, not knowing that the conservatory door had been left open for him.

"But there is no need to labour this point—we *know* that Captain Cathcart was in the study at that time, for we have seen in evidence the sheet of blotting-paper on which he blotted his letter to Simone Vonderaa, and Lord Peter Wimsey has told us how he himself removed that sheet from the study blotting-pad a few days after Cathcart's death.

"And let me here draw your attention to the significance of one point in the evidence. The Duke of Denver has told us that he saw the revolver in his drawer a short time before the fatal 13th, when he and Cathcart were together."

The Lord High Steward: "One moment, Sir Impey, that is not quite as I have it in my notes."

Counsel: "I beg your lordship's pardon if I am wrong."

L.H.S.: "I will read what I have. 'I was hunting for an old photograph of Mary to give Cathcart, and that was how I came across it.' There is nothing about Cathcart being there."

Counsel: "If your lordship will read the next sentence——"

L.H.S.: "Certainly. The next sentence is: 'I remember saying at the time how rusty it was getting.' "

Counsel: "And the next?"

L.H.S.: " 'To whom did you make that observation?' Answer: 'I really don't know, but I distinctly remember saying it.' "

Counsel: "I am much obliged to your lordship. When the noble peer made that remark he was looking out some photographs to give to Captain Cathcart. I think we may reasonably infer that the remark was made to the deceased."

L.H.S. (to the House): "My lords, your lordships will, of course, use your own judgment as to the value of this suggestion."

Counsel: "If your lordships can accept that Denis Cathcart may have known of the existence of the revolver, it is immaterial at what exact moment he saw it. As you have heard, the table-drawer was always left with the key in it. He might have seen it himself at any time, when searching for an envelope or sealing-wax or what not. In any case, I contend that the movements heard by Colonel and Mrs. Marchbanks on Wednesday night were those of Denis Cathcart. While he was writing his farewell letter, perhaps with the pistol before him on the table—yes, at that very moment the Duke of Denver slipped down the stairs and out through the conservatory door. Here is the incredible part of this affair—that again and again we find two series of events, wholly unconnected between themselves, converging upon the same point of time, and causing endless confusion. I have used the word 'incredible'—not because any coincidence is incredible, for we see more remarkable examples every day of our lives than any writer of fiction would dare to invent—but merely in order to take it out of the mouth of the learned Attorney-General, who is preparing to make it return, boomerang-fashion, against me. (Laughter.)

"My lords, this is the first of these incredible—I am not afraid of the word—coincidences. At 11:30 the Duke goes downstairs and Cathcart enters the study. The learned Attorney-General in his cross-examination of my noble client, very justifiably made what capital he could out of the discrepancy between witness's statement at the inquest—which was that he did not leave the house till 2:30—and his present statement—that he left it at half-past eleven. My lords, whatever interpretation you like to place upon the motives of the noble Duke in so doing, I must remind you once more that at the time when that first statement was made everybody supposed that the shot had been fired at three o'clock, and that the misstatement was then useless for the purpose of establishing an alibi.

"Great stress, too, has been laid on the noble Duke's inability to establish this alibi for the hours from 11:30 to 3 a.m. But my lords, if he is telling the truth in saying that he walked all that time upon the moors without meeting anyone, what alibi could he establish? He is not bound to supply a motive for all his minor actions during the twenty-four hours. No rebutting evidence has been brought to discredit his story. And it is perfectly reasonable that, unable to sleep after the scene with Cathcart, he should go for a walk to calm himself down.

"Meanwhile, Cathcart has finished his letter and tossed it into the post-bag. There is nothing more ironical in the whole of this case than that letter. While the body of a murdered man lay stark upon the threshold, and detectives and doctors searched everywhere for clues, the normal routine of an ordinary English household went, unquestioned, on. That letter, which contained the whole story, lay undisturbed in the post-bag, till it was taken away and put in the post as a matter of course, to be fetched back again, at enormous cost, delay, and risk of life, two months later in vindication of the great English motto: 'Business as usual.'

"Upstairs, Lady Mary Wimsey was packing her suitcase and writing a farewell letter to her people. At length Cathcart signs his name; he takes up the revolver and hurries out into the shrubbery. Still he paces up and down, with what thoughts God alone knows—reviewing the past, no doubt, racked with vain remorse, most of all, bitter against the woman who has ruined him. He bethinks him of the little love-token, the platinum-and-diamond cat which his mistress gave him for good luck! At any rate, he will not die with *that* pressing upon his heart. With a furious gesture he hurls it far from him. He puts the pistol to his head.

"But something arrests him. Not that! Not that! He sees in fancy his own hideously disfigured corpse—the shattered jaw—the burst eyeball—blood and brains horribly splashed about. No. Let the bullet go cleanly to the heart. Not even in death can he bear the thought of looking—*so!*

"He places the revolver against his breast and draws the trigger. With a little moan, he drops to the sodden ground. The weapon falls from his hand; his fingers scrabble at his breast.

"The gamekeeper who heard the shot is puzzled that poachers should come so close. Why are they not on the moors? He thinks of the hares in the plantation. He takes his lantern and searches in the thick drizzle. Nothing. Only soggy grass and dripping trees. He is human. He concludes his ears deceived him, and he returns to his warm bed. Midnight passes. One o'clock passes.

"The rain is less heavy now. Look! In the shrubbery—what was that? A movement. The shot man is moving—groaning a little—crawling to his feet. Chilled to the bone, weak from loss of blood, shaking with the fever of his wound, he but dimly remembers his purpose. His groping hands go to the wound in his breast. He pulls out a handkerchief and presses it upon the place. He drags himself up, slipping and stumbling. The handkerchief slides to the ground, and lies there beside the revolver among the fallen leaves.

"Something in his aching brain tells him to crawl back to the house. He is sick, in pain, hot and cold by turns, and horribly thirsty. There someone will take him in and be kind to him—give him things to drink. Swaying and starting, now falling on hands and knees, now reeling to and fro, he makes that terrible nightmare journey to the house. Now he walks, now he crawls, dragging his heavy limbs after him. At last, the conservatory door! Here there will be help. And water for his fever in the trough by the well. He crawls up to it on hands and knees, and strains to lift himself. It is growing very difficult to breathe—a heavy weight seems to be bursting his chest. He lifts himself—a frightful hiccuping cough catches him—the blood rushes from his mouth. He drops down. It is indeed all over.

"Once more the hours pass. Three o'clock, the hour of rendezvous, draws on. Eagerly the young lover leaps the wall and comes hurrying through the shrubbery to greet his bride to be. It is cold and wet, but his happiness gives him no time to think of his surroundings. He passes through the shrubbery without a thought. He reaches the conservatory door, through which in a few moments love and happiness will come to him. And in that moment he stumbles across —the dead body of a man!

"Fear possesses him. He hears a distant footstep. With but one idea—escape from this horror of horrors—he dashes into the shrubbery, just as, fatigued perhaps a little, but with a mind soothed by his little expedition, the Duke of Denver comes briskly up the path, to meet the eager bride over the body of her betrothed.

"My lords, the rest is clear. Lady Mary Wimsey, forced by a horrible appearance of things into suspecting her lover of murder, undertook—with what courage every man amongst you will realise—to conceal that George Goyles ever was upon the scene. Of this ill-considered action of hers came much mystery and perplexity. Yet, my lords, while chivalry holds its own, not one amongst us will breathe one word of blame against that gallant lady. As the old song says:

> God send each man at his end
> Such hawks, such hounds, and such a friend.

"I think, my lords, that there is nothing more for me to say. To you I leave the solemn and joyful task of freeing the noble peer, your companion, from this unjust charge. You are but human, my lords, and some among you will have grumbled, some will have mocked on assuming these mediaeval splendours of scarlet and ermine, so foreign to the taste and habit of a utilitarian age. You know well enough that

'Tis not the balm, the sceptre and the ball,
The sword, the mace, the crown imperial,
The intertissued robe of gold and pearl,
The farcèd title, nor the tide of pomp
That beats upon the high shores of the world

that can add any dignity to noble blood. And yet, to have beheld, day after day, the head of one of the oldest and noblest houses in England standing here, cut off from your fellowship, stripped of his historic honours, robed only in the justice of his cause–this cannot have failed to move your pity and indignation.

"My lords, it is your happy privilege to restore to his grace the Duke of Denver these traditional symbols of his exalted rank. When the clerk of this House shall address to you severally the solemn question: Do you find Gerald, Duke of Denver, Viscount St. George, guilty or not guilty of the dreadful crime of murder, every one of you may, with a confidence unmarred by any shadow of doubt, lay his hand upon his heart and say, 'Not guilty, upon my honour.' "

# 19

# WHO GOES HOME?

*Drunk as a lord? As a class they are really very sober.*

Judge Cluer, in court

WHILE THE Attorney-General was engaged in the ungrateful task of trying to obscure what was not only plain, but agreeable to everybody's feelings, Lord Peter hauled Parker off to a Lyons over the way, and listened, over an enormous dish of eggs and bacon, to a brief account of Mrs. Grimethorpe's dash to town, and a long one of Lady Mary's cross-examination.

"What are you grinning about?" snapped the narrator.

"Just natural imbecility," said Lord Peter. "I say, poor old Cathcart. She *was* a girl! For the matter of that, I suppose she still is. I don't know why I should talk as if she'd died away the moment I took my eyes off her."

"Horribly self-centred, you are," grumbled Mr. Parker.

"I know. I always was from a child. But what worries me is that I seem to be gettin' so susceptible. When Barbara turned me down——"

"You're cured," said his friend brutally. "As a matter of fact, I've noticed it for some time."

Lord Peter sighed deeply. "I value your candour, Charles," he said, "but I wish you hadn't such an unkind way of putting things. Besides—— I say, are they coming out?"

The crowd in Parliament Square was beginning to stir and spread. Sparse streams of people began to drift across the street. A splash of scarlet appeared against the grey stone of St. Stephen's. Mr. Murbles's clerk dashed in suddenly at the door.

"All right, my lord—acquitted—unanimously—and will you please come across, my lord?"

They ran out. At sight of Lord Peter some excited bystanders raised a cheer. The great wind tore suddenly through the Square, bellying out the scarlet robes of the emerging peers. Lord Peter was bandied from one to the other, till he reached the centre of the group.

"Excuse me, your grace."

It was Bunter. Bunter, miraculously, with his arms full of scarlet and ermine, enveloping the shameful blue serge suit which had been a badge of disgrace.

"Allow me to offer my respectful congratulations, your grace."

"Bunter!" cried Lord Peter. "Great God, the man's gone mad! Damn you, man, take that thing away," he added, plunging at a tall photographer in a made-up tie.

"Too late, my lord," said the offender, jubilantly pushing in the slide.

"Peter," said the Duke. "Er—thanks, old man."

"All right," said his lordship. "Very jolly trip and all that. You're lookin' very fit. Oh, don't shake hands—there, I knew it! I heard that man's confounded shutter go."

They pushed their way through the surging mob to the cars. The two Duchesses got in, and the Duke was following, when a bullet crashed through the glass of the window, missing Denver's head by an inch, and ricocheting from the windscreen among the crowd.

A rush and a yell. A big bearded man struggled for a moment with three constables; then came a succession of wild shots, and a fierce rush—the crowd parting, then closing in, like hounds on the fox, streaming past the Houses of Parliament, heading for Westminster Bridge.

"He's shot a woman—he's under that 'bus—no, he isn't—hi!—murder!—stop him!" Shrill screams and yells—police whistles blowing—constables darting from every corner-swooping down in taxis—running.

The driver of a taxi spinning across the bridge saw the fierce face just ahead of his bonnet, and jammed on the brakes, as the madman's fingers closed for the last time on the trigger. Shot and tyre exploded almost simultaneously; the taxi slewed giddily over to the right, scooping the fugitive with it, and crashed horribly into a tram standing vacant on the Embankment dead-end.

"I couldn't 'elp it," yelled the taxi-man, " 'e fired at me. Ow, Gawd, I couldn't 'elp it."

Lord Peter and Parker arrived together, panting.

"Here, constable," gasped his lordship; "I know this man. He has an unfortunate grudge against my brother. In connection with a poaching matter—up in Yorkshire. Tell the coroner to come to me for information."

"Very good, my lord."

"Don't photograph *that*," said Lord Peter to the man with the reflex, whom he suddenly found at his elbow.

The photographer shook his head.

"They wouldn't like to see that, my lord. Only the scene of the crash and the ambulance-men. Bright, newsy pictures, you know. Nothing gruesome"—with an explanatory jerk of the head at the great dark splotches in the roadway—"it doesn't pay."

A red-haired reporter appeared from nowhere with a notebook.

"Here," said his lordship, "do you want the story? I'll give it you now."

* * * * *

There was not, after all, the slightest trouble in the matter of Mrs. Grimethorpe. Seldom, perhaps, has a ducal escapade resolved itself with so little embarrassment. His grace, indeed, who was nothing if not a gentleman, braced himself gallantly for a regretful and sentimental interview. In all his rather stupid affairs he had never run away from a scene, or countered a storm of sobs with that maddening "Well, I'd better be going now" which has led to so many despairs and occasionally to cold shot. But, on this occasion, the whole business fell flat. The lady was not interested.

"I am free now," she said. "I am going back to my own people in Cornwall. I do not want anything, now that he is dead." The Duke's dutiful caress was a most uninteresting failure.

Lord Peter saw her home to a respectable little hotel in Bloomsbury. She liked the taxi, and the large, glittering shops, and the sky-signs. They stopped at Piccadilly Circus to see the Bonzo dog smoke his gasper and the Nestlé's baby consume his bottle of milk. She was amazed to find that the prices of the things in Swan & Edgar's window were, if anything, more reasonable than those current in Stapley.

"I should like one of those blue scarves," she said, "but I'm thinking 'twould not be fitting, and me a widow."

"You could buy it now, and wear it later on," suggested his lordship, "in Cornwall, you know."

"Yes." She glanced at her brown stuff gown. "Could I buy my blacks here? I shall have to get some for the funeral. Just a dress and a hat—and a coat, maybe."

"I should think it would be a very good idea."

"Now?"

"Why not?"

"I have money," she said; "I took it from his desk. It's mine now, I suppose. Not that I'd wish to be beholden to him. But I don't look at it that way."

"I shouldn't think twice about it, if I were you," said Lord Peter.

She walked before him into the shop—her own woman at last.

* * * * *

In the early hours of the morning Inspector Sugg, who happened to be passing Parliament Square, came upon a taxi-man apparently addressing a heated expostulation to the statue of Lord Palmerston. Indignant at this senseless proceeding, Mr. Sugg advanced, and then observed that the statesman was sharing his pedestal with a gentleman in evening dress, who clung precariously with one hand, while with the other he held an empty champagne-bottle to his eye, and surveyed the surrounding streets.

"Hi," said the policeman, "what are you doing there? Come off of it!"

"Hullo!" said the gentleman, losing his balance quite suddenly, and coming down in a jumbled manner. "Have you seen my friend? Very odd thing—damned odd. 'Spec you know where find him, what? When in doubt—tasker pleeshman, what? Friend of mine. Very dignified sort of man 'nopera-hat. Freddy—good ol' Freddy. Alwaysh answersh t'name—jush like jolly ol' bloodhound!" He got to his feet and stood beaming on the officer.

"Why, if it ain't his lordship," said Inspector Sugg, who had met Lord Peter in other circumstances. "Better be gettin' home, my lord. Night air's chilly-like, ain't it? You'll catch a cold or summat o' that. Here's your taxi–just you jump in now."

"No," said Lord Peter. "No. Couldn' do that. Not without frien'. Good ol' Freddy. Never–desert–friend! Dear ol' Sugg. Wouldn't desert Freddy." He attempted an attitude, with one foot poised on the step of the taxi, but, miscalculating his distance, stepped heavily into the gutter, thus entering the vehicle unexpectedly, head first.

Mr. Sugg tried to tuck his legs in and shut him up, but his lordship thwarted this movement with unlooked-for agility, and sat firmly on the step.

"Not my taxi," he explained solemnly. "Freddy's taxi. Not right–run away with frien's taxi. Very odd. Jush went roun' corner to fesh Fred'sh taxshi–Freddy jush went roun' corner fesh *my* taxi–fesh friend'sh taxshi–friendship sush a beautiful thing–don't you thing-so, Shugg? Can't leave frien'. Beshides–there'sh dear ol' Parker."

"Mr. Parker?" said the inspector apprehensively. "Where?"

"Hush!" said his lordship. "Don' wake baby, theresh good shoul. Neshle'sh baby–jush shee 'm neshle, don't he neshle nishely?"

Following his lordship's gaze, the horrified Sugg observed his official superior cosily tucked up on the far side of Palmerston and smiling a happy smile in his sleep. With an exclamation of alarm he bent over and shook the sleeper.

"Unkind!" cried Lord Peter in a deep, reproachful tone. "Dishturb poor fellow–poor hardworkin' pleeshman. Never getsh up till alarm goes. . . . 'Stra'or'nary thing," he added, as though struck by a new idea, "why hashn't alarm gone off, Shugg?" He pointed a wavering finger at Big Ben. "They've for-forgotten to wind it up. Dishgrayshful. I'll write to *The T-T-Timesh* about it."

Mr. Sugg wasted no words, but picked up the slumbering Parker and hoisted him into the taxi.

"Never–never–deshert——" began Lord Peter, resisting all efforts to dislodge him from the step, when a second taxi, advancing from Whitehall, drew up, with the Hon. Freddy Arbuthnot cheering loudly at the window.

"Look who's here!" cried the Hon. Freddy. "Jolly, jolly, jolly ol' Sugg. Let'sh all go home together."

"That'sh *my* taxshi," interposed his lordship, with dignity, staggering across to it. The two whirled together for a moment; then the Hon. Freddy was flung into Sugg's arms, while his lordship, with a satisfied air, cried "Home!" to the new taxi-man, and instantly fell asleep in a corner of the vehicle.

Mr. Sugg scratched his head, gave Lord Peter's address, and watched the cab drive off. Then, supporting the Hon. Freddy on his ample bosom, he directed the other man to convey Mr. Parker to 12a Great Ormond Street.

"Take me home," cried the Hon. Freddy, bursting into tears, "they've all gone and left me!"

"You leave it to me, sir," said the Inspector. He glanced over his shoulder at St. Stephen's, whence a group of Commons were just issuing from an all-night sitting.

"Mr. Parker an' all," said Inspector Sugg, adding devoutly, "Thank Gawd there weren't no witnesses."

# Murder Must Advertise

## AUTHOR'S NOTE

I do not suppose that there is a more harmless and law-abiding set of people in the world than the Advertising Experts of Great Britain. The idea that any crime could possibly be perpetrated on advertising premises is one that could only occur to the ill-regulated fancy of a detective novelist, trained to fasten the guilt upon the Most Unlikely Person. If, in the course of this fantasy, I have unintentionally used a name or slogan suggestive of any existing person, firm or commodity, it is by sheer accident, and is not intended to cast the slightest reflection upon any actual commodity, firm or person.

# CONTENTS


1 DEATH COMES TO PYM'S PUBLICITY 263
2 EMBARRASSING INDISCRETION OF TWO TYPISTS 274
3 INQUISITIVE INTERVIEWS OF A NEW COPY-WRITER 280
4 REMARKABLE ACROBATICS OF A HARLEQUIN 288
5 SURPRISING METAMORPHOSIS OF MR. BREDON 302
6 SINGULAR SPOTLESSNESS OF A LETHAL WEAPON 312
7 ALARMING EXPERIENCE OF A CHIEF-INSPECTOR 321
8 CONVULSIVE AGITATION OF AN ADVERTISING AGENCY 329
9 UNSENTIMENTAL MASQUERADE OF A HARLEQUIN 343
10 DISTRESSING DEVELOPMENTS OF AN OFFICE ROW 351
11 INEXCUSABLE INVASION OF A DUCAL ENTERTAINMENT 364
12 SURPRISING ACQUISITION OF A JUNIOR REPORTER 374
13 EMBARRASSING ENTANGLEMENT OF A GROUP-MANAGER 384
14 HOPEFUL CONSPIRACY OF TWO BLACK SHEEP 393
15 SUDDEN DECEASE OF A MAN IN DRESS CLOTHES 398
16 ECCENTRIC BEHAVIOUR OF A POST-OFFICE DEPARTMENT 412
17 LACHRYMOSE OUTBURST OF A NOBLEMAN'S NEPHEW 419
18 UNEXPECTED CONCLUSION OF A CRICKET MATCH 431
19 DUPLICATE APPEARANCES OF A NOTORIOUS PERSONALITY 441
20 APPROPRIATE EXIT OF AN UNSKILLED MURDERER 448
21 DEATH DEPARTS FROM PYM'S PUBLICITY 455

# 1

# DEATH COMES TO PYM'S PUBLICITY

"AND BY the way," said Mr. Hankin, arresting Miss Rossiter as she rose to go, "there is a new copy-writer coming in today."

"Oh, yes, Mr. Hankin?"

"His name is Bredon. I can't tell you much about him; Mr. Pym engaged him himself; but you will see that he is looked after."

"Yes, Mr. Hankin."

"He will have Mr. Dean's room."

"Yes, Mr. Hankin."

"I should think Mr. Ingleby could take him in hand and show him what to do. You might send Mr. Ingleby along if he can spare me a moment."

"Yes, Mr. Hankin."

"That's all. And, oh, yes! Ask Mr. Smayle to let me have the Dairyfields guard-book."

"Yes, Mr. Hankin."

Miss Rossiter tucked her note-book under her arm, closed the glass-panelled door noiselessly after her and tripped smartly down the corridor. Peeping through another glass-panelled door, she observed Mr. Ingleby seated on a revolving chair with his feet on the cold radiator, and talking with great animation to a young woman in green, perched on the corner of the writing-table.

"Excuse me," said Miss Rossiter, with perfunctory civility, "but Mr. Hankin says can you spare him a moment, Mr. Ingleby?"

"If it's Tom-Boy Toffee," replied Mr. Ingleby defensively, "it's being typed. Here! you'd better take these two bits along and make it so. That will lend an air of verisimilitude to an otherwise—"

"It isn't Tom-Boy. It's a new copy-writer."

"What, already?" exclaimed the young woman. "Before those shoes were old! Why, they only buried little Dean on Friday."

"Part of the modern system of push and go," said Mr. Ingleby. "All very distressing in an old-fashioned gentlemanly firm. Suppose I've got to put this blighter through his paces. Why am I always left with the baby?"

"Oh, rot!" said the young woman, "you've only got to warn him not to use the directors' lav., and not to tumble down the iron staircase."

"You are the most callous woman, Miss Meteyard. Well, as long as they don't put the fellow in with me–"

"It's all right, Mr. Ingleby. He's having Mr. Dean's room."

"Oh! What's he like?"

"Mr. Hankin said he didn't know, Mr. Pym took him on."

"Oh, gosh! friend of the management." Mr. Ingleby groaned.

"Then I think I've seen him," said Miss Meteyard. "Tow-coloured, supercilious-looking blighter. I ran into him coming out of Pymmie's room yesterday. Horn-rims. Cross between Ralph Lynn and Bertie Wooster."

"Death, where is thy sting? Well, I suppose I'd better push off and see about it."

Mr. Ingleby lowered his feet from the radiator, prised up his slow length from the revolving chair, and prowled unhappily away.

"Oh, well, it makes a little excitement," said Miss Meteyard.

"Oh, don't you think we've had rather too much of that lately? By the way, could I have your subscription for the wreath? You told me to remind you."

"Yes, rather. What is it? A bob? Here's half-a-crown, and you'd better take the sweep-money out of it as well."

"Thanks awfully, Miss Meteyard. I do hope you get a horse this time."

"High time I did. I've been five years in this beastly office and never even been placed. I believe you wangle the draw."

"Indeed we don't, Miss Meteyard, or we shouldn't let all the horses go to those people in the Printing. Wouldn't you like to come and draw for us this time? Miss Parton's just typing out the names."

"All right." Miss Meteyard scrambled down leggily and followed Miss Rossiter to the typists' room.

This was a small, inconvenient cubicle, crowded at the moment to bursting-point. A plump girl in glasses, with head tilted back and brows twisted to keep the smoke of a cigarette out of her eyes, was rattling off the names of Derby runners on her type-writer, assisted by a bosom-friend who dictated the list from the columns of the *Morning Star*.

A languid youth in shirt-sleeves was cutting the names of sweep-subscribers from a typed sheet, and twisting the papers into secretive little screws. A thin, eager young man, squatting on an upturned waste-paper basket, was turning over the flimsies in Miss Rossiter's tray and making sarcastic comments upon the copy to a bulky, dark youth in spectacles, immersed in a novel by P. G. Wodehouse and filching biscuits from a large tin. Draped against the door-posts and blocking the entrance to all comers, a girl and another young man, who seemed to be visitors from another department, were smoking gaspers and discussing lawn-tennis.

"Hullo, angels!" said Miss Rossiter, brightly. "Miss Meteyard's going to draw for us. And there's a new copy-writer coming."

The bulky young man glanced up to say "Poor devil!" and retreated again into his book.

"Bob for the wreath and sixpence for the sweep," went on Miss Rossiter, scrabbling in a tin cash-box. "Has anybody got two shillings for a florin? Where's your list, Parton? Scratch Miss Meteyard off, will you? Have I had your money, Mr. Garrett?"

"No money till Saturday," said the Wodehouse-reader.

"Hark at him!" cried Miss Parton, indignantly. "You'd think we were millionaires, the way we have to finance this department."

"Pick me a winner," replied Mr. Garrett, "and you can knock it off the prize-money. Hasn't that coffee come yet?"

"Have a look, Mr. Jones," suggested Miss Parton, addressing the gentleman on the door-post, "and see if you can see the boy. Just check these runners over with me, duckie. Meteor Bright, Tooralooral, Pheidippides II, Roundabout–"

"Roundabout's scratched," said Mr. Jones. "Here's the boy just coming."

"Scratched? No, when? What a shame! I put him down in the *Morning Star* competition. Who says so?"

"*Evening Banner* lunch special. Slip in the stable."

"Damn!" said Miss Rossiter, briefly. "There goes my thousand quid! Oh, well, that's life. Thank you, sonnie. Put it on the table. Did you remember the cucumber? Good boy. How much? One-and-five? Lend me a penny, Parton. There you are. Mind out a minute, Mr. Willis, do you mind? I want a pencil and rubber for the new bloke."

"What's his name?"

"Bredon."

"Where's he come from?"

"Hankie doesn't know. But Miss Meteyard's seen him. She says he's like Bertie Wooster in horn-rims."

"Older, though," said Miss Meteyard. "A well-preserved forty."

"Oh, gosh! When's he coming?"

" 'Smorning. If I'd been him I'd have put it off till tomorrow and gone to the Derby. Oh, here's Mr. Ingleby. He'll know. Coffee, Mr. Ingleby? Have you heard anything?"

"Star of Asia, Twinkletoes, Sainte-Nitouche, Duke Humphrey . . ."

"Forty-two," said Mr. Ingleby. "No sugar, thanks. Never been in advertising before. *Balliol.*"

"Golly!" said Miss Meteyard.

"As you say. If there is one thing more repulsive than another it is Balliolity," agreed Mr. Ingleby, who was a Trinity man.

"*Bredon went to Balliol*
*And sat at the feet of Gamaliel,*"

chanted Mr. Garrett, closing his book.

"*And just as he ought*
*He cared for nought,*"

added Miss Meteyard. "I defy you to find another rhyme for Balliol."

"Flittermouse, Tom Pinch, Fly-by-Night . . ."

*Add his language was sesquipedalial.*"

"It isn't sesquipedalial, it's sesquipedalian."

"Brother!"

"Twist those papers up tight, duckie. Put them in the lid of the biscuit-tin. Damn! that's Mr. Armstrong's buzzer. Stick a saucer over my coffee. Where's my note-book?"

". . . two double-faults running, so I said . . ."

". . . I can't find the carbon of that Magnolia wholetreble . . ."

". . . started at fifty to one . . ."

"Who's bagged my scissors?"

"Excuse me, Mr. Armstrong wants his Nutrax carbons . . ."

". . . and shake 'em up well . . ."

". . . hail you all, impale you all, jail you all . . ."

"Mr. Ingleby, can you spare me a moment?"

At Mr. Hankin's mildly sarcastic accents, the scene dislimned as by magic. The door-post drapers and Miss Parton's bosom-friend melted out into the passage, Mr. Willis, rising hurriedly with the tray of carbons in his hand, picked a paper out at random and frowned furiously at it, Miss Parton's cigarette dropped unostentatiously to the floor, Mr. Garrett, unable to get rid of his coffee-cup, smiled vaguely and tried to look as though he had picked it up by accident and didn't know it was there, Miss Meteyard, with great presence of mind, put the sweep counterfoils on a chair and sat on them, Miss Rossiter, clutching Mr. Armstrong's carbons in her hand, was able to look businesslike, and did so. Mr. Ingleby alone, disdaining pretence, set down his cup with a slightly impudent smile and advanced to obey his chief's command.

"This," said Mr. Hankin, tactfully blind to all evidences of disturbance, "is Mr. Bredon. You will–er–show him what he has to do. I have had the Dairyfields guard-books sent along to his room. You might start him on margarine. Er–I don't think Mr. Ingleby was up in your time, Mr. Bredon–he was at Trinity. Your Trinity, I mean, not ours." (Mr. Hankin was a Cambridge man.)

Mr. Bredon extended a well-kept hand.

"How do you do?"

"How do you do?" echoed Mr. Ingleby. They gazed at one another with the faint resentment of two cats at their first meeting. Mr. Hankin smiled kindly at them both.

"And when you've produced some ideas on margarine, Mr. Bredon, bring them along to my room and we'll go over them."

"Right-ho!" said Mr. Bredon, simply.

Mr. Hankin smiled again and padded gently away.

"Well, you'd better know everybody," said Mr. Ingleby, rapidly. "Miss Rossiter and Miss Parton are our guardian angels–type our copy, correct our grammar, provide us with pencils and paper and feed us on coffee and cake. Miss Parton is the blonde and Miss Rossiter the brunette. Gentlemen prefer blondes but personally I find them both equally seraphic."

Mr. Bredon bowed.

"Miss Meteyard–of Somerville. One of the brighter ornaments of our department. She makes the vulgarest limericks ever recited within these chaste walls."

"Then we shall be friends," said Mr. Bredon cordially.

"Mr. Willis on your right, Mr. Garrett on your left–both comrades in affliction. That is the whole department, except Mr. Hankin and Mr. Armstrong who are directors, and Mr. Copley, who is a man of weight and experience and does not come and frivol in the typists' room. He goes out for his elevenses, and assumes seniority though he hath it not."

Mr. Bredon grasped the hands extended to him and murmured politely.

"Would you like to be in on the Derby sweep?" inquired Miss Rossiter, with an eye to the cash-box. "You're just in time for the draw."

"Oh, rather," sald Mr. Bredon. "How much?"

"Sixpence."

"Oh, yes, rather. I mean, it's jolly good of you. Of course, absolutely–must be in on the jolly old sweep, what?"

"That brings the first prize up to a pound precisely," said Miss Rossiter, with a grateful sigh. "I was afraid I should have to take two tickets myself. Type Mr. Bredon's for him, Parton. B,R,E,D,O,N–like summer-time on Bredon?"

"That's right."

Miss Parton obligingly typed the name and added another blank ticket to the collection in the biscuit-box.

"Well, I suppose I'd better take you along to your dog-kennel," said Mr. Ingleby, with gloom.

"Right-ho!" said Mr. Bredon. "Oh, rather. Yes."

"We're all along this corridor," added Mr. Ingleby, leading the way. "You'll find your way about in time. That's Garrett's room and that's Willis's, and this is yours, between Miss Meteyard and me. That iron staircase opposite me goes down to the floor below; mostly group managers and conference rooms. Don't fall down it, by the way. The man whose room you've got tumbled down it last week and killed himself."

"No, did he?" said Mr. Bredon, startled.

"Bust his neck and cracked his skull," said Mr. Ingleby. "On one of those knobs."

"Why do they put knobs on staircases?" expostulated Mr. Bredon. "Cracking fellows' skulls for them? It's not right."

"No, it isn't," said Miss Rossiter, arriving with her hands full of scribbling-blocks and blotting-paper. "They're supposed to prevent the boys from sliding down the hand-rail, but it's the stairs themselves that are so–oh, I say, push on. There's Mr. Armstrong coming up. They don't like too much being said about the iron staircase."

"Well, here you are," said Mr. Ingleby, adopting this advice. "Much the same as the rest, except that the radiator doesn't work very well. Still, that won't worry you just at present. This was Dean's room."

"Chap who fell downstairs?"

"Yes."

Mr. Bredon gazed round the small apartment, which contained a table, two chairs, a rickety desk and a bookshelf, and said:

"Oh!"

"*It was* awful," said Miss Rossiter.

"It must have been," agreed Mr. Bredon, fervently.

"Mr. Armstrong was just giving me dictation when we heard the most *frightful* crash. He said, 'Good God, what's that?' I thought it must be one of the boys, because one of them fell down last year carrying an Elliot-Fisher typewriter and it sounded exactly like it, only worse. And I said, 'I think one of the boys must have fallen downstairs, Mr. Armstrong,' and he said, 'Careless little devil,' and went on dictating and my hand was so shaky I could hardly make my outlines and then Mr. Ingleby ran past and Mr. Daniels' door opened and then we heard the most terrific shriek, and Mr. Armstrong said, 'Better go and see what's happened,' so I went out and looked down and I couldn't see anything because there was such a bunch of people standing round and then Mr. Ingleby came tearing up, with *such* a look on his face–you were as white as a sheet, Mr. Ingleby, you really were."

"Possibly," said Mr. Ingleby, a little put out. "Three years in this soul-searing profession have not yet robbed me of all human feeling. But that will come in time."

"Mr. Ingleby said, 'He's killed himself!' And I said, 'Who?' and he said, 'Mr. Dean,' and I said, 'You don't mean that,' and he said, 'I'm afraid so,' and I went back to Mr. Armstrong and said, 'Mr. Dean's killed himself,' and he said, 'What do you mean, killed himself?' and then Mr. Ingleby came in and Mr. Armstrong gave one look at him and went out and I went down by the other staircase and saw them carrying Mr. Dean along to the board-room and his head was all hanging sideways."

"Does this kind of thing happen often?" inquired Mr. Bredon.

"Not with such catastrophic results," replied Mr. Ingleby, "but that staircase is definitely a death-trap."

"I fell down it myself one day," said Miss Rossiter, "and tore the heels off both my shoes. It was awfully awkward, because I hadn't another pair in the place and—"

"I've drawn a horse, darlings!" announced Miss Meteyard, arriving without ceremony. "No luck for you, Mr. Bredon, I'm afraid."

"I always was unlucky."

"You'll feel unluckier still after a day with Dairyfields Margarine," said Mr. Ingleby, gloomily. "Nothing for me, I suppose?"

"Nothing, I'm afraid. Of course Miss Rawlings has drawn the favourite—she always does."

"I hope it breaks its beastly leg," said Mr. Ingleby. "Come in, Tallboy, come in. Do you want me? Don't mind butting in on Mr. Bredon. He will soon become used to the idea that his room is a public place within the meaning of the act. This is Mr. Tallboy, group-manager for Nutrax and a few other wearisome commodities. Mr. Bredon, our new copy-writer."

"How do you do?" said Mr. Tallboy, briefly. "Look here, about this Nutrax 11-inch double. Can you possibly cut out about thirty words?"

"No, I can't," said Mr. Ingleby. "I've cut it to the bone already."

"Well, I'm afraid you'll have to. There isn't room for all this guff with a two-line sub-head."

"There's plenty of room for it."

"No, there isn't. We've got to get in the panel about the Fifty-six Free Chiming Clocks."

"Damn the clocks and the panel! How do they expect to display all that in a half-double?"

"Dunno, but they do. Look here, can't we take out this bit about 'When your nerves begin to play tricks on you,' and start off with 'Nerves need Nutrax'?"

"Armstrong liked that bit about playing tricks. Human appeal and all that. No, take out that rot about the patent spring-cap bottle."

"They won't stand for dropping that," said Miss Meteyard. "That's their pet invention."

"Do they think people buy nerve-food for the sake of the bottle? Oh, well! I can't do it straight away. Hand it over."

"The printer wants it by two o'clock," said Mr. Tallboy, dubiously.

Mr. Ingleby damned the printer, seized the proof and began cutting the copy, uttering offensive ejaculations between his teeth.

"Of all beastly days of the week," he observed, "Tuesday is the foulest. There's no peace till we get this damned 11-inch double off our chests. There! I've cut out twenty-two words, and you'll have to make it do. You can take that 'with' up into the line above and save a whole line, and that gives you the other eight words."

"All right, I'll try," agreed Mr. Tallboy. "Anything for a quiet life. It'll look a bit tight, though."

"Wish *I* was tight," said Mr. Ingleby. "Take it away, for God's sake, before I murder anybody."

"I'm going, I'm going," said Mr. Tallboy, and vanished hastily. Miss Rossiter had departed during the controversy, and Miss Meteyard now took herself out of the way, remarking, "If Pheidippides wins, you shall have a cake for tea."

"Now we'd better start you off," observed Mr. Ingleby. "Here's the guard-book. You'd better have a look through it to see the kind of thing, and then think up some headlines. Your story is, of course, that Dairyfields' 'Green Pastures' Margarine is everything that the best butter ought to be and only costs ninepence a pound. And they like a cow in the picture."

"Why? Is it made of cow-fat?"

"Well, I daresay it is, but you mustn't say so. People wouldn't like the idea. The picture of the cow suggests the taste of butter, that's all. And the name–Green Pastures–suggests cows, you see."

"It suggests Negroes to me," said Mr. Bredon. "The play, you know."

"You mustn't put Negroes in the copy," retorted Mr. Ingleby. "Nor, of course, religion. Keep Psalm 23 out of it. Blasphemous."

"I see. Just something about 'Better than Butter and half the price.' Simple appeal to the pocket."

"Yes, but you mustn't knock butter. They sell butter as well."

"Oh!"

"You can say it's as good as butter."

"But in that case," objected Mr. Bredon, "what does one find to say in favour of butter? I mean, if the other stuff's as good and doesn't cost so much, what's the argument for buying butter?"

"You don't need an argument for buying butter. It's a natural, human instinct."

"Oh, I see."

"Anyway, don't bother about butter. Just concentrate on Green Pastures Margarine. When you've got a bit done, you take it along and get it typed, and then you buzz off to Mr. Hankin with the result. See? Are you all right now?"

"Yes, thanks," said Mr. Bredon, looking thoroughly bewildered.

"And I'll push along about 1 o'clock and show you the decentest place for lunch."

"Thanks frightfully."

"Well, cheerio!" Mr. Ingleby returned to his own room.

"*He* won't stay the course," he said to himself. "Goes to a damned good tailor, though. I wonder–"

He shrugged his shoulders and sat down to concoct a small, high-class folder about Slider's Steel Office Tables.

Mr. Bredon, left alone, did not immediately attack the subject of margarine. Like a cat, which, in his soft-footed inquisitiveness, he rather resembled, he proceeded to make himself acquainted with his new home. There was not very much to see in it. He opened the drawer in his writing-table and found a notched and inky ruler, some bitten-looking pieces of india-rubber, a number of bright thoughts on tea and margarine scribbled on scraps of paper, and a broken fountain-pen. The book-case contained a dictionary, a repellent volume entitled *Directory of Directors*, a novel by Edgar Wallace, a pleasingly got-up booklet called *All about Cocoa*, *Alice in Wonderland*, Bartlett's *Familiar Quotations*, the *Globe* edition of the *Works of Wm. Shakespeare*, and five odd numbers of the *Children's Encyclopædia*. The interior of the sloping desk offered more scope for inquiry; it was filled with ancient and dusty papers, including a Government Report on the Preservatives in Food (Restrictions) Act of 1926, a quantity of rather (in every sense) rude sketches by an amateur hand, a bundle of pulls of advertisements for Dairyfields commodities, some private correspondence and some old bills. Mr. Bredon, dusting fastidious fingers, turned from this receptacle, inventoried a hook and a coat-hanger on the wall and a battered paperfile in a corner, and sat down in the revolving-chair before the table. Here, after a brief glance at a paste-pot, a pair of scissors, a new pencil and a blotting-pad, two scribbling-blocks and a grubby card-board box-lid full of oddments, he propped up the Dairyfields guard-book before him, and fell to studying his predecessor's masterpieces on the subject of Green Pastures Margarine.

An hour later, Mr. Hankin pushed open the door and looked in upon him.

"How are you getting on?" he inquired kindly.

Mr. Bredon sprang to his feet.

"Not frightfully well, I'm afraid. I don't seem to get the atmosphere altogether, if you follow me."

"It will come," said Mr. Hankin. He was a helpfully minded man, who believed that new copy-writers throve on encouragement. "Let me see what you are doing. You are starting with the headlines? Quite right. The headline is more than half the battle. IF YOU WERE A COW–no, no, I'm afraid we mustn't call the customer a cow. Besides, we had practically the same headline in–let me see–about 1923, I think. Mr. Wardle put it up, you'll find it in the last guard-book but three. It went 'IF YOU KEPT A COW IN THE KITCHEN you could get no better bread-spread than G. P. Margarine'–and so on. That was a good one. Caught the eye, made a good picture, and told the whole story in a sentence."

Mr. Bredon bowed his head, as one who hears the Law and the Prophets. The copy-chief ran a thoughtful pencil over the scribbled list of headlines, and ticked one of them.

"I like that."

BIGGER AND BUTTER
VALUE FOR MONEY

"That has the right feel about it. You might write copy for that, and perhaps for this one,

YOU'D BE READY TO BET
IT WAS BUTTER–

though I'm not quite sure about it. These Dairyfields people are rather strait-laced about betting."

"Oh, are they? What a pity! I'd done several about that, 'HAVE A BIT ON–' Don't you like that one?"

Mr. Hankin shook his head regretfully.

"I'm afraid that's too direct. Encouraging the working classes to waste their money."

"But they all do it–why, all these women like a little flutter."

"I know, I know. But I'm sure the client wouldn't stand for it. You'll soon find that the biggest obstacle to good advertising is the client. They all have their fads. That headline would do for Darling's, but it won't do for Dairyfields. We did very well with a sporting headline in '26–'PUT YOUR SHIRT ON Darling's Non-collapsible Towel-Horse'–sold 80,000 in Ascot week.

Though that was partly accident, because we mentioned a real horse in the copy and it came in at 50 to 1, and all the women who'd won money on it rushed out and bought Non-collapsible Towel-Horses out of sheer gratitude. The public's very odd."

"Yes," said Mr. Bredon. "They must be. There seems to be more in advertising than, so to speak, meets the eye."

"There is," said Mr. Hankin, a little grimly. "Well, get some copy written and bring it along to me. You know where to find my room?"

"Oh, yes—at the end of the corridor, near the iron staircase."

"No, no, that's Mr. Armstrong. At the other end of the corridor, near the other staircase—not the iron staircase. By the way—"

"Yes?"

"Oh, nothing," said Mr. Hankin, vaguely. "That is to say—no, nothing."

Mr. Bredon gazed after his retreating figure, and shook his fair head in a meditative manner. Then, applying himself to his task, he wrote out, rather quickly, a couple of paragraphs in praise of margarine and wandered out with them. Turning to the right. he paused opposite the door of Ingleby's room and stared irresolutely at the iron staircase. As he stood there, the glass door of a room on the opposite side of the corridor opened and a middle-aged man shot out. Seeing Bredon, he paused in his rush for the stairhead and inquired:

"Do you want to know how to get anywhere or anything?"

"Oh! thanks awfully. No—I mean, yes. I'm the new copy-writer. I'm looking for the typists' room."

"Other end of the passage."

"Oh, I see, thanks frightfully. This place is rather confusing. Where does this staircase go to?"

"Down to a whole lot of departments—mostly group-managers' rooms and board-rooms and Mr. Pym's room and several of the Directors' rooms and the Printing."

"Oh, I see. Thanks ever so. Where does one wash?"

"That's downstairs too. I'll show you if you like."

"Oh, thanks—thanks most awfully."

The other man plunged down the steep and rattling spiral as though released by a spring. Bredon followed more gingerly.

"A bit precipitous, isn't it?"

"Yes, it is. You'd better be careful. One fellow out of your department smashed himself up here the other day."

"No, really?'

"Broke his neck. Dead when we picked him up."

"No, did he? was he? How on earth did he come to do that? Couldn't he see where he was going?"

"Slipped, I expect. Must have been going too fast. There's nothing really wrong with the staircase. I've never had an accident. It's very well-lit."

"Well-lit?" Mr. Bredon gaped vaguely at the skylight and up and down the passage, surrounded, like the one on the floor above, with glass partitions. "Oh, yes, to be sure. It's very well-lit. Of course he must have slipped. Dashed easy thing to slip on a staircase. Did he have nails in his shoes?"

"I don't know. I wasn't noticing his shoes. I was thinking about picking up the pieces."

"Did you pick him up?"

"Well, I heard the racket when he went down, and rushed out and got there one of the first. My name's Daniels, by the way."

"Oh, is it? Daniels, oh, yes. But didn't it come out at the inquest about his shoes?"

"I don't remember anything about it."

"Oh! then I suppose he didn't have nails. I mean, if he had, somebody would have mentioned it. I mean, it would be a sort of excuse, wouldn't it?"

"Excuse for whom?" demanded Daniels.

"For the firm; I mean, when people put up staircases and other people come tumbling down them, the insurance people generally want to know why. At least, I'm told so. I've never fallen down any staircases myself–touch wood."

"You'd better not try," retorted Daniels, evading the question of insurance. "You'll find the wash-place through that door and down the passage on the left."

"Oh, thanks frightfully."

"Not at all."

Mr. Daniels darted away into a room full of desks, leaving Mr. Bredon to entangle himself in a heavy swing door.

In the lavatory, Bredon encountered Ingleby.

"Oh!" said the latter. "You've found your way. I was told off to show you, but I forgot."

"Mr. Daniels showed me. Who's he?"

"Daniels? He's a group-manager. Looks after a bunch of clients–Sliders and Harrogate Bros. and a few more. Sees to the lay-outs and sends the stereos down to the papers and all that. Not a bad chap."

"He seems a bit touchy about the iron staircase. I mean, he was quite matey till I suggested that the insurance people would want to look into that fellow's accident–and then he kind of froze on me."

"He's been a long time in the firm and doesn't like any nasturtiums cast at it. Certainly not by a new bloke. As a matter of fact, it's better not to throw one's weight about here till one's been ten years or so in the place. It's not encouraged."

"Oh? Oh, thanks awfully for telling me."

"This place is run like a Government office," went on Ingleby. "Hustle's not wanted and initiative and curiosity are politely shown the door."

"That's right," put in a pugnacious-looking red-headed man, who was scrubbing his fingers with pumice-stone as though he meant to take the skin off. "I asked them for £50 for a new lens–and what was the answer? Economy, please, in all departments–the Whitehall touch, eh?–and yet they pay you fellows to write more-you-spend-more-you-save copy! However, I shan't be here long, that's one comfort."

"This is Mr. Prout, our photographer," said Ingleby. "He has been on the point of leaving us for the last five years, but when it comes to the point he realizes that we couldn't do without him and yields to our tears and entreaties."

"Tcha!" said Mr. Prout.

"The management think Mr. Prout so precious," went on Ingleby, "that they have set his feet in a large room–"

"That you couldn't swing a kitten in," said Mr. Prout, "and no ventilation. Murder, that's what they do here. Black holes of Calcutta and staircases that break people's heads open. What we want in this country is a Mussolini to organize trade conditions. But what's the good of talking? All the same, one of these days, you'll see."

"Mr. Prout is our tame firebrand," observed Ingleby, indulgently. "You coming up, Bredon?"

"Yes, I've got to take this stuff to be typed."

"Right-ho! Here you are. Round this way and up this staircase by the lift, through the Dispatching and here you are—right opposite the home of British Beauty. Children, here's Mr. Bredon with a nice bit of copy for you."

"Hand it here," said Miss Rossiter, "and oh! Mr. Bredon, do you mind putting down your full name and address on this card—they want it downstairs for the file."

Bredon took the card obediently.

"Block letters please," added Miss Rossiter, glancing with some dismay at the sheets of copy she had just received.

"Oh, do you think my handwriting's awful? I always think it's rather neat, myself. Neat, but not gaudy. However, if you say so—"

"Block letters," repeated Miss Rossiter, firmly. "Hullo! here's Mr. Tallboy. I expect he wants you, Mr. Ingleby."

"What, again?"

"Nutrax have cancelled that half-double," announced Mr. Tallboy with gloomy triumph. "They've just sent up from the conference to say that they want something special to put up against the new Slumbermalt campaign, and Mr. Hankin says will you get something out and let him have it in half an hour."

Ingleby uttered a loud yell, and Bredon, laying down the index-card, gazed at him open-mouthed.

"Damn and blast Nutrax," said Ingleby. "May all its directors get elephantiasis, locomotor ataxy and ingrowing toenails!"

"Oh, quite," said Tallboy. "You'll let us have something, won't you? If I can get it passed before 3 o'clock the printer— Hullo!"

Mr. Tallboy's eye, roving negligently round, had fallen on Bredon's index-card. Miss Rossiter's glance followed his. Neatly printed on the card stood the one word

DEATH

"Look at that!" said Miss Rossiter.

"Oh!" said Ingleby, looking over her shoulder. "That's who you are, is it, Bredon? Well, all I can say is, your stuff ought to come home to everybody. Universal appeal, and so forth."

Mr. Bredon smiled apologetically.

"You startled me so," he said. "Pooping off that howl in my ear." He took up the card and finished his inscription:

DEATH BREDON,
12A, Great Ormond Street,
W.C.I.

# 2

# EMBARRASSING INDISCRETION OF TWO TYPISTS

FOR THE twentieth time, Mr. Death Bredon was studying the report of the coroner's inquest on Victor Dean.

There was the evidence of Mr. Prout, the photographer:

"It would be about tea-time. Tea is served at 3.30, more or less. I was coming out of my room on the top floor, carrying my camera and tripod. Mr. Dean passed me. He was coming quickly along the passage in the direction of the iron staircase. He was not running–he was walking at a good pace. He was carrying a large, heavy book under one arm. I know now that it was *The Times Atlas*. I turned to walk in the same direction that he was going. I saw him start down the iron staircase; it is rather a steep spiral. He had taken about half a dozen steps when he seemed to crumple together and disappear. There was a tremendous crash. You might call it a clatter–a prolonged crashing noise. I started to run, when Mr. Daniels' door opened and he came out and collided with the legs of my tripod. While we were mixed up together, Mr. Ingleby ran past us down the corridor. I heard a shrill scream from below. I put the camera down and Mr. Daniels and I went to the head of the staircase together. Some other people joined us–Miss Rossiter, I think, and some of the copy-writers and clerks. We could see Mr. Dean lying huddled together at the foot of the staircase. I could not say whether he had fallen down the stairs or through the banisters. He was lying all in a heap. The staircase is a right-handed spiral, and makes one complete turn. The treads are composed of pierced ironwork. The hand-rail has a number of iron knobs on it, about the size of small walnuts. The stairs are apt to be slippery. The stair is well lit. There is a sky-light above, and it receives light through the glass panels of Mr. Daniels' room and also from the glass-panelled corridor on the floor below. I have here a photograph taken by myself at 3.30 p.m. yesterday–that is the day after the accident. It shows the head of the spiral staircase. It was taken by ordinary daylight. I used an Actinax Special Rapid plate with the H & D number 450. The exposure was 1/5 second with the lens stopped down to *f*.16. The light was then similar to what it was at the time of Mr. Dean's death. The sun was shining on both occasions. The corridor runs, roughly, north and south. As deceased went down the staircase, the light would be coming from above and behind him; it is not possible that he could have the sun in his eyes."

Then came Mr. Daniels' account:

"I was standing at my desk consulting with Mr. Freeman about an advertising lay-out. I heard the crash. I thought one of the boys must have fallen down again. A boy did fall down that staircase on a previous occasion. I do not consider it a dangerous structure. I consider that the boy was going too fast. I do not recollect hearing Mr. Dean go along the passage. I did not see him. My back was to the door. People pass along that passage continuously; I should not be paying attention. I went quickly out when I heard the noise of the fall. I encountered Mr. Prout and tripped over his tripod. I did not exactly fall down, but I stumbled and had to catch hold of him to steady myself. There was nobody in the corridor when I came out except Mr. Prout. I will swear to that. Mr. Ingleby came past us while we were recovering from the collision. He did not come from his own room, but from the south end of the passage. He went down the iron staircase and Mr. Prout and I followed as quickly as we could. I heard somebody shriek downstairs. I think it was just before, or just after I ran into Mr. Prout. I was rather confused at the time and cannot say for certain. We saw Mr. Dean lying at the bottom of the staircase. There were a number of people standing round. Then Mr. Ingleby came up the stairs very hastily and called out: 'He's dead!' or 'He's killed himself.' I cannot speak to the exact words. I did not believe him at first; I thought he was exaggerating. I went on down the staircase. Mr. Dean was lying bundled together, head downwards. His legs were partly up the staircase. I think somebody had already tried to lift him before I got there. I have had some experience of death and accidents. I was a stretcher-bearer in the War. I examined him and gave it as my opinion that he was dead. I believe Mr. Atkins had already expressed a similar opinion. I helped to lift the body and carry it into the Board-room. We laid him on the table and endeavoured to administer first-aid, but I never had any doubt that he was dead. It did not occur to us to leave him where he was till the police were summoned, because, of course, he might not have been dead, and we could not leave him head downwards on the staircase."

Then came Mr. Atkins, who explained that he was a group-secretary, working in one of the downstairs rooms.

"I was just coming out of my room, the door of which commands a view of the iron staircase. It is not directly opposite the foot of the staircase, but it commands a view of the lower half of the staircase. Any one coming down the staircase would have his back turned to me as he stepped off. I heard a loud crash, and saw the deceased falling all of a heap down the stairs. He did not appear to make any attempt to save himself. He was clutching a large book in his arms. He did not loose his grip of the book as he fell. He seemed to cannon from one side of the staircase to the other and fall like a sack of potatoes, so to speak. He pitched on his head at the bottom. I was carrying a large tray full of glass jars. I set this down and ran towards him. I endeavoured to lift him up, but the moment I touched him I felt sure that he was dead. I formed the opinion that he had broken his neck. Mrs. Crump was in the passage at the time. Mrs. Crump is the head charwoman. I said to her: 'Good God! he's broken his neck,' and she screamed loudly. A number of other people arrived almost immediately upon the scene. Somebody said, 'Perhaps it's only dislocated.' Mr. Daniels said to me: 'We can't leave him here.' I think it was Mr. Armstrong who suggested that he should be taken into the Board-room. I assisted to carry him there. The book was held by the deceased in such a tight grip that we had difficulty in getting it away from him. He made no movement of any kind after he fell, and no attempt at speech. I never had the least doubt that he was dead from the moment that he fell."

Mrs. Crump confirmed this account to the best of her ability. She said: "I am head charwoman to the firm of Pym's Publicity, Ltd. It is my duty to take the tea-waggon round the office building at about 3:30 each afternoon. That is, I start my round at about 3:15 and finish at about 3:45. I had nearly finished doing the first floor, and was returning on my way to the lift to take tea up to the top floor. That would make the time about 3:30. I was coming along the corridor and was facing the foot of the iron staircase. I saw Mr. Dean fall. He fell all in a bunch-like. It was dreadful. He did not shout out or make any exclamation in falling. He fell like a dead thing. My heart seemed to stop. I was struck so I couldn't move for a minute or two. Then Mr. Atkins came running along to pick him up. He said: 'He's broke his neck,' and I let out a scream. I couldn't help myself, I was that upset. I think that staircase is a wicked dangerous place. I am always warning the other women against it. If you was to slip you couldn't hardly save yourself, not if you was carrying anything. People run up and downstairs on it all day, and the edges of the steps gets that polished you wouldn't believe, and some of them is wore down at the edges."

The medical evidence was given by Dr. Emerson. "I reside in Queen's Square, Bloomsbury. It is about five minutes from my house to the offices of Pym's Publicity in Southampton Row. I received a telephone message at 3.40 p.m. and went round immediately. Deceased was dead when I arrived. I concluded that he had then been dead about 15 minutes. His neck was broken at the fourth cervical vertebra. He also had a contused wound on the right temple which had cracked the skull. Either of these injuries was sufficient to cause death. I should say he had died instantly upon falling. He had also the tibia of the left leg broken, probably through catching in the banister of the staircase. There were also, of course, a quantity of minor scratches and contusions. The wound on the head is such as might be caused through pitching upon one of the knobs on the handrail in falling. I could not say whether this or the broken vertebra was the actual cause of death, but in either case, death would be instantaneous. I agree that it is not a matter of great importance. I found no trace of any heart disease or any other disease which might suggest that deceased was subject to vertigo or fainting-fits. I observed no traces of alcoholic tendency or of addiction to drugs. I have seen the staircase, and consider that it would be very easy to slip upon it. So far as I can tell, deceased's eyesight would appear to have been normal."

Miss Pamela Dean, sister of deceased, gave evidence that her brother had been in good health at the time of the accident and that he had never been subject to fits or fainting. He was not short-sighted. He occasionally suffered from liverish attacks. He was a good dancer and usually very neat and nimble on his feet. He had once sprained his ankle as a boy, but so far as she knew, no permanent weakness of the joint had resulted.

Evidence was also called which showed that accidents had occurred on several previous occasions to persons descending the staircase; other witnesses expressed the opinion that the staircase was not dangerous to anybody exercising reasonable care. The jury returned a verdict of accidental death, with a rider to the effect that they thought the iron spiral should be replaced by a more solid structure.

Mr. Bredon shook his head. Then he drew a sheet of paper from the rack before him and wrote down:

1. He seemed to crumple together.
2. He did not make any attempt to save himself.
3. He did not loose his grip of the book.
4. He pitched on his head at the bottom.
5. Neck broken, skull cracked; either injury fatal.
6. Good health; good sight; good dancer.

He filled himself a pipe and sat for some time staring at this list. Then he searched in a drawer and produced a piece of notepaper, which seemed to be an unfinished letter, or the abandoned draft of one.

"Dear Mr. Pym,—I think it only right that you should know that there is something going on in the office which is very undesirable, and might lead to serious—"

After a little more thought, he laid this document aside and began to scribble on another sheet, erasing and rewriting busily. Presently a slow smile twitched his lips.

"I'll swear there's something in it," he muttered, "something pretty big. But the job is, to handle it. One's got to go for the money–but where's it coming from? Not from Pym, I fancy. It doesn't seem to be his personal show, and you can't blackmail a whole office. I wonder, though. After all, he'd probably pay a good bit to prevent–"

He relapsed into silence and meditation.

"And what," demanded Miss Parton, spearing another chocolate éclair, "do you think of our Mr. Bredon?"

"The Pimlico Pet?" said Miss Rossiter. "You'll put on pounds and pounds if you eat all that sweet stuff, duckie. Well, I think he's rather a lamb, and his shirts are simply too marvellous. He won't be able to keep that up on Pym's salary, bonus or no bonus. Or the silk socks either."

"He's been brought up silk-lined all right," agreed Miss Parton. "One of the new poor, I expect. Lost all his money in the slump or something."

"Either that, or his family have got tired of supporting him and pushed him out to scratch for himself," suggested Miss Rossiter. She slimmed more strenuously than her colleague, and was less inclined to sentiment. "I sort of asked him the other day what he did before he came here, and he said, all sorts of things, and mentioned that he'd had a good bit to do with motors. I expect he's been one of these gilded johnnies who used to sell cars on commission, and the bottom's dropped out of that and he's got to do a job of work–if you call copy-writing work."

"I think he's very clever," said Miss Parton. "Did you see that idiotic headline he put up for Margarine yesterday: 'IT'S A FAR, FAR, BUTTER THING'? Hankie nearly sniggered himself sick. I think the Pet was pulling his leg. But what I mean is, he wouldn't think of a silly thing like that if he hadn't got brains."

"He'll make a copy-writer," declared Miss Rossiter, firmly. She had seen so many new copy-writers come and pass like ships in the night, that she was as well able to size them up as the copy-chiefs themselves. "He's got the flair if you know what I mean. He'll stay all right."

"I hope he does," said Miss Parton. "He's got beautiful manners. Doesn't chuck the stuff at you as if you were dirt like young Willis. And he pays his tea-bill like a little gentleman."

"Early days," said Miss Rossiter. "He's paid *one* tea-bill. Gives me the pip, the way some of them make a fuss about it. There's Garrett. He was quite rude when I went to him on Saturday. Hinted that I made money out of the teas. I suppose he thinks it's funny. I don't."

"He means it for a joke."

"No, he doesn't. Not altogether. And he's always grumbling. Whether it's Chelsea buns or jam roll, there's always something wrong with it. I said to him, 'Mr. Garrett,' I said, 'if *you* like to give up your lunch-time every day to trying to find something that *everybody* will enjoy, you're welcome to do it.' 'Oh, no,' he said, 'I'm not the office-boy.' 'And who do you think I am,' I said, 'the errand-girl?' So he told me not to lose my temper. It's all very well, but you get very tired of it, especially this hot weather, fagging round."

Miss Parton nodded. The teas were a perennial grievance.

"Anyhow," she said, "friend Bredon is no trouble. A plain biscuit and a cup of tea every day. That's his order. And he said he was quite ready to pay the same subscription as everybody else, though really he ought to be let off with sixpence. I do like a man to be generous and speak to you nicely."

"Oh, the Pet's tongue runs on ball-bearings," said Miss Rossiter. "And talk of being a nosey-parker!"

"They all are," replied Miss Parton. "But I say, do you know what I did yesterday? It was dreadful. Bredon came in and asked for Mr. Hankin's carbons. I was in an awful rush with some of old Copley's muck—he always wants everything done in five minutes—and I said, 'Help yourself.' Well, what do you think? Ten minutes afterwards I went to look for something on the shelf and I found he'd gone off with Mr. Hankin's private letter-file. He must have been blind, because it's marked PRIVATE in red letters an inch high. Of course Hankie'd be in an awful bait if he knew. So I hared off to Bredon and there he was, calmly reading Hankie's private letters, if you please! 'You've got the wrong file, Mr. Bredon,' I said. And he wasn't a bit ashamed. He just handed it back with a grin and said, 'I was beginning to think I might have. It's very interesting to see what salary everybody gets.' And, my dear, he was reading Hankie's departmental list. And I said, 'Oh, Mr. Bredon, you *oughtn't* to be reading that. It's frightfully confidential.' And he said, 'Is it?' He seemed quite surprised."

"Silly ass!" said Miss Rossiter. "I hope you told him to keep it to himself. They *are* all so sensitive about their salaries. I'm sure I don't know why. But they're all dying to find out what the others get and terrified to death anybody should find out what they get themselves. If Bredon goes round shooting his mouth off, he'll stir up some awful trouble."

"I warned him," said Miss Parton, "and he seemed to think it was awfully funny and asked how long it would take him to reach Dean's salary."

"Let's see, how much was Dean getting?"

"Six," replied Miss Parton, "and not worth much more in my opinion. The department will be better-tempered without him, I must say. He did rile 'em sometimes."

"If you ask me," said Miss Rossiter, "I don't think this business of mixing the University people with the other sort works very well. With the Oxford and Cambridge lot it's all give-and-take and bad language, but the others don't seem to fit in with it. They always think they're being sneered at."

"It's Ingleby upsets them. He never takes anything seriously."

"None of them do," said Miss Rossiter, putting an unerring and experienced finger on the point of friction. "It's all a game to them, and with Copley and Willis it's all deadly serious. When Willis starts on metaphysics, Ingleby recites limericks. Personally, I'm broad-minded. I rather like it. And I will say the 'varsity crowd don't quarrel like the rest of them. If Dean hadn't fallen downstairs, there'd have been a good old bust-up between him and Willis."

"I never could understand what that was all about," observed Miss Parton, thoughtfully stirring her coffee.

"*I* believe there was a girl in it," said Miss Rossiter. "Willis used to go about with Dean quite a lot at the week-end, and then it all stopped suddenly. They had an awful row one day last March. Miss Meteyard heard them going at it hammer and tongs in Dean's room."

"Did she hear what the fuss was?"

"No. Being Miss Meteyard, she first pounded on the partition and then went in and told them to shut up. She's no use for people's private feelings. Funny woman. Well, I suppose we'd better push off home, or we shan't be fit for anything in the morning. It was quite a good show, wasn't it? Where's the check? You had two cakes more than me. Yours is one-and-a-penny and mine's ninepence. If I give you a bob and you give me twopence and the waitress twopence and settle up at the desk, we shall be all square."

The two girls left the Corner House by the Coventry Street entrance, and turned to the right and crossed the Piccadilly merry-go-round to the Tube entrance. As they regained the pavement, Miss Rossiter clutched Miss Parton by the arm:

"Look! the Pet! got up regardless!"

"Go on!" retorted Miss Parton. "It isn't the Pet. Yes, it is! Look at the evening cloak and the gardenia, *and*, my dear, the monocle!"

Unaware of this commentary, the gentleman in question was strolling negligently towards them, smoking a cigarette. As he came abreast of them, Miss Rossiter broke into a cheerful grin and said, "Hullo!"

The man raised his hat mechanically and shook his head. His face was a well-bred blank. Miss Rossiter's cheeks became flooded with a fiery crimson.

"It isn't him. How *awful!*"

"He took you for a tart," said Miss Parton, with some confusion and perhaps a little satisfaction.

"It's an extraordinary thing," muttered Miss Rossiter, vexed. "I could have sworn—"

"He's not a bit like him, really, when you see him close to," said Miss Parton, wise after the event. "I told you it wasn't him."

"You said it was him." Miss Rossiter glanced back over her shoulder, and was in time to see a curious little incident.

A limousine car came rolling gently along from the direction of Leicester Square and drew up close to the kerb, opposite the entrance to the Criterion Bar. The man in dress-clothes stepped up to it and addressed a few words to the occupant, flinging his cigarette away as he did so, and laying one hand on the handle of the door, as though about to enter the car. Before he could do so, two men emerged suddenly and silently from a shop-entrance. One of them spoke to the chauffeur; the other put his hand on the gentleman's elegant arm. A brief sentence or two were exchanged; then the one man got up beside the chauffeur while the second man opened the door of the car. The man in dress-clothes got in, the other man followed, and the whole party drove off. The whole thing was so quickly done that almost before Miss Parton could turn round in answer to Miss Rossiter's exclamation, it was all over.

"An arrest!" breathed Miss Rossiter, her eyes shining. "Those two were detectives. I wonder what our friend in the monocle's been doing."

Miss Parton was thrilled.

"And we actually spoke to him and thought it was Bredon."

"*I* spoke to him," corrected Miss Rossiter. It was all very well for Miss Parton to claim the credit, but only a few minutes back she had rather pointedly dissociated herself from the indiscretion and she could not be allowed to have it both ways.

"You did, then," agreed Miss Parton. "I'm surprised at you, Rossie, trying to get off with a smart crook. Anyhow, if Bredon doesn't turn up tomorrow, we'll know it was him after all."

But it could hardly have been Mr. Bredon, for he was in his place the next morning just as usual. Miss Rossiter asked him if he had a double.

"Not that I know of," said Mr. Bredon. "One of my cousins is a bit like me."

Miss Rossiter related the incident, with slight modifications. On consideration, she thought it better not to mention that she had been mistaken for a lady of easy virtue.

"Oh, I don't think that would be my cousin," replied Mr. Bredon. "He's a frightfully proper person. Well known at Buckingham Palace, and all that."

"Go on," said Miss Rossiter.

"I'm the black sheep of the family," said Mr. Bredon. "He never even sees me in the street. It must have been some one quite different."

"Is your cousin called Bredon, too?"

"Oh, yes," said Mr. Bredon.

# 3

# INQUISITIVE INTERVIEWS OF A NEW COPY-WRITER

MR. BREDON had been a week with Pym's Publicity, and had learnt a number of things. He learned the average number of words that can be crammed into four inches of copy; that Mr. Armstrong's fancy could be caught by an elaborately-drawn lay-out, whereas Mr. Hankin looked on art-work as waste of a copy-writer's time; that the word "pure" was dangerous, because, if lightly used, it laid the client open to prosecution by the Government inspectors, whereas the words "highest quality," "finest ingredients," "packed under the best conditions" had no legal meaning, and were therefore safe; that the expression "giving work to umpteen thousand British employees in our model works at so-and-so" was not by any means the same thing as "British made throughout"; that the north of England liked its butter and margarine salted, whereas the south preferred it fresh; that the *Morning Star* would not accept any advertisements containing the word "cure," though there was no objection to such expressions as "relieve" or "ameliorate," and that, further, any commodity that professed to "cure" anything might find itself compelled to register as a patent medicine and use an expensive stamp; that the most convincing copy was always written with the tongue in the cheek, a genuine conviction of the commodity's worth producing—for some reason—poverty and flatness of style; that if, by the most far-fetched stretch of ingenuity, an indecent meaning could be read into a headline, that was the meaning that the great British Public would infallibly read into it; that the great aim and object of the studio artist was to crowd the copy out of the advertisement and that, conversely, the copy-writer was a designing villain whose ambition was to cram the space with verbiage and leave no room for the sketch; that the lay-out man, a meek ass between two burdens, spent a miserable life trying to reconcile these opposing parties; and further, that all departments alike united in hatred of the client, who persisted in spoiling good lay-outs by cluttering them up with coupons, free-gift offers, lists of local agents and realistic portraits of hideous and uninteresting cartons, to the detriment of his own interests and the annoyance of everybody concerned.

He also learned to find his way without assistance over the two floors occupied by the agency, and even up on to the roof, where the messenger boys did their daily physical jerks under the eye of the Sergeant, and whence a fine view of London might be obtained on a clear day. He became acquainted with a number of the group-managers, and was sometimes even able to remember off-hand which clients' accounts were in the control of which manager, while with most of the members of his own department he found himself established on a footing of friendly intimacy. There were the two copy-chiefs, Mr. Armstrong and Mr. Hankin, each brilliant in his own way and each with his own personal fads. Mr. Hankin, for example, would never accept a headline containing the word "magnificent"; Mr. Armstrong disliked any lay-out which involved the picture of a judge or a Jew, and was rendered so acutely wretched when the proprietors of "Whifflets" put out a new brand of smoke called "Good Judge" Mixture that he was obliged to hand the whole account over, lock, stock and barrel to Mr. Hankin. Mr. Copley, an elderly, serious-minded man, who had entered the advertising profession before the modern craze set in for public-school-and-University-trained copy-writers, was remarkable for a tendency to dyspepsia and a perfectly miraculous knack of writing appetizing copy for tinned and packeted foodstuffs. Anything that came out of a tin or a packet was poison to him, and his diet consisted of under-cooked beef-steak, fruit and whole-meal bread. The only copy he really enjoyed writing was that for Bunbury's Whole-Meal Flour, and he was perennially depressed when his careful eulogiums, packed with useful medical detail, were scrapped in favour of some light-headed foolishness of Ingleby's, on the story that Bunbury's Whole-Meal Flour took the Ache out of Baking. But on Sardines and Tinned Salmon he was unapproachable.

Ingleby specialized in snobbish copy about Twentyman's Teas ("preferred by Fashion's Favourites"), Whifflets ("in the Royal Enclosure at Ascot, in the Royal Yacht Club at Cowes, you find the discriminating men who smoke Whifflets") and Farley's Footwear ("Whether it's a big shoot or a Hunt Ball, Farley puts you on a sound footing"). He lived in Bloomsbury, was communistic in a literary way, and dressed almost exclusively in pull-overs and grey flannels. He was completely and precociously disillusioned and one of the most promising copy-writers Pym's had ever fathered. When released from Whifflets and fashionable footwear, he could be amusing on almost any subject, and had a turn for "clever" copy, wherever cleverness was not out of place.

Miss Meteyard, with a somewhat similar mental make-up, could write about practically anything except women's goods, which were more competently dealt with by Mr. Willis or Mr. Garrett, the former of whom in particular, could handle corsets and face-cream with a peculiar plaintive charm which made him more than worth his salary. The copy department on the whole worked happily together, writing each other's headlines in a helpful spirit and invading each other's rooms at all hours of the day. The only two men with whom Bredon was unable to establish genial relations were Mr. Copley, who held aloof from everybody, and Mr. Willis, who treated him with a reserve for which he was unable to account. Otherwise he found the department a curiously friendly place.

And it talked. Bredon had never in his life encountered a set of people with such active tongues and so much apparent leisure for gossip. It was a miracle that any work ever got done, though somehow it did. He was reminded of his Oxford days, when essays mysteriously wrote themselves in the intervals of club-meetings and outdoor sports, and when most of the people who took firsts boasted of never having worked more than three hours of any day. The atmosphere suited him well enough. He was a bonhomous soul, with the insatiable curiosity of a baby elephant, and nothing pleased him better than to be interrupted in his encomiums of Sopo ("makes Monday, Fun-day") or the Whoosh Vacuum-cleaner ("one Whoosh and it's clean") by a fellow-member of the department, fed-up with advertising and spoiling for a chat.

"Hullo!" said Miss Meteyard one morning. She had dropped in to consult Bredon about googlies—the proprietors of Tomboy Toffee having embarked upon a series of cricket advertisements which, starting respectively from "Lumme, what a Lob!" or "Yah! that's a Yorker!" led up by devious routes to the merits of Toffee–and had now reached the point when "Gosh! it's a Googly" had to be tackled. Bredon had demonstrated googlies with pencil and paper, and also in the corridor with a small round tin of Good Judge tobacco (whereby he had nearly caught Mr. Armstrong on the side of the head), and had further discussed the relative merits of "Gosh" and "Golly" in the headline; but Miss Meteyard showed no symptoms of departing. She had sat down at Bredon's table and was drawing caricatures, in which she displayed some skill, and was rummaging in the pencil-tray for an india-rubber when she remarked, as above mentioned, "Hullo!"

"What?"

"That's little Dean's scarab. It ought to have been sent back to his sister."

"Oh, that! Yes, I knew that was there, but I didn't know whom it belonged to. It's not a bad thing. It's real onyx, though of course it's not Egyptian and it's not even very old."

"Probably not, but Dean adored it. He thought it was a sure-fire mascot. He always had it in his waistcoat pocket or sitting in front of him while he worked. If he'd had it on him that day, he wouldn't have tumbled downstairs–at least, that's what he'd have said himself."

Bredon poised the beetle on the palm of his hand. It was as big as a man's thumb-nail, heavy and shallowly carved, smooth except for a slight chip at one side.

"What sort of chap was Dean?"

"Well. *De mortuis*, and all that, but I wasn't exactly keen on him. I thought he was rather an unwholesome little beast."

"What way?"

"For one thing, I didn't like the people he went about with. "

Bredon twitched an interrogative eyebrow.

"No," said Miss Meteyard, "I don't mean what you mean. At least, I mean, I can't tell you about that. But he used to tag round with that de Momerie crowd. Thought it was smart, I suppose. Luckily, he missed the famous night when that Punter-Smith girl did away with herself. Pym's would never have held its head up again if one of its staff had been involved in a notorious case. Pym's is particular."

"How old did you say this blighter was?"

"Oh, twenty-six or -seven, I should think."

"How did he come to be here?"

"Usual thing. Needed cash, I suppose. Had to have some sort of job. You can't lead a gay life on nothing, and he wasn't anybody, you know. His father was a bank-manager, or something, deceased, so I suppose young Victor had to push out and earn his keep. He knew how to look after himself all right."

"Then how did he get in with that lot?"

Miss Meteyard grinned at him.

"Somebody picked him up, I should think. He had a certain kind of good looks. There is a *nostalgie de la banlieue* as well as *de la boue*. And you're pulling my leg, Mr. Death Bredon because you know that as well as I do."

"Is that a compliment to my sagacity or a reflection on my virtue?"

"How *you* came here is a good deal more interesting than how Victor Dean came here. They start new copy-writers without experience at four quid a week–about enough to pay for a pair of your shoes."

"Ah!" said Bredon, "how deceptive appearances can be! But it is evident, dear lady, that you do not do your shopping in the true West End. You belong to the section of society that pays for what it buys. I revere, but do not imitate you. Unhappily, there are certain commodities which cannot be obtained without cash. Railway fares, for example, or petrol. But I am glad you approve of my shoes. They are suppied by Rudge in the Arcade and, unlike Farley's Fashion Footwear, are actually of the kind that is to be seen in the Royal Enclosure at Ascot and wherever discriminating men congregate. They have a ladies' department, and if you will mention my name—"

"I begin to see why you chose advertising as a source of supply." The look of doubt left Miss Meteyard's angular face, and was replaced by a faintly derisive expression. "Well, I suppose I'd better get back to Tomboy Toffee. Thanks for your dope about googlies."

Bredon shook his head mournfully as the door closed after her. "Careless," he muttered. "Nearly gave the game away. Oh, well, I suppose I'd better do some work and look as genuine as possible."

He pulled towards him a guard-book pasted up with pulls of Nutrax advertising and studied its pages thoughtfully. He was not left long in peace, however, for after a couple of minutes Ingleby slouched in, a foul pipe at full blast and his hands thrust deep into his trousers-pockets.

"I say, is Brewer here?"

"Don't know him. But," added Bredon, waving his hand negligently, "you have my permission to search. The priest's hole and the concealed staircase are at your service."

Ingleby rooted in the bookcase in vain.

"Somebody's bagged him. Anyway, how do you spell Chrononhotonthologos?"

"Oh! I can do that. And Aldiborontophoscophornio, too. Crossword? Torquemada?"

"No, headline for Good Judges. Isn't it hot? And now I suppose we're going to have a week's dust and hammering."

"Why?"

"The fiat has gone forth. The iron staircase is condemned."

"Who by?"

"The Board."

"Oh, rot! they mustn't do that."

"What d'you mean?"

"Admission of liability, isn't it?"

"Time, too."

"Well, I suppose it is."

"You looked quite startled. I was beginning to think you had some sort of personal feeling in the matter."

"Good lord, no, why should I? Just a matter of principle. Except that the staircase does seem to have had its uses in eliminating the unfit. I gather that the late Victor Dean was not universally beloved."

"Oh, I don't know. I never saw much harm in him, except that he wasn't exactly pukka and hadn't quite imbibed the Pym spirit, as you may say. Of course the Meteyard woman loathed him."

"Why?"

"Oh! she's a decent sort of female, but makes no allowances. My motto is, live and let live, but protect your own interests. How are you getting on with Nutrax?"

"Haven't touched it yet. I've been trying to get out a name for Twentyman's shilling tea. As far as I can make Hankin out, it has no qualities except cheapness to recommend it, and is chiefly made of odds and ends of other teas. The name must suggest solid worth and respectability."

"Why not call it 'Domestic Blend'? Nothing could sound more reliable and obviously nothing could suggest so much dreary economy."

"Good idea. I'll put it up to him." Bredon yawned. "I've had too much lunch. I don't think anybody ought to have to work at half-past two in the afternoon. It's unnatural."

"Everything's unnatural in this job. Oh, my God! Here's somebody with something on a tray! Go away! go a-*way!*"

"I'm sorry," said Miss Parton, brightly, entering with six saucers filled with a grey and steaming mess. "But Mr. Hankin says, will you please taste these samples of porridge and report upon them?"

"My dear girl, look at the time!"

"Yes, I know, it's awful, isn't it? They're numbered A, B and C, and here's the questionnaire paper, and if you'll let me have the spoons back I'll get them washed for Mr. Copley."

"I shall be sick," moaned Ingleby. "Who's this? Peabody's?"

"Yes–they're putting out a tinned porridge, 'Piper Parritch.' No boiling, no stirring–only heat the tin. Look for the Piper on the label."

"Look here," sald Ingleby, "run away and try it on Mr. McAllister."

"I did, but his report isn't printable. There's sugar and salt and a jug of milk."

"What we suffer in the service of the public!" Ingleby attacked the mess with a disgusted sniff and a languid spoon. Bredon solemnly rolled the portions upon his tongue, and detained Miss Parton.

"Here, take this down while it's fresh in my mind. Vintage A: Fine, full-bodied, sweet nutty flavour, fully matured; a grand masculine porridge. Vintage B: extra-sec, refined, delicate character, requiring only–"

Miss Parton emitted a delighted giggle, and Ingleby, who hated gigglers, fled.

"Tell me, timeless houri," demanded Mr. Bredon, "what was wrong with my lamented predecessor? Why did Miss Meteyard hate him and why does Ingleby praise him with faint damns?"

This was no problem to Miss Parton.

"Why, because he didn't play fair. He was always snooping round other people's rooms, picking up their ideas and showing them up as his own. And if anybody gave him a headline and Mr. Armstrong or Mr. Hankin liked it, he never said whose it was."

This explanation seemed to interest Bredon. He trotted down the passage and thrust his head round Garrett's door. Garrett was stolidly making out his porridge report, and looked up with a grunt.

"I hope I'm not interrupting you at one of those moments of ecstasy," bleated Bredon, "but I just wanted to ask you something. I mean to say, it's just a question of etiquette, don't you know, and what's done, so to speak. I mean, look here! You see, Hankie-pankie told me to get out a list of names for a shilling tea and I got out some awful rotten ones, and then Ingleby came in and I said, 'What would you call this tea?' just like that, and he sald, 'Call it Domestic Blend,' and I said, 'What-ho! that absolutely whangs the nail over the crumpet.' Because it struck me, really, as being the caterpillar's boots."

"Well, what about it?"

"Well, just now I was chatting to Miss Parton about that fellow Dean, the one who fell downstairs you know, and why one or two people here didn't seem to be fearfully keen on him, and she said, it was because he got ideas out of other people and showed them up with his own stuff. And what I wanted to know was, isn't it done to ask people? Ingleby didn't say anything, but of course, if I've made a floater–"

"Well, it's like this," said Garrett. "There's a sort of unwritten law–at our end of the corridor, anyway. You take any help you can get and show it up with your initials on it, but if Armstrong or whoever it is simply goes all out on it and starts throwing bouquets about, you're rather expected to murmur that it was the other bird's suggestion really, and you thought rather well of it yourself."

"Oh, I see. Oh, thanks frightfully. And if, on the other hand, he goes right up in the air and says it's the damn-silliest thing he's seen since 1919, you stand the racket, I suppose."

"Naturally. If it's as silly as that you ought to have known better than to put it up to him anyway."

"Oh, yes."

"The trouble with Dean was that he first of all snitched people's ideas without telling them, and then didn't give them the credit for it with Hankin. But, I say, I wouldn't go asking Copley or Willis for too much assistance if I were you. They weren't brought up to the idea of lending round their lecture notes. They've a sort of board-school idea that everybody ought to paddle his own canoe."

Bredon thanked Garrett again.

"And if I were you," continued Garrett, "I wouldn't mention Dean to Willis at all. There's some kind of feeling–I don't know quite what. Anyway, I just thought I'd warn you."

Bredon thanked him with almost passionate gratitude.

"It's so easy to put your foot in it in a new place, isn't it? I'm really most frightfully obliged to you."

Clearly Mr. Bredon was a man of no sensibility, for half an hour later he was in Willis's room, and had introduced the subject of the late Victor Dean. The result was an unequivocal request that Mr. Bredon would mind his own business. Mr. Willis did not wish to discuss Mr. Dean at all. In addition to this, Bredon became aware that Willis was suffering from an acute and painful embarrassment, almost as though the conversation had taken some indecent turn. He was puzzled, but persisted. Willis, after sitting for some moments in gloomy silence, fidgeting with a pencil, at last looked up.

"If you're on Dean's game," he said, "you'd better clear out. I'm not interested."

He might not be, but Bredon was. His long nose twitched with curiosity.

"What game? I didn't know Dean. Never heard of him till I came here. What's the row?"

"If you didn't know Dean why bring him up? He went about with a gang of people I didn't care about, that's all, and from the look of you, I should have said you belonged to the same bright crowd."

"The de Momerie crowd?"

"It's not much use your pretending you don't know all about it, is it?" said Willis, with a sneer.

"Ingleby told me Dean was a hanger-on of that particular bunch of Bright Young People," replied Bredon, mildly. "But I've never met any of them. They'd think me terribly ancient. They would, really. Besides, I don't think they're nice to know. Some of them are really naughty. Did Mr. Pym know that Dean was a Bright Young Thing?"

"I shouldn't think so, or he'd have buzzed him out double quick. What business is Dean of yours, anyway?"

"Absolutely none. I just wondered about him, that's all. He seems to have been a sort of misfit here. Not quite imbued with the Pym spirit, if you see what I mean."

"No, he wasn't. And if you take my advice, you'll leave Dean and his precious friends alone, or you won't make yourself too popular. The best thing Dean ever did in his life was to fall down that staircase."

"Nothing in life became him like the leaving it? But it seems a bit harsh, all the same. Somebody must have loved him. 'For he must be somebody's son,' as the dear old song says. Hadn't he any family? There is a sister, at least, isn't there?"

"Why the devil do you want to know about his sister?"

"I don't. I just asked, that's all. Well, I'd better tootle off, I suppose. I've enjoyed this little talk."

Willis scowled at his retreating form, and Mr. Bredon went away to get his information elsewhere. As usual, the typists' room was well informed.

"Only the sister," said Miss Parton. "She's something to do with Silkanette Hosiery. She and Victor ran a little flat together. Smart as paint, but rather silly, I thought, the only time I saw her. I've an idea our Mr. Willis was a bit smitten in that direction at one time, but it didn't seem to come to anything."

"Oh, I see," said Mr. Bredon, much enlightened.

He went back to his own room and the guard-books. But his attention wandered. He paced about, sat down, got up, stared out of the window, came back to the desk. Then, from a drawer, he pulled out a sheet or paper. It bore a list of dates in the previous year, and to each date was appended a letter of the alphabet, thus:

Jan. 7 G
14 O?
21 A
28 P
Feb. 5 G

There were other papers in the desk in the same handwriting—presumably Victor Dean's—but this list seemed to interest Mr. Bredon unaccountably. He examined it with an attention that one would have thought it scarcely deserved, and finally folded it carefully away in his pocketbook.

"Who dragged whom, how many times, at the wheels of what, round the walls of where?" demanded Mr. Bredon of the world at large. Then he laughed. "Probably some sublime scheme for selling Sopo to sapheads," he remarked, and this time set himself soberly to work upon his guard-books.

Mr. Pym, the presiding genius of Pym's Publicity, Ltd., usually allowed a week or so to elapse before interviewing new members of his staff. His theory was that it was useless to lecture people about their work till they had acquired some idea of what the work actually was. He was a conscientious man, and was particularly careful to keep before his mind the necessity for establishing a friendly personal relation with every man, woman and child in his employment, from the heads of departments down to the messenger-boys and, not being gifted with any spontaneous ease and charm of social intercourse, had worked out a rigid formula for dealing with this necessity. At the end of a week or so, he sent for any newly-joined recruits, interrogated them about their work and interests, and delivered his famous sermon on Service in Advertising. If they survived this frightful ordeal, under which nervous young typists had been known to collapse and give notice, they were put on the list for the monthly tea-party. This took place in the Little Conference Room. Twenty persons, selected from all ranks and departments, congregated under Mr. Pym's official eye to consume the usual office tea, supplemented by ham sandwiches from the canteen, and cake supplied at cost by Dairyfields, Ltd., and entertained one another for an exact hour. This function was supposed to promote inter-departmental cordiality, and by its means the entire staff, including the Outside Publicity, passed under scrutiny once in every six months. In addition to these delights there were, for department and group managers, informal dinners at Mr. Pym's private residence, where six victims were turned off at a time, the proceedings being hilariously concluded by the formation of two bridge-tables, presided over by Mr. and Mrs. Pym respectively. For the group-secretaries, junior copy-writers and junior artists, invitations were issued to an At Home twice a year, with a band and dancing till 10 o'clock; the seniors were expected to attend these and exercise the functions of stewards. For the clerks and typists, there was the Typists' Garden-Party, with tennis and badminton; and for the office-boys, there was the Office-Boys' Christmas Treat. In May of every year there was the Grand Annual Dinner and Dance for the whole staff, at which the amount of the staff bonus was announced for the year, and the health of Mr. Pym was drunk amid expressions of enthusiastic loyalty.

In accordance with the first item on this onerous programme, Mr. Bredon was summoned to the Presence within ten days of his first appearance at Pym's.

"Well, Mr. Bredon," said Mr. Pym, switching on an automatic smile and switching it off again with nervous abruptness, "and how are you getting on?"

"Oh, pretty well, thank you, sir."

"Find the work hard?"

"It is a little difficult," admitted Bredon, "till you get the hang of it, so to speak. A bit bewildering, if you know what I mean."

"Quite so, quite so," said Mr. Pym. "Do you get on all right with Mr. Armstrong and Mr. Hankin?"

Mr. Bredon said he found them very kind and helpful.

"They give me very good accounts of you," said Mr. Pym. "They seem to think you will make a good copy-writer." He smiled again and Bredon grinned back impudently.

"That's just as well, under the circumstances, isn't it?"

Mr. Pym rose suddenly to his feet and threw open the door which separated his room from his secretary's cubicle.

"Miss Hartley, do you mind going along to Mr. Vickers and asking him to look up the detailed appropriation for Darling's and let me have it? You might wait and bring it back with you."

Miss Hartley, realizing that she was to be deprived of hearing Mr. Pym's discourse on Service in Advertising, which—owing to the thinness of the wooden partition and the resonant quality of Mr. Pym's voice—was exceedingly familiar to her, rose and departed obediently. This meant that she would be able to have a nice chat with Miss Rossiter and Miss Parton while Mr. Vickers was getting his papers together. And she would not hurry herself, either. Miss Rossiter had hinted that Mr. Willis had hinted all kinds of frightful possibilities about Mr. Bredon, and she wanted to know what was up.

"Now," said Mr. Pym, passing his tongue rapidly across his lips and seeming to pull himself together to face a disagreeable interview. "What have you got to tell me?"

Mr. Bredon, very much at his ease, leaned across with his elbows on the Managing Director's desk, and spoke for some considerable time in a low tone, while Mr. Pym's cheek grew paler and paler.

# 4

# REMARKABLE ACROBATICS OF A HARLEQUIN

IT HAS already been hinted that Tuesday was a day of general mortification in Pym's copy-department. The trouble was caused by Messrs. Toule & Jollop, proprietors of Nutrax, Maltogene, and Jollop's Concentrated Lactobeef Tablets for Travellers. Unlike the majority of clients who, though all tiresome in their degree, exercised their tiresomeness by post from a reasonable distance and at reasonable intervals, Messrs. Toule & Jollop descended upon Pym's every Tuesday for a weekly conference. While there, they reviewed the advertising for the coming week, rescinding the decisions taken at the previous week's conference, springing new schemes unexpectedly upon Mr. Pym and Mr. Armstrong, keeping those two important men shut up in the Conference Room for hours on end, to the interruption of office-business, and generally making nuisances of themselves. One of the items discussed at this weekly séance was the Nutrax 11-inch double for Friday's *Morning Star*, which occupied an important position in that leading news-organ on the top right-hand corner of the Home page, next to the special Friday feature. It subsequently occupied other positions in other journals, of course, but Friday's *Morning Star* was the real matter of importance.

The usual procedure in respect of this exasperating advertisement was as follows. Every three months or so, Mr. Hankin sent out an S O S to the copy-department to the effect that more Nutrax copy was urgently required. By the united ingenuity of the department, about twenty pieces of copy were forthwith produced and submitted to Mr. Hankin. Under his severely critical blue-pencil, these were reduced to twelve or so, which went to the Studio to be laid out and furnished with illustrative sketches. They were then sent or handed to Messrs. Toule & Jollop, who fretfully rejected all but half-a-dozen, and weakened and ruined the remainder by foolish alterations and additions. The copy-department was then scourged into producing another twenty efforts, of which, after a similar process of elimination and amendment, a further half-dozen contrived to survive criticism, thus furnishing the necessary twelve half-doubles for the ensuing three months. The department breathed again, momentarily, and the dozen lay-outs were stamped in purple ink "Passed by Client," and a note was made of the proposed order of their appearance.

On Monday of each week, Mr. Tallboy, group-manager for Nutrax, squared his shoulders and settled down to the task of getting Friday's half-double safely into the *Morning Star*. He looked out the copy for the week and sent round to collect the finished sketch from the Studio. If the finished sketch was really finished (which seldom happened), he sent it down to the block-makers, together with the copy and a carefully drawn lay-out. The block-makers, grumbling that they never were allowed proper time for the job, made a line-block of the sketch. The thing then passed to the printers, who set up the headlines and copy in type, added a name-block of the wrong size, locked the result up in a forme, pulled a proof and returned the result to Mr. Tallboy, pointing out in a querulous note that it came out half an inch too long. Mr. Tallboy corrected the misprints, damned their eyes for using the wrong name-block, made it clear to them that they had set the headlines in the wrong fount, cut the proof to pieces, pasted it up again into the correct size and returned it. By this time it was usualiy 11 o'clock on Tuesday morning, and Mr. Toule or Mr. Jollop, or both of them, were closeted in the Conference Room with Mr. Pym and Mr. Armstrong, calling loudly and repeatedly for their 11-inch double. As soon as the new proof arrived from the printer's, Mr. Tallboy sent it down to the Conference Room by a boy, and escaped, if he could, for his elevenses. Mr. Toule or Mr. Jollop then pointed out to Mr. Pym and Mr. Armstrong a great number of weaknesses in both sketch and copy. Mr. Pym and Mr. Armstrong, sycophantically concurring in everything the client said, confessed themselves at a loss and invited suggestions from Mr. Toule (or Mr. Jollop). The latter, being, as most clients are, better at destructive than constructive criticism, cudgelled his brains into stupor, and thus reduced himself to a condition of utter blankness, upon which the persuasiveness of Mr. Pym and Mr. Armstrong could work with hypnotic effect. After half an hour of skilled treatment, Mr. Jollop (or Mr. Toule) found himself returning with a sense of relief and refreshment to the rejected lay-out. He then discovered that it was really almost exactly what he required. It only needed the alteration of a sentence and the introduction of a panel about gift-coupons. Mr. Armstrong then sent the lay-out up again to Mr. Tallboy, with a request that he would effect these necessary alterations. Mr. Tallboy, realizing with delight that these involved nothing more drastic than the making of a new lay-out and the complete re-writing of the copy, sought out the copy-writer whose initials appeared on the original typescript, instructing him to cut out three lines and incorporate the client's improvements, while he himself laid the advertisement out afresh.

When all this had been done, the copy was returned to the printer to be re-set, the forme was sent to the block-makers, a complete block was made of the whole advertisement, and a fresh proof was returned. If, by any lucky chance, there turned out to be no defects in the block, the stereotypers got to work and made a sufficient number of stereos to be sent out to the other papers carrying the Nutrax advertising, with a proof to accompany each. On Thursday afternoon, the stereos were distributed by the despatching department to the London papers by hand, and to the provincial papers by post and train, and if nothing went wrong with these arrangements, the advertisement duly appeared in Friday's *Morning Star* and in other papers on the dates provided for. So long and arduous a history it is, that lies behind those exhortations to "Nourish your Nerves with Nutrax," which smite the reader in the eye as he opens his *Morning Star* in the train between Gidea Park and Liverpool Street.

On this particular Tuesday, exasperation was intensified. To begin with, the weather was exceptionally close, with a thunderstorm impending, and the top floor of Pym's Publicity was like a slow oven beneath the broad lead roof and the great glass skylights. Secondly, a visit was expected from two directors of Brotherhoods, Ltd., that extremely old-fashioned and religiously-minded firm who manufacture boiled sweets and non-alcoholic liquors. A warning had been sent round that all female members of the staff must refrain from smoking, and that any proofs of beer or whisky advertising must be carefully concealed from sight. The former restriction bore hardly upon Miss Meteyard and the copy-department typists, whose cigarettes were, if not encouraged, at least winked at in the ordinary way by the management. Miss Parton had been further upset by a mild suggestion from Mr. Hankin that she was showing rather more arm and neck than the directors of Brotherhoods, Ltd., would think seemly; out of sheer perversity, she had covered the offending flesh with a heavy sweater, and was ostentatiously stewing and grumbling and snapping the head off every one who approached her. Mr. Jollop, who was, if anything, slightly more captious than Mr. Toule, had arrived particularly early for the weekly Nutrax conference, and had distinguished himself by firmly killing no less than three advertisements which Mr. Toule had previously passed. This meant that Mr. Hankin had been obliged to send out his S O S nearly a month earlier than usual. Mr. Armstrong had toothache, and had been exceptionally short with Miss Rossiter, and something had gone wrong with Miss Rossiter's type-writer, so that its spacing was completely unreliable.

To Mr. Ingleby, perspiring over his guard-books, entered the detested form of Mr. Tallboy, a sheet of paper in his hand.

"Is this your copy?"

Mr. Ingleby stretched out a languid hand, took the paper, glanced at it and returned it.

"How often have I got to tell you blasted incompetents," he demanded amiably, "that those initials are on the copy for the purpose of identifying the writer? If you think my initials are DB you're either blind or potty."

"Who is DB anyway?"

"New fellow, Bredon."

"Where is he?"

Mr. Ingleby jerked his thumb in the direction of the next room.

"Empty," announced Mr. Tallboy, after a brief excursion.

"Well, have a look for him," suggested Ingleby.

"Yes, but look here," said Mr. Tallboy, persuasively, "I only want a suggestion. What the devil are the Studio to do with this? Do you mean to say Hankin passed that headline?"

"Presumably," said Ingleby.

"Well, how does he or Bredon or anybody suppose we're going to get it illustrated? Has the client seen it? They'll never stand for it. What's the point in laying it out? I can't think how Hankin came to pass it."

Ingleby stretched his hand out again.

"Brief, bright and brotherly," he observed. "What's the matter with it?"

The headline was:

——————!

IF LIFE'S A BLANK
TAKE NUTRAX

"And in any case," grumbled Tallboy, "the *Morning Star* won't take it. They won't put in anything that looks like bad language."

"Your look-out," said Ingleby. "Why not ask 'em?"

Tallboy muttered something impolite.

"Anyway, if Hankin's passed it, it'll have to be laid out, I suppose," said Ingleby. "Surely the Studio–oh! hullo! here's your man. You'd better worry him. Bredon!"

"That's me!" said Mr. Bredon. "All present and correct!"

"Where've you been hiding from Tallboy? You knew he was on your tail."

"I've been on the roof," admitted Bredon, apologetically. "Cooler and all that. What's the matter. What have I done?"

"Well, this headline of yours, Mr. Bredon. How do you expect them to illustrate it?"

"I don't know. I left it to their ingenuity. I always believe in leaving scope to other people's imagination."

"How on earth are they to draw a blank?"

"Let 'em take a ticket in the Irish Sweep. That'll larn 'em," said Ingleby.

"I should think it would be rather like a muchness," suggested Bredon. "Lewis Carroll, you know. Did you ever see a drawing of a muchness?"

"Oh, don't fool," growled Tallboy. "We've got to do something with it. Do you really think it's a good headline, Mr. Bredon?"

"It's the best I've written yet," said Bredon enthusiastically, "except that beauty Hankie wouldn't pass. Can't they draw a man looking blank? Or just a man with a blank face, like those 'Are these missing features yours?' advertisements?"

"Oh, I suppose they *could*," admitted Tallboy, discontentedly. "I'll put it up to them anyhow. Thanks," he added, belatedly, and bounced out.

"Cross, isn't he?" said Ingleby. "It's this frightful heat. Whatever made you go up on the roof? It must be like a gridiron."

"So it is, but I thought I'd just try it. As a matter of fact, I was chucking pennies over the parapet to that brass band. I got the bombardon twice. The penny goes down with a tremendous whack, you know, and they look up all over the place to see where it comes from and you dodge down behind the parapet. It's a tremendous high parapet, isn't it? I suppose they wanted to make the building look even higher than it is. It's the highest in the street in any case. You do get a good view from up there. 'Earth hath not anything to show more fair.' It's going to rain like billy-ho in about two ticks. See how black it's come over."

"You seem to have come over pretty black if it comes to that," remarked Ingleby. "Look at the seat of your trousers."

"You do want a lot," complained Bredon, twisting his spine alarmingly. "It is a bit sooty up there. I was sitting on the skylight."

"You look as if you'd been shinning up a pipe."

"Well, I did shin down a pipe. Only one pipe–rather a nice pipe. It took my fancy."

"You're loopy," said Ingleby, "doing acrobatics on dirty pipes in this heat. Whatever made you?"

"I dropped something," said Mr. Bredon, plaintively. "It went down on to the glass roof of the wash-place. I nearly put my foot through. Wouldn't old Smayle have been surprised if I'd tumbled into the wash-basin on top of him? And then I found I needn't have gone down the pipe after all; I came back by the staircase–the roof-door was open on both floors."

"They generally keep them open in hot weather," said Ingleby.

"I wish I'd known. I say, I could do with a drink."

"All right, have a glass of Sparkling Pompayne."

"What's that?"

"One of Brotherhood's non-alcoholic refreshers," grinned Ingleby. "Made from finest Devon apples, with the crisp, cool sparkle of champagne. Definitely anti-rheumatic and nonintoxicant. Doctors recommend it."

Bredon shuddered.

"I think this is an awfully immoral job of ours. I do, really. Think how we spoil the digestions of the public."

"Ah, yes–but think how earnestly we strive to put them right again. We undermine 'em with one hand and build 'em up with the other. The vitamins we destroy in the canning, we restore in Revito, the roughage we remove from Peabody's Piper Parritch we make up into a package and market as Bunbury's Breakfast Bran; the stomachs we ruin with Pompayne, we re-line with Peplets to aid digestion. And by forcing the damn-fool public to pay twice over–once to have its food emasculated and once to have the vitality put back again, we keep the wheels of commerce turning and give employment to thousands–including you and me."

"This wonderful world!" Bredon sighed ecstatically. "How many pores should you say there were in the human skin, Ingleby?"

"Damned if I know. Why?"

"Headline for Sanfect. Could I say, at a guess, ninety million? It sounds a good round number. 'Ninety Million Open Doors by which Germs can Enter–Lock Those Doors with Sanfect.' Sounds convincing, don't you think? Here's another: 'Would you Leave your Child in a Den of Lions?' That ought to get the mothers."

"It'd make a good sketch– Hullo! here comes the storm and no mistake."

A flash of lightning and a tremendous crack of thunder broke without warning directly over their heads.

"I expected it," said Bredon. "That's why I did my roofwalk."

"How do you mean, that's why?"

"I was on the look-out for it," explained Bredon. "Well, it's here. Phew! that was a good one. I do adore thunderstorms. By the way, what has Willis got up against me?"

Ingleby frowned and hesitated.

"He seems to think I'm not nice to know," explained Bredon.

"Well–I warned you not to talk to him about Victor Dean. He seems to have got it into his head you were a friend of his, or something."

"But what *was* wrong with Victor Dean?"

"He kept bad company. Why are you so keen to know about Dean, anyway?"

"Well, I suppose I'm naturally inquisitive. I always like to know about people. About the office-boys, for instance. They do physical jerks on the roof, don't they? Is that the only time they're allowed on the roof?"

"They'd better not let the Sergeant catch 'em up there in office-hours. Why?"

"I just wondered. They're a mischievous lot, I expect; boys always are. I like 'em. What's the name of the redheaded one? He looks a snappy lad."

"That's Joe–they call him Ginger, of course. What's he been doing?"

"Oh, nothing. I suppose you get a lot of cats prowling about this place."

"Cats? I've never seen any cats. Except that I believe there's a cat that lives in the canteen, but she doesn't seem to come up here. What do you want a cat for?"

"I don't–anyway, there must be dozens of sparrows, mustn't there?"

Ingleby began to think that the heat had affected Bredon's brain. His reply was drowned in a tremendous crash of thunder. A silence followed, in which the street noises came thinly up from without; then heavy drops began to spit upon the panes. Ingleby got up and shut the window.

The rain came down like rods and roared upon the roof. In the lead gutters it danced and romped, rushing in small swift rivers into the hoppers. Mr. Prout, emerging from his room in a hurry, received a deluge of water down his neck from the roof and yelled for a boy to run along and shut the skylights. The oppression of heat and misery lifted from the office like a cast-off eiderdown. Standing at the window of his own room, Bredon watched the hurrying foot-passengers six stories below, open their umbrellas to the deluge, or, caught defenceless, scurry into shop doorways. Down below, in the Conference Room, Mr. Jollop suddenly smiled and passed six lay-outs and a three-colour folder, and consented to the omission of the Fifty-six Free Chiming Clocks from the current week's half-double. Harry, the lift-man, ushering a dripping young woman into the shelter of the cage, expressed sympathy with her plight, and offered her a wipedown with a duster. The young woman smiled at him, assured him that she was quite all right and asked if she could see Mr. Bredon. Harry handed her on to Tompkin, the reception clerk, who said he would send up, and what was her name, please?

"Miss Dean—Miss Pamela Dean—on private business."

The clerk became full of sympathetic interest.

"Our Mr. Dean's sister, miss?"

"Yes."

"Oh, yes, miss. A dreadful sad thing about Mr. Dean, miss. We were all very sorry to lose him like that. If you'll just take a seat, miss, I'll tell Mr. Bredon you're here."

Pamela Dean sat down and looked about her. The reception-hall was on the lower floor of the agency and contained nothing but the clerk's semi-circular desk, two hard chairs, a hard settle and a clock. It occupied the space which, on the upper floor, was taken up by the Dispatching, and just outside the door was the lift and the main staircase, which wound round the lift-shaft and went the whole way to the roof, though the lift itself went no further than the top floor. The clock pointed to 12:45, and already a stream of employees was passing through the hall, or clattering down from the floor above for a wash and brush-up before going out to lunch. A message from Mr. Bredon arrived to say that he would be down in a moment, and Pamela Dean entertained herself by watching the various members of the staff as they passed. A brisk, neat young man, with an immaculate head of wavy brown hair, a minute dark moustache and very white teeth (Mr. Smayle, had she known it, group-manager for Dairyfields, Ltd.); a large, bald man with a reddish, clean-shaven face and a masonic emblem (Mr. Harris of the Outdoor Publicity); a man of thirty-five, with rather sulky good looks and restless light eyes (Mr. Tallboy, brooding on the iniquities of Messrs. Toule & Jollop); a thin, prim, elderly man (Mr. Daniels); a plump little man with a good-natured grin and fair hair, chatting to a square-jawed, snub-nosed red-head (Mr. Cole, group-manager for Herrogate Bros. of soap fame, and Mr. Prout, the photographer); a handsome, worried, grey-haired man in the forties, accompanying a prosperous baldpate in an overcoat (Mr. Armstrong escorting Mr. Jollop away to a mollifying and expensive lunch); an untidy, saturnine person with both hands in his trousers-pockets (Mr. Ingleby); a thin, predatory man with a stoop and jaundiced eyeballs (Mr. Copley, wondering whether his lunch was going to agree with him); then a lean, fair-haired, anxious-looking youth, who, at sight of her, stopped dead in his tracks, flushed, and then passed on. This was Mr. Willis; Miss Dean gave him a glance and a cool nod, which was as coolly returned. Tompkin, the reception clerk, who missed nothing, saw the start, the flush, the glance and the nods and mentally added another item to his fund of useful knowledge. Then came a slim man of forty or so, with a long nose and straw-coloured hair, wearing horn-rimmed glasses and a pair of well-cut grey trousers which seemed to have received recent ill-treatment; he came up to Pamela and said, more as a statement than as a question:

"Miss Dean."

"Mr. Bredon?"

"Yes."

"You ought not to have come here," said Mr. Bredon, shaking his head reproachfully, "it's a little indiscreet, you know. However–hullo, Willis, want me?"

It was evidently not Mr. Willis' lucky day. He had conquered his nervous agitation and turned back with the obvious intention of addressing Pamela, just in time to find Bredon in possession. He replied, "Oh, no, not at all"–with such patent sincerity that Tompkin made another ecstatic mental note, and was, indeed, forced to dive hurriedly behind his counter to conceal his radiant face. Bredon grinned amiably and Willis, after a moment's hesitation, fled through the doorway.

"I'm sorry," said Miss Dean. "I didn't know–"

"Never mind," said Bredon, and then, in a louder tone: "You've come for those things of your brother's, haven't you? I've got them here; I'm working in his room, don't you know. I say, er, how about, er, coming out and honouring me by taking in a spot of lunch with me, what?"

Miss Dean agreed; Bredon fetched his hat and they passed out.

"Ho!" said Tompkin in confidence to himself. "Ho! what's the game, I wonder? She's a smart jane all right, all right. Given the youngster a chuck and now she's out after the new bloke, I shouldn't be surprised. *And* I don't know as I blame her."

Mr. Bredon and Miss Dean went sedately down together in silence, affording no pasture for the intelligent ears of Harry the liftman, but as they emerged into Southampton Row, the girl turned to her companion:

"I was rather surprised when I got your letter . . ."

Mr. Willis, lurking in the doorway of a neighbouring tobacconist's shop, heard the words and scowled. Then, pulling his hat over his eyebrows and buttoning his mackintosh closely about him, he set out in pursuit. They walked through the lessening rain to the nearest cab-rank and engaged a taxi. Mr. Willis, cunningly waiting till they were well started, engaged the next.

"Follow that taxi," he said, exactly like somebody out of a book. And the driver, nonchalant as though he had stepped from the pages of Edgar Wallace, replied, "Right you are, sir," and slipped in his clutch.

The chase offered no excitement, ending up in the tamest possible manner at Simpson's in the Strand. Mr. Willis paid off his taxi, and climbed, in the wake of the couple, to that upper room where ladies are graciously permitted to be entertained. The quarry found a table near the window; Mr. Willis, ignoring the efforts of a waiter to pilot him to a quiet corner, squeezed in at the table next to them, where a man and woman, who obviously wanted to lunch alone, made way for him indignantly. Even so, he was not very well placed, for, though he could see Bredon and the girl, they had their backs to him, and their conversation was perfectly inaudible.

"Plenty of room at the next table, sir," suggested the waiter.

"I'm all right here," replied Willis, irritably. His neighbour glared, and the waiter, with a glance as much as to say, 'Loopy—but what can a man do?' presented the bill of fare. Willis vaguely ordered saddle of mutton and red-currant jelly with potatoes and gazed at Bredon's slim back.

". . . very nice today, sir."

"What?"

"The cauliflower, sir—very nice today."

"Anything you like."

The little black hat and the sleek yellow poll seemed very close together. Bredon had taken some small object out of his pocket and was showing it to the girl. A ring? Willis strained his eyes—

"What will you drink, sir?"

"Lager," said Willis, at random.

"Pilsener, sir, or Barclay's London Lager?"

"Oh, Pilsener."

"Light or dark, sir?"

"Light—dark—no, I mean light."

"Large light Pilsener, sir?"

"Yes, yes."

"Tankard, sir?"

"Yes, no—damn it! Bring it in anything that's got a hole in the top." There seemed no end to the questions that could be asked about beer. The girl had taken the object, and was doing something with it. What? For heaven's sake, what?

"Roast or new potatoes, sir?"

"New." The man had gone, thank goodness. Bredon was holding Pamela Dean's hand—no, he was turning over the object that lay on her palm. The woman opposite Willis was stretching across for the sugar-basin—her head obstructed his view—deliberately, as it seemed to him. She moved back. Bredon was still examining the object—

A large dinner-wagon, laden with steaming joints under great silver covers was beside him. A lid was lifted—the odour of roast mutton smote him in the face.

"A little more fat, sir? You like it underdone?"

Great God! What monster helpings they gave one at this place! What sickening stuff mutton was! How vile were these round yellow balls of potato that the man kept heaping on his plate! What disgusting stuff cauliflower could be—a curdle of cabbage! Willis, picking with nauseated reluctance at the finest roast saddle in London, felt his stomach cold and heavy, his feet a-twitch.

The hateful meal dragged on. The indignant couple finished their gooseberry pie and went their affronted way without waiting for coffee. Now Willis could see better. The other two were laughing now and talking eagerly. In a sudden lull a few words of Pamela's floated clearly back to him: "It's to be fancy dress, so you'll slip in all right." Then she dropped her voice again.

"Will you take any more mutton, sir?"

Try as he would, Willis could catch nothing more. He sat on in Simpson's until Bredon, glancing at his watch, appeared to remind himself and his companion that advertising copy-writers must work sometimes. Willis was ready for them. His bill was paid. He had only to shelter behind the newspaper he had brought in with him until they had passed him and then—what? Follow them out? Pursue them again in a taxi, wondering all the time how closely they were clasped together, what they were saying to one another, what appointments they were making, what new devilment there was still in store for Pamela, now that Victor Dean was out of the way, and what he would or could do next to make the world safe for her to live in?

He was spared the decision. As the two came abreast of him, Bredon, suddenly popping his head over the Lunch Edition of the *Evening Banner*, observed cheerfully:

"Hullo, Willis! enjoyed your lunch? Excellent saddle, what? But you should have tried the peas. Can I give you a lift back to the tread-mill?"

"No, thanks," growled Willis; and then realized that if he had said, "Yes, please," he would at least have made an ardent tête-à-tête in the taxi impossible. But ride in the same taxi with Pamela Dean and Bredon he could not.

"Miss Dean, unhappily, has to leave us," went on Bredon. "You might come and console me by holding my hand."

Pamela was already half-way out of the room. Willis could not decide whether she knew to whom her escort was speaking and had studied to avoid him, or whether she supposed him to be some friend of Bredon's unknown to her. Quite suddenly he made up his mind.

"Well," he said, "it is getting a bit late. If you're having a taxi, I'll share it with you."

"That's the stuff," said Bredon. Willis rose and joined him and they moved on to where Pamela was waiting.

"I think you know our Mr. Willis?"

"Oh, yes," Pamela smiled a small, frozen smile. "Victor and he were great friends at one time."

The door. The stairs. The entrance. They were outside at last.

"I must be getting along now. Thank you so much for my lunch, Mr. Bredon. And you won't forget?"

"I certainly will not. 'Tisn't likely, is it?"

"Good afternoon, Mr. Willis."

"Good afternoon."

She was gone, walking briskly in her little, high-heeled shoes. The roaring Strand engulfed her. A taxi purred up to them.

Bredon gave the address and waved Willis in before him.

"Pretty kid, young Dean's sister," he remarked, cheerfully.

"See here, Bredon; I don't know quite what your game is, but you'd better be careful. I told Dean and I tell you–if you get Miss Dean mixed up with that dirty business of yours–"

"What dirty business?"

"You know well enough what I mean."

"Perhaps I do. And what then? Do I get my neck broken, like Victor Dean?"

Bredon slewed round as he spoke and looked Willis hard in the eye.

"You'll get–" Willis checked himself. "Never mind," he said darkly, "you'll get what's coming to you. I'll see to that."

"I've no doubt you'll do it very competently, what?" replied Bredon. "But do you mind telling me exactly where you come into it? From what I can see, Miss Dean does not seem to welcome your championship with any great enthusiasm."

Willis flushed a dusky red.

"It's no business of mine, of course," went on Bredon, airily, while their taxi chugged impatiently in a traffic jam at Holborn Tube Station, "but then, on the other hand, it doesn't really seem to be any business of yours, does it?"

"It is my business," retorted Willis. "It's every decent man's business. I heard Miss Dean making an appointment with you," he went on, angrily.

"What a detective you would make," said Bredon, admiringly. "But you really ought to take care, when you are shadowing anybody, that they are not sitting opposite a mirror, or anything that will serve as a mirror. There is a picture in front of the table where we were sitting, that reflects half the room. Elementary, my dear Watson. No doubt you will do better with practice. However, there is no secret about the appointment. We are going to a fancy dress affair on Friday. I am meeting Miss Dean for dinner at Boulestin's at 8 o'clock and we are going on from there. Perhaps you would care to accompany us?"

The policeman dropped his arm, and the taxi lurched forward into Southampton Row.

"You'd better be careful," growled Willis, "I might take you at your word."

"I should be charmed, personally," replied Bredon. "You will decide for yourself whether Miss Dean would or would not be put in an embarrassing position if you joined the party. Well, well, here we are at our little home from home. We must put aside this light badinage and devote ourselves to Sopo and Pompayne and Peabody's Piper Parritch. A delightful occupation, though somewhat lacking in incident. But let us not complain. We can't expect battle, murder and sudden death more than once a week or so. By the way, where were you when Victor Dean fell downstairs?"

"In the lavatory," said Willis, shortly.

"Were you, indeed?" Bredon looked at him once more attentively. "In the lavatory? You interest me strangely."

The atmosphere of the copy-department was much less strained by tea-time. Messrs. Brotherhood had been and gone, having seen nothing to shock their sense of propriety; Mr. Jollop, mellowed by his lunch, had passed three large poster designs with almost reckless readiness and was now with Mr. Pym, being almost persuaded to increase his appropriation for the autumn campaign. The suffering Mr. Armstrong, released from attendance on Mr. Jollop, had taken himself away to visit his dentist. Mr. Tallboy, coming in to purchase a stamp from Miss Rossiter for his private correspondence, announced with delight that the Nutrax half-double had gone to the printer's.

"Is that 'KITTLE CATTLE'?" asked Ingleby. "You surprise me. I thought we should have trouble with it."

"I believe we did," said Tallboy. "Was it Scotch, and would people know what it meant? Would it suggest that we were calling women cows? And wasn't the sketch a little modernistic? But Armstrong got it shoved through somehow. May I drop this in your 'Out' basket, Miss Rossiter?"

"Serpently," replied the lady, with gracious humour, presenting the basket to receive the latter. "All billy-doos receive our prompt attention and are immediately forwarded to their destination by the quickest and surest route."

"Let's see," said Garrett. "I bet it's to a lady, and him a married man, too! No, you don't, Tallboy, you old devil—stand still, will you? Tell us who it is, Miss Rossiter."

"K. Smith, Esq.," said Miss Rossiter. "You lose your bet."

"What a swizz! But I expect it's all camouflage. I suspect Tallboy of keeping a harem somewhere. You can't trust these handsome blue-eyed men."

"Shut up, Garrett. I never," said Mr. Tallboy, extricating himself from Garrett's grasp and giving him a playful punch in the wind, "in my life, met with such a bunch of buttinskis as you are in this department. Nothing is sacred to you, not even a man's business correspondence."

"How should anything be sacred to an advertiser?" demanded Ingleby, helping himself to four lumps of sugar. "We spend our whole time asking intimate questions of perfect strangers and it naturally blunts our finer feelings. 'Mother! has your Child Learnt Regular Habits?' 'Are you Troubled with Fullness after Eating?' 'Are you satisfied about your Drains?' 'Are you *Sure* that your Toilet-Paper is Germ-free?' 'Your most Intimate Friends dare not Ask you this question.' 'Do you Suffer from Superfluous Hair?' 'Do you Like them to Look at your Hands?' 'Do you ever ask yourself about Body-Odour?' 'If anything Happened to you, would your Loved Ones be Safe?' 'Why Spend so much Time in the Kitchen?' 'You think that Carpet is Clean—but is it?' 'Are you a Martyr to Dandruff?' Upon my soul, I sometimes wonder why the long-suffering public doesn't rise up and slay us."

"They don't know of our existence," said Garrett. "They all think advertisements write themselves. When I tell people I'm in advertising, they always ask whether I design posters—they never think about the copy."

"They think the manufacturer does it himself," said Ingleby.

"They ought to see some of the suggestions the manufacturer does put up when he tries his hand at it."

"I wish they could." Ingleby grinned. "That reminds me. You know that idiotic thing Darling's put out the other day—the air-cushion for travellers with a doll that fits into the middle and sits up holding an 'ENGAGED' label?"

"What for?" asked Bredon.

"Well, the idea is, that you plank the cushion down in the railway carriage and the doll proclaims that the place is taken."

"But the cushion would do that without the doll."

"Of course it would, but you know how silly people are. They like superfluities. Well, anyway, they—Darling's, I mean—got out an ad. for the rubbish all by their little selves, and were fearfully pleased with it. Wanted us to put it through for them, till Armstrong burst into one of his juicy laughs and made them blush."

"What was it?"

"Picture of a nice girl bending down to put the cushion in the corner of a carriage. And the headline? 'DON'T LET THEM PINCH YOUR SEAT.' "

"Attaboy!" said Mr. Bredon.

The new copy-writer was surprisingly industrious that day. He was still in his room, toiling over Sanfect ("Wherever there's Dirt there's Danger!" "The Skeleton in the Water-closet," "Assassins Lurk in your Scullery!" "Deadlier than Shell-Fire—GERMS!!!") when Mrs. Crump led in her female army to attack the day's accumulated dirt—armed, one regrets to say, not with Sanfect, but with plain yellow soap and water.

"Come in, come in!" cried Mr. Bredon, genially, as the good lady paused reverently at his door. "Come and sweep me and my works away with the rest of the rubbish."

"Well, I'm sure, sir," said Mrs. Crump, "I've no need to be disturbing you."

"I've finished, really," said Bredon. "I suppose there's an awful lot of stuff to clear out here every day."

"That there is, sir—you'd hardly believe. Paper—well, I'm sure paper must be cheap, the amount they waste. Sackfuls and sackfuls every evening goes out. Of course, it's disposed of to the mills, but all the same it must be a dreadful expense. And there's boxes and boards and odds and ends—you'd be surprised, the things we picks up. I sometimes think the ladies and gentlemen brings up all their cast-offs on purpose to throw 'em away here."

"I shouldn't wonder."

"And mostly chucked on the floor," resumed Mrs. Crump, warming to her theme, "hardly ever in the paper-baskets, though goodness knows they makes 'em big enough."

"It must give you a lot of trouble."

"Lor', sir, we don't think nothing of it. We just sweeps the lot up and sends the sacks down by the lift. Though sometimes we has a good laugh over the queer things we finds. I usually just give the stuff a look through to make sure there's nothing valuable got dropped by mistake. Once I found two pound-notes on Mr. Ingleby's floor. He's a careless one and no mistake. And not so long ago–the very day poor Mr. Dean had his sad accident, I found a kind of carved stone lying round in the passage–looked as though it might be a charm or a trinket or something of that. But I think it must have tumbled out of the poor gentleman's pocket as he fell, because Mrs. Doolittle said she'd seen it in his room, so I brought it in here, sir, and put it in that there little box."

"Is this it?" Bredon fished in his waistcoat pocket and produced the onyx scarab, which he had unaccountably neglected to return to Pamela Dean.

"That's it, sir. A comical-looking thing, ain't it? Like it might be a beedle or such. It was lying in a dark corner under the iron staircase and at first I thought it was just a pebble like the other one."

"What other one?"

"Well, sir, I found a little round pebble in the very same place only a few days before. I said at the time, 'Well,' I said, 'that's a funny thing to find there.' But I reckon that one must have come from Mr. Atkins's room, him having taken his seaside holiday early this year on account of having been ill, and you know how people do fill up their pockets with sea-shells and pebbles and such."

Bredon hunted in his pocket again.

"Something like that, was it?" He held out a smooth, water-rounded pebble, about the size of his thumbnail.

"Very like it, sir. Did that come out of the passage, sir, might I ask?"

"No–I found that up on the roof."

"Ah!" said Mrs. Crump. "It'll be them boys up to their games. When the Sergeant's eye is off them you never know what they're after."

"They do their drill up there, don't they? Great stuff. Hardens the muscles and develops the figure. When do they perform? In the lunch-hour?"

"Oh, no, sir. Mr. Pym won't have them running about after their dinners. He says it spoils their digestions and gives them the colic. Very particular, is Mr. Pym. Half-past eight regular they has to be on duty, sir, in their pants and singlets. Twenty minutes they has of it and then changed and ready for their dooties. After dinner they sets a bit in the boys' room and has a read or plays something quiet, as it might be, shove ha'penny or tiddley-winks or such. But in their room they must stay, sir; Mr. Pym won't have nobody about the office in the dinner-hour, sir, not without, of course, it's the boy that goes round with the disinfectant, sir."

"Ah, of course! Spray with Sanfect and you're safe."

"That's right, sir, except that they uses Jeyes' Fluid."

"Oh, indeed," said Mr. Bredon, struck afresh by the curious reluctance of advertising firms to use the commodities they extol for a living. "Well, we're very well looked after here, Mrs. Crump, what?"

"Oh, yes, sir. Mr. Pym pays great attention to 'ealth. A very kind gentleman, is Mr. Pym. Next week, sir, we has the Charwomen's Tea, down in the canteen, with an egg-and-spoon race and a bran-tub, and bring the kiddies. My daughter's little girls always look forward to the tea, sir."

"I'm sure they must," said Mr. Bredon, "and I expect they'd like some new hair-ribbons or something of that sort–"

"It's very kind of you, sir," said Mr. Crump, much gratified.

"Not at all." A couple of coins clinked. "Well, I'll push off now and leave you to it."

A very nice gentleman, in Mrs. Crump's opinion, and not at all proud.

It turned out precisely as Mr. Willis had expected. He had tracked his prey from Boulestin's, and this time he felt quite certain he had not been spotted. His costume–that of a member of the Vehmgericht, with its black cossack and black, eyeleted hood covering the whole head and shoulders–was easily slipped on over his every-day suit. Muffled in an old burberry, he had kept watch behind a convenient van in Covent Garden until Bredon and Pamela Dean came out; his taxi had been in waiting just round the corner. His task was made the easier by the fact that the others were driving, not in a taxi, but in an enormous limousine, and that Bredon had taken the wheel himself. The theatre rush was well over before the chase started, so that there was no need to keep suspiciously close to the saloon. The trail had led westward through Richmond and still west, until it had ended at a large house, standing in its own grounds on the bank of the river. Towards the end of the journey they were joined by other cars and taxis making in the same direction; and on arrival they found the drive a parking-place for innumerable vehicles. Bredon and Miss Dean had gone straight in, without a glance behind them.

Willis, who had put on his costume in the taxi, anticipated some difficulty about getting in, but there was none. A servant had met him at the door and asked if he was a member. Willis had replied boldly that he was and given the name of William Brown, which seemed to him an ingenious and plausible invention. Apparently the club was full of William Browns, for the servant raised no difficulty, and he was ushered straight in to a handsomely furnished hall. Immediately in front of him, on the skirts of a crowd of people drinking cocktails, was Bredon, in the harlequin black and white which had been conspicuous as he stepped into his car after dinner. Pamela Dean, in an exiguous swan's-down costume representing a powder-puff, stood beside him. From a room beyond resounded the strains of a saxophone.

"The place," said Mr. Willis to himself, "is a den of iniquity." And for once, Mr. Willis was not far wrong.

He was amazed by the slackness of the organization. Without question or hesitation, every door was opened to him. There was gambling. There was drink in oceans. There was dancing. There were what Mr. Willis had heard described as orgies. And at the back of it all, he sensed something else, something that he did not quite understand; something that he was not precisely kept out of, but to which he simply had not the key.

He was, of course, partnerless, but he soon found himself absorbed into a party of exceedingly bright young people, and watching the evolutions of a *danseuse* whose essential nakedness was enhanced and emphasized by the wearing of a top hat, a monocle and a pair of patent-leather boots. He was supplied with drinks–some of which he paid for, but the majority of which were thrust upon him, and he suddenly became aware that he would have made a better detective had he been more hardened to mixed liquors. His head began to throb, and he had lost sight of Bredon and Pamela. He became obsessed with the idea that they had departed into one of the sinister little cubicles he had seen—each heavily curtained and furnished with a couch and a mirror. He broke away from the group surrounding him and began a hurried search through the house. His costume was hot and heavy, and the sweat poured down his face beneath the stifling black folds of his hood. He found a conservatory full of amorous drunken couples, but the pair he was looking for was not among them. He pushed open a door and found himself in the garden. Cries and splashes attracted him. He plunged down a rose-scented alley beneath a pergola and came out upon an open space with a round fountain-pool in the centre.

A man with a girl in his arms came reeling past him, flushed and hiccuping with laughter, his leopard-skin tunic half torn from his shoulders and the vine-leaves scattering from his hair as he ran. The girl was shrieking like a steam-engine. He was a broad-shouldered man, and the muscles of his back gleamed in the moonlight as he swung his protesting burden from him and tossed her, costume and all, into the pool. Yells of laughter greeted this performance, renewed as the girl, draggled and dripping, crawled back over the edge of the basin and burst into a stream of abuse. Then Willis saw the black-and-white harlequin.

He was climbing the statue-group in the centre of the pool—an elaborate affair of twined mermaids and dolphins, supporting a basin in which crouched an amorino, blowing from a conch-shell a high spout of dancing water. Up and up went the slim chequered figure, dripping and glittering like a fantastic water-creature. He caught the edge of the upper basin with his hands, swung for a moment and lifted. Even in that moment, Willis felt a pang of reluctant admiration. It was the easy, unfretted motion of the athlete, a display of muscular strength without jerk or effort. Then his knee was on the basin. He was up and climbing upon the bronze cupid. Yet another moment and he was kneeling upon the figure's stooped shoulders—standing upright upon them, the spray of the fountain blowing about him.

"Good God!" thought Willis, "the fellow's a tight-rope walker—or he's too drunk to fall." There were yells of applause, and a girl began to shriek hysterically. Then a very tall woman, in a moonlight frock of oyster satin, who had made herself the centre of the most boisterous of all the parties, pushed past Willis and stood out on the edge of the basin, her fair hair standing out like a pale aureole round her vivid face.

"Dive!" she called out, "dive in! I dare you to! Dive in!"

"Shut up, Dian!" One of the soberer of the men caught her round the shoulders and put his hand over her mouth. "It's too shallow—he'll break his neck."

She pushed him away.

"You be quiet. He shall dive. I want him to. Go to hell, Dickie. You wouldn't dare do it, but he will."

"I certainly wouldn't. Stow it."

"Come on, Harlequin, dive!"

The black and white figure raised its arms above its fantastic head and stood poised.

"Don't be a fool, man," bawled Dickie.

But the other women were fired with the idea and their screams drowned his voice.

"Dive, Harlequin, dive."

The slim body shot down through the spray, struck the surface with scarcely a splash and slid through the water like a fish. Willis caught his breath. It was perfectly done. It was magnificent. He forgot his furious hatred of the man and applauded with the rest. The girl Dian ran forward and caught hold of the swimmer as he emerged.

"Oh, you're marvellous, you're marvellous!" She clung to him, the water soaking into her draggled satin.

"Take me home, Harlequin—I adore you!"

The Harlequin bent his masked face and kissed her. The man called Dickie tried to pull him away, but was neatly tripped and fell with a jerk into the pool, amid a roar of laughter. The Harlequin tossed the tall girl across his shoulder.

"A prize!" he shouted. "A prize!"

Then he swung her lightly to her feet and took her hand. "Run," he called, "run! Let's run away, and let them catch us if they can."

There was a sudden stampede. Willis saw the angry face of Dickie as he lurched past him and heard him swearing. Somebody caught his hand. He ran up the rose-alley, panting. Something caught his foot, and he tripped and fell. His companion abandoned him, and ran on, hooting. He sat up, found his head enveloped in his hood and struggled to release himself.

A hand touched his shoulder.

"Come on, Mr. Willis," said a mocking voice in his ear, "Mr. Bredon says I am to escort you home."

He succeeded in dragging the black cloth from his head and scrambled to his feet.

Beside him stood Pamela Dean. She had taken off her mask, and her eyes were alight with mischief.

# 5

# SURPRISING METAMORPHOSIS OF MR. BREDON

LORD PETER Wimsey had paid a call upon Chief-Inspector Parker of Scotland Yard, who was his brother-in-law.

He occupied a large and comfortable arm-chair in the Chief-Inspector's Bloomsbury flat. Opposite him, curled upon the chesterfield, was his sister, Lady Mary Parker, industriously knitting an infant's vest. On the window-seat, hugging his knees and smoking a pipe, was Mr. Parker himself. On a convenient table stood a couple of decanters and a soda siphon. On the hearthrug was a large tabby cat. The scene was almost ostentatiously peaceful and domestic.

"So you have become one of the world's workers, Peter," said Lady Mary.

"Yes; I'm pulling down four solid quid a week. Amazin' sensation. First time I've ever earned a cent. Every week when I get my pay-envelope, I glow with honest pride."

Lady Mary smiled, and glanced at her husband, who grinned cheerfully back. The difficulties which are apt to arise when a poor man marries a rich wife had, in their case, been amicably settled by an ingenious arrangement, under which all Lady Mary's money had been handed over to her brothers in trust for little Parkers to come, the trustee having the further duty of doling out each quarter to the wife a sum precisely equal to the earnings of the husband during that period. Thus a seemly balance was maintained between the two principals; and the trifling anomaly that Chief-Inspector Parker was actually a mere pauper in comparison with small Charles Peter and still smaller Mary Lucasta, now peacefully asleep in their cots on the floor above, disturbed nobody one whit. It pleased Mary to have the management of their moderate combined income, and incidentally did her a great deal of good. She now patronized her wealthy brother with all the superiority which the worker feels over the man who merely possesses money.

"But what *is* the case all about, exactly?" demanded Parker.

"Blest if I know," admitted Wimsey, frankly. "I got hauled into it through Freddy Arbuthnot's wife–Rachel Levly that was, you know. She knows old Pym, and he met her at dinner somewhere and told her about this letter that was worrying him, and she said, Why not get somebody in to investigate it, and he said, Who? So she said she knew somebody–not mentioning my name, you see–and he said would she ask me to buzz along, so I buzzed and there I am."

"Your narrative style," said Parker, "though racy, is a little elliptical. Could you not begin at the beginning and go on until you come to the end, and then, if you are able to, stop?"

"I'll try," said his lordship, "but I always find the stopping part of the business so difficult. Well, look! On a Monday afternoon–the 25th of May, to be particular, a young man, Victor Dean by name, employed as a copy-writer in the firm of Pym's Publicity, Ltd., Advertising Agents, fell down an iron spiral staircase on their premises, situated in the upper part of Southampton Row, and died immediately of injuries received, to wit: one broken neck, one cracked skull, one broken leg and minor cuts and contusions, various. The time of this disaster was, as nearly as can be ascertained, 3.30 in the afternoon."

"Hum!" said Parker. "Pretty extensive injuries for a fall of that kind."

"So I thought, before I saw the staircase. To proceed. On the day after this occurrence, the sister of deceased sends to Mr. Pym a fragment of a half-finished letter which she has found on her brother's desk. It warns him that there is something of a fishy nature going on in the office. The letter is dated about ten days previous to the death, and appears to have been laid aside as though the writer wanted to think over the wording a bit more carefully. Very good. Now, Mr. Pym is a man of rigid morality–except, of course, as regards his profession, whose essence is to tell plausible lies for money–"

"How about truth in advertising?"

"Of course, there is *some* truth in advertising. There's yeast in bread, but you can't make bread with yeast alone. Truth in advertising," announced Lord Peter sententiously, "is like leaven, which a woman hid in three measures of meal. It provides a suitable quantity of gas, with which to blow out a mass of crude misrepresentation into a form that the public can swallow. Which incidentally brings me to the delicate and important distinction between the words 'with' and 'from.' Suppose you are advertising lemonade, or, not to be invidious, we will say perry. If you say 'Our perry is made from fresh-plucked pears only,' then it's got to be made from pears only, or the statement is actionable; if you just say it is made 'from pears,' without the 'only,' the betting is that it is probably made chiefly of pears; but if you say, 'made *with* pears,' you generally mean that you use a peck of pears to a ton of turnips, and the law cannot touch you–such are the niceties of our English tongue."

"Make a note, Mary, next time you go shopping, and buy nothing that is not 'from, only.' Proceed, Peter–and let us have a lIttle less of your English tongue."

"Yes. Well, here is a young man who starts to write a warning letter. Before he can complete it, he falls downstairs and is killed. Is that, or is it not, a darned suspicious circumstance?"

"So suspicious that it is probably the purest coincidence. But since you have a fancy for melodrama, we will allow it to be suspicious. Who saw him die?"

"I, said the fly. Meaning one Mr. Atkins and one Mrs. Crump, who saw the fall from below, and one Mr. Prout who saw it from above. All their evidence is interesting. Mr. Prout says that the staircase was well-lit, and that deceased was not going extra fast, while the others say that he fell all of a heap, forwards, clutching *The Times Atlas* in so fierce a grip that it could afterwards hardly be prised from his fingers. What does that suggest to you?"

"Only that the death was instantaneous, which it would be if one broke one's neck."

"I know. But look here! You are going downstairs and your foot slips. What happens? Do you crumple forwards and dive down head first? Or do you sit down suddenly on your tail and do the rest of the journey that way?"

"It depends. If it was actually a slip, I should probably come down on my tail. But if I tripped, I should very likely dive forwards. You can't tell, without knowing just how it happened."

"All right. You always have an answer. Well now–do you clutch what you're carrying with a deathly grip–or do you chuck it, and try to save yourself by grabbing hold of the banisters?"

Mr. Parker paused. "I should probably grab," he said, slowly, "unless I was carrying a tray full of crockery, or anything. And even then . . . I don't know. Perhaps it's an instinct to hold on to what one's got. But equally it's an instinct to try and save one's self. I don't know. All this arguing about what you and I would do and what the reasonable man would do is very unsatisfactory."

Wimsey groaned. "Put it this way, doubting Thomas. If the death-grip was due to instantaneous rigor, he must have been dead so quickly that he couldn't think of saving himself. Now, there are two possible causes of death–the broken neck, which he must have got when he pitched on his head at the bottom, and the crack on the temple, which is attributed to his hitting his skull on one of the knobs on the banisters. Now, falling down a staircase isn't like falling off a roof–you do it in installments, and have time to think about it. If he killed himself by hitting the banisters, he must have fallen first and hit himself afterwards. The same thing applies, with still more force, to his breaking his neck. Why, when he felt himself going, didn't he drop everything and break his fall?"

"I know what you want me to say," said Parker. "That he was sandbagged first and dead before he fell. But I don't see it. I say he could have caught his toe in something and tripped forwards and struck his head straight away and died of that. There's nothing impossible about it."

"Then I'll try again. How's this? That same evening, Mrs. Crump, the head charwoman, picked up this onyx scarab in the passage, just beneath the iron staircase. It is, as you see, rounded and smooth and heavy for its size, which is much about that of the iron knobs on the staircase. It has, as you also see, a slight chip on one side. It belonged to the dead man, who was accustomed to carry it in his waistcoat pocket or keep it sitting on the desk beside him while he worked. What about it?"

"I should say it fell from his pocket when he fell."

"And the chip?"

"If it wasn't there before–"

"It wasn't; his sister says she's sure it wasn't."

"Then it got chipped in falling."

"You think that?"

"I do."

"I think you were meant to think that. To continue: some few days earlier, Mrs. Crump found a smooth pebble of much the same size as the scarab lying in the same passage at the foot of the same iron staircase."

"Did she?" said Parker. He uncurled himself from the window-seat and made for the decanters. "What does she say about it?"

"Says that you'd scarcely believe the queer odds and ends she finds when she's cleaning out the office. Attributes the stone to Mr. Atkins, he having taken his seaside holiday early on account of ill-health."

"Well," said Parker, releasing the lever of the soda-siphon, "and why not?"

"Why not, indeed? This other pebble, which I here produce, was found by me on the roof of the lavatory. I had to shin down a pipe to get it, and ruined a pair of flannel bags."

"Oh, yeah?"

"Okay, captain. That's where I found it. I also found a place where the paint had been chipped off the skylight."

"What skylight?"

"The skylight that is directly over the iron staircase. It's one of those pointed things, like a young greenhouse, and it has windows that open all round–you know the kind I mean–which are kept open in hot weather. It was hot weather when young Dean departed this life."

"The idea being that somebody heaved a stone at him through the skylight?"

"You said it, chief. Or, to be exact, not *a* stone, but *the* stone. Meaning the scarab."

"And how about the other stones?"

"Practice shots. I've ascertained that the office is always practically empty during the lunch-hour. Nobody much ever goes on the roof, except the office-boys for their P.J.'s at 8.30 ack emma."

"People who live in glass skylights shouldn't throw stones. Do you mean to suggest that by chucking a small stone like this at a fellow, you're going to crack his skull open and break his neck for him?"

"Not if you just throw it, of course. But how about a sling or a catapult?"

"Oh, in that case, you've only got to ask the people in the neighbouring offices if they've seen anybody enjoying a spot of David and Goliath exercise on Pym's roof, and you've got him."

"It's not as simple as that. The roof 's quite a good bit higher than the roofs of the surrounding buildings, and it has a solid stone parapet all round about three feet high–to give an air of still greater magnificence, I suppose. To sling a stone through on to the iron staircase you'd have to kneel down in a special position between that skylight and the next, and you can't be seen from anywhere–unless somebody happened to be *on* the staircase looking up–which nobody obviously was, except Victor Dean, poor lad. It's safe as houses."

"Very well, then. Find out if any member of the staff has frequently stayed in at lunch-time."

Wimsey shook his head.

"No bon. The staff clock in every morning, but there are no special tabs kept on them at 1 o'clock. The reception clerk goes out to his lunch, and one of the elder boys takes his place at the desk, just in case any message or parcel comes in, but he's not there necessarily every moment of the time. Then there's the lad who hops round with Jeyes' Fluid in a squirt, but he doesn't go on to the roof. There's nothing to prevent anybody from going up, say at halfpast twelve, and staying there till he's done his bit of work and then simply walking out down the staircase. The liftman, or his locum tenens, would be on duty, but you've only to keep on the blind side of the lift as you pass and he couldn't possibly see you. Besides, the lift might quite well have gone down to the basement. All the bloke would have to do would just be to bide his time and walk out. There's nothing in it. Similarly, on the day of the death. He goes through towards the lavatory, which is reached from the stairs. When the coast is clear, he ascends to the roof. He lurks there, till he sees his victim start down the iron staircase, which everybody does, fifty times a day. He whangs off his bolt and departs. Everybody is picking up the body and exclaiming over it, when in walks our friend, innocently, from the lav. It's as simple as pie."

"Wouldn't it be noticed, if he was out of his own room all that time?"

"My dear old man, if you knew Pym's! Everybody is always out of his room. If he isn't chatting with the copy-department, or fooling round the typists, he's in the studio, clamouring for a lay-out, or in the printing, complaining about a folder, or in the press-department, inquiring about an appropriation, or in the vouchers, demanding back numbers of something, or if he isn't in any of those places, he's somewhere else–slipping out for surreptitious coffee or haircuts. The word alibi has no meaning in a place like Pym's."

"Youre going to have a lovely time with it all, I can see that," said Parker. "But what sort of irregularity could possibly be going on in a place like that, which would lead to murder?"

"Now we're coming to it. Young Dean used to tag round with the de Momerie crowd–"

Parker whistled.

"Sinning above his station in life?"

"Very much so. But you know Dian de Momerie. She gets more kick out of corrupting the bourgeois–she enjoys the wrestle with their little consciences. She's a bad lot, that girl. I took her home last night, so I ought to know."

"Peter!" said Lady Mary. "Quite apart from your morals, which alarm me, how did you get into that gang? I should have thought they'd as soon have taken up with Charles, here, or the Chief Commissioner."

"Oh, I went incog. A comedy of masks. And you needn't worry about my morals. The young woman became incapably drunk on the way home, so I pushed her inside her dinky little maisonette in Garlic Mews and tucked her up on a divan in the sitting-room to astonish her maid in the morning. Though she's probably past being astonished. But the point is that I found out a good bit about Victor Dean."

"Just a moment," interrupted Parker, "did he dope?"

"Apparently not, though I'll swear it wasn't Dian's fault if he didn't. According to his sister, he was too strong-minded. Possibly he tried it once and felt so rotten that he didn't try it again. . . . Yes–I know what you're thinking. If he was dopey, he might have fallen downstairs on his own account. But I don't think that'll work. These things have a way of coming out at post-mortems. The question was raised . . . no; it wasn't that."

"Did Dian have any opinion on the subject?"

"She said he wasn't a sport. All the same, she seems to have kept him in tow from about the end of November to the end of April—nearly six months, and that's a long time for Dian. I wonder what the attraction was. I suppose the whelp must have had something engaging about him."

"Is that the sister's story?"

"Yes; but she says that Victor 'had great ambitions.' I don't quite know what she thinks he meant by that."

"I suppose she realized that Dian was his mistress. Or wasn't she?"

"Must have been. But I rather gather his sister thought he was contemplating matrimony."

Parker laughed.

"After all," said Lady Mary, "he probably didn't tell his sister everything."

"Damned little, I should imagine. She was quite honestly upset by last night's show. Apparently the party Dean took her to wasn't quite so hot. Why did he take her? That's another problem. He said he wanted her to meet Dian, and no doubt the kid imagined she was being introduced to a future-in-law. But Dean—you'd think he'd want to keep his sister out of it. He couldn't, surely, really have wanted to corrupt her, as Willis said."

"Who is Willis?"

"Willis is a young man who foams at the mouth if you mention Victor Dean, who was once Victor Dean's dearest friend, who is in love with Victor Dean's sister, is furiously jealous of me, thinks I'm tarred with the same brush as Victor Dean, and dogs my footsteps with the incompetent zeal of fifty Watsons. He writes copy about face-cream and corsets, is the son of a provincial draper, was educated at a grammar school and wears, I deeply regret to say, a double-breasted waistcoast. That is the most sinister thing about him—except that he admits to having been in the lavatory when Victor Dean fell downstairs, and the lavatory, as I said before, is the next step to the roof."

"Who else was in the lavatory?"

"I haven't asked him yet. How can I? It's horribly hampering to one's detective work when one isn't supposed to be detecting, because one daren't ask any questions, much. But if whoever it was knew I was detecting, then whatsoever questions I asked, I shouldn't get any answers. It wouldn't matter if only I had the foggiest notion whom or what I was detecting, but looking among about a hundred people for the perpetrator of an unidentified crime is rather difficult."

"I thought you were looking for a murderer."

"So I am—but I don't think I shall ever get the murderer till I know why the murder was done. Besides, what Pym engaged me to do was to look for the irregularity in the office. Of course, murder is an irregularity, but it's not the one I'm commissioned to hunt for. And the only person I can fix a motive for the murder on to is Willis—and it's not the sort of motive I'm looking for."

"What was Willis's row with Dean?"

"Damn silliest thing in the world. Willis used to go home with Dean at week-ends. Dean lived in a flat with his sister, by the way—no parents or anything. Willis fell in love with sister. Sister wasn't sure about him. Dean took sister to one of Dian's hot parties. Willis found out. Willis, being a boob, talked to sister like a Dutch uncle. Sister called Willis a disgusting, stuck-up, idiotic, officious prig. Willis rebuked Dean. Dean told Willis to go to hell. Loud row. Sister joined in. Dean family united in telling Willis to go and bury himself. Willis told Dean that if he (Dean) persisted in corrupting his

(Dean's) sister he (Willis) would shoot him like a dog. His very words, or so I am told."

"Willis," said Mary, "appears to think in clichés."

"Of course he does—that's why he writes such good corset-copy. Anyhow, there it was. Dean and Willis at daggers drawn for three months. Then Dean fell downstairs. Now Willis has started on me. I told off Pamela Dean to take him home last night, but I don't know what came of it. I've explained to her that those hot-stuff parties are genuinely dangerous, and that Willis has some method in his madness, though a prize juggins as regards tact and knowledge of the sex. It was frightfully comic to see old Willis sneaking in after us in a sort of Ku Klux Klan outfit—incredibly stealthy, and wearing the same shoes he wears in the office and a seal-ring on his little finger that one could identify from here to the Monument."

"Poor lad! I suppose it wasn't Willis who tipped friend Dean down the staircase?"

"I don't think so, Polly—but you never know. He's such a melodramatic ass. He might consider it a splendid sin. But I don't think he'd have had the brains to work out the details. And if he had done it, I fancy he'd have gone straight round to the police-station, smitten the double-breasted waistcoat a resounding blow and proclaimed 'I did it, in the cause of purity.' But against that, there's the undoubted fact that Dean's connection with Dian and Co. definitely came to an end in April—so why should he wait till the end of May to strike the blow? The row with Dean took place in March."

"Possibly, Peter, the sister has been leading you up the garden. The connection may not have stopped when she said it did. She may have kept it up on her own. She may even be a drug-taker or something herself. You never know."

"No; but generally one can make a shrewd guess. No; I don't think there's anything like that wrong with Pamela Dean. I'll swear her disgust last night was genuine. It was pretty foul, I must say. By the way, Charles, where the devil do these people get their stuff from? There was enough dope floating about that house to poison a city."

"If I knew that," said Mr. Parker, sourly, "I should be on velvet. All I can tell you is, that it's coming in by the boat-load from somewhere or other, and is being distributed broadcast from somewhere or other. The question is, where? Of course, we could lay hands tomorrow on half a hundred of the small distributors, but where would be the good of that? They don't know themselves where it comes from, or who handles it. They all tell the same tale. It's handed to them in the street by men they've never seen before and couldn't identify again. Or it's put in their pockets in omnibuses. It isn't always that they won't tell; they honestly don't know. And if you did catch the man immediately above them in the scale, he would know nothing either. It's heartbreaking. Somebody must be making millions out of it."

"Yes. Well, to go back to Victor Dean. Here's another problem. He was pulling down six pounds a week at Pym's. How does one manage to run with the de Momerie crowd on £300 a year? Even if he wasn't much of a sport, it couldn't possibly be done for nothing."

"Probably he lived on Dian."

"Possibly he did, the little tick. On the other hand, I've got an idea. Suppose he really did think he had a chance of marrying into the aristocracy—or what he imagines to be the aristocracy. After all, Dian is a de Momerie, though her people have shown her the door, and you can't blame them. Put it that he was spending far more than he could afford in trying to keep up the running. Put it that it took longer than he thought and that he had got heavily dipped. And then see what that half-finished letter to Pym looks like in the light of that theory."

"Well," began Parker.

"Oh, do step on the gas!" broke in Mary. "How you two darlings do love going round and round a subject, don't you? Blackmail, of course. It's perfectly obvious. I've seen it coming for the last hour. This Dean creature is looking round for a spot of extra income and he discovers somebody at Pym's doing something he shouldn't—the head-cashier cooking the accounts, or the office-boy pilfering from the petty cash, or something. So he says, 'If you don't square me, I'll tell Pym,' and starts to write a letter. Probably, you know, he never meant that letter to get to Mr. Pym, at all; it was just a threat. The other man stops him for the moment by paying up something on account. Then he thinks: 'This is hopeless, I'd better slug the little beast.' So he slugs him. And there you are."

"Just as simple as that," said Wimsey.

"Of course it's simple, only men love to make mysteries."

"And women love to jump to conclusions."

"Never mind the generalizations," said Parker, "they always lead to bad reasoning. Where do I come into all this?"

"You give me your advice, and stand by ready to rally round with your myrmidons in case there's any rough-housing. By the way, I can give you the address of that house we went to last night. Dope and gambling to be had for the asking, to say nothing of nameless orgies."

He mentioned the address and the Chief-Inspector made a note of it. "Though we can't do much," he admitted. "It's a private house, belonging to a Major Milligan. We've had our eye on it for some time. And even if we could get in on it, it probably wouldn't help us to what we want. I don't suppose there's a soul in that gang who knows where the dope comes from. Still, it's something to have definite evidence that that's where it goes. By the way, we got the goods on that couple you helped us to arrest the other night. They'll probably get seven years."

"Good. I was pretty nearly had that time, though. Two of Pym's typists were fooling round and recognized me. I gave them a fishy stare and explained next morning that I had a cousin who closely resembled me. That notorious fellow Wimsey, of course. It's a mistake to be too well known."

"If the de Momerie crowd get wise to you, you'll find yourself in Queer Street," said Parker. "How did you get so pally with Dian?"

"Dived off a fountain into a fish-pond. It pays to advertise. She thinks I'm the world's eighth wonder. Absolutely the lobster's dress-shirt."

"Well, don't kill yourself," said Mary, gently. "We rather like you, and small Peter couldn't spare his best uncle."

"It will do you no end of good," remarked his brother-in-law, callously, "to have a really difficult case for once. When you've struggled for a bit with a death that might have been caused by anybody for any imaginable motive, you may be less sniffy and superior about the stray murders all over the country that the police so notoriously fail to avenge. I hope it will be a lesson to you. Have another spot?"

"Thanks; I'll try to profit by it. In the meantime, I'll go on gulling the public and being Mr. Bredon, to be heard of at your address. And let me know of any developments with the Momerie-Milligan lot."

"I will. Should you care to make one in our next dope-raid?"

"Sure thing. When do you expect it?"

"We've had information about cocaine-smuggling on the Essex coast. Worst thing the Government ever did was to abolish the coast-guard service. It doubles our trouble, especially with all these privately-owned motor-boats about. If you're out for an evening's fun any time, you could come along–and you might bring that car of yours. It's faster than anything we've got."

"I see. Two for yourselves and one for me. Right you are. I'm on. Send me a line any time. I cease work at 5:30."

In the meantime, three hearts were being wrung on Mr. Death Bredon's account.

Miss Pamela Dean was washing a pair of silk stockings in her solitary flat.

"Last night was rather marvellous. . . . I suppose I oughtn't to have enjoyed it, with poor old Victor only just buried, the darling . . . but, of course, I really went for Victor's sake . . . I wonder if that detective man will find out anything about it . . . he didn't say much, but I believe he thinks there was something funny about Victor being killed like that . . . anyhow, Victor suspected there was something wrong, and he'd *want* me to do everything I could to ferret it out. . . . I didn't know private detectives were like that. . . . I thought they were nasty, furtive little men . . . vulgar . . . I like his voice . . . and his hands . . . oh, dear! there's a hole . . . I'll have to catch it together before it runs up the instep . . . and beautiful manners, only I'm afraid he was cross with me for coming to Pym's . . . he must be fearfully athletic to climb up that fountain . . . he swims like a fish . . . my new bathing-dress . . . sun-bathing . . . thank goodness I've got decent legs . . . I'll really have to get some more stockings, these won't go on much longer . . . I wish I didn't look so washed-out in black. . . . Poor Victor! . . . I wonder what I can possibly do with Alec Willis . . . if only he wasn't such a prig. . . . I don't mind Mr. Bredon . . . he's quite right about that crowd being no good, but then he really knows what he's talking about, and it isn't just prejudice. . . . Why will Alec be so jealous and tiresome? . . . And looking so silly in that black thing . . . following people about. . . . Incompetent–I do like people to be competent. . . . Mr. Bredon looks terribly competent . . . no, he doesn't exactly look it, but he is . . . he looks as though he never did anything but go to dinner-parties. . . . I suppose high-class detectives have to look like that. . . . Alec would make a rotten detective. . . . I don't like ill-tempered men . . . I wonder what happened when Mr. Bredon went off with Dian de Momerie . . . she is beautiful . . . damn her, she's lovely . . . she does drink an awful lot . . . they say it makes you look old before your time . . . you get coarse . . . my complexion's all right, but I'm not the fashionable type . . . Dian de Momerie is perfectly crazy about people who do mad things . . . I don't like aluminium blondes . . . I wonder if I could get an aluminium bleach. . . ."

Alec Willis, hammering a rather hard pillow into a more comfortable shape in his boarding-house bedroom, sought slumber in vain:

"Gosh! what a head I had this morning . . . that damned, sleek brute! . . . there's something up between Pamela and him . . . helping her with some business of Victor's my foot! . . . He's out to make trouble . . . and going off with that white-headed bitch . . . it's a damned insult . . . of course Pamela would lick his boots . . . women . . . put up with anything . . . wish I hadn't had all those drinks . . . damn this bed! damn this foul place . . . I'll have to chuck Pym's . . . it isn't safe. . . . Murder? . . . anybody interfering with Pamela . . . Pamela. . . . She wouldn't let me kiss her . . . that swine

Bredon . . . down the iron staircase . . . get my hands on his throat. . . . What a hope! damned posturing acrobat . . . Pamela . . . I'd like to show her . . . money, money, money . . . if I wasn't so damned hard up . . . Dean was a little squirt anyway . . . I only told her the truth . . . blast all women! . . . They like rotters . . . I haven't paid for that last suit . . . oh, hell! I wish I hadn't had those drinks . . . I forgot to get any bicarbonate . . . I haven't paid for those boots . . . all those naked women in the swimming-pool . . . black and silver . . . he spotted me, damn his eyes! . . . 'Hullo, Willis!' this morning, as cool as a fish . . . dives like a fish . . . fish don't dive . . . fish don't sleep . . . or do they? . . . I can't sleep . . . 'Macbeth hath murdered sleep.' . . . Murder . . . down the iron staircase . . . get my hands on his throat . . . oh, damn! damn! damn! . . . "

Dian de Momerie was dancing:

"My God! I'm bored. . . . Get off my feet, you clumsy cow. . . . Money, tons of money . . . but I'm bored. . . . Can't we do something else? . . . I'm sick of that tune . . . I'm sick of everything . . . he's working up to get all mushy . . . suppose I'd better go through with it . . . I was sozzled last night . . . wonder where the Harlequin man went to . . . wonder who he was . . . that little idiot Pamela Dean . . . these women . . . I'll have to make up to her, I suppose, if I'm ever to get his address . . . I got him away from her, any old how . . . wish I hadn't been so squiffy . . . I can't remember . . . climbing up the fountain . . . black and silver . . . he's got a lovely body . . . I think he could give me a thrill . . . my God! how bored I am . . . he's exciting . . . rather mysterious . . . I'll have to write to Pamela Dean . . . silly little fool . . . expect she hates me . . . rather a pity I chucked little Victor . . . fell downstairs and broke his silly neck . . . damn good riddance . . . ring her up . . . she's not on the 'phone . . . so suburban not to be on the 'phone . . . if this tune goes on, I shall scream . . . Milligan's drinks are rotten . . . why does one go there? . . . Must do something . . . Harlequin . . . don't even know his name. . . . Weedon . . . Leader . . . something or other . . . oh, hell! perhaps Milligan knows . . . I can't stand this any longer . . . black and silver . . . thank God! that's over!"

All over London the lights flickered in and out, calling on the public to save its body and purse: SOPO SAVES SCRUBBING—NUTRAX FOR NERVES—CRUNCHLETS ARE CRISPER—EAT PIPER PARRITCH—DRINK POMPAYNE—ONE WHOOSH AND IT'S CLEAN—OH, BOY! IT'S TOMBOY TOFFEE—NOURISH NERVES WITH NUTRAX—FARLEY'S FOOTWEAR TAKES YOU FURTHER—IT ISN'T DEAR, IT'S DARLING—DARLING'S FOR HOUSEHOLD APPLIANCES—MAKE ALL SAFE WITH SANFECT—WHIFFLETS FASCINATE. The presses, thundering and growling, ground out the same appeals by the million: ASK YOUR GROCER—ASK YOUR DOCTOR—ASK THE MAN WHO'S TRIED IT—MOTHER'S! GIVE IT TO YOUR CHILDREN—HOUSEWIVES! SAVE MONEY—HUSBANDS! INSURE YOUR LIVES—WOMEN! DO YOU REALIZE?—DON'T SAY SOAP, SAY SOPO! Whatever you're doing, stop it and do something else! Whatever you're buying, pause and buy something different! Be hectored into health and prosperity! Never let up! Never go to sleep! Never be satisfied. If once you are satisfied, all our wheels will run down. Keep going—and if you can't, Try Nutrax for Nerves!

Lord Peter Wimsey went home and slept.

# 6

# SINGULAR SPOTLESSNESS OF A LETHAL WEAPON

"YOU KNOW," said Miss Rossiter to Mr. Smayle, "our newest copy-writer is perfectly potty."

"Potty?" Mr. Smayle, showing all his teeth in an engaging smile, "you don't say so, Miss Rossiter? How, potty?"

"Well, loopy," explained Miss Rossiter. "Goofy. Blah. He's always up on the roof, playing with a catapult. I don't know *what* Mr. Hankin would say if he knew."

"With a catapult?" Mr. Smayle looked pained. "That doesn't seem quite the thing. But we in other spheres, Miss Rossiter, always envy, if I may say so, the happy youthful spirit of the copy-department. Due, no doubt," added Mr. Smayle, "to the charming influence of the ladies. Allow me to get you another cup of tea."

"Thanks awfully, I wish you would." The monthly tea was in full swing, and the Little Conference Room was exceedingly crowded and stuffy. Mr. Smayle edged away gallantly in pursuit of tea, and against the long table, presided over by Mrs. Johnson (the indefatigable lady who ruled the Dispatching, the office-boys and the first-aid cupboard) found himself jostled by Mr. Harris of the Outdoor Publicity.

"Pardon, old fellow," said Mr. Smayle.

"Granted," said Mr. Harris, "fascinating young fellows like you are privileged to carry all before them. Ha, ha, *ha!* I saw you doing the polite to Miss Rossiter–getting on like a house afire, eh?"

Mr. Smayle smirked deprecatingly.

"Wouldn't you like three guesses at our conversation?" he suggested. "One milk and no sugar and one milk and sugar, Mrs. J., please."

"Three's two too many," replied Mr. Harris. "I can tell you. You were talking about Miss Rossiter and Mr. Smayle, hey? Finest subjects of conversation in the world–to Mr. Smayle and Miss Rossiter, hey?"

"Well, you're wrong," said Mr. Smayle, triumphantly. "We were discussing another member of this community. The new copy-writer, in fact. Miss Rossiter was saying he was potty."

"They're all potty in that department, if you ask me," said Mr. Harris, waggling his chins. "Children. Arrested development."

"It looks like it," agreed Mr. Smayle. "Cross-words I am not surprised at, for everybody does them, nor drawing nursery pictures, but playing with catapults on the roof is really childish. Though what with Miss Meteyard bringing her Yo-Yo to the office with her–"

"I'll tell you what it is, Smayle," pronounced Mr. Harris, taking his colleague by the lapel and prodding him with his forefinger, "it's all this University education. What does it do? It takes a boy, or a young woman for that matter, and keeps him in leading-strings in the playground when he ought to be ploughing his own furrow in the face of reality–Hullo, Mr. Bredon! Was that your toe? Beg pardon, I'm sure. This room's too small for these social gatherings. I hear you are accustomed to seek the wide, open spaces on the roof."

"Oh, yes. Fresh air and all that, you know. Exercise. Do you know, I've been taking pot-shots at the sparrows with a catapult. Frightfully good training for the eye and that sort of thing. Come up one day and we'll have a competition."

"Not for me, thanks," replied Mr. Harris. "Getting too old for that kind of thing. Though when I was a boy I remember putting a pebble through my old aunt's cucumber-frame. Lord! how she did scold, to be sure!"

Mr. Harris suddenly looked rather wistful.

"I haven't had a catapult in my hand for thirty years, I don't suppose," he added.

"Then it's time you took it up again." Mr. Bredon half pulled a tangle of stick and rubber from his side-pocket and pushed it back again, with a wink and a grimace at the back of Mr. Pym, who now came into view, talking condescendingly to a lately-joined junior. "Between you and me, Harris, don't you find this place a bit wearisome at times?"

"Wearisome?" put in Mr. Tallboy, extricating himself from the crowd at the table, and nearly upsetting Mr. Smayle's two cups of tea, now at length achieved, "wearisome? You people don't know the meaning of the word. Nobody but a lay-out man knows what a lay-out man's feelings is."

"You should frivol with us," said Mr. Bredon. "If the lay-out lays you out, rejuvenate your soul in Roof Revels with Copy-writers. I bagged a starling this morning."

"What do you mean, bagged a starling?"

"Father, I cannot tell a lie. I did it with my little catapult. But if it's found," added Mr. Bredon earnestly, "I expect they will lay the blame on the canteen cat."

"–apult," said Mr. Harris. He looked at Mr. Tallboy to see if this play upon words had been appreciated, and seeing that that gentleman looked more than ordinarily blank and unreceptive, he proceeded to rub it in.

"Like the old joke, eh? 'O take a pill! O take a pill! O take a pilgrim home!' "

"What do you say?" asked Mr. Tallboy, frowning in the effort to concentrate.

'O blame the cat, don't you see," persisted Mr. Harris, "O blame the cat! O blame the catapult! Got me?"

"Ha, ha! very good!" said Mr. Tallboy.

"There was another," Mr. Harris went on, "O for a man! O for a–"

"Are you a good hand with a catapult, Tallboy?" inquired Mr. Bredon, rather hastily, as though he feared something might explode unless he caused a diversion.

"I haven't the eye for it." Mr. Tallboy shook his head, regretfully.

"Eye for what?" demanded Miss Rossiter.

"For a catapult."

"Oh, go on, Mr. Tallboy! And you such a tennis champion!"

"It's not quite the same thing," explained Mr. Tallboy.

"A games' eye is a games' eye, surely!"

"An eye's an eye for a' that," said Mr. Harris, rather vaguely. "Ever done anything at darts, Mr. Bredon?"

"I won the pewter pot three years running at the Cow and Pump," replied that gentleman, proudly. "With right of free warren–I mean free beer every Friday night for a twelvemonth. It came rather expensive, though, because every time I had my free pot of beer I had to stand about fifteen to the pals who came to see me drink it. So I withdrew myself from the competition and confined myself to giving exhibition displays."

"What's that about darts?"

Mr. Daniels had roamed into view. "Have you ever seen young Binns throw darts? Really quite remarkable."

"I haven't yet the pleasure of Mr. Binns' acquaintance," acknowledged Mr. Bredon. "I am ashamed to say that there are still members of this great staff unknown to me except by sight. Which, of all the merry faces I see flitting about the passages, is the youthful Mr. Binns?"

"You wouldn't have seen him, I don't expect," said Miss Rossiter. "He helps Mr. Spender in the Vouchers. Go along there one day and ask for a back number of some obscure periodical, and Mr. Binns will be sent to fetch it. He's a terrific dab at any sort of game."

"Except bridge," said Mr. Daniels, with a groan. "I drew him one night at a tournament–you remember, Miss Rossiter, the last Christmas party but two, and he went three no trumps on the ace of spades singleton, five hearts to the king, queen and–"

"What a memory you have, Mr. Daniels! You'll never forget or forgive those three no trumps. Poor Mr. Binns! He must miss Mr. Dean–they often lunched together."

Mr. Bredon seemed to pay more attention to this remark than it deserved, for he looked at Miss Rossiter as though he were about to ask her a question, but the conclave was broken up by the arrival of Mrs. Johnson, who, having served out the tea and handed the teapot over to the canteen cook felt that the time had come for her to join in the social side of the event. She was a large, personable widow, with a surprising quantity of auburn hair and a high complexion, and being built on those majestic lines was, inevitably and unrelentingly, arch.

"Well, well," she said, brightly. "And how is Mr. Daniels day?"

Mr. Daniels, having suffered this method of address for nearly twelve years, bore up tolerably well under it, and merely replied that he was quite well.

"This is the first time you have been at one of our monthly gatherings, Mr. Bredon," pursued the widow. "You're *supposed* to make the acquaintance of the rest of the staff, you know, but I see you haven't strayed far from your own department. Ah, well, when we're fat and forty"–here Mrs. Johnson giggled–"we can't expect the same attention from the gentlemen that these young things get."

"I assure you," said Mr. Bredon, "that nothing but an extreme awe of your authority has hitherto prevented me from forcing my impertinent attentions upon you. To tell you the truth, I've been misbehaving myself, and I expect you would give me a rap over the knuckles if you knew what I'd been doing."

"Not unless you've been upsetting my boys," returned Mrs. Johnson, "the young scamps! Take your eye off them a minute and they're up to their games. Would you believe it, that little wretch they call Ginger brought a Yo-Yo to the office with him and broke the window in the boys' room practising 'Round the World' in his lunch-hour. That'll come out of young Ginger's wages."

"I'll pay up when I break a window," promised Mr. Bredon handsomely. "I shall say: I did it with my little catapult–"

"Catapult!" cried Mrs. Johnson "I've had quite enough of catapults. There was that Ginger, not a month ago– Let me catch you at it once again, I said."

Mr. Bredon, with raised and twisted eyebrows, exhibited his toy.

"You've been at my desk, Mr. Bredon!"

"Indeed I have not; I shouldn't dare," protested the accused. "I'm far too pure-minded to burgle a lady's desk."

"I should hope so," said Mr. Daniels. "Mrs. Johnson keeps all her letters from her admirers in that desk."

"That's quite enough of that, Mr. Daniels. But I really did think for a moment that was Ginger's catapult, but I see now it's a bit different."

"Have you still got that poor child's catapult? You are a hard-hearted woman."

"I have to be."

"That's bad luck on all of us," said Mr. Bredon. "Look here, let the kid have it back. I like that boy. He says 'Morning, sir,' in a tone that fills me with a pleasant conceit of myself. And I like red hair. To oblige *me*, Mrs. Johnson, let the child have his lethal weapon."

"Well," said Mrs. Johnson, yielding, "I'll hand it over to *you*, Mr. Bredon, and if any more windows are broken it's you will be responsible. Come along to me when the teaparty's over. Now I must go and talk to that other new member."

She bustled away, no doubt to tell Mr. Newbolt, Mr. Hamperley, Mr. Sidebotham, Miss Griggs and Mr. Woodhurst about the childish proclivities of copy-writers. The tea party dwindled to its hour's end, when Mr. Pym, glancing at the Greenwich-controlled electric clock-face on the wall, bustled to the door, casting vague smiles at all and sundry as he went. The chosen twenty, released from durance, surged after him into the corridor. Mrs. Johnson found Mr. Bredon's slim form drooping deprecatingly beside her.

"Shall I come for the catapult before we both forget about it?"

"Certainly, if you like; you *are* in a hurry," said Mrs. Johnson.

"It promises me a few more minutes in your company," said Mr. Bredon.

"You *are* a flatterer," said Mrs. Johnson, not altogether ill-pleased. After all, she was not very much older than Mr. Bredon, and a plump widowhood has its appeal. She led the way upstairs to the Dispatching department, took a bunch of keys from her handbag and opened a drawer.

"You're careful with your keys, I see. Secrets in the drawer and all that, I suppose?"

"Stamp-money, that's all," said Mrs. Johnson, "and any odds and ends I have to confiscate. Not but what anybody *might* get at my keys if they wanted to, because I often leave my bag on the desk for a few moments. But we've got a very honest set of boys here."

She lifted out a sheet of blotting-paper and a cash-box and began to rummage at the back of the drawer. Mr. Bredon detained her by laying his left hand on hers.

"What a pretty ring you're wearing."

"Do you like it? It belonged to my mother. Garnets, you know. Old-fashioned, but quaint, don't you think?"

"A pretty ring, and it suits the hand," said Mr. Bredon, gallantly. He held the hand pensively in his. "Allow me." He slipped his right hand into the drawer and brought out the catapult. "This appears to be the engine of destruction—a good, strong one, from the look of it."

"Have you cut your finger, Mr. Bredon?"

"It's nothing; my penknife slipped and it's opened up again. But I think it has stopped bleeding."

Mr. Bredon unwound his handkerchief from his right hand, wrapped it carelessly round the catapult, and dropped both together into his pocket. Mrs. Johnson inspected the finger he held out to her.

"You'd better have a bit of sticking-plaster for that," she pronounced. "Wait a moment, and I'll get you some from the first-aid cupboard." She took up her keys and departed. Mr. Bredon, whistling thoughtfully to himself, looked round. On a bench at the end of the room sat four messenger-boys, waiting to be sent upon any errand that might present itself. Conspicuous among them was Ginger Joe, his red head bent over the pages of the latest *Sexton Blake*.

"Ginger!"

"Yessir."

The boy ran up and stood expectantly by the desk.

"When do you get off duty tonight?"

" 'Bout a quarter to six, sir, when I've taken the letters down and cleared up here."

"Come along then and find me in my room. I've got a small job for you. You need not say anything about it. Just a private matter."

"Yessir." Ginger grinned confidentially. A message to a young lady, his experience told him. Mr. Bredon waved him back to his bench as Mrs. Johnson's footsteps approached.

The sticking-plaster was fixed in its place.

"And now," said Mrs. Johnson, playfully, "you must run away, Mr. Bredon. I see Mr. Tallboy's got a little spot of trouble for me, and I've got fifty stereos to pack and dispatch."

"I want this got down to the printer urgently," said Mr. Tallboy, approaching with a large envelope.

"Cedric!" cried Mrs. Johnson.

A boy ran up. Another lad, arriving from the staircase, dumped a large tray full of stereo-blocks on the desk. The interlude was over. Mrs. Johnson addressed herself briskly to the important task of seeing that the right block went to the right newspaper, and that all were safely packed in corrugated cardboard and correctly stamped.

Punctually at a quarter to six, Ginger Joe presented himself at Mr. Bredon's door. The office was almost empty; the cleaners had begun their rounds, and the chink of pails, the slosh of soap and water and the whirr of the vacuum-cleaner resounded through the deserted corridors.

"Come in, Ginger; is this your catapult?"

"Yessir."

"It's a good one. Made it yourself?"

"Yessir."

"Good shot with it?"

"Pretty fair, sir."

"Like to have it back?"

"Yes, please, sir."

"Well, don't touch it for the moment. I want to see whether you're the sort of fellow to be trusted with a catapult."

Ginger grinned a little sheepishly.

"Why did Mrs. Johnson take it away from you?"

"We ain't supposed to carry them sort of things in our uniform pockets, sir. Mrs. Johnson caught me a-showin' it to the other fellows, sir, and con-stickated it."

"Confiscated."

"Confiscated it, sir."

"I see. Had you been shooting with it in the office, Ginger?"

"No, sir."

"H'm. You're the bright lad who's broken a window, aren't you?"

"Yessir. But that wasn't with a catapult. It was a Yo-Yo, sir."

"Quite so. You're sure you've never used a catapult in the office?"

"Oh, no, sir, never, sir."

"What made you bring this thing to the office at all?"

"Well, sir—" Ginger stood on one leg. "I'd been telling the other chaps about me shooting me Aunt Emily's tomcat, sir, and they wanted to see it, sir."

"You're a dangerous man, Ginger. Nothing is safe from you. Tom-cats and windows and maiden aunts—they're all your victims, aren't they?"

"Yessir." Understanding this to be in the nature of a jest, Joe sniggered happily.

"How long ago did this bereavement take place, Ginger?"

"Bereavement, sir? Did you mean Auntie's cat?"

"No, I meant, how long ago was your catapult confiscated?"

"Bit over a month ago, it would be, sir."

"About the middle of May?"

"That's right, sir."

"And you've never laid hands on it since?"

"No, sir."

"Have you any other catapult?"

"No, sir."

"Has any of the other boys got a catapult?"

"No, sir."

"Or a sling, or any other infernal machine for projecting stones?"

"No, sir; leastways, not here, sir. Tom Faggott has a pea-shooter at home, sir."

"I said stones, not peas. Did you ever shoot with this, or any other catapult, on the roof?"

"On the roof of the office, sir?"

"Yes."

"No, sir."

"Or anybody else that you know of?"

"No, sir."

"Are you absolutely sure?"

"Nobody that I know of, sir."

"Now, look here, son; I've got an idea that you're a straight sort of fellow, that mightn't like to split on a pal. You're quite sure there isn't anything at all about this catapult that you know and don't like to tell me? Because, if there is, I shall quite understand, and I'll explain to you exactly why it would be better that you should tell me."

Ginger's eyes opened very wide in bewilderment.

"Honest injun, sir," he said, with earnest sincerity, "I don't know nothing at all about no catapult, bar Mrs. Johnson taking that one and putting it away in her desk. Cross me heart and wish I may die, sir."

"All right. What was that book I saw you reading just now?"

Ginger, accustomed to the curious habit grown-up people have of interrogating their youngers and betters on any unrelated subjects that happen to strike a roving fancy, replied without hesitation or surprise:

"*The Clue of the Crimson Star*, sir. About Sexton Blake; he's a detective, you know, sir. It's a top-hole yarn."

"Like detective-stories, Ginger?"

"Oh, yes, sir. I reads a lot of them. I'm going to be a detective one day, sir. My eldest brother's in the police, sir."

"Is he? Splendid fellow. Well, the first thing a detective has to learn to do is to keep his mouth shut. You know that?"

"Yessir."

"If I show you something now, can you keep quiet about it?"

"Yessir."

"Very well. Here's a ten-bob note. Hop out to the nearest chemist and get me some grey powder and an insufflator."

"What sort of powder, sir?"

"Grey powder–mercury powder–the man will know. And an insufflator; it's a little rubber bulb with a nozzle to it."

"Yessir."

Ginger Joe hopped with speed.

"An ally," said Mr. Bredon to himself, "an ally–indispensable, I fear, and I fancy I've picked the right one."

Ginger came panting back in record time. He scented adventure. Mr. Bredon, in the meantime, had attached a discreet curtain of brown paper to the glass panel of his door. Mrs. Crump was not surprised. That proceeding was familiar to her. It usually meant that a gentleman was going out, and wished to change his trousers in a decent privacy.

"Now," said Mr. Bredon, shutting the door, "we will see whether your catapult can tell us anything about its adventures since it left your hands." He filled the insufflator with the grey powder and directed an experimental puff upon the edge of the desk. On blowing away the surplus powder, he thus disclosed a surprising collection of greasy finger-prints. Ginger was enthralled.

"Coo!" he said, reverently. "Are you going to test the catapult for prints, sir?"

"I am. It will be interesting if we find any, and still more interesting if we find none."

Ginger, goggle-eyed, watched the proceedings. The catapult appeared to have been well polished by use and presented an admirable surface for finger-prints, had there been any, but though they covered every half-inch of the thick Y-fork with powder, the result was a blank. Ginger looked disappointed.

"Ah!" said Bredon. "Now is it that it will not, or that it cannot speak? We will make that point clear. Catch hold of the thing, Ginger, as though you were whanging a shot off."

Ginger obeyed, clutching grimly with his greasy little paw.

"That ought to give 'em," said his new friend, "the whole of the palms of the fingers round the handle and the ball of the thumb in the fork. Now we'll try again."

The insufflator came once more into play, and this time a noble set of markings sprang into view.

"Ginger," said Mr. Bredon, "what do you, as a detective, deduce from this?"

"Mrs. Johnson must a-wiped it, sir."

"Do you think that's very likely, Ginger?"

"No, sir."

"Then go on deducing."

"Somebody else must a-wiped it, sir."

"And why should somebody else do that?"

Ginger knew where he was now.

"So that the police couldn't fix nothing on him, sir."

"The police, eh?"

"Well, sir, the police–or a detective–or somebody like as it might be yourself, sir."

"I can find no fault with that deduction, Ginger. Can you go further and say why this unknown catapult artist should have gone to all that trouble?"

"No, sir."

"Come, come."

"Well, sir, it ain't as though he stole it–and besides, it ain't worth nothing."

"No; but it looks as though somebody had borrowed it, if he didn't steal it. Who could do that?"

"I dunno, sir. Mrs. Johnson keeps that drawer locked."

"So she does. Do you think Mrs. Johnson has been having a little catapult practice on her own?"

"Oh, no, sir. Women ain't no good with catapults."

"How right you are. Well, now, suppose somebody had sneaked Mrs. Johnson's keys and taken the catapult and broken a window or something with it, and was afraid of being found out?"

"There ain't been nothing broke in this office, not between Mrs. Johnson pinching my catapult and me breaking the window with the Yo-Yo. And if one of the boys had took the catapult, I don't think they'd think about fingerprints, sir."

"You never know. He might have been playing burglars or something and just wiped his finger-prints away out of dramatic instinct, if you know what that is."

"Yessir," agreed Ginger, in a dissatisfied tone.

"Particularly if he'd done some really bad damage with it. Or of course, it might be more than dramatic instinct. Do you realize, Ginger, that a thing like this might easily kill anybody, if it happened to catch him in just the right spot?"

"Kill anybody? Would it, sir?"

"I wouldn't like to try the experiment. Was your aunt's tom-cat killed?"

"Yessir."

"That's nine lives at a blow, Ginger, and a man has only one. You're quite sure, sonnie, that nobody you know of was larking about with this catapult the day Mr. Dean fell downstairs?"

Ginger flushed and turned pale; but apparently only with excitement. His small voice was hoarse as he answered:

"No, sir. Wish I may die, sir, I never see nothing of that. You don't think somebody catapulted Mr. Dean, sir?"

"Detectives never 'think' anything," replied Mr. Bredon, reprovingly. "They collect facts and make deductions–God forgive me!" The last three words were a whispered lip-service to truth. "Can you remember who might have happened to be standing round or passing by when Mrs. Johnson took that catapult from you and put it in her desk?"

Ginger considered.

"I couldn't say right off, sir. I was just coming upstairs to the Dispatching when she spotted it. She was behind me, you see, sir, and it made me pocket stick out, like. A-jawing me, she was, all up the stairs, and took it off of me at the top and sent me down again with the basket to Mr. 'Ornby. I never see her put it away. But some of the other boys may have. 'Course, I knowed it was there, because all the things as is confisticated–"

"Confiscated."

"Yessir–confiscated, gets put in there. But I'll ask round, sir."

"Don't let them know why you're asking."

"No, sir. Would it do if I said I believed somebody had been borrowing of it and spiled the elastic for me?"

"That would do all right, provided–"

"Yessir. Provided I recollecks to spile the elastic."

Mr. Bredon, who had already jabbed a penknife into his own finger that afternoon in the sacred cause of verisimilitude, smiled lovingly upon Ginger Joe.

"You are the kind of man I am proud to do business with," he said. "Here's another thing. You remember when Mr. Dean was killed. Where were you at the time?"

"Sittin' on the bench in the Dispatching, sir. I got an alibi." He grinned.

"Find out for me, if you can, how many other people had alibis."

"Yessir."

"It's rather a job, I'm afraid."

"I'll do me best, sir. I'll make up somefin', don't you worry. It's easier for me to do it than it is for you, I see that, sir. I say, sir!"

"Yes?"

"Are you a Scotland Yard 'tec?"

"No, I'm not from Scotland Yard."

"Oh! Begging your pardon for asking, sir. But I thought, if you was, you might be able, excuse me, sir, to put in a word for my brother."

"I might be able to do that, all the same, Ginger."

"Thank you, sir."

"Thank *you,*" replied Mr. Bredon, with the courtesy which always distinguished him. "And mum's the word, remember."

"Wild 'orses," declared Ginger, finally and completely losing his grasp of the aitches with which a careful nation had endowed him at the expense of the tax-payer, "wild 'orses wouldn't get a word out o' me when I've give me word to 'old me tongue."

He ran off. Mrs. Crump, coming along the passage with a broom, was surprised to find him still hanging about the place. She challenged him, received an impudent answer, and went her way, shaking her head. A quarter of an hour later, Mr. Bredon emerged from his seclusion. As she had expected, he was in evening dress and looking, she thought, very much the gentleman. She obliged by working the lift for him. Mr. Bredon, the ever-polite, expanded and assumed his gibus during the descent, apparently for the express purpose of taking it off to her when he emerged.

In a taxi rolling south-west, Mr. Bredon removed his spectacles, combed out his side-parting, stuck a monocle in his eye, and by the time he reached Piccadilly Circus was again Lord Peter Wimsey. With a vacant wonder he gazed upon the twinkling sky-signs, as though, ignorant astronomer, he knew nothing of the creative hands that had set these lesser lights to rule the night.

# 7

# ALARMING EXPERIENCE OF A CHIEF-INSPECTOR

On that same night, or rather in the early hours of the following morning, a very disagreeable adventure befell Chief-Inspector Parker. He was the more annoyed by it, in that he had done absolutely nothing to deserve it.

He had had a long day at the Yard—no thrills, no interesting disclosures, no exciting visitors, not so much as a dis-diamonded rajah or a sinister Chinaman—only the reading and summarizing of twenty-one reports of interviews with police narks, five hundred and thirteen letters from the public in response to a broadcast S O S about a wanted man, and a score or so of anonymous letters, all probably written by lunatics. In addition, he had had to wait for a telephone call from an inspector who had gone down to Essex to investigate some curious movements of motor-boats in and about the estuary of the Blackwater. The message, if favourable, might call for immediate action, on which account Mr. Parker thought it better to wait for it in his office than go home to bed, with the prospect of being hawked out again at 1 o'clock in the morning. There, then, he sat, as good as gold, collating information and drawing up a schedule of procedure for the following day's activities, when the telephone duly rang. He glanced at the clock, and saw that it pointed to 1.10. The message was brief and unsatisfactory. There was nothing to report; the suspected boat had not arrived with that tide; no action was therefore called for; Chief-Inspector Parker could go home and get what sleep he could out of the small hours.

Mr. Parker accepted disappointment as philosophically as the gentleman in Browning's poem, who went to the trouble and expense of taking music lessons just in case his lady-love might demand a song with lute *obbligato*. Waste of time, as it turned out, but—suppose it hadn't been. It was all in the day's work. Putting his papers tidily away and locking his desk, the Chief-Inspector left the building, walked down to the Embankment, took a belated tram through the subway to Theobald's Road and thence walked soberly to Great Ormond Street.

He opened the front door with his latch-key and stepped inside. It was the same house in which he had long occupied a modest bachelor flat, but on his marriage he had taken, in addition, the flat above his own, and thus possessed what was, in effect, a seven-roomed maisonette, although, on account of a fiddling L.C.C. regulation about access to the roof for the first-floor tenants in case of fire, he was not permitted to shut his two floors completely off by means of a door across the staircase.

The front hall, common to all the tenants, was in darkness when he got in. He switched on the light and hunted in the little glass-fronted box labelled "Flat 3—Parker" for letters. He found a bill and a circular and deduced, quite correctly, that his wife had been at home all evening and too tired or too slack to go down to fetch the 9:30 post. He was turning to go upstairs, when he remembered that there might be a letter for Wimsey, under the name of Bredon, in the box belonging to Flat 4. As a rule, of course, this box was not used, but when Wimsey had begun his impersonation at Pym's, his brother-in-law had provided him with a key to fit it and had embellished the box itself with a written label "Bredon," for the better information of the postman.

There was one letter in the "Bredon" box—the kind that novelists used to call a "dainty missive"; that is to say, the envelope was tinted mauve, had a gilt deckle-edge and was addressed in a flourishing feminine handwriting. Parker took it out, intending to enclose it with a note which he was sending to Wimsey in the morning, pushed it into his pocket and went on up to the first floor. Here he switched out the hall-light which, like the staircase lights, was fitted with two-way wiring, and proceeded to the second floor, containing Flat 3, which comprised his living-room, dining-room and kitchen. Here he hesitated, but, rather unfortunately for himself, decided that he did not really want soup or sandwiches. He switched off the lower light behind him and pressed down the switch that should have supplied light to the top flight. Nothing happened. Parker growled but was not surprised. The staircase lights were the affair of the landlord, who had a penurious habit of putting in cheap bulbs and leaving them there till the filament broke. By this means he alienated his tenants' affections, besides wasting more in electricity than he saved in bulbs, but then he was that kind of man. Parker knew the stairs as well as he knew the landlord's habits; he went on up in the dark, not troubling to light a match.

Whether the little incident had, however, put his professional subconsciousness on the alert, or whether some faint stir of breath or movement gave him last-minute warning, he never afterwards knew. He had his key in his hand, and was about to insert it in the lock when he dodged suddenly and instinctively to the right, and in that very instant the blow fell, with murderous violence, on his left shoulder. He heard his collar-bone crack as he flung himself round to grapple with the villainous darkness, and even as he did so he found himself thinking: "If I hadn't dodged, my bowler would have broken the blow and saved my collar-bone." His right hand found a throat, but it was protected by a thick muffler and a turned-up collar. He struggled to get his fingers inside this obstacle, at the same time that, with his semi-disabled left arm, he warded off the second blow which he felt was about to descend upon him. He heard the other man panting and cursing. Then the resistance suddenly gave way, and, before he could loose his grip he was lurching forward, while a jerked knee smote him with brutal violence in the stomach, knocking the wind out of him. He staggered, and his opponent's fist crashed upon his jaw. In his last seconds of consciousness before his head struck the ground, he thought of the weapon in the other's hand and gave up hope.

Probably his being knocked out saved his life. The crash of his fall woke Lady Mary. For a stunned moment she lay, wondering. Then her mind rushed to the children, asleep in the next room. She turned on the light, calling out as she did so to ask whether they were all right. Receiving no answer, she sprang up, threw on a dressing-gown and ran into the nursery. All was peace. She stood puzzled, and asking herself whether she had dreamed the crash. Then she heard feet running down the staircase at headlong speed. She ran back into the bedroom, pulled out the revolver which always lay loaded in the dressing-table drawer and flung open the door which gave upon the landing. The light streaming from behind her showed her the crumpled body of her husband, and as she stared aghast at this unnerving sight, she heard the street-door slam heavily.

"What you ought to have done," said Mr. Parker, acidly, "was not to have bothered about me, but dashed to the window and tried to get a squint at the bloke as he went down the street."

Lady Mary smiled indulgently at this absurd remark, and turned to her brother.

"So that's all I can tell you about it, and he's uncommonly lucky to be alive, and ought to be jolly well thankful instead of grumbling."

"You'd grumble all right," said Parker, "with a bust collar-bone and a headache like nothing on earth and a feeling as though bulls of Bashan had been trampling on your tummy."

"It beats me," said Wimsey, "the way these policemen give way over a trifling accident. In the Sexton Blake book that my friend Ginger Joe has just lent me, the great detective, after being stunned with a piece of lead-piping and trussed up for six hours in ropes which cut his flesh nearly to the bone, is taken by boat on a stormy night to a remote house on the coast and flung down a flight of stone steps into a stone cellar. Here he contrives to release himself from his bonds after three hours' work on the edge of a broken wine-bottle, when the villain gets wise to his activities and floods the cellar with gas. He is most fortunately rescued at the fifty-ninth minute of the eleventh hour and, pausing only to swallow a few ham sandwiches and a cup of strong coffee, instantly joins in a prolonged pursuit of the murderers by aeroplane, during which he has to walk out along the wing and grapple with a fellow who has just landed on it from a rope and is proposing to chuck a hand-grenade into the cockpit. And here is my own brother-in-law–a man I have known for nearly twenty years–giving way to bad temper and bandages because some three-by-four crook has slugged him one on his own comfortable staircase."

Parker grinned ruefully.

"I'm trying to think who it could have been," he said. "It wasn't a burglar or anybody like that–it was a deliberate attempt at murder. The light-bulb had been put out of action beforehand and he had been hiding for hours dehind the coal-bunker. You can see the marks of his feet. Now, who in the name of goodness have I got it in for to that extent? It can't be Gentleman Jim or Dogsbody Dan, because that's not their line of country at all. If it had happened last week, it might well have been Knockout Wally–he uses a cosh–but we jailed him good and hard for that business down in Limehouse on Saturday night. There are one or two bright lads who have it in for me one way or another, but I can't exactly fit it on to any of them. All I know is, that whoever it was, he must have got in here before 11 p.m., when the housekeeper shuts the street door and puts out the hall light. Unless, of course, he had a latch-key, but that's not so likely. He wasn't obliging enough to leave anything behind to identify him, except a Woolworth pencil."

"Oh, he left a pencil, did he?"

"Yes–one of those pocket propelling things–not a wooden one–you needn't hope for a handy mould of his front teeth on it, or anything like that."

"Show, show!" pleaded Wimsey.

"All right; you can see it if you like. I've tried it for finger-prints, but I can't get much–only vague smudges, very much superimposed. I've had our finger-print wallah round to look at 'em, but he doesn't seem to have made anything of 'em. See if you can find the pencil, Mary dear, for your little brother. Oh, and by the way, Peter, there's a letter for you. I've only just remembered. In my left coat-pocket, Mary. I'd just taken it out of the Flat 4 box when all this happened."

Mary sped away, and returned in a few minutes with the pencil and the coat.

"I can't find any letter."

Parker took the coat and, with his available hand, searched all the pockets carefully.

"That's funny," he said. "I know it was there. One of those fancy long-shaped mauve envelopes with gilt edges, and a lady's fist, rather sprawly."

"Oh!" said Wimsey, "the letter's gone, has it?" His eyes glinted with excitement. "That's very remarkable. And what's more, Charles, this isn't a Woolworth pencil—it's one of Darling's."

"I meant Darling's—same thing. Anybody might carry one of them."

"Ah!" said Wimsey, "but this is where my expert knowledge comes in. Darling's don't sell these pencils—they give them away. Anybody buying more than a pound's worth of goods gets a pencil as a good-conduct prize. You observe that it carries an advertising slogan: IT ISN'T DEAR, IT'S DARLING. (One of Pym's best efforts, by the way.) The idea is that, every time you make a note on your shopping list, you are reminded of the superior economy of purchasing your household goods from Darling's. And a very remarkable firm it is, too," added his lordship, warming to the subject. "They've carried the unit system to the pitch of a fine art. You can sit on a Darling chair, built up in shilling and sixpenny sections and pegged with patent pegs at sixpence a hundred. If Uncle George breaks the leg, you buy a new leg and peg it in. If you buy more clothes than will go into your Darling chest of drawers, you unpeg the top, purchase a new drawer for half a crown, peg it on and replace the top. Everything done by numbers, and kindness. And, as I say, if you buy enough, they give you a pencil. If you mount up to five pounds' worth, they give you a fountain pen."

"That's very helpful," said Parker, sarcastically. "It ought to be easy to identify a criminal who has bought a pound's worth of goods at Darling's within the last six months or so."

"Wait a bit; I said I had expert knowledge. This pencil—a natty scarlet, as you observe, with gold lettering—didn't come from any of Darling's branches. It's not on the market yet. There are only three places it could have come from: one, from the pencil manufacturer's; two, from Darling's head office; three, from our place."

"Do you mean Pym's?"

"I do. This is the new pencil design, with an improved propelling mechanism. The old ones only propelled; this repels also, with a handy twist of the what-d'ye-call. Darling's obligingly presented us with half a gross of them to try out."

Mr. Parker sat up so suddenly that he jarred his shoulder and his head, and groaned dismally.

"I think it highly improbable," went on Lord Peter, lusciously, "that you have a deadly enemy at the pencil manufacturer's or at Darling's head office. It seems to me much more likely that the gentleman with the cosh, or knuckle-duster, or sand-bag, or lead-piping, in short, the blunt instrument, came from Pym's, guided by the address which, with your usual amiability, you kindly allowed me to give as mine. Observing my name neatly inscribed on the letter-box of Flat 4, he mounted confidently, armed with his cosh, knuckle—"

"Well, I'm dashed!" exclaimed Lady Mary, "do you mean to say that it's really you, you devil, who ought to be lying there mangled and bruised in the place of my afflicted husband?"

"I think so," said Wimsey, with satisfaction, "I certainly do think so. Particularly as the assailant seems to have walked off with my private correspondence. I know who–or to be grammatical, whom–that letter was from, by the way."

"Who?" demanded Parker, disregarding the grammatical nicety.

"Why, from Pamela Dean, to be sure. I recognize your description of the envelope."

"Pamela Dean? The victim's sister?"

"As you say."

"Willis's young woman?"

"Precisely."

"But how should he know about the letter?"

"I don't suppose he did. I rather fancy this is the result of a little bit of self-advertisement I put in yesterday afternoon at the office tea-party. I made it clear to all and sundry that I had been experimenting on the roof with a catapult."

"Did you? Who, exactly, were the all and sundry?"

"The twenty people taking tea and all the other people they mentioned it to."

"Rather a wide limit."

"M'm, yes. I thought I might get some reaction. What a pity it reacted on you and not on me."

"A very great pity," agreed Mr. Parker, with feeling.

"Still, it might have been worse. We've got three lines to go upon. The people who heard about the catapult. The people who knew, or inquired for, my address. And, of course, the bloke who's lost his pencil. But, I say–" Wimsey broke off with a shout of laughter–"what a shock it must have been for whoever it was when I turned up this morning without so much as a black eye! Why in the name of creation didn't you let me have all the details first thing this morning, so that I could have kept a look-out?"

"We were otherwise employed," said Lady Mary.

"Besides, we didn't think it had anything to do with you."

"You should have guessed. Wherever trouble turns up, there am I at the bottom of it. But I'll overlook it this time. You have been sufficiently punished, and no one shall say that a Wimsey could not be magnanimous. But this blighter–you didn't manage to mark him, Charles, did you?"

"Afraid not. I got a clutch on his beastly throat, but he was all muffled up."

"You did that badly, Charles. You should have socked him one. But, as I said before, I forgive you. I wonder if our friend will have another shot at me."

"Not at this address, I hope," said Mary.

"*I* hope not. I'd like to have him under my own eye next time. He must have been pretty smart to get that letter. Why in the world–ah! now I understand."

"What?"

"Why nobody fainted at the sight of me this morning. He must have had a torch with him. He knocks you down and turns on the torch to see if you're properly dead. The first thing he spots is the letter. He grabs that–why? Because–we'll come back to that. He grabs it and then looks at your classic features. He realizes that he's slugged the wrong man, and at that very moment he hears Mary making a hullabaloo. So he clears. That's perfectly plain now. But the letter? Would he have taken any letter that happened to be there, or did he know the writing? When was that letter delivered? Yes, of course, the 9:30 post. Suppose, when he came in to look for my flat, he saw the letter in the box and recognized whom it was from. That opens up a wide field of speculation, and possibly even offers us another motive."

"Peter," said Lady Mary, "I don't think you ought to sit here exciting Charles with all this speculation. It'll send his temperature up."

"So it will, by Jove! Well, look here, old boy, I'm really fearfully sorry you copped that packet that was meant for me. It's perfectly damnable luck and I'm dashed thankful it was no worse. I'll buzz off now, I've got to, anyhow. I've got a date. So-long."

Wimsey's first action after leaving the flat was to ring up Pamela Dean, whom he fortunately found at home. He explained that her letter had been lost in transmission, and asked what was in it.

"Only a note from Dian de Momerie. She wants to know who you are. You seem to have made a remarkable hit."

"We aim to please," said Peter. "What have you done about it?"

"Nothing. I didn't know what you would like me to do."

"You didn't give her my address?"

"No. That was what she was asking for. I didn't want to make another mistake, so I passed it all on to you."

"Quite right."

"Well?"

"Tell her—does she know that I'm at Pym's?"

"No, I was very careful to say absolutely nothing about you. Except your name. I did tell her that, but she seems to have forgotten it."

"Good. Listen, now. Tell bright Dian that I'm a most mysterious person. You never know where to find me yourself. Hint that I'm probably miles away—in Paris or Vienna, or anything that sounds fruity. You can convey the right impression, I know. Phillips Oppenheim, with a touch of Ethel M. Dell and Elinor Glyn."

"Oh, yes, I can do that."

"And you might say that she will probably see me some time when she least expects it. Suggest, if you don't mind being so vulgar, that I am a sort of yellow-dog dingo, very truly run after and hard to catch. Be stimulating. Be intriguing."

"I will. Am I at all jealous, by the way?"

"Yes, if you like. Give the impression that you're sort of putting her off. It's a hard chase and you're not keen on competitors."

"All right. That won't be difficult."

"What did you say?"

"Nothing. I said I could manage that all right."

"I know you'll do it beautifully. I rely on you very much."

"Thank you. How is the enquiry getting on?"

"So-so."

"Tell me all about it some time, won't you?"

"Rather! As soon as there's anything to report."

"Will you come to tea one Saturday or Sunday?"

"I should love to."

"I'll keep you to that."

"Oh, yes, rather! Well, goodnight."

"Goodnight—Yellow-Dog Dingo."

"Bung-ho!"

Wimsey put down the receiver. "I hope," he thought, "she isn't going to make an awkwardness. You cannot trust these young women. No fixity of purpose. Except, of course, when you particularly want them to be yielding."

He grinned with a wry mouth, and went out to keep his date with the one young woman who showed no signs of yielding to him, and what he said or did on that occasion is in no way related to this story.

Ginger Joe hoisted himself cautiously up in bed and looked round the room.

His elder brother—not the policeman, but sixteen-year-old Bert, the nosey one—was reassuringly asleep, curled up dog-fashion, and dreaming, no doubt, of motor-cycles. The faint light from the street lamp outlined the passive hump he made in the bedclothes, and threw a wan gleam across Ginger's narrow bedstead.

From beneath his pillow, Ginger drew out a penny exercise book and a stubby pencil. There was very little privacy in Ginger's life, and opportunities had to be seized when they occurred. He licked the pencil, opened the book, and headed a page in a large, round hand: "Report."

There he paused. It was desirable to do this thing really creditably, and the exercises in English composition they had given him at school did not seem to help. "My Favourite Book," "What I Should Like to Do when I Grow Up," "What I Saw at the Zoo"—very good subjects but not of great assistance to a rising young detective. He had once been privileged to take a glimpse at Wally's note-book (Wally being the policeman), and remembered that the items had all begun somewhat in this fashion: "At 8:30 p.m., as I was proceeding along Wellington Street"—a good opening, but not applicable to the present case. The style of *Sexton Blake*, also, though vigorous, was more suited for the narration of stirring adventures than for the compilation of a catalogue of names and facts. And on the top of all this, there was the awkward question of spelling—always a stumbling-block. Ginger felt vaguely that an ill-spelt report would have an untrustworthy appearance.

In this emergency, he consulted his native commonsense, and found it a good guide.

"I better just begin at the beginning," he said to himself, and, pressing heavily upon the paper and frowning desperately, began to write.

"REPORT
by Joseph L. Potts
(aged 14 ½)"

On consideration, he thought this needed a little more corroborative detail, and added his address and the date. The report then proceeded:

"I had a talk with the boys about the *catter* (erased) cattapult. Bill Jones says he reckollects of me standing in the Dispatch and Mrs. Johnson collering of the cattapult. Sam Tabbit and George Pyke was there too. What I says to them was as Mr. Bredon give me back the cattapult and it have the bit of leather tore and I wants to know who done it. They all says they never been to Mrs. Johnson's draw and I think they was tellin the truth sir because Bill and Sam is good sorts and you can always tell if George is fibbing because of the way he looks and he was looking alright. So then I says could it have been any of the others and they says they have not seen none of them with cattapults so I makes out to be very angry and says it's a pitty a boy can't have his cattapult *confist* confiskcated without somebody goes and tears of it. And then Clarence Metcalfe comes along which he is head boy sir and asks what's up so I tells him and he says if anybody's been at Mrs. Johnsons draw its very serious. So he gets arsking them all and they all says no but Jack Bolter remembers of Mrs. Johnson leaving her bag on the desk one day and Miss Parton picking it up and taking of it down to the canteen. I says when? And he says it was about two days after my cattapult was *confik* took away, and the time just after lunch sir. So you see sir it would have been laying there an hour sir when nobody was about.

Now sir about who else was there and might have seen it took. Now I comes to think I remember Mr. Prout was there at the head of the stairs because he passed a remark to Mrs. Johnson and pulled my ear and there was one of the young ladies I think it was Miss Hartley waiting to get a messenger. And after I gone down to Mr. Hornby Sam says as Mr. Wedderburn came along and him and Mrs. Johnson had a bit of a joke about it. But sir I expecks lots of people knew about it because Mrs. Johnson would tell them in the canteen. She is always telling tales on we boys sir I suppose she thinks its funny.

This is all I has to report about the cattapult sir. I has not yet made any inquiry about the other matter thinking one was enough at a time or they might think I was askin a lot of questions but I have thought of a plan for that.

Yours respeckfully

J. Potts.

"What the devil are you doing there, Joe?"

Ginger, too absorbed in his report to have kept a proper look-out upon Bert, started violently, and thrust the exercise book under his pillow.

"Never you mind," he said, nervously. "It's private."

"Oh, is it?"

Bert flung the bedclothes aside and advanced, a threatening figure.

"Writing poitry?" he demanded, with contempt.

"It's nothing to do with you," retorted Ginger. "You leave me be."

" 'And that there book over," said Bert.

"No, I won't."

"You won't, won't you?"

"No, I won't. Get out!"

Ginger clasped the document with agitated hands.

"I'm going to 'ave a look—leggo!"

Ginger was a wiry child for his years and spirited, but his hands were hampered by the book, and the advantages of height, weight and position were with Bert. The struggle was noisy.

"Let me go, you beastly great bully."

"I'll teach you to call names! Cheeky little beast."

"Ow!" wailed Ginger. "I won't, I won't, I tell you! it's private!"

Whack! wallop!

"Nah then!" said a stately voice, "wot's all this?"

"Wally, tell Bert to leave me be."

"He didn't oughter cheek me. I only wanted ter know wot he was doin', sittin' up writin' poitry w'en he oughter a-bin asleep."

"It's private," persisted Ginger. "Really and truly, it's frightfully private."

"Can't yer leave the kid alone?" said P. C. Potts, magisterially, "makin' all this noise. You'll wake Dad and then you'll both get a 'iding. Now both of you 'op back to bed or I'll 'ave ter take you up for disturbing the peace. And you did oughter be asleep, Joe, and not writing poitry."

"It ain't poitry. It's something I was doing for a gentleman at the office and he said I wasn't to tell nobody."

"Well, see here," said Wally Potts, extending a vast official fist. "You 'and over that there book to me, see? I'll put it away in my drawer and you can 'ave it again in the morning. And now go to sleep for goodness' sake, both on yer."

"You won't read it, will yer, Wally?"

"All right, I won't read it if you're so bloomin' perticler."

Ginger, reluctant but confident of Wally's honour, reluctantly released the exercise-book.

"That's right," said Wally, "and if I 'ear any more larkin' about you're for it, both of yer. See wot I mean?"

He stalked away, gigantic in his striped pyjamas.

Ginger Joe, rubbing the portions of himself which had suffered in the assault, rolled the bed-clothes about him and took comfort in telling himself a fresh instalment of that nightly narrative of which he was both author and hero.

"Bruised and battered, but unshaken in his courage, the famous detective sank back on his straw pallet in the rat-ridden dungeon. In spite of the pain of his wounds, he was happy, knowing that the precious documents were safe. He laughed to think of the baffled Crime King, gnashing his teeth in his gilded oriental saloon. 'Foiled yet again, Hawkeye!' growled the villainous doctor, 'but it will be my turn next!' Meanwhile . . ."

The life of a detective is a hard one.

# 8

# CONVULSIVE AGITATION OF AN ADVERTISING AGENCY

It was on the Friday of the week in which all these stirring incidents occurred that Pym's Publicity, Ltd. became convulsed by the Great Nutrax Row, which shook the whole office from the highest to the lowest, turned the peaceful premises into an armed camp and very nearly ruined the Staff Cricket Match against Brotherhood's, Ltd.

The hardworking and dyspeptic Mr. Copley was the prime mover of all the trouble. Like most fomenters of schism, he acted throughout with the best intentions–and indeed, when one looks back upon the disturbance in the serene perspective of distance and impartiality, it is difficult to see what he could have done, other than what he did. But as Mr. Ingleby observed at the time, "It isn't what Copley *does*, it's the way he does it"; and in the heat and fury of the battle, when the passions of strong men are aroused, judgment easily becomes warped.

The thing started in this way:

At a quarter past six on the Thursday evening, the office was deserted, except for the cleaners and Mr. Copley, who, by an altogether exceptional accident, was left working overtime upon a rush series of cut-price advertisements for Jamboree Jellies. He was getting along nicely, and hoped to be through by half-past six and home in good time for 7:30 supper, when the telephone in the Dispatching rang violently and insistently.

"Dash it!" said Mr. Copley, annoyed by the din, "they ought to know the office is closed. You'd think they expected us to work all night."

He went on working, trusting that the nuisance would cease of itself. Presently it did cease, and he heard the shrill voice of Mrs. Crump informing the caller that there was nobody in the office. He took a soda-mint tablet. His sentence was shaping itself beautifully. "The authentic flavour of the fresh home-grown orchard fruit—of apricots ripening in the sunny warmth of an old, walled garden . . ."

"Excuse me, sir."

Mrs. Crump, shuffling apologetically in her carpet slippers, poked a nervous head round the door.

"What is it now?" said Mr. Copley.

"Oh, if you please, sir, it's the *Morning Star* on the telephone very urgent, asking for Mr. Tallboy. I told them they was all gone 'ome, but they says it's very important, sir, so I thought I'd better ask you."

"What's it all about?"

"Somethink about the advertisement for tomorrow morning, sir—somethink's gone wrong and they say, did it ought to be left out altogether or can we send them somethink else, sir?"

"Oh, well!" said Mr. Copley, resigned, "I suppose I'd better come and speak to them."

"I dunno whether I done right, sir," continued Mrs. Crump, anxiously pattering after him, "but I thought, sir, if there *is* a gentleman in the office I ought to tell him about it, because I didn't know but what it mightn't be important—"

"Quite right, Mrs. Crump, quite right," said Mr. Copley. "I daresay I can settle it."

He strode competently to the telephone and grasped the receiver.

"Hullo!" he said, petulantly, "Pym's here. What's the matter?"

"Oh!" said a voice. "Is that Mr. Tallboy?"

"No. Mr. Tallboy's gone home. Everybody's gone home. You ought to know that by this time. What is it?"

"Well," said the voice, "it's about that Nutrax half-double for tomorrow's feature page."

"What about it? Haven't you had it?"

(Just like Tallboy, thought Mr. Copley. No organization. You never could trust these younger men.)

"Yes, we've got it," said the voice, doubtfully, "but Mr. Weekes says we can't put it in. You see—"

"Can't put it in?"

"No. You see, Mr.—"

"I'm Mr. Copley. It's not in my department. I really know nothing about it. What's the matter with it?"

"Well, if you had it there before you, you'd see what I mean. You know the headline—"

"No, I don't," snapped Mr. Copley, exasperated. "I tell you it's not my business and I've never seen the thing."

"Oh!" said the voice, with irritating cheerfulness. "Well, the headline is: ARE YOU TAKING TOO MUCH OUT OF YOURSELF? And, taken in conjunction with the sketch, Mr. Weekes thinks it might lay itself open to an unfortunate interpretation. If you had it there before you, I think you'd see what he means."

"I see," said Mr. Copley, thoughtfully. Fifteen years' experience told him that this was disaster. There was no arguing with it. If the *Morning Star* got it into their heads that an advertisement contained some lurking indelicacy, that advertisement would not be printed, though the skies fell. Indeed, it was better that it should not. Errors of this kind lowered the prestige of the product and of the agency responsible. Mr. Copley had no fancy for seeing copies of *Morning Star* sold at half-a-crown a time in the Stock Exchange to provide a pornographer's holiday.

In the midst of his annoyance, he felt the inward exultation of the Jeremiah whose prophecies have come true. He had always said that the younger generation of advertising writers were No Good. Too much of the new-fangled University element. Feather-headedness. No solid business sense. No thought. But he was well-trained. He carried the war instantly into the enemy's camp.

"You ought to let us know earlier," he said, severely. "It's ridiculous to ring up at a quarter past six, when the office is closed. What do you expect us to do about it?"

"Not our fault," said the voice, brightly. "It only came in ten minutes ago. We're always asking Mr. Tallboy to let us have the blocks in better time, just to prevent this kind of situation."

More and more confirmation of Mr. Copley's prophecies. General slackness–that was what it was. Mr. Tallboy had left promptly at 5:30. Mr. Copley had seen him go. Clock-watchers, the whole lot of them. Tallboy had no business to leave before he had got an assurance from the paper that the block was received and that all was in order. Moreover, if the messenger had not delivered the parcel to the *Morning Star* till 6.5, he had either started too late, or had dawdled on the way. More bad management. That Johnson woman–no control, no discipline. Before the War there would have been no women in advertising offices, and none of these silly mistakes.

Still, something must be done.

"Very unfortunate," said Mr. Copley. "Well, I'll see if I can get hold of somebody. What's your last moment for making an alteration?"

"Must have it down here by 7 o'clock," said the voice, ineluctably. "As a matter of fact, the foundry is waiting for that sheet now. We only want your block to lock the forme. But I've spoken to Wilkes, and he says he can give you till seven."

"I'll ring you," said Mr. Copley, and rang off.

Rapidly his mind raced over the list of people who were fitted to cope with the situation. Mr. Tallboy, the Group-manager; Mr. Wedderburn, his Group-secretary; Mr. Armstrong, the copy-chief responsible; the writer of the copy, whoever he was; in the last resort, Mr. Pym. It was a most unfortunate moment. Mr. Tallboy lived at Croydon, and was probably still swaying and sweltering in the train; Mr. Wedderburn–he really had no idea where he lived, except that it was probably in some still more remote suburb. Mr. Armstrong lived in Hampstead; he was not in the telephone-book, but his private number would doubtless be on the telephone-clerk's desk; there was some hope of catching him. Mr. Copley hurried downstairs, found the list and the number and rang up. After two wrong numbers, he got the house. Mr. Armstrong's housekeeper replied. Mr. Armstrong was out. She could not say where he had gone or when he would return. Could she take a message? Mr. Copley replied that it didn't matter and rang off again. Half-past six.

He consulted the telephonist's list again. Mr. Wedderburn did not appear upon it and presumably was not on the 'phone. Mr. Tallboy's name was there. Without much hope, Mr. Copley got on to the Croydon number, only to hear, as he expected, that Mr. Tallboy had not yet returned. His heart sinking, Mr. Copley rang up Mr. Pym's house. Mr. Pym had just that minute left. Where for? It was urgent. Mr. and Mrs. Pym were dining at Frascati's with Mr. Armstrong. This sounded a little more hopeful. Mr. Copley rang up Frascati's. Oh, yes. Mr. Pym had engaged a table for 7:30. He had not yet arrived. Could they give a message when he did arrive? Mr. Copley left a message to ask Mr. Pym or Mr. Armstrong to ring him up at the office before 7 o'clock if possible, but he felt convinced that nothing could possibly come of it. No doubt these gadding directors had gone to a cocktail party somewhere. He looked at the clock. It was 6:45. As he looked, the telephone rang again.

It was, as he had expected, the *Morning Star*, impatient for instructions.

"I can't get hold of anybody," explained Mr. Copley.

"What are we to do? Leave it out altogether?"

Now, when you see in a newspaper a blank white space, bearing the legend: "THIS SPACE RESERVED FOR SO-AND-SO LTD.," it may mean nothing very much to you, but to those who know anything of the working of advertising agencies, those words carry the ultimate, ignominious brand of incompetency and failure. So-and-so's agents have fallen down on their job; nothing can be alleged in mitigation. It is the Thing That Must Not Happen.

Mr. Copley, therefore, while savagely reflecting that it would serve the whole bunch of slackers and half-wits right if the space *was* left blank, ejaculated hastily: "No, no! on no account. Hold the line one moment. I'll see what I can do." In so doing he acted very properly, for it is the first and almost the only rule of business morality that the Firm must come first.

Dashing hastily along the passage, he entered Mr. Tallboy's room, which was on the same floor as the Dispatching and Copy departments, on the far side of the iron staircase. One minute brought him there; another minute, spent rummaging in Mr. Tallboy's drawers, gave him what he wanted—an advance proof of the wretched Nutrax half-double. A glance showed him that Mr. Weekes's doubts were perfectly justified. Each harmless enough in itself, sketch and headline together were deadly. Without waiting to wonder how so obvious a gaffe had escaped the eagle eyes of the department chiefs, Mr. Copley sat down and pulled out his pocket pencil. Nothing now could be done about the sketch; it must stand; his job was to find a new headline which would suit the sketch and the opening line of the copy, and contain approximately the same number of letters as the original.

Hurriedly he jotted down ideas and crossed them out. 'WORK AND WORRY SAP NERVE-STRENGTH"—that was on the right lines, but was a few letters short. It was rather flat, too; and besides, it wasn't quite true. Not work—over-work was what the copy was talking about. "WORRY AND OVERWORK"—no good, it lacked rhythm. "OVERWORK AND OVERWORRY"—far better, but too long. As it stood, the headllne filled three lines (too much, thought Mr. Copley, for a half-double), being spaced thus:

ARE YOU TAKING
TOO MUCH OUT
OF YOURSELF?

He scribbled desperately, trying to save a letter here and there. "NERVOUS FORCE"? "NERVE-FORCE"? "NERVE-POWER"? The minutes were flying. Ah? how about this?

OVER-WORK &
OVER-WORRY—
waste Nerve-Power!

Not brilliant, but dead on the right note, unexceptionable and offering no difficulties about spacing. On the point of rushing back to the 'phone it occurred to him that the instrument on Mr. Tallboy's desk might have been left connected to the switchboard. He removed the receiver; a reassuring buzz assured him that it was so. He spoke urgently:

"Are you there?"

"Yes."

"Look here. Can you cut away the headline and re-set in Goudy Bold?"

"Ye-es—Yes, we can just do that if we get it at once."

"I'll dictate it."

"Right-ho! Fire away."

"Start exactly where you start now with 'ARE YOU TAKING.' First line in caps, same size as the caps you've got there for 'TOO MUCH OUT.' Right. This is the line: 'OVER-WORK &'—with hyphen in Over-work and an ampersand. Got that?"

"Yes."

"Next line. Same size. Start two ems further in. 'OVER-WORRY,' Hyphen. Dash. Got that?"

"Yes."

"Now, third line, Goudy 24-point upper and lower. Start under the W. 'Waste Nerve-Power!' Capital N, capital P, and screamer. Got that?"

"Yes; I'll repeat. First line Goudy caps., starting level with cap A of present headline. O,V,E,R, hyphen, W,O,R,K, ampersand; second line, same fount, 2 ems to the right, O,V,E,R, hyphen, W,O,R,R,Y, dash. Third line. Start under W, Goudy 24 point upper and lower: lower-case w,a,s,t,e, capital N,e,r,v,e hyphen, capital P,o,w,e,r, screamer. That O.K.?"

"That's right. Much obliged."

"Not at all. Much obliged to you. Sorry to bother you. Good-bye."

"Good-bye."

Mr. Copley sank back, mopping his brow. It was done. The firm was saved. Men had been decorated for less. When it came to an emergency, when all the jumped-up jacks-in-office had deserted their posts, it was on him, Mr. Copley, the old-fashioned man of experience, that Pym's Publicity had to depend. A man who could grapple with a situation. A man not afraid of responsibility. A man whose heart and soul were wrapped up in his job. Suppose he had rushed off home on the stroke of half-past five, like Tallboy, caring nothing whether his work was done or not—what would have happened? Pym's would have been in the cart. He would have something to say about it in the morning. He hoped it would be a jolly good lesson to them.

He pulled the roll-top of Mr. Tallboy's desk down again over the disgracefully untidy set of pigeon-holes and the cluttered mass of paper that it nightly concealed, and as he did so, received fresh proof of the disorderliness of Mr. Tallboy's habits. From some mysterious nook where it had become caught up, a registered envelope dislodged itself, and fell with a plump little flop to the floor.

Mr. Copley stooped at once and picked it up. It was addressed in block letters to J. Tallboy, Esq., at the Croydon address, and had already been opened. Peeping in at the slit end, Mr. Copley observed what could be nothing but a thickish wad of green currency notes. Yielding to a not unnatural impulse, Mr. Copley pulled them out, and counted, to his astonishment and indignation, no less than fifty of them.

If there was one action more than another which Mr. Copley condemned as Thoughtless and Unfair (long advertising practice had given him a trick of thinking in capital letters), it was Putting Temptation in People's Way. Here was the colossal sum of Fifty Pounds, so carelessly secured that the mere opening of the desk sent it skittering to the floor, for Mrs. Crump and her corps of charladies to find. No doubt they were all very honest women, but in these Hard Times, a working woman could hardly be blamed if she succumbed. Worse still, suppose the precious envelope had got swept up and destroyed. Suppose it had fallen into the wastepaper basket and thence made its way to the sack and the paper-makers, or, still worse, to the furnace. Some innocent person might have been Falsely Accused, and laboured for the rest of her life under a Stigma. It was intolerable of Mr. Tallboy. It was Really Wicked.

Of course, Mr. Copley realized exactly what had happened. Mr. Tallboy had received this Large Sum (from whom? there was no covering letter; but that was hardly Mr. Copley's business. Possibly these were winnings on dog-races, or something equally undesirable) and had brought it to the office, intending to bank it at the Metropolitan & Counties Bank at the corner of Southampton Row, where the majority of the staff kept their accounts. By some accident, he had been prevented from doing this before the Bank closed. Instead of bestowing the envelope safely in his pocket, he hat thrust it into his desk, and at 5:30 had rushed off home in his usual helter-skelter way, and forgotten all about it. And if he had since given another thought to it, reflected Mr. Copley indignantly, it was probably only to assume that it would be "perfectly all right." The man really ought to be given a lesson.

Very well, he *should* be given a lesson. The notes should be placed in safe custody and he, Mr. Copley, would give Mr. Tallboy a good talking-to in the morning. He hesitated for a moment as to the best plan. If he took the notes away with him, there was the possibility that he might have his pocket picked on the way home, which would be very unfortunate and expensive. It would be better to take them to his own room and lock them securely in the bottom drawer of his own desk. Mr. Copley congratulated himself upon the conscientious foresight that had prompted him to ask for a drawer with a proper lock.

He accordingly carried the packet to his room, put it safely away underneath a quantity of confidential papers dealing with future campaigns for tinned food and jellies, tidied up his own desk and locked it, pocketed the keys, brushed his hat and coat and took his virtuous departure, not forgetting to replace the telephone receiver upon its hook as he passed through the Dispatching.

He emerged from the doorway into the street, and crossed the road before turning south to the Theobalds Road tram-terminus. On gaining the opposite pavement, he happened to glance back, and saw the figure of Mr. Tallboy coming up on the other side from the direction of Kingsway. Mr. Copley stood still and watched him. Mr. Tallboy turned into Pym's entrance and disappeared.

"Aha!" said Mr. Copley to himself, "he's remembered about the money after all."

It is at this point that Mr. Copley's conduct is perhaps open to censure. A charitable fellow-feeling would, one imagines, have prompted him to dodge back through the traffic, to return to Pym's, to take the lift to the top floor, to seek out the anxious Mr. Tallboy and to say to him: "Look here, old man, I found a registered packet of yours sculling about and put it away in safety and, by the bye, about that half-double for Nutrax—" But he did not.

Let us remember, in mitigation, that it was now half-past seven, that there was no chance of his getting back to his evening meal much before half-past eight, that he was of dyspeptic habit and dependent upon regular hours, and that he had had a long day, concluding with an entirely unnecessary piece of worry and hustle occasioned by Mr. Tallboy's tiresomeness.

"Let him suffer for it," said Mr. Copley, grimly. "It serves him right."

He caught his tram and departed on his tedious way to a remote northern suburb. As he jolted and ground along, he planned to himself how, next day, he would score over Mr. Tallboy and earn commendations from the powers that were.

There was one factor with which Mr. Copley, in his anticipatory triumph, had failed to reckon; namely, that to obtain the full effect and splendour of his *coup de théâtre* it was necessary for him to get to the office before Mr. Tallboy. In his day-dream, he had taken this for granted—naturally so, since he was a punctual man at all times, and Mr. Tallboy was apt to be more punctual in departing than in arriving. Mr. Copley's idea was that, after making a stately report to Mr. Armstrong at 9 o'clock, in the course of which Mr. Tallboy would be called in and admonished, he should then take the repentant Group-manager privately to one side, read him a litile lecture on orderliness and thought for others, and hand him over his fifty pounds with a paternal caution. Meanwhile, Mr. Armstrong would mention the Nutrax incident to the other directors, who would congratulate themselves on having so reliable, experienced, and devoted a servant. The words sang themselves into a little slogan in Mr. Copley's head: "You can Count on Copley in a Crisis."

But things did not turn out that way. To begin with, Mr. Copley's late arrival on the Thursday night plunged him into a domestic storm which lasted into the night and still muttered with thunderous reverberations on the following morning.

"I suppose," said Mrs. Copley, acidly, "that while you were telephoning to all these people, it was too much trouble to think of your *wife*. I don't count at all, naturally. It's nothing to *you* that I should be left imagining all kinds of things. Well, don't blame *me* if the chicken is roasted to a chip and the potatoes are sodden, and you get indigestion."

The chicken *was* roasted to a chip; the potatoes *were* sodden; and, in consequence, Mr. Copley did get a violent indigestion, to which his wife was obliged to minister with soda-mint and bismuth and hot-water bottles, voicing her opinion of him at every application. Not until six o'clock in the morning did he fall into a heavy and unrefreshing slumber, from which he was aroused at a quarter to eight by hearing Mrs. Copley say:

"If you are going to the office today, Frederick, you had better get up. If you are *not* going, you may as well say so, and I will send a message. I have called you three times, and your breakfast is getting cold."

Mr. Copley, with a bilious headache over his right eye and a nasty taste in his mouth, would gladly have authorized her to send the message—gladly have turned over upon his pillow and buried his woes in sleep, but the recollection of the Nutrax half-double and the fifty pounds rushed over him in a flood and swept him groaning from between the sheets. Seen in the morning light, to the accompaniment of black spots dancing before his eyes, the prospect of his triumph had lost much of its glamour. Still, he could not let it go with a mere explanation by telephone. He must be on the spot. He shaved hastily, with a shaking hand and cut himself. The flow of blood would not be staunched. It invaded his shirt. He snatched the garment off, and called to his wife for a clean one. Mrs. Copley supplied it—not without reprimand. It seemed that the putting on of a clean shirt on a Friday morning upset the entire economy of the household. At ten minutes past eight, he came down to a breakfast he could not eat, his cheek ludicrously embellished with a tuft of cottonwool and his ears ringing with migraine and conjugal rebuke.

It was impossible, now, to catch the 8:15. Sourly, he caught the 8:25.

At a quarter to nine, the 8:25 was hung up for twenty minutes outside Kings Cross on account of an accident to a goods train.

At 9:30, Mr. Copley crawled drearily into Pym's, wishing he had never been born.

As he entered the office from the lift, the reception-clerk greeted him with a message that Mr. Armstrong would like to see him at once. Mr. Copley, savagely signing his name far away below the red line which divided the punctual from the dilatory, nodded, and then wished he had not, as a pang of agony shot through his aching head. He mounted the stair and encountered Miss Parton, who said brightly:

"Oh, *here* you are, Mr. Copley! We thought you were lost. Mr. Armstrong would like to see you."

"I'm just going," said Mr. Copley, savagely. He went to his room and took off his coat, wondering whether a phenacetin would cure his headache or merely make him sick. Ginger Joe knocked at the door.

"If you please, sir, Mr. Armstrong says, could you spare him a moment."

"All right, all right," said Mr. Copley. He tottered out into the passage, and nearly fell into the arms of Mr. Ingleby.

"Hullo!" said the latter, "you're wanted, Copley! We were just sending out the town-crier. You'd better nip along to Armstrong pronto. Tallboy's out for your blood."

"Ar'rh!" said Mr. Copley.

He shouldered Mr. Ingleby aside and went on his way, only to encounter Mr. Bredon, lurking at the door of his own room, armed with an imbecile grin and a jew's harp.

"See the conquering hero comes," cried Mr. Bredon, following up this remark with a blast upon his instrument.

"Jackanapes!" said Mr. Copley. Whereupon, to his horror, Mr. Bredon executed three handsome cart-wheels before him down the passage, finishing up accurately before Mr. Armstrong's door, and just out of Mr. Armstrong's line of sight.

Mr. Copley knocked upon the glass panel, through which he could see Mr. Armstrong, seated at his desk, Mr. Tallboy, upright and indignant, and Mr. Hankin standing, with his usual air of mild hesitation, on the far side of the room. Mr. Armstrong looked up and beckoned Mr. Copley in.

"Ah!" said Mr. Armstrong, "here's the man we want. Rather late this morning, aren't you, Mr. Copley?"

Mr. Copley explained that there had been an accident on the line.

"Something must be done about these accidents on the line," said Mr. Armstrong. "Whenever Pym's staff travels, the trains break down. I shall have to write to the Superintendent of the line. Ha, ha!"

Mr. Copley realized that Mr. Armstrong was in one of his frivolous and tiresome moods. He said nothing.

"Now, Mr. Copley," said Mr. Armstrong, "what's all this about the Nutrax half-double? We've just had an agitated telegram from Mr. Jollop. I can't get hold of the *Morning Star* man–what's his name?"

"Weekes," said Mr. Tallboy.

"Weekes–golly, what a name! But I understand–or Mr. Tallboy understands–from somebody or other, that you altered the Nutrax headline last night. I've no doubt you've got an excellent explanation, but I should like to know just what we've got to say to Mr. Jollop."

Mr. Copley pulled himself together and embarked on an account of the previous night's crisis. He felt that he was not doing himself justice. Out of the tail of his eye, he could see the dab of cotton-wool on his cheek waggling absurdly as he spoke. He pointed out with emphasis and acerbity the extremely unfortunate suggestion conveyed by the sketch and the original headlline.

Mr. Armstrong burst into a hoot of laughter.

"My God!" he shouted. "They've got us there, Tallboy! Ho, ho, ho! Who wrote the headline? I must tell Mr. Pym about this. Why the devil didn't you catch it, Tallboy?"

"It never occurred to me," said Mr. Tallboy, unaccountably crimson in the face. Mr. Armstrong hooted again.

"I think Ingleby wrote it," added Mr. Tallboy.

"Ingleby, of all people!" Mr. Armstrong's mirth was not to be restrained. He pushed the buzzer on his desk. "Miss Parton, ask Mr. Ingleby to step in here."

Mr. Ingleby arrived, cool and insolent as ever. Mr. Armstrong, half speechless with joy, thrust the original pull of the advertisement at him, with a comment so barbarically outspoken that Mr. Copley blushed.

Mr. Ingleby, unabashed, capped the comment with a remark still more immodest, and Miss Parton, lingering, notebook in hand, gave a refined snigger.

"Well, sir," said Ingleby, "it's not my fault. My original rough was illustrated with a very handsome sketch of a gentleman overwhelmed with business cares. If the innocents in the Studio choose to turn down my refined suggestion in favour of a (male epithet) and a (female epithet) who look as though they'd been making a night of it, I refuse to be responsible."

"Ha, ha!" said Mr. Armstrong. "That's Barrow all over. I don't suppose Barrow–"

The end of the sentence was more complimentary to the Studio-chief's virtue than to his virility. Mr. Hankin suddenly exploded into a loud snicker of laughter.

"Mr. Barrow is rather fond of cashiering any suggestion put forward by the Copy Department," said Mr. Copley. "I hardly like to suggest that there is any inter-departmental jealousy behind it, but the fact remains–"

But Mr. Armstrong was feeling hilarious, and paid no attention. He recited a limerick, amid applause.

"Well, it's all right, Mr. Copley," he said, when he had partially recovered himself. "You did quite right. I'll send an explanation to Mr. Jollop. He'll have a fit."

"He'll be surprised that *you* passed it," said Mr. Hankin.

"Well, he may be," agreed Mr. Armstrong, pleasantly. "It isn't often I overlook anything indecent. I must have been off-colour that day. So must you, Tallboy, Oh, dear! Mr. Pym will have something to say about it. I shall enjoy seeing his face. I only wish it had gone through. He'd have sacked the whole department."

"It would have been very serious," said Mr. Copley.

"Of course it would. I'm very glad the *Morning Star* spotted it. All right. Now that's settled. Mr. Hankin, about that whole page for Sopo–"

"I hope," said Mr. Copley, "you are satisifed with what I did. There wasn't much time–"

"Quite all right, quite all right," said Mr. Armstrong. "Very much obliged to you. But, by the way, you might have let somebody know. I was left rather up in the air this morning."

Mr. Copley explained that he had endeavoured to get into touch with Mr. Pym, Mr. Armstrong, Mr. Tallboy and Mr. Wedderburn, but without success.

"Yes, yes, I see," said Mr. Armstrong. "But why didn't you ring up Mr. Hankin?"

"I am always at home by six," added Mr. Hankin, "and it is very seldom that I go out. When I do, I always leave directions where I am to be found." (This was a dig at Mr. Armstrong.)

Dismay seized upon Mr. Copley. He had clean forgotten Mr. Hankin, and he knew well enough that Mr. Hankin, mild as were his manners, was quick to resent anything in the nature of a slight.

"Of course," he stammered. "Of course, yes, I might have done that. But Nutrax being your client, Mr. Armstrong–I thought–it never occurred to me that Mr. Hankin–"

This was a bad tactical error. It was, to begin with, contrary to the great Pym Principle that any member of the Copy Department was supposed to be ready to carry on with any part of the work at any time, if called upon. And it also suggested that Mr. Hankin was, in that respect, less versatile than Mr. Copley himself.

"Nutrax," said Mr. Hankin, in a thin manner, "is certainly not a favourite account of mine. But I have coped with it in my time." (This was another side-blow at Mr. Armstrong, who had temperamental periods when he was apt to hand all his clients over to Mr. Hankin, pleading nervous exhaustion.) "It is really no further outside my scope than that of the junior copy-writers."

"Well, well," said Mr. Armstrong, perceiving that Mr. Hankin was on the point of doing the undesirable thing, and ticking off a member of the department before a member of another department, "it's not of any great consequence, and you did your best in an awkward crisis. Nobody can think of everything. Now, Mr. Hankin"–he dismissed the small fry with a nod–"let's get this Sopo question settled once and for all. Don't go, Miss Parton, I want you to take a note. I'll see to Nutrax, Mr. Tallboy. Don't worry."

The door closed behind Mr. Copley, Mr. Ingleby and Mr. Tallboy.

"My God!" said Ingleby, "what a howl! Went with a bang from start to finish. It only wanted Barrow to make it complete. That reminds me, I'll have to go and pull his leg. This'll teach him to turn down my intelligent suggestions. Hullo! there's the Meteyard. I must tell her what Armstrong said about old Barrow."

He dived into Miss Meteyard's room, from which unladylike shouts of mirth were soon heard to proceed. Mr. Copley, feeling as though his head were filled with hard knobs of spinning granite that crashed with sickening thuds against his brain-pan, walked stiffly away to his own quarters. As he passed the Dispatching, he had a vision of Mrs. Crump, in tears, standing before Mrs. Johnson's desk, but he paid no attention. His one agonized yearning was to shake off Mr. Tallboy, who padded grimly at his heels.

"Oh, Mr. Tallboy!"

Mrs. Johnson's rather shrill voice came to Mr. Copley like an order of release. He shot home like a bolting rabbit. He must try phenacetin and chance the consequences. Hastily he swallowed three tablets without even troubling to fetch a glass of water, sat down in his revolving chair and closed his eyes.

Crash, crash, crash, went the lumps of granite in his brain. If only he could remain where he was, quite quietly, for half an hour–

The door was flung violently open.

"Look here, Copley," said Mr. Tallboy, in a voice like a pneumatic drill, "when you were hugger-muggering round with my desk last night did you have the unprintable bloody impertinence to interfere with my private belongings?"

"For heaven's sake," moaned Mr. Copley, "don't make such a row. I've got a splitting headache."

"I don't care a highly-coloured damn if you've got a headache or not," retorted Mr. Tallboy, flinging the door to behind him with a slam like the report of an 11-inch gun. "There was an envelope in my desk last night with fifty pounds in it, and it's gone, and that old (epithet) Mrs. Crump says she saw you (vulgar word)-ing about among my papers."

"I have your fifty pounds here," replied Mr. Copley, with as much dignity as he could muster. "I put it away safely for you, and I must say, Tallboy, that I consider it extremely thoughtless of you to leave your property about for the charwomen to find. It's not fair. You should have more consideration. And I did not rummage about in your desk as you suggest. I merely looked for the pull of the Nutrax half-double, and when I was closing the desk, this envelope fell out upon the floor."

He stooped to unlock the drawer, experiencing a ghastly qualm as he did so.

"You mean to tell me," said Mr. Tallboy, "that you had the all-fired cheek to take my money away to your own damned room–"

"In your own interests," said Mr. Copley.

"Interests be damned! Why the devil couldn't you leave it in a pigeon-hole and not be so blasted interfering?"

"You do not realize–"

"I realize this," said Mr. Tallboy, "that you're an expurgated superannuated interfering idiot. What you wanted to come poking your blasted nose in for–"

"Really, Mr. Tallboy–"

"What business was it of yours, anyway?"

"It was anybody's business," said Mr. Copley–so angry that he almost forgot his headache–"who had the welfare of the firm at heart. I am considerably older than you, Tallboy, and in my day, a Group-manager would have been ashamed to leave the building before ascertaining that all was well with his advertisement for the next day's paper. How you came to let such an advertisement pass in the first place is beyond my understanding. You were then late with the block. Perhaps you do not know that it was not received by the *Morning Star* till five minutes past six–*five minutes past six*. And instead of being at your post to consider any necessary corrections–"

"I don't want you to teach me my job," said Mr. Tallboy.

"Pardon me, I think you do."

"Anyhow, what's that got to do with it? The point is, you stick your nose into my private affairs–"

"I did not. The envelope fell out–"

"That's a bloody lie."

"Pardon me, it is the truth."

"Don't keep saying 'pardon me' like a bloody kitchenmaid."

"Leave my room!" shrieked Mr. Copley.

"I'm not going to leave your damned room till I get an apology."

"I think I ought to receive the apology."

"*You?*" Mr. Tallboy became almost inarticulate. "You–! Why the hell couldn't you have had the decency to ring me up and tell me, anyway?"

"You weren't at home."

"How do you know? Did you try?"

"No. I knew you were out, because I saw you in Southampton Row."

"You saw me in Southampton Row, and you hadn't the ordinary common decency to get hold of me and tell me what you'd been after? Upon my word, Copley, I believe you jolly well *meant* to get me into a row. And collar the cash for yourself, too, I shouldn't wonder."

"How dare you suggest any such thing?"

"And all your rot about consideration for the charwomen! It's sheer damned hypocrisy. Of course I thought one of them had had it. I told Mrs. Crump–"

"You accused Mrs. Crump?"

"I didn't accuse her. I told her I had missed fifty pounds."

"That just shows you," began Mr. Copley.

"And fortunately she'd seen you at my desk. Otherwise, I suppose I should never have heard anything more about my money."

"You've no right to say that."

"I've a damn sight more right to say it than you had to steal the money."

"Are you calling me a thief?"

"Yes, I am."

"And I call you a scoundrel," gasped Mr. Copley, beside himself, "an insolent scoundrel. And I say that if you came by the money honestly, which I doubt, sir, which I very much doubt–"

Mr. Bredon poked his long nose round the door.

"I say," he bleated anxiously, "sorry to butt in, and all that, but Hankie's compliments and he says, would you mind talking a little more quietly? He's got Mr. Simon Brotherhood next door."

A pause followed, in which both parties realized the thinness of the beaverboard partition between Mr. Hankin's room and Mr. Copley's. Then Mr. Tallboy thrust the recovered envelope into his pocket.

"All right, Copley," he said. "I shan't forget your kind interference." He bounced out.

"Oh, dear, oh, dear," moaned Mr. Copley, clasping his head in his hands.

"Is anything up?" queried Mr. Bredon.

"Please go away," pleaded Mr. Copley, "I'm feeling horribly ill."

Mr. Bredon withdrew on catlike feet. His inquisitive face beamed with mischief. He pursued Mr. Tallboy into the Dispatching, and found him earnestly talking to Mrs. Johnson.

"I say, Tallboy," said Mr. Bredon, "what's wrong with Copley? He looks jolly fed-up. Have you been twisting his tail?"

"It's no affair of yours, anyway," retorted Mr. Tallboy, sullenly. "All right, Mrs. J., I'll see Mrs. Crump and put it right with her."

"I hope you will, Mr. Tallboy. And another time, if you have any valuables, I should be obliged if you would bring them to me and let me put them in the safe downstairs. These upsets are not pleasant, and Mr. Pym would be greatly annoyed if he knew about it."

Mr. Tallboy fled for the lift without vouchsafing any reply.

"Atmosphere seems a bit hectic this morning, Mrs. Johnson," observed Mr. Bredon, seating himself on the edge of the good lady's desk. "Even the presiding genius of the Dispatching looks a trifle ruffled. But a righteous indignation becomes you. Gives sparkle to the eyes and a clear rosiness to the complexion."

"Now that'll do, Mr. Bredon. What will my boys think if they hear you making fun of me? Really, though, some of these people are *too* trying. But I must stand up for my women, Mr. Bredon, and for my boys. There isn't one of them that I wouldn't trust, and it isn't right to bring accusations with nothing to support them."

"It's simply foul," agreed Mr. Bredon. "Who's been bringing accusations?"

"Well, I don't know if I ought to tell tales out of school," said Mrs. Johnson, "but it's really only justice to poor Mrs. Crump to say–"

Naturally, in five minutes' time, the insinuating Mr. Bredon was in possession of the whole story.

"But you needn't go and spread it all round the office," said Mrs. Johnson.

"Of course I needn't," said Mr. Bredon. "Hullo! is that the lad with our coffee?"

He sprang alertly from his perch and hastened into the typists' room, where Miss Parton was detailing to a prick-eared audience the more juicy details of the morning's scene with Mr. Armstrong.

"That's nothing," announced Mr. Bredon. "You haven't heard the latest development."

"Oh, *what* is it?" cried Miss Rossiter.

"I've promised not to tell," said Mr. Bredon.

"Shame, shame!"

"At least, I didn't exactly promise. I was asked not to."

"Is it about Mr. Tallboy's money?"

"You do know, then? What a disappointment!"

"I know that poor little Mrs. Crump was crying this morning because Mr. Tallboy had accused her of taking some money out of his desk."

"Well, if you know that," said Mr. Bredon artlessly, "in justice to Mrs. Crump–"

His tongue wagged busily.

"Well, I think it's too bad of Mr. Tallboy," said Miss Rossiter. "He's always being rude to poor old Copley. It's a shame. And it's rotten to accuse the charwomen."

"Yes, it is," agreed Miss Parton, "but I've no patience with that Copley creature. He's a tiresome old sneak. He went and told Hankie once that he'd seen me at the dog-races with a gentleman friend. As if it was any business of his what a girl does out of business hours. He's too nosey by half. Just because anybody's a mere typist it doesn't mean one's a heathen slave. Oh! here's Mr. Ingleby. Coffee, Mr. Ingleby? I say, *have* you heard about old Copley pinching Mr. Tallboy's fifty quid?"

"You don't say so," exclaimed Mr. Ingleby, shooting a miscellaneous collection of oddments out of the waste-paper basket as a preliminary to up-turning it and sitting upon it. "Tell me quickly. Golly! what a day we're having!"

"Well," said Miss Rossiter, lusciously taking up the tale, "somebody sent Mr. Tallboy fifty pounds in a registered envelope–"

"What's all this?" interrupted Miss Meteyard, arriving with some sheets of copy in one hand and a bag of bulls' eyes in the other. "Here are some lollipops for my little ones. Now let's hear it all from the beginning. I only wish people would send *me* fifty poundses in registered envelopes. Who was the benefactor?"

"I don't know. Do you know, Mr. Bredon?"

"Haven't the foggiest. But it was all in currency notes, which is suspicious, for a start."

"And he brought them to the office, meaning to take them to the Bank."

"But he was busy," chimed in Miss Parton, "and forgot all about them."

"Catch me forgetting about fifty pounds," said Miss Parton's bosom-friend from the Printing.

"Oh, we're only poor hardworking typists. Fifty pounds or so is nothing to Mr. Tallboy, obviously. He put them in his desk–"

"Why not in his pocket?"

"Because he was working in his shirt-sleeves, and didn't like to leave all that wealth hanging on a coat-peg–"

"Yes; well, he forgot them at the lunch-hour. And in the afternoon, he found that the blockmaker had done something silly with the Nutrax block–"

"Was that what delayed it?" inquired Mr. Bredon.

"Yes, that was it. And, I say, I've found out something else. Mr. Drew–"

"Who's Mr. Drew?"

"That stout man from the Cormorant Press. He said to Mr. Tallboy he thought the headline was a bit hot. And Mr. Tallboy said he had a nasty mind and anyhow, everybody had passed it and it was too late to alter it then–"

"Jiminy!" said Mr. Garrett, suddenly bursting into speech, "it's a good thing Copley didn't get hold of that. He'd have rubbed it in, all right. I must say, I think Tallboy ought to have done something about it."

"Who told you that?"

"Mr. Wedderburn. Drew asked him about it this morning. Said he noticed they'd thought better of it after all."

"Well, get on with the story."

"By the time Mr. Tallboy had had the block put right, the Bank was shut. So he forgot about it again, and went off, leaving the fifty quid in his desk."

"Does he often do that sort of thing?"

"Goodness knows. And old Copley was working late on his jellies–"

Clack, clack, clack. The story lost nothing in the telling.

"–poor old Mrs. Crump was weeping like a sponge–"

"–Mrs. Johnson was in *such* a bait–"

"–making a most *awful* row. Mr. Bredon heard them. What did he call him, Mr. Bredon?"

"–accused him of stealing the money–"

"–thief and scoundrel–"

"—what Mr. Brotherhood must have thought—"

"—give them the sack, I shouldn't wonder—"

"—my dear, the *thrills* we get in this place!"

"And, by the way," observed Mr. Ingleby, maliciously, "I pulled Barrow's leg all right about that sketch."

"You *didn't* tell him what Mr. Armstrong said?"

"No. At least, I didn't tell him Mr. Armstrong said it. But I gave him a hint to that effect off my own bat."

"You are awful!"

"He's out for the blood of this department—especially Copley's."

"Because Copley went to Hankie last week about a Jamboree display and complained that Barrow didn't follow his directions, and so now he thinks this business is a plot of Copley's to—"

"Shut up!"

Miss Rossiter leapt at her typewriter and began to pound the keys deafeningly.

Amid a pointed silence of tongues, Mr. Copley made his entrance.

"Is that Jelly copy of mine ready, Miss Rossiter? There doesn't seem to be much work being done here this morning."

"You've got to take your turn, Mr. Copley. I have a report of Mr. Armstrong's to finish."

"I shall speak to Mr. Armstrong about the way the work is done," said Mr. Copley. "This room is a bear-garden. It's disgraceful."

"Why not give Mr. Hankin a turn?" snapped Miss Parton, unpleasantly.

"No, but really, Copley, old sport," pleaded Mr. Bredon, earnestly. "You mustn't let these little things get your goat. It's not done, old thing. Positively not done. You watch me squeeze copy out of Miss Parton. She eats out of my hand. A little kindness and putting her hair in papers will work wonders with her. Ask her nicely and she'll do anything for you."

"A man of your age, Bredon, should know better," said Mr. Copley, "than to hang round here all day. Am I the only person in this office with work to do?"

"If you only knew it," replied Mr. Bredon, "I'm working away like anything. Look here," he added, as the unhappy Mr. Copley withdrew, "do the poor old blighter's muck for him. It's a damned shame to tease him. He's looking horribly green about the gills."

"Right-ho!" said Miss Parton, amiably, "I don't mind if I do. May as well get it over."

The typewriters clacked again.

# 9

# UNSENTIMENTAL MASQUERADE OF A HARLEQUIN

DIANE DE Momerie was holding her own. True, the big Chrysler and the Bentley ahead of her had more horsepower, but young Spenlow was too drunk to last out, and Harry Thorne was a notoriously rotten driver. She had only to tail them at a safe distance till they came to grief. She only wished

"Spot" Lancaster would leave her alone. His clumsy grabs at her waist and shoulders interfered with her handling of the car. She eased the pressure of her slim sandal on the accelerator, and jabbed an angry elbow into his hot face.

"Shut up, you fool! you'll have us into the ditch, and then they'd beat us."

"I say!" protested Spot, "don't do that. It hurts."

She ignored him, keeping her eye on the road. Everything was perfect tonight. There had been a most stimulating and amusing row at Tod Milligan's, and Tod had been very definitely told where he got off. All the better. She was getting tired of Tod's hectoring. She was keyed up just enough and not too much. The hedges flashed and roared past them; the road, lit by the raking headlights, showed like a war-worn surface of holes and hillocks, which miraculously smoothed themselves out beneath the spinning wheels. The car rode the earth-waves like a ship. She wished it were an open car and not this vulgar, stuffy saloon of Spot's.

The Chrysler ahead was lurching perilously, thrashing her great tail like a fighting salmon. Harry Thorne had no business with a car like that; he couldn't hold it on the road. And there was a sharp S-bend coming. Dian knew that. Her senses seemed unnaturally sharpened—she could see the road unrolled before her like a map. Thorne was taking the first bend—far too wide—and young Spenlow was cutting in on the left. The race was hers now—nothing could prevent it. Spot was drinking again from a pocket-flask. Let him. It left her free. The Chrysler, wrenched brutally across the road, caught the Bentley on the inner edge of the bend, smashing it against the bank and slewing it round till it stood across the road. Was there room to pass? She pulled out, her off wheels bumping over the grass verge. The Chrysler staggered on, swaying from the impact—it charged the bank and broke through the hedge. She heard Thorne yell—saw the big car leap miraculously to earth without overturning, and gave an answering cry of triumph. And then the road was suddenly lit up as though by a searchlight, whose powerful beam swallowed her own headlights like a candle in sunlight.

She leant over to Spot.

"Who's that behind us?"

"Dunno," grunted Spot, twisting ineffectually to stare through the small pane at the rear of the car. "Some blighter or other."

Dian set her teeth. Who the hell, who the *hell* had a car like that? The driving mirror showed only the glare of the enormous twin lights. She drove the accelerator down to its limit, and the car leaped forward. But the pursuer followed easily. She swung out on the crown of the road. Let him crash if he wanted to. He held on remorselessly. A narrow, hump-backed bridge sprang out of the darkness. She topped it and seemed to leap the edge of the world. A village, with a wide open square. This would be the man's chance. He took it. A great dark shape loomed up beside her, long, low and open. Out of the tail of her eye she sought the driver. For five seconds he held beside her, neck and neck, and she saw the black mask and skull-cap and the flash of black and silver. Then, in the narrowing of the street, he swept ahead. She remembered what Pamela Dean had told her:

"You will see him when you least expect him."

Whatever happened, she must hold on to him. He was running ahead now, lightly as a panther, his red tail-lamp tantalizingly only a few yards away. She could have cried with exasperation. He was playing with her.

"Is this all your beastly Dutch-oven will do?"

Spot had fallen asleep. His head rolled against her arm and she shook it off violently. Two miles, and the road plunged beneath over-arching trees, with a stretch of woodland on either side. The leading car turned suddenly down a side-road and thence through an open gate beneath the trees; it wound its way into the heart of the wood, and then abruptly stopped; all its lights were shut off.

She jammed on her brakes and was out upon the grass. Overhead the treetops swung together in the wind. She ran to the other car; it was empty.

She stared round. Except for the shaft of light thrown by her own head-lamps, the darkness was Egyptian. She stumbled over her long skirts among briars and tufts of bracken. She called:

"Where are you? Where are you hiding? Don't be so *silly!*"

There was no answer. But presently, far off and mockingly, there came the sound of a very high, thin fluting. No jazz tune, but one which she remembered from nursery days:

*Tom, Tom the piper's son*
*Learned to play when he was young,*
*And the only tune that he could play*
*Was: "Over the hills and far away–"*

"It's too *stupid*," said Dian.

*Over the hills and a great way off*
*The wind is blowing my top-knot off.*

The sound was so bodiless that it seemed to have no abiding-place. She ran forward, and it grew fainter; a thick bramble caught her, tearing her ankles and her sheer silk stockings. She wrenched herself pettishly away and started off in a new direction. The piping ceased. She suddenly became afraid of the trees and the darkness. The good, comforting drinks were taking back the support they gave and offering her instead a horrible apprehensiveness. She remembered Spot's pocket-flask and began scrambling back towards the car. Then the beaconing lights went out, leaving her alone with the trees and the wind.

The high spirits induced by gin and cheerful company do not easily survive siege by darkness and solitude. She was running now, desperately, and screaming as she ran. A root, like a hand about her ankles, tripped her, and she dropped, cowering.

The thin tune began again.

*Tom, Tom the piper's son–*

She sat up.

"The terror induced by forests and darkness," said a mocking voice from somewhere over her head, "was called by the Ancients, Panic fear, or the fear of the great god Pan. It is interesting to observe that modern progress has not altogether succeeded in banishing it from ill-disciplined minds."

Dian gazed upwards. Her eyes were growing accustomed to the night, and in the branches of the tree above her she caught the pale gleam of silver.

"What do you want to behave like an idiot for?"

"Advertisement, chiefly. One must be different. I am always different. That is why, my dear young lady, I am the pursued and not the pursuer. You may say it is a cheap way of producing an effect, and so it is; but it is good enough for gin-soaked minds. On such as you, if you will pardon my saying so, subtlety would be wasted."

"I wish you would come down."

"Possibly. But I prefer to be looked up to."

"You can't stay there all night. Think how silly you would look in the morning."

"Ah! but by comparison with yourself I shall retain an almost bandbox perfection of appearance. My costume is better suited than yours to acrobatic exercise in a wood at midnight."

"Well, what are you doing it for, anyway?"

"To please myself–which is the only reason you would admit for doing anything."

"Then you can sit up there and do it all alone. I'm going home."

"Your shoes aren't very suitable for a long walk–but if it amuses you, go home by all means."

"Why should I have to walk?"

"Because I have the ignition keys of both cars in my pocket. A simple precaution, my dear Watson. Nor do I think it will be very much good to try to send a message by your companion. He is plunged in the arms of Morpheus–an ancient and powerful god, though not so ancient as Pan."

"I hate you," said Dian.

"Then you are on the high road to loving me–which is only natural. We needs must love the highest when we see it. Can you see me?"

"Not very well. I could see you better if you came down."

"And love me better, perhaps?"

"Perhaps."

"Then I am safer where I am. Your lovers have a knack of coming to bad ends. There was young Carmichael–"

"I couldn't help that. He drank too much. He was an idiot."

"And Arthur Barrington–"

"I told him it wasn't any good."

"Not a bit of good. But he tried, all the same, and blew his brains out. Not that they were very good brains, but they were all the brains he had. And Victor Dean–"

"The little rotter! That wasn't anything to do with me."

"Wasn't it?"

"Why, he fell down a staircase, didn't he?"

"So he did. But why?"

"I haven't the faintest idea."

"Haven't you? I thought you might have. Why did you send Victor Dean about his business?"

"Because he was a silly little bore and just like all the rest."

"You like them to be different?"

"I like everything to be different."

"And when you find them different, you try to make them all alike. Do you know anybody who is different?"

"Yes; you're different."

"Only so long as I stay on my branch, Circe. If I come down to your level, I should be just like all the rest."

"Come down and try."

"I know when I am well off. You had better come up to me."

"You know I can't."

"Of course you can't. You can only go down and down."

"Are you trying to insult me?"

"Yes, but it's very difficult."

"Come down, Harlequin–I want you here."

"That's a new experience for you, isn't it? To want what you can't get. You ought to be grateful to me."

"I always want what I can't get."

"What do you want?"

"Life–thrills–"

"Well, you're getting them now. Tell me all about Victor Dean."

"Why do you want to know about him?"

"That's a secret."

"If I tell you, will you come down?"

"Perhaps."

"What a funny thing to want to know about."

"I'm famous for being funny. How did you pick him up?"

"We all went out one night to some frightful sort of suburban dancing place. We thought it would be such a scream."

"And was it?"

"No, it was rather dull really. But he was there, and he fell for me and I thought he was rather a pet. That's all."

"A simple story in words of one syllable. How long was he your pet?"

"Oh, about six months. But he was terribly, terribly boring. And such a prig. Imagine it, Harlequin darling. He got all cross and wanted bread and cheese and kisses. Are you laughing?"

"Hilariously."

"He wasn't any fun. He was all wet."

"My child, you are telling this story very badly. You made him drink and it upset his little tummy. You made him play high, and he said he couldn't afford it. And you tried to make him take drugs and he didn't like it. Anything else?"

"He was a little beast, Harlequin, really he was. He was out for what he could get."

"Aren't you?"

"Me?" Dian was really surprised. "I'm terribly generous. I gave him everything he wanted. I'm like that when I'm fond of anybody."

"He took what he could get but didn't spend it like a gentleman?"

"That's it. Do you know, he actually called himself a gentleman. Wouldn't that make you laugh? Like the middle ages, isn't it? Ladies and Gentlemen. He said we needn't think he wasn't a gentleman because he worked in an office. Too mirth-making, Harlequin, darling, wasn't it?"

She rocked herself backwards and forwards in amusement.

"Harlequin! Listen! I'll tell you something funny. One night Tod Milligan came in and I told him: 'This is Victor Dean, and he's a gentleman, and he works for Pym's Publicity.' Tod said: 'Oh, you're the chap, are you?' and looked too utterly murderous. And afterwards he asked me, just like you, how I got hold of Victor. That's queer. Did Tod send you out here to ask me?"

"No. No one ever sends me. I go where I like."

"Well, then, why do you all want to know about Victor Dean?"

"Too mystery-making, isn't it? What did Milligan say to Dean?"

"Nothing much, but he told me to string him along. And afterwards, quite suddenly, he told me to give him the push."

"And you did as you were told, like a good girl?"

"I was fed up with Victor, anyhow. And it doesn't do to get wrong with Tod."

"No—he might cut off supplies, mightn't he? Where does he get it from?"

"Coke, do you mean? I don't know."

"No, I suppose you don't. And you can't get him to tell you, either. Not with all your charms, Circe."

"Oh, Tod! he doesn't give anything away. He's a dirty swine. I loathe him. I'd do anything to get away from Tod. But he knows too much. And besides, he's got the stuff. Lots of people have tried to chuck Tod, but they always go back again—on Fridays and Saturdays."

"That's when he hands it out, is it?"

"Mostly. But—" she began to laugh again—"you weren't there tonight, were you? It was too amusing. He'd run short, or something. There was a hellish row. And that septic woman Babs Woodley was screaming all over the place. She scratched him. I do hope he gets blood-poisoning. He promised it would be there tomorrow, but he looked the most perfect idiot, with blood running down his chin. She said she'd shoot him. It was too marvellous."

"Rabelaisian, no doubt."

"Fortunately I'd got enough, so I gave her enough to keep her quiet, and then we thought we'd have a race. I won—at least, I should have, if it hadn't been for you. How did you happen along?"

"Oh, I just happened along. I always happen."

"You don't. You only seem to happen occasionally. You aren't one of Tod's regular lot, are you?"

"Not at present."

"Do you want to be? Because, don't. I'll get the stuff for you if you want it. But Tod's a beast. You'd better keep clear of him."

"Are you warning me for my good?"

"Yes, I am."

"What devotion!"

"No, I mean it. Life's hell, anyway, but it's worse if you get mixed up with Tod."

"Then why don't you cut loose from Tod?"

"I can't."

"Afraid of him?"

"Not so much of him. It's the people behind him. Tod's afraid too. He'd never let me go. He'd kill me first."

"How fascinating! I think I must know Tod better."

"You'd end by being afraid, too."

"Should I? Well, there's a kick in being afraid."

"Come down here, Harlequin, and I'll show you how to get a kick out of life."

"Could you?"

"Try and see."

There was a rustle among the leaves, and he slid down to stand beside her.

"Well?"

"Lift me up. I'm all cramped."

He lifted her, and she felt his hands hard as iron under her breast. She was tall, and as she turned to look at him she could see the glint of his eyeballs, level with her own.

"Well, will I do?"

"For what?"

"For you?"

"For me? What are you good for, to me?"

"I'm beautiful."

"Not so beautiful as you were. In five years' time you will be ugly."

"Five years? I wouldn't want you for five years."

"I wouldn't want you for five minutes."

The cold daybreak was beginning to filter through the leaves; it showed her only a long, implacable chin and the thin curl of a smiling mouth. She made a snatch at his mask, but he was too quick for her. Very deliberately he turned her towards him, putting both her arms behind her back and holding them there.

"What next?" she demanded, mockingly.

"Nothing. I shall take you home."

"You will? Ah, you will, then?"

"Yes, as I did once before."

"Exactly as you did before?"

"Not exactly, because you were drunk then. You are sober now. With that trifling difference, the programme will be carried out according to precedent."

"You might kiss me, Harlequin."

"Do you deserve kissing? Once, for your information. Twice, for your disinterested effort to save me from the egregious Mr. Milligan. And the third time, because the fancy takes me that way."

He bestowed the kisses like deliberate insults. Then he picked her up bodily, still holding her arms imprisoned, and dumped her into the back of the open car.

"Here's a rug for you. You'll need it."

She said nothing. He started up the engine, turned the car and drove it slowly along the path. As they came abreast of the saloon, he leaned out and tossed the ignition key on to the knees of Spot Lancaster, happily snoring in his seat. In a few minutes, they had turned out from the wood into the main road. The sky was faintly streaked with the ghostly glimmer of the false dawn.

Dian de Momerie slid from under the rug and leaned forward. He was driving easily, slumped down in his seat, his black poll leaning carelessly back, his hand slack on the wheel. With a twist, she could send him and herself into the ditch, and he would deserve it.

"Don't do it," he said, without turning his head.

"You devil!"

He stopped the car.

"If you don't behave, I shall leave you by the roadside, sitting on a milestone, like the bailiff's daughter of Islington. Or, if you prefer it, I can tie you up. Which is it to be?"

"Be kind to me."

"I am being kind. I have preserved you from boredom for two solid hours. I beg you not to plunge us both into the horrors of an anti-climax. What are you crying for?"

"I'm tired—and you won't love me."

"My poor child, pull yourself together. Who would believe that Dian de

Momerie could fall for a fancy-dress and a penny whistle?"

"It isn't that. It's you. There's something queer about you. I'm afraid of you. You aren't thinking about me at all. You're thinking of something horrible. What is it? What is it? Wait!"

She put out a cold hand and clutched his arm.

"I'm seeing something that I can't make out. I've got it now. Straps. They are strapping his elbows and dropping a white bag over his head. The hanged man. There's a hanged man in your thoughts. Why are you thinking of hanging?"

She shrank away from him and huddled into the farthest corner of the car. Wimsey re-started the engine and let in the clutch.

"Upon my word," he thought, "that's the oddest after-effect of drink and drugs I've met yet. Very interesting. But not very safe. Quite a providential interposition in one way. We may get home without breaking our necks. I didn't know I carried such a graveyard aura about with me."

Dian was fast asleep when he lifted her out of the car. She half woke, and slipped her arms round his neck.

"Darling, it's been lovely." Then she came to with a little start. "Where have we got to? What's happened?"

"We're home. Where's your latch-key?"

"Here. Kiss me. Take that mask off."

"Run along in. There's a policeman thinking we look rather disreputable." He opened the door.

"Aren't you coming in?"

She seemed to have forgotten all about the hanged man.

He shook his head.

"Well, good-bye then."

"Good-bye."

He kissed her gently this time and pushed her into the house. The policeman, stumping inquisitively nearer, revealed a face that Wimsey knew. He smiled to himself as the official gaze swept over him.

"Good morning, officer."

"Morning, sir," said the policeman, stolidly.

"Moffatt, Moffatt," said his lordship, reprovingly, "you will never get promotion. If you don't know me, you should know the car."

"Good lord, your lordship, I beg your pardon. Didn't somehow expect to see you here."

"Not so much of the lordship. Somebody might be listening. You on your beat?"

"Just going home, my–sir."

"Jump in and I'll drive you there. Ever see a fellow called Milligan round this way?"

"Major Tod Milligan? Yes, now and then. He's a bad hat, he is, if ever there was one. Runs that place down by the river. Mixed up with that big drug-gang as Mr. Parker's after. We could pull him in any day, but he's not the real big noise."

"Isn't he, Moffatt?"

"No, my lord. This car's a treat, ain't she? Shouldn't think there's much catches *you* on the road. No. What Mr. Parker wants is to get him to lead us to the top man of all, but there don't seem to be much chance of it. They're as cunning as weasels, they are. Don't suppose he knows himself who the other fellow is."

"How's it worked, Moffatt?"

"Well, my lord, as far as we've been told, the stuff is brought in from the coast once or twice a week and run up to London. We've had a try at catching it on the way more than once, that is to say, Mr. Parker's special squad have, but they've always given us the slip. Then it'll be taken somewhere, but where we don't know, and distributed out again to the big distributors. From them it goes to all kinds of places. We could lay hands on it there—but lord! what's the use? It'd only be in another place next week."

"And whereabouts does Milligan come into it?"

"We think he's one of the high-up distributors, my lord. He hands it out at that house of his, and in other places."

"In the place where you found me, for instance?"

"That's one of them."

"But the point is, where does Milligan get his supplies?"

"That's it, my lord."

"Can't you follow him and find out?"

"Ah! but he don't fetch it for himself, my lord. There's others does that. And you see, if we was to open his parcels and search his tradesmen and so on, they'd just strike him off their list, and we'd be back where we was before."

"So you would. How often does he give parties in that house of his?"

"Most evenings, my lord. Seems to keep open house, like."

"Well, keep an eye open on Friday and Saturday nights, Moffatt."

"Fridays and Saturdays, my lord?"

"Those are the nights when things happen."

"Is that so, my lord? I'm much obliged to you. We didn't know that. That's a good tip, that is. If you'll drop me at the next corner, my lord, that'll do me champion. I'm afraid I've took your lordship out of your way."

"Not a bit, Moffatt, not a bit. Very glad to have seen you. And, by the way, you have not seen me. Not a question of my morals, you understand, but I've a fancy that Major Milligan might not approve of my visiting that particular house."

"That's all right, my lord. Not being on duty at the time, I ain't bound to put it in a report. Good morning, my lord, and thank you."

# 10

# DISTRESSING DEVELOPMENTS OF AN OFFICE ROW

All very well for you to talk, Bill Jones," said Ginger Joe, "but bet you sixpence if you was called as a witness in a case, you'd get into a 'owling mess. Why, they might ask you what you was doin' a month ago and what'd you know about that?"

"Bet you I'd know all right."

"Bet you you wouldn't."

"All right, bet you anything I would."

"Bet you if I was a 'tec—"

"Cor lumme, you'd be a good 'tec, you would."

"Bet you I would, anyhow."

" 'Oo ever 'eard of a carrotty-'eaded 'tec?"

This objection appeared to Ginger to be irrelevant. He replied, however, automatically:

"Bet you I'd be a better 'tec 'or you."

"Bet you you wouldn't."

"Bet you if I was a 'tec and arst you w'ere you was when Mr. Dean fell downstairs, you wouldn't 'ave no alleybi."

"That's silly, that is," said Bill Jones. "I wouldn't want no alleybi for Mr. Dean falling downstairs, 'cause it was accidental death."

"All right, Suet-face. I was only sayin', supposin' I *was* a 'tec an' I was investigatin' Mr. Dean's fallin' downstairs, and I arst you wot you was a-doin' of, you wouldn't be able to tell me."

"Bet you I would, then. I was on the lift, that's where I was, and 'Arry could prove it. So just you stick that in your silly face and shut up."

"Oh, you was on the lift, was you? 'Ow d'you know that was when it was?"

"When wot was?"

"When Mr. Dean fell downstairs?"

" 'Cos the first thing I 'ears when I comes off of the lift is Mr. Tompkin a-telling Sam there all about it. Didn't I, Sam?"

Sam Tabbitt glanced up from a copy of *Radio for Amateurs* and nodded briefly.

"That don't prove nothing," persisted Ginger. "Not without you know 'ow long it took Mr. Tompkin to shoot 'is mouth off."

"Not long it didn't," said Sam. "I'd just come out of the Big Conference room—takin' tea to Mr. Pym and two clients, I was—Muggleton's, if you want ter know—and I hears an awful screeching and I says to Mr. Tompkin, 'Coo, lumme!' I says, 'wot's up?' An' he says as Mr. Dean's fallen down and broke 'is neck an' they've jest rung up for a doctor."

"That's right," added Cyril, who was the boy in attendance on the Executive and the Switchboard. "Mr. Stanley comes running along full pelt into our place and says, 'Oh, Miss Fearney, Mr. Dean's fell downstairs and we're afraid he's killed himself and you're to telephone for a doctor.' So Miss Fearney tells Miss Beit to put the call through and I hops out quick through the other door so as Miss Fearney can't see me—that's the door behind Mr. Tompkin's desk—and I says, 'Mr. Dean's tumbled down and killed hisself,' and he says, 'Run and see what's happened, Cyril.' So I runs and I see Sam jest a-comin' out from the Big Conference room. Didn't I, Sam?"

Sam agreed.

"And that's when I heard the screeching," he added.

"Who was a-screeching?"

"Mrs. Crump was a-screeching in the Executive. Said she'd just seen Mr. Dean fall down and kill hisself and they was a-bringin' 'im along. So I looked into the passage and there they was, a-carryin' of him. He did look awful."

"And that was when I come up," said Bill, sticking to the point at issue. "I hears Mr. Tompkin telling Sam about it, and I runs after Sam and I calls to Mr. Tompkin as they're a-bringing him through, and he comes and looks on too. So they takes him into the Board-room, and Miss Fearney says, 'What about telling Mr. Pym?' and Mr. Tompkin says, 'He's still in the conference,' and she says, 'I know he is. We don't want the clients to hear about it.' So Mr. Tompkin says, 'Better telephone through to him.' So she does and then she gets hold of me and says, 'Bill, get a sheet of brown paper and run along to the Board-room and tell them to put it over the glass door,' and just as I was a-going, Mr. Atkins comes along and says, 'Is there any dust-sheets?' he says. 'He's gone,' he says, 'and we got to have somethink to put over him.' And Miss Fearney says, sharp-like, 'Dust-sheets is nothing to do with this department,' she says, 'what are you thinking about? Go up and ask Mrs. Johnson.' Coo! that was a set-out, that was." Bill grinned, as one who looks back to a grand gala-day, a brilliant green oasis in a desert of drudgery. Then he remembered once more what the dispute had been about.

"So where's your blinkin' alleybi?" he demanded, sternly. "Where's yours, Ginger, if it comes to that?"

By such methods, serpentine but effective, Ginger Joe pursued his inquiries. The eyes of the office-boy are everywhere, and his memory is retentive. Five days of inquiry brought the whole inside staff of Pym's under review—all that was necessary, since the day of Dean's death had not been the day that brought the Outside Publicity men into the office.

Out of the ninety-odd inside members of the staff, only ten remained unaccounted or partially unaccounted for. These were: in the Copy Department:

*Mr. Willis.* He had arrived from the outside staircase about five minutes after the accident, had gone straight through the hall, up the stair to the Dispatching and so into his own room, speaking to nobody. About a quarter of an hour later, he had gone to Mr. Dean's room and, not finding him, had gone back to the typists' room. Here, on asking for Mr. Dean, he had been greeted with the news, which appeared to startle and horrify him. (Witness: the boy George Pyke, who had heard Miss Rossiter telling Mrs. Johnson all about it.)

*Mr. Hankin.* He had been absent from the office since half-past two, on private business, and did not return till half-past four. Harry had informed him of the catastrophe as soon as he came in, and, as soon as he stepped out of the lift, Mr. Tompkin had requested him to go and see Mr. Pym. (Witnesses: Harry and Cyril.)

*Mr. Copley.* Presumably in his room all the time, but this could not be substantiated, since he never took tea and was accustomed to work at his "slope," which was set against the inner wall and not visible to any one casually passing his door. He was an assiduous worker, and was not likely to emerge from his room, however much noise or running about there might be in the passages. At a quarter to five, he had walked in the most ordinary way into the typists' room to ask why his copy had not been typed. Miss Parton had told him, rather tartly, that she didn't see how he could expect anything to be ready under the circumstances. He had then asked what circumstances and, on being told about Mr. Dean's fatal accident, had expressed astonishment and regret, but added that he could see no reason why the work of the department should not be carried on. (Witnesses: four boys who, on separate occasions, had heard this shocking exhibition of callousness discussed with and by Mrs. Johnson.)

In the Vouchers:

*Mr. Binns.* An elegant youth who had gone out at 3 o'clock to inquire for last September's number of the *Connoissseur* for Mr. Armstrong, and had unaccountably taken an hour and a half over the transaction. (Witness: Sam, whose elder sister was a typist in the Vouchers, and had given it as her opinion that young Binns had had a date for tea with his best girl.) (Note: Mr.

Binns was already known to Mr. Bredon as the darts expert who had often lunched with Victor Dean.)

In the various Group-managers' offices:

*Mr. Haagedorn* (Sopo and allied products). Leave of absence all day to attend aunt's funeral. But said to have been seen during the afternoon attending a matinée at the Adelphi. (Witnesses: Jack Dennis, the boy who thought he had seen him, and Mr. Tompkin's attendance-register consulted by Cyril.)

*Mr. Tallboy*. Exact location at the moment of the action not quite certain. At 3:30 or thereabouts, Mr. Wedderburn had come down to the Vouchers to ask for certain back numbers of the *Fishmonger's Gazette*, saying that Mr. Tallboy wanted them in a hurry. On returning ten minutes later, after having the required numbers sorted out for him, Mr. Wedderburn had run into all the excitement about Mr. Dean and had forgotten the *Fishmonger's Gazette*. He had, in fact, been talking to Miss Fearney in the Executive, when Mr. Tallboy had come in and rather abruptly asked whether he was expected to wait all night for them. Mr. Wedderburn had explained that the alarm about Mr. Dean had put the matter out of his head, and Mr. Tallboy had replied that the work had got to be done, notwithstanding. (Witnesses: Horace, the messenger-boy in the Vouchers, and Cyril.)

*Mr. McAllister*. Group-secretary to Dairyfields, Ltd., under Mr. Smayle. Absent all afternoon on visit to dentist. (Witness: Mr. Tompkin's register.)

In the Studio:

*Mr. Barrow*. At British Museum, studying Greek vases with view to advertising display for Klassika Corsets. (Witness: Mr. Barrow's time-sheet.)

*Mr. Vibart*. Supposed to be at Westminster, making a sketch of the Terrace of the House of Commons for Farley's Footwear. ("The feet that tread this historic pavement are more often than not, clad in Farley Fashion Footwear.") Absent 2:30-4:30. (Witnesses: Mr. Vibart's time-sheet and the sketch itself.)

*Wilfred Cotterill*. At 3 o'clock complained of nose-bleeding and sent to lie down by himself in the Boys' Room, the other boys being told to leave him alone. Completely forgotten by everybody till 5 o'clock, when he was discovered, asleep, by the boys going in to change their tunics. Alleged that he had slept through the whole of the excitement. (Witnesses: All the other boys.) Wilfred Cotterill was a small, pale, excitable child of fourteen, but looking much younger. When told what he had missed he merely remarked "Oo-er!"

A very creditable piece of work on Ginger Joe's part, thought Mr. Bredon, if we may continue so to call him during office-hours, but leaving much room for further inquiry. His own investigations were not going too well. In his search for Darling Special Pencils he had been brought face to face with the practical communism of office life. The Copy Department preferred 5B or even 6B drawing-pencils for writing its roughs, and was not much interested in Darling's product, except, of course, Mr. Garrett, who had been drawing up a little panel for display in Darling's advertisements, calling attention to the generous offer of the pencil. He had two specimens, and four, in various stages of decay, were found in the typists' room. There was one on Mr. Armstrong's desk. Mr. Hankin had none. Mr. Ingleby admitted to having thrown his out of the window in a fit of temper, and Miss Meteyard said she thought she had one somewhere if Mr. Bredon really wanted it, but he had better ask Miss Parton. The other departments were even worse. The pencils had been taken home, lost, or thrown away. Mr. McAllister, mysteriously but characteristically, said he had no less than six. Mr. Wedderburn had lost his, but produced one which he had bagged from Mr. Tallboy. Mr. Prout said he couldn't be bothered; the pencil was a silly, gimcrack thing anyway; if Bredon really wanted a propelling pencil he ought to get an Eversharp. He (Mr. Prout) had never seen the thing since he'd had it to photograph; he added that for a first-class photographer to spend his life photographing tin pencils and jelly cartons was enough to drive any sensitive person to suicide. It was heart-breaking work.

In the matter of his own address, Bredon did get one piece of information. Mr. Willis had asked for it one day. Discreet questioning fixed the date to within a day or so, one way or another, of Chief-Inspector Parker's unfortunate encounter on the stairs. Nearer than this, Miss Beit (the telephonist, who also presided over the office address-book) could not go. It was all rather unnerving as well as exasperating. Mr. Bredon hoped that the assailant would have been sufficiently alarmed by the failure of his first attempt to forswear blunt instruments and violence for the future; nevertheless, he developed a habit of keeping a careful lookout for following footsteps whenever he left the office. He went home by circuitous routes, and when engaged on his daily duties, found himself avoiding the iron staircase.

Meanwhile, the great Nutrax row raged on with undiminished vigour, developing as it went an extraordinary number of offshoots and ramifications, of which the most important and alarming was a violent breach between Mr. Smayle and Mr. Tallboy.

It began, rather absurdly, at the bottom of the lift, where Mr. Tallboy and Miss Meteyard were standing, waiting for Harry to return and waft them to their sphere of toil above. To them, enter Mr. Smayle, fresh and smiling, his teeth gleaming as though cleaned with Toothshine, a pink rosebud in his buttonhole, his umbrella neatly rolled.

"Morning, Miss Meteyard, morning, morning," said Mr. Smayle, raising his bowler, and replacing it at a jaunty angle. "Fine day again."

Miss Meteyard agreed that it was a fine day. "If only," she added, "they wouldn't spoil it with income-tax demands."

"Don't talk about income-tax," replied Mr. Smayle with a smile and a shudder. "I said to the wife this morning, 'My dear, we shall have to take our holiday in the back garden, I can see.' And I'm sure it's a fact. Where the money for our usual little trip to Eastbourne is to come from, I don't know."

"The whole thing's iniquitous," said Mr. Tallboy. "As for this last budget–"

"Ah! *you* must be paying super-tax, old man," said Mr. Smayle, giving Mr. Tallboy a prod in the ribs with his umbrella.

"Don't do that," said Mr. Tallboy.

"Tallboy needn't worry," said Mr. Smayle, with a rallying air. "He's got more money than he knows what to do with. We all know that, don't we, Miss Meteyard?"

"He's luckier than most, then," said Miss Meteyard.

"He can afford to chuck his quids over the office, fifty at a time," pursued Mr. Smayle. "Wish I knew where he gets it from. Daresay the income-tax authorities would like to know too. I'll tell you what, Miss Meteyard, this man's a dark horse. I believe he runs a dope-den or a bucket-shop on the sly, eh? You're a one, you are," said Mr. Smayle, extending a roguish forefinger and jabbing it into Mr. Tallboy's second waistcoat button. At this moment the lift descended and Miss Meteyard stepped into it. Mr. Tallboy, rudely thrusting Mr. Smayle aside, stepped in after her.

"Here!" said Mr. Smayle "manners, manners! The trouble with you, old man," he went on, "is that you can't take a joke. No offence meant, I'm sure–and none taken, I hope."

He clapped Mr. Tallboy on the shoulder.

"Do you mind keeping your hands off me, Smayle," said Mr. Tallboy.

"Oh, all right, all right, your Highness. Got out of bed the wrong side, hasn't he?" He appealed to Miss Meteyard, being troubled by an obscure feeling that men should not quarrel before ladies, and that it was somehow up to him to preserve the decencies by turning the whole thing into a joke.

"Money's a sore point with us all, I'm afraid, Mr. Smayle," replied Miss Meteyard. "Let's talk about something jollier. That's a nice rose you've got there."

"Out of my own garden," replied Mr. Smayle, with pride. "Mrs. Smayle's a wonder with the roses. I leave it all to her, bar the digging and mulching, of course." They emerged from the lift and signed their names at the desk. Miss Meteyard and Mr. Smayle passed on through the anteroom and turned by common consent to the left up the stair by the Dispatching. Mr. Tallboy shouldered past them and took a lone and frosty course down the main corridor to ascend by the iron staircase.

"I'm reelly very sorry," said Mr. Smayle, "that Tallboy and I should have indulged in anything approaching to words in your presence, Miss Meteyard."

"Oh, that's nothing. He seems a little irritable. I don't think he likes that little upset of his with Mr. Copley to be talked about."

"No, but reelly," said Mr. Smayle, lingering at the door of Miss Meteyard's room, "if a man can't take a harmless joke, it's a great pity, isn't it?"

"It is," said Miss Meteyard. "Hullo! What are all you people doing here?"

Mr. Ingleby and Mr. Bredon, seated on Miss Meteyard's radiator with a volume of the *New Century Dictionary* between them, looked up unabashed.

"We're finishing a Torquemada cross-word," said Ingelby, "and naturally the volume we wanted was in your room. Everything always is."

"I forgive you," said Miss Meteyard.

"But I do wish you wouldn't bring Smayle in here with you," said Mr. Bredon. "The mere sight of him makes me think of Green Pastures Margarine. You haven't come to dun me for that copy, have you? Because don't, there's a good fellow. I haven't done it and I can't do it. My brain has dried up. How you can live all day with Margarine and always look so fresh and cheerful passes my understanding."

"I assure you it's an effort," said Mr. Smayle, displaying his teeth. "But it reelly is a great refreshment to see you copy-writers all so cheerful and pleasant together. Not like some people I could name."

"Mr. Tallboy has been unkind to Mr. Smayle," said Miss Meteyard.

"I like to be agreeable with everybody," said Mr. Smayle, "but reelly, when it comes to shoving your way past a person into the lift as if one wasn't there and then telling you to keep your hands off as if a person was dirt, a man may be excused for taking offence. I suppose Tallboy thinks I'm not worth speaking to, just because he's been to a public school and I haven't."

"Public school," said Mr. Bredon, "first I've heard of it. What public school?"

"He was at Dumbleton," said Mr. Smayle, "but what I say is, I went to a Council School and I'm not ashamed of it."

"Where's Dumbleton?" demanded Ingleby. "I shouldn't worry, Smayle. Dumbleton isn't a public school, within the meaning of the act."

"Isn't it?" said Mr. Smayle, hopefully. "Well, you and Mr. Bredon have had college educations, so you know all about it. What schools do *you* call public schools?"

"Eton," said Mr. Bredon, promptly, "—and Harrow," he added, magnanimously, for he was an Eton man.

"Rugby," suggested Mr. Ingleby.

"No, no," protested Bredon, 'that's a railway junction."

Ingleby delivered a brisk left-hander to Bredon's jaw, which the latter parried neatly.

"And I've heard," Bredon went on, "that there's a decentish sort of place at Winchester, if you're not too particular."

"I once met a man who'd been to Marlborough," suggested Ingleby.

"I'm sorry to hear that," said Bredon. "They get a terrible set of hearty roughs down there. You can't be too careful of your associates, Ingleby."

"Well," said Mr. Smayle, "Tallboy always says that Dumbleton is a public school."

"I daresay it is—in the sense that it has a Board of Governors," said Ingleby, "but it's nothing to be snobbish about."

"What is, if you come to that?" said Bredon. "Look here, Smayle, if only you people could get it out of your heads that these things matter a damn, you'd be a darn sight happier. You probably got a fifty times better education than I ever did."

Mr. Smayle shook his head. "Oh, no," he said, "I'm not deceiving myself about that, and I'd give anything to have had the same opportunities as you. There's a difference, and I know there's a difference, and I don't mind admitting it. But what I mean is, some people make you feel it and others don't. I don't feel it when I'm talking to either of you, or to Mr. Armstrong or Mr. Hankin, though you've been to Oxford and Cambridge and all that. Perhaps it's just because you've been to Oxford and Cambridge."

He struggled with the problem, embarrassing the other two men by his wistful eyes.

"Look here," said Miss Meteyard, "I know what you mean. But it's just that these two here never think twice about it. They don't have to. And you don't have to, either. But the minute anybody begins to worry about whether he's as good as the next man, then he starts a sort of uneasy snobbish feeling and makes himself offensive."

"I see," said Mr. Smayle. "Well, of course, Mr. Hankin doesn't have to try and prove that he's better than me, because he is and we both know it."

"Better isn't the right word, Smayle."

"Well, better educated. You know what I mean."

"Don't worry about it," said Ingleby. "If I were half as good at my job as you are at yours, I should feel superior to everybody in this tom-fool office."

Mr. Smayle shook his head, but appeared comforted.

"I do wish they wouldn't start that kind of thing," said Ingleby when he had gone, "I don't know what to say to them."

"I thought you were a Socialist, Ingleby," said Bredon, "it oughtn't to embarrass you."

"So I am a Socialist," said Ingleby, "but I can't stand this stuff about Old

Dumbletonians. If everybody had the same State education, these things wouldn't happen."

"If everybody had the same face," said Bredon, "there'd be no pretty women."

Miss Meteyard made a grimace.

"If you go on like that, I shall be getting an inferiority complex too."

Bredon looked at her gravely.

"I don't think you'd care to be called pretty," he said, "but if I were a painter I should like to make a portrait of you. You have very interesting bones."

"Good God!" said Miss Meteyard. "I'm going. Let me know when you've finished with my room."

There was a mirror in the typists' room, and in this Miss Meteyard curiously studied her face.

"What's the matter, Miss Meteyard?" asked Miss Rossiter. "Got a spot coming?"

"Something of the sort," said Miss Meteyard, absently. "Interesting bones indeed!"

"Pardon?" said Miss Rossiter.

"Smayle is getting unbearable," grumbled Mr. Tallboy to Mr. Wedderburn. "Vulgar little tick. I hate a fellow who digs you in the ribs."

"He means no harm," rejoined Mr. Wedderburn. "He's quite a decent sort, really."

"Can't stand those teeth," grumbled Mr. Tallboy. "And why must he put that stinking stuff on his hair?"

"Oh, well," said Mr. Wedderburn.

"I'm not going to have him playing in the cricket match, anyhow," pursued Mr. Tallboy, viciously. "Last year he wore white suède shoes with crocodile vamps, and an incredible blazer with Old Borstalian colours."

Mr. Wedderburn looked up, rather startled.

"Oh, but you're not going to leave him out? He's quite a good bat and very nippy on the ball in the field."

"We can do without him," said Mr. Tallboy, firmly. Mr. Wedderburn said no more. There was no regular cricket eleven at Pym's, but every summer a scratch team was got together to play a couple of matches, the selection being entrusted to Mr. Tallboy, who was energetic and had once carried his bat out for 52 against Sopo. He was supposed to submit a list of cricketers for Mr. Hankin's final decision, but Mr. Hankin seldom questioned his selection, for the sufficient reason that there were seldom more than eleven candidates available to choose from. The important point was that Mr. Hankin should bat third, and field at mid-on. If these points were taken note of, he raised no further objections.

Mr. Tallboy pulled out a list.

"Ingleby," he said, "and Garrett. Barrow. Adcock. Pinchley. Hankin. Myself. Gregory can't play; he's going away for the week-end, so we'd better have McAllister. And we can't very well leave out Miller. I wish we could, but he's a Director. Yourself."

"Leave me out," said Mr. Wedderburn. "I haven't touched a bat since last year and I didn't put up much of a show then."

"We've nobody else who can bowl slow spinners," said Mr. Tallboy. "I'll put you down No. 11."

"All right," said Mr. Wedderburn, gratified by the recognition accorded to his bowling, but irrationally provoked by being put down No. 11. He had expected his companion to say, "Oh, but that was just a fluke," and send him in higher up the list. "How about a wicket-keeper? Grayson says he won't do it again, not after getting his front tooth knocked out last year. He seems to have got the wind up properly."

"We'll make Haagedorn do it. He's got hands like a pair of hams. Who else? Oh, that chap in the printing—Beeseley—he's not much good with a bat, but we can rely on him for a few straight balls."

"What about that new fellow in the Copy Department? Bredon? He's a public school man. Is he any good?"

"Might be. He's a bit ancient, though. We've got two aged stiffs already in Hankin and Miller."

"Aged stiff be blowed. That chap can move, I've seen him do it. I wouldn't be surprised if he could show us a bit of style."

"Well, I'll find out. If he's any good, we'll stick him in instead of Pinchley."

"Pinchley can swipe 'em up," said Mr. Wedderburn.

"He never does anything but swipe. He's jam for the fielders. He gave them about ten chances last year and was caught both innings."

Mr. Wedderburn agreed that this was so.

"But he'll be awfully hurt if he's left out," he said.

"I'll ask about Bredon," said Mr. Tallboy.

He sought out that gentleman, who was, for once, in his own room, singing soup-slogans to himself.

*A meal begun with Blagg's Tomato*
*Softens every husband's heart-oh!*

*Hubbies hold those wives most dear*
*Who offer them Blagg's Turtle Clear.*

*Fit for an Alderman—serve it up quick—*
Rum-ti-ty, tum-ti-ty, *Blagg's Turtle Thick.*

"Rum-ti-ty, tum-ti-ty," said Mr. Bredon. "Hullo, Tallboy, what's the matter? Don't say Nutrax has developed any more innuendos."

"Do you play cricket?"

"Well, I used to play for—" Mr. Bredon coughed; he had been about to say, "for Oxford," but remembered in time that these statements could be checked. "I've played a good deal of country-house cricket in the old days. But I'm rapidly qualifying to be called a Veteran. Why?"

"I've got to scrape up an eleven for a match against Brotherhood's. We play one every year. They always beat us, of course, because they have their own playing-fields and play together regularly, but Pym likes it to be done. He thinks it fosters fellow-feeling between client and agent and all that sort of thing."

"Oh! when does it come off?"

"Saturday fortnight."

"I daresay I might keep my end up for a bit, if you can't get anybody better."

"You anything of a bowler?"

"Nothing."

"Better with the willow than the leather, eh?"

Mr. Bredon, wincing a little at this picturesqueness, admitted that, if he was anything, he was a batsman.

"Right. You wouldn't care to open the ball with Ingleby, I suppose?"

"I'd rather not. Put me down somewhere near the tail."

Tallboy nodded.

"Just as you like."

"Who captains this Eleven?"

"Well, I do, as a rule. At least, we always ask Hankin or Miller, just out of compliment, but they generally decline with thanks. Well, righty-ho; I'll just buzz round and see that the others are O.K."

The selected team went up on the office notice-board at lunch-time. At ten minutes past two, the trouble began with Mr. McAllister.

"I observe," said he, making a dour appearance in Mr. Tallboy's room, "that ye're no askin' Smayle to play for ye, and I'm thinkin' it'll be a wee bit awkward for me if I play and he does not. Workin' in his room all day and under his orders, it will make my poseetion not just so very comfortable."

"Position in the office has nothing to do with playing cricket," said Mr. Tallboy.

"Ay, imph'm, that's so. But I just do not care for it. So ye'll oblige me by leavin' my name oot."

"Just as you like," said Tallboy, annoyed. He struck Mr. McAllister's name off the list, and substituted that of Mr. Pinchley. The next defection was that of Mr. Adcock, a stolid youth from the Voucher Department. He inconsiderately fell off a step-ladder in his own home, while assisting his mother to hang a picture, and broke the small bone of his leg.

In this extremity, Mr. Tallboy found himself compelled to go and eat humble pie to Mr. Smayle, and request him to play after all. But Mr. Smayle had been hurt in his feelings by being omitted from the first list, and showed no eagerness to oblige.

Mr. Tallboy, who was, indeed, a little ashamed of himself, endeavoured to gloss the matter over by making it appear that his real object in leaving out Mr. Smayle had been to make room for Mr. Bredon, who had been to Oxford and was sure to play well. But Mr. Smayle was not deceived by this specious reasoning.

"If you had come to me in the first instance," he complained, "and put the matter to me in a friendly way, I should say nothing about it. I like Mr. Bredon, and I appreciate that he has had advantages that I haven't had. He's a very gentlemanly fellow, and I should be happy to make way for him. But I do not care for having things done behind my back in a hole-and-corner fashion."

If Mr. Tallboy had said at this point, "Look here, Smayle, I'm sorry; I was rather out of temper at the time over that little dust-up we had, and I apologize"—then Mr. Smayle, who was really an amiable creature enough, would have given way and done anything that was required of him. But Mr. Tallboy chose to take a lofty tone. He said:

"Come, come, Smayle. You're not Jack Hobbs, you know."

Even this might have passed over with Mr. Smayle's ready admission that he was not England's premier batsman, had not Mr. Tallboy been unhappily inspired to say:

"Of course, I don't know about you, but *I* have always been accustomed to have these things settled by whoever was appointed to select the team, and to play or not, according as I was put down."

"Oh, yes," retorted Mr. Smayle, caught on his sensitive point, "you would say that. I am quite aware, Tallboy, that I never was at a public school, but that is no reason why I shouldn't be treated with ordinary, common courtesy. And from those who have been to real public schools, I get it, what's more. You may think a lot of Dumbleton, but it isn't what *I* call a public school."

"And what do *you* call a public school?" inquired Mr. Tallboy.

"Eton," retorted Mr. Smayle, repeating his lesson with fatal facility, "and Harrow, and—er—Rugby, and Winchester and places like those. Places where they send gentlemen's sons to."

"Oh, do they?" said Mr. Tallboy. "I suppose you are sending *your* family to Eton, then."

At this, Mr. Smayle's narrow face became as white as a sheet of paper.

"You cad!" he said, choking. "You unspeakable swine. Get out of here or I'll kill you."

"What the devil's the matter with you, Smayle?" cried Mr. Tallboy, in considerable surprise.

"Get out!" said Mr. Smayle.

"Now, I'd just like a word wi' ye, Tallboy," interposed Mr. McAllister. He laid a large, hairy hand on Mr. Tallboy's arm and propelled him gently from the room.

"What on airth possessed ye to say such a thing to him?" he asked, when they were safely in the passage. "Did ye not know that Smayle has but the one boy and him feebleminded, the poor child?"

Mr. Tallboy was really aghast. He was stricken with shame, and, like many shame-stricken people, took refuge in an outburst of rage against the nearest person handy.

"No, I didn't know. How should I be expected to know anything about Smayle's family? Good God! I'm damned sorry and all that, but why must the fellow be such an ass? He's got a mania about public schools. Eton, indeed! I don't wonder the boy's feeble-minded if he takes after his father."

Mr. McAllister was deeply shocked. His Scottish sense of decency was outraged.

"Ye ought to be damn well ashamed o' yersel'," he said, severely, and releasing Tallboy's arm, stepped back into the room he shared with Mr. Smayle and slammed the door.

Now, it is not very clear at the first glance what this disagreement between Mr. Tallboy and Mr. Smayle about a cricket match had to do with the original disagreement between the former and Mr. Copley. True, one may trace a remote connection at the beginning of things, since the Tallboy-Smayle row may be said to have started with Mr. Smayle's indiscreet jest about Mr. Tallboy's fifty pounds. But this fact has no very great importance. What is really important is that as soon as Mr. McAllister made known all the circumstances of the Tallboy-Smayle affair (which he did as soon as he could find a listener), public opinion, which, in the Tallboy-Copley dispute had been largely on Mr. Tallboy's side, veered round. It was felt that since Mr. Tallboy could behave with so much unkindness to Mr. Smayle, he was probably not guiltless towards Mr. Copley. The office staff was divided like the Red Sea and rose up in walls on either hand. Only Mr. Armstrong, Mr. Ingleby, and Mr. Bredon, sardonic Gallios, held themselves apart, caring little, but fomenting the trouble for their own amusement. Even Miss Meteyard, who abominated Mr. Copley, experienced an unwonted uprush of feminine pity for him, and pronounced Mr. Tallboy's behaviour intolerable.

Old Copley, she said, might be an interfering old nuisance, but he wasn't a cad. Mr. Ingleby said he really didn't think Tallboy could have meant what he said to Smayle. Miss Meteyard said: "Tell that to the marines," and, having said so, noted that the phrase would make a good headline for something-or-other. But Mr. Ingleby said, "No, that had been done."

Miss Parton, of course, was an anti-Copleyite whom nothing could move, and therefore smiled on Mr. Tallboy when he happened into the typists' room to borrow a stamp. But Miss Rossiter, though superficially more peppery, prided herself on possessing a well-balanced mind. After all, she insisted, Mr. Copley had probably meant well over the matter of the fifty pounds and, when you came to think of it, he had got Tallboy and all the rest of the Nutrax contingent out of a very tiresome sort of mess. She thought that Mr. Tallboy thought rather a lot of himself, and he had certainly had no business to speak as he had done to poor Mr. Smayle.

"And," said Miss Rossiter, "I don't like his lady friends."

"Lady friends?" said Miss Parton.

"Well, I'm not one to talk, as you know," replied Miss Rossiter, "but when you see a married man coming out of a restaurant at past midnight with somebody who is obviously not his wife—"

"No!" exclaimed Miss Parton.

"My dear! and got up regardless . . . one of those little hats with an eye-veil . . . three-inch diamanté heels . . . such bad taste with a semi-toilette . . . fish-net stockings and all. . . ."

"Perhaps it was his sister."

"My *dear!* . . . And his wife's having a baby, too . . . He didn't see me. . . . Of course, I wouldn't say a word, but I do think . . ."

Thus the typewriters clacked.

Mr. Hankin, though officially impartial, was a Tallboyite. Himself a precise and efficient man, he was nevertheless perennially irritated by the precision and efficiency of Mr. Copley. He suspected, what was quite true, that Mr. Copley criticized the conduct of the department and would have liked to be given a measure of authority. Mr. Copley had a way of coming to him with suggestions: "Would it not be better, Mr. Hankin, if . . ." "If you will excuse my making a suggestion, Mr. Hankin, could not a stricter control be kept . . . ?" "Of course, I know I am in an entirely subordinate position here, Mr. Hankin, but I have had over thirty years' experience of advertising, and in my humble opinion . . ."—excellent suggestions, always, and having only the one drawback that they threatened either to annoy Mr. Armstrong, or to involve a quantity of tedious and time-wasting supervision, or to embroil the whole temperamental Copy Department and put it off its stroke. Mr. Hankin grew weary of saying: "Quite so, Mr. Copley, but Mr. Armstrong and I find it works better, on the whole, to have as few restrictions as possible." Mr. Copley had a way of saying that he quite understood, which always left Mr. Hankin with the impression that Mr. Copley thought him weak and ineffectual, and this impression had been confirmed by the Nutrax incident. When a point had arisen about which Mr. Hankin might, and ought to, have been consulted, Mr. Copley had passed him over—conclusive proof to Mr. Hankin that all Mr. Copley's valuable suggestions about departmental management were so much window-dressing, put forward to show how brilliant Mr. Copley was, and not in the least with the desire of aiding Mr. Hankin or the department. In this, Mr. Hankin's shrewdness saw much more clearly into Mr. Copley's motives than did Mr. Copley himself. He was quite right. Consequently, he was not inclined to bother himself about Mr. Copley, and was determined to give any necessary support to Mr. Tallboy. The Smayle incident was, naturally, not reported to him; he therefore made no comment upon the Cricket Eleven except to ask, mildly, why Mr. Smayle and Mr. McAllister were excluded. Mr. Tallboy replied briefly that they were unable to play, and that was the end of the matter.

Mr. Tallboy had a further ally in Mr. Barrow, who disliked the whole Copy Department on principle, because, as he complained, they were a conceited lot who were always trying to interfere with his artists and dictate to him about his displays. He admitted that, as a general proposition, the sketch was supposed to illustrate the copy, but he maintained (and with truth) that the displays suggested by the copy-writers were often quite impracticable and that the copy-writers took unnecessary offence over the very necessary modifications which he had to make in their "roughs." Further, he had been deeply insulted by Mr. Armstrong's remarks about himself, too faithfully reported by Mr. Ingleby, whom he detested. In fact, he was within an ace of refusing altogether to play in the same match as Mr. Ingleby.

"Oh, but, look here!" protested Mr. Tallboy, "you simply can't let me down like that! You're the best bat we've got."

"Can't you leave Ingleby out?"

This was more than awkward, for in fact Mr. Barrow, though a good and reliable bat, was by no means so good a bat as Mr. Ingleby. Mr. Tallboy hesitated:

"I don't quite see how I can do that. He made 63 last year. But I'll tell you what. I'll put him in fourth and leave you to open with somebody else—say Pinchley. Will you start with Pinchley?"

"You can't put Pinchley in first. He's nothing but a slogger."

"Who else is there?"

Mr. Barrow scanned the list mournfully.

"It's a weak bunch, Tallboy. Is that really the best you can do?"

"Afraid so."

"Pity you've managed to get across Smayle and McAllister."

"Yes—but that can't be helped now. You'll *have* to play, Mr. Barrow, or we'll have to scratch—one or the other!"

"I know what you'd better do. Put yourself in first with me."

"They won't like that. They'll think it's swank."

"Then put Garrett in."

"Very well. You'll play, then?"

"I suppose I must."

"That's very sporting of you, Mr. Barrow."

Mr. Tallboy ran down, sighing, to pin the revised list on the board:

MATCH AGAINST BROTHERHOOD'S

1. Mr. Barrow
2. Mr. Garrett
3. Mr. Hankin
4. Mr. Ingleby
5. Mr. Tallboy (Captain)
6. Mr. Pinchley
7. Mr. Miller
8. Mr. Beeseley
9. Mr. Bredon
10. Mr. Haagedorn
11. Mr. Wedderburn

He stood for a moment looking at it rather hopelessly. Then he went back to his room and took up a large sheet of foolscap, with the intention of marking off the figures for a client's appropriation over the next three months. But his mind was not on the figures. Presently he pushed the sheet aside, and sat staring blankly out of the window across the grey London roofs.

"What's up, Tallboy?" inquired Mr. Wedderburn.

"Life's the devil," said Mr. Tallboy. Then, in a sudden outburst:

"My God! how I hate this blasted place. It gets on my nerves."

"Time you had your holiday," said Mr. Wedderburn, placidly. "How's the wife?"

"All right," rejoined Mr. Tallboy, "but we shan't be able to get away till September."

"That's the worst of being a family man," replied Mr. Wedderburn. "And that reminds me. Have you done anything about that series for *The Nursing Times* about 'Nutrax for Nursing Mothers'?"

Mr. Tallboy thoughtlessly cursed the nursing mothers, dialled Mr. Hankin's room on the inter-office 'phone and in a mournful tone put in a requisition for six 4-inch doubles on that inspiring subject.

# 11

# INEXCUSABLE INVASION OF A DUCAL ENTERTAINMENT

TO LORD Peter Wimsey, the few weeks of his life spent in unravelling the Problem of the Iron Staircase possessed an odd dreamlike quality, noticeable at the time and still more insistent in retrospect. The very work that engaged him—or rather, the shadowy simulacrum of himself that signed itself on every morning in the name of Death Bredon—wafted him into a sphere of dim platonic archetypes, bearing a scarcely recognizable relationship to anything in the living world. Here those strange entities, the Thrifty Housewife, the Man of Discrimination, the Keen Buyer and the Good Judge, for ever young, for ever handsome, for ever virtuous, economical and inquisitive, moved to and fro upon their complicated orbits, comparing prices and values, making tests of purity, asking indiscreet questions about each other's ailments, household expenses, bed-springs, shaving cream, diet, laundry work and boots, perpetually spending to save and saving to spend, cutting out coupons and collecting cartons, surprising husbands with margarine and wives with patent washers and vacuum cleaners, occupied from morning to night in washing, cooking, dusting, filing, saving their children from germs, their complexions from wind and weather, their teeth from decay and their stomachs from indigestion, and yet adding so many hours to the day by labour-saving appliances that they had always leisure for visiting the talkies, sprawling on the beach to picnic upon Potted Meats and Tinned Fruit, and (when adorned by So-and-so's Silks, Blank's Gloves, Dash's Footwear, Whatnot's Weatherproof Complexion Cream and Thingummy's Beautifying Shampoos), even attending Ranelagh, Cowes, the Grand Stand at Ascot, Monte Carlo and the Queen's Drawing-Rooms. Where, Bredon asked himself, did the money come from that was to be spent so variously and so lavishly? If this hell's-dance of spending and saving were to stop for a moment, what would happen? If all the advertising in the world were to shut down tomorrow, would people still go on buying more soap, eating more apples, giving their children more vitamins, roughage, milk, olive oil, scooters and laxatives, learning more languages by gramophone, hearing more virtuosos by radio, re-decorating their houses, refreshing themselves with more non-alcoholic thirst-quenchers, cooking more new, appetizing dishes, affording themselves that little extra touch which means so much? Or would the whole desperate whirligig slow down, and the exhausted public relapse upon plain grub and elbow-grease? He did not know. Like all rich men, he had never before paid any attention to advertisements. He had never realized the enormous commercial importance of the comparatively poor. Not on the wealthy, who buy only what they want when they want it, was the vast superstructure of industry founded and built up, but on those who, aching for a luxury beyond their reach and for a leisure for ever denied them, could be bullied or wheedled into spending their few hardly won shillings on whatever might give them, if only for a moment, a leisured and luxurious illusion. Phantasmagoria–a city of dreadful day, of crude shapes and colours piled Babel-like in a heaven of harsh cobalt and rocking over a void of bankruptcy–a Cloud Cuckoo-land, peopled by pitiful ghosts, from the Thrifty Housewife providing a Grand Family Meal for Fourpence with the aid of Dairyfields Butter Beans in Margarine, to the Typist capturing the affections of Prince Charming by a liberal use of Muggins's Magnolia Face Cream.

Among these phantasms, Death Bredon, driving his pen across reams of office foolscap, was a phantasm too, emerging from this nightmare toil to a still more fantastical existence amid people whose aspirations, rivalries and modes of thought were alien, and earnest beyond anything in his waking experience. Nor, when the Greenwich-driven clocks had jerked on to half-past five, had he any world of reality to which to return; for then the illusionary Mr. Bredon dislimned and became the still more illusionary Harlequin of a dope-addict's dream; an advertising figure more crude and fanciful than any that postured in the columns of the *Morning Star;* a thing bodiless and absurd, a mouthpiece of stale clichés shouting in dull ears without a brain. From this abominable impersonation he could not now free himself, since at the sound of his name or the sight of his unmasked face, all the doors in that other dream-city–the city of dreadful night–would be closed to him.

From one haunting disquietude, Dian de Momerie's moment of inexplicable insight had freed him. She no longer desired him. He thought she rather dreaded him; yet, at the note of the penny whistle she would come out and drive with him, hour after hour, in the great black Daimler, till night turned to daybreak. He sometimes wondered whether she believed in his existence at all; she treated him as though he were some hateful but fascinating figure in a hashish-vision. His fear now was that her unbalanced fancy might topple her over the edge of suicide. She asked him once what he was and what he wanted, and he told her stark truth, so far as it went.

"I am here because Victor Dean died. When the world knows how he died, I shall go back to the place from which I came."

"To the place from which you came. I've heard that said before, but I can't remember where."

"If you ever heard a man condemned to death, then you heard it said then."

"My God, yes! That was it. I went to a murder trial once. There was a horrible old man, the Judge—I forget his name. He was like a wicked old scarlet parrot, and he said it as though he liked it. 'And may the Lord have mercy upon your soul.' Do we have souls, Harlequin, or is that all nonsense? It is nonsense, isn't it?"

"So far as you are concerned, it probably is."

"But what have I got to do with Victor's death?"

"Nothing, I hope. But you ought to know."

"Of course I had nothing to do with it."

And indeed, she might not have. This was the most phantasmal part of the illusion—the border where daydream and night-dream marched together in an eternal twilight. The man had been murdered—of that he was now certain; but what hand had struck the blow and why was still beyond all guessing. Bredon's instinct told him to hold fast to Dian de Momerie. She was the guardian of the shadow-frontier; through her, Victor Dean, surely the most prosaic denizen of the garish city of daylight, had stepped into the place of bright flares and black abysses, whose ministers are drink and drugs and its monarch death. But question her as he might, he could get no help from her. She had told him one thing only, and over and over again he pondered it, wondering how it fitted into the plot. Milligan, the sinister Milligan, knew something about Pym's, or somebody who worked at Pym's. He had known of this before he met Dean, for he had said on meeting him: "So you're the chap, are you?" What connection was there? What had Dean, at Pym's, had to do with Milligan, before Milligan knew him? Was it merely that Dian had boasted, laughing, of having a lover from that respectable agency? Had Victor Dean died merely because of Dian's fancy for him?

Wimsey could not believe it; the fancy had died first, and the death of Dean was, after that, surely superfluous. Besides, when they of the city of night slay for passion's sake, they lay no elaborate schemes, wipe off no finger-prints and hold no discreet tongues before or after. Brawls and revolver-shots, with loud sobs and maudlin remorse, are the signs and tokens of fatal passion among leaders of the bright life.

One other piece of information Dian had indeed given him, but at that moment he could not interpret it, and was not even aware that he held it. He could only wait, like a cat at a mouse-hole, till something popped out that he could run after. And so he passed his nights very wearily, driving the car and playing upon a penny whistle, and snatching his sleep in the small hours, before taking up the daily grind at Pym's.

Wimsey was quite right about Dian de Momerie's feeling for him. He excited her and frightened her, and, on the whole, she got a sensation of rather titillating horror at the sound of the penny whistle. But the real reason of her anxiety to propitiate him was founded on a coincidence that he could not have known and that she did not tell him.

On the day after their first encounter, Dian had backed an outsider called Acrobat, and it had come in at 50 to 1. Three days after the adventure in the woods, she had backed another outsider called Harlequin, each way, and it had come in second at 100 to 1. Thereafter, she had entertained no doubt whatever that he was a powerful and heaven-sent mascot. The day after a meeting with him was her lucky day, and it was a fact that on those days she usually succeeded in winning money in one way or another. Horses, after those first two brilliant coups, had been rather disappointing, but her fortune with cards had been good. How much of this good fortune had been due to sheer self-confidence and the will to win, only a psychologist could say; the winnings were there, and she had no doubt at all about the reason for them. She did not tell him that he was a mascot, from a superstitious feeling that to do so would be to break the luck, but she had been to a crystal-gazer, who, reading her mind like a book, had encouraged her in the belief that a mysterious stranger would bring her good fortune.

Major Milligan, sprawling upon the couch in Dian's flat with a whisky-and-soda, turned on her a pair of rather bilious eyes. He was a large, saturnine man, blank as to morals but comparatively sober in his habits, as people must be who make money out of other people's vices.

"Ever see anything of that Dean girl nowadays, Dian?"

"No, darling," said Dian, absently. She was getting rather tired of Milligan, and would have liked to break with him, if only he had not been so useful, and if she had not known too much to make a break-away healthy.

"Well, I wish you would."

"Oh, why? She's one of Nature's worst bores, darling."

"I want to know if she knows anything about that place where Dean used to work."

"The advertising place? But, Tod, how too yawn-making. Why do you want to know about advertising?"

"Oh, never mind why. I was on to something rather useful there, that's all."

"Oh!" Dian considered. This, she thought, was interesting. Something to be made out of this, perhaps. "I'll give her a ring if you like. But she's about as wet as a drowned eel. *What* do you want to know?"

"That's my business."

"Tod, I've often wanted to ask you. Why did you say I'd got to chuck Victor? Not that I cared about him, the poor fish, but I just wondered, especially after you'd told me to string him along."

"Because," replied Major Milligan, "the young what-not was trying to double-cross me."

"Good heavens, Tod—you ought to go on the talkies as Dog-faced Dick the Dope-King of the Underworld. Talk sense, darling."

"That's all very well, my girl, but your little Victor was getting to be a nuisance. Somebody had been talking to him—probably you."

"Me? that's good! There wasn't anything I could tell him. You never tell me anything, Tod."

"No—I've got some sense left."

"How rude you are, darling. Well, you see, I couldn't have split to Victor. Did you bump Victor off, Tod?"

"Who says he was bumped off?"

"A little bird told me."

"Is that your friend in the black and white checks?"

Dian hesitated. In an expansive and not very sober moment, she had told Tod about her adventure in the woods, and now rather wished she had not. Milligan took her silence for consent and went on:

"Who is that fellow, Dian?"

"Haven't the foggiest."

"What's he want?"

"He doesn't want me, at any rate," said Dian. "Isn't that humiliating, Tod?"

"It must be." Milligan grinned. "But what's the big idea?"

"I think he's on Victor's lay, whatever that was. He said he wouldn't be here if Victor hadn't popped off. Too thrilling, don't you think?"

"Um," said Milligan. "I think I'd like to meet this friend of yours. When's he likely to turn up?"

"Damned if I know. He just arrives. I don't think I'd have anything to do with him, Tod, if I were you. He's dangerous—queer, somehow. I've got a hunch about him."

"Your brain's going to mush, sweetest," said Milligan, "and he's trading on it, that's all."

"Oh, well," said Dian, "he amuses me, and you don't any more. You're getting to be a bit feeding, Tod." She yawned and trailed over to the looking-glass, where she inspected her face narrowly. "I think I'll give up dope, Tod. I'm getting puffy under the eyes. Do you think it would be amusing to go all good?"

"About as amusing as a Quaker meeting. Has your friend been trying to reform you? That's damn good."

"Reform me, nothing. But I'm looking horribly hag-like tonight. Oh hell; what's the odds, anyway? Let's do something."

"All right. Come on round to Slinker's. He's throwing a party."

"I'm sick of Slinker's parties. I say, Tod, let's go and gate-crash something really virtuous. Who's the stickiest old cat in London that's got anything on?"

"Dunno."

"Tell you what. We'll scoop up Slinker's party and go round and look for striped awnings, and crash the first thing we see."

"Right-ho! I'm on."

Half an hour later, a noisy gang, squashed into five cars and a taxi, were whooping through the quieter squares of the West End. Even today, a few strongholds of the grimly aristocratic are left in Mayfair, and Dian, leaning from the open window of the leading car, presently gave tongue before a tall, old-fashioned house, whose entrance was adorned with a striped awning, a crimson carpet and an array of hothouse plants in tubs upon the steps.

"Whoopee! Hit it up, boys! Here's something! Whose is it?"

"My God!" said Slinger Braithwaite. "We've hit the bull, all right. It's Denver's place."

"You won't get in there," said Milligan. "The Duchess of Denver is heaven's prize frozen-face. Look at the chuckerout in the doorway. Better try something easier."

"Easier be damned. We said the first we came to, and this is the first. No ratting, darlings."

"Well, look here," said Milligan, "we'd better try the back entrance. There's a gate into the garden round the other side, opening on the car-park. We've more chance there."

From the other side, the assault turned out to be easy enough. The cars were parked in a back street, and on approaching the garden gate, they found it wide open, displaying a marquee, in which supper was being held. A bunch of guests came out just as they arrived, while, almost on their heels, two large cars drove up and disgorged a large party of people.

"Blow being announced," said an immaculate person, "we'll just barge right in and dodge the Ambassadors."

"Freddy, you can't."

"Can't I? You watch me." Freddy tucked his partner's arm firmly under his own and marched with determination up to the gate. "We're certain to barge into old Peter or somebody in the garden."

Dian nipped Milligan's arm, and the pair of them fell in behind the new arrivals. The gate was passed—but a footman just inside presented an unexpected obstacle.

"Mr. and Mrs. Frederick Arbuthnot," said the immaculate gentleman. "And party," he added, waving a vague hand behind him.

"Well, *we're* in, anyhow," exulted Dian.

Helen, Duchess of Denver, looked round with satisfaction upon her party. It was all going very nicely indeed. The Ambassador and his wife had expressed delight at the quality of the wine. The band was good, the refreshments more than adequate. A tone of mellow decorum pervaded the atmosphere. Her own dress, she thought, became her, although her mother-in-law, the Dowager Duchess, had said something rather acid about her spine. But then, the Dowager was always a little tiresome and incalculable. One must be fashionable, though one would not, of course, be vulgarly immodest. Helen considered that she was showing the exact number of vertebrae that the occasion demanded. One less would be incorrect; one more would be over-modern. She thanked Providence that at forty-five she still kept her figure—as indeed, she did, having been remarkably flat on both aspects the whole of her life.

She was just raising a well-earned glass of champagne to her lips when she paused, and set it down again. Something was wrong. She glanced hurriedly round for her husband. He was not there, but a few paces off an elegant black back and smooth, straw-coloured head of hair announced the presence of her brother-in-law, Wimsey. Hastily excusing herself to Lady Mendip, with whom she had been discussing the latest enormities of the Government, she edged her way through the crowd and caught Wimsey's arm.

"Peter! Look over there. Who are those people?"

Wimsey turned and stared in the direction pointed by the Duchess' fan.

"Good God, Helen! You've caught a pair of ripe ones this time! That's the de Momerie girl and her tame dope-merchant."

The Duchess shuddered.

"How horrible! Disgusting woman! How in the world did they get in? . . . Do you know them?"

"Not officially, no."

"Thank goodness! I was afraid you'd let them in. I never know what you're going to do next; you know so many impossible people."

"Not guilty this time, Helen."

"Ask Bracket how he came to let them in."

"I fly," said Wimsey, "to obey your behest."

He finished the drink he had in his hand, and set off in a leisurely manner in pursuit of the footman. Presently he returned.

"Bracket says they came with Freddy Arbuthnot."

"Find Freddy."

The Hon. Freddy Arbuthnot, when found, denied all knowledge of the intruders. "But there was a bit of a scrum at the gate, you know," he admitted, ingenuously, "and I daresay they barged in with the crowd. The de Momerie girl, eh, what? Where is she? I must have a look at her. Hot stuff and all that, what?"

"You will do nothing of the sort, Freddy. Where in the world is Gerald? Not here. He never is when he's wanted. You'll have to go and turn them out, Peter."

Wimsey, who had had time for a careful calculation, asked nothing better.

"I will turn them out," he announced, "like one John Smith. Where are they?"

The Duchess, who had kept a glassy eye upon them, waved a stern hand in the direction of the terrace. Wimsey ambled off amiably.

"Forgive me, dear Lady Mendip," said the Duchess, returning to her guest. "I had a little commission to give to my brother-in-law."

Up the dimly-lit terrace steps went Wimsey. The shadow of a tall pillar-rose fell across his face and chequered his white shirt-front with dancing black; and as he went he whistled softly: "Tom, Tom, the piper's son."

Dian de Momerie clutched Milligan's arm as she turned.

Wimsey stopped whistling.

"Er–good evening," he said, "excuse me. Miss de Momerie, I think."

"Harlequin!" cried Dian.

"I beg your pardon?"

"Harlequin. So here you are. I've got you this time. And I'm going to see your face properly if I die for it."

"I'm afraid there is some mistake," said Wimsey.

Milligan thought it time to interfere.

"Ah!" said he, "the mysterious stranger. I think it's time you and I had a word, young man. May I ask why you have been tagging round after this lady in a mountebank get-up?"

"I fear," said Wimsey, more elaborately, "that you are labouring under a misapprehension, sir, whoever you are. I have been dispatched by the Duchess on a–forgive me–somewhat distasteful errand. She regrets that she has not the honour of this lady's acquaintance, nor, sir, of yours, and wishes me to ask you by whose invitation you are here."

Dian laughed, rather noisily.

"You do it marvellously, darling," she said. "We gate-crashed on the dear old bird–same as you did, I expect."

"So the Duchess inferred," replied Wimsey. "I am sorry. I'm afraid I must ask you to leave at once."

"That's pretty good," said Milligan, insolently. "I'm afraid it won't work. It may be a fact that we weren't invited here, but we aren't going to turn out for a nameless acrobat who's' afraid to show his face."

"You must be mistaking me for a friend of yours," said Wimsey. "Allow me." He stepped across to the nearest pillar and pressed a switch, flooding that end of the terrace with light. "My name is Peter Wimsey; I am Denver's brother, and my face–such as it is, is entirely at your service."

He fixed his monocle in his eye and stared unpleasantly at Milligan.

"But aren't you my Harlequin?" protested Dian. "Don't be such an ass–I know you are. I know your voice perfectly well–and your mouth and chin. Besides, you were whistling that tune."

"This is very interesting," said Wimsey. "Is it possible–I fear it is–I think you must have encountered my unfortunate cousin Bredon."

"That was the name–" began Dian, uncertainly, and stopped.

"I am glad to hear it," replied Wimsey. "Sometimes he gives mine, which makes it very awkward."

"See here, Dian," broke in Milligan, "you seem to have dropped a brick. You'd better apologize and then we'll clear. Sorry we crashed in, and all that–"

"One moment," said Wimsey. "I should like to hear more about this. Be good enough to come into the house for a moment. This way."

He ushered them courteously round the corner of the terrace, up a side path and by way of a French window into a small ante-room, laid out with tables and a cocktail bar.

"What will you drink? Whiskies? I might have known it. The abominable practice of putting whisky on top of mixed drinks late at night is responsible for more ruined complexions and reputations than any other single cause. There is many a woman now walking the streets of London through putting whisky on top of gin cocktails. Two stiff whiskies, Tomlin, and a liqueur brandy."

"Very good, my lord."

"You perceive," said Wimsey, returning with the drinks, "the true object of this hospitable gesture. I have established my identity, by the evidence of the reliable Tomlin. Let us now seek a spot less open to interruption. I suggest the library. This way. My brother, being an English gentleman, possesses a library in all his houses, though he never opens a book. This is called fidelity to ancient tradition. The chairs, however, are comfortable. Pray be seated. And now, tell me all about your encounter with my scandalous cousin."

"One moment," said Milligan, before Dian could speak. "I think I know the stud-book pretty well. I was not aware that you had a cousin Bredon."

"It is not every puppy that appears in the kennel-book," replied Wimsey carelessly, "and it is a wise man that knows all his own cousins. But what matter? Family is family, though indicated by the border compony (or gobony if you prefer that form of the word) or by the bend or baton sinister, called by most writers of fiction the bar sinister, for reasons which I am unable to determine. My regrettable cousin Bredon, having no particular right to one family name more than another, makes it his practice to employ them all in turn, thus displaying a happy absence of favouritism. Please help yourselves to smokes. You will find the cigars passable, Mr.–er–"

"Milligan."

"Ah the notor–the well-known Major Milligan? You have a residence on the river, I fancy. Charming, charming. Its fame has reached me from time to time through my good brother-in-law, Chief-Inspector Parker of Scotland Yard. A beautiful, retired spot, I believe?"

"Just so," said Milligan. "I had the pleasure of entertaining your cousin there one night."

"Did he gate-crash on you? That is exactly what he would do. And you have retorted upon my dear sister-in-law. Poetic justice, of course. I appreciate it–though possibly the Duchess will take a different view of the matter."

"No; he was brought by a lady of my acquaintance."

"He is improving. Major Milligan, painful though it may be to me, I feel that I ought to warn you against that cousin of mine. He is definitely not nice to know. If he has been thrusting his attentions upon Miss de Momerie, it is probably with some ulterior object. Not," added Wimsey, "that any man would need an ulterior object for such attentions. Miss de Momerie is an object in herself—"

His eye wandered over Dian, scantily clothed and slightly intoxicated, with a cold appraisement which rendered the words almost impertinent.

"But," he resumed, "I know my cousin Bredon—too well. Few people know him better. And I must confess that he is the last man to whom I should look for a disinterested attachment. I am unhappily obliged, in self-defence, to keep an eye on Cousin Bredon's movements, and I should be deeply grateful to be informed of the details of his latest escapade."

"All right, I'll tell you," said Dian. The whisky had strung her up to recklessness, and she became suddenly voluble, disregarding Milligan's scowls. She poured out the tale of her adventures. The incident of the fountain-dive seemed to cause Lord Peter Wimsey acute distress.

"Vulgar ostentation!" he said, shaking his head. "How many times have I implored Bredon to conduct himself in a quiet and reasonable manner."

"I thought he was too marvellous," said Dian, and proceeded to relate the encounter in the wood.

"He always plays 'Tom, Tom, the piper's son,' so of course, when you came along whistling it, I thought it was him."

Wimsey's face darkened in a most convincing manner.

"Disgusting," he said.

"Besides, you are so much alike—the same voice and the same face as far as one can see it, you know. But of course he never took off his mask—"

"No wonder," said Wimsey, "no wonder." He heaved a deep sigh. "The police are interested in my cousin Bredon."

"How thrilling!"

"What for?" demanded Milligan.

"For impersonating me, among other things," said Wimsey, now happily launched and well away. "I cannot tell you in the brief time at our disposal, the distress and humiliation I have been put to on Bredon's account. Bailing him out at police stations—honouring cheques drawn in my name—rescuing him from haunts of infamy—I am telling you all these distressing details in confidence, of course."

"We won't split," said Dian.

"He trades upon our unfortunate resemblance," went on Wimsey. "He copies my habits, smokes my favourite brand of cigarettes, drives a car like mine, even whistles my favourite air—one, I may say, peculiarly well adapted for performance upon the penny whistle."

"He must be pretty well off," said Dian, "to drive a car like that."

"*That*," said Wimsey, "is the most melancholy thing of all. I suspect him—but perhaps I had better not say anything about that."

"Oh, do tell," urged Dian, her eyes dancing with excitement. "It sounds too terribly breath-taking."

"I suspect him," said Wimsey, in solemn and awful tones, "of having to do with—*smug-druggling*—I mean, dash it all—drug-smuggling."

"You don't say so," said Milligan.

"Well, I can't prove it. But I have received warnings from a certain quarter. You understand me." Wimsey selected a fresh cigarette and tapped it, with the air of one who has closed the coffin-lid upon a dead secret and is nailing it down securely. "I don't want to interfere in your affairs in any way at all, Major Milligan. I trust that I shall never be called upon to do so." Here he transfixed Milligan with another hard stare. "But you will perhaps allow me to give you, and this lady, a word of warning. Do not have too much to do with my cousin Bredon."

"I think you're talking rot," said Dian. "Why, you can't even get him to–"

"Cigarette, Dian?" interrupted Milligan, rather sharply.

"I do not say," resumed Wimsey, raking Dian slowly with his eyes, and then turning again to Milligan, "that my deplorable cousin is himself an addict to cocaine or heroin or anything of that description. In some ways, it would be almost more respectable if he were. The man or woman who can batten on the weaknesses of his fellow-creatures without sharing them is, I admit, to me a singularly disgusting object. I may be old-fashioned, but there it is."

"Quite so," said Milligan.

"I do not know, and do not wish to know," went on Wimsey, "how you came to allow my cousin Bredon into your house, nor what, on his side, can have brought him there. I prefer not to suppose that he found there any other attraction than good drinks and good company. You may think, Major Milligan, that because I have interested myself in certain police cases, I am a consistent busybody. That is not the case. Unless I am forced to take an interest in another man's business, I greatly prefer to let him alone. But I think it only fair to tell you that I *am* forced to take an interest in my cousin Bredon and that he is a person whose acquaintance might prove–shall I say, embarrassing?–to any one who preferred to live a quiet life. I don't think I need say any more, need I?"

"Not at all," said Milligan. "I am much obliged to you for the warning, and so, I am sure, is Miss de Momerie."

"Of course, I'm frightfully glad to know all about it," said Dian. "Your cousin sounds a perfect lamb. I like 'em dangerous. Pompous people are too terribly moribund, aren't they?"

Wimsey bowed.

"My dear lady, your choice of friends is entirely at your own discretion."

"I'm glad to hear it. I got the impression that the Duchess wasn't too fearfully anxious to have both arms round my neck."

"Ah! the Duchess–no. There, I fear, all the discretion is on the other side, what? Which reminds me–"

"Quite right," said Milligan. "We have trespassed on your hospitality too long. We must really apologize and remove ourselves. By the way, there were some other members of our party–"

"I expect my sister-in-law will have dealt with them by now," said Wimsey with a grin. "If not, I will make a point of seeing them and telling them that you have gone on to–where shall I say?"

Dian gave her own address.

"You'd better come round and have a drink, too," she suggested.

"Alas!" said Wimsey, "duty and all that sort of thing, what? Can't leave my sister-in-law in the lurch, greatly as I should enjoy the entertainment." He rang the bell. "You will excuse me now, I trust. I must see to our other guests. Porlock, show this lady and gentleman out."

He returned to the garden by way of the terrace, whistling a passage of Bach, as was his way when pleased.

"Nun gehn wir wo der Tudelsack, der Tudel, tudel, tudel, tudelsack . . ."

"I wonder, was the fly too big and gaudy? Will he rise to it? We shall see."

"My dear Peter," said the Duchess, fretfully, "what a terrible time you have been. Please go and fetch Mme. de Framboise-Douillet an ice. And tell your brother I want him."

# 12

# SURPRISING ACQUISITION OF A JUNIOR REPORTER

VERY EARLY one morning, a junior reporter on the *Morning Star*, of no importance to anybody except himself and his widowed mother, walked out of that great newspaper's palatial new offices and into the affairs of Chief-Inspector Parker. This nonentity's name was Hector Puncheon, and he was in Fleet Street at that time because a fire had broken out the previous night in a large City warehouse, destroying a great deal of valuable property and involving the spectacular escapes of three night watchmen and a cat from the roofs of the adjacent buildings. Hector Puncheon, summoned to the scene for the excellent reason that he had lodgings in the West Central district and could be transported to the scene of action in a comparatively brief time, had written a short stop-press notice of the disaster for the early country editions, a longer and more exciting account for the London edition, and then a still longer and more detailed report, complete with the night-watchmen's and eye-witnesses' stories and a personal interview with the cat, for the early editions of the *Evening Comet*, twin-organ to the *Morning Star* and housed in the same building.

After completing all this toil, he was wakeful and hungry. He sought an all-night restaurant in Fleet Street, accustomed to catering for the untimely needs of pressmen, and, having previously armed himself with a copy of the *Morning Star* as it poured out damp from the machines, sat down to a 3 a.m. breakfast of grilled sausages, coffee and rolls.

He ate with leisurely zest, pleased with himself and his good fortune, and persuaded that not even the most distinguished of the senior men could have turned in a column more full of snap, pep and human interest than his own. The interview with the cat had been particularly full of appeal. The animal was, it seemed, an illustrious rat-catcher, with many famous deeds to her credit. Not only that, but she had been the first to notice the smell of fire and had, by her anguished and intelligent mewings, attracted the attention of night-watchman number one, who had been in the act of brewing himself a cup of tea when the outbreak took place. Thirdly, the cat, an ugly black-and-white creature with a spotted face, was about to become a mother for the tenth time, and Hector Puncheon by a brilliant inspiration had secured the reversion of the expected family for the *Morning Star*, so that half a dozen or so fortunate readers might, by applying to their favourite paper and enclosing a small donation for the Animals' Hospital, become the happy owners of kittens with a prenatal reputation and a magnificent rat-catching pedigree. Hector Puncheon felt that he had done well. He had been alert and courageous, offering the night-watchman ten shillings on his own responsibility the very moment the big idea occurred to him, and the night-editor had okayed the stunt and even remarked that it would do quite well.

Filled with sausages and contentment, Hector Puncheon lingered over his paper, reading the Special Friday Feature with approval and appreciating the political cartoon. At length, he folded the sheet, stuffed it in his pocket, tipped the waiter extravagantly with sixpence and emerged into Fleet Street.

The morning was fine, though chilly, and he felt that after his night's labours, a little walk would do him good. He strolled happily along, past the Griffin at Temple Bar and the Law Courts and the churches of St. Clement Danes and St. Mary-le-Strand, and made his way up Kingsway. It was only when he got to the turning into Great Queen Street that he became aware of something lacking in an otherwise satisfactory universe. Great Queen Street led into Long Acre; off Long Acre lay Covent Garden; already the vans and lorries laden with fruit and flowers were rumbling in from all over the country and rumbling out again. Already the porters were unloading their stout sacks, huge crates, round baskets, frail punnets and long flat boxes filled with living scent and colour, sweating and grumbling over their labours as though their exquisite burdens were so much fish or pig-iron. And for the benefit of these men the pubs would be open, for Covent Garden interprets the London licensing regulations to suit its own topsy-turvy hours of labour. Hector Puncheon had had a successful night and had celebrated his success with sausages and coffee; but there are, dash it all! more suitable methods of celebration.

Hector Puncheon, swinging blithely along in his serviceable grey flannel bags and tweed jacket, covered by an old burberry, suddenly realized that he owned the world, including all the beer in Covent Garden Market. He turned into Great Queen Street, traversed half the length of Long Acre, dodged under the nose of a van horse at the entrance to the Underground Station, and set his face towards the market, picking his way cheerfully between the boxes and baskets and carts and straw that littered the pavement. Humming a lively tune, he turned in through the swing doors of the White Swan.

Although it was only a quarter past four, the Swan was already doing a brisk trade. Hector Puncheon edged his way up to the bar between two enormous carters and waited modestly for the landlord to finish serving his habitual customers before calling attention to himself. A lively discussion was going on about the merits of a dog named Forked Lightning. Hector, always ready to pick up a hint about anything that was, or might conceivably be turned into news, pulled his early *Morning Star* from his pocket and pretended to read it, while keeping his ears open.

"And what I say is," said Carter the First, "—same again, Joe—what I say is, when a dawg that's fancied like that dawg is, stops dead 'arf way round the course like as if 'e'd a-bin shot, wot I say is, I likes to know wot's at the back of it."

"Ar," said Carter the Second.

"Mind you," went on Carter the First, "I ain't sayin' as animals is always to be relied on. They 'as their off-days, same as you an' me, but wot I says is—"

"That's a fact," put in a smaller man, from the other side of Carter the Second, "that's a fact, that is. An' wot's more, they 'as their fancies. I 'ad a dawg once as couldn't abide the sight of a goat. Or maybe it was the smell. I dunno. But show 'im a goat any time, and 'e got a fit of the trembles. Couldn't run all day. I remember one time when I was bringin' 'im up to run at the White City, there was a bloke in the street leadin' two goats on a string—"

"Wot did a bloke want with two goats?" demanded Carter the Second, suspiciously.

" 'Ow should I know wot 'e wanted with goats?" retorted the little man, indignantly. "They wasn't my goats, was they? Well, that there dawg–"

"That's different," said Carter the First. "Nerves is nerves, and a thing like a goat might 'appen to anybody, but wot I says is–"

"What's yours, sir?" inquired the landlord.

"Oh, I think I'll have a Guinness," said Hector. "Guinness is good for you–particularly on a chilly morning. Perhaps," he added, feeling pleased with himself and the world, "these gentlemen will join me."

The two carters and the little man expressed their gratification, and ordered beer.

"It's a queer thing, this business of nerves," said the little man. "Talking of Guinness, now, my old aunt had a parrot. Some bird it was, too. Learnt to speak from a sailor. Fortunately the old lady couldn't 'ear 'alf of wot it said, and didn't understand the other 'alf. Now, that there bird–"

"You seem to have had a wide experience with livestock," observed Hector Puncheon.

"I 'ave that," said the little man. "That there bird, as I was going to say, got fits of nerves as would surprise you. 'Unched 'isself up on 'is perch like, and shivered fit to shake 'isself to pieces. And wot was the reason of that, do you think?"

"Beggared if I know," said Carter the Second. "Your 'ealth, sir."

"Mice," said the little man, triumphantly. "Couldn't stand the sight of a mouse. And wot do you think we 'ad to give it to pull it round, like?"

"Brandy," suggested Carter the First. "Nothing like brandy for parrots. We got one at 'ome–one o' them green sort. My wife's brother brought it 'ome with 'im–"

"They ain't such good talkers as the grey ones," said Carter the Second. "There was a parrot at the old Rose & Crown dahn Seven Dials way–"

"Brandy?" scoffed the little man, "not 'im. 'E wouldn't look at brandy."

"Wouldn't 'e now?" said Carter the First. "Now, you show our old bird brandy, an' 'e'll 'op right out of 'is cage for it same as a Christian. Not too much, mind you, but give it 'im neat in a teaspoon–"

"Well, it wasn't brandy," persisted the little man. "Aunt's was a teetotal bird, 'e was. Now, I'll give you three guesses, an' if you gets it right, I'll stand drinks all round, and I can't say fairer 'an that."

"Aspirin?" suggested the landlord, anxious that the round of drinks should be stood by somebody.

The little man shook his head.

"Ginger," said Carter the Second. "Birds is sometimes wonderful fond o' ginger. Stimulates the innards. Though, mind you, some says it's too 'eatin', an' brings their fevvers aht."

"Nutrax for Nerves," suggested Hector Puncheon, a little wildly, his eye having been caught by that morning's half-double, which carried the intriguing headline: "WHY BLAME THE WOMAN?"

"Nutrax nothing," snorted the little man, "nor none o' yer patent slops. No. Strong coffee wiv' cayenne pepper in it–that's wot that bird liked. Put 'im right in a jiff, it did. Well, seein' as the drinks ain't on me this time–"

He looked wistful, and Hector obliged again with the same all round. Carter the Second, jerking his beer off at one gulp and offering a general salute to the company, shouldered his way out, and the little man moved up closer to Hector Puncheon to make way for a florid person in evening dress, who had just shot his way in through the door and now stood swaying a little uncertainly against the bar.

"Scotch-and-soda," said this person, without preface, "double Scotch and not too bloody much soda."

The landlord looked at him keenly.

"Thass all right," said the newcomer, "I know what you're thinking, my boy, but I'm not drunk. Norra bittovit. Nerves a liddleoutavorder, 'tsall." He paused, evidently conscious that his speech was getting a little ahead of itself. "Been sittin' up with a sick friend," he explained, carefully. "Very trying to the system, sittin' up all night. Very hard on the conshi-conshishu-shion—excuse me—slight acshident to my dental plate, mush gettit-sheento."

He leaned one elbow on the bar, pawed vaguely with his foot for the brass rail, pushed his silk hat well to the back of his head and beamed pleasantly upon the company.

The landlord of the Swan looked at him again with a practised eye, calculated that his customer could probably carry one more Scotch-and-soda without actual disaster, and fulfilled his order.

"Thanks verrimush, old feller," said the stranger. "Well, goo' luck, all. What are these gentlemen taking?"

Hector Puncheon excused himself politely, explaining that he had really had all he wanted and must now be going home.

"No, no," said the other, hurt. "Mustn't say that. Nottime to gome yet. Night yet young." He flung an affectionate arm round Hector's neck. "I like your face. You're the sortafeller I like. You must come along one day 'n see my little place. Roses roun' the porch an' all that. Give you my card." He hunted in his pockets and produced a note-case, which he flapped open on the bar-counter. A quantity of small pieces of paper flew out right and left.

"Dashitall," said the gentleman in dress clothes, "what I mean, dashit." Hector stooped to pick up some of the scattered oddments, but the little man was before him.

"Thanks, thanks," said the gentleman. "Wheresh card? Thatsh not card, thatsh my wife's shopping-list—you gorrawife?"

"Not yet," admitted Hector.

"Lucky devil," replied the stranger with emphasis. "No wife, no damned shopping-list." His vagrant attention was caught and held by the shopping-list, which he held up in one hand and tried, unsuccessfully, to focus with a slightly squinting gaze. "Alwaysh bringing home parcels like a blurry errand-boy. Where'd I put that parcel now?"

"You 'adn't no parcel when you come in 'ere, guv'nor," said Carter the First. The question of drinks seemed to have been shelved, and the worthy man no doubt felt it was time to remind the gentleman that there were others in the bar, besides the abstemious Mr. Puncheon. "Dry work," he added, "cartin' parcels round."

"Damn dry," said the married gentleman. "Mine's a Scotch-and-soda. Whaddid you say you'd have, ol' boy?" He again embraced Hector Puncheon, who gently disentangled himself.

"I really don't want—" he began; but, seeing that this reiterated refusal might give offence, he gave way and asked for a half-tankard of bitter.

"Talking about parrots," said a thin voice behind them. Hector started and, looking round, observed a dried-up old man seated at a small table in the corner of the bar, absorbing a gin-and-potash. He must have been there all the time, thought Hector.

The gentleman in dress clothes swung round upon him so sharply that he lost his balance and had to cling to the little man to save himself.

"I never mentioned parrots," he said, enunciating the words very distinctly. "I shouldn't think of talking about parrots."

"I once knowed a parson wot 'ad a parrot," continued the old man. "Joey, they called 'im."

"Wot, the parson?" asked the little man.

"No, the parrot," said the old fellow, mildly, "and that there parrot hadn't ever been out of the parson's family. Joined in family prayers, he did and said 'Amen' like a Christian. Well, one day this here parson–"

A rush of customers entering from the market drew the landlord's attention away and drowned the next sentence or so of the story. The carter hailed some acquaintances and joined them in a fresh round of beer. Hector, shaking off the intoxicated gentleman, who seemed now to be inviting him to join a cozy little fishing party in Scotland, turned to go, but found himself caught and held by the old man.

"–and old parson found the bishop sitting over the cage with a lump of sugar in his fingers, saying, 'Come on, Joey, say it! B . . . b . . . b . . .!' And that, mind you," said the old man, "was a Church of England bishop. And what do you think the bishop did then?"

"I can't imagine," said Hector.

"Made the parson a canon," said the old man, triumphantly.

"Never!" said Hector.

"But that's nothing," pursued the old man. "There was a parrot I knew down in Somerset–"

Hector felt he really could not bear to hear about the parrot down in Somerset. He extricated himself politely and fled.

His next activity was to go home and have a bath, after which he coiled himself up on his bed and slept placidly till his normal breakfast-time at nine.

He breakfasted in his dressing-gown, and it was when he was transferring his various possessions from his grey flannels to his navy lounge suit that he came upon the little packet. It was neatly done up with sealing-wax in white paper, and bore the innocent label "Bicarbonate of Soda." He stared at it in surprise.

Hector Puncheon was a young man with a hearty and healthy digestion. He had heard, of course, of sodium bicarb, and its virtues, but only as a wealthy man hears of hire-purchase. For the moment he thought he must have accidentally picked the little package up in the bathroom and slipped it into his pocket unaware. Then he remembered that he had not taken his coat into the bathroom that morning, and that he had emptied out the pockets the previous night. He distinctly recollected that, when the summons to the fire had reached him, he had had to tumble hurriedly into them the few odds and ends he habitually carried about him–handkerchief, keys, loose cash, pencils and what-not, taken from his dressing-table. It was quite inconceivable that there should have been any bicarbonate on his dressing-table.

Hector Puncheon was puzzled. A glance at the clock, however, reminded him that he had no time for puzzlement just then. He had to get down to St. Margaret's, Westminster, by 10:30 to report the wedding of a fashionable beauty who was being married in the strictest secrecy at that unfashionable hour. He had then to hasten back to report a political meeting in Kingsway

Hall, and thence he must gallop round the corner to attend a luncheon given to a distinguished airman in the Connaught Rooms. If the speeches were over by 3 o'clock, he could then make a dash for a train and get out to Esher, where a royalty was opening a new school and inaugurating it with a children's tea-party. After which, if he were still alive, and had contrived to get his copy written up in the train, he could turn it in at the office and find time to think.

This strenuous programme was carried out without more than the usual number of exasperating hitches, and not until he had pushed the last sheet of copy over to the sub-editor, and was sitting, tired but conscious of work well done, in the Cock Tavern, tackling a beef-steak, did he give another thought to the mysterious packet of sodium bicarb. And now, the more he thought about it, the odder the incident became.

He ran over in his mind the various activities of the previous night. At the fire, he remembered now quite distinctly, he had put on his burberry and buttoned it up, by way of protecting his light grey flannels against showers of smuts and the spray of the firemen's hoses. The mysterious package could hardly have been placed in his jacket-pocket then. After that, there had been interviews with various people—including the cat—the writing of his copy in the *Morning Star* offices and his breakfast in the Fleet Street eating-house. To suppose that he had accidentally found and pocketed four ounces of bicarbonate on any of these occasions seemed to him fantastic. Unless, of course, one of his newspaper colleagues had put the thing there for a joke. But who? And why?

He went on to consider the walk home and the conversation in the White Swan. His exhilarated acquaintance in dress clothes was the kind of man, he thought, who might from time to time require the assistance of a mild digestive and carminative. Possibly in one of his more affectionate moments he might have slipped the packet into Hector's coat-pocket by mistake for his own. The two carters would not, Mr. Puncheon felt sure, be carrying drugs round with them. . . .

Drugs. As the word shaped itself in his mind—for Hector Puncheon usually thought articulately, and often, indeed, conversed quite sensibly aloud with his own soul—an enormous query shot up in his brain. Bicarbonate of soda, hell! He was ready to stake his journalistic reputation it was nothing of the sort. His fingers sought the packet, which he had thrust back into the pocket where he had found it, and he was on the point of opening it and investigating the contents when a better idea struck him. Leaving his rump-steak half finished, and muttering to the astonished waiter that he would be back in a minute, he ran out hatless to the establishment of the nearest chemist, one Mr. Tweedle, who knew him well.

Mr. Tweedle's shop was shut, but a light still burned within, and Hector hammered violently until the door was opened by an assistant. Was Mr. Tweedle in? Yes, he was in, but he was just going. On being assured that Mr. Puncheon wanted to see Mr. Tweedle personally, the assistant volunteered to see what could be done.

Mr. Tweedle, hatted and coated, appeared from the inner recesses of the shop with just enough delay to make Hector feel that he had acted with some precipitation and had probably started out upon a wild-goose chase. Once started, however, he had to go through with it.

"Look here, Tweedle," he said, "I'm sorry to bother you, and there's probably nothing in it, but I wish you'd have a look at this for me. It came into my hands in rather a curious way."

The chemist received the packet and held it balanced in his hand for a moment.

"What's wrong with it?"

"I don't know that anything's wrong with it. I want you to tell me."

"Bicarbonate of soda," said Mr. Tweedle, glancing at the label and at the sealed flaps of the package. "No chemist's name—the ordinary printed label. You don't seem to have opened it."

"No, I haven't, and I want you to bear witness to that, if necessary. It appears to be just as it came from the chemist, doesn't it?"

"It appears to be, certainly," rejoined Mr. Tweedle in some surprise. "The label seems to be the original label and the ends have apparently only been sealed once, if that is what you want to know."

"Yes, and I couldn't have sealed it up like that, could I? I mean, it looks professional."

"Quite."

"Well, now, if you're quite satisfied about that, open it."

Mr. Tweedle carefully inserted a penknife beneath one flap, broke the wax and opened up the paper. The packet was, as might have been expected, filled with a fine white powder.

"What next?" inquired Mr. Tweedle.

"Well, is it bicarbonate of soda?"

Mr. Tweedle shook some of the powder out into the palm of his hand, looked closely at it, smelt it, moistened his finger and took up a few grains, and then carried them to his tongue. Then his face changed. He took out his handkerchief, wiped his mouth, poured the powder from his palm carefully back into the paper and asked:

"How did you get hold of this?"

"I'll tell you in a moment," said Hector. "What is it?"

"Cocaine," said Mr. Tweedle.

"Are you sure?"

"Positive."

"My God!" cried Hector, jubilantly. "I'm on to something! What a day! Here, Tweedle, can you spare a moment? I want you to come round to our place and tell Hawkins about this."

"Where? What?" demanded Mr. Tweedle.

Hector Puncheon wasted no more words, but grabbed him by the arm. Thus, on Mr. Hawkins, news-editor of the *Morning Star*, there burst an agitated member of his own staff, with a breathless witness in tow, and an exhibit of cocaine.

Mr. Hawkins was a keen newspaper man and rejoiced in a stunt. He had, nevertheless, a certain conscience in such matters, so far as giving information to the police was concerned. For one thing, it does a newspaper no good to be on bad terms with the police, and, for another, there had only recently been trouble about another case in which information had been held up. Having, therefore, heard Hector Puncheon's story and scolded him soundly for having waited so long before examining the mysterious package, he telephoned to Scotland Yard.

Chief-Inspector Parker, with his arm in a sling and his nerves very much on edge, received the information in his own home, just as he thought his day's work was happily done with. He grumbled horribly; but there had been a good deal of fuss made lately at the Yard about dope-gangs, and things had been said which he resented. He irritably called a taxi and trundled down to the *Morning Star* offices, accompanied by a morose person called Sergeant Lumley, who disliked him, and whom he disliked, but who happened to be the only sergeant available.

By this time, Hector Puncheon's excitement had rather worn off. He was getting sleepy and stupid after a broken night and a hard day's work. He could not control his yawns, and the Chief-Inspector snapped at him. In answer to questions he managed, however, to give a fairly complete account of his movements during the night and early morning.

"Actually, then," said Parker, when the tale was finished, "you can't say with any certainty when you received this packet?"

"No, I can't," said Hector, resentfully. He could not help feeling that it was very clever of him to have received the packet at all, and that everybody ought, somehow, to be grateful to him. Instead of which, they almost seemed to think he was to blame for something.

"You say you found it in your right hand coat-pocket. Did you at no time previously to that put your hand in that pocket for anything?"

"I should think I must have," said Hector. He yawned. "But I can't exactly remember." He yawned again, uncontrollably.

"What do you keep in that pocket?"

"Odds and ends," said Hector. He dipped into the pocket and drew out a mixed collection—a pencil, a box of matches, a pair of nail-scissors, some string, a thing for opening beer-bottles with patent caps, a corkscrew for opening ordinary beer-bottles, a very dirty handkerchief and some crumbs.

"If you could remember using any of those things during the night—" suggested Parker.

"I must have used the handkerchief," said Hector, gazing at it in some dismay. "I meant to take a clean one out this morning. I did, too. Where is it? Oh, in my trousers-pocket. Here it is. But of course," he added, helpfully, "this isn't the suit I wore last night. I had my old tweed jacket on then. I must have put the dirty handkerchief in this pocket with the other things instead of into the clothesbasket. I know it's the one I had at the fire. Look at the soot on it."

"Quite so," said Parker, "but can you remember *when* you used this handkerchief last night? Surely, if you had felt in your pocket at any time, you couldn't have failed to come on the packet if it was there."

"Oh, yes, I could," said Hector, brightly. "I shouldn't notice. I'm so accustomed to having a lot of junk in my pocket. I can't help you there, I'm afraid."

Another frightful yawn attacked him. He stifled it manfully, and it forced itself painfully out at his nose, nearly breaking his ear-drums on the way. Parker gazed crossly at his grimacing countenance.

"Do try to keep your mind on what I am asking you, Mr. Firkin," he said. "If only—"

"Puncheon," said Hector, annoyed.

"Puncheon," said Parker, "I beg your pardon. Did you at any time, Mr. Puncheon—?"

"I don't know," interrupted Hector. "I honestly don't know. It's no good asking. I can't tell you. I would if I could, but I simply can't."

Mr. Hawkins, looking from one to the other, discovered in himself a little elementary knowledge of human nature.

"I think," he said, "a small drink is indicated."

He fetched a bottle of Johnnie Walker and some glasses from a locker and set them on the desk, together with a siphon. Parker thanked him and, suddenly ashamed of himself and his bad temper, apologized.

"I'm sorry," he said. "I'm afraid I was a bit curt. I got my collar-bone broken a little time ago and it still aches a bit and makes me abominably peevish. Let's go about this business another way. Why do you suppose, Mr. Puncheon, that anybody should have picked you out to take charge of this hefty dose of dope?"

"I thought whoever it was must have mistaken me for some one else."

"So I should imagine. And you think that's more likely to have happened at the pub than anywhere else?"

"Yes; unless it was in the crowd at the fire. Because in the other places–I mean in this office and when I was interviewing people, everybody knew me, or at least they knew what I was there for."

"That seems sound," agreed Parker. "How about this restaurant where you had your sausages?"

"There's that, of course. But I can't recollect anybody coming near enough to me to shove things in my pocket. And it couldn't have been during the fire either, because I had my burberry on, buttoned up. But in the pub, I had my burberry open, and there were at least four people barging up against me–one of two carters who were there before me, and a little man who looked like a bookmaker's tout or something, and the drunken chap in dress clothes and the old boy sitting in the corner. I don't think it can have been the carter, though; he looked quite genuine."

"Had you ever been to the White Swan before?"

"Once, I think, ages ago. Certianly not often. And I think there's a new landlord since then."

"Well, then," said Parker, "what is there about you, Mr. Puncheon, that induces people to hand you out valuable cargoes of dope on sight and without payment?"

"Goodness knows," said Hector.

The desk telephone buzzed furiously, and Mr. Hawkins, snatching the receiver, plunged into a long conversation with some unknown person. The two policemen with their witness retired into a distant corner and carried on the inquiry in low tones.

"Either," said Parker, "you must be the dead spit of some habitual dope-peddler, or you must have led them in some way to imagine that you were the person they expected to see. What did you talk about?"

Hector Puncheon racked his brains.

"Greyhounds," he said at last, "and parrots. Chiefly parrots. Oh, yes–and goats."

"Greyhounds, parrots and goats?"

"We were swapping stories about parrots," said Hector Puncheon. "No, wait, we began about dogs. The little tout person said he'd had a dog that couldn't abide goats and that led on to parrots and mice (I'd forgotten the mice)–and doping parrots with coffee and cayenne."

"Doping?" said Parker, quickly. "Was that word used?"

"No, I don't know that it was. The parrot was frightened of mice, and they had to cure it of shock by giving it coffee."

"Whose parrot?"

"The little fellow's aunt's, I think. The old boy knew a parrot, too, but that belonged to a clergyman, and the bishop tried to teach it to swear and promoted the parson. I don't know whether it was blackmail, or just that he liked the parrot."

"But what did you contribute to the conversation?"

"Hardly anything. I just listened and paid for the drinks."

"And the man in dress clothes?"

"Oh, he talked about his wife's shopping-list and a parcel—yes, there was something about a parcel he ought to have brought with him."

"Was the parcel produced?"

"No, he never had a parcel."

"All right," said Parker, after a little more of this unsatisfactory conversation. "We'll go into the matter, Mr. Puncheon. We're very much obliged to you and Mr.—er—Hawkins for having called our attention to the matter. We will take charge of the packet, and if we want you again, we'll let you know."

He rose to his feet. Mr. Hawkins shot across from his desk.

"Got all you want? You don't want this story to go in, I suppose?" he added, wistfully.

"No; you mustn't say anything about it at present," said Parker, firmly. "But we're very much indebted to you, and if anything comes of it, you shall have the story first with all the details we can give you. I can't say fairer than that."

He left the office with Sergeant Lumley, mournful and silent, at his heels.

"It's a thousand pities, Lumley, that we didn't get this information earlier. We could have put a man in at that pub for the rest of the day. It's too late to do anything now."

"Yes, sir, it is," said Sergeant Lumley.

"The pub's the place, I fancy."

"Very likely, sir."

"The cargo of dope was a pretty large one. That means that it was meant for some one who distributes the stuff on a fairly extensive scale. And it didn't have to be paid for. That suggests to me that the man they expected to see was only a messenger for this distributor, who, no doubt, settles up direct with the top man by some other route."

"Very possibly, sir," said Sergeant Lumley, in an unbelieving tone.

"The thing is, what are we to do? We could raid the place, of course, but I don't think that would be advisable. We probably shouldn't find anything, and we should merely give the alarm to no purpose."

"That wouldn't be anything unusual," grunted the Sergeant, disagreeably.

"Too true. We haven't anything against the White Swan so far, have we?"

"Not that I know of, sir."

"We shall have to make certain about it first. The landlord may or may not be concerned in the business. Quite possibly he isn't, but we shall have to make sure. You had better arrange for at least two men to investigate the Swan. They mustn't make themselves conspicuous. They can drop in from time to time and talk about parrots and goats and see if anything peculiar happens to them. And they can try and get a line on those people—the little chap, and the old man, and the fellow in the boiled shirt. It ought not to be difficult. Put on two sensible, tactful men who are not teetotallers, and if they don't get anything in the course of a day or two, change them for two others. And see that they look like what they're supposed to be and don't wear regulation boots or anything foolish."

"Very well, sir."

"And for God's sake, Lumley, look a little more cheerful about it," said the Chief-Inspector. "I like to see duties undertaken in a pleasant spirit."

"I do my best," replied Sergeant Lumley, offended.

Chief-Inspector Parker went resolutely home to bed.

# 13

# EMBARRASSING ENTANGLE-MENTS OF A GROUP-MANAGER

EXCUSE ME, miss," said Tompkin, the reception-clerk, to Miss Rossiter, "but do you happen to have seen Mr. Wedderburn anywhere? He's not in his room."

"I think I saw him in with Mr. Ingleby."

"Thank you very much, miss."

Tompkin's cheerful face looked worried; and all the more so, when he reached Mr. Ingleby's room and found nobody there but Mr. Ingleby himself and Mr. Bredon.

He repeated his inquiry.

"He's just gone down to Bream's Buildings about an insertion in some magazine or other," said Ingleby.

"Oh!" Tompkin looked so non-plussed that Ingleby added, "Why, what's up?"

"Well, sir, as a matter of fact and strictly between you and I, a rather awkward thing has happened. I don't quite know what to do about it."

"In all social difficulties," said Bredon, "ask Uncle Ugly. Do you want to know how many buttons there should be on a dress waistcoat? how to eat an orange in public? how to introduce your first-wife-that-was to your third-wife-to-be? Uncle Ugly will put you right."

"Well, sir, if you will treat the matter in confidence, you and Mr. Ingleby—"

"Say on, Tompkin. We will be silent as a pre-talkie movie. Any sum from £5 to £5,000 advanced on your note of hand alone. No embarrassing investigations. No security required—or offered. What's your trouble?"

"Not mine, sir. As a matter of fact, sir, there's a young woman here, asking for Mr. Tallboy, and he's in conference with Mr. Armstrong and Mr. Toule, and I don't like to send a message."

"Well," said Ingleby, "tell her to wait."

"That's just it, sir, I did, and she said I was only saying that to put her off, while Mr. Tallboy got out of the building, and she took on terribly and said she was going to speak to Mr. Pym. Well, sir, of course I don't know what the trouble is"—here Tompkin looked unnaturally blank and innocent—"but I don't think Mr. Tallboy would care for that, nor Mr. Pym neither. So I thought, seeing that Mr. Wedderburn is the gentleman who sees most of Mr. Tallboy, so to speak—"

"I see," said Ingleby. "Where is the young woman?"

"Well, I've put her in the Little Conference Room," said Tompkin, dubiously, with an accent on the "put," "but of course, if she was to come out again (and there's nothing to stop her) and was to go to Mr. Pym, or even to Miss Fearney— You see, sir, when parties like Miss Fearney are in an official position, they have to take notice of things, as you may say, whether they like to or not. It isn't the same as you or me, sir." Tompkins glanced from Ingleby to Bredon, dividing the "sir" impartially between them.

Bredon, who was drawing patterns on his blotter, looked up.

"What is she like?" he asked. "I mean"—as Tompkin hesitated—"do you think she is genuinely in distress or merely out to make trouble?"

"Well, sir," said Tompkin, "since you ask me, I should say she was a tough jane."

"I'll go and keep her quiet," said Bredon. "Be sure you tell Mr. Tallboy the moment he is free."

"Very good, sir."

"And try not to let it get round the office. It may be nothing at all."

"Quite so, sir. I'm not one to talk. But there's the boy on the desk, sir—"

"Oh! Well, tell him to hold his tongue."

"Yes, sir."

Bredon went out, looking as though he did not care for his self-imposed task. By the time he arrived at the door of the Little Conference Room, however, his face bore nothing but an expression of amiable helpfulness. He entered briskly, and in the first glance his practised eye took in every detail about the young woman who sprang up to face him, from her hard eyes and shrewish mouth to her blood-red, pointed fingernails and over-elaborate shoes.

"Good afternoon," he said, brightly. "You want Mr. Tallboy, I think. He won't be long, but he's been called in to a conference with some clients and we can't rescue him, so they've sent me down to entertain you till he comes. Will you smoke, Miss—er—the clerk didn't mention your name?"

"It's Vavasour—Miss Ethel Vavasour. Who're you? Are you Mr. Pym?"

Bredon laughed.

"Good lord, no. I'm a very unimportant person—one of the junior copy-writers, that's all."

"Oh, I see. You a pal of Jim's?"

"Of Tallboy's? Not specially. I just happened to be there, so I came along, don't you know. They told me there was a very beautiful young lady asking for Tallboy, and I thought, What-ho! Why not buzz along and cheer her weary hours of waiting?"

"I'm sure it's frightfully good of you," said Miss Vavasour, laughing rather shrilly. "I expect what you mean is, that Jim's sent you along to see if you can talk me round. That's just like Jim. I suppose he's sneaked off the back way."

"I assure you, my dear young lady, that I haven't seen or spoken to Tallboy this afternoon. And I expect, when he hears that I've been along to have a chat with you, he'll be very fed-up with me. And no wonder. If you'd come to see me, I should loathe any other blighter who came and barged in."

"You can can that stuff," retorted Miss Vavasour. "I know your sort. You'd talk the hind leg off a donkey. But I can tell you this: if Jim Tallboy thinks he's going to get round me by sending his flash friends to shoot off a lot of hot air, he's mistaken."

"My dear Miss Vavasour, will nothing rid you of this misapprehension? In other words, you got me all wrong. I'm not here to forward Tallboy's interests in any way—except, perhaps, by offering the suggestion that this office is possibly not the most suitable spot for interviews of a personal and confidential kind. If I might presume to advise you, would not an appointment for some other place and time—?"

"Ah!" said Miss Vavasour. "I dare say. But if a fellow won't answer your letters or come and see you, and you don't even know where he lives, what is a girl to do? I'm sure I don't want to make trouble."

Here Miss Vavasour sniffed and applied a small handkerchief carefully to her made-up eye-lashes.

"Good heavens!" said Bredon. "How unkind and abominable!"

"You may well say so," said Miss Vavasour. "It's not what anybody would expect of a gentleman, is it? But there! When a fellow's telling the tale to a girl it's one thing, and when he's got her into trouble it's another. A girl doesn't hear so much about him marrying her then. Well, you tell him he's got to do it, see? Or I'll scream my way into old Pym's office and make him. A girl's got to look after herself these days. I'm sure I only wish I had somebody to do it for me, and now poor Auntie's dead, I haven't got a soul to stick up for me."

The handkerchief came into play again.

"But, my dear girl," said Bredon, "even Mr. Pym, great autocrat as he is, couldn't make Tallboy marry you. He's married already."

"Married?" Miss Vavasour took away the handkerchief revealing a pair of perfectly dry and very angry eyes, "the dirty beast! So *that's* why he never asked me to his home. Talking a lot of eye-wash about only one room and his landlady being very particular. I don't care, though. He's got to do it. His wife can divorce him. Goodness knows she's got cause. I've got his letters."

Her eyes turned, irresistibly, to her large and ornate handbag. It was a false move and she realized it instantly and gazed appealingly at Bredon, but he knew where he was now.

"So you've got them there with you. That was very–farsighted of you. See here, Miss Vavasour, what's the use of talking like this? You may just as well be frank with me. Your idea was to threaten to show those letters to Mr. Pym if Tallboy didn't pay up, wasn't it?"

"No, of course it wasn't."

"You're so devoted to Tallboy that you always carry his correspondence about with you?"

"Yes–no. I never said I'd got the letters with me."

"No? But you've admitted it now, you know. Now, you take the advice of a man double your age." (This was a generous estimate, for Miss Vavasour was an easy twenty-eight.) "If you make a disturbance here, nothing will happen, except that Tallboy will possibly lose his job and have no money at all for you or anybody. And if you try to sell him those letters–there's a name for that, and it's not a pretty one."

"That's all very well," said Miss Vavasour, sullenly, "but how about this trouble he's got me into? I'm a mannequin, see? And if a girl's got to chuck her job, and her figure ruined for life–"

"Are you sure you're not mistaken about that?"

" 'Course I'm sure. What do you take me for? An innocent?"

"Surely not," said Bredon. "No doubt Tallboy will be ready to come to a suitable arrangement. But–if I may presume to advise you–no threats and no disturbance. And–forgive me–there are other people in the world."

"Yes, there are," said Miss Vavasour, frankly, "but they're not so keen to take over a girl with encumbrances, if you know what I mean. You wouldn't yourself now, would you?"

"Oh, me? I'm not in the running," said Bredon, with perhaps more promptness and emphasis than was quite complimentary. "But, speaking generally, I'm sure you'll find it better not to make an explosion–not here, at any rate. I mean to say, you know, that's the point. Because this is one of those old-fashioned firms that don't like anything unpleasant or–er–undesirable to happen on their premises."

"You bet they don't," said Miss Vavasour, shrewdly, "that's why I'm here."

"Yes, but take it from me, you'll do no good by making a fuss. Really not. And—ah! here is the missing gentleman. I'll be pushing along. Hullo, Tallboy—I've just been entertaining the lady in your absence."

Tallboy, his eyes burning in a very white face and his lips twitching, looked at Bredon for a moment or two in silence. Then:

"Thanks very much," he said, in a stifled tone.

"No, don't thank me," said Bredon. "The gratification is entirely on my side."

He went out and shut the door upon the pair of them.

"Now, I wonder," said Mr. Bredon, reverting to his own detective personality as he went slowly upstairs to his room, "I wonder if it's possible that I'm all wrong about our friend Victor Dean. Can it be that he was merely a common or garden blackmailer, intent on turning his colleague's human weaknesses to his own advantage? Would that be worth cracking a fellow's skull for him and hurling him down a staircase, iron, one, murderers for the use of? The chap who could probably tell me is Willis, but somehow the good Willis is deaf as an adder to my well-known charm of speech. Is it any use sounding him again? If only I could be sure that he was not the gentleman who sandbagged my poor brother-in-law Charles and that he was not still harbouring designs upon my unworthy carcase. Not that I mind having designs harboured on me, but I don't want to make a confidant of the fellow I'm after, like the fat-headed hero in one of those detective stories where the detective turns out to be the villain. If only I had ever seen Willis engaged in any game or sport, I should know better where I stood, but he seems to despise the open-air life—and that in itself, if you come to think of it, is sinister."

After a little more thought, he went along to Willis' room.

"Oh, I say, Willis," he said, "am I disturbing you?"

"No. Come in."

Willis looked up from a sheet of paper which bore the engaging headlines: "MAGNOLIA-WHITE, MAGNOLIA-SOFT—that's what they'll say of your hands." He looked depressed and ill.

"See here, Willis," said Bredon, "I want your advice. I know we don't seem to hit it off very well—"

"No—it's my fault," said Willis. He seemed to struggle with himself for a moment, and then brought his words out with a rush, as though they had been violently forced from him: "I fancy I owe you some sort of apology. I appear to have been mistaken."

"What exactly did you have against me? I never could make out what it was, to tell you the truth."

"I thought you belonged to Victor Dean's beastly doping and drinking crowd, and thought you were trying to get Pamela—Miss Dean—in among them again. She tells me that's not the case. But I saw you there with her, and now she tells me it's my fault that you—that you—oh, hell!"

"What *is* the matter?"

"I'll tell you what's the matter," said Willis, violently. "You went and forced yourself on Miss Dean—God knows what you told her, and she won't tell me. You made out you were a friend of her brother's, or something—was that true, to start with?"

"Not quite, as you put it. I made Miss Dean's acquaintance over a matter connected with her brother, but I had never met him, and she knows that."

"What had it got to do with him, then?"

"I'm afraid I can't tell you that."

"It sounds damned queer to me," said Willis, his face darkening with suspicion. Then he seemed to recollect that he was supposed to be making an apology, and went on:

"Well, anyway, you took her to that disgusting place down there by the river."

"That's not altogether true, either. I asked her to take me, because I couldn't very well have got in without an introduction."

"That's a lie; I got in all right."

"Miss Dean told them to let you in."

"Oh!" Willis was disconcerted for a moment. "Well, in any case, you had no business to ask a decent girl to do anything of the kind. That was exactly what Dean and I had trouble about. A house like that is no fit place for her, and you know it."

"I do; and I regretted the necessity which compelled me to ask her to go there. You may have noticed that I took care nothing should happen to her."

"I don't know that," grumbled Willis.

"You aren't a very good detective," said Bredon with a smile. "You must take my word for it that she was quite safe."

"I won't take your word, but I'd take hers. She says so, and I suppose I've got to believe it. But if you're not an out-and-out rotter yourself, why did you want to be taken there?"

"That's another thing I can't tell you. But I can offer you one or two reasonable explanations that might fit the case. I might be a journalist, commissioned to write an inside story about the newest kind of night-club. Or I might be a detective, engaged in tracking down dope-smugglers. Or I might be a zealot with a new brand of religion, trying to save the souls of post-war society sinners. Or I might be in love with somebody–say, if you like, the notorious Dian de Momerie–and threatening to commit suicide unless I got an introduction to her. I present you with those four solutions on the spur of the moment, and I dare say I could think of others, if I was put to it."

"You might be a dope-merchant yourself," said Willis.

"I hadn't thought of that. But if I were, I doubt if I should need Miss Dean's introduction to that particular crowd."

Willis muttered something unintelligible.

"But I gather," said Bredon, "that Miss Dean has more or less absolved me of being anything hopelessly corrupt. So what's the trouble?"

"The trouble is," groaned Willis, "that you've–my God! you swine –you've thrown her over and she says it's my fault."

"You oughtn't to say a thing like that, old son," said Bredon, really distressed. "It's not done."

"No–I dare say I'm not quite a gentleman. I've never been–"

"If you tell me you've never been to a public school," said Bredon, "I shall scream. What with Copley and Smayle, and all the other pathetic idiots who go about fostering inferiority complexes, and weighing up the rival merits of this place and that place, when it doesn't matter a damn anyway, I'm fed up. Pull yourself together. Anybody, wherever he's been educated, ought to know better than to say a thing like that about any girl. Particularly when there isn't the slightest foundation for it."

"Ah, but there is," said Willis. "You don't realize it, but I do. I know a man's a man for a' that and all the rest of it, but people like you have a sort of glamour about them and women fall for it, every time. I know I'm as good a man as you are, but I don't look it, and that's where it is."

"I can only assure you, Willis–"

"I know, I know. You've never made love to Miss Dean–that's what you're going to say–never by word, look or deed and so forth and so on, given her the slightest ground–bah! I know it. She admits it. It makes it all the worse."

"I am afraid," said Mr. Bredon, "that you are a very foolish pair of people. And I really think you must be quite mistaken in Miss Dean's feelings."

"That's damned likely."

"I think so. In any case, you oughtn't to have said anything to me about it. And in any case, there's nothing I can do."

"She asked me," said Willis, miserably, "to apologize to you and bring you–and ask you–and put the matter right."

"There's nothing to put right. Miss Dean knows quite well that my interviews with her were merely a matter of business. And all I can say is, Willis, if you accepted any such commission, she must think you as soft as a pancake. Why on earth didn't you tell her you'd see me at the devil first? That's probably what she expected you to do."

"Do you think so?"

"Sure of it," said Bredon, who was not sure at all, but thought it best to appear so. "You mustn't go about creating intolerable situations, you know. It's very awkward for me, and I'm sure Miss Dean would be horribly upset if she knew what you'd been saying about her. All she meant was, I expect, that you'd taken quite a wrong view of a perfectly ordinary business acquaintanceship and been unnecessarily antagonistic and so on, and that she wanted you to put the thing straight, so that, if I needed her help again, there wouldn't be any awkwardness about it. Isn't that, in other words, what she said to you?"

"Yes," said Willis. It was a lie, and he knew that Bredon knew that it was a lie, but he lied manfully. "Of course that was what she actually said. But I'm afraid I put another interpretation on it."

"All right," said Bredon, "that's settled. Tell Miss Dean that my business is progressing very well, and that when I need her kind help again I shall have no hesitation in calling her to my assistance. Now, is that all?"

"Yes, that's all."

"You're sure–while you are about it–that there's nothing else you want to get off your chest?"

"N-no."

"You don't sound very sure about it. You've been trying to say all this to me for some time, I dare say."

"No, not very long. A few days."

"Since the day of the monthly tea-party, shall we say?"

Willis started violently. Bredon, with a wary eye on him, followed up his advantage.

"Was that what you came round to Great Ormond Street that night to tell me?"

"How do you know about that?"

"I didn't know, I guessed. As I have said before, you would not make a good detective. You lost a pencil on that occasion, I believe?"

He drew the pencil from his pocket and held it out.

"A pencil? Not that I know of. Where did you find that?"

"In Great Ormond Street."

"I don't think it's mine. I don't know. I think I've still got mine."

"Well, never mind. You came round that night intending to apologize?"

"No–I didn't. I came round to have an explanation with you. I wanted to bash your face in, if you must know. I went round there just before ten–"

"Did you ring the bell of my flat?"

"No, I didn't. I'll tell you why. I looked in your letterbox, and I saw a letter there from Miss Dean, and I–I didn't dare go upstairs. I was afraid I might let myself go. I felt like murdering you. So I went off and wandered about till I was too done-up to think."

"I see. You didn't make any attempt to get hold of me at all?"

"No."

"Oh, well, that's that." Bredon dismissed the matter with a wave of the hand. "It's quite all right. It doesn't matter. I was only a little bit puzzled about the pencil."

"The pencil?"

"Yes. I found it on the top landing, you see, just outside my door. I couldn't quite understand how it got there, that's all."

"It wasn't me. I didn't go upstairs."

"How long did you stay in the house?"

"Only a few minutes."

"In the front hall downstairs all the time?"

"Yes."

"Oh, well then, it can't have been your pencil. It's very odd, because those pencils aren't on the market, as you know."

"Perhaps you dropped it yourself."

"Well, perhaps I did. That seems the likeliest explanation, doesn't it? It's not of any importance."

There was a short and rather uncomfortable pause. Willis broke it by asking in a constrained tone:

"What did you want to ask my advice about?"

"About the old subject," said Bredon; "perhaps, now that we've had this little explanation, you may find it easier to tell me what I want to know. Circumstances have brought me up against the Dean family, and I feel a certain amount of curiosity about the late lamented Victor. From his sister I gather that he was a good, kind brother, but unfortunately a little wild in his morals–which means, I take it, that he became infatuated with Dian de Momerie. According to her, he took his sister to various places to meet the fair Dian; you interfered; Miss Dean then realized what the situation was, and withdrew from the association, while quite naturally and illogically resenting your interference; and finally Dian de Momerie shut down on Victor and sent him off home. That's true, as far as it goes, I imagine?"

"Yes," said Willis, "except that I don't believe Dean ever was really infatuated with the de Momerie woman. I think he was flattered, and I think he thought he could make something out of her. As a matter of fact, he was a mean little beast."

"Did she give him money?"

"Yes, she did; but he didn't get much out of that, because he found that crowd so expensive to run with. He wasn't naturally one of that sort. He didn't enjoy gambling, though he had to do it, to keep in with them; and he wasn't a drinker. In some ways, I'd have liked him better if he had been. He wouldn't dope, either. I expect that's why Miss de Momerie got tired of him. The worst of that crowd, you know, is that they can't rest tlll they've made everybody they have to do with as bad as themselves. If they'd only drug themselves into their graves and have done with it, the sooner they did it the better it would be for every one. I'd cheerfully hand the stuff over to them by the cartload. But they get hold of quite decent people and ruin them for life.

That's why I got so worried about Pamela."

"But you say that Victor managed to remain undefiled."

"Yes, but Pamela's different. She's rather impulsive and easily—no, not easily led, but easily excited about things. She's high-spirited and likes to try everything once. If she once gets a sort of enthusiasm for a person, she wants to do the same as they do. She needs somebody—well, never mind that. I don't want to discuss Pamela. I only mean that Victor was just the opposite. He was very careful of himself, and he had a very good eye for the main chance."

"Do you mean that he was the sort of man who makes what he can out of his friends?"

"He was the kind of man who never has his own cigarettes, and never happens to be there, if he can help it, when it's his turn to stand the drinks. And he'd pick your brains every time."

"He must have had a pretty good reason, then, for going round with Dian de Momerie's lot. As you say, they're expensive."

"Yes; he must have seen something remunerative in the distance. And when it came to sacrificing his sister—"

"Exactly. Well, that's all rather by the way. What I wanted to know from you was this: supposing he found out that somebody—say somebody in this office—as it might be yourself—had a skeleton in the closet, to use the pretty old metaphor, was Victor Dean the kind of fellow to—er—to dispose of that skeleton to an anatomist?"

"Blackmail, do you mean?" asked Willis, bluntly.

"That's a strong word. But call it that."

"I don't quite know," said Willis, after a few moments' consideration. "It's a devil of a thing to suggest about anybody, isn't it? But I can only say that the question gives me no shock. If you were to tell me that he had blackmailed somebody, it wouldn't surprise me very much. Only, as it's a pretty serious offence, it would have to be a very safe kind of blackmail, with the sort of victim who couldn't possibly afford to face a court of law. Mind you, I haven't the least reason to suppose he ever did anything of the kind. And he certainly never seemed to be particularly flush of cash. Not that that's much to go by, with a careful fellow like him. *He* wouldn't have let wads of bank-notes come tumbling out his desk."

"You think the tumbling about of notes affords a presumption of innocence?"

"Not a bit. Only of carelessness, and Dean certainly wasn't careless."

"Well, thanks for speaking so frankly."

"That's all right. Only, for goodness' sake, don't let Pamela know what I've been saying about Victor. I've had trouble enough about that."

Bredon assured him that he need not fear any such fantastic indiscretion, and took his leave, polite but still puzzled.

Mr. Tallboy was lying in wait for him at the end of the passage.

"Oh, Bredon, I'm very much obliged to you, of course. I'm sure I can rely on you not to spread the thing any further than it's gone already. All quite absurd, of course. That fool Tompkin seems to have lost his head completely. I've ticked him off properly."

"Oh, yes, absolutely," replied Bredon. "Just so. Much ado about nothing. No real necessity for me to have butted in at all. But you never know. I mean to say, if you'd been detained and Miss Vavasour had got tired of waiting or—well, you know what I mean."

"Yes." Tallboy licked his dry lips. "It might have been very awkward.

When girls get hysterical and so on, they sometimes say more than they mean. I've been a bit of a fool, as I dare say you've gathered. I'm cutting it all out now. I've settled everything all right. Worrying, of course, but nothing really desperate." He laughed uncomfortably.

"You're looking a bit over-done."

"I feel it. The fact is, I was up all night. My wife—well, the fact is, my wife had a baby last night. That was partly why—oh, hell, what's it matter, anyhow?"

"I quite understand," said Bredon. "Very wearing business. Why didn't you take the day off?"

"I didn't want to do that. It's my busy day. Much better to occupy one's mind. Besides, there wasn't any necessity. Everything went all right. I suppose you think I'm an awful swine."

"You're not the first, by any means," said Bredon.

"No—it's rather usual, I believe. It's not going to happen again, I can tell you."

"It must have put you in a hell of a hole—all this."

"Yes—at least—not so bad. As you say, I'm not the only man it's ever happened to. It doesn't do to let one's self be upset, does it? Well, as I said, thanks very much and—that's all, isn't it?"

"Absolutely. There's nothing whatever to thank me about. Well, sonnie, what do you want?"

"Any letters to go, sir?"

"No, thanks," said Bredon.

"Oh, stop a minute," said Tallboy. "Yes, I've got one." He searched in his breast-pocket and pulled out an envelope, all ready sealed. "Lend me a pen one moment, Bredon. Here, boy, take this penny-halfpenny and run along to Miss Rossiter and ask her for a stamp."

He took the pen Bredon held out, and bending over the desk addressed the envelope hurriedly to "T. Smith, Esq." Bredon, idly watching him, was caught by his eye in the act, and apologized.

"I beg your pardon; I was snooping. Beastly habit. One catches it in the typists' room."

"All right—it's only a note to a stockbroker."

"Lucky man to have anything to stockbroke."

Tallboy laughed, stamped the letter and tossed it to the waiting boy.

"And so ends an exhausting day," he observed.

"Toule very tiresome?"

"Not more so than usual. He turned down 'Like Niobe, all Tears.' Said he didn't know who Niobe was and he didn't suppose anybody else did either. But he passed this week's 'Tears, Idle Tears,' because when he was a boy his father used to read Tennyson aloud to the family circle."

"That's one saved from the wreck, anyhow."

"Oh, yes. He liked the general idea of the poetical quotations. Said he thought they gave his advertisements class. You'll have to think up some more. He likes the ones that illustrate well."

"All right. 'Like Summer Tempest came her Tears.' That's Tennyson, too. Picture of the nurse of ninety years setting his babe upon her knee. Babies always go well. (Sorry, we don't seem able to get off babies.) Start the copy, 'Tears are often a relief to overwrought nerves, but when they flow too often, too easily, it is a sign that you need Nutrax.' I'll do that one. Bassanio and Antonio: 'I know not Why I am so Sad.' Carry the quote on into the copy.

'Causeless depression, like Antonio's, wearies both the sufferer and his friends. Go to the root of the matter and tone up the overstrung Nerves with Nutrax.' I can do that sort of thing by the hour."

Mr. Tallboy smiled wanly.

"It's a pity we can't cure ourselves with our own nostrums, isn't it?"

Mr. Bredon surveyed him critically.

"What *you* need," he said, "is a good dinner and a bottle of fizz."

# 14

# HOPEFUL CONSPIRACY OF TWO BLACK SHEEP

THE GENTLEMAN in the harlequin costume removed his mask with quiet deliberation, and laid it on the table.

"Since," he said, "my virtuous cousin Wimsey has let the cat out of the bag, I may as well take this off. I am afraid" –he turned to Dian–"my appearance will disappoint you. Except that I am handsomer and less rabbity-looking, the woman who has seen Wimsey has seen me. It is a heavy handicap to carry, but I can't help it. The resemblance, I am happy to say, is only skin-deep."

"It's almost incredible," said Major Milligan. He bent forward to examine the other's face more closely, but Mr. Bredon extended a languid arm and, without apparently using any force at all, pushed him back into his seat.

"You needn't come too close," he observed, insolently. "Even a face like Wimsey's is better than yours. Yours is spotty. You eat and drink too much."

Major Milligan, who had, indeed, been distressed that morning by the discovery of a few small pimples on his forehead, but had hoped they were not noticeable, grunted angrily. Dian laughed.

"I take it," pursued Mr. Bredon, "that you want to get something out of me. People of your sort always do. What is it?"

"I've no objection to being frank with you," replied Major Milligan.

"How nice it is to hear anybody say that. It always prepares one for a lie to follow. Fore-warned is fore-armed, isn't it?"

"If you choose to think so. But I think you'll find it to your advantage to listen."

"Financial advantage?"

"What other kind is there?"

"What indeed? I begin to like your face a trifle better."

"Oh, do you? Perhaps you may like it well enough to answer a few questions?"

"Possibly."

"How do you come to know Pamela Dean?"

"Pamela? A charming girl, isn't she? I obtained an introduction to her through what the great public–seduced by the unfortunate example of that incomparable *vulgari-sateur*, Charles Dickens–abominably calls a mutual friend. I admit that my object in obtaining the introduction was a purely business one; I can only say that I wish all business acquaintances were so agreeable."

"What was the business?"

"The business, my dear fellow, was concerned with another mutual friend of us all–with the late Victor Dean, who died, deeply regretted, upon a staircase. A remarkable young man, was he not?"

"In what way?" asked Milligan, quickly.

"Don't you know? I thought you did. Otherwise, why am I here?"

"You two idiots make me tired," broke in Dian. "Where's the sense of going round and round each other like this? Your pompous cousin told us all about you, Mr. Bredon–I suppose you've got a Christian name, by the way?"

"I have. It's spelt Death. Pronounce it any way you like. Most of the people who are plagued with it make it rhyme with teeth, but personally I think it sounds more picturesque when rhymed with breath. What did my amiable cousin say about me?"

"He said you were a dope-runner."

"Where my cousin Wimsey gets his information from, I am damned if I know. Sometimes he is correct."

"And you know perfectly well that one can get what one wants at Tod's place. So why not come to the point?"

"As you say, why not? Is that the particular facet of my brilliant personality that interests you, Milligan?"

"Is that the particular facet of Victor Dean's personality that interests *you?*"

"One point to me," said Mr. Bredon. "Till this moment, I was not sure that it was a facet of his personality. Now I do. Dear me! How interesting it all is, to be sure."

"If you can find out exactly how Victor Dean was involved in that show," said Mr. Milligan, "it might be worth something to you and to me."

"Say on."

Major Milligan reflected a little and seemed to make up his mind to lay his cards on the table.

"Did you learn from Pamela Dean what her brother's job was?"

"Yes, of course. He wrote advertising copy at a place called Pym's. There's no secret about that."

"That's just what there is. And if that infernal young fool hadn't gone and got killed, we might have found out what it was and done ourselves a lot of good. As it is–"

"But look here, Tod," said Dian. "I thought it was the other way round. I thought you were afraid of *his* finding out too much."

"That's true," said Milligan, scowling. "What would be the use of it if he found out first?"

"I don't follow all this," said Bredon. "Wasn't it his secret? Why not stop talking like a sensation novel and give us the dope straight?"

"Because I don't believe you know even as much as I do about the fellow."

"I don't. I never met him in my life. But I know a good deal about Pym's Publicity, Ltd."

"How?"

"I work there."

"What?"

"I work there."

"Since when?"

"Since Dean's death."

"Because of Dean's death, do you mean?"

"Yes."

"How did that happen?"

"I received information, as my dear cousin Wimsey's police pals would say, that Dean was on to something fishy about Pym's. So, since most fish have gold in their mouths like St. Peter's, I thought it wouldn't do any harm to try a cast or two over that particular pool."

"And what did you find?"

"My dear Milligan, you would make a cat laugh. I don't give away information. I dispose of it–advantageously."

"So do I."

"As you like. You invited me here tonight. I wasn't looking for you. But there's one thing I don't mind telling you, because I've already told Miss de Momerie, and that is, that Victor Dean was bumped off deliberately to prevent him from talking. So far, the only person I can discover who wanted him out of the way was yourself. The police might be interested to know that fact."

"The police?"

"Oh! I quite agree. I don't like the police. They pay very badly and ask a hell of a lot of questions. But it might be useful, for once, to get on the right side of them."

"That's all punk," said Milligan. "You're barking up the wrong tree. I didn't kill the fellow. I didn't want him killed."

"Prove that," said the other, coolly.

He watched Milligan's impassive face, and Milligan watched his.

"Give it up," suggested Bredon, after a few minutes of this mutual scrutiny. "I can play poker just as well as you. But this time I fancy I hold a straight flush."

"Well, what do you want to know?"

"I want to know what you think Dean was in a position to find out."

"I can tell you that. He was trying to find out–"

"Had found out."

"How do you know?"

"If you want instruction in detective methods, you must pay extra. I say he had found out."

"Well, then, he had found out who was running the show from Pym's end."

"The dope-show?"

"Yes. And he may have found out, too, the way it's worked."

"*Is* worked?"

"Yes."

"It's still being worked the same way, then?"

"So far as I know."

"So far as you know? You don't seem to know much."

"Well, how much do you know about the way your own gang run the show?"

"Nothing whatever. Instructions are issued–"

"By the way, how did you get into it?"

"Sorry. Can't tell you that. Not even if you pay extra."

"How do I know I can trust you, then?"

Bredon laughed.

"Perhaps you'd like me to supply you," he said. "If you're not satisfied with your distribution, you can inscribe yourself upon the roll of my customers. Deliveries Sunday and Thursday. Meanwhile—and as a sample—you may be interested in the collar of my cloak. It is handsome, is it not? A rich velvet. A little ostentatious, perhaps you think—a little overmuch buckram? Possibly you are right. But very well made. The opening is almost invisible. We delicately insert the forefinger and thumb, pull the tab gently, and produce this dainty bag of oiled silk—fine as an onion-skin, but remarkably tough. Within it, you will discover sufficient inspiration for quite a number of enthusiasts. A magician's cloak. Such stuff as dreams are made on."

Milligan examined the contents of the little bag in silence. They were, in fact, a portion of the famous packet obtained by Mr. Hector Puncheon at the White Swan.

"All right, so far. Where do you get it from?"

"I got it in Covent Garden."

"Not at Pym's?"

"No."

Milligan looked disappointed.

"What day did you get it?"

"Friday morning. Like yourself, I get it on a Friday."

"Look here," said Milligan, 'you and I have got to be together on this. Dian, my child, run away and play. I'm going to talk business with your friend."

"That's a nice way to treat me in my own house," grumbled Miss de Momerie, but, seeing that Milligan meant what he said, she gathered up herself and her wraps and retreated into the bedroom. Milligan leaned forwards over the table.

"I'm going to tell you what I know," he said. "If you double-cross me, it's at your own risk. I don't want any funny business with that damned cousin of yours."

Mr. Bredon expressed his opinion of Lord Peter Wimsey in a few well-chosen words.

"All right," said Milligan. "You have been warned. Now, see here. If we can find out who works this thing and how it's worked, we can get in at the top. It pays fairly well as it is, in one way, but it's a devil of a risk and a lot of trouble, and it's expensive. Look at that place I have to keep up. It's the man in the centre of the ring that makes the big profits. I know, and you know, what we pay for the stuff, and then there's the bore of handing it out to all these fools and collecting the cash. Now, here's what I know. The whole stunt is worked from that advertising place of yours—Pym's. I found that out from a man who's dead now. I won't tell you how I fell in with him—it's a long story. But I'll tell you what he told me. I was dining with him one night at the Carlton, and he was a bit lit-up. A chap came in with a party, and this man said to me: 'Know who that is?'—'Not from Adam,' I said. He said: 'Well, it's old Pym, the publicity agent.' And then he laughed and said: "If he only knew what his precious agency was doing, he'd have a fit.' 'How's that?' I said. 'Why,' said he, 'didn't you know? All this dope-traffic is worked from there.' Naturally, I started to ask him how he knew and all about it, but he suddenly got an attack of caution and started to be mysterious, and I couldn't get another word out of him."

"I know that brand of drunkenness," said Bredon. "Do you think he really knew what he was talking about?"

"Yes, I think so. I saw him again next day, but he was sober then, and got the shock of his life when I told him what he'd said. But he admitted it was true, and implored me to keep quiet about it. That was all I could get out of him, and the same evening he was run over by a lorry."

"Was he? How remarkably well-timed."

"I thought so myself," said Milligan. "It made me rather nervous."

"But how does Victor Dean come into it?"

"There," admitted Milligan, "I dropped a bad brick. Dian brought him along one evening–"

"Just a minute. When did this conversation with your indiscreet friend take place?"

"Nearly a year ago. Naturally, I'd been trying to follow the matter up, and when Dian introduced Dean and said he worked at Pym's, I thought he must be the man. Apparently he wasn't. But I'm afraid he got an idea about the thing from me. After a bit, I found out he was trying to horn in on my show, and I told Dian to shut down on him."

"In fact," said Mr. Bredon, 'You tried to pump him, just as you are trying to pump me, and you found out that he was pumping you instead."

"Something like that," confessed Milligan.

"And shortly after that he fell down a staircase."

"Yes; but I didn't push him down it. You needn't think that. I didn't want him snuffed out. I only wanted him kept out of the way. Dian's too much of a chatterer, especially when she's ginned up. The trouble is, you're never safe with these people. You'd think common sense would tell them to keep quiet in their own interests, but they've got no more sense than a cageful of monkeys."

"Well," said Bredon, "if we fill them up with stuff that notoriously saps their self-control, I suppose we can't grumble at the consequences."

"I suppose not, but it's a damned nuisance sometimes. They're as cunning as weasels in one way, and sheer idiots in another. Spiteful, too."

"Yes. Dean never became an addict, did he?"

"No, if he had, we'd have had more control over him; but unfortunately, his head was screwed on the right way. All the same, he knew pretty well that he'd have been well paid for any information."

"Very likely. The trouble is that he was taking money from the other side as well–at least, I think he was."

"Don't you try that game," said Milligan.

"I've no wish to fall down staircases. What you want, I take it, is the way the trick's worked and the name of the man who works it. I dare say I can find that out for you. How about terms?"

"My idea is, that we use the information to get into the inside ring ourselves, and each strike our own bargain."

"Just so. Alternatively, I suppose, we put the screw on the gentleman at Pym's, when we've got him, and divide the spoil. In which case, as I'm doing most of the work and taking the biggest risk, I suggest I take 75 per cent."

"Not on your life. Fifty-fifty. I shall conduct the negotiations."

"Will you? That's pretty good. Why should I bring you into it at all? You can't negotiate till I tell you whom to negotiate with. You don't think I was born yesterday."

"No. But knowing what I do, I could get you shifted from Pym's tomorrow, couldn't I? If Pym knew who you were, do you suppose he'd keep you on his virtuous premises for another day?"

"Well, look here. We conduct the negotiations together, and I take 60 per cent."

Milligan shrugged his shoulders.

"Well, leave it at that for the moment. I'm hoping it won't pan out that way. What we want to aim at is getting the reins into our own hands."

"As you say. When we've done that, it will be time enough to decide which of us is going to crack the whip."

When he had gone, Tod Milligan went into the bedroom, and found Dian kneeling on the window-seat, staring down into the street.

"Have you fixed things up with him?"

"Yes. He's a twister, but I'll be able to make him see that it'll pay him to be straight with me."

"You had much better leave him alone."

"You're talking rubbish," said Milligan, using a coarser term.

Dian turned round and faced him.

"I've warned you," she said. "Not that I care a damn what happens to you. You're getting on my nerves, Tod. It's going to be great fun to see you come to smash. But you'd better keep off that man."

"Thinking of selling me, are you?"

"I shan't need to."

"You'd better not. Lost your head over this theatrical gentleman in tights, haven't you?"

"Why do you have to be so vulgar?" she asked, contemptuously.

"What's the matter with you, then?"

"I'm frightened, that's all. Unlike me, isn't it?"

"Frightened of that advertising crook?"

"Really, Tod, you're a fool sometimes. You can't see a thing when it's under your nose. It's written too big for you to see, I suppose."

"You're drunk," said Milligan. "Just because you haven't quite managed to get off with this joker of yours—"

"Shut up," said Dian. "Get off with him? I'd as soon get off with the public hangman."

"I dare say you would. Any new sensation would do for you. What do you want? A row? Because, if so, I'm afraid I can't be bothered to oblige you."

There is a dreary convention which decrees that the final collapse of a sordid liaison shall be preceded by a series of no less sordid squabbles. But on this occasion, Miss de Momerie seemed ready to dispense with convention.

"No. I'm through with you, that's all. I'm cold. I'm going to bed. . . . Tod, *did* you kill Victor Dean?"

"I did not."

Major Milligan dreamed that night that Death Bredon, in his harlequin dress, was hanging him for the murder of Lord Peter Wimsey.

# 15

# SUDDEN DECEASE OF A MAN IN DRESS CLOTHES

CHIEF-INSPECTOR PARKER continued to be disturbed in his mind. There had been another fiasco in Essex. A private motor-boat, suspected of being concerned in the drug-traffic, had been seized and searched without result–except, of course, the undesired result of giving the alarm to the parties concerned, if they were concerned. Further, a fast car, which had attracted attention by its frequent midnight excursions from the coast to the capital, had been laboriously tracked to its destination, and proved to belong to a distinguished member of the diplomatic corps, engaged on extremely incognito visits to a lady established in a popular seaside resort. Mr. Parker, still incapacitated from personal attendance upon midnight expeditions, was left with the gloomy satisfaction of saying that everything always went wrong when he wasn't there himself. He was also unreasonably annoyed with Wimsey, as the original cause of his incapacity.

Nor had the investigation at the White Swan so far borne very much fruit. For a week in succession, tactful and experienced policemen had draped themselves over its bar, chatting to all and sundry about greyhounds, goats, parrots and other dumb friends of man, without receiving any return in the shape of mysterious packets.

The old man with the parrot-story had been traced easily enough. He was an habitué. He sat there every morning and every afternoon, and had a fund of such stories. The patient police made a collection of them. The proprietor–against whose character nothing could be proved–knew this customer well. He was a superannuated Covent Garden porter, who lived on an old-age pension, and every corner of his inoffensive life was open to the day. This excellent old gentleman, when questioned, recalled the conversation with Mr. Hector Puncheon, but was positive that he had never seen any of the party before, except the two carters, whom he knew well enough. These men also agreed that the gentleman in dress clothes and the little man who had talked about greyhounds were equally unknown to them. It was not, however, unusual for gentlemen in dress clothes to drop in at the Swan by way of a good finish to a lively night–or for gentlemen without dress clothes, either. Nothing threw any light on the mystery of the packet of cocaine.

Parker was, however, roused to some enthusiasm by Wimsey's report of his conversations with Milligan.

"What incredible luck you do have, Peter. People who, in the ordinary way, would avoid you like the plague, gate-crash into your parties at the psychological moment and offer you their noses to lead them by."

"Not so much luck, old man," said Wimsey. "Good guidance, that's all. I sent the fair Dian an anonymous letter, solemnly warning her against myself and informing her that if she wanted to know the worst about me, she had only to inquire at my brother's address. It's a curious thing, but people *cannot* resist anonymous letters. It's like free sample offers. They appeal to all one's lower instincts."

"You are a devil," said Parker. "One of these days you'll get into trouble. Suppose Milligan had recognized you."

"I prepared his mind to accept a striking resemblance."

"I wonder he didn't see through it. Family resemblances don't usually extend to details of teeth and so on."

"I never let him get close enough to study details."

"That ought to have made him suspicious."

"No, because I was rude to him about it. He believed me all the time, simply because I was rude. Everybody suspects an eager desire to curry favour, but rudeness, for some reason, is always accepted as a guarantee of good faith. The only man who ever managed to see through rudeness was St. Augustine, and I don't suppose Milligan reads the *Confessions*. Besides, he wanted to believe in me. He's greedy."

"Well, no doubt you know your own business. But about this Victor Dean affair. Do you really believe that the head of this particular dope-gang is on Pym's staff? It sounds quite incredible."

"That's an excellent reason for believing it. I don't mean in a *credo quia impossible* sense, but merely because the staff of a respectable advertising agency would be such an excellent hiding-place for a big crook. The particular crookedness of advertising is so very far removed from the crookedness of dope-trafficking."

"Why? As far as I can make out, all advertisers are dope-merchants."

"So they are. Yes, now I come to think of it, there is a subtle symmetry about the thing which is extremely artistic. All the same, Charles, I must admit that I find it difficult to go the whole way with Milligan. I have carefully reviewed the staff of Pym's, and I have so far failed to find any one who looks in the least like a Napoleon of crime."

"But you seem convinced that the murder of Victor Dean was an inside job. Or do you now think that some stranger was hiding on the roof and did away with Dean because he was on the point of splitting on the gang? I suppose an outsider could get access to Pym's roof?"

"Oh, easily. But that wouldn't explain the catapult in Mrs. Johnson's desk."

"Nor the attack on me."

"Not if the same person that killed Dean attacked you too."

"Meaning that it might have been Willis? I take it that Willis is not the Napoleon of crime, anyhow."

"Willis isn't a Napoleon of anything. Nor, I fancy, is the chap with the catapult. If he had been, he'd have had the common sense to use his own catapult and burn it afterwards. As I see him, he is a person of considerable ingenuity but limited foresight; a person who snatches at the first thing that is offered him and does his best with it, but lacks just that little extra bit of consideration that would make the thing a real success. He lies from hand to mouth, as you may say. I dare say I could spot him without much difficulty—but that's not what you want, is it? You'd rather have the Napoleon of the dope-traffic, wouldn't you? If he exists, that is."

"Certainly I should," said Parker, emphatically.

"That's what I thought. What, if you come to think of it, is a trifle like an odd murder or assault, compared with a method of dope-running that baffles Scotland Yard? Nothing at all."

"It isn't, really," replied Parker, seriously. "Dope-runners are murderers, fifty times over. They slay hundreds of people, soul and body, besides indirectly causing all sorts of crimes among the victims. Compared with that, slugging one inconsiderable pip-squeak over the head is almost meritorious."

"Really, Charles! for a man of your religious upbringing, your outlook is positively enlightened."

"Not so irreligious, either. Fear not him that killeth, but him that hath power to cast into hell. How about it?"

"How indeed? Hang the one and give the other a few weeks in jail—or, if of good social position, bind him over or put him on remand for six months under promise of good behaviour."

Parker made a wry mouth.

"I know, old man, I know. But where would be the good of hanging the wretched victims or the smaller fry? There would always be others. We want the top people. Take even this man, Milligan, who's a pest of the first water–with no excuse for it, because he isn't an addict himself–but suppose we punish him here and now. They'd only start again, with a new distributor and a new house for him to run his show in, and what would anybody gain by that?"

"Exactly," said Wimsey. "And how much better off will you be, even if you catch the man above Milligan? The same thing will apply."

Parker made a hopeless gesture.

"I don't know, Peter. It's no good worrying about it. My job is to catch the heads of the gangs if I can, and, after that, as many as possible of the little people. I can't overthrow cities and burn the population."

" 'Tis the Last Judgment's fire must cure this place," said Wimsey, "calcine its clods and set its prisoners free. There are times, Charles, when even the unimaginative decency of my brother and the malignant virtue of his wife appear to me admirable. I could hardly say more."

"You have a certain decency of your own, Peter," replied Parker, "which I like better, because it is not negative." Having given voice to this atrocious outburst of sentiment, he became extremely red in the face, and hastened to cover up his lapse from good taste. "But at the present moment I must say you are not being very helpful. You have been investigating a crime–if it is a crime–for some weeks now, and the only tangible result is a broken collar-bone for me. If you could confine yourself to breaking your own collar-bone–"

"It has been broken before now," said Wimsey, "and in no less good a cause. You shouldn't shove your beastly collar-bone into my affairs."

At this moment, the telephone-bell rang.

It was half-past eight in the morning, and Wimsey had been consuming an early breakfast with his brother-in-law, prior to their departure each to his own place of business. Lady Mary, who had been supplying their bodily necessities and leaving them to their argument, took up the receiver.

"It's from the Yard, darling. Something about that man Puncheon."

Parker took the instrument and plunged into an animated discussion, which ended with his saying:

"Send Lumley and Eagles along at once, and tell Puncheon to keep in touch with you. I'm coming."

"What's up?" inquired Wimsey.

"Our little friend Puncheon has seen his bloke in dress clothes again," said Parker, cursing as he tried to get his coat over his damaged shoulder. "Saw him hanging about the *Morning Star* offices this morning, buying an early paper or something. Been chasing him ever since, apparently. Landed out at Finchley, of all places. Says he couldn't get on to the 'phone before. I must push off. See you later. Cheerio, Mary dear. Bung-ho, Peter."

He bounced out in a hurry.

"Well, well," said Wimsey. He pushed back his chair and sat staring vacantly at the wall opposite, on which hung a calendar. Then, emptying the sugar-bowl on the table-cloth with a jerk, he began, frowning hideously, to build a lofty tower with its contents. Mary recognized the signs of inspiration and stole quietly away to her household duties.

Forty-five minutes afterwards she returned. Her brother had gone, and the banging of the flat-door after him had flung his column of sugar-lumps in disorder across the table, but she could see that it had been a tall one. Mary sighed.

"Being Peter's sister is rather like being related to the public hangman," she thought, echoing the words of a lady with whom she had otherwise little in common. "And being married to a policeman is almost worse. I suppose the hangman's relatives are delighted when business is looking up. Still," she thought, being not without humour, "one might be connected with an undertaker, and rejoice over the deaths of the righteous, which would be infinitely worse."

Sergeant Lumley and P.C. Eagles found no Hector Puncheon at the small eating-house in Finchley from which he had telephoned. They did, however, find a message.

"He has had breakfast and is off again," said the note, written hurriedly on a page torn from the reporter's notebook. "I will telephone to you here as soon as I can. I'm afraid he knows I am following him."

"There," said Sergeant Lumley, gloomily. "That's an amachoor all over. 'Course 'e lets the bloke know 'e's bein' followed. If one of these newspaper fellows was a bluebottle and 'ad to follow an elephant, 'e'd get buzzin' in the elephant's ear, same as 'e'd know what 'e was up to."

P.C. Eagles was struck with admiration at this flight of fancy, and laughed heartily.

"Ten to one 'e'll lose 'im for keeps, now," pursued Sergeant Lumley. "Gettin' us pushed off 'ere without our breakfusses."

"There ain't no reason why we shouldn't have our breakfusses, seein' as we are here," said his subordinate, who was of that happy disposition that makes the best of things. " 'Ow about a nice pair o' kippers?"

"I don't mind if I do," said the sergeant, "if only we're allowed to eat 'em in peace. But you mark my words, 'e'll start ringin' up again afore we 'as time to swallow a bite. Which reminds me. I better ring up the Yard and stop me lord Parker from traipsin' up 'ere. 'E mustn't be put about. Oh, no!"

P.C. Eagles ordered the kippers and a pot of tea. He used his jaws more readily for eating than for talking. The sergeant got his call, and returned, just as the eatables were placed on the table.

"Says, if 'e rings up from anywhere else, we better take a taxi," he announced. "Save time, 'e says. 'Ow's 'e think we're goin' to pick up a taxi 'ere? Nothing but blinkin' trams."

"Order the taxi now," suggested Mr. Eagles, with his mouth full, "so's to be in readiness, like."

"And 'ave it tickin' up the thruppences for nothing? Think they'll call that legitimate expenses? Not 'arf. 'You pay that out of your own pocket, my man' that's what they'll say, the lousy skin-flints."

"Well, 'ave yer grub," suggested Mr. Eagles, pacifically.

Sergeant Lumley inspected his kipper narrowly.

" 'Ope it's a good one, that's all," he muttered. "Looks oily, it do. 'Ope it's cooked. Eat a kipper what ain't properly cooked through and you gets kipper on your breath for the rest of the day." He forked a large portion into his mouth without pausing to remove the bones, and was obliged to expend a painful minute rescuing them with his fingers. "Tcha! it beats me why Godamighty wanted to put such a lot of bones into them things."

P.C. Eagles was shocked.

"You didn't oughter question the ways of Godamighty," he said, reprovingly.

"You keep a civil tongue in your 'ed, my lad," retorted Sergeant Lumley, unfairly intruding his official superiority into this theological discussion, "and don't go forgettin' what's due to my position."

"There ain't no position in the eyes of Godamighty," said P.C. Eagles, stoutly. His father and his sister happened to be noted lights in the Salvation Army, and he felt himself to be on his own ground here. "If it pleases 'Im to make you a sergeant, that's one thing, but it won't do you no good when you comes before 'Im to answer to the charge of questionin' 'Is ways with kippers. Come to think of it, in 'Is sight you an' me is just the same as worms, with no bones at all."

"Not so much about worms," said Sergeant Lumley. "You oughter know better than to talk about worms when a man's eating his breakfuss. It's enough to take any one's appetite away. And let me tell you, Eagles, worm or no worm, if I have any more lip from you—Drat that telephone! What did I tell you?"

He pounded heavily across to the insanitary little cupboard that held the instrument, and emerged in a minute or two, dismally triumphant.

"That's 'im. Kensington, this time. You 'op out an' get that taxi, while I settle up 'ere."

"Wouldn't the Underground be quicker?"

"They said taxi, so you damn well make it taxi," said Sergeant Lumley. While Eagles fetched the taxi, the sergeant took the opportunity to finish his kipper, thus avenging his defeat in religious controversy. This cheered him so much that he consented to take the Underground at the nearest suitable point, and they journeyed in comparative amity as far as South Kensington Station, and thence to the point indicated by Hector Puncheon, which was, in fact, the entrance to the Natural History Museum.

There was nobody in the entrance-hall who resembled Hector Puncheon in the least.

"Suppose 'e's gone on already?" suggested P. C. Eagles.

"Suppose 'e 'as," retorted the sergeant. "I can't 'elp that. I told 'im to telephone 'ere if 'e did or to let them know at the Yard. I can't do no more, can I? I better take a walk round, and you sit 'ere to see as they don't come out. If they do, you be ready to take up this other bird's trail and tell Puncheon to set 'ere till I come. An' don't let your bird see you talking to Puncheon, neether. And if they comes out and you see me a-follerin' of them, then you foller on be'ind an' keep yourself outer sight, see?"

Mr. Eagles saw clearly—as indeed he well might, for he knew quite as much about his duties as Sergeant Lumley. But the worm still rankled in the sergeant's breast. Mr. Eagles strolled over to a case of humming-birds and gazed at it with absorbed interest, while Mr. Lumley went heavlly up the steps, looking as much as possible like a country cousin bent on seeing the sights.

He had been in the entrance-hall about ten minutes, and had almost exhausted the humming-birds, when he saw something reflected in the glass case which made him sidle softly round so as to command a view of the staircase. A portly person in an overcoat and a top-hat was coming slowly down, one hand thrust deep into his overcoat pocket, the other swinging carelessly at his side. P.C. Eagles looked past him up the stair; there was no sign, either of Hector Puncheon or of Sergeant Lumley, and for a moment the constable hesitated. Then something caught his eye. In the gentleman's left-hand overcoat pocket was a folded copy of the *Morning Star*.

There is nothing unusual about seeing a gentleman with a copy of the *Morning Star*. The readers of that great organ periodically write to the editor, giving statistics of the number of passengers on the 8:15 who read the *Morning Star* in preference to any other paper, and their letters are printed for all to read. Nevertheless, P. C. Eagles determined to take the risk. He scribbled a hasty note on the back of an envelope and walked across to the doorkeeper.

"If you see my friend that came in with me," he said, "you might give him that and tell him I can't wait any longer. I got to get along to my work."

Out of the corner of his eye, he saw the gentleman in the overcoat pass out through the swing-door. Unobtrusively, he followed him.

Upstairs, at the top of a dark staircase barred by a trestle bearing the words "No Entrance," Sergeant Lumley was bending anxiously over the inanimate form of Hector Puncheon. The reporter was breathing heavily in a way the sergeant did not like, and there was a nasty contused wound on his temple.

"Trust your amachoors to make a mess of it," reflected Sergeant Lumley, bitterly. "I only 'ope as that Eagles 'as got 'is 'ead screwed on the right way. But there you are. I can't be in two places at once."

The man in the overcoat walked quietly down the street towards the Underground Station. He did not look back. A few yards behind him, P.C. Eagles sauntered casually along in his wake. His eyes were on his quarry. Neither of them saw a third man, who emerged from nowhere in particular and followed a few yards behind P.C. Eagles. No passer-by gave so much as a second glance to the little procession as it crossed Cromwell Road and debouched upon the station.

The man in the overcoat glanced at the taxi-rank; then he seemed to change his mind. For the first time, he looked back. All he saw was P. C. Eagles purchasing a newspaper, and in this sight there was nothing alarming. The other follower he could not have seen, because, like the Spanish Fleet, he was not yet in sight, though P. C. Eagles might have seen him, had he been looking in his direction. The gentleman appeared to reject the notion of a taxi and turned into the station entrance. Mr. Eagles, his eyes apparently intent upon a headline about Food-Taxes, wandered in after him, and was in time to follow his example in taking a ticket for Charing Cross. Pursued and pursuer entered the lift together, the gentleman walking across to the farther gate, Eagles remaining modestly on the hither side. There were already about half a dozen people, mostly women, in the lift, and just as the gate was shutting, another man came in hurriedly. He passed Eagles and took up a central position among the group of women. At the bottom of the shaft, they all emerged in a bunch, the strange man pressing rather hastily past the man in the overcoat, and leading the way towards the platform, where an eastward-bound train was just running in.

What exactly happened then, P. C. Eagles was not quite clear about at the time, though, in the light of after events he saw plainly one or two things that were not obvious to him then. He saw the third man standing close to the edge of the platform, carrying a thin walking-stick. He saw the man in the overcoat walk past him and then suddenly stop and stagger in his walk. He saw the man with the stick fling out his hand and grasp the other by the arm, saw the two waver together on the edge and heard a shriek from a woman. Then both toppled together under the advancing train.

Through the uproar, Eagles shouldered his way.

" 'Ere," he said, "I'm an officer of the law. Stand aside, please."

They stood aside, with the exception of a porter and another man, who were hauling out something between the train and the platform. An arm came up and then a head—then the battered body of the third man, the one who had had the walking-stick. They laid him down on the platform bruised and bloody.

"Where's the other?"

"Gone, poor chap."

"Is that one dead?"

"Yes."

"No, he ain't."

"Oh, Betty, I'm going to faint."

"He's all right—see! He's opening his eyes."

"Yes, but how about the other?"

"Do stop shoving."

"Look out, that's a policeman."

"That's the live rail down there."

"Where's a doctor? Send for a doctor."

"Stand back, please. Stand right back."

"Why don't they shut off the electricity?"

"They have. That feller ran off to do it."

"How'll they get 'im out without moving the train?"

"Expect he's all in little bits, pore chap."

"That one tried to save 'im."

"Looked as if he was took ill, or drunk-like."

"Drunk, this time in the morning?"

"They ought to give 'im brandy."

"Clear all this lot out," said Eagles. "This one'll do all right. The other's done for, I suppose."

"Smashed all to blazes. 'Orrible."

"Then you can't do him any good. Clear the station and get an ambulance and another police officer."

"Right you are."

"This one's coming round," put in the man who had helped to haul the victim up. "How are you feeling now, sir?"

"Bloody," said the rescued man, faintly. Then, seeming to realize where he was, he added:

"What happened?"

"Why, sir, a poor gentleman fell off the platform and took you over with him."

"Yes, of course. Is he all right?"

"Afraid he's badly knocked about, sir. Ah!" as somebody ran up with a flask. "Take a pull at this, sir. Gently, you. Lift his head up. Don't jerk him. Now then."

"Ah!" said the man. "That's better. All right. Don't fuss. My spine's all right and I don't think anything's broken to speak of." He moved his arms and legs experimentally.

"Doctor'll be here in a minute, sir."

"Doctor be damned. I'm a doctor myself. Limbs all correct. Head apparently sound, though it aches like hell. Ribs—not so sure about those. Something gone there, I'm afraid. Pelvis intact, thank goodness."

"Very glad to hear that," said Eagles.

"It's the footboard of the train that got me, I fancy. I remember being rolled round and round like a pat of butter between two whatsinames," said the stranger, whose damaged ribs did not seem to impede his breathing altogether. "And I saw the wheels of the train get slower and stop, and I said to myself: 'This is it. You're for it, my lad. Time's stopped and this is Eternity.' But I see I was mistaken."

"Happily so, sir," said Eagles.

"Wish I'd been able to stop that other poor devil, though."

"I'm sure you did your best, sir." Eagles produced his notebook. "Excuse me, sir, but I'm a police-officer, and if you could manage to tell me just how it occurred—"

"Damned if I know myself," replied the other. "All I know is, I was standing just about here when the fellow passed me." He paused, catching his breath a little. "I noticed he was looking rather queer. Heart subject, I should think. He suddenly stopped and staggered and then came towards me. I caught hold of his arm and then he lurched over with all his weight and dragged me over with him. And then I can't remember anything but the noise of the train and the tremendous size of its wheels and the feeling of having the breath squeezed out of me. I must have dropped him, I suppose."

"And no wonder," said Eagles, sympathetically.

"My name's Garfield," went on the rescuer. "Dr. Herbert Garfield." He gave an address in Kensington and another in Harley Street. "I think I see one of my professional brethren arriving, and he'll probably say I'm not to talk." He grinned faintly. "Anyhow, I shall be filed for reference for the next few weeks, if you want more information."

P. C. Eagles thanked Dr. Garfield, and then turned to the body of the man in the overcoat, which had by now been disentangled from between the wheels of the train and laid upon the platform. It was an unpleasant sight. Even Eagles, accustomed as he was to casualties, felt a violent distaste for the necessary job of searching the dead man's pockets for evidence of identity. Curiously enough he found none in the shape of visiting cards or papers. There was a note-case with a few pound-notes, a silver cigarette-case filled with a popular brand of Turks, a little loose change, an unmarked handkerchief, and an H.T. & V. latch-key. Moreover—and this pleased him very much—in the overcoat pocket was a little rubber cosh, such as is sold for use against motor-bandits. He was in the act of hunting over the suit for the tailor's tab, when he was hailed by a local inspector of police, who had arrived with the ambulance.

Eagles was relieved to have the support of a colleague. He knew that he ought to get in touch with Sergeant Lumley and with Scotland Yard. An hour's energetic action on the part of all resulted in a happy reunion at the nearest police-station, where, in fact, Lumley had already arrived, after depositing the unconscious Mr. Puncheon in hospital. Chief-Inspector Parker came hot-foot to Kensington, heard the statements of Lumley and Eagles, reviewed the scene of the disaster and the remains of the mysterious man in dress clothes, and was annoyed. When a man whom you have been elaborately chasing all over London has the impudence to be killed just as you are on the point of catching him, and turns out have no tailor's name on his clothes and nothing to identify him by; when, moreover, he has thoughtlessly permitted his face to be smashed into pulp by an electric train, so that you cannot usefully circulate his photograph for recognition, your satisfaction in feeling that there is something wrong about him is cancelled by the thought of the weary work that his identification is going to involve.

"There's nothing for it," said Chief-Inspector Parker, "but his laundry-mark, I suppose. And, of course, his dentistry, if any."

Irritatingly enough, the deceased turned out to have an excellent set of teeth and at least three laundry-marks. Nor were his shoes helpful, being ready-made, though by an excellent and much-advertised firm. In fact, the wretched man had gone to meet his Maker in Farley's Footwear, thus upholding to the last the brave assertion that, however distinguished the occasion, Farley's Footwear will carry you through.

In this extremity, Mr. Parker—perhaps stimulated by the thought of Messrs. Farley's advertising—rang up Pym's Publicity and desired to speak with Mr. Bredon.

That gentleman was closeted with Mr. Armstrong when the call came through. Whifflets were causing trouble. The sales of Whifflets had been considerably affected by the publicity methods of a rival brand, Puffin Cigarettes. The manufacturers of Puffins had had a brain-wave. They were giving away aeroplanes. In every packet of Puffins they enclosed a coupon, bearing the name of a component part of a popular little touring 'plane, suitable for amateur use. When you had collected your complete set of parts (numbering one hundred) you sent up your coupons, together with a brief essay on the importance of air-mindedness for British boys. The writer of the best essay each day became the recipient of a private 'plane, and a course of free instruction enabling him or her to take out an air-pilot's certificate. This happy scheme was supported by heavy advertising of a modern and stimulating kind: "The Future is with the Air-Minded"—"The Highest Flight in Modern Cigarette Manufacture"—"Puff Puffins, and Reach the Height of your Ambition"—and so forth. If you were incapacitated, by reason of age or infirmity, from enjoying the ownership of an aeroplane, you received instead a number of shares in the new issue of the Aeroplane Company involved. The scheme had the support of several notable airmen, whose faces, adorned with flying helmets, stared and grinned from every page of the press in conjunction with their considered opinions that Puffins were doing a valuable work in helping to establish British Supremacy in the Air.

Whifflets were upset. They demanded, with some annoyance, why Pym's had not had this brilliant idea first. They clamoured for an aeroplane scheme of their own, with a larger plane and a hangar to keep it in. Mr. Armstrong pointed out to them that the sole result of this would be to confuse the public mind between Whifflets and Puffins, which were already quite sufficiently similar in quality and appearance to confuse anybody.

"They're all alike," he said to Bredon, not meaning the cigarettes, but the manufacturers. "They follow each other like sheep. If Whifflets use large heads of film-stars, Puffin's want to come out with still larger heads of still more important stars. If Gasperettes give away timepieces, Puffins follow on with grandfather clocks and Whifflets with chronometers. If Whifflets announce that they don't damage the lungs, Puffins claim that they strengthen the pulmonary system and Gasperettes quote doctors who recommend them in cases of tuberculosis. They will try to snatch each other's thunder—and what happens? The public smoke them all in turn, just as they did before."

"Isn't that a good thing for trade?" asked Mr. Bredon, innocently. "If one of them got all the sales, the others would go bankrupt."

"Oh, no, they wouldn't," said Mr. Armstrong. "They'd merely amalgamate. But it would be bad for us, because then they'd all use the same agency."

"Well, what about it, then?" queried Bredon.

"We've got to cope. We must head them off aeroplanes. For one thing, the boom won't last. The country isn't ready to be cluttered up with aeroplanes, and fathers of families are beginning to complain about it. Even today, few fathers care about having private aeroplanes delivered to their daughters in quiet suburban areas. What we want is a new scheme, on similar lines but with more family appeal. But it must boost Britain. We've got to have the patriotic note."

It was in that moment, and while Chief-Inspector Parker was arguing over the line with the office telephonist, that Mr. Death Bredon conceived that magnificent idea that everybody remembers and talks about today–the scheme that achieved renown as "Whiffling Round Britain"–the scheme that sent up the sales of Whifflets by five hundred per cent in three months and brought so much prosperity to British Hotel-keepers and Road and Rail Transport. It is not necessary to go into details. You have probably Whiffled yourself. You recollect how it was done. You collected coupons for everything–railway fares, charabancs, hotel-bills, theatre-tickets–every imaginable item in a holiday programme. When you had collected enough to cover the period of time you wished to spend in travelling, you took your coupons with you (no sending up to Whifflets, nothing to post or fill in) and started on your tour. At the railway station you presented coupons entitling you to so many miles of first-class travel and received your ticket to the selected town. You sought your hotel (practically all the hotels in Britain fell eagerly in with the scheme) and there presented coupons entitling you to so many nights' board and lodging on special Whifflet terms. For your charabanc outings, your sea-bathing, your amusements, you paid in Whifflet coupons. It was all exceedingly simple and trouble-free. And it made for that happy gregariousness which is the joy of the travelling middle-class. When you asked for your packet of Whifflets in the bar, your next-door neighbour was almost sure to ask, "Are you Whiffling too?" Whiffling parties arranged to Whiffle together, and exchanged Whifflet coupons on the spot. The great Whifflers' Club practically founded itself, and Whifflers who had formed attachments while Whiffling in company, secured special Whifflet coupons entitling them to a Whifflet wedding with a Whifflet cake and their photographs in the papers. When this had happened several times, arrangements were made by which Whiffler couples could collect for a Whifflet house, whose Whifflet furniture included a handsome presentation smoking cabinet, free from advertising matter and crammed with unnecessary gadgets. After this, it was only a step to a Whifflet Baby. In fact, the Whifflet Campaign is and remains the outstanding example of Thinking Big in Advertising. The only thing that you cannot get by Whiffling is a coffin; it is not admitted that any Whiffler could ever require such an article.

It is not to be supposed that the great Whiffle-Way, in all its comprehensive perfection, sprang fully armed from Mr. Bredon's brain when Mr. Armstrong uttered the words, Family Appeal. All that then happened was a mental association with the phrase Family Hotel, coupled with a faint consciousness of inner illumination. He replied, humbly, "Yes, I see; I'll try to work out something," gathered up some sheets of paper on which Mr. Armstrong had scribbled a few illegible notes and a thing that looked like a hedgehog, and made his way out. He had taken six steps down the passage when the idiotic slogan: "If that's what you want, you can Whiffle for it," took possession of his brain; two steps further on, this repellent sentence had recast itself as: "All you Want by Whiffling," and on the threshold of his own room, the first practical possibility of Whiffledom struck him like a sledgehammer. Fired with excitement, he hurled himself at his desk snatched a scribbling-block, and had written the word "WHIFFLE" in capitals an inch high, when Miss Rossiter arrived with the message that Mr. Parker urgently requested Mr. Bredon to ring him up on the Whitehall number. Lord Peter Wimsey was so intimately in the skin of Mr. Death Bredon that he said: "Damn!" loudly and heartily.

Nevertheless, he obeyed the call, presented himself with leave of absence on urgent private business, and went down to Scotland Yard, where he surveyed the clothes and effects of the man in the dress suit.

"No doubt we shall end by having to circularize the laundries," said Parker. "Perhaps a photograph in some of the London and provincial papers would be as well. I loathe newspapers, but they do advertise one's requirements, and some of these laundry-marks may come from outside London. . . ."

Wimsey looked at him.

"Advertisement, my dear Charles, may be desirable in the case of laundries, but for people like ourselves it does not exist. A gentleman whose clothes are so well cut, and who yet deprives his tailor of the credit for them is, like ourselves, not of the advertising sort. This, I see, is his top-hat, mysteriously uninjured."

"It had rolled beyond the train, on to the farther line."

"Quite. Here again the maker's golden imprint has been removed. How absurd, Charles! One does not–at least, you and I and this gentleman do not–consider the brand to be the guarantee of quality. For us, the quality guarantees the brand. There are two hatters in London who could have made this hat, and you have doubtless already observed that the crown is markedly dolichocephalic, while the curve of the brim is also characteristic. It is a thought behind the present fashion; yet the article is undoubtedly of recent manufacture. Send one of your sleuths to each of these two establishments and ask for the customer with the elongated head who has a fancy for this type of brim. Do not waste your time on laundry-marks, which are, at best, tedious and, at worst, deceptive."

"Thanks," said Parker. "I thought you might be able to put your finger either on the hatter or the tailor."

The first hatter they visited proved to be the right man. He directed their researches to the flat of a Mr. Horace Mountjoy, who lived in Kensington. They armed themselves with a search-warrant and visited the flat.

Mr. Mountjoy, they ascertained from the commissionaire, was a bachelor of quiet habits, except that he was frequently out rather late at night. He lived alone, and was waited upon and valeted by the staff belonging to the block of flats.

The commissionaire came on duty at 9 o'clock. There was no night porter. Between 11 p.m. and 9 a.m. the outer door was locked and could be opened by the tenants with their own keys, without disturbing him in his basement flat. He had seen Mr. Mountjoy go out the previous evening at about 7:45, in evening dress. He had not seen him return. Withers, the valet, would probably be able to say whether Mr. Mountjoy had been in that night.

Withers was able to say positively that he had not. Nobody had entered Mr. Mountjoy's flat but himself, and the chambermaid who did the rooms. The bed had not been slept in. That was nothing unusual with Mr. Mountjoy. He was frequently out all night, though he generally returned to breakfast at 9:30.

Parker displayed his official card, and they went upstairs to a flat on the third floor. Withers was about to open the door with his pass-key, which, as he explained, he was accustomed to use in the mornings, to avoid disturbing the tenants, but Parker stopped him and produced the two keys which had been taken from the corpse. One of them fitted the lock and established, without much doubt, that they had come to the right place.

Everything in the flat was in perfect order. There was a desk in the sitting-room, containing a few bills and some notepaper, but its drawers were all unlocked and it appeared to hold no secrets. Nor was there anything remarkable about the bedroom or the small dining-room. In the bathroom was a little cupboard containing the usual toilet articles and household medicines. Parker made a rapid inventory of these, pausing for a few minutes over a packet labelled "Bicarbonate of Soda," but touch and taste soon assured him that this contained exactly what it purported to contain. The only thing that could be considered in the slightest degree out of the ordinary in the whole establishment was the presence (also in the bathroom cupboard) of several packets of cigarette papers.

"Did Mr. Mountjoy roll his own cigarettes?"

"I never saw him do so," replied Withers. "He smoked Turkish Abdullas as a rule."

Parker nodded and impounded the cigarette-papers. A further search disclosed no loose tobacco. A number of boxes of cigars and cigarettes were retrieved from the dining-room sideboard. They looked innocent and a few, which Parker promptly slit open, proved to contain excellent tobacco and nothing else. Parker shook his head.

"You'll have to go through everything very carefully, Lumley."

"Yes, sir."

"Any letters by the first post?"

There were none.

"Any visitors today?"

"No, sir. Not unless you count the man from the post-office."

"Oh? What did *he* want?"

"Nothing," replied Withers, "except to bring the new telephone directory." He indicated the two clean volumes which lay upon the sitting-room desk.

"Oh!" said Parker. This did not sound promising. "Did he come into the room?"

"No, sir. He knocked at the door when Mrs. Trabbs and I were both here. Mrs. Trabbs was sweeping, sir, and I was brushing Mr. Mountjoy's lounge suit. I took the books in, sir, and handed him out the old ones."

"I see. All right. And beyond sweeping and brushing and so on, you disturbed nothing?"

"No, sir."

"Anything in the waste-paper basket?"

"I could not say, sir. Mrs. Trabbs would know."

Mrs. Trabbs, produced, said there had been nothing in the waste-paper basket except a wine-merchant's circular. Mr. Mountjoy wrote very little and did not receive many letters.

Satisfied that there had been no interference with the flat since the occupant had left two nights before, Parker turned his attention to the wardrobe and chest of drawers, where he found various garments, all properly marked with the names of the tailor or shirt-maker responsible for them. He noticed that all were by first-class artists in their own line. Another silk hat, similar to the one now resting at Scotland Yard, but with sweat-band and crown undisfigured, was found in a hat-box; there were also several felt hats and a bowler, all by first-class makers.

"Mr. Mountjoy was a rich man?"

"He appeared to be in very easy circumstances, sir. He did himself well; the best of everything. Especially during the last year or so."

"What was his profession?"

"I think he was a gentleman of independent means. I never heard of him being engaged in any business."

"Did you know that he had a silk hat from which the maker's name had been removed?"

"Yes, sir. He was very angry about it. Said that some friend of his had damaged the hat for a rag. I offered several times to get it put right, sir, but when he had cooled down he said it didn't matter. It wasn't a hat he very often used, sir. And besides, he said, why should he be a walking advertisement for his hatter?"

"Did you know that his dress suit had also lost the tailor's tab?"

"Had it indeed, sir? No, I can't say I noticed it."

"What sort of man was Mr. Mountjoy?"

"A very pleasant gentleman, sir. I'm very sorry to hear he has met with such a sad accident."

"How long has he lived here?"

"Six or seven years, I believe, sir. I've been here four years myself."

"When was the practical joke played on his silk hat?"

"About eighteen months ago, sir, if I remember rightly."

"As long ago as that? I fancied the hat looked newer."

"Well, sir, as I say, he didn't wear it above once or twice a week, sir. And Mr. Mountjoy didn't trouble about the fashion of his hats. There was one particular shape he fancied, and he had all his hats specially made to that pattern."

Parker nodded. He knew this already from the hatter and from Wimsey, but it was well to check matters up. He reflected that he had never yet caught Wimsey tripping in any fact pertaining to dress.

"Well," he said, "as you may have guessed, Withers, there will have to be an inquiry about Mr. Mountjoy's death. You had better say as little as possible to any outside person. You will give me all the keys of the flat, and I shall be leaving the police in charge here for a day or two."

"Very good, sir."

Parker waited to ascertain the name and address of the proprietor of the flats, and left Lumley to his investigations. From the proprietor he gained very little information. Mr. Mountjoy, of no profession, had taken the flat six years previously. He had paid his rent regularly. There had been no complaints. Nothing was known of Mr. Mountjoy's friends or relations. It was regrettable that so good a tenant should have come to so sudden and sad an end. It was much to be hoped that nothing would transpire of a scandalous nature, as those flats had always been extremely respectable.

Parker's next visit was to Mr. Mountjoy's bank. Here he encountered the usual obstructive attitude, but eventually succeeded in getting access to the books. There was a regular income of about a thousand a year derived from sound investments. No irregularities. No mysterious fluctuations. Parker came away with an uneasy impression that Mr. Hector Puncheon had discovered a mare's nest.

# 16

# ECCENTRIC BEHAVIOUR OF A POST-OFFICE DEPARTMENT

THE CHIEF-INSPECTOR voiced his opinion to Wimsey the same evening. His lordship, whose mind was still divided between detection and the new Whifflet campaign, which had taken clear shape during the afternoon, was curt with him:

"Mare's nest? Then what knocked Puncheon out? A kick from the mare's heel?"

"Perhaps Mountjoy merely got fed up with him. You'd get fed up yourself if you were pursued all over London by a Puncheon."

"Possibly. But I shouldn't knock him out and leave him to his fate. I should give him in charge. How is Puncheon?"

"Still unconscious. Concussion. He seems to have got a violent blow on the temple and a nasty crack on the back of the head."

"Um. Knocked up against the wall, probably, when Mountjoy got him with the cosh."

"No doubt you're right."

"I am always right. I hope you are keeping an eye on the man Garfield."

"He won't move for a bit. Why?"

"Well–it's odd that Mountjoy should have been snuffed out so inconveniently for you."

"You don't suppose that Garfield had anything to do with it? Why, the man was nearly killed himself. Besides, we've looked into him. He's a well-known Harley Street man, with a large West-end practice."

"Among the dope-maniacs, perhaps?"

"He specializes in nervous complaints."

"Exactly."

Parker whistled.

"That's what you think, is it?"

"See here," said Wimsey, "your grey matter isn't functioning as it ought. Are you tired at the end of the day? Do you suffer from torpor and lethargy after meals? Try Sparkletone, the invigorating vegetable saline that stimulates while it cleanses. Some accidents are too accidental to be true. When a gentleman removes his tailor's tab and takes the trouble to slice his hatter's imprint away with a razor, and goes skipping, for no reason at all, from Finchley to South Kensington Museum in his dress suit at unearthly hours in the morning, it's because he has something to hide. If he tops up his odd behaviour by falling under a train without the smallest apparent provocation, it's because somebody else is interested in getting the things hidden, too. And the more risks somebody else takes in the process, the more certain it is that the thing is worth hiding."

Parker looked at him and grinned quietly.

"You're a great guesser, Peter. Would you be surprised to hear that you're not the only one?"

"No, I shouldn't. You're holding something out on me. What is it? A witness to the assault, what? Somebody who was on the platform? Somebody you weren't inclined to pay much attention to? You old leg-puller, I can see it in your face. Out with it now—who was it? A Woman. A hysterical woman. A middle-aged, hysterical spinster. Am I right?"

"Curse you, yes."

"Go on, then. Tell me all about it."

"Well, when Eagles took the depositions of the witnesses at the station, they all agreed that Mountjoy had walked several paces past Garfield and then suddenly staggered; that Garfield had caught him by the arm and that both had fallen together. But this female, Miss Eliza Tebbutt by name, 52, umarried, housekeeper, living in Kensington, says that she was standing a little way beyond them both and that she distinctly heard what she describes as a 'dreadful voice' say, 'Punch away, you're *for* it!' That Mountjoy immediately stopped as though he had been shot, and that Garfield 'with a terrible face,' took him by the arm and tipped him up. It may increase your confidence in this good lady when you hear that she is subject to nervous disorders, has once been confined in a mental home and is persuaded that Garfleld is a prominent member of a gang whose object is to murder all persons of British birth and establish the supremacy of the Jews in England."

"Jews in England be damned. Because a person has a monomania she need not be wrong about her facts. She might have imagined or invented a good deal, but she couldn't possibly imagine or invent anything so fantastic as 'Punch away,' which is obviously her mishearing of the name 'Mountjoy.' Garfield's your man—though I admit that you're going to have some difficulty in fixing anything on him. But if I were you, I'd have his premises searched—if it isn't too late by now."

"I'm afraid it probably is too late. We didn't get any sense out of Miss Tebbutt for an hour or so; by which time the heroic Dr. Garfleld had, naturally, telephoned both to his home and to his consulting room to explain what had happened to him. Still, we'll keep an eye on him. The immediate matter of importance is Mountjoy. Who was he? What was he up to? Why did he have to be suppressed?"

"It's pretty clear what he was up to. He was engaged in the dope traffic and he was suppressed because he had been fool enough to let Puncheon recognize and follow him. Somebody must have been on the watch; this gang apparently keeps tabs on all its members. Or the wretched Mountjoy may have asked for help and been helped out of the world as the speediest method of disposing of the difficulty. It's a pity Puncheon can't talk—he could tell us whether Mountjoy had telephoned or spoken to anybody during his dash round town. Anyhow, he made a mistake, and people who make mistakes are not permitted to survive. The odd thing, to my mind, is that you heard nothing of any visit to the flat. You'd rather expect the gang to have made some sort of investigation there, just to make sure. I suppose those servants are to be trusted?"

"I think so. We've made inquiries. They've all got good histories. The commissionaire has an army pension and an excellent record. The valet and chambermaid are highly respectable—nothing whatever against them."

"H'm. And you've found nothing but a packet of cigarette-papers. Handy, of course, for wrapping up a grain or so of cocaine but, in themselves, no proof of anything."

"I thought you'd see the significance of the cigarette-papers."

"I am not yet blind or mentally deficient."

"But where is the dope?"

"The dope? Really, Charles! He was going to fetch the dope when friend

Puncheon butted in. Haven't you yet grasped that this is part of the Milligan crowd and that Friday is their day for distributing dope? The Milligans get it on Friday and give house-parties on Friday night and Saturday, when it goes into the hands of the actual addicts. Dian de Momerie told me so."

"I wonder," said Parker, "why they stick to one day? It must add to the risk."

"It's obviously an integral part of the system. The stuff comes into the country–say on Thursdays. That's your part of the story. You don't seem to have done much about that, by the way. It is taken to–somewhere or the other–that night. Next day it is called for by the Mountjoys and sent on to the Milligans, none of whom probably knows any of the others by sight. And by Saturday the whole lot is pushed out and everybody has a happy week-end."

"That sounds plausible. It certainly explains why we found no trace of anything either in the flat or on Mountjoy's body. Except cigarette-papers. By the way, is that right? If Mountjoy has the cigarette-papers, he ought to be the one who distributes to the addicts."

"Not necessarily. He gets it himself in bulk–done up as Bicarbonate of Soda or what not. He divides it into small packets and parcels them out–so many to Milligan, so many to the next retailer and so forth; when, or how, I don't know. Nor do I know how the payments are worked."

"Glad to hear there's something you don't know."

"I said I didn't know; not that I couldn't guess. But I won't bother you with guesses. All the same, it's rather surprising that Garfield & Co. left that flat alone."

"Perhaps Garfleld meant to go there afterwards, if he hadn't got knocked out."

"No; he'd not leave it so late. Tell me again about the flat."

Parker patiently repeated the account of his visit and the interviews with the servants. Before he was half-way through, Wimsey had sat up in his chair and was listening with fascinated attention.

"Charles! What imbeciles we are! Of course, that's it!"

"What's what?"

"The Telephone Directory, of course. The man who brought the new volumes and took the old away. Since when has the Post Office taken to getting *both* new volumes out at once?"

"By Jove!" exclaimed Parker.

"I should think it was, by Jove. Ring up now and find out whether two new volumes were sent round to Mountjoy's address today."

"It'll be a job to get hold of O.C. Directories at this time of night."

"So it will. Wait a moment. Ring up the flats and ask if anybody else received any Directories this morning. My experience is that even Government departments do these things in batches, and don't make a special journey to every subscriber."

Parker acted on this suggestion. After a little trouble, he succeeded in getting into touch with three other occupants in the same block as Mountjoy's flat. All three gave the same answer. They had received a new L-Z volume about a fortnight previously. The new A-K volume was not yet due to be issued. One man went further. His name was Barrington, and he had only recently moved in. He had inquired when the new A-K volume would be out with his new 'phone number, and had been told that it would probably be issued in October.

"That settles it," said Wimsey. "Our friend Mountjoy kept his secrets in the telephone directory. That great work contains advertisements, post-office regulations and names and addresses, but particularly names and addresses. May we conclude that the secret nestled among the names and addresses? I think we may."

"It seems reasonable."

"Very reasonable. Now, how do we set about discovering those names and addresses?"

"Bit of a job. We can probably get a description of the man who called for the books this morning—"

"And comb London's teeming millions for him? Had we but world enough and time. Where do good telephone directories go when they die?"

"The pulping-mills, probably."

"And the last exchange of the L-Z volume was made a fortnight ago. There's a chance that it hasn't been pulped yet. Get on to it, Charles. There's more than a chance that it, too, was marked, and that the markings were transferred at each exchange from the old book to the new one."

"Why? Mountjoy might easily have kept the old marked set by him."

"I fancy not, or we should have either found it or heard about it from the manservant. The stranger came; the two current volumes were handed to him and he went away satisfied. As I see the plan, the whole idea would be to use the current volume, so as to rouse no suspicion, have nothing to conceal and provide a convenient mechanism for getting rid of the evidence at short notice."

"You may be right. It's a chance, as you say. I'll get on to the telephone people first thing in the morning."

The tide of luck seemed to have turned. A morning's strenuous work revealed that the old directories had already been dispatched by the sackful to the pulping-mills, but had not, so far, been pulped. Six workers, toiling over the week-end among L-Z volumes collected from the Kensington District, brought to light the pleasing fact that nine people out of ten marked their directories in some way or another. Reports came pouring in. Wimsey sat with Parker in the latter's office at Scotland Yard and considered these reports.

Late on Sunday night, Wimsey raised his head from a sheaf of papers.

"I think this is it, Charles."

"What is it?" Parker was weary and his eyes blood-shot with strain, but a note of hope was in his voice.

"This one. A whole list of public-houses in Central London have been ticked off—three in the middle of the L's, two near the end of the M's, one in the N's, one in the O's, and so forth and so on, including two in the middle of the W's. The two in the W's are the White Stag in Wapping and the White Stoat off Oxford Street. The next W after that is the White Swan in Covent Garden. I would bet any money that in the new volume that was carried away, the White Swan was duly ticked off in its turn."

"I'm not quite sure what you're driving at."

"I'm making rather a long cast, but I suggest this. When the stuff comes up to London of a Thursday, I think it is taken to which ever pub. stands next on the list in the directory. One week it will be a pub. with a name in A—say the Anchor. Next week it will be a B—the Bull & Dog, or the Brickmaker's Arms. The week after that, it will be a C, and so on to W,X,Y,Z—if there are any. The people who have to call for their dope wander into the pub. indicated, where it is slipped to them by the head distributor and his agents, probably quite without the knowledge of the proprietor. And since it never comes twice to the same place, your pretty policemen can go and talk parrots and goats in the White Swan till they are blue in the face. They ought to have been at the Yellow Peril or the York & Lancaster."

"That's an idea, Peter. Let's look at that list again.

Wimsey handed it over.

"If you're right, then this week was W week, and next week will be X week. That's unlikely. Say Y week. The next Y after the last one ticked is the Yelverton Arms in Soho. Wait a minute, though. If they have been taking them in aphabetical order, why have they got right down to the end of the M's in one case and only to WH in the other?

"They must have been through the W's once, and be starting again."

"Yes–I suppose there are quite a lot of M's. But then there are hundreds of W's. Still, we'll try it, Peter, any way. What is it, Lumley?"

"Report from the hospital, sir. Puncheon has come round."

Parker glanced through the report.

"Much what we expected," he said, handing the paper to Wimsey. "Mountjoy evidently knew he was being followed. He put through a telephone call at Piccadilly Tube Station, and started off on a wild scamper across London."

"That was how the gang came to be ready for him."

"Yes. Finding he couldn't shake Puncheon off, he lured him into the Museum, got him into a quiet corner and laid him out. Puncheon thinks he was slugged with a weapon of some kind. So he was. He did not speak to Mountjoy. In fact, this report tells us nothing we didn't know, except that, when Puncheon first saw him, Mountjoy was buying an early copy of the *Morning Star* from a man outside the office."

"Was he? That's interesting. Well, keep your eye on the Yelverton Arms."

"And you keep your eye on Pym's. Do remember that what we want is the man at the top."

"So does Major Milligan. The man at the top is very much sought after. Well, cheerio! If I can't do anything more for you, I think I'll tootle off to bed. I've got my Whifflets scheme to get out tomorrow."

"I like this scheme. Mr. Bredon," said Mr. Pym, tapping his finger on the drafts submitted to him. "It has Breadth. It has Vision. More than anything else, Advertising needs Vision and Breadth. That is what determines Appeal. In my opinion, this scheme of yours has Appeal. It is going to be expensive, of course, and needs some working out. For instance, if all these vouchers were cashed in at once, it would send up the cost per packet issued to a figure that the profits could not possibly cover. But I think that can be got over."

"They won't all be cashed in at once," said Mr. Armstrong. "Not if we mix them up sufficiently. People will want time to collect and exchange. That will give us a start. They've got to look on the cost of the thing as so much advertising expenditure. We shall want a big press splash to start it, and after that, it will run itself quite happily in small spaces."

"That's all very well, Armstrong, but we've got to think of ourselves."

"That's all right. We make all the arrangements with the hotels and railways and so forth and charge our fee or commission on the work. All we've got to do is to average the thing out so that the claims won't amount to more than their estimated appropriation for the month. If the thing goes big they'll be willing enough to increase the appropriation. The other thing we've got to do is to see that each coupon bears more or less the same actual cash value, so as not to get into trouble with the Lottery Act. The whole thing comes down to this. How much of the profit on each shilling packet are they prepared to spend in advertising? Remembering that this scheme, if properly put through, is going to sweep every other fag off the market for the time being. Then we make our coupons up to that value minus an appropriation for the opening press campaign. At present their appropriation is sixty thousand and their sales . . . have we got that report on sales?"

The two directors plunged into a maze of facts and figures. Mr. Bredon's attention wandered.

"Printing costs . . . see that they have a sufficient distribution . . . bonus to the tobacconists . . . free displays . . . tackle the hotels first . . . news-value . . . get the *Morning Star* to give it a show . . . no, I know, but there's the Boost Britain side of it . . . I can wangle Jenks . . . reduce overheads by . . . call it £200 a day . . . Puffin's aeroplanes must be costing them that . . . front-page splash and five free coupons . . . well, that's a matter of detail. . . ."

"In any case, we've got to do *something*." Mr. Armstrong emerged from the argument with a slightly flushed face. "It's no use telling people that the cost of the advertising has to come out of the quality of the goods. They don't care. All they want is something for nothing. Pay? Yes, of course they pay in the end, but somebody's got to pay. You can't fight free gifts with solemn assertions about Value. Besides, if Whifflets lose their market they'll soon lose their quality too—or what are we here for?"

"You needn't tell me that, Armstrong." said Mr. Pym. "Whether people like it or not, the fact remains that unless you continually increase sales you must either lose money or cut down quality. I hope we've learnt that by this time."

"What happens," asked Mr. Bredon, "when you've increased sales to saturation point?"

"You mustn't ask those questions, Bredon," said Mr. Armstrong, amused.

"No, but really. Suppose you push up the smoking of every man and woman in the Empire till they must either stop or die of nicotine poisioning?"

"We're a long way off that," replied Mr. Pym, seriously. "And that reminds me. This scheme should carry a strong appeal to women. 'Give your children that seaside holiday by smoking Whifflets.' That sort of thing. We want to get women down to serious smoking. Too many of them play about with it. Take them off scented stuff and put them on to the straightforward Virginia cigarette—"

"The gasper, in fact."

"Whifflets," said Mr. Pym. "You can smoke a lot more of them in the day without killing yourself. And they're cheaper. If we increase women's smokes by 500 per cent—there's plenty of room for it—"

Mr. Bredon's attention wandered again.

"—all right, date the coupons. Let them run for three months only. That will give us plenty of duds to play with. And they'll have to see that their stockists are kept up to date with fresh goods. By the way, that makes a selling point—"

Mr. Bredon fell into a dream.

"—but you must have a good press campaign as well. Posters are good and cheap, but if you really want to tell people something, you've got to have a press campaign. Not a big one, necessarily, after the first big bang. But a good, short, snappy reminder week by week—"

"Very well, Mr. Bredon." The creator of the Whifflet scheme came out of his doze with a start. "We'll put this up to Whifflets. Will you see if you can get out some copy? And you'd better put a few other people on to it as well, Armstrong. Ingleby–it's rather his line. And Miss Meteyard. We want to get something out by the end of the week. Tell Mr. Barrow to put everything else aside and rough out some really striking displays." Mr. Pym gave the signal of dismissal, and then, as a thought struck him, called Bredon back.

"I want a word with you, Bredon. I'd almost forgotten what you were really here for. Has any progress been made in that matter?"

"Yes." The Whifflets campaign receded from Lord Peter Wimsey, dying along the distance of his mind. "In fact, the investigation is turning out to be of so much importance that I don't quite know how I can take even you into my confidence."

"That's nonsense," said Mr. Pym. "I am employing you–"

"No. There's no question of employment. I'm afraid it's a police job."

The shadows of disquiet gathered and deepened in Mr. Pym's eyes.

"Do you mean that those earlier suspicions you mentioned to me were actually justified?"

"Oh, yes. But it's a bigger thing than that."

"I don't want any scandal."

"Possibly not. But I don't quite see how it's to be avoided, if the thing comes to trial."

"Look here, Bredon," said Mr. Pym, "I don't like your behaviour. I put you in here as my private inquiry agent. I admit that you have made yourself very useful in other capacities, but you are not indispensable. If you insist on going beyond your authority–"

"You can sack me. Of course. But would that be wise?"

Mr. Pym mopped his forehead.

"Can you tell me this," he inquired anxiously, after a silence in which he seemed to be digesting the meaning of his employee's question. "Do your suspicions point to any particular person? Is it possible to remove that person promptly from our staff? You see my point. If, before this scandal breaks–whatever it is–and I really think I ought to be told–but so long as we can say that the person is no longer on the staff, it makes a difference. The firm's name might even be kept out of it–mightn't it? The good name of Pym's means a great deal to me, Mr. Bredon–"

"I can't tell you," said Wimsey; "a few days ago, I thought I knew, but just lately, other facts have come to my knowledge which suggest that the man I originally suspected may not be the right one. And until I know definitely, I can't do or say anything. At the moment it might be anybody. It might even be yourself."

"This is outrageous," cried Mr. Pym. "You can take your money and go."

Wimsey shook his head.

"If you get rid of me, the police will probably want to put somebody in my place."

"If I had the police here," retorted Mr. Pym, "I should at least know where I was. I know nothing about you, except that Mrs. Arbuthnot recommended you. I never cared for the idea of a private detective, though I certainly thought at first that you were of a somewhat superior type to the usual inquiry agent. But insolence I cannot and will not put up with. I shall communicate at once with Scotland Yard, and they will, I imagine, require you to state plainly what you imagine yourself to have discovered."

"They know it."

"Do they? You do not seem to be a model of discretion, Mr. Bredon." He pressed his buzzer. "Miss Hartley, will you please get Scotland Yard on the 'phone, and ask them to send up a reliable detective."

"Very well, Mr. Pym."

Miss Hartley danced away. This was meat and drink. She had always said there was something funny about Mr. Bredon, and now he had been caught. Pinching the cash, perhaps. She dialled the switch-board and asked for Whitehall 1212.

"Just one moment," said Wimsey, when the door had closed upon her. "If you really want Scotland Yard tell her to ask for Chief-Inspector Parker and say that Lord Peter Wimsey would like to speak to him. Then he'll know what it's about."

"You are—? Why didn't you tell me?"

"I thought it might raise difficulties about the salary and prove embarrassing. I took the job on because I thought advertising might be rather good fun. So it is," added Wimsey, pleasantly, "so it is."

Mr. Pym put his head into Miss Hartley's room.

"I'll take that call in here," he said, briefly.

They sat mute till the call came through. Mr. Pym asked for Chief-Inspector Parker.

"There is a man here on my staff, calling himself—"

The conversation was a brief one. Mr. Pym handed the receiver to Wimsey.

"They want to speak to you."

"Hullo, Charles! That you? Have you established my credit? All right. . . . No, no trouble, only Mr. Pym feels he ought to know what it's all about. . . . Shall I tell him? . . . Not wise? . . . Honestly, Charles, I don't think he's our man. . . . Well, that's a different question. . . . The Chief-Inspector wants to know whether you can hold your tongue, Mr. Pym."

"I only wish to God everybody could hold his tongue," groaned Mr. Pym.

Wimsey passed on the reply. "I think I'll risk it, Charles. If anybody is going to be slugged in the dark after this, it won't be you, and I can look after myself."

He rang off and turned to Mr. Pym.

"Here's the brutal fact," he said. "Somebody's running an enormous dope-traffic from this office. Who is there that has far more money than he ought to have, Mr. Pym? We're looking for a very rich man. Can you help us?"

But Mr. Pym was past helping anybody. He was chalk-white.

"Dope? From this office? What on earth will our clients say? How shall I face the Board? The publicity . . . "

"Pym's Publicity," said Lord Wimsey, and laughed.

# 17

# LACHRYMOSE OUTBURST OF A NOBLEMAN'S NEPHEW

THAT WEEK passed quietly. On Tuesday, Mr. Jollop passed, quite amiably, another of the new "Quotations" series for Nutrax "—And Kissed Again with Tears" ("But Tears, and Fallings-Out, however poetical, are nearly always a sign of Nerve-Strain"); on Wednesday, Green Pastures Margarine was Reduced in Price though Improved in Quality ("It might seem impossible to improve on Perfection but we have done it!"); Sopo adopted a new advertising figure ("Let Susan Sopo do the Dirty Work"); Tomboy Toffee finished up its Cricket Campaign with a huge display containing the portraits of a complete Eleven of Famous Cricketers all eating Tomboy; five people went on holiday; Mr. Prout created a sensation by coming to the office in a black shirt; Miss Rossiter lost a handbag containing her bonus money and recovered it from the Lost Property Office, and a flea was found in the ladies' cloak-room, causing dire upheaval, some ill-founded accusations and much heart-burning. In the typists' room, the subject of the flea almost ousted for the moment the juicier and more speculative topic of Mr. Tallboy's visitor. For, whether by the indiscretion of Tompkin or of the boy at the desk, or of some other person (though not of Mr. Ingleby or Mr. Bredon, who surely knew better) the tale had somehow seeped through.

"And how he does it on his salary I don't know," observed Miss Parton. "I do think it's a shame. His wife's a nice little woman. You remember, we met her last year at the Garden Party."

"Men are all alike," said Miss Rossiter, scornfully. "Even your Mr. Tallboy. I told you, Parton, that I didn't think old Copley was so much to blame as you thought in that other business, and now perhaps, you'll believe me. What I say is, if a man does one ungentlemanly thing, he'll do another. And as for doing it on his salary, how about that fifty pounds in an envelope? It's pretty obvious where *that* went to."

"It's always obvious where money goes to," said Miss Meteyard sardonically. "The point is, where does it come from?"

"That's what Mr. Dean used to say," said Miss Rossiter. "You remember how he used to chip Mr. Tallboy about his stockbrokers?"

"The famous firm of Smith," said Mr. Garrett. "Smith, Smith, Smith, Smith, Smith & Smith Unlimited."

"Money-lenders, if you ask me," said Miss Rossiter. "Are you going to the cricket-match, Miss Meteyard? In *my* opinion, Mr. Tallboy ought to resign and leave somebody else to captain it. You can't wonder that people aren't keen to play under him, with all these stories going about. Don't you feel the same, Mr. Bredon?"

"Not a bit of it," said Mr. Bredon. "Provided the man can captain, I don't care a bit if he has as many wives as Solomon, and is a forger and swindler into the bargain. What's it matter?"

"It would matter to me," said Miss Rossiter.

"How feminine she is," said Mr. Bredon, plaintively, to the world at large. "She *will* let the personal element come into business."

"I dare say," said Miss Rossiter, "but you bet, if Hankie or Pymmy knew, there'd soon be an end of Mr. Tallboy."

"Directors are the last people to hear anything about the staff. Otherwise," said Miss Meteyard, "they wouldn't be able to stand on their hind legs at the Staff Dinner and shoot off the speeches about co-operation, and all being one happy family."

"Family quarrels, family quarrels." Mr. Ingleby waved his hand. "Little children, love one another and don't be such little nosey-parkers. What's Hecuba's bank-balance to you, or yours to Hecuba?"

"Bank-balance? Oh, you mean Mr. Tallboy's. Well, *I* don't know anything, except what little Dean used to say."

"And how did Dean know so much about it?"

"He was in Mr. Tallboy's office for a few weeks. Learning the work of other departments, they call it. I expect you'll be pushed round the office before long, Mr. Bredon. You'll have to mind your P's and Q's in the Printing. Mr. Thrale's a perfect tartar. Won't even allow you to slip out for coffee."

"I shall have to come to you for it."

"They won't let Mr. Bredon out of this department for a bit," said Miss Meteyard. "They're all up in the air about his Whifflets stunt. Everybody always hoped Dean would do better somewhere else. He was like a favourite book–you liked him so well that you were always yearning to lend him to somebody else."

"What a savage woman you are," observed Ingleby, coolly amused. "It's that kind of remark that gets the university woman a bad name." He glanced at Willis, who said:

"It isn't the savagery. It's the fact that there's no animosity behind it. You are all like that."

"You agree with Shaw–whenever you beat your child, be sure that you do it in anger."

"Shaw's Irish," said Bredon. "Willis has put his finger on the real offensiveness of the educated Englishman–that he will not even trouble to be angry."

"That's right," said Willis. "It's that awful, bleak, blank–" he waved his hands helplessly–"the façade."

"Meaning Bredon's face?" suggested Ingleby, mischievously.

"Icily regular, splendidly null," said Bredon, squinting into Miss Rossiter's mirror. "Strange, to think that a whole Whifflets campaign seethes and burgeons behind this solid ivory brow."

"Mixed metaphor," said Miss Meteyard. "Pots seethe, plants burgeon."

"Of course; it is a flower of rhetoric culled from the kitchen-garden."

"It's no use, Miss Meteyard," said Ingleby, "you might as well argue with an eel."

"Talking of eels," said Miss Meteyard, abandoning the position, "what's the matter with Miss Hartley?"

"The hipless wonder? Why?"

"She came up the other day to inform the world that the police were coming to arrest somebody."

"What?" said Willis.

"You mean, whom?"

"Whom, then?"

"Bredon."

"Mr. Bredon?" said Miss Parton. "What next, I wonder."

"You mean, what for? Why don't you people say what you do mean?"

Miss Rossiter turned on her chair and gazed at Mr. Bredon's gently twitching mouth.

"That's funny," she said. "Do you know, Mr. Bredon, we never told you, but Parton and I thought we saw you actually being arrested one evening, in Piccadilly Circus."

"Did you?"

"It wasn't you, of course."

"Well, as a matter of fact, it wasn't. Still, cheer up–it may happen yet. Only I suppose Pymmy doesn't keep his millions in the office safe."

"Nor yet in registered envelopes," said Miss Meteyard casually.

"Don't say they're after our Mr. Copley!"

"I hope not. Bread-and-skilly wouldn't suit him at all."

"But what was Bredon being arrested for?"

"Loitering, perhaps," said a mild voice in the doorway. Mr. Hankin poked his head round the corner and smiled sarcastically. "I am sorry to interrupt you, but if Mr. Bredon could favour me with his attention for a moment on the subject of Twentyman's Teas–"

"I beg your pardon, sir," said Mr. Bredon, springing to attention and allowing himself to be marched off.

Miss Rossiter shook her head.

"You mark my words, there's a mystery about Mr. Bredon."

"He's a darling," objected Miss Parton, warmly.

"Oh, Bredon's all right," said Ingleby.

Miss Meteyard said nothing. She went downstairs to the Executive and borrowed the current volume of *Who's Who*. She ran her finger through the W's, till she came to the entry beginning: "WIMSEY, Peter Death Bredon (Lord), D.S.O., born 1890; second *s.* of Mortimer Gerald Bredon Wimsey, 15th Duke of Denver, and Honoria Lucasta, *d.* of Francis Delagardie of Bellingham Manor, Bucks. *Educ.* Eton College and Balliol." She read it through.

"So that's it," said Miss Meteyard to herself. "I thought so. And now what? Does one do anything? I think not. Better leave it alone. But there's no harm in putting out feelers for another job. One's got to look after one's self."

Mr. Bredon, unaware that his disguise had been penetrated, gave but a superficial consideration to the interests of Twentyman's Teas. He meekly accepted the instruction to prepare a window-bill with two streamers on the subject of a richer infusion with fewer spoonfuls, and a gentle rebuke in the matter of wasting time in the typists' room. His mind was in Old Broad Street.

"You are playing for us on Saturday, I see," said Mr. Hankin, at the conclusion of the interview.

"Yes, sir."

"I hope the weather will hold. You have played in first-class cricket, I believe?"

"A long time ago."

"You will be able to show them a bit of style," said Mr. Hankin, happily. "Style–one sees so little of it nowadays. I am afraid you will find us a scratch lot, and for some reason, several of our best players seem unable to attend this match. A pity. But you will find Mr. Tallboy very good. An excellent all-round man, and quite remarkable in the field."

Mr. Bredon said that it was all too rare to find proper attention given to fielding. Mr. Hankin agreed with him.

"Mr. Tallboy is excellent at all games; it's a pity he can't give more time to them. Personally, I should like to see more organization of the athletic side of our social functions here. But Mr. Pym thinks it would perhaps be too absorbing, and I dare say he is right. Still, I can't help feeling that the cultivation of the team-spirit would do this office good. I don't know whether you, as a newcomer, have noticed a certain tension from time to time–"

Bredon admitted that he had noticed something of the sort.

"You know, Mr. Bredon," said Mr. Hankin, a little wistfully, "it is sometimes difficult for the directors to get the atmosphere of situations in the office. You people keep us rather in cotton-wool, don't you? It can't be helped, naturally, but I sometimes fancy that there are currents beneath the surface. . . ."

Evidently, thought Bredon, Mr. Hankin had realized that something was on the point of breaking. He felt suddenly sorry for him. His eyes strayed to a strip poster, printed in violent colours and secured by drawing-pins to Mr. Hankin's notice-board:

EVERY ONE EVERYWHERE ALWAYS AGREES
ON THE FLAVOUR AND VALUE OF TWENTYMAN'S TEAS

No doubt it was because agreement on any point was so rare in a quarrelsome world, that the fantastical announcements of advertisers asserted it so strongly and so absurdly. Actually, there was no agreement, either on trivialities like tea or on greater issues. In this place, where from morning till night a staff of over a hundred people hymned the praises of thrift, virtue, harmony, eupepsia and domestic contentment, the spiritual atmosphere was clamorous with financial storm, intrigue, dissension, indigestion and marital infidelity. And, with worse things—with murder wholesale and retail, of soul and body, murder by weapon and by poison. These things did not advertise, or, if they did, they called themselves by other names.

He made some vague answer to Mr. Hankin.

At one o'clock he left the office and took a taxi citywards. He was suddenly filled with a curiosity to visit Mr. Tallboy's stockbroker.

At twenty minutes past one, he was standing on the pavement in Old Broad Street, and his blood was leaping with excitement which always accompanies discovery.

Mr. Tallboy's stockbroker inhabited a small tobacconist's shop, the name over which was not Smith but Cummings.

"An accommodation address," observed Lord Peter Wimsey. "Most unusual for a stockbroker. Let us probe this matter further."

He entered the shop, which was narrow, confined and exceedingly dark. An elderly man stepped forward to serve him. Wimsey went immediately to the point.

"Can I see Mr. Smith?"

"Mr. Smith doesn't live here."

"Then perhaps you would kindly let me leave a note for him."

The elderly man slapped his hand on the counter.

"If I've said it once, I've said it five hundred times," he snapped irritably. "There's no Mr. Smith here, and never was, to my knowledge. And if you're the gentleman that addresses his letters here, I'd be glad if you'd take that for an answer. I'm sick and tired of handing his letters back to the postman."

"You surprise me. I don't know Mr. Smith myself, but I was asked by a friend to leave a message for him."

"Then tell your friend what I say. It's no good sending letters here. None whatever. Never has been. People seem to think I've got nothing better to do than hand out letters to postmen. If I wasn't a conscientious man, I'd burn the lot of them. That's what I'd do. Burn 'em. And I will, if it goes on any longer. You can tell your friend that from me."

"I'm very sorry," said Wimsey. "There seems to be some mistake."

"Mistake?" said Mr. Cummings, angrily. "I don't believe it's a mistake at all. It's a stupid practical joke, that's what it is. And I'm fed up with it, I can tell you."

"If it is," said Wimsey, "I'm the victim of it. I've been sent right out of my way to deliver a message to somebody who doesn't exist. I shall speak to my friend about it."

"I should, if I were you," said Mr. Cummings. "A silly, tom-fool trick. You tell your friend to come here himself, that's all. I'll know what to say to him."

"That's a good idea," said Wimsey. "And you tell him off."

"You can lay your last penny I shall, sir." Mr. Cummings, having blown off his indignation seemed a little appeased. "If your friend should turn up, what name will he give, sir?"

Wimsey, on the point of leaving the shop, pulled up short. Mr. Cummings, he noticed, had a pair of very sharp eyes behind his glasses. A thought struck him.

"Look here," he said, leaning confidentially over the counter. "My friend's name is Milligan. That mean anything to you? He told me to come to you for a spot of the doings. See what I mean?"

That got home; a red glint in Mr. Cummings' eye told Wimsey as much.

"I don't know what you are talking about," was what Mr. Cummings actually said. "I never heard of a Mr. Milligan, and I don't want to. And I don't want any of your sauce, neither."

"Sorry, old thing, sorry," said Wimsey.

"And what's more," said Mr. Cummings, "I don't want you. See?"

"I see," said Wimsey. "I see perfectly. Good-morning."

"That's torn it," he thought. "I'll have to work quickly now. St. Martin's-le-Grand comest next, I fancy."

A little pressure at head-quarters produced what was required. The postmen who carried letters to Old Broad Street were found and interrogated. It was quite true that they frequently delivered letters for a Mr. Smith to Mr. Cummings' shop, and that these letters invariably were returned, and marked "Not known." Where did they go then? To the Returned Letter Office. Wirnsey rang up Pym's, explained that he was unavoidably detained, and sought the Returned Letter Office. After a little delay, he found the official who knew all about it.

The letters for Mr. Smith came regularly every week. They were never returned to the sender in the ordinary course. Why? Because they bore no sender's name. In fact, they never contained anything but a sheet of blank paper.

"Had they last Tuesday's letter there?" No; it had already been opened and destroyed. Would they keep the next one that arrived and send it on to him? Seeing that Lord Peter Wimsey had Scotland Yard behind him, they would. Wimsey thanked the official, and went his way, pondering.

On leaving the office at 5.30, he walked down Southampton Row to Theobald's Road. There was a newsvendor at the corner. Wimsey purchased an *Evening Comet* and glanced carelessly through the news. A brief paragraph in the Stop Press caught his eye.

CLUBMAN KILLED IN PICCADILLY

At 3 o'clock this afternoon a heavy lorry skidded and mounted the pavement in Piccadilly, fatally injuring Major "Tod" Milligan, the well-known clubman, who was standing on the kerb.

"They work quickly," he thought with a shudder. "Why, in God's name, am I still at large?" He cursed his own recklessness. He had betrayed himself to Cummings; he had gone into the shop undisguised; by now they knew who he was. Worse, they must have followed him to the General Post Office and to Pym's. Probably they were following him now. From behind the newspaper he cast a swift glance about the crowded streets. Any one of these loitering men might be *the* man. Absurd and romantic plans flitted through his mind. He would lure his assassins into some secluded spot, such as the Blackfriars subway or the steps beneath Cleopatra's Needle, and face them there and kill them with his hands. He would ring up Scotland Yard and get a guard of detectives. He would go straight home to his own flat in a taxi ("not the first nor the second that presents itself," he thought, with a fleeting recollection of Professor Moriarty), barricade himself in and wait—for what? For air-guns? . . . In this perplexity he suddenly caught sight of a familiar figure—Chief-Inspector Parker himself, apparently taking his early way home, and carrying a fish-monger's bag in one hand and an attache case in the other.

He lowered the paper and said, "Hullo!"

Parker stopped. "Hullo!" he replied, tentatively. He was obviously not quite certain whether he was being hailed by Lord Peter Wimsey or by Mr. Death Bredon. Wimsey strode forward and relieved him of the fish-bag.

"Well met. You come most carefully upon your cue, to prevent me from being murdered. What's this, lobster?"

"No, turbot," said Parker, placidly.

"I'm coming to eat it with you. They will hardly attack both of us. I've made a fool of myself and given the game away, so we may as well be open and cheerful about it."

"Good. I'd like to feel cheerful."

"What's wrong? Why so early home?"

"Fed-up. The Yelverton Arms is a wash-out, I'm afraid."

"Did you raid it?"

"Not yet. Nothing happened during the morning, but during the lunch-hour crush, Lumley saw something being smuggled into a fellow's hands by a chap who looked like a tout. They stopped the fellow and searched him. All they found was some betting-slips. It's quite possible that nothing is timed to happen before this evening. If nothing turns up, I'll have the place searched. Just before closing-time will be best. I'm going down there myself. Thought I'd step home for an early supper."

"Right. I've got something to tell you."

They walked to Great Ormond Street in silence.

"Cummings?" said Parker, when Wimsey had told his tale. "Don't know anything about him. But you say he knew Milligan's name?"

"He certainly did. Besides, here's the proof of it."

He showed Parker the stop-press item.

"But this fellow, Tallboy—is he the bird you're after?"

"Frankly, Charles, I don't understand it. I can't see him as the Big Bug in all this business. If he were, he'd be too well-off to get into difficulties with a cheap mistress. And his money wouldn't be coming to him in fifty-pound instalments. But there's a connection. There must be."

"Possibly he's only a small item in the account."

"Possibly. But I can't get over Milligan. According to his information, the whole show was run from Pyms."

"Perhaps it is. Tallboy may be merely the cat's paw for one of the others.

Pym himself—he's rich enough, isn't he?"

"I don't think it's Pym. Armstrong, possibly, or even quiet little Hankie. Of course, Pym's calling me in may have been a pure blind, but I don't somehow think he has quite that kind of brain. It was so unnecessary. Unless he wanted to find out, through me, how much Victor Dean really knew. In which case, he's succeeded," added Wimsey, ruefully. "But I can't believe that any man would be such a fool as to put himself in the power of one of his own staff. Look at the opportunities for blackmail! Twelve years' penal servitude is a jolly threat to hold over a man. Still—blackmail. Somebody was being blackmailed, that's almost a certainty. But Pym can't have slugged Dean; he was in conference at the time. No, I think we must acquit Pym."

"What I don't quite see," said Lady Mary, "is why Pym's is brought into it at all. Somebody *at* Pym's is one thing, but if you say that the show is 'run from Pym's,' it suggests something quite different—to me, anyhow. It sounds to me as though they were using Pym's organization for something—doesn't it to you?"

"Well, it does," agreed her husband. "But how? And why? What has advertising got to do with it? Crime doesn't want to advertise, far from it."

"I don't know," said Wimsey, suddenly and softly. "I don't know." His nose twitched, rabbit-fashion. "Pymmy was saying only this morning that to reach the largest number of people all over the country in the shortest possible time, there was nothing like a press campaign. Wait a second, Polly—I'm not sure that you haven't said something useful and important."

"Everything I say is useful and important. Think it over while I go and tell Mrs. Gunner how to cook turbot."

"And the funny thing is," said Parker, "she seems to like telling Mrs. Gunner how to cook turbot. We could perfectly well afford more servants—"

"My dear old boy," said Wimsey. "Servants are the devil. I don't count my man Bunter, because he's exceptional, but it's a treat to Polly to kick the whole boiling out of the house at night. Don't you worry. When she wants servants, she'll ask for them."

"I admit," said Parker, "I was glad myself when the kids were old enough to dispense with a resident nurse. But look here, Peter, it seems to me you'll be wanting a resident nurse yourself, if you want to avoid nasty accidents."

"That's just it. Here I am. Why? What are they keeping me for? Something unusually nasty?"

Parker moved quietly across to the window and peered out from a little gap in the short net blind.

"He's there, I think. A repellent-looking young man in a check cap, playing with a Yo-Yo on the opposite pavement. Playing darned well, too, with a circle of admiring kids round him. What a grand excuse for loitering. There he goes. Three-leaf clover, over the falls, non-stop lift, round the world. Quite masterly. I must tell Mary to have a look at him, and take a lesson. You'd better sleep here tonight, old man."

"Thanks. I think I will."

"And stop away from the office tomorrow."

"I should, in any case. I've got to play in a cricket match at Brotherhood's. Their place is down at Romford."

"Cricket-match be damned. I don't know, though. It's nice and public. Provided the fast bowler doesn't knock you out with a swift ball, it may be as safe as anywhere else. How are you going?"

"Office charabanc."

"Good. I'll see you round to the starting-point."

Wimsey nodded. Nothing further was said about dope or danger until supper was over and Parker had departed for the Yelverton Arms. Then Wimsey gathered up a calendar, the telephone directory, a copy of the official report on the volume retrieved from Mountjoy's flat, a scribbling-block and a pencil, and curled himself up on the couch with a pipe.

"You don't mind, do you, Polly? I want to brood."

Lady Mary dropped a kiss on the top of his head.

"Brood on, old thing. I won't disturb you. I'm going up to the nursery. And if the telephone rings, take care it isn't the mysterious summons to the lonely warehouse by the river, or the bogus call to Scotland Yard."

"All right. And if the door-bell rings, beware of the disguised gas-inspector and the plain-clothes cop without a warrant-card. I need scarcely warn you against the golden-haired girl in distress, the slit-eyed Chink or the distinguished grey-haired man wearing the ribbon of some foreign order."

He brooded.

He took from his pocket-book the paper he had removed, weeks earlier, from Victor Dean's desk, and compared the dates with the calendar. They were all Tuesdays. After a little further cogitation, he added the date of the previous Tuesday week, the day when Miss Vavasour had called at the office and Tallboy had borrowed his pen to address a letter to Old Broad Street. To this date he appended the initial "T." Then, his mind working slowly backwards, he remembered that he had come to Pym's on a Tuesday, and that Tallboy had come into the typists' room for a stamp. Miss Rossiter had read out the name of his addressee—what had the initial been? "K," of course. He wrote this down also. Then with rather more hesitation, he looked up the date of the Tuesday preceding Mr. Puncheon's historic adventure at the White Swan, and wrote "W?"

So far, so good. But from "K" to "T" there were nine letters—there had not been nine weeks. Nor should "W" have come between "K" and "T." What was the rule governing the letter-sequence? He drew thoughtfully at his pipe and sank into a reverie that was almost a pipe-dream, till he was aroused by a very distinct sound of yells and conflict from the floor above. Presently the door opened and his sister appeared, rather flushed.

"I'm sorry, Peter. Did you hear the row? Your young namesake was being naughty. He heard Uncle Peter's voice and refused to stay in bed. He wants to come down and see you."

"Very flattering," said Wimsey.

"But very exhausting," said Mary. "I do hate disciplining people. Why shouldn't he see his uncle? Why should uncle be busy with dull detective business when his nephew is so much more interesting?"

"Quite so," said Wimsey. "I have often asked myself the same question. I gather that you hardened your heart."

"I compromised. I said that if he was a good boy and went back to bed, Uncle Peter might come up to say good night to him."

"And has he been a good boy?"

"Yes. In the end. That is to say, he is in bed. At least, he was when I came down."

"Very well," said Wimsey, putting down his paraphernalia. "Then I will be a good uncle."

He mounted the stairs obediently and found Peterkin, aged three, technically in bed. That is to say, he was sitting bolt upright with the blankets cast off, roaring lustily.

"Hullo!" said Wimsey, shocked.

The roaring ceased.

"What is all this?" Wimsey traced the course of a fat, down-rolling drop with a reproachful finger. "Tears, idle tears? Great Scott!"

"Uncle Peter! I got a naeroplane." Peterkin tugged violently at the sleeve of a suddenly unresponsive uncle. "Look at my naeroplane, Uncle! Naeroplane, naeroplane!"

"I beg your pardon, old chap," said Wimsey, recollecting himself. "I wasn't thinking. It's a beautiful aeroplane. Does it fly? . . . Hi! you needn't get up and show me now. I'll take your word for it."

"Mummie make it fly."

It flew very competently, effecting a neat landing on the chest of drawers. Wimsey watched it with vague eyes.

"Uncle Peter!"

"Yes, son, it's splendid. Listen, would you like a speedboat?"

"What's peed-boat?"

"A boat that will run in the water–chuff, chuff–like that."

"Will it float in my barf?"

"Yes, of course. It'll sail right across the Round Pond."

Peterkin considered.

"Could I have it in my barf wiv' me?"

"Certainly, if Mummie says so."

"I'd like a boat in my barf."

"You shall have one, old man."

"When, now?"

"Tomorrow."

"Weally tomowwow?"

"Yes, promise."

"Say thank-you, Uncle Peter."

"Fank-you, Uncle Peter. Will it be tomowwow soon?"

"Yes, if you lie down down now and go to sleep."

Peterkin, who was a practically-minded child, shut his eyes instantly, wriggled under the bed-clothes, and was promptly tucked in by a firm hand.

"Really, Peter, you shouldn't bribe him to go to sleep. How about my discipline?"

"Discipline be blowed," said Peter, at the door.

"Uncle!"

"Good night!"

"Is it tomowwow yet?"

"Not yet. Go to sleep. You can't have tomorrow till you've been to sleep."

"Why not?"

"It's one of the rules."

"Oh! I'm asleep now, Uncle Peter."

"Good. Stick to it." Wimsey pulled his sister out after him and shut the nursery door.

"Polly, I'll never say kids are a nuisance again."

"What's up? I can see you're simply bursting with something."

"I've got it! Tears, idle Tears. That kid deserves fifty speed-boats as a reward for howling."

"Oh, dear!"

"I couldn't tell him that, though, could I? Come downstairs, and I'll show you something."

He dragged Mary at full speed into the sitting-room, took up his list of dates and jabbed at it with a jubilant pencil.

"See that date? That's the Tuesday before the Friday on which coke was being served out at the White Swan. On that Tuesday the Nutrax headline was finally passed for the following Friday. And what," asked Wimsey, rhetorically, "was that headline?"

"I haven't the faintest idea. I never read advertisements."

"You should have been smothered at birth. The headline was, 'Why Blame the Woman?' You will note that it begins with a 'W.' White Swan also begins with a 'W.' Got that?"

"I think so. It seems fairly simple."

"Just so. Now on this date, the Nutrax headline was 'Tears, idle Tears'—a quotation from the poets."

"I follow you so far."

"This is the date on which the headline was passed for press, you understand."

"Yes."

"Also a Tuesday."

"I have grasped that."

"On that same Tuesday, Mr. Tallboy, who is Group-manager for Nutrax, wrote a letter addressed to 'T. Smith, Esq.' You get that?"

"Yes."

"Very good. That advertisement appeared on a Friday."

"Are you trying to explain that these advertisements are all passed for press on a Tuesday and all appear on a Friday?"

"Exactly."

"Then why not say so, instead of continually repeating yourself?"

"All right. But now perpend. Mr. Tallboy has a habit of sending letters on a Tuesday, addressed to a Mr. Smith—who, by the way, doesn't exist."

"I know. You told us all about that. Mr. T. Smith is Mr. Cummings; only Mr. Cummings denies it."

"He denies it, said the King. Leave out that part. The point is that Mr. Smith isn't always Mr. T. Smith. Sometimes he's other kinds of Mr. Smith. But on the day that the Nutrax headline began with a 'T,' Mr. Smith was Mr. T. Smith."

"And what sort of Mr. Smith was he on the day that the Nutrax headline began with a 'W'?"

"Unfortunately I don't know. But I can guess that he was Mr. W. Smith. In any case, on this date here, which was the day I came to Pym's, the Nutrax headlIne was 'Kittle Cattle.' On that day, Mr. Smith—"

"Stop! I can guess this one. He was Mr. K. Smith."

"He was. Kenneth, perhaps, or Kirkpatrick, or Killarney. Killarney Smith would be a lovely name."

"And was coke distributed the next Friday from the King's Head?"

"I'm betting my boots it was. What do you think of that?"

"I think you want a little more evidence on that point. You don't seem to have any instance where you can point to the initial, the headline and the pub. all together."

"That's the weak point," confessed Wimsey. "But look here. This Tuesday which I now write down is the date on which the great Nutrax row occurred, and the headline was altered at the last moment on Thursday night. On the Friday of that week, something went wrong with the supply of dope to Major Milligan. It never turned up."

"Peter, I do believe you've got hold of something."

"Do you, Polly? Well, so do I. But I wasn't sure if it would sound plausible to anybody but me. And, look here! I remember another day." Wimsey began to laugh. "I forget which date it was, but the headline was simply a blank line and an exclamation mark, and Tallboy was horribly peeved about it. I wonder what they did that week. I should think they took the initial of the sub-head. What a joke!"

"But how is it worked, Peter?"

"Well, I don't know the details, but I imagine it's done this way. On the Tuesday, as soon as the headline is decided, Tallboy sends an envelope to Cummings' shop addressed to A. Smith, Esq., or B. Smith, Esq., according to the initial of the headline. Cummings looks at it, snorts at it and hands it back to the postman. Then he informs the head distributing agent, or agents. I don't know how. Possibly he advertises too, because the great point of this scheme, as I see it, is to have as little contact as possible between the various agents. The stuff is run across on Thursday, and the agent meets it and packets it up as Bicarbonate of Soda, or something equally harmless. Then he gets the London Telephone Directory and looks up the next pub. on the list whose name begins with the letter of which Cummings has advised him. As soon as the pub. opens on Friday morning, he is there. The retail agents, if we may call them so, have meanwhile consulted the *Morning Star* and the Telephone Directory. They hasten to the pub. and the packets are passed to them. The late Mr. Mountjoy must have been one of these gentry."

"How does the wholesaler recognize the retailer?"

"There must be some code or other, and our battered friend Hector Puncheon must have given the code-word by accident. We must ask about that. He's a *Morning Star* man, and it may be something to do with the *Morning Star*. Mountjoy, by the way, evidently believed in being early on the job, because he seems to have made a practice of getting his copy of the paper the second it was off the machine, which accounts for his having been in full working order at 4:30 a.m. in Covent Garden, and hanging round Fleet Street again in the small hours of the following Friday. He must have given the code-signal, whatever it was; Puncheon may remember about it. After that, he would make his supply up into smaller packets (hence his supply of cigarette-papers) and proceed with the distribution according to his own taste and fancy. Of course, there are a lot of things we don't know yet. How the payments are made, for instance. Puncheon wasn't asked for money. Tallboy seems to have got his particular share in Currency Notes. But that's a detail. The ingenuity of the thing is that the stuff is never distributed twice from the same place. No wonder Charles had difficulties with it. By the way, I've sent him to the wrong place tonight, poor devil. How he must be cursing me!"

Mr. Parker cursed solidly enough on his return.

"It's entirely my fault," said Wimsey, blithely. "I sent you to the Yelverton Arms. You ought to have been at the Anchor or the Antelope. But we'll pull it off next week–if we live so long."

"If," said Parker, seriously, "we live so long."

# 18

# UNEXPECTED CONCLUSION OF A CRICKET MATCH

THE PARTY from Pym's filled a large charabanc; in addition, a number of people attended in their own Austins. It was a two-innings match, starting at 10 a.m., and Mr. Pym liked to see it well attended. A skeleton staff was left to hold the fort at the office during the Saturday morning, and it was expected that as many of them as possible would trundle down to Romford by the afternoon train. Mr. Death Bredon, escorted by Lady Mary and Chief-Inspector Parker, was one of the last to scramble into the charabanc.

The firm of Brotherhood believed in ideal conditions for their staff. It was their pet form of practical Christianity; in addition to which, it looked very well in their advertising literature and was a formidable weapon against the trade unions. Not, of course, that Brotherhood's had the slightest objection to trade unions as such. They had merely discovered that comfortable and well-fed people are constitutionally disinclined for united action of any sort—a fact which explains the asinine meekness of the income-tax payer.

In Brotherhood's régime of bread and circuses, organized games naturally played a large part. From the pavilion overlooking the spacious cricket-field floated superbly a crimson flag, embroidered with the Brotherhood trademark of two clasped hands. The same device adorned the crimson blazers and caps of Brotherhood's cricket eleven. By contrast, the eleven advertising cricketers were but a poor advertisement for themselves. Mr. Bredon was, indeed, a bright spot on the landscape, for his flannels were faultless, while his Balliol blazer, though ancient, carried with it an air of authenticity. Mr. Ingleby also was correct, though a trifle shabby. Mr. Hankin, beautifully laundered, had rather spoilt his general effect by a brown felt hat, while Mr. Tallboy, irreproachable in other respects, had an unfortunate tendency to come apart at the waist, for which his tailor and shirt-maker were, no doubt, jointly responsible. The dress of the remainder varied in combining white flannels with brown shoes, white shoes with the wrong sort of shirt, tweed coats with white linen hats, down to the disgraceful exhibition of Mr. Miller, who, disdaining to put himself out for a mere game, affronted the sight in grey flannel trousers, a striped shirt and braces.

The day began badly with Mr. Tallboy's having lost his lucky half-crown and with Mr. Copley's observing, offensively, that perhaps Mr. Tallboy would prefer to toss with a pound-note. This flustered Mr. Tallboy. Brotherhood's won the toss and elected to go in first. Mr. Tallboy, still flustered, arranged his field, forgetting in his agitation Mr. Hankin's preference for mid-on and placing him at cover-point. By the time this error was remedied, it was discovered that Mr. Haagedorn had omitted to bring his wicket-keeper's gloves, and a pair had to be borrowed from the pavilion. Mr. Tallboy then realized that he had put on his two fast bowlers together. He remedied this by recalling Mr. Wedderburn from the deep field to bowl his slow "spinners," and dismissing Mr. Barrow in favour of Mr. Beeseley. This offended Mr. Barrow, who retired in dudgeon to the remotest part of the field and appeared to go to sleep.

"What's all the delay about?" demanded Mr. Copley.

Mr. Willis said he thought Mr. Tallboy must have got a little confused about the bowling order.

"Lack of organization," said Mr. Copley. "He should make out a list and stick to it."

The first Brotherhood innings passed off rather uneventfully. Mr. Miller missed two easy catches and Mr. Barrow, to show his resentment at the placing of the field, let a really quite ordinary ball go to the boundary instead of running after it. The eldest Mr. Brotherhood, a spry old gentleman of seventy-five, came doddering cheerfully round from the pavilion and sat down to make himself agreeable to Mr. Armstrong. He did this by indulging in reminiscences of all the big cricket matches he had ever seen in a long life, and as he had been devoted to the game since his boyhood, and had never missed a game of any importance, this took him some time and was excessively wearisome to Mr. Armstrong, who thought cricket a bore and only attended the staff match out of compliment to Mr. Pym's prejudices. Mr. Pym, whose enthusiasm was only equalled by his ignorance of the game, applauded bad strokes and good strokes indifferently.

Eventually the Brotherhoods were dismissed for 155, and the Pym Eleven gathered themselves together from the four corners of the field; Messrs. Garrett and Barrow, both rather ill-tempered, to buckle on their pads, and the remainder of the team to mingle with the spectators. Mr. Bredon, languid in movement but cheerful, laid himself down at Miss Meteyard's feet, while Mr. Tallboy was collared by the aged Mr. Brotherhood, thus releasing Mr. Armstrong, who promptly accepted the invitation of a younger Brotherhood to inspect a new piece of machinery.

The innings opened briskly. Mr. Barrow, who was rather a showy bat, though temperamental, took the bowling at the factory end of the pitch and cheered the spirits of his side by producing a couple of twos in the first over. Mr. Garrett, canny and cautious, stonewalled perseveringly through five balls of the following over and then cut the leather through the slips for a useful three. A single off the next ball brought the bowling back to Mr. Barrow, who, having started favourably, exhibited a happy superiority complex and settled down to make runs. Mr. Tallboy breathed a sigh of relief. Mr. Barrow, confident and successful, could always be relied upon for some good work; Mr. Barrow, put off his stroke by a narrowly missed catch, or the sun in his eyes, or a figure crossing the screens, was apt to become defeatist and unreliable. The score mounted blithely to thirty. At this point, Brotherhood's captain, seeing that the batsmen had taken the measure of the bowling, took off the man at the factory end and substituted a short, pugnacious-looking person with a scowl, at sight of whom Mr. Tallboy quaked again.

"They're putting on Simmonds very early," he said. "I only hope nobody gets hurt."

"Is this their demon bowler?" inquired Bredon, seeing the wicket-keeper hurriedly retire to a respectful distance from the wicket.

Tallboy nodded. The ferocious Simmonds wetted his fingers greedily, pulled his cap fiercely over his eyes, set his teeth in a snarl of hatred, charged like a bull and released the ball with the velocity of a 9-inch shell in Mr. Barrow's direction.

Like most fast bowlers, Simmonds was a little erratic in the matter of length. His first missile pitched short, rocketed up like a pheasant, whizzed past Mr. Barrow's ear and was adroitly fielded by long-stop, a man with a phlegmatic countenance and hands of leather. The next two went wide. The fourth was pitched straight and with a good length. Mr. Barrow tackled it courageously. The impact affected him like an electric shock; he blinked and shook his fingers, as though not quite sure whether his bones were still intact. The fifth was more manageable; he smote it good and hard and ran.

"Again!" yelled Mr. Garrett, already half-way down the pitch for the second time. Mr. Barrow accordingly ran and once again stood ready for the onslaught. It came; it ran up his bat llke a squirrel, caught him viciously on the knuckle and glanced off sharply, offering a chance to point, who, very fortunately, fumbled it. The field crossed over, and Mr. Barrow was able to stand aside and nurse his injuries.

Mr. Garrett, pursuing a policy of dogged-does-it, proceeded systematically to wear down the bowling by blocking the first four balls of the next over. The fifth produced two runs; the sixth, which was of much the same calibre, he contented himself with blocking again.

"I don't like this slow-motion cricket," complained the aged Mr. Brotherhood. "When I was a young man—"

Mr. Tallboy shook his head. He knew very well that Mr. Garrett suffered from a certain timidity when facing fast bowling. He knew, too, that Garrett had some justification, because he wore spectacles. But he knew equally well what Mr. Barrow would think about it.

Mr. Barrow, irritated, faced the redoubtable Simmonds with a sense of injury. The first ball was harmless and useless; the second was a stinger, but the third he could hit and did. He whacked it away lustily to the boundary for four, amid loud cheers. The next kept out of the wicket only by the grace of God, but the sixth he contrived to hook round to leg for a single. After which, he adopted Mr. Garrett's tactics, stonewalled through an entire over, and left Mr. Garrett to face the demon.

Mr. Garrett did his best. But the first ball rose perpendicularly under his chin and unnerved him. The second came to earth about half-way down the pitch and bumped perilously over his head. The third, pitched rather longer, seemed to shriek as it rushed for him. He stepped out, lost heart, flinched and was bowled as clean as a whistle.

"Dear, dear!" said Mr. Hankin. "It seems that it is up to me." He adjusted his pads and blinked a little. Mr. Garrett retired gloomily to the pavilion. Mr. Hankin with exasperating slowness, minced his way to the crease. He had his own methods of dealing with demon bowlers and was not alarmed. He patted the turf lengthily, asked three times for middle and off, adjusted his hat, requested that a screen might be shifted, asked for middle and off again and faced Mr. Simmonds with an agreeable smile and a very straight bat, left elbow well forward and his feet correctly placed. The result was that Simmonds, made nervous, bowled an atrocious wide, which went to the boundary, and followed it up by two mild balls of poor length, which Mr. Hankin very properly punished. This behaviour cheered Mr. Barrow and steadied him. He hit out with confidence, and the score mounted to fifty. The applause had scarcely subsided when Mr. Hankin, stepping briskly across the wicket to a slow and inoffensive-looking ball pitched rather wide to the off, found it unaccountably twist from under his bat and strike him on the left thigh. The wicket-keeper flung up his hands in appeal.

"Out!" said the umpire.

Mr. Hankin withered him with a look and stalked very slowly and stiffly from the field, to be greeted by a chorus of: "Bad luck, indeed, sir!"

"It *was* bad luck," replied Mr. Hankin. "I am surprised at Mr. Grimbold."

(Mr. Grimbold was the umpire, an elderly and impassive man from Pym's Outdoor Publicity Department.) "The ball was an atrocious wide. It could never have come anywhere near the wicket."

"It had a bit of a break on it," suggested Mr. Tallboy.

"It certainly had a break on it," admitted Mr. Hankin, "but it would have gone wide nevertheless. I don't think anybody can accuse me of being unsporting, and if I *had* been leg before, I should be the first to admit it. Did you see it, Mr. Brotherhood?"

"Oh, I saw it all right," said the old gentleman, with a chuckle.

"I put it to you," said Mr. Hankin, "whether I was l.b.w. or not."

"Of course not," said Mr. Brotherhood. "Nobody ever is. I have attended cricket matches now for sixty years, for sixty years, my dear sir, and that goes back to a time before you were born or thought of, and I've never yet known anybody to be really out l.b.w.—according to himself, that is." He chuckled again. "I remember in 1892 . . ."

"Well, sir," said Mr. Hankin, "I must defer to your experienced judgment. I think I will have a pipe." He wandered away and sat down by Mr. Pym.

"Poor old Brotherhood," he said, "is getting very old and doddery. Very doddery indeed. I doubt if we shall see him here another year. That was a very unfortunate decision of Grimbold's. Of course it is easy to be deceived in these matters, but you could see for yourself that I was no more l.b.w. than he was himself. Very vexing, when I had just settled down nicely."

"Shocking luck," agreed Mr. Pym, cheerfully. "There's Ingleby going in. I always like to watch him. He puts up a very good show, doesn't he, as a rule?"

"No style," said Mr. Hankin, morosely.

"Hasn't he?" said Mr. Pym, placidly. "You know best about that, Hankin. But he always hits out. I like to see a batsman hitting out, you know. There! Good shot! Good shot! Oh, dear!"

For Mr. Ingleby, hitting out a little too vigorously, was caught at cover-point and came galloping out rather faster than he had gone in.

"Quack, quack," said Mr. Bredon.

Mr. Ingleby threw his bat at Mr. Bredon, and Mr. Tallboy, hurriedly muttering, "Bad luck!" went to take his place.

"What a nuisance," said Miss Rossiter, soothingly. "I think it was very brave of you to hit it at all. It was a frightfully fast one."

"Um!" said Mr. Ingleby.

The dismissal of Mr. Ingleby had been the redoubtable Simmonds' swan-song. Having exhausted himself by his own ferocity, he lost his pace and became more erratic than usual, and was taken off, after an expensive over, in favour of a gentleman who bowled leg-breaks. To him, Mr. Barrow fell a victim, and retired covered with glory, with a score of twenty-seven. His place was taken by Mr. Pinchley, who departed, waving a jubilant hand and declaring his intention of whacking hell out of them.

Mr. Pinchley indulged in no antics of crease-patting or taking middle. He strode vigorously to his post, raised his bat shoulder-high and stood four-square to whatever it might please Heaven to send him. Four times did he loft the ball sky-high to the boundary. Then he fell into the hands of the Philistine with the leg-break and lofted the ball into the greedy hands of the wicket-keeper.

"Short and sweet," said Mr. Pinchley, returning with his ruddy face all grins.

"Four fours are very useful," said Mr. Bredon, kindly.

"Well, that's what I say," said Mr. Pinchley. "Make 'em quick and keep things going, that's my idea of cricket. I can't stand all this pottering and poking about."

This observation was directed at Mr. Miller, whose cricket was of the painstaking sort. A tedious period followed, during which the score slowly mounted to 83, when Mr. Tallboy, stepping back a little inconsiderately to a full-pitch, slipped on the dry turf and sat down on his wicket.

Within the next five minutes Mr. Miller, lumbering heavily down the pitch in gallant response to an impossible call by Mr. Beeseley, was run out, after compiling a laborious 12. Mr. Bredon, pacing serenely to the wicket, took counsel with himself. He reminded himself that he was still, in the eyes of Pym's and Brotherhood's at any rate, Mr. Death Bredon of Pym's. A quiet and unobtrusive mediocrity, he decided, must be his aim. Nothing that could recall the Peter Wimsey of twenty years back, making two centuries in successive innings for Oxford. No fancy cuts. Nothing remarkable. On the other hand, he had claimed to be a cricketer. He must not make a public exhibition of incompetence. He decided to make twenty runs, not more and, if possible, not less.

He might have made his mind easy; the opportunity was not vouchsafed him. Before he had collected more than two threes and a couple of demure singles, Mr. Beeseley had paid the penalty of rashness and been caught at mid-on. Mr. Haagedorn, with no pretensions to being a batsman, survived one over and was then spread-eagled without remorse or question. Mr. Wedderburn, essaying to cut a twisty one which he would have done well to leave alone, tipped the ball into wicket-keeper's gloves and Pym's were disposed of for 99, Mr. Bredon having the satisfaction of carrying out his bat for 14.

"Well played all," said Mr. Pym. "One or two people had bad luck, but of course, that's all in the game. We must try and do better after lunch."

"There's one thing," observed Mr. Armstrong, confidently to Mr. Miller, "they always do one very well. Best part of the day, to my thinking."

Mr. Ingleby made much the same remark to Mr. Bredon. "By the way," he added, "Tallboy's looking pretty rotten."

"Yes, and he's got a flask with him," put in Mr. Garrett, who sat beside them.

"He's all right," said Ingleby. "I will say for Tallboy, he can carry his load. He's much better off with a flask than with this foul Sparkling Pomayne. All wind. For God's sake, you fellows, leave it alone."

"Something's making Tallboy bad-tempered, though," said Garrett. "I don't understand him; he seems to have gone all to pieces lately, ever since that imbecile row with Copley."

Mr. Bredon said nothing to all this. His mind was not easy. He felt as though thunder was piling up somewhere and was not quite sure whether he was fated to feel or to ride the storm. He turned to Simmonds the demon bowler, who was seated on his left, and plunged into cricket talk.

"What's the matter with our Miss Meteyard today?" inquired Mrs. Johnson, archly, across the visitors' table. "You're very silent."

"I've got a headache. It's very hot. I think it's going to thunder."

"Surely not," said Miss Parton. "It's a beautiful clear day."

"*I* believe," asserted Mrs. Johnson, following Miss Meteyard's gloomy gaze, "*I* believe she's more interested in the *other* table. Now, Miss Meteyard, confess, who is it? Mr. Ingleby? I hope it's not my favourite Mr. Bredon. I simply *can't* have anybody coming between us, you know."

The joke about Mr. Bredon's reputed passion for Mrs. Johnson had become a little stale, and Miss Meteyard received it coldly.

"She's offended," declared Mrs. Johnson. "I believe it *is* Mr. Bredon. She's blushing! When are we to offer our congratulations, Miss Meteyard?"

"Do you," demanded Miss Meteyard, in a suddenly harsh and resonant voice, "recollect the old lady's advice to the bright young man?"

"Why, I can't say that I do. What was it?"

"Some people can be funny without being vulgar, and some can be both funny and vulgar. I should recommend you to be either the one or the other."

"Oh, really?" said Mrs. Johnson, vaguely. After a moment's reflection she gathered the sense of the ancient gibe and said, "Oh, really!" again, with a heightened colour. "Dear me, how rude we can be when we try. I do hate a person who can't take a joke."

Brotherhood's second innings brought some balm to the feelings of the Pymmites. Whether it was the Sparkling Pomayne, or whether it was the heat ("I do believe you were right about the thunder," remarked Miss Parton), more than one of their batsmen found his eye a little out and his energy less than it had been. Only one man ever looked really dangerous, and this was a tall, dour-faced person with whipcord wrists and a Yorkshire accent, whom no bowling seemed to daunt, and who had a nasty knack of driving extremely hard through gaps in the field. This infuriating man settled down grimly and knocked up a score of fifty-eight, amid the frenzied applause of his side. It was not only his actual score that was formidable, but the extreme exhaustion induced in the field.

"I've had—too much—gas," panted Ingleby, returning past Garrett after a mad gallop to the boundary, "and this blighter looks like staying till Christmas."

"Look here, Tallboy," said Mr. Bredon, as they crossed at the next over. "Keep your eye on the little fat fellow at the other end. He's getting pumped. If this Yorkshire tyke works him like this, something will happen."

It did happen in the next over. The slogger smote a vigorous ball from the factory end, a little too high for a safe boundary, but an almost certain three. He galloped and the fat man galloped. The ball was racing over the grass, and Tallboy racing to intercept it, as they galloped back.

"Come on!" cried the Yorkshireman, already half way down the pitch for the third time. But Fatty was winded; a glance behind showed him Tallboy stooping to the ball. He gasped "No!" and abode, like Dan, in his breaches. The other saw what was happening and turned in his tracks. Tallboy, disregarding the frantic signals of Haagedorn and Garrett, became inspired. He threw from where he stood, not to Garrett, but point-blank at the open wicket. The ball sang through the air and spread-eagled the Yorkshireman's stumps while he was still a yard from the crease, while the batsman, making a frantic attempt to cover himself, flung his bat from his hand and fell prostrate.

"Oh, pretty!" exulted old Mr. Brotherhood. "Oh, well played, sir, well played!"

"He must have taken marvellous aim," said Miss Parton.

"What's the matter with you, Bredon?" asked Ingleby, as the team lolled thankfully on the pitch to await the next man in. "You're looking very white. Touch of the sun?"

"Too much light in my eyes," said Mr. Bredon.

"Well, take it easy," advised Mr. Ingleby. "We shan't have much trouble with them now. Tallboy's a hero. Good luck to him."

Mr. Bredon experienced a slight qualm of nausea.

The remainder of the Brotherhood combination achieved nothing very remarkable, and the side was eventually got out for 114. at 4 o'clock, on a fiery wicket, Mr. Tallboy again sent out his batsmen, faced with the formidable task of making 171 to win.

At 5:30, the thing still looked almost feasible, four wickets having fallen for 79. Then Mr. Tallboy, endeavouring to squeeze a run where there was no run to be got, was run out for 7, and immediately afterwards, the brawny Mr. Pinchley, disregarding his captain's frantic appeals for care, chopped his first ball neatly into the hands of point. The rot had set in. Mr. Miller, having conscientiously blocked through two overs, while Mr. Beeseley added a hard-won 6 to the score, lost his off stump to the gentleman with the leg-break. With the score at 92 by the addition of a couple of byes, and three men to bat, including the well-meaning but inadequate Mr. Haagerdorn, defeat appeared to be unavoidable.

"Well," said Mr. Copley morosely, "it's better than last year. They beat us then by about seven wickets. Am I right, Mr. Tallboy?"

"No," said Mr. Tallboy.

"I beg your pardon, I'm sure," said Mr. Copley, "perhaps it was the year before. You should know, for I believe you were the captain on both occasions."

Mr. Tallboy vouchsafed no statistics, merely saying to Mr. Bredon:

"They draw stumps at 6:30; try and stick it out till then if you can."

Mr. Bredon nodded. The advice suited him excellently. A nice, quiet, defensive game was exactly the game least characteristic of Peter Wimsey. He sauntered tediously to the crease, expended some valuable moments in arranging himself, and faced the bowllng with an expression of bland expectation.

All would probably have gone according to calculation, but for the circumstance that the bowler at the garden end of the field was a man with an idiosyncrasy. He started his run from a point in the dim, blue distance, accelerated furiously to within a yard of the wicket, stopped, hopped, and with an action suggestive of a Catherine-wheel, delivered a medium-length, medium-paced, sound straight ball of uninspired but irreproachable accuracy. In executing this manoeuvre for the twenty-second time, his foot slipped round about the stop-and-hop period, he staggered, performed a sort of splits and rose, limping and massaging his leg. As a result, he was taken off, and in his place Simmonds, the fast bowler, was put on.

The pitch was by this time not only fast, but bumpy. Mr. Simmonds' third delivery rose wickedly from a patch of bare earth and smote Mr. Bredon violently upon the elbow.

Nothing makes a man see red like a sharp rap over the funny-bone, and it was at this moment that Mr. Death Bredon suddenly and regrettably forgot himself. He forgot his caution and his rôle, and Mr. Miller's braces, and saw only the green turf and the Oval on a sunny day and the squat majesty of the gas-works. The next ball was another of Simmonds' murderous short-pitched bumpers, and Lord Peter Wimsey, opening up wrathful shoulders, strode out of his crease like the spirit of vengeance and whacked it to the wide. The next he clouted to leg for three, nearly braining square-leg and so flummoxing deep-field that he flung it back wildly to the wrong end, giving the Pymmites a fourth for an overthrow. Mr. Simmonds' last ball he treated with the contempt it deserved, snicking it as it whizzed past half a yard wide to leg and running a single.

He was now faced by the merchant with the off-break. The first two balls he treated carefully, then drove the third over the boundary for six. The fourth rose awkwardly and he killed it dead, but the fifth and sixth followed number three. A shout went up, headed by a shrill shriek of admiration from Miss Parton. Lord Peter grinned amiably and settled down to hit the bowling all round the wicket.

As Mr. Haagedorn panted in full career down the pitch, his lips moved in prayer, "Oh, Lord, oh, Lord! don't let me make a fool of myself!" A four was signalled and the field crossed over. He planted his bat grimly, determined to defend his wicket if he died for it. The ball came, pitched, rose, and he hammered it down remorselessly. One. If only he could stick out the other five. He dealt with another the same way. A measure of confidence came to him. He pulled the third ball round to leg and, to his own surprise, found himself running. As the batsmen passed in mid-career, he heard his colleague call: "Good man! Leave 'em to me now."

Mr. Haagedorn asked nothing better. He would run till he burst, or stand still till he hardened into marble, if only he could keep this miracle from coming to an end. He was a poor bat, but a cricketer. Wimsey ended the over with a well-placed three, which left him still in possession of the bowling. He walked down the pitch and Haagedorn came to meet him.

"I'll take everything I can," said Wimsey, "but if anything comes to you, block it. Don't bother about runs. I'll see to them."

"Yes, sir," said Mr. Haagedorn, fervently. "I'll do anything you say. Keep it up, sir, only keep it up."

"All right," said Wimsey. "We'll beat the b—s yet. Don't be afraid of them. You're doing exactly right."

Six balls later, Mr. Simmonds, having been hit to the boundary four times running, was removed, as being too expensive a luxury. He was replaced by a gentleman who was known at Brotherhoods as "Spinner." Wimsey received him with enthusiasm, cutting him consistently and successfully to the off, till Brotherhood's captain moved up his fieldsmen and concentrated them about the off-side of the wicket. Wimsey looked at this grouping with an indulgent smile, and placed the next six balls consistently and successfully to leg. When, in despair, they drew a close net of fielders all round him, he drove everything that was drivable straight down the pitch. The score mounted to 150.

The aged Mr. Brotherhood was bouncing in his seat. He was in an ecstasy. "Oh, pretty, sir! Again! Oh, well played, indeed, sir!" His white whiskers fluttered like flags. "Why on earth, Mr. Tallboy," he asked, severely, "did you send this man in ninth? He's a cricketer. He's the only cricketer among the whole damned lot of you. Oh, well placed!" as the ball skimmed neatly between two agitated fielders who nearly knocked their heads together in the effort to retrieve it. "Look at that! I'm always telling these lads that placing is nine-tenths of the game. This man knows it. Who is he?"

"He's a new member of the staff," said Tallboy, "he's a public-school man and he said he'd done a good deal of country-house cricket, but I hadn't an idea he could play like that. Great Scott!" He paused to applaud a particularly elegant cut, "I never saw anything like it."

"Didn't you?" said the old gentleman with asperity. "Well, now, I've been watching cricket, man and boy, for sixty years, and I've seen something very like it. Let me see, now. Before the War, that would be. Dear, dear—I sometimes think my memory for names isn't what it was, but I fancy that in the 'varsity match of 1910, or it might be 1911—no, not 1910, that was the year in which—"

His tinkling voice was drowned in a yell as the 170 appeared on the score-board.

"One more to win!" gasped Miss Rossiter. "Oh!" For at that moment, Mr. Haagedorn, left for an unfortunate moment to face the bowling, succumbed to a really nasty and almost unplayable ball which curled round his feet like a playful kitten and skittled his leg-stump.

Mr. Haagedorn came back almost in tears, and Mr. Wedderburn, quivering with nervousness, strode forward into the breach. He had nothing to do but to survive four balls and then, except for a miracle, the game was won. The first ball rose temptingly, a little short; he stepped out, missed it, and scuttled back to his crease only just in time. "Oh, be careful! Be careful!" moaned Miss Rossiter, and old Mr. Brotherhood swore. The next ball, Mr. Wedderburn contrived to poke a little way down the pitch. He wiped his forehead. The next was a spinner and, in trying to block it, he tipped it almost perpendicularly into the air. For a moment that seemed like hours the spectators saw the spinning ball—the outstretched hand—then the ball dropped, missed by a hair.

"I'm going to scream," announced Mrs. Johnson to nobody in particular. Mr. Wedderburn, now thoroughly unnerved, wiped his forehead again. Fortunately, the bowler was also unnerved. The ball slipped in his sweating fingers and went down short and rather wide.

"Leave it alone! Leave it alone!" shrieked Mr. Brotherhood, hammering with his stick. "Leave it alone, you numbskull! You imbecile! You—"

Mr. Wedderburn, who had lost his head completely, stepped across to it, raised his bat, made a wild swipe, which missed its object altogether, heard the smack of the leather as the ball went into the wicket-keeper's gloves, and did the only possible thing. He hurled himself bodily back and sat down on the crease, and as he fell he heard the snick of the flying bails.

"How's that?"

"Not out."

"The nincompoop! The fat-headed, thick-witted booby!" yelled Mr. Brotherhood. He danced with fury, "Might have thrown the match away! Thrown it away! That man's a fool. I say he's a fool. He's a fool, I tell you."

"Well, it's all right, Mr. Brotherhood," said Mr. Hankin, soothingly. "At least, it's all wrong for your side, I'm afraid."

"Our side be damned," ejaculated Mr. Brotherhood. "I'm here to see cricket played, not tiddlywinks. I don't care who wins or who loses, sir, provided they play the game. Now, then!"

With five minutes to go, Wimsey watched the first ball of the over come skimming down towards him. It was a beauty. It was jam. He smote it as Saul smote the Philistines. It soared away in a splendid parabola, struck the pavilion roof with a noise like the crack of doom, rattled down the galvanized iron roofing, bounced into the enclosure where the scorers were sitting and broke a bottle of lemonade. The match was won.

Mr. Bredon, lolloping back to the pavillion at 6:30 with 83 runs to his credit, found himself caught and cornered by the ancient Mr. Brotherhood.

"Beautifully played, sir, beautifully played indeed," said the old gentleman. "Pardon me—the name has just come to my recollection. Aren't you Wimsey of Balliol?"

Wimsey saw Tallboy, who was just ahead of them, falter in his stride and look round, with a face like death. He shook his head.

"My name's Bredon," he said.

"Bredon?" Mr. Brotherhood was plainly puzzled. "Bredon? I don't remember ever hearing the name. But didn't I see you play for Oxford in 1911? You have a late cut which is exceedingly characteristic, and I could have taken my oath that the last time I saw you play it was at Lords in 1911, when you made 112. But I thought the name was Wimsey—Peter Wimsey of Balliol—Lord Peter Wimsey—and, now I come to think of it—"

At this very awkward moment an interruption occurred. Two men in police uniform were seen coming across the field, led by another man in mufti. They pushed their way through the crowd of cricketers and guests, and advanced upon the little group by the pavilion fence. One of the uniformed men touched Lord Peter on the arm.

"Are you Mr. Death Bredon?"

"I am," said Wimsey, in some astonishment.

"Then you'll have to come along of us. You're wanted on a charge of murder, and it is my duty to warn you that anything you say may be taken down and used in evidence."

"Murder?" ejaculated Wimsey. The policeman had spoken in unnecessarily loud and penetrating tones, and the whole crowd had frozen into fascinated attention. "Whose murder?"

"The murder of Miss Dian de Momerie."

"Good God!" said Wimsey. He looked round and saw that the man in mufti was Chief-Inspector Parker, who gave a nod of confirmation.

"All right," said Wimsey. "I'll come with you, but I don't know a thing about it. You'd better come with me while I change."

He walked away between the two officers. Mr. Brotherhood detained Parker as he was about to follow them.

"You say that man's called Bredon?"

"Yes, sir," replied Parker, with emphasis. "Bredon is his name. Mister Death Bredon."

"And you want him for murder?"

"For murder of a young woman, sir. Very brutal business."

"Well," said the old gentleman, "you surprise me. Are you sure you've got the right man?"

"Dead sure, sir. Well known to the police."

Mr. Brotherhood shook his head.

"Well," he said again, "his name may be Bredon. But he's innocent. Innocent as day, my good fellow. Did you see him play? He's a damned fine cricketer and he'd no more commit a murder than I would."

"That's as may be, sir," said Inspector Parker, stolidly.

"Just fancy that!" exclaimed Miss Rossiter. "I always *knew* there was *something*. Murder! Only think! We might all have had our throats cut! What do you think, Miss Meteyard? Were you surprised?"

"Yes, I was," said Miss Meteyard. "I was never so surprised in my life. Never!"

# 19

# DUPLICATE APPEARANCES OF A NOTORIOUS PERSONALITY

It's a fact, old man," said Parker, as the police-car sped Londonwards. "Dian de Momerie was found this morning with her throat cut in a wood near Maidenhead. Beside the body was a penny whistle and a few yards away there was a black mask caught on a bramble bush, as if some one had flung it away in a hurry. Inquiry among her friends elicited the fact that she had been going about at night with a masked harlequin, one Bredon by name. Strong suspicion was accordingly directed against the said Mr. Bredon, and Scotland Yard, acting with commendable promptitude, tracked the gentleman down to Romford and secured his person. Accused, when charged, replied—"

"I done it," said Wimsey, concluding the sentence for him. "And so, in a sense, I have, Charles. If that girl had never seen me, she'd be alive today."

"Well, she's no great loss," said the Chief-Inspector, callously. "I'm beginning to see their game. They've not yet tumbled to the fact that you're not Death Bredon, and their idea is to put you on ice quietly till they've had time to settle up their affairs. They know you can't get bail on a murder charge."

"I see. Well, they're not quite as smart as I took them to be, or they'd have identified me long since. What happens next?"

"My idea is, that we take immediate steps to establish that Mr. Death Bredon and Lord Peter Wimsey are not one person but two. Is that chap still following us, Lumley?"

"Yes, sir."

"Take care he doesn't lose us in the traffic through Stratford. We're taking you to be questioned at Scotland Yard, and this josser shall see you safely into the building. I've arranged for some pressmen to be there, and we'll prime them with full details of the arrest and a lot about your hideous past. You, as Mr. Bredon, will then telephone to yourself, as Lord Peter Wimsey, to come and see you, with a view to arranging your defence. You will be smuggled out by the back entrance—"

"Disguised as a policeman? Oh, Charles, do let me be a policeman! I should adore it."

"Well, you're a bit under the regulation height, but we might be able to manage it; the helmet is very disguising. Anyway, you go home, or else to your club—"

"Not my club; I couldn't go to the Marlborough dressed up as a cop. Stop a bit, though—the Egotists'—I could go there. I've got a room there, and the Egotists don't care what one does. I like this. Go on."

"All right. You change there, and come down to the Yard in a temper, grumbling loudly about the trouble Mr. Bredon puts you to. You can give an interview about it if you like. Then you go home. The Sunday papers have a long bit about you, with photographs of you both."

"Splendid!"

"And on Monday you go before the magistrate and reserve your defence.

It's a pity you can't be in court to hear yourself, but I'm afraid that's rather beyond our powers. Still, you can be seen immediately afterwards doing something conspicuous. You might ride in the Row and fall off—"

"No," said Wimsey. "I absolutely refuse to fall off. There are limits. I don't mind being run away with, and only saving myself by consummate horsemanship."

"Very well; I'll leave that to you. The point is that you must be in the papers."

"I will. I will advertise myself in some way. Advertising is my long suit. By the way, though, that'll mean I can't be at the office on Monday."

"Naturally."

"But that won't do. I've got to get that Whifflets campaign finished. Armstrong wants it particularly; I can't let him down. And besides, I've got interested in the thing."

Parker gazed at him in astonishment.

"Is it possible, Peter, that you are developing a kind of business morality?"

"Dash it all, Charles! You don't understand. It's a really big scheme. It'll be the biggest advertising stunt since the Mustard Club. But if that doesn't stir you, here's another thing. If I'm not at the office, you won't know the Nutrax headline next Tuesday, and won't catch the supplies being delivered."

"We can find that out without you, old man. It won't help us in the least to have you murdered, will it?"

"I suppose not. What I can't understand is, why they haven't murdered Tallboy yet."

"No: I can't understand that, either."

"I'll tell you what I think. They haven't matured their new plans yet. They're leaving him till after next Tuesday, because they've got to deliver one more consignment by the old route. They think that if I'm out of the way they can take the risk."

"Perhaps that's it. We must hope so, any way. Well, here we are. Out you come, and try and look as much like a baffled villain as possible."

"Right-ho!" said Wimsey, distorting his face into a disagreeable sneer. The car turned into the entrance to New Scotland Yard and drew up. The sergeant got out; Wimsey followed, and, glancing round, observed three obvious newspaper men hanging about the courtyard. Just as Parker emerged in his turn from the car, Wimsey tapped the sergeant lightly but efficiently under the chin and sent him staggering, tripped Parker neatly as he jumped from the running-board, and made for the gate like a hare. Two policemen and a reporter dived to intercept him; he dodged the bobbies, tackled the pressman and left him sprawling, swerved through the gateway and led a beautiful ding-dong chase down Whitehall. As he sped, he heard shouts and the blowing of whistles. Foot-passengers joined in the pursuit; motorists accelerated to cut him off; people in buses crowded to the windows and stared. He slipped nimbly into the whirl of traffic, dodged three times round the Cenotaph, doubled back on the opposite side of the street and finally staged a magnificent and sensational capture in the middle of Trafalgar Square. Parker and Lumley came up panting.

"'Ere 'e is, mister," said the man who had grabbed hold of him—a large and powerful navvy, with a bag of tools. " 'Ere 'e is. Wot's 'e done?"

"He's wanted for murder," announced Parker, briefly and loudly.

A murmur of admiration arose. Wimsey cast an offensively contemptuous glance at Sergeant Lumley.

"You ruddy bobbies are all too fat," he said. "You can't run."

"That's all right," said the sergeant, grimly. "Hold out your hands, my lad. We're taking no more chances."

"As you please, as you please. Are your hands clean? I don't want my cuffs dirtied."

"That's quite enough of it, my lad," said Parker, as the handcuffs snapped home, "we don't want any more trouble from you. Pass along there, please, pass along."

The little procession returned to Scotland Yard.

"Rather prettily done, I flatter myself," said Wimsey.

"Ar!" said Lumley, caressing his jaw. "You didn't need to have hit quite so hard, my lord."

"Verisimilitude," said Wimsey, "verisimilitude. You looked lovely as you went over."

"Ar!" said Sergeant Lumley.

A quarter of an hour later, a policeman whose uniform trousers were a little long for him and whose tunic was slightly too large in the waist, came out from Scotland Yard by a side-entrance, entered a car and was driven along Pall Mall to the discreet entrance of the Egotists' Club. Here he disappeared, and was never seen again, but presently an immaculately dressed gentleman, in evening dress and silk hat, tripped out and stood on the steps to await a taxi. An elderly gentleman of military appearance stood beside him.

"You will forgive me, Colonel? I shall not be many minutes. This fellow Bredon is an abominable nuisance, but what can one do? I mean to say, one has to do something."

"Quite, quite," said the Colonel.

"I only hope this is the last time. If he's done what they say he has, it *will* be the last."

"Oh, quite," said the Colonel, "my dear Wimsey, quite."

The taxi appeared.

"Scotland Yard," said Wimsey, in very audible tones.

The taxi sped away.

Miss Meteyard, skimming the papers in bed on Sunday morning, found her attention held by enormous headlines:

DE MOMERIE MURDER CASE ARREST

FAMOUS DUCAL HOUSE INVOLVED

INTERVIEW WITH LORD PETER WIMSEY

and again:

PENNY WHISTLE MURDER

ARREST OF MASKED MUMMER

CHIEF-INSPECTOR PARKER INTERVIEWED

and once more:

WHISTLING HARLEQUIN CAUGHT

DESPERATE MELEE IN WHITEHALL

PEER'S BROTHER VISITS SCOTLAND YARD

There followed lengthy and picturesque descriptions of the arrest; pictures of the place where the body was found; articles on Lord Peter Wimsey, on the Wimsey family, on their historic seat in Norfolk; on night-life in London and on penny whistles. The Duke of Denver had been interviewed, but refused to say anything; Lord Peter Wimsey, on the other hand, had said a good deal. Finally—and this puzzled Miss Meteyard very much, there was a photograph of Lord Peter and of Death Bredon standing side by side.

"It would be useless," said Lord Peter Wimsey in an interview, "in view of the remarkable resemblance between us, to deny that there is a relationship between this man and myself. In fact, he has on various occasions given trouble by impersonating me. If you were to see us together, you would notice that he is the darker of the two; there are also, of course, slight differences of feature; but, when we are seen separately, it is easy to mistake one of us for the other."

The Death Bredon of the photograph had certainly very much darker hair than the Peter Wimsey; his mouth was set in an unpleasing sneer, and he had that indefinable air of raffish insolence which is the hall-mark of the *chevalier d'industrie*. The newspaper article wandered on to give various unverifiable details.

"Bredon never went to a university, though he sometimes claims Oxford as his Alma Mater. He was educated at a public school in France where English sports are cultivated. He is a very fine natural cricketer, and was actually playing in a cricket match when arrested through the prompt and intelligent action of Chief-Inspector Parker. Under various names he is well known in the night-clubs of London and Paris. He is said to have met the unfortunate girl, with whose murder he is charged, at the house of the late Major Milligan, who met his death two days ago by being run down by a lorry in Piccadilly. Following representations by the Wimsey family as to his mode of life, he had recently taken a post in a well-known commercial firm, and was supposed to have turned over a new leaf, but . . ."

And so on, and so forth.

Miss Meteyard sat for a long time with the papers strewn about her, smoking cigarettes, while her coffee got cold. Then she went and had a bath. She hoped it might clear her brain.

The excitement at Pym's on the Monday morning was indescribable. The Copy Department sat in the typists' room and did no work at all. Mr. Pym telephoned that he was unwell, and could not come to the office. Mr. Copley was so unnerved that he sat for three hours with a blank sheet of paper before him and then went out for a drink—a thing he had never done in his life. Mr. Willis seemed to be on the verge of nervous collapse. Mr. Ingleby laughed at his colleagues' agitation and said that it was a grand new experience for them all. Miss Parton burst into tears and Miss Rossiter proclaimed that she had always known it. Mr. Tallboy then enlivened the proceedings by fainting in Mr. Armstrong's room, thus giving Mrs. Johnson (who was hysterically inclined) useful occupation for half an hour. And Ginger Joe, of the red head and sunny temper, astonished his companions by having a fit of the sulks and then suddenly cuffing Bill's head for no reason whatever.

At 1 o'clock Miss Meteyard went out to lunch, and read in the *Evening Banner* that Mr. Death Bredon had appeared before the magistrates at 10 a.m. on the murder charge, and had reserved his defence. At 10:30, Lord Peter Wimsey (picturesquely described as "the second protagonist in this drama of dope and death") had, while riding in the Row, narrowly escaped injury, owing to his horse's having been startled by a back-fire from a racing car; the animal had bolted and only Lord Peter's consummate horsemanship had averted a nasty accident. There was a photograph of Mr. Bredon entering the court at Bow Street in a dark lounge suit and soft hat; there was also a photograph of Lord Peter Wimsey returning from his ride in neat breeches and boots and a bowler; there was, needless to say, no photograph of the metamorphosis of the one gentleman into another, behind the drawn blinds of a Daimler saloon while traversing the quiet squares north of Oxford Street.

On Monday night, Lord Peter Wimsey attended a performance of *Say When!* at the Frivolity, companioning a Royal personage.

On Tuesday morning, Mr. Willis arrived at the office late and in a great state of excited importance. He beamed at everybody, presented the typists' room with a four-pound box of chocolates and an iced cake, and informed the sympathetic Miss Parton that he was engaged to be married. At coffee-time, the name of the lady was known to be Miss Pamela Dean. At 11:30, it was divulged that the ceremony would take place at the earliest possible moment, and at 11:45 Miss Rossiter was collecting subscriptions for a wedding-present. By 2 o'clock, the subscribers were already divided into two opinionated and bitterly hostile factions, the one advocating the purchase of a handsome dining-room clock with Westminster chimes, and the other voting with passion for a silver-plated electric chafing-dish. At 4 o'clock, Mr. Jollop had turned down successively, "Sigh no more, Ladies." "Oh, Dry those Tears" and "Weeping Late and Weeping Early," which Mr. Toule had previously passed, and rejected with derision the proposed substitution of "If you have Tears," "O Say, What are You Weeping For?" and "A Poor Soul Sat Sighing." Mr. Ingleby, stimulated by a frantic request for new headlines, had flown into a passion because the *Dictionary of Quotations* had mysteriously disappeared. At 4:30 Miss Rossiter, feverishly typing had completed "I Weep, I know not Why" and "In Silence and in Tears," while the distracted Mr. Ingleby was seriously contemplating "In that Deep Midnight of the Mind" (for, as he observed, "they'll never know it's Byron unless we tell them"), when Mr. Armstrong sent up word to say that he had persuaded Mr. Jollop to accept the copy of "O Say, What are you Weeping For?" combined with the headline "Flat, Stale, and Unprofitable," and would Mr. Ingleby kindly verify at once whether it was "Flat, Stale" or "Stale, Flat," and get the thing re-typed and hand it to Mr. Tallboy immediately.

"Isn't Mr. Armstrong marvellous?" said Miss Rossiter. "He aways finds a way out. Here you are, Mr. Ingleby—I've looked it up—it's 'Stale, Flat.' The first sentence will want altering, I suppose. You can't have this bit about 'Sometimes you are tempted to ask yourself, in the words of the old game,' can you?"

"I suppose not," grunted Ingleby. "Better make it: 'Sometimes you may be tempted, like Hamlet, to exclaim'—then the whole quote—and go on, 'yet if anybody were to ask you why—' and join it up there. That'll do. Courses of the world, please, not curses."

"T'chk!" said Miss Rossiter.

"Here's Wedderburn, panting for his copy. How's Tallboy, Wedder?"

"Gone home," said Mr. Wedderburn. "He didn't want to go, but he's fagged out. He oughtn't to have come to the office at all today, but he would do it. Is this the thing?"

"Yes. They'll want a new sketch, of course."

"Of course," said Mr. Wedderburn, gloomily. "How they ever expect things to look right when they chop and change like this— Oh, well! What is it? 'Picture of Hamlet.' Have the Studio got a reference for Hamlet?"

"Of course not; they never have anything. Who does these sketches? Pickering? You'd better take him my illustrated Shakespeare with my compliments, and request him not to cover it with Indian ink and rubber solution."

"All right."

"And to return it sometime before Christmas."

Wedderburn grinned and departed on his errand.

About ten minutes later, the telephone tinkled in the typists' room.

"Yes?" said Miss Rossiter, in mellifluous accents. "Who is it, please?"

"Tallboy speaking," said the telephone.

"Oh!" Miss Rossiter altered her voice from the tone reserved for clients and directors to a tarter one (for she was not too well pleased with Mr. Tallboy), modified by the sympathy due to ill-health:

"Oh, yes? Are you feeling better, Mr. Tallboy?"

"Yes, thanks. I've been trying to get Wedderburn, but he doesn't seem to be in his room."

"I expect he's in the Studio, making poor Mr. Pickering work overtime on a new Nutrax sketch."

"Oh! that's what I wanted to know. Did Jollop pass that copy?"

"No—he turned the whole lot down. It's a new one—at least, new headline with the 'What are you Weeping for?' copy."

"Oh, a new headline? What is it?"

"Stale, Flat and Unprofitable. Shakespeare, you know."

"Oh! Oh, good! Glad something managed to get through. It was worrying me."

"It's quite all right, Mr. Tallboy." Miss Rossiter rang off. "Touching devotion to business," she observed to Miss Parton. "As if the world would stop turning just because *he* wasn't here!"

"I expect he was afraid old Copley would be butting in again," said Miss Parton, with a snort.

"Oh, him!" said Miss Rossiter.

"Well, now, young man," said the policeman, "and what do *you* want?"

"I want to see Chief-Inspector Parker."

"Ho!" said the policeman. "Don't want much, do you? Sure you wouldn't rather see the Lord Mayor o' London? Or Mister Ramsay MacDonald?"

"I say, are you always as funny as that? Cor lumme, don't it 'urt yer sometimes? You better buy yourself a new pair o' boots or you'll be gettin' too big for wot yer wearin'. You tell Chief-Inspector Parker as Mr. Joe Potts wants ter see 'im about this 'ere 'Arlequin murder. And look snappy, 'cos I gotter git 'ome ter me supper."

"About the 'Arlequin murder, eh? And wot do you know about that?"

"Never you mind. Just tell 'im wot I say. Tell 'im it's Joe Potts as works at Pym's Publicity and you'll 'ave 'im steppin' aht ter meet me wiv' a crimson carpet and a bokay."

"Oh! you're from Pym's. Got something to say about this Bredon, is that it?"

"That's it. Now, you 'op it, and don't waste time."

"You'd better come in here, young Cocky—and be'ave yourself."

"Right-oh! it's all the same to me."

Mr. Joseph Potts wiped his boots neatly on the mat, took his seat upon a hard bench, drew out a Yo-Yo from his pocket, and began nonchalantly throwing a handsome series of loops, while the policeman retired defeated.

Presently he returned and, sternly commanding Mr. Joseph Potts to put his top away, conducted him through a series of passages to a door, upon which he knocked. A voice said "Come in," and Mr. Potts found himself in a good-sized room, furnished with two desks, a couple of comfortable arm-chairs and several other seats of penitential appearance. At the farther desk sat a man in mufti, writing, with his back to the door; at the nearer, facing the door, was another man in a grey suit, with a pile of documents before him.

"The boy, sir," announced the policeman, and retired.

"Sit down," said the man in grey, briefly, indicating one of the penitential chairs. "Now then, what's all this you've got to tell us, eh?"

"Excuse me, sir, are you Chief-Inspector Parker?"

"This is a very cautious witness," observed the man in grey to the world in general. "Why do you particularly want to see Chief-Inspector Parker?"

" 'Cos it's important and confidential, see?" said Mr. Joseph Potts, pertly. "Information, that's wot it is. I likes ter do business with the boss, especially if there's anythink ain't bein' 'andled as it should be."

"Oh!"

"I want to tell this Parker that this case ain't bein' 'andled right. See? Mr. Bredon ain't got nothink to do with it."

"Indeed. Well, I'm Chief-Inspector Parker. What do you know about Bredon?"

"This 'ere." Ginger Joe extended an inky forefinger. "You been 'ad. Mr. Bredon ain't no crook, 'e's a great detective, and I'm 'is assistant. We're 'ard on the track of a murderer, see? And this here is just a mashi—macki—I mean it's jest a bobby-trap set by the 'ideous gang as 'e's out ter track to its lair. You been boobies ter let yerselves be took in by it, see? 'E's a sport, is Mr. Bredon, and he ain't never murdered no young woman, let alone bein' such a fool as ter leave penny whistles be'ind 'im. If you wants a murderer, Mr. Bredon's got 'is eye on one now, and you're jest playin' into the 'ands of the Black Spider and 'is gang—meaning to say, 'oever done this. Wot I meantersay, the time 'as come fer me ter divulge wot I know, and I ain't agoin'—cor lumme!"

The man at the farther desk had turned round and was grinning at Ginger over the back of his chair.

"That'll do, Ginger," said this person. "We know all about that here. I am obliged to you for your testimonial. I hope you haven't been divulging anything in other directions."

"Me, sir? No, sir. I ain't said a word, Mr. Bredon, sir. But seein' as 'ow—"

"That's all right; I believe you. Now, Charles, I think this is just the lad we want. You can get that headline from him and save ringing up Pym's. Ginger, was the Nutrax headline passed this afternoon?"

"Yes, sir, 'Stale, Flat and Unprofitable,' that's what it was. And lor', wasn't there a to-do about it! Took 'em all afternoon, it did, and Mr. Ingleby wasn't 'arf wild."

"He would be," said Wimsey. "Now, you'd better cut along home, Ginger, and not a word, mind."

"No, sir."

"We're much obliged to you for coming," added Parker, "but you see, we aren't quite such boobies as you think. We know a good deal about Mr. Bredon here. And by the way, let me introduce you to Lord Peter Wimsey."

Ginger Joe's eyes nearly popped out of his head.

"Coo! Lord Peter–where's Mr. Bredon, then? This *is* Mr. Bredon. You're pulling my leg."

"I promise," said Wimsey, "to tell you all about it this time next week. Cut along now, there's a good chap. We're busy."

On Wednesday morning, Mr. Parker received a communication from St. Martin's-le-Grand. Inside the official envelope was another, addressed in Tallboy's hand to "S. Smith, Esq." at Cummings' address in Old Broad Street.

"That settles it," said Wimsey. He consulted the marked Telephone Directory. "Here you are. The Stag at Bay, Drury Lane. Make no mistake this time."

It was not until Thursday evening that Miss Meteyard made up her mind to speak to Mr. Tallboy.

# 20

# APPROPRIATE EXIT OF AN UNSKILLED MURDERER

"Is LORD Peter Wimsey at home?"

The manservant raked his questioner with a swift glance, which took in everything from his hunted eyes to his respectable middle-class boots. Then he said, inclining a respectful head:

"If you will be good enough to take a seat, I will ascertain if his Lordship is at leisure. What name shall I say, sir?"

"Mr. Tallboy."

"Who, Bunter?" said Wimsey. "Mr. Tallboy? This is a little embarrassing. What does he look like?"

"He looks, my lord, if I may so poetically express myself, as though the Hound of Heaven had got him, so to say, cornered, my lord."

"You are probably right. I should not be surprised if a hound of hell or so were knocking about the neighbourhood as well. Take a squint out of the window, Bunter."

"Very good, my lord. . . . I can observe nobody, but I retain a distinct impression that, when I opened the door to Mr. Tallboy, I overheard a footstep on the floor below."

"Very likely. Well, it can't be helped. Show him in."

"Very good, my lord."

The young man came in and Wimsey rose to greet him.

"Good evening, Mr. Tallboy."

"I have come," began Tallboy, and then broke off. "Lord Peter —Bredon—for God's sake, which are you?"

"Both," said Wimsey, gravely. "Won't you sit down?"

"Thanks, I'd rather . . . I don't want . . . I came . . . "

"You're looking rather rotten. I really think you'd better sit down, and have a spot of something."

Tallboy's legs seemed to give way under him, and he sat down without further protest.

"And how," inquired Wimsey, pouring him out a stiff whisky, "is the Whifflets campaign getting on without me?"

"Whifflets?"

"It doesn't matter. I only asked to show you that I really was Bredon. Put that straight down. Is that better?"

"Yes. I'm sorry to have made a fool of myself. I came to you—"

"You came to find out how much I knew?"

"Yes—no. I came because I couldn't stick it out any longer. I came to tell you all about it."

"Wait a minute. There's something I must tell you first. It's all out of my hands now. You understand? As a matter of fact, I don't think there's very much you can tell me. The game's up, old man. I'm sorry—I'm really sorry, because I think you've been having a perfectly bloody time. But there it is."

Tallboy had gone very white. He accepted another drink without protest, and then said:

"Well, I'm rather glad in a way. If it wasn't for my wife and the kid—oh, God!" He hid his face in his hands, and Wimsey walked over to the window and glanced at the lights of Piccadilly, pale in the summer dusk. "I've been a bloody fool," said Tallboy.

"Most of us are," said Wimsey. "I'm damned sorry, old chap."

He came back and stood looking down at him.

"Look here," he said, "you need not tell me a thing, if you don't want to. But if you do, I want you to understand that it won't really make any difference. I mean, if you feel like getting it off your chest, I don't think it will prejudice matters for you at all."

"I'd like to tell you," said Tallboy. "I think you might understand. I realize that it's all up, anyhow." He paused. "I say, what put you on to this?"

"That letter of Victor Dean's. You remember it? The one he threatened to write to Pym. He showed it to you, I fancy."

"The little swine. Yes, he did. Didn't he destroy it?"

"No, he didn't."

"I see. Well, I'd better begin at the beginning. It all started about two years ago. I was rather hard up and I wanted to get married. I'd been losing money on horses, as well, and things were not too good. I met a man in a restaurant."

"What restaurant?"

Tallboy gave the name. "He was a middle-aged, ordinary sort of person. I've never seen him since. But we got talking about one thing and another, and how tight money was and so on, and I happened to mention where I was working. He seemed to be thinking a bit after that, and asked a good many questions about how advertisements were put together and sent to the papers, and so on, and whether I was in a position to know beforehand what the headlines were going to be. So I said, of course, that there were some accounts I knew all about, such as Nutrax, and others I didn't. So then he mentioned the *Morning Star* half-double, and asked when I knew about the headlines of that, and I said, on Tuesday afternoon. Then he suddenly asked me if I could do with an extra thousand a year, and I said, 'Couldn't I? Lead me to it.' So then he came out with his proposal. It sounded pretty innocent. At least, it was quite obviously a dirty trick, but it wasn't criminal, the way he put it. He said, if I would let him know, every Tuesday, the initial letter of the headline for the following Friday, I should be well paid for it. Of course, I made a fuss about breach of confidence and so on and he raised his terms to twelve hundred. It sounded damned tempting, and I couldn't see, for the life of me, how it was going to harm the firm in any way. So I said I'd do it, and we fixed up a code–"

"I know all about that," said Wimsey. "It was very ingenious and simple. I suppose he told you that the address was simply an accommodation address."

"Yes. Wasn't it? I went to see the place once; it was a tobacconist's."

Wimsey nodded. "I've been there. It's not exactly an accommodation address, in the sense you mean. Didn't this man give you any reason for this rather remarkable request?"

"Yes, he did, and of course I oughtn't to have had anything to do with him after that. He said he was fond of having a bit of a bet with some friends of his about one thing and another, and his idea was to bet on the initial letter of each week's headline–"

"Oh, I see. And he would be betting on a certainty as often as he liked. Plausible; not criminal, but just dirty enough to explain the insistence on secrecy. Was that it?"

"Yes. I fell for it. . . . I was damned hard up. . . . I can't excuse myself. And I suppose I ought to have guessed that there was more to it than that. But I didn't want to guess. Besides, at first I thought it was all a leg-pull, but I wasn't risking anything, so I buzzed off the first two code-letters, and at the end of the fortnight I got my fifty pounds. I was heavily in debt, and I used it. After that–well, I hadn't the courage to chuck it."

"No, it would be rather hard, I should think."

"Hard? You don't know, Bredon–Wimsey–you don't know what it means to be stuck for money. They don't pay any too well at Pym's, and there are heaps of fellows who want to get out and find something better, but they daren't. Pym's is safe–they're kind and decent, and they don't sack you if they can help it–but you live up to your income and you simply daren't cut loose. The competition is so keen, and you marry and start paying for your house and furniture, and you must keep up the instalments, and you can't collect the capital to sit round for a month or two while you look for a new job. You've got to keep going, and it breaks your heart and takes all the stuffing out of you. So I went on. Of course, I kept hoping that I might be able to save money and get out of it, but my wife fell ill and one thing and another, and I was spending every penny of my salary and Smith's money on top of it. And then, somehow, that little devil Dean got hold of it; God knows how!"

"I can tell you that," said Wimsey, and told him.

"I see. Well, he started to put the screw on. First of all he wanted to go fifty-fifty, and then he demanded more. The devil of it was, that if he split on me, I should lose my job as well as Smith's money, and things were getting pretty awful. My wife was going to have a baby, and I was behind with the income-tax, and I think it was just because everything seemed too utterly hopeless that I got mixed up with the Vavasour girl. Naturally, that only made things worse in the long run. And then, one day I felt I couldn't stand it any longer and told Dean I was chucking the whole show and he could do as he damn well pleased. And it wasn't till then that he told me what it was all about, and pointed out that I might easily get twelve years' penal servitude for helping to run the dope-traffic."

"Dirty," said Wimsey, "very dirty. It never occurred to you, I suppose, to turn King's Evidence and expose the whole system."

"No; not at first. I was terrified and couldn't think properly. And even if I'd done that, there'd have been awful trouble. Still, I did think of it after a bit, and told Dean that that was what I would do. And then he informed me that he was going to get his shot in first, and showed me that letter he was sending to Pym. That finished me, and I begged him to hold off for a week or two, while I thought things over. What happened about that letter exactly?"

"His sister found it among his things and sent it on to Pym, and he engaged me, through a friend, to enquire into it. He didn't know who I was. I thought there probably wasn't much in it, but I took the job on for the experience."

Tallboy nodded.

"Well, you've had your experience. I hope you haven't paid as heavily for it as I have. I could see no way out of it–"

He stopped speaking, and glanced at Wimsey.

"Perhaps I'd better tell you the next bit," said the latter. "You thought it over, and decided that Victor Dean was a wart and a scab, and would be no great loss to the world. One day, Wedderburn came along to your room, chuckling because Mrs. Johnson had caught Ginger Joe with a catapult and had confiscated it and put it in her desk. You knew you were a wonderfully good shot with any sort of missile–the kind of man who could spread-eagle a wicket from the other end of a cricket-field–and you realized how easily a man could be plugged through the skylight as he went down the iron staircase. If the blow didn't kill him, then the fall might, and it was well worth trying."

"You really do know all about it, then?"

"Nearly. You pinched the catapult, opening the drawer with Mrs. Johnson's keys during the lunch-hour, and you did a few practice shots from day to day. You left a pebble there once, you know."

"I know. Somebody came along, before I could find it."

"Yes. Well, then, the day came for putting Dean away–a nice bright day, when all the skylights were open. You dodged about the building a good bit, so that nobody should know exactly where you were at any particular minute, and then you went up on the roof. How, by the way, did you ensure that Dean would go down the iron staircase at the right moment? Oh, yes, and the scarab? It was a very good idea to use the scarab, because if anybody found it, they would naturally think it had tumbled out of his pocket as he fell."

"I'd seen the scarab on Dean's desk after lunch; I knew he often kept it there. And I had *The Times Atlas* in my room. I sent Wedderburn down to the Vouchers for something or other, and then I rang up Dean on my telephone. I said I was speaking for Mr. Hankin from the Big Conference Room, and would Mr. Dean please come down about the Crunchlets copy and bring *The Times Atlas* with him from my room. While he went for it, I pinched the scarab and slipped up on to the roof. I knew it would take him a bit of time to find the atlas, because I'd buried it under a whole heap of files, and I was pretty sure he'd go by the iron staircase, because that was the nearest way from my room to the Conference Room. As a matter of fact, it might have gone wrong at that point because he didn't come that way at all. I think he must have gone back to his own room for something after getting the atlas, but of course, I don't know. Anyway, he came along all right and I shot at him through the skylight when he was about four steps down the staircase."

"How did you know so exactly where to hit him?"

"Curiously enough, I had a young brother who was accidentally killed by being hit in just that place with a golf-ball. But I went and looked it up in a book at the British Museum to make sure. Apparently he broke his neck as well; I hadn't expected that. I stayed up on the roof till the fuss was over, and then came down quietly by the stairs. I didn't meet a soul, of course, they were all holding post-mortems and hanging round the corpse. When I knew I'd succeeded, I didn't care. I was glad. And I tell you this, if I hadn't been found out, I shouldn't care now."

"I can sympathize with that," said Wimsey.

"They asked me for a shilling for the little beast's wreath." Tallboy laughed. "I'd gladly have given twenty shillings, or twenty pounds even. . . . And then you came along. . . . I didn't suspect anything . . . till you started to talk about catapults. . . . And then I got badly frightened, and I . . . and I . . ."

"We'll draw a veil over that," said Wimsey. "You must have got a bit of a shock when you found you'd slugged the wrong man. I suppose that was when you struck a light to look for Pamela Dean's letter."

"Yes. I knew her writing–I'd seen it in Dean's room–and I knew her writing-paper, too. I really came round to find out whether you knew anything or whether you were just drawing a bow at a venture–that's rather appropriate, isn't it? Drawing a catapult at a venture would be better. When I saw that letter I felt sure there must be something in it. And Willls, too–he'd told me that you and Pamela Dean were as thick as thieves. I thought the letter might be telling you all about Dean and me. I don't know quite what I thought, to tell you the truth. Then, when I'd found out my mistake, I got frightened and thought I'd better not try again."

"I was expecting you. When nothing came of it, I began to think it hadn't been you at all, but somebody else."

"Did you know by then that the other thing was me?"

"I didn't know it was you; you were one of several possibles. But after the Nutrax row and the £50 in notes–"

Tallboy looked up with a shy, fleeting smile.

"You know," he said, "I was horribly careless and incompetent all through. Those letters–I ought never to have sent them from the office."

"No; and the catapult. You should have taken the trouble to make your own. A catapult without fingerprints is something very unusual."

"So that was it. I'm afraid I've made an awful mess of everything. Couldn't even do a simple murder. Wimsey–how much of this will have to come out? Everything, I suppose? Even that Vavasour girl. . .?"

"Ah!" said Wimsey, without replying to the question. "Don't talk about the Vavasour girl. I felt a cad about that. You know, I did tell you not to thank me."

"You did, and it frightened me badly, because you sounded as if you meant it. I knew then that it hadn't been an accident about the catapult. But I hadn't an idea who you were till that infernal cricket match."

"I was careless then. But that damned fellow Simmonds rapping me on the funny-bone got my goat. You didn't fall for my impressive arrest then?"

"Oh, yes, I did. I believed in it implicitly and put up the most heartfelt thanksgivings. I thought I'd got off."

"Then what brought you round here tonight?"

"Miss Meteyard. She got hold of me last night. She said she'd believed first of all that you and Bredon were the same person, but now she thought you couldn't be. But she said that Bredon would be dead sure to split on me by way of currying favour with the police, and I had better get out in time."

"She said that? Miss Meteyard? Do you mean to say she knew all about it?"

"Not about the Nutrax business. But she knew about Dean."

"Good God!" Wimsey's natural conceit received a shattering blow. "How in Heaven's name did *she* know?"

"Guessed. Said she'd once seen me look at Dean when I didn't know she was there—and apparently he had once let out something to her. Apparently she'd always thought there was something odd about his death. She said she'd made up her mind not to interfere either way, but after your arrest she decided you were the bigger crook of the two. She could stand Lord Peter Wimsey doing a proper investigation, but not Mr. Dirty Bredon squealing to save his skin. She's an odd woman."

"Very. I'd better forget about all this, hadn't I? She seems to have taken the whole thing very coolly."

"She did. You see, she knew Dean. He tried to blackmail her once, about some man or the other. You wouldn't think it to look at her, would you?" said Tallboy, naïvely. "There was nothing much in it, she said, but it was the kind of thing old Pym would have been down on like a sledgehammer."

"And what did she do?" asked Wimsey, fascinated.

"Told him to publish and be damned. And I wish to God I'd done the same. Wimsey—how much longer is it going to hang on? I've been in torment—I've been trying to give myself up—I—my wife—why haven't I been arrested before this?"

"They've been waiting," said Wimsey, thoughtfully, for his mind was pursuing two trains of thought at the same time. "You see, you aren't really as important as this dope-gang. Once you were arrested, they would stop their little game, and we didn't want them to stop. I'm afraid you're being the tethered kid, left there to trap the tigers."

All this time, his ear was alert to catch the tinkle of the telephone, which would tell him that the raid on the Stag at Bay had succeeded. Once the arrests were made and the gang broken, the sinister watcher in the street would be harmless. He would fly for his life and Tallboy would be able to go home to whatever awaited him there. But if he were to go now—

"When?" Tallboy was saying urgently, "when?"

"Tonight."

"Wimsey—you've been frightfully decent to me—tell me—there's no way out? It isn't myself, exactly, but my wife and the kid. Pointed at all their lives. It's damnable. You couldn't give me twenty-four hours?"

"You would not pass the ports."

"If I were alone I'd give myself up. I would, honestly."

"There is an alternative."

"I know. I've thought about that. I suppose that's—" he stopped and laughed suddenly—"that's the public school way out of it. I—yes—all right. They'll hardly make a headline of it, though, will they? 'Suicide of Old Dumbletonian' wouldn't have much news-value. Never mind, damn it! We'll show 'em that Dumbleton can achieve the Eton touch. Why not?"

"Good man!" said Wimsey. "Have a drink. Here's luck!"

He emptied his glass and stood up.

"Listen!" he said. "I think there is one other way out. It won't help you, but it may make all the difference to your wife and your child."

"How?" said Tallboy, eagerly.

"They need never know anything about all this. Nothing. Nobody need ever know anything, if you do as I tell you."

"My God, Wimsey! What do you mean? Tell me quickly. I'll do anything."

"It won't save you."

"That doesn't matter. Tell me."

"Go home now," said Wimsey. "Go on foot, and not too fast. And don't look behind you."

Tallboy stared at him; the blood drained away from his face, leaving even his lips as white as paper.

"I think I understand. . . . Very well."

"Quickly, then," said Wimsey. He held out his hand.

"Good-night, and good luck."

"Thank you. Good-night."

From the window, Wimsey watched him come out into Piccadilly, and walk quickly away towards Hyde Park Corner. He saw the shadow slip from a neighbouring doorway and follow him.

"–and from thence to the place of execution . . . and may the Lord have mercy upon your soul."

Half an hour later, the telephone rang.

"Bagged the whole crew," said Parker's cheerful voice. "We let the stuff go up to town. What do you think it went as? Traveller's samples–one of those closed cars with blinds all round."

"That's where they made it into packets, then."

"Yes. We watched our man into the Stag; then we pulled in the motor-boat and the car. Then we kept our eye on the pub. and let the birds hop out into our arms, one after the other. It went off beautifully. No hitch at all. Oh, and by the way–their code-word. We ought to have thought of that. It was just anything to do with Nutrax. Some of them had the *Morning Star*, showing the ad., and some of them just mentioned Nutrax for Nerves. One chap had a bottle of the stuff in his pocket, another had it written on a shopping-list and so on. And one frightfully ingenious chap was bursting with information about some new tracks for greyhound racing. Simple as pie, wasn't it?"

"That explains Hector Puncheon."

"Hector–? Oh, the newspaper fellow. Yes. He must have had his copy of the *Morning Star* with him. We've got old Cummings, too, of course. He turns out to be the actual top-dog of the whole show, and as soon as we collared him he coughed up the whole story, the mangy little blighter. That doctor fellow who shoved Mountjoy under the train is in it–we've got definite information about him, and we've also got our hands on Mountjoy's loot. He's got a safe-deposit somewhere, and I think I know where to find the key. He kept a woman in Maida Vale, bless his heart. The whole thing is most satisfactory. Now we have only got to rake in your murderer chap, what's his name, and everything in the garden will be lovely."

"Lovely," said Wimsey, with a spice of bitterness in his tone, "simply lovely."

"What's the matter? You sound a bit peeved. Hang on a minute till I've cleared up here and we'll go round somewhere and celebrate."

"Not tonight," said Wimsey. "I don't feel quite like celebrating."

# 21

# DEATH DEPARTS FROM PYM'S PUBLICITY

"So you see" said Wimsey to Mr. Pym, "the thing need never come into the papers at all, if we're careful. We've plenty of evidence against Cummings without that, and there's no need to take the public into our confidence about the details of their distributing system."

"Thank Heaven!" said Mr. Pym. "It would have been a terrible thing for Pym's Publicity. How I have lived through this last week, I really don't know. I suppose you will be leaving the advertising?"

"I'm afraid so."

"Pity. You have a natural flair for copy-writing. You will have the satisfaction of seeing your Whifflets scheme go through."

"Splendid! I shall begin to collect coupons at once."

"Just fancy!" said Miss Rossiter. "Charge withdrawn."

"I always *said* Mr. Bredon was a darling," triumphed Miss Parton. "Of course the *real* murderer was one of those horrible dope-trafficking beasts. That was far more likely. I said so at the time."

"I didn't hear you, dear," snapped Miss Rossiter. "I say, Miss Meteyard, you've seen the news? You've seen that our Mr. Bredon is discharged and never did any murder at all?"

"I've done better," replied Miss Meteyard. "I've seen Mr. Bredon."

"No, where?"

"Here."

"*No!*"

"And he isn't Mr. Bredon, he's Lord Peter Wimsey."

"What! ! !"

Lord Peter poked his long nose round the door.

"Did I hear my name?"

"You did. She says you're Lord Peter Wimsey."

"Quite right."

"Then what were you doing here?"

"I came here," said his lordship, unabashed, "for a bet. A friend of mine laid me ten to one I couldn't earn my own living for a month. I did it, though, didn't I? May I have a cup of coffee?"

They would gladly have given him anything.

"By the way," said Miss Rossiter, when the first tumult had subsided, "you heard about poor Mr. Tallboy?"

"Yes, poor chap."

"Knocked down and killed on his way home—wasn't it dreadful? And poor Mrs. Tallboy with a small baby—it does seem awful! Goodness knows what they'll have to live on, because—well, you know! And that reminds me, while you're here, could I have your shilling for a wreath? At least, I suppose you'll be leaving Pym's now, but I expect you'd like to contribute."

"Yes, rather. Here you are."

"Thanks awfully. Oh, and I say! There's Mr. Willis' wedding-present. You know he's getting married?"

"No, I didn't. Everything seems to happen while I'm away. Whom is he marrying?"

"Pamela Dean."

"Oh, good work. Yes, of course. How much for Willis?"

"Well, most people are giving about two bob, if you can spare it."

"I think I can manage two bob. What are we giving him, by the way?"

"Well," said Miss Rossiter, "there's been *rather* a fuss about that. The Department was awfully keen on a clock, but Mrs. Johnson and Mr. Barrow went off on their own and bought an electric chafing-dish—such a silly thing, because I'm sure they'll never use it. And in any case, Mr. Willis did belong to the Copy Department and we ought to have had a voice in it, don't you think? So there are going to be two presents—the staff as a whole is giving the chafing-dish and the Department is giving its own present. I'm afraid we shan't be able to manage a chiming clock, though, because you can't very well ask people for more than two bob or so, though Hankie and Armstrong have been very decent and stumped up half a quid each."

"I'd better make it half a quid too."

"Oh, no," said Miss Rossiter. "You're a lamb, but it isn't fair."

"It's quite fair," said Wimsey. "There are excellent reasons why I should contribute largely to a wedding present for Mr. Willis."

"Are there? I thought you and he didn't get on very well. I expect I'm being tactless, as usual. If you're quite sure—oh, I forgot, I *am* a fool. Of course, if you're Lord Peter Wimsey, you're simply frightfully rich, aren't you?"

"Fair to middling," confessed Wimsey. "It might run to a cake for tea."

He had a word with Miss Meteyard.

"I'm sorry, you know," he said.

She shrugged her angular shoulders.

"It's not your fault. Things have to happen. You're one of the sort that pushes round and makes them happen. I prefer to leave them alone. You've got to have both kinds."

"Perhaps your way is wiser and more charitable."

"It isn't. I shirk responsibility, that's all. I just let things rip. I don't make it my business to interfere. But I don't blame the people who do interfere. In a way, I rather admire them. They do make something, even if it's only mischief. My sort make nothing. We exploit other people's folly, take the cash and sneer at the folly. It's not admirable. Never mind. You'd better run along now. I've got to get out a new series for Sopo. 'Sopo Day is Cinema Day.' 'Leave the Laundry to ruin itself while you addle your brains at the Talkies.' Muck! Dope! And they pay me £10 a week for that sort of thing. And yet, if we didn't do it, what would happen to the trade of this country? You've got to advertise."

Mr. Hankin tripped along the passage and encountered them.

"So you're leaving us, Mr. Bredon? In fact, I understand that we've been nursing a cuckoo in the nest."

"Not so bad as that, sir. I'm leaving a few of the original nestlings behind me."

Miss Meteyard evaporated quietly, and Mr. Hankin continued:

"A very sad business. Mr. Pym is very grateful for the discretion you have shown. I hope you will lunch with me some day. Yes, Mr. Smayle?"

"Excuse me, sir–about this window-bill for Green Pastures?"

Wimsey made his way out, exchanging mechanical handgrips and farewells. At the foot of the lift, in the lower vestibule, he found Ginger, with his arms full of parcels.

"Well, Ginger," said Wimsey, "I'm off."

"Oh, sir!"

"By the way, I've still got your catapult."

"I'd like you to keep it, please, sir. You see, sir–" Ginger struggled with a variety of emotions–"if I was ter keep that there catapult, I might get telling some of the boys about it, not meaning to, like. Wot I meantersay, it's 'istorical, like, ain't it, sir?"

"So it is." Wimsey sympathized with the temptation. It is not every fellow whose catapult has been borrowed for the purpose of committing a murder. "Well, I'll keep it, and thank you very much for all your help. Look here, I'll tell you what. I'll give you something in exchange. Which would you rather have–a model aeroplane, or the pair of scissors with which the steward of the *Nancy Belle* stabbed the captain and the purser?"

"Ooh, sir! 'As the scissors got the marks on 'em, sir?"

"Yes, Ginger. Genuine, original bloodstains."

"Then, please, sir, I'd like the scissors."

"You shall have them."

"Thank you *very* much, sir."

"And you'll never say one word to anybody about you know what?"

"Not if you was to roast me alive, sir."

"Right you are; good-bye, Ginger."

"Good-bye, sir."

Wimsey stepped out into Southampton Row. Facing him was a long line of hoardings. Enormous in its midst stretched a kaleidoscopic poster:

NUTRAX FOR NERVES

In the adjoining space, a workman with a broom and a bucket of paste was unfolding a still more vast and emphatic display in blue and yellow:

ARE YOU A WHIFFLER?
IF NOT, WHY NOT?

A 'bus passed, bearing a long ribbon display upon its side:

WHIFFLE YOUR WAY ROUND BRITAIN!

The great campaign had begun. He contemplated his work with a kind of amazement. With a few idle words on a sheet of paper he had touched the lives of millions. Two men, passing, stopped to stare at the hoarding.

"What's this Whiffling business, Alf?"

"I dunno. Some advertising stunt or other. Cigarettes, ain't it?"

"Oh, Whifflets?"

"I suppose so."

"Wonderful how they think of it all. What's it about, anyway?"

"Gawd knows. Here, let's get a packet and see."

"All right. I don't mind."

They passed on.

Tell England. Tell the world. Eat more Oats. Take Care of your Complexion. No More War. Shine your Shoes with Shino. Ask your Grocer. Children Love Laxamalt. Prepare to meet thy God. Bung's Beer is Better. Try Dogsbody's Sausages. Whoosh the Dust Away. Give them Crunchlets. Snagsbury's Soups are Best for the Troops. *Morning Star*, best Paper by Far. Vote for Punkin and Protect your Profits. Stop that Sneeze with Snuffo. Flush your Kidneys with Fizzlets. Flush your Drains with Sanfect. Wear Wool-fleece next the Skin. Popp's Pills Pep you Up, Whiffle your Way to Fortune. . . .

Advertise, or go under.

# Gaudy Night

*The University is a Paradise. Rivers of Knowledge are there. Arts and Sciences flow from thence. Counsell Tables are* Horti conclusi, (*as is said in the Canticles*) Gardens that are walled in, *and they are* Fontes signati. Wells that are sealed up; *bottomless depths of unsearchable Counsels there.*

JOHN DONNE

# AUTHOR'S NOTE

It would be idle to deny that the City and University of Oxford (*in aeternum floreant*) do actually exist, and contain a number of colleges and other buildings, some of which are mentioned by name in this book. It is therefore the more necessary to affirm emphatically that none of the characters which I have placed upon this public stage has any counterpart in real life. In particular, Shrewsbury College, with its dons, students and scouts, is entirely imaginary; nor are the distressing events described as taking place within its walls founded upon any events that have ever occurred anywhere. Detective-story writers are obliged by their disagreeable profession to invent startling and unpleasant incidents and people, and are (I presume) at liberty to imagine what might happen if such incidents and people were to intrude upon the life of an innocent and well-ordered community; but in so doing they must not be supposed to suggest that any such disturbance ever has occurred or is ever likely to occur in any community in real life.

Certain apologies are, however, due from me: first, to the University of Oxford, for having presented it with a Chancellor and Vice-Chancellor of my own manufacture and with a college of 150 women students, in excess of the limit ordained by statute. Next, and with deep humility, to Balliol College—not only for having saddled it with so wayward an alumnus as Peter Wimsey, but also for my monstrous impertinence in having erected Shrewsbury College upon its spacious and sacred cricket-ground. To New College, also to Christ Church, and especially to Queen's, I apologize for the follies of certain young gentlemen, to Brasenose for the facetiousness of a middle-aged one, and to Magdalen for the embarrassing situation in which I have placed an imaginary pro-Proctor. The Corporation Dump, on the other hand, is, or was, a fact, and no apology for it is due from me.

To the Principal and Fellows of my own college of Somerville, I tender my thanks for help generously given in questions of proctorial rules and general college discipline —though they are not to be held responsible for details of discipline in Shrewsbury College, many of which I have invented to suit my own purpose.

Persons curious in chronology may, if they like, work out from what they already know of the Wimsey family that the action of the book takes place in 1935; but if they do, they must not be querulously indignant because the King's Jubilee is not mentioned, or because I have arranged the weather and the moon's changes to suit my own fancy. For, however realistic the background, the novelist's only native country is Cloud-Cuckooland, where they do but jest, poison in jest: no offence in the world.

# 1

Thou blind man's mark, thou fool's self-chosen snare,
Fond fancy's scum, and dregs of scattered thought,
Band of all evils; cradle of causeless care;
Thou web of will, whose end is never wrought:
Desire! Desire! I have too dearly bought
With price of mangled mind, thy worthless ware.

Sir Philip Sidney

HARRIET VANE sat at her writing-table and stared out into Mecklenburg Square. The late tulips made a brave show in the Square garden, and a quartet of early tennis-players were energetically calling the score of a rather erratic and unpracticed game. But Harriet saw neither tulips nor tennis-players. A letter lay open on the blotting-pad before her, but its image had faded from her mind to make way for another picture. She saw a stone quadrangle, built by a modern architect in a style neither new nor old, but stretching out reconciling hands to past and present. Folded within its walls lay a trim grass plot, with flower-beds splashed at the angles, and surrounded by a wide stone plinth. Behind the level roofs of Cotswold slate rose the brick chimneys of an older and less formal pile of buildings—a quadrangle also of a kind, but still keeping a domestic remembrance of the original Victorian dwelling-houses that had sheltered the first shy students of Shrewsbury College. In front were the trees of Jowett Walk, and beyond them, a jumble of ancient gables and the tower of New College, with its jackdaws wheeling against a windy sky.

Memory peopled the quad with moving figures. Students sauntering in pairs. Students dashing to lectures, their gowns hitched hurriedly over light summer frocks, the wind jerking their flat caps into the absurd likeness of so many jesters' cockscombs. Bicycles stacked in the porter's lodge, their carriers piled with books and gowns twisted about their handlebars. A grizzled woman don crossing the turf with vague eyes, her thoughts riveted upon aspects of sixteenth-century philosophy, her sleeves floating, her shoulders cocked to the academic angle that automatically compensated the backward drag of the pleated poplin. Two male commoners in search of a coach, bareheaded, hands in their trousers-pockets, talking loudly about boats. The Warden—grey and stately—and the Dean—stocky, brisk, birdlike, a Lesser Redpoll—in animated conference under the archway leading to the Old

Quadrangle. Tall spikes of delphinium against the grey, quiveringly blue like flames, if flame were ever so blue. The college cat, preoccupied and remote, stalking with tail erect in the direction of the buttery.

It was all so long ago; so closely encompassed and complete; so cut off as by swords from the bitter years that lay between. Could one face it now? What would those women say to her, to Harriet Vane, who had taken her First in English and gone to London to write mystery fiction, to live with a man who was not married to her, and to be tried for his murder amid a roar of notoriety? That was not the kind of career that Shrewsbury expected of its old students.

She had never gone back; at first, because she had loved the place too well, and a clean break seemed better than a slow wrenching-away; and also because, when her parents had died and left her penniless, the struggle to earn a livelihood had absorbed all her time and thought. And afterwards, the stark shadow of the gallows had fallen between her and that sun-drenched quadrangle of grey and green. But now–?

She picked up the letter again. It was an urgent entreaty that she should attend the Shrewsbury Gaudy–an entreaty of the kind that it is difficult to disregard. A friend whom she had not seen since they went down together; married now and remote from her, but fallen sick, and eager to see Harriet once again before going abroad for a delicate and dangerous operation.

Mary Stokes, so pretty and dainty as Miss Patty in the Second-Year play; so charming and finished in manner; so much the social center of her year. It had seemed strange that she should take such a fancy to Harriet Vane, rough and gawky and anything but generally popular. Mary had led and Harriet had followed; when they punted up the Cher with strawberries and thermos flasks; when they climbed Magdalen tower together before sunrise on May-Day and felt it swing beneath them with the swing of the reeling bells; when they sat up late at night over the fire with coffee and parkin, it was always Mary who took the lead in all the long discussions about love and art, religion and citizenship. Mary, said all her friends, was marked for a First; only the dim, inscrutable dons had not been surprised when the lists came out with Harriet's name in the First Class and Mary's in the Second. And since then, Mary had married and scarcely been heard of; except that she haunted the College with a sick persistence, never missing an Old Students' Meeting or a Gaudy. But Harriet had broken all her old ties and half the commandments, dragged her reputation in the dust and made money, had the rich and amusing Lord Peter Wimsey at her feet, to marry him if she chose, and was full of energy and bitterness and the uncertain rewards of fame. Prometheus and Epimetheus had changed their parts, it seemed; but for one there was the box of troubles and for the other the bare rock and the vulture; and never, it seemed to Harriet, could they meet on any common ground again.

"But, by God!" said Harriet, "I won't be a coward. I'll go and be damned to it. Nothing can hurt me worse than I've been hurt already. And what does it matter after all?"

She filled up her invitation form, addressed it, stamped it with a sharp thump and ran quickly down to drop it in the pillar-box before she changed her mind.

She came back slowly across the Square garden, mounted the Adam stone stair to her flat and, after a fruitless rummage in a cupboard, came out and climbed up slowly again to a landing at the top of the house. She dragged out an ancient trunk, unlocked it and flung back the lid. A close, cold odor. Books. Discarded garments. Old shoes. Old manuscripts. A faded tie that had belonged to her dead lover—how horrible that that should still be hanging about! She burrowed to the bottom of the pile and dragged a thick, black bundle out into the dusty sunlight. The gown, worn only once at the taking of her M.A. degree, had suffered nothing from its long seclusion: the stiff folds shook loose with hardly a crease. The crimson silk of the hood gleamed bravely. Only the flat cap showed a little touch of the moth's tooth. As she beat the loose fluff from it, a tortoise-shell butterfly, disturbed from its hibernation beneath the flap of the trunk-lid, fluttered out into the brightness of the window, where it was caught and held by a cobweb.

Harriet was glad that in these days she could afford her own little car. Her entry into Oxford would bear no resemblance to those earlier arrivals by train. For a few hours longer she could ignore the whimpering ghost of her dead youth and tell herself that she was a stranger and a sojourner, a well-to-do woman with a position in the world. The hot road span away behind her; towns rose from the green landscape, crowded close about her with their inn-signs and petrolpumps, their shops and police and perambulators, then reeled back and were forgotten. June was dying among the roses, the hedges were darkening to a duller green; the blatancy of red brick sprawled along the highway was a reminder that the present builds inexorably over the empty fields of the past. She lunched in High Wycombe, solidly, comfortably, ordering a half-bottle of white wine and tipping the waitress generously. She was eager to distinguish herself as sharply as possible from that former undergraduate who would have had to be content with a packet of sandwiches and a flask of coffee beneath the bough in a by-lane. As one grew older, as one established one's self, one gained a new delight in formality. Her dress for the Garden-party, chosen to combine suitably with full academicals, lay, neatly folded, inside her suit-case. It was long and severe, of plain black georgette, wholly and unimpeachably correct. Beneath it was an evening dress for the Gaudy Dinner, of a rich petunia color, excellently cut on restrained lines, with no unbecoming display of back or breast; it would not affront the portraits of dead Wardens, gazing down from the slowly mellowing oak of the Hall.

Headington. She was very near now, and in spite of herself a chill qualm cramped her stomach. Headington Hill, up which one had toiled so often, pushing a decrepit bicycle. It seemed less steep now, as one made decorous descent behind four rhythmically pulsating cylinders; but every leaf and stone hailed one with the intrusive familiarity of an old schoolfellow. Then the narrow street, with its cramped, untidy shops, like the main street of a village; one or two stretches had been widened and improved, but there was little real change to take refuge in.

Magdalen Bridge. Magdalen Tower. And here, no change at all—only the heartless and indifferent persistence of man's handiwork. Here one must begin to steel one's self in earnest. Long Wall Street. St. Cross Road. The iron hand of the past gripping at one's entrails. The college gates; and now one must go through with it.

There was a new porter at the St. Cross lodge, who heard Harriet's name unmoved and checked it off upon a list. She handed him her bag, took her car round to a garage in Mansfield Lane,* and then, with her gown over her arm,

*For the purposes of this book, Mansfield Lane is deemed to run from Mansfield Road to St. Cross Road, behind Shrewsbury College and somewhere about the junction between the Balliol and Merton Cricket grounds as they stand at present.

passed through the New Quad into the Old, and so, by way of an ugly brick doorway, into Burleigh Building.

She met nobody of her year in the corridors or on the staircase. Three contemporaries of a far senior generation were greeting one another with effusive and belated girlishness at the door of the Junior Common Room; but she knew none of them, and went by unspeaking and unspoken to, like a ghost. The room allotted to her she recognized, after a little calculation, as one that had been occupied in her day by a woman she particularly disliked, who had married a missionary and gone to China. The present owner's short gown hung behind the door; judging by the bookshelves, she was reading History; judging by her personal belongings, she was a Fresher with an urge for modernity and very little natural taste. The narrow bed, on which Harriet flung down her belongings, was covered with drapery of a crude green color and ill-considered Futuristic pattern; a bad picture in the neo-archaic manner hung above it; a chromium-plated lamp of angular and inconvenient design swore acidly at the table and wardrobe provided by the college, which were of a style usually associated with the Tottenham Court Road; while the disharmony was crowned and accentuated by the presence, on the chest of drawers, of a curious statuette or three-dimensional diagram carried out in aluminium, which resembled a gigantic and contorted corkscrew, and was labelled upon its base: ASPIRATION. It was with surprise and relief that Harriet discovered three practicable dress-hangers in the wardrobe. The looking-glass, in conformity with established college use, was about a foot square, and hung in the darkest corner of the room.

She unpacked her bag, took off her coat and skirt, slipped on a dressing-gown and set out in search of a bathroom. She had allowed herself three-quarters of an hour for changing, and Shrewsbury's hot-water system had always been one of its most admirable minor efficiencies. She had forgotten exactly where the bathrooms were on this floor, but surely they were round here to the left. A pantry, two pantries, with notices on the doors: NO WASHING-UP TO BE DONE AFTER 11 P.M.; three lavatories, with notices on the doors: KINDLY EXTINGUISH THE LIGHT WHEN LEAVING; yes, here she was—four bathrooms, with notices on the doors: NO BATHS TO BE TAKEN AFTER 11 P.M., and, underneath, an exasperated addendum to each: IF STUDENTS PERSIST IN TAKING BATHS AFTER 11 P.M. THE BATHROOMS WILL BE LOCKED AT 10:30 P.M. *Some* CONSIDERATION FOR OTHERS IS NECESSARY IN COMMUNITY LIFE. Signed: L. MARTIN, DEAN. Harriet selected the largest bathroom. It contained a notice: REGULATIONS IN CASE OF FIRE, and a card printed in large capitals: THE SUPPLY OF HOT WATER IS LIMITED. PLEASE AVOID UNDUE WASTE. With a familiar sensation of being under authority, Harriet pushed down the waste-plug and turned on the tap. The water was boiling, though the bath badly needed a new coat of enamel and the cork mat had seen better days.

Once bathed, Harriet felt better. She was lucky again in returning to her room to meet no one whom she knew. She was in no mood for reminiscent gossipings in dressing-gowns. She saw the name "Mrs. H. Attwood" on the door next but one to hers. The door was shut, and she was grateful. The next door bore no name, but as she went by, someone turned the handle from within, and it began to open slowly. Harriet leapt quickly past it and into shelter. She found her heart beating absurdly fast.

The black frock fitted her like a glove. It was made with a small square yoke and long, close sleeves, softened by a wristfrill falling nearly to the knuckles. It outlined her figure to the waist and fell full-skirted to the ground, with a suggestion of the mediaeval robe. Its dull surface effaced itself, not outshining the dull gleam of the academic poplin. She pulled the gown's heavy folds forward upon her shoulders, so that the straight fronts fell stole-wise, serene. The hood cost her a small struggle, before she remembered the right twist at the throat which turned the bright silk outwards. She pinned it invisibly on her breast, so that it sat poised and balanced—one black shoulder and one crimson. Standing and stooping before the inadequate looking-glass (the present student who owned the room was obviously a very short woman), she adjusted the soft cap to lie flat and straight, peak down in the centre of the forehead. The glass showed her her own face, rather pale, with black brows fronting squarely either side of a strong nose, a little too broad for beauty. Her own eyes looked back at her—rather tired, rather defiant—eyes that had looked upon fear and were still wary. The mouth was the mouth of one who has been generous and repented of generosity; its wide corners were tucked back to give nothing away. With the thick, waving hair folded beneath the black cloth, the face seemed somehow stripped for action. She frowned at herself and moved her hands a little up and down upon the stuff of her gown; then, becoming impatient with the looking-glass, she turned to the window, which looked out into the Inner or Old Quad. This, indeed, was less a quad than an oblong garden, with the college buildings grouped about it. At one end, tables and chairs were set out upon the grass beneath the shade of the trees. At the far side, the new Library wing, now almost complete, showed its bare rafters in a forest of scaffolding. A few groups of women crossed the lawn; Harriet observed with irritation that most of them wore their caps badly, and one had had the folly to put on a pale lemon frock with muslin frills, which looked incongruous beneath a gown.

"Though, after all," she thought, "the bright colors are mediaeval enough. And at any rate, the women are no worse than the men. I once saw old Hammond walk in the Encaenia procession in a Mus. Doc. gown, a grey flannel suit, brown boots and a blue spotted tie, and nobody said anything to him."

She laughed suddenly, and for the first time felt confident.

"They can't take this away, at any rate. Whatever I may have done since, this remains. Scholar; Master of Arts; Domina; Senior Member of this University (*statutum est quod Juniores Senioribus debitam et congruam reverentiam tum in privato tum in publico exhibeant*); a place achieved, inalienable, worthy of reverence.

She walked firmly from the room and knocked upon the door next but one to her own.

The four women walked down to the garden together—slowly, because Mary was ill and could not move fast. And as they went, Harriet was thinking:

"It's a mistake—it's a great mistake—I shouldn't have come. Mary is a dear, as she always was, and she is pathetically pleased to see me, but we have nothing to say to one another. And I shall always remember her, *now*, as she is today, with that haggard face and look of defeat. And she will remember me as I am—hardened. She told me I looked successful. I know what that means."

She was glad that Betty Armstrong and Dorothy Collins were doing all the talking. One of them was a hardworking dog-breeder; the other ran a bookshop in Manchester. They had evidently kept in touch with one another, for they were discussing things and not people, as those do who have lively interests in common. Mary Stokes (now Mary Attwood) seemed cut off from them, by sickness, by marriage, by–it was no use to blink the truth–by a kind of mental stagnation that had nothing to do with either illness or marriage. "I suppose," thought Harriet, "she had one of those small, summery brains, that flower early and run to seed. Here she is–my intimate friend–talking to me with a painful kind of admiring politeness about my books. And I am talking with a painful kind of admiring politeness about her children. We ought *not* to have met again. It's awful."

Dorothy Collins broke in upon her thoughts by asking her a question about publishers' contracts, and the reply to this tided them over till they emerged into the quad. A brisk figure came bustling along the path, and stopped with a cry of welcome.

"Why, it's Miss Vane! How nice to see you after all this long time."

Harriet thankfully allowed herself to be scooped up by the Dean, for whom she had always had a very great affection, and who had written kindly to her in the days when a cheerful kindliness had been the most helpful thing on earth. The other three, mindful of reverence toward authority, passed on; they had paid their respects to the Dean earlier in the afternoon.

"It was splendid that you were able to come."

"Rather brave of me, don't you think?" said Harriet.

"Oh, nonsense!" said the Dean. She put her head on one side and fixed Harriet with a bright and birdlike eye. "You mustn't think about all that. Nobody bothers about it at all. We're not nearly such dried-up mummies as you think. After all, it's the work you are doing that really counts, isn't it? By the way, the Warden is longing to see you. She simply loved *The Sands of Crime.* Let's see if we can catch her before the Vice-Chancellor arrives. . . . How did you think Stokes was looking–Attwood, I mean? I never *can* remember all their married names."

"Pretty rotten, I'm afraid," said Harriet. "I came here to see her, really, you know–but I'm afraid it's not going to be much of a success."

"Ah!" said the Dean. "She's stopped growing, I expect. She was a friend of yours–but I always thought she had a head like a day-old chick. Very precocious, but no staying power. However, I hope they'll put her right. . . . Bother this wind–I can't keep my cap down. You manage yours remarkably well; how do you do it? And I notice that we are both decently sub-fusc. *Have* you seen Trimmer in that frightful frock like a canary lampshade?"

"That was Trimmer, was it? What's *she* doing?"

"Oh, lord! my dear, she's gone in for mental healing. Brightness and love and all that. . . . Ah! I thought we should find the Warden here."

Shrewsbury College had been fortunate in its wardens. In the early days, it had been dignified by a woman of position; in the difficult period when it fought for Women's degrees it had been guided by a diplomat; and now that it was received into the University, its behaviour was made acceptable by a personality. Dr. Margaret Baring wore her scarlet and French grey with an air. She was a magnificent figure-head on all public occasions, and she could soothe with tact the wounded breasts of crusty and affronted male dons. She greeted Harriet graciously, and asked what she thought of the new Library Wing, which would complete the North side of the Old Quad. Harriet duly admired what could be seen of its proportions, said it would be a great improvement and asked when it would be finished.

"By Easter, we hope. Perhaps we shall see you at the Opening."

Harriet said politely that she should look forward to it, and, seeing the

Vice-Chancellor's gown flutter into sight in the distance, drifted tactfully away to join the main throng of old students.

Gowns, gowns, gowns. It was difficult sometimes to recognize people after ten years or more. That in the blue-and-rabbit-skin hood must be Sylvia Drake—she had taken that B.Litt. at last, then. Miss Drake's B.Litt. had been the joke of the college; it had taken her so long; she was continually rewriting her thesis and despairing over it. She would hardly remember Harriet, who was so much her junior, but Harriet remembered her well—always popping in and out of the J.C.R. during her year of residence, and chattering away about mediaeval Courts of Love. Heavens! Here was that awful woman, Muriel Campshott, coming up to claim acquaintance. Campshott had always simpered. She still simpered. And she was dressed in a shocking shade of green. She was going to say, "How *do* you think of all your plots?" She did say it. Curse the woman. And Vera Mollison. She was asking: "Are you writing anything now?"

"Yes, certainly," said Harriet. "Are you still teaching?"

"Yes—still in the same place," said Miss Mollison. "I'm afraid my doings are very small beer compared with yours."

As there was no possible answer to this but a deprecating laugh, Harriet laughed deprecatingly. A movement took place. People were drifting into the New Quad, where a Presentation Clock was to be unveiled, and taking up their positions upon the stone plinth that ran round behind the flower-beds. An official voice was heard exhorting the guests to leave a path for the procession. Harriet used this excuse to disentangle herself from Vera Mollison and establish herself at the back of a group, all of whose faces were strange to her. On the opposite side of the Quad she could see Mary Attwood and her friends. They were waving. She waved back. She was *not* going to cross the grass and join them. She would remain detached, a unit in an official crowd.

From behind a drapery of bunting the clock, anticipating its official appearance in public, chimed and struck three. Footsteps crunched along the gravel. The procession came into sight beneath the archway; a small crocodile-walk of elderly people, dressed with the incongruous brilliance of a more sumptuous era, and moving with the slovenly dignity characteristic of university functions in England. They crossed the quad; they mounted the plinth beneath the clock; the male dons removed their Tudor bonnets and mortarboards in deference to the Vice-Chancellor; the female dons adopted a reverential attitude suggestive of a prayer-meeting. In a thin, delicate voice, the Vice-Chancellor began to speak. He spoke of the history of the college; he made a graceful allusion to achievements which could not be measured by the mere passing of time; he cracked a dry and nutty little jest about relativity and adorned it with a classical tag; he referred to the generosity of the donor and the beloved personality of the deceased Member of Council in whose memory the clock was presented; he expressed himself happy to unveil this handsome clock, which would add so greatly to the beauty of the quadrangle—a quadrangle, he would add, which, although a newcomer in point of time, was fully worthy to take its place among those ancient and noble buildings which were the glory of our University. In the name of the Chancellor and University of Oxford, he now unveiled the clock. His hand went out to the rope; an agitated expression came over the face of the Dean, resolving itself into a wide smile of triumph when the drapery fell away without any unseemly hitch or disaster; the clock was revealed, a few bold spirits started a round of applause; the Warden, in a short, neat speech, thanked the ViceChancellor for his kindness in coming and his friendly expressions; the golden hand of the clock moved on, and the quarter-chime rang out mellowly. The assembly heaved a sigh of satisfaction; the procession collected itself and made the return journey through the archway, and the ceremony was happily over.

Harriet, following with the throng, discovered to her horror that Vera Mollison had bobbed up again beside her, and was saying she supposed all mystery-writers must feel a strong personal interest in clocks, as so many alibis turned upon clocks and time-signals. There had been a curious incident one day at the school where she taught; it would, she thought, make a splendid plot for a detective-story, for anybody who was clever enough to work such things out. She had been longing to see Harriet and tell her all about it. Planting herself firmly on the lawn of the Old Quad, at a considerable distance from the refreshment-tables, she began to retail the curious incident, which required a good deal of preliminary explanation. A scout advanced, carrying cups of tea. Harriet secured one, and instantly wished she hadn't; it prevented swift movement, and seemed to nail her to Miss Mollison's side to all eternity. Then, with a heart-lifting surge of thankfulness, she saw Phoebe Tucker. Good old Phoebe, looking exactly the same as ever. She excused herself hurriedly to Miss Mollison, begging that she might hear the clock incident at a more leisured moment, made her way through a bunch of gowns and said, "Hullo!"

"Hullo?" said Phoebe. "Oh, it's you. Thank God! I was beginning to think there wasn't a soul of our year here, except Trimmer and that ghastly Mollison female. Come and get some sandwiches; they're quite good, strange to say. How are you these days; flourishing?"

"Not too bad."

"You're doing good stuff, anyhow."

"So are you. Let's find something to sit upon. I want to hear all about the digging."

Phoebe Tucker was a History student, who had married an archaeologist, and the combination seemed to work remarkably well. They dug up bones and stones and pottery in forgotten corners of the globe, and wrote pamphlets and lectured to learned societies. At odd moments they had produced a trio of cheerful youngsters, whom they dumped casually upon delighted grandparents before hastening back to the bones and stones.

"Well, we've only just got back from Ithaca. Bob is fearfully excited about a new set of burial-places, and has evolved an entirely original and revolutionary theory about funerary rites. He's writing a paper that contradicts all old Lambard's conclusions, and I'm helping by toning down his adjectives and putting in deprecatory footnotes. I mean, Lambard may be a perverse old idiot, but it's more dignified not to say so in so many words. A bland and deadly courtesy is more devastating, don't you think?"

"Infinitely."

Here at any rate was somebody who had not altered by a hair's-breadth, in spite of added years and marriage. Harriet was in a mood to be glad of that. After an exhaustive inquiry into the matter of funerary rites, she asked after the family.

"Oh, they're getting to be rather fun. Richard—that's the eldest—is thrilled by the burial-places. His grandmother was horrified the other day to find him very patiently and correctly excavating the gardener's rubbish-heap and making a collection of bones. Her generation always get so agitated about germs and dirt. I suppose they're quite right, but the offspring doesn't seem any the worse. So his father gave him a cabinet to keep the bones in. Simply encouraging him, Mother said. I think we shall have to take Richard out with us next time, only Mother would be so worried, thinking about no drainage and what he might pick up from the Greeks. All the children seem to be coming out quite intelligent, thank goodness. It would have been such a bore to be the mother of morons, and it's an absolute toss-up, isn't it? If one could only invent them, like characters in books, it would be much more satisfactory to a well-regulated mind."

From this the conversation naturally passed to biology, Mendelian factors and *Brave New World.* It was cut short by the emergence of Harriet's former tutor from a crowd of old students. Harriet and Phoebe made a concerted rush to greet her. Miss Lydgate's manner was exactly what it had always been. To the innocent and candid eyes of that great scholar, no moral problem seemed ever to present itself. Of a scrupulous personal integrity, she embraced the irregularities of other people in a wide, unquestioning charity. As any student of literature must, she knew all the sins of the world by name, but it was doubtful whether she recognized them when she met them in real life. It was as though a misdemeanour committed by a person she knew was disarmed and disinfected by the contact. So many young people had passed through her hands, and she had found so much good in all of them; it was impossible to think that they could be deliberately wicked, like Richard III or Iago. Unhappy, yes; misguided, yes; exposed to difficult and complicated temptations which Miss Lydgate herself had been mercifully spared, yes. If she heard of a theft, a divorce, even worse things, she would knit puzzled brows and think how utterly wretched the offenders must have been before they could do so dreadful a thing. Only once had Harriet ever heard her speak with unqualified disapproval of anyone she knew, and that was of a former pupil of her own who had written a popular book about Carlyle. "No research at all," had been Miss Lydgate's verdict, "and no effort at critical judgment. She has reproduced all the old gossip without troubling to verify anything. Slipshod, showy, and catchpenny. I am really ashamed of her." And even then she had added: "But I believe, poor thing, she is very hard up."

Miss Lydgate showed no signs of being ashamed of Miss Vane. On the contrary, she greeted her warmly, begged her to come and see her on Sunday morning, spoke appreciatively of her work, and commended her for keeping up a scholarly standard of English, even in mystery fiction.

"You give a lot of pleasure in the S.C.R.," she added, "and I believe Miss de Vine is also a fervent admirer of yours."

"Miss de Vine?"

"Ah, of course, you don't know her. Our new Research Fellow. She's such a nice person, and I know she wants to talk to you about your books. You must come and make her acquaintance. We've got her for three years, you know. That is, she only comes into residence next term but she's been living in Oxford for the last few weeks, working in Bodley. She's doing a great work on National Finance under the Tudors, and makes it perfectly fascinating, even for people like me, who are stupid about money. We are all so glad that the College decided to offer her the Jane Barraclough Fellowship, because she is a most distinguished scholar, and has had rather a hard time."

"I think I've heard of her. Wasn't she Head of one of the big provincial colleges?"

"Yes; she was Provost of Flamborough for three years; but it wasn't really her job; too much admistration, though of course she was marvellous on the financial side. But she was doing too much, what with her own work, and examining for doctorates and so on, and coping with students—the University and the College between them wore her out. She's one of those people who always *will* give of her best; but I think she found all the personal contacts uncongenial. She got ill, and had to go abroad for a couple of years. In fact, she has only just got back to England. Of course, having to give up Flamborough made a good deal of difference from the financial point of view; so it's nice to think that for the next three years she'll be able to get on with her book and not worry about that side of things."

"I remember about it now," said Harriet; "I saw the election announced somewhere or other, last Christmas or thereabouts."

"I expect you saw it in the Shrewsbury Year-Book. We are naturally very proud to have her here. She ought really to have a professorship, but I doubt if she could stand the tutorial side of it. The fewer distractions she has, the better, because she's one of the *real* scholars. There she is, over there—and, oh, dear! I'm afraid she's been caught by Miss Gubbins. You remember Miss Gubbins?"

"Vaguely," said Phoebe. "She was Third Year when we were freshers. An excellent soul, but rather earnest, and an appalling bore at College Meetings."

"She is a very conscientious person," said Miss Lydgate, "but she has rather an unfortunate knack of making any subject sound dull. It's a great pity, because she is exceptionally sound and dependable. However, that doesn't greatly matter in her present appointment; she holds a librarianship somewhere—Miss Hillyard would remember where—and I believe she's researching on the Bacon family. She's such a hard worker. But I'm afraid she's putting poor Miss de Vine through a cross-examination, which doesn't seem quite fair on an occasion like this. Shall we go to the rescue?"

As Harriet followed Miss Lydgate across the lawn, she was visited by an enormous nostalgia. If only one could come back to this quiet place, where only intellectual achievement counted; if one could work here steadily and obscurely at some close-knit piece of reasoning, undistracted and uncorrupted by agents, contracts, publishers, blurb-writers, interviewers, fan-mail, autograph-hunters, notoriety-hunters, and competitors; abolishing personal contacts, personal spites, personal jealousies; getting one's teeth into something dull and durable; maturing into solidity like the Shrewsbury beeches—then, one might be able to forget the wreck and chaos of the past, or see it, at any rate, in a truer proportion. Because, in a sense, it was not important. The fact that one had loved and sinned and suffered and escaped death was of far less ultimate moment than a single footnote in a dim academic journal establishing the priority of a manuscript or restoring a lost iota subscript. It was the hand-to-hand struggle with the insistent personalities of other people, all pushing for a place in the limelight, that made the accidents of one's own personal adventure bulk so large in the scheme of things.

But she doubted whether she were now capable of any such withdrawal. She had long ago taken the step that put the grey-walled paradise of Oxford behind her. No one can bathe in the same river twice, not even in the Isis. She would be impatient of that narrow serenity—or so she told herself.

Pulling her wandering thoughts together, she found herself being introduced to Miss de Vine. And, looking at her, she saw at once that here was a scholar of a kind very unlike Miss Lydgate, for example, and still more grotesquely unlike anything that Harriet Vane could ever become. Here was a fighter, indeed; but one to whom the quadrangle of Shrewsbury was a native and proper arena: a soldier knowing no personal loyalties, whose sole allegiance was to the fact. A Miss Lydgate, standing serenely untouched by the world, could enfold it in a genial warmth of charity; this woman, with infinitely more knowledge of the world, would rate it at a just value and set it out of her path if it incommoded her. The thin, eager face, with its large grey eyes deeply set and luminous behind thick glasses, was sensitive to impressions; but behind that sensitiveness was a mind as hard and immovable as granite. As the Head of a woman's college she must, thought Harriet, have had a distasteful task; for she looked as though the word "compromise" had been omitted from her vocabulary; and all statesmanship is compromise. She would not be likely to tolerate any waverings of purpose or woolliness of judgment. If anything came between her and the service of truth, she would walk over it without rancor and without pity—even if it were her own reputation. A formidable woman when pursuing the end in view—and the more so, for the deceptive moderation and modesty she would display in dealing with any subject of which she was not master. As they came up, she was saying to Miss Gubbins:

"I entirely agree that a historian ought to be precise in detail; but unless you take all the characters and circumstances concerned into account, you are reckoning without the facts. The proportions and relations of things are just as much facts as the things themselves; and if you get those wrong, you falsify the picture really seriously."

Here, just as Miss Gubbins, with a mulish look in her eye, was preparing to expostulate, Miss de Vine caught sight of the English tutor and excused herself. Miss Gubbins was obliged to withdraw; Harriet observed with regret that she had untidy hair, an ill-kept skin and a large white safetypin securing her hood to her dress.

"Dear me!" said Miss de Vine, "who is that very uninspired young woman? She seems very much annoyed with my review of Mr. Winterlake's book on Essex. She seems to think I ought to have torn the poor man to pieces because of a trifling error of a few months made in dealing, quite incidentally, with the early history of the Bacon family. She attaches no importance to the fact that the book is the most illuminating and scholarly handling to date of the interactions of two most enigmatic characters."

"Bacon family history is her subject," said Miss Lydgate, "so I've no doubt she feels strongly about it."

"It's a great mistake to see one's own subject out of proportion to its background. The error should be corrected, of course; I did correct it—in a private letter to the author, which is the proper medium for trifling corrections. But the man has, I feel sure, got hold of the master-key to the situation between those two men, and in so doing he has got hold of a fact of genuine importance."

"Well," said Miss Lydgate, showing her strong teeth in a genial grin, "you seem to have taken a strong line with Miss Gubbins. Now I've brought along somebody I know you're anxious to meet. This is Miss Harriet Vane—also an artist in the relating of details."

"Miss Vane?" The historian bent her brilliant, short-sighted eyes on Harriet, and her face lit up. "This is delightful. Do let me say how much I enjoyed your last book. I thought it quite the best thing you'd done—though of course

I'm not competent to form an opinion from the scientific point of view. I was discussing it with Professor Higgins, who is quite a devotee of yours, and he said it suggested a most interesting possibility, which had not before occurred to him. He wasn't quite sure whether it would work, but he would do his best to find out. Tell me, what did you have to go upon?"

"Well, I got a pretty good opinion," said Harriet, feeling a hideous qualm of uncertainty, and cursing Professor Higgins from the bottom of her heart. "But of course–"

At this point, Miss Lydgate espied another old pupil in the distance and ran away. Phoebe Tucker had already been lost on the way across the lawn. Harriet was left to her fate. After ten minutes, during which Miss de Vine ruthlessly turned her victim's brain inside out, shook the facts out of it like a vigorous housemaid shaking dust from a carpet, beat it, refreshed it, rubbed up the surface of it, relaid it in a new position and tacked it into place with a firm hand, the Dean mercifully came up and burst into the conversation.

"Thank *goodness*, the Vice-Chancellor's taking himself off. Now we can get rid of this filthy old bombazine and show off our party frocks. *Why* did we ever clamor for degrees and the fun of stewing in full academicals on a hot day? There! he's gone! Give me those anything-but-glad-rags and I'll shove them into the S.C.R. with mine. Has yours got a name on it, Miss Vane? Oh, good girl! I've got three unknown gowns sitting in my office already. Found lying about at the end of term. No clue to owners, of course. The untidy little beasts seem to think it's our job to sort out their miserable belongings. They strew them everywhere, regardless, and then borrow each other's; and if anybody's fined for being out without a gown, it's always because somebody pinched it. And the wretched things are always as dirty as dishclouts. They use them for dusters and drawing the fire up. When I think how our devoted generation *sweated* to get the right to these garments—–and these young things don't care *that* for them! They go about looking all bits and pieces, like illustrations to *Pendennis–so* out of date of them! But their idea of being modern is to imitate what male undergraduates were like half a century ago."

"Some of us old students aren't much to write home about," said Harriet. "Look at Gubbins, for instance."

"Oh, my dear! That crashing bore. And *all* held together with safety-pins. And I wish she'd wash her neck."

"I think," said Miss de Vine, with painstaking readiness to set the facts in a just light "that the color is natural to her skin."

"Then she should eat carrots and clear her system," retorted the Dean, snatching Harriet's gown from her. "No, don't you bother. It won't take me a minute to chuck them through the S.C.R. window. And don't you dare to run away, or I shall *never* find you again."

"Is my hair tidy?" inquired Miss de Vine, becoming suddenly human and hesitating with the loss of her cap and gown.

"Well," said Harriet, surveying the thick, iron-grey coils from which a quantity of overworked hair-pins stood out like croquet-hoops, "it's coming down just a trifle."

"It always does," said Miss de Vine, making vague dabs at the pins. "I think I shall have to cut it short. It must be much less trouble that way."

"I like it as it is. That big coil suits you. Let me have a go at it, shall I?"

"I wish you would," said the historian, thankfully submitting to having the pins thrust into place. "I am very stupid with my fingers. I do possess a hat somewhere," she added, with an irresolute glance round the quad, as though she expected to see the hat growing on a tree, "but the Dean said we'd better stay here. Oh, thank you. That feels much better —a marvellous sense of security. Ah! here's Miss Martin. Miss Vane has kindly been acting as hair-dresser to the White Queen—but oughtn't I to put on a hat?"

"Not now," said Miss Martin emphatically. "I'm going to have some proper tea, and so are you. I'm *ravenous*. I've been tagging after old Professor Boniface who's ninetyseven and practically gaga, and screaming in his deaf ear till I'm almost *dead*. What's the time? Well, I'm like Marjory Fleming's turkey—I do not give a single damn for the Old Students' Meeting; I simply must eat and drink. Let's swoop down upon the table before Miss Shaw and Miss Stevens collar the last ices." ..

## 2

'Tis proper to all melancholy men saith *Mercurialis, what conceit they have once entertained, to be most intent, violent and continually about it. Invitis occurrit*, do what they may, they cannot be rid of it, against their wills they must think of it a thousand times over, *perpetuo molestantur, nec oblivisci possunt*, they are continually troubled with it, in company, out of company; at meat, at exercise, at all times and places, *non desinunt ea, quae minime volunt, cogitare*; if it be offensive especially, they cannot forget it.

Robert Burton

So far, so good, thought Harriet, changing for dinner. There had been baddish moments, like trying to renew contact with Mary Stokes. There had also been a brief encounter with Miss Hillyard, the History tutor, who had never liked her, and who had said, with wry mouth and acidulated tongue, "Well, Miss Vane, you have had some very *varied* experiences since we saw you last." But there had been good moments too, carrying with them the promise of permanence in a Heraclitean universe. She felt it might be possible to survive the Gaudy Dinner, though Mary Stokes had dutifully bagged for her a place next herself, which was trying. Fortunately, she had contrived to get Phoebe Tucker on her other side. (In these surroundings, she thought of them still as Stokes and Tucker.)

The first thing to strike her, when the procession had slowly filed up to the High Table, and grace had been said, was the appalling noise in Hall. "Strike" was the right word. It fell upon one like the rush and weight of a shouting waterfall; it beat on the ear like the hammer-clang of some infernal smithy; it savaged the air like the metallic clatter of fifty thousand monotype machines casting type. Two hundred female tongues, released as though by a spring, burst into high, clamorous speech. She had forgotten what it was like, but it came back to her tonight how, at the beginning of every term, she had felt that if the noise were to go on like that for one minute more, she would go quite mad. Within a week, the effect of it had always worn off. Use had made her immune. But now it shattered her unaccustomed nerves with all and more than all its original violence. People screamed in her ear, and she found herself screaming back. She looked rather anxiously at Mary; could any invalid bear it? Mary seemed not to notice; she was more animated than she had been earlier in the day and was screaming quite cheerfully at Dorothy Collins. Harriet turned to Phoebe.

"Gosh! I'd forgotten what this row was like. If I scream I shall be as hoarse as a crow. I'm going to bellow at you in a fog-horn kind of voice. Do you mind?"

"Not a bit. I can hear you quite well. Why on earth did God give women such shrill voices? Though I don't mind frightfully. It reminds me of native workmen quarrelling. They're doing us rather well, don't you think? Much better soup than we ever got."

"They've made a special effort for Gaudy. Besides, the new Bursar's rather good, I believe; she was something to do with Domestic Economy. Dear old Straddles had a mind above food."

"Yes; but I liked Straddles. She was awfully decent to me when I got ill just before Schools. Do you remember?"

"What happened to Straddles when she left?"

"Oh, she's Treasurer at Brontë College. Finance was really her line, you know. She had a real genius for figures."

"And what became of that woman–what's her name?–Peabody? Freebody?–you know–the one who always said solemnly that her great ambition in life was to become Bursar of Shrewsbury?"

"Oh, my dear! She went absolutely potty on some new kind of religion and joined an extraordinary sect somewhere or other where they go about in loin-cloths and have agapemones of nuts and grape-fruit. That is, if you mean Brodribb?"

"Brodribb–I knew it was something like Peabody. Fancy her of all people! So intensely practical and sub-fusc."

"Reaction, I expect. Repressed emotional instincts and all that. She was frightfully sentimental inside, you know."

"I know. She wormed round rather. Had a sort of G.P. for Miss Shaw. Perhaps we were all rather inhibited in those days."

"Well, the present generation doesn't suffer from that, I'm told. *No* inhibitions of any kind."

"Oh, come, Phoebe. We had a good bit of liberty. Not like before Women's Degrees. We weren't monastic."

"No, but we were born long enough before the War to feel a few restrictions. We inherited some sense of responsibility. And Brodribb came from a fearfully rigid sort of household–Positivists or Unitarians or Presbyterians or something. The present lot are the real War-time generation, you know."

"So they are. Well, I don't know that I've any right to throw stones at Brodribb."

"Oh, my dear! That's entirely different. One thing's natural; the other's –I don't know, but it seems to me like complete degeneration of the grey matter. She even wrote a book."

"About agapemones?"

"Yes. And the Higher Wisdom. And Beautiful Thought. That sort of thing. Full of bad syntax."

"Oh, lord! Yes–that's pretty awful, isn't it? I can't think why fancy religions should have such a ghastly effect on one's grammar."

"It's a kind of intellectual rot that sets in, I'm afraid. But which of them causes the other, or whether they're both symptoms of something else, I don't know. What with Trimmer's mental healing, and Henderson going nudist–"

"No!"

"Fact. There she is, at the next table. That's why she's so brown."

"And her frock so badly cut. If you can't be naked, be as ill-dressed as possible, I suppose."

"I sometimes wonder whether a little normal, hearty wickedness wouldn't be good for a great many of us."

At this moment, Miss Mollison, from three places away on the same side of the table, leaned across her neighbors and screamed something.

"What?" screamed Phoebe.

Miss Mollison leaned still further, compressing Dorothy Collins, Betty Armstrong and Mary Stokes almost to suffocation.

"I hope Miss Vane isn't telling you anything *too* bloodcurdling!"

"No," said Harriet, loudly. "Mrs. Bancroft is curdling *my* blood."

"How?"

"Telling me the life-histories of our year."

"Oh!" screamed Miss Mollison, disconcerted. The service of a dish of lamb and green peas intervened and broke up the formation, and her neighbors breathed again. But to Harriet's intense horror, the question and reply seemed to have opened up an avenue for a dark, determined woman with large spectacles and rigidly groomed hair, who sat opposite to her, and who now bent over and said, in piercingly American accents:

"I don't suppose you remember me, Miss Vane? I was only in college for one term, but I would know you anywhere. I'm always recommending your books to my friends in America who are keen to study the British detective story, because I think they are just terribly good."

"Very kind of you," said Harriet, feebly.

"And we have a very dear mutooal acquaintance," went on the spectacled lady.

Heavens! thought Harriet. What social nuisance is going to be dragged out of obscurity now? And who is this frightful female?

"Really?" she said, aloud, trying to gain time while she ransacked her memory. "Who's that, Miss—"

"Schuster-Slatt" prompted Phoebe's voice in her ear.

"Schuster-Slatt." (Of course. Arrived in Harriet's first summer term. Supposed to read Law. Left after one term because the conditions at Shrewsbury were too restrictive of liberty. Joined the Home Students, and passed mercifully out of one's life.)

"How clever of you to know my name. Yes, well, you'll be surprised when I tell you, but in my work I see so many of your British aristocracy."

Hell! thought Harriet. Miss Schuster-Slatt's strident tones dominated even the surrounding uproar.

"Your marvellous Lord Peter. He was so kind to me, and terribly interested when I told him I was at college with you. I think he's just a lovely man."

"He has very nice manners," said Harriet. But the implication was too subtle. Miss Schuster-Slatt proceeded:

"He was just wonderful to me when I told him all about my work." (I wonder what it is, thought Harriet.) "And of course I wanted to hear all about his thrilling detective cases, but he was much too modest to say anything. Do tell me, Miss Vane, does he wear that cute little eyeglass because of his sight, or is it part of an old English tradition?"

"I have never had the impertinence to ask him," said Harriet.

"Now isn't that just like your British reticence!" exclaimed Miss Schuster-Slatt; when Mary Stokes struck in with :

"Oh, Harriet, do tell us about Lord Peter! He must be perfectly charming, if he's at all like his photographs. Of course you know him very well, don't you?"

"I worked with him over one case."

"It must have been frightfully exciting. Do tell us what he's like."

"Seeing," said Harriet, in angry and desperate tones, "seeing that he got me out of prison and probably saved me from being hanged, I am naturally bound to find him delightful."

"Oh!" said Mary Stokes, flushing scarlet, and shrinking from Harriet's furious eyes as if she had received a blow. "I'm sorry—I didn't think—"

"Well, there," said Miss Schuster-Slatt, "I'm afraid I've been very, very tactless. My mother always said to me, 'Sadie, you're the most tactless girl I ever had the bad luck to meet.' But I am enthusiastic. I get carried away. I don't stop to think. I'm just the same with my work. I don't consider my own feelings; I don't consider other people's feelings. I just wade right in and ask for what I want, and I mostly get it."

After which, Miss Schuster-Slatt, with more sensitive feeling than one might have credited her with, carried the conversation triumphantly away to the subject of her own work, which turned out to have something to do with the sterilization of the unfit, and the encouragement of matrimony among the intelligentsia.

Harriet, meanwhile, sat miserably wondering what devil possessed her to display every disagreeable trait in her character at the mere mention of Wimsey's name. He had done her no harm; he had only saved her from a shameful death and offered her an unswerving personal devotion; and for neither benefit had he ever claimed or expected her gratitude. It was not pretty that her only return should be a snarl of resentment. The fact is, thought Harriet, I have got a bad inferiority complex; unfortunately, the fact that I know it doesn't help me to get rid of it. I could have liked him so much if I could have met him on an equal footing. . . .

The Warden rapped upon the table. A welcome silence fell upon the Hall. A speaker was rising to propose the toast of the university.

She spoke gravely, unrolling the great scroll of history, pleading for the Humanities, proclaiming the Pax Academica to a world terrified with unrest. "Oxford has been called the home of lost causes: if the love of learning for its own sake is a lost cause everywhere else in the world, let us see to it that here at least, it finds its abiding home." Magnificent, thought Harriet, but it is not war. And then, her imagination weaving in and out of the spoken words, she saw it as a Holy War, and that whole wildly heterogeneous, that even slightly absurd collection of chattering women fused into a corporate unity with one another and with every man and woman to whom integrity of mind meant more than material gain—defenders in the central keep of Man-soul, their personal differences forgotten in face of a common foe. To be true to one's calling, whatever follies one might commit in one's emotional life, that was the way to spiritual peace. How could one feel fettered, being the freeman of so great a city, or humiliated, where all enjoyed equal citizenship? The eminent professor who rose to reply spoke of a diversity of gifts but the same spirit. The note, once struck, vibrated on the lips of every speaker and the ear of every hearer. Nor was the Warden's review of the Academic year out of key with it: appointments, degrees, fellowships—all these were the domestic details of the discipline without which the community could not function. In the glamour of one Gaudy night, one could realize that one was a citizen of no mean city. It might be an old and an old-fashioned city, with inconvenient buildings and narrow streets where the passersby squabbled foolishly about the right of way; but her foundations were set upon the holy hills and her spires touched heaven.

Leaving the Hall in this rather exalted mood, Harriet found herself invited to take coffee with the Dean.

She accepted, after ascertaining that Mary Stokes was bound for bed by doctor's orders and had therefore no claim upon her company. She therefore made her way along to the New Quad and tapped upon Miss Martin's door. Gathered together in the sitting-room she found Betty Armstrong, Phoebe Tucker, Miss de Vine, Miss Stevens the Bursar, another of the Fellows who answered to the name of Barton, and a couple of old students a few years senior to herself. The Dean, who was dispensing coffee, hailed her arrival cheerfully.

"Come along! Here's coffee that is coffee. Can *nothing* be done about the Hall coffee, Steve?"

"Yes, if you'll start a coffee-fund," replied the Bursar. "I don't know if you've ever worked out the finance of really first-class coffee for two hundred people."

"I know," said the Dean. "It's so trying to be grovellingly poor. I think I'd better mention it to Flackett. You remember Flackett, the rich one, who was always rather odd. She was in your year, Miss Fortescue. She has been following me round, trying to present the College with a tankful of tropical fish. Said she thought it would brighten the Science Lecture-Room."

"If it would brighten some of the lectures," said Miss Fortescue, "it might be a good thing. Miss Hillyard's Constitutional Developments were a bit gruesome in our day."

"Oh, my *dear!* Those Constitutional Developments! Dear me, yes–they still go on. She starts every year with about thirty students and ends up with two or three earnest black men, who take every word down solemnly in note-books. Exactly the same lectures; I don't think even fish would help them. Anyway, I said, 'It's very good of you, Miss Flackett, but I really don't think they'd thrive. It would mean putting in a special heating system, wouldn't it? And it would make extra work for the gardeners.' She looked so disappointed, poor thing; so I said she'd better consult the Bursar."

"All right," said Miss Stevens, "I'll tackle Flackett, and suggest the endowment of a coffee-fund."

"*Much* more useful than tropical fish," agreed the Dean. "I'm afraid we do turn out some oddities. And yet, you know, I believe Flackett is extremely sound upon the life-history of the liver-fluke. Would anybody like a Benedictine with the coffee? Come along, Miss Vane. Alcohol loosens the tongue, and we want to hear all about your latest mysteries."

Harriet obliged with a brief resume of the plot she was working on.

"Forgive me, Miss Vane, for speaking frankly," said Miss Barton, leaning earnestly forward, "but after your own terrible experience, I wonder that you care about writing that kind of book."

The Dean looked a little shocked.

"Well," said Harriet, "for one thing, writers can't pick and choose until they've made money. If you've made your name for one kind of book and then switch over to another, your sales are apt to go down, and that's the brutal fact." She paused. "I know what you're thinking–that anybody with proper sensitive feeling would rather scrub floors for a living. But I should scrub floors very badly, and I write detective stories rather well. I don't see why proper feeling should prevent me from doing my proper job."

"Quite right," said Miss de Vine.

"But surely," persisted Miss Barton, "you must feel that terrible crimes and the sufferings of innocent suspects ought to be taken seriously, and not just made into an intellectual game."

"I do take them seriously in real life. Everybody must. But should you say that anybody who had tragic experience of sex, for example, should never write an artificial drawing-room comedy?"

"But isn't that different?" said Miss Barton, frowning. "There is a lighter side to love; whereas there's no lighter side to murder."

"Perhaps not, in the sense of a comic side. But there is a purely intellectual side to the detection."

"You did investigate a case in real life, didn't you? How did you feel about that?"

"It was very interesting."

"And, in the light of what you knew, did you like the idea of sending a man to the dock and the gallows?"

"I don't think it's quite fair to ask Miss Vane that," said the Dean. "Miss Barton," she added, a little apologetically, to Harriet, "is interested in the sociological aspects of crime, and very eager for the reform of the penal code."

"I am," said Miss Barton. "Our attitude to the whole thing seems to me completely savage and brutal. I have met so many murderers when visiting prisons; and most of them are very harmless, stupid people, poor creatures, when they aren't definitely pathological."

"You might feel differently about it," said Harriet, "if you'd happened to meet the victims. They are often still stupider and more harmless than the murderers. But *they* don't make a public appearance. Even the jury needn't see the body unless they like. But I saw the body in that Wilvercombe case—I *found* it; and it was beastlier than anything you can imagine."

"I'm quite sure you must be right about that," said the Dean. "The description in the papers was more than enough for me."

"And," went on Harriet to Miss Barton, "you don't see the murderers actively engaged in murdering. You see them when they're caught and caged and looking pathetic. But the Wilvercombe man was a cunning, avaricious brute, and quite ready to go and do it again, if he hadn't been stopped."

"That's an unanswerable argument for stopping them," said Phoebe, "whatever the law does with them afterwards."

"All the same," said Miss Stevens, "isn't it a little coldblooded to catch murderers as an intellectual exercise? It's all right for the police—it's their duty."

"In law," said Harriet, "it is every citizen's obligation—though most people don't know that."

"And this man Wimsey," said Miss Barton, "who seems to make a hobby of it—does he look upon it as a duty or as an intellectual exercise?"

"I'm not sure," said Harriet, "but, you know, it was just as well for me that he did make a hobby of it. The police were wrong in my case—I don't blame them, but they were—so I'm glad it wasn't left to them."

"I call that a perfectly noble speech," said the Dean. "If anyone had accused me of doing something I hadn't done, I should be foaming at the mouth."

"But it's my job to weigh evidence," said Harriet, "and I can't help seeing the strength of the police case. It's a matter of a + b, you know. Only there happened to be an unknown factor."

"Like that thing that keeps cropping up in the new kind of physics," said the Dean. "Planck's constant, or whatever they call it."

"Surely," said Miss de Vine, "whatever comes of it, and whatever anybody feels about it, the important thing is to get at the facts."

"Yes," said Harriet; "that's the point. I mean, the fact is that I *didn't* do the murder, so that my feelings are quite irrelevant. If I had done it, I should probably have thought myself thoroughly justified, and been deeply indignant about the way I was treated. As it is, I still think that to inflict the agonies of poisoning on anybody is unpardonable. The particular trouble I got let in for was as much sheer accident as falling off a roof."

"I really ought to apologize for having brought the subject up at all," said Miss Barton. "It's very good of you to discuss it so frankly."

"I don't mind–now. It would have been different just after it happened. But that awful business down at Wilvercombe shed rather a new light on the matter–showed it up from the other side."

"Tell me," said the Dean, "Lord Peter–what is he like?"

"To look at, do you mean? or to work with?"

"Well, one knows more or less what he looks like. Fair and Mayfair. I meant, to talk to."

"Rather amusing. He does a good deal of the talking himself, if it comes to that."

"A little merry and bright, when you're feeling off-colour?"

"I met him once at a dog-show," put in Miss Armstrong unexpectedly. "He was giving a perfect imitation of the sillyass-about-town."

"Then he was either frightfully bored or detecting something," said Harriet, laughing. "I know that frivolous mood, and it's mostly camouflage–but one doesn't always know for what."

'There must be something behind it," said Miss Barton, "because he's obviously very intelligent. But is it only intelligence, or is there any genuine feeling?"

"I shouldn't," said Harriet, gazing thoughtfully into her empty coffee-cup, "accuse him of any lack of feeling. I've seen him very much upset, for instance, over convicting a sympathetic criminal. But he is really rather reserved, in spite of that deceptive manner."

"Perhaps he's shy," suggested Phoebe Tucker, kindly. "People who talk a lot often are. I think they are very much to be pitied."

"Shy?" said Harriet. "Well, hardly. Nervy, perhaps–that blessed word covers a lot. But he doesn't exactly seem to call for pity."

"Why should he?" said Miss Barton. "In a very pitiful world, I don't see much need to pity a young man who has everything he can possibly want."

"He must be a remarkable person if he has that," said Miss de Vine, with a gravity that her eyes belied.

"And he's not so young as all that," said Harriet. "He's forty-five." (This was Miss Barton's age.)

"I think it's rather an impertinence to pity people," said the Dean.

"Hear, hear!" said Harriet. "Nobody likes being pitied. Most of us enjoy self-pity, but that's another thing."

"Caustic," said Miss de Vine, "but painfully true."

"But what I should like to know," pursued Miss Barton, refusing to be diverted, "is whether this dilettante gentleman does anything, outside his hobbies of detecting crimes and collecting books, and, I believe, playing cricket in his offtime."

Harriet, who had been congratulating herself upon the way in which she was keeping her temper, was seized with irritation.

"I don't know," she said. "Does it matter? Why should he do anything else? Catching murderers isn't a soft job, or a sheltered job. It takes a lot of time and energy, and you may very easily get injured or killed. I dare say he does it for fun, but at any rate, he does do it. Scores of people must have as much reason to thank him as I have. You can't call that nothing."

"I absolutely agree," said the Dean. "I think one ought to be very grateful to people who do dirty jobs for nothing, whatever their reason is."

Miss Fortescue applauded this. "The drains in my weekend cottage got stopped up last Sunday, and a most helpful neighbour came and unstopped them. He got quite filthy in the process and I apologized profusely, but he said I owed him no thanks, because he was inquisitive and liked drains. He may not have been telling the truth, but even if he was, I certainly had nothing to grumble about."

"Talking of drains," said the Bursar–

The conversation took a less personal and more anecdotal turn (for there is no chance assembly of people who cannot make lively conversation about drains), and after a little time, Miss Barton retired to bed. The Dean breathed a sigh of relief.

"I hope you didn't mind too much," she said. "Miss Barton is the most terribly downright person, and she was determined to get all that off her chest. She is a splendid person, but hasn't very much sense of humour. She can't bear anything to be done except from the very loftiest motives."

Harriet apologized for having spoken so vehemently.

"I thought you took it all wonderfully well. And your Lord Peter sounds a most interesting person. But I don't see why you should be forced to discuss him, poor man."

"If you ask me," observed the Bursar, "we discuss everything a great deal too much in this university. We argue about this and that and why and wherefore, instead of getting the thing done."

"But oughtn't we to ask what things we want done," objected the Dean.

Harriet grinned at Betty Armstrong, hearing the familiar academic wrangle begin. Before ten minutes had passed, somebody had introduced the word "values." An hour later they were still at it. Finally the Bursar was heard to quote:

"God made the integers; all else is the work of man."

"Oh, bother!" cried the Dean. "Do let's keep mathematics out of it. And physics. I cannot cope with them."

"Who mentioned Planck's constant a little time ago?"

"I did, and I'm sorry for it. I call it a revolting little object."

The Dean's emphatic tones reduced everybody to laughter, and, midnight striking, the party broke up.

"I am still living out of College," said Miss de Vine to Harriet. "May I walk across to your room with you?"

Harriet assented, wondering what Miss de Vine had to say to her. They stepped out together into the New Quad. The moon was up, painting the buildings with cold washes of black and silver whose austerity rebuked the yellow gleam of lighted windows behind which old friends reunited still made merry with talk and laughter.

"It might almost be term-time," said Harriet.

"Yes." Miss de Vine smiled oddly. "If you were to listen at those windows, you would find it was the middle-aged ones who were making the noise. The old have gone to bed, wondering whether they have worn as badly as their contemporaries. They have suffered some shocks, and their feet hurt them. And the younger ones are chattering soberly about life and its responsiblities. But the women of forty are pretending they are undergraduates again, and finding it rather an effort. Miss Vane—I admired you for speaking as you did tonight. Detachment is a rare virtue, and very few people find it lovable, either in themselves or in others. If you ever find a person who likes you in spite of it—still more, because of it—that liking has very great value, because it is perfectly sincere and because, with that person, you will never need to be anything but sincere yourself."

"That is probably very true," said Harriet, "but what makes you say it?"

"Not any desire to offend you, believe me. But I imagine you come across a number of people who are disconcerted by the difference between what you do feel and what they fancy you ought to feel. It is fatal to pay the smallest attention to them."

"Yes," said Harriet, "but I am one of them. I disconcert myself very much. I never know what I do feel."

"I don't think that matters, provided one doesn't try to persuade one's self into appropriate feelings."

They had entered the Old Quad, and the ancient beeches, most venerable of all Shrewsbury institutions, cast over them a dappled and changing shadow-pattern that was more confusing than darkness.

"But one has to make some sort of choice," said Harriet. "And between one desire and another, how is one to know which things are really of overmastering importance?"

"We can only know that," said Miss de Vine, "when they have overmastered us."

The chequered shadow dropped off them, like the dropping of linked silver chains. Each after each, from all the towers of Oxford, clocks struck the quarter-chime, in a tumbling cascade of friendly disagreement. Miss de Vine bade Harriet good night at the door of Burleigh Building and vanished, with her long, stooping stride, beneath the Hall archway.

An odd woman, thought Harriet, and of a penetrating shrewdness. All Harriet's own tragedy had sprung from "persuading herself into appropriate feelings" towards a man whose own feelings had not stood up to the test of sincerity either. And all her subsequent instability of purpose had sprung from the determination that never again would she mistake the will to feel for the feeling itself. "We can only know what things are of overmastering importance when they have overmastered us." Was there anything at all that had stood firm in the midst of her indecisions? Well, yes; she had stuck to her work—and that in the face of what might have seemed overwhelming reasons for abandoning it and doing something different. Indeed, though she had shown cause that evening for this particular loyalty, she had never felt it necessary to show cause to herself. She had written what she felt herself called upon to write; and, though she was beginning to feel that she might perhaps do this thing better, she had no doubt that the thing itself was the right thing for her. It had overmastered her without her knowledge or notice, and that was the proof of its mastery.

She paced for some minutes to and fro in the quad, too restless to go in and sleep. As she did so, her eye was caught by a sheet of paper, fluttering untidily across the trim turf. Mechanically she picked it up and, seeing that it was not blank, carried it into Burleigh Building with her for examination. It was a sheet of common scribbling paper, and all it bore was a childish drawing scrawled heavily in pencil. It was not in any way an agreeable drawing–not at all the kind of thing that one would expect to find in a college quadrangle. It was ugly and sadistic. It depicted a naked figure of exaggeratedly feminine outlines, inflicting savage and humiliating outrage upon some person of indeterminate gender clad in a cap and gown. It was neither sane nor healthy; it was, in fact, a nasty, dirty and lunatic scribble.

Harriet stared at it for a little time in disgust, while a number of questions formed themselves in her mind. Then she took it upstairs with her into the nearest lavatory, dropped it in and pulled the plug on it. That was the proper fate for such things, and there was an end of it; but for all that, she wished she had not seen it.

## 3

They do best who, if they cannot but admit love, yet make it keep quarter, and sever it wholly from their serious affairs and actions of life; for if it check once with business it troubleth men's fortunes, and maketh men that they can no ways be true to their own ends.

Francis Bacon

SUNDAY, AS the S.C.R. always declared, was invariably the best part of a Gaudy. The official dinner and speeches were got out of the way; the old students resident in Oxford, and the immensely busy visitors with only one night to spare had all cleared off. People began to sort themselves out, and one could talk to one's friends at leisure, without being instantly collared and hauled away by a collection of bores.

Harriet paid her visit of state to the Warden, who was holding a small reception with sherry and biscuits, and then went to call upon Miss Lydgate in the New Quad. The English tutor's room was festooned with proofs of her forthcoming work on the Prosodic elements in English verse from Beowulf to Bridges. Since Miss Lydgate had perfected, or was in process of perfecting (since no work of scholarship ever attains a static perfection), an entirely new prosodic theory, demanding a novel and complicated system of notation which involved the use of twelve different varieties of type; and since Miss Lydgate's handwriting was difficult to read and her experience in dealing with printers limited, there existed at that moment five successive revises in galley form, at different stages of completion, together with two sheets in page-proof, and an appendix in typescript, while the important Introduction which afforded the key to the whole argument still remained to be written. It was only when a section had advanced to page-proof condition that Miss Lydgate became fully convinced of the necessity of transferring large paragraphs of argument from one chapter to another, each change of this kind naturally demanding expensive over-running on the page-proof, and the elimination of the corresponding portions in the five sets of revises; so that in the course of the necessary cross-reference, Miss Lydgate would be discovered by her pupils and colleagues wound into a kind of paper cocoon and helplessly searching for her fountain-pen amid the litter.

"I am afraid," said Miss Lydgate, rubbing her head, in response to Harriet's polite inquiries as to the magnum opus, "I am dreadfully ignorant about the practical side of book-making. I find it very confusing and I'm not at all clever at explaining myself to the printers. It will be a great help having Miss de Vine here. She has such an orderly mind. It's really an education to see her manuscript, and of course her work is far more intricate than mine—all sorts of little items out of Elizabethan pay-rolls and so on, all wonderfully sorted out and arranged in a beautiful clear argument. And she understands setting out footnotes properly, so that they fit in with the text. I always find that so difficult, and though Miss Harper is kindly doing all my typing for me, she really knows more about Anglo-Saxon than about compositors. I expect you remember Miss Harper. She was two years junior to you and took a second in English and lives in the Woodstock Road."

Harriet said she thought footnotes were always very tiresome, and might she see some of the book.

"Well, if you're really interested," said Miss Lydgate, "but I don't want to bore you." She extracted a couple of paged sheets from a desk stuffed with papers. "Don't prick your fingers on that bit of manuscript that's pinned on. I'm afraid it's rather full of marginal balloons and interlineations, but you see, I suddenly realized that I could work out a big improvement in my notation, so I've had to alter it all through. I expect," she added wistfully, "the printers will be rather angry with me."

Harriet privately agreed with her, but said comfortingly that the Oxford University Press was no doubt accustomed to deciphering the manuscripts of scholars.

"I sometimes wonder whether I am a scholar at all," said Miss Lydgate. "It's all quite clear in my head, you know, but I get muddled when I put it down on paper. How do you manage about your plots? All that time-table work with the alibis and so on must be terribly hard to bear in mind."

"I'm always getting mixed up myself," admitted Harriet. "I've never yet succeeded in producing a plot without at least six major howlers. Fortunately, nine readers out of ten get mixed up too, so it doesn't matter. The tenth writes me a letter, and I promise to make the correction in the second edition, but I never do. After all, my books are only meant for fun; it's not like a work of scholarship."

"You always had a scholarly mind, though," said Miss Lydgate, "and I expect you find your training a help in some ways, don't you? I used to think you might take up an academic career."

"Are you disappointed that I didn't?"

"No, indeed. I think it's so nice that our students go out and do such varied and interesting things, provided they do them well. And I must say, most of our students do do exceedingly good work along their own lines."

"What are the present lot like?"

"Well," said Miss Lydgate, "we've got some *very* good people up, and they work surprisingly hard, when you think of all the outside activities they manage to carry on at the same time. Only sometimes I'm afraid they rather overdo it, and don't get enough sleep at night. What with young men and motor-cars and parties, their lives are so much fuller than they were before the War—even more so than in your day, I think. I'm afraid our old Warden would be very greatly disconcerted if she saw the college as it is today. I must say that I am occasionally a little startled myself, and even the Dean, who is so broad-minded, thinks a brassiere and a pair of drawers rather unsuitable for sun-bathing in the quad. It isn't so much the male under-graduates—they're used to it—but after all, when the Heads of the men's colleges come to call on the Warden, they really ought to be able to get through the grounds without blushing. Miss Martin has really had to insist on bathing dresses—backless if they like, but proper bathing dresses made for the purpose, and not ordinary underwear."

Harriet agreed that this seemed only reasonable.

"I am so glad you think so," said Miss Lydgate. "It is rather difficult for us of the older generation to hold the balance between tradition and progress—if it is progress. Authority as such commands very little respect nowadays, and I expect that is a good thing on the whole, though it makes the work of running any kind of institution more difficult. I am sure you would like a cup of coffee. No, really—I always have one myself about this time. Annie!—I think I hear my scout in the pantry—Annie! Would you please bring in a second cup for Miss Vane."

Harriet was fairly well satisfied already with eatables and drinkables, but politely accepted the refreshment brought in by the smartly uniformed maid. She made some remark, when the door was shut again, as to the great improvements made since her own day in the staff and service at Shrewsbury, and again heard the praise awarded to the new bursar.

"Though I am afraid," added Miss Lydgate, "we may have to lose Annie from this staircase. Miss Hillyard finds her too independent; and perhaps she *is* a little absent-minded. But then, poor thing, she is a widow with two children, and really ought not to have to be in service at all. Her husband was in quite a good position, I believe, but he went out of his mind, or something, poor man, and died or shot himself, or something tragic of that kind, leaving her very badly off, so she was glad to take what she could. The little girls are boarded out with Mrs. Jukes—you remember the Jukeses, they were at the St. Cross Lodge in your time. They live down in St. Aldate's now, so Annie is able to go and see them at week-ends. It is nice for her and brings in a trifle extra for Mrs. Jukes."

"Did Jukes retire? He wasn't very old, was he?"

"Poor Jukes," said Miss Lydgate, her kind face clouding. "He got into sad trouble and we were obliged to dismiss him. He turned out to be not quite honest, I am sorry to say. But we found him work as a jobbing gardener," she went on more cheerfully, "where he wouldn't be exposed to so much temptation in the matter of parcels and so on. He was a most hardworking man, but he would put money on horse-races, and so, naturally, he found himself in difficulties. It was so unfortunate for his wife."

"She was a good soul," agreed Harriet.

"She was terribly upset about it all," went on Miss Lydgate. "And so, to do him justice, was Jukes. He quite broke down, and there was a sad scene with the Bursar when she told him he must go."

"Ye-es'" said Harriet. "Jukes always had a pretty glib tongue. "

"Oh, but I'm sure he was really very sorry for what he'd done. He explained how he'd slipped into it, and one thing led to another. We were all very much distressed about it. Except, perhaps, the Dean—but then she never did like Jukes very much. However, we made a small loan to his wife, to pay off his debts, and they certainly repaid it most honestly, a few shillings each week. Now that he's *put* straight I feel sure he will *keep* straight. But of course, it was impossible to keep him on here. One could never feel absolutely easy, and one must have entire confidence in the porter. The present man, Padgett, is most reliable and a very amusing character. You must get the Dean to tell you some of Padgett's quaint sayings."

"He looks a monument of integrity," said Harriet. "He may be less popular, on that account. Jukes took bribes, you know–if one came in late, and that sort of thing."

"We were afraid he did," said Miss Lydgate. "Of course, it's a responsible post for a man who isn't of very strong character. He'll do much better where he is."

"You've lost Agnes, too, I see."

"Yes–she was Head-Scout in your time; yes, she has left. She began to find the work too much for her and had to retire. I'm glad to say we were able to squeeze out a tiny pension for her–only a trifle, but as you know, our income has to be stretched very carefully to cover everything. And we arranged a little scheme by which she takes in odd jobs of mending and so on for the students and attends to the College linen. It all helps; and she's especially glad because that crippled sister of hers can do part of the work and contribute something to their small income. Agnes says the poor soul is so much happier now that she need not feel herself a burden."

Harriet marvelled, not for the first time, at the untiring conscientiousness of administrative women. Nobody's interests ever seemed to be overlooked or forgotten, and an endless goodwill made up for a perennial scarcity of funds.

After a little more talk about the doings of past dons and students, the conversation turned upon the new Library. The books had long outgrown their old home in Tudor Building, and were at last to be adequately housed.

"And when that is finished," said Miss Lydgate, "we shall feel that our College Buildings are substantially complete. It does seem rather wonderful to those of us who remember the early days when we only had the one funny old house with ten students, and were chaperoned to lectures in a donkey-carriage. I must say we rather wept to see the dear old place pulled down to make way for the Library. It held so many memories."

"Yes, indeed," said Harriet, sympathetically. She supposed that there was no moment of the past upon which this experienced and yet innocent soul could not dwell with unaffected pleasure. The entrance of another old pupil cut short her interview with Miss Lydgate, and she went out, vaguely envious, to encounter the persistent Miss Mollison, primed with every remorseless detail of the clock incident. It gave her pleasure to inform Miss Mollison that Mr. A. E. W. Mason had hit on the same idea earlier. Unquenchable, Miss Mollison proceeded to question her victim eagerly about Lord Peter Wimsey, his manners, customs and appearance; and when Miss Mollison was driven away by Miss Schuster-Slatt, the irritation was little relieved, for Harriet was subjected to a long harangue about the sterilization of the unfit, to which (it appeared) a campaign to encourage the marriage of the fit was a necessary corollary. Harriet agreed that intellectual women should marry and reproduce their kind; but she pointed out that the English husband had something to say in the matter and that, very often, he did not care for an intellectual wife.

Miss Schuster-Slatt said she thought English husbands were lovely, and that she was preparing a questionnaire to be circulated to the young men of the United Kingdom, with a view to finding out their matrimonial preferences.

"But English people won't fill up questionnaires," said Harriet.

"Won't fill up questionnaires?" cried Miss Schuster-Slatt, taken aback.

"No," said Harriet, "they won't. As a nation we are not questionnaire-conscious."

"Well, that's too bad," said Miss Schuster-Slatt. "But I do hope you will join the British Branch of our League for the Encouragement of Matrimonial Fitness. Our President, Mrs. J. Poppelhinken, is a wonderful woman. You would so much like to meet her. She will be coming to Europe next year. In the meantime I am here to do propaganda and study the whole question from the angle of British mentality."

"I'm afraid you will find it a very difilcult job. I wonder," added Harriet (for she felt she owed Miss Schuster-Slatt a riposte for her unfortunate observations of the night before), "whether your intentions are as disinterested as you make out. Perhaps you are thinking of investigating the loveliness of English husbands in a personal and practical way."

"Now you're making fun of me," said Miss Schuster-Slath with perfect good-humour. "No. I'm just the little workerbee, gathering honey for the queens to eat."

"How all occasions do inform against me!" muttered Harriet to herself. One would have thought that Oxford at least would offer a respite from Peter Wimsey and the marriage question. But athough she herself was a notoriety, if not precisely a celebrity, it was an annoying fact that Peter was a still more spectacular celebrity, and that, of the two, people would rather know about him than about her. As regards marriage—well, here one certainly had a chance to find out whether it worked or not. Was it worse to be a Mary Attwood (*nee* Stokes) or a Miss Schuster-Slatt? Was it better to be a Phoebe Bancroft (*nee* Tucker) or a Miss Lydgate? And would all these people have turned out exactly the same, married or single?

She wandered into the J.C.R., which was empty, but for one drab and ill-dressed woman who sat desolately reading an illustrated paper. As Harriet passed, this woman looked up and said, rather tentatively, "Hullo! it's Miss Vane, isn't it?"

Harriet racked her memory hastily. This was obviously someone very much senior to herself—she looked nearer fifty than forty. Who on earth?

"I don't suppose you remember me," said the other. "Catherine Freemantle."

(Catherine Freemantle, good God! But she had been only two years senior to Harriet. Very brllliant, very smart, very lively and the outstanding scholar of her year. What in Heaven's name had happened to her?)

"Of course I remember you," said Harriet, "but I'm always so stupid about names. What have you been doing?"

Catherine Freemantle, it seemed, had married a farmer, and everything had gone wrong. Slumps and sickness and tithe and taxes and the Milk Board and the Marketing Board, and working one's fingers to the bone for a bare living and trying to bring up children—Harriet had read and heard enough about agricultural depression to know that the story was a common one enough. She was ashamed of being and looking so prosperous. She felt she would rather be tried for life over again than walk the daily treadmill of Catherine's life. It was a saga, in its way, but it was preposterous. She broke in rather abruptly upon a complaint against the hardheartedness of the Ecclesiastical Commissioners.

"But, Miss Freemantle—I mean, Mrs.—Mrs. Bendick—it's absurd that you should have to do this kind of thing. I mean, pick your own fruit and get up at all hours to feed poultry and slave like a navvy. Surely to goodness it would have paid far better for you to take on some kind of writing or intellectual job and get someone else to do the manual work."

"Yes, it would. But at the beginning I didn't see it like that. I came down with a lot of ideas about the dignity of labour. And besides, at that time, my husband wouldn't have liked it much if I'd separated myself from his interests. Of course, we didn't think it would turn out like this."

What damned waste! was all Harriet could say to herself. All that brilliance, all that trained intelligence, harnessed to a load that any uneducated country girl could have drawn, and drawn far better. The thing had its compensations, she supposed. She asked the question bluntly.

Worth it? said Mrs. Bendick. Oh, yes, it was certainly worth it. The job was worth doing. One was serving the land. And that, she managed to convey, was a service harsh and austere indeed, but a finer thing than spinning words on paper.

"I'm quite prepared to admit that," said Harriet. "A ploughshare is a nobler object than a razor. But if your natural talent is for barbering, wouldn't it be better to *be* a barber, and a good barber—and use the profits (if you like) to speed the plough? However grand the job may be, is it *your* job?"

"It's got to be my job now," said Mrs. Bendick. "One can't go back to things. One gets out of touch and one's brain gets rusty. If you'd spent your time washing and cooking for a family and digging potatoes and feeding cattle, you'd know that that kind of thing takes the edge off the razor. You needn't think I don't envy you people your easy life; I do. I came to the Gaudy out of sentiment, and I wish I'd stopped away. I'm two years older than you, but I look twenty. None of you care in the least for my interests, and yours all seem to me to be mere beating the air. You don't seem to have anything to do with real life. You are going about in a dream." She stopped speaking, and her angry voice softened. "But it's a beautiful dream in its way. It seems queer to me now to think that once I was a scholar . . . I don't know. You may be right after all. Learning and literature have a way of outlasting the civilization that made them."

"The word and nought else
in time endures.
Not you long after,
perished and mute
will last, but the defter
viol and lute,"

quoted Harriet. She stared vaguely out into the sunshine. "It's curious—because I have been thinking exactly the same thing—only in a different connection. Look here! I admire you like hell, but I believe you're all wrong. I'm sure one should do one's own job, however trivial, and not persuade one's self into doing somebody else's, however noble."

As she spoke, she remembered Miss de Vine; here was a new aspect of persuasion.

"That's all very well," replied Mrs. Bendick. "But one's rather apt to marry into somebody else's job."

True; but Harriet was offered the opportunity of marrying into a job as near her own as made no great difference. And into money enough to make any job supererogatory. Again she saw herself unfairly provided with advantages which more deserving people desired in vain.

"I suppose," she said, "marriage is the really important job, isn't it?"

"Yes, it is," said Mrs. Bendick. "My marriage is happy as marriages go. But I often wonder whether my husband wouldn't have been better off with another kind of wife. He never says so, but I wonder. I think he knows I miss—things, and resents it sometimes. I don't know why I should say this to you—I've never said it to anybody and I never knew you very well, did I?"

"No; and I haven't been very sympathetic, either. In fact, I've been disgustingly rude."

"You have, rather," said Mrs. Bendick. "But you have such a beautiful voice to be rude in."

"Good gracious!" said Harriet.

"Our farm's on the Welsh border, and the people all speak in the most hideous local sing-song. Do you know what makes me feel most home-sick here? The cultured speech. The dear old much-abused Oxford accent. That's funny, isn't it?"

"I thought the noise in Hall was more like a cage full of peacocks."

"Yes; but out of Hall you can pick out the people who speak the right way. Lots of them don't, of course; but some do. You do; and you have a lovely voice into the bargain. Do you remember the old Bach Choir days?"

"Do I not. Do you manage to get any music on the Welsh border? The Welsh can sing."

"I haven't much time for music. I try to teach the children."

Harriet took advantage of this opening to make suitable domestic inquiries. She parted eventually from Mrs. Bendick with a depressed feeling that she had seen a Derby winner making shift with a coal-cart.

Sunday lunch in Hall was a casual affair. Many people did not attend it, having engagements in the town. Those who did, dropped in as and when they liked, fetched their food from the serving-hatches and consumed it in chattering groups wherever they could find seats. Harriet, having seized a plate of cold ham for herself, looked round for a lunch partner, and was thankful to see Phoebe Tucker just come in and being helped by the attendant scout to a portion of cold roast beef. The two joined forces, and sat down at the far end of a long table which ran parallel to the High and at right angles to the other tables. From there they commanded the whole room, including the High Table itself and the row of serving-hatches. As her eye wandered from one briskly occupied luncher to the next Harriet kept on asking herself, Which? Which of all these normal and cheerful-looking women had dropped that unpleasant paper in the quad the night before? Because you never knew; and the trouble of not knowing was that you dimly suspected everybody. Haunts of ancient peace were all very well, but very odd things could crawl and creep beneath lichen-covered stones. The Warden in her great carved chair was bending her stately head and smiling at some jest of the Dean's. Miss Lydgate was attending, with eager courtesy, to the wants of a very old student indeed, who was almost blind. She had helped her stumbling feet up the three steps of the dais, fetched her lunch from the hatch and was now putting salad on her plate for her. Miss Stevens the Bursar and Miss Shaw the Modern Language Tutor had collected about them three other old students of considerable age and attainments; their conversation was animated and apparently amusing. Miss Pyke, the Classical Tutor, was deep in a discussion with a tall, robust woman whom Phoebe Tucker had recognized and pointed out to Harriet as an eminent archaeologist, and in a momentary flash of comparative silence, the Tutor's high voice rang out unexpectedly: "The tumulus at Halos appears to be an isolated instance. The cist-graves of Theotokou . . ." Then the clamour again closed over the argument. Two other dons, whom Harriet did not recognize (they were new since her day) appeared from their gestures to be discussing millinery. Miss Hillyard, whose sarcastic tongue tended to isolate her from her colleagues, was slowly eating her lunch and glancing at a pamphlet she had brought in with her. Miss de Vine, arriving late, sat down beside Miss Hillyard and began to consume ham in a detached way with her eyes fixed on vacancy.

Then the Old Students in the body of the Hall—all types, all ages, all varieties of costume. Was it the curious roundshouldered woman in a yellow djibbah and sandals, with her hair coiled in two snail-shells over her ears? Or the sturdy, curly-headed person in tweeds, with a masculine-looking waistcoat and the face like the back of a cab? Or the tightly-corseted peroxide of sixty, whose hat would better have suited an eighteen-year-old debutante at Ascot? Or one of the innumerable women with "school-teacher" stamped on their resolutely cheery countenances? Or the plain person of indeterminate age who sat at the head of her table with the air of a chairman of committee? Or that curious little creature dressed in unbecoming pink, who looked as though she had been carelessly packed away in a drawer all winter and put into circulation again without being ironed? Or that handsome, well-preserved business woman of fifty with the well-manicured hands, who broke into the conversation of total strangers to inform them that she had just opened a new hairdressing establishment "just off Bond Street"? Or that tall, haggard, tragedy-queen in black silk marocain who looked like Hamlet's aunt, but was actually Aunt Beatrice who ran the Household Column in the *Daily Mercury?* Or the bony woman with the long horseface who had devoted herself to Settlement work? Or even that unconquerably merry and bright little dumpling of a creature who was the highly-valued secretary of a political secretary and had secretaries under her? The faces came and went, as though in a dream, all animated, all inscrutable.

Relegated to a remote table at the lower end of the Hall were half-a-dozen present students, still lingering in Oxford for viva voce examinations. They babbled continually among themselves, rather obviously ignoring the invasion of their college by all these quaint old freaks who were what they themselves would be in ten years' time, or twenty or thirty. They were a badly-turned-out bunch, Harriet thought, with an end-of-term crumpled appearance. There was an odd, shy-faced, sandy girl with pale eyes and restless fingers, and next to her a dark, beautiful one, for whose face men might have sacked cities, if it had had any sort of animation; and there was a gawky and unfinished-looking young person, very badly made up, who had a pathetic air of seeking to win hearts and never succeeding; and, most interesting of the bunch a girl with a face like eager flame who was dressed with a maddening perversity of wrongness, but who one day would undoubtedly hold the world in her hands for good or evil. The rest were nondescript, as yet undifferentiated—yet nondescripts, thought Harriet, were the most difficult of all human beings to analyze. You scarcely knew they were there, until—bang! Something quite unexpected blew up like a depth charge and left you marvelling, to collect strange floating débris.

So the Hall seethed, and the scouts looked on impassively from the serving-hatches. "And what they think of us all, God only knows," mused Harriet.

"Are you plotting an exceptionally intricate murder?" demanded Phoebe's voice in her ear. "Or working out a difficult alibi? I've asked you three times to pass the cruet."

"I'm sorry," said Harriet, doing as she was requested. "I was meditating on the impenetrability of the human countenance." She hesitated, on the verge of telling Phoebe about the disagreeable drawing, but her friend went on to ask some other question, and the moment passed by.

But the episode had troubled and unsettled her. Passing through the empty Hall, later in the day, she stopped to stare at the portrait of that Mary, Countess of Shrewsbury, in whose honor the college had been founded. The painting was a well-executed modern copy of the one in St. John's College, Cambridge, and the queer, strong-featured face, with its ill-tempered mouth and sidelong, secretive glance, had always exercised a curious fascination over her—even in her student days, a period when the portraits of dead and gone celebrities exposed in public places incur more sarcastic comment than reverential consideration. She did not know, and indeed had never troubled to inquire, how Shrewsbury College had come to adopt so ominous a patroness. Bess of Hardwick's daughter had been a great intellectual, indeed, but something of a holy terror; uncontrollable by her menfolk, undaunted by the Tower, contemptuously silent before the Privy Council, an obstinate recusant, a staunch friend and implacable enemy and a lady with a turn for invective remarkable even in an age when few mouths suffered from mealiness. She seemed, in fact, to be the epitome of every alarming quality which a learned woman is popularly credited with developing. Her husband, the "great and glorious Earl of Shrewsbury," had purchased domestic peace at a price; for, said Bacon, there was "a greater than he, which is my Lady of Shrewsbury." And that, of course, was a dreadful thing to have said about one. The prospect seemed discouraging for Miss Schuster-Slatt's matrimonial campaign, since the rule seemed to be that a great woman must either die unwed, to Miss Schuster-Slatt's distress, or find a still greater man to marry her. And that limited the great woman's choice considerably, since, though the world of course abounded in great men, it contained a very much larger number of middling and common-place men. The great man, on the other hand, could marry where he liked, not being restricted to great women; indeed, it was often found sweet and commendable in him to choose a woman of no sort of greatness at all.

"Though of course," Harriet reminded herself, "a woman may achieve greatness, or at any rate great renown, by merely being a wonderful wife and mother, like the mother of the Gracchi; whereas the men who have achieved great renown by being devoted husbands and fathers might be counted on the fingers of one hand. Charles I was an unfortunate king, but an admirable family man. Still, you would scarcely class him as one of the world's great fathers, and his children were not an unqualified success. Dear me! Being a great father is either a very difficult or a very sadly unrewarded profession. Wherever you find a great man, you will find a great mother or a great wife standing behind him—or so they used to say. It would be interesting to know how many great women have had great fathers and husbands behind them. An interesting thesis for research. Elizabeth Barrett? Well, she had a great husband, but he was great in his own right so to speak—and Mr. Barrett was not exactly—The Brontes? Well, hardly. Queen Elizabeth? She had a remarkable father, but devoted helpfulness towards his daughters was scarcely his leading characteristic. And she was so wrong-headed as to have no husband. Queen Victoria? You might make a good deal out of poor Albert, but you couldn't do much with the Duke of Kent."

Somebody passed through the Hall behind her; it was Miss Hillyard. With a mischievous determination to get some response out of this antagonistic personality, Harriet laid before her the new idea for a historical thesis.

"You have forgotten physical achievements," said Miss Hillyard. "I believe many female singers, dancers, Channel swimmers and tennis stars owe everything to their devoted fathers."

"But the fathers are not famous."

"No. Self-effacing men are not popular with either sex. I doubt whether even your literary skill would gain recognition for their virtues. Particularly if you select your women for their intellectual qualities. It will be a short thesis in that case."

"Gravelled for lack of matter?"

"I'm afraid so. Do you know any man who sincerely admires a woman for her brains?"

"Well," said Harriet, "certainly not many."

"You may think you know *one*," said Miss Hillyard with a bitter emphasis. "Most of us think at some time or other that we know *one*. But the man usually has some other little axe to grind."

"Very likely," said Harriet. "You don't seem to have a very high opinion of men–of the male character, I mean, as such."

"No," said Miss Hillyard, "not very high. But they have an admirable talent for imposing their point of view on society in general. All women are sensitive to male criticism. Men are not sensitive to female criticism. They despise the critics."

"Do you, personally, despise male criticism?"

"Heartily," said Miss Hillyard. "But it does damage. Look at this University. All the men have been amazingly kind and sympathetic about the Women's Colleges. Certainly. But you won't find them appointing women to big University posts. That would never do. The women might perform their work in a way beyond criticism. But they are quite pleased to see us playing with our little toys."

"Excellent fathers and family men," murmured Harriet.

"In that sense–yes," said Miss Hillyard, and laughed rather unpleasantly.

Something funny there, thought Harriet. A personal history, probably. How difficult it was not to be embittered by personal experience. She went down to the J.C.R. and examined herself in the mirror. There had been a look in the History Tutor's eyes that she did not wish to discover in her own.

Sunday evening prayers. The College was undenominational, but some form of Christian worship was held to be essential to community life. The chapel, with its stained glass windows, plain oak panelling and unadorned Communion Table was a kind of Lowest Common Multiple of all sects and creeds. Harriet, making her way towards it, remembered that she had not seen her gown since the previous afternoon, when the Dean had taken it to the S.C.R. Not liking to penetrate uninvited into that Holy of Holies, she went in search of Miss Martin, who had, it appeared, taken both gowns together to her own room. Harriet wriggled into the gown, one fluttering sleeve of which struck an adjacent table with a loud bang.

"Mercy!" said the Dean, "what's that?"

"My cigarette-case," said Harriet. "I thought I'd lost it. I remember now. I hadn't a pocket yesterday, so I shoved it into the sleeve of my gown. After all, that's what these sleeves are for, aren't they?"

"Oh, my dear! Mine are always a perfect dirty-clothes bag by the end of term. When I have absolutely *no* clean handkerchiefs left in the drawer, my scout turns out my gown sleeves. My best collection worked out at twenty-two—but then I'd had a bad cold one week. Dreadful insanitary garments. Here's your cap. Never mind taking your hood—you can come back here for it. What have you been doing today?—I've scarcely seen you."

Again Harriet felt an impulse to mention the unpleasant drawing, but again she refrained. She felt she was getting rather unbalanced about it. Why think about it at all? She mentioned her conversation with Miss Hillyard.

"Lor'!" said the Dean. "That's Miss Hillyard's hobby-horse. Rubbidge, as Mrs. Gamp would say. Of *course* men don't like having their poor little noses put out of joint—who does? I think it's perfectly noble of them to let us come trampling over their University at all, bless their hearts. They've heen used to being lords and masters for hundreds of years and they want a bit of time to get used to the change. Why, it takes a man months and *months* to reconcile himself to a new hat. And *just* when you're preparing to send it to the jumble sale, he says, 'That's rather a nice hat you've got on, where did you get it?' And you say, 'My dear Henry, it's the one I had last year and you said made me look like an organ-grinder's monkey.' My brother-in-law says that *every* time, and it does make my sister so wild."

They mounted the steps of the chapel.

It had not, after all, been so bad. Definitely not so bad as one had expected. Though it was melancholy to find that one had grown out of Mary Stokes, and a little tiresome, in a way, that Mary Stokes refused to recognize the fact. Harriet had long ago discovered that one could not like people any the better, merely because they were ill, or dead—still less because one had once liked them very much. Some happy souls could go through life without making this discovery, and they were the men and women who were called "sincere." Still, there remained old friends whom one was glad to meet again, like the Dean and Phoebe Tucker. And really, everybody had been quite extraordinarily decent. Rather inquisitive and silly about "the man Wimsey," some of them, but no doubt with the best intentions. Miss Hillyard might be an exception, but there had always been something a little twisted and uncomfortable about Miss Hillyard.

As the car wound its way over the Chilterns, Harriet grinned to herself, thinking of her parting conversation with the Dean and Bursar.

"Be sure and write us a new book soon. And remember, if ever we get a mystery at Shrewsbury we shall call upon you to come and disentangle it."

"All right," said Harriet. "When you find a mangled corpse in the buttery, send me a wire'—and be sure you let Miss Barton view the body, and then she won't so much mind my haling the murderess off to justice."

And suppose they actually did find a bloody corpse in the buttery, how surprised they would all be. The glory of a college was that nothing drastic ever happened in it. The most frightful thing that was ever likely to happen was that an undergraduate should "take the wrong turning." The purloining of a parcel or two by a porter had been enough to throw the whole Senior Common Room into consternation. Bless their hearts, how refreshing and soothing and good they all were, walking beneath their ancient beeches and meditating on 'òv xaì uǹ 'òv and the finance of Queen Elizabeth.

"I've broken the ice," she said aloud, "and the water wasn't so cold after all. I shall go back, from time to time. I shall go back."

She picked out a pleasant pub for lunch and ate with a good appetite. Then she remembered that her cigarette-case was still in her gown. She had brought the garment in with her on her arm, and, thrusting her hand down to the bottom of the long sleeve, she extracted the case. A piece of paper came out with it–an ordinary sheet of scribbling paper folded into four. She frowned at a disagreeable memory as she unfolded it.

There was a message pasted across it, made up of letters cut apparently from the headlines of a newspaper.

YOU DIRTY MURDERESS. AREN'T YOU
ASHAMED TO SHOW YOUR FACE?

"Hell!" said Harriet. "Oxford, thou too?" She sat very still for a few moments. Then she struck a match and set light to the paper. It burned briskly, till she was forced to drop it upon her plate. Even then, the letters showed grey upon the crackling blackness, until she pounded their spectral shapes to powder with the back of a spoon.

## 4

Thou canst not, Love, disgrace me half so ill,
  To set a form upon desired change,
As I'll myself disgrace: knowing thy will,
  I will acquaintance strangle and look strange,
Be absent from thy walks, and in my tongue
  My sweet beloved name no more shall dwell,
Lest I, too much profane, should do it wrong
  And haply of our old acquaintance tell.
William Shakespeare

THERE ARE incidents in one's life which, through some haphazard coincidence of time and mood, acquire a symbolic value. Harriet's attendance at the Shrewsbury Gaudy was of this kind. In spite of minor incongruities and absurdities, it had shown itself to have one definite significance; it had opened up to her the vision of an old desire, long obscured by a forest of irrelevant fancies, but now standing up unmistakable, like a tower set on a hill. Two phrases rang in her ears: the Dean's, "It's the work you're doing that really counts"; and that one melancholy lament for eternal loss: "Once, I was a scholar."

"Time is," quoth the Brazen Head; "time was; time is past." Philip Boyes was dead; and the nightmares that had haunted the ghastly midnight of his passing were gradually fading away. Clinging on, by blind instinct, to the job that had to be done, she had fought her way back to an insecure stability. Was it too late to achieve wholly the clear eye and the untroubled mind? And what, in that case, was she to do with one powerful fetter which still tied her ineluctably to the bitter past? What about Peter Wimsey?

During the past three years, their relations had been peculiar. Immediately after the horrible business that they had investigated together at Wilvercombe, Harriet–feeling that something must be done to ease a situation which was fast becoming intolerable–had carried out a long-cherished scheme, now at last made practicable by her increasing reputation and income as a writer. Taking a woman friend with her as companion and secretary, she had left England, and travelled slowly about Europe, staying now here, now there, as fancy dictated or a good background presented itself for a story. Financially the trip had been a success. She had gathered material for two full-length novels, the scenes laid respectively in Madrid and Carcassonne, and written a series of short stories dealing with detective adventures in Hitlerite Berlin, and also a number of travel articles; thus more than replenishing the treasury. Before her departure, she had asked Wimsey not to write. He had taken the prohibition with unexpected meekness.

"I see. Very well. *Vade in pace*. If you ever want me, you will find the Old Firm at the usual stand."

She had occasionally seen his name in the English papers, and that was all. At the beginning of the following June, she had returned home, feeling that, after so long a break, there should be little difficulty in bringing the relationship to a cool and friendly close. By this time he was probably feeling as much settled and relieved as she was. As soon as she got back to London, she moved to a new flat in Mecklenburg Square, and settled down to work at the Carcassonne novel.

A trifling incident, soon after her return, gave her the opportunity to test her own reactions. She went down to Ascot, in company with a witty young woman writer and her barrister husband—partly for fun and partly because she wanted to get local color for a short story, in which an unhappy victim was due to fall suddenly dead in the Royal Enclosure, just at the exciting moment when all eyes were glued upon the finish of a race. Scanning those sacred precincts, therefore, from without the pale, Harriet became aware that the local colour included a pair of slim shoulders tailored to swooning-point and carrying a well-known parrot profile, thrown into prominence by the acute backward slant of a pale-grey topper. A froth of summer hats billowed about this apparition, so that it resembled a slightly grotesque but expensive orchid in a bouquet of roses. From the expressions of the parties, Harriet gathered that the summer hats were picking long-priced and impossible outsiders, and that the topper was receiving their instructions with an amusement amounting to hilarity. At any rate, his attention was well occupied.

"Excellent," thought Harriet; "nothing to trouble about there." She came home rejoicing in the exceptional tranquility of her own spirits. Three days later, while reading in the morning paper that among the guests at a literary luncheon-party had been seen "Miss Harriet Vane, the well-known detective authoress," she was interrupted by the telephone. A familiar voice said, with a curious huskiness and uncertainty :

"Miss Harriet Vane? . . . Is that you, Harriet? I saw you were back. Will you dine with me one evening?"

There were several possible answers; among them, the repressive and disconcerting "*Who* is that speaking, please?" Being unprepared and naturally honest, Harriet feebly replied :

"Oh, thank you, Peter. But I don't know whether . . ."

"What?" said the voice, with a hint of mockery. "*Every* night booked from now till the coming of the Coqcigrues?"

"Of course not," said Harriet, not at all willing to pose as the swollen-headed and much-run-after celebrity.

"Then say when."

"I'm free tonight," said Harriet, thinking that the shortness of the notice might force him to plead a previous engagement.

"Admirable," said he. "So am I. We will taste the sweets of freedom. By the way, you have changed your telephone number."

"Yes; I've got a new flat."

"Shall I call for you? Or will you meet me at Ferrara's at 7 o'clock?"

"At Ferrara's?"

"Yes. Seven o'clock, if that's not too early. Then we can go on to a show, if you care about it. Till this evening, then. Thank you."

He hung up the receiver before she had time to protest. Ferrara's was not the place she would have chosen. It was both fashionable and conspicuous. Everybody who could get there, went there; but its charges were so high that, for the present at least, it could afford not to be crowded. That meant that if you went there you were seen. If one intended to break off a connection with anyone, it was perhaps not the best opening move to *afficher* one's self with him at Ferrara's.

Oddly enough, this would be the first time she had dined in the West End with Peter Wimsey. During the first year or so after her trial, she had not wanted to appear anywhere, even had she then been able to afford the frocks to appear in. In those days, he had taken her to the quieter and better restaurants in Soho, or, more often, carried her off, sulky and rebellious, in the car to such roadside inns as kept reliable cooks. She had been too listless to refuse these outings, which had probably done something to keep her from brooding, even though her host's imperturbable cheerfulness had often been repaid only with bitter or distressful words. Looking back, she was as much amazed by his patience as fretted by his persistence.

He received her at Ferrara's with the old, quick, sidelong smile and ready speech, but with a more formal courtesy than she remembered in him. He listened with interest, and indeed with eagerness, to the tale of her journeyings abroad; and she found (as was to be expected) that the map of Europe was familiar ground to him. He contributed a few amusing incidents from his own experience, and added some well-informed comments on the conditions of life in modern Germany. She was surprised to find him so closely acquainted with the ins-and-outs of international politics, for she had not credited him with any great interest in public affairs. She found herself arguing passionately with him about the prospects of the Ottawa Conference, of which he appeared to entertain no very great hopes; and by the time they got to the coffee she was so eager to disabuse his mind of some perverse opinions about Disarmament that she had quite forgotten with what intentions (if any) she had come to meet him. In the theatre she contrived to remind herself from time to time that something decisive ought to be said; but the conversational atmosphere remained so cool that it was difficult to introduce the new subject.

The play being over, he put her into a taxi, asked what address he should give the driver, requested formal permission to see her home and took his seat beside her. This, to be sure, was the moment; but he was babbling pleasantly about the Georgian architecture of London. It was only as they were running along Guilford Street that he forestalled her by saying (after a pause, during which she had been making up her mind to take the plunge) :

"I take it, Harriet, that you have no new answer to give me?"

"No, Peter. I'm sorry, but I can't say anything else."

"All right. Don't worry. I'll try not to be a nuisance. But if you could put up with me occasionally, as you have done tonight, I should be very grateful to you."

"I don't think that would be at all fair to you."

"If that's the only reason, I am the best judge of that." Then, with a return of his habitual self-mockery: "Old habits die hard. I will not promise to reform altogether. I shall, with your permission, continue to propose to you, at decently regulated intervals—as a birthday treat, and on Guy Fawkes Day and on the Anniversary of the King's Accession. But consider it, if you will, as a pure formality. You need not pay the smallest attention to it."

"Peter, it's foolish to go on like this."

"And, of course, on the Feast of All Fools."

"It would be better to forget all about it—I hoped you had."

"I have the most ill-regulated memory. It does those things which it ought not to do and leaves undone the things it ought to have done. But it has not yet gone on strike altogether."

The taxi drew up, and the driver peered round inquiringly. Wimsey handed her out and waited gravely while she disentangled her latch-key. Then he took it from her, opened the door for her, said good-night and was gone.

Mounting the stone staircase, she knew that, as far as this situation was concerned, her flight had been useless. She was back in the old net of indecision and distress. In him, it appeared to have worked some kind of change; but it had certainly not made him any easier to deal with.

He had kept his promise, and troubled her very little. He had been out of Town a good deal, hard at work upon cases, some of which trickled through into newspaper columns, while others appeared to settle themselves in discreet obscurity. For six months he had himself been out of the country, offering no explanation except "business." One summer, he had been involved in an odd affair, which had led him to take a post in an Advertising Agency. He had found office life entertaining; but the thing had come to a strange and painful conclusion. There had been an evening when he had turned up to keep a previously-made dinner appointment, but had obviously been unfit either to eat or talk. Eventually he had confessed to a splitting headache and a temperature and suffered himself to be personally conducted home. She had been sufficiently alarmed not to leave him till he was safely in his own flat and in the capable hands of Bunter. The latter had been reassuring: the trouble was nothing but reaction—of frequent occurrence at the end of a trying case, but soon over. A day or two later, the patient had rung up, apologized, and made a fresh appointment, at which he had displayed a quite remarkable effervescence of spirits.

On no other occasion had Harriet ever passed his threshold. Nor had he ever violated the seclusion of Mecklenburg Square. Two or three times, courtesy had moved her to invite him in; but he had always made some excuse, and she understood that he was determined to leave her that place, at least, free from any awkward associations. It was clear that he had no fatuous intention of making himself more valued by withdrawal: he had rather the air of trying to make amends for something. He renewed his offer of marriage on an average once in three months, but in such a way as to afford no excuse for any outbreak of temperament on either side. One First of April, the question had arrived from Paris in a single Latin sentence, starting off dispiritedly. "Num . . . ?"—a particle which notoriously "expects the answer No." Harriet rummaging the Grammar book for "polite negatives," replied, still more briefly, "Benigne."

Looking back upon her visit to Oxford, Harriet found that it had had an unsettling effect. She had begun to take Wimsey for granted, as one might take dynamite for granted in a munitions factory. But the discovery that the mere sound of his name still had the power to provoke such explosions in herself—that she could so passionately resent, at one and the same time, either praise or blame of him on other people's lips—awakened a misgiving that dynamite was perhaps still dynamite, however harmless it might come to look through long custom.

On the mantelpiece of her sitting-room stood a note, in Peter's small and rather difficult writing. It informed her that he had been called away by Chief-Inspector Parker, who was in difficulties over a murder in the north of England. He must therefore regretfully cancel their appointment for that week. Could she oblige him by making use of the tickets, of which he had no time to dispose otherwise?

Harriet pinched her lips over that last cautious sentence. Ever since one frightful occasion, during the first year of their acquaintance, when he had ventured to send her a Christmas present and she, in an access of mortified pride, had returned it to him with a stinging rebuke, he had been careful never to offer her anything that could possibly be looked upon as a material gift. Had he been wiped out of existence at any moment, there was nothing among her possessions to remind her of him. She now took up the tickets and hesitated over them. She could give them away, or she could go herself and take a friend. On the whole, she thought she would rather not sit through the performance with a kind of Banquo's ghost disputing possession of the next stall with somebody else. She put the tickets in an envelope, dispatched them to the married couple who had taken her to Ascot, and then tore the note across and deposited it in the wastepaper basket. Having thus disposed of Banquo, she breathed more freely, and turned to deal with the day's next nuisance.

This was the revision of three of her books for a new edition. The rereading of one's own works is usually a dismal matter; and when she had completed her task she felt thoroughly jaded and displeased with herself. The books were all right, as far as they went; as intellectual exercises, they were even brilliant. But there was something lacking about them; they read now to her as though they had been written with a mental reservation, a determination to keep her own opinions and personality out of view. She considered with distaste a clever and superficial discussion between two of the characters about married life. She could have made a much better thing of that, if she had not been afraid of giving herself away. What hampered her was this sense of being in the middle of things, too close to things, pressed upon and bullied by reality. If she could succeed in standing aside from herself she would achieve self-confidence and a better control. That was the great possession in which—with all his limitations—the scholar could account himself blessed: the single eye, directed to the object, not dimmed nor distracted by private motes and beams. "Private, indeed?" muttered Harriet to herself, as she smacked her proofs irritably into brown paper.

"*You not alone, when you are still alone,*
*O God, from you that I could private be!*"

She was exceedingly glad that she had got rid of the theatre tickets.

So that when Wimsey eventually got back from his expedition north, she went to meet him in a belligerent spirit. He had asked her to dine with him, this time, at the Egotists' Club—an unusual venue. It was a Sunday night and they had the room to themselves. She mentioned her Oxford visit and took the opportunity to recite to him a list of promising scholars, distinguished in their studies and subsequently extinguished by matrimony. He agreed mildly that such things did happen, far too often, and instanced a very brllliant painter who, urged on by a socially ambitious wife, had now become a slick machine for the production of Academy portraits.

"Sometimes, of course," he went on dispassionately, "the partner is merely jealous or selfish. But half the time it's sheer stupidity. They don't mean it. It's surprisin' how few people ever mean anything definite from one year's end to the other."

"I don't think they could help it, whatever they meant. It's the pressure of other people's personalities that does the mischief."

"Yes. Best intentions no security. They never are, of course. You may say you won't interfere with another person's soul, but you do—merely by existing. The snag about it is the practical difficulty, so to speak, of not existing. I mean, here we all are, you know, and what are we to do about it?"

"Well, I suppose some people feel themselves called to make personal relationships their life-work. If so, it's all right for them. But what about the others?"

"Tiresome, isn't it?" he said, with a gleam of amusement that annoyed her. "Do you think they ought to cut out human contacts altogether? It's not easy. There's always the butcher or the baker or the landlady or somebody one has to wrestle with. Or should the people with brains sit tight and let the people with hearts look after them?"

"They frequently do."

"So they do." For the fifth time he summoned the waiter to pick up Harriet's napkin for her. "Why do geniuses make bad husbands, and all that? But what are you going to do about the people who are cursed with both hearts and brains?"

"I'm sorry I keep on dropping things; this silk's so slippery. Well, that's just the problem, isn't it? I'm beginning to believe they've got to choose."

"Not compromise?"

"I don't think the compromise works."

"That I should live to hear any person of English blood blaspheme against compromise!"

"Oh, I'm not all English. I've got some bits of Scotch and Irish tucked away somewhere."

"That proves you're English. No other race ever boasts of being mongrel. I'm quite offensively English myself, because I'm one-sixteenth French, besides all the usual nationalities. So that compromise is in my blood. However. Should you catalogue me as a heart or a brain?"

"Nobody," said Harriet, "could deny your brain."

"Who denies of it? And you may deny my heart, but I'm damned if you shall deny its existence."

"You argue like an Elizabethan wit—two meanings under one word."

"It was your word. You will have to deny something, if you intend to be like Caesar's sacrifice."

"Caesar's . . . ?"

"A beat without a heart. Has your napkin gone again?"

"No—it's my bag this time. It's just under your left foot."

"Oh!" He looked round, but the waiter had vanished. "Well," he went on, without moving, "it is the heart's office to wait upon the brain, but in view of–"

"Please don't trouble," said Harriet, "it doesn't matter in the least."

"In view of the fact that I've got two cracked ribs, I'd better not try; because if I once got down I should probably never get up again."

"Good gracious!" said Harriet. "I thought you seemed a little stiff in your manner. Why on earth didn't you say so before, instead of sitting there like a martyr and inveigling me into misjudging you?"

"I don't seem able to do anything right," he said plaintively.

"How did you manage to do it?"

"Fell off a wall in the most inartistic manner. I was in a bit of a hurry; there was a very plain-looking bloke on the other side with a gun. It wasn't so much the wall, as the wheelbarrow at the bottom. And it isn't really so much the ribs as the sticking-plaster. It's strapped as tight as hell and itches infernally."

"How beastly for you. I'm so sorry. What became of the bloke with the gun?"

"Ah! I'm afraid personal complications won't trouble him any longer."

"If the luck had been the other way, I suppose they wouldn't have troubled *you* any longer?"

"Probably not. And then I shouldn't have troubled *you* any longer. If my mind had been where my heart was, I might have welcomed that settlement. But my mind being momentarily on my job, I ran away with the greatest rapidity, so as to live to finish the case."

"Well, I'm glad of that, Peter."

"Are you? That shows how hard it is for even the most powerful brain to be completely heartless. Let me see. It is not my day for asking you to marry me, and a few yards of sticking plaster are hardly enough to make it a special occasion. But we'll have coffee in the lounge, if you don't mind, because this chair is getting as hard as the wheelbarrow, and seems to be catching me in several of the same places."

He got up cautiously. The waiter arrived and restored Harriet's bag, together with some letters which she had taken from the postman as she left the house and thrust into the outer pocket of the bag without reading. Wimsey steered his guest into the lounge, established her in a chair and lowered himself with a grimace into one corner of a low couch.

"Rather a long way down, isn't it?"

"It's all right when you get there. Sorry to be always presenting myself in such a decrepit state. I do it on purpose, of course, to attract attention and awaken sympathy; but I'm afraid the manoeuvre's getting rather obvious. Would you like a liqueur with the coffee or a brandy? Two old brandies, James."

"Very good, my lord. This was found under the table in the dining room, madam."

"More of your scattered belongings?" said Wimsey, as she took the postcard; then, seeing her flush and frown of disgust, "What is it?"

"Nothing," said Harriet, pushing the ugly scrawl into her bag.

He looked at her.

"Do you often get that kind of thing?"

"What kind of thing?"

"Anonymous dirt."

"Not very often now. I got one at Oxford. But they used to come by every post. Don't worry; I'm used to it. I only wish I'd looked at it before I got here.

It's horrible of me to have dropped it about your club for the servants to read."

"Careless little devil, aren't you? May I see it?"

"No, Peter; please."

"Give it to me."

She handed it to him without looking up. "*Ask your boy friend with the title if he likes arsenic in his soup. What did you give him to get you off?*" it inquired, disagreeably.

"God, what muck!" said he, bitterly. "So that's what I'm letting you in for. I might have known it. I could hardly hope that it wasn't so. But you said nothing, so I allowed myself to be selfish."

"It doesn't matter. It's just part of the consequences. You can't do anything about it."

"I might have the consideration not to expose you to it. Heaven knows you've tried hard enough to get rid of me. In fact, I think you've used every possible lever to dislodge me, except that one."

"Well, I knew you would hate it so. I didn't want to hurt you."

"Didn't want to *hurt* me?"

She realized that this, to him, must sound completely lunatic.

"I mean that, Peter. I know I've said about every damnable thing to you that I could think of. But I have my limits." A sudden wave of anger surged up in her. "My God, do you really think that of me? Do you suppose there's no meanness I wouldn't stoop to?"

"You'd have been perfectly justified in telling me that I was making things more difficult for you by hanging round."

"Should I? Did you expect me to tell you that you were compromising my reputation, when I had none to compromise? To point out that you'd saved me from the gallows, thank you very much, but left me in the pillory? To say, my name's mud, but kindly treat it as lilies? I'm not quite such a hypocrite as that."

"I see. The plain fact is, that I am doing nothing but make life a little bitterer for you. It was generous of you not to say so."

"Why did you insist on seeing that thing?"

"Because," he said, striking a match and holding the flame to a corner of the postcard, "while I am quite ready to take flight from plug-uglies with guns, I prefer to look other kinds of trouble in the face." He dropped the burning paper on to the tray and crushed the ashes together, and she was again reminded of the message she had found in her sleeve. "You have nothing to reproach yourself with—you didn't tell me this; I found it out for myself. I will admit defeat and say good-bye. Shall I?"

The club waiter set down the brandies. Harriet, with her eyes on her own hands, sat plaiting her fingers together. Peter watched her for some minutes, and then said gently:

"Don't look so tragic about it. The coffee's getting cold. After all, you know, I have the consolation that 'not you but Fate has vanquished me.' I shall emerge with my vanity intact, and that's something."

"Peter. I'm afraid I'm not very consistent. I came here tonight with the firm intention of telling you to chuck it. But I'd rather fight my own battles. I—I—" she looked up and went on rather quaveringly—"I'm *damned* if I'll have you wiped out by plug-uglies or anonymous letter writers!"

He sat up sharply, so that his exclamation of pleasure turned half-way into an anguished grunt.

"Oh, curse this sticking-plaster! . . . Harriet, you have got guts, haven't you? Give me your hand, and we'll fight on until we drop. Here! none of that. You can't cry in this club. It's never been done, and if you disgrace me like this, I shall get into a row with the Committee. They'll probably close the Ladies' Rooms altogether."

"I'm sorry, Peter."

"And *don't* put sugar in my coffee."

Later in the evening, having lent a strong arm to extricate him, swearing loudly, from the difficult depths of the couch, and dispatched him to such rest as he might reasonably look for between the pains of love and sticking-plaster, she had leisure to reflect that if fate had vanquished either of them it was not Peter Wimsey. He knew too well the wrestler's trick of letting the adversary's own strength defeat itself. Yet she knew with certainty that if, when he had said, "Shall I go?" she had replied with firm kindness, "I'm sorry, but I think it would be better," there would have been the desired end of the matter.

"I wish," she said to the friend of the European trip, "he would take a firm line of some kind."

"But he has," replied the friend, who was a clear-headed Person. "He knows what he wants. The trouble is that you don't. I know it isn't pleasant putting an end to things, but I don't see why he should do all your dirty work for you, particularly as he doesn't want it done. As for anonymous letters, it seems to me quite ridiculous to pay any attention to them."

It was easy for the friend to say this, having no vulnerable points in her brisk and hard-working life.

"Peter says I ought to get a secretary and have them weeded out."

"Well," said the friend, "that's a practical suggestion, anyway. But I suppose, since it's his advice, you'll find some ingenious reason for not taking it."

"I'm not as bad as that," said Harriet; and engaged the secretary.

So matters went on for some months. She made no further effort to discuss the conflicting claims of heart and brain. That line of talk led to a perilous exchange of personalities, in which he, with a livelier wit and better self-control, could always drive her into a corner without exposing himself. It was only by sheer brutal hacking that she could beat down his guard; and she was beginning to be afraid of those impulses to savagery.

She heard no news of Shrewsbury College in the interval, except that one day in the Michaelmas Term there was a paragraph in one of the more foolish London dailies about an "Undergraduettes' Rag," informing the world that somebody had made a bonfire of gowns in Shrewsbury Quad and that the "Lady Head" was said to be taking disciplinary measures. Women, of course, were always news. Harriet wrote a tart letter to the paper, pointing out that either "undergraduate" or "woman student" would be seemlier English than "undergraduette," and that the correct method of describing Dr. Baring was "the Warden." The only result of this was to provoke a correspondence headed "Lady Undergrads," and a reference to "sweet girl-graduates."

She informed Wimsey—who happened to be the nearest male person handy for scarifying—that this kind of vulgarity was typical of the average man's attitude to women's intellectual interests. He replied that bad manners always made him sick; but was it any worse than headlining foreign monarchs by their Christian names, untitled?

About three weeks before the end of the Easter term, however, Harriet's attention was again called to college affairs in a way that was more personal and more disquieting.

February was sobbing and blustering its lachrymose way into March, when she received a letter from the Dean.

My dear Miss Vane,

I am writing to ask you whether you will be able to get up to Oxford for the opening of the New Library Wing by the Chancellor next Thursday. This, as you know, has always been the date for the official opening, though we had hoped that the buildings themselves would be ready for habitation at the beginning of this term. However, what with a dispute in the contractors' firm, and the unfortunate illness of the architect, we got badly held up, so that we shall only *just* be ready in time. In fact, the interior decoration of the ground floor isn't finished *yet*.—Still, we couldn't very well ask Lord Oakapple to change the date, as he is such a busy man; and after all, the Library is the chief thing, and not the Fellows' sets, however badly they may need a home to go to, poor dears.

We are particularly anxious—I am speaking for Dr. Baring as well as myself—that you should come, if you *can* manage to find time (though of course you have a lot of engagements). We should be very glad to have your advice about a most unpleasant thing that has been happening here. Not that one expects a detective novelist to be a practical policeman; but I know you have taken part in one real investigation, and I feel sure you know a lot more than we do about tracking down malefactors.

Don't think we are all getting murdered in our beds! In some ways I'm not sure that a "nice, clean murder" wouldn't be easier to deal with! The fact is, we are being victimized by a cross between a Poltergeist and a Poison-Pen, and you can imagine how disgusting it is for everybody. It seems that the letters started coming some time ago, but at first nobody took much notice. I suppose everyone gets vulgar anonymous communications from time to time; and though some of the beastly things didn't come by post, there's nothing in a place like this to prevent an outsider from dropping them at the Lodge or even inside the College. But wanton destruction of property is a different matter, and the last outbreak has been so abominable that something really must be done about it. Poor Miss Lydgate's *English Prosody*—you saw that colossal work in progress—has been defaced and mutilated in the most *revolting* manner, and some important manuscript portions completely destroyed, so that they will have to be done all over again. She was almost in tears, poor dear—and the alarming thing is that it now looks as though somebody in college *must* be responsible. We suppose that some student must have a grudge against the S.C.R.—but it must be more than a grudge—it must be a very horrid kind of pottiness.

One can scarcely call in the police—if you'd seen some of the letters you'd realize that the less publicity the better, and you know how things get about. I dare say you noticed there was a wretched newspaper paragraph about that bonfire in the quad last November. We never discovered who did that, by the way; we thought, naturally, it was a stupid practical joke; but we are now beginning to wonder whether it wasn't all part of the same campaign.

So if you could possibly snatch time to give us the benefit of your experience, we should be exceedingly grateful. There must he *some* way of coping—this sort of persecution simply CAN'T GO ON. But it's an awfully difficult job to pin anything down in a place like this, with 150 students and all doors open everywhere night and day.

I am afraid this is rather an incoherent letter, but I'm feeling *that* put about, with the Opening looming ahead and *all* the entrance and scholarship papers blowing about me like leaves in Vallombrosa! Hoping very much to see you next Thursday,

Yours very sincerely,

LETITIA MARTIN

Here was a pretty thing! Just the kind of thing to do the worst possible damage to University women–not only in Oxford, but everywhere. In any community, of course, one always ran the risk of harbouring somebody undesirable; but parents obviously would not care to send their young innocents to places where psychological oddities flourished unchecked. Even if the poison campaign led to no open disaster (and you never knew what people might be driven to under Persecution) a washing of dirty linen in public was not calculated to do Shrewsbury any good. Because, though nine-tenths of the mud might be thrown at random, the remaining tenth might quite easily be, as it usually was, dredged from the bottom of the well of truth, and would stick.

Who should know that better than herself? She smiled wryly over the Dean's letter. "The benefit of your experience"; yes, indeed. The words had, of course, been written in the most perfect innocence, and with no suspicion that they could make the galled jade wince. Miss Martin herself would never dream of writing abusive letters to a person who had been acquitted of murder, and it had undoubtedly never occurred to her that to ask the notorious Miss Vane for advice about how to deal with that kind of thing was to talk of rope in the house of the hanged. This was merely an instance of that kind of unworldly tactlessness to which learned and cloistered women were prone. The Dean would be horrified to know that Harriet was the last person who should, in charity, have been approached in the matter; and that, even in Oxford itself, in Shrewsbury College itself–

In Shrewsbury College itself: and at the Gaudy. That was the point. The letter she had found in her sleeve had been put there in Shrewsbury College *and at the Gaudy*. Not only that; there had been the drawing she had picked up in the quad. Was either, or were both of these, part only of her own miserable quarrel with the world? Or were they rather to be connected with the subsequent outbreak in the college itself? It seemed unlikely that Shrewsbury should have to harbour *two* dirty-minded lunatics in such quick succession. But if the two lunatics were one and the same lunatic, then the implication was an alarming one, and she herself must, at all costs, interfere at least so far as to tell what she knew. There did come moments when all personal feelings had to be set aside in the interests of public service; and this looked like being one of them.

Reluctantly, she reached for the telephone and put a call through to Oxford. While she waited for it, she thought the matter over in this new light. The Dean had given no details about the poison letters, except that they suggested a grudge against the S.C.R. and that the culprit appeared to belong to the college. It was natural enough to attribute destructive ragging to the undergraduates; but then, the Dean did not know what Harriet knew. The warped and repressed mind is apt enough to turn and wound itself. "Soured virginity"–"unnatural life"–"semi-demented spinsters"–"starved appetites and suppressed impulses"–"unwholesome atmosphere"–she could think of whole sets of epithets, ready-minted for circulation. Was this what lived in the tower set on the hill? Would it turn out to be like Lady Athaliah's tower in

*Frolic Wind*, the home of frustration and perversion and madness? "If thine eye be single, the whole body is full of light"—but was it physically possible to have the single eye? "What are you to do with the people who are cursed with both hearts and brains?" For them, stereoscopic vision was probably a necessity; as for whom was it not? (This was a foolish play on words, but it meant something.) Well, then, what about this business of choosing one way of life? Must one, after all, seek a compromise, merely to preserve one's sanity? Then one was doomed for ever to this miserable inner warfare, with confused noise and garments rolled in blood —and, she reflected drearily, with the usual war aftermath of a debased coinage, a lowered efficiency and unstable conditions of government.

At this point the Oxford call came through, with the Dean's voice sounding full of agitation. Harriet, after hurriedly disclaiming all pretence to detective ability in real life, expressed concern and sympathy and then asked the question that, to her, was of prime importance.

"How are the letter's written?"

"That's *just* the difficulty. They're mostly done by pasting together bits out of newspapers. So, you see, there's no handwriting to identify."

That seemed to settle it; there were not two anonymous correspondents, but only one. Very well, then:

"Are they merely obscene, or are they abusive or threatening too?"

"All three. Calling people names that poor Miss Lydgate didn't know existed—the worst she knows being Restoration Drama—and threatening everything from public exposure to the gallows."

Then the tower was Lady Athaliah's tower.

"Are they sent to anybody besides the S.C.R.?"

"It's difficult to say, because people don't always come and tell you things. But I believe one or two of the students here have had them."

"And they come sometimes by post and sometimes to the Lodge?"

"Yes. And they are beginning to come out on the walls now, and lately they've been pushed under people's doors at night. So it looks as though it *must* be somebody in college."

"When did you get the first one?"

"The first one I *definitely* know about was sent to Miss de Vine last Michaelmas Term. That was her first term here, and of course, she thought it must be somebody who had a personal grudge against her. But several people got them shortly afterwards, so we decided it couldn't be that. We'd never had anything of that sort happening before, so just at present we're inclined to check up on the First Year students."

The one set of people that it can't possibly be, thought Harriet. She only said however:

"It doesn't do to take too much for granted. People may go on quite all right for a time, till something sets them off. The whole difficulty with these things is that the person generally behaves quite normally in other respects. It might be anybody."

"That's true. I suppose it might even be one of ourselves. That's what's so horrible. Yes, I know—elderly virgins, and all that. It's awful to know that at any minute one may be sitting cheek by jowl with somebody who feels like that. Do you think the poor creature knows that she does it herself? I've been waking up with nightmares, wondering whether I didn't perhaps prowl round in my sleep, spitting at people. And, my dear! I'm so terrified about next week! Poor Lord Oakapple, coming to open the Library, with venomous asps simply *dripping* poison over his boots! Suppose they send *him* something!"

"Well," said Harriet, "I think I'll come along next week. There's a very good reason why I'm not quite the right person to handle this, but on the other hand, I think I ought to come. I'll tell you why when we meet."

"It's terribly good of you. I'm sure you'll be able to suggest something. I suppose you'll want to see all the specimens there are. Yes? Very well. Every fragment shall be cherished next our hearts. Do we handle them with the tongs for the better preservation of finger-prints?"

Harriet doubted whether finger-prints would be of much service, but advised that precautions should be taken on principle. When she had rung off, with the Dean's reiterated thanks still echoing from the other end of the line, she sat for a few moments with the receiver in her hand. Was there any quarter to which she might usefully turn for advice? There was; but she was not eager to discuss the subject of anonymous letters, still less the question of what lived in academic towers. She hung up resolutely, and pushed the instrument away.

She woke next morning with a change of heart. She had said that personal feeling ought not to stand in the way of public utility. And it should not. If Wimsey could be made useful to Shrewsbury College, she would use him. Whether she liked it or not, whether or not she had to put up with his saying "I told you so," she would put her pride in her pocket and ask him the best way to go about the job. She had her bath and dressed, glowing all the time with a consciousness of her own disinterested devotion to the cause of truth. She came into the sitting-room and enjoyed a good breakfast, still congratulating herself. As she was finishing her toast and marmalade, the secretary arrived, bringing in the morning's post. It contained a hurried note from Peter, sent off the previous evening from Victoria.

Hauled off abroad again at a moment's notice. Paris first, then Rome. Then God knows. If you should want me—*per impossible*—you can get me through the Embassies, or the post-office will forward letters from the Piccadilly address. In any case, you will hear from me on April 1st.

P.D.B.W.

*Post occasio calva.* One could scarcely bombard the Embassies with letters about an obscure and complicated little affair in an Oxford college, especially when one's correspondent was urgently engaged in investigating something else all over Europe. The call must have been urgent, for the note was very ill and hastily written, and looked, in fact as though it had been scribbled at the last moment in a taxi. Harriet amused herself with wondering whether the Prince of Ruritania had been shot, or the Master-Crook of the Continent had brought off a fresh *coup*, or whether this was the International Conspiracy to Wreck Civilization with a DeathRay—all those situations being frequent in her kind of fiction. Whatever it was all about, she would have to carry on unaided and find consolation in a proper independence of spirit.

# 5

Virginty is a fine picture, as *Bonaventure* calls it, a blessed thing in itself, and if you will believe a Papist, meritorious. And although there be some inconveniences, irksomeness, solitariness, etc., incident to such persons ... yet they are but toys in respect easily to be endured, if conferred to those frequent incumbrances of marriage .... And methinks sometime or other, amongst so many rich Bachelors, a benefactor should be found to build a monastical College for old, decayed, deformed, or discontented maids to live together in, that have lost their first loves, or otherwise miscarried, or else are willing howsoever to lead a single life. The rest I say, are toys in respect and sufficiently recompensed by those innumerable contents and incomparable privileges of Virginty.

Robert Burton

HARRIET DROVE out to Oxford through a vile downpour of sleet that forced its way between the joints of the all-weather curtains and kept the windscreen-wiper hard at work. Nothing could have been less like her journey of the previous June; but the greatest change of all was in her own feelings. Then, she had been reluctant and uneasy; a prodigal daughter without the romantic appeal of husks and very uncertain of the fatted calf. Now, it was the College that had blotted its copybook and had called her in as one calls in a specialist, with little regard to private morals but a despairing faith in professional skill. Not that she cared much for the problem, or had very much hope of solving it; but she was able by now to look upon it as pure problem and a job to be done. In June, she had said to herself, at every landmark on the way: "Plenty of time yet—thirty mlles before I need begin to feel uncomfortable—twenty miles more respite—ten miles is still a good way to go." This time, she was plainly and simply anxious to reach Oxford as quickly as possible—a state of mind for which the weather was perhaps largely responsible. She slithered down Headington Hill with no concern beyond a passing thought for possible skids, crossed Magdalen Bridge with only a caustic observation addressed to a shoal of pushcyclists, muttered "Thank God!" as she reached the St. Cross Road gate, and said "Good afternoon" cheerfully to Padgett the porter.

"Good afternoon, miss. Nasty day it's been. The Dean left a message, miss, as you was to be put in the Guest Room over at Tudor and she was out at a meeting but would be back for tea. Do you know the Guest Room, miss? That would be since your time, perhaps. Well, it's on the New Bridge, miss, between Tudor Building and the North Annexe where the Cottage used to be, miss, only of course that's all done away now and you has to go up by the main staircase past the West Lecture-Room, miss, what used to be the Junior Common Room, miss, before they made the new entrance and moved the stairs, and then turn right and it's half-way along the corridor. You can't mistake it, miss. Any of the Scouts would show you, miss, if you can find one about just now."

"Thank you, Padgett. I'll find it all right. I'll just take the car round to the garage."

"Don't you trouble, miss. Raining cats and dogs, it is. I'll take her round for you later on. She won't 'urt in the street for a bit. And I'll have your bag up in half a moment, miss; only I can't leave the gate till Mrs. Padgett comes back from running over to the Buttery, or I'm sure I'd show you the way myself."

Harriet again begged him not to trouble.

"Oh, it's quite easy when you know, miss. But what with pulling down here and building up there and altering this and that there's a many of our old ladies gets quite lost when they comes back to see us."

"I won't get lost Padgett." And she had, in fact, no difficulty in finding the mysterious Guest Room by the shifting stair and the non-existent Cottage. She noticed that its windows gave her a commanding view over the Old Quad, though the New Quad was out of range and the greater part of the new Library Building hidden by the Annexe Wing of Tudor.

Having had tea with the Dean, Harriet found herself seated in the Senior Common Room at an informal meeting of the Fellows and Tutors, presided over by the Warden. Before her lay the documents in the case—a pitiful little heap of dirty imaginations. Fifteen or so of them had been collected for inspection. There were half-a-dozen drawings, all much of a same kind with the one she had picked up on the Gaudy night. There were a number of messages, addressed to various members of the S.C.R., and informing them, with various disagreeable epithets, that their sins would find them out, that they were not fit for decent society and that unless they left men alone, various unpleasing things would occur to them. Some of these missives had come by post; others had been found on window-sills or pushed under doors; all were made up of the same cut-out letters pasted on sheets of rough scribbling-paper. Two other messages had been sent to undergraduates: one, to the Senior Student a very well-bred and inoffensive young woman who was reading Greats; the other to a Miss Flaxman, a brilliant Second Year scholar. The latter was rather more definite than most of the letters, in that it mentioned a name: "IF YOU DON'T LEAVE YOUNG FARRINGDON ALONE," it said, adding an abusive term, "IT WILL BE THE WORSE FOR YOU."

The remaining items in the collection consisted, first, of a small book written by Miss Barton: *The Position of Women in the Modern State*. The copy belonged to the Library, and had been discovered one Sunday morning merrily burning on the fire in the Junior Common Room in Burleigh House. Secondly, there were the proofs and manuscript of Miss Lydgate's *English Prosody*. The history of these was as follows. Miss Lydgate had at length transferred all her corrections in the text to the final page-proof and destroyed all the earlier revises. She had then handed the proofs, together with the manuscript of the Introduction, to Miss Hillyard, who had undertaken to go through them with a view to verifying certain historical allusions. Miss Hillyard stated that she had received them on a Saturday morning and taken them to her own rooms (which were on Miss Lydgate's staircase and on the floor immediately above). She had subsequently taken them into the Library (that is to say, the Library in Tudor, now about to be superseded by the New Library), and had there worked upon them for some time with the aid of some reference books. She said she had been alone in the Library at the time, except for someone, whom she had never seen, who was moving about in the bay at the far end. Miss Hillyard had then gone out to lunch in Hall, leaving the papers on the Library table. After lunch, she had gone on the river to put a group of First-Year students through a sculling-test. On her return to the Library after tea to resume work, she found that the papers had disappeared from the table. She had at first supposed that Miss Lydgate had come in and, seeing them there, carried them off to make a few more of her celebrated corrections. She went to Miss Lydgate's rooms to ask about them, but Miss

Lydgate was not there. She said she had been a little surprised that Miss Lydgate should have removed them without leaving a note to say what she had done; but she was not actually alarmed until, knocking again at Miss Lydgate's door shortly before Hall, she suddenly remembered that the English Tutor had said that she was leaving before lunch to spend a couple of nights in Town. An inquiry was, of course, immediately set on foot, but nothing had come of it until, on the Monday morning, just after Chapel, the missing proofs had been found sprawled over the table and floor of the Senior Common Room. The finder had been Miss Pyke, who had been the first don to enter the room that morning. The scout responsible for dusting the S.C.R. was confident that nothing of the kind had been there before Chapel; the appearance of the papers suggested that they had been tossed into the room by somebody passing the window, which would have been an easy enough thing for anybody to do. Nobody, however, had seen anything suspicious, though the entire college, particular late-comers to Chapel and those students whose windows overlooked the S.C.R., had been interrogated.

The proofs, when found, had been defaced throughout with thick copying-ink. All the manuscript alterations in the margins had been heavily blacked out and on certain pages offensive epithets had been written in rough block capitals. The manuscript Introduction had been burnt, and a triumphant note to this effect pasted in large printed letters across the first sheet of the proofs.

This was the news with which Miss Hillyard had had to face Miss Lydgate when the latter returned to College immediately after breakfast on the Monday. Some effort had been made to find out when, exactly, the proofs had been taken from the Library. The person in the far bay had been found, and turned out to have been Miss Burrows, the Librarian. She, however, said that she had not seen Miss Hillyard, who had come in after her and gone to lunch before her. Nor had she seen, or at any rate noticed, the proofs lying on the table. The Library had not been very much used on the Saturday afternoon; but a student who had gone in there at about 3 o'clock to consult Ducange's Late Latin Dictionary, in the bay where Miss Hillyard had been working, had said that she had taken the volume down and laid it on the table, and she *thought* that if the proofs had been there, she would have noticed them. This student was a Miss Waters, a second-year French student and a pupil of Miss Shaw's.

A slight awkwardness had been introduced into the situation by the Bursar, who had seen Miss Hillyard apparently entering the Senior Common Room just before Chapel on Monday morning. Miss Hillyard explained that she had only gone as far as the door, thinking that she had left her gown there; but remembering in time that she had hung it up in the cloakroom of Queen Elizabeth Building, had come out immediately without entering the S.C.R. She demanded, angrily, whether the Bursar suspected her of having done the damage herself. Miss Stevens said, "Of course not, but if Miss Hillyard had gone in, she could have seen whether the proofs were already in the room, and so provided a *terminus a quo*, or alternatively *ad quem*, for that part of the investigation."

This was really all the material evidence available, except that a large bottle of copying-ink had disappeared from the office of the College Secretary and Treasurer, Miss Allison. The Treasurer had not had occasion to enter the office during Saturday afternoon or Sunday; she could only say that the bottle had been in its usual place at one o'clock on Saturday. She did not lock the door of her office at any time, as no money was kept there, and all important papers were locked up in a safe. Her assistant did not live in college and had not been in during the week-end.

The only other manifestation of any importance had been an outbreak of unpleasant scribbling on the walls of passages and lavatories. These inscriptions had, of course, been effaced as soon as noticed and were not available.

It had naturally been necessary to take official notice of the loss and subsequent disfigurement of Miss Lydgate's proofs. The whole college had been addressed by Dr. Baring and asked whether anybody had any evidence to bring forward. Nobody offered any; and the Warden had thereupon issued a warning against making the matter known outside the college, together with an intimation that anybody sending indiscreet communications to either the University papers or the daily press might find herself liable to severe disciplinary action. Delicate interrogation among the other Women's Colleges had made it fairly clear that the nuisance was, so far, confined to Shrewsbury.

Since nothing, so far, had come to light to show that the persecution had started before the previous October, suspicion rather naturally centered upon the First-Year students. It was when Dr. Baring had reached this point of her exposition that Harriet felt obliged to speak.

"I am afraid, Warden," she said, "that I am in a position to rule out the First Year, and in fact the majority of the present students altogether."

And she proceeded, with some discomfort, to tell the meeting about the two specimens of the anonymous writer's work that she had discovered at and after the Gaudy.

"Thank you, Miss Vane," said the Warden, when she had finished. "I am extremely sorry that you should have had so unpleasant an experience. But your information of course narrows the field a great deal. If the culprit is someone who attended the Gaudy, it must have been either one of the few present students who were then waiting up for vivas, or one of the scouts, or—one of ourselves."

"Yes. I'm afraid that is the case."

The dons looked at one another.

"It cannot, of course," went on Dr. Baring, "be an old student, since the outrages have continued in the interim; nor can it be an Oxford resident outside the college, since we know that certain papers have been pushed under people's doors during the night, to say nothing of inscriptions on the walls which have been proved to have come into existence between, say, midnight and the next morning. We therefore have to ask ourselves who, among the comparatively small number of persons in the three categories I have mentioned, can possibly be responsible."

"Surely," said Miss Burrows, "it is far more likely to be one of the scouts than one of ourselves. I can scarcely imagine that a member of this Common Room would be capable of anything so disgusting. Whereas that class of persons—"

"I think that is a very unfair observation," said Miss Barton. "I feel strongly that we ought not to allow ourselves to be blinded by any sort of class prejudice."

"The scouts are all women of excellent character, so far as I know," said the Bursar, "and you may be sure that I take very great care in engaging the staff. The scrubbing-women and others who come in by the day are, naturally, excluded from suspicion. Also, you will remember that the greater number of the scouts sleep in their own wing. The outer door of this is locked at night and the ground-floor windows have bars. Besides this, there are the iron gates which cut off the back entrance from the rest of the college buildings. The only possible communication at night would be by way of the buttery, which is also locked. The Head Scout has the keys. Carrie has been with us fifteen years, and is presumably to be trusted."

"I have never understood," said Miss Barton, acidly, "why the unfortunate servants should be locked up at night as though they were dangerous wild beasts, when everybody else is free to come and go at pleasure. However, as things are, it seems to be just as well for them."

"The reason, as you very well know," replied the Bursar, "is that there is no porter at the tradesmen's entrance, and that it would not be difficult for unauthorized persons to climb over the outer gates. And I will remind you that *all* the ground-floor windows that open directly upon the street or the kitchen yard are barred, including those belonging to the Fellows. As for the locking of the buttery, I may say that it is done to prevent the students from raiding the pantry as they frequently did in my predecessor's time, or so I am informed. The precautions are taken quite as much against the members of the college as against the scouts."

"How about the scouts in the other buildings?" asked the Treasurer.

"There are perhaps two or three occupying odd bedrooms in each building," replied the Bursar. "They are all reliable women who have been in our service since before my time. I haven't the list here at the moment; but I think there are three in Tudor, three or four in Queen Elizabeth, and one in each of the four little dormer rooms in the New Quad. Burleigh is all students' rooms. And there is, of course, the Warden's own domestic staff, besides the Infirmary maid who sleeps there with the Infirmarian."

"I will take steps," said Dr. Baring, "to make sure that no mernber of my own household is at fault. You, Bursar, had better do the same by the Infirmary. And, in their own interests, the scouts sleeping in College had better be subjected to some kind of supervision."

"Surely, Warden—" began Miss Barton, hotly.

"In their own interests," said the Warden, with quiet emphasis. "I entirely agree with you, Miss Barton, that there is no greater reason for suspecting them than for suspecting one of ourselves. But that is the more reason why they should be cleared completely and at once."

"By all means," said the Bursar.

"As to the method used," went on the Warden, "to keep check upon the scouts, or upon anybody else, I feel strongly that the fewer people who know anything about that, the better. Perhaps Miss Vane will be able to put forward a good suggestion, in confidence to myself, or to . . ."

"Exactly," said Miss Hillyard, grimly. "To whom? So far as I can see, nobody among us can be taken on trust."

"That is unfortunately quite true," said the Warden, "and the same thing applies to myself. While I need not say that I have every confidence in the senior members of the College, both jointly and severally, it appears to me that, exactly as in the case of the scouts, it is of the highest importance that we should be safeguarded, in our own interests. What do you say, Sub-Warden?"

"Certainly," replied Miss Lydgate. "There should be no distinction made at all. I am perfectly willing to submit to any measures of supervision that may be recommended."

"Well, you at least can scarcely be suspected," said the Dean. "You are the greatest sufferer."

"We have nearly all suffered to some extent," said Miss Hillyard.

"I am afraid," said Miss Allison, "we shall have to allow for what I understand is the well-known practice of these unfortunate–um, ah–anonymous-letter writers, of sending letters to themselves to distract suspicion. Isn't that so, Miss Vane?" . . .

"Yes," said Harriet, bluntly. "It seems unlikely, on the face of it, that anybody would do herself the kind of material damage Miss Lydgate has received; but if we once begin to make distinctions it is difficult to know where to stop. I don't think anything but a plain alibi ought to be accepted as evidence."

"And I have no alibi," said Miss Lydgate. "I did not leave College on the Saturday till after Miss Hillyard had gone to lunch. What is more, I went over to Tudor during lunchtime, to return a book to Miss Chilperic's room before I left; so that I might quite easily have taken the manuscript from the Library then."

"But you have an alibi for the time when the proofs were put in the S.C.R.," said Harriet.

"No," said Miss Lydgate; "not even that. I came by the early train and arrived when everybody was in Chapel. I should have had to be rather quick to run across and throw the proofs into the S.C.R. and be back in my rooms again before the discovery was made; but I suppose I *could* have done it. In any case, I would much rather be treated on the same footing as other people."

"Thank you," said the Warden. "Is there anybody who does not feel the same?"

"I am sure we must all feel the same," said the Dean. "But there is one set of people we are overlooking."

"The present students who were up at the Gaudy," said the Warden. "Yes; how about them?"

"I forget exactly who they were," said the Dean, "but I think most of them were Schools people, and have since gone down. I will look up the lists and see. Oh, and, of course, there was Miss Cattermole who was up for Responsions–for the second time of asking."

"Ah!" said the Bursar. "Yes. Cattermole."

"And that woman who was taking Mods–what's her name? Hudson, isn't it? Wasn't she still up?"

"Yes," said Miss Hillyard, "she was."

"They will be in their Second and Third Years now, I suppose," said Harriet. "By the way, is it known who 'young Farringdon' is, in this note addressed to Miss Flaxman?"

"There's the point," said the Dean. "Young Farringdon is an undergraduate of–New College, I think it is–who was engaged to Cattermole when they both came up, but is now engaged to Flaxman."

"Is he, indeed?"

"Mainly, I understand, or partly, in consequence of that letter. I am told that Miss Flaxman accused Miss Cattermole of sending it and showed it to Mr. Farringdon; with the result that the gentleman broke off the engagement and transferred his affections to Flaxman."

"Not pretty," said Harriet.

"No. But I don't think the Cattermole engagement was ever anything much more than a family arrangement, and that the new deal was not much more than an open recognition of the *fait accompli*. I gather there has been some feeling in the Second Year about the whole thing."

"I see," said Harriet.

"The question remains," said Miss Pyke, 'What steps do we propose to take in the matter? We have asked Miss Vane's advice, and personally I am prepared to agree–particularly in view of what we have heard this evening–that it is abundantly necessary that some outside person should lend us assistance. To call in the police authorities is clearly undesirable. But may I ask whether, at this stage, it is suggested that Miss Vane should personally undertake an investigation? Or alternatively, would she propose our placing the matter in the hands of a private inquiry agent? Or what?"

"I feel I am in a very awkward position," said Harriet. "I am willing to give any help I can; but you do realize, don't you, that this kind of inquiry is apt to take a long time, especially if the investigator has to tackle it single-handed. A place like this, where people run in and out everywhere at all hours is almost impossible to police or patrol efficiently. It would need quite a little squad of inquiry agents–and even if you disguised them as scouts or students a good deal of awkwardness might arise."

"Is there no material evidence to be obtained from an examination of the documents themselves?" asked Miss Pyke. "Speaking for myself, I am quite ready to have my fingerprints taken or to undergo any other kind of precautionary measure that may be considered necessary."

"I'm afraid," said Harriet, "the evidence of finger-prints isn't quite so easy a matter as we make it appear in books. I mean, we could take finger-prints, naturally, from the S.C.R. and, possibly, from the scouts–though they wouldn't like it much. But I should doubt very much whether rough scribbling-paper like this would show distinguishable prints. And besides–"

"Besides," said the Dean, "every malefactor nowadays knows enough about finger-prints to wear gloves."

"And," said Miss de Vine, speaking for the first time, and with a slightly grim emphasis, "if we didn't know it before, we know it now."

"Great Scott!" cried the Dean, impulsively, "I'd forgotten all about its being us."

"You see what I meant," said the Warden, "when I said that it was better not to discuss methods of investigation too freely."

"How many people have handled all these documents already?" inquired Harriet.

"Ever so many, I should think," said the Dean.

"But could not a search be made for–" began Miss Chilperic. She was the most junior of the dons; a small, fair and timid young woman, assistant-tutor in English Language and Literature, and remarkable chiefly for being engaged to be married to a junior don at another college. The Warden interrupted her.

"Please, Miss Chilperic. That is the kind of suggestion that ought not to be made here. It might convey a warning."

"This," said Miss Hillyard, "is an intolerable position." She looked angrily at Harriet, as though she were responsible for the position; which, in a sense, she was.

"It seems to me," said the Treasurer, "that, now that we have asked Miss Vane to come and give us her advice, it is impossible for us to take it, or even to hear what it is. The situation is rather Gilbertian."

"We shall have to be frank up to a point," said the Warden. "Do you advise the private inquiry agent, Miss Vane?"

"Not the ordinary sort," said Harriet; "you wouldn't like them at all. But I do know of an organization where you could get the right type of person and the greatest possible discretion."

For she had remembered that there was a Miss Katherine Climpson, who ran what was ostensibly a Typing Bureau but was in fact a useful organization of women engaged in handling odd little investigations. The Bureau was self-supporting, though it had, she knew, Peter Wimsey's money behind it. She was one of the very few people in the Kingdom who did know it.

The Treasurer coughed.

"Fees paid to a Detective Agency," she observed, 'Will have an odd appearance in the Annual Audit."

"I think that might be arranged," said Harriet. "I know the organization personally. A fee might not be necessary."

"That," said the Warden, "would not be right. The fees would, of course, have to be paid. I would gladly be personally responsible."

"That would not be right either," said Miss Lydgate. "We certainly should not like that."

"Perhaps," suggested Harriet, "I could find out what the fees were likely to be." She had, in fact, no idea how this part of the business was worked.

"There would be no harm in inquiring," said the Warden. "In the meantime–"

"If I may make the suggestion," said the Dean, "I should propose, Warden, that the evidence should be handed over to Miss Vane, as she is the only person in this room who cannot possibly come under suspicion. Perhaps she would like to sleep upon the matter and make a report to you in the morning. At least, not in the morning, because of Lord Oakapple and the Opening; but at some time during tomorrow."

"Very well," said Harriet in response to an inquiring look from the Warden. "I will do that. And if I can think of any way in which I can be helpful, I'll do my best."

The Warden thanked her. "We all appreciate," she added, "the extreme awkwardness of the situation, and I am sure we shall all do what we can to co-operate in getting the matter cleared up. And I should like to say this: Whatever any of us may think or feel, it is of the very greatest importance that we should dismiss, as far as possible, all vague suspicions from our minds, and be particularly careful how we may say anything that might be construed as an accusation against anybody at all. In a close community of this kind, nothing can be more harmful than an atmosphere of mutual distrust. I repeat that I have the very greatest confidence in every Senior Member of the College. I shall endeavour to keep an entirely open mind, and I shall look to all my colleagues to do the same."

The dons assented; and the meeting broke up.

"*Well!*" said the Dean, as she and Harriet turned into the New Quad, "that is the most uncomfortable meeting I have ever had to sit through. My dear, you *have* thrown a bombshell into our midst!"

"I'm afraid so. But what could I do?"

"You couldn't possibly have done anything else. Oh, dear! It's all very well for the Warden to talk about an open mind, but we shall all feel perfectly ghastly wondering what other people are thinking about us, and whether our own conversation doesn't sound a little potty. It's the pottiness, you know, that's so awful."

"I know. By the way, Dean, I do absolutely refuse to suspect *you*. You're quite the sanest person I ever met."

"I don't think that's keeping an open mind, but thank you all the same for those few kind words. And one can't possibly suspect the Warden or Miss Lydgate, can one? But I'd better not say even that, I suppose. Otherwise, by a process of elimination–oh, lord! For Heaven's sake can't we find some handy outsider with a cast-iron alibi ready for busting?"

"We'll hope so. And of course there are those two students and the scouts to be disposed of." They turned in at the Dean's door. Miss Martin savagely poked up the fire in the sittingroom, sat down in an armchair and stared at the leaping flames. Harriet coiled herself on a couch and contemplated Miss Martin.

"Look here," said the Dean; "you had better not tell me too much about what *you* think, but there's no reason why any of us shouldn't tell *you* what *we* think, is there? No. Well. Here's the point. What is the object of all this persecution? It doesn't look like a personal grudge against anybody in particular. It's a kind of blind malevolence, directed against everybody in College. What's at the back of it?"

"Well, it might be somebody who thought the College as a body had injured her. Or it might be a personal grudge masking itself under a general attack. Or it might be just somebody with a mania for creating disturbance in order to enjoy the fun; that's the usual reason for this kind of outbreak, if you can call it a reason."

"That's sheer pottiness, in that case. Like those tiresome children who throw furniture about and the servants who pretend to be ghosts. And, talking of servants, do you think there's anything in that idea that it's more likely to be somebody of that class? Of course, Miss Barton wouldn't agree; but after all, some of the words used are very coarse."

"Yes," said Harriet; "but actually there isn't one that I, for example, don't know the meaning of. I believe, when you get even the primmest people under an anaesthetic, they are liable to bring the strangest vocabulary out of the subconscious–in fact, the primmer the coarser."

"True. Did you notice that there wasn't a single spelling mistake in the whole bunch of messages?"

"I noticed that. It probably points to a fairly well educated person; though the converse isn't necessarily true. I mean, educated people often put in mistakes on purpose, so that spelling mistakes don't prove much. But an absence of mistakes is a more difficult thing to manage, if it doesn't come natural. I'm not putting this very clearly."

"Yes, you are. A good speller could pretend to be a bad one; but a bad speller can't pretend to be a good one, any more than I could pretend to be a mathematician."

"She could use a dictlonary."

"But then she would have to know enough to be dictionary-conscious–as the new slang would call it. Isn't our poison-pen rather silly to get all her spelling right?"

"I don't know. The educated person often fakes bad spelling rather badly; misspells easy words and gets quite difficult ones right. It's not so hard to tell when people are putting it on. I think it's probably cleverer to make no pretence about it."

"I see. Does this tend to exclude the scouts? . . . But probably they spell far better than we do. They so often *are* better educated. And I'm sure they dress better. But that's rather off the point. Stop me when I dither."

"You're not dithering," said Harriet. "Everything you say is perfectly true. At present I don't see how anybody is to be excluded."

"And what," demanded the Dean, "becomes of the mutilated newspapers?"

"This won't do," said Harriet; "you're being a great deal too sharp about this. That's just one of the things I was wondering about."

"Well, we've been into that," said the Dean, in a tone of satisfaction. "We've checked up on all the S.C.R. and J.C.R. papers ever since this business came to our notice—that is, more or less, since the beginning of this term. Before anything goes to be pulped, the whole lot are checked up with the list and examined to see that nothing has been cut out."

"Who has been doing that?"

"My secretary, Mrs. Goodwin. I don't think you've met her yet. She lives in College during term. Such a nice girl—or woman, rather. She was left a widow, you know, very hard up, and she's got a little boy of ten at a prep. school. When her husband died—he was a schoolmaster—she set to work to train as a secretary and really did splendidly. She's simply invaluable to me, and most careful and reliable."

"Was she here at Gaudy?"

"Of course she was. She—good gracious! You surely don't think—my dear, that's *absurd*! The *most* straightforward and sane person. And she's very grateful to the College for having found her the job, and she certainly wouldn't want to run the risk of losing it."

"All the same, she's got to go on the list of possibles. How long has she been here?"

"Let me see. Nearly two years. Nothing at all happened till the Gaudy, you know, and she'd been here a year before that."

"But the S.C.R. and the scouts who live in College have been here still longer, most of them. We can't make exceptions along those lines. How about the other secretaries?"

"The Warden's secretary—Miss Parsons—lives at the Warden's Lodgings. The Bursar's and the Treasurer's secretaries both live out, so they can be crossed off."

"Miss Parsons been here long?"

"Four years."

Harriet noted down the names of Mrs. Goodwin and Miss Parsons.

"I think," she said, "for Mrs. Goodwin's own sake we'd better have a second check on those newspapers. Not that it really matters; because, if the poison-pen knows that the papers are being checked, she won't use those papers. And I suppose she must know, because of the care taken to collect them."

"Very likely. That's just the trouble, isn't it?"

"How about people's private newspapers?"

"Well, naturally, we couldn't check them. We've kept an eye on the waste-paper baskets as well as we can. Nothing is ever destroyed, you know. It's all thriftily collected in sacks and sent to the paper-makers or whoever it is that gives pence for old papers. The worthy Padgett is instructed to examine the sacks—but it's a terrific job. And then, of course, since there are fires in all the rooms, why *should* anybody leave evidence in the W.P.B.?"

"How about the gowns that were burnt in the quad? That must have taken some doing. Surely more than one person would have been needed to work that."

"We don't know whether that was part of the same business or not. About ten or a dozen people had left their gowns in various places–as they do, you know–before Sunday supper. Some were in the Queen Elizabeth portico, and some at the foot of the Hall stairs and so on. People bring them over and dump them, ready for evening Chapel." (Harriet nodded; Sunday evening Chapel was held at a quarter to eight and was compulsory; being also a kind of College Meeting for the giving-out of notices.) "Well, when the bell started, these people couldn't find their gowns and so couldn't go in to Chapel. Everybody thought it was just a rag. But in the middle of the night somebody saw a blaze in the quad, and it turned out to be a merry little bonfire of bombazine. The gowns had all been soaked in petrol and they went up beautifully."

"Where did the petrol come from?"

"It was a can Mullins keeps for his motor-cycle. You remember Mullins–the Jowett Lodge porter. His machine lies in a little outhouse in the Lodge garden. He didn't lock it up–why should he? He does *now*, but that doesn't help. Anybody could have gone and fetched it. He and his wife heard nothing, having retired to their virtuous rest. The bonfire happened bang in the middle of the Old Quad and burnt a nasty patch in the turf. Lots of people rushed out when the flare went up, and whoever did it probably mingled with the crowd. The victims were four M.A. gowns, two scholars' gowns and the rest commoners' gowns; but I don't suppose there was any selection; they just happened to be lying about."

"I wonder where they were put in the interval between supper and the bonfire. Anybody carrying a whole bunch of gowns round College would be a bit conspicuous."

"No; it was at the end of November, and it would be pretty dark. They could easlly have been bundled into a lectureroom to be left till called for. There wasn't a proper organized search over College, you see. The poor victims who were left gownless thought somebody was having a joke; they were very angry, but not very efficient. Most of them rushed round to accuse their friends."

"Yes; I don't suppose we can get much out of that episode at this time of day. Well–I suppose I'd better go and wash-and-brush-up for Hall."

Hall was an embarrassed meal at the High Table. The conversation was valiantly kept to matters of academic and world interest. The undergraduates babbled noisily and cheerfully; the shadow that rested upon the college did not seem to have affected their spirits. Harriet's eye roamed over them.

"Is that Miss Cattermole at the table on the right? In a green frock, with a badly made-up face?"

"That's the young lady," replied the Dean. "How did you know?"

"I remember seeing her at Gaudy. Where is the all-conquering Miss Flaxman?"

"I don't see her. She may not be dining in Hall. Lots of them prefer to boil an egg in their rooms, so as to avoid the bother of changing. Slack little beasts. And that's Miss Hudson, in a red jumper, at the middle table. Black hair and horn rims."

"She looks quite normal."

"So far as I know, she is. So far as I know, we all are."

"I suppose," said Miss Pyke, who had overheard the last remark, "even murderers look much like other people, Miss Vane. Or do you hold any opinions about the theories put forward by Lombroso? I understand that they are now to a considerable extent exploded."

Harriet was quite thankful to be allowed to discuss murderers.

After Hall, Harriet felt herself rather at a loose end. She felt she ought to be doing something or interviewing somebody; but it was hard to know where to begin. The Dean had announced that she would be busy with some lists, but would be open to receive visitors later on. Miss Burrows the Librarian was to be engaged in putting the final touches to the Library before the Chancellor's visit; she had been carting and arranging books the greater part of the day and had roped in a small band of students to assist her with the shelving of them. Various other dons mentioned that they had work to do; Harriet thought they seemed a little shy of one another's company.

Catching hold of the Bursar, Harriet asked whether it was possible to get hold of a plan of the College and a list of the various rooms and their occupants. Miss Stevens offered to supply the list and said she thought there was a plan in the Treasurer's office. She took Harriet across into the New Quad to get these things.

"I hope," said the Bursar, 'You wlll not pay too much attention to that unfortunate remark of Miss Burrows' about the scouts. Nothing would please me more, personally, than to transfer all the maids to the Scouts' Wing out of reach of suspicion, if that were practicable; but there is no room for them there. Certainly I do not mind giving you the names of those who sleep in College, and I agree, certainly, that precautions should be taken. But to my mind, the episode of Miss Lydgate's proofs definitely rules out the scouts. Very few of them would be likely to know or care anything about proof-sheets; nor would the idea of mutilating manuscripts be likely to come into their heads. Vulgar letters–yes, possibly. But damaging those proofs was an educated person's crime. Don't you think so?"

"I'd better not say what I think," said Harriet.

"No; quite right. But I can say what *I* think. I wouldn't say it to anybody but you. Still, I do not like this haste to make scapegoats of the scouts."

"The thing that seems so extraordinary," said Harriet, "is that Miss Lydgate, of all people, should have been chosen as a victim. How could *anybody*–particularly one of her own colleagues–have any grudge against *her*? Doesn't it look rather as though the culprit knew nothing about the value of the proofs, and was merely making a random gesture of defiance to the world in general?"

"That's possible, certainly. I must say, Miss Vane, that your evidence today has made matters very complicated. I would rather suspect the scouts than the S.C.R., I admit; but when these hasty accusations are made by the last person known to have been in the same room with the manuscript I can only say that–well, that it appears to me injudicious."

Harriet said nothing to this. The Bursar, apparently feeling that she had gone a little too far, added:

"I have no suspicions of anybody. All I say is, that statements ought not to be made without proof."

Harriet agreed, and, after marking off the relevant names upon the Bursar's list, went to find the Treasurer.

Miss Wilson produced a plan of the College, and showed the positions of the rooms occupied by various people.

"I hope this means," she said, "that you intend to undertake the investigation yourself. Not I suppose, that we ought to ask you to spare the time for any such thing. But I do most strongly feel that the presence of paid detectives in this college would be *most* unpleasant, however discreet they might be. I have served the College for a considerable number of years and I have its interests very much at heart. You know how undesirable it is that any outsider should be brought into a matter of this kind."

"It is; very," said Harriet. "All the same, a spiteful or mentally deficient servant is a misfortune that might occur anywhere. Surely the important thing is to get to the bottom of the mystery as quickly as possible; and a trained detective or two would be very much more efficient than I should be."

Miss Allison looked thoughtfully at her, and swayed her glasses to and fro slowly on their gold chain.

"I see you incline to the most comfortable theory. Probably we all do. But there is the other possibllity. Mind you I quite see that from your own point of view, you would not wish to take part in an exposure of a member of the Senior Common Room. But if it came to the point, I would put more faith in your tact than in that of an outside professional detective. And you start with a knowledge of the workings of the collegiate system, which is a great advantage."

Harriet said that she thought she would know better what to suggest when she had made a preliminary review of all the circumstances.

"If," said Miss Allison, "you do undertake an inquiry, it is probably only fair to warn you that you may meet with some opposition. It has already been said–but perhaps I ought not to tell you this."

"That is for you to judge."

"It has already been said that the narrowing-down of the suspects within the limits mentioned at today's meeting rests only upon your assertion. I refer, of course, to the two papers you found at the Gaudy."

"I see. Am I supposed to have invented those?"

"I don't think anybody would go as far as that. But you have said that you sometimes received similar letters on your own account. And the suggestion is that–"

"That if I found anything of the sort I must have brought it with me? That would be quite likely, only that the style of the things was so like the style of these others. However, I admit you have only my word for that."

"*I'm* not doubting it for a moment. What is being said is that your experience in these affairs is–if anything–a disadvantage. Forgive me. That is not what *I* say."

"That is the thing that made me very unwilling to have anything to do with the inquiry. It is absolutely true. I haven't lived a perfectly blameless life, and you can't get over it."

"If you ask me," said Miss Allison, "some people's blameless lives are to blame for a good deal. I am not a fool, Miss Vane. No doubt my own life has been blameless as far as the more generous sins are concerned. But there are points upon which I should expect you to hold more balanced opinions than certain people here. I don't think I need say more than that, need I?"

Harriet's next visit was to Miss Lydgate; her excuse being to inquire what she should do with the mutilated proofs in her possession. She found the English Tutor patiently correcting a small pile of students' essays.

"Come in, come in," said Miss Lydgate, cheerfully. "I have nearly done with these. Oh, about my poor proofs? I'm afraid they're not much use to me.

They're really quite undecipherable. I'm afraid the only thing is to do the whole thing again. The printers will be tearing their hair, poor souls. I shan't have very much difficulty with the greater part of it, I hope. And I have the rough notes of the Introduction, so it isn't as bad as it might have been. The worst loss is a number of manuscript footnotes and two manuscript appendices that I had to put in at the last moment to refute what seemed to me some very ill-considered statements in Mr. Elkbottom's new book on *Modern Verse-Forms*. I stupidly wrote those in on the blank pages of the proofs and they are quite irrecoverable. I shall have to verify all the references again in Elkbottom. It's so tiresome, especially as one is always so busy towards the end of term. But it's all my own fault for not keeping a proper record of everything."

"I wonder," said Harriet, "if I could be of any help to you in getting the proofs put together. I'd gladly stay up for a week or so if it would do any good. I'm quite used to juggling with proof-sheets, and I think I can remember enough of my Schools work to be reasonably intelligent about the Anglo-Saxon and Early English."

"That would be a tremendous help!" exclaimed Miss Lydgate, her face lighting up. "But wouldn't it be trespassing far too much on your time?"

Harriet said, No; she was well ahead with her own work and would enjoy putting in a little time on English Prosody. It was in her mind that, if she really meant to pursue inquiries at Shrewsbury, Miss Lydgate's proofs would offer a convenient excuse for her presence in College.

The suggestion was left there for the moment. As regards the author of the outrages, Miss Lydgate could make no suggestion; except that, whoever it was, the poor creature must be mentally afflicted.

As she left Miss Lydgate's room, Harriet encountered Miss Hillyard, who was descending the staircase from her own abode.

"Well," said Miss Hillyard, "how is the investigation progressing? But I ought not to ask that. You have contrived to cast the Apple of Discord among us with a vengeance. However, as you are so well accustomed to the receipt of anonymous communications, you are no doubt the fittest person to handle the situation."

"In my case," said Harriet, "I only got what was to some extent deserved. But this is a very different matter. It's not the same problem at all. Miss Lydgate's book could offend nobody."

"Except some of the men whose theories she has attacked," replied Miss Hillyard. "However, circumstances seem to exclude the male sex from the scope of the inquiry. Otherwise, this mass-attack on a woman's college would suggest to me the usual masculine spite against educated women. But you, of course, would consider that ridiculous."

"Not in the least. Plenty of men are very spiteful. But surely there are no men running about the college at night."

"I wouldn't be too sure of that" said Miss Hillyard, smiling sarcastically. "It is quite ridiculous for the Bursar to talk about locked gates. What is to prevent a man from concealing himself about the grounds before the gates are locked and escaping again when they are opened in the morning? Or climbing the walls, if it comes to that?"

Harriet thought the theory far-fetched; but it interested her, as evidence of the speaker's prejudice, which amounted almost to obsession.

"The thing that in my opinion points to a man," went on Miss Hillyard, "is the destruction of Miss Barton's book, which is strongly pro-feminist. I don't suppose you have read it; probably it would not interest you. But why else should that book be picked out?"

Harriet parted from Miss Hillyard at the corner of the quad and went over to Tudor Building. She had not very much doubt who it was that was likely to offer opposition to her inquiries. If one was looking for a twisted mind, Miss Hillyard's was certainly a little warped. And, when one came to think of it, there was no evidence whatever that Miss Lydgate's proofs had ever been taken to the Library or ever left Miss Hillyard's hands at all. Also, she had undoubtedly been seen on the threshold of the S.C.R. before Chapel on the Monday morning. If Miss Hillyard was sufficiently demented to inflict a blow of this kind on Miss Lydgate, then she was fit for a lunatic asylum. But, indeed, this would apply to whoever it was.

She went into Tudor and tapped on Miss Barton's door, asking, when she was admitted, whether she might borrow a copy of *Woman's Place in the Modern State*.

"The sleuth at work?" said Miss Barton. "Well, Miss Vane, here it is. By the way, I should like to apologize to you for some of the things I said when you were here last. I shall be very glad to see you handle this most unpleasant business, which can scarcely be an agreeable thing for you. I admire exceedingly anyone who can subordinate her own feelings to the common advantage. The case is obviously pathological –as all anti-social behaviour is, in my opinion. But here there is no question of legal proceedings, I imagine. At least, I hope not. I feel extremely anxious that it should *not* be brought into court; and on that account I am against hiring detectives of any kind. If you are able to get to the bottom of it, I am ready to give you any help I can."

Harriet thanked the Fellow for her good opinion and for the book.

"You are probably the best psychologist here," said Harriet. "What do you think of it?"

"Probably the usual thing: a morbid desire to attract attention and create a public uproar. The adolescent and the middle-aged are the most likely suspects. I should very much doubt whether there is much more to it than that. Beyond, I mean, that the incidental obscenities point to some kind of sexual disturbance. But that is a commonplace in cases of this kind. But whether you ought to look for a man-hater or a man-trap," added Miss Barton, with the first glimmer of humour Harriet had ever seen in her, "I can't tell you."

Having put away her various acquisitions in her own room, Harriet thought it was time to go and see the Dean. She found Miss Burrows with her, very tired and dusty after coping with the Library, and being refreshed with a glass of hot milk, to which Miss Martin insisted on adding just a dash of whisky to induce slumber.

"What new light one gets on the habits of the S.C.R. when one's an old student," said Harriet. "I always imagined that there was only one bottle of ardent spirits in the college, kept under lock and key by the Bursar for life-and-death emergencies."

"It used to be so," said the Dean, "but I'm gettlng frivolous in my old age. Even Miss Lydgate cherishes a small stock of cherry brandy, for high-days and holidays. The Bursar is even thinking of laying down a little port for the College."

"Great Scott!" said Harriet.

"The students are not supposed to imbibe alcohol," said the Dean, "but I shouldn't like to go bail for the contents of all the cupboards in College."

"After all," said Miss Burrows, "their tiresome parents bring them up to have cocktails and things at home, so it probably seems ridiculous to them that they shouldn't do the same thing here."

"And what can one do about it? Make a police search through their belongings? Well, I flatly refuse. We can't keep the place like a gaol."

"The trouble is," said the Librarian, "that everybody sneers at restrictions and demands freedom, till something annoying happens; then they demand angrily what has become of the discipline."

"You can't exercise the old kind of discipline in these days," said the Dean; "it's too bitterly resented."

"The modern idea is that young people should discipline themselves," said the Librarian. "But do they?"

"No; they won't. Responsibility bores 'em. Before the War they passionately had College Meetings about everything. Now, they won't be bothered. Half the old institutions, like the College debates and the Third Year Play, are dead or moribund. They don't want responsibility."

"They're all taken up with their young men," said Miss Burrows.

"Drat their young men," said the Dean. "In my day, we simply thirsted for responsibility. We'd all been sat on at school for the good of our souls, and came up bursting to show how brilliantly we could organize things when we were put in charge."

"If you ask me," said Harriet, "it's the fault of the schools. Free discipline and so on. Children are sick to death of running things and doing prefect duty; and when they get up to Oxford they're tired out and only want to sit back and let somebody else run the show. Even in my time, the people from the up-to-date republican schools were shy of taking office, poor brutes."

"It's all very difficult," said Miss Burrows with a yawn. "However, I did get my Library volunteers to do a job of work today. We've got most of the shelves decently filled, and the pictures hung and the curtains up. It looks very well. I hope the Chancellor will be impressed. They haven't finished painting the radiators downstairs, but I've bundled the paintpots and things into a cupboard and hoped for the best. And I borrowed a squad of scouts to clean up, so as not to leave anything to be done tomorrow."

"What times does the Chancellor arrive?" asked Harriet.

"Twelve o'clock; reception in the S.C.R. and show him round the College. Then lunch in Hall, and I hope he enjoys it. Ceremony at 2:30. And then push him off to catch the 3:45. Delightful man; but I am getting fed up with Openings. We've opened the New Quad, the Chapel (with choral service), the S.C.R. Dining-Room (with lunch to Former Tutors and Fellows), the Tudor Annexe (with Old Students' Tea), the Kitchens and Scouts' Wing (with Royalty), the Sanatorium (with address by the Lister Professor of Medicine), the Council-Chamber and the Warden's Lodgings, and we've unveiled the late Warden's Portrait, the Willett Memorial Sundial and the New Clock. And now it's the Library. Padgett said to me last term, when we were making those alterations in Queen Elizabeth, 'Excuse me, madam Dean, miss, but could you tell me, miss, the date of the Opening?' 'What Opening, Padgett?' said I. 'We aren't opening anything this term. What is there to open?' 'Well, miss,' says Padgett, 'I was thinking of these here new lavatories, if you'll excuse me, madam Dean, miss. We've opened everything there was to open up to the present, miss, and if there was to be a Ceremony, miss, it would be convenient if I was to know in good time, on account of arranging for taxis and parking accommodation.' "

"Dear Padgett!" said Miss Burrows. "He's the brightest spot in this academy." She yawned again. "I'm dead."

"Take her away to bed, Miss Vane," said the Dean, "and we'll call it a day."

# 6

Often when they were gone to Bed, the inner doors were flung open, as also the Doors of a Cupboard which stood in the Hall; and this with a great deal of Violence and Noise. And one Night the Chairs, which when they went to Bed stood all in the Chimney-corner, were all removed and placed in the middle of the Room in very good order, and a Meal-sieve hung upon one cut full of Holes, and a Key of an inner Door upon another. And in the Day-time, as they sate in the House spinning, they could see the Barn-doors often flung open, but not by whom. Once, as *Alice* sate spinning the Rock or Distaff leapt several times out of the Wheel into the middle of the room . . . with much more such ridiculous stuff as this is, which would be tedious to relate.

William Turner

"PETER," SAID Harriet. And with the sound of her own voice she came drowsing and floating up out of the strong circle of his arms, through a green sea of sun-dappled beechleaves into darkness.

"Oh, damn," said Harriet softly to herself. "Oh, damn. And I didn't want to wake up."

The clock in the New Quad struck three musically.

"This won't do," said Harriet. "This really will not do. My sub-conscious has a most treacherous imagination." She groped for the switch of her bedside lamp. "It's disquieting to reflect that one's dreams never symbolize one's real wishes, but always something Much Worse." She turned the light on and sat up.

"If I really wanted to be passionately embraced by Peter, I should dream of something like dentists or gardening. I wonder what are the unthinkable depths of awfulness that can only be expressed by the polite symbol of Peter's embraces. Damn Peter! I wonder what he would do about a case like this."

This brought her mind back to the evening in the Egotists' Club and the anonymous letter; and thence back to his absurd fury with the sticking-plaster.

". . . but my mind being momentarily on my job . . ."

You'd think he was quite bird-witted, sometimes, she thought. But he does keep his mind on the job, when he's doing it. One's mind on the job. Yes. What am I doing, letting my mind stray all over the place. Is this a job, or isn't it? . . . Suppose the Poison-Pen is on its rounds now, dropping letters at people's doors . . . Whose door, though? One can't watch all the doors . . . I ought to be sitting up at the window, keeping an eye open for creeping figures in the quad . . . Somebody ought to do it—but who's to be trusted? Besides, dons have their jobs to do; they can't sit up all night and work all day . . . The job . . . keeping one's mind on the job . . .

She was out of bed now and pulling the window curtains aside. There was no moon, and nothing at all to be seen. Not even a late essay-writer seemed to be burning the midnight lamp.

Anybody could go anywhere on a dark night like this, she thought to herself. She could scarcely see even the outline of the roofs of Tudor on her right or the dark bulk of the New Library jutting out on her left from behind the Annexe.

The Library; with not a soul in it.

She put on a dressing-gown and opened her door softly. It was bitterly cold. She found the wall-switch and went down the central corridor of the Annexe, past a row of doors behind which students were sleeping and dreaming of goodness knew what---examinations, sports, undergraduates, parties, all the queer jumble of things that are summed up as "activities." Outside their doors lay little heaps of soiled crockery for the scouts to collect and wash. Also shoes. On the doors were cards, bearing their names: Miss H. Brown, Miss Jones, Miss Colburn, Miss Szleposky, Miss Isaacson–so many unknown quantities. So many destined wives and mothers of the race; or, alternatively, so many potential historians, scientists, schoolteachers, doctors, lawyers; as you liked to think one thing of more importance than the other. At the end of the passage was a large window, hygienically open at top and bottom. Harriet gently pushed up the bottom sash and looked out, shivering.

And suddenly she knew that whatever reason or instinct had led her to look at the Library had taken a very just view of the situation. The New Library should have been quite dark. It was not. One of the long windows was split from top to bottom by a narrow band of light.

Harriet thought rapidly. If this was Miss Burrows, carrying on legitimately (though at an unreasonable and sacrificial hour) with her preparations, why had she troubled to draw the curtains? The windows had been curtained, because a Library that faces south must have some protection against strong sunlight. But it would be absurd for the Librarian to protect herself and her proper functions from scrutiny in the middle of a dark March night. College authorities were not so secretive as all that. Something was up. Should one go and investigate on one's own, or rouse somebody else?

One thing was clear; if it was a member of the S.C.R. lurking behind those curtains, it would not be politic to bring a student to witness the discovery. What dons slept in Tudor? Without consulting the list, Harriet remembered that Miss Barton and Miss Chilperic had rooms there, but on the far side of the building. Here was an opportunity to check up on them, at any rate. With a last glance at the Library window, Harriet made her way quickly back past her own room on the Bridge and through into the main building. She cursed herself for not having a torch; she was delayed by fumbling with the switches. Along the corridor, past the stair-head and round to the left. No don on that floor; it must be on the floor below. Back, and down the stairs and along to the left again. She was leaving all the passage-lights burning behind her, and wondered whether they would arouse attention in other buildings. At last. A door on her left labelled "Miss Barton." And the door stood open.

She knocked at it sharply, and went in. The sitting-room was empty. Beyond it, the bedroom door stood open too. "Gracious!" said Harriet. "Miss Barton!" There was no reply; and, looking in, she saw that the bedroom was as empty as the sitting-room. The bed-clothes were flung back and the bed had been slept in; but the sleeper had risen and gone.

It was easy to think of an innocent explanation. Harriet stood for a moment, considering; and then called to mind that the window of the room overlooked the quad. The curtains were drawn back; she looked out into the darkness. The light still shone in the Library window; but while she looked, it went out.

She ran back to the foot of the stair and through the entrance-hall. The front door of the building was ajar. She pulled it open and ran out and across the quad. As she ran, something seemed to loom up ahead of her. She made for it and closed with it. It caught her in a muscular grip.

"Who's that?" demanded Harriet, fiercely.

"And who's *that?*"

The grip of one hand was released and a torch was switched on into Harriet's face.

"Miss Vane! What are you doing here?"

"Is that Miss Barton? I was looking for you. I saw a light in the New Library."

"So did I. I've just been over to investigate. The door's locked."

"Locked?"

"And the key inside."

"Isn't there another way up?" asked Harriet.

"Yes, of course there is. I ought to have thought of that. Up through the Hall passage and the Fiction Library. Come along!"

"Wait a minute," said Harriet. "Whoever it is may be still there. You watch the main door, to see they don't get out that way. I'll go up through the Hall."

"Very well. Good idea. Here! haven't you got a torch? You'd better take mine. You'll waste time turning on lights."

Harriet snatched the torch and ran, thinking hard. Miss Barton's story sounded plausible enough. She had woken up (why?), seen the light (very likely she slept with her curtains drawn open) and gone out to investigate while Harriet was running about the upper floors hunting for the right room. In the meantime, the person in the Library had either finished what she was doing or, possibly, peeped out and been alarmed by seeing the lights go up in Tudor. She had switched out the light. She had not gone out by the main door; she was either still somewhere in the Hall-Library Wing, or she had crept out by the Hall stair while Miss Barton and Harriet were grappling with one another in the quad.

Harriet found the Hall stair and started up it, using her torch as little as possible and keeping the light low. It came forcibly into her mind that the person she was hunting was—must be—unbalanced, if not mad, and might possibly deliver a nasty swipe out of a dark corner. She arrived at the head of the stair, and pushed back the swinging glass double door that led to the passage between the Hall and the Buttery. As she did so, she fancied she heard a slight scuffling sound ahead, and almost simultaneously she saw the gleam of a torch. There ought to be a two-way switch just on the right, behind the door. She found it, and pressed it down. There was a quick flicker, and then darkness. A fuse? Then she laughed at herself. Of course not. The person at the other end of the passage had flicked the switch at the same moment as herself. She pushed the switch up again, and the lights flooded the passage.

On her left she saw the three doorways, with the serving-hatches between, that led into the Hall. On the right was the long blank wall between the passage and the kitchens. And ahead of her, at the far end of the passage, close to the Buttery door, stood somebody clutching a dressing-gown about her with one hand and a large jug in the other.

Harriet advanced swiftly upon this apparition, which came meeky enough to meet her. Its features seemed familiar, and in a moment she identified them. It was Miss Hudson, the Third Year student who had been up at Gaudy.

"What in the world are you doing here at this time of night?" demanded Harriet, severely. Not that she had any particular right to question students about their movements. Nor did she feel that her own appearance, in pajamas and a jaeger dressing-gown, suggested dignity or authority. Miss Hudson, indeed, seemed quite flabbergasted at being thus accosted by a total stranger at three in the morning. She stared, speechless.

"Why shouldn't I be here?" said Miss Hudson, at last defiantly. "I don't know who you are. I've as much right to walk about as you have . , . Oh, gosh!" she added, and burst out laughing. "I suppose you're one of the scouts. I didn't recognize you without your uniform."

"No," said Harriet "I'm an old student. You're Miss Hudson, aren't you! But your room isn't here. Have you been along to the Buttery?" Her eyes were on the jug; Miss Hudson blushed.

"Yes–I wanted some mllk. I've got an essay."

She spoke of it as though it were a disease. Harriet chuckled.

"So that still goes on, does it? Carrie's just as soft-hearted as Agnes was in my day." She went up to the Buttery hatch and shook it, but it was locked. "No, apparently she isn't."

"I asked her to leave it open," said Miss Hudson, "but I expect she forgot. I say–don't give Carrie away. She's awfully decent."

"You know quite well that Carrie isn't supposed to leave the hatch open. You ought to get your milk before ten o'clock"

"I know. But one doesn't always know if one will want it. You've done the same thing in your time, I expect."

"Yes," said Harriet. "Well, you'd better cut along. Wait a second. When did you come up here?"

"Just now. Just a few seconds before you did."

"Did you meet anybody?"

"No," Miss Hudson looked alarmed. "Why? Has anything happened?"

"Not that I know of. Get along to bed."

Miss Hudson escaped and Harriet tried the Buttery door which was as firmly locked as the hatch. Then she went on, through the Fiction Library, which was empty, and put her hand on the handle of the oak door that led to the New Library,

The door was immovable. There was no key in the lock. Harriet looked round the Fiction Library. On the window-sill lay a thin pencil, beside a book and a few papers. She pushed the pencil into the key-hole; it encountered no resistance.

She went to the window of the Fiction Library and pushed it up. It looked on to the roof of a small loggia. Two people were not enough for this game of hide-and-seek. She pulled a table across the Library door, so that if anybody tried to come out that way behind her back she should have notice of it; then she climbed out on to the loggia roof and leaned over the balcony. She could see nothing distinctly beneath her, but she pulled her torch from her pocket and signalled with it.

"Hullo!" said Miss Barton's voice, cautiously, from below.

"The other door's locked, and the key gone."

"That's awkward. If either of us goes, somebody may come out. And if we yell for help there'll be an uproar."

"That's about the size of it" said Harriet.

"Well, listen; I'll try and get in through one of the groundfloor windows, They all seem to be latched, but I might break a pane of glass."

Harriet waited. Presently she heard a faint tinkle. Then there was a pause, and presently the sound of a moving sash. There was a longer pause. Harriet came back into the Fiction Library and pulled the table away from the door. In about six or seven minutes' time she saw the door handle move and heard a tap on the other side of the oak. She stooped to the key-hole, and called: "What's up?" and bent her ear to listen.

"Nobody here," said Miss Barton's voice on the other side. "Keys gone. And the most ghastly mess-up."

"I'll come round."

She hurried back through the Hall and round to the front of the Library. Here she found the window that Miss Barton had opened, climbed through and ran on up the stairs into the Library.

"Well!'" said Harriet.

The New Library was a handsome, lofty room, with six bays on the South side, lit by as many windows running nearly from the floor to the ceiling. On the North side, the wall was windowless, and shelved to a height of ten feet. Above this was a space of blank wall, along which it would be possible, at some future time, to run an extra gallery when the books should become too many for the existent shelving. This blank space had been adorned by Miss Burrows and her party with a series of engravings, such as every academic community possesses, representing the Parthenon, the Colosseum Trajan's Column and other topographical and classical subjects.

All the books in the room had been dragged out and flung on the floor, by the simple expedient of removing the shelves bodily. The pictures had been thrown down. And the blank wall space thus exposed had been adorned with a frieze of drawings, roughly executed in brown paint, and with inscriptions in letters a foot high, all of the most unseemly sort. A pair of library steps and a pot of paint with a wide brush in it stood triumphantly in the midst of the wreckage, to show how the transformation had been accomplished.

"That's torn it," said Harriet.

"Yes," said Miss Barton. "A very nice reception for Lord Oakapple."

There was an odd note in her voice–almost of satisfaction. Harriet looked sharply at her.

"What are you going to do? What does one do? Go over the place with a magnifying glass? or send for the police?"

"Neither," said Harriet. She considered for a moment.

"The first thing," she said, "is to send for the Dean. The next is to find either the original keys or a spare set. The third, is to clean off these filthy inscriptions before anybody sees them. And the fourth is to get the room straight before twelve o'clock. There's plenty of time. Will you be good enough to wake the Dean and bring her with you. In the meantime, I'll have a look round for clues. We can discuss afterwards who did the job and how she got out. Please make haste."

"H'm!" said the Fellow. "I like people who know their own minds."

She went with surprising promptness.

"Her dressing-gown is all over paint," said Harriet aloud to herself. "But she may have got it climbing in." She went downstairs and examined the open window. "Yes, here's where she scrambled over the wet radiator. I expect I'm marked too. Yes, I am. Nothing to show whether it all came from there. Damp footmarks–hers and mine, no doubt. Wait a moment."

She traced the damp marks up to the top of the stairs, where they grew faint and ceased. She could find no third set; but the footmarks of the intruder would probably have had time to dry. Whoever it was must have begun operations very soon after midnight at latest. The paint had splashed about a good deal; if it were possible to search the whole college for paint-stained clothing, well and good. But it would cause a terrific scandal. Miss Hudson–had she shown any marks of paint anywhere? Harriet thought not.

She looked about her again, and realized unexpectedly that she had the lights full on, and that the curtains were drawn open. If anybody was looking across from one of the other bulldings, the interior of the room would show up like a lighted stage. She snapped the lights off, and drew the curtains again carefully before putting them on again.

"Yes," she said. "I see. That was the idea. The curtains were drawn while the job was done. Then the lights were turned off and the curtains opened. Then the artist escaped, leaving the doors locked. In the morning, everything would look quite ordinary from the outside. Who would have been the first to try and come in? An early scout, to do a final clean-round? She would find the door locked, think Miss Burrows had left it like that, and probably do nothing about it. Miss Burrows would probably have come up first. When? A little after Chapel, or a little before. She would not have been able to get in. Time would have been wasted hunting for the keys. When anybody did get in, it would have been two late to straighten things up. Everybody would have been about. The Chancellor–?"

Miss Burrows would have been the first to come up. She had also been the last to leave, and was the person who knew best where the paint pots had been put. Would she have wrecked her own job, any more than Miss Lydgate would have wrecked her own proofs? How far was that psychological premise sound? One would surely damage anything in the world, *except* one's own work. But on the other hand, if one were cunning enough to see that people would think exactly that, then one would promptly take the precaution of seeing that one's own work did suffer.

Harriet moved slowly about the Library. There was a big splash of paint on the parquet. And at the edge of it–oh, yes! it would be very useful to hunt the place over for paintstained clothes. But here was evidence that the culprit had worn no slippers. Why should she have worn anything? The radiators on this floor were working at full blast, and a complete absence of clothing would be not merely politic but comfortable.

And how had the person got away? Neither Miss Hudson (if she was to be trusted) nor Harriet had met anyone on the way up. But there had been plenty of time for escape, after the lights were put out. A stealthy figure creeping away under the Hall archway could not have been seen from the far side of the Old Quad. Or, if it came to that, there might quite well have been somebody lurking in the HW while Harriet and Miss Hudson were talking in the passage.

"I've mucked it a bit," said Harriet. "I ought to have turned on the Hall lights to make sure."

Miss Barton re-entered with the Dean, who took one look round and said "Mercy!" She looked like a stout little mandarin, with her long red pigtail and quilted blue dressing-gown sprawled over with green-and-scarlet dragons. "What *idiots* we were not to expect it. Of course, the *obvious* thing! If we'd only thought about it, Miss Burrows could have locked up before she went. And what do we do now?"

"My first reaction," said Harriet, "is turpentine. And the second is Padgett."

"My dear, you are perfectly right. Padgett will cope. He always does. Like charity, he never fails. What a mercy you people spotted what was going on. As soon as we get these disgusting inscriptions cleaned off, we can put on a coat of quick-drying distemper or something, or paper the wall over, and–goodness! I don't know where the turpentine will come from unless the painters have left a lot. It'll need a young bath: But Padgett will manage."

"I'll run over and get him," said Harriet "and at the same time I'll collar Miss Burrows. We'll have to get these books back into place. What's the time? Five to four. I think it can be done all right. Will you hold the fort till I come back?"

"Yes. Oh, and you'll find the main door open now. I had an extra key, fortunately. A beautiful *plated* key–all ready for Lord Oakapple. But we'll have to get a locksmith to the other door, unless the builders have a spare."

The most remarkable thing about that remarkable morning was the imperturbability of Padgett. He answered Harriet's summons attired in a handsome pair of striped pyjamas, and received her instructions with monumental stolidity.

"The Dean is sorry to say, Padgett, that somebody has been playing some very disagreeable tricks in the New Library."

"Have they indeed, miss?"

"The whole place has been turned upside down, and some very vulgar words and pictures scrawled on the wall."

"Very unfortunate, miss, that is."

"In brown paint."

"That's awkward, miss."

"It will have to be cleaned at once, before anybody sees it."

"Very good, miss."

"And then we shall have to get hold of the decorators or somebody to paper or wash it over before the Chancellor arrives."

"Very good, miss."

"Do you think you can manage it, Padgett?"

"Just you leave it to me, miss."

Harriet's next job was to collect Miss Burrows, who received the news with loud expressions of annoyance.

"How loathsome! And do you mean to say all those books have got to be done *again?* Now? Oh, lord, yes–I suppose there's no help for it. What a blessing I hadn't put the Folio Chaucer and the other valuables in the show-cases. Lord!"

The Librarian scrambled out of bed. Harriet looked at her feet. They were quite clean. But there was an odd smell in the bedroom. She traced it after a moment or two to the neighborhood of the permanent basin.

"I say–is that turps?"

"Yes," replied Miss Burrows, struggling into her stockings. "I brought it across from the library. I got paint on my hands when I moved those pots and things."

"I wish you'd lend it me. We had to scramble in through the window over a wet radiator,"

"Yes, rather."

Harriet went out, puzzled. Why should Miss Burrows have bothered to bring the can over to the New Quad, when she could have cleaned off the paint on the spot? But, she could well understand that if anyone had wanted to remove paint from her feet after being disturbed in the middle of a piece of dirty work, there might have been nothing for it but to snatch up the can and bolt for it.

Then she had another idea. The culprit could not have left the Library with her feet bare. She would have put on her slippers again. If you put paint-stained feet into slippers, the slippers ought to show signs of it.

She went back to her own room and dressed. Then she returned to the New Quad. Miss Burrows had gone. Her bedroom slippers lay by the bed. Harriet examined them minutely, inside and out, but they were quite free from paint.

On her way back again, Harriet overtook Padgett. He was walking sedately across the lawn, carrying a large can of turpentine in each hand.

"Where did you rake that up, Padgett, so early in the morning?"

"Well, miss, Mullins went on his motor-bike and knocked up a chap he knows what lives over his own oil-shop, miss."

As simple as that.

Some time later, Harriet and the Dean, decorously robed and gowned, found themselves passing along the East side of Queen Elizabeth Building in the wake of Padgett and the decorators' foreman.

"Young ladies," Padgett was heard to say, "will 'ave their larks, same as young gentlemen."

"When I was a lad," replied the foreman, "young ladies was young ladies. And young gentlemen was young gentlemen. If you get my meaning."

"Wot this country wants," said Padgett, "is a 'Itler."

"That's right," said the foreman. "Keep the girls at 'ome. Funny kind o' job you got 'ere, mate. Wot was you, afore you took to keepin' a 'en 'ouse?"

"Assistant camel 'and at the Zoo. Very interesting job it was, too."

"Wot made you chuck it?"

"Blood-poison. I was bit in the arm," said Padgett "by a female."

"Ah!" said the foreman decorator.

By the time Lord Oakapple arrived, the Library presented nothing unseemly to the eye, beyond a certain dampness and streakiness in its upper parts, where the new paper was drying unevenly. The glass had been swept up and the paint stains cleaned from the floor; twenty photographs of classical statuary had been unearthed from a store-cupboard to replace the Colosseum and the Parthenon; the books were back on their shelves, and the showcases duly displayed the Chaucer Folio, the Shakespeare First Quarto, the three Kelmscott Morrises, the autographed copy of *The Man of Property*, and the embroidered glove belonging to the Countess of Shrewsbury.

The Dean hovered about the Chancellor like a hen with one chick, in a martyrdom of nervous apprehension lest some indelicate missive should drop from his table-napkin or flutter out unexpectedly from the folds of his robes; and when, in the Senior Common Room after lunch, he took out a bunch of notes from his pocket and riffled them over with a puzzled frown, the tension became so acute that she nearly dropped the sugar-basin. It turned out, however, that he had merely mislaid a Greek quotation. The Warden, though the history of the Library was known to her, displayed her usual serene poise.

Harriet saw nothing of all this. She spent the whole interval, after the decorators had done their part, in the Library, watching the movements of everyone who came in or out, and seeing that they left nothing undesirable behind them.

Apparently, however, the College Poltergeist had shot its bolt. A cold lunch was brought up to the self-appointed invigilator. A napkin covered it; but nothing lurked beneath its folds beyond a plate of ham sandwiches and other such harmless matter. Harriet recognized the scout.

"It's Annie, isn't it? Are you on the kitchen staff now?"

"No, madam. I wait upon the Hall and Senior Common Room."

"How are your little girls getting on? I think Miss Lydgate said you had two little girls?"

"Yes, madam. How kind of you to ask." Annie's face beamed with pleasure. "They're splendid. Oxford suits them, after living in a manufacturing town, where we were before. Are you fond of children, madam?"

"Oh, yes," said Harriet. Actually, she did not care much about children; but one can scarcely say so, bluntly, to those possessed of these blessings.

"You ought to be married and have some of your own, madam. There! I oughtn't to have said that–it's not my place. But it seems to me a dreadful thing to see all these unmarried ladies living together. It isn't natural, is it?"

"Well, Annie, it's all according to taste. And one has to wait for the right person to come along."

"That's very true, madam." Harriet suddenly recollected that Annie's husband had been queer, or committed suicide, or something unfortunate, and wondered whether her commonplace had been a tactful one. But Annie seemed quite pleased with it. She smiled again; she had large, light blue eyes, and Harriet thought she must have been a good-looking woman before she got so thin and worried-looking. "I'm sure I hope he'll come along for you–or perhaps you are engaged to be married?"

Harriet frowned. She had no particular liking for the question, and did not want to discuss her private affairs with the college servants. But there seemed to be no impertinent intention behind the inquiry, so she answered Pleasantly, "Not just yet; but you never know. How do you like the new Library?"

"It's a very handsome room, isn't it madam? But it seems a great shame to keep up this big place just for women to study books in. I can't see what girls want with books. Books won't teach them to be good wives."

"What dreadful opinions!" said Harriet. "Whatever made you take a job in a women's college, Annie?"

The scout's face clouded. "Well, madam, I've had my misfortunes. I was glad to take what I could get."

"Yes, of course; I was only joking. Do you like the work?"

"It's quite all right. But some of these clever ladies are a bit queer, don't you think, madam? Funny, I mean. No heart in them."

Harriet remembered that there had been misunderstandings with Miss Hillyard.

"Oh, no," she said briskly. "Of course they are very busy people, and haven't much time for outside interests. But they are all very kind."

"Yes, madam; I'm sure they mean to be. But I always think of what it says in the Bible, about 'much learning hath made thee mad.' It isn't a right thing."

Harriet looked up sharply and caught an odd look in the scout's eyes.

"What do you mean by that, Annie?"

"Nothing at all, madam. Only funny things go on sometimes, but of course, being a visitor, you wouldn't know, and it's not my place to mention them –being only a servant, nowadays."

"I certainly," said Harriet, rather alarmed, "wouldn't mention anything of the kind you suggest to outside people or visitors. If you have any complaint to make, you should speak to the Bursar, or the Warden."

"I haven't any complaint, madam. But you may have heard about rude words being written up on the walls, and about the things that were burnt in the Quad–why, there was a bit in the papers about that. Well, you'll find, madam, they all happened since a certain person came into the college."

"What person?" said Harriet sternly.

"One of these learned ladies, madam. Well, perhaps I'd better not say anything more about that. You write detective books, don't you, madam? Well, you'll find something in that lady's past, you may be sure of it. At least that's what a good many people are saying. And it isn't a nice thing for anybody to be in the same place with a woman like that."

"I feel quite sure you must be mistaken, Annie; I should be very careful how you spread about a tale of that kind. You'd better run along back to the Hall, now; I expect they'll be needing you."

So that was what the servants were saying. Miss de Vine, of course; she was the "learned lady" whose arrival had coincided with the beginning of the disturbances–coincided more exactly than Annie could know, unless she too had seen that drawing in the quad at the Gaudy. A curious woman, Miss de Vine, and undoubtedly with a varied experience behind those disconcerting eyes. But Harriet was inclined to like her, and she certainly did not look mad in the way that the "Poison-Pen" was mad; though it would not be surprising to learn that she had a streak of fanaticism somewhere. What, by the way, had she been doing the previous night? She had rooms at the moment in Queen Elizabeth; there was probably little likelihood of proving an alibi for her now. Miss de Vine–well! she would have to be put on the same footing as everbody else.

The opening of the Library took place without a hitch. The Chancellor unlocked the main door with the plated key, unaware that the same key had opened it, under curious circumstances, the night before. Harriet watched carefully the faces of the assembled dons and scouts; none of them showed any sign of surprise, anger or disappointment at the decorous appearance of the Library. Miss Hudson was present looking cheerfully unconcerned; Miss Cattermole, too, was there. She looked as though she had been crying; and Harriet noticed that she stood in a corner by herself and talked to nobody until, at the conclusion of the ceremony, a dark girl in spectacles made her way through the crowd to her and they walked away together.

Later in the day, Harriet went to the Warden to make her promised report. She pointed out the difficulty of dealing with an outbreak like that of the previous night single-handed. A careful patrol of the quads and passages by a number of helpers would probably have resulted in the capture of the culprit; and the whole of the suspects could in any case have been checked up at an early moment. She strongly advised enlisting some women from Miss Climpson's Agency, the nature of which she explained.

"I see the point," replied the Warden; "but I find that at least two members of the Senior Common Room feel very strong objections to that course of action."

"I know," said Harriet. "Miss Allison and Miss Barton. Why?"

"I think, too," pursued the Warden, without answering this question, "that the matter presents certain difficulties. What would the students think of these strangers prowling about the college at night? They will wonder why police duties cannot be undertaken by ourselves, and we can hardly inform them that we ourselves are particularly under suspicion. And to perform such duties as you suggest, properly, quite a large number would be required—if all the strategic points are to be held. Then these persons would be quite ignorant of the conditions of college life, and might easily make unfortunate mistakes by following and questioning the wrong people. I do not see how we could avoid a very unpleasant scandal and some complaints."

"I see all that, Warden. But all the same, that is the quickest solution."

The Warden bent her head over a handsome piece of tapestry-work on which she was engaged.

"I cannot feel it to be very desirable. I know you will say that the whole situation is undesirable. I quite agree with you." She looked up. "I suppose, Miss Vane, you could not yourself spare the time to assist us?"

"I could spare the time," said Harriet, slowly. "But without help it is going to be very difficult. If there were only one or two people who were exonerated without a shadow of doubt, it would be very much easier."

"Miss Barton assisted you very ably last night."

"Yes," said Harriet; "but—how shall I put it? If I were writing a story about this, the person first on the spot would be the first person to be suspected."

The Warden selected an orange skein from her basket and threaded her needle deliberately.

"Will you explain that, please?"

Harriet explained carefully.

"That is very clearly put," said Dr. Baring. "I understand perfectly. Now, about this student, Miss Hudson. Her explanation does not seem to be satisfactory. She could not possibly have expected to get food from the Buttery at that hour; and in fact, she did not."

"No," said Harriet; "but I know quite well that in my day it wasn't too difficult to get round the right side of the Head Scout to leave the hatch open all night. Then, if one had a late essay or anything and felt hungry, one went down and got what one wanted."

"Dear me," said the Warden.

"We were always quite honourable about it," said Harriet, "and entered it all on the slate, so that it figured in our battels at the end of term. Though," she added thoughtfully, "there were some items of cold meat and dripping that must have been camouflaged a bit. Still—I think Miss Hudson's explanation will pass muster."

"Actually, the hatch was locked"

"Actually, it was. As a matter of fact, I have seen Carrie, and she assures me that it was locked at 10:30 last night as usual. She admits that Miss Hudson asked her to leave it open, but says she didn't do so, because, only last night, the Bursar had given special instructions about the locking of the hatch and Buttery. That would be after the meeting, no doubt. She also says she has been more particular this term than she used to be, because of a little trouble there was over the same thing last term."

"Well—I see there is no proof against Miss Hudson. I believe she is rather a lively young woman, however; so it may be as well to keep an eye on her. She is very able; but her antecedents are not particularly refined, and I dare say, it is possible that she might look upon even the disagreeable expressions found in the—er—the communications in the light of a joke. I tell you this, not to create any prejudice against the girl, but merely for whatever evidential value it may possess."

"Thank you. Well, then, Warden; if you feel it is impossible to call in outside help, I suggest that I should stay in College for a week or so, ostensibly to help Miss Lydgate with her book and to do some research on my own account in Bodley. I could then make a few more investigations. If nothing decisive results by the end of the term, I really think the question of engaging professionals will have to be faced."

"That is a very generous offer," said the Warden. "We shall all be exceedingly grateful to you."

"I ought to warn you" said Harriet, "that one or two of the Senior Members do not approve of me."

"That may make it a little more difficult. But if you are ready to put up with that unpleasantness in the interests of the College, it can only increase our sense of gratitude. I cannot too strongly emphasize how exceedingly important it is to avoid publicity. Nothing is more prejudicial to the College in particular and to University women in general than spiteful and ill-informed gossip in the press, The students, so far, seem to have been very loyal. If any of them had been indiscreet we should certainly have heard of it by now."

"How about Miss Flaxman's young man at New College?"

"Both he and Miss Flaxman have behaved quite well. At first, naturally, it was taken to be a purely personal matter. When the situation developed, I spoke to Miss Flaxman, and received her assurance that she and her fiancé would keep the whole thing to themselves until it could be properly cleared up."

"I see," said Harriet. "Well, we must do what we can. One thing I should like to suggest, and that is that some of the passage-lights should be left on at night. It is difficult enough to patrol a large set of buildings in the light: in the dark, it is impossible."

"That is reasonable," replied Dr. Baring. "I will speak to the Bursar about it."

And with this unsatisfactory arrangement, Harriet was obliged to be content.

# 7

O my deare *Cloris* be not sad,
  Nor with these Furies daunted,
But let these female fooles be mad,
  With Hellish pride inchanted;
Let not thy noble thoughts descend
  So low as their affections,
Whom neither counsell can amend,
  Nor yet the Gods corrections.
Michael Drayton

IT WAS a matter of mild public interest at Shrewsbury College that Miss Harriet Vane, the well-known detective novelist, was spending a couple of weeks in College, while engaged in research at the Bodleian upon the life and works of Sheridan Le Fanu. The excuse was good enough; Harriet really was gathering material, in a leisurely way, for a study of Le Fanu, though the Bodleian was not, perhaps, the ideal source for it. But there must be some reason given for her presence, and Oxford is willing enough to believe that the Bodleian is the hub of the scholar's universe. She was able to find enough references among the Periodical Publications to justify an optimistic answer to kindly inquiries about her progress; and if, in fact, she snoozed a good deal in the arms of Duke Humphrey by day, to make up for those hours of the night spent in snooping about the corridors, she was probably not the only Person in Oxford to find the atmosphere of old leather and central heating favorable to slumber.

At the same time, she devoted a good many hours to establishing order among Miss Lydgate's chaotic proofs. The introduction was re-written, and the obliterated passages restored, from the author's capacious memory; the disfigured pages were replaced from fresh proof-sheets; fifty-nine errors and obscurities in the cross-references were eliminated; the rejoinder to Mr. Elkbottom was incorporated in the text and made more vigorous and conclusive; and the authorities at the Press began to speak quite hopefully about the date of publication.

Whether because Harriet's night prowlings, or because the mere knowledge that the circle of suspects was so greatly narrowed, had intimidated the Poison-Pen, or from whatever cause, there were few outbreaks during the next few days. One tiresome episode was the complete stopping-up of the lavatory basin drain in the S.C.R. cloak-room. This was found to be due to some torn fragments of material, which had been rammed firmly down through the grid with the help of a fine rod, and which, when the plumber had got them out proved to be the remains of a pair of fabric gloves, stained with brown paint and quite unidentifiable as anybody's property. Another was the noisy emergence of the missing Library keys from the interior of a roll of photographs which Miss Pyke had left for half an hour in one of the lecture-rooms before using them to illustrate some remarks about the Parthenon Frieze. Neither of these episodes led to any discovery.

The Senior Common Room behaved to Harriet with that scrupulous and impersonal respect for a person's mission in life which the scholarly tradition imposes. It was clear to them that, once established as the official investigator, she must be allowed to investigate without interference. Nor did they hasten to her with protestations of innocence or cries of indignation. They treated the situation with a fine detachment, making little reference to it, and confining the conversation in Common Room to matters of general and University interest. In solemn and ritual order, they invited her to consume sherry or coffee in their rooms, and refrained from comment upon one another. Miss Barton, indeed, went out of her way to invite Harriet's opinions upon *Women in the Modern State* and to consult her on the subject of conditions in Germany. It is true that she flatly disagreed with many of the opinions expressed, but only objectively and without personal rancour; the vexed subject of the amateur's right to investigate crimes was decently shelved. Miss Hillyard also, setting aside animosity, took pains to interrogate Harriet about the technical aspect of such historical crimes as the murder of Sir Edmund Berry Godfrey and the alleged poisoning of Sir Thomas Overbury by the Countess of Essex. Such overtures might, of course, be policy; but Harriet was inclined to attribute them to a careful instinct for propriety.

With Miss de Vine she had many interesting conversations. The Fellow's personality attracted and puzzled her very much. More than with any other of the dons, she felt that with Miss de Vine the devotion to the intellectual life was the result, not of the untroubled following of a natural or acquired bias, but of a powerfull spiritual call, over-riding other possible tendencies and desires. She felt inquisitive enough, without any prompting, about Miss de Vine's past life; but inquiry was difficult, and she always emerged from an encounter with the feeling that she had told more than she had learnt. She could guess at a history of confiict; but she found it difficult to believe that Miss de Vine was unaware of her own repressions or unable to control them.

With a view to establishing friendly relations with the Junior Common Room, Harriet further steeled herself to compose and deliver a "talk" on "Detection in Fact and Fiction" for a College literary society. This was perilous work. To the unfortunate case in which she had herself figured as the suspected party she naturally made no allusion; nor in the ensuing discussion was anybody so tactless as to mention it. The Wilvercombe murder was a different matter. There was no obvious reason why she should not tell the students about that, and it seemed unkind to deprive them of a legitimate thrill on the purely personal grounds that it was a bore to have to mention Peter Wimsey in every second sentence. Her exposition, though perhaps erring slightly on the dry and academic side, was received with hearty applause, and at the end of the meeting the Senior Student, one Miss Millbanks, invited her to coffee.

Miss Millbanks had her room in Queen Elizabeth, and had furnished it with a good deal of taste. She was a tall, elegant girl, obviously well-to-do, much better dressed than the majority of the students, and carrying her intellectual attainments easily. She held a minor scholarship without emoluments, declaring publicly that she was only a scholar because she would not be seen dead in the ridiculous short gown of a commoner. As alternatives to coffee, she offered Harriet the choice of madeira or a cocktail, politely regretting that the inadequacy of college arrangements made it impossible to provide ice for the shaker. Harriet, who disliked cocktails after dinner, and had consumed madeira and sherry on an almost wearisome number of occasions since her arrival in Oxford, accepted the coffee, and chuckled as cups and glasses were filled. Miss Millbanks inquired courteously what the joke was.

"Only," said Harriet, "that I gathered the other day from an article in the *Morning Star* that 'undergraduettes,' in the journalist's disgusting phrase, lived entirely on cocoa."

"Journalists," said Miss Millbanks, condescendingly, "are always thirty years behind the times. Have you ever seen cocoa in College, Miss Fowler?"

"Oh, yes," said Miss Fowler. She was a dark, thick-set Third Year, dressed in a very grubby sweater which, as she had previously explained, she had not had time to change, having been afflicted with an essay up to the moment of attending Harriet's talk. "Yes, I've seen it in dons' rooms. Occasionally. But I've always looked on that as a kind of infantilism."

"Isn't it a re-living of the heroic past?" suggested Miss Millbanks. "*0 les beaux jours que ce siecle de fer*. And so on."

"Groupists drink cocoa," added another Third Year. She was thin, with an eager, scornful face, and made no apology for her sweater, apparently thinking such matters beneath her notice.

"But they are oh! so tender to the failings of others," said Miss Millbanks. "Miss Layton was 'changed' once, but she has now changed back. It was good while it lasted."

Miss Layton, curled on a pouffe by the fire, lifted a wicked little heart-shaped face alight with mischief.

"I did enjoy telling people what I thought of them. Too rapturous. Especially confessing in public the evil, evil thoughts I had had about that woman Flaxman."

"Bother Flaxman," said the dark girl, shortly. Her name was Haydock, and she was, as Harriet presently discovered, considered to be a safe History First. "She's setting the whole Second Year by the ears. I don't like her influence at all. And if you ask me, there's something very wrong with Cattermole. Goodness knows, I don't want any of this business of being my brother's keeper—we had quite enough of that at school—but it'll be awkward if Cattermole is driven into doing something drastic. As Senior Student, Lilian, don't you think you could do something about it?"

"My dear," protested Miss Millbanks, "what can anybody do? I can't forbid Flaxman to make people's lives a burden to them. If I could, I wouldn't. You don't surely expect me to exercise authority? It's bad enough hounding people to College Meetings. The S.C.R. don't understand our sad lack of enthusiasm."

"In their day," said Harriet, "I think people had a passion for meetings and organization."

"There are plenty of inter-collegiate meetings," said Miss Layton. "We discuss things a great deal, and are indignant about the Proctorial Rules for Mixed Parties. But our enthusiasm for internal affairs is more restrained."

"Well, I think," said Miss Haydock bluntly, "we sometimes overdo the *laisser-aller* side of it. If there's a big blow-up, it won't pay anybody."

"Do you mean about Flaxman's cutting-out expeditions? Or about the ragging affair? By the way, Miss Vane, I suppose you have heard about the College Mystery."

"I've heard something," replied Harriet, cautiously. "It seems to be all very tiresome."

"It will be extremely tiresome if it isn't stopped," said Miss Haydock. "I say we ought to do a spot of private investigation ourselves. The S.C.R. don't seem to be making much progress."

"Well, the last effort at investigation wasn't very satisfactory," said Miss Millbanks.

"Meaning Cattermole? I don't believe it's Cattermole. She's too obvious. And she hasn't the guts. She could and does make an ass of herself, but she wouldn't go about it so secretively."

"There's nothing against Cattermole," said Miss Fowler, "except that somebody wrote Flaxman an offensive letter on the occasion of her swiping Cattermole's young man. Cattermole was the obvious suspect then, but why should she do all these other things?"

"Surely," Miss Layton appealed to Harriet, "surely the obvious suspect is always innocent."

Harriet laughed; and Miss Millbanks said:

"Yes; but I do think Cattermole is getting to the stage when she'd do almost anything to attract attention."

"Well, I don't believe it's Cattermole," said Miss Haydock. "Why should she write letters to me?"

"Did you have one?"

"Yes; but it was only a kind of wish that I should plough in Schools. The usual silly thing made of pasted-up letters. I burnt it, and took Cattermole in to dinner on the strength of it."

"Good for you," said Miss Fowler.

"I had one too," said Miss Layton. "A beauty–about there being a reward in hell for women who went my way. So, acting on the suggestion given, I forwarded it to my future address by way of the fireplace."

"All the same," said Miss Millbanks, "it is rather disgusting. I don't mind the letters so much. It's the rags, and the writing on the wall. If any snoopy person from outside happened to get hold of it there'd be a public stink, and that would be a bore. I don't pretend to much public spirit, but I admit to some. We don't want to get the whole College gated by way of reprisals. And I'd rather not have it said that we were living in a madhouse."

"Too shame-making," agreed Miss Layton; "though of course, you may get an isolated queer specimen anywhere."

"There are some oddities in the First Year all right," said Miss Fowler. "Why is it that every year seems to get shriller and scrubbier than the last?"

"They always did," said Harriet.

"Yes," said Miss Haydock, "I expect the Third Year said the same about us when we first came up. But it's a fact that we had none of this trouble before we had this bunch of freshers in."

Harriet did not contradict this, not wishing to focus suspicion on either the S.C.R. or on the unfortunate Cattermole who (as everybody would remember) was up during the Gaudy, waging simultaneous war against despised love and Responsions. She did ask, however, whether any suspicion had fallen upon other students besides Miss Cattermole.

"Not definitely, no," replied Miss Millbanks. "There's Hudson, of course–she came up from school with a bit of a reputation for ragging, but in my opinion she's quite sound. I should call the whole of our year pretty sound. And Cattermole really has only herself to thank. I mean, she's asking for trouble."

"How?" asked Harriet.

"Various ways," said Miss Millbanks, with a caution which suggested that Harriet was too much in the confidence of the S.C.R. to be trusted with details. "She is rather inclined to break rules for the sake of it–which is all right if you get a kick out of it; but she doesn't."

"Cattermole's going in off the deep end," said Miss Haydock. "Wants to show young what's-his-name–Farringdon –he isn't the only pebble on the beach. All very well. But she's being a bit blatant. She's simply pursuing that lad Pomfret."

"That fair-faced goop at Queen's?" said Miss Fowler. "Well, she's going to be unlucky again, because Flaxman is steadily hauling him off."

"Curse Flaxman!" said Miss Haydock. "Can't she leave other people's men alone? She's bagged Farringdon; I do think she might leave Pomfret for Cattermole."

"She hates to leave anybody anything," said Miss Layton.

"I hope," said Miss Millbanks, "she has not been trying to collect your Geoffrey."

"I'm not giving her the opportunity," said Miss Layton, with an impish grin. "Geoffrey's sound–yes, darlings, definitely sound–but I'm taking no chances. Last time we had him to tea in the J.C.R., Flaxman came undulating in–*so* sorry, she had no idea anybody was there, and she'd left a book behind. With the Engaged Label on the door as large as life. I did not introduce Geoffrey."

"Did he want you to?" inquired Miss Haydock.

"Asked who she was. I said she was the Templeton Scholar and the world's heavyweight in the way of learning. That put him off."

"What'll Geoffrey do when you pull off your First, my child?"demanded Miss Haydock.

"Well, Eve–it *will* be awkward if I do that. Poor lamb! I shall have to make him believe I only did it by looking fragile and pathetic at the viva."

And Miss Layton did, indeed, contrive to look fragile and pathetic, and anything but learned. Nevertheless, on inquiry from Miss Lydgate, Harriet discovered that she was an exceptionally well-fancied favourite for the English School, and was taking, of all things, a Language Special. If the dry bones of Philology could be made to live by Miss Layton, then she was a very dark horse indeed. Harriet felt a respect for her brains; so unexpected a personality might be capable of anything.

So much for Third-Year opinion. Harriet's first personal encounter with the Second Year was more dramatic.

The College had been so quiet for the last week that Harriet gave herself a holiday from police-duty and went to a private dance given by a contemporary of her own, who had married and settled in North Oxford. Returning between twelve and one, she garaged the car in the Dean's private garage, let herself quietly through the grille dividing the Traffic Entrance from the rest of College and began to cross the Old Quad towards Tudor. The weather had turned finer, and there was a pale glimmer of cloudy moonlight. Against that glimmer, Harriet, skirting the corner of Burleigh Building, observed something humped and strange about the outline of the eastern wall, close to where the Principal's private postern led out into St. Cross Road. It seemed clear that here, in the words of the old song, was "a man where nae man should be."

If she shouted at him, he would drop over on the outer side and be lost. She had the key of the postern with her-having been trusted with a complete set of keys for patrol purposes. Pulling her black evening cloak about her face and stepping softly, Harriet ran quickly down the grass path between the Warden's House and the Fellows' Garden, let herself silently out into St. Cross Road and stood beneath the wall. As she emerged, a second dark form stepped out from the shadows and said urgently, "Oy!"

The gentleman on the wall looked round, exclaimed, "Oh, hell!" and scrambled down in a hurry. His friend made off at a smart pace, but the wall-climber seemed to have damaged himself in his descent, and made but poor speed. Harriet, who was nimble enough, for all she was over nine years down from Oxford, gave chase and came up a few yards from the corner of Jowett Walk. The accomplice, now well away, looked back, hesitating.

"Clear out, old boy!" yelled the captive; and then, turning to Harriet, remarked with a sheepish grin, "Well, it's a fair cop. I've bust my ankle or something."

"And what were you doing on our wall, sir?" demanded Harriet. In the moonlight she beheld a fresh, fair and ingenuous face, youthfully rounded and, at the moment, disturbed by an expression of mingled apprehension and amusement. He was a very tall and very large young man; but Harriet had clasped him in a wiry grip that he could scarcely shake off without hurting her, and he showed no disposition to use violence.

"Just having a beano," said the young man, promptly. "A bet, you know, and all that. Hang my cap on the tip-top branch of the Shrewsbury beeches. My friend there was the witness. I seem to have lost don't I?"

"In that case," said Harriet severely, "where's your cap? And your gown, if it comes to that? And, sir, your name and college?"

"Well," said the young man, impudently, "if it comes to that, where and what are yours?"

When one's thirty-second birthday is no more than a matter of months away, such a question is flattering. Harriet laughed.

"My dear young man, do you take me for an undergraduate?"

"A don—a female don, God help us!" exclaimed the young man, whose spirits appeared to be sustained, though not unduly exhalted, by spirituous liquors.

"Well?" said Harriet.

"I don't believe it," said the young man, scanning her face as closely as he could in the feeble light. "Not possible. Too young. Too charming. Too much sense of humour."

"A great deal too much sense of humour to let you get away with that, my lad. And no sense of humour at all about this intrusion."

"I say," said the young man, "I'm really most frightfully sorry. Mere lightheartedness and all that kind of thing. Honestly, we weren't doing any harm. Quite definitely not. I mean, we were just winning the bet and going away quietly. I say, do be a sport. I mean, you're not the Warden or the Dean or anything. I know them. Couldn't you overlook it?"

"It's all very well," said Harriet. "But we can't have this kind of thing. It doesn't do. You must see that it doesn't do."

"Oh, I do see," agreed the young man. "Absolutely. Definitely. Dashed silly thing to do. Open to misinterpretation." He winced, and drew up one leg to rub his injured ankle. "But when you do see a tempting bit of wall like that—"

"Ah, yes," said Harriet, "what *is* the temptation? Just come and show me, will you?" She led him firmly, despite his protests, towards the postern. "Oh, I see, yes. A brick or two out of that buttress. Excellent foothold. You'd almost think they'd been knocked out on purpose, wouldn't you? And a handy tree in the Fellows' Garden. The Bursar will have to see to it. Are you well acquainted with that buttress, young man?"

"It's known to exist," admitted her captive. "But, look here, we weren't —we weren't calling on anybody or anything of that kind, you know, if you know what I mean."

"I hope not," said Harriet.

"No, we were all on our own," explained the young man, eagerly. "Nobody else involved. Good Heavens, no. And, look here, I've bust my ankle and we shall be gated anyhow, and, dear, kind lady—"

At this moment, a loud groan resounded from within the College wall. The young man's face became filled with agonized alarm.

"What's that?" asked Harriet.

"I really couldn't say," said the young man.

The groan was repeated. Harriet grasped the undergraduate tightly by the arm and led him along to the postern.

"But look here," said the gentleman, limping dolefully beside her, "you mustn't—please don't think—"

"I'm going to see what's the matter," said Harriet.

She unlocked the postern, drew her captive in with her, and relocked the gate. Under the wall, just beneath the spot where the young man had been perched, lay a huddled figure, which was apparently suffering acute internal agonies of some kind.

"Look here," said the young man, abandoning all pretence, "I'm most frightfully sorry about this. I'm afraid we were a bit thoughtless. I mean, we didn't notice. I mean, I'm afraid she isn't very well, and we didn't notice how it was, you know."

"The girl's drunk," said Harriet, uncompromisingly.

She had, in the bad old days, seen too many young poets similarly afflicted to make any mistake about the symptoms.

"Well, I'm afraid—yes, that's about it," said the young man. "Rogers *will* mix 'em so strong. But look here, honestly, there's no harm done, and I mean—"

"H'm!" said Harriet. "Well, don't shout. That house is the Warden's Lodgings."

"Hell!" said the young man, for the second time. "I say—are you going to be sporting?"

"That depends," said Harriet. "As a matter of fact, you've been extraordinarily lucky. I'm not one of the dons. I'm only staying in College. So I'm a free agent."

"Bless you!" exclaimed the young man, fervently.

"Don't be in a hurry. You'll have to tell me about this. Who's the girl, by the way?"

The patient here gave another groan.

"Oh, dear!" said the undergraduate.

"Don't worry," said Harriet. "She'll be sick in a minute." She walked over and inspected the sufferer. "It's all right. You can preserve a gentlemanly reticence. I know her. Her name's Cattermole. What's yours?"

"My name's Pomfret—of Queen's."

"Ah!" said Harriet.

"We threw a party round in my friend's rooms," explained Mr. Pomfret. "At least it started as a meeting, but it ended as a party. Nothing wrong whatever. Miss Cattermole came along for a joke. All clean fun. Only there were a lot of us and what with one thing and another we had a few too many, and then we found Miss Cattermole was rather under the weather. So we got her collected up, and Rogers and I—"

"Yes, I see," said Harriet. "Not very creditable, was it?"

"No, it's rotten," admitted Mr. Pomfret.

"Had she got leave to attend the meeting? And late leave?"

"I don't know," said Mr. Pomfret, disturbed. "I'm afraid—look here! It's all rather tiresome. I mean, she doesn't belong to the Society—"

"What Society?"

"The Society that was meeting. I think she pushed in for a joke."

"Gate-crashed you? H'm. That probably means no late leave."

"Sounds serious," said Mr. Pomfret.

"It's serious for *her*," said Harriet. "You'll get off with a fine or a gating, I suppose; but we have to be more particular. It's a nasty-minded world, and our rules have to remember that fact."

"I know," said Mr. Pomfret. "As a matter of fact we were dashed worried. We had a devil of a job getting her along," he burst out confidentially. "Fortunately it was only from this end of Long Wall. Phew!"

He pulled out his handkerchief and wiped his forehead.

"Anyhow," he went on, "I'm thankful you aren't a don."

"That's all very well," said Harriet austerely; "but I'm a Senior Member of College and I must feel responsibility. This isn't the kind of thing one wants."

She turned a cold glance on the unfortunate Miss Cattermole, to whom the worst was happening.

"I'm sure *we* didn't want it," said Mr. Pomfret, averting his eyes; "but what could we do? It's no good trying to corrupt your porter," he added ingenuously; "it's been tried."

"Indeed?" said Harriet. "No; you wouldn't get much change out of Padgett. Was anybody else there from Shrewsbury?"

"Yes–Miss Flaxman and Miss Blake. But they had ordinary leave to come and went off at about eleven. So they're all right."

"They ought to have taken Miss Cattermole with them."

"Of course," said Mr. Pomfret. He looked gloomier than ever. Obviously, thought Harriet, Miss Flaxman would not mind at all if Miss Cattermole got into trouble. Miss Blake's motives were more obscure; but she was probably only weakminded. Harriet was fired with a quite unscrupulous determination that Miss Cattermole should not get into trouble if she could prevent it. She went across to the limp form and hauled it to its feet. Miss Cattermole groaned dismally. "She'll do now," said Harriet. "I wonder where the little fool's room is. Do *you* know?"

"Well, as a matter of fact, I do," replied Mr. Pomfret. "Sounds bad, but there–people do show people their rooms, you know, all regulations notwithstanding and all that. It's somewhere over there, through that archway."

He waved a vague hand towards the New Quad at the other end of nowhere.

"Heavens!" said Harriet, "it would be. I'm afraid you'll have to give me a hand with her. She's a bit too much for me, and she can't stay here in the damp. If anybody sees us, you'll have to go through with it. How's the ankle?"

"Better, thanks," said Mr. Pomfret. "I think I can make shift to stagger a bit. I say, you're being very decent."

"Get on with the job," said Harriet, grimly, "and don't waste time in speeches."

Miss Cattermole was a thickly-built young woman, and no inconsiderable weight. She had also reached the stage of complete inertia. For Harriet, hampered by high-heeled shoes, and to Mr. Pomfret, afflicted with a game ankle, the progress across the quads was anything but triumphal. It was also rather noisy, what with the squeak of stone and gravel under their feet, and the grunts and shufflings of the limp figure between them. At every moment, Harriet expected to hear a window thrust up, or to see the shape of an agitated don come rushing out to demand some explanation of Mr. Pomfret's presence at that early hour of the morning. It was with very great relief that she at last found the right doorway and propelled Miss Cattermole's helpless form through it.

"What next?" inquired Mr. Pomfret in a hoarse whisper.

"I must let you out. I don't know where her room is, but I can't have you wandering all over College. Wait a minute. We'll deposit her in the nearest bathroom. Here you are. Round the corner. Easy does it."

Mr. Pomfret again bent obligingly to the task.

"There!" said Harriet. She laid Miss Cattermole on her back on the bathroom floor, took the key from the lock and came out, securing the door behind her. "She must stay there for the moment. Now we'll get rid of you. I don't think anybody saw us. If we're met on the way back, you were at Mrs. Hemans' dance and saw me home. Get that? It's not very convincing, because you ought not to have done any such thing, but it's better than the truth."

"I only wish I *had* been at Mrs. Hemans' dance," said the grateful Mr. Pomfret. "I'd have danced every dance with you and all the extras. Do you mind telling me who you are?"

"My name's Vane. And you'd better not start being enthusiastic too soon. I'm not considering *your* welfare particularly. Do you know Miss Cattermole well?"

"Rather well. Oh, yes. Naturally. I mean, we know some of the same people and that sort of thing. As a matter of fact, she used to be engaged to an old schoolfellow of mine —New College man—only that fell through and all that. No affair of mine; but you know how it is. One knows people and one kind of goes on knowing them. And there you are."

"Yes, I see. Well, Mr. Pomfret I am not anxious to get either you or Miss Cattermole into a row—"

"I knew you were a sport!" cried Mr. Pomfret.

("Don't *shout*)—but this sort of thing cannot go on. There must be no more late parties and no more climbing over walls. You understand. Not with anybody. It's not fair. If I go to the Dean with this story, nothing much will happen to *you*, but Miss Cattermole will be lucky if she's not sent down. For God's sake, stop being an ass. There are much better ways of enjoying Oxford than fooling round at midnight with the women students."

"I know there are. I think it's all rather rot, really."

"Then why do it?"

"I don't know. Why does one do idiotic things?"

"Why?" said Harriet. They were passing the end of the Chapel, and Harriet stood still to give emphasis to what she was saying. "I'll tell you why, Mr. Pomfret. Because you haven't the guts to say No when somebody asks you to be a sport. That tom-fool word has got more people in trouble than all the rest of the dictionary put together. If it's sporting to encourage girls to break rules and drink more than they can carry and get themselves into a mess on your account, then I'd stop being a sport and try being a gentleman."

"Oh, I say," said Mr. Pomfret, hurt.

"I mean it," said Harriet.

"Well, I see your point," said Mr. Pomfret, shifting his feet uneasily. "I'll do my best about it. You've been dashed spor— I mean you've behaved like a perfect gentleman about all this—" he grinned—"and I'll try to—good Lord! here's somebody coming."

A quick patter of slippered feet along the passage between the Hall and Queen Elizabeth was approaching rapidly.

On an impulse, Harriet stepped back and pushed open the Chapel door.

"Get in," she said.

Mr. Pomfret slipped hastily in behind her. Harriet shut the door on him and stood quietly in front of it. The footsteps came nearer, came opposite the porch and stopped suddenly. The night-walker uttered a little squeak.

"Ooh!"

"What is it?" said Harriet.

"Oh miss it's you! You gave me such a start. Did you see anything?"

"See what? Who is it, by the way?"

"Emily, miss. I sleep in the New Quad, miss, and I woke up, and I made sure I heard a man's voice in the quadrangle, and I looked out and there he was, miss, as plain as plain, coming this way with one of the young ladies. So I slipped on my slippers, miss. . . ."

"Damn!" said Harriet to herself. Better tell part of the truth, though.

"It's all right, Emily. It was a friend of mine. He came in with me and wanted very much to see the New Quad by moonlight. So we just walked across and back again."

(A poor excuse, but probably less suspicious than a flat denial.)

"Oh, I see, miss. I beg your pardon. But I get that nervous, with one thing and another. And it's unusual, if you'll excuse me saying so, miss. . . ."

"Yes, very," said Harriet, strolling gently away in the direction of the New Quad, so that the scout was bound to follow her. "It was stupid of me not to think that it might disturb people. I'll mention it to the Dean in the morning. You did quite right to come down."

"Well, miss, of course I didn't know who it was. And the Dean is so particular. And with all these queer things happening. . . ."

"Yes, absolutely. Of course. I'm really very sorry to have been so thoughtless. The gentleman has gone now, so you won't get woken up again."

Emily seemed doubtful. She was one of those people who never feel they have said a thing till they have said it three times over. She paused at the foot of her staircase to say everything again. Harriet listened impatiently, thinking of Mr. Pomfret, fuming in the Chapel. At last she got rid of the scout and turned back.

Complicated, thought Harriet; silly situation, like a farce. Emily thinks she's caught a student: I think I've caught a poltergeist. We catch each other. Young Pomfret parked in the Chapel. He thinks I'm kindly shielding him and Cattermole. Having carefully hidden Pomfret, I have to admit he was there. But if Emily *had* been the Poltergeist–and perhaps she is–then I couldn't have had Pomfret helping to chase her. This kind of sleuthing is very confusion-making.

She pushed open the Chapel door. The porch was empty.

"Damn!" said Harriet, irreverently. "The idiot's gone. Perhaps he's gone inside, though."

She looked in through the inner door and was relieved to see a dark figure faintly outlined against the pale oak of the stalls. Then, with a sudden, violent shock, she became aware of a second dark figure, poised strangely, it seemed, in midair.

"Hullo!" said Harriet. In the thin light of the South windows she saw the flash of a white shirt-front as Mr. Pomfret turned. "It's only me. *What's that?*"

She took a torch from her handbag and recklessly switched it on. The beam showed a dismal shape dangling from the canopy above the stalls. It was swinging a little to and fro and turning slowly as it swung. Harriet darted forward.

"Morbid kind of imagination these girls have got, haven't they?" said Mr. Pomfret.

Harriet contemplated the M.A. cap and gown, arranged over a dress and bolster hitched by a thin cord to one of the terminals with which the architect had decorated the canopies.

"Bread-knife stuck through the tummy, too," pursued Mr. Pomfret. "Gave me quite a turn as my aunt would say. Did you catch the young woman?"

"No. Was she in here?"

"Oh, definitely," said Mr. Pomfret. "Thought I'd retreat a bit further, you know. So in I came. Then I saw that. So I came along to investigate and heard somebody scrambling out by the other door—over there."

He pointed vaguely towards the north side of the building, where a door led into the vestry. Harriet hastened to look. The door was open, and the outer vestry door, though shut, had been unlocked from within. She peered out. All was quiet.

"Bother them and their rags," said Harriet, returning. "No, I didn't meet the lady. She must have got away while I was taking Emily back to the New Quad. Just my luck!" She muttered the last exclamation under her breath. It was really sickening to have had the Poltergeist under her hand like that, and to have been distracted by Emily. She went up to the dummy again, and saw that a paper was pinned to its middle by the bread-knife.

"Quotation from the classics," said Mr. Pomfret, easily. "Looks as though somebody had a grouse against your dons."

"Silly young fools!" said Harriet. "Very convincing bit of work, though, come to look at it. If we hadn't found it first, it would have created quite a sensation when we all filed into prayers. A little investigation is indicated. Well, now, it's time you went quietly home and were gated for the good of your soul."

She led him down to the postern and let him out.

"By the way, Mr. Pomfret, I'd be obliged if you didn't mention this rag to anybody. It's not in the best of taste. One good turn deserves another."

"Just as you say," replied Mr. Pomfret. "And, look here —may I push round tomorrow—at least, it's this morning, isn't it?—and make inquiries and all that? Only proper, you know. When shall you be in? Please!"

"No visitors in the morning," said Harriet, promptly. "I don't know what I shall be doing in the afternoon. But you can aways ask at the Lodge."

"Oh, I may? That's top-hole. I'll call—and if you're not there I'll leave a note. I mean, you must come round and have tea or a cocktail or something. And I do honestly promise it shan't happen again, if I can help it."

"All right. By the way—what time did Miss Cattermole arrive at your friend's place?"

"Oh—about half-past nine, I think. Couldn't be sure. Why?"

"I only wondered whether her initials were in the porter's book. But I'll see to it. Good-night."

"Good-night," said Mr. Pomfret, "and thanks frightfully."

Harriet locked the postern behind him and returned across the quadrangle, feeling that, out of all this absurd tiresomeness, something had been most definitely gained. The dummy could scarcely have been put in position before 9:30; so that Miss Cattermole, through sheer folly, had contrived to give herself a cast-iron alibi. Harriet was so grateful to her for advancing the inquiry by even this small step that she determined the girl should, if possible, be let off the consequences of her escapade.

This reminded her that Miss Cattermole still lay on the bathroom floor, waiting to be dealt with. It would be awkward if she had come to her senses in the interval and started to make a noise. But on reaching the New Quad and unlocking the door, Harriet found her prisoner in the somnolent stage of her rake's progress. A little research along the corridors revealed that Miss

Cattermole slept on the first floor. Harriet opened the door of the room, and as she did so the door next it opened also, and a head popped out.

"Is that you, Cattermole?" whispered the head. "Oh, I'm sorry." It popped in again.

Harriet recognized the girl who had gone up and spoken to Miss Cattermole after the Opening of the Library. She went to her door, which bore the name of "C. I. Briggs," and knocked gently. The head reappeared.

"Were you expecting to see Miss Cattermole come in?"

"Well," said Miss Briggs, "I heard somebody at her door –oh! it's Miss Vane, isn't it?"

"Yes. What made you sit up and wait for Miss Cattermole?"

Miss Briggs, who was wearing a woolly coat over her pajamas, looked a little alarmed.

"I had some work to do. I was sitting up in any case. Why?"

Harriet looked at the girl. She was short and sturdily built, with a plain, strong, sensible face. She appeared trustworthy.

"If you're a friend of Miss Cattermole's," said Harriet, "You'd better come and help me upstairs with her. She's down in the bathroom. I found her being helped over the wall by a young man, and she's rather under the weather."

"Oh, dear!" said Miss Briggs. "Tight?"

"I'm afraid so."

"She *is* a fool," said Miss Briggs. "I knew there'd be trouble some day. All right, I'll come."

Between them they lugged Miss Cattermole up the noisy, polished stairs and dumped her upon her bed. In grim silence they undressed her and put her between the sheets.

"She'll sleep it off now," said Harriet. "I think, by the way, a little explanation wouldn't be a bad idea. How about it?"

"Come into my room," said Miss Briggs. "Would you like any hot milk or Ovaltine or coffee, or anything?"

Harriet accepted hot milk. Miss Briggs put a kettle on the ring in the pantry opposite, came in, stirred up the fire and sat down on a pouffe.

"Please tell me," said Miss Briggs, "what has happened."

Harriet told her, omitting the names of the gentlemen concerned. But Miss Briggs promptly supplied the omission.

"That was Reggie Pomfret of course," she observed. "Poor blighter. He *always* gets left with the baby. After all, what is the lad to do, if people go chasing him?"

"It's awkward," said Harriet. "I mean, you need some knowledge of the world to get out of it gracefully. Does the girl really care for him?"

"No," said Miss Briggs. "Not really. She just wants somebody or something. You know. She got a nasty knock when her engagement was broken. You see, she and Lionel Farringdon had been childhood friends and so on, and it was all settled before she came up. Then Farringdon got collared by our Miss Flaxman, and there was a frightful bust-up. And there were complications. And Violet Cattermole has gone all unnerved."

"I know," said Harriet. "Sort of desperate feeling–I must have a man of my own–that kind of thing."

"Yes. Doesn't matter who he is. I think it's a sort of inferiority complex, or something. One must do idiotic things and assert one's self. Am I making myself clear?"

"Oh, yes. I understand that perfectly. It happens so often. One just has to make one's self out no end of a little devil.... Has this kind of thing happened often?"

"Well," confessed Miss Briggs, "more often than I like. I've tried to keep Violet reasonable, but what's the good of preaching to people? When they get into that worked-up state you might as well talk to the man in the moon. And though it's very tiresome for young Pomfret, he's awfully decent and safe. If he were strong-minded, of course he'd get out of it. But I'm rather thankful he's not, because, if it wasn't for him it might be some frightful tick or other."

"Is anything likely to come of it?"

"Marriage, do you mean? No-o. I think he has enough sense of self-protection to avoid that. And besides– Look here, Miss Vane, it really is an awful shame. Miss Flaxman simply cannot leave anybody alone, and she's trying to get Pomfret away too, though she doesn't want him. If only she'd leave poor Violet alone, the whole thing would probably work itself out quite quietly. Mind you, I'm very fond of Violet. She's a decent sort, and she'd be absolutely all right with the right kind of man. She's no business to be up at Oxford at all, really. A nice domestic life with a man to be devoted to is what she really wants. But he'd have to be a solid, decided kind of man, and frightfully affectionate in a firm kind of way. But not Reggie Pomfret, who is a chivalrous young idiot."

Miss Briggs poked the fire savagely.

"Well," said Harriet "something has got to be done about all this. I don't want to go to the Dean, but–"

"Of course, something must be done," said Miss Briggs. "It's extraordinarily lucky it should have been you who spotted it and not one of the dons. I've been almost wishing that *something* might happen. I've been frightfully worried about it. It isn't the kind of thing I know how to cope with at all. But I had to stand by Violet more or less–otherwise I should simply have lost her confidence altogether and goodness knows what stupid thing she'd have done then."

"I think you're quite right" said Harriet. "But now, perhaps, I can have a word with her and tell her to mind her step. After all, she has got to give some guarantee of sensible behaviour if I'm not to report her to the Dean. A spot of benevolent blackmail is indicated, I fancy."

"Yes," agreed Miss Briggs. "You can do it. It's exceedingly decent of you. I'll be thankful to be relieved of the responsibility. It's all rather wearing–and it does upset one's work. After all, work's what one's here for. I've got Honor Mods. next term, and it's frightfully upsetting, never knowing what's going to happen next."

"I expect Miss Cattermole relies on you a lot."

"Yes," said Miss Briggs, "but listening to people's confidences does take such a time, and I'm not awfully good at wrestling with fits of temperament."

"The confidante has a very heavy and thankless task," said Harriet. "It's not surprising if she goes mad in white linen. It's more surprising if she keeps sane and sensible like you. But I agree that you ought to have the burden taken off your shoulders. Are you the only one?"

"Pretty well. Poor old Violet lost a lot of friends over the uproar."

"And the business of the anonymous letters?"

"Oh, you've heard about that? Well, of course, it wasn't Violet. That's ridiculous. But Flaxman spread the story all over the college, and once you've started an accusation like that it takes a lot of killing."

"It does. Well, Miss Briggs, you and I had better get to bed. I'll come along and see Miss Cattermole after breakfast. Don't worry too much. I dare say this upset will be a blessing in disguise. Well, I'll be going now. Can you lend me a strong knife?"

Miss Briggs, rather astonished, produced a stout pen-knife and said good-night. On her way over to Tudor, Harriet cut down the dangling dummy and carried it away with her for scrutiny and action at a later hour. She felt she badly needed to sleep on the situation.

She must have been weary, for she dropped off as soon as she was in bed, and dreamed neither of Peter Wimsey nor of anything else.

# 8

> Tho marking him with melting eyes
> A thrilling throbbe from her hart did aryse,
> And interrupted all her other speache
> With some old sorowe that made a newe breache:
> Seemed shee sawe in the younglings face
> The old lineaments of his fathers grace.
>
> Edmund Spenser

"THE FACT remains," said Miss Pyke, "that I have to lecture at nine. Can anybody lend me a gown?"

A number of the dons were breakfasting in the S.C.R dining-room. Harriet entered in time to hear the request, formulated in a high and rather indignant tone.

"Have you lost your gown, Miss Pyke?"

"You could have mine with pleasure, Miss Pyke," said little Miss Chilperic, mildly, "but I'm afraid it wouldn't be nearly long enough."

"It isn't safe to leave *anything* in the S.C.R. cloakroom these days," said Miss Pyke. "I *know* it was there after dinner, because I saw it."

"Sorry," said Miss Hillyard, "but I've got a 9 o'clock lecture myself."

"You can have mine," suggested Miss Burrows, "if you can get it back to me by 10 o'clock."

"Ask Miss de Vine or Miss Barton," said the Dean. "They have no lectures. Or Miss Vane—hers would fit you."

"Certainly," said Harriet, carelessly. "Do you want a cap as well?"

"The cap has *gone* as well," replied Miss Pyke. "I don't need it for the lecture; but it would be convenient to know where my property has gone to."

"It's surprising the way things disappear," said Harriet helping herself to scrambled eggs. "People are very thoughtless. Who, by the way, owns a black semi-evening crepe de Chine, figured with bunches of red and green poppies, with a draped cross-over front, deep hip-yoke and flared skirt and sleeves about three years out of date?"

She looked round the dining-room, which was by now fairly well filled with dons. "Miss Shaw—you have a very good eye for a frock. Can you identify it?"

"I might if I saw it," said Miss Shaw. "I don't recollect one like it from your description."

"Have you found one?" asked the Bursar.

"Another chapter in the mystery?" suggested Miss Barton.

"I'm sure none of my students has one like it," said Miss Shaw. "They like to come and show me their frocks. I think it's a good thing to take an interest in them."

"I don't remember a frock like that in the Senior Common Room," said the Bursar.

"Didn't Miss Wrigley have a black figured crepe de Chine?" asked Mrs. Goodwin.

"Yes," said Miss Shaw. "But she's left. And anyhow, hers had a square neck and no hip-yoke. I remember it very well."

"Can't you tell us what the mystery is, Miss Vane?" inquired Miss Lydgate. "Or is it better that you shouldn't say anything?"

"Well," said Harriet, "I don't see any reason why I shouldn't tell you. When I came in last night after my dance I–er–went the rounds a bit–"

"Ah!" said the Dean. "I thought I heard somebody going to and fro outside my window. And whispering."

"Yes–Emily came out and caught me. I think she thought I was the Practical Joker. Well–I happened to go into the Chapel."

She told her story, omitting all mention of Mr. Pomfret, and merely saying that the culprit had apparently left by the vestry door.

"And," she concluded, "as a matter of fact, the cap and gown were yours, Miss Pyke, and you can have them any time. The bread-knife was taken from the Hall, presumably, or from here. And the bolster–I can't say where they got that."

"I think I can guess," said the Bursar. "Miss Trotman is away. She lives on the ground floor of Burleigh. It would be easy to nip in and bag her bolster."

"Why is Trotman away?" asked Miss Shaw. "She never told me."

"Father taken ill," said the Dean. "She went off in a hurry yesterday afternoon."

"I can't think why she shouldn't have told me," said Miss Shaw. "My students always come to me with their troubles. It's rather upsetting, when you think your pupils value your sympathy–"

"But you were out to tea," said the Treasurer, practically.

"I put a note in your pigeon-hole," said the Dean.

"Oh," said Miss Shaw. "Well, I didn't see it. I knew nothing about it. It's very odd that nobody should have mentioned it."

"Who *did* know it?" asked Harriet.

There was a pause; during which everybody had time to think it strange and improbable that Miss Shaw should not have received the note or heard of Miss Trotman's departure.

"It was mentioned at the High last night, I think," said Miss Allison.

"I was out to dinner," said Miss Shaw. "I shall go and see if that note's there."

Harriet followed her out; the note was there–a sheet of paper folded together and not sealed in an envelope.

"Well," said Miss Shaw; "I never saw it."

"Anybody might have read that and put it back," said Harriet.

"Yes–including myself, you mean."

"I didn't say that, Miss Shaw. Anybody."

They returned gloomily to the Common Room.

"The–er–the joke was perpetrated between dinner-time, when Miss Pyke lost her gown, and about a quarter to one, when I found it out," said Harriet. "It would be convenient if anybody could produce a water-tight alibi for the whole of that time. Particularly for the time after 11.15. I suppose I can find out whether any students had late leave till midnight. Anybody coming in then might have seen something."

"I have a list," said the Dean. "And the porter could show you the names of those who came in after nine."

"That will be a help."

"In the meantime," said Miss Pyke, pushing away her plate and rolling her napkin, "the ordinary duties of the day must be proceeded with. Could I have my gown—or *a* gown?"

She went over to Tudor with Harriet, who restored the gown and displayed the crepe de Chine frock.

"I have never seen that dress to my knowledge before," said Miss Pyke; "but I cannot pretend to be observant in these matters. It appears to be made for a slender person of medium height."

"There's no reason to suppose it belongs to the person who put it there," said Harriet, "any more than your gown."

"Of course not," said Miss Pyke; "no." She gave Harriet an odd, swift glance from her sharp, black eyes. "But the owner might provide some clue to the thief. Would it not—pardon me if I am trespassing upon your province—would it not be possible to draw some deduction from the name of the shop where it was bought?"

"Obviously it would have been," said Harriet; "the tab has been removed."

"Oh," said Miss Pyke. "Well; I must go to my lecture. As soon as I can find leisure I will endeavour to provide you with a time-table of my movements last night. I fear, however, it will scarcely be illuminating. I was in my room after dinner and in bed by half-past ten."

She stalked out, carrying her cap and gown. Harriet watched her go, and then took out a piece of paper from a drawer. The message upon it was pasted up in the usual way, and ran:

*tristius haud illis monstrum nec saevior ulla pestis er ira deum Stygiis sese extulit undis. Virginei volucrum vultus foedissima ventris proluvies uncaeque manus et pallida semper ora fame.*

"Harpies," said Harriet aloud. "Harpies. That seems to suggest a train of thought. But I'm afraid we can't suspect Emily or any of the scouts of expressing their feelings in Virgilian hexameters."

She frowned. Matters were looking rather bad for the Senior Common Room.

Harriet tapped on Miss Cattermole's door, regardless of the fact that it bore a large notice: HEADACHE—DO NOT DISTURB. It was opened by Miss Briggs, whose brow was anxious, but cleared when she saw who the visitor was.

"I was afraid it might be the Dean," said Miss Briggs.

"No," said Harriet, "so far I have held my hand. How is the patient?"

"Not too good," said Miss Briggs.

"Ah! 'His lordship has drunk his bath and gone to bed again.' That's about it, I suppose." She strode across to the bed and looked down at Miss Cattermole, who opened her eyes with a groan. They were large, light, hazel eyes, set in a plump face that ought to have been of a pleasant rose-leaf pink. A quantity of fluffy brown hair tumbled damply about her brow, adding to the general impression of an Angora rabbit that had gone on the loose and was astonished at the result.

"Feeling bloody?" inquired Harriet, with sympathy.

"Horrible," said Miss Cattermole.

"Serve you right," said Harriet. "If you must take your drink like a man, the least you can do is to carry it like a gentleman. It's a great thing to know your own limitations."

Miss Cattermole looked so woebegone that Harriet began to laugh. "You don't seem to be a very practised hand at this kind of thing. Look here; I'll get you something to pull you together and then I'm going to talk to you."

She went out briskly and nearly fell over Mr. Pomfret in the outer doorway.

"You here?" said Harriet. "I told you, no visitors in the morning. It makes a noise in the quad and is contrary to regulations."

"I'm not a visitor," said Mr. Pomfret, grinning. "I've been attending Miss Hillyard's lecture on Constitutional Developments."

"God help you!"

"And seeing you cross the quad in this direction, I turned in that direction like the needle to the North. Dark," said Mr. Pomfret, with animation, "and true and tender is the North. That's a quotation. It's very nearly the only one I know, so it's a good thing it fits."

"It does not fit. I am not feeling tender."

"Oh! . . . how's Miss Cattermole?"

"Bad hang-over. As you might expect."

"Oh! . . . sorry . . . No row, I hope?"

"No."

"Bless you!" said Mr. Pomfret. "I was lucky too. Friend of mine has a dashed good window. All quiet on the Western Front. So–look here! I wish there was something I could do to–"

"You shall," said Harriet. She twitched his lecture notebook from under his arm and scribbled in it.

"Get that made up at the chemist's and bring it back. I'm damned if I want to go myself and ask for a recipe for hobnailed liver."

Mr. Pomfret looked at her with respect.

"Where did you learn that one?" said he.

"Not at Oxford. I may say I have never had occasion to taste it; I hope it's nasty. The quicker you can get it made up, the better, by the way."

"I know, I know," said Mr. Pomfret, disconsolately. "You're fed up with the sight of me, and no wonder. But I do wish you'd come round some time and meet old Rogers. He's incredibly penitent. Come and have tea. Or a drink or something. Come this afternoon. Do. Just to show there's no ill feeling."

Harriet was opening her mouth to say No, when she looked at Mr. Pomfret, and her heart softened. He had the appeal of a very young dog of a very large breed–a kind of amiable absurdity.

"All right," said Harriet. "I will. Thank you very much."

Mr. Pomfret exhausted himself in expressions of delight, and, still vocal, allowed himself to be shepherded to the gate, where, almost in the act of stepping out, he had to step back to allow the entrance of a tall, dark student wheeling a bicycle.

"Hullo Reggie!" cried the young woman, "looking for me?"

"Oh, good morning," said Mr. Pomfret, rather taken aback. Then, catching sight of a handsome leonine head over the student's shoulder, he added with more assurance, "Hullo, Farringdon!"

"Hullo, Pomfret!" replied Mr. Farringdon. The adjective "Byronic" fitted him well enough, thought Harriet. He had an arrogant profile, a mass of close chestnut curls, hot brown eyes and a sulky mouth, and looked less pleased to see Mr. Pomfret than Mr. Pomfret to see him.

Mr. Pomfret presented Mr. Farringdon of New College to Harriet, and murmured that of course Miss Flaxman was known to her. Miss Flaxman stared coolly at Harriet and said how much she had enjoyed her detective talk the other night.

"We're throwing a party at 6 o'clock," went on Miss Flaxman to Mr. Pomfret. She pulled off her scholar's gown and stuffed it unceremoniously into her bicycle-basket. "Care to come? In Leo's room. Six o'clock. I think we've room for Reggie, haven't we, Leo?"

"I suppose so," said Mr. Farringdon, rather ungraciously. "There'll be an awful crowd anyway."

"Then we can always stuff in one more," said Miss Flaxman. "Don't mind Leo, Reggie; he's mislaid his manners this morning."

Mr. Pomfret appeared to think that somebody else's manners had also been mislaid, for he replied with more spirit than Harriet had expected of him:

"I'm sorry; I'm afraid I'm engaged. Miss Vane is coming to tea with me."

"Another time will do for that," said Harriet.

"Oh, no," said Mr. Pomfret.

"Couldn't you both come along, then, afterwards?" said Mr. Farringdon. "Always room for one more, as Catherine says." He turned to Harriet. "I hope you will come, Miss Vane. We should be delighted."

"Well–" said Harriet. It was Miss Flaxman's turn to look sulky.

"I say," said Mr. Farringdon, suddenly putting two and two together, "are you *the* Miss Vane? the novelist . . . You *are!* Then, look here, you simply *must* come. I shall be the most envied man in New College. We're all detective fans there."

"What about it?" said Harriet, deferring to Mr. Pomfret.

It was so abundantly clear that Miss Flaxman did not want Harriet, that Mr. Farringdon did not want Mr. Pomfret, and that Mr. Pomfret did not want to go, that she felt the novelist's malicious enjoyment in a foolish situation. Since none of the party could now very well get out of the situation without open rudeness, the invitation was eventually accepted. Mr. Pomfret stepped into the street to join Mr. Farringdon; Miss Flaxman could scarcely get out of accompanying Miss Vane back through the quadrangle.

"I didn't know you knew Reggie Pomfret," said Miss Flaxman.

"Yes, we have met," said Harriet. "Why didn't you bring Miss Cattermole home with you last night? Especially as you must have seen she was unwell."

Miss Flaxman looked startled.

"It was nothing to do with me," she said. "Was there a row?"

"No; but did you do anything to prevent it? You might have done, mightn't you?"

"I can't be Violet Cattermole's guardian."

"Anyway," said Harriet, "you may be glad to know that some good has come of this stupid business. Miss Cattermole is now definitely cleared of all suspicion about the anonymous letters and other disturbances. So it would be quite a good idea to behave decently to her, don't you think?"

"I tell you," said Miss Flaxman, "that I don't care one way or the other about it."

"No; but you started the rumours about her; it's up to you to stop them, now you know. I think it would be only fair to tell Mr. Farringdon the truth. If you do not, I shall."

"You seem to be very much interested in my affairs, Miss Vane."

"They seem to have aroused a good deal of general interest," said Harriet, bluntly. "I don't blame you for the original misunderstanding, but now that it is cleared up—and you can take my word for it that it is—I am sure you will see it is unfair that Miss Cattermole should be made a scapegoat. You can do a lot with your own year. Will you do what you can?"

Miss Flaxman, perplexed and annoyed, and obviously not quite clear what status she was to accord to Harriet, said, rather grudgingly:

"Of course, if she didn't do it, I'm glad. Very well. I'll tell Leo."

"Thank you very much," said Harriet.

Mr. Pomfret must have run very fast both ways, for the prescription appeared in a remarkably short space of time, along with a large bunch of roses. The draught was a potent one, and enabled Miss Cattermole not only to appear in Hall, but to eat her lunch. Harriet pursued her as she was leaving and carried her off to her own room.

"Well," said Harriet, "You are a young idiot, aren't you?"

Miss Cattermole dismally agreed.

"What's the sense of it?" said Harriet. "You have contrived to commit every crime in the calendar and got dashed little fun out of it, haven't you? You've attended a meeting in a man's rooms after Hall without leave, and you oughtn't to have got leave, because you gate-crashed the meeting. That's a social crime as well as a breach of rules. In any case, you were out after nine, without putting your initials in the book. That would cost you two bob. You came back to College after 11.15 without extra late leave—which would be five shillings. You returned, in fact, after midnight, which would be ten shillings, even if you had had leave. You climbed the wall, for which you ought to be gated; and finally, you came in blotto, for which you ought to be sent down. Incidentally, that's another social crime. What have you got to say, prisoner at the bar? Is there any reason why sentence should not be passed upon you? Have a cigarette."

"Thank you," said Miss Cattermole, faintly.

"If," said Harriet, "you hadn't, by this silly piece of work, contrived to clear yourself of the suspicion of being the College lunatic, I should go to the Dean. As it is, the episode has had its usefulness, and I'm inclined to be merciful."

Miss Cattermole looked up.

"Did something happen while I was out?"

"Yes, it did."

"Oh—h—h!" said Miss Cattermole, and burst into tears.

Harriet watched her for a few minutes and then brought out a large clean handkerchief from a drawer and silently handed it over.

"You can forget all that," said Harriet, when the victim's sobs had died down a little. "But do chuck all this nonsense. Oxford isn't the place for it. You can run after young men any time—God knows the world's full of them. But to waste three years which are unlike anything else in one's lifetime is ridiculous. And it isn't fair to College. It's not fair to other Oxford women. Be a fool if you like—I've been a fool in my time and so have most people—but for Heaven's sake do it somewhere where you won't let other people down."

Miss Cattermole was understood to say, rather incoherently, that she hated College and loathed Oxford, and felt no responsibility towards those institutions.

"Then why," said Harriet, "are you here?"

"I don't want to be here; I never did. Only my parents were so keen. My mother's one of those people who work to get things open to women—you know—professions and things. And father's a lecturer in a small provincial University. And they've made a lot of sacrifices and things."

Harriet thought Miss Cattermole was probably the sacrificial victim.

"I didn't mind coming up, so much," went on Miss Cattermole; "because I was engaged to somebody, and he was up, too, and I thought it would be fun and the silly old Schools wouldn't matter much. But I'm not engaged to him any more and how on earth can I be expected to bother about all this dead-and-gone History?"

"I wonder they bothered to send you to Oxford, if you didn't want to go, and were engaged."

"Oh! but they said that didn't make any difference. Every woman ought to have a University education, even if she married. And *now*, of course, they say what a good thing it is I still have my College career. And I can't make them understand that I *hate* it! They can't see that being brought up with everybody talking education all round one is enough to make one loathe the sound of it. I'm sick of education."

Harriet was not surprised.

"What should you have liked to do? I mean, supposing the complication about your engagement hadn't happened?"

"I think," said Miss Cattermole, blowing her nose in a final manner and taking another cigarette, "I think I should have liked to be a cook. Or possibly a hospital nurse, but I think I should have been better at cooking. Only, you see, those are two of the things Mother's always trying to get people out of the way of thinking women's sphere ought to be restricted to."

"There's a lot of money in good cooking," said Harriet.

"Yes—but it's not an educational advance. Besides, there's no school of Cookery at Oxford, and it had to be Oxford, you see, or Cambridge, because of the opportunity of making the right kind of friends. Only I haven't made any friends. They all hate me. Perhaps they won't so much, now that the beastly letters—"

"Quite so," said Harriet, hastily, fearing a fresh outburst. "How about Miss Briggs? She seems to be a very good sort."

"She's awfully kind. But I'm always having to be grateful to her. It's very depressing. It makes me want to bite."

"How right you are," said Harriet, to whom this was a direct hit over the solar plexus. "I know. Gratitude is simply damnable."

"And now," said Miss Cattermole, with devastating candour, "I've got to be grateful to *you*."

"You needn't be. I was serving my own ends as much as yours. But I'll tell you what I'd do. I'd stop trying to do sensational things, because it's apt to get you into positions where you have to be grateful. And I'd stop chasing undergraduates, because it bores them to tears and interrupts their work. I'd tackle the History and get through Schools. And then I'd turn round and say,

'Now I've done what you want me to, and I'm going to be a cook.' And stick to it."

"Would you?"

"I expect you want to be very truly run after, like Old Man Kangaroo. Well, good cooks are. Still, as you've started here on History, you'd better worry on at it. It won't hurt you, you know. If you learn how to tackle one subject–any subject–you've learnt how to tackle all subjects."

"Well," said Miss Cattermole, in rather an unconvinced tone, "I'll try."

Harriet went away in a rage and tackled the Dean.

"Why do they send these people here? Making themselves miserable and taking up the place of people who *would* enjoy Oxford? *We* haven't got room for women who aren't and never will be scholars. It's all right for the men's colleges to have hearty passmen who gambol round and learn to play games, so that they can gambol and game in Prep. Schools. But this dreary little devil isn't even hearty. She's a wet mess."

"I *know*," said the Dean, impatiently. "But schoolmistresses and parents are such jugginses. We do our best, but we can't always weed out their mistakes. And here's my secretary–called away, just when we're all so busy, because her tiresome little boy's got chicken-pox at his infuriating school. Oh, dear! I oughtn't to talk like that, because he's a delicate child and naturally children must come first, but it is *too* crushing!"

"I'll be off," said Harriet. "It's a shame you should have to be working of an afternoon and a shame of me to interrupt. By the way, I may as well tell you that Cattermole had an alibi for last night's affair."

"Had she? Good! That's something. Though I suppose it means *more* suspicion on our miserable selves. Still, facts are facts. Miss Vane, what *was* the noise in the quad last night? And who was the young man you were bear-leading? I didn't ask this morning in Common-Room, because I had an idea you didn't want me to."

"I didn't," said Harriet.

"And you don't?"

"As Sherlock Holmes said on another occasion: 'I think we must ask for an amnesty in that direction.' "

The Dean twinkled shrewdly at her.

"Two and two make four. Well, I trust you."

"But I was going to suggest a row of revolving spikes on the wall of the Fellows' Garden."

"Ah!" said the Dean. "Well, I don't *want* to know things. And most of it's sheer cussedness. They want to make heroes and heroines of themselves. Last week of term's the worst for wall-climbing. They make bets. Have to work 'em off before the end of term. Tiresome little cuckoos. All the same, it can't be allowed."

"It won't happen again, I fancy, with this particular lot."

"Very well. I'll speak to the Bursar–in a general way–about spikes."

Harriet changed her frock, pondering on the social absurdities of the party to which she was invited. Clearly, Mr. Pomfret clung to her as a protection against Miss Flaxman, and Mr. Farringdon, as a protection against Mr. Pomfret, while Miss Flaxman, who was apparently her hostess, did not want her at all. It was a pity that she could not embark on the adventure of annexing Mr. Farringdon, to complete a neat little tail-chasing circle. But she was both too old and too young to feel any thrill over the Byronic profile of Mr. Farringdon; there was more amusement to be had out of remaining a buffer state. She did, however, feel sufficient resentment against Miss Flaxman for her handling of the Cattermole affair, to put on an excecdingly well-cut coat and skirt and a hat of unexceptionable smartness, before starting out for the first item in her afternoon's program.

She had little difficulty in finding Mr. Pomfret's staircase, and none whatever in finding Mr. Pomfret. As she wound her way up the dark and ancient stair, past the shut door of one, Mr. Smith, the sported oak of one, Mr. Banerjee, and the open door of one, Mr. Hodges, who seemed to be entertaining a large and noisy party of male friends, she became aware of an altercation going on upon the landing above, and presently Mr. Pomfret himself came into view, standing in his own doorway and arguing with a man whose back was turned towards the stair.

"You can go to the devil," said Mr. Pomfret.

"Very good, sir," said the back; "but how about me going to the young lady? If I was to go and tell her that I seen you a-pushing of her over the wall—"

"Blast you!" exclaimed Mr. Pomfret. "*Will* you shut up?"

At this point, Harriet set her foot upon the top stair, and encountered the eye of Mr. Pomfret.

"Oh!" said Mr. Pomfret, taken aback. Then, to the man, "Clear off now; I'm busy. You'd better come again."

"Quite a man for the ladies, ain't you, sir?" said the man, disagreeably.

At these words, he turned, and, to her amazement, Harriet recognized a familiar face.

"Dear me, Jukes," said she. "Fancy seeing you here!"

"Do you know this blighter?" said Mr. Pomfret.

"Of course I do," said Harriet. "He was a porter at Shrewsbury, and was sacked for petty pilfering. I hope you're going straight now, Jukes. How's your wife?"

"All right," said Jukes, sulkily. "I'll come again."

He made a move to slip down the staircase, but Harriet had set her umbrella so awkwardly across it as to bar the way pretty effectively.

"Hi!" said Mr. Pomfret. "Let's hear about this. Just come back here a minute, will you?" He stretched out a powerful arm, and yanked the reluctant Jukes over the threshold.

"You can't get me on that old business," said Jukes, scornfully, as Harriet followed them in, shutting oak and door after her with a bang. "That's over and done with. It ain't got nothing to do with that other little affair what I mentioned."

"What's that?" asked Harriet.

"This nasty piece of work," said Mr. Pomfret, "has had the blasted neck to come here and say that if I don't pay him to keep his mouth shut, he'll lay an information about what happened last night."

"Blackmail," said Harriet, much interested. "That's a serious offence."

"I didn't mention no money," said Jukes, injured. "I only told this genleman as I seen something as didn't ought to have happened and was uneasy in my mind about it. He says I can go to the devil, so I says in that case I'll go to the lady, being troubled in my conscience, don't you see."

"Very well," said Harriet. "I'm here. Go ahead."

Mr. Jukes stared at her.

"I take it," said Harriet, "you saw Mr. Pomfret help me in over the Shrewsbury wall last night when I'd forgotten my key. What were you doing out there, by the way? Loitering with intent? You then probably saw me come out again, thank Mr. Pomfret and ask him to come in and see the College Buildings by moonlight. If you waited long enough, you saw me let him out again. What about it?"

"Nice goings-on, I don't think," said Jukes, disconcerted.

"Possibly," said Harriet. "But if Senior Members choose to enter their own college in an unorthodox way, I don't see who's to prevent them. Certainly not you."

"I don't believe a word of it," said Jukes.

"I can't help that," said Harriet. "The Dean saw Mr. Pomfret and me, so she will. Nobody's likely to believe you. Why didn't you tell this man the whole story at once, Mr. Pomfret, and relieve his conscience? By the way, Jukes, I've just told the Dean she ought to have that wall spiked. It was handy for us, but it really isn't high enough to keep out burglars and other undesirables. So it's not much good your loitering about there any more. One or two things have been missed from people's rooms lately," she added, with some truth, "it might be as well to have that road specially policed."

"None of that," said Jukes. "I ain't a-going to have my character took away. If it's as you say, then I'm sure I'd be the last to want to make trouble for a lady like yourself."

"I hope you'll bear that in mind," said Mr. Pomfret. "Perhaps you'd like to have something to remember it by."

"No assault!" cried Jukes, backing towards the door. "No assault!" Don't you go to lay 'ands on me!"

"If ever you show your dirty face here again," said Mr. Pomfret, opening the door, "I'll kick you downstairs and right through the quad. Get that? Then get out!"

He flung the oak back with one hand and propelled Jukes vigorously through it with the other. A crash and a curse proclaimed that the swiftness of Jukes's exit had carried him over the head of the stairs.

"Whew!" exclaimed Mr. Pomfret, returning. "By jove! that was great! That was marvellous of you. How did you come to think of it?"

"It was fairiy obvious. I expect it was all bluff, really. I don't see how he could have known who Miss Cattermole was. I wonder how he got on to you."

"He must have followed me back when I came out. But I didn't get in through this window–obviously–so how did he–? Oh! yes, when I knocked Brown up I believe he stuck his head out and said, 'That you, Pomfret?' Careless blighter. I'll talk to him. . . .I say, you do seem to be everybody's guardian angel, don't you? It's marvellous, being able to keep your wits about you like that."

He gazed at her with dog-like eyes. Harriet laughed, as Mr. Rogers and the tea entered the room together.

Mr. Rogers was in his third year–tall, dark, lively and full of an easy kind of penitence.

"All this running round and busting rules is rot," said Mr. Rogers. "Why do we do it? Because somebody says it is fun, and one believes it. Why should one believe it? I can't imagine. One should look at these things more objectively. Is the thing beautiful in itself? No. Then let us not do it. By the way, Pomfret, have you been approached about debagging Culpepper?"

"I am all for it," said Mr. Pomfret.

"True, Culpepper is a wart. He is a disgusting object. But would he look any better debagged? No, Socrates, he would not. He would look much worse. If anybody is to be debagged, it shall be somebody with legs that will stand exposure—your own, Pomfret, for example."

"You try, that's all," said Mr. Pomfret.

"In any case," pursued Mr. Rogers, "debagging is otiose and out of date. The modern craze for exposing unaesthetic legs needs no encouragement from me. I shall not be a party to it. I intend to be a reformed character. From now on, I shall consider nothing but the value of the Thing-in-Itself, unmoved by any pressure of public opinion."

Having, in this pleasant manner, confessed his sins and promised amendment, Mr. Rogers gracefully led the conversation to topics of general interest, and, about 5 o'clock, departed, murmuring something in an apologetic way about work and his tutor, as though they were rather indelicate necessities. At this point, Mr. Pomfret suddenly went all solemn, as a very young man occasionally does when alone with a woman older than himself, and told Harriet a good deal about his own view of the meaning of life. Harriet listened with as much intelligent sympathy as she could command; but was slightly relieved when three young men burst in to borrow Mr. Pomfret's beer and remained to argue over their host's head about Komisarjevsky. Mr. Pomfret seemed faintly annoyed, and eventually asserted his right to his own guest by announcing that it was time to pop round to New College for old Farringdon's party. His friends let him go with mild regret and, before Harriet and her escort were well out of the room, took possession of their armchairs and continued the argument.

"Very able fellow, Marston," said Mr. Pomfret, amiably enough. "Great noise on O.U.D.S. and spends his vacations in Germany. I don't know how they contrive to get so worked up about plays. I like a good play, but I don't understand all this stuff about stylistic treatment and planes of vision. I expect you do, though."

"Not a word," said Harriet, cheerfully. "I dare say they don't, either. Anyhow, I know I don't like plays in which all the actors have to keep on tumbling up and down flights of steps, or where the lighting's so artistically done that you can't see anything, or where you keep on wondering all the time what the symbolical whirligig in the center of the stage is going to be used for, if anything. It distracts me. I'd rather go to the Holborn Empire and have my fun vulgar."

"Would you?" said Mr. Pomfret, wistfully. "You wouldn't come and do a show with me in Town in the vac, would you?"

Harriet made a vague kind of promise, which seemed to delight Mr. Pomfret very much, and they presently found themselves in Mr. Farringdon's sitting-room, packed like sardines among a mixed crowd of undergraduates and struggling to consume sherry and biscuits without moving their elbows.

The crowd was such that Harriet never set eyes on Miss Flaxman from first to last. Mr. Farringdon did, however, struggle through to them, bringing with him a bunch of young men and women who wanted to talk about detective fiction. They appeared to have read a good deal of this kind of literature, though very little of anything else. A School of Detective Fiction would, Harriet thought, have a fair chance of producing a goodly crop of Firsts. The fashion for psychological analysis had, she decided, rather gone out since her day: she was instinctively aware that a yearning for action and the concrete was taking its place. The pre-War solemnity and the post-War exhaustion were both gone; the desire now was for an energetic doing of something definite, though the definitions differed. The detective story, no doubt, was acceptable, because in it something definite was done, the "what" being comfortably decided beforehand by the author. It was borne in upon Harriet that all these young men and women were starting out to hoe a hardish kind of row in a very stony ground. She felt rather sorry for them.

Something definite done. Yes, indeed. Harriet, reviewing the situation next morning, felt deeply dissatisfied. She did not like this Jukes business at all. He could scarcely, she supposed, have anything to do with the anonymous letters: where could he have got hold of that passage from the *Aeneid?* But he was a man with a grudge, a nasty-minded man, and a thief; it was not pleasant that he should make a habit of hanging round the College walls after dark.

Harriet was alone in the Senior Common Room, everybody else having departed to her work. The S.C.R. scout came in, carrying a pile of clean ash-trays, and Harriet suddenly remembered that her children lodged with the Jukeses.

"Annie," she said, impulsively, "what does Jukes come down into Oxford for, after dark?"

The woman looked startled. "Does he, madam? For no good, I should think."

"I found him loitering in St. Cross Road last night, in a place where he might easily get over. Is he keeping honest, do you know?"

"I couldn't say, I'm sure, madam, but I have my doubts. I like Mrs. Jukes very much, and I'd be sorry to add to her troubles. But I never have trusted Jukes. I've been thinking I ought to put my little girls somewhere else. He might be a bad influence on them, don't you think?"

"I certainly do think so."

"I'm the last person to wish to put difficulties into the way of a respectable married woman," went on Annie, slapping an ash-tray smartly down, "and naturally she's right to stick by her husband. But one's own children must come first, mustn't they?"

"Of course," said Harriet, rather inattentively. "Oh, yes. I should find somewhere else for them. I suppose you haven't ever heard either Jukes or his wife say anything to suggest that he—well, that he was stealing from the College or cherishing bad feelings against the dons."

"I don't have much to say to Jukes, madam, and if Mrs. Jukes knew anything, she wouldn't tell me. It wouldn't be right if she did. He's her husband, and she has to take his part. I quite see that. But if Jukes is behaving dishonestly, I shall have to find somewhere else for the children. I'm much obliged to you for mentioning it, madam. I shall be going round there on Wednesday, which is my free afternoon, and I'll take the opportunity to give notice. May I ask if you have said anything to Jukes, madam?"

"I have spoken to him, and told him that if he hangs round here any more he will have to do with the police."

"I'm very glad to hear that, madam. It isn't right at all that he should come here like that. If I'd known about it, I really shouldn't have been able to sleep. I feel sure it ought to be put a stop to."

"Yes, it ought. By the way, Annie, have you ever seen anybody in the College in a dress of this description?"

Harriet picked up the black figured crepe de Chine from the chair beside her. Annie examined it carefully.

"No, madam, not to my recollection. Perhaps one of the maids that's been here longer than me might know. There's Gertrude in the dining-room; should you like to ask her?"

Gertrude, however, could give no help. Harriet asked them to take the dress and catechize the rest of the staff. This was done, but with no result. An inquiry among the students produced no identification, either. The dress was brought back, still unclaimed and unrecognized. One more puzzle. Harriet concluded that it must actually be the property of the Poison Pen; but if so, it must have been brought to College and kept in hiding till the moment of its dramatic appearance in Chapel; for if it had ever been worn in College, it was almost inconceivable that no one should be able to recognize it.

The alibis produced, meekly enough, by the members of the S.C.R. were none of them water-tight. That was not surprising; it would have been more surprising if they had been. Harriet (and Mr. Pomfret, of course) alone knew the exact time for which the alibi was required; and though many people were able to show themselves covered up to midnight or thereabouts, all had been, or claimed to have been, virtuously in their own rooms and beds by a quarter to one. Nor, though the porter's book and late-leave tickets had been examined, and all students interrogated who might have been about the quad at midnight, had anybody seen any suspicious behaviour with gowns or bolsters or bread-knives. Crime was too easy in a place like this. The College was too big, too open. Even if a form had been seen crossing the quad with a bolster, or indeed for that matter a complete set of bedding and a mattress, nobody would ever think anything of it. Some hardy fresh-air fiend sleeping out; that would be the natural conclusion.

Harriet, exasperated, went over to Bodley and plunged into her researches upon Le Fanu. There, at least, one did know what one was investigating.

She felt so much the need of a soothing influence that, in the afternoon, she went down to Christ Church to hear service at the Cathedral. She had been shopping–purchasing, among other things, a bag of meringues for the entertainment of some students she had asked to a small party in her room that evening–and it was only when her arms were already full of parcels that the idea of Cathedral suggested itself. It was rather out of her way; but the parcels were not heavy. She dodged across Carfax, angrily resenting its modern bustle of cars and complication of stop-and-go lights, and joined the little sprinkling of foot-passengers who were tripping down St. Aldate's and through Wolsey's great unfinished quadrangle, bound on the same pious errand as herself.

It was quiet and pleasant in Cathedral. She lingered in her seat for some little time after the nave had emptied and until the organist had finished the voluntary. Then she came slowly out, turning left along the plinth with a vague idea of once more admiring the great staircase and the Hall, when a slim figure in a grey suit shot with such velocity from a dark doorway that he cannoned full tilt against her, nearly knocking her down, and sending her bag and parcels flying in disorder along the plinth.

"Hell!" said a voice which set her heart beating by its unexpected familiarity, "have I hurt you? Me all over–bargin' and bumpin' about like a bumble-bee in a bottle. Clumsy lout! I say, do say I haven't hurt you.

Because, if I have, I'll run straight across and drown myself in Mercury."

He extended the arm that was not supporting Harriet in a vague gesture towards the pond.

"Not in the least, thank you," said Harriet, recovering herself.

"Thank God for that. This is my unlucky day. I've just had a most unpleasant interview with the Junior Censor. Was there anything breakable in the parcels? Oh, look! your bag's opened itself wide and all the little oojahs have gone down the steps. Please don't move. You stand there, thinkin' up things to call me, and I'll pick 'em all up one by one on my knees sayin' 'meâ cûlpa' to every one of 'em."

He suited the action to the words.

"I'm afraid it hasn't improved the meringues." He looked up apologetically. "But if you'll say you forgive me, we'll go and get some new ones from the kitchen–the real kind–*you* know–speciality of the House, and all that."

"Please don't bother," said Harriet.

It wasn't he, of course. This was a lad of twenty-one or two at the most, with a mop of wavy hair tumbling over his forehead and a handsome, petulant face, full of charm, though ominously weak about the curved lips and upwardslanting brows. But the color of the hair was right–the pale yellow of ripe barley; and the light drawling voice, with its clipped syllables and ready babble of speech; and the quick, sidelong smile; and above all, the beautiful, sensitive hands that were gathering the "oojahs" deftly up into their native bag.

"You haven't called me any names yet," said the young man.

"I believe I could almost put a name to you," said Harriet. "Isn't it–are you any relation of Peter Wimsey's?"

"Why, of course," said the young man, sitting up on his heels. "He's my uncle; and a dashed sight more accommodating than the Jewish kind," he added, as though struck by a melancholy association of ideas. "Have I met you somewhere? Or was it pure guesswork? You don't think I'm like him, do you?"

"When you spoke, I thought you were your uncle for the moment. Yes, you're very like him, in some ways."

"That'll break my mater's heart, all right," said the young man, with a grin. "Uncle Peter's not approved. I wish to God he was here, though. He'd come in uncommonly handy at the moment. But he seems to have beetled off somewhere as usual. Mysterious old tom-cat, isn't he? I take it you know him–I forgot the proper bromide about how small the world is, but we'll take it as read. Where *is* the old blighter?"

"I believe he's in Rome."

"He *would* be. That means a letter. It's awfully hard to be persuasive in a letter, don't you think? I mean, it all takes so much explaining, and the famous family charm doesn't seem to go over so well in black and white."

He smiled at her with engaging frankness as he recaptured a last straying copper.

"Do I gather," said Harriet, with some amusement, "that you anticipate an appeal to Uncle Peter's better feelings?"

"That's about it," said the young man. "He's quite human, really, you know, if you go about him the right way. Besides, you see, I've got the bulge on Uncle Peter. If the worst comes to the worst, I can always threaten to cut my throat and land him with the strawberry leaves."

"With the what?" said Harriet, fancying that this must be the latest Oxford version of giving the raspberry.

"The strawberry leaves," said the young man. "The balm, the sceptre, and the ball. Four rows of moth-eaten ermine. To say nothing of that dashed great barracks down at Denver, eating its mouldy head off." Seeing that Harriet still looked blankly at him, he explained further: "I'm sorry; I forgot. My name's Saint-George and the Governor forgot to provide me with any brothers. So the minute they write d.s.p. after me, Uncle Peter's for it. Of course, my father might outlive him; but I don't believe Uncle Peter's the sort to die young, unless one of his pet criminals manages to bump him off."

"That might easily happen," said Harriet, thinking of the plug-ugly.

"Well, that makes it all the worse for him," said Lord Saint-George, shaking his head. "The more risks he takes, the quicker he's got to toe the line for the matrimonial stakes. No more bachelor freedom with old Bunter in a Piccadilly flat. *And* no more spectacular Viennese singers. So you see, it's as much as his life's worth to let anything happen to me."

"Obviously," said Harriet, fascinated by this new light on the subject.

"Uncle Peter's weakness," went on Lord Saint-George, carefully disentangling the squashed meringues from their paper, "is his strong sense of public duty. You mightn't think it to look at him, but it's there. (Shall we try these on the carp? I don't think they're really fit for human consumption.) He's kept out of it so far—he's an obstinate old devil. Says he'll have the right wife or none."

"But suppose the right one says No."

"That's the story he puts up. I don't believe a word of it. Why should anybody object to Uncle Peter? He's no beauty and he'd talk the hind leg off a donkey; but he's dashed well-off and he's got good manners and he's in the stud-book." He balanced himself on the edge of Mercury and peered into its tranquil waters. "Look! there's the big old one. Been here since the foundation, by the looks of him—see him go? Cardinal Wolsey's particular pet." He tossed a crumb to the great fish, which took it with a quick snap and submerged again.

"I don't know how well you know my uncle," he proceeded, "but if you do get a chance, you might let him know that when you saw me I was looking rather unwell and hagridden and hinted darkly at felo-de-se."

"I'll make a point of it," said Harriet. "I will say you seemed scarcely able to crawl and, in fact, fainted into my arms, accidentally crushing all my parcels. He won't believe me, but I'll do my best."

"No—he isn't good at believing things, confound him. I'm afraid I shall have to write, after all, and produce the evidence. Still, I don't know why I should bore you with my personal affairs. Come on down to the kitchen."

The Christ Church cook was well pleased to produce meringues from the ancient and famous College oven; and when Harriet had duly admired the vast fireplace with its shining spits and heard statistics of the number of joints roasted and the quantity of fuel consumed per week in term-time, she followed her guide out into the quadrangle again with all proper expressions of gratitude.

"Not at all," said the viscount. "Not much return, I'm afraid, after banging you all over the place and throwing your property about. May I know, by the way, whom I have had the honour of inconveniencing?"

"My name's Harriet Vane."

Lord Saint-George stood still, and smote himself heavily over the forehead.

"My God, what have I done? Miss Vane, I do beg your pardon—and throw myself abjectly on your mercy. If my uncle hears about this he'll never forgive me, and I *shall* cut my throat. It is borne in upon me that I have said every possible thing I should not."

"It's my fault," said Harriet, seeing that he looked really alarmed, "I ought to have warned you."

"As a matter of fact, I've no business to say things like that to anybody. I'm afraid I've inherited my uncle's tongue and my mother's want of tact. Look here, for God's sake forget all that rot. Uncle Peter's a dashed good sort, and as decent as they come."

"I've reason to know it," said Harriet.

"I suppose so. By the way—hell! I seem to be putting my foot in it all round, but I ought to explain that I've never heard him talk about you. I mean, he's not that sort. It's my mother. She says all kinds of things. Sorry. I'm making things worse and worse."

"Don't worry," said Harriet. "After all, I *do* know your uncle, you know—well enough, anyhow, to know what sort he is. And I certainly won't give you away."

"For Heaven's sake, don't. It isn't only that I'd never get anything more out of him—and I'm in a devil of a mess—but he makes one feel such an appalling tick. I don't suppose you've ever been given the wrong side of my uncle's tongue—naturally not. But of the two, I recommend skinning."

"We're both in the same boat. I'd no business to listen. Good-bye—and many thanks for the meringues."

She was half-way up St. Aldate's when the viscount caught her up.

"I say—I've just remembered. That old story I was ass enough to rake up—"

"The Viennese dancer?"

"Singer—music's his line. Please forget that. I mean, it's got whiskers on it—it's six years old, anyway. I was a kid at school and I dare say it's all rot."

Harriet laughed, and promised faithfully to forget the Viennese singer.

# 9

Come hether freind, I am ashamed to hear that what I hear of you . . . . You have almost attayned to the age of nyne yeeres, at least to eight and a halfe, and seeing that you knowe your dutie, if you neglect it you deserve greater punishment then he which through ignorance doth it not. Think not that the nobilitie of your Ancestors doth free you to doe all that you list, contrarywise, it bindeth you more to followe vertue.

Pierre Erondell

"So," SAID the Bursar, coming briskly up to the High Table for lunch on the following Thursday; "Jukes has come to grief once more. . . ."

"Has he been stealing again?" asked Miss Lydgate. "Dear me, how disappointing!"

"Annie tells me she's had her suspicions for some time, and yesterday being her half-day she went down to tell Mrs. Jukes she would have to place the children somewhere else —when lo, and behold! in walked the police and discovered a whole lot of things that had been stolen a fortnight ago from an undergraduate's rooms in Holywell. It was most unpleasant for her–for Annie, I mean. They asked her a lot of questions."

"I always thought it was a mistake to put those children there," said the Dean.

"So that's what Jukes did with himself at night," said Harriet. "I heard he'd been seen outside the College here. As a matter of fact, I gave Annie the tip. It's a pity she couldn't have removed the children earlier."

"I thought he was doing quite well," said Miss Lydgate. "He had a job–and I know he kept chickens–and there was the money for the little Wilsons, Annie's children, I mean–so he ought not to have needed to steal, poor man. Perhaps Mrs. Jukes is a bad manager."

"Jukes is a bad lot," said Harriet. "A nasty bit of business altogether. He's much best out of the way."

"Had he taken much?" inquired the Dean.

"I gather from Annie," said the Bursar, "that they rather think they can trace a lot of petty thieving to Jukes. I understand it's a question of finding out where he sold the things."

"He'd dispose of them through a fence, I suppose," said Harriet; "some pawnbroker or somebody of that kind. Has he been inside–in prison –before?"

"Not that I know of," said the Dean; "though he *ought* to have been."

"Then I suppose he'll get off lightly as a first offender."

"Miss Barton will know all about that. We'll ask her. I do hope poor Mrs. Jukes isn't involved," said the Bursar.

"Surely not," cried Miss Lydgate, "she's such a nice woman."

"She must have known about it," said Harriet, "unless she was a perfect imbecile."

"What a dreadful thing, to know your husband was a thief!"

"Yes," said the Dean. "It would be very uncomfortable to have to live on the proceeds."

"Terrible," said Miss Lydgate. "I can't imagine anything more dreadful to an honest person's feelings."

"Then," said Harriet, "we must hope, for Mrs. Jukes's sake, she was as guilty as he was."

"What a horrible hope!" exclaimed Miss Lydgate.

"Well, she's got to be either guilty or unhappy," said Harriet, passing the bread to the Dean with a twinkle in her eye.

"I dissent altogether," said Miss Lydgate. "She must either be innocent and unhappy or guilty and unhappy–I don't see how she can be happy, poor creature."

"Let us ask the Warden next time we see her," said Miss Martin, "whether it is possible for a guilty person to be happy. And if so, whether it is better to be happy or virtuous."

"Come, Dean," said the Bursar, "we can't allow this sort of thing. Miss Vane, a bowl of hemlock for the Dean, if you please. To return to the subject under discussion, the police have not, so far, taken up Mrs. Jukes, so I suppose there's nothing against her."

"I'm very glad of that," said Miss Lydgate; and, Miss Shaw arriving at that moment, full of woe about one of her pupils who was suffering from perpetual headache, and an incapacity to work, the conversation wandered into other channels.

Term was drawing to a close, and the investigation seemed little farther advanced; but it appeared possible that Harriet's nightly perambulations and the frustration of the Library and Chapel scandals had exercised a restraining influence on the Poltergeist, for there was no further outbreak of any kind, not so much as an inscription in a lavatory or an anonymous letter, for three days. The Dean, exceedingly busy, was relieved by the respite, and also cheered by the news that Mrs. Goodwin the secretary would be back on the Monday to cope with the end-of-term rush. Miss Cattermole was seen to be more cheerful, and wrote a quite respectable paper for Miss Hillyard about the naval policy of Henry VIII. Harriet asked the enigmatic Miss de Vine to coffee. As usual, she had intended to lay bare Miss de Vine's soul, and, as usual, found herself laying bare her own.

"I quite agree with you," said Miss de Vine, "about the difficulty of combining intellectual and emotional interests. I don't think it affects women only; it affects men as well. But when men put their public lives before their private lives, it causes less outcry than when a woman does the same thing, because women put up with neglect better than men, having been brought up to expect it."

"But suppose one doesn't quite know which one wants to put first. Suppose," said Harriet, falling back on words which were not her own, "suppose one is cursed with both a heart and a brain?"

"You can usually tell," said Miss de Vine, "by seeing what kind of mistakes you make. I'm quite sure that one never makes *fundamental* mistakes about the thing one really wants to do. Fundamental mistakes arise out of lack of genuine interest. In my opinion, that is."

"I made a very big mistake once," said Harriet, "as I expect you know. I don't think that arose out of lack of interest. It seemed at the time the most important thing in the world."

"And yet you made the mistake. Were you really giving all your mind to it, do you think? Your *mind?* Were you really being as cautious and exacting about it as you would be about writing a passage of fine prose?"

"That's rather a difficult sort of comparison. One can't, surely, deal with emotional excitements in that detached spirit."

"Isn't the writing of good prose an emotional excitement?"

"Yes, of course it is. At least, when you get the thing dead right and know it's dead right, there's no excitement like it. It's marvellous. It makes you feel like God on the Seventh Day—for a bit, anyhow."

"Well, that's what I mean. You expend the trouble and you don't make any mistake—and *then* you experience the ecstasy. But if there's any subject in which you're content with the second-rate, then it isn't really your subject."

"You're dead right," said Harriet, after a pause. "If one's genuinely interested one knows how to be patient, and let time pass, as Queen Elizabeth said. Perhaps that's the meaning of the phrase about genius being eternal patience, which I always thought rather absurd. If you truly want a thing, you don't snatch; if you snatch, you don't really want it. Do you suppose that, if you find yourself taking pains about a thing, it's a proof of its importance to you?"

"I think it is, to a large extent. But the big proof is that the thing comes right, without those fundamental errors. One always makes surface errors, of course. But a fundamental error is a sure sign of not caring. I wish one could teach people nowadays that the doctrine of snatching what one thinks one wants is unsound."

"I saw six plays this winter in London," said Harriet, "all preaching the doctrine of snatch. I agree that they left me with the feeling that none of the characters knew what they wanted."

"No," said Miss de Vine. "If you are once sure what you do want, you find that everything else goes down before it like grass under a roller–all other interests, your own and other people's. Miss Lydgate wouldn't like my saying that, but it's as true of her as of anybody else. She's the kindest soul in the world, in things she's indifferent about, like the peculations of Jukes. But she hasn't the slightest mercy on the prosodical theories of Mr. Elkbottom. She wouldn't countenance those to save Mr. Elkbottom from hanging. She'd say she couldn't. And she couldn't, of course. If she actually *saw* Mr. Elkbottom writhing in humiliation, she'd be sorry but she wouldn't alter a paragraph. That would be treason. One can't be pitiful where one's own job is concerned. You'd lie cheerfully, I expect, about anything except–what?"

"Oh, anything!" said Harriet, laughing. "Except saying that somebody's beastly book is good when it isn't. I can't do that. It makes me a lot of enemies, but I can't do it."

"No, one can't," said Miss de Vine. "However painful it is, there's always one thing one has to deal with sincerely, if there's any root to one's mind at all. I ought to know, from my own experience. Of course, the one thing may be an emotional thing; I don't say it mayn't. One may commit all the sins in the calendar, and still be faithful and honest towards one person. If so, then that one person is probably one's appointed job. I'm not despising that kind of loyalty; it doesn't happen to be mine, that is all."

"Did you discover that by making a fundamental mistake?" asked Harriet, a little nervously.

"Yes," said Miss de Vine. "I once got engaged to somebody. But I found I was always blundering–hurting his feelings, doing stupid things, making quite elementary mistakes about him. In the end I realized that I simply wasn't taking as much trouble with him as I should have done over a disputed reading. So I decided he wasn't my job." She smiled. "For all that, I was fonder of him than he was of me. He married an excellent woman who is devoted to him and does make him her job. I should think he was a full-time job. He is a painter and usually on the verge of bankruptcy; but he paints very well."

"I suppose one oughtn't to marry anybody, unless one's prepared to make him a full-time job."

"Probably not; though there are a few rare people, I believe, who don't look on themselves as jobs but as fellow-creatures."

"I should think Phoebe Tucker and her husband were like that," said Harriet. "You met her at the Gaudy. That collaboration seems to work. But what with the wives who are jealous of their husbands' work and the husbands who are jealous of their wives' interests, it looks as though most of us imagined ourselves to be jobs."

"The worst of being a job," said Miss de Vine, "is the devastating effect it has on one's character. I'm very sorry for the person who is somebody else's job; he (or she, of course) ends by devouring or being devoured, either of which is bad for one. My painter has devoured his wife, though neither of them knows it; and poor Miss Cattermole is in great danger of being identified with her parents' job and being devoured."

"Then you're all for the impersonal job?"

"I am," said Miss de Vine.

"But you say you don't despise those who make some other person their job?"

"Far from despising them," said Miss de Vine; "I think they are dangerous."

Christ Church,
Friday.

Dear Miss Vane,

If you can forgive my idiotic behaviour the other day, will you come and lunch with me on Monday at 1 o'clock? Please do. I am still feeling suicidal, so it would really be a work of charity all round. I hope the meringues got home safely.

Very sincerely yours,
SAINT-GEORGE

My dear young man, thought Harriet, as she wrote an acceptance of this naive invitation, if you think I can't see through that, you're mightily mistaken. This is not for me, but for *les beaux yeux de la cassette de l'oncle Pierre.* But there are worse meals than those that come out of the House kitchen, and I will go. I should like to know how much money you're managing to get through, by the way. The heir of Denver should be rich enough in his own right without appealing to Uncle Peter. Gracious! when I think that I was given my college fees and my clothes and five pounds a term to make whoopee on! You won't get much sympathy or support from me, my lord.

Still in this severe mood, she drove down St. Aldate's on Monday and inquired of the porter beneath Tom Tower for Lord Saint-George; only to be told that Lord Saint-George was not in College.

"Oh!" said Harriet, disconcerted, "but he asked me to lunch."

"What a pity you weren't let know, miss. Lord Saint-George was in a nasty motor-accident on Friday night. He's in the Infirmary. Didn't you see it in the papers?"

"No, I missed it. Is he badly hurt?"

"Injured his shoulder and cut his head open pretty badly, so we hear," said the porter, with regret, and yet with a slight relish at the imparting of bad news. "He was unconscious for twenty-four hours; but we are informed that his condition is now improving. The Duke and Duchess have left for the country again."

"Dear me!" said Harriet. "I'm very sorry to hear this. I'd better go round and inquire. Do you know whether he is allowed to see anybody yet?"

The porter looked her over with a paternal eye, which somehow suggested to her that if she had been an undergraduate the answer would have been No.

"I believe, miss," said the porter, "that Mr. Danvers and Lord Warboys were permitted to visit his lordship this morning. I couldn't say further than that. Excuse me—there is Mr. Danvers just crossing the quadrangle. I will ascertain."

He emerged from his glass case and pursued Mr. Danvers, who immediately came running to the lodge.

"I say," said Mr. Danvers, "are you Miss Vane? Because poor old Saint-George has only just remembered about you. He's terribly sorry, and I was to catch you and give you some grub. No trouble at all—a great pleasure. We ought to have let you know, but he was knocked clean out, poor old chap. And then, what with the family fussing round—do you know the Duchess?—No?—Ah! Well, she went off this morning, and then I was allowed to go round and got my instructions. Terrific apologies and all that."

"How did it happen?"

"Driving a racing car to the danger of the public," said Mr. Danvers, with a grimace. "Trying to make it before the gates were shut. No police on the spot, as it happened, so we don't know exactly what *did* happen. Nobody killed, fortunately. Saint-George took a telegraph-pole in his stride, apparently, went out head first and pitched on his shoulder. Lucky he had the windscreen down, or he'd have had no face to speak of. The car's a total wreck, and I don't know why he isn't. But all those Wimseys have as many lives as cats. Come along in. These are my rooms. I hope you can eat the usual lamb cutlets—there wasn't time to think up anything special. But I had particular orders to hunt out Saint-George's Niersteiner '23 and mention Uncle Peter in connection with it. Is that right? I don't know whether Uncle Peter bought it or recommended it or merely enjoyed it, or what he had to do with it, but that's what I was told to say."

Harriet laughed. "If he did any of those things, it'll be all right."

The Niersteiner was excellent, and Harriet heartlessly enjoyed her lunch, finding Mr. Danvers a pleasant host.

"And do go up and see the patient," said Mr. Danvers, as he escorted her at length to the gate. "He's quite fit to receive company, and it'll cheer him up no end. He's in a private ward, so you can get in any time."

"I'll go straight away," said Harriet.

"Do," said Mr. Danvers. "What's that?" he added, turning to the porter, who had come out with a letter in his hand. "Oh, something for Saint-George. Right. Yes. I expect the lady will take it up, if she's going now. If not, it can wait for the messenger."

Harriet looked at the superscription. "The Viscount Saint-George, Christ Church, Oxford, Inghilterra." Even without the Italian stamp, there was no mistaking where that came from. "I'll take it," she said—"it might be urgent."

Lord Saint-George, with his right arm in a sling, his forehead and one eye obscured by bandages and the other eye black and bloodshot, was profuse in welcome and apology.

"I hope Danvers looked after you all right. It's frightfully decent of you to come along."

Harriet asked if he was badly hurt.

"Well, it might be worse. I fancy Uncle Peter had a near squeak of it this time, but it's worked out at a cut head and a busted shoulder. And shock and bruises and all that. Much less than I deserve. Stay and talk to me. It's dashed dull being all alone, and I've only got one eye and can't see out of that."

"Won't talking make your head ache?"

"It can't ache worse than it does already. And you've got a nice voice. Do be kind and stay."

"I've brought a letter along for you from College."

"Some dashed dun or other, I suppose."

"No. It's from Rome."

"Uncle Peter. Oh, my God! I suppose I'd better know the worst."

She put it into his left hand, and watched his fingers fumble across the broad red seal.

"Ugh! Sealing-wax and the family crest. I know what that means. Uncle Peter at his stuffiest."

He struggled impatiently with the tough envelope.

"Shall I open it for you?"

"I wish you would. And, look here—be an angel and read it to me. Even with two good eyes, his fist's a bit of a strain."

Harriet drew out the letter and glanced at the opening words.

"This looks rather private."

"Better you than the nurse. Besides, I can bear it better with a spot of womanly sympathy. I say, is there any enclosure?"

"No enclosure. No."

The patient groaned.

"Uncle Peter turns to bay. That's torn it. How does it start? If it's 'Gherkins' or 'Jerry,' or even 'Gerald,' there's hope yet."

"It starts, 'My dear Saint-George.' "

"Oh, gosh! Then he's really furious. And signed with all the initials he can rake up, what?"

Harriet turned the letter over.

"Signed with all his names in full."

"Unrelenting monster! You know, I had a sort of feeling he wouldn't take it very well. I don't know what the devil I'm going to do now."

He looked so ill that Harriet said, rather anxiously:

"Hadn't we better leave it till tomorrow?"

"No. I must know where I stand. Carry on. Speak gently to your little boy. Sing it to me. It'll need it."

My dear Saint-George,

If I have rightly understood your rather incoherent statement of your affairs, you have contracted a debt of honour for a sum which you do not possess. You have settled it with a cheque which you had no money to meet. As cover for this, you have borrowed from a friend, giving him a post-dated cheque which you have no reason to suppose will be met either. You suggest that I should accommodate you by backing your bill at six months; failing which, you will either (a) "try Levy again," or (b) blow your brains out. The former alternative would, as you admit, increase your ultimate liability; the second, as I will myself venture to point out, would not reimburse your friend but merely add disgrace to insolvency.

Lord Saint-George shifted restlessly upon his pillows. "Nasty clear-headed way he has of putting things."

You are good enough to say that you approach me rather than your father, because I am, in your opinion, more likely to be sympathetic to this dubious piece of finance. I cannot say I feel flattered by your opinion.

"I didn't mean that, exactly," groaned the viscount. "He knows quite well what I mean. The Governor would fly right off the handle. Damn it, it's his own fault! He oughtn't to keep me so short. What does he expect? Considering the money *he* got through in his giddy youth, he should know something about it. And Uncle Peter's rolling–it wouldn't hurt him to cough up a bit."

"I don't think it's the money so much as the dud cheques, is it?"

"That's the trouble. Well, why the devil does he go barging off to Rome just when he's wanted? He knows I wouldn't have given a dud if I could have got cover for it. But I couldn't get at him if he wasn't there. Well, read on. Let's hear the worst."

I am quite aware that your premature decease would leave me heir-presumptive to the title–

"Heir-presumptive? . . . Oh, I see. My mother might peg out and my father marry again. Calculating brute."

–heir-presumptive to the title and estate. Tedious as such an inheritance might be, you will forgive me for suggesting that I might prove a more honest steward than yourself.

"Hell! That's one in the eye," said the viscount. "If that line of defence has gone, it's all up."

You remind me that when you attain your majority next July, you will receive an increased allowance. Since, however, even the sum you have mentioned amounts to about a year's income on the higher scale of payment, your prospect of redeeming your bill in six months' time seems to be remote; nor do I understand what you propose to live on when you have anticipated your income to this extent. Further, I do not for one moment suppose that the sum in question represents the whole of your liabilities.

"Damned thought-reader!" growled his lordship. "Of course it doesn't. But how does *he* know?"

Under the circumstances, I must decline to back your bill or to lend you money.

"Well, that's flat. Why didn't he say so at once?"

Since, however, you have put your name to a cheque, and that name must not be dishonoured, I have instructed my bankers–"

"Come! that sounds a bit better. Good old Uncle Peter! You can always get him on the family name."

–instructed my bankers to arrange to cover your cheques–

"Cheque, or cheques?"

"Cheques, in the plural; quite distinctly."

–cover your cheques from now until the time of my return to England, when I shall come and see you. This will probably be before the end of the Trinity Term. I will ask you to see to it that the whole of your liabilities are discharged by that time, including your outstanding Oxford debts and your obligations to the children of Israel.

"First gleam of humanity," said the viscount.

May I offer you, in addition, a little advice? Bear in mind that the amateur professional is peculiarly rapacious. This applies both to women and to people who play cards. If you must back horses, back them at a reasonable price and both ways. And, if you insist on blowing out your brains, do it in some place where you will not cause mess and inconvenience.

Your affectionate Uncle,

PETER DEATH BREDON WIMSEY

"Whew!" said Lord Saint-George, "that's a stinker! I fancy I detect a little softening in the last paragraph. Otherwise, I should say that a nastier kind of letter never came to soothe the sufferer's aching brow. What do you think?"

Harriet privately agreed that it was not the kind of letter she should care to receive. It displayed, in fact, almost everything that she resented most in Peter; the condescending superiority, the arrogance of caste and the generosity that was like a blow in the face. However:—"He's done far more than you asked him," she pointed out. "So far as I can see, there's nothing to prevent you from drawing a cheque for fifty thousand and blueing the lot."

"That's the devil of it. He's got me by the short hairs. He's trusted me with the whole dashed outfit. I did think he might offer to settle up for me, but he's left me to do it and hasn't even asked for an account. That means it'll have to be done. I don't see how I can get out of it. He has the most ingenious ways of making a fellow feel a sweep. Oh, hell! my head's splitting."

"You'd better keep quiet and try to go to sleep. You've nothing to worry about now."

"No. Wait a minute. Don't go away. The cheque's all right, that's the chief thing. Just as well, because I'd have had a job to raise the wind elsewhere, laid up like this. There's one thing about it—I can't use this arm, so I shan't have to write a long screed full of grateful penitence."

"Does he know about your accident?"

"Not unless Aunt Mary's written to him. My grandmother's on the Riviera, and I don't suppose it would occur to my sister. She's at school. The Governor never writes to anybody, and my mother certainly wouldn't bother with Uncle Peter. Look here, I must do something. I mean, the old boy's been thoroughly decent, really. Couldn't you write a line for me, explaining all about it! I don't want to let my family in on this."

"I'll do that, certainly."

"Tell him I'll settle the blasted debts as soon as I can produce a recognizable signature. I say! think of having a free hand with Uncle Peter's pile and not being able to sign a cheque. Enough to make a cat laugh, isn't it? Say I—what's the phrase?—appreciate his confidence and won't let him down. Here! you might give me a spot of the stuff in that jug, would you? I feel like Dives in what's-his-name."

He gulped the iced drink down gratefully.

"No, damn it! I must do something. The old boy's really worried. I think I can work these fingers after a fashion. Find me a pencil and paper and I'll have a shot."

"I don't think you'd better."

"Yes, I had better. And I will if it kills me. Find me something, there's a darling."

She found writing materials, and held the paper in place while he scrawled a few staggering words. The pain made him sweat; a shoulder joint which has been dislocated and returned to position is no cushion of ease the day after; but he set his teeth and went through with it gamely.

"There," he said, with a faint grin, "that looks dashed pathetic. Now it's up to you. Do your best for me, won't you?"

Perhaps, thought Harriet, Peter knew the right way with his nephew. The boy was unblushingly ready to consider other people's money his own; and probably, if Peter had simply basked his bill, he would have thought his uncle easy game and proceeded to issue more paper on the same terms. As it was, he seemed inclined to stop and think. And he had, what she herself lacked, the grace of gratitude. His facile acceptance of favours might be a sign of shallowness; still, it had cost him something to scribble that painful note.

It was only when, in her own room after Hall, she set about writing to Peter, that she realized how awkward her own task was going to be. To put down a brief explanation of her own acquaintance with Lord Saint-George and a reassuring account of his accident was child's play. The difficulties began with the matter of the young man's finances. Her first draft ran easily; it was slightly humorous and rather gave the benefactor to understand that his precious balms were calculated to break the recipient's head, where other agents had not already broken it. She rather enjoyed writing this one. On reading it over, she was disappointed to find that it had an air of officious impertinence. She tore it up.

The students were making a vast noise of trampling and laughter in the corridor. Harriet briefly cursed them and tried again.

The second draft began stiffly: "Dear Peter–I am writing on behalf of your nephew, who has unfortunately–"

This one, when finished, conveyed the impression that she disapproved strongly of uncle and nephew alike, and was anxious to dissociate herself as far as possible from their affairs.

She tore it up, cursed the students again and made a third draft.

This, when completed, turned out to be a moving, and, indeed, powerful piece of special pleading on the young sinner's behalf, but contained remarkably little of the gratitude and repentance which she had been instructed to convey. The fourth draft, erring in the opposite direction, was merely fulsome.

"What the devil is the matter with me?" she said aloud. "(Damn those noisy brats!) Why can't I write a straightforward piece of English on a set subject?"

When she had once formulated the difficulty in this plain question, the detached intellect bent meekly to its academic task and produced the answer.

"Because, however you put it, all this is going to hurt his pride damnably."

Answer adjudged correct.

What she had to say, stripped of its verbiage, was: Your nephew has been behaving foolishly and dishonestly, and I know it; he gets on badly with his parents, and I know that, too; he has taken me into his confidence and, what is more, into yours, where I have no right to be; in fact, I know a great many things you would rather I did not know, and you can't lift a hand to prevent it.

In fact, for the first time in their acquaintance, she had the upper hand of Peter Wimsey, and could rub his aristocratic nose in the dirt if she wanted to. Since she had been looking for such an opportunity for five years, it would be odd if she did not hasten to take advantage of it.

Slowly and with extreme pains, she started on Draft No. 5.

Dear Peter,

I don't know whether you know that your nephew is in the Infirmary, recovering from what might have been a nasty motor accident. His right shoulder is dislocated and his head badly cut; but he is getting on all right and is lucky not to have been killed. Apparently he skidded into a telegraph pole. I don't know the details; perhaps you have already heard from his people. I met him by chance a few days ago, and only heard of the accident today, when I went round to see him.

So far, so good; now for the awkward bit.

One of his eyes was bandaged up and the other badly swollen, so he asked me to read him a letter he had just that moment received from you. (Please don't think his sight is damaged–I asked the nurse, and it's only cuts and bruises.) There was nobody else to read it to him, as his parents left Oxford this morning. As he can't write much himself, he asks me to send you the enclosed and to say he thanks you very much and is sorry. He appreciates your confidence and will do exactly as you ask him, as soon as he is well enough.

She hoped there was nothing there that could offend. She had started to write "honourably do as you ask," and then erased the first word: to mention honour was to suggest its opposite. Her consciousness seemed to have become all one exposed nerve-centre, sensitive to the lightest breath of innuendo in her own words.

I didn't stay long, as he was really a good bit under the weather, but they assure me he is doing very well. He insisted on writing this note himself, though I suppose I oughtn't to have let him. I'll look him up again before I leave Oxford–entirely for my own sake, because he is perfectly charming. I hope you don't mind my saying so, though I'm sure you don't need to be told it.

Yours,

HARRIET D. VANE

I seem to be taking a lot of trouble about this, she thought, as she carefully re-read it. If I believed Miss de Vine, I might begin to imagine–*damn* those students–Would anybody believe it could take one two hours to write a simple letter?

She put the letter resolutely into an envelope, and addressed and stamped it. Nobody, having put on a two-penny-half-penny stamp, was ever known to open the envelope again. That was *done*. For a couple of hours now she would devote herself to the affairs of Sheridan Le Fanu.

She worked away happily till half-past ten; the racket in the passage calmed down; words flowed smoothly. From time to time, she looked up from her paper, hesitating for a word, and saw through the window the lights of Burieigh and Queen Elizabeth burning back across the quad, counterparts of her own. Many of them, no doubt, illumined cheerful parties, like the one in the Annexe; others lent their aid to people who, like herself, were engaged in the elusive pursuit of knowledge, covering paper with ink and hesitating now and again over a word. She felt herself to be a living part of a community engaged in a common purpose. "Wilkie Collins," wrote Harriet, "was always handicapped in his treatment of the supernatural by the fatal itch" (could one be handicapped by an itch? Yes, why not? Let it go, anyway, for the moment)–"the fatal itch to explain everything. His legal training–" Bother! Too long. " . . . was handicapped by the lawyer's fatal habit of explaining everything. His ghaisties and ghoulies"–no; worn-out humour–"His dream-phantasies and apparitions are too careful to tuck their shrouds neatly about them and leave no loose ends to trouble us. It is in Le Fanu that we find the natural maker of–natural master of–the master of the uncanny whose mastery comes by nature. If we compare–"

Before the comparison could be instituted, the lamp went suddenly out.

"Curse!" said Harriet. She rose and pressed down the wall-switch. Nothing happened. "Fused!" said Harriet, opening the door to investigate. The corridor was in darkness, and a lamentable outcry on either side proclaimed that the lights were out in the whole of Tudor.

Harriet snatched her torch from the table and turned right towards the main block of the building. She was soon swept into a crowd of students, some with torches and some clinging to those that had them, all clamouring and wanting to know what was wrong with the lights.

"Shut *up!*" said Harriet, peering behind the barrier of the torch-lights to find anybody she recognized. "The main fuse must have gone. Where's the fuse-box?"

"I think it's under the stairs," said somebody.

"Stay where you are," said Harriet. "I'll go and see."

Nobody, naturally, stayed where she was. Everybody came helpfully and angrily downstairs.

"It's the Poltergeist," said somebody.

"Let's catch her this time," said somebody else.

"Perhaps it's only blown," suggested a timid voice out of the darkness.

"Blown be blowed!" exclaimed a louder voice, scornfully. "How often does a main fuse blow?" Then, in an agitated whisper, "Hellup, it's the Chilperic. Sorry I spoke."

"Is that you, Miss Chilperic?" said Harriet, glad to round up one member of the Senior Common Room. "Have you met Miss Barton anywhere?"

"No, I've only just got out of bed."

"Miss Barton isn't there," said a voice from the hall below, and then another voice chimed in:

"Somebody's pulled out the main fuse and taken it away!"

And then, in a shrill cry from someone at the end of the lower corridor: "There she goes! Look! running across the quad!"

Harriet was carried down the stairs with a rush of twenty or thirty students into the midst of those already milling in the hall. There was a cram in the doorway. She lost Miss Chilperic and was left behind in the struggle. Then, as she thrust her way through on to the terrace, she saw under the dim sky a string of runners stretched across thc quad. Voices were calling shrilly. Then, as the first half-dozen or so of the pursuers were outlined against the blazing lower windows of Burleigh, those lights too were blacked out.

She ran, desperately—not to Burleigh, where the uproar was repeating itself, but to Queen Elizabeth, which, she judged, would be the next point of attack. The side-doors would, she knew, be locked. She dashed past the hall stair and through to the portico, where she flung herself upon the main door. That was locked also. She stepped back and shouted through the nearest window: "Look out! There's somebody in here playing tricks. I'm coming in." A student put out a tousled head. Other heads appeared. "Let me get past," said Harriet, flinging the sash up, and hauling herself up over the sill. "They're putting out all the lights in College. Where's your fuse-box?"

"I'm sure I don't know," said the student, as Harriet plunged across the room.

"Of course you wouldn't!" said Harriet, unreasonably. She flung the door open and burst out—into Stygian blackness. By this time the hue-and-cry outside had reached Queen Elizabeth. Somebody found the front door and unlocked it, and the tumult increased, those within surging out and those outside surging in. A voice said: "Somebody came through my room and went out of the window, just after the lights went out." Torches appeared. Here and there a face—mostly unfamiliar—was momentarily lit up. Then the lights in the New Quad began to go out also, beginning on the South side. Everybody was running aimlessly. Harriet, dashing along the plinth, cannoned full tilt into somebody and flashed the torch in her face. It was the Dean.

"Thank God!" said Harriet. "Here's somebody in the right place." She held on to her.

"What's happening?" said the Dean.

"Stand still," said Harriet: "I'll have an alibi for you if I die for it." As she spoke, the lights on the North-East angle went out. "You're all right," said Harriet. "Now then! make for the West Staircase and we'll catch her."

The same idea seemed to have occurred to a number of other people, for the entrance to the West Staircase was blocked with a crowd of students, while a crowd of scouts, released by Carrie from their own Wing, added to the congestion. Harriet and the Dean forced a pathway through them, and found Miss Lydgate standing bewildered, and clasping her proof-sheets to her bosom, being determined that this time nothing should happen to them. They scooped her up with them—"like playing 'Staggie,'" thought Harriet—and made their way to the fuse-boxes under the stair. There they found Padgett, grimly on guard, with his trousers hastily pulled on over his pyjamas and a rolling-pin in his hand.

"They don't get this," said Padgett. "You leave it to me madam Dean, miss. Just turning into my bed I was, all the late-leave ladies being in. My wife's telephoning across to Jackson to fetch over some new fuses. Have you seen the boxes, miss? Wrenched open with a chisel, they was, or summat of that. A nice thing to happen. But they won't get this."

Nor did "they." In the West side of the New Quad, the Warden's House, the Infirmary, and the Scouts' Wing entrenched behind its relocked grille, the lights burned on steadily. But when Jackson arrived with the new fuses, every darkened building showed its trail of damage. While Padgett had sat by the mouse-hole, waiting for the mouse that did not come, the Poltergeist had passed through the college, breaking ink-bottles, flinging papers into the fire, smashing lamps and crockery and throwing books through the windowpanes. In the Hall, where the main fuse had also been taken, the silver cups on the High Table had been hurled at the portraits, breaking the glass, and the plaster bust of a Victorian benefactor pitched down the stone stair, to end in a fragmentary trail of detached side-whiskers and disintegrated features.

"*Well!*" said the Dean, surveying the wreckage. "That's *one* thing to be grateful for. We've seen the last of the Reverend Melchisedek Entwistle. But, oh, *lord!*"

# 10

Some say thy fault is youth, some wantonness,
Some say thy grace is youth and gentle sport:
Both grace and faults are loved of more and less;
Thou makst faults graces that to thee resort.

William Shakespeare

IT WOULD seem, at first sight, as though, in an episode witnessed by so many people and lasting altogether about an hour (counting, that is, from the first alarm in Tudor to the refitting of the final fuse) it should have been easy to find alibis for all the innocent. In practice, it was not so at all, chiefly owing to the stubborn refusal of human beings to stay where they are put. It was the very multiplicity of witnesses that made the difficulty; for it seemed likely that the culprit had mixed with the crowd over and over again in the dark. Some alibis were established for certain: Harriet and the Dean had been standing together when the lights were extinguished on the North-east angle of the New Quad; the Warden had not left her own house till after the uproar had started, as her household staff could attest; the two porters were vouched for by their respective wives, and had, in fact, never been suspected, since on various earlier occasions disturbances had occurred while they were at their posts; the Infirmarian and the Infirmary maid had also been together the whole time. Miss Hudson, the student who had been considered a "possible," had been at a coffee-party when the trouble began, and was clear; Miss Lydgate also, to Harriet's great relief, had been in Queen Elizabeth, enjoying the hospitality of a party of Third Years; she had just risen to say good-night, remarking that it was past her usual time, when the lights had gone out. She had then been caught up in the throng and, as soon as she could free herself, had run hastily up to her own room to rescue her proofs.

Other members of the S.C.R. were less fortunately placed. The case of Miss Barton was exciting and mysterious. According to her own account, she had been sitting working when the fuse was pulled out in Tudor. After trying the wallswitch, she had looked out of the window, seen the figure hastening across the quad, and gone immediately in pursuit. The figure had dodged her round Burleigh twice, and had then suddenly come upon her from behind, flung her against the wall "with extraordinary strength" and knocked her torch from her hand. Before she could recover herself, the evil-doer had extinguished the Burleigh lights and gone again. Miss Barton could give no description of this person, except that it wore "something dark" and ran very fast. She had not seen its face. The only proof of this story was that Miss Barton certainly had received a heavy bruise on the side of the face where, so she said, she had been flung against an angle of the building. She had remained where she lay for a few minutes after receiving the blow; by that time the excitement had spread to the New Quad. Here she had certainly been seen for a few seconds together by a pair of students. She had then run to look for the Dean, found her room empty, run out again and joined Harriet and the rest in the West Staircase.

Miss Chilperic's story was equally difficult of proof. When the cry of "There she goes!" had been raised at Tudor, she had been among the first to run out, but, having no torch, and being too much excited to notice where she was going, she had tripped and fallen down the steps of the terrace, twisting her foot slightly. This had made her late in arriving on the scene. She had come up with the crowd at Queen Elizabeth, been carried in with it through the portico and run straight into the New Quadrangle Buildings. She had thought she heard footsteps scurrying along to her right, and had followed them, when the lights had gone out and, not knowing the building at all well, she had wandered about in some confusion, till at last she found the way out into the Quad. Nobody seemed able to remember seeing Miss Chilperic at all after she left Tudor; she was that kind of person.

The Treasurer had been sitting up at work on the term's accounts. The lights in her building had been the last to go out, and her windows looked outward upon the road and not upon the quad, so that she had known nothing about the affair till a late stage in the proceedings. When the darkness fell on her she went (so she said) to the Bursar's set opposite, electrical replacements being in the Bursar's department. The Bursar was not in her bedroom or office; but as Miss Allison came out from looking for her, she emerged from the place where the fuse-boxes were, to announce the disappearance of the main fuse. Treasurer and Bursar had then joined the crowd in the quadrangle.

The account given by Miss Pyke of her movements seemed to be the most incredible of all. She lived above the Treasurer and had been working at an article for a learned Society's transactions. When her lights had gone out, she had said, "Bother!", taken a pair of candles from a stock which she kept for such emergencies, and gone quietly on working.

Miss Burrows asserted that she had been having a bath when the Burleigh Building lights failed, and, by an extraordinary coincidence, had found, on getting hastily out of it, that she had left her towel in her bedroom. She did not possess a self-contained set with a private bathroom, and so was obliged to grope, with her dressing-gown clutched about her dripping body, along the passage to her bedroom, and there dry and dress herself in the dark. This had taken a surprisingly long time and, when she came up with the main party, most of the fun was over. No proof, except the undoubted presence of soapy water in a bathroom on her floor.

Miss Shaw's set was over the Bursar's, and her bedroom looked out on St. Cross Road. She had gone to bed and to sleep, being very tired, and knew nothing about it till it was all over. The same story was told by Mrs. Goodwin, who had returned to College only that day, rather exhausted by sick-nursing. As for Miss Hillyard and Miss de Vine, living above Miss Lydgate; their lights had never gone out at all, and, their windows facing on the road, they had never known that anything was wrong, putting down a vague noise in the quad to the natural cussedness of undergraduates.

It had only been after Padgett had sat for about five minutes in vain at the mousehole, that Harriet had done what she should have done earlier, and attempted to make a count of the Senior Common Room. She had then found them all in the places where, by their subsequent accounts of themselves, they should have been. But to collect them all into one lighted room and keep them there was not so easy. She established Miss Lydgate in her own room and went to look for the rest, asking them to go straight down to Miss Lydgate's room and stay there. The Warden, meanwhile, had arrived and was addressing the students, imploring them also to stay where they were and keep quiet. Unfortunately, just as it began to seem possible to make sure of everbody's whereabouts, some inquisitive person, who had broken away from the rest had gone roaming through the Old Quad, arrived, breathless, to announce the tale of damage in the Hall. Instantly, pandemonium broke loose again. Dons who were trotting like lambs into the sheep-fold suddenly lost their heads and raced with the students into the darkness. Miss Burrows screamed "The Library!" and tore away, and the Bursar, with an anguished cry for the College property, dashed after her. The Dean called, "Stop them!" and Miss Pyke and Miss Hillyard, taking the command to themselves, rushed out and disappeared. In the resulting confusion, everybody got lost twenty times over; and by the time the fuses were replaced and the community at last gathered and numbered, the damage had all been done.

It is surprising how much can be done in a very few minutes. Harriet calculated that the Hall had probably been wrecked first of all, being in a detached wing, where noise was not likely to attract much attention; all that was done there could have been done in a couple of minutes. From the extinguishing of the first lights in Tudor to that of the last lights in the New Quad, rather less than ten minutes had elapsed. The third, and longest part of the business—the wrecking of the rooms in the darkened buildings, had taken anything from a quarter to half an hour.

The Warden addressed the College after Chapel, again enjoining discretion, begging the culprit to come forward, and promising that all possible measures should be taken to identify her in case she did not confess.

"I have no intention," said Dr. Baring, "of inflicting any restriction or punishment upon the college in general for the act of one irresponsible person. I will ask anyone who has any suggestion to make or any evidence to offer with regard to the identity of this foolish practical joker to come privately, either to the Dean or myself, and make the communication in strict confidence."

She added a few words about the solidarity of the College and departed with a grave face, her gown floating behind her.

The glaziers were already at work restoring damaged window-panes. In the Hall, the Bursar was affixing neat cards in the places of portraits whose glass had been broken: "Portrait of Miss Matheson: Warden 1899-1912. Removed for cleaning." Broken crockery was being swept from the grass of the Old Quad. The College was engaged in presenting a serene face to the world.

It did not improve anybody's temper to discover a printed message, consisting of "HA! HA!" and a vulgar epithet, pasted across the mirror in the Senior Common Room, shortly before lunch. The Common Room had been empty from 9 o'clock onwards, so far as was known. The Common Room maid, going in at lunch-time with the coffee-cups, had been the first to see the notice; and it had by then dried hard. The Bursar, who had missed her pot of Gloy after the night's excitement, found it placed neatly in the centre of the S.C.R. mantelpiece.

The feeling in the Senior Common Room after this episode underwent a subtle alteration. Tongues were sharpened; the veneer of detachment began to wear thin; the uneasiness of suspicion began to make itself felt; only Miss Lydgate and the Dean, being proved innocent, remained unmoved.

"Your bad luck seems to have repeated itself, Miss Barton," observed Miss Pyke, acidly. "Both in the Library affair and in this last outbreak, you seem to have been first on the spot and yet unhappily prevented from securing the culprit."

"Yes," said Miss Barton. "It's very unfortunate. If next time my gown gets taken as well, the College sleuth will begin to smell a rat."

"Very trying for you, Mrs. Goodwin," said Miss Hillyard, "to come back to all this upset, just when you needed a rest. I trust your little boy is better. It is particularly tiresome, because all the time you were away we had no disturbance at all."

"It's most annoying," said Mrs. Goodwin. "The poor creature who does these things must be quite demented. Of course these disorders do tend to occur in celibate, or chiefly celibate communities. It is a kind of compensation, I suppose, for the lack of other excitements."

"The great mistake," said Miss Burrows, "was, of course, our not keeping together. Naturally I wanted to see if any damage had been done in the Library—but why so many people should have come pelting after me—"

"The Hall was my concern," said the Bursar.

"Oh! you *did* get to the Hall? I completely lost sight of you in the quad."

"That," said Miss Hillyard, "was exactly the catastrophe I was trying to avoid when I pursued you. I called loudly to you to stop. You *must* have heard me."

"There was too much noise to hear anything," said Miss Stevens.

"I came to Miss Lydgate's room," said Miss Shaw, "the moment I could get dressed, understanding that everybody was to be there. But there was really nobody. I thought I must have misunderstood, so I tried to find Miss Vane, but she seemed to have gone off into the Ewigkeit."

"It must have taken you a remarkably long time to dress," said Miss Burrows. "Anybody could run three times round College in the time it takes you to pull your stockings on."

"Somebody," said Miss Shaw, "apparently *did*."

"They're beginning to get fractious," said Harriet to the Dean.

"What *can* you expect? The silly cuckoos! If they'd *only* sat tight on their little behinds last night, we could have cleared the whole business up. It's not *your* fault. You couldn't be everywhere at once. *How* we can expect discipline from the students, when a whole bunch of middle-aged seniors behave like a flock of *hens* in a crisis, I can't think. Who's that out there, conducting that strident conversation with a top window? Oh! I think it's Baker's young man. Well, discipline must be observed, I suppose. Give me the housetelephone, would you? Thanks. I don't see how we're to prevent this last outbreak from getting— Oh! Martha! The Dean's compliments, if you please, to Miss Baker, and will she kindly bear in mind the rule about morning visitors—And the students are getting rather annoyed about the destruction of their property. I think they're actually getting worked up to calling a J.C.R. meeting, and it's very unfair on them, poor lambs, to let *them* go on suspecting one another, but what *can* we do about it? Thank God, it's the last week of term! I suppose we're not making a ghastly mistake? It must be one of us, and not a student or a scout."

"We seem to have eliminated the students–unless it's a conspiracy between two of them. It might be that. Hudson and Cattermole together. But as for the scouts–I can show you this, now, I suppose. Would any of the scouts quote Virgil?"

"No," said the Dean, examining the "Harpy" passage. "No; it doesn't seem likely. Oh, dear!"

The reply to Harriet's letter arrived by return.

My dear Harriet,

It is exceedingly good of you to be bothered with my graceless nephew. I am afraid the episode must have left you with an unfortunate impression of both of us.

I am very fond of the boy, and he is, as you say, attractive; but he is rather easily led, and my brother is not, in my opinion, handling him in the wisest way. Considering his expectations, Gerald is kept absurdly short of money, and naturally he feels he has a right to anything he can lay hands on. Still, he must learn to draw the line between carelessness and dishonesty. I have offered to augment his allowance myself, but the suggestion was not well received at home. His parents, I know, feel that I am stealing his confidence from them; but if I refused to help him, he would go elsewhere and get himself into worse trouble. Though I do not like the position into which I am forced of "Codlin is the friend, not Short," I still think it better that he should turn to me than to an outsider. I call this family pride; it may be mere vanity; I know it is vexation of spirit.

Let me assure you that so far, when I have trusted Gerald with anything, he has not let me down. He is amenable to some of the shibboleths. But he is not amenable to a discipline of alternate indulgence and severity; and indeed I do not know who is.

I must again apologize for troubling you with our family affairs. What on earth are you doing in Oxford? Have you retired from the worid to pursue the contemplative life? I will not attempt to dissuade you now, but shall address you on the subject in the usual form on the 1st April next.

Yours in all gratitude,

P.D.B.W.

I had forgotten to say, thank you for telling me about the accident and reassuring me as to its results. It was the first I had heard of it–as old James Forsyte says, "Nobody ever tells me anything." I will oblige with a few kind words.

"Poor old Peter!" said Harriet.

The remark probably deserves to be included in an anthology of Great First Occasions.

Lord Saint-George, when she went to pay him a parting visit, was considerably improved in appearance; but his expression was worried. His bed strewn with untidy papers, he seemed to be trying to cope with his affairs and to be making but heavy weather of it. He brightened up considerably at sight of Harriet.

"Oh, look! You're just the person I've been praying for. I've no head for this kind of thing, and all the beastly bills keep sliding off the bed. I can write my name pretty well, but I can't keep track of things. I'm sure I've paid some of these brutes twice over."

"Let me help; can I?"

"I hoped you'd say that. It's so nice of you to spoil me, isn't it? I can't think how things mount up so. They rook one shockingly at these places. But one must have something to eat, mustn't one? And belong to a few clubs. And play a game or two. Of course polo comes a bit expensive, but it's rather done just now. It's nothing, really. Of course, the mistake was going round with that bunch in Town last vac. Mother imagines they're O.K. because they're in the studbook, but they're pretty hot, really. She'll be no end surprised if they end up in gaol, and her white-headed boy with them. Sad degeneracy of old landed families, and that kind of thing. Solemn rebuke by learned judge. I somehow got behindhand with things about the New Year, and never caught up again. It looks to me as though Uncle Peter was going to get a bit of a shock. He's written, by the way. Much more like himself."

He tossed the letter over.

Dear Jerry,

Of all the thundering nuisances that ever embittered the lives of their long-suffering relatives, you are the worst. For God's sake put down that racing car before you kill yourself; strange as it may appear, I still retain some lingering remnants of affection for you. I hope they take your licence away for life, and I hope you feel like hell. You probably do. Don't worry any more about the money.

I am writing to thank Miss Vane for her kindness to you. She is a person whose good opinion I value, so be merciful to my feelings as a man and an uncle.

Bunter has just found three silver threads among the gold. He is incredibly shocked. He begs to tender you his respectful commiseration, and advises scalp-massage (for me, I mean).

When you can manage it, send a line to report progress to your querulous and rapidly-decaying uncle

P. W.

"He'll get a whole crop of silver threads when he realizes that I hadn't paid up the insurance," said the viscount, callously, as he took the letter back.

"What!"

"Fortunately there was nobody else involved, and the police weren't on the spot. But I suppose I shall hear from the Post Office about their blasted telegraph pole. If I have to go before the magistrates and the Governor hears of it, he'll be annoyed. It'll cost a bit to get the car put right. I'd throw the damned thing away, only Dad gave it to me in one of his generous fits. And of course, about the first thing he asked when I came out from under was whether the insurance was all right. And being in no state to argue, I said Yes. If only it doesn't get into the papers about the insurance, we're all right—only the repairs will make a nice little item in Uncle Peter's total."

"Is it fair to make him pay for that?"

"Damned unfair," said Lord Saint-George, cheerfully. "The Governor ought to pay the insurance himself. He's like the Old Man of Thermopylae—never does anything properly. If you come to that, it isn't fair to make Uncle Peter pay for all the horses that fall down when one backs them. Or for all the rotten little gold-diggers one carts round either—I shall have to lump *them* together under 'Sundries.' And he'll say, 'Ah, yes! Postage stamps, telephone calls and live wires.' And then I shall lose my head and say, 'Well, Uncle—' I hate those sentences that start with 'Well, Uncle.' They always seem to go on and on and lead anywhere."

"I don't suppose he'll ask for details, if you don't volunteer them. Look! I've got all these bills sorted. Shall I write out the cheques for you to sign?"

"I wish you would. No, he won't ask. He'll only sit looking harmless till I tell him. I suppose that's the way he gets criminals to come across with it. It's not a nice characteristic. Have you got that note from Levy? That's the main thing. And there's a letter from a chap called Cartwright that's rather important. I borrowed a bit from him up in Town once or twice. What's he make it come to? . . . Oh, rot! It can't be as much as that . . . Let's see . . . Well, I suppose he's right . . . And Archie Campbell—he's my bookmaker—God! what a lot of screws! they oughtn't to allow the poor beasts out. And the odds-and-ends here? What a marvellously neat way you have with these things, haven't you? Shall we tot them all up and see where we get to? Then if I faint, you can ring the bell for Nurse."

"I'm not very good at arithmetic. You'd better check this up. It looks a bit unlikely, but I can't make it come any less."

"Add on, say a hundred and fifty, estimated repairs to car, and then we'll see. Oh, hell! what have we here?"

"The portrait of a blinking idiot," said Harriet, irresistibly.

"Amazing fellow, Shakespeare. The apt word for all occasions. Yes; there's a 'Well, Uncle' look about this, all right. Of course, I get my quarter's allowance at the end of the month, but there's the vac. to get through and all next term. One thing, I'll have to go home and be good; can't get about the place much like this. The Governor more or less hinted that I ought to pay my own doctor's bill, but I wasn't taking the hint. Mother blames Uncle Peter for the whole thing."

"Why on earth?"

"Setting me a bad example of furious driving. He is a bit hot, of course, but he never seems to get my foul luck."

"Can he possibly be a better driver?"

"Darling Harriet, that's unkind. You don't mind my calling you Harriet?"

"As a matter of fact, I do, rather."

"But I can't keep on saying 'Miss Vane' to a person who knows all my hideous secrets. Perhaps I'd better accustom myself to saying 'Aunt Harriet' . . . What's wrong with that? You simply can't refuse to be an adopted aunt to me. My Aunt Mary has gone all domestic and hasn't time for me, and my mother's sisters are the original gorgons. I'm dreadfully unappreciated and quite auntless for all practical purposes."

"You deserve neither aunts nor uncles, considering how you treat them. Do you mean to finish these cheques today? Because, if not, I have other things to do."

"Very well. We will continue to rob Peter to pay all. It's wonderful what a good influence you have over me. Unbending devotion to duty. If you'd only take me in hand I might turn out quite well after all."

"Sign, please."

"But you don't seem very susceptible. Poor Uncle Peter!"

"It will be poor Uncle Peter by the time you've finished."

"That's what I mean. Fifty-three, nineteen, four—it's shocking the way other people smoke one's fags, and I'm sure my scout bags half of them. Twenty-six, twelve, eight. Nineteen, seven, two. A hundred quid gone before you've time to look at it. Thirty-one, fourteen. Twelve, nine, six. Five, fifteen, three. What's all this tale about ghosts playing merry hell in Shrewsbury?"

Harriet jumped. "Damn! which of our little beasts told you about that?"

"None of 'em told *me*. I don't encourage women students. Nice girls, no doubt, but too grubby. There's a chap on my staircase who came up today with a story. . . . I forget, he told me not to mention it. What's it all about? and why the hush-hush?"

"Oh, dear! and they were implored not to talk. They never think of the harm this kind of thing does to the College."

"Well, but it's only a rag, isn't it?"

"I'm afraid it's a bit more than that. Look here, if I tell you why it's hush-hush, will you promise not to pass it on?"

"Well," said Lord Saint-George, candidly, "you know how my tongue runs away with me. I'm not very dependable."

"Your uncle says you are."

"Uncle Peter? Good lord! he must be potty. Sad to see a fine brain going to rack and ruin. Of course, he's not as young as he was. . . . You're looking very sober about it."

"It is rather grim, really. We're afraid the trouble's caused by somebody who's not quite right in her head. Not a student–but of course we can't very well tell the students that, especially when we don't know who it is."

The viscount stared. "Good lord! How beastly for you! I quite see your point. Naturally you don't want a thing like that to get about. Well, I'll not say a word–honestly, I won't. And if anybody mentions it I'll register a concentrated expression of no enthusiasm. I say! Do you know, I wonder if I've met your ghost."

"Met her?"

"Yes. I certainly met somebody who didn't seem quite all there. It scared me a bit. You'll be the first person I've told about it."

"When was this? Tell me about it."

"End of last term. I was awfully short of cash, and I'd had a bet with a man that I'd get into Shrewsbury and–" He stopped and looked up at her with the smile that was so uncannily not his own. "What do you know about that?"

"If you mean that bit of the wall by the private gate, it's having a set of spikes put on it. The revolving sort."

"Ah! all is known. Well, it wasn't an awfully good night for it–full moon and all that–but it seemed about the last chance to get that ten quid, so I hopped over. There's a bit of a garden there."

"The Fellows' Garden. Yes."

"Yes. Well, I was just pushing along there, when somebody hopped out from behind a bush and grabbed me. My heart nearly shot right out of my mouth on to the lawn. I wanted to do a bunk."

"What was the person like?"

"It was in black and had a bit of black stuff sort of twisted round its head. I couldn't see anything but its eyes, and they looked beastly. So I said, 'Oh, gosh!' and she said, 'Which of 'em do you want?' in a horrid voice, like glue. Well, that wasn't nice and not what I expected. I don't pretend to be a good boy, but such were not my intentions at the time. So I said, 'Nothing of that sort; I only made a bet I wouldn't be caught, and I have been caught, so I'll go away and I'm sorry.' So she said, 'Yes, go away. We murder beautiful boys like you and eat their hearts out.' So I said, 'Good God! how very unpleasant!' I didn't like it a bit."

"Are you making all this up?"

"Honestly, I'm not. Then she said, 'The other one had fair hair, too.' And I said, 'No, did he really?' And she said something, I forget what–it seemed to me she had a kind of hungry look about her, if you know what I mean–and anyhow, it was all most uncomfortable, and I said, 'Excuse me, I think I'd better be getting along,' and I pulled free (she was uncommonly strong in the wrists) and legged it over the wall like one, John Smith."

Harriet looked at him, but he appeared to be perfectly serious.

"How tall was she?"

"About your height, I should think, or a bit less. Honestly, I was too scared to notice much. I couldn't recognize her again, I don't think. She didn't give me the impression of being a young thing, and that's about all I can tell you."

"And you say you've kept this remarkable story to yourself?"

"Yes. Doesn't sound like me, does it? But there was something about it–I don't know. If I'd told any of the men, they'd have thought it howlingly funny. But it wasn't. So I didn't mention it. It didn't seem the right thing, somehow."

"I'm glad you didn't want it laughed at."

"No. The boy has quite nice instincts. Well, that's all. Twenty-five, eleven, nine; that blasted car simply eats oil and petrol–all those big engines do. It's going to be awfully awkward about that insurance. Please, dear Aunt Harriet, need I do any more of these? They depress me."

"You can leave them till I've gone, and write all the cheques and envelopes yourself."

"Slave-driver. I shall burst into tears."

"I'll fetch you a handkerchief."

"You are the most unwomanly woman I ever met. Uncle Peter has my sincere sympathy. Look at this! Sixty-nine, fifteen–account rendered; I wonder what it was all about."

Harriet said nothing, but continued to make out the cheques.

"One thing, there doesn't seem to be much at Blackwell's. A mere trifle of six pounds twelve."

"One halfpennyworth of bread to this intolerable deal of sack."

"Did you catch that habit of quotation from Uncle Peter?"

"You needn't lay any *more* burdens on your uncle's shoulders."

"Must you rub it in? There's practically nothing at the wine-merchant's either. Hard drinking has quite gone out. Isn't that satisfactory? Of course, the Governor obliges with a bottle or two from time to time. Did you like that Niersteiner the other day? Uncle Peter obliged with that. How many more of these things are there?"

"Quite a few."

"Oh! My arm aches horribly."

"If you're really too tired–"

"No, I can manage."

Half an hour later, Harriet said, "That's the lot."

"Thank God! Now talk prettily to me."

"No; I must get back now. I'll post these on my way."

"You're not really going? Right away?"

"Yes; right away to London."

"Wish I was you. Shall you be up next term?"

"I don't know."

"Oh, dear, oh, dear! Well, kiss me good-bye nicely."

Since she could think of no form of refusal that might not provoke some nerve-shattering comment, Harriet sedately complied. She was turning to go, when the nurse arrived to announce another visitor. This was a young woman, dressed in the more foolish extreme of the current fashion, with an intoxicated-looking hat and bright purple finger-nails, who advanced, crying sympathetically:

"Oh, darling Jerry! How too ruinously shattering!"

"Good lord, Gillian!" said the viscount, without very much enthusiasm. "How did you–?"

"My lamb! You don't sound very pleased to see me."

Harriet escaped, and found the nurse in the passage, putting an armful of roses in a bowl.

"I hope I haven't tired your patient too much with all that business."

"I'm glad you came to help him out with it; it was on his mind. Aren't these roses beautiful? The young lady brought them from London. He gets a lot of visitors. But you can't wonder, can you? He's a dear boy, and the things he says to Sister! It's as much as one can do to keep a straight face. He's looking a lot better now, don't you think? Mr. Whybrow's made a beautiful job of the cut on his head. He's got his stitches out now–oh, yes! it'll hardly show at all. It is a mercy, isn't it? Because he's ever so handsome."

"Yes; he's a very good-looking young man."

"He takes after his father. Do you know the Duke of Denver? He's ever so handsome, too. I shouldn't call the Duchess good-looking; more distinguished. She was terribly afraid he might be disfigured for life, and it *would* have been a pity. But Mr. Whybrow's a splendid surgeon. You'll see he'll be quite all right. Sister's ever so pleased–we tell her she's quite lost her heart to Number Fifteen. I'm sure we shall all be sorry to say good-bye to him; he keeps us all lively."

"I expect he does."

"And the way he pulls Matron's leg. Impudent young monkey, she calls him, but she can't help laughing at his ways. Oh, dear! there's Number Seventeen ringing again. I expect she wants a bed-pan. You know your way out, don't you?"

Harriet departed; feeling that it might be rather an onerous position to be aunt to Lord Saint-George.

"Of course," said the Dean, "if anything should happen in vacation–"

"I rather doubt if it will," said Harriet. "Not a big enough audience. A public scandal is the thing aimed at, I imagine. But if another episode should occur, it will narrow the field."

"Yes; most of the S.C.R. will be away. Next term, what with the Warden, Miss Lydgate and myself definitely clear of suspicion, we ought to be able to patrol the place better. What are you going to do?"

"I don't know. I've been rather thinking of coming back to Oxford altogether for a time, to do some work. This place gets you. It's so completely uncommercial. I think I'm getting a little shrill in my mind. I need mellowing."

"Why not work for a B.Litt.?"

"That would be rather fun. I'm afraid they wouldn't accept Le Fanu, would they? It would have to be somebody duller. I should enjoy a little dullness. One would have to go on writing novels for bread and butter, but I'd like an academic and meaty egg to my tea for a change."

"Well, I hope you'll come back for part of next term, anyway. You can't leave Miss Lydgate now till those proofs are in the printer's hands."

"I'm almost afraid to set her loose this vac. She is dissatisfied with her chapter on Gerard Manley Hopkins; she feels she may have attacked him from the wrong angle altogether."

"Oh, *no!*"

"I'm afraid it's Oh, yes! . . . Well, I'll cope with that, anyway. And the rest–well, we shall see what happens."

Harriet left Oxford just after lunch. As she was putting her suit-case in the car, Padgett came up to her.

"Excuse me, miss, but the Dean thinks you would like to see this, miss. In Miss de Vine's fireplace it was found this morning, miss."

Harriet looked at the half-burnt sheet of crumpled newspaper. Letters had been cut out from the advertising columns.

"Is Miss de Vine still in College?"

"She left by the 10.10, miss."

"I'll keep this, Padgett, thank you. Does Miss de Vine usually read the *Daily Trumpet?*"

"I shouldn't think so, miss. It would be more likely the *Times* or *Telegraph*. But you could easy find out."

"Of course, anybody might have dropped this in the fireplace. It proves nothing. But I'm very glad to have seen it. Good morning, Padgett."

"Good morning, miss."

# 11

Leave me, O Love, which reachest but to dust;
And thou, my mind, aspire to higher things;
Grow rich in that which never taketh rust,
Whatever fades, but fading pleasures brings.
Draw in thy beams, and humble all thy might
To that sweet yoke where lasting freedoms be;
Which breaks the clouds, and opens forth the light
That doth both shine and give us sight to see.

Sir Philip Sidney

TOWN SEEMED remarkably empty and uninteresting. Yet a lot of things were going on. Harriet saw her agent and publisher, signed a contract for serial rights, heard the inner history of the quarrel between Lord Gobbersleigh, the newspaper proprietor and Mr. Adrian Cloot, the reviewer, entered warmly into the triangular dispute raging among Gargantua Colour-Talkies Ltd., Mr. Garrick Drury, the actor, and Mrs. Snell-Wilmington, author of *Passion-flower Pie*, and into the details of Miss Sugar Toobin's monstrous libel action against the *Daily Headline*, and was, of course, passionately interested to learn that Jacqueline Squills had made a malicious expose of her second divorced husband's habits and character in her new novel, *Gas-Filled Bulbs*.

Yet, somehow, these distractions failed to keep her amused. To make matters worse, her new mystery novel had got somehow stuck. She had five suspects, neatly confined in an old water-mill with no means of entrance or egress except by a plank bridge, and all provided with motives and alibis for a pleasantly original kind of murder. There seemed to be nothing fundamentally wrong with the thing. But the permutations and combinations of the five people's relationships were beginning to take on an unnatural, an incredible symmetry. Human beings were not like that; human problems were not like that; what you really got was two hundred or so people running like rabbits in and out of a college, doing their work, living their lives, and actuated all the time by motives unfathomable even to themselves, and then, in the midst of it all—not a plain, understandable murder, but an unmeaning and inexplicable lunacy.

How could one, in any case, understand other people's motives and feelings, when one's own remained mysterious? Why did one look forward with irritation to the receipt of a letter on April lst, and then feel alarmed and affronted when it did not arrive by the first post? Very likely the letter had been sent to Oxford. There was no possible urgency about it, since one knew what it would contain and how it had to be answered; but it was annoying to sit about, expecting it.

Ring. Enter secretary with telegram (this was probably it). Wordy and unnecessary cable from American magazine representative to say she was shortly arriving in England and very anxious to talk to Miss Harriet Vane about a story for their publication. Cordially. What on earth did these people want to talk about? You did not write stories by talking about them.

Ring. Second post. Letter with Italian stamp. (Slight delay in sorting, no doubt.) Oh, thank you, Miss Bracey. Imbecile, writing very bad English, was eager to translate Miss Vane's works into Italian. Could Miss Vane inform the writer of what books she had composed? Translators were all like that—no English, no sense, no backing. Harriet said briefly what she thought of them, told Miss Bracey to refer the matter to the agent and returned to her dictation.

"Wilfrid stared at the handkerchief. What was it doing there in Winchester's bedroom? With a curious feeling of . . . "

Telephone. Hold on a moment, please. (It couldn't very well be that; it would be ridiculous to put through an expensive foreign call.) Hullo! Yes. Speaking. Oh?

She might have known it. There was a kind of mild determination about Reggie Pomfret. Would Miss Vane, could Miss Vane put up with his company for dinner and the new show at the Palladium? That night? the next night? Any night? That very night? Mr. Pomfret was inarticulate with pleasure. Thank you. Ring off. Where were we, Miss Bracey?

"With a curious feeling of— Oh, yes, Wilfrid. Very distressing for Wilfrid to find his young woman's handkerchief in the murdered man's bedroom. Agonizing. A curious feeling of— What should you feel like under the circumstances, Miss Bracey?"

"I should think the laundry had made a mistake, I expect."

"Oh, Miss Bracey! Well—we'd better say it was a lace handkerchief. *Winchester* couldn't have mistaken a lace handkerchief for one of his own, whatever the laundry sent him."

"But would Ada have used a lace handkerchief, Miss Vane? Because she's been made rather a boyish, out-door person. And it's not as if she was in evening dress, because it was so important she should turn up in a tweed costume."

"That's true. Well—well, better make the handkerchief small, but not lace. Plain but good. Turn back to the description of the handkerchief . . . Oh, dear! No, I'll answer it. Yes? *Yes?* YES! . . . No, I'm afraid I can't possibly. No, really. Oh? Well, you had better ask my agents. Yes, that's right. Good-bye . . . Some club wanting a debate on 'Should Genius Marry?' The question's not likely to concern any of their members personally, so why do they bother? . . . Yes, Miss Bracey? Oh, yes, Wilfrid. Bother Wilfrid! I'm taking quite a dislike to the man."

By tea-time, Wilfrid was behaving so tiresomely that Harriet put him away in a rage and sallied out to attend a literary cocktail party. The room in which it was held was exceedingly hot and crowded, and all the assembled authors were discussing (a) publishers, (b) agents, (c) their own sales, (d) other people's sales, and (e) the extraordinary behavior of the Book of the Moment selectors in awarding their ephemeral crown to Tasker Hepplewater's *Mock Turtle*. "I finished this book," one distinguished adjudicator had said, "with the tears running down my face." The author of *Serpent's Fang* confided to Harriet over a *petite saucisse* and a glass of sherry that they must have been tears of pure boredom; but the author of *Dusk and Shiver* said, No—they were probably tears of merriment, called forth by the unintentional humour of the book; had she ever met Hepplewater? A very angry young woman, whose book had been passed over, declared that the whole thing was a notorious farce. The Book of the Moment was selected from each publisher's list in turn, so that her own *Ariadne Adams* was automatically excluded from benefit, owing to the mere fact that her publisher's imprint had been honoured in the previous January. She had, however, received private assurance that the critic of the *Morning Star* had sobbed like a child over the last hundred pages of *Ariadne*, and would probably make it his Book of the Fortnight, if only the publisher could be persuaded to take advertising space in the paper. The author of *The Squeezed Lemon* agreed that advertising was at the bottom of it: had they heard how the *Daily Flashlight* had tried to blackmail Humphrey Quint into advertising with them? And how, on his refusal, they had said darkly, "Well, you know what will happen, Mr. Quint?" And how no single Quint book had received so much as a review from the *Flashlight* ever since? And how Quint had advertised that fact in the *Morning Star* and sent up his net sales 50 per cent. in consequence? Well, by some fantastic figure, anyhow. But the author of *Primrose Dalliance* said that with the Book of the Moment crowd, what counted was Personal Pull—surely they remembered that Hepplewater had married Walton Strawberry's latest wife's sister. The author of *Jocund Day* agreed about the Pull, but thought that in this instance it was political, because there was some powerful anti-Fascist propaganda in *Mock Turtle* and it was well known that you could always get old Sneep Fortescue with a good smack at the Blackshirts.

"But what's *Mock Turtle* about?" inquired Harriet.

On this point the authors were for the most part vague; but a young man who wrote humorous magazine stories, and could therefore afford to be wide-minded about novels, said he had read it and thought it rather interesting, only a bit long. It was about a swimming instructor at a watering-place, who had contracted such an unfortunate anti-nudity complex through watching so many bathing-beauties that it completely inhibited all his natural emotions. So he got a job on a whaler and fell in love at first sight with an Eskimo, because she was such a beautiful bundle of garments. So he married her and brought her back to live in a suburb, where she fell in love with a vegetarian nudist. So then the husband went slightly mad and contracted a complex about giant turtles, and spent all his spare time staring into the turtle-tank at the Aquarium, and watching the strange, slow monsters swimming significantly round in their encasing shells. But of course a lot of things came into it—it was one of those books that reflect the author's reactions to Things in General. Altogether, significant was, he thought, the word to describe it.

Harriet began to feel that there might be something to be said even for the plot of *Death 'twixt Wind and Water*. It was, at least, significant of nothing in particular.

Harriet went back, irritated, to Mecklenburg Square. As she entered the house, she could hear her telephone ringing apoplectically on the first floor. She ran upstairs hastily—one never knew with telephone calls. As she thrust her key into the lock, the telephone stopped dead.

"Damn!" said Harriet. There was an envelope lying inside the door. It contained press cuttings. One referred to her as Miss Vines and said she had taken her degree at Cambridge; a second compared her work unfavorably with that of an American thriller-writer; a third was a belated review of her last book, which gave away the plot; a fourth attributed somebody else's thriller to her and stated that she "adopted a sporting outlook on life" (whatever that might mean). "This," said Harriet, much put out, "is one of those days! April the First, indeed! And now I've got to dine with this dashed undergraduate, and be made to feel the burden of incalculable age."

To her surprise, however, she enjoyed both the dinner and the show. There was a refreshing lack of complication about Reggie Pomfret. He knew nothing about literary jealousies; he had no views about the comparative importance of personal and professional loyalties; he laughed heartily at obvious jokes; he did not expose your nerve-centres or his own; he did not use words with double meanings; he did not challenge you to attack him and then suddenly roll himself into an armadillo-like ball, presenting a smooth, defensive surface of ironical quotations; he had no overtones of any kind; he was a good-natured, not very clever, young man, eager to give pleasure to someone who had shown him a kindness. Harriet found him quite extraordinarily restful.

"Will you come up for a moment and have a drink or anything?" said Harriet, on her own doorstep.

"Thanks awfully," said Mr. Pomfret, "if it isn't too late."

He instructed the taxi to wait and galumphed happily up. Harriet opened the door of the flat and switched the light on. Mr. Pomfret stooped courteously to pick up the letter lying on the mat.

"Oh, thank you," said Harriet.

She preceded him into the sitting-room and let him remove her cloak for her. A moment or two later, she became aware that she was still holding the letter in her hand and that her guest and she were still standing.

"I beg your pardon. Do sit down."

"Please—" said Mr. Pomfret, with a gesture that indicated, "Read it and don't mind me."

"It's nothing," said Harriet, tossing the envelope on the table. "I know what's in it. What will you have? Will you help yourself?"

Mr. Pomfret surveyed such refreshments as offered themselves and asked what he might mix for her. The drink question being settled, there was a pause.

"Er—by the way," said Mr. Pomfret, "is Miss Cattermole all right? I haven't seen very much of her since—since that night when I made your acquaintance, you know. Last time we met she said she was working rather hard."

"Oh, yes. I believe she is. She's got Mods next term."

"Oh, poor girl! She has a great admiration for you."

"Has she? I don't know why. I seem to remember ticking her off rather brutally."

"Well, you were fairly firm with me. But I agree with Miss Cattermole. Absolutely. I mean, we agree about having a great admiration for you."

"How nice of you," said Harriet, inattentively.

"Yes, really. Rather. I'll never forget the way you tackled that fellow Jukes. Did you see he got himself into trouble only a week or so later?"

"Yes. I'm not surprised."

"No. A most unpleasant wart. Thoroughly scaly."

"He always was."

"Well, here's to a long stretch for comrade Jukes. Not a bad show tonight, don't you think?"

Harriet pulled herself together. She was all at once tired of Mr. Pomfret and wished he would go; but it was monstrous of her not to behave politely to him. She exerted herself to talk with bright interest of the entertainment to which he had kindly taken her and succeeded so well that it was nearly fifteen minutes before Mr. Pomfret remembered his waiting taxi, and took himself off in high spirits.

Harriet took up the letter. Now that she was free to open it, she did not want to. It had spoilt the evening for her.

Dear Harriet,

I send in my demand notes with the brutal regularity of the income-tax commissioners; and probably you say when you see the envelopes, 'Oh, God! I know what this is.' The only difference is that, some time or other, one *has* to take notice of the income-tax.

*Will you marry me?*–It's beginning to look like one of those lines in a farce–merely boring till it's said often enough; and after that, you get a bigger laugh every time it comes.

I should like to write you the kind of words that burn the paper they are written on–but words like that have a way of being not only unforgettable but unforgivable. You will burn the paper in any case; and I would rather there should be nothing in it that you cannot forget if you want to.

Well, that's over. Don't worry about it.

My nephew (whom you seem, by the way, to have stimulated to the most extraordinary diligence) is cheering my exile by dark hints that you are involved in some disagreeable and dangerous job of work at Oxford about which he is in honour bound to say nothing. I hope he is mistaken. But I know that, if you have put anything in hand, disagreeableness and danger will not turn you back, and God forbid they should. Whatever it is, you have my best wishes for it.

I am not my own master at the moment, and do not know where I shall be sent next or when I shall be back–soon, I trust. In the meantime may I hope to hear from time to time that all is well with you?

Yours, more than my own,

PETER WIMSEY

After reading that letter, Harriet knew that she could not rest till it was answered. The bitter unhappiness of its opening paragraphs was readily explained by the last two. He probably thought—he could not possibly help thinking—that she had known him all these years, only to confide in the end, not in him, but in a boy less than half his age and his own nephew, whom she had known only a couple of weeks and had little reason to trust. He had made no comment and asked no questions—that made it worse. More generously still, he had not only refrained from offers of help and advice which she might have resented; he had deliberately acknowledged that she had the right to run her own risks. "Do be careful of yourself"; "I hate to think of your being exposed to unpleasantness"; "If only I could be there to protect you"; any such phrase would express the normal male reaction. Not one man in ten thousand would say to the woman he loved, or to any woman: "Disagreeableness and danger will not turn you back, and God forbid they should." That was an admission of equality, and she had not expected it of him. If he conceived of marriage along those lines, then the whole problem would have to be reviewed in that new light; but that seemed scarcely possible. To take such a line and stick to it, he would have to be, not a man but a miracle. But the business about Saint-George must be cleared up immediately. She wrote quickly, without stopping to think too much.

Dear Peter,

No. I can't see my way to it. But thank you all the same. About the Oxford business—I would have told you all about it long ago, only that it is not my secret. I wouldn't have told your nephew, only that he had stumbled on part of it and I had to trust him with the rest to keep him from making unintentional mischief. I wish I could tell you; I should be very glad of your help; if ever I get leave to, I will. It is rather disagreeable but not dangerous, I hope. Thank you for not telling me to run away and play—that's the best compliment you ever paid me.

I hope your case, or whatever it is, is getting on all right. It must be a tough one to take so long.

HARRIET

Lord Peter Wimsey read this letter while seated upon the terrace of an hotel overlooking the Pincian Gardens, which were bathed in brilliant sunshine. It astonished him so much that he was reading it for the fourth time, when he became aware that the person standing beside him was not the waiter.

"My dear Count! I beg your pardon. What manners! My head was in the clouds. Do me the favour to sit down and join me. *Servitore!*"

"I beg you will not apologize. It is my fault for interrupting you. But fearing that last night might have somewhat entangled the situation—"

"It is foolish to talk so long and so late. Grown men behave like tired children who are allowed to sit up till midnight. I admit that we were all very fractious, myself not least."

"You are always the soul of amiability. That is why I thought that a word with you alone— We are both reasonable men."

"Count, Count, I hope you have not come to persuade me to anything. I should find it too difficult to refuse you." Wimsey folded the letter away in his pocket-book. "The sun is shining, and I am in the mood to make mistakes through over-confidence."

"Then, I must take advantage of the good moment." The Count set his elbows on the table and leaned forward, thumb-tip to thumb-tip and little-finger-tip to little-finger-tip, smiling, irresistible. Forty minutes later, he took his leave, still smiling, having ceded, without noticing it, rather more than he had gained, and told in ten words more than he had learned in a thousand.

But of this interlude Harriet naturally knew nothing. On the evening of the same day, she was dining alone, a little depressed, at Romano's. She had nearly finished, when she saw a man, just leaving the restaurant, who was sketching a vague gesture of recognition. He was in the forties, going a little bald, with a smooth, vacant face and a dark moustache.

For a moment she could not place him; then something about his languid walk and impeccable tailoring brought back an afternoon at Lord's. She smiled at him, and he came up to her table.

"Hullo–ullo! Hope I'm not bargin' in. How's all the doings and all that?"

"Very well, thanks."

"That's grand. Thought I must just ooze over and pass the time of day. Or night. Only I was afraid you wouldn't remember me, and might think I was bein' a nuisance."

"Of course I remember you. You're Mr. Arbuthnot–the Honourable Frederick Arbuthnot–and you're a friend of Peter Wimsey's, and I met you at the Eton and Harrow match two years ago, and you're married and have two children. How are they?"

"Fair to middlin', thanks. What a brain you've got! Yes, ghastly hot afternoon that was, too. Can't think why harmless women should be dragged along to be bored while a lot of little boys play off their Old School Ties. (That's meant for a joke.) You were frightfully well-behaved, I remember."

Harriet said sedately that she always enjoyed a good cricket match.

"Do you? I thought it was politeness. It's pretty slow work, if you ask me. But I was never any good at it myself. It's all right for old Peter. He can always work himself into a stew thinking how much better he'd have done it himself."

Harriet offered him coffee.

"I didn't know anybody ever got into a stew at Lord's. I thought it wasn't done."

"Well, the atmosphere doesn't exactly remind one of the Cup Final; but mild old gentlemen do sometimes break out into a spot of tut-tuttery. How about a brandy? Waiter, two liqueur brandies. Are you writing any more books?"

Suppressing the rage that this question always rouses in a professional writer, Harriet admitted that she was.

"It must be splendid to be able to write," said Mr. Arbuthnot. "I often think I could spin a good yarn myself if I had the brains. About the odd things that happen, you know. Queer deals, and that kind of thing."

A dim recollection of something Wimsey had once said lit up the labyrinth of Harriet's mind. Money. That was the connection between the two men. Mr. Arbuthnot, moron as he might be in other respects, had a flair for money. He knew what that mysterious commodity was going to do; it was the one thing he did know, and he only knew that by instinct. When things were preparing to go up or down, they rang a little warning bell in what Freddy Arbuthnot called his mind, and he acted on the warning without being able to explain why. Peter had money, and Freddy understood money; that must be the common interest and bond of mutual confidence that explained an otherwise inexplicable friendship. She admired the strange nexus of interests that unites the male half of mankind into a close honeycomb of cells, each touching the other on one side only, and yet constituting a tough and closely adhering fabric.

"Funny kind of story popped up the other day," went on Mr. Arbuthnot. "Mysterious business. Couldn't make head or tail of it. It would have amused old Peter. How is old Peter, by the way?"

"I haven't seen him for some time. He's in Rome. I don't know what he's doing there, but I suppose he's on a case of some kind."

"No. I expect he's left his country for his country's good. It's usually that. I hope they manage to keep things quiet. The exchanges are a bit nervy."

Mr. Arbuthnot looked almost intelligent.

"What's Peter got to do with the exchange?"

"Nothing. But if anything blows up, it's bound to affect the exchange."

"This is Greek to me. What is Peter's job out there?"

"Foreign Office. Didn't you know?"

"I hadn't the slightest idea. He's not permanently attached there, is he?"

"In Rome, do you mean?"

"To the Foreign Office."

"No; but they sometimes push him out when they think he's wanted. He gets on with people."

"I see. I wonder why he never mentioned it."

"Oh, everybody knows; it's not a secret. He probably thought it wouldn't interest you." Mr. Arbuthnot balanced his spoon across his coffee-cup in an abstracted way. "I'm damned fond of old Peter," was his next, rather irrelevant, contribution. "He's a dashed good sort. Last time I saw him, I thought he seemed a bit under the weather. . . . Well, I'd better be toddling."

He got up, a little abruptly, and said good-night.

Harriet thought how humiliating it was to have one's ignorance exposed.

Ten days before the beginning of term, Harriet could bear London no longer. The final touch was put to her disgust by the sight of an advance notice of *Death 'twixt Wind and Water*, embodying an exceptionally fulsome blurb. She developed an acute homesickness for Oxford and for the *Study of Le Fanu*—a book which would never have any advertising value, but of which some scholar might some day moderately observe, "Miss Vane has handled her subject with insight and accuracy." She rang up the Bursar, discovered that she could be accommodated at Shrewsbury, and fled back to Academe.

College was empty, but for herself, the Bursar and Treasurer, and Miss Barton, who vanished daily into the Radcliffe Camera and was only seen at meals. The Warden was up, but remained in her own house.

April was running out, chilly and fickle, but with the promise of good things to come; and the city wore the withdrawn and secretive beauty that wraps her about in vacation. No clamour of young voices echoed along her ancient stones; the tumult of flying bicycles was stilled in the narrow strait of the Turl; in Radcliffe Square the Camera slept like a cat in the sunshine, disturbed only by the occasional visit of a slow-footed don; even in the High, the roar of car and charabanc seemed minished and brought low, for the holiday season was not yet; punts and canoes, new-fettled for the summer term, began to put forth upon the Cherwell like the varnished buds upon the horse-chestnut tree, but as yet there was no press of traffic upon the shining reaches; the mellow bells, soaring and singing in tower and steeple, told of time's flight through an eternity of peace; and Great Tom, tolling his nightly hundred-and-one, called home only the rooks from off Christ Church Meadow.

Mornings in Bodley, drowsing among the worn browns and tarnished gilding of Duke Humphrey, snuffing the faint, musty odour of slowly perishing leather, hearing only the discreet tippety-tap of Agag-feet along the padded floor; long afternoons, taking an outrigger up the Cher, feeling the rough kiss of the sculls on unaccustomed palms, listening to the rhythmical and satisfying ker-klunk of the rowlocks, watching the play of muscle on the Bursar's sturdy shoulders at stroke, as the sharp spring wind flattened the thin silk shirt against them; or, if the day were warmer, flicking swiftly in a canoe under Magdalen walls and so by the twisting race at King's Mill by Mesopotamia to Parson's Pleasure; then back, with mind relaxed and body stretched and vigorous, to make toast by the fire; and then, at night, the lit lamp and the drawn curtain, with the flutter of the turned page and soft scrape of pen on paper the only sounds to break the utter silence between quarter and quarter chime. Now and again, Harriet took out the dossier of the poison-pen and looked it over; yet, viewed by that solitary lamp, even the ugly, printed scrawls looked harmless and impersonal, and the whole dismal problem less important than the determining of a first edition date or the settlement of a disputed reading.

In that melodious silence, something came back to her that had lain dumb and dead ever since the old, innocent undergraduate days. The singing voice, stifled long ago by the pressure of the struggle for existence, and throttled into dumbness by that queer, unhappy contact with physical passion, began to stammer a few uncertain notes. Great golden phrases, rising from nothing and leading to nothing, swam up out of her dreaming mind like the huge, sluggish carp in the cool waters of Mercury. One day she climbed up Shotover and sat looking over the spires of the city, deep-down, fathom-drowned, striking from the round bowl of the river-basin, improbably remote and lovely as the towers of Tir-nan-Og beneath the green sea-rollers. She held on her knee the looseleaf note-book that contained her notes upon the Shrewsbury scandal; but her heart was not in that sordid inquiry. A detached pentameter, echoing out of nowhere, was beating in her ears—seven marching feet—a pentameter and a half:—

*To that still centre where the spinning world*
*Sleeps on its axis—*

Had she made it or remembered it? It sounded familiar, but in her heart she knew certainly that it was her own, and seemed familiar only because it was inevitable and right.

She opened the note-book at another page and wrote the words down. She felt like the man in the *Punch* story: "Nice little barf-room, Liza—what shall we do with it?" Blank verse? . . . No . . . it was part of the octave of a sonnet . . . it had the feel of a sonnet. But what a rhyme-sound! Curled? furled? . . . she fumbled over rhyme and metre, like an unpracticed musician fingering the keys of a disused instrument.

Then, with many false starts and blank feet, returning and filling and erasing painfully as she went, she began to write again, knowing with a deep inner certainty that somehow, after long and bitter wandering, she was once more in her own place.

*Here, then, at home . . .*

the centre, the middle sea, the heart of the labyrinth . . .

*Here, then, at home, by no more storms distrest,*
*Stay we our steps—course—flight—hands folded and wings furled.*

*Here, then at home, by no more storms distrest,*
*Folding laborious hands we sit, wings furled;*
*Here in close perfume lies the rose-leaf curled,*
*Here the sun stands and knows not east nor west,*
*Here no tide runs; we have come, last and best,*
*From the wide zone through dizzying circles hurled,*
*To that still centre where the spinning world*
*Sleeps on its axis, to the heart of rest.*

Yes; there was something there, though the metre halted monotonously, lacking a free stress-shift, and the chime "dizzying-spinning" was unsatisfactory. The lines swayed and lurched in her clumsy hands, uncontrollable. Still, such as it was, she had an octave.

And there it seemed to end. She had reached the full close, and had nothing more to say. She could find no turn for the sestet to take, no epigram, no change of mood. She put down a tentative line or two and crossed them out. If the right twist would not come of itself, it was useless to manufacture it. She had her image—the world sleeping like a great top on its everlasting spindle—and anything added to that would be mere verse-making. Something might come of it some day. In the meanwhile she had got her mood on to paper—and this is the release that all writers, even the feeblest, seek for as men seek for love; and, having found it, they doze off happily into dreams and trouble their hearts no further.

She shut up the note-book, scandal and sonnet together, and began to make her way slowly down the steep path. Halfway down, she met a small party coming up: two small, flaxen-haired girls in charge of a woman whose face seemed at first only vaguely familiar. Then, as they came close, she realized that it was Annie, looking strange without her cap and apron, taking the children for a walk.

As in duty bound, Harriet greeted them and asked where they were living now.

"We've found a very nice place in Headington, madam, thank you. I'm stopping there myself for my holiday. These are my little girls. This one's Beatrice and this is Carola. Say how do you do to Miss Vane."

Harriet shook hands gravely with the children and asked their ages and how they were getting on.

"It's nice for you having them so close."

"Yes, madam. I don't know what I should do without them." The look of quick pride and joy was almost fiercely possessive. Harriet got a glimpse of a fundamental passion that she had, as it were, forgotten when she made her reckoning; it blazed across the serenity of her sonnet-mood like an ominous meteor.

"They're all I have—now that I've lost their father."

"Oh, dear, yes," said Harriet, a little uncomfortably. "Has he—how long ago was that, Annie?"

"Three years, madam. He was driven to it. They said he did what he ought not, and it preyed on his mind. But I didn't care. He never did any harm to anybody, and a man's first duty is to his wife and family, isn't it? I'd have starved with him gladly, and worked my fingers to the bone to keep the children. But he couldn't get over it. It's a cruel world for anyone with his way to make and so much competition."

"Yes, indeed," said Harriet. The elder child, Beatrice, was looking up at her mother with eyes that were too intelligent for her eight years. It would be better to get off the subject of the husband's wrongs and iniquities, whatever they might be. She murmured that the children must be a great comfort.

"Yes, madam. There's nothing like having children of your own. They make life worth living. Beatrice here is her father's living image, aren't you, darling? I was sorry not to have a boy; but now I'm glad. It's difficult to bring up boys without a father."

"And what are Beatrice and Carola going to be when they grow up?"

"I hope they'll be good girls, madam, and good wives and mothers–that's what I'll bring them up to be."

"I want to ride a motor-cycle when I'm bigger," said Beatrice, shaking her curls assertively.

"Oh, no, darling. What things they say, don't they, madam?"

"Yes, I do," said Beatrice. "I'm going to have a motor-cycle and keep a garage."

"Nonsense," said her mother, a little sharply. "You mustn't talk so. That's a boy's job."

"But lots of girls do boys' jobs nowadays," said Harriet.

"But they ought not, madam. It isn't fair. The boys have hard enough work to get jobs of their own. Please don't put such things into her head, madam. You'll never get a husband, Beatrice, if you mess about in a garage, getting all ugly and dirty."

"I don't want one," said Beatrice, firmly. "I'd rather have a motor-cycle."

Annie looked annoyed; but laughed when Harriet laughed.

"She'll find out some day, won't she, madam?"

"Very likely she will," said Harriet. If the woman took the view that any husband was better than none at all, it was useless to argue. And she had rather got into the habit of shying at all discussion that turned upon men and marriage. She said good-afternoon pleasantly and strode on, a little shaken in her mood, but not unduly so. Either one liked discussing these matters or one did not. And when there were ugly phantoms lurking in the corners of one's mind, skeletons that one dared not show to anybody, even to Peter–

Well, of course not to Peter; he was the last person. And he, at any rate, had no niche in the grey stones of Oxford. He stood for London, for the swift, rattling, chattering, excitable and devilishly upsetting world of strain and uproar. Here, at the still centre (yes, that line was definitely good), he had no place. For a whole week, she had scarcely given him a thought.

And then the dons began to arrive, full of their vacation activities and ready to take up the burden of the most exacting, yet most lovable term of the academic year. Harriet watched them come, wondering which of those cheerful and determined faces concealed a secret. Miss de Vine had been consulting a library in some ancient Flemish town, where was preserved a remarkable family correspondence dealing with trade conditions between England and Flanders under Elizabeth. Her mind was full of statistics about wool and pepper, and it was difficult to get her to think back to what she had done on the last day of the Hilary Term. She had undoubtedly burnt some old papers—there might have been newspapers among them—certainly she never read the *Daily Trumpet*—she could throw no light on the mutilated newspaper found in the fireplace.

Miss Lydgate—as Harriet had expected—had contrived in a few short weeks to make havoc of her proofs. She was apologetic. She had spent a most interesting long week-end with Professor Somebody, who was a great authority upon Greek quantitative measures; and he had discovered several passages that contained inaccuracies and thrown an entirely fresh light upon the argument of Chapter Seven. Harriet groaned dismally.

Miss Shaw had taken five of her students for a reading-party, had seen four new plays and bought a rather exciting summer outfit. Miss Pyke had spent an enthralling time assisting the curator of a local museum to put together the fragments of three figured pots and a quantity of burial-urns that had been dug up in a field in Essex. Miss Hillyard was really glad to be back in Oxford; she had had to spend a month at her sister's house while the sister was having a baby; looking after her brother-in-law seemed to have soured her temper. The Dean, on the other hand, had been helping to get a niece married and had found the whole business full of humour. "One of the bridesmaids went to the wrong church and only turned up when it was all over, and there were at *least* two hundred of us squeezed into a room that would only hold fifty, and I only got half a glass of champagne and no wedding-cake, my tummy was flapping against my spine; and the bridegroom lost his hat at the last moment, and, my *dear!* would you believe it? people *still* give plated biscuit-barrels!" Miss Chilperic had gone with her fiance and his sister to a number of interesting places to study mediaeval domestic sculpture. Miss Burrows had spent most of her time playing golf. There arrived also a reinforcement in the person of Miss Edwards, the Science tutor, just returned from taking a term's leave. She was a young and active woman, square in face and shoulder, with bobbed hair and a stand-no-nonsense manner. The only member missing from the Senior Common Room was Mrs. Goodwin, whose small son (a most unfortunate child) had come out with measles immediately upon his return to school and again required his mother's nursing.

"Of course she can't help it," said the Dean, "but it's a very great nuisance, just at the beginning of the Summer Term. If I'd only known, I could have come back earlier."

"I don't see," observed Miss Hillyard, grimly, "what else you can expect, if you give jobs to widows with children. You have to be prepared for these perpetual interruptions. And for some reason, these domestic pre-occupations always have to be put before the work."

"Well," said the Dean, "one must put work aside in a case of serious illness."

"But all children get measles."

"Yes; but he's not a very strong child, you know. His father was tubercular, poor man—in fact, that's what he died of—and if measles should turn to pneumonia, as it so often does, the consequences might be serious."

"But *has* it turned to pneumonia?"

"They're afraid it may. He's got it very badly. And, as he's a nervous little creature, he naturally likes to have his mother with him. And in any case, she'll *be* in quarantine."

"The longer she stays with him, the longer she'll *be* in quarantine."

"It's very tiresome, of course," put in Miss Lydgate, mildly. "But if Mrs. Goodwin had isolated herself and come back at the earliest possible moment—as she very bravely offered to do—she would have been suffering a great deal of anxiety."

"A great many of us have to suffer from anxiety in one way or another," said Miss Hillyard, sharply. "I have been very anxious about my sister. It is always an anxious business to have a first baby at thirty-five. But if the event had happened to occur in term-time, it would have had to take place without my assistance."

"It is always difficult to say which duty one should put first," said Miss Pyke. "Each case must be decided individually. I presume that, in bringing children into the world one accepts a certain responsibility towards them."

"I'm not denying it," said Miss Hillyard. "But if the domestic responsibility is to take precedence of the public responsibility, then the work should be handed over to someone else to do."

"But the children must be fed and clothed," said Miss Edwards.

"Quite so. But the mother should not take a resident post."

"Mrs. Goodwin is an excellent secretary," said the Dean. "I should be very sorry to lose her. And it's nice to think that we are able to help her in her very difficult position."

Miss Hillyard lost patience.

"The fact is, though you will never admit it, that everybody in this place has an inferiority complex about married women and children. For all your talk about careers and independence, you all believe in your hearts that we ought to abase ourselves before any woman who has fulfilled her animal functions."

"That is absolute nonsense," said the Bursar.

"It is natural, I suppose, to feel that married women lead a fuller life," began Miss Lydgate.

"And a more useful one," retorted Miss Hillyard. "Look at the fuss that's made over 'Shrewsbury grandchildren'! Look how delighted you all are when old students get married! As if you were saying 'Aha! education doesn't unfit us for real life after all!' And when a really brilliant scholar throws away all her prospects to marry a curate, you say perfunctorily, 'What a pity! But of course her own life must come first.'"

"I've *never* said such a thing," cried the Dean indignantly. "I always say they're perfect *fools* to marry."

"I shouldn't mind," said Miss Hillyard, unheeding, "if you said openly that intellectual interests were only a second-best; but you pretend to put them first in theory and are ashamed of them in practice."

"There's no need to get so heated about it," said Miss Barton, breaking in upon the angry protest of Miss Pyke. "After all, *some* of us may have deliberately chosen not to marry. And, if you will forgive my saying so—"

At this ominous phrase, always the prelude to something quite unforgivable, Harriet and the Dean broke hastily into the discussion.

"Considering that we are devoting our whole lives—"

"Even for a man, it is not always easy to say—"

Their common readiness confounded their good intention. Each broke off and begged the other's pardon, and Miss Barton went on unchecked:

"It is not altogether wise—or convincing—to show so much animus against married women. It was the same unreasonable prejudice that made you get that scout removed from your staircase—"

"I object," said Miss Hillyard, with a heightened colour, "to this preferential treatment. I do not see why we should put up with slackness on duty because a servant or a secretary happens to be a widow with children. I do not see why Annie should be given a room to herself in the Scouts' Wing, and charge over a corridor, when servants who have been here for longer than she has have to be content to share a room. I do not–"

"Well," said Miss Stevens, "I think she is entitled to a little consideration. A woman who has been accustomed to a nice home of her own–"

"Very likely," said Miss Hillyard. "At any rate, it was not *my* lack of consideration that led to her precious children being placed in the charge of a common thief."

"I was always against that," said the Dean.

"And why did you give in? Because poor Mrs. Jukes was such a nice woman and had a family to keep. She *must* be considered and rewarded for being fool enough to marry a scoundrel. What's the good of pretending that you put the interests of the College first, when you hesitate for two whole terms about getting rid of a dishonest porter, because you're so sorry for his family?"

"There," said Miss Allison, "I entirely agree with you. The College ought to come first in a case like that."

"It ought always to come first. Mrs. Goodwin ought to see it, and resign her post if she can't carry out her duties properly." She stood up. "Perhaps, however, it is as well that she should be away and stay away. You may remember that, *last* time she was away, we had no trouble from anonymous letters or monkey-tricks."

Miss Hillyard put down her coffee-cup and stalked out of the room. Everybody looked uncomfortable.

"Bless my heart!" said the Dean.

"Something very wrong there," said Miss Edwards, bluntly.

"She's so prejudiced," said Miss Lydgate. "I always think it's a very great pity she never married."

Miss Lydgate had a way of putting into language that a child could understand things which other people did not say, or said otherwise.

"I should be sorry for the man, I must say," observed Miss Shaw; "but perhaps I am showing an undue consideration for the male sex. One is almost afraid to open one's mouth."

"Poor Mrs. Goodwin!" exclaimed the Bursar. "The very last person!"

She got up angrily and went out. Miss Lydgate followed her. Miss Chilperic, who had said nothing, but looked quite alarmed, murmured that she must get along to work. The Common Room slowly cleared, and Harriet was left with the Dean.

"Miss Lydgate has the most terrifying way of hitting the nail on the head," said Miss Martin; "because it is obviously much more likely that–"

"A great deal more likely," said Harriet.

Mr. Jenkyn was a youngish and agreeable don whom Harriet had met the previous term at a party in North Oxford-the same party, in fact, which had led to her acquaintance with Mr. Reginald Pomfret. He resided at Magdalen, and was incidentally one of the pro-Proctors. Harriet had happened to say something to him about the Magdalen May-day ceremony, and he had promised to send her a ticket for the Tower. Being a scientist and a man of scrupulously exact mind, he remembered his promise; and the ticket duly arrived.

None of the Shrewsbury S.C.R. was going. Most of them had been up on May mornings before. Miss de Vine had not; but though she had been offered tickets, her heart would not stand the stairs. There were students who had received invitations; but they were not students whom Harriet knew. She therefore set off alone, well before sunrise, having made an appointment to meet Miss Edwards when she came down and take an outrigger down to the Isis for a pipe-opener before having breakfast on the river.

The choristers had sung their hymn. The sun had risen, rather red and angry, casting a faint flush over the roofs and spires of the waking city. Harriet leaned over the parapet, looking down upon the heart-breaking beauty of the curved High Street, scarcely disturbed as yet by the roar of petrol-driven traffic. Under her feet, the tower began to swing to the swinging of the bells. The little group of bicyclists and pedestrians far below began to break up and move away. Mr. Jenkyn came up, said a few pleasant words, remarked that he had to hurry off to go bathing with a friend at Parson's Pleasure; there was no need for her to hurry—could she get down the stairs all right alone?

Harriet laughed and thanked him, and he took leave of her at the stair-head. She moved to the East side of the tower. There lay the river and Magdalen Bridge, with its pack of punts and canoes. Among them, she distinguished the sturdy figure of Miss Edwards, in a bright orange jumper. It was wonderful to stand so above the world, with a sea of sound below and an ocean of air above, all mankind shrunk to the proportions of an ant-heap. True, a cluster of people still lingered upon the tower itself—her companions in this airy hermitage. They too, spell-bound with beauty—

Great Scott! What was that girl trying to do?

Harriet made a dive at the young woman who was just placing one knee on the stonework and drawing herself up between two crenellations of the parapet.

"Here!" she said, "you mustn't do that. It's dangerous."

The girl, a thin, fair, frightened-looking child, desisted at once.

"I only wanted to look over."

"Well, that's very silly of you. You might get giddy. You'd better come along down. It would be very unpleasant for the Magdalen authorities if anyone fell over. They might have to stop letting people come up."

"I'm so sorry. I didn't think."

"Well, you should think. Is anybody with you?"

"No."

"I'm going down now; you'd better come too."

"Very well."

Harriet shepherded the girl down the dark spiral. She had no proof of anything but rash curiosity, but she wondered. The girl spoke with a slightly common accent, and Harriet would have put her down for a shop-assistant, but for the fact that tickets for the Tower were more likely to be restricted to University people and their friends. She might be an undergraduate, come up with a County Scholarship. In any case, one was perhaps attaching too much importance to the incident.

They were passing the bell-chamber now, and the brazen clamour was loud and insistent. It reminded her of a story that Peter Wimsey had told her, years ago now, one day when only a resolute determination to talk on and on had enabled him to prevent a most unfortunate outing from ending in a quarrel. Something about a body in a belfry, and a flood, and the great bells bawling the alarm across three counties.

The noise of the bells died down behind her as she passed, and the recollection with it; but she had paused for a moment in the awkward descent, and the girl, whoever she was, had got ahead of her. When she reached the foot of the stair and came out into clear daylight, she saw the slight figure scurrying off through the passage into the quad. She was doubtful whether to pursue it or not. She followed at a distance, watched it turn downwards up the High, and suddenly found herself almost in the arms of Mr. Pomfret, coming down from Queen's in a very untidy grey flannel suit, with a towel over his arm.

"Hullo!" said Mr. Pomfret. "You been saluting the sunrise?"

"Yes. Not a very good sunrise, but quite a good salute."

"*I* think it's going to rain" said Mr. Pomfret. "But I said I would bathe and I am bathing."

"Much the same here," said Harriet. "I said I'd scull, and I'm sculling."

"Aren't we a pair of heroes?" said Mr. Pomfret. He accompanied her to Magdalen Bridge, was hailed by an irritable friend in a canoe, who said he had been waiting for half an hour, and went off up-river, grumbling that nobody loved him and that he knew it was going to rain.

Harriet joined Miss Edwards, who said, on hearing about the girl:

"Well, you might have got her name, I suppose. But I don't see what one could do about it. It wasn't one of our people, I suppose?"

"I didn't recognize her. And she didn't seem to recognize me."

"Then it probably wasn't. Pity you didn't get the name, all the same. People oughtn't to do that kind of thing. Inconsiderate. Will you take bow or stroke?"

# 12

As a Tulipant to the Sun (which our herbalists call *Narcissus*) when it shines, is *admirandus flos ad radios solis se pandens*, a glorious Flower exposing itself; but when the Sun sets, or a tempest comes, it hides itself, pines away, and hath no pleasure left . . . do all Enamoratoes to their Mistress.

Robert Burton

The mind most effectually works upon the body, producing by his passions and perturbations miraculous alterations, as melancholy, despair, cruel diseases, and sometimes death itself . . . . They that live in fear are never free, resolute, secure, never merry, but in continual pain . . . . It causeth oft-times sudden madness.

ID.

THE ARRIVAL of Miss Edwards, together with the rearrangements of residences due to the completion of the Library Building, greatly strengthened the hands of authority at the opening of the Trinity Term. Miss Barton, Miss Burrows and Miss de Vine moved into the three new sets on the groundfloor of the Library; Miss Chilperic was transferred to the New Quad, and a general redistribution took place; so that Tudor and Burleigh Buildings were left entirely denuded of dons. Miss Martin, Harriet, Miss Edwards and Miss Lydgate established a system of patrols, by which the New Quad, Queen Elizabeth and the Library Building could be visited nightly at irregular intervals and an eye kept on all suspicious movements.

Thanks to this arrangement, the more violent demonstrations of the Poison-Pen received a check. It is true that a few anonymous letters continued to arrive by post, containing scurrilous insinuations and threats of revenge against various persons. Harriet was carefully docketing as many of these as she could hear of or lay hands on—she noticed that by this time every member of the S.C.R. had been persecuted, with the exception of Mrs. Goodwin and Miss Chilperic; in addition, the Third Year taking Schools began to receive sinister prognostications about their prospects, while Miss Flaxman was presented with an ill-executed picture of a harpy tearing the flesh of a gentleman in a mortar-board. Harriet had tried to eliminate Miss Pyke and Miss Burrows from suspicion, on the ground that they were both fairly skilful with a pencil, and would therefore be incapable of producing such bad drawings, even by taking thought; she discovered, however, that, though both were dexterous, neither of them was ambidexterous, and that their left-handed efforts were quite as bad as anything produced by the Poison-Pen, if not worse. Miss Pyke, indeed, on being shown the Harpy picture, pointed out that it was, in several respects, inconsistent with the classical conception of this monster; but there again it was clearly easy enough for the expert to assume ignorance; and perhaps the eagerness with which she drew attention to the incidental errors told as much against her as in her favour.

Another trifling but curious episode, occurring on the third Monday in term, was the complaint of an agitated and conscientious First-Year that she had left a harmless modern novel open upon the table in the Fiction Library, and that on her return to fetch it after an afternoon on the river, she had found several pages from the middle of the book—just where she was reading—ripped out and strewn about the room. The First-Year, who was a County Council Scholar, and as poor as a church mouse, was almost in tears; it really wasn't her fault; should she have to replace the book? The Dean, to whom the question was addressed, said, No; it certainly didn't seem to be the First-Year's fault. She made a note of the outrage: "*The Search* by C. P. Snow, pp. 327 to 340 removed and mutilated, May 13th," and passed the information on to Harriet, who incorporated it in her diary of the case, together with such items as: "March 7—abusive letter by post to Miss de Vine," "March 11, do. to Miss Hillyard and Miss Layton," "April 29—Harpy drawing to Miss Flaxman," of which she had now quite a formidable list.

So the Summer Term set in, sun-flecked and lovely, a departing April whirled on wind-spurred feet towards a splendour of May. Tulips danced in the Fellows' Garden; a fringe of golden green shimmered and deepened upon the saecular beeches; the boats put out upon the Cher between the budding banks, and the wide reaches of the Isis were strenuous with practising eights. Black gowns and summer frocks fluttered up and down the streets of the city and through the College gates, making a careless heraldry with the green of smooth turf and the silver-sable of ancient stone; motor-car and bicycle raced perilously side by side through narrow turnings and the wail of gramophones made hideous the water-ways from Magdalen Bridge to far above the new By-pass. Sunbathers and untidy tea-parties desecrated Shrewsbury Old Quad, newly-whitened tennis-shoes broke out like strange, unwholesome flowers along plinth and window-ledge, and the Dean was forced to issue a ukase in the matter of the bathing-dresses which flapped and fluttered, flag-fashion, from every coign of vantage. Solicitous tutors began to cluck and brood tenderly over such ripening eggs of scholarship as were destined to hatch out damply in the Examination Schools after their three years' incubation; candidates, realizing with a pang that they had now fewer than eight weeks in which to make up for cut lectures and misspent working hours, went flashing from Bodley to lecture-room and from Camera to coaching; and the thin trickle of abuse from the Poison-Pen was swamped and well-nigh forgotten in that stream of genial commination always poured out from the lips of examinees elect upon examining bodies. Nor, in the onset of Schools Fever, was a lighter note lacking to the general delirium. The draw for the Schools Sweep was made in the Senior Common Room, and Harriet found herself furnished with the names of two "horses," one of whom, a Miss Newland, was said to be well fancied. Harriet asked who she was, having never to her knowledge seen or heard of her.

"I don't suppose you have," said the Dean. "She's a shy child. But Miss Shaw thinks she's pretty safe for a First."

"She isn't looking well this term, though," said the Bursar. "I hope she isn't going to have a break-down or anything. I told her the other day she ought not to cut Hall so often."

"They *will* do it," said the Dean. "It's all very well to say they can't be bothered to change when they come off the river and prefer pyjamas and an egg in their rooms; but I'm sure a boiled egg and a sardine aren't sustaining enough to do Schools on."

"And the mess it all makes for the scouts to clear up," grumbled the Bursar. "It's almost impossible to get the rooms done by eleven when they're crammed with filthy crockery."

"It isn't being out on the river that's the matter with Newland," said the Dean. "That child works."

"All the worse," said the Bursar. "I distrust the candidate who swots in her last term. I shouldn't be a bit surprised if your horse scratched, Miss Vane. She looks nervy to me."

"That's very depressing," said Harriet. "Perhaps I'd better sell half my ticket while the price is good. I agree with Edgar Wallace, 'Give me a good stupid horse who will eat his oats.' Any offers for Newland?"

"What's that about Newland?" demanded Miss Shaw, coming up to them. They were having coffee in the Fellows' Garden at the time. "By the way, Dean, couldn't you put up a notice about sitting on the grass in the New Quad? I have had to chase two parties off. We cannot have the place looking like Margate Beach."

"Certainly not. They know quite *well* it isn't allowed. *Why* are women undergraduates so sloppy?"

"They're always exceedingly anxious to be like the men," said Miss Hillyard, sarcastically, "but I notice the likeness doesn't extend to showing respect for the College grounds."

"Even you must admit that men have some virtues," said Miss Shaw.

"More tradition and discipline, that's all," said Miss Hillyard.

"I don't know," said Miss Edwards. "I think women are messier by nature. They are naturally picnic-minded."

"It's nice to sit out in the open air in this lovely weather," suggested Miss Chilperic, almost apologetically (for her student days were not far behind her), "and they don't think how awful it looks."

"In hot weather," said Harriet, moving her chair back into the shade, "men have the common sense to stay indoors, where it's cooler."

"Men," said Miss Hillyard, "have a passion for frowst."

"Yes," said Miss Shaw, "but what were you saying about Miss Newland? You weren't offering to sell your chance, Miss Vane, were you? Because, take it from me, she's a hot favourite. She's the Latymer Scholar, and her work's brilliant."

"Somebody suggested she was off her feed and likely to be a non-starter."

"That's very unkind," said Miss Shaw, with indignation. "Nobody's any right to say such things."

"I think she looks harassed and on edge," said the Bursar. "She's too hard-working and conscientious. She hasn't got the wind-up about Schools, has she?"

"There's nothing wrong with her work," said Miss Shaw. "She does look a little pale, but I expect it's the sudden heat."

"Possibly she's worried about things at home," suggested Mrs. Goodwin. She had returned to College on the 9th May, her boy having taken a fortunate turn for the better, though he was still not out of the wood. She looked anxious and sympathetic.

"She'd have told me if she had been," said Miss Shaw. "I encourage my students to confide in me. Of course she's a very reserved girl, but I have done my best to draw her out, and I feel sure I should have heard if there was anything on her mind."

"Well," said Harriet, "I must see this horse of mine before I decide what to do about my sweep-stake ticket. Somebody must point her out."

"She's up in the Library at this moment, I fancy," said the Dean; "I saw her stewing away there just before dinner-cutting Hall as usual. I nearly spoke to her. Come and stroll through, Miss Vane. If she's there, we'll chase her out for the good of her soul. I want to look up a reference, anyhow."

Harriet got up, laughing, and accompanied the Dean.

"I sometimes think," said Miss Martin, "that Miss Shaw would get more real confidence from her pupils if she wasn't always probing into their little insides. She likes people to be fond of her, which I think is rather a mistake. Be kind, but leave 'em alone, is my motto. The shy ones shrink into their shells when they're poked, and the egotistical ones talk a lot of rubbish to attract attention. However, we all have our methods."

She pushed open the Library door, halted in the end bay to consult a book and verify a quotation, and then led the way through the long room. At a table near the centre, a thin, fair girl was working amid a pile of reference books. The Dean stopped.

"You still here, Miss Newland? Haven't you had any dinner?"

"I'll have some later, Miss Martin. It was so hot, and I want to get this language paper done."

The girl looked startled and uneasy. She pushed the damp hair back from her forehead. The whites of her eyes showed like those of a fidgety horse.

"Don't you be a little juggins," said the Dean. "All work and no play is simply silly in your Schools term. If you go on like this, we'll have to send you away for a rest-cure and forbid work altogether for a week or so. Have you got a headache? You look as if you had."

"Not very much, Miss Martin."

"For goodness' sake," said the Dean, "chuck that perishing old Ducange and Meyer-Lubke or whoever it is and go away and play. I'm always having to chase the Schools people off to the river and into the country," she added, turning to Harriet. "I wish they'd all be like Miss Camperdown–she was after your time. She frightened Miss Pyke by dividing the whole of her Schools term between the river and the tenniscourts, and she ended up with a First in Greats."

Miss Newland looked more alarmed than ever.

"I don't seem able to think," she confessed. "I forget things and go blank."

"Of course you do," said the Dean, briskly. "Sure sign you're doing too much. Stop it at once. Get up now and get yourself some food and then take a nice novel or something, or find somebody to have a knock-up with you."

"Please don't bother, Miss Martin. I'd rather go on with this. I don't feel like eating and I don't care about tennis–I *wish* you wouldn't bother!" she finished, rather hysterically.

"All right," said the Dean; "bless you, *I* don't want to fuss. But do be sensible."

"I will, really, Miss Martin. I'll just finish this paper. I couldn't feel comfortable if I hadn't. I'll have something to eat then and go to bed. I promise I will."

"That's a good girl." The Dean passed on, out of the Library, and said to Harriet:

"I don't like to see them getting into that state. What do you think of your horse's chance?"

"Not much," said Harriet. "I do know her. That is, I've seen her before. I saw her last on Magdalen Tower."

"What?" said the Dean. "Oh, lord!"

Of Lord Saint-George, Harriet had not seen very much during that first fortnight of term. His arm was out of a sling; but a remaining weakness in it had curbed his sporting activities, and when she did see him, he informed her that he was working. The matter of the telegraph pole and the insurance had been safely adjusted and the parental wrath avoided. "Uncle Peter," to be sure, had had something to say about it, but Uncle Peter, though scathing, was as safe as houses. Harriet encouraged the young gentleman to persevere with his work and refused an invitation to dine and meet "his people." She had no particular wish to meet the Denvers, and had hitherto successfully avoided doing so.

Mr. Pomfret had been assiduously polite. He and Mr. Rogers had taken her on the river, and had included Miss Cattermole in the party. They had all been on their best behaviour, and a pleasant time had been enjoyed by all, the mention of previous encounters having, by common consent, been avoided. Harriet was pleased with Miss Cattermole; she seemed to have made an effort to throw off the blight that had settled upon her, and Miss Hillyard's report had been encouraging. Mr. Pomfret had also asked Harriet to lunch and to play tennis; on the former occasion she had truthfully pleaded a previous engagement and, on the second, had said, with rather less truth, that she had not played for years, was out of form and was not really keen. After all, one had one's work to do (*Le Fanu, 'Twixt Wind and Water*, and the *History of Prosody* among them made up a fairly full programme), and one could not spend all one's time idling with undergraduates.

On the evening after her formal introduction to Miss Newland, however, Harriet encountered Mr. Pomfret accidentally. She had been to see an old Shrewsburian who was attached to the Somerville Senior Common Room, and was crossing St. Giles on her way back, shortly before midnight, when she was aware of a group of young men in evening dress, standing about one of the trees which adorn that famous thoroughfare. Being naturally inquisitive, Harriet went to see what was up. The street was practically deserted, except for through traffic of the ordinary kind. The upper branches of the tree were violently agitated, and Harriet, standing on the outskirts of the little group beneath, learned from their remarks that Mr. Somebody-or-the-other had undertaken, in consequence of an after-dinner bet, to climb every tree in St. Giles without interference from the Proctor. As the number of trees was large and the place public, Harriet felt the wager to be rather optimistic. She was just turning away to cross the street in the direction of the Lamb and Flag, when another youth, who had evidently been occupying an observation-post, arrived, breathless, to announce that the Proggins was just coming into view round the corner of Broad Street. The climber came down rather hastily, and the group promptly scattered in all directions–some running past her, some making their way down side-streets, and a few bold spirits fleeing towards the small enclosure known as the Fender, within which (since it belongs not to the Town but to St. John's) they could play at tig with the Proctor to their hearts' content. One of the young gentlemen darting in this general direction passed Harriet close, stopped with an exclamation, and brought up beside her.

"Why, it's you!" cried Mr. Pomfret, in an excited tone.

"Me again," said Harriet. "Are you always out without your gown at this time of night?"

"Practically always," said Mr. Pomfret, falling into step beside her. "Funny you should always catch me at it. Amazing luck, isn't it? . . . I say, you've been avoiding me this term. Why?"

"Oh, no," said Harriet; "only I've been rather busy."

"But you *have* been avoiding me," said Mr. Pomfret. "I know you have. I suppose it's ridiculous to expect you to take any particular interest in me. I don't suppose you ever think about me. You probably despise me."

"Don't be so absurd, Mr. Pomfret. Of course I don't do anything of the sort. I like you very much, but–"

"Do you? ... Then why won't you let me see you? Look here, I *must* see you. There's something I've got to tell you. When can I come and talk to you?"

"What about?" said Harriet, seized with a sudden and awful qualm.

"What *about*? Hang it, don't be so unkind. Look here, Harriet– No, stop, you've got to listen. Darling, wonderful Harriet–"

"Mr. Pomfret, please–"

But Mr. Pomfret was not to be checked. His admiration had run away with him, and Harriet, cornered in the shadow of the big horse-chestnut by the Lamb and Flag, found herself listening to as eager an avowal of devotion as any young gentleman in his twenties ever lavished upon a lady considerably his senior in age and experience.

"I'm frightfully sorry, Mr. Pomfret. I never thought– No, really, it's quite impossible. I'm at least ten years older than you are. And besides–"

"What does that matter?" With a large and clumsy gesture Mr. Pomfret swept away the difference of age and plunged on in a flood of eloquence, which Harriet, exasperated with herself and him, could not stop. He loved her, he adored her, he was intensely miserable, he could neither work nor play games for thinking of her, if she refused him he didn't know what he should do with himself, she must have seen, she must have realized–he wanted to stand between her and all the world–

Mr. Pomfret was six feet three and broad and strong in proportion.

"Please don't do that," said Harriet, feeling as though she were feebly saying "Drop it, Caesar," to somebody else's large and disobedient Alsatian. "No, I mean it. I can't let you–" And then in a different tone:

"Look out, juggins! Here's the Proctor."

Mr. Pomfret, in some consternation, gathered himself together and turned as to flee. But the Proctor's bull-dogs, who had been having a lively time with the tree-climbers in St. Giles, and were now out for blood, had come through the archway at a smart trot, and seeing a young gentleman not only engaged in nocturnal vagation without his gown but actually embracing a female (*mulier vel meretrix, cujus consortio Christianis prorsus interdictum est*) leapt gleefully upon him, as upon a lawful prey.

"Oh, blast!" said Mr. Pomfret. "Here, you–"

"The Proctor would like to speak to you, sir," said the Bull-dog, grimly.

Harriet debated with herself whether it might not be more tactful to depart, leaving Mr. Pomfret to his fate. But the Proctor was close on the heels of his men; he was standing within a few yards of her and already demanding to know the offender's name and college. There seemed to be nothing for it but to face the matter out.

"Just a moment, Mr. Proctor," began Harriet, struggling, for Mr. Pomfret's sake, to control a rebellious uprush of laughter. "This gentleman is with me, and you can't– Oh! good evening, Mr. Jenkyn."

It was, indeed, that amiable pro-Proctor. He gazed at Harriet, and was struck dumb with embarrassment.

"I say," broke in Mr. Pomfret, awkwardly, but with a gentlemanly feeling that some explanation was due from him; "it was entirely my fault. I mean, I'm afraid I was annoying Miss Vane. She–I–"

"You can't very well prog him, you know," said Harriet, persuasively, "can you now?"

"Come to think of it," replied Mr. Jenkyn, "I suppose I can't. You're a Senior Member, aren't you?" He waved his bull-dogs to a distance. "I beg your pardon," he added, a little stiffly.

"Not at all," said Harriet. "It's a nice night. Did you have good hunting in St. Giles?"

"Two culprits will appear before their dean tomorrow," said the pro-Proctor, rather more cheerfully. "I suppose nobody came through here?"

"Nobody but ourselves," said Harriet; "and I can assure you that we haven't been climbing trees."

A wicked facility in quotation tempted her to add "except in the Hesperideas"; but she respected Mr. Pomfret's feelings and restrained herself.

"No, no," said Mr. Jenkyn. He fingered his bands nervously and hitched his gown with its velvet facings protectively about his shoulders. "I had better be away in pursuit of those that have."

"Good-night," said Harriet.

"Good-night," said Mr. Jenkyn, courteously raising his square cap. He turned sharply upon Mr. Pomfret. "Goodnight, sir."

He stalked away with brisk steps between the posts into Museum Road, his long liripipe sleeves agitated and fluttering. Between Harriet and Mr. Pomfret there occurred one of those silences into which the first word spoken falls like the stroke of a gong. It seemed equally impossible to comment on the interruption or to resume the interrupted conversation. By common consent, however, they turned their backs upon the pro-Proctor and moved out once more into St. Giles. They had turned left and were passing through the now-deserted Fender before Mr. Pomfret found his tongue.

"A nice fool I look," said Mr. Pomfret, bitterly.

"It was very unfortunate," said Harriet, "but I must have looked much the more foolish. I very nearly ran away altogether. However, all's well that ends well. He's a very decent sort and I don't suppose he'll think twice about it."

She remembered, with another disconcerting interior gurgle of mirth, an expression in use among the irreverent: "to catch a Senior girling." "To boy" was presumably the feminine equivalent of the verb "to girl"; she wondered whether Mr. Jenkyn would employ it in Common Room next day. She did not grudge him his entertainment; being old enough to know that even the most crashing social bricks make but a small ripple in the ocean of time, which quickly dies away. To Mr. Pomfret, however, the ripple must inevitably appear of the dimensions of a maelstrom. He was muttering sulkily something about a laughing-stock.

"Please," said Harriet, "don't worry about it. It's of no importance. I don't mind one bit."

"Of course not," said Mr. Pomfret. "Naturally, you can't take me seriously. You're treating me like a child."

"Indeed I'm not. I'm very grateful—I'm very much honoured by everything you said to me. But really and truly, it's quite impossible."

"Oh, well, never mind," said Mr. Pomfret, angrily.

It was too bad, thought Harriet. To have one's young affections trampled upon was galling enough; to have been made an object of official ridicule as well was almost unbearable. She must do something to restore the young gentleman's self-respect.

"Listen, Mr. Pomfret. I don't think I shall ever marry anybody. Please believe that my objection isn't personal at all. We have been very good friends. Can't we—?"

Mr. Pomfret greeted this fine old bromide with a dreary snort.

"I suppose," he said, in a savage tone, "there's somebody else."

"I don't know that you've any right to ask that."

"Of course not," said Mr. Pomfret, affronted. "I've no right to ask you anything. I ought to apologize for asking you to marry me. And for making a scene in front of the Proggins—in fact, for existing. I'm exceedingly sorry."

Very clearly, the only balm that could in the least soothe the wounded vanity of Mr. Pomfret would be the assurance that there *was* somebody else. But Harriet was not prepared to make any such admission; and besides, whether there was anybody else or not, nothing could make the notion of marrying Mr. Pomfret anything but preposterous. She begged him to take a reasonable view of the matter; but he continued to sulk; and indeed, nothing that could possibly be said could mitigate the essential absurdity of the situation. To offer a lady one's chivalrous protection against the world in general, and to be compelled instead to accept her senior standing as a protection for one's self against the just indignation of the Proctor is, and remains, farcical.

Their ways lay together. In resentful silence they paced the stones, past the ugly front of Balliol and the high iron gates of Trinity, past the fourteen-fold sneer of the Caesars and the top-heavy arch of the Clarendon Building, till they stood at the junction of Cat Street and Holywell.

"Well," said Mr. Pomfret, "if you don't mind, I'd better cut along here. It's just going twelve."

"Yes. Don't bother about me. Good-night. . . . And thank you again very much."

"Good-night."

Mr. Pomfret ran hurriedly in the direction of Queen's College, pursued by a yelping chorus of chimes.

Harriet went on down Holywell. She could laugh now if she wanted to; and she did laugh. She had no fear of any permanent damage to Mr. Pomfret's heart; he was far too cross to be suffering in anything but his vanity. The incident had that rich savour of the ludicrous which neither pity nor charity can destroy. Unfortunately, she could not in decency share it with anybody; she could only enjoy it in lonely ecstasies of mirth. What Mr. Jenkyn must be thinking of her she could scarcely imagine. Did he suppose her to be an unprincipled cradle-snatcher? or a promiscuous sexual maniac? or a disappointed woman eagerly grasping at the rapidly disappearing skirts of opportunity? or what? The more she thought about her own part in the episode, the funnier it appeared to her. She wondered what she should say to Mr. Jenkyn if she ever met him again.

She was surprised to find how much Mr. Pomfret's simpleminded proposal had elated her. She ought to have been thoroughly ashamed of herself. She ought to be blaming herself for not having seen what was happening to Mr. Pomfret and taken steps to stop it. Why hadn't she? Simply, she supposed, because the possibility of such a thing had never occurred to her. She had taken it for granted that she could never again attract any man's fancy, except the eccentric fancy of Peter Wimsey. And to him she was, of course, only the creature of his making and the mirror of his own magnanimity. Reggie Pomfret's devotion, though ridiculous, was at least singleminded; *he* was no King Cophetua; she had not to be humbly obliged to *him* for kindly taking notice of her. And that reflection, after all, was pleasurable. However loudly we may assert our own unworthiness, few of us are really offended by hearing the assertion contradicted by a disinterested party.

In this unregenerate mood she reached the College, and let herself in by the postern. There were lights in the Warden's Lodgings, and somebody was standing at the gate, looking out. At the sound of Harriet's footsteps, this person called out, in the Dean's voice:

"Is that you, Miss Vane? The Warden wants to see you."

"What's the matter, Dean?"

The Dean took Harriet by the arm.

"Newland hasn't come in. You haven't seen her anywhere?"

"No—I've been round at Somerville. It's only just after twelve. She'll probably turn up. You don't think—?"

"We don't know what to think. It's not like Newland to be out without leave. And we've found things."

She led Harriet into the Warden's sitting-room. Dr. Baring was seated at her desk, her handsome face stern and judicial. In front of her stood Miss Haydock, with her hands thrust into her dressing-gown pockets; she looked excited and angry. Miss Shaw, curled dismally in a corner of the big couch, was crying; while Miss Millbanks the Senior Student, half-frightened and half-defiant, hovered uneasily in the background. As Harriet came in with the Dean, everybody looked hopefully towards the door and then away again.

"Miss Vane," said the Warden, "the Dean tells me that you saw Miss Newland behaving in a peculiar manner on Magdalen Tower last May-Day. Can you give me any more exact details about that?"

Harriet told her story again.

"I am sorry," she added in conclusion, "that I didn't get her name at the time; but I didn't recognize her as one of our students. As a matter of fact, I don't remember ever noticing her at all, until she was pointed out to me yesterday by Miss Martin."

"That's quite right," said the Dean. "I'm not at all surprised you shouldn't have known her. She's very quiet and shy and seldom comes in to Hall or shows herself anywhere. I think she works nearly all day at the Radcliffe. Of course, when you told me about the May-Day business, I decided that somebody ought to keep an eye on her. I informed Dr. Baring and Miss

Shaw, and I asked Miss Millbanks whether any of the Third Year had noticed that she seemed to be in any trouble."

"I can't understand it," cried Miss Shaw. "Why couldn't she have come to me about it? I always encourage my pupils to give me their full confidence. I asked her again and again. I really thought she had a real affection for me. . . ."

She sniffed hopelessly into a damp handkerchief.

"I knew something was up," said Miss Haydock, bluntly. "But I didn't know what it was. The more questions you asked, the less she'd tell you—so I didn't ask many."

"Has the girl no friends?" asked Harriet.

"I thought she looked on me as a friend," complained Miss Shaw.

"She didn't make friends," said Miss Haydock.

"She's a very reserved child," said the Dean. "I don't think anybody could make much out of her. I know I couldn't."

"But what has happened, exactly?" asked Harriet.

"When Miss Martin spoke to Miss Millbanks about her," said Miss Haydock, cutting in without respect of persons upon the Warden's reply, "Miss Millbanks mentioned the matter to me, saying she couldn't see that we could be expected to do anything."

"But I scarcely knew her . . ." began Miss Millbanks.

"Nor did I," said Miss Haydock. "But I thought something had better be done about it. I took her out on the river this afternoon. She said she ought to work, but I told her not to be an idiot, or she'd crack up. We took a punt up over the Rollers and had tea along by the Parks. She seemed all right then. I brought her back and persuaded her to come and dine properly in Hall. After that, she said she wanted to go and work at the Radder. I had an engagement, so I couldn't go with her—besides, I thought she'd think it funny if I trailed after her all day. So I told Miss Millbanks that somebody else had better carry on."

"Well, I carried on myself," said Miss Millbanks, rather defiantly. "I took my own work across there. I sat in a desk where I could see her. She was there till half-past nine. I came away at ten and found she'd gone."

"Didn't you see her go?"

"No. I was reading and I suppose she slipped out. I'm sorry; but how was I to know? I've got Schools this term. It's all very well to say I oughtn't to have taken my eyes off her, but I'm not a nurse or anything—"

Harriet noticed how Miss Millbanks's self-assurance had broken down. She was defending herself angrily and clumsily like a school-girl.

"On returning," pursued the Warden, "Miss Millbanks—"

"But has anything been done about it?" interrupted Harriet, impatient with this orderly academic exposition. "I suppose you asked whether she'd been up to the gallery of the Radcliffe."

"I thought of that later on," replied the Warden, "and suggested that a search should be made there. I understand that it has been made, without result. However, a subsequent—"

"How about the river?"

"I am coming to that. Perhaps I had better continue in chronological order. I can assure you that no time has been wasted."

"Very well, Warden."

"On returning," said the Warden, taking up her tale exactly where she had left it, "Miss Millbanks told Miss Haydock about it, and they ascertained that

Miss Newland was not in College. They then, very properly, informed the Dean, who instructed Padgett to telephone through as soon as she came in. At 11.15 she had not returned, and Padgett reported that fact. He mentioned at the same time that he had himself been feeling uneasy about Miss Newland. He had noticed that she had taken to going about alone, and that she looked strained and nervous."

"Padgett is pretty shrewd," said the Dean. "I often think he knows more about the students than any of us."

"Up till tonight," wailed Miss Shaw, "I should have said I knew all my pupils intimately."

"Padgett also said he had seen several of the anonymous letters arrive at the Lodge for Miss Newland."

"He ought to have reported that," said Harriet.

"No," said the Dean. "It was after you came last term that we instructed him to report. The ones he saw came before that."

"I see."

"By that time," said the Warden, "we were beginning to feel alarmed, and Miss Martin rang up the police. In the meantime, Miss Haydock made a search in Miss Newland's room for anything that might throw light on her state of mind; and found–these."

She took a little sheaf of papers from her desk and handed them to Harriet, who said, "Good God."

The Poison-Pen, this time, had found a victim ready made to her hand. There were the letters, thirty or more of them ("and I don't suppose that's the lot, either," was the Dean's comment)–menancing, abusive, insinuating–all hammering remorselessly upon the same theme. "You needn't think you will get away with it"–"What will you do when you fail in Schools?"–"You deserve to fail and I shall see that you do"–then more horrible suggestions: "Don't you feel your brain going?"–"If they see you are going mad they will send you down"–and finally, in a sinister series: "You'd better end it now"–;'Better dead than in the loony-bin"–"In your place I should throw myself out of the window"–"Try the river"–and so on; the continuous, deadly beating on weak nerves that of all things is hardest to resist.

"If only she had shown them to me!" Miss Shaw was crying.

"She wouldn't, of course," said Harriet. "You have to be very well balanced to admit that people think you're going mad. That's what's done the mischief."

"Of all the wicked things–" said the Dean. "Think of that unfortunate child collecting all these horrors and brooding over them! I'd like to kill whoever it is!"

"It's a definite effort at murder," said Harriet. "But the point is, has it come off?"

There was a pause. Then the Warden said in an expressionless voice:

"One of the boat-house keys is missing."

"Miss Stevens and Miss Edwards have gone up-stream in the Water-fly," said the Dean, "and Miss Burrows and Miss Barton have taken the other sculler down to the Isis. The police are searching too. They've been gone about three-quarters of an hour. We didn't discover till then that the key was gone."

"Then there's not much we can do," said Harriet, suppressing the angry comment that the boat-house keys should have been checked the moment Miss Newland's absence had been remarked. "Miss Haydock–did Miss Newland say anything to you–anything at all–while you were out, that might suggest where she was likely to go in case she wanted to drown herself?"

The blunt phrase, spoken openly for the first time, shook everybody. Miss Haydock put her head in her hands.

"Wait a minute," she said. "I do remember something. We were well up through the Parks– Yes– It was after tea, and we went a bit further before turning. I struck a bad bit of water and nearly lost the pole. I remember saying it would be a nasty place to go in, because of the weeds. It's a bad bottom–all mud with deep holes in it. Miss Newland asked if that wasn't the place where a man had been drowned last year. I said I didn't know, but I thought it was near there. She didn't say anything more, and I'd forgotten it till this moment."

Harriet looked at her watch.

"Half-past nine, she was last seen. She'd have to get to the boat-house. Had she a bicycle? No? Then it would take her nearly half an hour. Ten. Say another forty minutes to the Rollers, unless she was very quick–"

"She's not a quick punter. She'd take a canoe."

"She'd have the wind and stream against her. Say 10.45. And she'd have to get the canoe over the Rollers by herself. That takes time. But she would still have over an hour. We may be too late, but it's just worth trying."

"But she might have gone in anywhere."

"Of course she might. But there's just the chance. People get an idea and stick to it. And they don't always make their minds up instantly."

"If I know anything of the girl's psychology," began Miss Shaw.

"What's the good of arguing?" said Harriet. "She's either dead or alive and we've got to risk a guess. Who'll come with me? I'll get the car–we shall go quicker by road than by river. We can commandeer a boat somewhere above the Parks–if we have to break open a boat-house. Dean–"

"I'm with you," said Miss Martin.

"We want torches and blankets. Hot coffee. Brandy. Better get the police to send up a constable to meet us at Timms's. Miss Haydock, you're a better oar than I am–"

"I'll come," said Miss Haydock. "Thank God for something to do."

Lights on the river. The plash of sculls. The steady chock of the rowlocks. The boat crept slowly down-stream. The constable, crouched in the bows, swept the beam of a Powerful torch from bank to bank. Harriet holding the rudder-lines, divided her attention between the dark current and the moving light ahead. The Dean, setting a slow and steady stroke, kept her eyes before her and her wits on the job.

At a word from the policeman, Harriet checked the boat and let her drift down towards a dismal shape, black and slimy on the black water. The boat lurched as the man leaned out. In the silence came the answering groan, plash, chuck of oars on the far side of the next bend.

"All right," said the policeman. "Only a bit o' sacking."

"Ready? Paddle!"

The sculls struck the water again.

"Is that the Bursar's boat coming up?" said the Dean.

"Very likely," said Harriet.

Just as she spoke, someone in the other boat gave a shout. There was a heavy splash and a cry ahead, and an answering shout from the constable:

"There she goes!"

"Pull like blazes," said Harriet. As she drew on the rudderlines to bring their nose round the bend, she saw, across stroke's shoulder in the beam of the torch, the thing they had come to find–the shining keel of a canoe adrift in midstream, with the paddles floating beside it; and all around it the water ran, ringed and rippling with the shock of the plunge.

"Look out, ladies. Don't run her down. She can't be far off."

"Easy!" said Harriet. And then, "Back her! Hold her!"

The stream chuckled and eddied over the reversed oarblades. The constable shouted to the up-coming sculler, and then pointed away towards the left bank.

"Over by the willow there."

The light caught the silver leaves, dripping like rain towards the river. Something swirled below them, pale and ominous.

"Easy. Paddle. One on bow. Another on bow. Another. Easy. Paddle. One. Two. Three. Easy. Paddle on stroke, backwater on bow. One. Two. Easy. Look out for your bow oars."

The boat swung across the stream and turned, following the policeman's signal. He was kneeling and peering into the water on the bow side. A white patch glimmered up to the surface and sank again.

"Fetch her round a bit more, miss."

"Ready? One on stroke, paddle. Another. Easy. Hold her." He was leaning out, groping with both hands among the ribbon-weed. "Back a little. Easy. Keep those bow oars out of the water. Trim the boat. Sit over to stroke. Have you got her?"

"I've got her–but the weeds are cruel strong."

"Mind you don't go over or there'll be two of you. Miss Haydock–ready, ship! See if you can help the constable. Dean–paddle one very gentle stroke and sit well over."

The boat rocked periloualy as they heaved and tore at the clinging weeds, razor-sharp and strong as grave-bands. The Water-fly had come up now and was pulling across the stream. Harriet yelled to Miss Stevens to keep her sculls out of mischief. The boats edged together. The girl's head was out of the water, dead-white and lifeless, disfigured with black slime and dark stripes of weed. The constable was supporting the body. Miss Haydock had both hands in the stream, slashing with a knife at the ribbon-weed that was wrapped viciously about the legs. The other boat, hampered by its own lightness, was heeling over to stroke with gunwales awash, as her passengers reached and grappled.

"Trim your boat, damn you!" said Harriet, not pleased at the idea of having two fresh corpses to see to, and forgetting in her wrath to whom she was speaking. Miss Stevens paid no attention; but Miss Edwards threw her weight over; and as the boat lifted the body lifted too. Harriet, keeping her torch steady so that the rescuers could see what they were doing, watched the reluctant weeds loose their last coils and slip back.

"Better get her in here," said the constable. Their boat had the less room in it, but the stronger arms and the better balance. There was a strong heave and a violent lurch as the dead weight was hauled over the side and rolled in a dripping heap at Miss Haydock's feet.

The constable was a capable and energetic young man. He took the first-aid measures in hand with admirable promptness. The women, gathered on the bank, watched with anxious faces. Other help had now arrived from the boat-house. Harriet took it upon herself to stem the stream of questions.

"Yes. One of our students. Not a good waterman. Alarmed to think she had taken a canoe out alone. Reckless. Yes, we were afraid there might be an accident. Wind. Strong current. Yes. No. Quite against the rules." (If there was going to be an inquest, other explanations might have to be made there. But not here. Not now.) "Very unwise. High spirits. Oh, yes. Most unfortunate. Taking risks. . . ."

"She'll do now," said the constable.

He sat up and wiped the sweat from his eyes.

Brandy. Blankets. A melancholy little procession along the fields to the boat-house, but less melancholy than it might have been. Then an orgy of telephoning. Then the arrival of the doctor. Then Harriet found herself, suddenly shaking with nerves, being given whisky by some kindly person. The patient was better. The patient was quite all right. The capable policeman and Miss Haydock and Miss Stevens were having their hands dressed, where the sharp weeds had slashed them to the bone. People were talking and talking; Harriet hoped they were not talking foolishly.

"Well, said the Dean in her ear, "we *are* having a night!"

"Who's with Miss Newland?"

"Miss Edwards. I've warned her not to let the child say anything if she can help it. And I've muzzled that nice policeman. Accident, my dear, accident. It's quite all right. We've taken your cue. You kept your head wonderfully. Miss Stevens lost hers a bit, though. Started to cry and talk about suicide. I soon shut *her* up."

"Damn!" said Harriet. "What did she want to do that for?"

"What indeed? You'd think she *wanted* to make a scandal."

"Somebody obviously does."

"You don't think Miss Stevens–? She did her bit with the rescue-work, you know."

"Yes, I know. All right, Dean. I don't think. I won't try to think. I thought she and Miss Edwards would have that boat over between them."

"Don't let's discuss it now. Thank Heaven the worst hasn't happened. The girl's safe and that's all that matters. What we've got to do now is to put the best face on it."

It was nearly five in the morning when the rescuers, weary and bandaged, sat once again in the Warden's house. Everybody was praising everybody else.

"It was so clever of Miss Vane," said the Dean, "to realize that the wretched child would go up to that particular place. What a mercy that we arrived just when we did."

"I'm not so sure about that," sald Harriet. "We may have done more harm than good. Do you realize that it was only when she saw us coming that she made up her mind to do it?"

"Do you mean she mightn't have done it at all if we hadn't gone after her?"

"Difficult to say. She was putting it off, I think. What really sent her in was that shout from the other boat. Who shouted, by the way?"

"I shouted," said Miss Stevens. "I looked over my shoulder and saw her. So I shouted."

"What was she doing when you saw her?"

"Standing up in the canoe."

"No she wasn't " said Miss Edwards. "I looked round when you shouted, and she was just getting to her feet then."

"You're quite mistaken," contradicted Miss Stevens. "I say she was standing up when I saw her, and I shouted to stop her. You couldn't have seen past me."

"I saw perfectly plainly," said Miss Edwards. "Miss Vane is quite right. It was when she heard the shout that she got up."

"I know what I saw," said the Bursar, obstinately.

"It's a pity you didn't take somebody to cox," said the Dean. "Nobody can see clearly what's going on behind her back."

"It is hardly necessary to argue about it," said the Warden, a little sharply. "The tragedy has been prevented, and that is all that matters. I am exceedingly grateful to everybody."

"I resent the suggestion," said Miss Stevens, "that I drove the unfortunate girl to destroy herself. And as for saying that we ought not to have gone in search of her–"

"I never said that," said Harriet, wearily. "I only said that *if* we had not gone it *might* not have happened. But of course we had to go."

"What does Newland say herself?" demanded the Dean.

"Says, why couldn't we leave her alone?" replied Miss Edwards. "I told her not to be an inconsiderate little ass."

"Poor child!" said Miss Shaw.

"If I were you," said Miss Edwards, "I shouldn't be too soft with these people. Bracing up is what does them good. You let them talk too much about themselves–"

"But she didn't talk to me," said Miss Shaw. "I tried very hard to make her."

"They'd talk much more if you'd only leave them alone."

"I think we'd better all go to bed," said Miss Martin.

"What a night," said Harriet, as she rolled, dog-weary, between the sheets. "What a gaudy night!" Her memory, thrashing round her brain like a cat in a sack, brought up the images of Mr. Pomfret and the pro-Proctor. They seemed to belong to another existence.

# 13

My sad hurt it shall releeve,
When my thoughts I shall disclose,
For thou canst not chuse but greeve,
When I shall recount my woes:
There is nothing to that friend,
To whose close uncranied breast,
We our secret thoughts may send,
And there safely let it rest;
And thy faithfull counsell may
My distressed case assist,
Sad affliction else may sway
Me a woman as it list.

Michael Drayton

"You must see," said Harriet, "that it's impossible to go on like this. You've got to call in expert help and risk the consequences. Any scandal is better than a suicide and an inquest."

"I think you are right," said the Warden.

Only Miss Lydgate, the Dean and Miss Edwards sat with Dr. Baring in the Warden's sitting-room. The brave pretence at confidence had been given up. In the Senior Common Room, members averted their eyes from one another and set a guard upon their lips. They were no longer angry and suspicious. They were afraid.

"The girl's parents are not likely to keep quiet about it," went on Harriet, remorselessly. "If she had succeeded in drowning herself, we should have the police and the reporters in at this moment. Next time, the attempt may come off."

"Next time–" began Miss Lydgate.

"There will be a next time," said Harriet. "And it may not be suicide; it may be open murder. I told you at the beginning that I did not think the measures adequate. I now say that I refuse to take any further share in the responsibility. I have tried, and I have failed, every time."

"What could the police do?" asked Miss Edwards. "We did have them in once–about those thefts, you remember, Warden. They made a great deal of fuss and arrested the wrong person. It was a very troublesome business."

"I don't think the police are the right people at all," said the Dean. "Your idea was a firm of private detectives, wasn't it?"

She turned to Harriet.

"Yes; but if anybody else has anything better to suggest–"

Nobody had any very helpful suggestion. The discussion went on. In the end:

"Miss Vane," said the Warden, "I think your idea is the best. Will you get into communication with these people?"

"Very well Warden. I will ring up the head of the firm.

"You will use discretion."

"Of course," said Harriet. She was becoming a little impatient; the time for discretion seemed to her to be past. "If we call people in, we shall have to give them a free hand, you know," she added.

This was obviously an unpalatable reminder, though its force had to be admitted. Harriet could foresee endless hampering restrictions placed upon the investigators, and felt the difficulties that went with a divided authority. The police were answerable to nobody but themselves, but paid private detectives were compelled to do more or less as they were told. She looked at Dr. Baring, and wondered whether Miss Climpson or any of her underlings was capable of asserting herself against that formidable personality.

"And now," said the Dean, as she and Harriet crossed the quad together, "I've got to go and tackle the Newlands. I'm *not* looking forward to it. They'll be terribly upset, poor things. He's a very minor civil servant, and their daughter's career means everything to them. Quite apart from the personal side of it, it'll be a frightful blow if this ruins her Schools. They're very poor and hard-working, and so proud of her–"

Miss Martin made a little despairing gesture, squared her shoulders and went to face her task.

Miss Hillyard, in her gown, was making for one of the lecture-rooms. She looked hollow-eyed and desperate, Harriet thought. Her glance shot from side to side, as though she were pursued.

From an open window on the ground floor of Queen Elizabeth came the voice of Miss Shaw, giving a coaching:

"You might have quoted also from the essay *De la Vanité*. You remember the passage. *Je me suis couche mille fois chez moi, imaginant qu'on me trahirait et assomeroit cette nuitlà*—his morbid preoccupation with the idea of death and his—"

The academic machine was grinding on. At the entrance leading to their offices, the Bursar and Treasurer stood together, their hands full of papers. They seemed to be discussing some question of finance. Their glances were secretive and mutually hostile; they looked like sullen dogs, chained together and forced into a grumbling amity by the reprimand of their master.

Miss Pyke came down her staircase and passed them without a word. Still without a word she passed Harriet and turned along the plinth. Her head was held high and defiantly. Harriet went in and along to Miss Lydgate's room. Miss Lydgate, as she knew, was lecturing; she could use her telephone undisturbed. She put her call through to London.

A quarter of an hour later, she hung up the receiver with a sinking heart. Why she should be surprised to learn that Miss Climpson was absent from Town "engaged on a case" she could not have said. It seemed vaguely monstrous that this should be so; but it was so. Would she like to speak to anyone else? Harriet had asked for Miss Murchison, the only other member of the firm who was personally known to her. Miss Murchison had left a year ago to be married. Harriet felt this as almost a personal affront. She did not like to pour all the details of the Shrewsbury affair into the ears of a complete stranger. She said she would write, rang off, and sat feeling curiously helpless.

It is all very well to take a firm line about things, and rush to the telephone, determined to "do something" without delay; other people do not sit with folded hands waiting upon the convenience even of our highly interesting and influential selves. Harriet laughed at her own annoyance. She had made up her mind to instant action, and now she was furious because a business firm had affairs of its own to attend to. Yet to wait any longer was impossible. The situation was becoming a nightmare. Faces had grown sly and distorted overnight; eyes fearful; the most innocent words charged with suspicion. At any moment some new terror might break bounds and carry all before it.

She was suddenly afraid of all these women: *horti conclusi*, *fontes signati*, they were walled in, sealed down, by walls and seals that shut her out. Sitting there in the clear light of morning, staring at the prosaic telephone on the desk, she knew the ancient dread of Artemis, moon-goddess, virgin-huntress, whose arrows are plagues and death.

It struck her then as a fantastic idea that she should fly for help to another brood of spinsters; even if she succeeded in getting hold of Miss Climpson, how was she to explain matters to that desiccated and elderly virgin? The very sight of some of the poison letters would probably make her sick, and the whole trouble would be beyond her comprehension. In this, Harriet did the lady less than justice; Miss Climpson had seen many strange things in sixty-odd years of boardinghouse life, and was as free from repressions and complexes as any human being could very well be. But, in fact, the atmosphere of Shrewsbury was getting on Harriet's nerves. What she wanted was someone with whom she did not need to mince her words, somebody who would neither show nor feel surprise at any manifestation of human eccentricity, somebody whom she knew and could trust.

There were plenty of people in London—both men and women—to whom the discussion of sexual abnormalities was a commonplace; but most of them were very little to be trusted. They cultivated normality till it stood out of them all over in knobs, like the muscles upon professional strong men, and scarcely looked normal at all. And they talked interminably and loudly. From their bouncing mental health ordinary ill-balanced mortals shrank in alarm. She ran over various names in her mind, but found none that would do.

"The fact is," said Harriet to the telephone, "I don't know whether I want a doctor or a detective. But I've got to have somebody."

She wished—and not for the first time—that she could have got hold of Peter Wimsey. Not, of course, that this was the kind of case he could very suitably have investigated himself; but he would probably have known the right person. He at least would be surprised at nothing, shocked at nothing; he had far too wide an experience of the world. And he was completely to be trusted. But he was not there. He had vanished from view at the very moment when the Shrewsbury affair had first come to her notice; it seemed almost pointed. Like Lord Saint-George, she began to feel that Peter really had no right to disappear just when he was wanted. The fact that she had spent five years angrily refusing to contract further obligations towards Peter Wimsey had no weight with her now; she would readily have contracted obligations towards the devil himself, if she could have been sure that the prince of darkness was a gentleman of Peter's kidney. But Peter was as far beyond reach as Lucifer.

Was he? There was the telephone at her elbow. She could speak to Rome as easily as to London—though at a trifle more expense. It was probably only the financial modesty of the person whose income is all earned by work that made it seem more momentous to ring somebody up across a continent than across a city. At any rate, it could do no harm to fetch Peter's last letter and find the telephone number of his hotel. She went out quickly, and encountered Miss de Vine.

"Oh!" said the Fellow. "I was coming to look for you. I thought I had better show you this."

She held out a piece of paper; the sight of the printed letters was odiously familiar:

YOUR TURN'S COMING

"It's nice to be warned," said Harriet, with a lightness she did not feel. "Where? when? and how?"

"It fell out of one of the books I'm using," said Miss de Vine, blinking behind her glasses at the questions, "just now."

"When did you use the book last?"

"That," said Miss de Vine, blinking again, "is the odd thing about it. I didn't. Miss Hillyard borrowed it last night, and Mrs. Goodwin brought it back to me this morning."

Considering the things Miss Hillyard had said about Mrs. Goodwin, Harriet was faintly surprised that she should have chosen her to run her errands. But in certain circumstances the choice might, of course, be a wise one.

"Are you sure the paper wasn't there yesterday?"

"I don't think it could have been. I was referring to various pages, and I think I should have seen it."

"Did you give it directly into Miss Hillyard's own hands?"

"No; I put it in her pigeon-hole before Hall."

"So that anybody might have got hold of it."

"Oh, yes."

Exasperating. Harriet took possession of the paper and passed on. It was now not even clear against whom the threat was directed, much less from whom it came. She fetched Peter's letter, and discovered that in the interval she had made up her mind. She had said she would ring up the head of the firm; and so she would. If he was not technically the head, he was certainly the brains of it. She put the call through. She did not know how long it would take, but left instructions at the Lodge that when it came she was to be searched for and found without fail. She felt abominably restless.

The next piece of news was that a violent quarrel had taken place between Miss Shaw and Miss Stevens, who were normally the closest of friends. Miss Shaw, having heard the full story of the previous night's adventure, had accused Miss Stevens of frightening Miss Newland into the river; Miss Stevens had in her turn accused Miss Shaw of deliberately playing on the girl's feelings, so as to work her up into a state of nerves.

The next disturber of the peace was Miss Allison. As Harriet had discovered the previous term, Miss Allison had a way of passing on to people the things other people had said of them. In a spirit of candour she had now chosen to pass on to Mrs. Goodwin the hints thrown out by Miss Hillyard. Mrs. Goodwin had tackled Miss Hillyard about it; and there had been a most unpleasant scene, in which Miss Allison, the Dean and poor little Miss Chilperic, who had been drawn into the discussion by malignant chance, took sides with Mrs. Goodwin against Miss Pyke and Miss Burrows, who, though they thought Miss Hillyard had spoken ill-advisedly, resented any aspersions cast against the unmarried state as such. This unpleasantness took place in the Fellows' Garden.

Finally, Miss Allison had further inflamed the situation by passing on a vivid account of the matter to Miss Barton, who had gone away indignantly to tell Miss Lydgate and Miss de Vine exactly what she thought of the psychology both of Miss Hillyard and Miss Allison.

It was not an agreeable morning.

Between the married (or about-to-be-married) and the unmarried, Harriet felt herself to be like Aesop's bat between the birds and beasts; an odd result, she felt, of having sown her wild oats in public. Lunch was a strained meal. She came into Hall rather late, to find that the High Table had sorted itself out into opposing camps, with Miss Hillyard at one end and Mrs. Goodwin at the other. She found an empty chair between Miss de Vine and Miss Stevens, and amused herself by drawing them and Miss Allison, who was next to Miss de Vine on the other side, into a discussion of currency and inflation. She knew nothing of the subject, but they, naturally, knew a great deal, and her tact was rewarded. Conversation spread; the table presented a less sullen front to the assembled students, and Miss Lydgate beamed approval. Things were moving nicely when a scout, leaning between Miss Allison and Miss de Vine, murmured a message.

"From Rome?" said Miss de Vine. "Who can that be, I wonder?"

"Telephoning from Rome?" said Miss Allison, in piercing accents. "Oh, one of your correspondents, I suppose. He must be better off than most historians."

"I think it's for me," said Harriet, and turned to the scout. "Are you sure they said de Vine and not Vane?"

The scout was not very sure.

"If you're expecting it, it must be for you," said Miss de Vine. Miss Allison made some rather sharp observation about writers of international celebrity and Harriet left the table, flushing uncomfortably and angry with herself for doing so.

As she went down to the public call-box in Queen Elizabeth, to which the call had been put through, she tried to arrange in her own mind what to say. A brief sentence of apology; another brief sentence of explanation; and a request for advice; into whose hands should the case be put? There was, surely, nothing difficult about that.

The voice from Rome spoke English very well. It did not think Lord Peter Wimsey was in the hotel, but would inquire. A pause, during which she could hear feet passing to and fro on the other side of the continent. Then the voice again, suave and apologetic.

"His lordship left Rome three days ago."

Oh! Did they know for what destination?

They would inquire. Another pause, and voices speaking Italian. Then the same voice again.

"His lordship left for Warsaw."

"Oh! Thank you very much."

And that was that.

At the thought of ringing up the British Embassy at Warsaw, her heart failed her. She replaced the receiver and went upstairs again. She did not seem to have gained very much by taking a firm line.

Friday afternoon. Crises always, thought Harriet, occurred at the week-end, when there were no posts. If she wrote now to London and they replied by return, she would still, in all probability, be able to take no action till Monday. If she wrote to Peter, there might be an Air-Mail—but suppose he wasn't at Warsaw after all. He might by now have gone on to Bucharest or Berlin. Could she possibly ring up the Foreign Office and demand to know his whereabouts? Because, if the letter got to him over the week-end and he wired a reply, she would not be losing so very much time. She was not sure if she would be very good at dealing with the Foreign Office. Was there anybody who could? How about the Hon. Freddy?

It took a little time to locate Freddy Arbuthnot, but eventually she ran him down, by 'phone, at an office in Throgmorton Street. He was definitely helpful. He had no idea where old Peter was, but he would take steps to find out, and if she liked to send a letter care of him (Freddy) he would see that it was forwarded on at the earliest possible moment. No trouble at all. Charmed to be of use.

So the letter was written, and despatched so as to reach Town first post on the Saturday morning. It contained a brief outline of the case, and finished up:

"Can you tell me whether you think Miss Climpson's people could handle it? And who, in her absence, is the most competent person there? Or, if not, can you suggest anybody else I could ask? Perhaps it should be a psychologist and not a detective. I know that anybody you recommend will be trustworthy. Would you mind wiring as soon as you get this? I should be immensely grateful. We are all getting rather worked up, and I'm afraid something drastic may happen if we don't cope with it quickly."

She hoped that last sentence did not sound as panicky as she felt.

"I rang up your hotel in Rome and they said you had gone on to Warsaw. As I don't know where you may be by this time, I'm getting Mr. Arbuthnot to forward this through the Foreign Office."

That sounded faintly reproachful, but it couldn't be helped. What she really wanted to say was, "I wish to God you were here and could tell me what to do"; but she felt that that might make him feel uncomfortable, since he obviously couldn't be there. Still, it could do no harm to ask, "How soon do you think you will be back in England?" And with this addition, the letter was finished and posted.

"And to put the lid on things," said the Dean, "there's this man coming to dinner."

"This man" was Dr. Noel Threep, a very worthy and important man, a Fellow of a distinguished college and a member of the Council by which Shrewsbury was governed. Friends and benefactors of this kind were not infrequently entertained in College, and as a rule the High Table was glad of their presence. But the moment was scarcely auspicious. However, the engagement had been made early in the term and it was quite impossible to put Dr. Threep off. Harriet said she thought his visit might be a good thing, and help to keep the minds of the S.C.R. off their troubles.

"We'll hope so," said the Dean. "He's a very nice man, and talks very interestingly. He's a political economist."

"Hard-boiled or soft-boiled?"

"Hard, I think."

This question had no reference to Dr. Threep's politics or economics, but only to his shirt-front. Harriet and the Dean had begun to collect shirt-fronts. Miss Chilperic's "young man" had started the collection. He was extremely tall and thin and rather hollow-chested; by way of emphasizing this latter defect, he always wore a soft pleated dress-shirt, which made him look (according to the Dean) like the scooped-out rind of a melon. By way of contrast, there had been an eminent and ample professor of chemistry–a visitor from another university–who had turned up in a front of intense rigdity, which stood out before him like the chest of a pouter pigeon, bulging out of all control and displaying a large area of the parent shirt at either side. A third variety of shirt fairly common among the learned was that which escaped from the centre stud and gaped in the middle; and one never-to-be-forgotten happy day a popular poet had arrived to give a lecture on his methods of composition and the future of poetry, whereby, at every gesticulation (and he had used a great many), his waistcoat had leapt in the air, allowing a line of shirt, adorned with a little tab, to peep out, rabbit-like, over the waist-line of the confining trouser. On this occasion, Harriet and the Dean had disgraced themselves badly.

Dr. Threep was a large, agreeable, talkative person, who at first sight appeared to present no loophole for sartorial criticism. But he had not been seated at table three minutes before Harriet realized that he was doomed to form one of the most notable additions to the collection. For he popped. When he bent over his plate, when he turned to pass the mustard, when he courteously inclined himself to catch what his neighbour was saying, his shirt-front exploded with a merry little report like the opening of ginger-beer.

The clamour in Hall seemed louder than usual that night, so that the poppings were inaudible beyond a few places to right and left of him; but the Warden and the Dean, who sat beside him, heard them, and Harriet, sitting opposite, heard them; she dared not catch the Dean's eye. Dr. Threep was too well-bred, or perhaps too much embarrassed, to allude to the matter; he talked on imperturbably, raising his voice more and more to be heard above the din of the undergraduates. The Warden was frowning.

"–the excellent relations between the Women's Colleges and the University," said Dr. Threep. "All the same–"

The Warden summoned a scout, who presently went down to the Junior High and thence to the other tables, with the usual message :

"The Warden's compliments, and she would be obliged if there could be rather less noise."

"I beg your pardon, Dr. Threep. I didn't quite catch."

"All the same," repeated Dr. Threep, with a polite bend and pop, "it is curious to see how traces of the old prejudice linger. Only yesterday the Vice-Chancellor showed me a remarkably vulgar anonymous letter sent to him that very morning . . ."

The noise in Hall was dying down gradually; it was like a lull in the intervals of a storm.

". . . making the most absurd accusations–oddly enough against your own Senior Common Room in particular. Accusations of murder, of all things. The Vice-Chancellor . . ."

Harriet missed the next few words; she was watching how, as Dr. Threep's voice rang out in the comparative quiet, the heads at the High Table jerked towards him, as though pulled by wires.

". . .pasted on paper–quite ingenious. I said, 'My dear Mr. Vice-Chancellor, I doubt whether the police can do much; it is probably the work of some harmless crank.' But is it not curious that such peculiar delusions should exist–and *persist*–at this day?"

"Very curious indeed," said the Warden, with stiff lips.

"So I advised against police interference–for the moment, at any rate. But I said I would put the matter before you, since Shrewsbury was particularly mentioned. I defer, of course, to your opinion."

The dons sat spell-bound; and in that moment, Dr. Threep, bowing to the Warden's decision, popped–with so loud and violent an explosion that it resounded from end to end of the table, and the major embarrassment was swallowed up in the minor. Miss Chilperic suddenly broke out into a spasm of high, nervous laughter.

How dinner ended, Harriet could never properly recall. Dr. Threep went over to have coffee with the Warden, and Harriet found herself in the Dean's room, helpless between mirth and alarm.

"It's really very serious," said Miss Martin.

"Horribly.' I said to the Vice-Chancellor–' "

"Pop!"

"No; but honestly, what are we to do about it?"

"I defer to your opinion."

"Pop!"

"I can't imagine what makes shirts do that. Can you?"

"I've no idea. And I meant to be so clever this evening. Here, said I, is a Man come among us; I will watch everybody's reactions–and then it all went Pop!"

"It's no good watching reactions to Dr. Threep," said the Dean. "Everyone's too used to him. And anyhow, he has half a dozen children. But it's going to be very awkward if the Vice-Chancellor–"

"Very."

Saturday dawned dull and lowering.

"I believe it's going to thunder," said Miss Wlison.

"Rather early in the year for that," said Miss Hillyard.

"Not at all," retorted Mrs. Goodwin; "I've known plenty of thunderstorms in May."

"There is certainly something electrical in the atmosphere," said Miss Lydgate.

"I agree with you," said Miss Barton.

Harriet had slept badly. She had, in fact, been walking about College half the night, a prey to imaginary alarms. When at length she had gone to bed, she had had the tiresome dream about trying to catch a train, hampered all the time by a quantity of luggage which she strove vainly to pack in misty and unmanageable suit-cases. In the morning, she struggled desperately with the proofs of Miss Lydgate's chapter on Gerard Manley Hopkins, finding it as unmanageable as the suit-cases and very nearly as misty. In the intervals of disentangling the poet's own system of sprung, counterpoint and logaoedic rhythm, with its rove-over lines and outrides, from Miss Lydgate's rival system of scansion (which required five alphabets and a series of pothooks for its expression), she wondered whether Freddy Arbuthnot had succeeded in doing what he had promised and whether she ought to leave it at that or do something else: in which case, what? In the afternoon, she could bear herself no longer and set out, under a threatening sky, to wander about Oxford, and walk herself, if possible, into exhaustion. She started up the High, pausing for a few moments to stare into the window of an Antique shop; there was a set of carved ivory chessmen there, for which she had conceived an unreasonable affection. She even played with the idea of going boldly in and buying them; but she knew they would cost too much. They were Chinese, and each piece was a complicated nest of little revolving balls, delicate as fine lace. It would be jolly to handle them, but idiotic to buy them; she was not even a good chessplayer, and in any case, one couldn't play chess comfortably with pieces like that. She put temptation aside and moved on. There was a shop full of wooden objects embellished with the painted shields of colleges: book-ends, match-stands, pens shaped like oars and horribly top-heavy, cigarette-boxes, inkpots and even powder-compacts. Did it add a zest to facial repairs to have them watched over by the lions of Orlel or the martlets of Worcester? To be reminded during the process that one had a betrothed among the tripping stags of Jesus or a brother nourished by the pious pelican of Corpus? She crossed the street before she came to Queen's (for Mr. Pomfret might conceivably pop out of the gate, and she was rather avoiding an encounter with Mr. Pomfret) and went on up the other side. Books and prints–fascinating at most times, but insufficiently exciting to hold her attention. Robes and gowns, colorful, but too academic for her mood. A chemist's shop. A stationer's, with more college bric-a-brac, this time in glass and pottery. A tobacconist's, with more coats of arms, on ash-trays and tobacco-jars. A jeweller's, with college arms on spoons and brooches and napkin-rings. She grew weary of college arms and turned down a side-street into Merton Street. In this untouched and cobbled thoroughfare there should be peace, if anywhere. But peace is in the mind, and not in streets, however old and beautiful. She passed through the iron gate into Merton Grove, and so, crossing over Dead Man's Walk, into the Broad Walk of Christ Church and along this and round to the towing path where the New Cut meets the Isis. And there, to her horror, she was hailed by a well-known voice. Here, by special interposition of all the powers of evil, was Miss Schuster-Slatt, whose presence in Oxford she had till that moment mercifully forgotten, convoying a party of American visitors, all eager for information. Miss Vane was the very person to tell them everything. Did she know which of these barges belonged to which college? Were those cute little blue-and-gold heads griffins or phoenixes and were there three of them to symbolize the Trinity or was that just accident? Were those the Magdalen lilies? If so, why was there the initial "W" painted all round the barge and what did it stand for? Why did Pembroke have the English rose and the Scotch thistle at the top of the shield? Were the roses of New College English roses, too? Why was it called New when it was so old, and why mustn't you call it "New" but always "New College"? Oh! look, Sadie—are those geese flying across? Swans? How interesting! Were there many swans on the river? Was it true that all the swans in England belonged to the King? Was that a swan on that barge? Oh, an eagle. Why did some barges have figure-heads and some not? Did the boys ever have tea-parties on the barges? Could Miss Vane explain about those bumping races, because nobody had been able to understand from Sadie's description. Was that the University barge? Oh, the University *College* barge. Was the University College the place where all the classes were held?

And so forth and so on—all along the towing path, all the way up the long avenue to the Meadow Buildings and all the way round Christ Church, from Hall to Kitchen, from Cathedral to Library, from Mercury to Great Tom, while all the time the sky brooded lower and the weather became more oppressive, until Harriet, who had started out feeling as though her skull were stuffed with wool, ended up with a raging headache.

The storm held off till after Hall, except for threatenings and grumblings of thunder. At 10 o'clock the first great flash went across the sky like a search-light, picking out roof and treetop violet-blue against the blackness, and followed by a clap that shook the walls. Harriet flung her window open and leaned out. There was a sweet smell of approaching rain. Another flash and crash; a swift gust of wind; and then the swish and rush of falling water, the gurgle of overflowing gutters, and peace.

# 14

Truce gentle love, a parly now I crave,
Me thinks, 'tis long since first these wars begun,
Nor thou nor I, the better yet can have:
Bad is the match where neither party won.
I offer free conditions of faire peace,
My hart for hostage, that it shall remaine,
Discharge our forces heere, let malice cease,
So for my pledge, thou give me pledge againe.

Michael Drayton

"It was a good storm," said the Dean.

"First-class," said the Bursar, dryly, "for those that like it and don't have to cope with those that don't. The scouts' quarters were a pandemonium; I had to go over. There was Carrie in hysterics, and Cook thinking her last hour had come, and Annie shrieking to Heaven that her darling children would be terrified and wanting to rush off to Headington then and there to comfort them–"

"I wonder you didn't send her there at once in the best car available," put in Miss Hillyard in sarcastic tones.

"–and one of the kitchen-maids having an outbreak of religious blues," went on Miss Stevens, "and confessing her sins to an admiring circle. I can't think why people have so little self-control."

"I'm horribly afraid of thunder," said Miss Chilperic.

"The wretched Newland was all upset again," said the Dean. "The Infirmarian was quite frightened about her. Said the Infirmary maid was hiding in the linen-cupboard and she didn't like to be left alone with Newland. However, Miss Shaw obligingly coped."

"Who were the four students who were dancing in the quad in bathing-dresses?" inquired Miss Pyke. "They had quite a ritual appearance. I was reminded of the ceremonial dances of the–"

"I was afraid the beeches were going to be struck," said Miss Burrows. "I sometimes wonder whether it's safe to have them so near the buildings. If they came down–"

"There's a bad leak in my ceiling, Bursar," said Mrs. Goodwin. "The rain came in like a water-spout–just over my bed. I had to move all the furniture, and the carpet is quite–"

"Anyhow," repeated the Dean, "it was a good storm, and it's cleared the air. Look at it. Could anybody want a better and brighter Sunday morning?"

Harriet nodded. The sun was brilliant on the wet grass and the wind blew fresh and cool.

"It's taken my headache away, thank goodness! I'd like to do something calm and cheerful and thoroughly Oxonian. Isn't everything a lovely colour? Like the blues and scarlets and greens in an illuminated missal!"

"I'll tell you what we'll do," said the Dean, brightly. "We'll toddle along like two good little people and hear the University Sermon. I can't think of anything more soothingly normal and academic than that. And Dr. Armstrong's preaching. He's always interesting."

"The University Sermon?" said Harriet, amused. "Well, that's the last thing I should have thought of for myself. But it's an idea; definitely an idea. We'll go."

Yes; the Dean was right; here was the great Anglican compromise at its most soothing and ceremonial. The solemn procession of doctors in hood and habit; the Vice-Chancellor bowing to the preacher, and the beadles tripping before them; the throng of black gowns and the decorous gaiety of the summer-frocked wives of dons; the hymn and the biddingprayer; the gowned and hooded preacher austere in cassock and bands; the quiet discourse delivered in a thin, clear, scholarly voice, and dealing gently with the relations of the Christian philosophy to atomic physics. Here were the Universities and the Church of England kissing one another in righteousness and peace, like the angels in a Botticelli Nativity: very exquisitely robed, very cheerful in a serious kind of way, a little mannered, a little conscious of their fine mutual courtesy. Here, without heat, they could discuss their common problem, agreeing pleasantly or pleasantly agreeing to differ. Of the grotesque and ugly devil-shapes sprawling at the foot of the picture these angels had no word to say. What solution could either of them produce, if challenged, for the Shrewsbury problem? Other bodies would be bolder: the Church of Rome would have its answer, smooth, competent and experienced; the queer, bitterly-jarring sects of the New Psychology would have another, ugly, awkward, tentative and applied with a passionate experimentalism. It was entertaining to imagine a Freudian University indissolubly wedded to a Roman Establishment: they certainly would not live so harmoniously together as the Anglican Church and the School of Litterae Humaniores. But it was delightful to believe, if only for an hour, that all human difficulties could be dealt with in this detached and amiable spirit. "The University is a Paradise"–true, but–"then saw I that there was a way to hell even from the gates of Heaven" . . .

The blessing was given; the voluntary rolled out–something fugal and pre-Bach; the procession re-formed and dispersed again, passing out south and north; the congregation rose to their feet and began to stream away in an orderly disorder. The Dean, who was fond of early fugues, remained quietly in her place and Harriet sat dreamily beside her, with eyes fixed on the softly-tinted saints in the rood-screen. At length they both rose and made their way to the door. A mild, clear gust of wind met them as they passed between the twisted columns of Dr. Owen's porch, making the Dean clutch at the peak of her rebellious cap and bellying out their gowns into wide arcs and volutes. The sky, between pillow and pillow of rounded cloud, was the pale and transparent blue of aquamarine.

Standing at the corner of Cat Street was a group of gowns, chatting with animation–among them, two Fellows of All Souls and a dignified figure which Harriet recognized as that of the Master of Balliol. Beside him was another M.A. who, as Harriet and the Dean went by, conversing of counterpoint, turned suddenly and lifted his mortar-board.

For a long moment, Harriet simply could not believe her eyes. Peter Wimsey. Peter, of all people. Peter, who was supposed to be in Warsaw, planted placidly in the High as though he had grown there from the beginning. Peter, wearing cap and gown like any orthodox Master of Arts, presenting every appearance of having piously attended the University Sermon, and now talking mild academic shop with two Fellows of All Souls and the Master of Balliol.

"And why not?" thought Harriet, after the first second of shock. "He is a Master of Arts. He was at Balliol. Why shouldn't he talk to the Master if he likes? But how did he get here? And why? And when did he come? And why didn't he let me know?"

She found herself confusedly receiving introductions and presenting Lord Peter to the Dean.

"I rang up yesterday from Town," Wimsey was saying, "but you were out." And then more explanations–something about flying over from Warsaw, and "my nephew at the House," and "the Master's kind hospitality," and sending a note round to College. Then, out of the jumble of polite nothings, a sentence she grasped clearly.

"If you are free and in College during the next half-hour or so, may I come round and look you up?"

"Yes, do," said Harriet, lamely, "that would be delightful." She pulled herself together. "I suppose it's no good asking you to lunch?"

It appeared that he was lunching with the Master, and that one of the All Souls men was lunching also. In fact, a little lunch-party with, she gathered, some kind of historical basis, with mention of somebody's article for the Proceedings of Something or Other, which Wimsey was going to "step into All Souls and look at–it won't take you ten minutes," and references to the printing and distribution of Reformation polemical pamphlets–to Wimsey's expert knowledge–to the other man's expert knowledge–and to the inexpert pretence at knowledge of some historian from another university.

Then the whole group broke up. The Master raised his cap and drifted away, reminding Wimsey and the historian that lunch would be at 1:15; Peter said something to Harriet about being "round in twenty minutes," and then vanished with the two Fellows into All Souls, and Harriet and the Dean were walking together again.

"Well!" said the Dean, "so that's the man."

"Yes," said Harriet weakly, "that's him."

"My dear, he's perfectly charming. You never said he was coming to Oxford."

"I didn't know. I thought he was in Warsaw. I knew he was supposed to be coming up some time this term to see his nephew, but I'd no idea he could get away so soon. As a matter of fact, I wanted to ask him–only I don't suppose he could have got my letter–"

She felt that her efforts at explanation were only darkening counsel. In the end she made a clean breast of the whole affair to the Dean.

"I don't know whether he got my letter and knows already, or whether, if he doesn't, I ought to tell him. I know he's absolutely safe. But whether the Warden and the S.C.R.– I didn't expect him to turn up like this."

"I should think it was the wisest thing you could have done," said Miss Martin. "I shouldn't say too much at College. Bring him along if he'll come, and let him turn the whole lot of us inside out. A man with manners like that could twist the whole High Table round his little finger. What a mercy he's a historian–that will put him on the right side of Miss Hillyard."

"I never thought of him as a historian."

"Well, he took a First, anyway . . . didn't you know?"

She had not known. She had not even troubled to wonder. She had never consciously connected Wimsey and Oxford in her mind. This was the Foreign Office business all over again. If he had realized her thoughtlessness it must have hurt him.

She saw herself as a monster of callous ingratitude.

"I'm told he was looked upon as one of the ablest scholars of his year," pursued the Dean. "A. L. Smith thought highly of him. It's a pity, in a way, he didn't stick to History–but naturally, his chief interests wouldn't be academic."

"No," said Harriet.

So the Dean had been making inquiries. Naturally, she would. Probably the whole S.C.R. could by now give her detailed information about Wimsey's University career. That was comprehensible enough: they thought along those lines. But she herself might surely have found the energy for two minutes' study of the Calendar.

"Where shall I put him when he comes? I suppose if I take him off to my own room it will set a bad example to the students. And it is a bit cramped."

"You can have my sitting-room. Much better than any of the public rooms, if you're going to discuss this beastly business. I wonder if he *did* get that letter. Perhaps the eager interest behind that penetrating eye was due to his suspicions of me. And I put it all down to my personal fascination! The man's dangerous, though he doesn't look it."

"That's why he's dangerous. But if he read my letter, he'll know that it isn't you."

Some minor confusions were cleared up when they reached College and found a note from Peter in Harriet's pigeon-hole. It explained that he had reached London early on Saturday afternoon and found Harriet's letter waiting for him at the Foreign Office. "I tried to ring you, but left no name, as I did not know whether you wanted me to appear personally in this matter." He had been engaged in London that afternoon, motored to Oxford for dinner, been captured by some Balliol friends and kindly invited by the Master to stay the night, and would call "some time tomorrow" in the hope of finding her in.

So she waited in the Dean's room, idly watching the summer sun play through the branches of the plane-tree in the New Quad and make a dancing pattern upon the plinth, until she heard his knock. When she said "Come in!" the commonplace formula seemed to take on a startling significance. For good or evil, she had called in something explosive from the outside world to break up the ordered tranquillity of the place; she had sold the breach to an alien force; she had sided with London against Oxford and with the worid against the cloister.

But when he entered, she knew that the image had been a false one. He came into the quiet room as though he belonged there, and had never belonged to any other place.

"Hullo-ullo!" he said, with a faint echo of the old, flippant manner. Then he stripped off his gown and tossed it on the couch beside her own, laying his mortar-board on the table.

"I found your note when I got back. So you did get my letter?"

"Yes; I'm sorry you should have had all this bother. It seemed to me, as I was coming to Oxford in any case, I had better push along and see you. I meant to come round yesterday evening, but I got tied up with people–and I thought perhaps I had better announce myself first."

"It was good of you to come. Sit down."

She pulled an arm-chair forward, and he dropped into it rather heavily. She noticed, with a curious little prick of anxiety, how the clear light picked out the angles of the skull on jaw and temple.

"Peter! You look tired to death. What have you been doing with yourself?"

"Talking," he said, discontentedly. "Words, words, words. All these interminable weeks. I'm the professional funny man of the Foreign Office. You didn't know that? Well, I am. Not often, but waiting in the wings if wanted. Some turn goes wrong–some Under-Secretary's secretary with small discretion and less French uses an ill-considered phrase in an after-dinner speech, and they send on the patter-comedian to talk the house into a good humour again. I take people out to lunch and tell them funny stories and work them up to mellowing point. God! what a game!"

"I didn't know this, Peter. I've just discovered that I've been too selfish even to try and know anything. But it isn't like you to sound so dreadfully discouraged. You look–"

"Spare me, Harriet. Don't say I'm getting to look my age. That won't do. An eternal childishness is my one diplomatic asset."

"You only look as though you hadn't slept for weeks."

"I'm not sure that I have, now you mention it. I thought–at one point we all thought–something might be going to happen. All the old, filthy uproar. I got as far as saying to Bunter one night: 'It's coming; it's here; back to the Army again, sergeant.' . . . But in the end, you know, it made a noise like a hoop and rolled away–for the moment."

"Thanks to the comic cross-talk?"

"Oh, no. Great Scott, no. Mine was a very trivial affair. Slight frontier skirmish. Don't get it into your head that I'm the man who saved the Empire."

"Then who did?"

"Dunno. Nobody knows. Nobody ever does know, for certain. The old bus wobbles one way, and you think, 'That's done it!' and then it wobbles the other way and you think, 'All serene'; and then, one day, it wobbles over too far and you're in the soup and can't remember how you got there."

"That's what we're all afraid of, inside ourselves."

"Yes. It terrifies me. It's a relief to get back and find you here–and all this going on as it used to do. Here's where the real things are done, Harriet–if only those bunglers out there will keep quiet and let it go on. God! how I loathe haste and violence and all that ghastly, slippery cleverness. Unsound, unscholarly, insincere–nothing but propaganda and special pleading and 'what do we get out of this?' No time, no peace, no silence; nothing but conferences and newspapers and public speeches till one can't hear one's self think. . . . If only one could root one's self in here among the grass and stones and do something worth doing, even if it was only restoring a lost breathing for the love of the job and nothing else."

She was astonished to hear him speak with so much passion.

"But, Peter, you're saying exactly what I've been feeling all this time. But can it be done?"

"No; it can't be done. Though there are moments when one comes back and thinks it might."

" 'Ask for the old paths, where is the good way, and walk therein, and ye shall find rest for your souls.' "

"Yes," said he bitterly, "and it goes on: 'But they said: we will not walk therein.' Rest? I had forgotten there was such a word."

"So had I."

They sat silent for a few minutes. Wimsey offered her his cigarette-case and struck a match for them both.

"Peter, it's queer we should sit here and talk like this. Do you remember that horrible time at Wilvercombe when we could find nothing to throw at one another but cheap wit and spiteful remarks? At least, I was spiteful: you never were."

"It was the watering-place atmosphere," said Wimsey. "One is always vulgar at watering-places. It is the one haunting terror of my life that some day some perfectly irresistible peach of a problem will blossom out at Brighton or Blackpool, and that I shall be weak-minded enough to go and meddle with it." The laughter had come back to his voice and his eyes were tranquil. "Thank Heaven, it's extremely difficult to be cheap in Oxford–after one's second year, at any rate. Which reminds me that I haven't yet properly thanked you for being so kind to Saint-George."

"Have you seen him yet?"

"No; I have threatened to descend on him on Monday, and show him a damned disinheriting countenance. He has gone off somewhere today with a party of friends. I know what that means. He's getting thoroughly spoilt."

"Well, Peter, you can't wonder. He's terribly good-looking."

"He's a precocious little monkey," said his uncle, without enthusiasm. "Though I can't blame him for that; it runs in the blood. But it's characteristic of his impudence that he should have gate-crashed your acquaintance, after you had firmly refused to meet any of my people."

"I found him for myself, you see, Peter."

"Literally, or so he says. I gather that he nearly knocked you down, damaged your property and generally made a nuisance of himself, and that you instantly concluded he must be some relation to me."

"That's– If he said that, you know better than to believe it. But I couldn't very well miss the likeness."

"Yet people have been known to speak slightingly of my personal appearance! I congratulate you on a perception worthy of Sherlock Holmes at his keenest."

It amused and touched her to discover this childish streak of vanity in him. But she knew that he would see through her at once if she tried to pander to it by saying anything more flattering than the truth.

"I recognized the voice before I looked at him at all. And he has your hands; I shouldn't think anybody has ever spoken slightingly about those."

"Confound it, Harriet! My one really shameful weakness. My most jealously guarded bit of personal conceit. Dragged into the light of day and remorselessly exposed. I am idiotically proud of having inherited the Wimsey hands. My brother and my sister both missed them, but they go back in the family portraits for three hundred years." His face clouded for a moment. "I wonder all the strength hasn't been bred out of them by this time; our sands are running down fast. Harriet, will you come with me one day to Denver and see the place before the new civilization grows in on it like the jungle? I don't want to go all Galsworthy about it. They'll tell you I don't care a damn for the whole outfit, and I don't know that I do. But I was born there, and I shall be sorry if I live to see the land sold for ribbon-building and the Hall turned over to a Hollywood Colour-Talkie king."

"Lord Saint-George wouldn't do that, would he?"

"I don't know, Harriet. Why shouldn't he? Our kind of show is dead and done for. What the hell good does it do anybody these days? But he may care more than he thinks he does."

"You care, don't you, Peter?"

"It's very easy for me to care, because I'm not called upon to do a hand's turn in the matter. I am the usual middle-aged prig, with an admirable talent for binding heavy burdens and laying them on other men's shoulders. Don't think I envy my nephew his job. I'd rather live at peace and lay my bones in the earth. Only I have a cursed hankering after certain musty old values, which I'm coward enough to deny, like my namesake of the Gospels. I never go home if I can help it, and I avoid coming here; the cocks crow too long and too loudly."

"Peter, I'd no idea you felt like that. I'd like to see your home."

"Would you? Then we'll go, one of these days. I won't inflict the family on you–though I think you'd like my mother. But we'll choose a time when they're all away–except a dozen or so harmless dukes in the family vault. All embalmed, poor devils, to linger on dustily to the Day of Judgment. Typical, isn't it, of a family tradition that it won't even let you rot."

Harriet could find nothing to say to him. She had fought him for five years, and found out nothing but his strength; now, within half an hour, he had exposed all his weaknesses, one after the other. And she could not in honesty say: "Why didn't you tell me before?" because she knew perfectly well what the answer ought to be. Fortunately, he did not seem to expect any comment.

"Great Scott!" was his next remark, "look at the time! You've let me maunder on, and we've never said a word about your problem."

"I've been only too thankful to forget it for a bit."

"I dare say you have," he said, looking thoughtfully at her. "Listen, Harriet, couldn't we make today a holiday? You've had enough of this blasted business. Come and be bothered with me for a change. It'll be a relief for you–like getting a nice go of rheumatism in exchange for toothache. Equally damnable, but different. I've got to go to this lunch-party, but it needn't take too long. How about a punt at 3:o'clock from Magdalen Bridge?"

"There'll be an awful crowd on the river. The Cherwell's not what it was, especially on a Sunday. More like Bank Holiday at Margate, with gramophones and bathing-dresses and everybody barging into everybody else."

"Never mind. Let's go and do our bit of barging along with the happy populace. Unless you'd rather come in the car and fly with me to the world's end. But the roads will be worse than the river. And if we find a quiet spot, either I shall make a pest of myself or else we shall start on the infernal problem. There's safety in publicity."

"Very well, Peter. We'll do exactly as you like."

"Then we'll say Magdalen Bridge at three. Trust me, I'm not shirking the problem. If we can't see our way through it together, we'll find somebody who can. There are no seas innavigable nor lands unhabitable."

He got up and held out a hand.

"Peter, what a rock you are! The shadow of a great rock in a weary land. My dear, what are you thinking about? One doesn't shake hands at Oxford."

"The elephant never forgets." He kissed her fingers gently. "I have brought my formal cosmopolitan courtesy with me. My God! talk of courtesy–I'm going to be late for lunch."

He snatched up cap and gown and was gone before she had time even to think of seeing him down to the Lodge.

"But it's just as well," she thought, watching him run across the quad like an undergraduate, "he hasn't too much time as it is. Bless the man, if he hasn't taken my gown instead of his own! Oh, well, it doesn't matter. We're much of a height and mine's pretty wide on the shoulders, so it's exactly the same thing."

And then it struck her as strange that it should be the same thing.

Harriet smiled to herself as she went to change for the river. If Peter was keen on keeping up decayed traditions he would find plenty of opportunity by keeping to a pre-War standard of watermanship, manners and dress. Especially dress. A pair of grubby shorts or a faded regulation suit rolled negligently about the waist was the modern version of Cherwell fashions for men; for women, a sun-bathing costume with (for the tender-footed) a pair of gaily-coloured beach-sandals. Harriet shook her head at the sunshine, which was now hot as well as bright. Even for the sake of startling Peter, she was not prepared to offer a display of grilled back and mosquito-bitten legs. She would go seemly and comfortable.

The Dean, meeting her under the beeches, gazed with exaggerated surprise at her dazzling display of white linen and pipe-clay.

"If this were twenty years ago I should say you were going on the river."

"I am. Hand in hand with a statelier past."

The Dean groaned gently. "I'm afraid you are making yourself conspicuous. That kind of thing is not done. You are clothed, clean and cool. On a Sunday afternoon, too. I am ashamed of you. I hope, at least, the parcel under your arm contains the records of crooners."

"Not even that," said Harriet.

Actually, it contained her diary of the Shrewsbury scandal. She had thought that the best thing would be to let Peter take it away and study it for himself. Then he could decide what was best to be done about it.

She was punctual at the bridge, but found Peter there before her. His obsolete politeness in this respect was emphasized by the presence of Miss Flaxman and another Shrewsburian, who were sitting on the raft, apparently waiting for their escort, and looking rather hot and irritable. It amused Harriet to let Wimsey take charge of her parcel, hand her ceremoniously into the punt and arrange the cushions for her, and to know, by his ironical eyes, that he perfectly well understood the reason of her unusual meekness.

"Is it your pleasure to go up or down?"

"Well, going up there's more riot but a better bottom; going down you're all right as far as the fork, and then you choose between thick mud and the Corporation dump."

"It appears to be altogether a choice of evils. But you have only to command. My ear is open like a greedy shark to catch the tunings of a voice divine."

"Great heavens! Where did you find that?"

"That, though you might not believe it, is the crashing conclusion of a sonnet by Keats. True, it is a youthful effort; but there are some things that even youth does not excuse."

"Let us go down-stream. I need solitude to recover from the shock."

He turned the punt out into the stream and shot the bridge accurately. Then:

"Admirable woman! You have allowed me to spread the tail of vanity before that pair of deserted Ariadnes. Would you now prefer to be independent and take the pole? I admit it is better fun to punt than to be punted, and that a desire to have all the fun is nine-tenths of the law of chivalry."

"Is it possible that you have a just and generous mind? I will not be outdone in generosity. I will sit like a perfect lady and watch you do the work. It's nice to see things well done."

"If you say that, I shall get conceited and do something silly."

He was, in fact, a pretty punter to watch, easy in action and quite remarkably quick. They picked their way at surprising speed down the crowded and tortuous stream until, in the narrow reach above the ferry, they were checked by another punt, which was clumsily revolving in mid-stream and cramming a couple of canoes rather dangerously against the bank.

"Before you come on this water," cried Wimsey, thrusting the offenders off with his heel and staring offensively at the youth in charge (a stringy young man, naked to the waist and shrimp-pink with the sun), "you should learn the rule of the river. Those canoes have the right of way. And if you can't handle a pole better than that, I recommend you to retire up the back-water and stay there till you know what God gave you feet for."

Whereat a middle-aged man, whose punt was moored a little way further on, turned his head sharply and cried in ringing tones:

"Good lord! Wimsey of Balliol!"

"Well, well, well," said his lordship, abandoning the pink youth, and ranging up alongside the punt. "Peake of Brasenose, by all that's holy. What brings you here?"

"Dash it," said Mr. Peake, "I live here. What brings *you* here is more to the point. You haven't met my wife—Lord Peter Wimsey, my dear—the cricket blue, you know. The rest is my family."

He waved his hand vaguely over a collection of assorted offspring.

"Oh, I thought I'd look the old place up," said Peter, when the introductions were completed all round. "I've got a nephew here and all that. What are you doing? Tutor? Fellow? Lecturer?"

"Oh, I coach people. A dog's life, a dog's life. Dear me! A lot of water has flowed under Folly Bridge since we last met. But I'd have known your voice anywhere. The moment I heard those arrogant, off-hand, go-to-blazes tones I said 'Wimsey of Balliol.' Wasn't I right?"

Wimsey shipped the pole and sat down.

"Have pity, old son, have pity! Let the dead bury their dead."

"You know," said Mr. Peake to the world at large, "when we were up together—shocking long time ago that is—never mind! If anyone got landed with a country cousin or an American visitor who asked, as these people will, 'What is this thing called the Oxford manner?' we used to take 'em round and show 'em Wimsey of Balliol. He fitted in very handily between St. John's Gardens and the Martyrs' Memorial."

"But suppose he wasn't there, or wouldn't perform?"

"That catastrophe never occurred. One never failed to find Wimsey of Balliol planted in the centre of the quad and laying down the law with exquisite insolence to somebody."

Wimsey put his head between his hands.

"We were accustomed to lay bets," went on Mr. Peake, who seemed to have preserved an undergraduate taste in humour, owing, no doubt, to continuous contact with First-Year mentality, "upon what they would say about him afterwards. The Americans mostly said, 'My, but isn't he just the perfect English aristocrat!' but some of them said, 'Does he need that glass in his eye or is it just part of the costoom?' "

Harriet laughed, thinking of Miss Schuster-Slatt.

"My dear—" said Mrs. Peake, who seemed to have a kindly nature.

"The country cousins," said Mr. Peake remorselessly, "invariably became speechless and had to be revived with coffee and ices at Buol's."

"Don't mind me," said Peter, whose face was invisible, except for the tip of a crimson ear.

"But you're wearing very well, Wimsey," pursued Mr. Peake, benevolently. "Kept your waist-line. Still good for a sprint between the wickets? say I'm much use now, except for the Parents' Match, eh, Jim? That's what marriage does for a man—makes him fat and lazy. But *you* haven't changed. Not an atom. Not a hair. Absolutely unmistakable. And you're quite right about these louts on the river. I'm sick and tired of being barged into and getting their beastly punts over my bows. They don't even know enough to apologize. Think it's dashed funny. Stupid oafs. And gramophones bawling in your ears. And look at 'em! Just look at 'em! Enough to make you sick. Like the monkey-house at the Zoo!"

"Noble and nude and antique?" suggested Harriet.

"I don't mean that. I mean the pole-climbing. Watch that girl–hand over hand, up she goes! And turning round to shove as if she was trying to clear a drain. She'll be in if she isn't careful."

"She's dressed for it," said Wimsey.

"I'll tell you what," said Mr. Peake, confidentially. "That's the real reason for the costume. They *expect* to fall in. It's all right to come out with those beautiful creases down your flannels, but if you do go in it makes it all the funnier."

"How true that is. Well, we're blocking the river. We'd better be getting on. I'll look you up one day, if Mrs. Peake will allow me. So long."

The punts parted company.

"Dear me," said Peter, when they were out of earshot; "it's pleasant to meet old friends. And very salutary."

"Yes; but don't you find it depressing when they go on making the same joke they were making about a hundred years ago?"

"Devilish depressing. It's the one great drawback to living in this place. It keeps you young. Too young."

"It's rather pathetic, isn't it?"

The river was wider here, and by way of answer he bent his knees to the stroke, making the punt curtsey and the water run chuckling under the bows.

"Would you have your youth back if you could, Harriet?"

"Not for the world."

"Nor I. Not for anything you could give me. Perhaps that's an exaggeration. For one thing you could give me I might want twenty years of my life back. But not the same twenty years. And if I went back to my twenties, I shouldn't be wanting the same thing."

"What makes you so sure of that?" said Harriet, suddenly reminded of Mr. Pomfret and the pro-Proctor.

"The vivid recollection of my own follies . . . Harriet! Are you going to tell me that all young men in their twenties are not fools?" He stood, trailing the pole, and looking down at her; his raised eyebrows lent his face a touch of caricature.

"Well, well, well . . . . I hope it is not Saint-George, by the way. That would be a most unfortunate domestic complication."

"No, not Saint-George."

"I thought not; his follies are less ingenuous. But somebody. Well, I refuse to be alarmed, since you have sent him about his business."

"I like the rapidity of your deductions."

"You are incurably honest. If you had done anything drastic you would have told me so in your letter. You would have said 'Dear Peter, I have a case to submit to you; but before doing so I think it only right to inform you that I am engaged to Mr. Jones of Jesus.' Should you not?"

"Probably. Should you have investigated the case all the same?"

"Why not? A case is a case. What is the bottom like in the Old River?"

"Foul. You're pulled back two strokes for every stroke you make."

"Then we will stick to the New Cut. Well, Mr. Jones of Jesus has my sincere sympathy. I hope his troubles will not affect his class."

"He is only in his Second year."

"Then he has time to get over it I should like to meet him. He is probably the best friend I have in the worid."

Harriet said nothing. Peter's intelligence could always make rings round her own more slowly-moving wits. It was quite true that the spontaneous affections of Reggie Pomfret had, somehow, made it easier to believe that Peter's own feelings might be something more than an artist's tenderness for his own achievement. But it was indecent of Peter to reach that conclusion so rapidly. She resented the way in which he walked in and out of her mind as if it was his own flat.

"Good God!" said Peter, suddenly. He peered with an air of alarm into the dark green water. A string of oily bubbles floated slowly to the surface, showing where the pole had struck a patch of mud; and at the same moment their nostrils were assaulted by a loathsome stench of decay.

"What's the matter?"

"I've struck something horrible. Can't you smell it? It's scandalous the way corpses pursue me about. Honestly, Harriet . . ."

"My dear idiot, it's only the Corporation garbage dump."

His eye followed her pointing hand to the farther bank, where a cloud of flies circled about a horrid mound of putrefaction.

"Well, of all the–! What the devil do they mean by doing a thing like that?" He passed a wet hand across his forehead. "For a moment I really thought I *had* run across Mr. Jones of Jesus. I was beginning to be sorry I had spoken so lightheartedly about the poor chap. Here! Let's get out of this!"

He drove the punt vigorously forward.

"The Isis for me. There is *no* romance left on this river." ..

# 15

Do but consider what an excellent thing sleep is: it is so inestimable a jewel that, if a tyrant would give his crown for an hour's slumber, it cannot be bought: of so beautiful a shape is it, that though a man lie with an Empress, his heart cannot beat quiet till he leaves her embracements to be at rest with the other: yea, so greatly indebted are we to this kinsman of death, that we owe the better tributary, half of our life to him: and there is good cause why we should do so: for sleep is that golden chain that ties health and our bodies together. Who complains of want? of wounds? of cares? of great men's oppressions? of captivity? whilst he sleepeth? Beggars in their beds take as much pleasure as kings: can we therefore surfeit on this delicate Ambrosia? Can we drink too much of that whereof to taste too little tumbles us into a churchyard, and to use it but indifferently throws us into Bedlam? No, no, look upon Endymion, the moon's minion, who slept three score and fifteen years, and was not a hair the worse for it.

Thomas Dekker

"YOU WILL find the tea-basket," said Wimsey, "behind you in the bows."

They had put in under the dappled shade of an overhanging willow a little down the left bank of the Isis. Here there was less crowd, and what there was could pass at a distance. Here, if anywhere, they might hope for comparative peace. It was, therefore, with more than ordinary irritation that Harriet, with the thermos yet in her hand, observed a heavily-laden punt approaching.

"Miss Schuster-Slatt and her party. Oh, God! and she says she knows you."

The poles were firmly driven in at either end of the boat; escape was impossible. Ineluctably the American contingent advanced upon them. They were alongside. Miss Schuster-Slatt was crying out excitedly. It was Harriet's turn to blush for her friends. With incredible coyness Miss Schuster-Slatt apologized for her intrusion, effected introductions, was sure they were terribly in the way, reminded Lord Peter of their former encounter, recognized that he was far too pleasantly occupied to wish to be bothered with her, poured out a flood of alarming enthusiasm about the Propagation of the Fit, again drew strident attention to her own tactlessness, informed Lord Peter that Harriet was a lovely person and just too sympathetic, and favoured each of them with an advance copy of her new questionnaire. Wimsey listened and replied with imperturbable urbanity, while Harriet, wishing that the Isis would flood its banks and drown them all, envied his self-command. When at length Miss Schuster-Slatt removed herself and her party, the treacherous water wafted back her shrill voice from afar:

"Well, girls! Didn't I tell you he was just the perfect English aristocrat?"

At which point the much-tried Wimsey lay down among the tea-cups and became hysterical.

"Peter," said Harriet, when he had finished crowing like a cock, "your unconquerable sweetness of disposition is very shaming. I lose my temper with that harmless woman. Have some more tea."

"I think," said his lordship, mournfully, "I had better stop being the perfect English aristocrat and become the great detective after all. Fate seems to be turning my one-day romance into a roaring farce. If that is the dossier, let me have it. We'll see," he added with a faint chuckle, "what kind of a detective you make when you're left to yourself."

Harriet handed him the loose-leaf book and an envelope containing the various anonymous documents, all endorsed, where possible, with the date and manner of publication. He examined the documents first, separately and carefully, without manifesting surprise, disgust, or, indeed, any emotion beyond meditative interest. He then put them all back in the envelope, filled and lit a pipe, curled himself up among the cushions and devoted his attention to her manuscript. He read slowly, turning back every now and again to verify a date or a detail. At the end of the first few pages he looked up to remark:

"I'll say one thing for the writing of detective fiction: you know how to put your story together; how to arrange the evidence."

"Thank you," said Harriet drily; "praise from Sir Hubert is praise indeed."

He read on.

His next observation was:

"I see you have eliminated all the servants in the Scouts' Wing on the strength of one locked door."

"I'm not so simple-minded as that. When you come to the Chapel episode, you'll find that it eliminates them all, for another reason."

"I beg your pardon; I was committing the fatal error of theorizing ahead of my data."

Accepting rebuke, he relapsed into silence, while she studied his half-averted face. Considered generally, as a facade, it was by this time tolerably familiar to her, but now she saw details, magnified as it were by some glass in her own mind. The flat setting and fine scroll-work of the ear, and the height of the skull above it. The glitter of closecropped hair where the neck-muscles lifted to meet the head. A minute sickle-shaped scar on the left temple. The faint laughter-lines at the corner of the eye and the droop of the lid at its outer end. The gleam of gold down on the cheekbone. The wide spring of the nostril. An almost imperceptible beading of sweat on the upper lip and a tiny muscle that twitched the sensitive corner of the mouth. The slight sunreddening of the fair skin and its sudden whiteness below the base of the throat. The little hollow above the points of the collar-bone.

He looked up; and she was instantly scarlet, as though she had been dipped in boiling water. Through the confusion of her darkened eyes and drumming ears some enormous bulk seemed to stoop over her. Then the mist cleared. His eyes were riveted upon the manuscript again, but he breathed as though he had been running.

So, thought Harriet, it has happened. But it happened long ago. The only new thing that has happened is that now I have got to admit it to myself. I have known it for some time. But does he know it? He has very little excuse, after this, for not knowing it. Apparently he refuses to see it, and that may be new. If so, it ought to be easier to do what I meant to do.

She stared out resolutely across the dimpling water. But she was conscious of his every movement, of every page he turned, of every breath he drew. She seemed to be separately conscious of every bone in his body. At length he spoke, and she wondered how she could ever have mistaken another man's voice for his.

"Well, Harriet, it's not a pretty problem."

"It's not. And it simply mustn't go on, Peter. We can't have any more people frightened into the river. Publicity or no publicity, it's got to be stopped. Otherwise, even if nobody else gets hurt, we shall all go mad."

"That's the devil of it."

"Tell me what we are to do, Peter."

She had once again lost all consciousness of him except as the familiar intelligence that lived and moved so curiously behind an oddly amusing set of features.

"Well—there are two possibilities. You can plant spies all over the place and wait to pounce on this person when the next outbreak occurs."

"But you don't know what a difficult place it is to police. And it's ghastly waiting for the outbreak. And suppose we don't catch her and something horrible happens."

"I agree. The other and I think the better, way is to do what we can to frighten this lunatic into keeping quiet while we dig out the motive behind the whole thing. I'm sure it's not mere blind malignity; there's a method in it."

"Isn't the motive only too painfully obvious?"

He stared pensively at her, and then said:

"You remind me of a charming old tutor, now dead, whose particular subject of research was the relations of the Papacy to the Church in England between certain dates which I do not precisely recall. At one time, a special subject on these lines was set for the History School, and undergraduates taking that subject were naturally sent to the old boy for coaching and did very well. But it was noticed that no man from his own college ever entered for that particular special—the reason being that the tutor's honesty was such that he would earnestly dissuade his pupils from taking his own subject for fear lest his encouragement might influence their decision."

"What a charming old gentleman! I'm flattered by the comparison, but I don't see the point."

"Don't you? Isn't it a fact that, having more or less made up your mind to a spot of celibacy you are eagerly peopling the cloister with bogies? If you want to do without personal relationships, then do without them. Don't stampede yourself into them by imagining that you've got to have them or qualify for a Freudian case-book."

"We're not talking about me and my feelings. We're talking about this beastly case in College."

"But you can't keep your feelings out of the case. It's no use saying vaguely that sex is at the bottom of all these phenomena—that's about as helpful as saying that human nature is at the bottom of them. Sex isn't a separate thing functioning away all by itself. It's usually found attached to a person of some sort."

"That's rather obvious."

"Well, let's have a look at the obvious. The biggest crime of these blasted psychologists is to have obscured the obvious. They're like a man packing for the week-end and turning everything out of his drawers and cupboards till he can't find his pyjamas and toothbrush. Take a few obvious points to start with. You and Miss de Vine met at Shrewsbury for the first time at the Gaudy, and the first letter was put into your sleeve at that time; the people attacked are nearly all dons or scholars; a few days after your tea-party with young Pomfret, Jukes goes to prison; all the letters received by post come either on a Monday or a Thursday; all the communications are in English except the Harpy quotation; the dress found on the dummy was never seen in College: do all those facts taken together suggest nothing to you beyond a general notion of sex repression?"

"They suggest a lot of things separately, but I can't make anything of them taken together."

"You are usually better than that at a synthesis. I wish you could clear this personal preoccupation out of your mind. My dear, what are you afraid of? The two great dangers of the celibate life are a forced choice and a vacant mind. Energies bombinating in a vacuum breed chimaeras. But *you* are in no danger. If you want to set up your everlasting rest, you are far more likely to find it in the life of the mind than the life of the heart."

"*You* say that?"

"I say that. It is *your* needs we are considering, you know; not anybody else's. That is my opinion as an honest scholar, viewing the question academically and on its merits."

She had the old sensation of being outwitted. She grasped again at the main theme of the discussion:

"Then you think we can solve the problem by straight detection, without calling in a mental specialist?"

"I think it can be solved by a little straight and unprejudiced reasoning."

"Peter. I seem to be behaving very stupidly. But the reason why I want to—to get clear of people and feelings and go back to the intellectual side is that that is the only side of life I haven't betrayed and made a mess of."

"I know that," he said, more gently. "And it's upsetting to think that it may betray you in its turn. But why should you think that? Even if much learning makes one person mad it need not make everybody mad. All these women are beginning to look abnormal to you because you don't know which one to suspect, but actually, even you don't suspect more than one."

"No; but I'm beginning to feel that almost any one of them might be capable of it."

"That, I fancy, is where your fears are distorting your judgment. If every frustrate person is heading straight for the asylum I know at least one danger to Society who ought to be shut up."

"Damn you, Peter. Will you keep to the point!"

"Meaning: what steps ought we to take? Will you give me tonight to think it over? If you will trust me to deal with it, I fancy I see one or two lines that might be followed up with profit."

"I would rather trust you than anybody."

"Thank you, Harriet. Shall we now resume our interrupted holiday? . . . Oh, my lost youth. Here are the ducks coming up for the remains of our sandwiches. Twenty-three years ago I fed these identical ducks with these identical sandwiches."

"Ten years ago, I too fed them to bursting-point."

"And ten and twenty years hence the same ducks and the same undergraduates will share the same ritual feast, and the ducks will bite the undergraduates' fingers as they have just bitten mine. How fleeting are all human passions compared with the massive continuity of ducks. . . . Be off, cullies, that's the lot."

He tossed the last crumbs of bread into the water, rolled over among the cushions and lay watching the ripples with half-shut eyes . . . . A punt went past, full of silent, sunstupefied people, with a plop and a tinkle alternately as the pole entered and left the water; then a noisy party with a gramophone bawling "Love in Bloom"; then a young man in spectacles, by himself in a canoe, and paddling as though for dear life; then another punt, paddled at a funeral pace by a whispering man and girl; then a hot and energetic party of girls in an outrigger; then another canoe, driven swiftly by two Canadian undergraduates kneeling to their work; then a very small canoe, punted dangerously by a giggling girl in a bathing-dress, with a jeering young man crouched in the bows, costumed, and obviously prepared, for the inevitable plunge; then a very sedate and fully-clothed party in a punt—mixed undergraduates being polite to a female don; then a bunch of both sexes and all ages in an inrigger with another gramophone whining "Love in Bloom"—the Town at play; then a succession of shrill cries which announced the arrival of a hilarious party teaching a novice to punt; then, in ludicrous contrast, a very stout man in a blue suit and linen hat, solemnly propelling himself all alone in a twopair tub, and a slim, singleted youth shooting contemptuously past him in a pair-oar skiff; then three punts side by side, in which everybody seemed to be asleep except those actually responsible for pole and paddle. One of these passed within a paddle's length of Harriet: a tousle-headed, rather paunchy young man lay with his knees cocked up, his mouth slightly open and his face flushed with the heat; a girl sprawled against his shoulder, while the man opposite, his hat over his face and his hands clasped over his chest with the thumbs beneath his braces, had also given up all interest in the outer world. The fourth passenger, a woman, was eating chocolates. The punter had a crumpled cotton frock and bare legs, much bitten. Harriet was reminded of a third-class railway compartment in an excursion train on a hot day; it was fatal to sleep in public; and how tempting to throw something at the paunchy youth. At that moment, the chocolate-eater screwed her remaining lollipops tightly in the bag and did throw it at the paunchy youth. It caught him in the midriff, and he woke with a loud snort. Harriet took a cigarette from her case and turned to ask her companion for a match. He was asleep.

It was a neat and noiseless kind of sleep; the posture might be described as the half-hedgehog, and offered neither mouth nor stomach as a target for missiles. But asleep he undoubtedly was. And here was Miss Harriet Vane, gone suddenly sympathetic, afraid to move for fear of waking him and savagely resenting the approach of a boatload of idiots whose gramophone was playing (for a change) "Love in Bloom."

"How wonderful," says the poet, "is Death, Death and his brother Sleep!" And, having asked whether Ianthe will wake again and being assured that she will, he proceeds to weave many beautiful thoughts about Ianthe's sleep. From this we may fairly deduce that he (like Henry who kneeled in silence by her couch) felt tenderly towards Ianthe. For another person's sleep is the acid test of our own sentiments. Unless we are savages, we react kindly to death, whether of friend or enemy. It does not exasperate us; it does not tempt us to throw things at it; we do not find it funny. Death is the ultimate weakness, and we dare not insult it. But sleep is only an illusion of weakness and, unless it appeals to our protective instincts, is likely to arouse in us a nasty, bullying spirit. From a height of conscious superiority we look down on the sleeper, thus exposing himself in all his frailty, and indulge in derisive comment upon his appearance, his manners and (if the occasion is a public one) the absurdity of the position in which he has placed his companion, if he has one, and particularly if we are that companion.

Harriet, thus cozened into playlng Phoebe to the sleeping Endymion, had plenty of opportunity to examine herself. After careful consideration, she decided that what she most needed was a box of matches. Peter had used matches to light his pipe: where were they? He had gone to sleep on the whole outfit, confound him! But his blazer was beside him on the cushions; had anybody ever known a man to carry only *one* box of matches in his pockets?

To take possession of the blazer was ticklish work, for the punt rocked at every movement and she had to lift the garment over his knees; but his sleep was the deep sleep of physical fatigue, and she crawled back in triumph without having wakened him. With a curious sense of guilt she ransacked his pockets, finding three boxes of matches, a book and a corkscrew. With tobacco and literature one could face out any situation, provided, of course, that the book was not written in an unknown tongue. The spine was untitled, and as she turned back the worn calf cover the first thing she saw was the engraved book-plate with its achievement of arms: the three silver mice on a field sable and the "domestick Catt" couched menacingly on the helmet-wreath. Two armed Saracens supported the shield, beneath which ran the mocking and arrogant motto: "As my Whimsy takes me." She turned on to the title-page. *Religio Medici*. Well! . . . Well? Was that so very unexpected?

Why did he travel about with that? Did he fill in the spare moments of detection and diplomacy with musing upon the "strange and mystical" transmigrations of silkworms and the "legerdemain of changelings"? or with considering how "we vainly accuse the fury of guns and the new inventions of death"? "Certainly there is no happiness within this circle of flesh; nor is it in the opticks of these eyes to behold felicity. The first day of our jubilee is death." She had no wish to suppose that he could find any personal application for that; she would rather have him secure and happy in order that she might resent his happy security. She flicked the pages over hurriedly. "When I am from him, I am dead till I be with him. United souls are not satisfied with embraces, but desire to be truly each other; which being impossible, these desires are infinite, and must proceed without a possibility of satisfaction." That was a most uncomfortable passage, whichever way you looked at it. She turned back to the first page and began to read steadily, with critical attention to grammar and style, so as to occupy the upper current of her mind without prying too closely into what might be going on beneath the surface.

The sun moved down the sky and the shadows lengthened upon the water. There were fewer craft on the river now; the tea-parties were hurrying home to dinner and the supperparties had not yet put out. Endymion had the air of being settled for the night; it was really time to harden her heart and pull up the poles. She put off decision from moment to moment, till a loud shriek and a bump at her end of the punt came to spare her the trouble. The incompetent novice had returned with her crew and, having left her pole in the middle of the river had let her craft drift across their stern. Harriet pushed the intruders off with more vigour than sympathy and turned to find her host sitting up and grinning rather sheepishly.

"Have I been asleep?"

"Getting on for two hours," said Harriet, with a pleased chuckle.

"Good lord, what disgusting behaviour! I'm frightfully sorry. Why didn't you give me a shout? What time is it? My poor girl, you'll get no dinner tonight if we don't hurry up. Look here, I do apologize most abjectly."

"It doesn't matter a bit. You were awfully tired."

"That's no excuse." He was on his feet now, extricating the punt-poles from the mud. "We might make it by doublepunting–if you'll forgive the infernal cheek of asking you to work to make up for my soul-destroying sloth."

"I'd love to punt. But, Peter!" She suddenly liked him enormously. "What's the hurry? I mean, is the Master expecting you, or anything?"

"No; I've removed myself to the Mitre. I can't use the Master's Lodgings as a hotel; besides, they've got people coming in."

"Then couldn't we get something to eat somewhere along the river and make a day of it? I mean, if you feel like it. Or must you have a proper dinner?"

"My dear, I would gladly eat husks for having behaved like a hog. Or thistles. Preferably thistles. You are a most forgiving woman."

"Well, give me the pole. I'll stay up in the bows and you can do the steering."

"And watch you bring the pole up in three."

"I promise to do that."

She was conscious, nevertheless, of Wimsey of Balliol's critical eye upon her handling of the heavy pole. For either you look graceful or you look ghastly; there is no middle way in punting. They set their course towards Iffley.

"On the whole," said Harriet, as they took boat again some little time later, "thistles would have been preferable."

"That kind of food is provided for very young people whose minds are elsewhere. Men of passions but no parts. I am glad to have dined on apricot flan and synthetic lemonade; it enlarges one's experience. Shall I, you or we pole? Or shall we abandon aloofness and superiority and paddle in beauty side by side?" His eyes mocked her. "I am tame; pronounce."

"Whichever you prefer."

He handed her gravely to the stern seat and coiled himself down beside her.

"What the devil am I sitting on?"

"Sir Thomas Browne, I expect. I'm afraid I rifled your pockets."

"Since I was such a bad companion, I'm glad I provided you with a good substitute."

"Is he a constant companion of yours?"

"My tastes are fairly catholic. It might easily have been *Kai Lung* or *Alice in Wonderland* or Machiavelli–"

"Or Boccaccio or the Bible?"

"Just as likely as not. Or Apuleius."

"Or John Donne?"

He was silent for a moment, and then said in a changed voice:

"Was that a bow drawn at a venture?"

"A good shot?"

"Whang in the gold. Between the joints of the harness . . . If you would paddle a little on your side it would make it handier to steer."

"Sorry . . . . Do you find it easy to get drunk on words?"

"So easy that, to tell you the truth, I am seldom perfectly sober. Which accounts for my talking so much."

"And yet, if anybody had asked me, I should have said you had a passion for balance and order–no beauty without measure.

"One may have a passion for the unattainable."

"But you do attain it. At least, you appear to attain it."

"The perfect Augustan? No; I'm afraid it's at most a balance of opposing forces . . . . The river's filling up again."

"Lots of people come out after supper."

"Yes–well, bless their hearts, why shouldn't they? You're not feeling cold?"

"Not the least bit."

That was the second time within five minutes that he had warned her off his private ground. His mood had changed since the early hours of the afternoon and all his defences were up once more. She could not again disregard the "No Thoroughfare" sign; so she left it to him to start a fresh subject.

He did so, courteously enough, by asking how the new novel was getting on.

"It's gone sticky."

"What's happened to it?"

This involved a full rehearsal of the plot of *Death 'twixt Wind and Water*. It was a complicated story, and the punt had covered a good deal of water before she reached the solution.

"There's nothing fundamentally wrong with that," said he; and proceeded to offer a few suggestions about detail.

"How intelligent you are, Peter. You're quite right. Of course that would be much the best way to get over the clock difficulty. But why does the whole story sound so dead and alive?"

"If you ask me," said Wimsey, "it's Wilfrid. I know he marries the girl–but must he be such a mutt? Why does he go and pocket the evidence and tell all those unnecessary lies?"

"Because he thinks the girl's done it."

"Yes—but why should he? He's dotingly in love with her—he thinks she's absolutely the cat's pyjamas—and yet, merely because he finds her handkerchief in the bedroom he is instantly convinced, on evidence that wouldn't hang a dog, that she not only is Winchester's mistress but has also murdered him in a peculiarly diabolical way. That may be one way of love, but—"

"But, you would like to point out, it isn't yours—and in fact, it wasn't yours."

There it was again—the old resentment, and the impulse to hit back savagely for the pleasure of seeing him wince.

"No," he said, "I was considering the question impersonally."

"Academically, in fact."

"Yes—please . . . . From a purely constructional point of view, I don't feel that Wilfrid's behaviour is sufficiently accounted for."

"Well," said Harriet, recovering her poise, "academically speaking, I admit that Wilfrid is the world's worst goop. But if he doesn't conceal the handkerchief, where's my plot?"

"Couldn't you make Wilfrid one of those morbidly conscientious people, who have been brought up to think that anything pleasant must be wrong—so that, if he *wants* to believe the girl an angel of light she is, for that very reason, all the more likely to be guilty. Give him a puritanical father and a hell-fire religion."

"Peter, that's an idea."

"He has, you see, a gloomy conviction that love is sinful in itself, and that he can only purge himself by taking the young woman's sins upon him and wallowing in vicarious suffering . . . . He'd still be a goop, and a pathological goop, but he would be a bit more consistent."

"Yes—he'd be interesting. But if I give Wilfrid all those violent and lifelike feelings, he'll throw the whole book out of balance."

"You would have to abandon the jig-saw kind of story and write a book about human beings for a change."

"I'm afraid to try that, Peter. It might go too near the bone."

"It might be the wisest thing you could do."

"Write it out and get rid of it?"

"Yes."

"I'll think about that. It would hurt like hell."

"What would that matter, if it made a good book?"

She was taken aback, not by what he said, but by his saying it. She had never imagined that he regarded her work very seriously, and she had certainly not expected him to take this ruthless attitude about it. The protective male? He was being about as protective as a can-opener.

"You haven't yet," he went on, "written the book you could write if you tried. Probably you couldn't write it when you were too close to things. But you could do it now, if you had the—the—"

"The guts?"

"Exactly."

"I don't think I could face it."

"Yes, you could. And you'll get no peace till you do. I've been running away from myself for twenty years, and it doesn't work. What's the good of making mistakes if you don't use them? Have a shot. Start on Wilfrid."

"Damn Wilfrid! . . . All right. I'll try. I'll knock the sawdust out of Wilfrid, anyhow."

He took his right hand from the paddle and held it out to her, deprecatingly.

" 'Always laying down the law with exquisite insolence to somebody.' I'm sorry."

She accepted the hand and the apology and they paddled on in amity. But it was true, she thought, that she had had to accept a good deal more than that. She was quite surprised by her own lack of resentment.

They parted at the postern.

"Good-night, Harriet. I'll bring back your manuscript tomorrow. Would some time in the afternoon suit you? I must lunch with young Gerald, I suppose, and play the heavy uncle."

"Come round about six, then. Good-night—and thank you very much."

"I am in your debt."

He waited politely while she shut and locked the heavy grille against him.

"And so-o-o" (in saccharine accents), "the co-onvent gates closed behind So-o-onia!"

He smote his forehead with a theatrical gesture and an anguished cry and reeled away almost into the arms of the Dean, who was coming up the road at her usual brisk trot.

"Serve him right," said Harriet, and fled up the path without waiting to see what happened.

As she got into bed she recalled the extempore prayer of a well-meaning but incoherent curate, heard once and never forgotten:

"Lord, teach us to take our hearts and look them in the face, however difficult it may be."

# 16

From noise of Scare-fires rest ye free,
From Murders *Benedicite*.
From all mischances, they may fright
Your pleasing slumbers in the night:
Mercie secure ye all, and keep
The Goblins from ye, while ye sleep.

Robert Herrick

"Oh, Miss!"

"We are so sorry to disturb you, madam."

"Good gracious, Carrie, what is it?"

When you have been lying awake for an hour or so wondering how to reconstruct a Wilfrid without inflicting savage mayhem upon your plot, and have just tumbled into an uneasy slumber haunted by the embalmed bodies of dukes, it is annoying to be jerked into consciousness again by two excited and partly hysterical maid-servants in dressing-gowns.

"Oh, miss, the Dean said to come and tell you. Annie and me have been so frightened. We nearly caught it."

"Caught what?"

"Whatever it is, miss. In the Science lecture-room, miss. We saw it there. It was awful."

Harriet sat up, dazed.

"And it's gone off, miss, rampaging something horrible, and nobody knows what it mayn't be up to, so we thought we ought to tell somebody."

"For goodness' sake, Carrie, *do* tell me. Sit down, both of you, and begin from the beginning."

"But, miss, didn't we ought to see what's gone with it? Out through the dark-room window, that's where it went, and it may be murdering people at this very minute. And the room locked and the key inside–there might be a dead body lying there, all blood."

"Don't be ridiculous," said Harriet. But she got out of bed, none the less, and began to hunt for her slippers. "If somebody's playing another practical joke, we must try and stop it. But don't let's have any nonsense about blood and bodies. Where did it go to?"

"We don't know, miss."

Harriet looked at the stout and agitated Carrie, whose face was puckered and twitching and her eyes bolting with imminent hysteria. She had never thought the present head scout any too dependable, and was inclined to put down her abundant energy to an excess of thyroid.

"Where is the Dean, then?"

"Waiting by the lecture-room door, miss. She said to fetch you–"

"All right."

Harriet put her torch into her dressing-gown pocket and hustled her visitors out.

"Now tell me quickly what's the matter, and don't make a noise."

"Well, miss, Annie comes to me and says–"

"When was this?"

"About a quarter of an hour ago, miss, or it might be more or less."

"About that, madam."

"I was in bed and asleep, never dreaming of nothing, and Annie says, 'Have you got the keys, Carrie? There's something funny going on in the lecture-room.' So I says to Annie–"

"Just a minute. Let Annie tell her part first."

"Well, madam, you know the Science lecture-room at the back of the New Quad, and how you can see it from our wing. I woke up about half-past one and happened to look out of my window and I saw a light in the lecture-room. So I thought, that's funny, as late as this. And I saw a shadow on the curtain, like somebody moving about."

"The curtains were drawn, then?"

"Yes, madam; but they're only buff casement-cloth, you know, so I could see the shadow as plain as plain. So I watched a bit, and the shadow went away but the light stayed on and I thought it was funny. So I went and woke Carrie and said to her to give me the keys so as I could go and look in case it was something that wasn't quite right. And she saw the light, too. And I said, 'Oh, Carrie, come with me; I don't like to go alone.' So Carrie came down with me."

"Did you go through the Hall or across the yard?"

"Across the yard, madam. We thought it would be quicker. Through the yard and the iron gate. And we tried to look through the window, but it was tight shut and the curtains pulled close."

They were out of Tudor Building now; its corridors as they passed through had seemed quiet enough. Nor did there seem to be any disturbace in the Old Quad. The Library Wing was dark, except for a lamp burning in Miss de Vine's window and the dim illumination of the passage lights.

"When we came to the lecture-room door, it was locked and the key in it, because I stooped down to look through the hole, but I couldn't see anything.

And then I saw that the curtain wasn't quite drawn across the door—it has glass panels, you know, miss. So I looked through the crack and saw something all in black, madam. And I said, 'Oh, there it is!' And Carrie said, 'Let me see,' and she gave me a bit of a push and my elbow bumped against the door and that must have frightened it, because the light went out."

"Yes, miss," said Carrie, eagerly. "And I said, 'There now!' and then there was a most awful crash inside—dreadful, it was, and something bumping, and I calls out, 'Oh, it's coming out after us!' "

"And I said to Carrie, 'Run and fetch the Dean! We've got it in here.' So Carrie went for the Dean and I heard whoever it was moving about a bit, and then I didn't hear anything more."

"And the Dean came along and we waited a bit, and I said 'Ooh! do you think it's lying in there with its throat cut?' and the Dean said, 'There, now! How silly we've been. It'll have gone out through the window.' And I says, 'But all them windows are barred,' I says. And the Dean says, 'The darkroom window, that's where it's gone.' The dark-room door was locked too, so we run round outside and sure enough, there's the window wide open. So the Dean says, 'Fetch Miss Vane.' So we comes for you, miss."

By this time they had reached the east angle of the New Quad, where Miss Martin stood waiting.

"Our friend's vanished, I'm afraid," said the Dean. "We ought to have been quick enough to think of that window. I've been round this quad, but I can't find anything wrong there. Let's hope the creature's gone back to bed."

Harriet examined the door. It was certainly locked from the inside, and the curtain over the glass panel did not fit quite closely. But everything within was dark and silent.

"What does Sherlock Holmes do now?" inquired the Dean.

"I think we go in," said Harriet. "I suppose you haven't such a thing as a pair of long-nosed pliers? No. Well, it's probably just as good to break the glass."

"Don't cut yourself."

How many times, thought Harriet, had her detective, Robert Templeton, broken through doors to discover the dead body of the murdered financier! With a ludicrous feeling that she was acting a part, she laid a fold of her dressing-gown across the panel and delivered a sharp blow upon it with her closed fist. Rather to her astonishment, the panel broke inwards exactly as it should have done, to the accompaniment of a modest tinkle of glass. Now—a scarf or handkerchief wrapped round to protect the hand and wrist, and prevent leaving extra finger-prints on key and handle. The Dean obligingly fetched this needful accessory, and the door was opened.

Harriet's first glance by torch-light was for the switch. It stood in the "Off" position, and she struck it down with the handle of the torch. The room stood revealed.

It was a rather bare, uncomfortable place, furnished with a couple of long tables, a quantity of hard chairs and a blackboard. It was called the Science lecture-room partly because Miss Edwards occasionally used it for coachings that needed little in the way of apparatus, but chiefly because some dead-and-damned benefactor had left to the College a sum of money, together with a quantity of scientific books, anatomical casts, portraits of deceased scientists and glass cases filled with geological specimens; saddling this already sufficiently embarrassing bequest with the condition that all the bric-a-brac should be housed in one room together. Otherwise there was nothing that particularly fitted the room for scientific study, except that it communi cated on one side with a closet containing a sink. The closet was occasionally used by photographic enthusiasts as a dark-room, and was so called.

The cause of the crash and bumping heard by the two scouts was plain enough as soon as the light was turned on. The blackboard had been flung to the ground and a few chairs displaced, as though somebody, hurriedly making her way from the room in the dark, had become entangled among the furniture. The most interesting thing about the room was the collection of things that lay on one of the tables. There was a spread sheet of newspaper, on which stood a paste-pot with a brush in it, part of a cheap scribbling block and the lid of a cardboard box, filled with cut-out letters. Also, laid out upon the table were several messages, couched in the Poison-Pen's now familiar style, and pasted together in the usual way; while a half-finished work in the same style of art had fluttered to the floor, showing that the Pen had been interrupted in the middle of her work.

"So here's where she does it!" cried the Dean.

"Yes," said Harriet. "I wonder why. It seems unnecessarily public. Why not her own room? . . . I say, Dean–don't pick that up, if you don't mind. Better leave everything as it is."

The door into the dark-room was open. Harriet went in and examined the sink, and the open window above it. Marks in the dust showed clearly where something had scrambled over the sill.

"What's underneath this window outside?"

"It's a flagged path. I'm afraid you won't find much there."

"No; and it happens to be a spot that's overlooked by absolutely nothing except those bathroom windows in the corridor. It's very unlikely that the person should have been seen getting out. If the letters *had* to be concocted in a lectureroom, this is as good a place as any. Well! I don't see that we can do much here at the moment." Harriet turned sharply on the two scouts. "You say you saw the person, Annie."

"Not exactly saw her, madam, not to recognize. She had on something black and was sitting at the far table with her back to the door. I thought she was writing."

"Didn't you see her face when she got up and came across to turn off the light?"

"No, madam. I told Carrie what I saw and Carrie asked to look and bumped the door, and while I was telling her not to make a noise the light went out."

"Didn't you see anything, Carrie?"

"Well, I don't hardly know, miss. I was in such a fluster. I saw the light, and then I didn't see nothing."

"Perhaps she crept round the wall to get to the light," said the Dean.

"Must have, Dean. Will you go in and sit at the table on the chair that's pulled out a bit, while I see what I can see from the door. Then, when I knock on the glass, will you get up and out of sight as quickly as you can and work round to the switch and turn it off? Is the curtain much as it was, Annie, or did I disarrange it when I broke the glass?"

"I think it's much the same, madam."

The Dean went in and sat down. Harriet shut the door and put her eye to the chink in the curtain. This was at the hinge side of the door, and gave her a sight of the window, the ends of the two tables and the place where the blackboard had stood beneath the window.

"Have a look, Annie; was it like that?"

"Yes, madam. Only the blackboard was standing up then, of course."

"Now–do as you did then. Say to Carrie whatever it was you said, and Carrie, you knock on the door and then look in as you did the first time."

"Yes, madam. I said, 'There she is! we've got her.' And I jumped back like this."

"Yes, and I said, 'Oh, dear- Let's have a look!'–and then I sort of caught against Annie and knocked–like that."

"And I said, 'Look out–now you've done it.' "

"And I says, 'Coo!' or something like that, and I looked in and I didn't see nobody–"

"Can you see anybody now?"

"No, miss. And I was trying to see when the light went out all of a sudden."

The light went out.

"How did that go off?" asked the Dean, cautiously, with her mouth at the hole in the panel.

"First-rate performance," said Harriet. "Dead on time."

"The second I heard the knock, I just nipped away to the right and crept round the wall. Did you hear me?"

"Not a sound. You've got soft slippers on, haven't you?"

"We didn't hear the other one either, miss."

"She'd be wearing soft slippers, too. Well, I suppose that settles that. We'd better have a look round College to see that all's well and get back to bed. You two can be off now, Carrie–Miss Martin and I can see to things."

"Very good, miss. Come along, Annie. Though I'm sure I don't know how anybody's to get to sleep–"

"*Will* you stop making that filthy row!"

An exasperated voice heralded the appearance of an exceedingly angry student in pyjamas.

"Do remember some people want to get a bit of rest at night. This corridor's a– Oh, I'm sorry, Miss Martin. Is anything wrong?"

"Nothing at all, Miss Perry. I'm so sorry we disturbed you. Somebody left the lights on in the lecture-room and we came to see if it was all right."

The student vanished, with a jerk of a tousled head that showed what she thought of the matter. The two servants went their way. The Dean turned to Harriet.

"Why all that business of reconstructing the crime?"

"I wanted to find out whether Annie could really have seen what she said she saw. These people sometimes let their imagination run away with them. If you don't mind, I'm going to lock these doors and remove the keys. I'd rather like a second opinion."

"Aha!" said the Dean. "The exquisite gentleman who kissed my feet in St. Cross Road, crying, *Vera incessu patuit dean?*"

"That sounds characteristic. Well, Dean, you have got pretty feet. I've noticed them."

"They have been admired," said the Dean, complacently, "but seldom in so public a place or after five minutes' acquaintance. I said to his lordship, 'You are a foolish young man.' He said, 'A man, certainly; and sometimes foolish enough to be young.' 'Well,' I said, 'please get up; you can't be young here.' So then he said, very nicely, I beg your pardon for behaving like a mountebank; I have no excuse to offer, so will you forgive me?' So I asked him to dinner."

Harriet shook her head.

"I'm afraid you're susceptible to fair hair and a slim figure. That in the slender's but a humorous word which in the stout is flat impertinence."

"It might have been extremely impertinent, but actually it was not. I shall be interested to know what he makes of tonight's affair. We'd better go and see if there's been any more funny business."

Nothing unusual was, however, to be observed.

Harriet rang up the Mitre before breakfast.

"Peter, could you possibly come round this morning instead of at six o'clock?"

"Within five minutes, when and where you will. 'If she bid them, they will go barefoot to Jerusalem, to the great Cham's court, to the East Indies, to fetch her a bird to wear in her hat.' Has anything happened?"

"Nothing alarming; a little evidence *in situ*. But you may finish the bacon and eggs."

"I will be at the Jowett Walk Lodge in half an hour."

He came accompanied by Bunter and a camera. Harriet took them into the Dean's room and told them the story, with some assistance from Miss Martin, who asked whether he would like to interview the two scouts.

"Not for the moment. You seem to have asked all the necessary questions. We'll go and look at the room. There's no way to it, I take it, except along this passage. Two doors on the left–students' rooms, I suppose. And one on the right. And the rest bathrooms and things. Which is the door of the dark-room? This? In full view of the other door–so there was no escape except by the window. I see. The key of the lecture-room was inside and the curtain left exactly like that? You're sure? All right. May I have the key?"

He threw the door open and glanced in.

"Get a photograph of this, Bunter. You have very nice, well-fitting doors in this building. Oak. No paint, no polish."

He took a lens from his pocket and ran it, rather perfunctorily, over the light-switch and the door-handle.

"Am I really going to see finger-prints discovered?" asked the Dean.

"Why, of course," said Wimsey. "It won't tell us anything, but it impresses the spectator and inspires confidence. Bunter, the insufflator. You will now see," he pumped the white powder rapidly over the frame and handle of the door, "how inveterate is the habit of catching hold of doors when you open them." An astonishing number of superimposed prints sprang into view above the lock as he blew the superfluous powder away. "Hence the excellent old-fashioned institution of the finger-plate. May I borrow a chair from the bathroom? . . . Oh, thank you, Miss Vane; I didn't mean *you* to fetch it."

He extended the blowing operations right up to the top of the door and the upper edge of the frame.

"You surely don't expect to find finger-prints up there," said the Dean.

"Nothing would surprise me more. This is merely a shopwindow display of thoroughness and efficiency. All a matter of routine, as the policeman says. Your college is kept very well dusted; I congratulate you. Well, that's that. We will now direct our straining eyes to the dark-room door and do the same thing there. The key? Thank you. Fewer prints here, you see. I deduce that the room is usually approached by way of the lecture-room. That probably also accounts for the presence of dust along the top of the door. Something always gets overlooked, doesn't it? The linoleum, however, has been honourably swept and polished. Must I go down on my knees and do the floor-walk for footprints? It is shockingly bad for one's trousers and seldom useful. Let us rather examine the window. Yes—somebody certainly seems to have got out here. But we knew that already. She climbed over the sink and knocked that beaker off the draining-board."

"She trod in the sink," said Harriet, "and left a damp smear on the sill. It's dried up now, of course."

"Yes; but that proves she really did get out this way and at that time. Though it scarcely needed proving. There is no other way out. This isn't the old problem of a hermetically-sealed chamber and a body. Have you finished in there, Bunter?"

"Yes, my lord; I have made three exposures."

"That ought to do. You might clean those doors, would you?" He turned, smiling, on the Dean. "You see, even if we did identify all those finger-prints, they would all belong to people who had a perfect right to be here. And in any case, our culprit, like everybody else these days, probably knows enough to wear gloves."

He surveyed the lecture-room critically.

"Miss Vane!"

"Yes?"

"Something worried you about this room. What was it?"

"You don't need to be told."

"No; I am convinced that our two hearts beat as one. But tell Miss Martin."

"When the Poison-Pen turned off the light, she must have been close to the door. Then she went out by way of the dark-room. Why did she knock over the blackboard, which is right out of the line between the two doors?"

"Exactly."

"Oh!" cried the Dean, "but that's nothing. One often loses one's way in a dark room. My reading-lamp fused one night, and I got up to try and find the wall-switch and brought up with my nose against the wardrobe."

"There!" said Wimsey. "The chill voice of common-sense falls on our conjectures like cold water on hot glass, and shatters them to bits. But I don't believe it. She had only to feel her way along the wall. She must have had some reason for going back into the middle of the room."

"She'd left something on one of the tables."

"That's more likely. But what? Something identifiable."

"A handkerchief or something that she'd been using to press down the letters as she pasted them on."

"We'll say it was that. These papers are just as you found them, I imagine. Did you test them to see if the paste was still wet?"

"I just felt this unfinished one on the floor. You see how it's done. She drew a line of paste right across the paper and then dabbed the letters on. The unfinished line was just tacky, but not wet. But then, you see, we didn't get in till after she'd been gone five or ten minutes."

"You didn't test any of the others?"

"I'm afraid not."

"I only wondered how long she'd been working here. She's managed to get through a good bit. But we may be able to find out another way." He took up the box-lid containing the odd letters.

"Rough brown cardboard; I don't think we'll bother to look for finger-prints on this. Or to trace it; it might have come from anywhere. She'd nearly finished her job; there are only a couple of dozen letters left, and a lot of them are Q's and K's and Z's and such-like unhandy consonants. I wonder how this last message was meant to end."

He picked the paper from the floor and turned it over.

"Addressed to you, Miss Vane. Is this the first time you have been honoured?"

"The first time—since the first time."

"Ah! 'You needn't think you'll get me, you make me laugh, you . . .' Well, the epithet remains to be supplied—from the letters in the box. If your vocabulary is large enough you may discover what it was going to be."

"But . . . Lord Peter—"

It was so long since she had addressed him by his title that she felt self-conscious about it. But she appreciated his formality.

"What I want to know is, why she came to this room at all."

"That is the mystery, isn't it?"

There was a shaded reading-lamp on the table, and he stood idly clicking the light on and off. "Yes. Why couldn't she do it in her own room? Why invite discovery?"

"Excuse me, my lord."

"Yes, Bunter?"

"Would this be any contribution to the inquiry?"

Bunter dived beneath the table and came up, holding a long black hairpin.

"Good heavens, Bunter! This is like a leaf out of a forgotten story. How many people use these things?"

"Oh, quite a number, nowadays," said the Dean. "Little buns in the neck have come back. I use them myself, but mine are bronze ones. And some of the students. And Miss Lydgate—but I think hers are bronze, too."

"I know who uses black ones this shape," said Harriet. "I once had the pleasure of sticking them in for her."

"Miss de Vine, of course. Always the White Queen. And she *would* drop them all over the place. But I should think she was about the only person in College who would never, by any chance, come into this room. She gives no lectures or classes and never uses the dark-room or consults scientific works."

"She was working in her room when I came across last night," said Harriet.

"Did you see her?" said Wimsey, quickly.

"I'm sorry. I'm an idiot. I only meant that her reading-lamp was on, close to her window."

"You can't establish an alibi on the strength of a reading-lamp," said Wimsey. "I'm afraid I shall have to do the floor-walk after all."

It was the Dean who picked up a second hairpin—in the place where one might most reasonably expect to find it—in a corner near the sink in the dark-room. She was so pleased with herself as a detective that she almost forgot the implications of the discovery, till Harriet's distressed exclamation forced them upon her.

"We haven't identified the hairpins for certain," said Peter, comfortingly. "That will be a little task for Miss Vane." He gathered up the papers. "I'll take these and add them to the dossier. I suppose there's no message for us on the blackboard?"

He picked up the board, which contained only a few chemical formulae, scribbled in chalk, in Miss Edwards's handwriting, and restored the easel to an upright position, on the far side of the window.

"Look!" said Harriet, suddenly. "I know why she went round that way. She meant to get out by the lecture-room window, and had forgotten the bars. It was only when she pulled the curtain aside and saw them that she remembered the dark-room and plunged away in a hurry, knocking over the blackboard and tumbling into the chairs on the way. She must have been between the window and the easel, because the board *and* the easel fell forward into the room, and not backwards towards the wall."

Peter looked at her thoughtfully. Then he went back into the dark-room and lowered and raised the window-sash. It moved easily and almost in silence.

"If this place wasn't so well built," he said, almost accusingly, to the Dean, "somebody would have heard this window go up and run round in time to catch the lady. As it is, I wonder that Annie didn't notice the noise of the beaker falling into the sink . . . . But if she did, she probably thought it was something in the lecture-room–one of those glass cases or what not. *You* didn't hear anything after you arrived, did you?"

"Not a thing."

"Then she must have got out while Carrie was fetching you out of bed. I suppose nobody saw her go."

"I've asked the only three students whose windows overlook that wall, and they saw nothing," said Harriet.

"Well, you might ask Annie about the beaker. And ask both of them whether they noticed, as they came past, if the dark-room window was open or shut. I don't suppose they noticed anything, but you never can tell."

"What does it matter?" asked the Dean.

"Not very much. But if it was shut, it rather supports Miss Vane's idea about the blackboard. If it was open, it would suggest that a retreat had been planned in that direction. It's a question of whether we're dealing with a short-sighted or a long-sighted person–mentally, I mean. And you might inquire at the same time whether any of the other women in the Scouts' Wing saw the light in the lecture-room, and if so, how early."

Harriet laughed.

"I can tell you that at once. None of them. If they had, there would have been an eager rush to tell us all about it. You may be perfectly certain that Annie's and Carrie's adventure formed the staple of conversation in the servants' hall this morning."

"That," said his lordship, "is very true indeed."

There was a pause. The lecture-room seemed to offer no further field for research. Harriet suggested that Wimsey might like to look round the College.

"I was about to suggest it," said he, "if you can spare the time."

"Miss Lydgate is expecting me in half an hour for a fresh attack on the *Prosody*," said Harriet. "I mustn't cut that, because her time is so precious, poor dear, and she's suddenly thought of a new appendix."

"Oh, *no!*" cried the Dean.

"Alas, yes! But we could just go round and view the more important battlefields."

"I should like particularly to see the Hall and Library and the connection between them, the entrance to Tudor Building, with Miss Barton's former room, the lay-out of the Chapel with reference to the postern and the place where, with the help of God, one leaps over the wall, and the way from Queen Elizabeth into the New Quad."

"Great heavens!" said Harriet. "Did you sit up all night with the dossier?"

"Hush! no, I woke rather early. But don't let Bunter hear, or he will start being solicitous. Men have died and the worms have eaten them, but not for early rising. In fact, it is said that it's the early worm that gets the bird."

"You remind me," said the Dean, "that there are half-a-dozen worms waiting in my room to get the bird this minute. Three late-without-leaves, two gramophones-out-of-hours, and an irregular motor-vehicle. We shall meet again at dinner, Lord Peter."

She ran briskly away to deal with the malefactors, leaving Peter and Harriet to make their tour. From Peter's comments, Harriet could make out little of his mind; she fancied, indeed, that he was somewhat abstracted from the matter in hand.

"I fancy," he said at last, as they came to the Jowett Walk Lodge, where he had left the car, "that you will have very little more trouble at night."

"Why?"

"Well, for one thing, the nights are getting very short, and the risks very great. . . . All the same—shall you be offended if I ask you—if I suggest that you should take some personal precautions?"

"What sort of precautions?"

"I won't offer you a revolver to take to bed with you. But I have an idea that from now on you and at least one other person may be in some danger of attack. That may be imagination. But if this joker is alarmed and bottled up for a bit—and I think she has been alarmed—the next outrage may be a serious one—when it comes."

"Well," said Harriet, "we have her word for it that she finds me merely funny."

His attention seemed to be attracted by something among the dashboard fittings, and he said, looking not at her but at the car:

"Yes. But without any vanity, I wish I were your husband or your brother or you lover, or anything but what I am."

"You mean, your being here is a danger—to me?"

"I dare say I'm flattering myself."

"But it wouldn't stop *you* to damage *me*."

"She may not think very clearly about that."

"Well, I don't mind the risk, if it is one. And I don't see why it would be any less if you were a relation of mine."

"There'd be an innocent excuse for my presence, wouldn't there? . . . Don't think I'm trying to make capital out of this on my own account. I'm being careful to observe the formalities, as you may have noticed. I'm only warning you that I'm sometimes a dangerous person to know."

"Let's have this clear, Peter. You think that your being here may make this person desperate and that she may try to take it out of me. And you are trying to tell me, very delicately, that it might be safer if we camouflaged your interest in the case as another kind of interest."

"Safer for you."

"Yes—though I can't see why you think so. But you're sure I'd rather die than make such an embarrassing pretence."

"Well, wouldn't you?"

"And on the whole you'd rather see me dead than embarrassed."

"That is probably another form of egotism. But I am entirely at your service."

"Of course, if you're such a perilous ally, I could tell you to go away."

"I can see you urging me to go away and leave a job undone."

"Well, Peter, I'd certainly rather die than make any sort of pretence to you or about you. But I think you're exaggerating the whole thing. You don't usually get the wind up like this."

"I do, though; quite often. But if it's only my own risk, I can afford to let it blow. When it comes to other people–"

"Your instinct is to clap the women and children under hatches."

"Well," he admitted, deprecatingly, "one can't suppress one's natural instincts altogether; even if one's reason and self-interest are all the other way."

"Peter, it's a shame. Let me introduce you to some nice little woman who adores being protected."

"I should be wasted on her. Besides, she would always be deceiving me, in the kindest manner, for my own good; and that I could not stand. I object to being tactfully managed by somebody who ought to be my equal. If I want tactful dependents, I can hire them. And fire them if they get too tactful. I don't mean Bunter. He braces me by a continual cold shower of silent criticism. I don't protect him; he protects me, and preserves an independent judgment . . . . However; without presuming to be protective, may I yet suggest that you should use a reasonable caution? I tell you frankly, I don't like your friend's preoccupation with knives and strangling."

"Are you serious?"

"For once."

Harriet was about to tell him not to be ridiculous; then she remembered Miss Barton's story about the strong hands that had seized her from behind. It might have been quite true. The thought of perambulating the long corridors by night was suddenly disagreeable.

"Very well; I'll be careful."

"I think it would be wise. I'd better push off now. I'll be round in time to face the High Table at dinner. Seven o'clock?"

She nodded. He had interpreted strictly her injunction to come "this morning instead of at six." She went, feeling a little blank, to cope with Miss Lydgate's proofs.

# 17

He that questioneth much shall learn much, and content much; but especially if he apply his questions to the skill of the persons whom he asketh; for he shall give them occasion to please themselves in speaking, and himself shall continually gather knowledge. But let his questions not be troublesome, for that is fit for a poser; and let him be sure to leave other men their turns to speak.

Francis Bacon

"You look," said the Dean, "like a nervous parent whose little boy is about to recite *The Wreck of the Hesperus* at a School Concert."

"I feel," said Harriet, "more like the mother of Daniel.

*King Darius said to the lions:–*
*Bite Daniel. Bite Daniel.*
*Bite him. Bite him. Bite him."*

"G'rrrrr!" said the Dean.

They were standing at the door of the Senior Common Room, which conveniently overlooked the Jowett Walk Lodge. The Old Quad was animated. Late-comers were hurrying over to change for dinner; others, having changed, were strolling about in groups, waiting for the bell; some were still playing tennis; Miss de Vine emerged from the Library Building, still vaguely pushing in hairpins (Harriet had checked up on those hairpins and identified them); an elegant figure paraded towards them from the direction of the New Quadrangle.

"Miss Shaw's got a new frock," said Harriet.

"So she has! How posh of her!

*And she was as fine as a melon in the corn-field,*
*Gliding and lovely as a ship upon the sea.*

That, my dear, is meant for Daniel."

"Dean, darling, you're being a cat."

"Well, aren't we all? This early arrival of everybody is exceedingly sinister. Even Miss Hillyard is arrayed in her best black gown with a train to it. We all feel there's safety in numbers."

It was not out of the way for the Senior Common Room to collect outside their own door before dinner of a fine summer's day, but Harriet, glancing round, had to admit that there were more of them there that evening than was usual before 7 o'clock. She thought they all seemed apprehensive and some, even hostile. They tended to avoid one another's eyes; yet they gathered together as though for protection against a common menace. She suddenly found it absurd that anybody should be alarmed by Peter Wimsey; she saw them as a harmless collection of nervous patients in a dentist's waiting-room.

"We seem," said Miss Pyke's harsh voice in her ear, "to be preparing a somewhat formidable reception for our guest. Is he of a timid disposition?"

"I should say he was completely hard-boiled," said Harriet.

"That reminds me," said the Dean. "In the matter of shirtfronts–"

"Hard, of course," said Harriet, indignantly. "And if he pops or bulges, I will pay you five pounds."

"I have been meaning to ask you," said Miss Pyke. "How is the popping sound occasioned? I did not like to ask Dr. Threep so personal a question, but my curiosity was very much aroused."

"You'd better ask Lord Peter," said Harriet.

"If you think he will not be offended," replied Miss Pyke, with perfect seriousness, "I will do so."

The chimes of New College, rather out of tune, played the four quarters and struck the hour.

"Punctuality," said the Dean, her eyes turned towards the Lodge, "seems to be one of the gentleman's virtues. You'd better go and meet him and settle his nerves before the ordeal."

"Do you think so?" Harriet shook her head. "Ye'll no fickle Tammas Yownie."

It may, perhaps, be embarrassing for a solitary man to walk across a wide quadrangle under a fire of glances from a collection of collegiate females; but it is child's play compared, for example, with the long trek from the pavilion at Lord's to the far end of the pitch, with five wickets down and ninety needed to save the follow-on. Thousands of people then alive might have recognized that easy and unhurried stride and confident carriage of the head. Harriet let him do threequarters of the journey alone, and then advanced to meet him.

"Have you cleaned your teeth and said your prayers?"

"Yes, mamma; and cut my nails and washed behind the ears and got a clean handkerchief."

Looking at a bunch of students who happened to pass at the moment, Harriet wished she could have said the same of them. They were grubby and dishevelled and she felt unexpectedly obliged to Miss Shaw for having made an effort in the matter of dress. As for her convoy, from his sleek yellow head to his pumps she distrusted him; his mood of the morning was gone, and he was as ready for mischief as a wilderness of monkeys.

"Come along, then, and behave prettily. Have you seen your nephew?"

"I have seen him. My bankruptcy will probably be announced tomorrow. He asked me to give you his love, no doubt thinking I can still be lavish in that commodity. It all returned from him to you, though it was mine before. That colour is very becoming to you."

His tone was pleasantly detached and she hoped he was referring to her dress; but she was not sure. She was glad to relinquish him to the Dean, who came forward to claim him and to relieve her of the introductions. Harriet watched in some amusement. Miss Lydgate, far too unselfconscious to have any attitude at all, greeted him exactly as she would have greeted anybody else, and asked eagerly about the situation in Central Europe; Miss Shaw smiled with a graciousness that emphasized Miss Stevens's brusque "How-d'you do" and immediate retreat into animated discussion of college affairs with Miss Allison; Miss Pyke pounced on him with an intelligent question about the latest murder; Miss Barton, advancing with an evident determination to put him right about capital punishment, was disarmed by the blank amiability of the countenance offered for her inspection and observed instead that it had been a remarkably fine day.

"Comedian!" thought Harriet, as Miss Barton, finding she could make nothing of him, passed him on to Miss Hillyard.

"Ah!" said Wimsey instantly, smiling into the History Tutor's sulky eyes, "this is delightful. Your paper in the *Historical Review* on the diplomatic aspects of the Divorce . . ."

(Heavens! thought Harriet, I hope he knows his stuff.)

". . . really masterly. Indeed, I felt that, if anything, you had slightly underestimated the pressure brought to bear upon Clement by . . ."

". . . consulted the unedited dispatches in the possession of . . ."

". . . you might have carried the argument a trifle further. You very rightly point out that the Emperor . . ."

(Yes; he had read the article all right.)

". . .disfigured by prejudice, but a considerable authority on the Canon Law . . ."

". . . needing to be thoroughly overhauled and re-edited. Innumerable mistranscriptions and at least one unscrupulous omission. . . ."

". . . if at any time you require access, I could probably put you into touch with . . . official channels . . . personal introduction . . . raise no difficulties . . . "

"Miss Hillyard," said the Dean to Harriet, "looks as though she had been given a birthday present."

"I think he's offering her access to some out-of-the-way source of information." (After all, she thought, he is Somebody, though one never seems able to remember it.)

". . . not so much political as economic."

"Ah!" said Miss Hillyard, "when it comes to a question of national finance, Miss de Vine is the real authority."

She effected the introduction herself, and the discussion continued.

"Well," said the Dean, "he has made a complete conquest of Miss Hillyard."

"And Miss de Vine is making a complete conquest of him."

"It's mutual, I fancy. At any rate, her back hair's coming down, which is a sure sign of pleasure and excitement."

"Yes," said Harriet. Wimsey was arguing with intelligence about the appropriation of monastic funds, but she had little doubt that the back of his mind was full of hairpins.

"Here comes the Warden. We shall have to separate them forcibly. He's *got* to face Dr. Baring and take her in to dinner .... All's well. She has collared him. That firm assertion of the Royal Prerogative! ... Do you want to sit next him and hold his hand?"

"I don't think he needs any assistance from me. You're the person for him. Not a suspect, but full of lively information."

"All right; I'll go and prattle to him. You'd better sit opposite to us and kick me if I say anything indiscreet."

By this arrangement, Harriet found herself placed a little uncomfortably between Miss Hillyard (in whom she always felt an antagonism to herself) and Miss Barton (who was obviously still worried about Wimsey's detective hobbies), and face to face with the two people whose glances were most likely to disturb her gravity. On the other side of the Dean sat Miss Pyke; on the other side of Miss Hillyard was Miss de Vine, well under Wimsey's eye. Miss Lydgate, that secure fortress, was situated at the far end of the table, offering no kind of refuge.

Neither Miss Hillyard nor Miss Barton had much to say to Harriet, who was thus able to follow, without too much difficulty, the Warden's straightforward determination to size up Wimsey and Wimsey's diplomatically veiled but equally obstinate determination to size up the Warden; a contest carried on with unwavering courtesy on either side.

Dr. Baring began by inquiring whether Lord Peter had been conducted over the College and what he thought of it, adding, with due modesty, that architecturally, of course, it could scarcely hope to compete with the more ancient foundations.

"Considering," said his lordship plaintively, "that the architecture of my own ancient foundation is mathematically compounded of ambition, distraction, uglification and derision, that remark sounds like sarcasm."

The Warden, almost seduced into believing herself guilty of a breach of manners, earnestly assured him that she had intended no personal allusion.

"An occasional reminder is good for us," said he. "We are mortified in nineteenth-century Gothic, lest in our overweening Balliolity we forget God. We pulled down the good to make way for the bad; you, on the contrary, have made the world out of nothing—a more divine procedure."

The Warden, manoeuvring uneasily on this slippery ground between jest and earnest, found foothold:

"It is quite true that we have had to make what we can out of very little—and that, you know, is typical of our whole position here."

"Yes; you are practically without endowments?"

The question was so offered as to include the Dean, who said cheerfully:

"Quite right. All done by cheeseparing."

"That being so," he said, seriously, "even to admire seems to be a kind of impertinence. This is a very fine hall—who is the architect?"

The Warden supplied him with a little local history, breaking off to say:

"But probably you are not specially interested in all this question of women's education."

"Is it still a question? It ought not to be. I hope you are not going to ask me whether I approve of women's doing this and that."

"Why not?"

"You should not imply that I have any right either to approve or disapprove."

"I assure you," said the Warden, "that even in Oxford we still encounter a certain number of people who maintain their right to disapprove."

"And I had hoped I was returning to civilization."

The removal of fish-plates caused a slight diversion, and the Warden took the opportunity to turn her inquiries upon the situation in Europe. Here the guest was on his own ground. Harriet caught the Dean's eye and smiled. But the more formidable challenge was coming. International politics led to history, and history—in Dr. Baring's mind—to philosophy. The ominous name of Plato suddenly emerged from a tangle of words, and Dr. Baring moved out a philosophical speculation, like a pawn, and planted it temptingly *en prise*.

Many persons had plunged to irretrievable disaster over the Warden's philosophic pawn. There were two ways of taking it: both disastrous. One was to pretend to knowledge; the other, to profess an insincere eagerness for instruction. His lordship smiled gently and refused the gambit:

"That is out of my stars. I have not the philosophic mind."

"And how would you define the philosophic mind, Lord Peter?"

"I wouldn't, definitions are dangerous. But I know that philosophy is a closed book to me, as music is to the tone-deaf."

The Warden looked at him quickly; he presented her with an innocent profile, drooping and contemplative over his plate, like a heron brooding by a pond.

"A very apt illustration," said the Warden; "as it happens, I am tone-deaf myself."

"Are you? I thought you might be," he said, equably.

"That is very interesting. How can you tell?"

"There is something in the quality of the voice." He offered candid grey eyes for examination. "But it's not a very safe conclusion to draw, and, as you may have noticed, I didn't draw it. That is the art of the charlatan—-to induce a confession and present it as the result of deduction."

"I see," said Dr. Baring. "You expose your technique very frankly."

"You would have seen through it in any case, so it is better to expose one's self and acquire an unmerited reputation for candour. The great advantage about telling the truth is that nobody ever believes it—that is at the bottom of the *ψευδῆ λέγειν ὡς δεῖ*."

"So there is one philosopher whose books are not closed to you? Next time, I will start by way of Aristotle."

She turned to her left-hand neighbor and released him.

"I am sorry," said the Dean, "we have no strong drink to offer you."

His face was eloquent of mingled apprehension and mischief.

"The toad beneath the harrow knows where every separate tooth-point goes. Do you always prove your guests with hard questions?"

"Till they show themselves to be Solomons. You have passed the test with great credit."

"Hush! there is only one kind of wisdom that has any social value, and that is the knowledge of one's own limitations."

"Nervous young dons and students have before now been carried out in convulsions through being afraid to say boldly that they did not know."

"Showing themselves," said Miss Pyke across the Dean, "less wise than Socrates, who made the admission fairly frequently."

"For Heaven's sake," said Wimsey, "don't mention Socrates. It might start all over again."

"Not now," said the Dean. "She will ask no questions now except for instruction."

"There is a question on which I am anxious to be instructed," said Miss Pyke, "if you will not take it amiss."

Miss Pyke, of course, was still worried about Dr. Threep's shirt-front, and determined on getting enlightenment. Harriet hoped that Wimsey would recognize her curiosity for what it was: not skittishness, but the embarrassing appetite for exact information which characterizes the scholarly mind.

"That phenomenon," he said, readily, "comes within my own sphere of knowledge. It occurs because the human torso possesses a higher factor of variability than the ready-made shirt. The explosive sound you mention is produced when the shirt-front is slightly too long for the wearer. The stiff edges, being forced slightly apart by the inclination of the body, come back into contact with a sharp click, similar to that emitted by the elytra of certain beetles. It is not to be confused, however, with the ticking of the Death-watch, which is made by tapping with the jaws and is held to be a love-call. The clicking of the shirt-front has no amatory significance, and is, indeed, an embarrassment to the insect. It may be obviated by an increased care in selection or, in extreme cases, by having the garment made to measure."

"Thank you so much," said Miss Pyke. "That is a most satisfactory explanation. At this time of day, it is perhaps not improper to adduce the parallel instance of the old-fashioned corset, which was subject to a similar inconvenience."

"The inconvenience," added Wimsey, "was even greater in the case of plate armour, which had to be very well tailored to allow of movement at all."

At this point, Miss Barton captured Harriet's attention with some remark or other, and she lost track of the conversation on the other side of the table. When she picked up the threads again, Miss Pyke was giving her neighbours some curious details about Ancient Minoan civilization, and the Warden was apparently waiting till she had finished to pounce on Peter again. Turning to her right, Harriet saw that Miss Hillyard was watching the group with a curiously concentrated expression. Harriet asked her to pass the sugar, and she came back to earth with a slight start.

"They seem to be getting on very well over there," said Harriet.

"Miss Pyke likes an audience," said Miss Hillyard, with so much venom that Harriet was quite astonished.

"It's good for a man to have to do the listening sometimes," she suggested.

Miss Hillyard agreed absently. After a slight pause, during which dinner proceeded without incident, she said:

"Your friend tells me he can obtain access for me to some private collections of historical documents in Florence. Do you suppose he means what he says?"

"If he says so, you may be sure he can and will."

"That is a testimonial," said Miss Hillyard. "I am very glad to hear it."

Meanwhile, the Warden had effected her capture, and was talking to Peter in a low tone and with some earnestness. He listened attentively, while he peeled an apple, the narrow coils of the rind sliding slowly over his fingers. She concluded with some question; and he shook his head.

"It is very unlikely. I should say there was no hope of it at all."

Harriet wondered whether the subject of the Poison-Pen had risen at last to the surface; but presently he said:

"Three hundred years ago it mattered comparatively little. But now that you have the age of national self-realization, the age of colonial expansion, the age of the barbarian invasions and the age of the decline and fall, all jammed cheek by jowl in time and space, all armed alike with poison-gas and going through the outward motions of an advanced civilization, principles have become more dangerous than passions. It's getting uncommonly easy to kill people in large numbers, and the first thing a principle does—if it really is a principle—is to kill somebody."

"'The real tragedy is not the conflict of good with evil but of good with good; that means a problem with no solution."

"Yes. Afflicting, of course, to the tidy mind. One may either hulloo on the inevitable, and be called a bloodthirsty progressive; or one may try to gain time and be called a bloodthirsty reactionary. But when blood is their argument, all argument is apt to be—merely bloody."

The Warden passed the adjective at its face-value.

"I sometimes wonder whether we gain anything by gaining time."

"Well—if one leaves letters unanswered long enough, some of them answer themselves. Nobody can prevent the Fall of Troy, but a dull, careful person may manage to smuggle out the Lares and Penates—even at the risk of having the epithet *pius* tacked to his name."

"The Universities are always being urged to march in the van of progress."

"But epic actions are all fought by the rearguard—at Roncevaux and Thermopylae."

"Very well," said the Warden, laughing, "let us die in our tracks, having accomplished nothing but an epic."

She collected the High Table with her eye, rose, and made a stately exit. Peter effaced himself politely against the panelling while the dons filed past him, arriving at the edge of the dais in time to pick up Miss Shaw's scarf as it slipped from her shoulders. Harriet found herself descending the staircase between Miss Martin and Miss de Vine, who remarked:

"You are a courageous woman."

"Why?" said Harriet lightly. "To bring my friends here and have them put to the question?"

"Nonsense," interrupted the Dean. "We all behaved beautifully. Daniel is still uneaten—in fact, at one point he bit the lion. Was that genuine, by the way?"

"About tone-deafness? Probably just a little more genuine than he made out."

"Will he lay traps all evening for us to walk into?"

Harriet realized for a moment how queer the whole situation was. Once again, she felt Wimsey as a dangerous alien and herself on the side of the women, who, with so strange a generosity, were welcoming the inquisitor among them. She said, however:

"If he does, he will display all the mechanism in the most obliging manner."

"After one is inside. That's very comforting."

"That," said Miss de Vine, brushing aside these surface commentaries, "is a man able to subdue himself to his own ends. I should be sorry for anyone who came up against *his* principles—whatever they are, and if he has any."

She detached herself from the other two, and went on into the Senior Common Room with a sombre face.

"Curious," said Harriet. "She is saying about Peter Wimsey exactly what I have always thought about herself."

"Perhaps she recognizes a kindred spirit."

"Or a foe worthy of—I ought not to say that."

Here Peter and his companion caught them up, and the Dean, joining Miss Shaw, went on in with her. Wimsey smiled at Harriet, an odd, interrogative smile.

"What's worrying you?"

"Peter—I feel exactly like Judas."

"Feeling like Judas is part of the job. No job for a gentleman, I'm afraid. Shall we wash our hands like Pilate and be thoroughly respectable?"

She slid her hand under his arm.

"No; we're in for it now. We'll be degraded together."

"That will be nice. Like the lovers in that Strohheim film, we'll go and sit on the sewer." She could feel his bone and muscle, reassuringly human, under the fine broadcloth. She thought: "He and I belong to the same world, and all these others are the aliens." And then: "Damn it all! this is our private fight—why should they have to join in?" But that was absurd.

"What do you want me to do, Peter?"

"Chuck the ball back to me if it runs out of the circle. Not obviously. Just exercise your devastating talent for keeping to the point and speaking the truth."

"That sounds easy."

"It is—for you. That's what I love you for. Didn't you know? Well, we can't stop to argue about it now; they'll think we're conspiring about something."

She released his arm and went into the room ahead of him, feeling suddenly embarrassed and looking, in consequence, defiant. The coffee was already on the table, and the S.C.R. were gathered about it, helping themselves. She saw Miss Barton advance upon Peter, with a courteous offer of refreshment on her lips but the light of determination in her eye. Harriet did not for the moment care what happened to Peter. He had given her a new bone to worry. She provided herself with coffee and a cigarette, and retired with them and the bone into a corner. She had often wondered, in a detached kind of way, what it was that Peter valued in her and had apparently valued from that first day when she had stood in the dock and spoken for her own life. Now that she knew, she thought that a more unattractive pair of qualities could seldom have been put forward as an excuse for devotion.

"But do you really feel comfortable about it, Lord Peter?"

"No—I shouldn't recommend it as a comfortable occupation. But is your or my or anybody's comfort of very great importance?"

Miss Barton probably took that for flippancy; Harriet recognized the ruthless voice that had said, "What does it matter if it hurts . . . ?" Let them fight it out . . . . Unattractive; but if he meant what he said, it explained a great many things. Those were qualities that could be recognized under the most sordid conditions . . . . "Detachment . . . if you ever find a person who likes you because of it, that liking is sincere." That was Miss de Vine; and Miss de Vine was sitting not very far away, her eyes, behind their thick glasses, fixed on Peter with a curious, calculating look.

Conversations, carried on in groups, were beginning to falter and fall into silence. People were sitting down. The voices of Miss Allison and Miss Stevens rose into prominence. They were discussing some collegiate question, and they were doing it intently and desperately. They called upon Miss Burrows to give an opinion. Miss Shaw turned to Miss Chilperic and made a remark about the bathing at "Spinsters' Splash." Miss Chilperic replied elaborately—too elaborately; her answer took too long and attracted attention; she hesitated, became confused, and stopped speaking. Miss Lydgate, with a troubled face, was listening to an anecdote that Mrs. Goodwin was telling about her little boy; in the middle of it, Miss Hillyard, who was within earshot, rose pointedly, stabbed out her cigarette on a distant ash-tray, and moved slowly, and as though despite herself, to a window-seat close to where Miss Barton was still standing. Harriet could see her angry, smouldering glance fix itself on Peter's bent head and then jerk away across the quad, only to return again. Miss Edwards, close to Harriet and a little in front of her on a low chair, had her hands set squarely and rather mannishly on her knees, and was leaning forward; she had the air of waiting for something. Miss Pyke, on her feet, lighting a cigarette, was apparently looking for an opportunity to engage Peter's attention; she appeared eager and interested, and more at her ease than most of the others. The Dean, curled on a humpty, was frankly listening to what Peter and Miss Barton were saying. They were all listening, really, and at the same time most of them were trying to pretend that he was there as an ordinary guest—that he was not an enemy—not a spy. They were trying to prevent him from becoming openly the centre of attention as he was already the centre of consciousness.

The Warden, seated in a deep chair near the fireplace, gave nobody any help. One by one, the spurts of talk failed and died, leaving the one tenor floating, like a solo instrument executing a cadenza when the orchestra has fallen silent:

"The execution of the guilty is unpleasant—but not nearly so disturbing as the slaughter of the innocents. If you are out for my blood, won't you allow me to hand you a more serviceable weapon?"

He glanced round and, finding that everybody but Miss Pyke and themselves was sitting down silent, made a brief, interrogative pause, which looked like politeness, but which Harriet mentally classed as "good theatre."

Miss Pyke led the way to a large sofa near Miss Hillyard's window-seat and said, as she settled herself in the corner of it:

"Do you mean the murderer's victims?"

"No," said Peter, "I meant my own victims."

He sat down between Miss Pyke and Miss Barton, and went on in a pleasantly conversational tone:

"For example; I happened to find out that a young woman had murdered an old one for her money. It didn't matter much: the old woman was dying in any case, and the girl (though she didn't know that) would have inherited the money in any case. As soon as I started to meddle, the girl set to work again, killed two innocent people to cover her tracks and murderously attacked three others. Finally she killed herself. If I'd left her alone, there might have been only one death instead of four."

"Good gracious!" said Miss Pyke. "But the woman would have been at large."

"Oh, yes. She wasn't a nice woman, and she had a nasty influence on certain people. But who killed those other two innocents–she or society?"

"They were killed," said Miss Barton, "by her fear of the death-penalty. If the unfortunate woman had been medically treated, they and she would still be alive today."

"I told you it was a good weapon. But it isn't as simple as all that. If she hadn't killed those others, we should probably never have caught her, and so far from being medically treated she would be living in prosperity–and incidentally corrupting one or two people's minds, if you think that of any importance."

"You are suggesting, I think," said the Warden, while Miss Barton rebelliously grappled with this problem, "that those innocent victims died for the people; sacrificed to a social principle."

"At any rate, to *your* social principles," said Miss Barton.

"Thank you. I thought you were going to say, to my inquisitiveness."

"I might have done so," said Miss Barton, frankly. "But you lay claim to a principle, so we'll stick to that."

"Who were the other three people attacked?" asked Harriet. (She had no fancy to let Miss Barton get away with it too easily.)

"A lawyer, a colleague of mine and myself. But that doesn't prove that I have any principles. I'm quite capable of getting killed for the fun of the thing. Who isn't?"

"I know," said the Dean. "It's funny that we get so solemn about murders and executions and mind so little about taking risks in motoring and swimming and climbing mountains and so on. I suppose we *do* prefer to die for the fun of the thing."

"The social principle seems to be," suggested Miss Pyke, "that we should die for our own fun and not other people's."

"Of course I admit," said Miss Barton, rather angrily, "that murder must be prevented and murderers kept from doing further harm. But they ought not to be punished and they certainly ought not to be killed."

"I suppose they ought to be kept in hospitals at vast expense, along with other unfit specimens," said Miss Edwards. "Speaking as a biologist, I must say I think public money might be better employed. What with the number of imbeciles and physical wrecks we allow to go about and propagate their species, we shall end by devitalizing whole nations."

"Miss Schuster-Slatt would advocate sterilization," said the Dean.

"They're trying it in Germany, I believe," said Miss Edwards.

"Together," said Miss Hillyard, "with the relegation of woman to her proper place in the home."

"But they execute people there quite a lot," said Wimsey, "so Miss Barton can't take over their organization lock, stock and barrel."

Miss Barton uttered a loud protest against any such suggestion, and returned to her contention that *her* social principles were opposed to violence of every description.

"Bosh!" said Miss Edwards. "You can't carry through any principle without doing violence to somebody. Either directly or indirectly. Every time you disturb the balance of nature you let in violence. And if you leave nature alone you get violence in any case. I quite agree that murderers shouldn't be hanged–it's wasteful and unkind. But I don't agree that they should be comfortably fed and housed while decent people go short. Economically speaking, they should be used for laboratory experiments."

"To assist the further preservatlon of the unfit?" asked Wimsey, drily.

"To assist in establishing scientific facts," replied Miss Edwards, more drily still.

"Shake hands," said Wimsey. "Now we have found common ground to stand on. Establish the facts, no matter what comes of it."

"On that ground, Lord Peter," said the Warden, "your inquisitiveness becomes a principle. And a very dangerous one."

"But the fact that A killed B isn't necessarily the whole of the truth," persisted Miss Barton. "A's provocation and state of health are facts, too."

"Nobody surely disputes that," said Miss Pyke. "But one can scarcely ask the investigator to go beyond his job. If we mayn't establish any conclusion for fear somebody should make an injudicious use of it, we are back in the days of Galileo. There would be an end to discovery."

"Well," said the Dean, "I wish we could stop discovering things like poison-gas."

"There can be no objection to the making of discoveries," said Miss Hillyard; "but is it always expedient to publish them? In the case of Galileo, the Church—"

"You'll never get any scientist to agree there," broke in Miss Edwards. "To suppress a fact is to publish a falsehood."

For a few minutes Harriet lost the thread of the discussion, which now became general. That it had been deliberately pushed to this point, she could see; but what Peter wanted to make of it, she had no idea. Yet he was obviously interested. His eyes, under their half-closed lids, were alert. He was like a cat waiting at a mouse-hole. Or was she half-consciously connecting him with his own blazon? "Sable: three mice courant argent; a crescent for difference. The crest a domestick catt . . . . "

"Of course," said Miss Hillyard in a hard, sarcastic voice, "if you think private loyalties should come before loyalty to one's job . . . . "

("Couched as to spring, proper.") That was what he had been waiting for, then. One could almost see the silken fur ripple.

"Of course, I don't say that one should be disloyal to one's job for private reasons," said Miss Lydgate. "But surely, if one takes on personal responsibilities, one owes a duty in that direction. If one's job interferes with them, perhaps one should give up the job."

"I quite agree," said Miss Hillyard. "But then, my private responsibilities are few, and possibly I have no right to speak. What is your opinion, Mrs. Goodwin?"

There was a most unpleasant pause.

"If you mean that personally," said the Secretary, getting up and facing the Tutor, "I am so far of your opinion that I have asked Dr. Baring to accept my resignation. Not because of any of the monstrous allegations that have been made about me, but because I realize that under the circumstances I can't do my work as well as I ought. But you are all very much mistaken if you think *I* am at the bottom of the trouble in this college. I'm going now, and you can say what you like about me—but may I say that anybody with a passion for facts will do better to collect them from unprejudiced sources. Miss Barton at least will admit that mental health is a fact like another."

Into the horrified silence that followed, Peter dropped three words like lumps of ice.

"Please don't go."

Mrs. Goodwin stopped short with her hand on the door.

"It would be a great pity," said the Warden, "to take anything personally that is said in a general discussion. I feel sure Miss Hillyard meant nothing of that kind. Naturally, some people have better opportunities than others for seeing both sides of a question. In your own line of work, Lord Peter, such conflicts of loyalty must frequently occur."

"Oh, yes. I once thought I had the agreeable choice between hanging either my brother or my sister. Fortunately, it came to nothing."

"But supposing it had come to something?" demanded Miss Barton, pinning the *argumentum ad hominem* with a kind of relish.

"Oh, well– What does the ideal detective do then, Miss Vane?"

"Professional etiquette," said Harriet, "would suggest an extorted confession, followed by poison for two in the library."

"You see how easy it is, when you stick to the rules," said Wimsey. "Miss Vane feels no compunction. She wipes me out with a firm hand, rather than damage my reputation. But the question isn't always so simple. How about the artist of genius who has to choose between letting his family starve and painting pot-boilers to keep them?"

"He's no business to have a wife and family," said Miss Hillyard.

"Poor devil! Then he has the further interesting choice between repressions and immorality. Mrs. Goodwin, I gather, would object to the repressions and some people might object to the immorality."

"That doesn't matter," said Miss Pyke. "You have hypothesized a wife and family. Well–he could stop painting. That, if he really is a genius, would be a loss to the world. But he mustn't paint bad pictures–that would be really immoral."

"Why?" asked Miss Edwards. "What do a few bad pictures matter, more or less?"

"Of course they matter," said Miss Shaw. She knew a good deal about painting. "A bad picture by a good painter is a betrayal of truth–his own truth."

"That's only a relative kind of truth," objected Miss Edwards.

The Dean and Miss Burrows fell headlong upon this remark, and Harriet, seeing the argument in danger of getting out of hand, thought it time to retrieve the ball and send it back. She knew now what was wanted, though not why it was wanted.

"If you can't agree about painters, make it someone else. Make it a scientist."

"I've no objection to scientific pot-boilers," said Miss Edwards. "I mean, a popular book isn't necessarily unscientific."

"So long," said Wimsey, "as it doesn't falsify the facts. But it might be a different kind of thing. To take a concrete instance–somebody wrote a novel called *The Search*–"

"C. P. Snow," said Miss Burrows. "It's funny you should mention that. It was the book that the–"

"I know," said Peter. "That's possibly why it was in my mind."

"I never read the book," said the Warden.

"Oh, I did," said the Dean. "It's about a man who starts out to be a scientist and gets on very well till, just as he's going to be appointed to an important executive post, he finds he's made a careless error in a scientific paper. He didn't check his assistant's results, or something. Somebody finds out, and he doesn't get the job. So he decides he doesn't really care about science after all."

"Obviously not," said Miss Edwards. "He only cared about the post."

"But," said Miss Chilperic, "if it was only a mistake–"

"The point about it," said Wimsey, "is what an elderly scientist says to him. He tells him: 'The only ethical principle which has made science possible is that the truth shall be told all the time. If we do not penalize false statements made in error, we open up the way for false statements by intention. And a false statement of fact, made deliberately, is the most serious crime a scientist can commit.' Words to that effect. I may not be quoting quite correctly."

"Well, that's true, of course. Nothing could possibly excuse deliberate falsification."

"There's no sense in deliberate falsification, anyhow," said the Bursar. "What could anybody gain by it?"

"It has been done," said Miss Hillyard, "frequently. To get the better of an argument. Or out of ambition."

"Ambition to be what?" cried Miss Lydgate. "What satisfaction could one possibly get out of a reputation one knew one didn't deserve? It would be horrible."

Her innocent indignation upset everybody's gravity.

"How about the Forged Decretals . . . Chatterton . . . Ossian . . . Henry Ireland . . . those Nineteenth-Century Pamphlets the other day . . .?"

"I know," said Miss Lydgate, perplexed. "I know people do it. But *why?* They must be mad."

"In the same novel," said the Dean, "somebody deliberately falsifies a result–later on, I mean–in order to get a job. And the man who made the original mistake finds it out. But he says nothing, because the other man is very badly off and has a wife and family to keep."

"These wives and families!" said Peter.

"Does the author approve?" inquired the Warden.

"Well," said the Dean, "the book ends there, so I suppose he does."

"But does anybody here approve? A false statement is published and the man who could correct it lets it go, out of charitable considerations. Would anybody here do that? There's your test case, Miss Barton, with no personalities attached."

"Of course one couldn't do that," said Miss Barton. "Not for ten wives and fifty children."

"Not for Solomon and all his wives and concubines? I congratulate you, Miss Barton, on striking such a fine, unfeminine note. Will nobody say a word for the women and children?"

("I knew he was going to be mischievous," thought Harriet.)

"You'd like to hear it, wouldn't you?" said Miss Hillyard.

"You've got us in a cleft stick," said the Dean. "If we say it, you can point out that womanliness unfits us for learning; and if we don't, you can point out that learning makes us unwomanly."

"Since I can make myself offensive either way," said Wimsey, "you have nothing to gain by not telling the truth."

"The truth is," said Mrs. Goodwin, "that nobody could possibly defend the indefensible."

"It sounds, anyway, like a manufactured case," said Miss Allison, briskly. "It could very seldom happen; and if it did–"

"Oh, it happens," said Miss de Vine. "It has happened. It happened to me.

I don't mind telling you—without names, of course When I was at Flamborough College, examining for the professorial these in York University, there was a man who sent in a very interesting paper on a historical subject. It was a most persuasive piece of argument; only I happened to know that the whole contention was quite untrue, because a letter that absolutely contradicted it was actually in existence in a certain very obscure library in a foreign town. I'd come across it when I was reading up something else. That wouldn't have mattered, of course. But the internal evidence showed that the man must have had access to that library. So I had to make an inquiry, and I found that he really had been there and must have seen the letter and deliberately suppressed it."

"But how could you be so sure he had seen the letter?" asked Miss Lydgate anxiously. "He might carelessly have overlooked it. That would be a very different matter."

"He not only had seen it," replied Miss de Vine; "he stole it. We made him admit as much. He had come upon that letter when his thesis was nearly complete, and he had no time to re-write it. And it was a great blow to him apart from that, because he had grown enamoured of his own theory and couldn't bear to give it up."

"That's the mark of an unsound scholar, I'm afraid," said Miss Lydgate in a mournful tone, as one speaks of an incurable cancer.

"But here is the curious thing," went on Miss de Vine. "He was unscrupulous enough to let the false conclusion stand; but he was too good a historian to destroy the letter. He kept it."

"You'd think," said Miss Pyke, "it would be as painful as biting on a sore tooth."

"Perhaps he had some idea of rediscovering it some day," said Miss de Vine, "and setting himself right with his conscience. I don't know, and I don't think he knew very well himself."

"What happened to him?" asked Harriet.

"Well, that was the end of him of course. He lost the professorship, naturally, and they took away his M.A. degree as well. A pity, because he was brilliant in his own way—and very good-looking, if that has anything to do with it."

"Poor man!" said Miss Lydgate. "He must have needed the post very badly."

"It meant a good deal to him financially. He was married and not well off. I don't know what became of him. That was about six years ago. He dropped out completely. One was sorry about it, but there it was."

"You couldn't possibly have done anything else," said Miss Edwards.

"Of course not. A man as undependable as that is not only useless, but dangerous. He might do anything."

"You'd think it would be a lesson to him," said Miss Hillyard. "It didn't pay, did it? Say he sacrificed his professional honour for the women and children we hear so much about—but in the end it left him worse off."

"But that," said Peter, "was only because he committed the extra sin of being found out."

"It seems to me," began Miss Chilperic, timidly—and then stopped.

"Yes?" said Peter.

"Well," said Miss Chilperic, "oughtn't the women and children to have a point of view? I mean—suppose the wife knew that her husband had done a thing like that for her, what would she feel about it?"

"That's a very important point," said Harriet. "You'd think she'd feel too ghastly for words."

"It depends," said the Dean. "I don't believe nine women out of ten would care a dash."

"That's a monstrous thing to say," cried Miss Hillyard.

"You think a wife might feel sensitive about her husband's honour–even if it was sacrificed on her account?" said Miss Stevens. "Well–I don't know."

"I should think," said Miss Chilperic, stammering a little in her earnestness, "she would feel like a man who–I mean, wouldn't it be like living on somebody's immoral earnings?"

"There," said Peter, "if I may say so, I think you are exaggerating. The man who does that–if he isn't too far gone to have any feelings at all–is hit by other considerations, some of which have nothing whatever to do with ethics. But it is extremely interesting that you should make the comparison." He looked at Miss Chilperic so intently that she blushed.

"Perhaps that was rather a stupid thing to say."

"No. But if it ever occurs to people to value the honour of the mind equally with the honour of the body, we shall get a social revolution of a quite unparalleled sort–and very different from the kind that is being made at the moment."

Miss Chilperic looked so much alarmed at the idea of fostering a social revolution that only the opportune entry of two Common Room scouts to remove the coffee-cups and relieve her of the necessity of replying seemed to have saved her from sinking through the floor.

"Well," said Harriet, "I agree absolutely with Miss Chilperic. If anybody did a dishonourable thing and then said he did it for one's own sake, it would be the last insult. How could one ever feel the same to him again?"

"Indeed," said Miss Pyke, "it must surely vitiate the whole relationship."

"Oh, nonsense!" cried the Dean. "How many women care two hoots about anybody's intellectual integrity? Only overeducated women like us. So long as the man didn't forge a check or rob the till or do something socially degrading, most women would think he was perfectly justified. Ask Mrs. Bones the Butcher's Wife or Miss Tape the Tailor's Daughter how much they would worry about suppressing a fact in a mouldy old historical thesis."

"They'd back up their husbands, in any case," said Miss Allison. "My man, right or wrong, they'd say. Even if he *did* rob the till."

"Of course they would," said Miss Hillyard. "That's what the man wants. *He* wouldn't say thank you for a critic on the hearth."

"He must have the womanly woman, you think?" said Harriet. "What is it, Annie? My coffee-cup? Here you are . . . . Somebody who will say, 'The greater the sin the greater the sacrifice–and consequently the greater devotion.' Poor Miss Schuster-Slatt! . . . I suppose it is comforting to be told that one is loved whatever one does."

"Ah, yes," said Peter, in his reediest wood-wind voice:

*"And these say: 'No more now my knight*
*Or God's knight any longer–you,*
*Being than they so much more white,*
*So much more pure and good and true*

*"Will cling to me for ever–*

William Morris had his moments of being a hundred-percent manly man."

"Poor Morris!" said the Dean.

"He was young at the time," said Peter, indulgently. "It's odd, when you come to think of it, that the expressions 'manly' and 'womanly' should be almost more offensive than their opposites. One is tempted to believe that there may be something indelicate about sex after all."

"It all comes of this here eddication," pronounced the Dean, as the door shut behind the last of the coffee-service. "Here we sit round in a ring, dissociating ourselves from kind Mrs. Bones and that sweet girl, Miss Tape–"

"Not to mention," put in Harriet, "those fine, manly fellows, the masculine Tapes and Boneses–"

"And clacking on in the *most* unwomanly manner about intellectual integrity."

"While I," said Peter, "sit desolate in the midst, like a lodge in a garden of cucumbers."

"You look it," said Harriet, laughing. "The sole relic of humanity in a cold, bitter and indigestible wilderness."

There was a laugh, and a momentary silence. Harriet could feel a nervous tension in the room–little threads of anxiety and expectation strung out, meeting, crossing, quivering. Now, they were all saying to themselves, now something is going to be said about IT. The ground has been surveyed, the coffee has been cleared out of the road, the combatants are stripped for action–now, this amiable gentleman with the well-filed tongue will come out in his true colours as an inquisitor, and it is all going to be very uncomfortable.

Lord Peter took out his handkerchief, polished his monocle carefully, readjusted it, looked rather severely at the Warden, and lifted up his voice in emphatic, pained and querulous complaint about the Corporation dump.

The Warden had gone, expressing courteous thanks to Miss Lydgate for the hospitality of the Senior Common Room, and graciously inviting his lordship to call upon her in her own house at any convenient time during his stay in Oxford. Various dons rose up and drifted away, murmuring that they had essays to look through before they went to bed. The talk had ranged pleasantly over a variety of topics. Peter had let the reins drop from his hands and let it go whither it would, and Harriet, realizing this, had scarcely troubled to follow it. In the end, there remained only herself and Peter, the Dean, Miss Edwards (who seemed to have taken a strong fancy to Peter's conversation), Miss Chilperic, silent and half-hidden in an obscure position and, rather to Harriet's surprise, Miss Hillyard.

The clocks struck eleven. Wimsey roused himself and said he thought he had better be getting along. Everybody rose. The Old Quad was dark, except for the glean of lighted windows; the sky had clouded, and a rising wind stirred the boughs of the beech-trees.

"Well, good-night," said Miss Edwards. "I'll see that you get a copy of that paper about blood-groups. I think you'll find it of interest."

"I shall, indeed," said Wimsey. "Thank you very much."

Miss Edwards strode briskly away.

"Good-night, Lord Peter."

"Good-night, Miss Chilperic. Let me know when the social revolution is about to begin and I'll come to die upon the barricades."

"I think you would," said Miss Chilperic, astonishingly, and, in defiance of tradition, gave him her hand.

"Good-night," said Miss Hillyard, to the world in general, and whisked quickly past them with her head high.

Miss Chilperic flitted off into the darkness like a pale moth, and the Dean said, "Well!" And then, interrogatively, "Well?"

"Pass, and all's well," said Peter, placidly.

"There were one or two moments, weren't there?" said the Dean. "But on the whole–as well as could be expected."

"I enjoyed myself very much," said Peter, with the mischievous note back in his voice.

"I bet you did," said the Dean. "I wouldn't trust you a yard. Not a yard."

"Oh, yes, you would," said he. "Don't worry."

The Dean, too, was gone.

"You left your gown in my room yesterday," said Harriet "You'd better come and fetch it."

"I brought yours back with me and left it at the Jowett Walk Lodge. Also your dossier. I expect they've been taken up."

"You didn't leave the dossier lying about!"

"What do you take me for? It's wrapped up and sealed."

They crossed the quad slowly.

"There are a lot of questions I want to ask, Peter."

"Oh, yes. And there's one I want to ask you. What is your second name? The one that begins with a D?"

"Deborah, I'm sorry to say. Why?"

"Deborah? Well, I'm damned. All right. I won't call you by it. There's Miss de Vine, I see, still working."

The curtains of the Fellows' window were drawn back this time, and they could see her dark, untidy head, bent over a book.

"She interests me very much," said Peter.

"I like her, you know."

"So do I."

"But I'm afraid those are her kind of hairpins."

"I know they are," said he. He took his hand from his pocket and held it out. They were close under Tudor, and the light from an adjacent window showed a melancholy, spraddle-legged hairpin lying across his palm. "She shed this on the dais after dinner. You saw me pick it up."

"I saw you pick up Miss Shaw's scarf."

"Always the gentleman. May I come up with you, or is that against the regulations?"

"You can come up."

There were a number of students scurrying about the corridors in undress, who looked at Peter with more curiosity than annoyance. In Harriet's room, they found her gown lying on the table, together with the dossier. Peter picked up the book, examined the paper and string and the seals which secured them, each one stamped with the crouching cat and arrogant Wimsey motto.

"If that's been opened, I'll make a meal of hot sealingwax."

He went to the window and looked out into the quad.

"Not a bad observation post–in its way. Thanks. That's all I wanted to look at."

He showed no further curiosity, but took the gown she handed to him and followed her downstairs again.

They were half-way across the quad when he said suddenly:

"Harriet. Do you really prize honesty above every other thing?"

"I think I do. I hope so. Why?"

"If you don't, I am the most blazing fool in Christendom. I am busily engaged in sawing off my own branch. If I am honest, I shall probably lose you altogether. If I am not–"

His voice was curiously rough, as though he were trying to control something; not, she thought, bodily pain or passion, but something more fundamental.

"If you are not," said Harriet, "then *I* shall lose *you*, because you wouldn't be the same person, should you?"

"I don't know. I have a reputation for flippant insincerity. You think I'm honest?"

"I know you are. I couldn't imagine your being anything else."

"And yet at this moment I'm trying to insure myself against the effects of my own honesty. 'I have tried if I could reach that great resolution, to be honest without a thought of heaven or hell.' It looks as though I should get hell either way, though; so I need scarcely bother about the resolutlon. I believe you mean what you say–and I hope I should do the same thing if I didn't believe a word of it."

"Peter, I haven't an idea what you're talking about."

"All the better. Don't worry. I won't behave like this another time. 'The Duke drained a dipper of brandy-and-water and became again the perfect English gentleman.' Give me your hand."

She gave it to him, and he held it for a moment in a firm clasp, and then drew her arm through his. They moved on into the New Quad, arm in arm, in silence. As they passed the archway at the foot of the Hall stairs, Harriet fancied she heard somebody stir in the darkness and saw the faint glimmer of a watching face; but it was gone before she could draw Peter's attention to it.

Padgett unlocked the gate for them; Wimsey, stepping preoccupied over the threshold, tossed him a heedless goodnight.

"Good-night, Major Wimsey, sir!"

"Hullo!" Peter brought back the foot that was already in St. Cross Road, and looked closely into the porter's smiling face.

"My God, yes! Stop a minute. Don't tell me. Caudry–1918–I've got it! Padgett's the name. Corporal Padgett."

"Quite right, sir."

"Well, well, well. I'm damned glad to see you. Looking dashed fit, too. How are you keeping?"

"Fine, thank you, sir." Padgett's large and hairy paw closed warmly over Peter's long fingers. "I says to my wife, when I 'eard you was 'ere, 'I'll lay you anything you like,' I says, 'the Major won't have forgotten.' "

"By jove, no. Fancy finding you here! Last time I saw you, I was being carried away on a stretcher."

"That's right, sir. I 'ad the pleasure of 'elping to dig you out."

"I know you did. I'm glad to see you now, but I was a dashed sight gladder to see you then."

"Yes, sir. Gorblimey, sir–well, there! We thought you was gone that time. I says to Hackett–remember little Hackett, sir?"

"The little red-headed blighter? Yes, of course. What's become of him?"

"Driving a lorry over at Reading, sir, married and three kids. I says to Hackett, 'Lor' lumme!' I says, 'there's old Winderpane gawn'–excuse me, sir–and he says, ' 'Eli! wot ruddy luck!' So I says, 'Don't stand there grizzlin'–maybe 'e ain't gawn after all.' So we–"

"No," said Wimsey. "I fancy I was more frightened than hurt. Unpleasant sensation, being buried alive."

"Well, sir! W'en we finds yer there at the bottom o' that there old Boche dug-out with a big beam acrost yer, I says to Hackett, 'Well,' I says, ' 'e's all 'ere, anyhow.' And he says, 'Thank gawd for Jerry!' 'e says—meanin', if it 'adn't been for that there dug-out—"

"Yes," said Wimsey, "I had a bit of luck there. We lost poor Mr. Danbury, though."

"Yes, sir. Bad thing, that was. A nice young gentleman. Ever see anything of Captain Sidgwick nowadays, sir?"

"Oh, yes. I saw him only the other day at the Bellona Club. He's not very fit these days, I'm sorry to say. Got a dose of gas, you know. Lungs groggy."

"Sorry to hear that, sir. Remember how put about 'e was over that there pig—"

"Hush, Padgett. The less said about that pig, the better."

"Yes, sir. Nice bit o' crackling that pig 'ad on 'im. Coo!" Padgett smacked reminiscent lips. "You 'eard wot 'appened to Sergeant-Major Toop?"

"Toop? No—I've quite lost sight of him. Nothing unpleasant, I hope. Best sergeant-major I ever had."

"Ah! he was a one." Padgett's grin widened. "Well, sir, 'e found 'is match all right. Little bit of a thing—no 'igher than that, but, lummy!"

"Go on, Padgett. You don't say so."

"Yes, sir. When I was workin' in the camel 'ouse at the Zoo—"

"Good God, Padgett!"

"Yes, sir—I see them there and we passed the time o' day. Went round to look 'em up afterwards. Well, there! She give 'im sergeant-major all right. Put 'im through the 'oop proper. You know the old song: Naggin' at a feller as is six foot three—"

"And her only four foot two! Well, well! How are the mighty fallen! By the bye, I'll tell you who I ran into the other day—now, this will surprise you—"

The stream of reminiscence ran remorselessly on, till Wimsey, suddenly reminded of his manners, apologized to Harriet and plunged hastily out, with a promise to return for another chat over old times. Padgett, still beaming, swung the heavy gate to, and locked it.

"Ah!" said Padgett, "he ain't changed much, the major 'asn't. He was a lot younger then, o' course—only just gazetted—but he was regular good officer for all that—and a terror for eye-wash. *And* shavin'—lummy!"

Padgett supporting himself with one hand against the brickwork of the lodge, appeared lost in the long ago.

"'Now, men,' 'e'd say, when we was expectin' a bit of a strafe, 'if you gotter face your Maker, fer gawd's sake, face 'Im with a clean chin.' An! Winder-pane, we called 'im, along of the eyeglass, but meanin' no disrespect. None on us wouldn't 'ear a word agin 'im. Now, there was a chap came to us from another unit—'ulkin' foul-mouthed fellow, wot nobody took to much—'Uggins, that was the name, 'Uggins. Well, this bloke thinks 'e's goin' to be funny, see—and 'e starts callin' the major Little Percy, and usin' opprobrious epithets—"

Here Padgett paused, to select an epithet fit for a lady's ear, but, failing, repeated:

"Opprobrious epithets, miss. And I says to 'im—mind you, this was afore I got my stripes; I was jest a private then, same as 'Uggins—I says to 'im, 'Now, that's quite enough o' that.' And 'e says to me— Well, anyway, the end of it was, we 'ad a lovely scrap, all round the 'ouses."

"Dear me," said Harriet.

"Yes, miss. We was in rest at the time, and next morning, when the sergeant-major falls us in for parade—coo, lummy! we was a pair o' family portraits. The sergeant-major—Sergeant-Major Toop, that was, 'im wot got married like I was sayin'—'e didn't say nothin'—'e knew. And the adjutant, 'e knew too, and 'e didn't say nothin' neither. And blest if, in the middle of it all, we don't see the Major comin' strollin' out. So the adjutant forms us up into line, and I stands there at attention, 'oping as 'Uggins's face looked worse nor what mine did. 'Mornin',' says the Major; and the adjutant and Sergeant-Major Toop says, 'Morning, sir.' So 'e starts to chat casual-like to the sergeant-major, and I see 'is eye goin' up and down the line. 'Sergeant-major!' says he, all of a sudden. 'Sir!' says the sergeant-major. 'What's that man there been doin' to 'imself?' says 'e, meanin' me. 'Sir?' says the sergeant-major, starin' at me like 'e was surprised to see me. 'Looks as if he'd had a nasty accident,' says the Major. 'And what about that other fellow? Don't like to see that sort of thing. Not smart. Fall 'em out.' So the sergeant-major falls us both out. 'H'm,' says the Major, 'I see. What's this man's name?' 'Padgett, sir,' says the sergeant-major. 'Oh,' says he. 'Well, Padgett, what have you been doing to get yourself into a mess like that?' 'Fell over a bucket, sir,' says I, starin' 'ard over 'is shoulder with the only eye I could see out of, 'Bucket?' says 'e, 'very awkward things, buckets. And this other man—I suppose he trod on the mop, eh, sergeant-major?' 'Major wants to know if you trod on the mop,' says Sergeant-Major Toop. 'Yessir,' says 'Uggins, talkin' like 'is mouth 'urt 'im. 'Well,' says the Major, 'when you've got this lot dismissed, give these two men a bucket and a mop apiece and put 'em on fatigue. That'll learn 'em to 'andle these dangerous implements.' 'Yessir,' says Sergeant-Major Toop. 'Carry on,' says the Major. So we carries on. 'Uggins says to me arterwards, 'D'you think 'e knew?' 'Knew?' says I, 'course 'e knew. Ain't much 'e don't know.' Arter that, 'Uggins kep' 'is epithets to 'isself."

Harriet expressed due appreciation of this anecdote, which was delivered with a great deal of gusto, and took leave of Padgett. For some reason, this affair of a mop and a bucket seemed to have made Padgett Peter's slave for life. Men were very odd.

There was nobody under the Hall arches as she returned, but as she passed the West end of the Chapel, she thought she saw something dark pass like a shadow into the Fellows' Garden. She followed it. Her eyes were growing accustomed to the dimness of the summer night and she could see the figure walking swiftly up and down, up and down, and hear the rustle of its long skirt upon the grass.

There was only one person in College who had worn a trailing frock that evening, and that was Miss Hillyard. She walked in the Fellows' Garden for an hour and a half.

## 18

Go tell that witty fellow, my godson, to get home. It is no season to fool it here!

Queen Elizabeth

"LOR'!" SAID the Dean.

She gazed with interest from the Senior Common Room window, teacup in hand.

"What's the matter?"inquired Miss Allison.

"*Who* is that incredibly beautiful young man?"

"Flaxman's fiance, I expect, isn't it?"

"A beautiful young man?" said Miss Pyke. "I should like to see him." She moved to the window.

"Don't be ridiculous," said the Dean. "I know Flaxman's Byron by heart. This is an ash-blond in a House blazer."

"Oh, dear me!" said Miss Pyke. "Apollo Belvedere in spotless flannels. He appears to be unattached. Remarkable."

Harriet put down her cup and rose from the depths of the largest armchair.

"Perhaps he belongs to that bunch playing tennis," hazarded Miss Allison.

"Little Cooke's scrubby friends? My *dear!*"

"Why all the excitement, anyway?" asked Miss Hillyard.

"Beautiful young men are always exciting," said the Dean.

"That," said Harriet, at length getting a glimpse of the wonder-youth over Miss Pyke's shoulder, "is Viscount Saint-George."

"Another of your aristocratic friends?" asked Miss Barton.

"His nephew," replied Harriet; not very coherently.

"Oh!" said Miss Barton. "Well, I don't see why you need all gape at him like a lot of schoolgirls."

She crossed over to the table, cut herself a slice of cake and glanced casually out of the farther window.

Lord Saint-George stood, with a careless air of owning the place, at the corner of the Library Wing, watching a game of tennis being played between two bare-backed students and two young men whose shirts kept on escaping from their belts. Growing tired of this, he sauntered past the windows towards Queen Elizabeth, his eye roving over a group of Shrewsburians a-sprawl under the beeches, like that of a young Sultan inspecting a rather unpromising consignment of Circassian slaves.

"Supercilious little beast!" thought Harriet; and wondered if he was looking for her. If he was, he could wait, or ask properly at the Lodge.

"Oho!" said the Dean. "So *that's* how the milk got into the coco-nut!"

From the door of the Library Wing there issued slowly Miss de Vine, and behind her, grave and deferential, Lord Peter Wimsey. They skirted the tennis-court in earnest conversation. Lord Saint-George, viewing them from afar, advanced to meet them. They joined forces on the path. They stood for a little time talking. They moved away towards the Lodge.

"Dear me!" said the Dean. "Abduction of Helen de Vine by Paris and Hector."

"No, no," said Miss Pyke. "Paris was the brother of Hector, not his nephew. I do not think he had any uncles."

"Talking of uncles," said the Dean, "is it true, Miss Hillyard, that Richard III– I thought she was here."

"She *was* here," said Harriet.

"Helen is being returned to us," said the Dean. "The siege of Troy is postponed."

The trio were returning again up the path. Half-way along Miss de Vine took leave of the two men and returned towards her own room.

At that moment, the watchers in the S.C.R. were petrified to behold a portent. Miss Hillyard emerged from the foot of the Hall stair, bore down upon the uncle and nephew, addressed them, cut Lord Peter neatly off from his convoy and towed him firmly away towards the New Quad.

"Glory *alleluia!*" said the Dean. "Hadn't you better go out and rescue your young friend? He's been deserted again."

"You could offer him a cup of tea," suggested Miss Pyke. "It would be an agreeable diversion for us."

"I'm surprised at you, Miss Pyke," said Miss Barton. "No man is safe from women like you."

"Now, where have I heard that sentiment before?" said the Dean.

"In one of the Poison-letters," said Harriet.

"If you're suggesting—" began Miss Barton.

"I'm only suggesting," said the Dean, "that it's a bit of a cliche."

"I meant it for a joke," retorted Miss Barton, angrily. "Some people have no sense of humour."

She went out and slammed the door. Lord Saint-George had wandered back and was sitting in the loggia leading up to the Library. He rose politely as Miss Barton stalked past him on the way to her room, and made some remark, to which the Fellow replied briefly, but with a smile.

"Insinuating men, these Wimseys," said the Dean. "Vamping the S.C.R. right and left."

Harriet laughed, but in Saint-George's quick, appraising glance at Miss Barton she had again seen his uncle look for a moment out of his eyes. These family resemblances were unnerving. She curled herself into the window-seat and watched for nearly ten minutes. The viscount sat still, smoking a cigarette, and looking entirely at his ease. Miss Lydgate, Miss Burrows and Miss Shaw came in and began to pour out tea. The tennis-party finished the set and moved away. Then, from the left, came a quick, light step along the gravel walk.

"Hullo!" said Harriet to the owner of the step.

"Hullo!" said Peter. "Fancy seeing you here!" He grinned. "Come and talk to Gerald. He's in the loggia."

"I see him quite plainly," said Harriet. "His profile has been much admired."

"As a good adopted aunt, why didn't you go and be kind to the poor lad?"

"I never was one to interfere. I keep myself *to* myself."

"Well, come now."

Harriet got down from the window-seat and joined Wimsey outside.

"I brought him here," said Peter, "to see if he could make any identifications. But he doesn't seem able to."

Lord Saint-George greeted Harriet enthusiasticaliy.

"There was another female went past me," he said, turning to Peter. "Grey hair badly bobbed. Earnest manner. Dressed in sack-cloth. Institutional touch about her. I got speech of her."

"Miss Barton," said Harriet.

"Right sort of eyes; wrong sort of voice. I don't think it's her. It might be the one that collared you, Uncle. She had a kind of a lean and hungry look."

"H'm!" said Peter. "How about the first one?"

"I'd like to see her without her glasses."

"If you mean Miss de Vine," said Harriet, "I doubt whether she could see very far without them."

"That's a point," said Peter, thoughtfully.

"I'm sorry to be so vague and all that," said Lord Saint-George. "But it's not easy to identify a hoarse whisper and a pair of eyes seen once by moonlight."

"No," said Peter, "it needs a good deal of practice."

"Practice be blowed," retorted his nephew. "I'm not going to make a practice of it."

"It's not a bad sport," said Peter. "You might take it up till you can start games again."

"How's the shoulder getting on?" inquired Harriet.

"Oh, not too bad, thanks. The massage bloke is working wonders with it. I can lift the old arm shoulder-high now. It's quite serviceable–for some things."

By way of demonstratlon he threw the damaged arm round Harriet's shoulders, and kissed her rapidly and expertly before she could dodge him.

"Children, children!" cried his uncle, plaintively, "remember where you are."

"It's all right for *me*," said Lord Saint-George. "*I'm* an adopted nephew. Isn't that right, Aunt Harriet?"

"Not bang underneath the windows of the S.C.R.," said Harriet.

"Come round the corner, then," said the viscount, impenitently, "and I'll do it again. As Uncle Peter says, these things need a good deal of practice."

He was inpudently set upon tormenting his uncle, and Harriet felt extremely angry with him. However, to show annoyance was to play into his hands. She smiled upon him pityingly and uttered the Brasenose porter's classic rebuke:

"It's no good you making a noise, gentlemen. The Dean ain't a-coming down tonight."

This actually silenced him for the moment. She turned to Peter, who said:

"Have you any commissions in Town?"

"Why, are you going back?"

"I'm running up tonight and on to York in the morning. I expect to get back on Thursday."

"York?"

"Yes; I want to see a man there–about a dog, and all that."

"Oh, I see. Well–if it wouldn't be out of your way to call at my flat, you might take up a few chapters of manuscript to my secretary. I'd rather trust you than the post. Could you manage it?"

"With very great pleasure," said Wimsey, formally.

She ran up to her room to get the papers, and from the window observed that the Wimsey family was having the matter out with itself. When she came down with the parcel, she found the nephew waiting at the door of Tudor, rather red in the face.

"Please, I am to apologize."

"I should think so," said Harriet, severely. "I can't be disgraced like this in my own quad. Frankly, I can't afford it."

"I'm most frightfully sorry," said Lord Saint-George. "It was rotten of me. Honestly, I wasn't thinking of anything except getting Uncle Peter's goat. And if it's any satisfaction to you," he added, ruefully, "I got it."

"Well, be decent to him; he's very decent to you."

"I will be good," said Peter's nephew, taking the parcel from her, and they proceeded amicably together till Peter rejoined them at the Lodge.

"Damn that boy!" said Wimsey, when he had sent Saint-George ahead to start up the car.

"Oh, Peter, don't worry about every little thing so dreadfully. What does it matter? He only wanted to tease you."

"It's a pity he can't find some other way to do it. I seem to be a perfect mill-stone tied round your neck, and the sooner I clear out the better."

"Oh, for goodness' sake!" said Harriet irritated. "If you're going to be morbid about it, it certainly would be better for *you* if you *did* clear out. I've told you so before."

Lord Saint-George, finding his elders dilatory, blew a cheerful "hi-tiddley-hi-ti, pom, pom" on the horn.

"Damn and blast!" said Peter. He took gate and path at a bound, pushed his nephew angrily out of the driving-seat, jerked the door of the Daimler to noisily and shot off up the road with a bellowing roar. Harriet, finding herself unexpectedly possessed of a magnificent fit of bad temper, went back, determined to extract the last ounce of enjoyment out of it; an exercise in which she was greatly helped by the discovery that the little episode on the loggia had greatly intrigued the Senior Common Room, and by learning from Miss Allison, after Hall, that Miss Hillyard, when she heard of it, had made some very unpleasant observations, which it was only right that Miss Vane should know about.

Oh, God! thought Harriet, alone in her room, what have I done, more than thousands of other people, except have the rotten luck to be tried for my life and have the whole miserable business dragged out into daylight? . . . Anybody would think I'd been punished enough. . . . But nobody can forget it for a moment. . . . I can't forget it. . . . Peter can't forget it. . . . If Peter wasn't a fool he'd chuck it. . . . He must see how hopeless it all is. . . . Does he think I like to see him suffering vicarious agonies? . . . Does he really suppose I could ever marry him for the pleasure of seeing him suffer agonies?. . .Can't he see that the only thing for me to do is to keep out of it all? . . . What the devil possessed me to bring him to Oxford? . . . Yes—and I thought it would be so nice to retire to Oxford . . . to have "unpleasant observations" made about me by Miss Hillyard, who's half potty, if you ask me. . . . Somebody's potty, anyhow . . . that seems to be what happens to one if one keeps out of the way of love and marriage and all the rest of the muddle. . . . Well if Peter fancies I'm going to "accept the protection of his name" and be grateful, he's damn well mistaken. . . . A nice, miserable business that'd be for him. . . . It's a nice, miserable business for him, too, if he really wants me—if he does—and can't have what he wants because I had the rotten luck to be tried for a murder I didn't do. . . . It looks as if he was going to get hell either way. . . . Well, let him get hell, it's his lookout. . . . It's a pity he saved me from being hanged—he probably wishes by now he'd left me alone. . . . I suppose any decently grateful person would give him what he wants. . . . But it wouldn't be much gratitude to make him miserable. . . . We should both be perfectly miserable, because neither of us could ever forget. . . . I very nearly did forget the other day on the river. . . . And I had forgotten this afternoon, only he remembered it first. . . . Damn that impudent little beast! how horribly cruel the young can be to the middle-aged!. . . I wasn't frightfully kind myself. . . . And I did know what I was doing. . . . It's a good thing Peter's gone . . . but I wish he hadn't gone and left me in this ghastly place where people go off their heads and write horrible letters. . . . "When I am from him I am dead till I be with him." . . . No, it won't do to feel like that. . . . I won't get mixed up with that kind of thing again. . . . I'll stay out of it. . . . I'll stay here . . . where people go queer in their heads. . . . Oh, God, what have I done, that I should be such a misery to myself and other people? Nothing more than thousands of women . . .

Round and round, like a squirrel in a cage, till at last Harriet had to say firmly to herself: This won't do, or I shall go potty myself. I'd better keep my mind on the job. What's taken Peter to York? Miss de Vine? If I hadn't lost my temper I might have found out, instead of wasting time in quarrelling. I wonder if he's made any notes on the dossier.

She took up the loose-leaf book, which was still wrapped in its paper and string and sealed all over with the Wimsey crest. "As my Whimsy takes me"—Peter's whimsies had taken him into a certain amount of trouble. She broke the seals impatiently; but the result was disappointing. He had marked nothing—presumably he had copied out anything he wanted. She turned the pages, trying to piece some sort of solution together, but too tired to think coherently. And then—yes; here was his writing, sure enough, but not on a page of the dossier. This was the unfinished sonnet—and of all the idiotic things to do, to leave half-finished sonnets mixed up with one's detective work for other people to see! A schoolgirl trick, enough to make anybody blush. Particularly since, from what she remembered of the sonnet, its sentiments had become remarkably inappropriate to the state of her feelings.

But here it was: and in the interval it had taken to itself a sestet and stood, looking a little unbalanced, with her own sprawling hand above and Peter's deceptively neat script below, like a large top on a small spindle.

Here then at home, by no more storms distrest,
　Folding laborious hands we sit, wings furled;
　Here in close perfume lies the rose-leaf curled,
Here the sun stands and knows not east nor west,
Here no tide runs; we have come, last and best,
　From the wide zone in dizzying circles hurled
　To that still centre where the spinning world
Sleeps on its axis, to the heart of rest.

Lay on thy whips, O Love, that we upright,
　Poised on the perilous point, in no lax bed
　　May sleep, as tension at the verberant core
Of music sleeps; for, if thou spare to smite,
　Staggering, we stoop, stooping, fall dumb and dead,
　　And, dying so, sleep our sweet sleep no more.

Having achieved this, the poet appeared to have lost countenance; for he had added the comment:

"A very conceited, metaphysical conclusion!"

So. So there was the turn she had vainly sought for the sestet! Her beautiful, big, peaceful humming-top turned to a whip-top, and sleeping, as it were, upon compulsion. (And, damn him! how *dared* he pick up her word "sleep" and use it four times in as many lines, and each time in a different foot, as though juggling with the accent-shift were child's play? And drag out the last half-line with those great, heavy, drugged, drowsy monosyllables, contradicting the sense so as to deny their own contradiction? It was not one of the world's great sestets, but it was considerably better than her own octave: which was monstrous of it.)

But if she wanted an answer to her questions about Peter, there it was, quite appallingly plain. He did not want to forget, or to be quiet, or to be spared things, or to stay put. All he wanted was some kind of central stability, and he was apparently ready to take anything that came along, so long as it stimulated him to keep that precarious balance. And of course, if he really felt like that, everything he had ever said or done, as far as she was concerned, was perfectly consistent. "Mine is only a balance of opposing forces." . . ."What does it matter if it hurts like hell, so long as it makes a good book?" . . . "What is the use of making mistakes if you don't make use of them?" . . . "Feeling like Judas is part of the job.". . ."The first thing a principle does is to kill somebody." . . . If that was his attitude, it was clearly ridiculous to urge him, in kindly tones, to stand aside for fear he might get a rap over the shins.

He had tried standing aside. "I have been running away from myself for twenty years, and it doesn't work." He no longer believed that the Ethiopian could change his skin to rhinoceros hide. Even in the five years or so that she had known him, Harriet had seen him strip off his protections, layer by layer, till there was uncommonly little left but the naked truth.

That, then, was what he wanted her for. For some reason, obscure to herself and probably also to him, she had the power to force him outside his defences. Perhaps, seeing her struggling in a trap of circumstance, he had walked out deliberately to her assistance. Or perhaps the sight of her struggles had warned him what might happen to him, if he remained in a trap of his own making.

Yet with all this, he seemed willing to let her run back behind the barriers of the mind, provided—yes, he was consistent after all—provided she would make her own way of escape through her work. He was, in fact, offering her the choice between himself and Wilfrid. He did recognize that she had an outlet which he had not.

And that, she supposed, was why he was so morbidly sensitive about his own part in the comedy. His own needs were (as he saw the matter) getting between her and her legitimate way of escape. They involved her in difficulties which he could not share, because she had consistently refused him the right to share them. He had nothing of his nephew's cheerful readiness to take and have. Careless, selfish little beast, thought Harriet (meaning the viscount), can't he leave his uncle alone?

. . . It was just conceivable, by the way, that Peter was quite plainly and simply and humanly jealous of his nephew—not, of course, of his relations with Harriet (which would be disgusting and ridiculous), but of the careless young egotism which made those relations possible.

And, after all, Peter had been right. It was difficult to account for Lord Saint-George's impertinence without allowing people to assume that she was on terms with Peter which would explain that kind of thing. It had undoubtedly made an awkwardness. It was easy to say, "Oh, yes. I knew him slightly and went to see him when he was laid up after a motor accident." She did not really very much mind if Miss Hillyard supposed that with a person of her dubious reputation all and any liberties might be taken. But she did mind the corollary that might be drawn about Peter. That after five years' patient friendship he should have acquired only the right to look on while his nephew romped in public went near to making him look a fool. But anything else would not be true. She had placed him in exactly that imbecile position, and she admitted that that was not very pretty conduct.

She went to bed thinking more about another person than about herself. This goes to prove that even minor poetry may have its practical uses.

On the following night, a strange and sinister thing happened.

Harriet had gone, by appointment, to dine with her Somerville friend, and to meet a distinguished writer on the mid-Victorian period, from whom she expected to gain some useful information about Le Fanu. She was sitting in the friend's room, where about half a dozen people were gathered to do honour to the distinguished writer, when the telephone rang.

"Oh, Miss Vane," said her hostess. "Somebody wants you from Shrewsbury."

Harriet excused herself to the distinguished guest, and went out into the small lobby in which the telephone was placed. A voice which she could not quite recognize answered her "Hullo!"

"Is that Miss Vane?"

"Yes—who's that speaking?"

"This is Shrewsbury College. Could you please come round quickly. There's been another disturbance."

"Good heavens! What's happened? Who is speaking, please?"

"I'm speaking for the Warden. Could you please—?"

"Is that Miss Parsons?"

"No, miss. This is Dr. Baring's maid."

"But what has happened?"

"I don't know, miss. The Warden said I was to ask you to come at once."

"Very well. I'll be there in about ten or fifteen minutes. I haven't got the car. I'll be there about eleven."

"Very good, miss. Thank you."

The connection was severed. Harriet hurriedly got hold of her friend, explained that she had been called away suddenly, said her good-byes and hurried out.

She had crossed the Garden Quad and was just passing between the Old Hall and the Maitland Buildings, when she was visited with an absurd recollection. She remembered Peter's saying to her one day:

"The heroines of thrillers deserve all they get. When a mysterious voice rings them up and says it is Scotland Yard, they never think of ringing back to verify the call. Hence the prevalence of kidnapping."

She knew where Somerville kept its public call-box; presumably she could get a call from there. She went in; tried it; found that it was through to the Exchange; dialled the Shrewsbury number, and on getting it asked to be put through to the Warden's Lodgings.

A voice answered her; not the same person's that had rung her up before.

"Is that Dr. Baring's maid?"

"Yes, madam. Who is speaking, please?"

("Madam"—the other voice had said "miss." Harriet knew now why she had felt vaguely uneasy about the call. She had subconsciously remembered that the Warden's maid said "Madam.")

"This is Miss Harriet Vane, speaking from Somerville. Was it you who rang me up just now?"

"No, madam."

"Somebody rang me up, speaking for the Warden. Was it Cook, or anybody else in the house?"

"I don't think anybody has telephoned from here, madam."

(Some mistake. Perhaps the Warden had sent her message from somewhere in College and she had misunderstood the speaker or the speaker her.)

"Could I speak to the Warden?"

"The Warden isn't in College, madam. She went out to the theatre with Miss Martin. I'm expecting them back any minute."

"Oh, thank you. Never mind. There must have been some mistake. Would you please put me back to the Lodge?"

When she heard Padgett's voice again she asked for Miss Edwards, and while the connection was being made, she thought fast.

It was beginning to look very much like a bogus call. But why, in Heaven's name? What would have happened if she had gone back to Shrewsbury straight away? Since she had not the car with her, she would have gone in by the private gate, past the thick bushes by the Fellows' Garden—the Fellows' Garden, where people walked by night— "Miss Edwards isn't in her room, Miss Vane."

"Oh! The scouts are all in bed, I suppose."

"Yes, miss. Shall I ask Mrs. Padgett to see if she can find her?"

"No—see if you can get Miss Lydgate."

Another pause. Was Miss Lydgate also out of her room? Was every reliable don in College out, or out of her room? Yes—Miss Lydgate was out, too; and then it occurred to Harriet that, of course, they were dutifully patrolling the College before turning in to bed. However, there was Padgett. She explained matters as well as she could to him.

"Very good, miss," said Padgett, comfortingly. "Yes, miss—I can leave Mrs. Padgett on the Lodge. I'll get down to the private gate and have a look round. Don't you worry, miss. If there's anybody a-laying in wait for you, miss, I'm sorry for 'em, that's all. No, miss, there ain't been no disturbance tonight as I knows on; but if I catches anybody a-laying in wait, miss, then the disturbance will proceed according to schedule, miss, trust me."

"Yes, Padgett; but don't make a row about it. Slip down quietly and see if there's anybody hanging round—but don't let them see you. If anybody attacks me when I come in, you can come to the rescue; but if not, keep out of sight."

"Very good, miss."

Harriet hung up again and stepped out of the call-box. A center light burned dimly in the entrance-hall. She looked at the clock. Seven minutes to eleven. She would be late. However, the assailant, if there was one, would wait for her. She knew where the trap would be—must be. Nobody would start a riot just outside the Infirmary or the Warden's Lodgings, where people might overhear and come out. Nor would anyone hide under or behind the walls on that side of the path. The only reasonable lurking-place was the bushes in the Fellows' Garden, near the gate, on the right side of the path as you went up.

One would be prepared, and that was an advantage; and Padgett would be somewhere at hand; but there would be a nasty moment when one had to turn one's back and lock the private gate from the inside. Harriet thought of the bread-knife in the dummy, and shuddered.

If she bungled it and got killed—melodramatic, but possible, when people weren't quite sane—Peter would have something to say about it. Perhaps it would be only decent to apologize beforehand, in case. She found somebody's notebook astray on a window-seat, borrowed a sheet of it, scribbled half a dozen words with the pencil from her bag, folded the note, addressed it and put it away with the pencil. If anything happened, it would be found.

The Somerville porter let her out into the Woodstock Road. She took the quickest way: by St. Giles' Church, Blackhall Road, Museum Road, South Parks Road, Mansfield Road, walking briskly, almost running. When she turned into Jowett Walk, she slowed down. She wanted her breath and her wits.

She turned the corner into St. Cross Road, reached the gate and took out her key. Her heart was thumping.

And then, the whole melodrama dissipated itself into polite comedy. A car drew up behind her; the Dean deposited the Warden and drove on round to the tradesmen's entrance to garage her Austin, and Dr. Baring said pleasantly:

"Ah! it's you, Miss Vane? Now I shan't have to look for my key. Did you have an interesting evening? The Dean and I have been indulging in a little dissipation. We suddenly made up our minds after dinner . . ."

She walked on up the path with Harriet, chatting with great amiability about the play she had seen. Harriet left her at her own gate, refusing an invitation to come in and have coffee and sandwiches. Had she, or had she not, heard something stir behind the bushes? At any rate, the opportunity was by now lost. She had offered herself as the cheese, but, owing to the slight delay in setting the trap, the Warden had innocently sprung it.

Harriet stepped into the Fellows' Garden, switched on her torch and looked round. The garden was empty. She suddenly felt a complete fool. Yet, when all was said and done, there must have been some reason for that telephone call.

She made her way towards the St. Cross Lodge. In the New Quad she met Padgett.

"Ah!" said Padgett, cautiously. "She was there right enough, miss." His right hand moved at his side, and Harriet fancied it held something suspiciously like a cosh. "Sittin' on the bench be'ind them laurels near the gate. I crep' along careful, like it was a night reconnaissance, miss, and 'id be'ind them centre shrubs. She didn't tumble to me, miss. But when you an' Dr. Baring come through the gate a-talking, she was up and orf like a shot."

"Who was it, Padgett?"

"Well, miss, not to put too fine a point upon it, miss, it was Miss 'Illyard. She come out at the top end of the Garden, miss, and away to her own rooms. I follered 'er and see 'er go up. Going very quick, she was. I stepped out o' the gate, and I see the light go up in her window."

"Oh!" said Harriet. "Look here, Padgett. I don't want anything said about this. I know Miss Hillyard does sometimes take a stroll in the Fellows' Garden at night. Perhaps the person who sent the telephone call saw her there and went away again."

"Yes, miss. It's a funny thing about that there telephone call. It didn't come through the Lodge, miss."

"Perhaps one of the other instruments was through to the Exchange."

"No, they wasn't, miss. I 'ad a look to see. Afore I goes to bed at 11 o'clock, I puts the Warden, the Dean, and the Infirmary and the public box through, miss, for the night. But they wasn't through at 10:40, miss, that I'll swear."

"Then the call must have come from outside."

"Yes, miss. Miss 'Illyard come in at 10:50, miss, jest afore you rang up."

"Did she? Are you sure?"

"I remember quite well, miss, because of Annie passing a remark about her. There's no love lost between her and Annie," added Padgett, with a chuckle. "Faults o' both sides, that's what I say, miss, and a 'asty temper–"

"What was Annie doing in the Lodge at that hour?"

"Jest come in from her half-day out, miss. She set in the Lodge a bit with Mrs. Padgett."

"Did she? You didn't say anything about this business to her, did you, Padgett? She doesn't like Miss Hillyard, and if you ask me, I think she's a mischief-maker."

"I didn't say one word, miss, not even to Mrs. Padgett, and nobody could 'ave 'eard me on the 'phone, because, after I couldn't find Miss Lydgate and Miss Edwards and you begins to tell me, I shuts the door between me an' the settin'room. Then I jest puts me 'ead in afterwards and says to Mrs. Padgett, 'Look after the gate, would you?' I says, 'I jest got to step over and give Mullins a message.' So this here remains wot I might call confidential between you an' me, miss."

"Well, see that it stays confidential, Padgett. I may have been imagining something quite absurd. The 'phone call was certainly a hoax, but there's no proof that anybody meant mischief. Did anybody else come in between 10.40 and 11?"

"Mrs. Padgett will know, miss. I'll send you up a list of the names. Or if you like to step into the Lodge now–"

"Better not. No–give me the list in the morning."

Harriet went away and found Miss Edwards, of whose discretion and common-sense she had a high opinion, and told her the story of the 'phone call.

"You see," said Harriet, "if there *had* been any disturbance, the call might have been intended to prove an alibi, though I don't quite see how. Otherwise, why try to get me back at eleven? I mean, if the disturbance was due to start then, and I was brought there as a witness, the person might have wangled something so as to appear to be elsewhere at the time. But why was it necessary to have me as a witness?"

"Yes–and why say the disturbance had already happened, when it hadn't? And why wouldn't you do as a witness when you had the Warden with you?"

"Of course," said Harriet, "the idea might have been to make a disturbance and bring me on to the scene in time to be suspected of having done it myself."

"That would be silly; everybody knows *you* can't be the Poltergeist."

"Well, then, we come back to my first idea. I was to be attacked. But why couldn't I be attacked at midnight or any other time? Why bring me back at eleven?"

"It couldn't have been something timed to go off at eleven, while the alibi was being established?"

"Nobody could know to a moment the exact time I should take coming from Somerville to Shrewsbury. Unless you are thinking of a bomb or something that would go off when the gate was opened. But that would work equally well at any time."

"But if the alibi was fixed for eleven–"

"Then why didn't the bomb go off? As a matter of fact, I simply can't believe in a bomb at all."

"Nor can I–not really," said Miss Edwards. "We're just being theoretical. I suppose Padgett saw nothing suspicious?"

"Only Miss Hillyard," replied Harriet, lightly, "sitting in the Fellows' Garden."

"Oh!"

"She does go there sometimes at night; I've seen her. Perhaps she frightened away–whatever it was."

"Perhaps," said Miss Edwards. "By the way, your noble friend seems to have overcome her prejudices in a remarkable manner. I don't mean the one who saluted you in the quad–the one who came to dinner."

"Are you trying to make a mystery out of yesterday afternoon?" asked Harriet, smiling. "I think it was only a matter of introductions to some man in Italy who owns a library."

"So she informed us," said Miss Edwards. Harriet realized that, when her own back was turned, a good deal of chaff must have been flying about the History Tutor's ears. "Well," Miss Edwards went on, "I promised him a paper on bloodgroups, but he hasn't started to badger me for it yet. He's an interesting man, isn't he?"

"To the biologist?"

Miss Edwards laughed. "Well, yes–as a specimen of the pedigree animal. Shockingly overbred, but full of nervous intelligence. But I didn't mean that."

"To the woman, then?"

Miss Edwards turned a candid eye on Harriet.

"To many women, I should imagine."

Harriet met the eye with a level gaze.

"I have no information on that point."

"Ah!" said Miss Edwards. "In your novels, you deal more in material facts than in psychology, don't you?"

Harriet readily admitted that this was so.

"Well, never mind," said Miss Edwards; and said goodnight rather brusquely.

Harriet asked herself what all this was about. Oddly enough, it had never yet occurred to her to wonder what other women made of Peter, or he of them. This must argue either very great confidence or very great indifference on her own part; for, when one came to think of it, eligibility was his middle name.

On reaching her room, she took the scribbled note from her bag and destroyed it without re-reading it. Even the thought of it made her blush. Heroics that don't come off are the very essence of burlesque.

Thursday was chiefly remarkable for a violent, prolonged and wholly inexplicable row between Miss Hillyard and Miss Chilperic, in the Fellows' Garden after Hall. How it started or what it was about, nobody could afterwards remember. Somebody had disarranged a pile of books and papers on one of the Library tables, with the result that a History Schools candidate had arrived for a coaching with a tale of a set of notes mislaid or missing. Miss Hillyard, whose temper had been exceedingly short all day, was moved to take the matter personally and, after glowering all through dinner, burst out–as soon as the Warden had gone–into a storm of indignation against the world in general.

"Why *my* pupils should always be the ones to suffer from other people's carelessness, I don't know," said Miss Hillyard.

Miss Burrows said she didn't see that they suffered more than anybody else. Miss Hillyard angrily adduced instances extending over the past three terms of History students whose work had been interfered with by what looked like deliberate persecution.

"Considering," she went on, "that the History School is the largest in the College and certainly not the least important–"

Miss Chilperic pointed out, quite correctly, that in that particular year there happened to be more candidates for the English School than any other.

"Of course you would say that," said Miss Hillyard. "There may be a couple more this year–I dare say there may–though why we should need an extra English tutor to cope with them, when I have to grapple single-handed–"

It was at that point that the origin of the quarrel became lost in a fog of personalities, in the course of which Miss Chilperic was accused of insolence, arrogance, inattention to her work, general incompetence and a desire to attract notice to herself. The extreme wildness of these charges left poor Miss Chilperic quite bewildered. Indeed, nobody seemed to be able to make anything of it, except, perhaps, Miss Edwards, who sat with a grim smile knitting herself a silk jumper. At length the attack extended itself from Miss Chilperic to Miss Chilperic's fiancé, whose scholarship was submitted to scathing criticism.

Miss Chilperic rose up, trembling.

"I think, Miss Hillyard," she said, "you must be beside yourself. I do not mind what you say about me, but I cannot sit here while you insult Jacob Peppercorn." She stumbled a little over the syllables of this unfortunate name, and Miss Hillyard laughed unkindly. "Mr. Peppercorn is a very fine scholar," pursued Miss Chllperic, with rising anger as of an exasperated lamb, "and I insist that–"

"I'm glad to hear you say so," said Miss Hillyard. "If I were you, I should make do with him."

"I don't know what you mean," cried Miss Chilperic.

"Perhaps Miss Vane could tell you," retorted Miss Hillyard, and walked away without another word.

"Good gracious!" cried Miss Chilperic, turning to Harriet, "Whatever is she talking about?"

"I haven't the least idea," said Harriet.

"I don't know, but I can guess," said Miss Edwards. "If people will bring dynamite into a powder factory, they must expect explosions." While Harriet was rooting about in the back of her mind for some association that these words called up, Miss Edwards went on:

"If somebody doesn't get to the bottom of these disturbances within the next few days, there'll be murder done. If we're like this now, what's going to happen to us at the end of term? You ought to have had the police in from the start, and if I'd been here, I'd have said so. I'd like to deal with a good, stupid sergeant of police for a change."

Then she, too, got up and stalked away, leaving the rest of the dons to stare at one another.

# 19

O well-knit Samson! strong-jointed Samson! I do excel thee in my rapier, as much as thou didst excel me in carrying gates. I am in love, too.

William Shakespeare

HARRIET HAD been only too right about Wilfrid. She had spent portions of four days in altering and humanizing Wilfrid, and today, after a distressful morning with him, had reached the dismal conclusion that she would have to rewrite the whole thing from the beginning. Wilfrid's tormented humanity stood out now against the competent vacuity of the other characters like a wound. Moreover, with the reduction of Wilfrid's motives to what was psychologically credible, a large lump of the plot had fallen out, leaving a gap through which one could catch glimpses of new and exciting jungles of intrigue. She stood aimlessly staring into the window of the antique shop. Wilfrid was becoming like one of those coveted ivory chessmen. You probed into his interior and discovered an intricate and delicate carved sphere of sensibilities, and, as you turned it in your fingers, you found another inside that, and within that, another again.

Behind the table where the chessmen stood was a Jacobean dresser in black oak, and, as she stood at gaze, a set of features limned themselves pallidly against the dark background, like Pepper's ghost.

"What is it?" asked Peter over her shoulder; "Toby jugs or pewter pots or the dubious chest with Brummagem handles?"

"The chessmen," said Harriet. "I have fallen a victim to them. I don't know why. I have no possible use for them. It's just one of those bewitchments."

" 'The reason no man knows, let it suffice What we behold is censured by our eyes.' To be possessed is an admirable reason for possessing."

"What would they want for them, I wonder?"

"If they're complete and genuine, anything from forty to eighty pounds."

"Too much. When did you get back?"

"Just before lunch. I was on my way to see you. Were you going anywhere in particular?"

"No—just wandering. Have you found out anything useful?"

"I have been scouring England for a man called Arthur Robinson. Does the name mean anything to you?"

"Nothing whatever."

"Nor to me. I approached it with a refreshing absence of prejudice. Have there been any developments in College?"

"Well, yes. Something rather queer happened the other night. Only I don't quite understand it."

"Will you come for a run and tell me about it? I've got the car, and it's a fine afternoon."

Harriet looked round, and saw the Daimler parked by the kerb.

"I'd love to."

"We'll dawdle along the lanes and have tea somewhere," he added, conventionally, as he handed her in.

"How original of you, Peter!"

"Isn't it?" They moved decorously down the crowded High Street. "There's something hypnotic about the word tea. I am asking you to enjoy the beauties of the English countryside, to tell me your adventures and hear mine, to plan a campaign involving the comfort and reputation of two hundred people, to honour me with your sole presence and bestow upon me the illusion of Paradise—and I speak as though the pre-eminent object of all desire were a pot of boiled water and a plateful of synthetic pastries in Ye Olde Worlde Tudor Tea Shoppe."

"If we dawdle till after opening-time," said Harriet, practically, "we can get bread-and-cheese and beer in the village pub."

"Now you have said something.

*The crystal springs, whose taste illuminates*
*Refinèd eyes with an eternal sight,*
*Like trièd silver, run through Paradise*
*To entertain divine Zenocrate."*

Harriet could find no adequate reply to this, but sat watching his hands as they lay lightly on the driving-wheel. The car passed on through Long Marston out to Marston and Elsfield. Presently he turned it into a side-road and thence into a lane and there drew up.

"There comes a moment when one must cease voyaging through strange seas of thought alone. Will you speak first, or shall I?"

"Who is Arthur Robinson?"

"Arthur Robinson is the gentleman who behaved so strangely in the matter of a thesis. He was an M.A. of York University, held various tutorships from time to time in various seats of learning, applied for the Chair of Modern History at York, and there came up against the formidable memory and detective ability of your Miss de Vine, who was then Head of Flamborough College and on the examining body. He was a fair, handsome man, aged about thirty-five at the time, very agreeable and popular, though hampered a little in his social career by having in a weak moment married his landlady's daughter. After the unfortunate episode of the thesis, he disappeared from academic circles, and was no more heard of. At the time of his disappearance he had one female child of two years of age and another expected. I managed to hunt up a former friend of his, who said that he had heard nothing of Robinson since the disaster, but fancied that he had gone abroad and changed his name. He referred me to a man called Simpson, living in Nottingham. I pursued Simpson, and found that he had, in the most inconvenient way, died last year. I returned to London and dispatched sundry members of Miss Climpson's Bureau in search of other friends and colleagues of Mr. Arthur Robinson, and also to Somerset House to hunt through the Marriage and Birth Registers. That is all I have to show for two days of intensive activity—except that I honourably delivered your manuscript to your secretary."

"Thank you very much. Arthur Robinson. Do you think he can possibly have anything to do with it?"

"Well, it's rather a far cry. But it's a fact that until Miss de Vine came here there were no disturbances, and the only thing she has ever mentioned that might suggest a personal enmity is the story of Arthur Robinson. It seemed just worth while following up."

"Yes, I see . . . . I hope you're not going to suggest that Miss Hillyard is Arthur Robinson in disguise, because I've known her for ten years."

"Why Miss Hillyard? What's she been doing?"

"Nothing susceptible of proof."

"Tell me."

Harriet told him the story of the telephone call, to which he listened with a grave face.

"Was I making a mountain out of a mole-hill?"

"I think not. I think our friend has realized that you are a danger and is minded to tackle you first. Unless it is a quite separate feud—which is just possible. On the whole it's as well that you thought of ringing back."

"You may take the credit for that. I hadn't forgotten your scathing remarks about the thriller-heroine and the bogus message from Scotland Yard."

"Hadn't you? . . . Harriet, will you let me show you how to meet an attack if it ever does come?"

"Meet a—? Yes, I should like to know. Though I'm fairly strong, you know. I think I could cope with most things, except a stab in the back. That was what I rather expected."

"I doubt if it will be that," said he, coolly. "It makes a mess and leaves a messy weapon to be disposed of. Strangling is cleaner and quicker and makes no noise to speak of."

"Yeough!"

"You have a nice throat for it," pursued his lordship, thoughtfully. "It has a kind of arum-lily quality that is in itself a temptation to violence. I do not want to be run in by the local bobby for assault; but if you will kindly step aside with me into this convenient field, it will give me great pleasure to strangle you scientificaliy in several positions."

"You're a gruesome companion for a day's outing."

"I'm quite serious." He had got out of the car and was holding the door open for her. "Come, Harriet. I am very civilly pretending that I don't care what dangers you run. You don't want me to howl at your feet, do you?"

"You're going to make me feel ignorant and helpless," said Harriet, following him nevertheless to the nearest gate. "I don't like it."

"This field will do charmingly. It is not laid down for hay, it is reasonably free from thistles and cow-pats, and there is a high hedge to screen us from the road."

"And it is soft to fall on and has a pond to throw the corpse into if you get carried away by your enthusiasm. Very well. I have said my prayers."

"Then kindly imagine me to be an unpleasant-faced thug with designs on your purse, your virtue and your life."

The next few minutes were rather breathless.

"Don't thrash about," said Peter, mildly. "You'll only exhaust yourself. Use *my* weight to upset me with. I'm putting it entirely at your disposal, and I can't throw it about in two directions at once. If you let my vaulting ambition overleap itself, I shall fall on the other side with the beautiful precision of Newton's apple."

"I don't get that."

"Try throttling me for a change, and I'll show you."

"Did I say this field was soft?" said Harriet, when her feet had been ignominiously hooked from under her. She rubbed herself resentfully. "Just let me do it to you, that's all."

And this time, whether by skill or favour, she did contrive to bring him off his balance, so that he only saved himself from sprawling by a complicated twist suggestive of an eel on a hook.

"We'd better stop now," said Peter, when he had instructed her in the removal of the thug who leaps from in front, the thug who dives in from behind, and the more sophisticated thug who starts operations with a silk scarf. "You'll feel tomorrow as if you'd been playing football."

"I think I shall have a sore throat."

"I'm sorry. Did I let my animal nature get the better of me? That's the worst of these rough sports."

"It would be a good bit rougher if it was done in earnest. I shouldn't care to meet *you* in a narrow lane on a dark night, and I only hope the Poison-Pen hasn't been making a study of the subject. Peter, you don't seriously think—"

"I avoid serious thought like the plague. But I assure you I haven't been knocking you about for the fun of it."

"I believe you. No gentleman could throttle a lady more impersonally."

"Thank you for the testimonial. Cigarette?"

Harriet took the cigarette, which she felt she had deserved, and sat with her hands about her knees, mentally turning the incidents of the last hour into a scene in a book (as is the novelist's unpleasant habit) and thinking how, with a little vulgarity on both sides, it could be worked up into a nice piece of exhibitionism for the male and provocation for the female concerned. With a little manipulation it might come in for the chapter where the wart Everard was due to seduce the glamorous but neglected wife, Sheila. He could lock her to him, knee to knee and breast to breast in an unbreakable grip and smile challengingly into her flushed face; and Sheila could go all limp—at which point Everard could either rain fierce kisses on her mouth, or say, "My God! don't tempt me!" which would come to exactly the same thing in the end. "It would suit them very well," thought Harriet, "the cheap skates!" and passed an exploring finger under the angle of her jaw, where the pressure of a relentless thumb had left its memory.

"Cheer up," said Peter. "It'll wear off."

"Do you propose to give Miss de Vine lessons in self-defence?"

"I'm rather bothered about her. She's got a groggy heart, hasn't she?"

"She's supposed to have. She wouldn't climb Magdalen Tower."

"And presumably she wouldn't rush round College and steal fuses or climb in and out of windows. In which case the hairpins would be a plant. Which brings us back to the Robinson theory. But it's easy to pretend your heart is worse than it is. Ever seen her have a heart-attack?"

"Now you mention it, I have not."

"You see," said Peter, "she put me on to Robinson. I gave her the opportunity to tell a story, and she told it. Next day, I went to see her and asked for the name. She made a good show of reluctance, but she gave it. It's easy to throw suspicion on people who owe you a grudge, and that without telling any lies. If I wanted you to believe that somebody was having a smack at me, I could give you a list of enemies as long as my arm."

"I suppose so. Do they ever try to do you in?"

"Not very often. Occasionally they send silly things by post. Shaving-cream full of nasty bugs and so on. And there was a gentleman with a pill calculated to cure lassitude and debility. I had a long correspondence with him, all in plain envelopes. The beauty of his system was that he made you pay for the pill, which still seems to me a very fine touch. In fact, he took me in completely; he only made the one trifling miscalculation of supposing that I wanted the pill—and I can't really blame him for that, because the list of symptoms I produced for him would have led anybody to suppose I needed the whole pharmacopoeia. However, he sent me a week's supply—seven pills—at shocking expense; so I virtuously toddled round with them to my friend at the Home Office who deals with charlatans and immoral advertisements and so on, and he was inquisitive enough to analyze them. 'H'm,' said he, 'six of 'em would neither make nor mar you; but the other would cure lassitude all right.' So I naturally asked what was in it. 'Strychnine,' said he. 'Full lethal dose. If you want to go rolling round the room like a hoop with your head touching your heels, I'll guarantee the result.' So we went out to look for the gentleman."

"Did you find him?"

"Oh, yes. Dear old friend of mine. Had him in the dock before on a cocaine charge. We put him in jug—and I'm dashed if, when he came out, he didn't try to blackmail me on the strength of the pill correspondence. I never met a scoundrel I liked better . . . . Would you care for a little more healthy exercise, or shall we take the road again?"

It was when they were passing through a small town that Peter caught sight of a leather-and-harness shop, and pulled up suddenly.

"I know what you want," he said. "You want a dog-collar. I'm going to get you one. The kind with brass knobs."

"A dog-collar? Whatever for? As a badge of ownership?"

"God forbid. To guard against the bites of sharks. Excellent also against thugs and throat-slitters."

"My dear man!"

"Honestly. It's too stiff to squeeze and it'll turn the edge of a blade—and even if anybody hangs you by it, it won't choke you as a rope would."

"I can't go about in a dog-collar."

"Well, not in the day-time. But it would give confidence when patrolling at night. And you could sleep in it with a little practice. You needn't bother to come in—I've had my hands round your neck often enough to guess the size."

He vanished into the shop and was seen through the window conferring with the proprietor. Presently he came out with a parcel and took the wheel again.

"The man was very much interested," he observed, "in my bull-terrior bitch. Extremely plucky animal, but reckless and obstinate fighter. Personally, he said, he preferred greyhounds. He told me where I could get my name and address put on the collar, but I said that could wait. Now we're out of the town, you can try it on."

He drew in to the side of the road for this purpose, and assisted her (with, Harriet fancied, a touch of self-satisfaction), to buckle the heavy strap. It was a massive kind of necklace and quite surprisingly uncomfortable. Harriet fished in her bag for a hand-mirror and surveyed the effect.

"Rather becoming, don't you think?" said Peter. "I don't see why it shouldn't set a new fashion."

"I do," said Harriet. "Do you mind taking it off again."

"Will you wear it?"

"Suppose somebody grabs at it from behind."

"Let go and fall back on them—heavily. You'll fall soft, and with luck they'll crack their skull open."

"Bloodthirsty monster. Very well. I'll do anything you like if you'll take it off now."

"That's a promise," said he, and released her. "That collar," he added, wrapping it up again and laying it on her knee, "deserves to be put in a glass case."

"Why?"

"It's the only thing you've ever let me give you."

"Except my life—except my life—except my life."

"Damn!" said Peter, and stared out angrily over the windscreen. "It must have been a pretty bitter gift, if you can't let either of us forget it."

"I'm sorry, Peter. That was ungenerous and beastly of me. You *shall* give me something if you want to."

"May I? What shall I give you? Roc's eggs are cheap today."

For a moment her mind was a blank. Whatever she asked him for, it must be something adequate. The trivial, the commonplace or the merely expensive would all be equally insulting. And he would know in a moment if she was inventing a want to please him . . . .

"Peter—give me the ivory chessmen."

He looked so delighted that she felt sure he had expected to be snubbed with a request for something costing seven-and-sixpence.

"My dear—of course! Would you like them now?"

"This instant! Some miserable undergraduate may be snapping them up. Every day I go out I expect to find them gone. Be quick."

"All right. I'll engage not to drop below seventy, except in the thirty-mile limit."

"Oh, God!" said Harriet, as the car started. Fast driving terrified her, as he very well knew. After five breath-taking miles, he shot a glance sideways at her, to see how she was standing it, and slacked his foot from the accelerator.

"That was my triumph song. Was it a bad four minutes?"

"I asked for it" said Harriet with set teeth. "Go on."

"I'm damned if I will. We will go at a reasonable pace and risk the undergraduate, damn his bones!"

The ivory chessmen were, however, still in the window when they arrived. Peter subjected them to a hard and monocled stare, and said:

"They *look* all right."

"They're lovely. Admit that when I do do a thing, I do it handsomely. I've asked you now for thirty-two presents at once."

"It sounds like *Through the Looking-Glass*. Are you coming in, or will you leave me to fight it out by myself?"

"Of course I'm coming in. Why?—Oh! Am I looking too keen?"

"Much too keen."

"Well, I don't care. I'm coming in."

The shop was dark, and crowded with a strange assortment of first-class stuff, junk, and traps for the unwary. The proprietor, however, had all his wits about him and, recognizing after a preliminary skirmish of superlatives that he had to do with an obstinate, experienced and well-informed customer, settled down with something like enthusiasm to a prolonged siege of the position. It had not previously occurred to Harriet that anybody could spend an hour and forty minutes in buying a set of chessmen. Every separate carved ball in every one of thirty-two pieces had to be separately and minutely examined with finger-tips and the naked eye and a watchmaker's lens for signs of damage, repair, substitution or faulty workmanship; and only after a sharp catechism directed to the "provenance" of the set, and a long discussion about trade conditions in China, the state of the antique market generally and the effect of the American slump on prices, was any figure mentioned at all; and when it was mentioned, it was instantly challenged, and a further discussion followed, during which all the pieces were scrutinized again. This ended at length in Peter's agreeing to purchase the set at the price named (which was considerably above his minimum, though within his maximum estimate) provided the board was included. The unusual size of the pieces made it necessary that they should have their own board; and the dealer rather reluctantly agreed, after having it firmly pointed out to him that the board was sixteenth-century Spanish—clean out of the period—and that it was therefore almost a condescension on the purchaser's part to accept it as a gift.

The combat being now brought to an honourable conclusion, the dealer beamed pleasantly and asked where the parcel should be sent.

"We'll take it with us," said Peter, firmly. "If you'd rather have notes than a cheque—"

The dealer protested that the cheque would be quite all right but that the parcel would be a large one and take some time to make up, since the pieces ought all to be wrapped separately.

"We're in no hurry," said Peter. "We'll take it with us"; thus conforming to the first rule of good nursery behaviour, that presents must always be taken and never delivered by the shop.

The dealer vanished upstairs to look for a suitable box, and Peter turned apologetically to Harriet.

"Sorry to be so long about it. You've chosen better than you knew. I'm no expert, but I'm very much mistaken if that isn't a very fine and ancient set, and worth a good bit more than he wants for it. That's why I haggled so much. When a thing looks like a bargain, there's usually a snag about it somewhere. If one of those dashed pawns wasn't the original, it would make the whole lot worthless."

"I suppose so." A disquieting thought struck Harriet. "If the set hadn't been perfect, should you have bought it?"

"Not at any price."

"Not if I still wanted it?"

"No. That's the snag about *me*. Besides, you wouldn't want it. You have the scholarly mind and you'd always feel uncomfortable knowing it was wrong, even if nobody else knew."

"That's true. Whenever anybody admired it I should feel obliged to say, 'Yes, but one of the pawns is modern'—and that would get so tedious. Well, I'm glad they're all right, because I love them with a perfectly idiotic passion. They have been haunting my slumbers for weeks. And even now I haven't said thank you."

"Yes, you have—and anyway, the pleasure is all mine.... I wonder whether that spinet's in order."

He threaded his way through the dark backward and abysm of the antique shop, clearing away a spinning-wheel, a Georgian wine-cooler, a brass lamp and a small forest of Burmese idols that stood between him and the instrument. "Variations on a musical-box," he said, as he ran his fingers over the keys, and, disentangling a coffin-stool from his surroundings, sat down and played, first a minuet from a Bach suite and then a gigue, before striking into the air of *Greensleeves*.

*"Alas! my love, you do me wrong*
*To cast me off discourteously,*
*And I have loved you so long,*
*Delighting in your company."*

He shall see that I don't mind that, thought Harriet, and raised her voice cheerfully in the refrain:

> "*For O Greensleeves was all my joy,*
> *And O Greensleeves was my delight*–"

He stopped playing instantly.

"Wrong key for you. God meant you for a contralto." He transposed the air into E minor, in a tinkling cascade of modulations. "You never told me you could sing. . . . No, I can hear you're not trained . . .chorus-singer? Bach Choir? . . . of course–I might have guessed it. . . . 'And O Greensleeves was my heart of gold And who but my Lady Greensleeves' . . . Do you know any of Morley's *Canzonets for Two Voices?* . . . Come on, then, 'When lo! by Break of Morning' . . . Whichever part you like–they're exactly the same. . . . 'My love herself adorning.' . . . G natural, my dear, G natural. . . ."

The dealer, descending with his arms full of packing materials, paid no attention to them. He was well accustomed to the eccentricities of customers; and, moreover, probably cherished hopes of selling them the spinet.

"This kind of thing," said Peter, as tenor and alto twined themselves in a last companionable cadence, "is the body and bones of music. Anybody can have the harmony, if they will leave us the counterpoint. What next? . . . 'Go to Bed, sweet Muse'? Come, come! Is it true? is it kind? is it necessary? . . . 'Love is a fancy, love is a frenzy.' . . . Very well, I owe you one for that," and with a mischievous eye he played the opening bars of "Sweet Cupid, Ripen Her Desire."

"No," said Harriet, reddening.

"No. Not in the best of taste. Try again."

He hesitated; ran from one tune to another; then settled down to that best-known of all Elizabethan love-songs.

> "*Fain would I change that note*
> *To which fond love hath charmed me* . . . ."

Harriet, with her elbows on the lid of the spinet and her chin propped on her hands, let him sing alone. Two young gentlemen, who had strayed in and were talking rather loudly in the front part of the shop, abandoned a half-hearted quest for brass candlesticks and came stumbling through the gloom to see who was making the noise.

> "*True house of joy and bliss*
> *Where sweetest pleasure is*
> *I do adore thee;*
> *I see thee what thou art,*
> *I love thee in my heart*
> *And fall before thee.*"

Tobias Hume's excellent air rises to a high-pitched and triumphant challenge in the penultimate line, before tumbling with a clatter to the key-note. Too late, Harriet signed to the singer to moderate his voice.

"Here, you!" said the larger of the two young gentlemen, belligerently. "You're making a filthy row. Shut up!"

Peter swung round on the stool.

"Sir?" He polished his monocle with exaggerated care, adjusted it and let his eye travel up the immense tweedy form lowering over him. "I beg your pardon. Was that obligin' observation addressed to me?"

Harriet started to speak, but the young man turned to her.

"Who," he demanded loudly, "is this effeminate bounder?"

"I have been accused of many things," said Wimsey, interested; "but the charge of effeminacy is new to me. Do you mind explaining yourself?"

"I don't like your song," said the young man, rocking slightly on his feet, "and I don't like your voice, and I don't like your tom-fool eye-glass."

"Steady on, Reggie," said his friend.

"You're annoying this lady," persisted the young man. "You're making her conspicuous. Get out!"

"Good God!" said Wimsey, turning to Harriet. "Is this by any chance Mr. Jones of Jesus?"

"Who are you calling a bloody Welshman?" snarled the young man, much exasperated. "My name's Pomfret."

"Mine's Wimsey," said Peter. "Quite as ancient though less euphonious. Come on, son, don't be an ass. You mustn't behave like this to senior members and before ladies."

"Senior member be damned!" cried Mr. Pomfret, to whom this unfortunate phrase conveyed only too much. "Do you think I'm going to be sneered at by you? Stand up, blast you! why can't you stand up for yourself?"

"First," replied Peter, mildly, "because I'm twenty years older than you are. Secondly, because you're six inches taller than I am. And thirdly, because I don't want to hurt you."

"Then," said Mr. Pomfret, "take that, you sitting rabbit!"

He launched an impetuous blow at Peter's head, and found himself held by the wrist in an iron grip.

"If you don't keep quiet," said his lordship, "you'll break something. Here, you, sir. Take your effervescent friend home, can't you? How the devil does he come to be drunk at this time of the day?"

The friend offered a confused explanation about a lunchparty and subsequent cocktail binge. Peter shook his head.

"One damn gin after another," he said, sadly. "Now, sir. You had better apologize to the lady and beetle off."

Mr. Pomfret, much subdued and tending to become lachrymose, muttered that he was sorry to have made a row. "But why did you make fun of me with that?" he asked Harriet, reproachfully.

"I didn't, Mr. Pomfret. You're quite mistaken."

"Damn your senior members!" said Mr. Pomfret.

"Now, don't begin all over again," urged Peter, kindly. He got up, his eyes about on a level with Mr. Pomfret's chin. "If you want to continue the discussion, you'll find me at the Mitre in the morning. This way out."

"Come on, Reggie," said the friend.

The dealer, who had returned to his packing after assuring himself that it would not be necessary to send for the police or the proctors, leapt helpfully to open the door, and said "*Good* afternoon, gentlemen," as though nothing out of the way had happened.

"I'm damned if I'll be sneered at," said Mr. Pomfret, endeavoring to stage a come-back on the doorstep.

"Of course not, old boy," said his friend. "Nobody's sneering at you. *Come* on! You've had quite enough fun for one afternoon."

The door shut them out.

"Well, well!" said Peter.

"Young gentlemen will be lively," said the dealer. "I'm afraid it's a bit bulky, sir. I've put the board up separate."

"Stick 'em in the car," said Peter. "They'll be all right."

This was done; and the dealer, glad enough to get his shop cleared, began to put up his shutters, as it was now long past closing-time.

"I apologize for my young friend," said Harriet.

"He seems to have taken it hard. What on earth was there so infuriating about my being a senior?"

"Oh, poor lamb! He thought I'd been telling you about him and me and the proctor. I suppose I *had* better tell you now."

Peter listened and laughed a little ruefully.

"I'm sorry," he said. "That kind of thing hurts like hell when you're his age. I'd better send him a note and set that right. I say!"

"What?"

"We never had that beer. Come round and have one with me at the Mitre, and we'll concoct a salve for wounded feelings."

With two half-pint tankards on the table before them, Peter produced his epistle.

The Mitre Hotel,
Oxford

To Reginald Pomfret, Esq.

Sir,

I am given to understand by Miss Vane that in the course of our conversation this afternoon I unhappily made use of an expression which might have been misconstrued as a reference to your private affairs. Permit me to assure you that the words were uttered in complete ignorance, and that nothing could have been farther from my intentions than to make any such offensive allusion. While deprecating very strongly the behaviour you thought fit to use, I desire to express my sincere regret for any pain I may have inadvertently caused you, and beg to remain,

Your obedient servant,

PETER DEATH BREDON WIMSEY

"Is that pompous enough?"

"Beautiful," said Harriet. "Scarcely a word under three syllables and all the names you've got. What your nephew calls 'Uncle Peter at his stuffiest.' All it wants is the crest and sealing-wax. Why not write the child a nice, friendly note?"

"He doesn't want friendliness," said his lordship, grinning. "He wants satisfaction." He rang the bell and sent the waiter for Bunter and the sealing-wax. "You're right about the beneficial effects of a red seal–he'll think it's a challenge. Bunter, bring me my seal ring. Come to think of it, that's an idea. Shall I offer him the choice of swords or pistols on Port Meadow at daybreak?"

"I think it's time you grew up," said Harriet.

"Is it?" said Peter, addressing the envelope. "I've never challenged anybody. It would be fun. I've been challenged three times and fought twice; the third time the police butted in. I'm afraid that was because my opponent didn't fancy my choice of weapon .... Thanks, Bunter .... A bullet, you see, may go anywhere, but steel's almost bound to go somewhere."

"Peter," said Harriet, looking gravely at him, "I believe you're showing off."

"I believe I am," said he, setting the heavy ring accurately down upon the wax. "Every cock will crow upon his own dung-hill." His grin was half petulant, half deprecating. "I hate being loomed over by gigantic undergraduates and made to feel my age."

# 20

For, to speak in a word, envy is naught else but *tristitia de bonis alienis*, sorrow for other men's good, be it present, past, or to come: and *gaudium de adversis*, and joy at their harms .... 'Tis a common disease, and almost natural to us, as *Tacitus* holds, to envy another man's prosperity.

Robert Burton

It is said that love and a cough cannot be hid. Nor is it easy to hide two-and-thirty outsize ivory chessmen; unless one is so inhuman as to leave them swaddled in their mummyclothes of wadding and entombed within the six sides of a wooden sarcophagus. What is the use of acquiring one's heart's desire if one cannot handle and gloat over it, show it to one's friends and gather an anthology of envy and admiration? Whatever awkward deductions might be drawn about the giver–and, after all, was that anybody's business?–Harriet knew that she must needs display the gift or burst in solitary ecstasy.

Accordingly, she put a bold face on it, marched her forces openly into the Senior Common Room after Hall, and deployed them upon the table, with the eager assistance of the dons.

"But where are you going to keep them?" asked the Dean, when everybody had sufficiently exclaimed over the fineness of the carving, and had taken her turn at twisting and examining the nests of concentric globes. "You can't just leave them in the box. Look at those fragile little spears and things and the royal head-dresses. They ought to be put in a glass case."

"I know," said Harriet. "It's just like me to want something completely impracticable. I shall have to wrap them all up again."

"Only then," said Miss Chilperic, "you won't be able to look at them. I know, if they were mine, I shouldn't be able to take my eyes off them for a moment."

"You can have a glass case if you like," said Miss Edwards. "Out of the Science Lecture-Room."

"The very thing," said Miss Lydgate. "But how about the terms of the bequest? I mean, the glass cases–"

"Oh, blow the bequest!" cried the Dean. "Surely one can *borrow* a thing for a week or two. We can lump some of those hideous geological specimens together and have one of the small cases taken up to your room."

"By all means," said Miss Edwards. "I'll see to it."

"Thank you," said Harriet; "that will be lovely."

"Aren't you simply aching to play with the new toy?" asked Miss Allison. "Does Lord Peter play chess?"

"I don't know," said Harriet. "I'm not much of a player. I just fell in love with the pieces."

"Well," said Miss de Vine, kindly, "let us have a game. They are so beautiful, it would be a pity not to use them."

"But I expect you could play my head off."

"Oh, do play with them!" cried Miss Shaw, sentimentally. "Think how they must be longing for a little life and movement after sitting all that time in a shop-window."

"I will give you a pawn," suggested Miss de Vine.

Even with this advantage, Harriet suffered three humiliating defeats in quick succession: first, because she was but a poor player; secondly, because she found it difficult to remember which piece was which; thirdly, because the anguish of parting at one fell swoop with a fully-armed warrior, a prancing steed and a complete nest of ivory balls was such that she could scarcely bear to place so much as a pawn in jeopardy. Miss de Vine, viewing with perfect equanimity the disappearance even of a robed counsellor with long moustaches or an elephant carrying a castleful of combatants, soon had Harriet's king penned helplessly among his own defenders. Nor was the game made any easier for the weaker party by being played under the derisive eye of Miss Hillyard, who, pronouncing chess to be the world's most wearisome amusement, yet would not go away and get on with her work, but sat staring at the board as though fascinated and (what was worse) fiddling with the captured pieces and putting Harriet into an agony for fear she would drop one.

Moreover, when the games were finished, and Miss Edwards had announced that a glass case had been dusted and taken up to Harriet's room by a scout, Miss Hillyard insisted on helping to carry the pieces over, grasping for the purpose the white king and queen, whose headgear bore delicate waving ornaments like antennae, extremely liable to damage. Even when the Dean had discovered that the pieces could be more safely transported standing upright in their box, Miss Hillyard attached herself to the party that escorted them across the quad, and was officious in helping to set the glass case in a convenient position opposite the bed, "so that," as she observed, "you can see them if you wake up in the night."

The following day happened to be the Dean's birthday. Harriet, going shortly after breakfast to purchase a tribute of roses in the Market, and coming out into the High Street with the intention of making an appointment at the hair-dresser's, was rewarded by the rather unexpected sight of two male backs, issuing from the Mitre and proceeding, apparently in perfect amity, in an easterly direction. The shorter and slighter of the two she could have singled out from a million backs anywhere; nor was it easy to mistake the towering bulk and breadth of Mr. Reginald Pomfret. Both parties were smoking pipes, and she concluded from this that the object of their excursion could scarcely be swords or pistols on Port Meadow. They were strolling in a leisurely after-breakfast manner, and she took care not to catch them up. She hoped that what Lord Saint-George called the "famous family charm" was being exerted to good purpose; she was too old to enjoy the sensation of being squabbled over–it made all three of them ridiculous. Ten years ago, she might have felt flattered; but it seemed that the lust to power was a thing one grew out of. What one wanted, she thought, standing amid the stuffy perfumes of the hair-dresser's establishment, was peace, and freedom from the pressure of angry and agitated personalities. She booked an appointment for the afternoon and resumed her way. As she passed Queen's, Peter came down the steps alone.

"Hullo!" said he. "Why the floral emblems?"

Harriet explained.

"Good egg!" said his lordship. "I like your Dean." He relieved her of the roses. "Let me also be there with a gift.

"*Make her a goodly chapilet of azur'd Colombine,*
*And wreathe about her coronet with sweetest Eglantine,*
*With roses damask, white, and red, and fairest flower delice,*
*With Cowslips of Jerusalem, and cloves of Paradice.*

Though what Cowslips of Jerusalem may be I do not know, and they are probably not in season."

Harriet turned back with him marketwards.

"Your young friend came to see me," pursued Peter.

"So I observed. Did you 'fix a vacant stare and slay him with your noble birth'?"

"And he my own kin in the sixteenth degree on the father's mother's side? No; he's a nice lad, and the way to his heart is through the playing-fields of Eton. He told me all his griefs and I sympathized very kindly, mentioning that there were better ways of killing care than drowning it in a butt of malmsey. But, O God, turn back the universe and give me yesterday! He was beautifully sozzled last night, and had one breakfast before he came out and another with me at the Mitre. I do not envy the heart of youth, but only its head and stomach."

"Have you heard anything fresh about Arthur Robinson?"

"Only that he married a young woman called Charlotte Ann Clarke, and had by her a daughter, Beatrice Maud. That was easy, because we know where he was living eight years ago, and could consult the local registers. But they're still hunting the registers to find either his death–supposing him to be dead, which is rather less likely than otherwise–or the birth of the second child, which–if it ever occurred–might tell us where he went to after the trouble at York. Unfortunately, Robinsons are as plentiful as blackberries, and Arthur Robinsons not uncommon. And if he really did change his name, there may not be any Robinson entries at all. Another of my searchers has gone to his old lodgings–where, you may remember, he very imprudently married the landlady's daughter; but the Clarkes have moved, and it's going to be a bit of a job finding them. Another line is to inquire among the scholastic agencies and the small and inferior private schools, because it seems probable– You're not attending."

"Yes, I am," said Harriet, vaguely. "He had a wife called Charlotte and you're looking for him in a private school." A rich, damp fragrance gushed out upon them as they turned into the Market, and she was overcome by a sense of extravagant well-being. "I love this smell–it's like the cactus-house in the Botanical Gardens."

Her companion opened his mouth to speak, looked at her, and then, as one that will not interfere with fortune, let the name of Robinson die upon his lips.

"*Mandragorae dederunt odorem.*"

"What do you say, Peter?"

"Nothing. The words of Mercury are harsh after the songs of Apollo." He laid his hand gently upon her arm. "Let us interview the merchant with the sops-in-wine."

And when both roses and carnations had been despatched —this time by a messenger—to their destination, it seemed natural, since the Botanical Gardens had been mentioned, to go there. For a garden, as Bacon observes, is the purest of human pleasures and the greatest refreshment to the spirit of man; and even idle and ignorant people who cannot distinguish *Leptosiphon hybridus* from *Kaulfussia amelloides* and would rather languish away in a wilderness than break their backs with dibbling and weeding may get a good deal of pleasant conversation out of it, especially if they know the old-fashioned names of the commoner sorts of flowers and are both tolerably well acquainted with the minor Elizabethan lyrists.

It was only when they had made the round of the Gardens and were sitting idly on the bank of the river that Peter, wrenching his attention back to the sordid present, remarked suddenly:

"I think I shall have to pay a visit to a friend of yours. Do you know how Jukes came to be caught with the stuff on him?"

"I've no idea."

"The police got an anonymous letter."

"Not—?"

"Yes. One of them there. By the way, did you ever try and find out what was to have been the last word of that message to you? The one we found in the Science LectureRoom?"

"No—she couldn't have finished it, anyhow. There wasn't a single vowel left in the box. Not even a B and a dash!"

"That was an oversight. I thought so. Well, Harriet, it's easy to put a name to the person we want, isn't it? But proofs a different matter. We've tied the thing up so tight. That lecture-room episode was meant to be the last of the nocturnal prowls, and it probably will be. And the best bit of evidence will be at the bottom of the river by this time. It's too late to seal the doors and set a watch."

"On whom?"

"Surely you know by this time? You *must* know, Harriet, if you're giving your mind to the thing at all. Opportunity, means, motive—doesn't it stand out a mile? For God's sake, put your prejudices aside and think it out. What's happened to you that you can't put two and two together?"

"I don't know."

"Well," said he drily, "if you really don't know, it's not for me to tell you. But if you will turn your attention for one moment to the matter in hand and go through your own dossier of the case carefully—"

"Undeterred by any casual sonnets I may find by the way?"

"Undeterred by any personal consideration whatever," he burst out, almost angrily. "No; you're quite right. That was a stupidity. My talent for standing in my own light amounts to genius, doesn't it? But when you have come to a conclusion about all this, will you remember that it was *I* who asked *you* to take a dispassionate view and *I* who told *you* that of all devils let loose in the world there was no devil like devoted love . . . . I don't mean passion. Passion's a good, stupid horse that will pull the plough six days a week if you give him the run of his heels on Sundays. But love's a nervous, awkward, over-mastering brute; if you can't rein him, it's best to have no truck with him."

"That sounds very topsy-turvy," said Harriet, mildly. But his unwonted excitement had already flickered out.

"I'm only walking on my head, after the manner of clowns. If we went along to Shrewsbury now, do you think the Warden would see me?"

Later in the day, Dr. Baring sent for Harriet.

"Lord Peter Wimsey has been to see me," she said, "with a rather curious proposition which, after a little consideration, I refused. He told me that he was almost certain in his own mind of the identity of the—the offender, but that he was not in a position at the moment to offer a complete proof. He also said that the person had, he thought, taken the alarm, and would be doubly careful from now on to escape detection. The alarm might, in fact, be sufficient to prevent farther outbreaks until the end of the term at any rate; but as soon as our vigilance was relaxed, the trouble would probably break out again in a more violent form. I said that that would be very unsatisfactory, and he agreed. He asked whether he should name the person to me, in order that a careful watch might be kept upon her movements. I said I saw two objections to that: first, that the person might discover that she was being spied upon and merely increase her caution, and secondly, that if he happened to be mistaken as to the offender's identity, the person spied upon would be subjected to the most intolerable suspicions. Supposing, I said, the persecutions merely ceased, and we were left suspecting this person—who might be quite innocent—without proof either way. He replied that those were precisely the objections that had occurred to him. Do you know the name of the person to whom he alludes, Miss Vane?"

"No," said Harriet, who had been exercising her wits in the interval. "I am beginning to have an idea; but I can't make it fit. In fact, I simply can't believe it."

"Very well. Lord Peter then made a very remarkable proposition. He asked whether I would allow him to interrogate this person privately, in the hope of surprising her into some admission. He said that if this bluff, as he called it, came off, the culprit could then make her confession to me and be suffered to depart quietly, or be dealt with medically, as we might decide was advisable. If, however, it did not come off and the person denied everything, we might be placed in a very disagreeable position. I replied that I quite saw that and could not possibly consent to have such methods used upon anybody in this College. To which he replied that that was exactly what he had expected me to say.

"I then asked him what evidence, if any, he had against this person. He said that all his evidence was circumstantial; that he hoped to have more of it in the course of the next few days, but that in default of a fresh outbreak and the capture of the culprit red-handed, he doubted whether any direct evidence could be produced at this stage. I inquired whether there was any reason why we should not at least wait for the production of the additional evidence."

Dr. Baring paused and looked keenly at Harriet.

"He replied that there was only one reason, and that was that the culprit, instead of becoming more cautious, might throw caution to the winds and proceed to direct violence. 'In which case,' he said, 'we should very likely catch her, but only at the cost of somebody's death or serious injury.' I asked what persons were threatened with death or injury. He said the most probable victims were—yourself, Miss de Vine and another person whom he could not name, but whose existence, he said, he deduced. He also surprised me by saying that an abortive attack had already been made upon you. Is that true?"

"I shouldn't have put it as strongly as that," said Harriet. She briefly outlined the story of the telephone call. At the name of Miss Hillyard, the Warden looked up:

"Do I understand that you entertain a definite suspicion of Miss Hillyard?"

"If I did," said Harriet, cautiously, "I shouldn't be the only person to do so. But I'm bound to say that she doesn't seem to fit in at all with the line of Lord Peter's inquiries, so far as I am acquainted with them."

"I am glad to hear you say that," replied Dr. Baring. "Representations have been made to me which—in default of evidence—I have been very unwilling to listen to."

So Dr. Baring had kept abreast of the feeling in the S.C.R. Miss Allison and Mrs. Goodwin had probably been talking. Well!

"In the end," pursued the Warden, "I informed Lord Peter that I thought it would be better to wait for the further evidence. But that decision must, of course, be subject to the willingness of yourself and Miss de Vine to face the risks involved. The willingness of the unknown third party cannot, naturally, be ascertained."

"I don't in the least mind what risks *I* take," said Harriet. "But Miss de Vine ought to be warned, I suppose."

"That is what I said. Lord Peter agreed."

So, thought Harriet, something has decided him to acquit Miss de Vine. I'm glad. Unless this is a Machiavellian ruse to throw her off her guard.

"Have you said anything to Miss de Vine, Warden?"

"Miss de Vine is in Town, and will not return till tomorrow evening. I propose to speak to her then."

So there was nothing to do but to wait. And in the meantime, Harriet became aware of a curious change in the atmosphere of the Senior Common Room. It was as though they had lost sight of their mutual distrust and their general apprehensions and had drawn together like spectators at the ringside to watch another kind of conflict, in which she was one of the principals. The curious tension thus produced was scarcely relieved by the Dean's announcement to a few select spirits that in her opinion, Flaxman's young man had given her the chuck and serve her right; to which Miss Flaxman's tutor sourly replied that she wished people wouldn't have these upheavals in the Summer Term, but that, fortunately, Miss Flaxman didn't take her final Schools till next year. This prompted Harriet to ask Miss Shaw how Miss Newland was getting on. It appeared that Miss Newland was doing well, having completely got over the shock of her immersion in the Cherwell, so that her chances for a First looked pretty good.

"Splendid!" said Harriet. "I've ear-marked my winnings already. By the way, Miss Hillyard, how is our young friend Cattermole?"

It seemed to her that the room waited breathlessly for the answer. Miss Hillyard replied, rather shortly, that Miss Cattermole seemed to have recovered such form as she had ever possessed, thanks, as she understood from the young woman herself, to Miss Vane's good advice. She added that it was very kind of Harriet, amid her many preoccupations, to interest herself in the History students. Harriet made some vague reply and the room, as it seemed to her, breathed again.

Later in the day, Harriet took an outrigger on the river with the Dean, and, rather to her surprise, observed Miss Cattermole and Mr. Pomfret sharing a punt. She had received the "penitent letter" from Mr. Pomfret, and waved a cheerful hand as the boats passed, in token of peace restored. If she had known that Mr. Pomfret and Miss Cattermole had found a bond of sympathy in devotion to herself, she might have speculated on what may happen to rejected lovers who confide their troubles to willing ears; but this did not occur to her, because she was wondering what, exactly, had happened that morning at the Mitre; and her thoughts had strayed away into the Botanical Gardens before the Dean pointed out, rather sharply, that she was setting a very irregular and leisurely stroke.

It was Miss Shaw who innocently precipitated a flare-up.

"That's a very handsome scarf," she said to Miss Hillyard. The dons were assembling, as usual, for Hall, outside the S.C.R.; but the evening was dull and chilly and a thick silk scarf was a grateful addition to evening dress.

"Yes," said Miss Hillyard. "Unfortunately it isn't mine. Some careless person left it in the Fellows' Garden last night and I rescued it. I brought it along to be identified–but I'm ready to admit that I can do with it this evening."

"I don't know whose it can be," said Miss Lydgate. She fingered it admiringly. "It looks more like a man's scarf," she added.

Harriet, who had not been paying much attention, turned round, conscience-stricken.

"Good lord!" she said, "that's mine. At least, it's Peter's. I couldn't think where I'd left it."

It was, in fact, the very scarf that had been used for a strangling demonstration on the Friday, and been brought back to Shrewsbury by accident together with the chessmen and the dog-collar. Miss Hillyard turned brick-red and snatched it off as though it were choking her.

"I beg your pardon, Miss Vane," she said, holding it out.

"It's all right. I don't want it now. But I'm glad to know where it is. I'd have got into trouble if I'd lost it."

"Will you kindly take your property," said Miss Hillyard.

Harriet, who was already wearing a scarf of her own, said:

"Thank you. But are you sure you won't–"

"I will *not*," said Miss Hillyard, dropping the scarf angrily on the steps.

"Dear me!" said the Dean, picking it up. "Nobody seems to want this nice scarf. I shall borrow it. I call it a nasty, chilly evening, and I don't know why we can't all go inside."

She twisted the scarf comfortably round her neck and, the Warden mercifully arriving at that moment, they went in to dinner.

At a quarter to ten, Harriet, after an hour or so spent with Miss Lydgate on her proofs–now actually nearing the stage when they might really be sent to the printer–crossed the Old Quad to Tudor Building. On the steps, just coming out, she met Miss Hillyard.

"Were you looking for me?" asked Harriet, a little aggressively.

"No," said Miss Hillyard, "I wasn't. Certainly not." She spoke hurriedly, and Harriet fancied that there was something in her eyes both furtive and malicious; but the evening was dark for the middle of May, and she could not be sure.

"Oh!" said Harriet. "I thought you might be."

"Well, I wasn't," said Miss Hillyard again. And as Harriet passed her she turned back and said, almost as though the words were forced out of her:

"Going to work—under the inspiration of your beautiful chessmen?"

"More or less," said Harriet, laughing.

"I hope you will have a pleasant evening," said Miss Hillyard.

Harriet went on upstairs and opened the door of her room.

The glass case had been shattered, and the floor was strewn with broken glass and with smashed and trampled fragments of red and white ivory.

For about five minutes, Harriet was the prey of that kind of speechless rage which is beyond expression or control. If she had thought of it, she was at that moment in a mood to sympathize with the Poltergeist and all her works. If she could have beaten or strangled anybody, she would have done it and felt the better for it. Happily, after the first devastating fury, she found the relief of bad language. When she found she could keep her voice steady, she locked her bedroom door behind her and went down to the telephone.

Even so, she was at first so incoherent that Peter could hardly understand what she said. When he did understand, he was maddeningly cool about it, merely asking whether she had touched anything or told anybody. When assured that she had not, he replied cheerfully that he would be along in a few minutes.

Harriet went out and raged distractedly about the New Quad till she heard him ring—for the gates were just shut—and only a last lingering vestige of self-restraint prevented her from rushing at him and pouring out her indignation in the presence of Padgett. But she waited for him in the middle of the quad.

"Peter—oh Peter!"

"Well," said he, "this is rather encouraging. I was afraid we might have choked off these demonstrations for good and all."

"But my chessmen! I could kill her for that."

"My dear, it's sickening that it should be your chessmen. But don't let's lose all sense of proportion. It might have been you."

"I wish it had been. I could have hit back."

"Termagant. Let's go and look at the damage."

"It's horrible, Peter. It's like a massacre. It's—it's rather frightening, somehow—they've been hit so hard."

When he saw the room, Wimsey looked grave enough.

"Yes," he said, kneeling amid the wreckage. "Blind, bestial malignity. Not only broken but ground to powder. There's been a heel at work here, as well as the poker; you can see the marks on the carpet. She hates you, Harriet. I didn't realize that. I thought she was only afraid of you . . . . Is there yet any that is left of the house of Saul? . . . Look! one poor warrior hiding behind the coal-scuttle—remnant of a mighty army."

He held up the solitary red pawn, smiling; and then scrambled hurriedly to his feet.

"My dear girl, don't cry about it. What the hell does it matter?"

"I loved them," said Harriet, "and you gave them to me."

He shook his head.

"It's a pity it's that way round. 'You gave them to me, and I loved them' is all right, but 'I loved them and you gave them to me' is irreparable. Fifty thousand rocs' eggs won't supply their place. 'The Virgin's gone and I am gone; she's gone, she's gone and what shall I do?' But you needn't weep over the chest of drawers while I have a shoulder at your disposal, need you?"

"I'm sorry. I'm being a perfect idiot."

"I told you love was the devil and all. Two-and-thirty chessmen, baked in a pie. 'And all the powerful kings and all the beautiful queens of this world were but as a bed of flowers' . . ."

"I might have had the decency to take care of them."

"That's foolish," said he, with his mouth muffled in her hair. "Don't talk so soft, or I shall get foolish too. Listen. When did all this happen?"

"Between Hall and a quarter to ten."

"Was anybody absent from Hall? Because this must have made a bit of a noise. After Hall, there'd be students about, who might hear the glass smash or notice if anybody unusual was wandering about."

"There might be students here all through Hall–they often have eggs in their rooms. And–good God!–there was somebody unusual– She said something about the chessmen, too. And she was queer about them last night."

"Who was that?"

"Miss Hillyard."

"Again!"

While Harriet told her story he fidgeted restlessly about the room, avoiding the broken glass and ivory on the floor with the automatic precision of a cat, and stood at length in the window with his back to her. She had drawn the curtains together when she had brought him up, and his gaze at them seemed purely preoccupied.

"Hell!" he said, presently. "That's a devil of a complication." He still had the red pawn in his hand, and he now came back, and set it with great precision in the centre of the mantelpiece. "Yes. Well, I suppose you'll have to find out–"

Somebody knocked at the door, and Harriet went to open it.

"Excuse me, madam, but Padgett sent over to the Senior Common Room to see if Lord Peter Wimsey was there, and seeing he thought you might know–"

"He's here, Annie. It's for you, Peter."

"Yes?" said Peter, coming to the door.

"If you please, sir, they've rung up from the Mitre to say there's a message come from the Foreign Office and would you kindly ring up at once."

"What? Oh, Lord, that *would* happen! Very well, thank you, Annie. Oh, one moment. Was it you who saw the–er–the person who was playing tricks in the Lecture-Room?"

"Yes, sir. Not to know her again, sir."

"No; but you did see her, and she may not know you couldn't recognize her. I think if I were you I'd be rather careful how you go about the College after dark. I don't want to frighten you, but you see what's happened to Miss Vane's chessmen?"

"Yes, I see, sir. What a pity, isn't it?"

"It would be more than a pity if anything unpleasant happened to you personally. Now, don't get the wind up—but if I were you, I'd take somebody with me when I went out after sunset. And I should give the same advice to the scout who was with you."

"To Carrie? Very well, I'll tell her."

"It's only a precaution, you know. Good-night, Annie."

"Good-night, sir. Thank you."

"I shall have to make quite an issue of dog-collars," said Peter. "You never know whether to warn people or not. Some of them get hysterics, but she looks fairly level-headed. Look here, my dear, this is all very tiresome. If it's another summons to Rome, I shall have to go. (I should lock that door.) Needs must when duty calls, and all that. If it *is* Rome, I'll tell Bunter to bring round all the notes I've got at the Mitre and instruct Miss Climpson's sleuths to report direct to you. In any case, I'll ring you up this evening as soon as I know what it's all about. If it isn't Rome, I'll come round again in the morning. And in the meantine, don't let anybody into your room. I think I'd lock it up and sleep elsewhere tonight."

"I thought you didn't expect any more night disturbances."

"I don't; but I don't want people walking over that floor." He stopped on the staircase to examine the soles of his shoes. "I haven't carried away any bits. Do you think you have?"

Harriet stood first on one leg and then another.

"Not this time. And the first time I didn't walk into the mess at all. I stood in the doorway and swore."

"Good girl. The paths in the quad are a bit damp, you know, and something might have stuck. As a matter of fact, it's raining a little now. You'll get wet."

"It doesn't matter. Oh, Peter! I've got that white scarf of yours."

"Keep it till I come again—which will be tomorrow, with luck, and otherwise, God knows when. Damn it! I knew there was trouble coming." He stood still under the beech-trees. "Harriet, don't choose the moment my back's turned to get yourself wiped out or anything—not if you can help it; I mean, you're not very good at looking after valuables."

"I might have the decency to take care? All right, Peter. I'll do my best this time. Word of honour."

She gave him her hand and he kissed it. Once again Harriet thought she saw somebody move in the darkness, as on the last occasion they had walked through the shadowy quads. But she dared not delay him and so again said nothing. Padgett let him out through the gate and Harriet, turning away, found herself face to face with Miss Hillyard.

"Miss Vane, I should like to speak to you."

"Certainly," said Harriet. "I should rather like to speak to *you*."

Miss Hillyard, without another word, led the way to her own rooms. Harriet followed her up the stairs and into the sitting-room. The tutor's face was very white as she shut the door after them and said, without asking Harriet to sit down:

"Miss Vane. What are the relations between that man and you?"

"What do you mean by that?"

"You know perfectly well what I mean. If nobody else will speak to you about your behaviour, I must. You bring the man here, knowing perfectly well what his reputation is—"

"I know what his reputation as a detective is."

"I mean his moral reputation. You know as well as I do that he is notorious all over Europe. He keeps women by the score—"

"All at once or in succession?"

"It's no use being impertinent. I suppose that to a person with your past history, that kind of thing is merely amusing. But you must try to conduct yourself with a little more decency. The way you look at him is a disgrace. You pretend to be the merest acquaintance of his and call him by his title in public and his Christian name in private. You take him up to your room at night–"

"Really, Miss Hillyard, I can't allow–"

"I've seen you. Twice. He was there tonight. You let him kiss your hands and make love to you–"

"So that was you, spying about under the beeches."

"How dare you use such a word?"

"How dare you say such a thing?"

"It's no affair of mine how you behave in Bloomsbury. But if you bring your lovers here–"

"You know very well that he is not my lover. And you know very well why he came to my room tonight."

"I can guess."

"And *I* know very well why *you* came there."

"I came there? I don't know what you mean."

"You do. And you know that he came to see the damage you did in my room."

"I never went into your room."

"You didn't go into my room and smash up my chessmen?"

Miss Hillyard's dark eyes flickered.

"Certainly I did not. I told you I hadn't been anywhere near your room tonight."

"Then," said Harriet, "you told a lie."

She was too angry to be frightened, though it did cross her mind that if the furious white-faced woman attacked her, it might be difficult to summon assistance on this isolated staircase, and she thought of the dog-collar.

"I know it's a lie," said Harriet, "because there's a piece of broken ivory on the carpet under your writing-table and another stuck on the sole of your right shoe. I saw it, coming upstairs."

She was prepared for anything after that, but to her surprise, Miss Hillyard staggered a little, sat down suddenly, and said, "Oh, my God!"

"If you had nothing to do with smashing those chessmen," went on Harriet, "or with the other pranks that have been played in this College, you'd better explain those pieces of ivory."

(Am I a fool, she thought, showing my hand like this? But if I didn't, what would become of the evidence?)

Miss Hillyard, in a bewildered way, pulled off her slipper and looked at the sliver of white that clung to the heel, embedded in a little patch of damp gravel.

"Give it to me," said Harriet, and took slipper and all.

She had expected an outburst of denial, but Miss Hillyard said, faintly:

"That's evidence . . . incontrovertible . . . ."

Harriet thanked Heaven, with grim amusement, for the scholarly habit; at least, one did not have to argue about what was or was not evidence.

"I did go into your room. I went there to say to you what I said just now. But you weren't there. And when I saw the mess on the floor I thought–I was afraid you'd think–"

"I did think."

"What did he think?"

"Lord Peter? I don't know what he thought. But he'll probably think something now."

"You've no evidence that I did it," said Miss Hillyard, with sudden spirit. "Only that I was in the room. It was done when I got there. I saw it, I went to look at it. You can tell your lover that I saw it and was glad to see it. But he'll tell you that's no proof that I did it."

"Look here, Miss Hillyard," said Harriet, divided between anger, suspicion and a dreadful kind of pity, 'You must understand, once and for all, that he is not my lover. Do you really imagine that if he were, we should—" here her sense of the ludicrous overcame her and made it difficult to control her voice—"we should come and misbehave ourselves in the greatest possible discomfort at Shrewsbury? Even if I had no respect for the College—where would be the point of it? With all the world and all the time there is at our disposal, why on earth should we come and play the fool down here? It would be silly. And if you really were down there in the quad just now, you must know that people who are lovers don't treat each other like that. At least," she added rather unkindly, "if you knew anything about it at all, you'd know that. We're very old friends, and I owe him a great deal—"

"Don't talk nonsense," said the tutor roughly. "You know you're in love with the man."

"By God!" said Harriet, suddenly enlightened, "if I'm not, I know who is."

"You've no right to say that!"

"It's true, all the same," said Harriet. "Oh, damn! I suppose it's no good my saying I'm frightfully sorry." (Dynamite in a powder factory? Yes, indeed, Miss Edwards, you saw it before anybody else. Biologically interesting!) "This kind of thing is the devil and all." ("That's the devil of a complication," Peter had said. He'd seen it, of course. Must have. Too much experience not to. Probably happened scores of times—scores of women—all over Europe. Oh, dear! Oh, dear! And was that a random accusation, or had Miss Hillyard been delving into the past and digging up Viennese singers?)

"For Heaven's sake," said Miss Hillyard, "go away!"

"I think I'd better," said Harriet.

She did not know how to deal with the situation at all. She could no longer feel outraged or angry. She was not alarmed. She was not jealous. She was only sorry, and quite incapable of expressing any sympathy which would not be an insult. She realized that she was still clutching Miss Hillyard's slipper. Had she better give it back? It was evidence—of something. But of what? The whole business of the Poltergeist seemed to have retreated over the horizon, leaving behind it the tormented shell of a woman staring blindly into vacancy under the cruel harshness of the electric light. Harriet picked up the other fragment of ivory from under the writingtable—the little spearhead from a red pawn.

Well, whatever one's personal feelings, evidence was evidence. Peter—she remembered that Peter had said he would ring up from the Mitre. She went downstairs with the slipper in her hand, and in the New Quad ran into Mrs. Padgett, who was just coming to look for her.

The call was switched through to the box in Queen Elizabeth.

"It's not so bad after all," said Peter's voice. "It's only the Grand Panjandrum wanting a conference at his private house. Sort of Pleasant Sunday Afternoon in Wild Warwickshire. It may mean London or Rome after that but we'll hope not. At any rate, it'll do if I'm there by half-past eleven, so I'll pop round and see you about nine."

"Please do. Something's happened. Not alarming, but upsetting. I can't tell you on the 'phone."

He again promised to come, and said good-night. Harriet, after locking the slipper and the piece of ivory carefully away, went to the Bursar, and was accommodated with a bed in the Infirmary.

# 21

Thus she there wayted until eventyde,
Yet living creature none she saw appeare.
And now sad shadows gan the world to hyde
From mortall vew, and wrap in darkenes dreare;
Yet nould she d'off her weary armes, for feare
Of secret daunger, ne let sleepe oppresse
Her heavy eyes with nature's burdein deare,
But drew her self aside in sickernesse,
And her wel-pointed wepons did about her dresse.

Edmund Spenser

HARRIET LEFT word at the Lodge that she would wait for Lord Peter Wimsey in the Fellows' Garden. She had breakfasted early, thus avoiding Miss Hillyard, who passed through the New Quad like an angry shadow while she was talking to Padgett.

She had first met Peter at a moment when every physical feeling had been battered out of her by the brutality of circumstance; by this accident she had been aware of him from the beginning as a mind and spirit localized in a body. Never—not even in those later dizzying moments on the river—had she considered him primarily as a male animal, or calculated the promise implicit in the veiled eyes, the long, flexible mouth, the curiously vital hands. Nor, since of her he had always asked and never demanded, had she felt in him any domination but that of intellect. But now, as he advanced towards her along the flower-bordered path, she saw him with new eyes—the eyes of women who had seen him before they knew him—saw him, as they saw him, dynamically. Miss Hillyard, Miss Edwards, Miss de Vine, the Dean even, each in her own way had recognized the same thing: six centuries of possessiveness, fastened under the yoke of urbanity. She herself, seeing it impudent and uncontrolled in the nephew, had known it instantly for what it was; it astonished her that in the older man she should have been blind to it so long and should still retain so strong a defence against it. And she wondered whether it was only accident that had sealed her eyes till it was too late for realization to bring disaster.

She sat still where she was till he stood looking down at her.

"Well?" he said, lightly, "how doth my lady? What, sweeting, all amort? . . . Yes, something has happened; I see it has. What is it, domina?"

Though the tone was half-jesting, nothing could have reassured her like that grave, academic title. She said, as though she were reciting a lesson:

"When you left last night, Miss Hillyard met me in the New Quad. She asked me to come up to her room because she wanted to speak to me. On the way up, I saw there was a little piece of white ivory stuck on the heel of her slipper. She—made some rather unpleasant accusations; she had misunderstood the position—"

"That can and shall be put right. Did you say anything about the slipper?'

"I'm afraid I did. There was another bit of ivory on the floor. I accused her of having gone into my room, and she denied it till I showed her the evidence. Then she admitted it; but she said the damage was already done when she got there.

"Did you believe her?"

"I might have done . . . if . . . if she hadn't shown me a motive."

"I see. All right. You needn't tell me."

She looked up for the first time into a face as bleak as winter, and faltered:

"I brought the slipper away with me. I wish I hadn't."

"Are you going to be afraid of the facts?" he said. "And you a scholar?"

"I don't think I did it in malice. I hope not. But I was bitterly unkind to her."

"Happily," said he, "a fact is a fact, and your state of mind won't alter it by a hair's breadth. Let's go now and have the truth at all hazards."

She led him up to her room, where the morning sun cast a long rectangle of brilliance across the ruin on the floor. From the chest near the door she took out the slipper and handed it to him. He lay down flat, squinting sideways along the carpet in the place where neither he nor she had trodden the night before. His hand went to his pocket, and he smiled up sideways into her troubled face.

"If all the pens that ever poets held had had the feeling of their masters' thoughts, they could not write as much solid fact as you can hold in a pair of callipers." He measured the heel of the slipper in both directions, and then turned his attention to the pile of the carpet. "She stood here, heels together, looking." The callipers twinkled over the sunlit rectangle. "And here is the heel that stamped and trampled and ground beauty to dust. One was a French heel and one was a Cuban heel—isn't that what the footwear specialists call them?" He sat up and tapped the sole of the slipper lightly with the callipers. "Who goes there? France— Pass, France, and all's well."

"Oh, I'm glad," said Harriet, fervently. "I'm glad."

"Yes. Meanness isn't one of your accomplishments, is it?" He turned his eyes to the carpet again, this time to a place near the edge.

"Look! now that the sun's out you can see it. Here's where Cuban Heel wiped her soles before she left. There are very few flies on Cuban Heel. Well, that saves us a back-breaking search all over the college for the dust of kings and queens." He picked the sliver of ivory from the French heel, put the slipper in his pocket and stood up. "This had better go back to its owner, furnished with a certificate of innocence."

"Give it to me. I must take it."

"No, you will not. If anybody has to face unpleasantness, it shan't be you this time."

"But, Peter—you won't—"

"No," he said, "I won't. Trust me for that."

Harriet was left staring at the broken chessman. Presently she went out into the corridor, found a dustpan and brush in a scout's pantry and returned with them to sweep up the debris. As she was replacing the brush and pan in the pantry, she ran into one of the students from the annexe.

"By the way, Miss Swift," said Harriet, "you didn't happen to hear any noise in my room like glass being smashed last night, did you? Some time during or after Hall?"

"No, I didn't, Miss Vane. I was in my own room all evening. But wait a moment. Miss Ward came along about halfpast nine to do some Morphology with me and"—the girl's mouth dimpled into laughter—"she asked if you were a secret toffee-eater, because it sounded as though you were smashing up toffee with the poker. Has the College Ghost been visiting you?"

"I'm afraid so," said Harriet. "Thank you; that's very helpful. I must see Miss Ward."

Miss Ward, however, could help no farther than by fixing the time a little more definitely as "certainly not later than half-past nine."

Harriet thanked her, and went out. Her very bones seemed to ache with restlessness—or perhaps it was with having slept badly in an unfamiliar bed and with a disturbed mind. The sun had scattered diamonds among the wet grass of the quadrangle, and the breeze was shaking the rain in a heavy spatter of drops from the beeches. Students came and went. Somebody had left a scarlet cushion out all night in the rain; it was sodden and mournful-looking; its owner came and picked it up, with an air between laughter and disgust; she threw it on a bench to dry in the sunshine.

To do nothing was intolerable. To be spoken to by any member of the Senior Common Room would be still more intolerable. She was penned in the Old Quad, for she was sensitive to the mere neighbourhood of the New Quad as a person that has been vaccinated is sensitive to everything that lies on the sore side of his body. Without particular aim or intention, she skirted the tennis-court and turned in at the Library entrance. She had intended to go upstairs but, seeing the door of Miss de Vine's set stand open, she altered her mind; she could borrow a book from there. The little lobby was empty, but in the sitting-room a scout was giving the writing-table a Sunday morning flick with the duster. Harriet remembered that Miss de Vine was in town, and that she was to be warned when she returned.

"What time does Miss de Vine get back tonight? Do you know, Nellie?"

"I think she gets in by the 9:39, miss."

Harriet nodded, took a book from the shelves at random, and went to sit on the steps of the loggia, where there was a deck-chair. The morning, she told herself, was getting on. If Peter had to get to his destination by 11:30, it was time he went. She vividly remembered waiting in a nursing-home while a friend underwent an operation; there had been a smell of ether, and in the waiting-room, a large black Wedgwood jar, filled with delphiniums.

She read a page without knowing what was in it, and looked up at an approaching footstep into the face of Miss Hillyard.

"Lord Peter," said Miss Hillyard, without preface, "asked me to give you this address. He was obliged to leave quickly to keep his appointment."

Harriet took the paper and said, "Thank you."

Miss Hillyard went on resolutely: "When I spoke to you last night I was under a misapprehension. I had not fully realized the difficulty of your position. I am afraid I have unwittingly made it harder for you, and I apologize."

"That's all right," said Harriet, taking refuge in formula. "I am sorry too. I was rather upset last night and said a great deal more than I should. This wretched business has made everything so uncomfortable."

"Indeed it has," said Miss Hillyard, in a more natural voice. "We are all feeling rather overwrought. I wish we could get at the truth of it. I understand that you now accept my account of my movements last night."

"Absolutely. It was inexcusable of me not to have verified my data."

"Appearances can be very misleading," said Miss Hillyard.

There was a pause.

"Well," said Harriet at last, "I hope we may forget all this." She knew as she spoke that one thing at least had been said which could never be forgotten: she would have given a great deal to recall it.

"I shall do my best," replied Miss Hillyard. "Perhaps I am too much inclined to judge harshly of matters outside my experience."

"It is very kind of you to say that," said Harriet. "Please believe that I don't take a very self-satisfied view of myself either."

"Very likely not. I have noticed that the people who get opportunities always seem to choose the wrong ones. But it's no affair of mine. Good morning."

She went as abruptly as she had come. Harriet glanced at the book on her knee and discovered that she was reading *The Anatomy of Melancholy.*

"*Fleat Heraclitus an rideat Democritus?* in attempting to speak of these Symptoms, shall I laugh with *Democritus* or weep with *Heraclitus?* they are so ridiculous and absurd on the one side, so lamentable and tragical on the other."

Harriet got the car out in the afternoon and took Miss Lydgate and the Dean for a picnic in the neighbourhood of Hinksey. When she got back, in time for supper, she found an urgent message at the Lodge, asking her to ring up Lord Saint-George at the House as soon as she got back. His voice, when he answered the call, sounded agitated.

"Oh, look here! I can't get hold of Uncle Peter—he's vanished again, curse him! I say, I saw your ghost this afternoon, and I do think you ought to be careful."

"Where did you see her? When?"

"About half-past two—walking over Magdalen Bridge in broad daylight. I'd been lunching with some chaps out Iffley way, and we were just pulling over to put one of 'em down at Magdalen, when I spotted her. She was walking along, muttering to herself, and looking awfully queer. Sort of clutching with her hands and rolling her eyes about. She spotted me, too. Couldn't mistake her. A friend of mine was driving and I tried to catch his attention, but he was pulling round behind a bus and I couldn't make him understand. Anyhow, when we stopped at Magdalen gate, I hopped out and ran back, but I couldn't find her anywhere. Seemed to have faded out. I bet she knew I was on to her and made tracks. I was scared. Thought she looked up to anything. So I rang up your place and found you were out and then I rang up the Mitre and that wasn't any good either, so I've been sitting here all evening in a devil of a stew. First I thought I'd leave a note, and then I thought I'd better tell you myself. Rather devoted of me, don't you think? I cut a supper-party so as not to miss you."

"That was frightfully kind of you," said Harriet. "What was the ghost dressed in?"

"Oh—one of those sort of dark-blue frocks with spriggy bits on it and a hat with a brim. Sort of thing most of your dons wear in the afternoon. Neat, not gaudy. Not smart. Just ordinary. It was the eyes I recognized. Made me feel all goose flesh. Honest. That woman's not safe, I'll swear she isn't."

"It's very good of you to warn me," said Harriet again. "I'll try and find out who it could have been. And I'll take precautions."

"Please do," said Lord Saint-George. "I mean, Uncle Peter's getting the wind up horribly. Gone clean off his oats. Of course I know he's a fidgety old ass and I've been doing my best to soothe the troubled beast and all that, but

I'm beginning to think he's got some excuse. For goodness' sake, Aunt Harriet, do something about it. I can't afford to have a valuable uncle destroyed under my eyes. He's getting like the Lord of Burleigh, you know—walking up and pacing down and so on—and the responsibility is very wearing."

"I'll tell you what," said Harriet. "You'd better come and dine in College tomorrow and see if you can spot the lady. It's no good this evening, because so many people don't turn up to Sunday supper."

"Right-ho!" said the viscount. "That's a dashed good idea. I'd get a dashed good birthday-present out of Uncle Peter if I solved his problem for him. So long and take care of yourself."

"I ought to have thought of that before," said Harriet, retailing this piece of news to the Dean; "but I never imagined he'd recognize the woman like that after only seeing her once."

The Dean, to whom the whole story of Lord Saint-George's ghostly encounter had come as a novelty, was inclined to be sceptical. "Personally, I wouldn't undertake to identify anybody after one glimpse in the dark—and I certainly wouldn't trust a young harum-scarum like that. The only person here I know of with a navy sprigged foulard is Miss Lydgate, and I absolutely refuse to believe *that!* But ask the young man to dinner by all means. I'm all for excitement, and he's even more ornamental than the other one."

It was borne in upon Harriet that things were coming to a crisis. "Take precautions." A nice fool she would look, going about with a dog-collar round her neck. Nor would it be any defence against pokers and such things. . . . The wind must be in the south-west, for the heavy boom of Tom tolling his hundred-and-one came clearly to her ears as she crossed the Old Quad.

"Not later than half-past nine," Miss Ward had said. If the peril had ceased to walk by night, it was still abroad of an evening.

She went upstairs and locked the door of her room before opening a drawer and taking out the heavy strap of brass and leather. There was something about the description of that woman walking wild-eyed over Magdalen Bridge and "clutching with her hands" that was very unpleasant to think of. She could feel Peter's grip on her throat now like a band of iron, and could hear him saying serenely, like a textbook:

"*That* is the dangerous spot. Compression of the big blood-vessels there will cause almost instant unconsciousness. And then, you see, you're done for."

And at the momentary pressure of his thumbs the fire had swum in her eyes.

She turned with a start as something rattled the door-handle. Probably the passage-window was open and the wind blowing in. She was getting ridiculously nervous.

The buckle was stiff to her fingers. (Is thy servant a dog that she should do this thing?) When she saw herself in the glass, she laughed. "An arum-lily quality that is in itself an invitation to violence." Her own face, in the drowned evening light, surprised her—softened and startled and drained of colour, with eyes that looked unnaturally large under the heavy black brows, and lips a little parted. It was like the head of someone who had been guillotined; the dark band cut it off from the body like the stroke of the headsman's steel.

She wondered whether her lover had seen it like that, through that hot unhappy year when she had tried to believe that there was happiness in surrender. Poor Philip—tormented by his own vanities, never loving her till he had killed her feeling for him, and yet perilously clutching her as he went down into the slough of death. It was not to Philip she had submitted, so much as to a theory of living. The young were always theoretical; only the middle-aged could realize the deadliness of principles. To subdue one's self to one's own ends might be dangerous, but to subdue one's self to other people's ends was dust and ashes. Yet there were those, still more unhappy, who envied even the ashy saltness of those dead sea apples.

Could there ever be any alliance between the intellect and the flesh? It was this business of asking questions and analyzing everything that sterilized and stultified all one's passions. Experience perhaps had a formula to get over this difficulty: one kept the bitter, tormenting brain on one side of the wall and the languorous sweet body on the other, and never let them meet. So that if you were made that way, you could argue about loyalties in an Oxford common-room and refresh yourself elsewhere with—say—Viennese singers, presenting an unruffled surface on both sides of yourself. Easy for a man, and possible even for a woman, if one avoided foolish accidents like being tried for murder. But to seek to force incompatibles into a compromise was madness; one should neither do it nor be a party to it. If Peter wanted to make the experiment, he must do it without Harriet's connivance. Six centuries of possessive blood would not be dictated to by a bare forty-five years of over-sensitized intellect. Let the male animal take the female and be content; the busy brain could very well be "left talking" like the hero of *Man and Superman*. In a long monologue, of course; for the female animal could only listen without contributing. Otherwise one would get the sort of couple one had in *Private Lives*, who rolled on the floor and hammered one another when they weren't making love, because they (obviously) had no conversational resources. A vista of crashing boredom, either way.

The door rattled again, as a reminder that even a little boredom might be welcome by way of change from alarms. On the mantelpiece, a solitary red pawn mocked all security. . . . How quietly Annie had taken Peter's warning. Did she take it seriously? Was she looking after herself? She had been her usual refined and self-contained self when she brought in the Common-room coffee that night—perhaps a little brighter-looking than usual. Of course, she had had her afternoon off with Beatie and Carola. . . . Curious, thought Harriet, this desire to possess children and dictate their tastes, as though they were escaping fragments of one's self, and not separate individuals. Even if the taste ran to motor-bikes. . . . Annie was all right. How about Miss de Vine, traveling down from Town in happy ignorance?—With a start, Harriet saw that it was nearly a quarter to ten. The train must be in. Had the Warden remembered about warning Miss de Vine? She ought not to be left to sleep in the ground-floor room without being fore-armed. But the Warden never forgot anything.

Nevertheless, Harriet was uneasy. From her window she could not see whether any lights were on in the Library Wing. She unlocked the door and stepped out (yes—the passage-window was open; nobody but the wind had rattled the handle). A few dim figures were still moving at the far end of the quad as she passed along beside the tennis-court. In the Library Wing, all the ground-floor windows were dark except for the dim glow of the passage-light. Miss Barton, at any rate, was not in her room; nor was Miss de Vine back yet. Or—yes, she must be; for the window-curtains were drawn in her sitting-room, though no light shone as yet behind them.

Harriet went into the building. The door of Miss Burrows's set stood open, and the lobby was dark. Miss de Vine's door was shut. She knocked, but there was no answer–and it suddenly struck her as odd that the curtains should be drawn and no light on. She opened the door and pressed down the wall-switch in the lobby. Nothing happened. With a growing sense of disquiet, she went on to the sitting-room door and opened that. And then, as her fingers went out to the switch, the fierce clutch took her by the throat.

She had two advantages: she was partly prepared, and the assailant had not expected the dog-collar. She felt and heard the quick gasp in her face as the strong, cruel fingers fumbled on the stiff leather. As they shifted their hold, she had time to remember what she had been taught–to catch and jerk the wrists apart. But as her feet felt for the other's feet, her high heels slipped on the parquet–and she was falling–they were falling together and she was undermost; they seemed to take years to fall; and all the time a stream of hoarse, filthy abuse was running into her ears. Then the world went black in fire and thunder.

Faces–swimming confusedly through crackling waves of pain–swelling and diminishing anxiously–then resolving themselves into one–Miss Hillyard's face, enormous and close to her own. Then a voice, agonizingly loud, blaring unintelligibly like a fog-horn. Then, suddenly and quite clearly, like the lighted stage of a theatre, the room, with Miss de Vine, white as marble, on the couch and the Warden bending over her, and in between, on the floor, a white bowl filled with scarlet and the Dean kneeling beside it. Then the fog-horn boomed again, and she heard her own voice, incredibly faroff and thin: "Tell Peter,–" Then nothing.

Somebody had a headache–a quite unbearably awful headache. The white bright room in the Infirmary would have been very pleasant, if it hadn't been for the oppressive neighbourhood of the person with the headache, who was, moreover, groaning very disagreeably. It was an effort to pull one's self together and find out what the tiresome person wanted. With an effort like that of a hippopotamus climbing out of a swamp, Harriet pulled herself together and discovered that the headache and the groans were her own, and that the Infirmarian had realized what she was about and was coming to lend a hand.

"What in the world–?" said Harriet.

"Ah!" said the Infirmarian, "that's better. No–don't try to sit up. You've had a nasty knock on the head, and the quieter you keep the better."

"Oh, I see," said Harriet. "I've got a beast of a headache." A little thought located the worst part of the headache somewhere behind the right ear. She put up an exploratory hand and encountered a bandage. "What happened?"

"That's what we'd all like to know," said the Infirmarian.

"Well, I can't remember a thing," said Harriet.

"It doesn't matter. Drink this."

Like a book, thought Harriet. They always said, "Drink this." The room wasn't really so bright after all; the Venetian shutters were closed. It was her own eyes that were extraordinarily sensitive to light. Better shut them.

"Drink this" must have had something helpfully potent about it, because when she woke up again, the headache was better and she felt ravenously hungry. Also, she was beginning to remember things–the dog-collar and the lights that wouldn't go on–and the hands that had come clutching out of the darkness. There, memory obstinately stopped short. How the headache had come into existence she had no idea. Then she saw again the picture of Miss de Vine stretched on the couch. She asked after her.

"She's in the next room," said the Infirmarian. "She's had rather a nasty heart-attack, but she's better now. She would try to do too much, and of course, finding you like that was a shock to her."

It was not till the evening, when the Dean came in and found the patient fretting herself into a fever of curiosity, that Harriet got a complete story of the night's adventures.

"Now, if you'll keep quiet," said the Dean, "I'll tell you. If not, not. And your beautlful young man has sent you a young gardenful of flowers and will call again in the morning. Well, now! Poor Miss de Vine got here about 10 o'clock—her train was a bit late—and Mullins met her with a message to go and see the Warden *at* once. However, she thought she'd better take her hat off first, so she went along to her rooms—all in a hurry, so as not to keep Dr. Baring waiting. Well, of course, the first thing was that the lights wouldn't go on; and then to her horror she heard *you*, my dear, snorting on the floor in the dark. So then she tried the table-lamp and that worked—and there you were, a nasty bluggy sight for a respectable female don to find in her sitting-room. You've got two beautiful stitches in you, by the way; it was the corner of the bookcase did that. . . . So Miss de Vine rushed out calling for help, but there wasn't a soul in the building, and then, my dear, she ran like fury over to Burleigh and some students tore out to see what was happening and then somebody fetched the Warden and somebody else fetched the Infirmarian and somebody else fetched Miss Stevens and Miss Hillyard and me who were having a quiet cup of tea in my room, and we rang up the doctor, and Miss de Vine's groggy heart went back on her, what with shock and running about, and she went all blue on us—we had a lovely time."

"You must have. One other gaudy night! I suppose you haven't found who did it?"

"For quite a long time we hadn't a moment to think about that part of it. And then, just as we were settling down, all the fuss started again about Annie."

"Annie? What's happened to her?"

"Oh, didn't you know? We found her in the coal-hole, my dear, in such a state, what with coal-dust and hammering her fists on the door; and I wonder she wasn't clean off her head, poor thing, locked up there all that time. And if it hadn't been for Lord Peter we mightn't even have begun to look for her till next morning, what with everything being in such an uproar."

"Yes—he warned her she might be attacked....How did he—? Did you get him on the 'phone, or what?

"Oh, yes. Well, after we'd got you and Miss de Vine to bed and had made up our minds you wouldn't either of you peg out yet awhile, somebody brightly remembered that the first thing you said when we picked you up was 'Tell Peter.' So we rang up the Mitre and he wasn't there; and then Miss Hillyard said she knew where he was and 'phoned through. That was after midnight. Fortunately, he hadn't gone to bed. He said he'd come over at once, and then he asked what had happened to Annie Wilson. Miss Hillyard thought the shock had affected his wits, I think. However, he insisted that she ought to be kept an eye on, so we all started to look for her. Well, you know what a job it is tracking anybody down in this place, and we hunted and hunted and nobody had seen anything of her. And then, just before two, Lord Peter arrived, looking like death, and said we were to turn the place upside down if we didn't want a corpse on our hands. Nice and reassuring *that* was!"

"I wish I hadn't missed it all," said Harriet. "He must have thought I was an awful ass to let myself be knocked out like that."

"He didn't say so," said the Dean, drily. "He came in to see you, but of course you were well under the weather. And of course he explained about the dog-collar, which had puzzled us all dreadfully."

"Yes. She went for my throat. I do remember that. I suppose she really meant to get Miss de Vine."

"Obviously. And with her weak heart—and no dog-collar—she wouldn't have had much chance, or so the doctor said. It was very lucky for her you happened to go in there. Or did you know?"

"I think," said Harriet, her memory still rather confused, "I went to tell her about Peter's warning and—oh, yes! there was something funny about the window-curtains. And the lights were all off."

"The bulbs had been taken out. Well, anyway, somewhere about four o'clock, Padgett found Annie. She was locked up in the coal-cellar under the Hall Building, at the far end of the boiler-house. The key'd been taken away and Padgett had to break in the door. She was pounding and shouting—but of course, if we hadn't been searching for her she might have yelled till Doomsday, especially as the radiators are off, and we're not using the furnace. She was in what they call a state of collapse and couldn't give us a coherent story for ever so long. But there's nothing really the matter with her except shock and bruises where she was flung down on the coal-heap. And of course her hands and arms were pretty well skinned with battering on the door and trying to climb out of the ventilator."

"What did she say happened?"

"Why, she was putting away the deck chairs in the loggia about half-past nine, when somebody seized her round the neck from behind and frog's-marched her off to the cellar. She said it was a woman, and very strong—"

"She was," said Harriet. "I can bear witness to that. Grip like steel. And a most unfeminine vocabulary."

"Annie says she never saw who it was, but she thought that the arm that was round her face had a dark sleeve on. Annie's own impression was that it was Miss Hillyard; but she was with the Bursar and me. But a good many of our strongest specimens haven't got alibis—particularly Miss Pyke, who says she was in her room, and Miss Barton, who claims to have been in the Fiction Library, looking for a 'nice book to read.' And Mrs. Goodwin, and Miss Burrows aren't very well accounted for, either. According to their own story, they were each seized at the same moment with an unaccountable desire to wander. Miss Burrows went to commune with Nature in the Fellows' Garden and Mrs. Goodwin to commune with a higher Authority in the Chapel. We are looking rather askance at one another today."

"I wish to goodness," said Harriet, "I'd been a trifle more efficient." She pondered a moment. "I wonder why she didn't stay to finish me off."

"Lord Peter wondered that, too. He said he thought she must either have thought you were dead, or been alarmed by the blood and finding she'd got the wrong person. When you went limp, she'd probably feel about and she'd know you were not Miss de Vine—short hair and no spectacles, you see—and she'd hurry off to get rid of any bloodstains before somebody came along. At least, that was his theory. He looked pretty queer about it."

"Is he here now?"

"No; he had to go back. . . . Something about getting an early 'plane from Croydon. He rang up and made a great to-do, but apparently it was all settled and he had to go. If any of his prayers are heard, I shouldn't think anybody in the Government would have a whole place in his body this morning. So I comforted him with hot coffee and he went off, leaving orders that neither you nor Miss de Vine nor Annie was to be left alone for a single moment. And he's rung up once from London and three times from Paris."

"Poor old Peter!" said Harriet. "He never seems to get a night's rest."

"Meanwhile, the Warden is valiantly issuing an unconvincing statement to the effect that somebody played a foolish practical joke on Annie, that you accidentally slipped and cut your head and that Miss de Vine was upset by the sight of blood. And the College gates are shut to all comers, for fear they should be reporters in disguise. But you can't keep the scouts quiet—goodness knows what reports are going out by the tradesmen's entrance. However, the great thing is that nobody's killed. And now I must be off, or the Infirmarian will have my blood and there really *will* be an inquest."

The next day brought Lord Saint-George. "My turn to visit the sick," he said. "You're a nice, restful aunt for a fellow to adopt, I don't think. Do you realize that you've done me out of a dinner?"

"Yes," said Harriet. "It's a pity– Perhaps I'd better tell the Dean. You might be able to identify—"

"Now don't you start laying plots," said he, "or your temperature will go up. You leave it to Uncle. He says he'll be back tomorrow, by the way, and the evidence is rolling in nicely and you're to keep quiet and not worry. Honour bright. Had him on the 'phone this morning. He's all of a doodah. Says anybody could have done his business in Paris, only they've got it into their heads he's the only person who can get on the right side of some tedious old mule or other who has to be placated or conciliated or something. As far as I can make out, some obscure journalist has been assassinated and somebody's trying to make an international incident of it. Hence the pyramids. I told you Uncle Peter had a strong sense of public duty; now you see it in action."

"Well, he's quite right."

"What an unnatural woman you are! He ought to be here, weeping into the sheets and letting the international situation blow itself to blazes." Lord Saint-George chuckled "I wish I'd been on the road with him on Monday morning. He collected five summonses in the round trip between Warwickshire and Oxford and London. My mother will be delighted. How's your head?"

"Doing fine. It was more the cut than the bump, I think."

"Scalp-wounds do bleed, don't they? Completely pig-like. Still, it's as well you're not a 'corpse in the case with a sad, swelled face.' You'll be all right when they get the stitches out. Only a bit convict-like that side of the head. You'll have to be cropped all round to even matters up and Uncle Peter can wear your discarded tresses next his heart."

"Come, come," said Harriet. "He doesn't date back to the seventies."

"He's aging rapidly. I should think he'd nearly got to the sixties by now. With beautiful, golden side-whiskers. I really think you ought to rescue him before his bones start to creak and the spiders spin webs over his eyes."

"You and your uncle," said Harriet, "should be set to turn phrases for a living."

# 22

O no, there is no end: the end is death and madness! As I am never better than when I am mad: then methinks I am a brave fellow; then I do wonders: but reason abuseth me, and there's the torment, there's the hell. At the last, sir, bring me to one of the murderers: were he as strong as Hector, thus would I tear and drag him up and down.

Ben Jonson

THURSDAY. A heavy, gloomy and depressing Thursday, pouring down uninteresting rain from a sky like a grey box-lid. The Warden had called a meeting of the Senior Common Room for half-past two—an unconsoling hour. All three invalids were up and about again. Harriet had exchanged her bandages for some very unbecoming and unromantic strappings, and had not exactly a headache, but the sensation that a headache might begin at any moment. Miss de Vine looked like a ghost. Annie, though she had suffered less than the others physically, seemed to be still haunted by nervous terrors, and crept unhappily about her duties with the other Common Room maid always closely in attendance.

It was understood that Lord Peter Wimsey would attend the S.C.R. meeting in order to lay certain information before the staff. Harriet had received from him a brief and characteristic note, which said:

"Congratulations on not being dead yet. I have taken your collar away to have my name put on."

She had already missed the collar. And she had had, from Miss Hillyard, a strangely vivid little picture of Peter, standing at her bedside between night and dawn, quite silent, and twisting the thick strap over and over in his hands.

All morning she had expected to see him; but he arrived only at the last moment so that their meeting took place in the Common Room, under the eyes of all the dons. He had driven straight from Town without changing his suit, and above the dark cloth his head had the bleached look of a faint water-colour. He paid his respects politely to the Warden and the Senior dons before coming over and taking her hand.

"Well, and how are you?"

"Not too bad, considering."

"That's good."

He smiled and went to sit by the Warden. Harriet, at the opposite side of the table, slipped into a place beside the Dean. Everything that was alive in him lay in the palm of her hand, like a ripe apple. Dr. Baring was asking him to begin and he was doing so, in the flat voice of a secretary reading the minutes of a company meeting. He had a sheaf of papers before him, including (Harriet noticed) her dossier, which he must have taken away on the Monday morning. But he went on without referring to so much as a note, addressing himself to a bowl filled with marigolds that stood on the table before him.

"I need not take up your time by going over all the details of this rather confusing case. I will first set out the salient points as they presented themselves to me when I came to Oxford last Sunday week, so as to show you the basis upon which I founded my working theory. I will then formulate that theory, and adduce the supporting evidence which I hope and think you will consider conclusive. I may say that practically all the data necessary to the formation of the theory are contained in the very valuable digest of the events prepared for me by Miss Vane and handed to me on my arrival. The rest of the proof was merely what the police call routine work."

(This, thought Harriet, is suiting your style to your company with a vengeance. She looked round. The Common Room had the hushed air of a congregation settling down to a sermon, but she could feel the nervous tension everywhere. They did not know what they might be going to hear.)

"The first point to strike an outsider," went on Peter, "is the fact that these demonstrations began at the Gaudy. I may say that that was the first bad mistake the perpetrator made. By the way, it will save time and trouble if I refer to the perpetrator in the time-honoured way as X. If X had waited till term began, we should have had a much wider field for suspicion. I therefore asked myself what it was that so greatly excited X at the Gaudy that she could not wait for a more suitable time to begin.

"It seemed unlikely that any of the Old Students present could have roused X's animosity, because the demonstrations continued in the following term. But they did not continue during the Long Vacation. So my attention was immediately directed to any person who entered the College for the first time at Gaudy and was in residence the following term. Only one person answered these requirements, and that was Miss de Vine."

The first stir went round the table, like the wind running over a cornfield.

"The first two communications came into the hands of Miss Vane. One of them, which amounted to an accusation of murder, was slipped into the sleeve of her gown and might, by a misleading coincidence, have been held to apply to her. But Miss Martin may remember that she placed Miss Vane's gown in the Senior Common Room side by side with that of Miss de Vine. I believe that X, misreading 'H. D. Vane' as 'H. de Vine' put the note in the wrong gown. This belief is, of course, not susceptible of proof; but the possibility is suggestive. The error, if it was one, distracted attention at the start from the central object of the campaign."

Nothing altered in the level voice as he lifted the old infamy into view only to cast it in the next breath into oblivion, but the hand that had held hers tightened for a moment and relaxed. She found herself watching the hand as it moved now among the sheaf of papers.

"The second communicatlon, picked up accidentally by Miss Vane in the quad, was destroyed like the other; but from the description I gather that it was a drawing similar to this." He slipped out a paper from under the clip and passed it to the Warden. "It represents a punishment inflicted by a naked female figure upon another, which is clothed in academical dress and epicene. This appears to be the symbolic key to the situation. In the Michaelmas Term, other drawings of a similar kind appear, together with the motif of the hanging of some academical character—a motif which is repeated in the incident of the dummy found later on suspended in the Chapel. There were also communications of a vaguely obscene and threatening sort which need not be particularly considered. The most interesting and important one, perhaps, is the message addressed to (I think) Miss Hillyard. 'No man is safe from women like you'; and the other, sent to Miss Flaxman, demanding that she should leave another student's fiance alone. These suggested that the basis of X's grievance was sexual jealousy of the ordinary kind—a suggestion which, again, I believe to be entirely erroneous and to have obscured the issue in a quite fantastic manner.

"We next come (passing over the episode of the bonfire of gowns in the quad) to the more serious matter of Miss Lydgate's manuscript. I do not think it is a coincidence that the portions most heavily disfigured and obliterated were those in which Miss Lydgate attacked the conclusions of other scholars, and those scholars, men. If I am right, we see that X is a person capable of reading, and to some extent understanding, a work of scholarship. Together with this outrage we may take the mutilation of the novel called *The Search* at the exact point where the author upholds, or appears for the moment to uphold, the doctrine that loyalty to the abstract truth must over-ride all personal considerations; and also the burning of Miss Barton's book in which she attacks the Nazi doctrine that woman's place in the State should be confined to the 'womanly' occupations of *Kinder, Kirche, Kuche.*

"In addition to these personal attacks upon individuals, we get the affair of the bonfire and the sporadic outbursts of obscenity upon the walls. When we come to the disfigurement of the Library, we get the generalized attack in a more spectacular form. The object of the campaign begins to show itself more clearly. The grievance felt by X, starting from a single person, has extended itself to the entire College, and the intention is to provoke a public scandal, which may bring the whole body into disrepute."

Here for the first time the speaker lifted his gaze from the bowl of marigolds, let it travel slowly round the table, and brought it to rest upon the Warden's intent face.

"Will you let me say, here and now, that the one thing which frustrated the whole attack from first to last was the remarkable solidarity and public spirit displayed by your college as a body. I think that was the last obstacle that X expected to encounter in a community of women. Nothing but the very great loyalty of the Senior Common Room to the College and the respect of the students for the Senior Common Room stood between you and a most unpleasant publicity. It is the merest presumption in me to tell you what you already know far better than I do; but I say it, not only for my own satisfaction, but because this particular kind of loyalty forms at once the psychological excuse for the attack and the only possible defence against it."

"Thank you," said the Warden. "I feel sure that everybody here will know how to appreciate that."

"We come next," resumed Wimsey, his eyes once more on the marigolds, "to the incident of the dummy in the Chapel. This merely repeats the theme of the early drawings, but with a greater eye to dramatic effect. Its evidential importance lies in the 'Harpy' quotation pinned to the dummy; the mysterious appearance of a black figured frock which nobody could identify; the subsequent conviction of the ex-porter Jukes for theft; and the finding of the mutilated newspaper in Miss de Vine's room, which closed that sequence of events. I will take up those points later.

"It was about this time that Miss Vane made the acquaintance of my nephew Saint-George, and he mentioned to her that, under circumstances into which we need not, perhaps, inquire, he had met a mysterious woman one night in your Fellows' Garden, and that she had told him two things. One: that Shrewsbury College was a place where they murdered beautiful boys like him and ate their hearts out; secondly: that 'the other had fair hair, too.'"

This piece of information was new to most of the Senior Common Room, and caused a mild sensation.

"Here we have the 'murder-motif' emphasized, with a little detail about the victim. He is a man, fair, handsome and comparatively young. My nephew then said he would not undertake to recognize the woman again; but on a subsequent occasion he saw and did recognize her."

Once again the tremor passed round the table.

"The next important disturbance was the affair of the missing fuses."

Here the Dean could contain herself no longer and burst out:

"What a lovely title for a thriller!"

The veiled eyes lifted instantly, and the laughter-lines gathered at the corners.

"Perfect. And that was all it was. X retired, having accomplished nothing but a thriller with good publicity value."

"And it was after *that*," said Miss de Vine, "that the newspaper was found in my room."

"Yes," said Wimsey; "mine was a rational, not a chronological, grouping. ... That brings us to the end of the Hilary Term. The Vacation passed without incident. In the Summer Term, we are faced with the cumulative effect of long and insidious persecution upon a scholar of sensitive temperament. That was the most dangerous phase of X's activities. We know that other students besides Miss Newland had received letters wishing them bad luck in their Schools; happily, Miss Layton and the rest were of tougher fibre. But I should like particularly to draw your attention to the fact that, with a few unimportant exceptions, the animus was all directed against dons and scholars."

Here the Bursar, who had been manifesting irritation for some time, broke in:

"I cannot imagine why they are making all that noise underneath this building. Do you mind, Warden, if I send out and stop it?"

"I am sorry," said Wimsey. "I am afraid I am responsible for that. I suggested to Padgett that a search in the coal-cellar might be profitable."

"Then," pronounced the Warden, "I fear we must put up with it, Bursar." She inclined her head towards Wimsey, who went on:

"That is a brief summary of the events as presented to me by Miss Vane, when, with your consent, Warden, she laid the case before me. I rather gathered"—here the right hand became restless and began to beat out a silent tattoo upon the tabletop—"that she and some others among you were inclined to look upon the outrages as the outcome of repressions sometimes accompanying the celibate life and issuing in an obscene and unreasoning malice directed partly against the conditions of that life and partly against persons who enjoyed or had enjoyed or might be supposed to enjoy a wider experience. There is no doubt that malice of that kind exists. But the history of the case seemed to me to offer a psychological picture of an entirely different kind. One member of this Common Room has been married, and another is engaged to be married; and neither of these, who ought to have been the first victims, were (so far as I know) persecuted at all. The dominance of the naked female figure in the early drawing is also highly significant. So is the destruction of Miss Barton's book. Also, the bias displayed by X seemed to be strongly anti-scholastic, and to have a more or less rational motive, based on some injury amounting in X's mind to murder, inflicted upon a male person by a female scholar. The grievance seemed, to my mind, to be felt principally against Miss de Vine, and to be extended, from her, to the whole College and possibly to educated women in general. I therefore felt we should look for a woman either married or with sexual experience, of limited education but some acquaintance with scholars and scholarship, whose past was in some way linked with that of Miss de Vine, and (though this was an assumption) who had probably come into residence later than last December."

Harriet twisted her glance away from Peter's hand, which had ceased its soft drumming and now lay flat on the table, to estimate the effect of this on his hearers. Miss de Vine was frowning as though her mind, running back over the years, were dispassionately considering her claim to have done murder; Miss Chilperic's face wore a troubled blush, and Mrs. Goodwin's an air of protest; in Miss Hillyard's eyes was an extraordinary mixture of triumph and embarrassment; Miss Barton was nodding quiet assent, Miss Allison smiling, Miss Shaw faintly affronted; Miss Edwards was looking at Peter with eyes that said frankly, "You are the sort of person I can deal with." The Warden's grave countenance was expressionless. The Dean's profile gave no clue to her feelings, but she uttered a little, quick sigh that sounded like relief.

"I will now come," said Peter, "to the material clues. First, the printed messages. It seemed to me extremely unlikely that these could have been produced, in such quantity, within the College walls, without leaving some trace of their origin. I was inclined to look for an outside source. Similarly with the figured dress found on the dummy; it seemed very strange that nobody should ever have set eyes on it before, though it was several seasons old. Thirdly, there was the odd circumstance that the letters which came by post were always received either on a Monday or a Thursday, as though Sunday and Wednesday were the only days on which letters could conveniently be posted from a distant post-office or box. These three considerations might have suggested someone living at a distance, who visited Oxford only twice a week. But the nightly disturbances made it plain that the person actually lived within the walls, with fixed days for going outside them and a place somewhere outside, where clothes could be kept and letters prepared. The person who would fulfill these conditions best would be one of the scouts."

Miss Stevens and Miss Barton both stirred.

"The majority of the scouts, however, seemed to be ruled out. Those who were not confined within the Scouts' Wing at night were trusted women of long service here–most unlikely to fulfill any of the other conditions. Most of those in Scouts' Wing slept two in a room, and therefore (unless two of them were in collusion) could not possibly escape into the College night after night without being suspected. This left only those who had separate bedrooms: Carrie, the head Scout; Annie, the scout attached first to Miss Lydgate's staircase and subsequently to the Senior Common Room, and a third scout, Ethel, an elderly and highly reputable woman. Of these three, Annie corresponded most closely to the psychological picture of X; for she had been married and had the afternoon of Sunday and the afternoon and evening of Wednesday free; she also had her children domiciled in the town and therefore a place where she could keep clothes and prepare letters."

"'But–" began the Bursar, indignantly.

"This is only the case as I saw it last Sunday week," said Wimsey. "Certain powerful objections at once presented themselves. The Scouts' Wing was shut off by locked doors and gates. But it was made clear at the time of the Library episode that the buttery hatch was occasionally left open for the convenience of students wishing to obtain supplies late at night. Miss Hudson had, in fact, expected to find it open that very night. When Miss Vane tried it, it was, in fact, locked. But that was *after* X had left the Library, and you will remember that X was shown to have been trapped in the Hall Building by Miss Vane and Miss Hudson at one end and Miss Barton at the other. The assumption made at the time was that she had been hiding in the Hall.

"After that episode, greater care was taken to see that the buttery hatch was kept locked, and I learn that the key, which was previously left on the inner side of the hatch, was removed and placed on Carrie's key-ring. But a key can very readily be cut in a single day. Actually, it was a week before the next nocturnal episode occurred, which carries us over the following Wednesday, when a key abstracted from Carrie's bunch might readily have been copied and returned. (I know for a fact that such a key was cut on that Wednesday by an ironmonger in the lower part of the town, though I have not been able to identify the purchaser. But that is merely a routine detail.) There was one consideration which inclined Miss Vane to exonerate all the scouts, and that was, that no woman in that position would be likely to express her resentment in the Latin quotation from the *Aeneid* found attached to the dummy.

"This objection had some weight with me, but not a great deal. It was the only message that was not in English, and it was one to which any school child might easily have access. On the other hand, the fact that it was unique among the other scripts made me sure that it had some particular significance. I mean, it wasn't that X's feelings habitually expressed themselves in Latin hexameters. There must be something special about that passage besides its general applicability to unnatural females who snatch the meat from men's mouths. *Nec saevior ulla pestis.*"

"When I first heard of that," broke in Miss Hillyard, "I felt sure that a man was behind all this."

"That was probably a sound instinct," said Wimsey. "I feel sure that a man did write that . . . . Well, I need not take up time with pointing out how easy it was for anybody to wander about the College at night and play tricks on people. In a community of two hundred people, some of whom scarcely know one another by sight, it is harder to find a person than to lose her. But the intrusion of Jukes upon the situation at that moment was rather awkward for X. Miss Vane showed and announced, a disposition to inquire rather too closely into Jukes's home-life. As a result somebody who knew a good deal about Jukes's little habits laid an information and Jukes was removed to gaol. Mrs. Jukes took refuge with her relations and Annie's children were sent away to Headington. And in order that we should feel quite sure that the Jukes household had nothing to do with the matter, a mutilated newspaper appeared shortly afterwards in Miss de Vine's room."

Harriet looked up.

"I did work that out—eventually. But what happened last week seemed to make it quite impossible."

"I don't think," said Peter, "you approached the problem—forgive me for saying so—with an unprejudiced mind and undivided attention. Something got between you and the facts."

"Miss Vane has been helping me so generously with my books," murmured Miss Lydgate, contritely; "and she has had her own work to do as well. We really ought not to have asked her to spare any time for our problems."

"I had plenty of time," said Harriet. "I was only stupid."

"At any rate," said Wimsey, "Miss Vane did enough to make X feel she was dangerous. At the beginning of this term, we find X becoming more desperate and more deadly in intention. With the lighter evenings, it becomes more difficult to play tricks at night. There is the psychological attempt on Miss Newland's life and reason and, when that fails, an effort is made to create a stink in the University by sending letters to the Vice-Chancellor. However, the University proved to be as solid as the College; having let the women in, it was not prepared to let them down. This was no doubt exasperating to the feelings of X. Dr. Threep acted as intermediary between the Vice-Chancellor and yourselves, and the matter was presumably dealt with."

"I informed the Vice-Chancellor," said the Warden, "that steps were being taken."

"Quite so; and you complimented me by asking me to take those steps. I had very little doubt from the start as to the identity of X; but suspicion is not proof, and I was anxious not to cast any suspicion that could not be justified. My first task was obviously to find out whether Miss de Vine had actually ever murdered or injured anybody. In the course of a very interesting after-dinner conversation in this room, she informed me that, six years ago, she had been instrumental in depriving a man of his reputation and livelihood–and we decided, if you remember, that this was an action which any manly man or womanly woman might be disposed to resent."

"Do you mean to say," cried the Dean, "that all that discussion was intended merely to bring out that story?"

"I offered an opportunity for the story's appearance, certainly; but if it hadn't come out then, I should have asked for it. Incidentally, I established for a certainty, what I was sure of in my own mind from the start, that there was not a woman in this Common Room, married or single, who would be ready to place personal loyalties above professional honour. That was a point which it seemed necessary to make clear–not so much to me, as to yourselves."

The Warden looked from Miss Hillyard to Mrs. Goodwin and back at Peter.

"Yes," she said, "I think it was wise to establish that."

"The next day," said Peter, "I asked Miss de Vine for the name of the man in question, whom we already knew to be handsome and married. The name was Arthur Robinson; and with this information I set out to find what had become of him. My working theory was that X was either the wife or some relation of Robinson: that she had come here when Miss de Vine's appointment was announced, with the intention of revenging his misfortunes upon Miss de Vine, the College and academic women in general; and that in all probability X was a person who stood in some close relation to the Jukes family. This theory was strengthened by the discovery that information was laid against Jukes by an anonymous letter similar to those circulated here.

"Now, the first thing that happened after my arrival was the appearance of X in the Science Lecture Room. The idea that X was courting discovery by preparing letters in that public and dangerous manner was patently absurd. The whole thing was a clear fake, intended to mislead, and probably to establish an alibi. The communications had been prepared elsewhere and deliberately planted–in fact, there were not enough letters left in the box to finish the message that had been begun to Miss Vane. The room chosen was in full view of the Scouts' Wing, and the big ceiling light was conspicuously turned on, though there was a reading-lamp in the room, in good working order; it was Annie who drew Carrie's attention to the light in the window;

Annie was the only person who claimed to have actually seen X; and while the alibi was established for both scouts, Annie was the one who most closely corresponded to the conditions required to X."

"But Carrie heard X in the room," said the Dean.

"Oh, yes," said Wimsey, smiling. "And Carrie was sent to fetch you while Annie removed the strings that had switched out the light and overturned the blackboard from the other side of the door. I pointed out to you, you know, that the top of the door had been thoroughly dusted, so that the mark of the string shouldn't show."

"But the marks on the dark-room window-sill–" said the Dean.

"Quite genuine. She got out there the first time, leaving the doors locked on the inside and strewing a few of Miss de Vine's hairpins about to produce conviction. Then she let herself into the Scouts' Wing through the Buttery, called up Carrie and brought her along to see the fun . . . . I think, by the way, that some one of the scouts must have had her suspicions. Perhaps she had found Annie's bedroom door mysteriously locked on various occasions, or had met her in the passage at inconvenient times. Anyhow, the time had obviously arrived for establishing an alibi. I hazarded the suggestion that nocturnal ramblings would cease from that time on; and so they did. And I don't suppose we shall ever find that extra key to the Buttery."

"All very well," said Miss Edwards. "But you still have no proof."

"No. I went away to get it. In the meantime, X–if you don't like my identification–decided that Miss Vane was dangerous, and laid a trap to catch her. This didn't come off, because Miss Vane very sensibly telephoned back to College to confirm the mysterious message she had received at Somerville. The message was sent from an outside call-box on the Wednesday night at 10:40. Just before eleven, Annie came in from her day off and heard Padgett speak to Miss Vane on the 'phone. She didn't hear the conversation, but she probably heard the name.

"Although the attempt had not come off, I felt sure that another would be made, either on Miss Vane, Miss de Vine or the suspicious scout–or on all three. I issued a warning to that effect. The next thing that happened was that Miss Vane's chessmen were destroyed. That was rather unexpected. It looked less like alarm than personal hatred. Up till that time, Miss Vane had been treated with almost as much tenderness as though she had been a womanly woman. Can you think of anything that can have given X that impression, Miss Vane?"

"I don't know," said Harriet, confused. "I asked kindly after the children and spoke to Beatie–good heavens, yes, Beatie!–when I met them. And I remember once agreeing politely with Annie that marriage might be a good thing if one could find the right person."

"That was politic if unprincipled. And how about the attentive Mr. Jones of Jesus? If you will bring young men into the College at night and hide them in the Chapel–"

"Good gracious!" exclaimed Miss Pyke.

"–you must be expected to be thought a womanly woman. However; that is of no great importance. I fear the illusion was destroyed when you publicly informed me that personal attachments must come second to public duties."

"But," said Miss Edwards, impatiently, "what happened to Arthur Robinson?"

"He was married to a woman called Charlotte Ann Clarke, who had been his landlady's daughter. His first child, born eight years ago, was called Beatrice. After the trouble at York, he changed his name to Wilson and took a post as junior master in a small prepatory school, where they didn't mind taking a man who had been deprived of his M.A., so long as he was cheap. His second daughter, born shortly afterwards, was named Carola. I'm afraid the Wilsons didn't find life too easy. He lost his first job—drink was the reason, I'm afraid—took another—got into trouble again and three years ago blew his brains out. There were some photographs in the local paper. Here they are, you see. A fair, handsome man of about thirty-eight—irresolute, attractive, something of my nephew's type. And here is the photograph of the widow."

"You are right," said the Warden. "That is Annie Wilson.

"Yes. If you read the report of the inquest, you will see that he left a letter, saying that he had been hounded to death—rather a rambling letter, containing a Latin quotation, which the coroner obligingly translated."

"Good gracious!" said Miss Pyke. *"Tristius haud illis monstrum—?"*

"*Ita.* A man wrote that after all, you see; so Miss Hillyard was so far right. Annie Wilson, being obliged to do something to support her children and herself, went into service."

"I had very good references with her," said the Bursar.

"No doubt; why not? She must somehow have kept track of Miss de Vine's movements; and when the appointinent was announced last Christmas, she applied for a job here. She probably knew that, as an unfortunate widow with two small children, she would receive kindly consideration—"

"What did I tell you?" cried Miss Hillyard. "I always said that this ridiculous sentimentality about married women would be the ruin of all discipline in this College. Their minds are not, and cannot be, on their work."

"Oh, dear!" said Miss Lydgate. "Poor soul brooding over that grievance in this really unbalanced way! If only we had known, we could surely have done something to make her see the thing in a more rational light. Did it never occur to you, Miss de Vine, to inquire what happened to this unhappy man Robinson?"

"I am afraid it did not."

"Why should you?" demanded Miss Hillyard.

The noise in the coal-cellar had ceased within the last few minutes. As though the silence had roused a train of association in her mind, Miss Chilperic turned to Peter and said, hesitatingly:

"If poor Annie really did all these dreadful things, how did she get shut up in the coal-hole?"

"Ah!" said Peter. "That coal-hole very nearly shook my faith in my theory; especially as I didn't get the report from my research staff till yesterday. But when you come to think of it, what else could she do? She laid a plot to attack Miss de Vine on her return from Town—the scouts probably knew which train she was coming by."

"Nellie knew," said Harriet.

"Then she could have told Annie. By an extraordinary piece of good fortune, the attack was delivered—not against Miss de Vine, who would have been taken unawares and whose heart is not strong, but against a younger and stronger woman, who was, up to the certain point, prepared to meet it. Even so, it was serious enough, and might easily have proved fatal. I find it difficult to forgive myself for not having spoken earlier—with or without proof—and put the suspect under observation."

"Oh, nonsense!" said Harriet, quickly. "If you had, she might have chucked the whole thing for the rest of the term, and we should still not know anything definite. I wasn't much hurt."

"No. But it might not have been you. I knew you were ready to take the risk; but I had no right to expose Miss de Vine."

"It seems to me," said Miss de Vine, "that the risk was rightly and properly mine."

"The worst responsibility rests on me," said the Warden. "I should have telephoned the warning to you before you left Town."

"Whosever fault it was," said Peter, "it was Miss Vane who was attacked. Instead of a nice, quiet throttling, there was a nasty fall and a lot of blood, some of which, no doubt, got on to the assailant's hands and dress. She was in an awkward position. She had got the wrong person, she was bloodstained and dishevelled, and Miss de Vine or somebody else might arrive at any moment. Even if she ran quickly back to her own room, she might be seen–her uniform was stained–and when the body was found (alive or dead) she would be a marked woman. Her only possible chance was to stage an attack on herself. She went out through the back of the Loggia, threw herself into the coal-cellar, locked the door on herself and proceeded to cover up Miss Vane's bloodstains with her own. By the way, Miss Vane, if you remembered anything of your lesson, you must have marked her wrists for her."

"I'll swear I did," said Harriet.

"But any amount of bruising may be caused by trying to scramble through a ventilator. Well. The evidence, you see, is still circumstantial–even though my nephew is prepared to identify the woman he saw crossing Magdalen Bridge on Wednesday with the woman he met in the garden. One can catch a Headington bus from the other side of Magdalen Bridge. Meanwhile, you heard this fellow in the cellarage? If I am not mistaken, somebody is arriving with something like direct proof."

A heavy step in the passage was followed by a knock on the door; and Padgett followed the knock almost before he was told to come in. His clothes bore traces of coal-dust, though some hasty washing had evidently been done to his hands and face.

"Excuse me, madam Warden, miss," said Padgett. "Here you are, Major. Right down at the bottom of the 'eap. 'Ad to shift the whole lot, I had."

He laid a large key on the table.

"Have you tried it in the cellar-door?"

"Yes, sir. But there wasn't no need. 'Ere's my label on it. 'Coal-cellar' –see?"

"Easy to lock yourself in and hide the key. Thank you, Padgett."

"One moment, Padgett," said the Warden. "I want to see Annie Wilson. Will you please find her and bring her here."

"Better not," said Wimsey, in a low tone.

"I certainly shall," said the Warden, sharply. "You have made a public accusation against this unfortunate woman and it is only right that she should be given an opportunity to answer it. Bring her here at once, Padgett."

Peter's hands made a last eloquent gesture of resignation as Padgett went out.

"I think it is *very* necessary," said the Bursar, "that this matter should be cleared up completely and at once."

"Do you really think it wise, Warden?" asked the Dean.

"Nobody shall be accused in this Coliege," said the Warden "without a hearing. Your arguments, Lord Peter, appear to be most convincing; but the evidence may bear some other interpretation. Annie Wilson is, no doubt, Charlotte Ann Robinson; but it does not follow that she is the author of the disturbances. I admit that appearances are against her, but there may be falsification or coincidence. The key, for example, may have been put into the coal-cellar at any time within the last three days."

"I have been down to see Jukes," began Peter; when the entrance of Annie interrupted him. Neat and subdued as usual, she approached the Warden:

"Padgett said you wished to see me, madam." Then her eye fell on the newspaper spread out upon the table, and she drew in her breath with a long, sharp hiss, while her eyes went round the room like the eyes of a hunted animal.

"Mrs. Robinson," said Peter, quickly and quietly. "We can quite understand how you came to feel a grievance—perhaps a justifiable grievance—against the persons responsible for the sad death of your husband. But how could you bring yourself to let your children help you to prepare those horrible messages? Didn't you realize that if anything had happened they might have been called upon to bear witness in court?"

"No, they wouldn't," she said quickly. "They knew nothing about it. They only helped to cut out the letters. Do you think I'd let them suffer? ... My God! You can't do that .... I say you can't do it .... You beasts, I'd kill myself first."

"Annie," said Dr. Baring, "are we to understand that you admit being responsible for all these abominable disturbances? I sent for you in order that you might clear yourself of certain suspicions which—"

"Clear myself! I wouldn't trouble to clear myself. You smug hypocrites—I'd like to see you bring me into court. I'd laugh in your faces. How would you look, sitting there while I told the judge how that woman there killed my husband?"

"I am exceedingly disturbed," said Miss de Vine, "to hear about all this. I knew nothing of it till just now. But indeed I had no choice in the matter. I could not foresee the consequences—and even if I had—"

"You wouldn't have cared. You killed him and you didn't care. I say you murdered him. What had he done to you? What harm had he done to anybody? He only wanted to live and be happy. You took the bread out of his mouth and flung his children and me out to starve. What did it matter to you? You had no children. You hadn't a man to care about. I know all about you. You had a man once and you threw him over because it was too much bother to look after him. But couldn't you leave my man alone? He told a lie about somebody else who was dead and dust hundreds of years ago. Nobody was the worse for that. Was a dirty bit of paper more important than all our lives and happiness? You broke him and killed him—all for nothing. Do you think that's a woman's job?"

"Most unhappily," said Miss de Vine, "it was my job."

"What business had you with a job like that? A woman's job is to look after a husband and children. I wish I had killed you. I wish I could kill you all. I wish I could burn down this place and all the places like it—where you teach women to take men's jobs and rob them first and kill them afterwards."

She turned to the Warden.

"Don't you know what you're doing? I've heard you sit round snivelling about unemployment—but it's you, it's women like you who take the work away from the men and break their hearts and lives. No wonder you can't get men for yourselves and hate the women who can. God keep the men out of your hands, that's what I say. You'd destroy your own husbands, if you had any, for an old book or bit of writing . . . . I loved my husband and you broke his heart. If he'd been a thief or a murderer, I'd have loved him and stuck to him. He didn't mean to steal that old bit of paper—he only put it away. It made no difference to anybody. It wouldn't have helped a single man or woman or child in the world—it wouldn't have kept a cat alive; but you killed him for it."

Peter had got up and stood behind Miss de Vine, with his hand over her wrist. She shook her head. Immovable, implacable, thought Harriet; this won't make her pulse miss a single beat. The rest of the Common Room looked merely stunned.

"Oh, no!" said Annie, echoing Harriet's thoughts. "*She* feels nothing. None of them feel anything. You brazen devils—you all stand together. You're only frightened for your skins and your miserable reputations. I scared you all, didn't I? God! how I laughed to see you all look at one another! You didn't even trust each other. You can't agree about anything except hating decent women and their men. I wish I'd torn the throats out of the lot of you. It would have been too good for you, though. I wanted to see you thrown out to starve, like us. I wanted to see you all dragged into the gutter. I wanted to see you—you—sneered at and trampled on and degraded and despised as we were. It would do you good to learn to scrub floors for a living as I've done, and use your hands for something, and say 'madam' to a lot of scum . . . . But I made you shake in your shoes, anyhow. You couldn't even find out who was doing it—that's all your wonderful brains come to. There's nothing in your books about life and marriage and children, is there? Nothing about desperate people—or love—or hate or anything human. You're ignorant and stupid and helpless. You're a lot of fools. You can't do anything for yourselves. Even you, you silly old hags—you had to get a man to do your work for you.

"*You* brought him here." She leaned over Harriet with her fierce eyes, as though she would have fallen on her and torn her to pieces. "And you're the dirtiest hypocrite of the lot. I know who you are. You had a lover once, and he died. You chucked him out because you were too proud to marry him. You were his mistress and you sucked him dry, and you didn't value him enough to let him make an honest woman of you. He died because you weren't there to look after him. I suppose you'd say you loved him. You don't know what love means. It means sticking to your man through thick and thin and putting up with everything. But you take men and use them and throw them away when you've finished with them. They come after you like wasps round a jam-jar, and then they fall in and die. What are you going to do with that one there? You send for him when you need him to do your dirty work, and when you've finished with him you'll get rid of him. You don't want to cook his meals and mend his clothes and bear his children like a decent woman. You'll use him, like any other tool, to break me. You'd like to see me in prison and my children in a home, because you haven't the guts to do your proper job in the world. The whole bunch of you together haven't flesh and blood enough to make you fit for a man. As for *you*—"

Peter had come back to his place and was sitting with his head in his hands. She went over and shook him furiously by the shoulder, and as he looked up, spat in his face. "You! you dirty traitor! You rotten little white-faced rat! It's men like you that make women like this. You don't know how to do anything but talk. What do you know about life, with your title and your money and your clothes and motor-cars? You've never done a hand's turn of honest work. You can buy all the women you want. Wives and mothers may rot and die for all you care, while you chatter about duty and honour. Nobody would sacrifice anything for you—why should they? That woman's making a fool of you and you can't see it. If she marries you for your money she'll make a worse fool of you, and you'll deserve it. You're fit for nothing but to keep your hands white and father other men's children . . . . What are you going to do now, all of you? Run away and squeal to the magistrate because I made fools of you all? You daren't. You're afraid to come out into the light. You're afraid for your precious college and your precious selves. *I'm* not afraid. I did nothing but stand up for my own flesh and blood. Damn you! I can laugh at you all! You daren't touch me. You're afraid of me. I had a husband and I loved him—and you were jealous of me and you killed him. Oh, God! You killed him among you, and we never had a happy moment again."

She suddenly burst out crying—half dreadful and half grotesque, with her cap crooked and her hands twisting her apron into a knot.

"For Heaven's sake," muttered the Dean, desperately, "can't this be stopped?"

Here Miss Barton got up.

"Come, Annie," she said, briskly. "We are all very sorry for you, but you mustn't behave in this foolish and hysterical way. What would the children think if they saw you now? You had better come and lie down quietly and take some aspirin. Bursar! will you please help me out with her?"

Miss Stevens, galvanized, got up and took Annie's other arm, and all three went out together. The Warden turned to Peter, who stood mechanically wiping his face with his handkerchief and looking at nobody.

"I apologize for allowing this scene to take place. I ought to have known better. You were perfectly right."

"Of course he was right!" cried Harriet. Her head was throbbing like an engine. "He's always right. He said it was dangerous to care for anybody. He said love was a brute and a devil. You're honest, Peter, aren't you? Damned honest—Oh, God! let me get out of here. I'm going to be sick."

She stumbled blindly against him as he held the door open for her, and he had to steer her with a firm hand to the cloak-room door. When he came back, the Warden had risen, and the dons with her. They looked stupefied with the shock of seeing so many feelings stripped naked in public.

"Of course, Miss de Vine," the Warden was saying, "no sane person could possibly think of blaming you."

"Thank you, Warden," said Miss de Vine. "Nobody, perhaps, but myself."

"Lord Peter," said the Warden, "a little later on, when we are all feeling more ourselves, I think we should all like to say—"

"Please don't," said he. "It doesn't matter at all."

The Warden went out, and the rest followed her like mutes at a funeral, leaving only Miss de Vine, sitting solitary beneath the window. Peter shut the door after them and came up to her. He was still passing his handkerchief across his mouth. Becoming aware of this, he tossed the linen into the wastepaper basket.

"I do blame myself," said Miss de Vine, less to him than to herself. "Most bitterly. Not for my original action, which was unavoidable, but for the sequel. Nothing you can say to me could make me feel more responsible than I do already."

"I can have nothing to say," said he. "Like you and every member of this Common Room, I admit the principle and the consequences must follow."

"That won't do," said the Fellow, bluntly. "One ought to take some thought for other people. Miss Lydgate would have done what I did in the first place; but she would have made it her business to see what became of that unhappy man and his wife."

"Miss Lydgate is a very great and a very rare person. But she could not prevent other people from suffering for her principles. That seems to be what principles are for, somehow . . . . I don't claim, you know," he added, with something of his familiar diffidence, "to be a Christian or anything of that kind. But there's one thing in the Bible that seems to me to be a mere statement of brutal fact—I mean, about bringing not peace but a sword."

Miss de Vine looked up at him curiously.

"How much are *you* going to suffer for this?"

"God knows," he said. "That's my lookout. Perhaps not at all. In any case, you know, I'm with you—every time."

When Harriet emerged from the cloak-room, she found Miss de Vine alone.

"Thank Heaven, they've gone," said Harriet. "I'm afraid I made an exhibition of myself. It was rather—shattering, wasn't it? What's happened to Peter?"

"He's gone," said Miss de Vine.

She hesitated, and then said:

"Miss Vane—I've no wish to pry impertinently into your affairs. Stop me if I am saying too much. But we have talked a good deal about facing the facts. Isn't it time you faced the facts about that man?"

"I have been facing one fact for some time," said Harriet, staring out with unseeing eyes into the quad, "and that is, that if I once gave way to Peter, I should go up like straw."

"That," said Miss de Vine, drily, "is moderately obvious. How often has he used that weapon against you?"

"Never," said Harriet, remembering the moments when he might have used it. "Never."

"Then what are you afraid of? Yourself?"

"Isn't this afternooon warning enough?"

"Perhaps. You have had the luck to come up against a very unselfish and a very honest man. He has done what you asked him without caring what it cost him and without shirking the issue. He hasn't tried to disguise the facts or bias your judgment. You admit that, at any rate."

"I suppose he realized how I should feel about it?"

"Realized it?" said Miss de Vine, with a touch of irritation. "My dear girl, give him the credit for the brains he's got. They are very good ones. He is painfully sensitive and far more intelligent than is good for him. But I really don't think you can go on like this. You won't break his patience or his control or his spirit; but you may break his health. He looks like a person pushed to the last verge of endurance."

"He's been rushing about and working very hard," said Harriet, defensively. "I shouldn't be at all a comfortable person for him to live with. I've got a devilish temper."

"Well, that's his risk, if he likes to take it. He doesn't seem to lack courage."

"I should only make his life a misery."

"Very well. If you are determined that you're not fit to black his boots, tell him so and send him away."

"I've been trying to send Peter away for five years. It doesn't have that effect on him."

"If you had really tried, you could have sent him away in five minutes. . . . Forgive me. I don't suppose you've had a very easy time with yourself. But it can't have been easy for him, either–looking on at it, and quite powerless to interfere."

"Yes. I almost wish he had interfered, instead of being so horribly intelligent. It would be quite a relief to be ridden over rough-shod for a change."

"He will never do that. That's *his* weakness. He'll never make up your mind for you. You'll have to make your own decisions. You needn't be afraid of losing your independence; he will always force it back on you. If you ever find any kind of repose with him, it can only be the repose of very delicate balance."

"That's what he says himself. If you were me, should you like to marry a man like that?"

"Frankly," said Miss de Vine, "I should not. I would not do it for any consideration. A marriage of two independent and equally irritable intelligences seems to me reckless to the point of insanity. You can hurt one another so dreadfully."

"I know. And I don't think I can stand being hurt any more."

"Then," said Miss de Vine, "I suggest that you stop hurting other people. Face the facts and state a conclusion. Bring a scholar's mind to the problem and have done with it."

"I believe you're quite right," said Harriet. "I will. And that reminds me. Miss Lydgate's *History of Prosody* was marked PRESS with her own hand this morning. I fled with it and seized on a student to take it down to the printers. I'm almost positive I heard a faint voice crying from the window about a footnote on page 97–but I pretended not to hear."

"Well," said Miss de Vine, laughing, "thank goodness, *that* piece of scholarship has achieved a result at last!"

# 23

The last refuge and surest remedy, to be put in practice in the utmost place, when no other means will take effect, is, to let them go together and enjoy one another; *potissima cura est ut heros amasia sua portiatur,* saith *Guianerius. . . . Aesculapius* himself, to this malady, cannot invent a better remedy, *quam ut amanti cedat amatum* . . . than that a Lover his desire.

Robert Burton

THERE WAS no word from Peter in the morning. The Warden issued a brief and discreet announcement to the College that the offender had been traced and the trouble ended. The Senior Common Room, recovering a little from its shock, went quietly about the business of the term. They were all normal again. They had never been anything else. Now that the distorting-glass of suspicion was removed, they were kindly, intelligent human beings—not seeing, perhaps, very much farther beyond their own interests than the ordinary man beyond his job or the ordinary woman beyond her own household—but as understandable and pleasant as daily bread.

Harriet, having got Miss Lydgate's proofs off her mind, and feeling that she could not brace herself to deal with Wilfrid, took her notes on Le Fanu, and went down to put in a little solid work at the Camera.

Shortly before noon, a hand touched her shoulder.

"They told me you were here," said Peter. "Can you spare a moment? We can go up on to the roof."

Harriet put down her pen and followed him across the circular chamber with its desks full of silent readers.

"I understand," he said, pushing open the swing-door that leads to the winding staircase, "that the problem is being medically dealt with."

"Oh, yes. When the academic mind has really grasped a hypothesis—which may take a little time—it copes with great thoroughness and efficiency. Nothing will be overlooked."

They climbed in silence, and came out at length through the little turret upon the gallery of the Camera. The previous day's rain had passed and left the sun shining upon a shining city. Stepping cautiously over the slatted flooring towards the south-east segment of the circle, they were a little surprised to come upon Miss Cattermole and Mr. Pomfret, who were seated side by side upon a stone projection and rose as they approached, in a flutter, like daws disturbed from a belfry.

"Don't move," said Wimsey, graciously. "Plenty of room for all of us."

"It's quite all right, sir," said Mr. Pomfret. "We were just going. Really. I've got a lecture at twelve."

"Dear me!" said Harriet, watching them disappear into the turret. But Peter had already lost interest in Mr. Pomfret and his affairs. He was leaning with his elbows on the parapet, looking down into Cat Street. Harriet joined him.

There, eastward, within a stone's throw, stood the twin towers of All Souls, fantastic, unreal as a house of cards, clear-cut in the sunshine, the drenched oval in the quad beneath brilliant as an emerald in the bezel of a ring. Behind them, black and grey, New College frowning like a fortress, with dark wings wheeling about her belfry louvres; and Queen's with her dome of green copper; and, as the eye turned southward, Magdalen, yellow and slender, the tall lily of towers; the Schools and the battlemented front of University; Merton, square-pinnacled, half-hidden behind the shadowed North side and mounting spire of St. Mary's. Westward again, Christ Church, vast between Cathedral spire and Tom Tower; Brasenose close at hand; St. Aldate's and Carfax beyond; spire and tower and quadrangle, all Oxford springing underfoot in living leaf and enduring stone, ringed far off by her bulwark of blue hills.

*Towery City, and branchy between towers,*
*Cuckoo-echoing, bell-swarmd, lark-charmèd,*
*rook-racked, river rounded,*
*The dapple-eared lily below.*

"Harriet," said Peter; "I want to ask your forgiveness for these last five years."

"I think," said Harriet, "it ought to be the other way round."

"I think not. When I remember how we first met—"

"Peter, don't think about that ghastly time. I was sick of myself, body and soul. I didn't know what I was doing."

"And I chose that time, when I should have thought only of you, to thrust myself upon you, to make demands of you, like a damned arrogant fool—as though I had only to ask and have. Harriet, I ask you to believe that, whatever it looked like, my blundering was nothing worse than vanity and a blind, childish impatience to get my own way."

She shook her head, finding no words.

"I had found you," he went on, a little more quietly, "beyond all hope or expectation, at a time when I thought no woman could ever mean anything to me beyond a little easy sale and exchange of pleasure. And I was so terrified of losing you before I could grasp you that I babbled out all my greed and fear as though, God help me, you had nothing to think of but me and my windy self-importance. As though it mattered. As though the very word of love had not been the most crashing insolence a man could offer you."

"No, Peter. Never that."

"My dear—you showed me what you thought of me when you said you would live with me but not marry me."

"Don't. I am ashamed of that."

"Not so bitterly ashamed as I have been. If you knew how I have tried to forget it. I told myself that you were only afraid of the social consequences of marriage. I comforted myself with pretending that it showed you liked me a little. I bolstered up my conceit for months, before I would admit the humiliating truth that I ought to have known from the beginning—that you were so sick of my pestering that you would have thrown yourself to me as one throws a bone to a dog, to stop the brute from yelping."

"Peter, that isn't true. It was myself I was sick of. How could I give you base coin for a marriage-portion?"

"At least I had the decency to know that I couldn't take it in settlement of a debt. But I have never dared to tell you what that rebuke meant to me, when at last I saw it for what it was . . . . Harriet; I have nothing much in the way of religion, or even morality, but I do recognize a code of behaviour of sorts. I do know that the worst sin—perhaps the only sin—passion can commit, is to be joyless. It must lie down with laughter or make its bed in hell—there is no middle way . . . . Don't misunderstand me. I have bought it, often—but never by forced sale or at 'stupendous sacrifice.' . . . Don't, for God's sake, ever think you owe me anything. If I can't have the real thing, I can make do with the imitation. But I will not have surrenders or crucifixions . . . . If you have come to feel any kindness for me at all, tell me that you would never make me that offer again."

"Not for anything in the world. Not now or at any time since. It isn't only that I have found a value for myself. But when I made you the offer, it meant nothing to me—now it would mean something."

"If you have found your own value," he said, "that is immeasurably the greatest thing . . . . It has taken me a long time to learn my lesson, Harriet. I have had to pull down, brick by brick, the barriers I had built up by my own selfishness and folly. If, in all these years, I have managed to get back to the point at which I ought to have started, will you tell me so and give me leave to begin again? Once or twice in the last few days I have fancied that you might feel as though this unhappy interval might be wiped out and forgotten."

"No; not that. But as though I could be glad to remember it."

"Thank you. That is far more than I expected or deserved."

"Peter–it's not fair to let you talk like this. It's I who ought to apologize. If I owe you nothing else, I owe you my self-respect. And I owe you my life–"

"Ah!" said he, smiling. "But I have given you that back by letting you risk it. That was the last kick that sent my vanity out of doors."

"Peter, I did manage to appreciate that. Mayn't I be grateful for that?"

"I don't want gratitude–"

"But won't you take it, now that I want to give it you?"

"If you feel like that about it, then I have no right to refuse. Let that clear all scores, Harriet. You have given me already far more than you know. You are free now and for ever, so far as I am concerned. You saw yesterday what personal claims might lead to–though I didn't intend you to see it in quite that brutal way. But if circumstances made me a little more honest than I meant to be, still, I did mean to be honest up to a point."

"Yes," said Harriet, thoughtfully. "I can't see you burking a fact to support a thesis."

"What would be the good? What could I ever have gained by letting you imagine a lie? I set out in a lordly manner to offer you heaven and earth. I find that all I have to give you is Oxford–which was yours already. Look! Go round about her and tell the towers thereof. It has been my humble privilege to clean and polish your property and present her for your inspection upon a silver salver. Enter into your heritage and do not, as is said in another connection, be afraid with any amazement."

"Peter dear," said Harriet. She turned her back upon the shining city, leaning back against the balustrade, and looking at him. "Oh, *damn!*"

"Don't worry," said Peter. "It's quite all right. By the way, it looks as though it was Rome again for me next week. But I shan't leave Oxford till Monday. On Sunday there's a Balliol Concert. Will you come to it? We'll have one other gaudy night, and comfort our souls with the Bach Concerto for two violins. If you will bear with me so far. After that, I shall be clearing off and leaving you to–"

"To Wilfrid and Co.," said Harriet, in a kind of exasperation.

"Wilfrid?" said Peter, momentarily at a loss, with his mind scampering after rabbits.

"Yes, I'm re-writing Wilfrid."

"Good God, yes. The chap with the morbid scruples. How's he getting on?"

"He's better, I think. Almost human. I shall have to dedicate the book to you, I think. 'To Peter, who made Wilfrid what he is'–that sort of thing. . . . Don't laugh like that. I'm really *working* at Wilfrid."

For some reason, that anxious assurance shook him as nothing else had done.

"My dear–if anything I have said . . . If you have let me come as far as your work and your life . . . Here! I think I'd better remove myself before I do anything foolish. . . . I shall be honoured to go down to posterity in the turn-up of Wilfrid's trouser. . . . You will come on Sunday? I am dining with the Master, but I will meet you at the foot of the stairs. . . . Till then."

He slipped away along the gallery and was gone. Harriet was left to survey the kingdom of the mind, glittering from Merton to Bodley, from Carfax to Magdalen Tower. But her eyes were on one slight figure that crossed the cobbled Square, walking lightly under the shadow of St. Mary's into the High. All the kingdoms of the world and the glory of them.

Masters, undergraduates, visitors; they sat huddled closely together on the backless oak benches, their elbows on the long tables, their eyes shaded with their fingers, or turned intelligently towards the platform where two famous violinists twisted together the fine, strong strands of the Concerto in D Minor. The Hall was very full; Harriet's gowned shoulder touched her companion's, and the crescent of his long sleeve lay over her knee. He was wrapt in the motionless austerity with which all genuine musicians listen to genuine music. Harriet was musician enough to respect this aloofness; she knew well enough that the ecstatic rapture on the face of the man opposite meant only that he was hoping to be thought musical, and that the elderly lady over the way, waving her fingers to the beat, was a musical moron. She knew enough, herself, to read the sounds a little with her brains, laboriously unwinding the twined chains of melody link by link. Peter, she felt sure, could hear the whole intricate pattern, every part separately and simultaneously, each independent and equal, separate but inseparable, moving over and under and through, ravishing heart and mind together.

She waited till the last movement had ended and the packed hall was relaxing its attention in applause.

"Peter—what did you mean when you said that anybody could have the harmony if they would leave us the counterpoint?"

"Why," said he, shaking his head, "that I like my music polyphonic. If you think I meant anything else, you know what I meant."

"Polyphonic music takes a lot of playing. You've got to be more than a fiddler. It needs a musician."

"In this case, two fiddlers—both musicians."

"I'm not much of a musician, Peter."

"As they used to say in my youth: 'All girls should learn a little music—enough to play a simple accompaniment.' I admit that Bach isn't a matter of an autocratic virtuoso and a meek accompanist. But do you want to be either? Here's a gentleman coming to sing a group of ballads. Pray silence for the soloist. But let him be soon over, that we may hear the great striding fugue again."

The final Chorale was sung, and the audience made their way out. Harriet's way lay through the Broad Street gate; Peter followed her through the quad.

"It's a beautiful night—far too good to waste. Don't go back yet. Come down to Magdalen Bridge and send your love to London River."

They turned along the Broad in silence, the light wind fluttering their gowns as they walked.

"There's something about this place," said Peter presently, "that alters all one's values." He paused, and added a little abruptly: "I have said a good deal to you one way and another, lately; but you may have noticed that since we came to Oxford I have not asked you to marry me."

"Yes," said Harriet, her eyes fixed upon the severe and delicate silhouette of the Bodleian roof, just emerging between the Sheldonian and the Clarendon Building. "I had noticed it."

"I have been afraid," he said, simply; "because I knew that from anything you said to me here, there could be no going back . . . . But I will ask you now, and if you say No, I promise you that this time I will accept your answer. Harriet; you know that I love you: will you marry me?"

The traffic lights winked at the Holywell Corner: Yes; No; Wait. Cat Street was crossed and the shadows of New College walls had swallowed them up before she spoke:

"Tell me one thing, Peter. Will it make you desperately unhappy if I say No?"

"Desperately? . . . My dear, I will not insult either you or myself with a word like that. I can only tell you that if you will marry me it will give me very great happiness."

They passed beneath the arch of the bridge and out into the pale light once more.

"Peter!"

She stood still; and he stopped perforce and turned towards her. She laid both hands upon the fronts of his gown, looking into his face while she searched for the word that should carry her over the last difficult breach.

It was he who found it for her. With a gesture of submission he bared his head and stood gravely, the square cap dangling in his hand.

"*Placetne, magistra?*"

"*Placet.*"

The Proctor, stumping grimly past with averted eyes, reflected that Oxford was losing all sense of dignity. But what could he do? If Senior Members of the University chose to stand–in their gowns, too–closely and passionately embracing in New College Lane right under the Warden's windows, he was powerless to prevent it. He primly settled his white bands and went upon his walk unheeded; and no hand plucked his velvet sleeve.